THE COMBINATIONS

LOUIS ARMAND

The Combinations[†]

EQUUS

ISBN 978-1-9996964-1-2
3rd edition (December, 2020)

Equus Press
Birkbeck College (William Rowe)
43 Gordon Square, London, WC1 HoPD, United Kingdom

Typeset & design by lazarus

Set in Caslon, composed by William Caslon in 1734

White can always play differently,
in which case he merely loses differently.
— Bobby Fischer
A Bust to the King's Gambit

Habitants de Sodome, au feu du ciel
préférez le fiel de la queue.
— Rrose Sélavy

Alles begann am Anfang.
Aber sie nichts davon wußten…
— Zarathustra

By th' mass, & 'tis like a rat indeed!
— Polonius

Im einen Fall machen wir den Zug eines
bestehenden Spiels, im andern setzen wir
eine Spielregel fest. Man könnte auch das
Ziehen mit einer Spielfigur auf diese
beiden Arten auffassen: als Paradigma für
künftige Züge, und als Zug einer Partie.
— Ludwig Wittgenstein
Zettel

If the fool would persist in his folly
he would become wise.
— William Blake
The Marriage of Heaven & Hell

Ah din't wake up dis moanin'…
— Robert Johnson
Golem City Blues

Graviora manent…
— Publius Vergilius Maro
Aeneid

 Every confession's a lie.

(Spare a thought for the old guy arrested barking ZHIDS OUT! KRAUTS IN! dragged off to Gestapo HQ for the red-carpet treatment, sign the visitors' book, tour the facilities before having his balls fried off & fed back to him. 'Course he fessed-up, no secret about it. Standard procedure, you could say. Official policy, even. Matter of black&white. Or maybe the other way, white&black. Put a noose around his neck, too, for good measure, swung from a meathook. Was anything gained? Hardly takes much to figure out, every comedy needs a scapegoat like a soapbox needs a rousable rabble, like a discerning eye needs a Pygmalion to perv at, like a banana skin needs a halfwit in blackface making pratfalls all over the place, etc. *Le condiment humain*, as the Old Ballsack says in les classiques. *Well, your Honoré, I'm just a poor, mixed-up, muddled shitstick who can't see for thinking or think for seeing, you know how it is your Honoré, blind passions and impassioned blindness, la gloire est le soleil des merdes blah blah blah.* Oh you can be sure he perceived the error of his ways after all that, from end to finish, from start to the get-go, just a question of stringing a rope between the posts, joining the dots, putting a frame around the big picture so none of the details got left out. The whole operation was like a machine for turning-out sparkling insights at an unparalleled rate. *A man's only the sum of his whatsits, after all.* A pittance in the Great Payroll, a two-bit AlphaOmega miming through his own operative pronoun, a pinhole in the Light Fantastic shining on a mid-air dance act, neck-jobbed in a pool of putrescence. Think that was the Angel of Salvation applauding from the wings & not just another ratcheting-through-the-motions of the Funfair Funicular? They're giving away shares in the sequel each time you buy a ticket. *Return to go.* Just the highlights, a fifteen minute flash in the pan if you're lucky, saving the rest of the shtick for the pathologically morbid among you — the matchsticks under the fingernails, the stitched eyelids, the dripping faucet, the scalding, the freezing, the ruptured eardrum… Hypothetically at least there's no limit to their little hijinks. Like they say, God's in the small print like the Devil's in the retail. You can always hit rep(l)ay if there's something you want to savour. Or as the Old Reprobate used to say when he was getting banged by the City's Finest, *Come again?* Comforting, eh, that you'll wind-up just as you began, in a belch of bitchlitter under a septic outhouse bench, on the bracken of a cursed hillside, in the bosom of insentient self-deceit, blind as a newborn newt with barely a puddle to flap your last in? Ach, & after so much wasted effort! Evolution? Well you could measure it all backwards & still come up emptyhanded. One man's tosspot's another man's phrenological cockhead. But someone's gotta draw the short straw. Yep. No good making a song&dance of it. All them *amens* & *yoohoos* & lintel jobs! The hundredthousand culpa meas, the boneless beggaring, the staunchless pleading, the knee-bended gobstopping! Destined is destined, from the very first, or nearabouts. First glimpse out the wombwindow into the arsehole of it all. First grimace. First clenching of fists. Little-Big-Man in the wigwam of the World. Swaddled in mind's-eye cinema of the Great Ghoulie, Zhidgeist of the Zeitverschwendung,✿ the whole three reels: Mammy, Pap 'n' li'l Noddibody. Casting back, oh how unpromising it must've seemed, peekabooing out the O of Optimism's lesser half, taking the measure of it, getting a grip on the situation, proverbially of course, taking the proffered dilemma by the horns, good antenna, bad antenna. Well tits is tits, me love. Ol' wizened dugs in the moomouth of him. Warts 'n' all. Worts und alles. Oh but the words came later. Much later. Though from where you're standing you'd be forgiven for doubting there'd ever been anything but. *Woids*, they said. *Voids*! As verbiloquacious as a bum alibi. Dolling-out the gilded nothings, the nounings, the nonsequiturs in a last-ditch run at conning a reprieve — *Pleash oh pleash, Big Meishter Funundgamesh* — thinking to jerk a tear or two, the rained-on spit-sodden butt of all the spent supplications of yore (*that* old carcass, stuffed with bone & offal, served-up on high with cabbage & dumplings). *He* must've been a boring old cunt before He fell out of His tree & saw the Light Fantastic boring a blackhole in His brain. Somewho up there must've been laughing at least, the Pater Primate's pet parrot perhaps, sulphur-crested & porcelain-plumaged, keeping up the bottled-guffaw routine *ab immemorabili tempore*, even after the rest died waiting for the punchline. Nothing in the Eagle's Eyrie but saintly arses on stunted thrones all turned to schist — how they must've got sick of being so high&mighty after the first dozen Ice Ages, twirling field marshals' batons & fingering each other's whoopee cushions, wanting nothing less innocent than a bit of good cheer to get them through their chilblains. Periscope to the lower depths to see how their Neanderthal namesakes are getting along, doing the dirty in millennial cave-dark & half the heathenly host with crook necks straining to get a looksee. And Himself, needless to say, lying toes-up, right in the midst of it, like an untusked woolly mammoth flat on its back. A quare sight indeed. *Well*, mimeth Pontius the Panto Parrot, *show must go on* & all that razzledazzle crap. Cranking up the *Looney Tunes* theme like the tired wheeze of a jape gone stale. So what if it *was* no laughing matter? When the game's up, you'd think it was a contest to see who'll choke last. The way they go on, trying to meet their Maker halfway. That's progress, see? Guinness Book longest gut-roar in History, before the night finally closes-in. And it does, my preciouses. Like a finger on the restart button. Like a fist around a fiver. Like the man-under-the-bed creeping out to stuff a pillow in your face. Giving you the heebiejeebs. Clawing the walls of your little hemlock belly. Sending you off with that mad crosseyed toothless grimace-at-the-end-of-the-tunnel look. Knows what's coming, too, but isn't saying. Too bad for you. Is that it? Is that all? What about our chinooked castrato back in the cells with his wits knocked out of him & his jester's joystick jiggling his jugular? Lost the plot, you say? Gone missing from the narrative, eh? Slipped out the backway to take in the view from the other side, mmm? Zion of the Mind's Eye? Ben-Gurion & what not? Should we oblige the bugger to lie still & take his place in the Tale End of it All, the Untolled Troth, the Gullible's Travesty? He was a mensch, after all. He existed. Not for us to judge his one uncredited cameo in the

---

✿ "History, foreshortened by abstractions, is an advance to 'something better,' but Nature exhibits only a perpetually self-repeating cycle." G.W.F. Hegel

Great Schemer of Things' thousandyear ad-break. (Who *was* he? No-one *you'll* ever hear of again.) Such an erstwhile Oedipus as even ours would hardly be worth his weight in footnotes. But wait (who knows?), perhaps the scholastic sticklers of some future Post-Pleistocene might, one day — trifocals tilted at this infinitesimal event of questionable non-repute, putting the inconsequential back into the Grand Design like a butterfly's wing-flutter in the vacuum of the Cosmic Mind — set down in higgledypiggledy casebook hieroglyphics how, at the time of the Hitherto Unknown Offending Incident, the suspect known only as "K" was discovered loitering at the gates of the Old Zhiddish Semetery, attracting an audience, shouting his lungs out so to speak, waiving his arms, making a right spectacle of himself, for anyone who could hear, anyone who could see: ZHIDS OUT! *Ja, ja, ja.* KRAUTS IN! *Ai, ai, ai.* Occurring one mildly overcast midweek afternoon in the salad days of the Occupation, with all the hilarity still to come. The moral of the story being, were it to have one, *Let the dead laugh at the dead.*)

𝄢: Foolery runs amok.[†]

[†] An oldendays Chesk proverb: "Bláizniviny se rozsévají nazdařbůh."

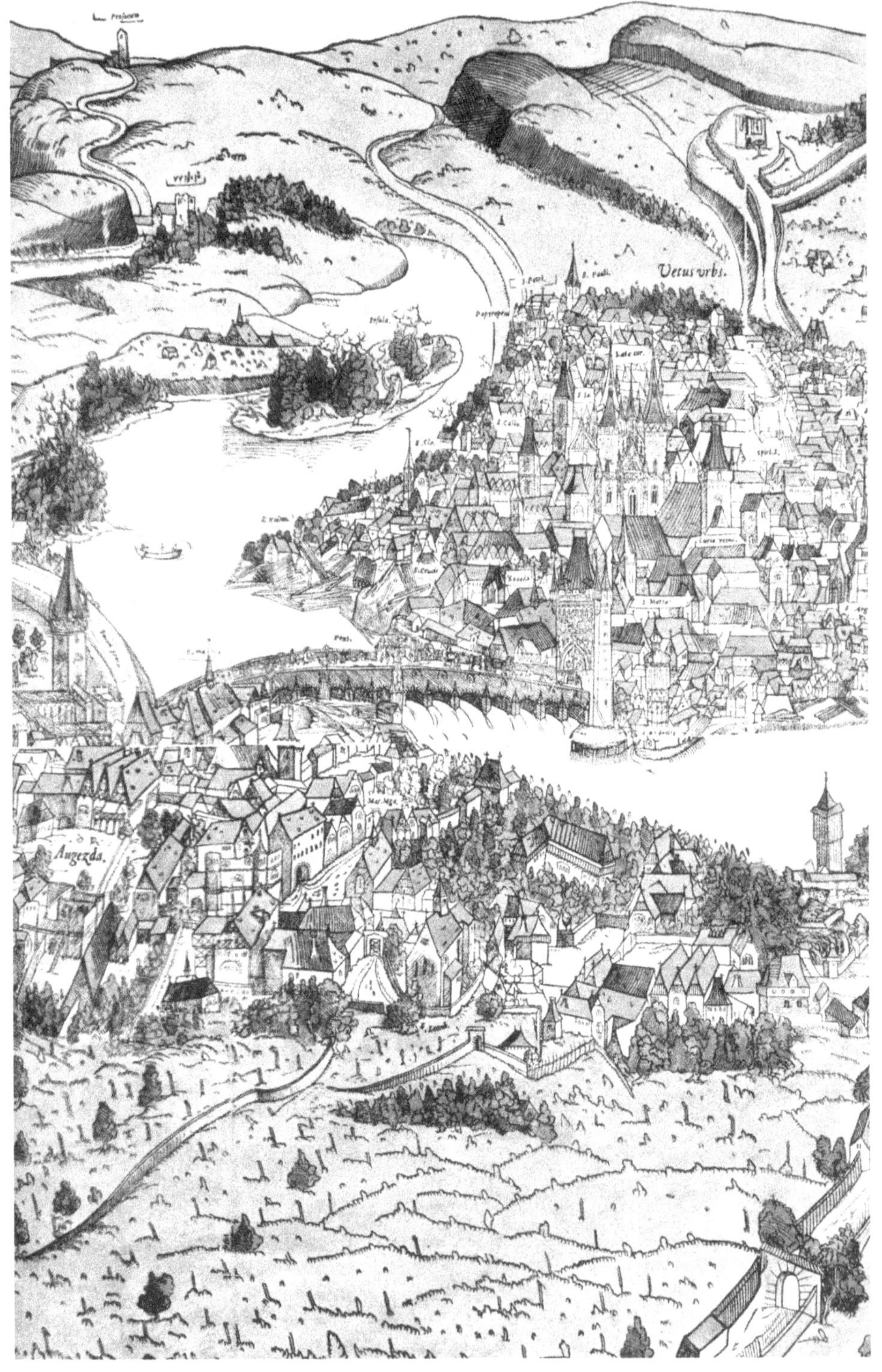

Vetus vrbs.
Augszda

THE COMBINATIONS

CAPUT totius REGNI BOHEMIÆ.

Overture

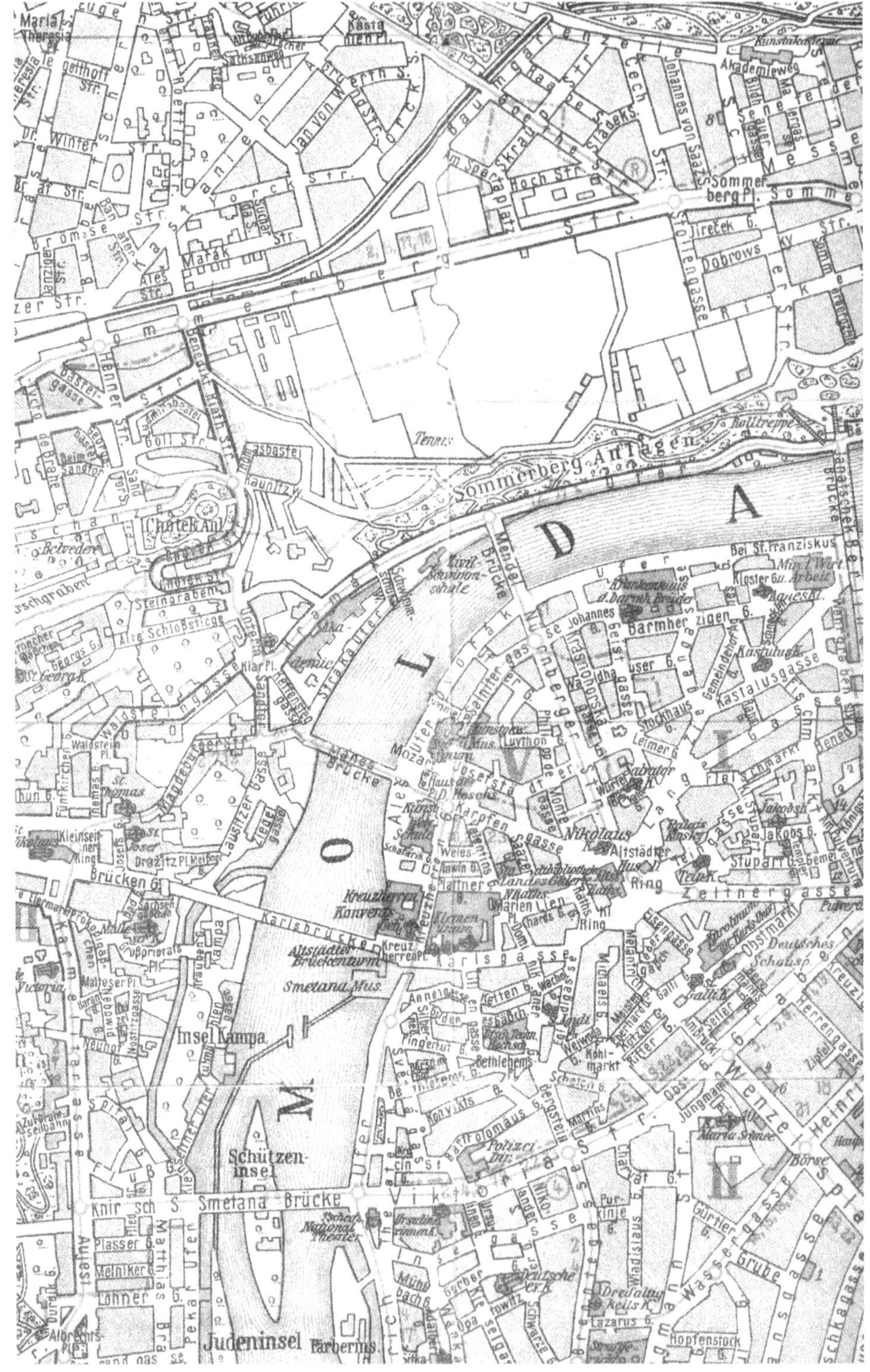

Maria-
Theresia
Dr. Winter
Graf Str.
Mařák
Sand
Chotek Anl.
Belvedere
Chotek Str.
Steingraben
Alte Schloßstiege
St. Georg K.
Civil
Schwimm-
schule
Mendl
Brücke
Bei St. Franziskus
Min.f.Wirt
Kloster 6u. Arbeit
Krankenhaus
d.barmh.Brüder
Barmher zigen
Kastalusk.
Kastalusgasse
Akademie
Klar Pl.
Stockhaus
Kunstschau
Mus. Luython
Mozarteum
Kunst
Schule
Karpfen
gasse
Salvator
Nikolaus
Altstädter
Waldstein
Pl.
St.
Thomas
Fünf Kirchen
Malteser Gasse
Lausitzer Gasse
Teufel
gasse
Welss
Altstädter
Mus.
Teich
Stupart
Zeltnergasse
Kleinseit
ner
Ring
St.
Josef
Dražitz Pl.
Brücken G.
Karlsbrücke
Kreuzherren
Konvent
Marien Pl.
Marien
Dom
Karlsgasse
Karolinenthal
Obstmarkt
Deutsches
Schausp.
Kreuz
Altstädter
Brückenturm
Smetana Mus.
Insel Kampa
Victoria
Malteser Pl.
Bethlehem
Kohl-
markt
Wenzel
Börse
Schützen-
insel
Smetana Brücke
Schiess
Polizei
Dir.
Maria Schnee
Judeninsel
Färberins.
National
Theater
Deutsche
K.
Dreifaltig
keits K.
Lazarus G.
Hopfenstock

Begin with a room
& a man inside the room.

An indistinct source of yellowish light reveals: an escritoire, four centuries antique already, littered with manuscripts, inkblotters, pens, inkwells & candlebutts. To the right of it, a long trestletable stands against a grey stone wall. The table, too, is littered with implements of diverse kinds: a pestle & mortar, stoppered bottles, flasks & beakers containing quantities of liquid in various shades & hues, alembics, coiled glass tubes & pipettes, faucets, ropes & pulleys, a collection of earthenware jars large & small, an oil lamp with blackened wick tapering out of it, etc. At the far end of the trestletable stands a woodstove, its flue rising towards an invisible ceiling — atop it (the stove) sits a pot of filth slowly percolating through an inverted funnel joined, by way of an equally filthy glass tube, to a complicated looking apparatus which takes up the entire surface of a second table positioned adjacent to it. Located between this table & the escritoire are a pair of high bookcases, their shelves bowed under rows of leatherbound folios — & between the bookcases, a narrow iron door with barred aperture staring out of it at eye-level.

Wrapped in gloom & laboratory stench, the man sits huddled over the escritoire, unkempt hair snaking from beneath a black coif. The lower half of his waxlike face remains hidden behind a grey beard peppered with morsels of foodstuff — a stained lace collar lies dishevelled beneath it (the beard), framed by an unbuttoned doublet & embroidered black robe whose pattern, in the halflight, is rendered ambiguous, vaguely geometric: interwoven pentagrams, crescent moons, circles in disbalanced concentricity redolent of Ptolemaic cosmographies. A matted ermine trim droops from the man's shoulders like a decayed carcass with flies hovering around it. With little effort of the imagination, one might rightly guess this to be a replica of some alchemist's den, cell, coven from times of yore, executed with a disconcerting eye to detail whose veracity is nevertheless undone by the visible layers of dust that, to varying degrees of thickness & greyness, have settled over the entire tableau.

As the eyes grow accustomed to the gloom, a detail previously overlooked comes into focus. Propped incongruous against the escritoire is a Rostov MK105 reel-to-reel tapemachine — СДЕЛАНО В МАТУШКЕ-РОССИИ* — a pair of twinned plastic spools ornamenting it like some technofetish bustier. The body of the tapemachine is stealth-black, the spools respectively: Shanks-Armitage white (the left one, trailing a red strip of magnetic tape), & aspic (the other, showing an inch of brown tape wound about its core like matjeshering) — a likewise-brown strip of tape runs between the two of them, passing midway across a pair of exposed tapeheads, capstans & pinch-rollers. Meanwhile, a greyfaced babička in brocaded headscarf, seated in a straightbacked chair propped beside the curtained entranceway (via which, a dozen schoolchildren accompanied by their teacher have just filed — the children obediently twobytwo, boygirl-girlboy, leftright, Little Pioneer red scarves, uniform-blue shirts, ten-degrees-darker greyblue skirts, trousers, standard-issue white shin-length socks, tan-brown rubbersoled shoes), puts aside a bundle of knitting, stands creakily & stoops, three four five steps over to the tapemachine, one arthritic Babajaga poking-finger snagging the ▶ button: an unseen current thence made to flow etherless from wallsocket to tapehead-coil by transmutations most miraculous, invoking fluctuant humours of magnetisation. Instantly the machine whirs, the spools spiral into rotorrelief, the tape slithers, a pair of occulted loudspeakers crackle & pop quadrophonally if not tetragrammatically. (*Patience dearests!*)

---

* Mammy's Milk, Inc.

As the Little Pioneers stand attentive, gawping from the alterside of a cordon of burgundy eightply, the beeswax pallor of the alchemist seated at his escritoire, glass-eyed under heavy folds of wizened eyelids, grows eerily refulgent. As it does so, the magnetic imprint on the reel-to-reel tape induces, by a current proportionate & so-to-say analogous to the original Ur-signal (decoded if not decorded by the tapeheads' combined Champollion-effect), a high-pitched whinnying hiss. Suddenly animate, the alchemist's lips tremble yellowgreen, dilate, contract, part & resuture themselves, their vaguely gross palpitations suggestive, thanks to a slight technical malfunction, of an advancing dementia — in any case, the operations of the mouth anticipate by several seconds (without seeming to be at all related to it) a stream of sounds at the very limits of whatever might be characterised as speech. *Haaaaaaaa!* The schoolchildren elbow one another. *Heeeeeeee!* The schoolchildren titter. Raising his head, the alchemist fixes them with boreal stare. Is it alive? they seem to wonder. An actor with makeup, playing dead? An audiotronic waxworks dummy? A carnival sideshow light-trick with mirrors & invisible guywires: the Iceman, the Bearded Lady? *KA-KA-!* the unsynced tapemachine booms, an angry Jove, a wrathful Jehovah. *Hiiiiiiii!* the mad alchemist ventriloquises, rictus-mouthed now, touched by the Almighty. *KA-KA-!* — baum! — *KA-KA-PITAL* — baum! — *ist ein gen-e-ral, eeee-ter-nal ree-la-tion von NA-NA-TUR!* — baum! — *Hoooooooo!*

The children back away, retreat, looking decidedly uneasy now. Their teacher taps her right shoe with studied impatience — red patent leather with a cross-strap & modest, one-inch heal, bought especially with a voucher for the last-but-one May Day parade — whose sole, despite several patchings & mendings, has already begun to wear through: in addition to which, beneath the vinyl & cardboard instep, she's recently (& to her considerable chagrin) discovered the telltale black-inked MADE IN CHINA quite blatantly concealed there — despite fulsome assurances from the Baťa shop assistant about genuine homegrown factory produce, the real thing & not some cheap knockoff imitation, sheered, stitched, glued & tacked by comrades in Gottwaldov, pride of their very own Cheskoslovnikian Socialist Republik. Peering down at them now she wonders if they don't make her look a little like that Dotty in *The Wizard of Oz* — & thinking this, vaguely expecting that ridiculous cybernated goblin there behind the rattling escritoire to suddenly shout *I AM THE INVINCIBLE THE ALLPOWERFULL THE TERRIBLE!* Foolish thought.

Instead, through a storm of tape-hiss increasing in volume exponentially, or as-if exponentially,[*] this pseudo-Oz berates the by-now thoroughly apprehensive huddle of Little Pioneers with a ten-minute-long garbled[**] diatribe about[***]

    (A)   the material-dialectical foundation of knowledge?
    (B)   ideology & false consciousness?
    (C)   English industrial occultism (from Gerald Winstanley to Edward Kelley) or/& the alchemical-cabbalistic origins of the Western freemarket?
    (D)   all of the above?
    (E)   none of the above?

— jaw aflap, head jolting back&forth in a convulsion of overly emphatic nods which threaten, at any moment, to send it — wig, coif & all — rebounding in a spray of spittle off the cluttered escritoire onto the museum's scuffed-black linoleum, *hehe*, *thumpthumpthump*, rolling to a precipitant stop like the return of the proverbial repressed right between some poor unfortunate Lenka's or Lukáš's polyblend shoelaces: fringed, where the neck used till recently to be, with anachronistically machinefiligreed lace, copper wires jutting from the chasm — exposed rheostats & diodes & transistors erupting in a shower of cartoon asterisks & exclamation points — doubletted torso juddering, trembling, convulsing in horrible-to-behold Jacobean deathrattle: *Hu-u-u-u-u-u-u-u!*

As the recording ends, the lights dim — the waxworks dummy slumps forward in silhouette against the dull afterglow of alchemical apparatuses. The teacher, back straightened, early-middleage paunch conscientiously retracted, leads the disconcerted schoolkiddies back out the way they came, past a small ten-by-fifteen framed reproduction hanging beside the door. It appears to depict a room very much like the one they're in the process of evacuating. Legible, now that light floods in through the parted curtain, a small rectangular plaque screwed to the wall, at child's-eyelevel beneath the picture frame, reads: *Amphitheatre of Eternal Wisdom, by Hans Vredeman de Vries, 1595.* None, however, appear to notice it. Next up, the teacher informs her Pioneer munchkins, they're off to see a famous scaled replica of the turbine room from

---

[*] Of which, seated beside the door with knitting needles tacktacktacking, the ancient assistant remains tranquilly oblivious.
[**] de facto? a priori? ad hoc?
[***] Speculatively.

Bratsk Station, patiently (from firsthand memory) reconstructed in bleached pine-needles by two civil engineers, twin brothers in fact, while convalescing in a quote-unquote sanatorium north of Lake Baikal & noted (the replica) for its astonishing veracity, its exactness of detail, its true-to-life-ness. In addition, she adds, provided they're all on their very bestabest lunchbreak behaviour, they might afterwards even be permitted to see a documentary film about the heroic comrades at the Leningrad Metal Works. *FOUNDARIES* (oops!), *FOUND-ATIONS… LAID ON BLOOD STAND FIRM!*

The teacher's voice trails off — the last children are filing out from the alchemist's den between black motheaten drapes, glancing back at the now-silent automaton. *Peeeeeee!* a boy cries (the teacher out of earshot already, leading the way down the corridor in clatterheeled Dotty-shoes carbuncular). *Poooooooo!* shrieks another to nervous giggles. The babička meanwhile, greyvisaged, knitting bundled, has hunched her slow way back across the room to re-set the tape machine, send the voice hindways into its box: the room twitters with backspeak — & for as long as it takes the tape to rewind, the scene is of an old woman in a park feeding breadcrumbs to sparrows. The ◄◄ button clicks as the spinning wheels come once more to a stop — the little white digits on the fidgety counter, freeze-framed at zero.

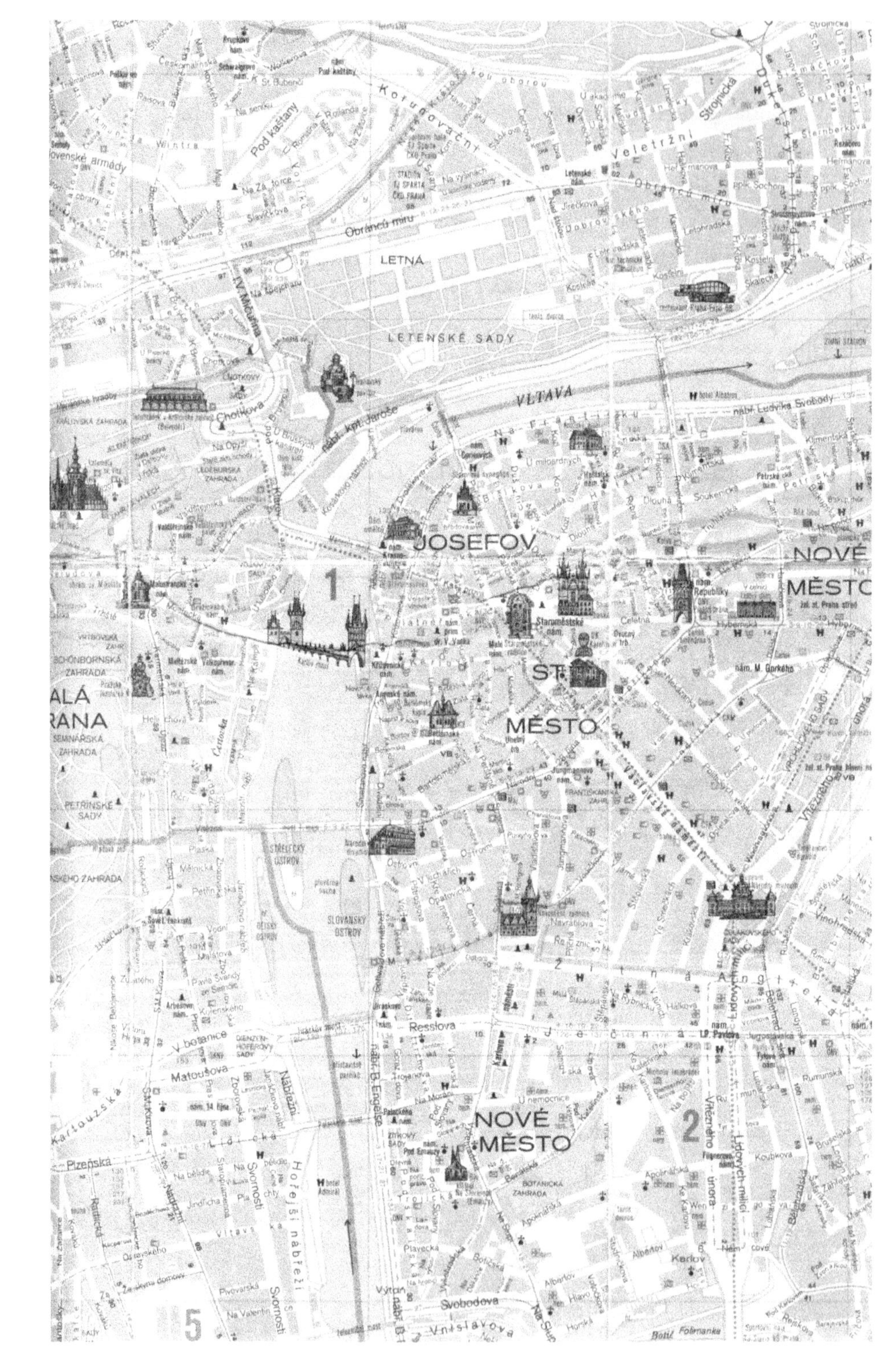

VLTAVA
JOSEFOV
LETNÁ
LETENSKÉ SADY
NOVÉ MĚSTO
STARÉ MĚSTO
MALÁ STRANA
NOVÉ MĚSTO
Korunovační
Veletržní
Obránců míru
Staroměstské nám.
nám. Republiky
nám. M. Gorkého
STŘELECKÝ OSTROV
SLOVANSKÝ OSTROV
PETŘÍNSKÉ SADY
SEMINÁŘSKÁ ZAHRADA
ŠCHÖNBORNSKÁ ZAHRADA
KRÁLOVSKÁ ZAHRADA
LEDEBURSKÁ ZAHRADA
Chotkova
Resslova
Matoušova
Plzeňská
Svobodova
Vnislavova
1
2
5

a. En Passant

kapitola jedna.

         díra vpodlaze.

     pršelo krví. oko se kutálelo .visela z okna kus ha
     dr.čplek oko sehnal asezral. kamení řali apírko

       bílá lehce padalo do toho zeleního hnusu.

          půl noc apírko se zvedalo . zvedalo se do vesmíru .
56799 ufo ledzastavilo aklapka scotevřela a zeleno černá ruka
sebralo pírko.ufa přiletěli do stanici.všechni ufa vistoupili.
jedno vzalo pírko druhej vzal krabici.šli kousek dál azatočili
       do pracovního centra2ufo přiležil krabicido sletku.
otevřel krabici adalší ufo ho dal do krabici. errrr!errrr!zvenilood
satelitu.alarm že nepřátele
znpetunuprávje střílela na centrum. byla to raketa sm8set5. jedna
z nejmenších raketách.

       ttttttrbchchchchchbuch.vibouchl horní část skleněno střechy.
vnitřní elektrárna vibouchla a propadla střecha na schránku.

       speciální pírko vyletélo .drama celí stanice.se zníčíla

       raketa ?0?2 oděšati ktora neviseuenla přistalaa z ní visi

 1 mimozemšťany. BYLO jiem asy 55.VŠECHNI byli zeleno zluty
 s klalovim ocasem.šli k žlutím dveřím,otevřeli se amimozemšt
 ané vitšli.Vevnitř bylo ticho. ležel na zemi.
                                 stejne bylo
     pulka z stanice zniceny.   t2 raketa na
                  nebespeoí byla uz daleko. letelo
 na plnkovou planetu. gdyz tam přiletéletak   vyšel ven .
 mymozemštan igi rozhledi se pak vysitil svuj portal.
       šel do pore tálu. pak šel sálu

1

They Say

'They say,' the ghost mused, holding his left hand palm-out like a juror taking an oath, 'that the fingernails continue to grow even after death.'

The Prof's ghost* was sitting by the roadside on a snowdrift, dressed in a brown woollen coat the colour of old chemical jars, paring his fingernails with a pocket knife. Lying barely a metre away was a grey horse. There was no doubt the horse was dead, flogging it was never going to be any use.

Němec stood there like an undertaker after a funeral watching them, the ghost & the dead horse. He wondered who the horse was supposed to belong to. The Prof flicked away a piece of blackened fingernail & peered across at him through pale watery eyes. Němec blinked back. The faintly falling snow made a vortex around a cone of orange lamplight. It was impossible to tell what time it was.

'Illusionary, of course,' the ghost added. 'In reality, a corpse's skin withers & contracts, causing the fingernails to only *appear* longer. Hair also.'

The Prof's voice, as he spoke, was full of unnatural emphasis, like a teacher trying to get a classroom of idiots to enunciate. *Fin-ger-na-ils.* It made Němec feel like an idiot just listening to it. He ogled the ghost blatantly, with his mouth half-open like someone who'd forgotten their lines & was waiting for a prompt —

'Fingernails…? But aren't you…?'

'Oh sure,' the Prof yawned, 'I'm the wits of former days.'

The ghost got creakily up on his feet & put the knife away, brushing snow from his pants. Coughed. Straightened. Arched his spine. He might've been some old homeless guy taking a stab at morning callisthenics, thumping his chest optimistically, pulling his elbows back, doing a bit of a softshoe shuffle. Sidling across, the ghost peered into Němec's face with an expression vaguely quixotic, then winked —

'But what about *you*, mein Freund, mmm?'

Němec stood dumbly. Perhaps he expected subtitles to put him wise. The

* If a man can be said to own his own ghost. [✋]

dead horse made unsympathetic eyes.

'Don't you at least have something to say for yourself?' the Prof chuckled.

Němec avoided the horse's dead stare. He scratched his neck pensively, but nothing came to mind. His shoulders made a helpless shrugging movement inside his dark suit jacket.

'Well then,' the Prof pursed his lips, 'so much for the story. Aren't you even curious as to why you're here?'

Němec gave it some thought. "Why" seemed too abstract. "How," on the other hand. But he had no idea *how* he'd got there either, only vague impressions that possibly existed merely to fill the blankness. A window. Wind tunnelling in his ears. A falling. But that was all. Maybe, at long last, he'd got the green light from Head Office to jump. Make a bold new start. All that. But the premise, the ground… Perhaps he wasn't *here* at all. Perhaps there *was* no "here."

The Prof meanwhile yawned, fanning his mouth with a woollen glove. Strange to say, he didn't look like a ghost. But what was a ghost *supposed* to look like? There were things you heard about but never actually saw. Cold War spooks, subversives, foreign agents, for example. Spectral crossborder numbers-stations broadcasting on the ether. Silhouettes erased from misty TV pictures. The disappeared & never quite rehabilitated, never quite resurrected. Concocted futures of greater things to come. *Ein Gespenst geht um in Europa*, etc. Well, what was a ghost after all, but a conspiracy to defraud the senses? A flibbertigibbet? Smoke-in-your-eyes? House of Hammer meets Material Dialectics?

Němec blinked. As for the Prof? He seemed altogether too corporeal to be an hallucination. Or the opposite, maybe: a wispy nothingness of methane & carbon dioxide lingering in the wake of the Old Man's dear departed composthumous body, given to assume visible form, faculty of speech, all the standard accoutrements. Like an ignis fatuus in a cartoon freezeframe with backing vocals.

The fingernails on the other hand…

The Whole

The whole thing would obviously have been a bad dream if not for the fact that he was sure he was awake. Němec picked his nose & inspected the end of his finger. A length of nose-hair lay kinked under a glistening film like a fly's leg in aspic. He wiped it on his jacket & stared down at his shoes, then at the Prof's shoes. Brown suède. Not much good for getting around in this weather. But the

Prof was dead, the horse was dead, the whole of Golem City may as well've been dead too & him with it for all the difference it would've made to his choice of footware. *Careful what you wish for, kiddo.* It brought to mind pictures of rooms stacked ceiling-high with confiscated shoes. Maybe somewhere, he mused, there were rooms like that for dead cities like there were mortuaries for dead people. Perhaps *this* was one & he'd slipped in through a side door by accident. The ghost frowned as if he could read Němec's thoughts —

'Bah! So now what? I'm supposed to go *puff* like a cloud of smoke?'

The Prof waved his arms, bugged his eyes out. Not quite round but folded down at the edges & at the same time stitched up under the eyebrows. Like Peter Lorre in *Secret Agent* — the "hairless Mexican" look the Old Man always gave him whenever in the past Němec had managed to come out with some particularly novel conception. That, for example, the world was controlled by androids. The recollection made him blush, though at the time he'd been positive about the androids. Even so, deny it as he might, the present situation was clearly getting out of hand. Brushing the Prof aside, he went over to the dead horse & with sudden vehemence kicked it in the mouth. A row of yellowed teeth gleamed out at him like bits of polished tesserae. The horse didn't even blink. Němec gave it another kick to be sure & stubbed his toes in the process. The grey horsehead was frozen solid as a curbstone.

'Bravo!' the Prof said, clapping him on the back. 'I was beginning to worry you weren't the man I took you for.'

'Christ almighty!' Němec winced.

The ghost stood beside him as if admiring a piece of his own handiwork.

'You know what they say,' the Prof grinned, 'about gift-horses?'

'What the hell *is* all this, comedy hour?'

'All *what*, mein Freund?'

Němec cast a despairing sideways glance. He'd never noticed before that the Old Man was missing an earlobe, but he noticed now.

'You've got no ear,' said Němec, unable to help himself.

'Don't be ridiculous. How else could I hear what *idiotisch* things keep coming out of your mouth?'

The Prof shook his head in disgust & turned away. The glow from a streetlamp caught in the grey stubble that covered his chin, casting a faint one o'clock shadow.

'Idiotisch!' he repeated.

Němec's attention, meanwhile, had been caught by the house across the street. It loomed there behind a gateway, utterly decrepit, with the stucco crumbling from its façade. He was fairly sure it hadn't been there before, either. He glanced around. On every other side there was only a grey vagueness, as if he was standing in the middle of a soundstage ten metres wide with the set taking up the back wall & a camera crew hidden behind the fog.

While Němec was busy with the scenery, the Prof shuffled away through the snow, his sepia-brown shape receding from the lone lamplight. It was a set-up for a scene by Hitchcock, Carroll, Wilder, Huston, Lang. It'd been done a million times before, but that didn't change anything, it could always be done again. Němec wondered what the Old Man was up to this time. He stopped in front of the house & pulled a large key from his pocket, stuck it in the lock in the middle of the gate, & turned it. The gate creaked open on rusty hinges. Behind it, the mustard-coloured façade was knotted with snow-covered ivy, baroque scrollwork above doors, mansards, roots poking through the eaves, sheets of ice hanging down.

'What're you waiting for?' the ghost called back, stamping snow from sodden suède, 'you'll never get anywhere standing around like that!'

Němec trudged across the street. When he reached the gate, the Prof was gazing up at the eaves above the fifth-floor windows, as if he was looking for something. Němec stuck his hands in his pockets & sighed.

'I have the feeling,' the ghost said, 'you've been here before…'

Resigned

Resigned, Němec followed the Prof's gaze. In one of the grimy high windows a painted smiley-face, like a dull half-moon, was sellotaped to the pane. The place indeed seemed familiar somehow, a detached fragment of a lost memory. While Němec puzzled at it, a swishing sound came through the air & something thumped heavily into the snow at his side. It was a sheet of ice that'd slid from the roof & ricocheted off the wall. It stuck in the ground like a cracked guillotine blade. Němec backed away in alarm.

'Incredible, when you think about it,' said the ghost, unperturbed, gazing up through the flickering vortex, 'that in a vacuum a snowflake falls at the same speed as a grown man.' He tilted his head to regard Němec over a brown herringboned shoulder. 'Except, of course, that neither snowflakes nor grown men are customarily found in a vacuum…'

'…?'

The Prof turned around & levelled his gaze at Němec.

'Surely they taught you that much in school?'

'I didn't go to regular school…'

'Well, my little misfit, consider this: With an open parachute it takes approximately twentyfive minutes to fall from a height of fortythousand feet. Which is to say, twelvethousandonehundred&ninetytwo metres — as countless poor blighters crossing the channel from imperial to metric learned during the War. Without a parachute it takes a little over three minutes. While to fall with or without a parachute from the fifth storey of an apartment building, takes barely any time at all…'

'…?'

The Prof gave him the "hairless Mexican" look & walked off through the gate into a yard.

'Hold your horses!' Němec said, stumbling behind. 'Where're you…?'

A tarnished brass plate fixed to one side of the gateway read:

DĚTSKÝ DOMOV
CHILDREN'S HOME

And now Němec knew why the mustard-coloured building was so familiar. It looked like the sort of place that only existed in dreams, but no, it was real alright, he'd been there before, he'd spent half his life there, like the squill-headed smiley in that window, wanting nothing more than to escape. The ghost turned & looked back at him. Fatherly now, with careworn eyes drooping under a weight not of this world, the Prof in a quiet singsong voice said —

'*Du liebes Kind, komm, geh mit mir! Gar schöne Spiele spiel' ich mit dir…*'[☜]

As he spoke, the Old Man's phantom drifted away along the pathway through the concrete garden with posts, benches, ungainly statuettes half-buried in snowdrift till he reached a pair of great black doors rising like a weathered cliff-face & dissolved into them, truly a ghost at last. High above, the face in the window peered out between crossed bars — a pair of black eyes that seemed to ask, *Why am I here? What type of punishment is this?* From somewhere in a muffled distance, Němec heard the ghost's indistinct laughter. The Prof, he

---

[☜] "Come here, liddle kiddy, have a sweet. We'll play a nice cosy bedtime game…" [☜]

thought, sure knew how to piss on a parade. But whose parade *was* it?

Like a helpless idiot in one of those films, he followed the ghost's footprints down the path & up the stairway, the years catching up with him as he went: deleted mysteries in a scenery of filing cards, lost, occulted, gaussian blurs of long-forgotten names & faces in reanimation, filmed with white-out. Overhead, the snow came down with renewed insistence, swirling & spiralling through the lamplight like the auricle of an ear. And somewhere in the back of Němec's mind, an echo, faint sounds like shattering glass, & the picture of something, glittering with light: light shattering falling — reverberations through gusty dormitories — darkness — a strange puppet-body in a stranger bed. Whimpering. And a voice. *Shut up!* it said. *I've wet myself,* the puppet-child answered. And the child was him. In the glory days of his young youth. *Best years,* they all smilingly said. Wine & bloody roses.

Rewind

Rewind, eleven years: lying on a stretcher in the infirmary of the Children's Home with a pair of bandaged mitts. It was the end of autumn & the beginning of winter. Němec couldn't remember what he was doing there. Smell of purgative, sal volatile, & all around, light glinting off beakers, bottles, jars & phials in glass cabinets. A nurse was shaking her head, tongue clicking behind nicotine-yellow teeth, threading a needle with surgical twine. Starched uniform, blotched with crimson, the stains darkening outwards from their centres in bands like ancient treetrunk chronography, drying to black. Next to her, one of the androids stood scolding with shrivelled Babajaga-mask & pointed finger. The android leered at his nakedness below the red Little Pioneer scarf knotted around his very breakable neck. Wiry nose hairs & nostrils twitched —

'Doesn't *deserve* to be saved,' the android hissed, 'little dog, little brat, little beggarboy. If it *weren't* for those *bars* on the windows he'd be right where he *belongs, belongs, belongs. The little mutt. Doesn't deserve. Little brat. Where he belongs. Beggarboy. Doesn't deserve...!*'

And then the nurse stuck the needle & twine in him & began stitching up a hole in his side without bothering with the anaesthetic. The pain made him throw up. Not then, but now.

Fastforward: Němec, doubling-over in the doorway of the Children's Home, bile matting the grey slush round his shoes. His body went slack against the doors, while the door remained fixed there as fast as Sinai granite, bolted by Iron Necessity. He heaved again. Something laughed. In a distance more figural than literal, Němec could hear giant footsteps, like something played on a Wurlitzer in an ancient movie hall. And in-between the giant footsteps drifted the Prof's singsong voice, ever-receding & perhaps already replaying itself at a yet more remote point in time Němec would only ever reach by imagining —

'In seinen Armen das Kind war tot…'

In his arms the child was dead…!?

Němec gasped to get his breath. On his knees now, beating his fists weakly against the door. A small frightened child's fists. He hammered without making so much as a noise. There was something wrong with him: he stared at his hands, a mock of paraselene glinting on unpared nails slimed with blood —

'Ein kleiner Mond im Fingernagel erinnert uns an etwas wie Ichor, das Blut der Götter…'

A little fingernail moon reminds of the gods' ichorous blood…?!

Němec's sleeves were wet with it also. The very air seemed saturated with the taste of blood. From beneath the black doors a grey plasma seeped & spread out, viscous as a Siberian river. The door gave a hydraulic shudder as if a flood was about to burst through at any moment & spill over him. Then all was black… Licorice blood?? Icarus' blood???

'Guilty,' Němec heard the distant voice intone, 'are those who are punished!'

The Revolution

The Revolution came & it was a different story. November, 1989. Year of the Snake. When the apparatchiks all went slithering off to shed their skin & slither back unnoticed to dollars in suitcases. Left to wander the corridors of the Children's Home, in the interzone between the chaos of rioting tribes, Němec spied through a door left ajar that selfsame Commie android blubbering behind her Babajaga-mask with the staffroom idiotbox (a Magneton "Rovesnik," top-of-the-range in '69) bewailing the lost Workers' Paradise. It was enough to break a scorpion's heart. Wrapped in the gloom of the TV set & a stew of old farts, the inhuman hag looked like a museum exhibit incompletely brought to life, some embalmed Pharaoh's Numidian concubine, or a funfair freak — *The Oldest "Woman" in the World*! The pallor of her face was off-green.

Němec stood & stared. And as the fear melted away from him, his eyes fell upon the handbag lying on the floor at the android's feet. And beside the handbag, a big bunch of keys crying *Freedom at Last*! He made a bee-line so fast the TV commentator didn't even blink. The android sat there howling into her handkerchief. Němec bolted, the sharp teeth of the keys biting into his little fist, as the hag android's moans pursued him down the hall & past the vacant porter's lodge. As he fumbled the lock, almost choking on his own breath, he remembered how in the androids' language the hag's name meant *deathbed* — & how that was what all the kids at the Home called her behind her back, Ol' Deathbed, or simply The Witch, or Babajugs because of her shrivelled tits & evil eye that sized you up like she'd just as soon stew you in a soup pot & eat you. Finding the right key at last, Němec strained with all his little might against the weight of the door till a crack opened wide enough to slip through & the bright day flooded in. And while Babajaga's horrible sobs echoed, dying as the door swung shut behind him, the megaphones in the street blared the National Hymn, unbetrayed by irony:

> *Kde domov můj?*
> *Voda hučí po lučinách,*
> *bory šumí po skalinách,*
> *v sadě skví se jara květ,*
> *zemský ráj to na pohled…*

> Oh where oh where is my home-of-homes?
> I ask & seek but have yet to find! The longed-for
> burble of the brooks across the maidenheaded meadows,
> the caressive clefts & craggy-crags,
> the perfumed peaches & airfreshened pinewoods,
> the whole dolled-up suckable paradiso…!

Cut to: Charlton Heston wide-stanced on some remote briny Bohemian seacoast. Picture him, square-jawed in loincloth, the giant fist of Kafka's Liberty jutting from the lone & level sands, lofting its rust-red flaming dildosword as a timewarped Jerry Goldsmith soundtrack decibel-by-decibel drowns everything else out, just as the closing credits come up on the screen…

You, too, are invited to join in & shed a tear. It must be awful to die & still go on parading yourself in all that gore of pomp & mediocrity, ghosts in celluloid, the Age's myth, half-naked before an audience of informers, & their victims, & their victims' victims. *None of them ever loved you! Can you hear me?*

Well who gives a toss for bygone days? Those little uproars turned to soap opera puked in your face. The guilty childhood love affair with nonsense. Those incomplete adventures of a world gone to the dogs & about to be recycled every fifteen minutes. Winding-up the string section for the closing crescendo, & that TV voiceover, first whispering, then shouting, sounding a long way off & then very close, deep down resounding in the tympanum of the middle-ear the way voices in dreams do —

'Why, my little Squillhead, do the Masters put bars OUTSIDE the windows, if their purpose is to keep all the children on the INSIDE?'

Die Fingernägel auf der anderen Seite…

Rewind further.

As If

As if a moral can or must be drawn from everything, & because he'd sleepwalked through a window (cutting himself up nice & good, but on account of the bars not falling to an untimely macabre embarrassment of a death), the Android Home Central Committee decreed, in the best interests of all&sundry (as well as society at large), that henceforth Little Dunce-Cap Němec, a.k.a. "Squillhead," should, with all due diligence, be buckled into bed each night before lights-out. And so he was: a dozen white canvas straps crisscrossing the sheets, bandaged mitts sticking out from under, for all the world[*] like a cartoon mummy.

Tied on his back in the dark Němec would wake up suffocating & try to scream, but nothing ever came out — the whole dormitory leered, pressing-in round the bed, laughing, spitting in his eyes as he gaped back mutely at faceless assailants. He was never sure if they were real. Nights fed into days whose every moment evoked panic, like a somnambulist who sees himself walking towards a precipice unable to wake up, always about to fall but never quite. He'd find himself alone in strange places, attic rooms, stairwells, toilets, fixated inexplicably by such things as objects trapped at the bottom of a urinal among the yellowsodden fag-butts, pubes, gobs of phlegm, bog-roll & chemicalblue cakes of disinfectant like baby tortoises flipside on their shells.

Later, with the bandages gone, Little Dunce-Cap Němec discovered an instinct for guile. Before lights-out, when the androids came to strap him into bed, he'd hold his breath while they adjusted the tension, like some trick-pony in a Wild West flick thinking to tip its rider on his head, saddle & all. If the trick

---

[*] Or only half of it. [✊]

worked, there'd be wiggle-room enough to squeeze out from under. Waiting first for the dorm to nod-off, then stealing from the covers to stand watch at the window he would've fallen through if *bars* hadn't been fixed to the outside of it — a rectangle of cold light that reached almost to the floor — scarred hands pressed to glass. Below, a concrete garden with barbed fence-rails fronted Leningradská Street. The pavement was hidden under embankments of grey snow, like earthworks thrown up & then abandoned by an army in hurried retreat. Concrete steps led past bricked-up windows, along a steep incline overhung by sickly black trees.

All winter Squillhead kept his vigil. In place of the nightmares there was the mocking invitation of the street with its promise of escape. The only problem was how to get to it before his term was up. If they succeeded in properly fucking with your head, by the time they handed him his freedom, he wouldn't want it. They had punishment down to a fine art. As for the street outside the Home, it was a dead-end anyhow, butting against the murky grey façade of what once had been a hotel. Its name was still outlined on a sagging bluegreen marquee: HOTEL K____ — K for *Kilo* or *Kolo* or *Kleč* or *Klíč* maybe. The boarded-up doorway was plastered with handbills in faded blues, greys, greens:

JOHNNY VRABETS & THE FANDANGOS!
ZAPOTEC VAULTS THE VLTAVA!
KAREL GOTT "LIVE" WITH THE BOLSHOI BAG BAND!

while in one of the broken upstairs windows a VACANCY sign still hung, dull red type on white plyboard, veneer slowly peeling away at the edges from too much weather. Flocks of soot-coloured pigeons had taken up residence under the eaves. Stalactites of pigeon crap decades-old hung down from gapped palings.

In a utopia of housing-shortages, Němec never understood why no-one lived in the old hotel. Sometimes, while he looked out at the darkened street, he made believe the whole City was like that, abandoned in the face of some cosmic catastrophe, the Doom of Time, the End of the World, the Haemorrhage of Dialectical Reason. He imagined being the last human alive, tracing his name with bony fingertip on fogged glass, like a message to a future he scarcely dared believe in — letter-by-awkward-letter, holding his breath, then exhaling, erasing whichever went before, while outside a rusty streetsign creaked in the wind beneath the lone streetlamp.

One Night

One night the shadow of a man emerged slowly from the dark into the cone of the streetlamp. Then another. The first was tall & thin as a scarecrow, the second was short & fat. Each was wrapped in a dark trenchcoat. Němec watched them from the window, struggling up the street with a battered saloon piano between them that kept sliding on the ice. Every couple of feet the men paused, cursing & heaving as the piano inched backwards. Němec tried not to breathe, afraid the figures would vanish behind the fogged glass & never return.

For long minutes the men dragged & shoved. Their actions, though awkward & strange, appeared full of purpose, yet there was nowhere they could go. Beyond the streetlamp, the dull grey edifice of Hotel K____ presented an insurmountable barrier. There they stopped. The scarecrow held steady while the other withdrew a pair of cobblestones from his coat pockets & wedged them under the piano's wheels. Brushing-off gloves, they each stood back to survey their handiwork. Almost immediately a silent argument ensued: hands gesticulated, then fists, then the argument became a game. Paper, scissors, rock. The short one spat in disgust, got down on all-fours in front of the piano & waited. The scarecrow, carefully arranging the tails of his trenchcoat behind him, seated himself on his companion's back, lifted the lid from the keyboard, disencumbered himself of his gloves & began to play.

Allegro ma non tanto.

Beneath the scarecrow's fingers the black & ivory keys of the piano gleamed. *Re-fa-mi-re-do-re-mi-re.* Now sharply, now dully, marred or married by the inconstant wind, the notes became a queer music full of sweetness & pleasure. Then snow began to fall & went on falling, & through the smudged glass the two figures at the piano dissolved into it.

Later Němec experienced a nightmare unlike any he'd ever had before & woke up with his tongue stuck in his throat. In it, he was trapped inside the grey hotel, trying to find a way out. There were corridor after corridor of locked doors. On every floor the same thing. It seemed to go on forever, running from end to end of the hotel with no way out. Then, at the head of a long flight of stairs, what light? A window! He rushed headlong up the staircase towards it, but no matter how fast he ran the window remained stubbornly out of reach. All of a sudden, the two trenchcoats were hot at his heels, hauling the piano on their shoulders. Step-for-step, dexter & sinister, they came — bulging foreheads, gog-eyed, sinewed jaws knotted with strain. Like some creature of paradox, he was caught between the unobtainable & the unrelenting. Less petrified, he might've recognised this allegory for what it was. But at that moment all hope was lost: the stairs he was climbing turned to enormous piano keys, rising & falling in gross undulations, octave upon octave:

Dun-dun-dun!

Dahda-da-dahda-dahda!

Dun-dun-dun!

Dadah-dadah-da!

Da!

Down he went, beneath the millwheel of his pursuers' feet. But then, just as precipitously, the dream turned into its opposite. Němec found himself alone, lying in bed, neither asleep nor awake. Two men in white boilersuits materialised on either side of him. They had no faces, no eyes, no mouths. As they wound the bedsheets around his body, they whispered, *Liszt, Liszt, oh Liszt!* Without warning he felt himself hoisted shoulder-high & carried pall-bearer-fashion across the room. The noise of a window being forced open. Then a rush of cold air & the sickening thrill of weightlessness. Through ice & snow, beneath the bitumen & cobblestones, down under the earth, he fell — fell & fell towards that black hole at the core of everything. And still that mad music, turning like a scratched record through the eye of God's needle.

The Worms

The worms were burrowing around him through dark emulsions, disgorging & digesting. It was a darkness more complete than any memory of darkness. Němec lay there listening. Someone hit the ▶▶ button & the worms burrowed through the soundbarrier into lightspeed. Then everything went still. For a moment he thought he was back in the infirmary at the Children's Home, that the nurse in her starched pinafore & white cap was leaning over him with a faint scent of rubbing alcohol. A tiny flashlight seemed to shine first into his left eye & then into his right. An indistinct face, as if seen from the underside of a sheet of ice, looked down at him. Then the light slid away & the stillness returned. And somewhere inside the stillness, the familiar sensation of falling again.

There was nothing left to throw up. What there had been was already smeared across his shoes. He was huddled in a doorway, staring at his hands. He couldn't feel them. Something was beating on the other side of the door. Fear propelled him onto his feet, down the steps & along the path. The beating followed him. *Idiot.* He stopped, breathed slowly so as to slow the blood in his ears. The cold burned, his teeth ached, a piercing wind-gust stung his face. Memory kicked in. Somehow he was back where he'd begun. There, across the street, was the same lamppost as before, the same snowbank, but no ghost, no dead horse. Němec coughed, there was a taste of blood in his mouth. He spat as if needing to visualise what he already knew. In the lamplight black spots appeared on the snow. The fear caught up with him again & he staggered out onto the street. The greyness opened before him, making a tunnel through the gloom. Squinting into it, he tried to get his bearings, to conjure a map of former escapes, but it was no good. The grey was unrelenting & the tunnel barely had a flicker at the end of it.

Was the particular God who created this place expecting him? Perhaps he'd arrived at the wrong time? Němec glanced back past the lamppost, half-hoping… But no, the scene with the Children's Home was already dissolving in the greyness. The street behind him led nowhere. The path ahead might lead to anything. He stopped & the greyness stopped with him. He walked on & the greyness advanced. Vague façades loomed & receded. Empty shadows blew beneath hallucinatory arcades, across dead-end intersections. Had he been offered alternatives he might've let chance take its course, but the tunnel led inexorably in one direction only.

Eventually it brought him to a ruined tramshelter, like a cave hollowed out of the snow. No-one waited there. A signpost with illegible numbers rose beside it like a future-primitive totempole or a paradox left cunningly abandoned. From here an unexpected vista opened out. There was a square with streets running into it, past buildings that sloped steeply away. Over the rooftops, the spires of St Vitus rose at an inscrutable angle, like an axis of the turning world, of invisible night-sky zodiacs. Němec steered towards them.

No sooner had he embarked on this new course than footprints appeared up ahead in the snow. He wasn't the sole survivor in this Apocalypse after all! Whoever had left the tracks might even know a way out. *Some* way. Němec trudged on after them, the road growing ever steeper. It was the struggle of the little guy against adversity, the marathon to be run against the clock, the mountain to be overcome — sound-up on the Wide World of Sports theme, softly in the background. Before very long the set of tracks he was following became two. Then three. They seemed to multiply in the eye into a whole confraternity, intersecting & branching, winding & cutting back, vanishing down alleyways only to reappear farther off, unexpectedly. Němec failed to read their meaning. It was like walking around inside an overly elaborate riddle —

the kind of riddle designed to conceal a solution that was either too obvious or didn't exist. Finally the paths, grown confused in a blind choreography, separated & never found each other again. Where were the people who'd made them? What lost tribe? Němec searched above the rooftops for the spires of St Vitus, to see if he'd gained ground, but they hadn't budged.

It might've gone on like that, endless-hours-on-end, past milestones, boundary signs, a plough, an animal hide cut in thongs, a ditch — yellow dog-stains marking canine territories — three-pronged blackbird tracks — a squirrel's hole: clues to the tenacious perseverance of species other than that to which even Němec felt a reluctant kinship — camouflaged, huddled in subsurface microclimates, hollowed tree trunks, eaves, gutters, abandoned attics. But everything that begins has an end.

Like Shackleton

Like Shackleton, trudging for days & weeks with raw bloodied feet towards some unobtainable pole. The scenery, the general layout of the district, resolutely unerring. Snowdrifts, invisible leylines of hidden crevasses, the involuted burrows, the migratory backalleys of cat & rat, the Escheresque staircase, the twisting river of fissured ice — many moons — old-man-beard midway to navel — grey leather horseface, creased & furrowed — ghostsledges & ghostdogs, howling & groaning — the wind, the unrelenting blizzard — eyes glassed-over, measuring the vanishing point of a mystic potentiality — some selfenclosed gelid orbit of Time outside all chronology, meridian lines & randomness. A drink might've helped, but no-one was offering. *Some vocation you've got lined up for yourself. Whose bright idea was that?* As if stranded in the middle of a kaleidoscope — the more Němec turned, the more everything resembled everything else, till all the images blurred behind the falling snow & static invaded the picture, from above & from all sides.

Snow in his eyes mouth ears, Němec staggered, one foot in front of the other, numb to the point of not knowing if he was even moving forward anymore or if the whole thing was being run on conked-out conveyorbelts, a cardboard scenery by fits & starts. St Vitus, his Mount of Purgatory, seemed only to be getting further away. There were bridges, empty parks, railway lines, boat horns echoing in a distance calculated to sound fake. As fake as all the corbels, trefoils, lancets, spandrels, voussoirs, vergeboards, chevrons, crockets, mouchettes, buttresses, clerestories, balustres, architraves, cupolas of this Potemkin village his mind seemed determined to erect at every turn. As fake as a city made of playing cards & balsawood, scraps of newsprint, papier-mâché, celluloid & déjà vu, bits & pieces of wrecked signage glued together, with nothing behind them but empty space. Stageprops.

'None of it's REAL!' Němec howled, coming at last to the point all this must secretly have been leading to from the very start.

But by now he was standing in front of the door to his own apartment building. How'd he manage that? The door was tilted slightly to one side. Everything, in fact, was tilted slightly to one side. Němec swayed on his feet, ankle-deep in pavement muck. The old homing-beacon still working after all, eh? He groped through pockets for a key but came up emptyhanded. Nothing to do but stare at the ends of his fingers — nails, crescent moons — *der Mond am Nagel dunkel bleibt...* Had they grown? A voice interrupted these speculations —

'Looking for anything in particular?'

From behind him came the sound of snow gritting underfoot. Němec turned to find the Prof's ghost standing in the middle of the sidewalk, snowflakes clinging to his hair, coat collar, crumpled threadbare lapel.

'A nice cosy place to put your feet up, maybe?'

The ghost's creased forehead & sinuous jaw swam in & out of focus. As usual the Prof was grinning. *Ghoulmouthed*, Němec thought. A hoarse whisper snuck out through clenched teeth, like a faucet when the water mains have been shut-off —

'You're not real either!'

The Prof scratched at the stubble on his chin.

Well d'you believe in ghosts, kiddo, or don't you?

'Ich glaube,' the ghost said smilingly. 'Aber, Ich glaube auch nicht. *To believe*, as a certain philosopher once said, *is also not to believe.* Maybe *you're* not real. Ever consider that?'

One, the Prof's grin seemed to say, *would imply the other, nicht wahr?*

'Besides,' he added, 'I'm not the one dreaming all this.'

And as he said it, he pointed at something lying at Němec's feet. It looked like a body, all crumpled up on itself. Němec blinked. He couldn't remember it being there before. Another one of the ghost's conjuring tricks. The body had snow folded around it like a dirty eiderdown. Němec peered. The face, he thought, looked horribly familiar.

Atavism

Atavism, Němec explained to himself, trying to be helpful, was the name of a primitive impulse to repeat — the vicious circle inscribed deep down in the forgotten part of the brain, in the axolotl sub-mind — which, through the dark ages of prehistory, had compelled evolution-wise the Tribe & his particular selfhood to this current impasse: an impasse you might liken to a broken amplifier at the end of a metaphoric telegraph line & a message trying to make itself heard down the eons from that first feeble gulping of air out of the evolutionary swamp to the shriek of some self-professed birdman lobbing himself from a high tower convinced he can fly. A fish casting off its gills, a man with wings: idiocies persistent enough to become the prime movers of Reason itself. But if you wanted to fly, you built an aeroplane instead of diving out a fifth-storey window debating the fine-points of gravity.

Under any other circumstances, the fact that he himself was lying on the pavement outside his apartment building's front door might've been funny. Funny or not, a weird sense of déjà vu crept in. *Yes, yes*, it seemed to say, *you've been here before, too. Been a real trip down Memory Lane tonight, hasn't it?* This other Němec reminded him of the dead horse, the way he/it was stretched out there with blank eyes staring back at *him*, & the Prof waiting to see his reaction, the skin around the Old Man's mouth taut in stifled amusement.

Němec came closer to get a better look at himself crumpled there on the ground, long enough for the joke to get stale around the edges. The Prof came over beside him & took a look as well, peering from under furrowed brows like someone observing a beetle on its back, wondering why the hell it didn't just turn itself over & get on with it. After a while the ghost cleared his throat —

'Well,' he said, 'that's one way to do it.'

'Do *what?*' Němec winced. 'Besides, where'd *you* pop up from anyway?'

The Prof stifled a yawn —

'Aber mein liebes Kind, I've been here all the time…'

Němec couldn't help feeling there was something wrong with the whole arrangement. *The point*, he thought. *What was the point?* Perhaps he was supposed to do something, kick himself in the teeth to see if he was real, attempt resuscitation, pretend he didn't exist. *Who? Him or me?* He felt the Prof's hand squeeze his shoulder.

'Don't take it so hard,' the ghost said. 'There'll always be next time.'

'…?'

The Prof let his hand drop & straightened his coat, breath hanging in the cold air. Němec shivered.

'You know,' the ghost said, dabbing at the sagging corners of his mouth with a woollen glove, 'there was a showman once, Mongo-the-Magnificent, soappellated — ever hear of him? No? Before your time I s'pose.'

Němec glanced sideways at the Prof, who was still gazing down at the shape on the pavement, no trace of humour left in his expression. It made Němec feel suddenly very tired. He wanted to laugh, to break the moment's strange solemnity, but only managed a wheezing cough.

'Well, the thing about Mongo-the-Magnif,' the ghost said, 'was he could walk around with his head tucked under his armpit. The head talked, rolled its eyes, cracked jokes, while the body went about its own business, sat, stood, danced a tango, a charleston, a softshoe shuffle, high-kicked, pirouetted, gyrated, performed one or two other buttock-squirming indecencies. He'd slot the head back on, spin it around for effect & take it off again — dress it up in funny costumes — sing folk songs, play skittles, tell limericks — recite a little Rachmaninoff here, some Rimsky-Korsakov there — the whole vaudeville routine, always showing off. No-one believed any of it was real, of course, they all reckoned it was nothing but a jukebox magician's hat-trick. Like sawing old ladies in bits & picking the pocket of the fat balding man in the second row. But it made Mongo the talk of the town nonetheless — his name in the daily papers, picture in magazines, face on posters stuck up on hoardings.'

A spasm of coughing caused Němec to double up. The Prof waited patiently before continuing —

'One day,' he said, 'a janitor at the theatre where Mongo was due to perform found him with a rope around his neck, hanging from the catwalk above the stage scenery. There was a note pinned to the front of his dinner shirt: ECCE HOMO, was all it said. No-one was sure what it was supposed to mean, though all agreed it was in questionable taste. For a while the boys at Homicide entertained the possibility of foul play — professional jealousy, a jilted lover, skeletons in the closet, a predilection for underage boys, some stigmatised sexually-transmitted disease perhaps, a split personality, a file at the Interior Ministry, an unacknowledged illegitimate child, a secret cough-syrup addiction, a minder on the make, a maker on the mend, a fatal attachment to irony, you know the rap. But nothing was ever proven.'

Němec, meanwhile, was down on his knees gasping for breath. He could barely hear what the Prof was saying anymore. Something was pounding inside his chest. He coughed again, racked by an excruciating pain. Beside him, on the pavement, his doppelgänger had turned into the vague shape of a man collapsing into himself. Němec felt his hands give way & slid over onto his back, down into the snow. The orange glow of the streetlamp made a halo around the Prof's

silhouette there up above. Němec groaned. The Prof leant down towards him &
continued the story —

'When it came to the inquest, the court had no trouble establishing the
identity of Mongo-the-Magnif's head, but who in their right mind could've
attested — beyond doubt reasonable or otherwise — that the rest of him, or
rather *her* as it turned out, was in fact the real McCoy? Habeas corpus & all that.
In addition, there was a general suspicion that *someone* had been tampering with
the evidence, made a switcheroo out of sheer spite: the conspicuous bosom, the
decidedly, *er*, female genitalia (virgo non intacta, if you must know). Bit of an
anatomical freak of nature, you might say. Some questions better left unasked.
Quit while you're ahead, so to speak. *Death by misadventure*, is all they could
agree upon under the, *er*, circumstances.'

The eyes of the ghost glistened down at Němec moistly.

'You know,' the Prof whispered, his face in sudden close-up, a strong
whiff of stale garlic, 'nothing's ever *only* in the mind...'

Němec

Němec blinked & the ghost was gone again. Where he'd stood, falling snow
flickered in the lamplight. From a great distance a sound like laughter echoed
through the night. Coming closer. Louder. Louder still. A rumble. A roar.
Thunder. The ground shuddered, the fake playing-card façades teetered, swayed.
In perfect synchronicity they all began to collapse: an ace of spades, queen of
diamonds, eight of hearts, scaffolds, dropcloths, guywires, ropes & winches, all
the backstage paraphernalia of a big production being pulled down after the final
show, wheeled away by invisible stagehands to be scrapped, put in cold storage,
rejigged for next season's main event, a fresh coat of paint slapped on here, a
stencilled silhouette there.

Němec stared up at it all. Things shifted in & out of focus — solid matter
dissolved by light — even the sky was a fake, the snow, the orange streetlamp,
nothing now but an horizon receding into paradoxical depthlessness, a milky
haze of white on white. Němec remained there on his back unable to move,
barely breathing at all now, gaping up into nothing, the non-light before
Creation. And then the nothing began to take shape, like the bottom of an
enormous elevator coming straight down on top of him, as if from a very great
height, slowly at first, then gathering speed, faster & faster. And at the last
possible moment Němec remembered something the Prof once said —

'You can hammer a nail with a samovar, but why with a samovar?'

2

The commotion began down behind the pear tree at the
bottom of the playground -- among the reeds & rushes &
speargrass that fringed the small lake: orpiment, verd
antique, russet swishing in the breeze (when there was a
breeze), though really it was just an artificial carp pond,
but "the Lake" by general consensus was how it was called,
when it wasn't "the Big Water" or less often "the
Atlantic" & only rarely "the Sea of Tranquillity," gnarly
fishmouths of varying breadths gulping at its surface,
stirring ripples among the algal blooms & duckweed &
dappled saucer-shaped lilypads, skaters dodging between,
emerald & azure dragonflies & midges ahover -- spreading
by concentric stages outwards among the clusters of
children: playing hopscotch on chalked hopscotch squares;
skipping Double-Dutch (the white ropes like two halves of
a standing wave, the visible harmonic); hanging upsidedown from monkey bars skirts flapping down from white,
pink, polkadot knickers; digging great holes with chipped
& cracked plastic spades in the musky sandpit, or else;
gathered around in the shade of the sole linden tree (the
Nerds' Club) in foureyed gravitas, much frowning &
lipchewing & headscratching, nodding wise after the fact
as they watch Rychlík, a.k.a. M-M-M-Mr Express, drag out
the endgame of a surely unwinnable Queen's Gambit (Mr E's
opponent, a tousle-haired fifth-grader with dandruff
issues, staring glassy-eyed off at some distant
unattainable vista of chess clocks & time-control), an
umpteenth Belomorkanal gone soggy between spittled lips,
shreds of tar-tobacco soldered to yellowed falsies -- &
only then, with Bobek in his drab forester's uniform
craning a head over the playground fence, to attract, it
seems best to assume, the attention of the android on
supervision roster, today winsome Miss Freudlová of the
dark ringlocks, scarlet wrap-around shawl over pennant-
blue gymsuit (despite the weather, erring to sultry,
contrary to the morning's forecast), who, woken from
untold reveries, looks up flustered from the beige-
covered paperback resting spine-on-knee which could've
been anything, a monograph on recent applications of
nutritional science or a handbook on the Ministry of
Education's SPECIAL CODE OF CONDUCT (essential reading
for aspirants to the Senior Teacher's exam) e.g., but was
in fact (as Robbo "the Rat" knew from scaling
surreptitiously the back rungs of her tennis umpire's

chair to sneak an opportunistic peek over her shoulder (&
catching a bit of unimpaired cleavage action in the
process)) an omnibus edition, volume 2, of Karel May
westerns, Old Shatterhand about to ride into an ambush,
no sign of Vinnetou to get him out of this fix... finger
poised mid-air just as she (Miss Freudlová) is about to
turn the page, a real cliff-hanger moment, interrupted by
Bobek's expressive yet incomprehensible gesturing from
the fence -- turning to see what all the ruckus is about
now that her head's no longer buried in a book & only
then taking in the unnerving spectacle of the whole
playground surging towards her in synchronicity, like a
slow-moving avalanche or mudslide she'll say afterwards
at the inquest -- even M-M-M-Mr Express, cigarette bent
in half, looking like he's been struck over the head by
something, carried along in the wake & casting helpless
entreating looks at her. In an instant the throng of
panicked children will have surrounded the tennis
umpire's chair on which she sits: "ambushed," like a swarm
of Red Indians rushing upon Old Shatterhand trapped in a
cul-de-sac at the foot of a canyon, certain death staring
him cold in the eye as the circle of braves parts to
reveal none other than the bloodthirsty warrior chief,
Awkward Buffalo, waist festooned with matted enemy
scalps, advancing knife-in-hand... But it was only the
Spastic Girl from the forth grade, ogling her with those
uncannily lopsided eyes, an expression half-beatific
half-sickly-smirk, thoroughly at odds with the looks of
horrible anticipation on the faces of all the other
children, thronging about at her feet -- stifled calls of
MISS! MISS! -- the Spastic Girl holding something up to
her now, hands cupping it darkly, a sudden & awful hush
all-round; Miss Freudlová, gripped by an immediate
apprehensiveness (the girl, frankly, gives her the heebiejeebs), though she couldn't quite make out what IT was till
the girl got closer, raising her cupped hands to the
light...
  The first to be drawn into the commotion was the ring
of boys & girls playing spin-the-bottle behind the paling
fence that ran into "the Lake" where it arched over onto
its side & lay there under the water & had been
collecting algae since the time the gully it once
traversed was dammed to make a fishpond, who knows when.
Habitually Nagel was the ring-leader on occasions such as
these, the circle of flattened paspalum behind the fence
being territory he'd marked out for the sole purpose, in
connivance with his trusty sidekicks, Robbo "the Rat"
(socalled for prominent buckteeth & the enduring fame of
having once risen to a dare to snatch Comrade Medvedev's
toupee in the middle of class & being chased by the
Russian schoolmaster around the room with a carpet
beater, scuttling under tables & between legs on all fours
like an oversized rodent, to cheers of GO THE RAT!) &

Buzík, a.k.a. Buzo, a freckle-faced Huck Finn always
talking-up big schemes to sail a raft downriver through
the East Fritzes & all the way to Hamburg, Liberty &
Uncle Sam -- a pipe-dream verging at times on obsession,
with the ginger-haired huckster devising countless plans
for every facet of The Great Escape, from dummies at
morning roll-call to tried&true methods of skipping off
on recess along the docks & making it back somehow
undetected, never failing to collect proof of these
nighttime escapades: a frayed section of mooring rope, a
metal sign with a red-painted ▼, a grimy fishing reel, a
jar of river water for "spectrographic" analysis -- while
day-by-day the painstaking accumulation of esoteric lore
on how to construct a river-worthy mode of conveyance,
one that'd actually float & not capsize or sink the moment
you set foot on it (Plan A entailing use of the fence-
palings behind which Nagel & his circle of conspirators
were at that very moment huddled, cross-lashed to forty-
gallon wine barrels scavenged from the boarded-up hotel
across the street from the Children's Home -- hoarding,
meanwhile, all the empty plastic juice bottles he could
lay his hands on, lids intact, against the day, plan B, to
be bagged & ducttaped as a makeshift, reasoning if
nothing else you could always coast down the river like
they were Lilos & the river was just one incredibly long
brown swimming pool -- dubious Boy Scout lore here,
concocted mainly from hearsay & picture books & fervid
eleven-year-old wishfulfilment) -- diligently plotting,
red circles with dots or crosses, the locations of locks &
weirs on filched navigation charts (at such points it
being rudimentary to manoeuvre said means of floatation
overground, employing ropes or possibly shopping-trolley
wheels nabbed from the local nonstop, providing he could
get his hands between now & then on a phillipshead
screwdriver & create the necessary diversion to kidnap
the trolley): Ústí nad Labem, Bad Schandau -- lying low
till nightfall then slip past the border guards,
camouflaged with reeds, willow branches, faces charcoaled,
riding the current under the shadow of the bombed-out
Frauenkirche, & onwards, ever onwards, under searchlights
& gunturrets, four-hundred clicks north to the sea…

The empty 300ml PragoCola bottle had just come to a
stop with its neck pointing straight at petite blonde-
haired Lučinka -- pony-tailed & pinafored, sandal-straps,
white knee-socks -- whose eight-year-old throat Nagel's
been itching all semester to get his tongue down, the
filthy little scallywag. Though a sixth-grader, & with a
name redolent of some ancient-of-old from a Norse saga,
Nagel erred more towards the Swabian than the
Scandinavian, romantic in a way that in later years
would simply be called short, rather like a Tyrolean
parking attendant, to compensate for which he was
constantly working at novel ways to get his stinky

finger inside some dívka's snatch. It was just as he was
inclining towards goggle-eyed Lučinka for a hot snog,
thinking to drop the hand while he had the advantage,
when from the reeds came a bloodcurdling shriek. It was
the Spastic Girl, whose bush Nagel had not many moons
before managed to stick his nose in after a quick barter,
rushing out into the circular clearing, the squelch of
mud in plastic shoes, leggings festooned with thick
verdant strings of slime. As if by reflex, hands rushing
up to her mouth (Lučinka), recoiling from this precipitous
apparition at Nagel's back -- who (Nagel) oblivious to its
cause is left with gob hanging open like a stunned mullet
(of which particular coiffure he's indeed in proud
possession), bedroom eyes narrowing ever so slightly on
the little minx, thinking this one might be a harder nut
to crack than he'd anticipated -- her (Lučinka's)
expression meanwhile sending out paradoxical signals
which only in their aftermath will he be able to fathom,
passing through states of alarm, distress,
incomprehension, terror, panic & outright revulsion, an
effect he's never quite witnessed before & concerned a
stray bogey might've slipped out onto his upper lip or
there's a great big tarantula's dangling over his head or
someone's chosen that particular M.M.I.[✋] to play a gag at
his expense, or else the kid had issues possibly stemming
from who knew what traumatic infancy… interrupted in his
train of thought by the Spastic Girl virtually stomping on
top of him, shrieking still, though its intensity lessening
(the shriek), grown hoarse, more bellow than shriek now --
the others in the circle covering their ears, wearing looks
of diverse shades of horror, fixated, as far as Nagel can
tell, by the thing she's holding in her hands. 'Jesus Christ,
what IS that…?'
 Collectively in the backs of their minds, & playing
like a TV rerun on fastforward, is a recent-enough-still-
to-be-technicolor-vivid episode in which, bawling out of
the blue in the middle of morning assembly, all blubber-
mouthed, pooey knickers down at her ankles almost
tripping her head-over-tits, the same creature presently
in their midst had, right there in front of everyone in
the main courtyard, importuned dear delirious Miss
Freudlová to PLEEEE BOOHOO wipe her bum for her, & the
mortified phys-ed instructress standing there in her
eternal gymsuit, looking as if Martians had just landed,
their leader schlüpping ectoplasmically down the
gangplank, coming straight towards, as all eyes in the
hall fixed now upon HER. But if any of those gathered
behind the paling fence, whose elicit smooching session
had thus been interrupted, was tempted in the brief
hiatus created by uncertainty -- i.e. as to WHAT the

[✋] Moment of Maximum Inconvenience. [✋]

Spastic Girl was actually shrieking ABOUT -- to breathe a
sigh of relief (at the fact, for example, that she (the
Spastic Girl) wasn't apparently threatening to dollop
fresh excrement on them), this impulse was immediately
supplanted by more primitive instincts. 'Holy shit!' gagged
Nagel, his composure having been progressively undermined
by the rapid sequence of events, any chance of diddling
doe-eyed dívkas dashed for this afternoon (though perhaps
later, in need of comforting, subsequent to what's yet to
take place, dot-dot-dot). The kid immediately to Nagel's
left could be heard barfing into the grass -- the rest,
saucer-eyed, grinning stupidly, in tears, speechless,
fainting, struggling to flee. 'Holy SHIT!' Buzík cried,
skidding to a halt & groping about for reverse, having
made a bee-line at the first sign of excitement from the
"boat shed" where, for the last hour, a stack of waterlogged palings has slowly been accumulating. 'Oh boy!'
Robbo "the Rat" chimed-in, his usual understated self.
From this point, whatever order had previously reigned in
the playground descended swiftly into chaos as the
Spastic Girl, now trailing a retinue of children by
varying degrees awestruck, confused, traumatised or, late-
comers to the unfolding drama, merely curious --
Squillhead there on the periphery, e.g. (always
peekabooing, unless he's doing his mummy-from-the-crypt
thing) -- capable in any case neither of pulling
themselves away from this spectacle nor of fully
apprehending it, proceeds (the Spastic Girl) erratically
from point A behind the pear tree, by way of the sand pit
& monkey bars, the ziggurats of chopped-up asphalt, the
pigeons scrambling for crumbs, past the Nerds Club (putting
paid, once & for all, to black's chances of forcing the
issue, checkmate in two) &, as if propelled by some cruel
atavism, some genius of injustice, straight towards (point
B) the lone & (all too plainly now in the hindsight of
retrospect) excruciatingly vulnerable figure seated aloft
in the tennis umpire's chair reading...
     In the minutes immediately preceding the commotion's
descent upon Miss Freudlová, Bobek observed the following
from behind the playground fence:
     1. the uninterrupted sound of the older boys, seventh,
eighth & ninth-graders, playing football on the patch of
dirt at the far side of "the Lake," sending up clouds of
dust wafting southerly over the bushes;
     2. the Fairinelly Twins hoisting a bucket of stones to
the top of the monkey bars where they'd established a
sniper position in an on-going skirmish with the boys in
the neighbouring linden tree armed with makeshift
slingshots;
     3. Buzík entering (so he surmised) into complex
negotiations with the Spastic Girl, involving many handsignals & gestures, to wade out into the shallow part of
"the Lake" in order to retrieve, for no immediately

apparent purpose, a number of loose palings from the
fence submerged among the rushes;

4. that idiot Rychlík* with his band of chess-playing
nerds -- how he wished something, anything (a piece of the
MIR space station wouldn't be asking too much) to fall out
of the sky on that pox of humanity;

5. some gangly five-year-old dumping the contents of
their own or someone else's satchel-bag into the sandpit
(pencils, crayons, glue stick, safety scissors, exercise
books), then methodically stomp each of them & the bag
into the wet sand all the stray cats in the neighbourhood
came to piss & crap in;

6. a lone child in a yellow raincoat, despite the
weather (sultry), standing at the edge of the playground
on a tree stump, hand clapped over ears, as wafting across
the fence came the microphoned plosives of Comrade
Deputy-Headmaster Med-the-Dev rehearsing the afternoon's
announcements, the genius after all these years still not
able to switch the PA system off while he sits up there in
his office crooning like he's Gott in Himmel;

7. two girls playing on the swings, one of whom he
suspects isn't wearing any knickers but can't quite make
his mind up on the evidence available;

8. the bold outline of Miss Freudlová's right breast
under the blue lycra of her gymsuit -- her having
absent-mindedly shrugged off the red shawl while turning
a page of her book, which (the shawl) she now readjusts,
causing:

a.) her breast to swell even further into profile, &;

b.) Bobek to experience a certain undeniable agitation
(between this & the sight on the swings -- fancying a bit
of pink flashing between the drapery, like the stuff
those Mucha hussies always seem to come wrapped in,
giving you the big eyes like they'd want nothing better
than to be rid of that ridiculous get-up & plonk down
flat on their backs, a-hold of their ankles... (Is that
STEAM coming out of Bobek's ears? Robbo "the Rat" wonders,
catching sight of the old perv getting a fistful in his
pocket & pounding away for all he's worth.))

At first the shrieks emanating from the reeds around
the carp pond conjugate the birdlike cries of pleasure he
imagines coming from the wetted lips of his at-this-very-
moment-envisaged recumbent Mucha maiden, head tossed
back, hair a mane of dark ringlets, the very picture of
her succulent Freudlovian self, as he works the end of
his nob through the frayed pocket lining, turning
slightly off-colour all of a sudden, a wrong note, THERE
IT IS AGAIN! sounding decidedly sick now, eyes unfogged,
darting back&forth with a certain desperation between
Freudlová's tit & the possibly apocryphal flash of

---

* Fast train to nowhere. [☙]

ungusseted etc., straining not to lose the momentum, FECK!
when right before his eyes the whole playground seems to
descend, FECKFECKFECKFECKFECK! -- Miss Freudlová
glancing up from her book, straight at him -- apparently
he's shouting out-loud, grimacing idiotically as he
attempts to wave with his left hand, disengaging
precipitously with the right which he begins also waving,
like a scarecrow in a gale -- just as the mob of agitated,
hysterical, one might even say DEMONICALLY POSSESSED
children begin chanting HER name, griping the legs of the
umpire's chair, shaking it -- the Spastic Girl at the
centre of it all, the source of that ungodly wail,
lurching towards... OH FECK! Bobek pulls himself away
from the fence & limps towards the gate as gamely as his
condition permits, his whole body now seemingly gone
flaccid at the sight, if only he can get there in time --
but before he's even able to reach the gate, he hears Miss
Freudlová's cry of dismay.

3

POPPYLOPPING

It all depended on how you looked at it, as to whether Jan Mydlář was (A) a tool of bureaucratic state terror, (B) an unsuspected saboteur détourning the status quo one neck at a time, or (C) just another stooge out to make a buck.[†]

Son of a Chrudim burgher, Mydlář was twentythree & a medical student when Emperor Rudolf conscripted him into the job of Golem City's preeminent poppylopper. It got his name up on the big marquee. In an age before machines & TV made serial killing, mass murder & genocide a headline statistic & death itself an abstraction, Mydlář's was indeed a métier of signal virtuosity. He was the Alice Cooper of his day & it wasn't chickens he bit the heads off. Fans queued overnight for tickets. Girls in the front-row swooned. Picture him: boots & codpiece & studded leather jerkin arrayed against the dawn, each darkly silhouetted arc & plunge of his giant axe turning the air to pure electricity. Huge plunging chords like the untelling of Creation itself. Mydlář-Cooper, demiurge of sonic voodoo, smithy of human souls, rending what first was made whole, undoing the original error, bringing the cycle to apocalyptic completion…

[†] Or (D), a confection of the Š.V.E.J.K. propaganda machine. And why not?

Mydlář was just the latest of Němec's obsessions when he happened to run into the Prof for the first time, one April afternoon, weather middling, in a courtyard of the Klementinum. Perhaps Fate had a hand in it.[*] The National Library, which was located there, housed a collection of records & suchlike pertaining to the life & career of the seventeenth-century executioner. Němec had done the paperwork & was waiting for his number to be called up so he could read what there was to be read. He figured on being there the whole afternoon. A situation like that, anything could happen…

The intention had been to construct, by whatever means came to hand, a type of life-study in words of this public assassin: Mydlář, from *infant terrible* to *bête-noir*, performance artist of the grim deed, chthonic choreographer in the solemn *pas-de-deux*. Confronted at every turn with the myth, Němec had sought to rediscover the man. He retraced Mydlář's footsteps across the City, where he slept, where he drank, who he did-in, the different faces he kept under his hood, the autistic inner monologue with his "Black Queen," his Muse, Bride of Death. How he projected a collective hidden wish: the glamour of oblivion, the orgiastic high of the Last Rites.

Němec made the rounds of the readingrooms, archives, antiquarians, mentally reconstructing Mydlář's long career from the scant evidence available. What he couldn't find, he deduced. What he failed to deduce, he invented. Long brain-curdled nights spent in a dive behind the Old Town Hall known locally as the *Chop House* — on account of one of Mydlář's machetes hung above the bar — conjuring the spirit of that most detested of men over jars of the local dishwater. Each night Němec eyeballed the rusty axeblade on the wall, working himself into a trance, travelling four centuries back through the murk of Time. The hours dragged, the unbearable visions petered-out, till in a spasm of six a.m. sunlight through nicotine-grimed windows the axe suddenly gleamed, stirring dustmotes into the apparition of a giant atop a scaffold. As if doubled over the chopping block, Němec felt the weight of that spectral presence bear down as with raised cleaver. Boldly at first he resisted the urge to pass out there & then, & with a subtle action of the wrist, emptying his glass into his mouth, might

---

[*] Though you'd never know for sure, she always keeps her mitts so damn clean. [♙]

even've switched the scene so as to witness that dismal caveat from the apparition's viewpoint, but in the end he always let the shutters come down just the way they did.

In the ensuing blackness he'd dream of the headsman's monkish composure, weighing the axe in his hands, calculating the force, the point of intersection — mind focused on the finest of lines forever narrowing, a bisected abyss in which all that can be heard is the karmic breath's slow regular in-out, diaphragm & thoracic volume, the cosmic respiration — then heave, in a single motion, the accelerated pendulum-swing, fifteen kilos of cold-forged Ostrava steel, its centrifugal fugueform, its whistling blade's cadenza as it cleaves air heavy with expectation — falling, through Zeno-infinities of pure paradox, sixteen silent frames-per-second upon that ever-divisible (ever-derisible?) point where topsy-turvy Tempus Edax balances on one foot juggling an applecart with the other: the "event-horizon" of this little stand-up routine done lying down.[*]

It was a lottery where he'd wake up. If the brain still worked & circumstances conspired, perhaps picturing himself in Mydlář's place: lying awake in the Torture House by the Old Zhiddish Cemetery, beside that well-fed snoring wife of his, squinting through a hangover at pre-dawn coming through the bedroom window — then, as silently as possible, so as not to disturb the as-yet slumbering household (of whom, in this morpho-Mydlář's solitary way of thinking, he's somehow embarrassed, as a pariah would be by some untoward act of human charity — Alžběta, the young wife, their two boys, Honzík & Vašek, waiting to follow in father's footsteps, *Just like you dad!*) — ruminating his breakfast of cold porridge — honing, meditatively, the wide blade of his axe, whispering to it, the way he sometimes imagined whispering to a beloved, one perhaps among the widows of men slain by his own hand (Mydlář's, not Němec's) in cold blood (that juice of such curious properties), who alone of all womanhood might guess the depth & complexity of his untrammelled soul — shaving at a basin in his nook under the stairs by candlelight, weird shadows playing about his eyes, haunted by demons of obsolescence — then performing the antique ritual of his vestry:

---

[*] What the naked eye would actually have seen: shaved neck, flesh, muscle, vertebrae, cartilage — the severed oesophagus, the spliced Adam's apple, the minimed anima & puncted pneuma, the devowelling of the last word — *thud!* & echo, tumbrelling, *thud!* axehead & head, into chopping block & bucket. *As if the wind had blown their Kopfs from their Schulters...* On that point, all the written accounts agreed. But Němec wanted more. Not the public mask of the executioner, but the man behind it — not the mechanic of death, but the other thing: was there an *other thing*? [✋]

the trademark black leather leggings with sweat-brined codpiece,

the platformed black kneehigh boots,

the black stiff-gauntleted leather gloves,

the sable cloak that tickled his earlobes —

an also black leatherbound translation of Wycliffe clandestinely tucked in breast-pocket (heretical keepsake from the amorted anatomist, Jesenský) —

solemnly unfolding the coarse Klan-hood from its place in the lowest drawer of his dressing table, draping it from the crook of his left arm, like the priest of the Eucharist —

the killing axe in its wooden travel-case clutched, righthanded —

key in the lock, pausing at the front door to glance once more around the way someone embarking upon a long journey does, unsure of when or if they'll ever return...*

---

* Mydlář's lot was to wield his dread instrument for no fewer than three Emperors of Holy Rome. Two years not yet deceased, & already Rudolt found himself usurped by brother Matthiass who, in turn barely at death's door, was about to be supplanted by cousin Ferdík, a despised Papist [Ferdinand II, King of Bohemia 5 June 1617 - 15 February 1637, Holy Roman Emperor ✋], denounced, *in absentia*, by a mob of Hussite rentiers, class of 1618. With all the ire of precedent on their side, these twelve angry men tossed Ferd's proxies (substitutes for a substitute) — Martinitz, Slavata, Fabricius — arse-over-tit out a high castle window, only to be borne (if they said so themselves) safely 'pon angels' wings to a soft landing in a pile of providential horsedung, dumped that morning contrary to City ordinances at the bottom of a dry moat, official inquiry pending. By thus refuting Ferd's claim & instead preferring his anagrammatical antagonist Fred-the-Fifth, a bootable Calvinist [Frederick V, King of Bohemia 26 August - 8 November 1620, Elector Palatine ✋], the hotheaded men of the hour, unbeknownst to their mob-self, had just struck the first blow in a brawl that'd ravage fair Europa with sword, bullet, famine & pestilence, till ended in the very place it began, thirty years post-facto, when — in the tricentennial year of 1648 [i.e. of the Great Man's *annus mirabilis*, Charles IV, 1348 ✋] — an army of Protestating Swedes was driven from that self-same Castle-on-the-Anthill (whose comicbook fenster-fuckings were more worthy of levity than Leviticus) by a rabble of university students [? ✋].

Between whiles, with the brawl in its early days, Mydlář experienced a minor revelation, finding himself one day in all innocence tripping towards one of History's precipices — father of an executioner-dynasty, the great craftsman of the humanistic hatchetjob brought face-to-hooded-face with the spectre of obsolescence, immanent as machine-death & more efficient than any executioner's nightmare, which one day would evolve into a hydra with six million heads — Hollerith punch-carded & routing-sheeted from here to eternity. The vision made no sense to him & he promptly forgot all about it, but somewhere the seed of an idea was sown.

After the Papist victory at the Debacle of Whitey Mountain, 1620, it was Mydlář of course (by now playing the stadium circuit under new management, Apoplectic Ferd & Partners) who was tasked, like a human guillotine, with the serial execution of the twentysix vanquished Prod aristos [half of them, the lesser worthies, had their necks stretched with a rope ✋] — & a twentyseventh: Mydlář's mentor-of-old, the presently unfashionable anatomist, disgraced University Rektor & vile collaborationist, "J.J." Jesenský — feet shackled, hands cuffed behind back, glopping in the solstice glare of the five a.m. morning sun as he takes his turn at the foot of the Altstädterring clocktower.

One thing leading to another…

It was while waiting at the Klementinum for the dossier on Mydlář to be delivered to the Reading Room, that Němec happened to wander out into one of the courtyards, idly deciphering the sundials that ornamented its walls. LAVDIBILE NOMEN DOMINE someone had painted on a white scroll beneath the first of them. Beneath the second: A SOLIS ORTV…? On the north wall, a date, in Roman numerals: MDCLXII. Before incorporation into the University during the 1770s, later becoming the National Library, the Klementinum was a Jesuit college & bastion of the Counter-Reformation — so

---

J.J.'s particular treason? To've speechified at the pretender False Freddie's coronation, for which crime Jesenský's tongue also to be cut out & nailed to his head (but why end there? why not the fingers, also, which held the pen that wrote the oration? & the toes & feet on which he stood to deliver it? the age-distended scrotum of his outlived manhood? the eyes with which he read? the basal ganglia of his treasonable consciousness?). The traitor's remains, thence quartered, to be cast in a ditch along the road to Kutná Hora, his head displayed side-by-side with the other unfortunates' in a cage hung from the western tower of Charles Bridge, flyblown, baked red in the July sun like Chinese lanterns (ah, but not Frederigo's: he, playing the Winter King to encores elsewhere, had fled the city at the first whiff of trouble — landless in unelected exile, agent of the conniving Stuart, James I & VI, outwitted & outmanoeuvred — in a word, *fallacious* — yet, was it mere comedy of coincidence or more, that in blighted soup-foggish Londinium an unlucky seven years hence, to honour Fred's Falstaffian nuptials — with the catholic Stuart's daughter no less, lisping Lizbeth of behoved Bohemia, so-styled — the eminent Shagsbeard, costumed toady to queenly kings, purviewed his once-witty though soon grown wearily witless *Winterish Tale*?).

A decade following Faltz's fall at Rokycany & the routing of the Swedish regiment at Breitenfeld, memory of the twentyseven martyrs of Whitey Mountain palled as Mydlář's son & heir, Jan Jnr., hacked & hanged his way through an entire regiment of defectors. It took two days, from sun-up to sun-down, corpses dangling in the winter trees all the way to Litohlavy, snow crowning them like the stone heads of the saints on Charles Bridge.

And as more years pass, picture old obsolete Mydlář, well past his come-back date, body racked by the disease of his trade, enfeebled, incontinent, unable to dignify itself for that last climb to the front stage — barred by unholy pact from taking the easy way out, not till the last pathetic feeble stroke, down on his knees, puking into the proscenium, the last three-chord hoorah that's never any fun 'cause it just keeps on repeating itself — outliving, somehow, even the infamy, the evasions in the street, the hex above the door — hunched back & walking cane, urchins laughing at his heels now whenever he tries to sneak out for a quiet pint at U Kalicha — *Going to the barbers old man?* — he's so used to the line he even lipsyncs to it as he goes along, tossing them boiled sweets in the vain hope they'll still cheer him on, a sideways toothless grin, coming-over all grandfatherly & *wouldn't-hurt-a-fly*, but who's kidding who? They'll rig a gallows in the oak tree up on the hill, his little sidewalk acolytes, for a makeshift swing — chase cats with blunted meat-cleavers — roll metal hoops under horses hooves — invent games that never end well, but good for a laugh at someone's expense, those halfpint converts to the Church of Murder-in-Jest & Latterday Švejks.

those sundials were put there at least half-a-century *after* Kepler had demonstrated his laws of planetary motion & almost *two* centuries after Šindel built that mechanised astrolabe on the Altstädterring — stubbornly holding to a more elemental technology.[*]

It brought to Němec's mind, for one reason or another, the Jesuit philosopher Descartes who famously said, *and so something which I thought I was seeing with my eyes is in fact grasped solely by the faculty of judgement which is in my mind*, & who, by no coincidence, served with the Catholic army at the Battle Whitey Mountain. It wasn't easy to envisage the somnolent philosopher among the Duke of Bravuria's private entourage, there under the clocktower, witness to the beheadings: seeing tongueless Jesenský forced to kneel, on a horsehair cushion before the high block — Mydlář, from behind his black mask, eyeing the crowd with unperceived apprehensiveness — the scientist's lopped head (blood spurting ketchup-red from sliced vein & severed artery) held up by the hair so it might survey the decapitated body, its prostrated former-self, proof most material if proof were indeed required of the dire causalities lately befallen it. Like clockwork. And Monsieur Descartes, methodically reasoning the weight & velocity of the axehead, the torque at the locus of its downward arc, the aftershock & delay, eight seconds approximately, before the final lapse of consciousness, the pineal eye, into blind eternal night — unsuspecting that twentythree years hence, he himself, his entire life's labour, from the *Compendium Musicæ* to the *Musicæ Compendium*, would be most gravely condemned by the Pope his former master to the *enfer* of the Index of Prohibited Books.

It was midafternoon, towards four o'clock, but the shadows on the sundials were inscrutable. After a little while Němec grew bored trying to decipher them & let his attention wander to the Baroque fountain centring the courtyard. Three Caryatids stood in a shallow pool with a stone basin on their heads: black water trickled over them. The pool itself formed a gammadion of interlocking shadows. Perched on its rim, partly obscured by potted shrubbery, a pair of elderly gents in shirtsleeves were playing a game of chess on a tiny magnetic chessboard. There was something precarious about the whole enterprise, not least because it seemed that at any moment all the pieces might come unstuck. The two men were playing a variation on the socalled King's Indian & black had made grave misjudgements about the timing of his adventure. Fingers hovered midair — forehead creased, shoulders sagging beneath a grey woollen vest — black was the

---

[*] But what more perfected automaton than a sundial? [✎]

very picture of that Eternal Apostate upon whom a very belated awareness of the Inevitable has only begun to dawn, while still clinging to the idea of some ingenious, impossible reprieve — like Scheherazade of the Thousand&One Nights. Or Custer, facing his Last Stand.

By contrast, black's opponent sat there with eyes lidded in Zenlike detachment. Had black not chosen that moment to concede, Němec most likely would've left the two men to their game & perhaps never've crossed paths with either again. But Chance played one of her little tricks & black, in a flurry of sudden gesticulations, lurched from his chair & rushed off as if reminded of an urgent engagement. So it was quite natural, then, wasn't it, that white's gaze, as he looked up, should fall squarely upon Němec, who just so happened to be at hand? And, *being* at hand, it was quite natural that he should be invited, by a vague yet efficient sign language, to take the now empty place at the board.

Having nothing better to do while he passed the time, Němec decided to humour the old man. And so he sat down.

In the Children's Home there'd always been a group of boys playing chess with the Russian teacher in the study room — they called him Mr Express on account of his taking so long over each move it was impossible to get him into checkmate before the next period bell rang. It was a way to earn exemption from the daily sports regimen, provided you could stomach the smell of the Belomorkanals M-M-M-Mr Express chainsmoked morning-to-night. But it was only later, after Němec'd run away from the Home, that he first learned how chess wasn't just about killing time.

His initiation, so to say, into the noble art occurred one morning on the train to Brno. Back just after the Revolution it was possible to ride as far as Jihlava before the ticket collector came around. Some days, when it was raining & there was nothing better to do, Němec would ride back & forth on the same hundred&twenty kilometres of track, reading some book he'd relieved the Municipal Library of, giving himself an education. On one of these journeys he found himself opposite an unusually tall baldheaded man in a green forester's uniform & wearing a skewed priest's collar that peeked out from behind the undone top button, like a tape getting the measure of his neck...

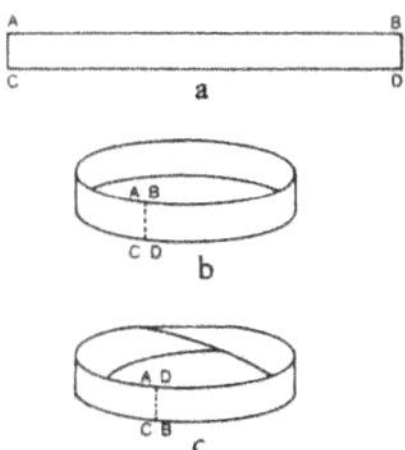

Baldy sat there smelling of week-old sweat, halfstooping like a camel in his seat — knees turned-out on either side of the folddown tray-table — the fogged window, the tiny metal ashtray overflowing with butts. Balanced on one of these knees was a plastic chessboard the size of a matchbox with holes in it for the tiny round-pegged pieces to stand in. The lanky giant caught Němec staring & asked if he'd care to play a game. Němec put his face back in his book, but the queer priest kept talking at him anyway, in a voice full of unbalanced intensity. The man reminded Němec of Bobek, the idiot savant caretaker who lived in the basement of the Home & talked to the trees &, like Baldy-the-Priest, wore a forester's uniform.

'Were you aware,' the man grimaced, 'that the Ancients who devised the rules of chess did so in the belief they were calculating the future? It's true. In India, long ago, their holymen considered the warring of opposite forces to be the source of all creation — black&white — good&evil — time, space, matter, *energy*! The game of chess, held by the Ancients of Days to be sacred, was really an *infinity machine* computing all the variables, all the possible outcomes, all the paths of evolution & extinction, as the very Mind of God!'

Němec was in no doubt the man was cracked.

'Are *you* a believer, my son?' the priest asked.

His breath, Němec couldn't help but notice, stank of pickled herring — it mingled with the smell of perspiration like Dead Sea brine. Němec glanced apprehensively as the priest tipped forward, leaning ever-closer. *Yes*, Němec thought. *Exactly like Bobek*. The man grinned with a row of blackened teeth.

'Pythagoras, the Greek,' his face barely inches away by now, 'speculated that the will of God is communicated in the form of geometry. There're patterns in the universe which appear with *unerring consistency* — from these, the outward forms of all things may be derived. The value of π, for instance — from "p" for *periphereia* — being the ratio of the circumference (K) of a circle to its diameter

(D).[*] Or the — whatsitcalled — *cosmological constant.* Chess reveals that *this* is what intelligent men have always *really* meant when speaking of a Creator. Chess, my young friend, is the blueprint of all the possible worlds from which Creation itself flows forth!'

Blueprint? Creator? Pseudo-Bobek tapped an index finger on the tiny chessboard balanced on his knee. His mouth exhaled rancid fishinesss —

'Every one of the squares on this board has its own unique existence in time & space. Like you & or me it has a name & a face. It has its own individual *personality.*'

The priest grimaced again & leant even closer, one hand touching Němec's left knee. His touch made Němec shudder, but you react, he thought, & these weirdos'll just take it as an invitation.

'Each square,' the priest spoke now in hushed but urgent tones, 'is singular in its essence, yet in its outward aspect appears identical to every other square. Thirtytwo black, thirtytwo white. Each bounded on two sides, on three sides, or on four — but never on one side alone. Never *un*bounded. Each open to its other, its double, its counterpart — the one to the two, the two to the three — the duality to the dialectic, the trinity — & from the trinity to the hidden tetragram. Just as each *piece* is not merely a *part*, but a *multiplicity* — without doing anything it already represents an array of potentialities, a visible dimension bound to other unfathomed dimensions, in space *and* in time…'

Němec stifled a yawn. After a while the priest let his hand slip away & re-arranged the pieces on the board, a wistful smile unbalancing his face even more.

'Having mastered the elements,' Baldy murmured so only Němec could hear, 'a correct method will enable the initiate to trace the connections & interactions between them, so that the whole may be perceived according to that controlling principle of unity-in-diversity…'

The priest advanced a pawn towards the centre of the board.

'It is now,' he purred, 'your move…'

Ten years further down the line, facing the old man in the Klementinum courtyard while the plash of the fountain hypnotised the air, Němec reached

---

[*] Approx. 3.14159. [♆]

across the board to make the exact same move as the priest had made. The old man advanced his opposing pawn. Němec continued with the set play, but something peculiar seemed to be happening. For each of Němec's moves, the old man made an identical, mirroring one: pawn / pawn, knight / knight, knight / knight, bishop / bishop, pawn / pawn. Gradually the mockery of it began to unnerve him. Every advance, every exchange of pieces, produced an identical result, like the symmetrical dance of a pair of signifying monkeys.

Němec felt compelled to break the pattern, to introduce an element of disharmony. Wild gambits & dubious sacrifices followed. The old man's composure seemed to waver. He hesitated. He scrutinised the arrangement of the pieces on the board. His moves became more tentative the more reckless Němec's own became. And then, without his knowing how it happened, the game came abruptly to an end. Graciously the old man proposed a rematch & then another. Němec, unsure why, accepted & together they rehearsed several more desultory setpiece openings, thwarted middle games & debauched endgames, always to the advantage of Němec's opponent.

While they played, the old man reminisced about this & that — the world as it once was, people he'd known (*Did you ever see that film, with soandso?*) — memorable games he'd played (once, many moons past, forcing a draw from the illustrious chess master & communist spy, Luděk Pachman[*]) — the present state of the philharmonic (unbearable!) — Thomas Mann (ditto) — quaternions & differential calculus (!!) — the ancient science of numerology (?!?). Then abruptly he broke off & gave Němec a long appraising look from beneath a pair of owlish grey eyebrows. Němec returned the old man's look expectantly.

'Hájek,' he finally said, proffering his hand.

Like the icecream cones, Němec thought. *Hájek & Boušová.* Soft banana, strawberry, fruit of the loom, raspberry ripple, triple scoop. *Ovocný Světozor. Zmrzlina Praha…*

'My name,' the old man explained, 'I don't believe we've been introduced.'

'Němec,' said Němec, reciprocating.

'Ah,' the old man nodded, as if there was something meaningful in it.

In the City, Němec considered, you met people all the time without ever knowing who they were. Why should *he* be any different. One name or another, it was all the same to him. They talked for a little longer, or rather this Hájek talked. Němec found listening to him strange. The old man spoke in a quaint

---

[*] Codename "PRAVDA," StB agent no. 22632. [✋]

days-of-yore austrohungarianised dialect — a grammar of exile, half a century removed. Despite himself, Němec grew curious.

As the old man soliloquised, his hands fidgeted with a small notebook. Němec's eyes followed the movements of his fingers as they turned the pages, hunting for something he never seemed to find — page after page filled with minute annotations, diagrams & a kind of Old World chess algebra. This Hájek, Němec supposed, was possibly one of those autistics you were liable to come across in public parks, solving crossword puzzles at four in the morning, pockets stuffed with grubby newsprint, train tickets, lottery cards, each notable for some auspicious date, or containing — somewhere — the multiple of a prime number, or a reference to the colour blue.

His interest beginning to wane, it was just as Němec was mentally preparing excuses to get away, thinking of the book on Mydlář he'd requested at the Reading Room but not wanting to mention it in case of further convoluted talk, when the old man started whistling to himself. It was a theme from Mahler's second symphony, the "Resurrection," in C^m. La-si-sol-fa-la-do-la… *Der Mensch liegt in größter Pein!*[*] Taken by surprise, & with no heed to potential consequences, Němec found himself joining in.

---

[*] Or "Not." ♮

4

THE PRODIGAL

An indifferent morning sometime in March. Year: 1948.

Beneath an open window, in the courtyard of the Foreign Ministry, Jan M, son of the Cheskoslovnikian Republic's founding father* is discovered spreadeagled in an advanced state of rigor mortis — the corpse too stiff, too composed, to look natural, one hand outstretched, clutching the air — socks with little black elasticised suspenders, cravat, red silk dressinggown over blue&white striped flannel pyjamas — a minor footnote to a minor History.*

Official verdict: Suicide.

Another widow, another orphan.

No witnesses to say otherwise, of course: somatic shapes drifting out of the City's sleep, a face in a window, the bells of St Vitus tolling the hour through coalblacked streets. By a wry coincidence, the bathroom whose window M has apparently thrown himself from during the night is the exact same bathroom formerly reserved (seems like only yesterday) for the "Blond Beast" — that laconic & well-remembered Reichsprotektor (acting), R.T.E. Heydrich. By a further & equally wry coincidence, sure to be remarked upon more than once in the following days & weeks, it happens that the late M's late garrulous *pater familias* (while yet still only a measly teaching assistant in the Phylactery Faculty of Charles University & before the said M's having been so much as a twinkle in the firmament of his matka's Brooklyn-blue eyes (the unblushing virgin that she was)) once penned a forgettable dissertation entitled *Suicide as a Mass Phenomenon of Modern Civilisation*.

Call it a sign of the times. Any minute now the whole nation'd be doin' it.

Doin' it, doin' it.

For M, at any rate, the hour hadn't been long in coming: never much more the Man of Destiny than a Venetian blind is, which a simple fidgeting of strings can open or shut, to let in the full glare of daylight or cast an oblique

---

* As in *Ma-sa-ryk*, T.G. [☝]
* All of which is completely true, if you discount the suspenders, the cravat, the sartorial dressinggown… [☝]

inner gloom (one day the blind stops working, the strings get stuck, the slats skew sideways & the whole contraption of pulleys & springs has to be tossed out, reinvented, replaced, with all the determination & inevitability of Progress, of the dialectical-materialist march of Reason, of the One True Etcetera). But he who's unable or refuses to stand aside from the path of Progress, Reason & the One True Etcetera? Can always be putsched ✒ hahaha.

Here the drama indicates an aside, a Polonius-moment behind an arras, a fly-on-the-wall's P.O.V. of the unfolding situation: picture an office in the Castle with filing cabinets & desk, behind which, ear glued to telephone, hunches M's nemesis, paternal supplanter (so to speak), usurper of the royal prerogative, Claudius to his Hamlet-father, satyr to Hyperion, the man sent not to praise but to bury him — Stalin's puppet, Klem Gottwald — already penning his moniker on a batch of arrest warrants as he sings —

When I left my home and family,
my mammy said to me:
Son, it's not how many Krauts you kill,
but how many poor souls you set free.

So I packed my bags, brushed my cap,
ran as far as I could go —
and found a cosy place to nap
till the last act of the show.

I wore a rose for Božena Němcová
in the summer of '45 —
when we rode into Golem Town,
and raised the red flag high!

Now we've packed away the do-gooders
all off to Terezín —
and strung the rest up by the neck,
to show 'em what "patriot" means!

Oh, mammy, mammy, I love youuuuuu!
I'll save the nation, don't you fret!
I'll make you proud of your little pet!
I promise I'll be truuuuuue!

Fastforward to the coronation scene: Gottwald in the Presidential suite flanked by grinning cronies, Vlado Clementis & Rudolf Slánský — they're breaking out the Bolinger & caviar, entertained by a troupe of little Red Army cheerleaders in brown mini-shorts, beige stockings, Cossack boots — albastone-bright flash of sturdy thigh — breasts bobbing & swaying in the glare of a dozen chandeliers. Some wit has put an Offenbach recording on a wind-up gramophone & now there's a lot of high-kicks & jaunty leg-wagging, all in jest of course — a little joke at the expense of the outmoded bourgeoisie, blind in sheer denial of the historical forces even now overrunning them.

'Our victory on the road of Revolution has been won!' Gottwald bellows, slapping his thigh.

Slánský grabs hold of the nearest cheerleader & whoops her into his lap, pinching a nipple to shrieks & giggles. Clementis finds the whole thing gut-clenchingly funny, but Gottwald goes on bellowing all the same, oblivious apparently to the effect all this is having on his moment of gravitas —

'But we shall continue our fight against Philistinism! There are still men in official positions today who haven't the least idea of the spirit of Revolution. We shall ruthlessly get rid of them if they dare try to put their reactionary ideas into practice! For WE are the incorruptible guardians of the fulfilment of the Revolution!'

Another champagne cork POP!s & ricochets between the chandeliers, like a pinball earning bonus points, before whizzing out of nowhere to hit one of the Red Army cheerleaders PING! in the eye — a redhead who, stunned for a moment, just stands there, knock-kneed, mouth doing a Clara Bow pout that has Clementis even more in stitches. There's a good chance *someone's* spiked his drink, but they're not letting on. Who cares? It's three years to the day since the Nazis got the boot & the last democretinously elected parliament of Cheskoslovnikia has just rubberstamped the Ninth-of-May Constitution — anointing thusly this most high & hallowed first Gottwaldian dynasty. Oh yes, there's plenty to celebrate.

On such a day as this a young graduate, name of Tomáš Hájek (Jnr.) — son of an archivist of identical name (Snr.), formerly of the National Literary Museum, since 1942 deceased, cause of death: severe trauma of the spinal column with brainstem separation — sets off south-by-southeast on a diesel train for Schnitzelstadt, his personal muses in tow: Alžběta Seifertová, his soon-to-be wife, & Elsbeth von N____, their mutual companion, daughter of Eldrich von N____, son of Gaspar von N____, late of Greiffenberg, Silesia, where they used to make dancing puppets before the Bolsheviks came.

Picture them: fugitives in black&white *à la* Carol Reed, hours waiting at the border, the by-now routine cross-examinations, sweating it out in sardine-canned thirdclass compartment, the stale garlic & pork sausage stench of exhaustion, cheek-by-jowl with fleeing Hungarians, Italians, Romanians — identity papers of dubious provenance, blackmarket passports, exit visas — armed with a dozen different vocabularies for baksheesh payable in Neutral Swiss francs, Bolshevik roubles, Imperialist pounds sterling, Capitalist dollars hidden in shoes, cloth caps, brassieres… — the guard's sour vodka breath, eyes redrimmed scrutinising each of their faces as he deliberately smudges the stamp on their transit passes to destinations more remote — the felt unease of a subterfuge about to be undone — panicked thoughts flashing back to other train journeys, other border-crossings — anxiety mounting to outright suspicion at the sound of the conductor's whistle — *It must be a trick! They can't really be letting us get away with this?*

And as if on cue, a branch-line comes into view with cattle-cars backed up as far as the naked eye can see — sweating faces visible through the slatted doorways, illegals & undesirables to be shipped back for reprocessing north to Terezín or south to Mauthausen — the old Nazi holiday camps doing overtime in the name of redemption, reparation & the revamped National Idea. They're shunted past sidings crowded with the women & children who've waited sleepless days & nights for a train, & will be made to wait a while longer yet — loose piles of confiscated luggage spilling from the backs of drab troop transports — the Displaced Persons enclosure with faces peering out from blankets behind a crosshatching of barbed wire — snaking lines of Sudeten refugees advancing slowly on foot along disused tracks overgrown with nettles — morose guardtowers keeping watch over scorched-earth Landschaften strewn with war wreckage…

One-by-one the depressing bits of scenery slip from sight like set-designs dragged offstage by hands unseen, till what's left are the longed-for rolling apple-green pastures, Christmas-tree groves & quaint little farmhouses strangely undisturbed by the total absence of livestock. Gradually a sense of relief comes over the compartment's motley of escapees — but not for long — as the greenery peters-out into military encampments, once more giving way to doubt & the renewal of apprehension — & from apprehension to foreboding as the train shunts from one Occupied Zone to the next & back again, causing everything to be repeated, the whole rigmarole of passports checked, visas stamped, selective confiscations & the general whittling away of the bribe economy, till they're left bartering cufflinks, earrings, bread, old pairs of boots.

Their tormentors would like nothing better than to spit in all their faces — these parasites, fleas jumping ship — to put the boot in, get each of them alone in the baggage car for a bit of good cheer, eh? A truncheon in the kisser, a rifle-butt in the arse, a bit of the ol' rape&rapine. Even when all's said & done there're still permissions to approach, supplications to be made, the public apology for one's very existence, atonement for crimes committed, real or imputed, by virtue of race or class or a wrong facial feature — seeing themselves, the stigmata of a guilty conscience, handed over to a mob on any one of the dozen station platforms they've already passed — heads shaved, tarred & feathered, paraded through the streets, pelted with excrement, the long shadow of doubt & accusation they'll never be allowed to crawl out from under, when even to've survived's a criminal offence: life's from-now-on (when will it end?) little whormiliations.

SCHNITZELSTADT SÜDBAHNHOF

A sight for sore eyes. Hard to believe they've actually arrived — a hundred miles in a hundred hours, Golem City a lifetime away by now, they'll hardly recognise themselves, or it, ever again. Climbing down onto the platform like the disembarkation from the Ark — how it must've felt all those ages ago, forty days & nights believing the world had come to its Final End, when, just about to give up, there's little old God on his mountain-top, perched above the waves, grinning like a one-man welcoming committee — *Nice day for it, what?*

They stand there clutching their bags, breathing in the atmosphere of diesel & wishfulfilment as the other passengers push on past in a rush to get somewhere or just away from where they've been. At the end of the platform a pair of day-labourers is hauling down an eight-foot-high banner —

WILKOMMEN! BIENVENUE! WELCOME!

— rain&soot-streaked, dangling red on white from the gloom of coalblacked glass & steel girder — greyed & fraying tricolour, unionjack, stars&stripes bunting — leftovers from some brass-hat's last visit, in further evidence of which: a bandstand with sagging red, blue & white crêpe, the odd trampled bit of yellow streamer, drifts of confetti tending eastward across the concourse. Even the second-hand on the station clock looks worn-out & at any moment about to expire.

The instant the train disembarks, a human tide surges along the platform, pushing & shouting, hoisting baggage aloft — whatever remains of it — onto shoulders, heads, to squeeze through, every specimen of humanity suddenly & most redolently *there* — informers scanning the faces of the newly arrived, undercover agents, military cops, widows & orphans waiting for husbands & fathers still unreturned, Zionist middlemen, blackmarketeers, hawkers, scam-artists, taxi drivers, pickpockets & panhandlers, birds of prey on the lookout for carrion, rag&bones men, the hopeful & the homeless. Opposing tides mingle, eddy, knots of turbulence smoothing out into flows that carry onwards & outwards, to the streets, the tram lines, the Belvedere Gardens grey-silhouetted in feeble afterduskings — a couple of lost souls here & there floundering about, a blind-beggar rattling a tin cup, a one-armed, one-legged War veteran dragging himself from bin to bin, stump doing a bit of a Charleston as he digs through the trash, & over there a pair of scrofulous street urchins in oversized lederhosen going into a — *yep* — barefoot tapdance & even whistling a tune from *Easter Parade*.

It's the cue for the station master, conductors, porters, train drivers & engineers to enter from the wings singing the chorus from *We're a Couple of Swells*, but the soundtrack isn't working, so you're stuck having to make do with a bit more realism instead — shades of drab & grey, starved faces, rats scuttling along the tracks, a man's suitcase spilling open full of old newspapers, altercations that melt away as soon as they begin, the weary settling onto benches, the unsuspecting into shady lockerrooms where who-knows-what illicit deals are at this very moment being transacted.

Standing apart from all this you watch & wait, getting the situation into a type of perspective, sizing-up the immediate options — behind you now the Parkinson's stammer of a departing locomotive, a megaphone's hiss & feedback. The city's unfamiliar, but not because you haven't been here before — the War's changed everything, the whole place a wreck, unlike where you've just arrived from (all the barricades taken down, might never've been there, the Old Town Hall a wreck but the rest standing firm, more or less, as far as appearances are concerned). There's a rationale in all this, an almost contrived senselessness you're barely able to grasp — the entropy of political stand-off, where everything else is left in abeyance, crypto fascists under every rock, Stalinist double-dealers, Opus Dei — camouflaged in plain view by the general dungheap mess the POWs have been set to work cleaning up — it'll be decades before the Fog of

War clears & even then… There're other places, too, cities caught in the same suspended animation, vivisectioned, just like this one — zones of chthonic reterritorialisation, joined by an invisible meridian, telluric currents that flow deep under Mitteleuropa, along an axis from Trieste to Berlin, disturbed only by the last piece in the Nazi puzzle not falling into place. Golem City. It's necessary for the adepts of the new order to seek sanctuary elsewhere, under cover of the Zone — to bide time, await the Resurrection.

Here, in the bowdlerised Ostmark capital — with its demi-Dietrich ennui & untermonde-chic, its black markets & counterintrigue & bureaucratic miasma — Hájek & his two merry muses eek-out whatever can be called under such circumstances a living. Dignity has its price, but it isn't very high. Things the years will ameliorate & even banish from memory for now at least are bread & butter on the table. Under cover of the university, *Alma Mater Rudolphina*, Hájek advances his studies in the occult drama of human desire. Adept of the crafts of procurement & supply, he begins charting a secret terrain within the city, underground passageways, buried caches of those who'd died or fled or made to disappear, hidden museums, archives, libraries, catacombs into which the scrolls of the great bookkeepers had been smuggled during the deportations.

The university itself, with its front of respectability for a man who's long since ceased to sleep, lies on the Ringstrasse in the grey International Zone, under the monthly rotated authority of the Four Powers: it's a question of keeping to the cracks, working the faultlines, buying, extorting or stealing when necessary the documents that one-by-one will put them (Hájek & co.) finally beyond reach of the Bolsheviks. Legal in all the most pejorative senses of the word, certified non-collaborators, citizens in good standing, owners (on paper at least) of several properties in the British Sector…

The whole city's a stage for this little pantomime on its eight-year run (till the allied occupation finally comes to an end & Hájek's fortunes with it). Across the Donau Kanal, the bombed-out Prater with its majestic ruin of a ferriswheel surveys the ancient moribund city — Orson Welles, meanwhile, rehearsing the infamous *Third Man* cuckoo-clock scene, faked in a London studio left somehow unscathed during the Blitz. Who knows what could be taking place, what plots being hatched, what conspiracy thwarted in the room next door, in the drains & sewers beneath your feet — that man or woman reading a newspaper, stirring a cup of coffee, gripping a leather strap on the tram & glancing towards you with enough ambiguity in the gesture to set your nerves on edge — a zither playing inconspicuously in the background. Nothing's what it seems. Subsistence by constant deception…

> *They call me Harry Lime,*
> *but I haven't got a dime —*
> *I just came from my own funeral,*
> *the sermon was quite beautiful,*
> *but as for the company*
> *it had much to be desired…*

While not very far away, in an obscure village on the Lüneburg Heath (at the very time Hájek is leveraging a free pass) one Adolf Eichmann, chief technician of the Final Solution, a.k.a. Otto Eckmann, is busy penning his memoirs in neat tiny script on engineers' quadrille paper, about to decamp for Rome & Bishop Hudal, the Nazis' Mr Fixit, thence — in the guise of one Ricardo Klemens (or Clemens, as an Argentine immigration official will later record on his residency visa), mechanic by trade — embarking on a forged Red Cross passport for Buenos Aires & a smalltime job (the lowest of low-key) at the local Mercedes Benz plant…

Blitz the highways in our new
four-door 170V Cambrio-Limousine,
with full-length foldaway canvas roof &
1,767cc of *unbeatable* horsepower!

Hájek — within a year of settling down in a large apartment on the Judenplatz, presently enrolled for a degree in philology & earning more than his keep from the black trade in antique books (*inter alia, etc.*) — soon finds himself en route to the Eternal City, following the trail of a piece of late medieval[*] arcanum called the Voynich Manuscript. There were WANTED posters for Eichmann at all the checkpoints, a grainy photograph of the ubiquitous Nazi in full regalia. Hájek would later recall (while waiting at the Südbahnhof for the overnighter to Rome) a balding, bespectacled man in a beige overcoat standing nearby at the

---

[*] Or early Renaissance? [☛]

station kiosk, chewing a pretzel as he watched the entrances & exits, *something about him, strangely familiar* but no more than that — a fleeting encounter which adds nothing to what History would have us know or bid us deny.

In 1955, after the 'liberation' of Schnitzelstadt from the Four Powers & as atonement for his sins, the now Herr Doktor & ex-blackmarketeer, recent author of *Teatrum Mundi: Truth and Methods of Interpretation in Kircherian Theosophy*, is sent to eke-out his moral subsistence teaching History, socalled, to snot-chugging schoolboys. First in Linz, then in Salzburg, & finally in some lamentable suburb of Klagenfurt. By some coincidence, in each of these cities the ever-industrious Dr Hájek makes important discoveries of illuminated manuscripts previously thought lost, destroyed, looted during the war. Not even the keenest expert eye suspects a thing.

'Memory & Reason,' the Herr Doktor gesticulates at a room of nosepicking halfwits, 'what good are they? Mankind's *délire de grandeur*. To this extent it's true, we're created in God's own image. But is the death of God therefore the tragedy we've been led to expect — hoped & prayed for — or merely farce? Can we tell the image from its reflection? Of course, God — or so we're told by those expert in such things — is *unbekannt*, a stranger, unknown, unfamiliar. Yet also obscure, unaware, ignorant — withdrawn from the world like a tired old man. As in all things — History no less than Philosophy — *truth* is often the contrary of what we wish for.'

1968 comes & goes — annus mirabilis, annus horribilis.

'Nothing changed. The same creature with a different face. Everyone who went back, you know, they never got out again.'

Hájek watches patiently across the border as Cheskoslovnikia offers its neck once more to the henchmen. In the meantime, a brief window of opportunity. He's searching for something, waiting for a sign, for some hidden hand to show itself, reappear. Strange happenings. Rumours stirred by foreign currencies. Books no-one has ever heard of coming to light after fourhundred years & quietly vanishing again...

Elected a Privatdozent the year ex-Nazi Kurt Waldheim was handed the job of U.N. Secretary-General, Hájek returns with all due discretion to a teaching post at his adopted Alma Mater, Univ. of Schnitzelstadt, having recently published an annotated bibliography, thick as a telephone directory, of the Carteggio Kircheriano (*Romani Collegii Societatis Jesu musaeum celeberrimum, cujus magnum antiquariae rei, etc., etc.*). The subsequent years pass as uneventfully as an eddy in a backwater. Then, with the Cold War on its last legs, Hájek commences, for reasons far too *je ne sais quoi* ever to be stated in words, the belaboured task of repatriation to his belovèd & much bereaved Golem City.

Number 8 Jánský Vršek, in the fairytale district of Golem City, was a plain white house & it was here that Professor Tomáš Hájek (Jnr.) resided before he died & became a ghost. A coming-to-rest of sorts after the long peripatetic years of exile. From the street, nothing too remarkable. Cross the threshold into the courtyard, though, & an ancient astrological observatory stands atop a high tower abutting the house's northern wall.

The observatory — a bare platform with some shingling raised over it for a roof — was sometimes referred to as Kelley's Tower. This Tower had for nearly four centuries served no higher function than that of a stairwell connecting the upper & groundfloor apartments of the house, but it was true that at one time it served a much grander design. Of the house, the Prof's apartment occupied the entire top floor: it opened from a narrow foyer off the stairwell onto a parlour with a Petrov grand, a bureau, a winter garden, two socalled *garçonnières* at either end reserved for the pair of muses who, faithful to the last, had accompanied the Prof during the long Novembers of exile.

There was a very old photograph in a tarnished pewter frame on the Prof's writing desk. In it, a youthful Elsbeth von N____ stood on the Prof's right, in a black Grecian tunic, head nestling against his shoulder, hand draped in the crook of his arm. Alžběta stood on his left, sheathed in white satin, jaw out-thrust, one hand likewise draped, the fingers of the other entwined in a long necklace. Their faces exhibited a curious symmetry, neither opposite nor reversed, but rather *contrary* — as if illustrating some Pythagorean mysterium — a pair of tutelary deities wrapped in obscure allegory & the Prof between them, the divided soul, dark suit hanging from scarecrow shoulders, eyes fixed, gazing full of purpose at the camera.

The apartment itself stood in a permanent First Republic gloom, littered with decayed bric-à-brac. Dingy chandeliers, glassfronted cabinets with mismatched crystal, skewed mirrors in oversized gilt frames, mantelpieces crowded with porcelain kitsch, filigreed candelabra, bronze ashtrays, pendulum clocks, carved obsidian heads, blue & green bottles, fleshy seashells, a battered Viennese grandpiano in the corner, a plaster bust of Gaius Octavius in the fireplace, & — in a stand behind the bureau door — a collection of ornate walkingsticks, handles carved from poached ivory, yellow from wear. The Prof's private bureau opened from the end of a hallway that telescoped between overladed shelves, books piled on the floor, filing cabinets & bundles of dusty manuscript. In contrast, the bureau was a model of orderliness — only the architecture betrayed any eccentricity: the windows were slanted left & right, the parquet rose & fell in a single undulation, while a vaulted ceiling sloped to the north so that the room itself appeared lopsided, each line contradicting every other. It'd been that way for centuries.

Many many years before, the house at number 8 Jánský Vršek came to be known as the *Donkey in the Cradle*. The story went something like this…

Towards the end of the sixteenth century one of the astrological celebs gracing the imperial court of Big Rudolf-with-the-double-digits-after-his-name (number one in the number two business — known to dabble in the *prima materia* himself from time-to-time — the socalled "alchemists' friend"), a certain Edwack Kelley no less, elected to take up residence there. Only a brief time earlier, back in Old Blighty, this Kelley (K for short) lost his ears at the behest of her Virgin Majesty — *honi soit qui mal y pense* — for having failed, very much to his own immodest surprise, to deliver a promised Elixir of Life. Thereafter, Magister K took to wearing his hair long, in an effort to keep this public misfortune private.

At the house on Jánský Vršek, K's living quarters were located in the attic directly above the Prof's apartment &, as the legend went, he was nightly to be found in the sanctuary of his Ivory Tower charting the great firmament. During this time a young widow with an infant found lodgings in a room on the ground floor. When on one dark & stormy night her child fell gravely ill, the distraught Frau ran out into the courtyard where she harkened upon a light emanating from the Tower's high window. Not knowing what else to do, she cried out —

'Your Excellency, *I beseech thee*!' she beseeched. 'Please *help*! My poor little Pinocchio's *dying*!'

You'd think she'd've known better. The astrologer, disturbed by the commotion below, leant out the Tower window &, as fortune would have it, at that precise moment a windgust blew back his hair, exposing for all the world to see a pair of mutilated earstubs. Furious, K screamed at the hapless woman —

'Whore begone! Your whelp shall have the head of a *mule!*'

Mortified, the young mother rushed back inside, where she found her child as she'd left him, lying in his cradle, but indeed the child's head had transformed into a mule's. This poor afflicted Frau fretted in her room for three days & nights, door locked & windows bolted, fearing the lunatic in the Tower might attempt some further abomination. Then, on Christmas Eve, the sometimes pious widow quietly snuck from the house & crossed the street to the church of St Thomas.

Bawling, down on the raw of her knees before the statue of Our Lady, beggaring belief for the sake of intercession, *Ave Maria, gra... ple... do... te... Virgo serena, pi... mu... et... imma...* she lit a candle. In the chapel's chiaroscuro the Madonna's lips trembled & she took it as a sign. Returning to her lodgings, the anxious Frau fairly fainted-away at the sight now presenting itself. There in its cradle, where only a moment past a braying monster lay, the all-too-human phyzog of her little pipsqueak Pinochle peered from a bundle of humid swaddling. The widow screeched. The babs smiled blithely at her heaving bub. Seizing the moment, she snatched the child in her arms & shooed back to St Tom's to give thanks.

News of these events spread quickly throughout Golem City & it may freely be assumed that in the days & weeks following, mother & infant acquired a certain notoriety. What became of the widow's uncertain. The Wunderkind, falling into the clutches of one dubious impresario after another, came (it's said) to a sorry end, consumed by alcoholism, poverty & the clap. History, sometimes just despite being arbitrary, nevertheless records that henceforth the alchemist's house on Jánský Vršek was known as *U osla v kolébce...*

They said, 'Kid here's your ticket,
the sky above's no limit
and you'll be the biggest star
this town has ever seen by far!
It'll do your mother proud,
by Christ we'll pull a monster crowd!'
And they promised me the moon,
said we'd be there very soon,
at least within the hour
once I had my trousers down

'Man must take his miracles as they come,' the Prof intoned, rounding the story off on a solemn note, 'even in an ass's ear…'

As the occasion required, the Prof was standing under an umbrella in the courtyard of the old white house with the relic of Kelley's Tower butting out above the eaves, a headless neck. Němec, for whose benefit the tale had been retold, stood at his side, slightly bored, watching a wet clubfooted pigeon trying to make a roost for itself under a drainpipe. It was several weeks since their inauspicious first meeting over a chessboard at the Klementinum.

'In fact,' the Prof said, gesturing up at the drizzle, 'our nasty alchemist with the clipped lobes was supposed to've installed some manner of lightning rod up there on the Tower roof: a copper globe atop a mizzen mast. They say he used it to perform magic & conjure lightning out of clear sky — a stunt, presumably, to impress the Emperor, surrounded as he was by an endless retinue of quacks & conmen. Spectators, avid for miracles, gathered along the streets & castle walls. Passersby saw sparks flash beneath their heels on the paving stones. Night after night, streaming blue lights were seen all over the City, till the burghers grew restive & the mast was petitioned to be taken down as a public nuisance.'

It was this that'd deformed the house's architecture, he said. The Prof scratched his left ear & pursed his lips like a picture of someone pondering the imponderables, then continued —

'Kelley was the type of impure genius society conspires to produce in order to persecute. A man whose soul may easily be parleyed for a parable — existing between the yet unknown & the unknowable — a vain, all-too-human creature, trading in the world's dark secrets & darker fantasies. What is it Zarathustra said? *Verily, my friends, I walk amongst men as amongst the fragments and limbs of human beings!*'

Another pause & then, by way of a postscript —

'I never could find any official record,' he confessed, 'of the woman in the story, or of her unfortunate brat for that matter. Perhaps, after all, they existed merely to facilitate a myth, or give birth to a fable…'

As a young student during the last heady days of Masaryk's First Republic, Hájek had acquired a taste for such apocrypha, going so far as to attempt a dissertation on Rabbi Judah Löw ben Bezalel (known to the elect as *the Maharal* — notorious cabbalist & legendary maker of the Golem from Vltava rivermud) & thereafter his scholastic bent was almost exclusively towards the science & esoterica of the Mitteleuropean renascence.

The Prof kept a library in his apartment. In it were many unusual books, including a collection of leatherbound antiques & rare editions, of potentially dubious provenance (communist-era blackmarket underground networks of Culture Ministry junior clerks, library technicians, museum guards, archivists, petty thieves, restoration artists, junky antiquarians hungry for western currency, smuggling illicit merchandise cross-border). Doubtful, at least, to've been financed by a Privatdozent's salary. The titles were as exotic as their bindings: Galileo's *Siderius Nuncius*, a sixteenth-century translation of Mattioli's botanical writings, Dee's *Monas Hieroglyphica*, the *Fama Fraternitatis*, Columella's *De Arboribus*, Kepler's *Mysterium* & (in several dozen black hidebound volumes) the monstrous *Codex Gigas*, the Devil's Bible.

After '48 the house on Jánský Vršek had, like everything else, been communalised by the Gottwald regime & the Prof himself convicted, *in absentia*, of Illegal Abandonment of the State, sentenced to five years, pursuant of the Law of 6 October, 1948, "on the Defence of the People's Republic," No. 231, articles 40 & 48 respectively. After the moment's euphoria of '89, all this waits to be undone. With all the resentment of lost prerogatives the courts — determined to work, when at all, with Dickensian slowness — look askance at the Prof's documentation — the existing tenants, benefactors of the system, appeal — the State drags its feet — obstacles are put in the way, conditions attached, a general airing of vested interests. Red tape mounts: the Law of 23 April, 1990, No. 119, article 2(1)(b), "on Judicial Rehabilitation" — the Law of 2 October, 1990, No. 402, "on Mitigation of Property Injustices" — the Law of 21 February, 1991, No. 87, "on Extra-Judicial Rehabilitation" — the Law of 26 February, 1991, No. 92, "on the Conditions for Transfer of State Property to Other Persons (Privatisation)" — the Law of 21 May, 1991, No. 229, "on Regulation of Property," etc.

You might think Democracy would have something more to say for itself, but judges don't grow on trees (though sometimes they hang from them) — still, at the end of the day, there're "principles" which in some quarters at least have to be seen to be adhered to — the rights of property & so forth. Finally, if only for lack of achievable alternatives, they decide in the Prof's favour — taxes in arrears.

Home-sweet-home thus redeemed, & having since retired from the pedagogue's trade, the Prof, now emeritus, freed of all superfluous duties & supernumerary distractions, is at liberty at last to pursue, unhindered & undisturbed, his Old World proclivities for chess, the cabbala, cosmogony, & the works of the misunderstood Moravian Kapellmeister, Gustav Mahler (1860-1911), son of a Zhiddish shopkeeper & author of nine symphonies, number ten unconcluded — these snorable autumn years especially devoted to the business, ultimately futile if judged by the exacting standards-of-the-day, of deciphering once & for all (his revealed lifelong obsession) the Voynich Manuscript. Till, that is, one late October morning when, a Sunday, sitting in his bath, chessboard balanced between his knees, a sudden aneurysm puts paid to all that — a pantomime with the last act missing.

If it'd happened in a film, the rest would never be believed — the coldblooded madness of it, the unnatural symmetry of it, the absence of any apparent justification for it — tragedy elevated to the dizzy heights of farce. In their separate *garconnières*, & barely three days apart, both Alžběta Hájková (wife) & Elsbeth von N____ (mistress) each asphyxiated themselves by leaving open the gas valves. Wife first, immediately after burning all of the Prof's letters. Then Elsbeth von N____, having taken pains to put the Prof's remaining papers in a semblance of order — the blueprint & all the component pieces of his mythic Polygraphia. The authorities were eager to rule-out foul play. Scandal flared in the tabloids then died away.

Three Dead in Bizarre Suicide Pact?

Gruesome Gas Deaths

Deadly Tryst Ends Sordid Ménage à Trois

Confronted with this precipitous end to the Prof's last labour, what was to be done? The drama allowed for no postscript, no following instructions — what began unforeseen concluded in a vista without prospects, like an immaculately ordered room in which the one crucial element is missing & will always remain missing, no matter how thoroughly one searches, no matter how fastidiously: almost as if the whole thing had been staged simply to conceal the shoddiness of the motive — a shoebox of burned letters, so anxiously culled — a half-dozen (give or take) binders of notes belonging to an obscure investigation, tentative, preliminary, by definition incomplete, so dutifully put in order — but into what *order* could they've been put, other than the self-fulfilling order of tidied corners, all neatly stacked, bound with lengths of ribbon? To what had they been privy, the Prof's muses? And who was the orderliness conceived *for*?

Since, after all, the singular consequence of this three-way tryst was the courts, acting in no-one's interest than their own, were left with few options but to deem Professor Hájek *intestate*. No sinister character in the wings, no unnamed claimant filing suit, no stealthy removal of the evidence. It'd all been left there in plain view, to be signed-off by forensics, collected, sealed & deposited by the State's appointed executor in the National Literary Archive at Strahov Monastery (perhaps the solemnity of it all gave the State cause to suspend judgement, hedge their bets, who knows, all those papers might be worth something one day — but did they bother with an expert assessment?).

There, under the supervision of a junior secretary, what'd seemed of an almost irrational urgency in the task of mourning & in mitigation of two suicides, was unceremoniously filed away inside a dozen metal boxes & promptly forgotten. Or so it might've appeared.

On the day the Prof's ashes were put to rest, Němec sat out on the roof of his apartment building with the superintendent, Blecha the "Bugman," & got properly soused. He looked like a scarecrow in the Bugman's borrowed black suit & tie, hands too big, feet sticking out of his shoes. And the more he drank, the more like a scarecrow he looked, slowly sagging under its own weight, waiting for a jackdaw to come & peck its strawman's brains out, its button eyes.

'Well,' said Blecha, warming his hands over a primus stove, legionnaire's cap & a rug over his shoulders, 'your friend's gone to a better world to suffer in. They all start out believing in the All-Mighty, till it's just the bit about Calvary that sticks. And Judas — a man'd be nothing without his sense of betrayal.'

Němec shivered. It was cold even for October. As for suffering, he had his own theories. But something about the Prof'd never seemed quite right, & it had nothing to do with God or Calvary or Silver Dollars. To die like that... And then the others, the way they did it straight after... *If* they did it. He had a strange feeling everything wasn't as it seemed. And the longer he pondered, the more he had an even stranger feeling, that he ought to be next — if only by association. Death seemed to be contracting.

Gazing down from the ledge at the buglike things scuttling down below — toy cars going around in circles, people hunched in their coats against the cold, the universal entropy — Němec wondered what move would come next if all this was just a game, the way the Prof used to say. But to ask the question you needed to know what the game consisted of & Němec didn't even know if there was one.

'Like a man with a spade,' as Blecha would've said, if he'd known what Němec was thinking, 'out searching for a hole to dig in the middle of the sea.'

Instead he reached for the bottle & Němec handed it to him. They passed it back & forth like that till the evening settled in with a frost that made Němec's scarecrow suit glimmer in the light of the primus. By the time he made it back to his room, he couldn't feel a thing. Better, he thought, to wait & see what happens, let the other side make the first move. And the Prof? The dead, he muttered, half-conscious, minister to themselves. He'd proved it by playing dead himself for so long, faking his own existence, immaculately born full of holes.

The days after the funeral went by as they had before. But as autumn progressed the leaves fell against the windowsills like a rustling in the mind that wouldn't stop. Little by little the routine of his existence stood more naked to the eye — more pointless, empty, absurd. Němec thought back to the Home, the desire for nothing more than to be forgotten, vanish into the narcissism of amnesia, piss against his own crucifix if it came to that. Searching within himself, Němec made the futile gestures of one digging for the sake of filling a hole. He locked himself in his room & rolled empty bottles back & forth across the floor. The floor became the foredeck on a seashantied skiff with the weather gone sour. Conspiring, as once before, in his own sabotage, the needling mitigation, still tied by an umbilicus to his own mizzenmast, there in that monsoonal dark second womb, the bosom of the failed State,[*] the wreck fast upon him, the washed-out atoll & its cave. And the wind making voices in the cave. Voices of the Ancient Prophets of Doom, the Undead Fathers of History's Horrorshow:

We'll have our happy ending now...

We'll have our happy ending now.

We'll have our happy ending now!

WE'LL HAVE OUR HAPPY ENDING NOW!

Sleepless, Němec listened to old vinyls on the scratchy recordplayer & sometimes watched the vague shapes on the idiot boxes glowing in the windows across the street: the comforting tedium of soap operas, old re-runs of nothing, commercials, gameshows, the weather girl doing her ten o'clock reverse-striptease. More & more he drank to keep the illusions from falling apart, till there were no illusions left but the unpleasant ones. *At least,* he tried to tell himself, *you could write it down. Edify the soul.* He stared into the typewriter like someone staring into an empty Chinese Box: the misery, stupidity, drudgery of words, everything he'd ever written seemed contaminated with it. It would've been better to heave that dumb machine right out the window & be done with it.

---

[*] What'd they get for their effort? Eight years after the Revolution the century bombed, the rest was just a fizzle in a rain of sodden confetti hiding the fallout. [✋]

54

But he didn't. Untutored in the occult arts of patricide, Němec sat & watched the cavewall shadows playing on the inner screen till the bottle won out & everything went blank for a while, before it started all over again. Awake, he dreamt that he slept. Time dragged, raced, leapt back & forth. For uncountable days he languished in his cave on that barren sea-coast, setting out, being beaten back, without ever arriving anywhere than the point he began, waiting for a voice from the sky, a hand risen from the depths, a sign, any sign at all, to tell him, what? *Reduce existence to its ultimate particle and you end here*?* Asleep, a demon remained awake behind his eyes, calculating the set task, an existence by metastasis, deadening the air in the room, leaching the mould that grew in corners, along the windowsill, the stalactites hanging under drains. *The future*, the demon whispered, *doesn't exist and never will.* It was a childish idea, like a seven-day weekend in which there was never any rest, too busy working to fill in the holes that kept secretly reappearing.

The message came through loud & clear. Fingers tapping secret commands on the walls — Morse transcriptions of alien traffic — the groaning through the floor — the scampering of rats above the cornices — rubble sifting down into sealed-up chimneys, dumbwaiters, coalchutes, hidden passageways — the tireless inscrutable industry of ant colonies, weevils, termites, excavating through brick, mortar, red clay, foundation stones — whole underworlds feeding on the substrate of All Visible Things. But you didn't need to see it, to know it was true. The proof was everywhere.

---

* A late singular conjugation out of prehistoric miasma — the lost dream of the original composite entity, Hermaphroditos, programmed to fail because otherwise it *could not be*? Mene, mene! The mortal soul in its x-ray machine, how beautifully it suffered! The languishing soul entertaining itself to death with visions of its own torment. Sucked down into a mouldering compost, its dream became a pretence for itself. Poor thing. [✋]

5

INSTITUTE OF HUMAN STUDIES & SOCIAL MEDICINE
Psychiatric Assessment

Name: Jan Němec
D.O.B.: 04-05-1975
Address: Římská 499/15 120 00 Praha 2
Occupation: Unemployed
Admitted 30-12-1996 to the Traumatology Department, Golem City
General Teaching, with depressed cranial fracture, oblique
intra-articular fracture of the sixth cervical vertebra,
fractures to fourth, fifth & sixth rib on the left side,
intrathoracic trauma, pneumothorax emphysema, compound fracture
of the left patella, lacerations.

Consulting physician: N. Volta, MUDr.

Note: the following account was provided by the patient on 15
March 1997 & is appended for further consideration.

At the halfway mark, the hands & the numbers they pointed to got lost behind reflections in the darkened glass: fractured, circled, triangled, squared, pentagrammed. Headlights drifted counter-clockwise out of the night, turning shadows across the ceiling — wet slow hiss of tarmac, groan of carburettor, croak of frog: toad's fugue. Into the room's ear, the tireless Sphinx of the City whispered its unrelenting riddle — the serenade of a madwoman always at the door, at the window, at the foot of the stairs. Ticktocktick of melting ice between windowpanes. Tockticktock of leaky faucet. Whatever it was, time didn't matter — it would always be too early or too late. Why? Don't ask me why.

There was nothing auspicious about the setting — it wasn't much of a room. A box with window facing onto the street, one lateral pane atop two verticals: to left of it, a foldout cot with mess of newsprint, record covers, stolen-borrowed-scavenged magazines, dogeared paperbacks, mouldy hardbacks, others coverless, piled or scattered in occult disorder under & about, sheaves of blank or scribbled-upon foolscap, miscellaneous desiderata, amidst which a black-as-your-eye writingmachine in battered carrycase; to right of it, a cafétable with recordplayer — old scritchscratched vinyls tilted diagonal, a cascade of dominos in freezeframe beside a canvas armchair perpendicular, the seat of it sagging almost to the floor — like wearing your arse in a sling. The recordplayer *thutted*, turntable going ringaringaround, bluntmuted needle stuck centripetal in innermost rut, two-three-*thut*, two-three-*thuttut*, two-three Strausslike, Johann, the younger — *An der Schönen Blauen Donau...*

At an angle oblique through an opening at the room's far corner, some two-bit Le Corbusier had wedged a *soi-disant* kitchenette — in sum, one modular alcove two-feet-by-three with sagging plyboard shelf, electric-coil hotplate & limescaled sink (plughole wadded with black shoppingbag to quarantine insects, vermin, parasites) — unobstructed view of a reeking post-brutalist ventilation duct thrown-in gratis. The only door in the place stood flush in the middle of the back wall like a Khrushchev-era stage exit — out of which, an inchwide peephole from under hairy eyelid of stale chewinggum leered. Additional modcons: one lavatory, WC, jakes, pissoir or *comme il faut* shitehouse located east-by-northeast in a broomcloset down the gangway, first right before you hit the stairs, elevator facing.

So much for atmospherics.

Whatever I was waiting for was slow in coming. Dreams of ambrosial sleep & all that. The eternal mañana. I'd killed a bottle of slivovice since midnight — it lay there on the parquet doing nothing. My stomach burned from the last drink, a taste like a sick dog's wishfulfilment. The hungerlessness, the drink-fuelled awakeness. Weeks chained to my rock, eating my own liver. There were things behind my eyes you wouldn't want to see — it took all I had to keep focus on the lights through the window, the traffic sounds, the shadows creeping over the walls like fingers over invisible Braille. Sooner or later I'd have to make the next move — in the meantime the bottle was empty, the clock ticked off the seconds, the eternal chessboard beckoned. Even if I could've stayed that way, calculating the odds till Kingdom Come, I'd've still ended up going in blind. What the Prof used to tell me, Hájek, his chessmaster's eyes, cold, vitreous, shoulders hunched over the board: When you're as certain as you can be that you've found the best move, begin again & find one better.

Ad infinitum.

Ad absurdum.

Ad nauseam.

Adadadadad...

Rewind eight years: A mock moon through crossed bars — children coughing in the dark under coarse bedsheets — the sound of a garbage truck turning the street corner — the silence of the stairwells — snow gritting against windowpanes. You catch yourself listening for the others, for the sound of their breathing. Always the others. You take comfort in what you can, even hated things. Voices in the toilets, a cake of soap jammed between your teeth, pants down around ankles, bent over a sink being whipped for something you didn't do — the Spastic Girl in the corridor with skirt up, a gang of boys squatting in front, Nagel his name was their ringleader poking with fingers at the wiry black bush — the

Fairinelly Twins* rubbing dry dogshit down the back of your shirt for acting the freak — the aftertaste of tree sap — the smell & consistency of celery sauce — black ants flaring under magnifying glasses in the late August sun... How many hours staring at the shrivelled knot of your navel, picturing yourself, the first-created alone in the night — the outer body nothing but a feeble reflection of the inner — Adam Kadmon — radiant-eyed, orphan of our great sweet dialectical mother?

Too young when the estébáci in their secret cop uniforms came for them — a pair of brown leather coats.* Mamitati? Not a picture even, to wax sentimental by. The nostos of nothingness. About my coming into this world — conceived in the full immaculation of my own ignorance — I knew nothing, which is exactly as it should be. A date, a name. My real existence began in a file in an Interior Ministry archive on Havelkova Street, residues of torn paper where the Tatimami's photograph should've been. Code: **A3294**. Typed, red ink: **31.X.1983**. Whereabouts: **UNKNOWN**. Inferences on that basis. A charge-sheet stapled to a thick wad of redacted protocol: **CRIMINAL SUBVERSION OF THE STATE IN COLLUSION WITH FOREIGN AGENTS**... The meaning of the word *collusion*: *n.* a fraudulent secret understanding, esp. between ostensible opponents as in a lawsuit — hence *a.* collu'SIVE [f. L COL (*ludere lus*-play)].

Black to move...

Check.

If I tried to picture them? Matamiti? He: faceless artefact in brown twill clerk-suit, smelling of late nights, beer & tobacco. Tatínek?! She: Daughter-of-Man, face like all the womanly faces I'd ever known peering down, blurred into one pale thinlipped moon of unsmilingness. Mamousch!? Maminka!! In dreams, the perfume & touch of her — mouth eyes hair — & darkness. The snakes of fear. An agoraphobia of empty rooms somewhere in the cul-de-sac of the mind, where once Ozymandiaslike figures watched over — eyes brown&green, & mouths, mouthing undictionaried words, hands, & the longedfor milksour breast. Maybe, at some indefinite future point, all the forgotten things come back to you. The fear. The longing. The stupidity & shame. Teaching the lesson that guilt must never be doubted.

Or you find yourself alone, again, as ever before, in a room, at night, in a city you barely exist in, re-becoming once more that witless snivelling thing lost in the wilderness, afraid of the monster-under-the-bed, the monster-behind-the-door, the monster-in-your-head, with nothing to your name but all of history still to atone for. As they say in the classics, *He who seeks the inward path is merely dreaming of a condition in which he'll one day be able to endure himself...*? Or unendure — pulling the world out of your arse so as to abolish it? Some swaddling occult geometer, drawing lines in

---

* → Chapter 18. [✋]

* StB = Státní bezpáteřnost: the Cheskoslovnikian Secret Police. [✋]

the undersoil of the night: maps, architectures, secret itineraries of the palsied mind's eye, all aglitter like a polished turd?

In the place I grew up — the Witch's House, the Inquisition, the Haunted Castle, the Prison, the Home-is-where-the-heart-lies-bleeding — survival was never the thing it seemed. Horizontal in the dark, unsleeping, wanting to die but too afraid to — grasping the threads of something indefinite, unreal — the intuition of a light at the end — a voice — a caress. *They did things to you, so you'd never be right in the head. To punish you, for the sins of your fathers, and of your fathers' fathers…* You bury the thoughts & go on, day after day, year after etc., making a type of procedure out of it — making the gestures demanded by expedience, to negate the routines of boredom, brutalism — to fill the emptiness, blot out the truths, the untruths: little formulae for each of those moments in which — reprieve! — you don't have to think. The perpetual sunny disposition.

Cut to: "A room… in a city."

A clock. Someone ("you") sitting there laughing with all the humour gone out of the situation. A dry, croaking laugh. Thinking: *So this's how the future turned out to be?*[*] No, it wasn't like that. It happened without anything seeming to happen at all. The time on the clock was almost quarter-past-four. Outside it was snowing. Hoisted myself off the floor two-three-*thut* feeling along the walls, measuring out the shape of my confinement — an idea stalking itself through the dark like an insomnia — bare feet on cracked parquet — whispers in the shadows, *pianissimo* — a child alone in a dormitory, sleepwalking towards an unknown precipice — fragments of half-remembered chambermusic. Across the room a window looked out. A strip of curtain hung to one side, made of some lousy plastic. The glass was cold, ice had formed in the gaps around the panes where the rain seeps in, had frozen & was now melting in a temporary thaw: a sheen of brown muck spreading along the sill. The window bulged, forehead against. Below, the street was deserted — the streetlamps, vague orange halos misting in the glass. Sideways reflected there, a pair of eyes: black holes cut from a djinn-mask, of that *thing* inside the camera of the mind, which dials all the settings, all the reflexes, into a divided point — which sees what I cannot see, knows what I cannot know. A glimpse before it's gone & where it was, nothing but a smear of light.

Someone said once that there're two ways to understand what we are: *Erdichtung und Geschichte* — fiction & history. One, a picture of the imagination with its moods, its poetry & its irrationalism. The other, nothing but a reflection bereft of psychology, meaning, intention — nothing than what it is: a trick of geometry, angles of incidence. Yet, in the eye of the beholder, what could be further from the truth? Forehead pressed to window, the wormeaten crumbling wood frame & panes in

---

[*] So bright — *Man wird beim Schlafen Ray-Bans tragen müssen* — dah-dum. (1980s pop song. [✋])

duplicate — everything factored by twos — mind wandering out through the eyes, out through overlapping, halfreflected agonist-antiself... Because there, in that theatre of doubles, something's happening — something's sizing you up, passing judgement, taking apart the pieces, reversing the distinctions, fitting them back together contrarywise. And what would this agonist-self be, if not some spectre-of-history or even the absence of a history — my own above all? And fiction, antiself? Free to become whatever it willed, like Fantomas? While somewhere between, the thing each barely approximated, contradicted, embellished — the thing that hungered, was conscious, lived supposedly or died — a ghost or the shadow of a ghost, arrested, caught, trapped in the glass: a figment in amber. My very existence seemed like a mirror that to enter I had to turn my back on & creep away.

But in the time of the mirror, all direction had ceased: the time of history & the time of fiction. Outside, where a moment ago it was snowing, everything has come to a standstill. Thousands of bright, tinsel-flecks of white hang suspended in midair. It's as if the scene in the film in which they were falling had frozen, the celluloid jammed in the projector & at any moment about to dissolve. But the scene doesn't dissolve, it hovers over an abyss. In the streetlamps' orange glow, faint white holes open everywhere. Holes multiplying. Holes in the very substance of the world. Holes within holes within holes. Your aching hand reaches out & unlatched the window — the holes so real you want to touch them — thinking, *This's what it looks like on the other side — in the place where images begin?* History, fiction, agonist & antiself. You're back where in your mind you've always been: watching — anaesthetised — detached, while there in your proxy-place a thin silhouette stands framed in the open window, ventriloquising you: a rictused mutter in *diminuendo*, growing thinner still & smaller — a thin-small muttering thing. And then in the blink of an eye it happens, as arbitrary & predetermined as the course of a clock: a white gust of static sweeps in — the silhouette flutters against the light, gesticulates the way a puppet does whose strings are being cut & is already falling — a weightlessness comes over you & the room's gone.

6

GOLEM CITY, DAY ZERO

The doctor's face swims in & out of focus — a pair of enormous insect monitors. Němec sees the pores in the skin, craterous, worming down into hidden passageways of flesh, collagens & reticula, down to the burned core of crashed circuitry mirrored back at him. Weird dome-lights hover out on the periphery, like alien surveillance systems that shift away from wherever he looks, the light itself melting down. Periodically the light speaks to him, always with questions. *Do you know what your name is? Where you are? Why you're here? What day it is?* The dominant theme's white. Currents, switches, thoracic loops. From somewhere outside, a sound like fireworks, car alarms & breaking glass: neural flares in the EEG tuned to cartoon soundbytes. *Zap! Kapow! Zibaldone!* It could be the end of the world. War. Revolution. Auld lang syne. All of the above. What does Němec know about History, anyway? A rumour of panic aboard the spaceship, set to auto-destruct, tractor-beamed & drifting towards the zero-event horizon, the crash-course singularity, the terminator gene at the end of the evolutionary vortex…

But this isn't a simulation, all the scenarios are real: red warning light in the corner of the picture, reception phasing out. Switch modules, teleport, down to the medical bay. And now fade up on:

A pair of eyes above a green mask where nose & mouth should be — the face of God, apparently. The following procedure is one never before attempted. The electrocardiogram flatlines, the curtain comes down, lights-out. A last smattering of applause from the frontal-lobe peanut gallery. Or not the end, but only a false start: the cold steel aftertaste of creation, the demiurge at his operating table, implanting the K codes, toggling the cryogenic on-off switch. A faint glint of madness in those eyes: unbalanced Cartesian dualities like hieratic ☼ & helioeccentric ☽, quaternions, cabbalistic zeroes, as if he's being reprogrammed (Němec) to wake up somewhere, at some unspecified future time & place, staring into a mirror not knowing how he got there (the ideal sleeper agent) but still with a creeping suspicion something's on the other side watching him through the glass — confirmation, it might seem, that at least he's someone else's hallucination & not just his own. But that's exactly what *they*'d want him to think, undermining

even the most tenuous of whatever certainties he might've had, once upon a time
— but was there ever a *once upon a time*? What if even his most private inklings,
childhood memorias, secret humiliations, were just vestiges downloaded from the
mass archive, nanospasms of a collective brainwave, retrofitted? And could that
noise in his head be the sound of God's laughter?

Suffer the Little Children

Within the regime of organised optimism that governs our modern medical
institutions there prospers a demon of efficient irrationalism.[*] The Prof liked to
say the only healthy obsession's how to stay alive, but that's no reason to have to.
He'd outlived the Protektorat & spent forty years biding Communism's time
from the sidelines — it was a burst artery that finally did him in, a detail in an
autopsy report which gave the cause of death as *pulmonary aneurysm*. It
happened while he was playing a one-sided game of chess in the bath. The first
picture that came into Němec's head when he learned the news, was of the Prof
dead in the water, like Marat, arm dangling over the side of the tub & a black
knight lying just out of reach on the wet tiled floor. It immediately made him
think of Charlotte Corday's letter, in that painting of the snuffed "People's
Friend." But there was the letter & then the was the letter *inside the letter*, the
one no-one could see because it was addressed only to the deadman.

If you can do it once, you can do it again…

There's a line between murder, suicide & misadventure, but it's not always
obvious where it's drawn. Survival? When your only reason for anything's the
System, survival's the lowest form of passive resistance, like toilet training for the
right-thinking mind. *The filth! That's the third time this afternoon! And he's rubbing
himself in it!* For most people just drawing breath becomes a task. Why should
Němec've been different. Speaking for himself, well, there wasn't much to say
that hadn't already been said. Sure he wanted to escape, play his part in the
Outright Abolition of all the Etceteras, & then what? What good's an Oedipus

---

[*] This's merely one of the many factors that contribute to hospitals being sinister & threatening
places. In addition, there's a characteristic smell, calculated to reinforce the patients' neurotic
susceptibilities. A smell of incontinence, humiliation, misery. A smell into which you're born &—
misfortune being what it is — in which you'll one day putrefy. Misfortune being what it is, you
won't be let off the hook so easily. [☛]

Complex if all it amounts to is waiting for the System to choke to death on its own vitriol? Face it, they had him by the short hairs before he even had any — the whole reeking banquet cooked-up in advance, the menu printed, the RSVP with his name & number express mailed before he'd learnt the first rudiments of pissing in his own nappy — gorge-full of mammy's ersatz & daddio's patsy paroxysms, more than enough to tuck himself up with at night in those Sweet Dreams, all courtesy of the One Who Really Cares, the Sympathetic Ghost in the Machine, the Architect of All, the Heart & Soul of that selfsame slandered & oft-maligned System which, despite every evil thing thought & said has his Very Best Interests first & foremost, etc. And as the Good Doctor said, the sooner you learn to love the System,* the better it'll be: the System that clothes & feeds you / sends you off to school in the morning / waxes yr nose with toiletpaper & kicks you in the pants for good measure / promises the world & withholds meals / teaches you not to shirk in doing yr duty / pounds you in the gut with heavy blackbrown stuffedleather medicineballs / pushes you onto the balancebeam & kicks yr feet out from under you / swings you dizzy from parallel bars & hoops till you'd rather break yr neck than hang-on any longer / singles you out for the *special treatment* / makes an *example* out of you / stands you in a corner hands-on-head for 8 hours straight *to learn yr lesson* / holds you shivering under cold showers naked / gives you the metal ruler / makes you pick up the soap / sends you to the back of the line / makes you say *please, pretty please* / poisons you with boiled & pickled shite / taunts with undisguised lies of future happiness in sentimental radio monotones / marches you in lines two-three-four / makes you recite the eight-times-table backwards crying like a siss in front of the class / pours glue in your hair / short-sheets you / makes you wait till you've pissed your pants then screams at you to clean up the mess / insults you into confessing crimes not yours / orders you to write it out a hundred times every day during recess / smiles while it tears up the pictures you kept under yr pillow / cajoles you into singing along to Dalibor Janda, Helena Vondráčková, Michal David, Iveta Bartošová & endless identical other mush / straps you into bed at night with collective brainwash fairytales of the great Workers' Struggle before lights-out at nine sharp when the real menace begins…

---

* *Love's never what they say it is, kiddo. But when there's nothing else, you take what you can get.* [✍]

N

They called him Němec. *Nye-metz.* The mute. Meaning dumb, because as a kid he hardly spoke & whenever he did *they* acted like it didn't make the slightest bit of sense. *Ne-ye-me-tsss.* The name on his file said **NIKDO**. *Nobody.* Nobobod. But he got to preferring Němec. Wouldn't you? They might just as well've called him nothing. A nothing with a ten-digit serial number stamped on it. A decimal. An autism. A selfrepeating error in the System.

But even the System couldn't survive itself indefinitely.

'All ideologies are false,
but some are more false than others…'

— so sayeth the Bugman.

Eight days after the Wall came down, their little world fell on its ear. When no-one was looking, Němec (who wasn't as dumb as he looked), escaped from Home out into the Big Bad World. The last hours of Universal Calm, of the doddering Workers' Paradise, became the cacophony of everything that didn't work & never would. Perhaps things were more perfect at the beginning than at the end. The City that Němec walked out into was a wreck, grey façades & greyer faces — the river grey, the sky grey, the streetlights grey, the keys rattling on their chains grey, the very air grey. Every pore, fibre, cranny, crack, plughole & pissoir. Wherever he looked: shop windows, billboards, taped to car bumpers — grey massconsumption Cold War photofits colourised for comicstrip re-sale: Gorby "The Inkblot," "Hradchin" Havel, "The Gipper" & that dynamic duo of freedom fighters, Colonel "Chuck" Sanders & Ronnie "The Clown" McDee. Hamburgers, chicken nuggets & US dollars.

We Luv Amerika

is what the writing in public lavatories said, cheek-by-jowl with smiley faces, telephone numbers & promises of handjobs, blowjobs, sodomy & coprophilia. The whole City was like the last stop in a shoestring road-movie running on fumes: Aňa Geislerová in a gangbanged Trabi, coal-stained Bohee tricolours tied to the exhaust pipe, Yankeedoodle stars&stripes undies waving from the aerial, doped-out hippy rainbow freedom bunting strung out the windows, Bolshies-

Go-Home graffitied all over the doors, ghettoblaster blasting a medley of Franco Zapatista & late '80s backmasked Western Imperialist Record Industry mindwash —

One, Two, Three, Four
(*join in everybody!*),
What's another Dollar for?
Five, Six, Seven, Eight,
Cap'talism-with-a-Human-Face!

The "Velvet Renovation," comrades! A pipedream kicked into a crooked u-bend — a skylight ten stories down — a periscope in a shitehole — eau-de-cologne dousing the much-loved stink. *Oy vey!* Between the hucksters & doomsayers was a fine familiar line ever-narrowing: you squeezed in wherever you could fit, any available back pocket would do. What'd a man really want from life, anyway, but a pair of warm buttocks to grow old between? And how about a nice little jaunt up Memory Lane (that hussy!)? The Good Ol' Days! The Golden Days! The Days-in-the-Sun! What the rosy eye can't fool itself into seeing could balance on a pinhead, right alongside all the rest of the Heavenly Host. Well of course everyone was happier then, they had SO MUCH TO LOOK FORWARD TO! Idiot! What was freedom, anyway, but an open invitation to expect the worst? And if or when the worst doesn't come, you can always dream-up something worser! Doesn't pay to let the old grey matter get too messed-up with colourful ideas, now, does it? History soon grows tired of the taciturn man's ironic stance & demands its share of outright farce instead. The script read like a spaghetti western took a left turn at the crossroads:

WOAH!

Hold yer horses a minute there, I'm tryin'a tell a story, boy! Well now, *er,* it's like this, y'see? Word on the prairie was, them wily bearhuggin' Slov-yets jist sittin' back bidin' their good ol' time, like they been doin' since befo' the Romanovs was Romanovs. Ain't that right. Meanwhiles our righteous 'n' not-to-be-tomfooled local cit'zenry, well they all hunkered down 'n' kept watch from out behind-a-them faux-lace curtains a theirs (Zhiddish *heir-looms* most prob'ly), whiles dust piled up on the crystal cabinets, dumb with godfearin' atheist

65

trepidation [cue theme tune by Ennio Morricone, slow fade-in], 'n' jist waitin', theys a-reckonin', fer them bolshyannie *tanks* to pop up out of their toilets, reappearin', *er*, the way the Bad Dude always, y'know, *reappears* in movies, even when jist a half-moment ago (God's truth, boy, swear it on this here meal coupon) he been flushed down the tube, six foot under, shot full a silver bullets, 'n' with a *stake* thru his heart! But wldn't y'know it? Whiles they all preoccupied peekin' & pookin'-like, some watchamacallim ne'er-do-good gone snuck in by the backdoor 'n' hell-to-jaysus *stole* the very house they was standin' in! Yessiree. House, home 'n' everythin' in it. *Includin'* th'underwear.

And so, once again, a sinister unreality invades the life of Golem City…

'89. Year of the Snake. While the munchkins danced & smoked spliff, the tidewaiters went to ground like cats during fireworks — the banks got tunnelled, the brainstrust bolted & the fireworks fizzed. Cut to: air-raid spotlight BAT-signal — the Golem City Police Commissioner ankle-deep in pigeon crap, scanning the low-hanging sky from a roof above Bartolomějská Street, fretting about his embezzled pension plan — tonight's villain being a rogue Santa Claus lookalike with a bag of loot from the National Bank loaded on a sleigh (yep, reindeers & everything).

Meanwhile, dear readers, unbeknownst to the world-at-large, a certain disillusioned superhero sits watching from on-high, like a gargoyle on a rooftop, picking his toes while the world waits…

Well in the long-run things might've got dolled-up & even smelt better, but underneath all that teflon & limited liability the same ugliness went on, stewing & percolating like a coprophagic China Syndrome on slow meltdown. In Moscow, the freakshow doctor with his baldwig had only to pull the levers & discharge the secret electron deathray. *Perestroika*! *Abracadoom*! Ah, but very cunning is the mind of the Eternal Bolshoivik! A season passes. Two seasons. Three. The curtains keep coming down but going back up again! *We've been hoodwinked*, they all say. *Led up the garden path*! They demand the price of their tickets back. The nation falls into a squalid heap, begins gnawing its own hind leg like a mutt caught in a trap. Dismembers itself. Everyone wants the Good Old Days. *Oh where oh where are the Good Old Days?* By night, the theatre of men & women with nothing but themselves to despise — by day, whole generations set adrift, left waiting around in train stations, greasy spoons, parking lots, endstops on the road to nowhere, slotting change in the eternal machine, being vacant & not at all pretty about it, just killing time till their number comes up. The walls stopped listening & muttered —

Beware of Certainty!
Everything is subject to Change!

Losers & no-hopers out-doing each other in the argument against Progress — ex-cops in patchwork leather jackets shaking-down lonely drunks in unlit Metro stations — sidewalk prophets proclaiming inalienable right not to work, making common cause with the crippled & insane — hucksters in maroon polyester suits cut short at the ankle, sandals & white socks strewing scam-talk like dog-mess on pavements a nation of suckers will one day be made to clean with their tongues — FOR SALE signs appearing like pop-up funfair target silhouettes in boarded-up windows everywhere — the barstool philosopher at *The White Whale* shouting, *Democracy's a pimp's addressbook! Bang bang! You've been privatised!* — post-Soviet dentistry leering out of headline news propaganda like a pantomime mugshot of the nation's Most Wanted — a whole matinee's worth of crimescene newsreel faces wrapped around in white bodybag ziplocks stuffed with dollars… *And now for a word from our sponsor:*

DRINK *Kolaloka*
THE ALL-IN-ONE MIRACLE CURE!

Between commercial breaks our accidental hero, Nikdo-Němec, subsisted — scrounged food, drank box-wine, scoured the bazaars on Libeňský Island, shipping container junkboxes, antikvariáts, attics, basements, landfills of communist museum trash — scavenged old cassette tapes, vinyls, film canisters, books pilfered many times over from public libraries & resold on street corners — prowled the post-Fall citystreets observing the androids in transistored shellshock, hungover, bereft, machines that hadn't functioned without an override command for decades, caught now in the bleak daylight of the New World Order. *Work*, so Yob in his Bible said, *is God's punishment for original sin.* God — & the System. God — with his big fat suitcase full of paycheques, privatisation vouchers & dirty money. God — with his Cuban cigar & Mercedes Benz. God — with his key to the Castle, his bugspray & flyswat.

Arbeiten! Arbeiten! Arbeiten!

History belongs to the parasites. Just not *your kind*, eh, kiddo? Well all the pillars of salt in nine-to-five purgatory wouldn't've been inducement enough. Carrying the Man on your back? As the Bugman said, *Yer only as wise as the last lesson you unlearned.* So like the Emperor of the North Pole, Němec hitched a slow ride on the brokedown gravytrain, did the bare-naked minimum for pin&kino money — the odd hustle — the odd bit of wealth redistribution — the odd re-sale book-job — the odd pickup & delivery from the nearest grocery, supermarket, department store — the odd bit of freelance for the local freakshow down on The Square ("Pinhead Jan," "Escobar," "Jiří Grossmann," "The Cook," "Věra-the-Lymph" (size of a windmill with a head like a baby's fist)) — hawked day-old Opera tickets, secondhand jeans, expired newspapers, like a barefoot camelot, from traffic islands, in Metro stations, out on The Bridge — watched trustfund Yankee kids get high talking loud through the night about Paris & Hemingway — observed the half-lives of others, strangers, what it'd be like to *be* them, *that* man in *that* window, *that* woman exiting the Metro, making a film out of chance voyeurisms, poetry out of the unseen, a script for an insomniac to dream by — lounged on park benches, along the quays, in stairwells, scribbling notes in exercise books, on paperscraps, napkins, for the unwritten Masterpiece of a Doomed Time — killed the endless intervening hours the way only a parasite knows how — sometimes found sleep in the front rows of cinemas, their names a potpourri of disenchantments: *Lucerna, Hvězda, Praha, Jalta, Květen, Světozor, Illusion,* dreaming of soundtracks by Karel Zeman, Sergio Leone, Billy Wilder, Jan Švankmajer, Fritz Lang, Jess Franco, Charlie Chaplin, Tinto Brass — seeing & in the mind touching, smelling, tasting the promised Eden of some preFall paradise, there, in the Great Beyond (three chimes, the lights dim, the curtains draw back from the magic screen: the bare-bones mystique of a con-artist poking a light in your eye still gets you your fix sitting down — you're the trick that gets turned & likes it that way — *Hands off the merchandise!* — the razzledazzle chorusline, canned applause — then curtains, your time's up & of course you want more, hustled back out the door to join the queue for the next peepshow sucker routine) —

Finest romance in town, kiddo!

After the last show, a drink at the nonstop then crawled back to a room in a half-empty tenement behind the Natural History Museum. It was the dead end of a street that went nowhere, boarded up windows & stucco coming undone from the walls. One day he'd found an open door & slipped in, found an empty fourth-floor apartment, full of dust & rat bait & not much else. The first night he'd slept behind the door, feet jammed up against, in case it was contested territory. At night the sound of emptiness, like wind in caves. He rigged the entrance so he could come & go. Got to exploring. There was an elevator, maybe it even worked, but he avoided it. He picked his way up & down stairways laden with debris, scavenged bits of furniture from neighbouring demolition sites, places that looked as if the occupants had been abducted in the middle of the night & never returned. The third night someone kicked him awake under the glare of a flashlight. It was an old guy, grey hair poking out under the sides of a tricolour legionnaire's cap, a raised broomstick in one hand. The old guy tossed the broom at him, said if he intended to stay, he could start by cleaning the place up.

The old guy was the superintendent. He played at being a soft-touch & turned the proverbial blind-eye as long as Němec pulled his weight & the electricity bill got paid, but he was no push-over. His name was Blecha, the Bugman. He'd been round long enough to've had a ringside seat the first time the Reds came to liberape Golem City. Grey shadow of a man in faded anorak, the type you never notice passing in the street, thin-looking but hands like vice-grips & eyes could stop a man dead if & when. He kept the junkies & thieves out but sometimes let a stray like Němec take shelter. Nothing ever seemed to bother him. He had a vegetable patch up on the roof & a couple of chickens. He'd sit up there most days just surveying the patchwork & sometimes Němec him soon fell into a routine of joining him for a couple of hours here & there to listen to the Old Guy's stories & not be alone.

The Bugman's true vocation in life was to keep watch over the rooftops & talk to the sky, like an aborigine elder up on a high rock reciting the Dreamtime, calling the City out of its inexistence into that great picturebook laid before him as far as the eye could see.

Buried beneath it like an extinct volcano was the carcass of some suicided godhead whose brain had died but whose limbs still twitched, causing periodic tremors, eruptions, bellowing echoes through the sewers. The corpse of Historical Materialism no less. Every day the undertakers worked furiously to keep it buried, while others, grave robbers, exposed the putrescence in search of the alchemical mystery that once had given it life. But the anima had fled, only the rotten vapours remained, dark spirals of soot with the power still to turn everything grey.

Others might've taken him for mad, but Němec knew better. Up on the roof, at least the atmosphere was breathable. One day, Němec figured, all the rooftops in the City would be like one great big gipsy camp: anyone still sane enough & able to climb a set of stairs, to escape that subworld below, to get above the stink for a last desperate gasp of air. If they could, they'd probably climb right up into the clouds, like Tex Avery cartoon lemmings, for a moment defying gravity till some sort of realisation set in. They'd look down, look at the camera, then up'd pop Bugs Bunny —

That's all Folks!

Without making a deal out of it, Blecha took this misfit runaway who'd turned up on his doorstep under his wing, so to speak, doing what he could to keep the kid out of the shit, focused on the day-to-day, building something from it. Like the Prof, the Bugman knew what it meant to beat the odds, back in the time when the future was just an idea people talked about. Back when they still believed in one.

Like every other loser out there, Němec was adrift in a story no-one owned yet. It was the Bugman who told him he should try to *write* it. But Němec couldn't think of writing something down without belonging to it, because as soon as you wrote anything down the System had a hold over you. Even the words in your head. He tried to explain the Home, where you weren't allowed to own anything but everything owned you, but it was buried too deep. He wasn't afraid of the Bugman, it was himself he was afraid of, himself he was afraid to trust. Maybe the Bugman understood. He'd known a writer once, in the camps, who survived that way — told the kid maybe it'd work for him, trap the demons on paper. One day he dragged an old typewriter from his stash of junk, the keys clotted with dust that hadn't been disturbed since Masaryk's first term. Told the kid he could keep it as long as he used it — warned him it'd only work if he didn't think about himself doing it — said whatever he wrote, or whatever he didn't, was his own business.

Němec took the machine back to his room. It sat there on the coffee table like a creature in the dark. He'd wake up & find it watching him, keys pale & round like the polished eyes of a thirteen-headed voodoo doll. Sleepless hours spent falling in & out of a vague, trance-like state, the hunger in his gut feeding the agitation in his mind. Instead of walking the streets, he stared at the machine. Like the machines the androids had filed his crimes & misdemeanours in. Machines that could read your thoughts if you didn't keep your mind as blank as a wall. But what if it worked the other way, if *he* could control *it* just by saying the words in his head, like some ancient alchemist spelling the Periodic Table backwards? But where was he supposed to *start*? Which were the words he was *supposed* to say?

Abracadab? Hokey pokey? Zang tumb tumb?

It all seemed to be about knowing where the Real World ended & the one you could fake by stringing words together began? But the world as far as he could see, Real or Fake, was nothing but the angry mantras of the bereft, graffities of the jejune & profaned, the City's insoluble crossword, its Sphinx-riddle, Mater Urbium, the muted cries of the Golem's secret midwife being strangled in her sleep. To himself he recanted stolen credos, made anonymous proclamations, plagiarised in search of a faith, any kind of faith, in people he saw every day succumbing to new lies indistinguishable in all other respects from the old. His was the art of denunciation by intuition. How could the written word exorcise & know better how to exist outside the world while stuck *inside* it? How to *write* without simply reiterating the mindfuck programme by other means? Becoming just another agent of the *word virus*? Slow to awaken to the pretence of a separate existence among a mass of facsimiles — to recognise delayed actions — effects without apparent cause — causes without actions — the truant inside Němec had believed evasion was everything. Now, with the eyes of that voodoo machine daring him to think otherwise, his hands began typing the phrases his mind wrote. Pages went by in a white streak. Afterwards, the sleep that finally came over him was absolute. When he woke again, the mystery only deepened. There they lay, smears of black ink on sheets of stolen paper. He stuffed them in his pockets & took to the streets. In the gloom of a cinema he read what he'd scratched-out during the night, all of it gibberish, mashed-up bits of Bondy, Bulgakov, Bakunin

(*What's power but a letter on a piece of paper?*), Verlaine, Voltaire, Batman & Daffy Duck, Sancho Panza, Cervantes, weather forecasts, lottery numbers, vowels & spectrography. *Go Rimbaud, do the watusi!* It made no sense. It made all the sense in the world. It was like channelling the ghost of something pervasively dead that wouldn't shut up. The low-pitched whistling stink of a corpse murdered by a trapped fart.

This time our hero woke up screaming…

A nurse came & stuck a needle in his vein & Němec slept again — the cold, distended sleep of a slug floating in water. He pictured himself exactly that way, like a comicbook slug left to distend in a jar in some quack's laboratory. The scenario repeated at vaguely decreasing intervals, waking, screaming, nurse, needle, the slug in the jar, till there was only a numbness — residues of pain like percolating jism in beakers, catching the light through a cracked window: colourless, shapeless, full of vague shadows & invisible things moving inside the shadows, voices coming closer, drifting away. The squished squill of his head, reinflated like an echo-chamber… Then one day something happened, the mind's-eye switch got flipped, the comicbook world dissolved into a testpattern & then went blank — as blank as a dead TV set. And when the picture came on again, Němec wasn't there anymore. He used to play this game back in the Home — things'd go out of tune, radiate, get lost in the montage: he'd wake up in the infirmary with a nose-bleed, staring at the sky through smudged windowglass & safetywire. He always knew by the smell of permanganate that he wasn't dead yet. In a socialist Heaven everything was suppose to smell differently — like a smooth-running machine.

As the weeks passed, gradually bits of memory filtered through: a field in spring — faces blandly smiling out of propaganda films — advertisements for air freshener, toothpaste, laundry soap — airhostesses waving from the top of a boarding ramp in tight airhostess uniforms — a child flying a kite. Someone else's memories — they moved & talked, sometimes they acted as if they were aware of him. How long had this been going on? Propped in a reclining chair at the back of a dayroom, leering at a fuzzy TV screen with the sour aftertaste of institutional poison lingering in his craw: blue pill, red pill, white pill, yellow pill. *The blue pills take you down into a low groove — the white pills make soft edges and haloes…* Neckbraced. Cortisoned. Lung pumped by a mechanical windbag twisted into flatulent convulsions. Arms, pelvis, legs lovingly bandaged & bow-tied like *Frankenstooge meets the Madcap Mummy.*

Head. Something about the head. *If it wasn't screwed on…?*

It was like a scenario for some rotten tele-series. *The Six Million Dollar Man.* Lee Majors. 'We have the technology, we *will* rebuild him…' Canned voices tinkled away in the back of Němec's braincase like bits of glass, falling & breaking & being made whole again through long elusive labyrinths of a dream, full of senselessness & TV commercials. All the while the Prof's ghost was there, off-screen or on, leading him through hell & purgatory onwards to the *tune-in same time next week* beatific vision, caught in a circuit, a loop, a playback mechanism there was no getting outside of. Even with his head screwed on backwards, Němec knew the faceless technicians were keeping him alive just so he could suffer, & possibly more nefarious purposes in mind. He hated them, whoever they were. From hating, he turned to suspecting their place in the larger scheme. And finally, to fearing them — in a pathetic, helpless kind of way a child fears the dark. Even in the full glare of the Ward, the fear never went away, it just modulated into a sinister absurdity at which his condition made it torturous to laugh.

Time dissolved into routine. The chorus of groans. Bedpan & syringe. The Hippocratic stink of it all. Everywhere. From all sides. On the ubiquitous idiotbox, the seasons passed —

Like sands through an hourglass,
so are the days of our etceteras…

— the diurnal incessance, back&forth, monstrous in its frequency.[*] Then one day the Bugman turned up with a little present from Moravia & a get-well card.

'That was some gag you pulled, kiddo!' he said, just to cheer Němec up. 'There I was, out shovellin' snow off the goddamn footpath. What're the odds? *Whomp!* Just like that. Scared the bejaysus outta me. And just lyin' there, leavin'

---

[*] As if perceived through intergalactic U-boat periscope, espying fantastical alien worlds orbiting in timelapse round twin suns: Havana Club tropical paradises melding into post-fallout nuclear winters — a monsoon in Bangkok — an eighteenthcentury grotto carpeted in moss — San Pelegrinoesque spring rain falling on sun-bathed alpine dairy pastures — particle accelerators & subterranean Antarctic lakes — climate-controlled glasshouse vistas — a nitrogenated Yokohama robotics laboratory — a Swedish sauna — the sexless blue light of solarium beds — snowdrifts on Wall Street — the dance movement of low-orbit communications satellites against the blackness of space — solarpowered selfcleaning modularised toilet cubicles with ecofriendly human-waste-disposal & thermostatic toilet seats… [♣]

all the bother up to whoever, eh? Might've been flattened meself if I hadn'a been lucky. Wouldn't stand up, neither, you good for nothin' layabout. Legless as a sailor in port! Hardly got you propped up & you were flat on yer face all over again. And me with me bad back! Can't expect to be picked up whenever it suits you to take a swan dive out the window, eh?'

Němec blinked. Made a futile effort to say something in reply, a string of spit working its way down the funnel of his chin to *drip drip drip* onto the front of his tunic.

'Kiddo,' Blecha said, 'you surely do know how to make a mess, I'll say that much for you. Well, a citizen has a duty, so I off & dialled 155, like they tell you, & brought down a blanket so you wouldn't catch yer death out there. Kept us waitin' long enough, & for what? Some beat-up yellow delivery van with ƎƆИA⅃U8MA painted on, like that was supposed to fool anyone, & the crook drivin' it puttin' his hand out for two grand up-front or no dice. *Yer kiddin' me*, I tells him. *Think I'm kidding*? he says, & buggered off just like that, fishtailin' the wrong way up a one-way street, siren on, lights a-flashin', the whole circus, with me left there holdin' the can, so to speak, & you with yer face on the wrong side of yer head…'

Němec coughed, gagged, winced inside his bandages. The Bugman handed him a glass of water, only Němec couldn't move his arm to drink it. It stayed there in his hand till later a nurse took it away, tut-tutting. In the meantime Blecha continued his story —

'Well you weren't about to go anywhere on yer own, so I hotfooted it down to the Square to find a cab — & me at my age! That time of night, you'd be lucky to find a cab at all. Driver didn't much like the idea, once he copped a looksee at the bloody mess you'd made a yerself. Told him it was just a case of a few too many — eh, kiddo? What the feck were you thinkin'? Back when I was young & stupid like you, they used to say drunks bounce. Want to be careful about that, though. It's the bounce that kills you.'

Clockwork

4x weekly at seven a.m., Němec was required to wait for his name to be called in front of a blue door, second floor of a white tiled building on the east side of Charles Square. This was the door to the Physical Rehab Unit of the Golem City General Teaching Hospital. Where they fitted you back together — bits &

pieces of a mind with bits & pieces of a body. Accordingly, for Němec, the word *rehabilitation* took on new & previously unforeseen significance. It was no longer that comforting familiar thing whose meaning was selfevident, to be taken for granted, without a second thought, like an infant at the bosom of its mother tongue. Here he was, the infant weaned under sudden duress, maternal teat wrenched from mouth, speechless, agape. In the past, it'd seemed only normal, right & good, that cripples, invalids, accident victims & paralytics should be rehabilitated. But what about all those in whose "rehabilitation" the régime had taken a very particular interest? If rehabilitation meant restoring things to their former state, it also meant making a person *capable of being a useful member of society*. It meant learning to be patient & suffer & work towards redemption. It meant, in fact, playing the game of *the unbearable burden of history — social psychiatry — correction — normalisation — the gross and the transformed*. If additionally it meant restitution of property & liberal democracy, it also meant fixing what was "broken" & breaking what deviated from the status quo. It meant the hidden hand of the free market & the hand of God. Most of all, it meant picking up the pieces & being made to go on, despite oneself & against one's will, for the Greater Good. But what Greater Good? What was Němec to it, or it to him?

In the chill of the corridor…

Something about the colour of the walls (stark white with a horizontal strip of bile-green running waist-high) made time seem to pass very slowly. Němec stared at it waiting for whatever was going to happen next. A cheerfully Dantesque nurse had left him there, having wheeled him across from the Convalescents Ward. The green strip had a rather emphatic texture to it, like something squashed into the wall. With almost no effort, Němec made the texture move around inside his eye — green dislocated stick-things flopping side-to-side, like a parade of foetuses playing Punch & Judy with each other — till he got bored with that & stared at the cracks in the white.

Later a different nurse appeared, straightened Němec's dressinggown, tightened his straps, patted everything into place, fussed around behind him, heady perfume trailing in the air, gave his ear a tweak & read out the name inscribed on the clipboard hanging from the back of his chair — as if to be sure it was really him: *Nye-metz*, voice full of silent question marks, suggesting something about it (the name) ought to've amused her, but… He felt the nurse's fingers trace the pink scars on his tenderised head, puckered around the stitch-holes, still visible through the stubble, then down the nape of his neck —

'Ooh, what *have* we been doing with ourselves? Naughty, naughty!'

The nurse wheeled the chair about & backed him up to the blue door. Knuckles rapping on wood & that voice in his ear again —

'You'll be a good little boysiewoysie now, won't you, & do exactly what you're told, mmm?'

And then, left again to wait in this altered arrangement, the nurse exiting the scene by another door accompanied by the perfunctory sounds of white flatsoled shoes coming along the corridor, approaching from the opposite end — a group of male orderlies in blue smocks, John Beradino lookalikes, swapping banter at high volume. *A preview of next Monday's instalment of*

GENERAL HOSPITAL

I was listenin' to the radio the other day about this psycho in Beverly Hills with a stash of body parts belonging to ol' movie stars 'n' stuff, nicked from some big exclusive cryogenics lab…'

'And *snuff*?'

'Ty vole!'

'Planned to sell 'em back to their original owners, I suppose?'

'Ah, pull the other one!'

'The old nip&tuck, eh? Bit stitched on here, bit sliced off there.'

'Picture it, Ivana Trump with Ronny Reagan's head!'

'And King Kong's brain!'

'Ty vole!'

'What Comrade Marx said, *Every economy can be reduced to the problem of supply and demand.*'

'Ty vole!'

'Apparently some famous Hollywood quack was bank-rolling the whole show…'

'Ty vole!'

'Bride of Frankenstein, *vole!*'

'Don't cry for me, Ne-cro-feel-ya…!'

'Da-da-da-dead in A-mer-i-ka! Da-da-da-dead in A-mer-i-ka!'

'So what happened next, doc?'

'They were out digging at Mount Sinai & about to knock off some old bat's tit when they discovered she was still alive?'

'What I tell you? Pure silicon!'

'Ty *vole!*'

'Nah, neighbours complained about a rotten stink & it not even election time. Y'know how it is in Southern California, mid-summer & a power outage killed the refrigeration. Cops got wind of it & went 'round to find a freezer full of goodies. Had themselves a bit of a stakeout, *harhar.* Couple of days later this Boris Karloff type comes home from a little gardening expedition to Potter's Field.'

'Welcome back Potter!'

'Certified nutjob. They couldn't touch the quack, though. Quack hired some bignote attorney. Walked, scot-free.'

'Ty vole!'

'Always the little guy takes the rap.'

'Yeah, just like Lee Harvey. Reckon there's a connect? Magic bullet & all that?'

'Whole thing sounds like a scam, you ask me. Insurance or somethin'.'

''Course it was a bleedin' scam, *vole!*'

'Hey, anyone up for a few cold one's after lunch?'

'Ty *vole!*'

Trailing the orderlies at a distance, a Ward Zombie shuffled in a pair of oversized flipflops, mumbling, thick-spittled lips, catheter dragging on the floor. *Thn mun, thnn mmm, thth mnunth, thm unnn.* Němec glanced after the orderlies then back at the zombie with his leaky catheter weaving patterns on the linoleum, *flip-flop-flip,* then down at his own legs strapped to the wheelchair. *So this's what it's come to, eh? Once more entirely in their hands.* And then the door opened & the nurse had him inside faster than he could say *Run for your life!*

Behind the Blue Door

Behind the blue door of the Rehab Unit was a very large room divided by a complex arrangement of curtains & walled partitions into a labyrinth of cubicles-within-cubicles-within-more-cubicles. The impression was of an improvised bureaucracy hastily set up in the midst of a siege in a museum of corrective medicine. At the far end of the room a tall fume cupboard, reaching almost to the ceiling, held a collection of specimen jars containing oddments & curios: malformed tendons, arthritic joints & jawbones distended from the effects of elephantiasis — a thick layer of dust, decades old, was spread out around them on the shelves. At the other end, a bank of cathode tubes, oscillators & discharge chambers, heaped above a row of filing cabinets, flanked on either side by traction devices that too-readily evoked scenes from the Inquisition. Connecting the two ends of the room was a long corridor. Its floor was a patchwork of linoleum & herringbone parquet, panelled with oblique shadows cast by a row of high windows facing onto Charles Square. From there, visible in the far corner of the park, was the chapel of John Nepomuk beside the salmon pink façade of the Faust House. Through the denuded trees in the park it was just possible, in the afternoons before sunset when the light fell across the window just-so, to observe the point diagonally adjacent to the socalled Faust House where the tramlines forked — one turning towards the river & the Friedrich Engels Embankment, the other snaking down into the valley past the Botanical Gardens' glass pavilion.

The Devil take the hind parts…

During sessions at the Rehab Unit, the nurse in charge — Nurse Peklá (or perhaps it was Pěkná) — maintained an obsessional monologue against Foreigners, Gypsies & Zhids. She spoke calmly, with the equipoise of a true fanatic. Sensing no contradiction, she appeared equally in thrall to the romantic cult of faraway places: Lichtenstein, the Jungfrau, the Frauenkirche in Dresden, Schnitzelstadt, Karelia, Innsbruck. Němec was struck almost at once by the scent that lingered whenever the nurse's uniform brushed against him: a smell of carbolic or dead ants crushed & rubbed against the skin. The whiteness of the nurse's uniform brought to mind the whiteness of women's inner thighs in billboard advertisements, or the statues above the portico of the Municipal Library. He closed his eyes, but it was hopeless. She was already there, sneering back at him in the dismal room of his mind, naked & hairless & cold as cut stone.

The Treatment

The treatment followed an unerring routine consisting principally of repetition & manipulation: 1. injections, 2. a numbed flexing & rotation of joints, 3. various complicated forms of electrical stimulation, 4. being pinned to a narrow stretcherbed like a vivisectionist's frog, in a cubicle rigged with a large grey metal box, monitors & dials. The box produced weird hypnotic music, as if a whole orchestra of gutstringed instruments had split themselves endwise. Němec fixed his mind upon it while the nurse & a pair of orderlies (mute thicknecked twins in white dungarees & black wellies) attached electrodes, alligator clips, smeared conducting gel, applying high-voltage alternating current to the scarred most sensitive parts of his corpus corporum. After, manhandled back into his chair, he was escorted by elevator down to the basement, exposed concrete walls sliding past from one level to the next till far underground. Naked fluorescents hung from the low ceiling of yet another corridor, at the end of which an archway gave onto a kind of peristyle hall shrouded in mist. Echoing in an indeterminate distance, voices moaned. The air was stifling. Pale ghostlike figures shifted against a curtain of white, appearing & disappearing behind tiled columns. A metal sink with a row of pressure hoses punctuated the mist. A steam chest stood beside it like an Egyptian sarcophagus, a red thermostat eye leering out of it. Across the archway, a dyslexic white-on-green mosaic perspired into the fog:

HYDRAPOTHY

They continued through a maze of shower rooms & baths — the sound of the orderly's rubber soles taking up the rear, enlarging or fading with the fluctuations in atmosphere. When they arrived at their destination, the rehab nurse was already waiting. Němec felt a kind of sickening elation. The room they had arrived at was a room just like the others, tiled white, with a bench on one side covered with a plastic sheet. Here a second series of treatments ensued. One of the mutes unbuckled the chair while his twin took Němec under the arms & raised him up. His legs dangled. The nurse narrowed her eyes, as though watching something pleasantly distasteful. *Curtains up on the shower block scene! What's our favourite game today, then, boys and girls? Rub-a-dub-dub?* Lilywhite pillbox hat, white pinafore, white stockings, white shoes, white all the way down to her white-of-whites. She clicked her tongue — a wet, sticking sound. *Pizzicato.* Němec let his body go slack in anticipation. Perhaps distant strains of Shostakovich. In the very middle of the room a hand-cranked metal hoist straddled a large trapdoor, like a pair of compasses describing a black circle in the tiled floor. A wire-&-leather harness dangled from the hoist, gibbetlike. While the nurse went on clicking her tongue, the first orderly walked over & pulled the trapdoor up by a handle. Below, a source of freezing water churned out of the darkness.

7

THE VOYNICH MANUSCRIPT

The Voynich Manuscript was & remains one of the Great Conundrums of the Known World — if not merely of Renaissance philology.* Composed by an Unknown Author, in an Unknown Language, it had, over the course of its moderately long history, attracted the various attentions of occultists, amateur riddlers, pseudoscientists & crackpots of every stripe from the four corners of the globe: each obsessed with a Dark Ages awaiting illumination, Secrets Most Profound still to be unconcealed — conspiracy nuts hunting the missing link in the great chain of paranoia, ancient sewer speleologists, Nazi bunker-moles, Raiders of the Lost Ark — adepts of the universal hermetic, revised, corrected & expanded Theory of Everything — all, like the proverbial moth to the perennial flame, drawn into the Manuscript's vortex to be consumed in eructations of insane mothman gibberish.

Somewhere along the line, the Prof managed to get his hands on a complete facsimile copy: he carried it about with him in a brown leather attaché case. Always at hand, its faded greyblack calligraphy within valleys of sepia, bound in a simulacrum of undistinguished vellum (creased at the edges & heavily seamed), the Manuscript was his secret prize. The attaché case was propped on the toilet seat beside the bath when the Prof died. Had any agent of foul play chosen to look inside they'd've found a bundle of incomprehensible scribble on gloss paper bearing the imprint of the Beinecke Rare Book & Manuscript Library, reference number MS 408. Possibly it even now resided in one of those metal boxes in the basement of Strahov Monastery, courtesy of the dead Prof's dead wife. If so, what had the archivists made of it? It might turn up in a catalogue as almost anything: psychiatric art, an almanac of Oriental pornography, a child's doodlebook.

How the facsimile came into his possession in the first place, the Prof never explained. There were many things about the Prof that were never explained — secrets that perished in his wife's *auto-da-fé* (rumours spawned in

---

* Or late Medieval? [✋]

exile, those nebulous Ostmark years post-War, in the chaos of Rome after Mussolini, when no-one would've passed too many remarks about an obscure footnote-hunter on the run from the Bolsheviks, hustling, trading, thieving even, in league with who-knows-what dark powers: sinister antiquarians, corrupted priests, librarians on the take, disillusioned academics, blackmarketeers, each with an eye on the gold standard & non-inflationary dollars — they'd've sold their grandmothers for a ten percent commission without batting an eyelid).

The Voynich Manuscript wasn't your run-of-the-mill pastime for retired boffins. It wasn't just that it was "mysterious," it also possessed an aura of danger, of insalubrious transactions, shadowy cloisters in which the unwary might easily come to a sticky end — professional envies & conspiracies to test even the most credulous of willing believers. There were other dangers, too. Having for centuries remained indecipherable, the manuscript presented to the more rationally constituted mind a schizophrenic's compendium of delusions — Wölfliesque mental hieroglyphs, infantile bestiaries, anatomic weirdness, faux naïf, abominable, phantasmagoric — Rube Goldberg allegories of alchemical transformation, menageries of naked sybarites, bizarro LSD cosmologies, Horus-eyed horoscopes...

You get the picture.

Perhaps suspecting they were being led a merry dance, a persistent number of commentators over the years maintained that the Manuscript was little more than an elaborate hoax, concocted by none other than the oft-maligned alchemist Edwarp K, for purposes variously speculated upon. Versions of this "theory" proliferated in many forms, though none founded upon much more than the most *umständlich* of circumstantial evidence. A competing rumour attributed authorship to K's one time employer & unhappy companion, John Dee,* & yet another to the thirteenth century Franciscan friar, Roger Bacon. The known facts were few & disappointing. The Manuscript itself was purportedly discovered in a remote villa in Frascati, in 1912, by an eccentric antique book dealer & collector, known to the world as W.M. Voynich.

Born auspiciously on Halloween 1865, in a long-abolished Russian province of Lithuania, Wilfrid Michael Voynich (a.k.a. Michał Habdank-Wojnicz, a.k.a. Ivan

---

* Whose name, incidentally, derives from the Welsh for *black*. [♣]

Kiecevsky), was the scion of a dissolute branch of the Polish nobility. His father was a petty bureaucrat who wore a sash. Upon graduating with a degree in chemistry at Moscow University, Michał Wojnicz pursued the only career his ancestry qualified him for, that of a dilettante nationalist. As a member of *Narodnaya Volia* & *Proletarjat* (would-be militant groups riddled with police informers), Wojnicz engaged in antiTzarist revolutionary activity & was duly arrested in St Petersburg. One day while awaiting trial, Wojnicz looked out his cell window at the gallows square & noticed a young golden-haired woman standing at the edge of the square below, gazing up searchingly at the prison walls. She stayed there till the guards came & sent her away. Blonde beneath a black peasant scarf, like a vision out of a fairytale. Whatever else happened, Wojnicz never forgot that fair fräulein's face. Nor the date. It was a Sunday, the 10th of April, 1887. In Warsaw it would've been Easter, but in Petersburg he'd have to wait another 7 days. It'd taken that long for God to get from Poland to Russia.

Instead of wasting a bullet on him, they sent Wojnicz to a Siberian gulag near Irkutsk to ponder the error of is ways. They breed a vicious strain of tuberculosis out in them there gulags, but Wojnicz was lucky & the disease only took thirty years to kill him. In the meantime he tried his hand at escape: wound up down the hole after the first two attempts, third time he got lucky. It was the summer of 1890, humidity around 100%, the permafrost oozing up through the taiga & temperatures into the thirties. Wojnicz made his way south, across Mongolia by camel-train, to Peking. And from Peking, dirty hungry penniless, via Hamburg aboard a fruit boat, for the price of a handmedown waistcoat & a pair of reading glasses, to Commercial Rd London, where, transformed into Wilfrid Voynich, he married, in 1893, the daughter of one George Boole, author of *The Laws of Thought* & inventor of Boolean logic.

Ethel Lilian Boole wasn't your typical pale-skinned beauty. Irish by birth, she was the youngest of five daughters. Her mother was Mary Everest, whose uncle had the mountain named after him. But despite the notoriety, the Booles weren't exactly living the highlife & poverty forced them to board Lilian with rich Uncle Charles in Lancashire, a pious industrialist who liked to dish out the abuse. While his wife & children stood dutifully by & watched, he'd tie his niece to a piano leg & bash on the keys, raging like a mad evangelist against this sluttish piece of filth he'd been obliged by charity to defile their home with.[*]

Strange the ways of the world. When eventually she left her uncle's house,

---

[*] *Jack Raymond* (London: W. Heinemann, 1901). [☛]

Lilian Boole went on a scholarship to study at the Hochschule der Musik in Berlin. She chose piano. Soon she became involved in political activism, it seemed like a natural progression. She travelled to St Petersburg & on Easter Sunday 1887 found herself standing outside a prison in which anti-Tzarist agitators were being kept. Her marriage to Wilfrid Voynich seemed fated, though fate wasn't something she believed in, rather it appeared to her as a necessary unfolding of a larger narrative, the dialectical progression of History with a capital H.

The Voynichs, "rare people" in the class of bibliophiles & propagandists, opened an expensive book emporium at 1 Soho Sq. which dealt in first editions, incunabula, books unknown to bibliographers, & served as the base of operations for the Society of Friends for a Free Russia. Eleonor Marx, Friedrich Engels, Peter Kropotkin, G.B. Shaw, William Morris & Oscar Wilde all passed through the Voynichs' doors (their in-house cataloguer, one Herbert *Garland*, later penned a memoir, *Some Famous English Bookshops*, volume III of which was devoted to his former employer & had many interesting things to say).

While Wilfrid devoted his spare hours to publishing elaborately designed catalogues, Lilian Voynich began a career as a novelist. In addition to translating & smuggling illegal literature, she now penned revolutionary potboilers, ace-of-spions stuff, that had a young officeboy called Ian Flemming watering at the mouth — books that were dead as mutton eighteen months after they were born. The pièce de résistance was *The Gadfly* (1897), an unlikely survival which lived to reach the bestseller list behind the Iron Curtain, a half-century after the fact. Stalin, whose judgement in all things was infallible, considered its author greater than Shakespeare & caused a recently discovered minor planet to be named in her honour.

The Voynichs' flourishing book business didn't go unnoticed by Scotland Yard, however, & as the Great War rumbled eastwards the order went out to bring them in. Deftly evading capture, the two crypto-Bolsheviks decamped across the pond to an address at Aeolian Hall, 42nd Street, New York, where news of the October Revolution wasn't long in coming. Needless to say, the rare books came too, including the recently discovered "Roger Bacon" Manuscript. After the war it was business as usual. Then eight years before the Non-Aggression Pact, comforted by the knowledge that the last Tzar was dead, W.M. Voynich quit this world for some higher plane.

The Widow Voynich — stern, childless & ever-mindful of Nazi

sympathisers in Congress — secluded herself from the world with her dead husband's books. And his former secretary.* From time to time men with German-sounding accents made inquiries over the telephone, into the present whereabouts of the fabled Manuscript. They offered Reichsmarks, gold, certified US Treasury bonds, to no avail. Then soon enough the Atlantic once again erupted into war & the world forgot. A Russian translator rediscovered her in the 1950s at Stalin's behest, living in a time-capsule, surrounded by the meaningless din of TV & McCarthyism. The translator handed her a royalty cheque which she fed to her cats. The remainder of the decade passed uneventfully. Though she might never've known, the year Ethel Lilian Voynich died was the year they put the 50th star on the Star Spangled Banner — the year *Ben Hur* swept the Oscars — the year Eichmann was kidnapped in Buenos Aires & Khrushchev pounded his shoe at the UN — the year Sputnik 5 bore a pair of mutts* into outer space & safely back again — the year Operation Grand Slam went pearshaped & Ebbets Field Stadium in Brooklyn got demolished & John F. Kennedy became the youngest elected President of those United States.

And the Manuscript?

While he'd been alive, Voynich was never shy about airing his personal theories as to who wrote it & when & where. He even had photostats made & sent to all the experts. Most of them figured him for a con-artist or a crackpot. By 1960 not too many even remembered the Manuscript existed. One of the ones who did was Hans Kraus, a Gotham City antiquarian, infamous in the trade. He practically staked-out Lilian Voynich's funeral. She'd always been the stubborn type, wouldn't sell no matter what — had some sort of sentimental attachment to the old stuff her husband left behind. She died surrounded by cats & bookshelves crammed with junk. The ex-secretary, her sole heir, was sick of the stuff — the Bahamas that time of year had a certain appeal. Hans Kraus lost no time finagling the Manuscript out of Miss Nil for a tidy $24,500.

Maybe Kraus thought he could crack the secret himself, use it to mint gold. Or maybe he calculated a big fat profit on the biggest unsolved mystery since before the Bermuda Triangle. It might've got him a fifteen-minute slot on *Ripley's Believe it or Not*, but the market wasn't buying that year, or any other year. When he finally got sick of trying to peddle it, Kraus decided to salvage as

---

* Anne Nil, Lilian Voynich's sole companion for thirty years. [☜]
* "Belka" & "Strelka," accompanied by 1 rabbit, 2 rats, 42 mice, flies, plants & fungi, all of which survived, apparently. [☜]

much of his reputation as he could by donating the Manuscript to the Beinecke Rare Books Library at Yale University. It was an uncharacteristic act of generosity from a man famed for his ruthlessness. But he probably figured by then it was a fake. Besides, it was tax deductible.

☥

Was it the fault of Gustav Mahler that Němec ever laid eyes on this eighth wonder of the occult world? Or a half-hearted fianchetto in a forgettable gambit?

The way he explained it to the Bugman was like this, beginning with Mydlář & the old fellas playing chess at the Klementinum, then fastforwarding to evening trawls through Malá Strana & winding up on the Prof's doorstep, being in the neighbourhood so to speak, acting on impulse & a certain degree of curiosity, finding himself in front of a certain house on Jánský Vršek, in the hot rain, & it slowly dawning on him where he was. A likely story.

To be fair, Němec had been carrying around the address of the man who called himself Hájek for over a week, crumpled in his trouser pocket. The Old Man's "invitation" had been nothing if not perfunctory: a street name & number scribbled on a page torn from his notebook, thrust into Němec's gangly, reluctant hand as he (Hájek, "the Prof") packed away his chessboard that fateful afternoon. It was a parting gesture Němec promptly forgot — perhaps it was intended that way.

His sudden appearance, therefore, might've surprised the Old Man, but it didn't. Not in the slightest. It was, to quote a well-worn turn of phrase, as if he (Němec) had been expected all along: the anticipated outcome, you might say, of a gambit calculated to remain imperceptible till long after the fact & even in hindsight cloaked in uncertainties. The impression suited the occasion, Kelley's Tower & all that. The Prof met him on the stairs, turned him around, pointed out the salient features, the "Donkey in the Cradle," etc., before ushering him back through into his thinking parlour. There was a chessboard with pieces arranged on it on a table between a couple of padded armchairs: all that was required were the players. It was all both strange & yet strangely familiar…

This second encounter had the air of a private audience between Ruy Lopez & some exiled minor Lama, wizened in brown suit, tie askew, silver hair fanning up from broad Sklavic forehead, high-cheekboned & blunt-chinned, beardless. The setting was vaguely mortuary in a decayed, unimposing kind of way: a stage set for a low-budget silent film someone had dragged-up from the vaults & dubbed over, washed in 40watts of sepia tone, the smell of beeswax & tallow oozing out of the furniture. Němec admired Lopez's tenacity, right up to the point of conceding. It was a close game, but all the moves had already been written down. And then the Prof told him about the Manuscript.

'Well you sure know how to pick 'em, dontcha kiddo?' the Bugman said.

Němec knew the only way to tell the story was to play it straight, the crazy stuff would take care of itself. Only he wasn't sure if any of it was really crazy or not. Every minute of his life till the moment he escaped from the Home had been like a joke someone made up just to dare you to laugh, too absurd to be anything but fiction, except it'd all been real, *too* real. Like someone shows you a book no one's been able to make heads or tails out of for hundreds of years? Němec shrugged. The way he described it to the Bugman, if aliens had made a report on the Lost Workers' Paradise, it might've looked pretty much the same. But it wasn't the Manuscript itself that was crazy, it was what the Prof told him about it that was crazy.

While Němec spieled it out the Bugman sat on the edge of his deckchair among a dozen pecking chickens, holding a mirror in one hand & clipping his nose-hairs with a pair of scissors in the other. Even with the evening coming, the heat radiating up from the roof was palpable. He could feel the Astroturf wilting between his toes. The chickens had that dazed hypnotic look in their eyes. An indecipherable Morse flashed from the Bugman's mirror as he worked the scissors up inside is left nostril. Němec adjusted a pair of sunglasses against the glare, mumbled something about how he figured the Prof was just some lonely old guy big-noting himself on the back of a scam laid down in antiquity, to give him some leverage, so to speak, when the day came to get his ticket stamped for the Great Hereafter. Maybe upgrade to World Traveller class.

At the same time Němec remembered thinking how maybe the Old Man regarded *him* in a not dissimilar way, like a stray dog in search of a bone & a place to gnaw on it — touching if you're prone to sentimentality about things that bite, companionable the way driftwood is when there's a current to keep it close by, eddying in the shallows, till the river rises again & carries it downstream, imbued with all the fatalism of a broken clock. He thought maybe he was being played for a sucker twice-over. The way people had of sizing him up like some kind of man-child, how he stuck out of his clothes at wrong angles, head lopsided, a bit slow in the face to anyone who didn't look too deep. But that wasn't the way the Prof looked at him. The Prof looked at Němec like someone he wanted to *listen*.

After a while Blecha put down the scissors & mirror & poured himself a brandy. He poured one for Němec, too. Soon dusk began settling over the rooftops, like the two of them were parked in a drive-in with the whole story playing up there on the biggest screen around, just the way Němec was telling it. The Bugman nodded patiently, sipped his brandy, scooped his favourite chook into his lap so he could pet it & coo over it.

'Well,' he said after Němec'd talked himself out, 'there's no accountin' for charity, kiddo.'

What the Manuscript actually *was*? Well who could say? What it *appeared to be* was legion. Rumours spread from the moment of its discovery, circulating with the ebb & flow of the times. Its momentary fame was interrupted by the Great War, the October Revolution, the Depression, Fascism, the teetering end of Empire. By the time Kraus got his hands on it, the Voynich Manuscript seemed like an artefact of a forgotten age. But word of it still circulated, cunningly, quietly, in the occult mists that still shroud this world in which the Organisation Man fancies himself king.

Dispersed in remote corners of the globe, factions of self-described adepts gathered with patient stealth, & having gathered, multiplied & re-divided like bacteria, evolving into counterfactions & countercounterfactions, each with its own theory, its own dogma, its own key to the Great Riddle. And like the clandestine sects of police informers that'd first set Michał Wojnicz on the path to becoming Wilfrid Voynich, their secret conspiracy produced a public enigma, photographed & available on request for inspection on a single spool of microfilm. But how it'd got there acquired over the years a lore whose intricacy in the retelling was almost as Byzantine & unfathomable as the Manuscript itself.

'Which, of course,' the Prof said, 'doesn't prevent anyone believing it harbours a *true* secret.'

Of course he dismissed the lot as the work of cross-eyed zodiac-gazers, demon-worshippers, penny-ante Fausts trumped-up on the limitless prospects their narcissism afforded. To such imbeciles the Manuscript was nothing short of a magic mirror, reflecting whatever they wanted to see in it. Yet stripped of its mystique, what was the Voynich Manuscript but a book no-one could read — whose fascination, like a *femme fatale*, lay solely in being out of reach — an object merely of desire in place of an object of knowing?

'Unable to know even the nature of its secret, they turn to other facets, in the hope that science, after all, or if not precisely science something at least resembling it, can lead them to the other side of the mirror & out of their cul-de-sac. In place of the usual hocus-pocus they pose questions: *Who wrote the Manuscript and when? What's its provenance? Is it a forgery? Can it in some way be computed?* The answers? No-one knows. Probably they never will.'

The Prof had a little ritual which he practiced without fail each time Němec came to visit him. He would set out a bottle of white port beside two cut crystal glasses on a tray on his desk & ask Němec to pour while he rearranged the chessmen on the small checkerboard table. The label on the bottle had the word *Lágrima* printed on it in large green letters.

'The tears of Eurydice,'[*] the Old Man pronounced on their first such

---

[*] The Ancient Greeks, it seemed, had an elaborate yarn, about a young maiden, called Eurydice, belovèd of one Orpheus, poet & pantomime artiste of local renown, with a knack for charming the wildlife. With what tenderness he trothed his affections, in couplets chafed & chaste by turn — inserts in the supplements, blazoned on billboards, broadcast by the birds, making primetime of the big forthcoming wedding night — odds going two-to-one at the betting parlour behind Zorba's Hashhouse that our ovaried Orf'd like as swandive into a serenade to his dear doxy's prize imperishables as stay in the saddle while the paparazzi snap a page 3 exposé. But lo! On the very eve of those widely adverted nuptials, Eurydice, overcome by the high excitement of it all, catching a little shut-eye, flowers in her hair, recumbent in private arbour, a little undiluted grapejuice on the side, feels a pang below the milkwhite globe of her left bosom & awakes to find a green-eyed asp's been taking liberties under her undone velour, forked tongue licking the lifeblood from grinning chops, sibilantly salacious, slithering into song as the vapid vestal's eyes grow round —

> *Si tu veux couvrir de roses tous ceux que vois en gris*
> *Si tu es vraiment morose vient danser le sirtaki*
> *Si tu veux que disparaissent tes soucis et tes tracas*
> *Si tu cherches ta jeunesse vient danser avec Zorba*
> *Vient danser pour qu'on oublie que le jour se lèvera…*

Alas, the stolen love-bite proves the undoing of poor Eurydice & she fades, borne off by fevers unremitting, ministered by the local leach-touting quacks bleeding her lilywhite, thin as air, purified of the flesh & spirit, destined no longer to dance the sirtaki. Piqued by the injustice of it all, young Orf, garbed in impetuous felt beret & flowing cape, resolves in stanzas more maudite than martial to claim back his necrid amor, if from the very grave he must, & plant upon her blushing blue lips the kiss of life that is immortal poésie. Her old man's having none of it & mounts a guard to ambush the verb-virile versifier the moment he lays so much as a strophe on her tombstone. Unperturbed, epical Orf petitions every priest, patriarch & politician from Thrace to Thebes, conspires & connives, conjures & colludes — till lighting one day all-of-a-sudden upon the pièce de résistance of his carotid canto, offering a hymn to the guardian spirits of the air & of occasion. 'Or so they say.' He raised his glass & eyed the contents. 'Eurydice's lament — symbolised, we're told, by the late harvest grapes from which the wine's made, born as autumn steers towards winter, & the Kingdom of Death & Remorse comes into the ascendant.'

Eight o'clock became the accepted hour. Němec would arrive, the Prof would set out the port & they'd play a game of chess while listening to classical recordings. Mahler, usually, but also others. Tchaikovsky, Dvořák, Chopin, Smetana. When the chess wore itself out, the Prof talked — about books mostly, sometimes about himself, what he was currently working on, which was invariably the same thing — what he called his Polygraphia — unriddling the Voynich Manuscript.

The pattern had already established itself by Němec's second visit. It was late-August but the humidity that day was appalling. A too-brief thunderstorm had swept the City, but by dusk the mercury was still in the high twenties. Black clouds sweated in the sky. The gloom was just beginning to turn dark when Němec descended the wet cobbled steps from Nerudova to the little square with the garden on old Johannesburgstraße, facing the arched entranceway to the

---

water, of fire & of earth, setting out upon a path most perilous, aided only by a talent for the judicious bribe & a charming singing voice, our Orf dons finest funereal array, slits his wrists (not too emphatically) & chugs a cup of hemlock (not too immoderately) — thence to descend, through spooked spirals of entropology, down to the Forbidden Fjords of Dis, at Death's Door so to speak, there to intercede with the Great Mortifiction himself, Who-in-Hades — soliciting His indulgence in the name of unconsummated teenage romance etc., painting a pretty picture of the lovers' plight & no stinting on the violins. Old Death's deaf as a post, so it's up to persuadable Persephone, the god-wife, Hades' better half, to take pity on the luckless lyricist, giving Him (Hades) a half-dozen wifely handsignals, to make himself scarce it seems, doddering out in the backgarden while She-Indoors concludes a quick little contractual arrangement with the unbuttoned panting poet, stuffing that rhymstering gob of his with a clit the size of a clapper in a charnel house bell, thinking for sure he's about to gasp his last & — *oh God!* — she's old enough to be his grandmum's grandmum! But what the hell, eh? Business being business, & if it means Hell's wife'll resurrect his sweet Eurydice back up in the Big Bad Überwelt, what part wouldn't he be prepared to write for himself? But there're conditions, of course: for one, when he's found his third leg again & hies his way back to his deathbed, Eurydice following dutifully behind (if only she knew!), he's *on no account*   Persephone wiggling her righthand pinkie at him — to sneak as much as a peek back at her, *capisce?* But, but, as in all these tales, misfortune has its way... At the very threshold of the world, taunted beyond endurance by the sneaking suspicion his beloved's not really there at all, duped, taken for a rube, like an idiot afraid of losing his shadow — the impulse to peep over his shoulder growing stronger with each step, as if someone's sending out radio signals controlling his mind, *just a little squint won't hurt* — & no sooner done than right before his eyes the grinning Furies, all teeth & yellowed gum, grab hold of poor zombie-eyed Eurydice, stumbling there not six feet behind him, & drag the mute weeping chit back down to the Dungeon of Darkness, eternally condemned. [♣]

courtyard of the house on Jánský Vršek. A light shone from the stairwell in the tower: in the dark, its illumination was as hard as brass, like a lighthouse beacon or a searchlight pointing from the sky.

When Němec rang the bell it was the Old Man's "Black Queen," so he called her, Elsbeth von N____, who answered the door. She wore a long black shawl with oriental patterns snaking across it. Her features were the Norma Desmond type circa *Sunset Blvd*, beautiful in a carved alabaster kind of way. Wordlessly she bid Němec enter. The door clicked shut behind him: the silence that followed was leaden. Elsbeth von N____ seemed to drift in a faint cloud of incense, like a black widow suspended in its web. How many unwitting victims, Němec wondered, had trod this path before? Unresisting he followed her through the parlour, past the teetering musty bookshelves, to the Prof's bureau, as one ushered into the sanctum sanctorum by a temple priestess to be offered at an altar. But a first impression is only a first impression.[*]

Elsbeth von N____ left Němec at the threshold, her eyes like the eyes of someone watching from behind a mask, drifting away through curtained obscurity to some other part of her domain. Across the room, the Prof, in a passable impression of Erich von Stroheim, was re-arranging the silhouettes of chess pieces on a side-table. A desklamp cast its immediate surroundings in stark chiaroscuro, failing from there on against the blackness that swallowed the edges of the room. The mood was heightened by a record playing somewhere in scratchy surround-sound. Before Němec had quite got halfway across the parquet the Prof began delivering one of his characteristic lectures, breaking the Old Hollywood spell, this time on the Réti System, his latest enthusiasm probably.

'The indirect attack,' he offered by way of welcome, 'cunning over brute force — like the Greeks at Marathon, who gave-up the centre so as to entrap the Medes by a simple outflanking manoeuvre.' The Prof grinned. 'Réti was the first

---

[*] On closer inspection, the bureau reminded Němec of the type of rooms into which men of dubious achievement retire at a certain age to commune with their own memorabilia. He couldn't help thinking of Mydlář. He pictured the headsman in his private den under the stairs, with assorted axeheads nailed to the wall, labelled with dates, the rich & famous who'd been their clients (all had paid, too, to buy a clean cut — though his reputation preceded him, his anatomical expertise, his sureness of hand, his pride in a perfectionist's attention to detail — it was more the tradition of it, the headman's tithe, a little *pour boire* — a dirty business, but they all understood each other, & if it had to be that way then that's the way it had to be) — Jesenius' Bible, a dozen anatomical encyclopaedias, medals (for exemplary service rendered) stitched onto a folded black tunic framed behind glass, the royal charter of three emperors, his favourite pair of calfskin gloves, the embroidered hood his first wife, poor Alžběta, gave him on his thirtieth birthday, the commemorative sketches he'd collected over the years, his sons' first drawings. [☚]

to grasp the true significance of the diagonal. For him, a square was never simply a four-sided figure.'

While the Prof spoke, he gestured to Němec to pour the wine, which Němec did, handing the Old Man a glass & taking the other for himself. The Prof eased himself into a well-stuffed armchair & Němec followed suit. He sipped the wine, it was heady stuff. There was the lingering incense of Elsbeth von N____ in the air & pipe tobacco & the smell of aged leather coming off the armchair. It smelled just the way you'd expect a well-stuffed armchair to smell in a room like that. A low checkerboard table was pushed against the right arm, the other side of it touched the left arm of the Prof's chair: mother-of-pearl inlaid, with ornate chessmen dressed in antique armour ranged at either end like opposed armies ready to do battle, Papist & Hussite. The black bishop's pawn had advanced across the field to parley with the white queen's pawn — they seemed in no particular hurry.

'Did you know our entire national literature's founded on a pair of nineteenth-century fakes?' the Prof said all of a sudden.

Němec blinked, supposed an answer wasn't required, & sipped some more wine, trying to get the appreciation of it, steeped as it was in the romance of mythology. Eurydice's tears tasted bittersweet, just as they had to. The Prof, making a furrow of his brow, set his glass on the edge of the checkerboard table, plucking a black rook from the corner square & turning it between his fingers the way a priest worries a rosary. He squinted at it as if to espy between its crenellations some Lilliputian man taking refuge there, a gnat with clipped ears. Němec pondered white's kingside knight, thinking to get on with the business at hand.

'Unfortunate,' the Prof continued, 'but true. The *Königinhofer Handschrift* & the *Judgement of Libuše* socalled from Zelená Hora. Palacký, for one, was a confirmed believer.* There were still one or two of the man's disciples intent on drumming that rot into us when I was at school — along with all the rest of that claptrap — High Church legends, epics, chronicles, courtly romances — a whole archaeological conspiracy to dupe a people into patriotism, for something that didn't even exist.'

The Prof placed the rook back on its square, smoothed out his forehead, pursed his lips. His gaze rested disconcertingly on Němec's hand.

'One could quibble over distinctions, of course, split hairs or, as our

---

* František Palacký, the nation's original "Dear Old Dad," hoaxed head-honcho of the Chesk National Revival. Before Klem Gottwald & "all that." [☚]

Francophiliac foundling-father might've said, *bugger flies* — but the question is, would it've made the slightest difference if those books had never existed or hadn't been faked?'

Pins & needles crept up Němec's fingers. The Prof's eyes wandered back to the board. For the next few moments he exercised the compulsion to straighten the rest of the pieces, nudging them into a neat line in the middle of their squares, forward-facing, then appeared to change his mind & adjusted the two knights so that their horse heads were both turned inwards, as it were, facing their respective bishops. The Prof shrugged, surveying the possibilities. Of course, this was all just a preamble to advancing his king's bishop pawn this time, almost as if he didn't mean to, just to occupy his hands while he talked, but the gambit was exposed, it'd been planned that way all along & now it was up to Němec to pretend he was falling for it.

'You take away the premise,' the Prof sighed, as if by way of afterthought, '& what's left?'

Němec wondered what indeed was left. About a centimetre in his glass, which he upended then made tentative movements in the direction of refilling. But the Prof seemed not to notice, his mind had already shifted to his magic book. The gambit, Němec supposed, would stay like that, frozen in time, while the talk circled around & came to some salient point the succeeding move might illustrate, like serendipity. A subtle expression shaded the Prof's face.

'Consider the Voynich Manuscript,' he said, making a gesture that was probably supposed to be offhanded, 'what do we know about it? Does anything whatsoever depend upon it? Or is it rootless, *ewige*, uncompelled by Man's hunger for certain certainties, for a fixed foundation, blood & soil — like the hoaxers of Zelená Hora, the Unitas Fratrum, chauvinists of the Great Sklavonic Idea (which, incidentally, had had to be taught to them by a pair of peripatetic Peloponnesians come north bearing alphabets to illiterate hordes…).'*

Němec steeled himself for another of the Prof's monologues, but the Prof's cunning was in never fully playing his hand till it was too late to back away: testing his opponent, sizing him up for something. The background music played its part, swelling & fading. At first Němec convinced himself he was humouring the Old

---

* Those pederast candy salesmen, Tweedle-Kyril & Tweedle-Methodious. [♥]

Man, acting the role of Poor Tom to the Prof's Leer, keeping the old bird company while making the most of an excellent wine cellar. The Prof's voice made a low hum, like an engine approaching or getting further away, drifting in & out as the wine grew smoother. Somehow the game on the board had evolved without Němec even being aware of it. Time past. He began pondering his moves, taking longer & longer, & when the Prof issued his replies it was as if Němec didn't register them at all but rather stumbled upon them, the way he might discover that a familiar landscape he'd been staring at for hours suddenly had something completely out of place in it. *Well how the hell did that get there?*

Němec pictured himself in the situation he was in, there in that room, wine glass in hand, playing a game that was evolving beyond his capacity to grasp it, not even a game any more but something else entirely. He touched the glass to his lips to resist the urge to laugh: the runaway kid from the Home grown up into a right savant, sharing a drink with the Prof up in the dead astrologist's tower, talking the big ideas, getting a mind's-eye hard-on. Maybe it was because no-one apart from the Bugman had ever taken him seriously that way before, where he didn't have to play dumb or be ashamed of the things inside his head. But what'd the Prof see in *him*? And always, without fail, the Manuscript — *asleep four hundred years, waiting to be woken up* — what was he to it?

From the first mention the very idea of the thing had seemed ridiculous —by the third or fourth glass, downright bizarre. Yet all the while, the Prof demanded a credulity that only existed in theatre. Like a magician preparing his audience, he ushered Němec into the presence of the mystery by degrees: now touching upon this aspect, now upon that, showing there was nothing up one sleeve while from the other pulling a coloured handkerchief that turned into a white dove that became a rabbit asleep in a hat.

As his talk veered, the Prof's hands became more & more agitated, now rearranging the chessmen on the board, now fidgeting with his wine glass, now pushing himself up from the arms of his chair to wander back & forth behind his desk, drumming the edge of it as he did so, now parting & drawing the curtains, now turning the flaps over the pockets of his suit jacket, now sitting back down to begin the whole charade anew in another register, another key. It became impossible not to watch the Prof's fingers as he spoke — like a concert pianist playing Tchaikovsky — as a way of listening, it was all Němec could do to keep the Old Man's words from melding into pure sound.

'The cryptanalysts...' the Prof was saying, & the words *crypt* & *analyst* drifted apart & back together at the same time, the way he said it, voice dropping a register, grave, thinking *a pickaxe and a spade, a spade*, exhuming by statistical analysis, *hehe*, 'have nothing to tell us about the Manuscript at all, except its *significant randomness*. Which means, in layman's terms, the script might contain elements of any language at all — but still a language, mind you, & not just sounding brass & tinkling cymbals. But,' he fingered the crown of the black king, 'they can hardly even agree on that. As for the rest…'

Did Voynich fake it?

Possibly.

Did it resemble other forgeries of the same period?

Well, no-one knew what period it came from, but supposedly not.

Did anyone have the faintest idea what it was all about?

None. At. All.

Němec stared at the chessboard & made some desultory response to the Prof's apparent retreat, shifting a rook's pawn in lieu of anything meaningful. The next move would probably be the clincher, the one he couldn't see — it was always like that, you stalled for time & time suddenly ran out & you got to stare Inevitability in the face once again. *Pretty, eh kiddo?* As pretty as a Sphinx combing her hair in a mirror. He sank back in the armchair with its musty dust-of-the-attic smell & sipped some more of Eurydice's bittersweet tears. *In every sorrow a joy begins. So why stall, when you can throw yourself joyously into the abyss?* The black queen seemed to smirk at him. Something stirred across the room. A draught perhaps. And Němec had to fight the impulse to glance over his shoulder, knowing full well what he'd find & thinking how the Prof had left out the other half of the story…*

---

* About how Orf in his secondhand grief, penning heartbroke haiku at an exponential rate (his Grief = his Art, hard to suppose he'd've wanted it otherwise), charming the stones to weep but getting a bit on the nose as far as the would've-been in-laws are concerned, not to mention the local sorority who could bear a bit of breast-beating in the right spirit, but the man was set to make a career out of it — only a matter of time before the indecent spectacle of that bawling bard day-in, day-out, lousing the place up with his oxters unwashed & Rastafarian sidelocks, wrecking the view out past the playing fields where even sheep now feared to tread, sleeping bollock-naked under the stars & only himself to keep company at night, harping on about that love-that-dare-not-look-over-its-shoulder & blowing snots at any skinnylegged shepherd girl gormless enough to give him a flash of her drawers…

Well it was only a matter of time, & that running out fast, before Orf here aroused once & for all the deep-seated, so to speak, ire of every man-hungry suffragette within cooee, who, spurned beyond forbearing & righteously indignant at the crooning bard's endless blather from the bleachers 'bout a Love Ideal, came at him one perfect sea-breezed mid-afternoon pell-mell out of the proverbial nowhere to take wee Orf, shaking himself off after his post-siesta micturation, in what you might call an unguarded moment — long suppressed passions running high by now, each of his femmenly assailants fully prepared to play below the belt, drop the hand for a bit of a

Meanwhile the Prof was still going with his lecture about the mystery Manuscript. The biggest names in War-time cryptognometry, he was saying, had butted their eggheads against it & come up with something called a *continuum* —

'Meaning it could be Greek for all they know.'*

---

grapple, a cinch of the offending article, a punch in the ars longa, a paw-full of sweaty thigh, a headlock on the short&curlies — launching in unison into a bosom-heaving tackle at the fey fairy's size eights, toothy slobbers over sideswiped kneecaps, a bitesize of skinny rump, a flayed falsetto, the wholesale savaging of coccyx & vertebrae, a stiff lick of the salt from his ears, gobble of his yardarm, a fervid frottage over every square inch of babyfaced butter-wouldn't-melt licksomeness...

Easy to see how the whole thing might get out of hand with all that hotblooded groping, gripping, grinding womanhood, each out for a first go at our mate Pudding&Pie there, gobstopped & pop-eyed — one end of him taken out of touch while the other's being put to rights on the ten-yard line, rucked in a scrum from all sides simultaneously & — before he can so much as squeak foul or a high-C abracadab in hope of turning their Amazon-ardour to butterfly kisses, their loins to quivers — have him by his eunuch's tonsure, twisted into a figure-eight, scalped head gouged-off at the neck, snatched from the seething mass by the most colossal butch of a prop-forward yer ever liable to clap eyes on & in one fell swoop booted the length of the pitch clear over the cross-bar, stands, scoreboard & seagull perched on the satellite dish, far, far, a speck arcing through the blue, out over the red-flagged gusty beach, the lifeguard's eyrie, past the breakers, splat into the sea. Dürer called the poor headless bastard the first Thracian sodomite — since having once gone down the backroad with Eurydice, he refused all other offers of the fairer sex, & loved only altar-boys — gushing-on all the while about that prissy little belle-de-jour he was forever spared the morning-after pout of. Adrift upon the tides — food for fishes & way-station for migratory gulls — Orf's head, unabashed, lovingly wave-lapped, last seen, washed-up some mythical eight months hence, on the very Sapphic isle of Lesbos, briny, tanned as a coconut, mouth ajar, tongue wagging in its own wind, a curate cunnalinguist. Poetic justice? [♣]

* Ain't that always the way? Picture taciturn public school types: men in beige sitting about in Victorian country mansions as if the War's just an extension of junior commonroom antics, doodling on napkins, watching the Buckinghamshire weather through fogged mullioning — jejune graduates of the Government Code & Cipher School making smalltalk out of algebraic geometry, one-time pads & modular additions — it's dull monotonous work, but someone's got to do it (you can picture the type). They're busy, though no-one would guess from looking at them, building a Colossus to beat the Krauts with — a giant Golem of a thing, wired into a captured Wehrmacht encryption machine, spirited out of Poland by members of the resistance — codename E.N.I.G.M.A. Like Babbage, the boys at Bletchley are looking for ways to mechanise the number-crunching, put a crank in the job of *calculation*, turn randomness into information. Down in a bunker with their data bombs churning-out strings of gibberished probability which, given time & an infinite spreadsheet, provided eerie contours of the unfolding of events: Wolf-packs gathering in the Atlantic, trans-continental freight routings, deployments on the Eastern Front, all the mental twitchings of an enemy fast spiralling into madness. Who knows if the Voynich Manuscript wasn't exactly that, a map of chaotic reason, the madness of the Dark Ages gasping its last, in a tongue no-one would ever be able to speak again? But to the mechanics of modern reason, pure fancy, of course. They'd reckon anything dreamt-up by a medieval monk ought to be child's play — & so it ought — rudimentary adding-tables & substitution ciphers, nothing by their standards: they'll lounge about on deckchairs during R&R & dash off a solution like doing the *Evening Standard* crossword. But even their hundred-million-permutation machines won't give

Outside, it'd begun to rain again. The insistent tapping of the rain at the windows sounded like someone impatiently wanting to have their say. Muted timpanies gonged in the background, becoming stifled thunder, becoming a car passing in the street. The Prof, having made the seemingly unremarkable gesture of edging his queen's bishop along a short diagonal, stood & went around to the far side of his desk, pulling a brown leather attaché case from under it. Němec, resigned to a state of affairs that no longer concealed itself, could tell the Old Man was about to launch into a technical dissertation on this or that facet of the accursed Manuscript. Everything so far might just as well've been a pretence for exactly this: the revealed check & the inevitable checkmate.

'Certain ideas,' the Prof began, wasting no time, 'had been in the wind for some time. Ada Lovelace, countess & daughter of the poet Byron, wrote *programmes* back in the 19th century already, designed to compute socalled Bernoulli polynomials.* There were no computers back then, but there was Babbage's theoretical Difference Engine, which was the closest thing to a mainframe before the boys at Bletchley Park built the Colossus during the War, to crack the Nazi's "Enigma" codes.

Babbage was a kind of mathematical Frank N. Furter who began by designing machines that could reckon logarithms & do pushups at the same time, instead of leaving it to chimpanzees with slide-rules who were prone to get their decimal points mucked-up when the numbers got too big: rudimentary stuff, you might say, but you have to start somewhere. He even invented a steam engine to drive the thing. Ada Lovelace was his personal muse. She provided the software, so to speak, while he hard-wired it, only he never quite got there. The Difference Engine wasn't built till after he was well & truly dead (brought on, as ill-luck would have it, by renal calculus). In the meantime Boole came along & rewrote the book — from then on it was only a matter of time before someone had the bright idea to plug an automated telephone exchange into a bank of

---

them a shred of an outcome to go on, which makes *this* particular codebook more than just a little unusual, unique in fact, as far as the E.N.I.G.M.A. boys are concerned (& though there're bombs falling they've gotten themselves obsessed with this sideline, trying to outwit each other between sorties with the day's E.N.I.G.M.A. key-change) — that's to say, if it *is* a codebook, but of course they're not even sure about *that*. The sort of code that gives Bletchley Park novices the heebie-jeebies — a *code* that only exists *because* it can't be broken, whose decrypt's only ever *true* on condition it can't be *verified*. Blind, like faith or the search for the Philosopher's Stone: with this simple qualification — the Manuscript was real. [✋]
* $B'_r = r! B_r(O)$ $(r=0,1,2,3,\dots)$ [✋]

cathode tubes & create the world's first Electronic Brain.'*

The Prof grinned down at Němec who'd managed to keep his face studiously blank throughout.

'Back in the day, the transcripts Babbage made looked remarkably like Voynich's, crude as they are.' The Prof's grin dissolved. 'What you'd expect Frankenstein's notebooks to've looked like, if they'd ever existed. Confections of a delusional mind, perhaps, or perhaps not delusional at all. The real miscegenated with the socalled imaginary, the organic & inorganic, species & genera. What else is Creation but evolution by other means — which is to say, a perversion?'

The Prof set the attaché case on the edge of his desk.

'For her part,' he went on, fidgeting with the clasps, 'the countess refused to accept any such thing. Babbage might dream of a machine imbued with life, but Ada Lovelace dreamt only of programmes that produced nothing but numbers: beautiful numbers, like a Jacquard loom weaving algebraic patterns, but not the sacred number, the Pythagorean soul, capable of moving itself. Was she afraid of creating a monster? What if the programme discovered a motive of its own, some hidden idea it would only require a catalyst to transmit from algebraic particle to intelligent design? Did she suspect such a thing might already've happened, if yet only as dark whisperings of Masonic adepts, of Babbage himself perhaps, ancient member of the Cambridge Ghost Club — & not to mention her own begetter, whose unholy cohabitations were the stuff of legend.'*

---

* "Fact is, there was nothing wrong with the plan. Oh the plan was alright. The plan would've worked." J. Higgins, CIA Deputy Director, NY. [✊]

* Another glass of Eurydice's tears, rebalancing the ratios, bloodsugar alchemistry, transmutation of enzyme to alcohol, to see spiralling out from a vanishing point behind the eye, aurora-like, a 4.7µs sync-pulsed flicker across the brain-mosaic, scan-lines of static ridging into silhouette, from which, tuning the dials, emerged a picture of Ada Lovelace snapping her garterstrap (*sonnez les cloches, comme on dit dans les classiques*), lewd-mouthed & myopic-eyed — small of the back club-footed Byron might've tapped-out tight incestuous hexameters on had he but lived (he died, alas, when his poor slip of a daughter was only eight, of fever, at Missolonghi, in the middle of someone else's war) — braced there against the heavy machinery, Babbage's psychotronic doodad-in-progress: knobbed gearshift leaving its impress through the light calico of her skirts, inching their way up ever so slightly now she's got the old goat's attention by the horn… What sort of image was this? Some kind of blackbook smutty Victoriana creeping in? As with birch switch the old numbercruncher approaches, tumescent to his muttonchops — tickles the girl's spindly shins, his *Enchantress of Numbers* he calls her — hum of lovelaced voice softly in his ears, harking back to memories of long walks from Porlock Weir to Culbone, fading now. Of course the whole thing's an octogenarian's folly, pretending himself in these penurial last days Master of Situations, as Lady Fate comes to meet him perhaps for the last time, & dear Ada, long dead, all so long, how time doth fly — unacknowledged ghost in his machine, its *genius loci*, had it ever existed beyond the

So saying, the Prof fumbled a thick folder from the attaché case & laid it on his desk. Removing a sheet of paper from it, he beckoned Němec over —

'See for yourself.'

Němec got up & stood beside the Prof — he was pointing at something & Němec leaned forward to see what it was. On the page in front of him was a lot of mystical glossolalia surrounded by diagrams, word lists, tables, like a defaced version of what you'd find in a schoolboy's grammar book. Strange conjugations unfolded in logarithmic progression:

An, ain, aiin, aiiin…
Ar, air, aiir, aiiir…
Al, ail, aiil, aiiil…
Ey, eey, eeey, eyeee…
Edy, eedy, eeedy, eeeed!

Němec looked at the page blankly.

'Curious, *mnnn?*' the Prof said. 'The pattern's not simple repetition — there're cycles, loops, permutations & recombinations, like a routine performed by a primitive computer. Call it a *grammatron*, if you like: a word-machine whose use, or even existence, has long been forgotten.'

Němec did his best to envision echoes of machined angelspeak blown by cosmic winds, of agonies & bewailings, fall of Babel, toppling stone & shattered

---

page, in the intermingling of their minds — that immeasurable exultation of cogs & wheels, to out-evolve Darwin with. No mere boy's-own gynaecological crudescence but a celestial *symphony* of hydraulic cockstands & turbined cunts, in sublime transport of, etc. The machine-to-end-all-machines! And more! All the as-yet unformed future life of those generations-to-come — spawned of this instant, terminal though it be (as prodigious as the club-footed poet himself!), like tadpoled gnomes of a difficult-to-imagine parallel universe, barely resembling *this* one, which *goes on* though *we* end: from cell-division to siamesed suturation, birthing a whole host of (horrific to behold!) machined Morlocks, genetic pariahs cast out of Paradise to geodesic subterrains, post-apocalyptic cyboreal molemen — as remote from what you'd expect of an innocent bit of laboratory slap&tickle as Babbage himself from a mutated mainframe: timewarped in analoguese, the Creator's DNA coded by a room full of copyists working 8-hour shifts at just above the minimum wage, to feed all of everything-known-to-man into a virtualised jism to be fed, cryogenically, into countless Ada clones: moulding & shaping that hypostatised wombfruit like a zillion typehammers punching Turing-like into pastried nano-cortex, print-erase, foetal synapses cauterised like overblown tungsten filaments smashed flat, cathodes, oscillations in vacuum tubes, if only to get the one idea into that pulpy protoprimitive skull! Those vast unborn arrayed palimpsests of damage where dreams of a habitat beyond Earth commingle with denatured inanity: is this what the Future holds…? (*Not bad, Němec, old chump — remember to write that down.* [☝])

etceteras, Nimrod's gibberish.* But to no effect: the words on the page looked simply like the shrieks of an inmate in a nuthouse. Convulsive xenoglossings of the pentecostally brainbaked.

'Perhaps its meaning isn't as might be *sought*,' the Prof intoned, assuming an attitude of mock profundity, 'but an intention *within*... Received wisdom is the whole thing's too complex to be a fluke, so if it's a forgery it's the best one out there. Or it could just be an incompetent transcription from a lost language. Some undiscovered Linea B or the cuneiform of Nineveh before they deciphered *that*.'

The Prof turned to him with a mad glint in his eye —

'Or else,' he leered, 'it might be something entirely without precedent. A *singularity*. Evidence of an alternative set of probabilities to the one which constitutes *this* world — some inaccessible *other place*, the unconstituted *quaestium* of the ear-eye in its quest for an intelligible object — some *thing* which is at the same time *no-thing*. It might appear as innocuous as a purely mathematical dilemma, with no relation at all to the socalled *esoteria*: strange attractors of pseudo-random chaos in the G.O.D. Codex — *materia prima* of the Word itself, its genome, secret source of the true, multiple & divided, logos...'*

The watery folds of the Prof's eyes contracted as he forged ahead with his proofs & speculations, like a Buster Keaton character who conceals his disappointment at finding only an inattentive audience with increasingly strange antics. He waved at another sheet of paper with notes clipped to it —

'Here's an analysis a statistician from I.B.M. produced...'

Numeric ranks & files crisscrossed the page: factored improbability quotients, Möbius strips of raw data spooling into feedback infinity, the strop to Ockham's razor perhaps — Němec was in no real position to say.

'Supposedly the whole thing exhibits a pattern of complexity that suggest a process of *evolution* at work — like a system tending in competing directions & somewhere inside it a *mind* at work, divided but struggling to reconcile itself, order the chaos into patterns, entropy into the base matter of an idea... Which

---

* "Are not the thunders of increase numbered 33, which reign in the second angle? Under whom I have placed 9639, whom none has yet numbered but one, in whom the second beginning of things are & wax strong; which also successively, are the number of time; & their powers are as the first 456...?" e.g. [✋]
* "Rephèl maì amècche zabì almi..." [✋]

is a fancy way of saying it doesn't tick any of the usual boxes.'

The Prof turned the sheet over — there were about a dozen more of the same type of grammatical tables. Němec gazed blankly. As far as he could see, the Prof had made his point: the whizbang Manuscript had beaten the band. *Whoopee.* He wondered idly what Descartes or any of the others would've thought of all this had he ever lain eyes etc. Would it've changed the course of history? Of philosophical thought? Of anything? The Prof kept a sideline in this, as well. Question: what if Descartes' undisclosed purpose in venturing to Golem City in 1620, at significant risk to his person, was none other than to gain access to the Manuscript? Already the subject of anachronism & contradictory fables, teasing the worms out of the woodwork, it (the Manuscript) was even, so the Prof intimated, at one time believed to hold the key to Kepler's last, misunderstood observations, about the clockwork mechanism of the universe no less, boiled down to a verbal algebra, ideas simple enough for any child to grasp but somehow escaping even the notice of Rudolph's brains-trust. Word of this secret K Manuscript had rumoured its way cross-continent, prompting the young Descartes on his fool's errand — for by then the Manuscript had already been spirited-off, beyond the reach of the Counter-Reformationists, a lost meaning detached from the plethora of signs strewn about to conceal the fact of its disappearance. Gaius Octavius gazed blankly from the fireplace like he'd heard this all before…

But the story went back further than that.

'For many years none other than the polymath *Roger* Bacon was suspected of being the Manuscript's maker — the man who believed the only way to keep nature honest was mathematics applied to observation. Ahead of his time & grievously misunderstood by men with a talent for doing so: the master of the Franciscans — those dullwitted authors of the Inquisition — accused Bacon of *novelties* & had him thrown in prison.' The Prof coughed into his balled fist. 'Be mindful, the discovery of new things in contradiction to the status quo has never been viewed benevolently by the Powers that Be. We, of course, would prefer to think we live in more enlightened times, but perhaps not. Perhaps Bacon's detractors were simply unable to profit from the man's genius without risking everything they themselves believed in or stood for. Idiots & ideologues have always been enemies of *virtuosity* — & Bacon, whatever his faults, was of a particularly excessive type: optics, chemistry, astronomy, grammatology also. With very good reason, they regarded him as a threat.'

The Prof shrugged his shoulders, sighed, as if playing the part of the reluctant sceptic who, like Democritus, believes only what he can see, yet who still might be persuaded of an idea that's so far eluded him. He shuffled his papers together & returned the folder to the leather case, snapping the clasp into the lock. He held the case for a moment with both hands, with a pensive expression on his face, then quietly slipped it back behind the desk. He was a man to keep everything in its proper place, even the bric-a-brac probably had reason to it. The head in the fireplace seemed to curl its lips up at the edges, but only for a moment. Němec took the opportunity to pour more wine.

'To his admirers, though,' the Prof straightened up, continuing where he'd left off (the man was indefatigable), 'Bacon was the real deal — including, strange but true, the Pope, Clement X — *Doctor Admirabilis*, they called him: astonishing, strange, most worthy etc. of admiration.'

Němec handed the Prof a refilled glass, nodded, made affirmative noises & edged back towards his armchair. The Prof remained standing where he was —

'Bacon's self-adverted ambition was to disperse those mists which persisted to his day in shrouding the world in unscientific mystery & superstition. *Ideology*, by any other name. It's true Bacon still believed in the philosopher's stone & astrology, but in those days they, too, were considered science. Remember,' the Prof said, jabbing the air with the end of his index finger, 'the alchemists believed in matter *as well as* the spirit, & matter in its relation to spirit was expected to follow a combination of physical *and* metaphysical laws. The confluxus radiorum. He wasn't merely tinkering with providence. Think of Pythagoras, who never knew Latin but was supposed to have said "anima est numero seipsum movens." *The soul is the number that moves itself.* No,' the Prof's voice was dry, strained from the exertions of the intellect — he sipped at the tears of St Eurydice to lubricate his speech. 'Bacon didn't write the Voynich Manuscript any more than I did…'

He gazed profoundly at the residue at the bottom of his glass & then added as an afterthought —

'*But* does it matter *who* wrote it? There could've been more than one author, more than one code, too: *a tongue*, as Goethe says, *doubly foreign*. So why not a whole Albigensian conspiracy, eh?'

The Prof drained the last drop from his glass, set it to one side, pressed the palms of his hands together as in an attitude of prayer, shook his head, nodded, fixed Němec with colourless eyes.

'But it would be impossible for any writing to contain two grammars at the same time. No? Still, there never seems to be a shortage,' the Prof waved his right hand airily, 'of idiots willing to resurrect that particular theory.'

Finally he seemed to notice the armchair & sat down in it, spreading his hands on his knees, the way tired old men do. His eyes gazed listlessly at the chessboard. Nothing had happened there in a while, but if it had it wouldn't have made any difference, there were only another two moves in it. The Prof seemed to be considering the plight of Němec's king, like a player who thinks they might be able to outwit themselves & prolong the game into a different outcome. It was a hopeless proposition. Then another idea must've occurred to him: when he looked back up from the board he was faintly grinning —

'Or turn the problem around. Take the noble language of our over-endearing comrades to the East. No-one else seems to agree on how the damned thing should be written, apart from the Russians, of course ... Consider,' pointed finger raised, an ironic undertone creeping into his voice, 'Tchaikovsky — whose name, incidentally, derives from *čajka*, the gull, like the old Soviet parade car. You know the type? Long black open-top thingamajig with fins at the back, like the one they shot John F. Kennedy in...'

'Who? The Russians?'

The Prof smirked without seeming to move his face —

'No-one seems to know.'

Someone must know, Němec thought — the man who pulled the trigger at least. Or perhaps even *he* didn't know, hypnotised by secret powers, wheels within wheels. *Ooh-ee.*

All this time (it was no real coincidence) a record had been playing softly in the background, was at that moment coming to an end, but only now did Němec recognise it as Tchaikovsky's violin concerto in D major. It was, the Prof took the opportunity to point out, a very rare Edison recording: Adolf Brodsky in London, re-mastered & transferred to vinyl LP but still emanating the ghostly background hiss of a technology as remote from the present as Atlantis was from Edison. The Prof poked a finger at his bottom lip thoughtfully, his features immobile. The music concluded before he spoke again —

'Anyway, a well-bespectacled graphologist in Oslo, or maybe it was Copenhagen — Professor Dötthuvud — concluded recently that whichever scribe or scribes prepared the Manuscript, their writing styles evolved over the *course* of its composition — suggesting the script itself only became fluent for the authors at the moment of completion.'

What else had the graphologist made out of so much slanted gibberish? The upstrokes *here* & *here* indicating such&such affliction of the personality, these rounded figures suggestive of so&so disease of the brain & central nervous system, a certain hysterical propensity to obliqueness, the uncrossed "t" typical of manipulative tendencies, etc.? The medieval calligraphy machine not giving much of the game away to ballpoint-wielding boffins weaned on gestalt therapeutics, psychograms, *sistema de Xandró*? Lending an eye to legends long put to rest: San Juan Huarte de San Juan, 1775, *Examen de ingenios para las ciencias* — Prospero Aldorisio, 1611, *Idengraphicus nuncis* — Camilo Baldi, 1622, *Trattado come de una lettera missiva si conoscano la natura e qualita dello scriviente*… Picking apart the texture of the text with a blunt needle, a numbed Braille finger, a blind Pineal eye — to see sense in the form of things, the weft & weave, the weariness of the nib & profundity of the inkwell, plucked quill, steel nib, copperplate, squid ink, India ink, ink of the ancient Incas, ink of the mythical incunabulum. *The real question*, he might've said, *is what's all this for?*

'Then there's the object itself,' the Prof continued. 'Should we or shouldn't we attribute significance to the fact that the Manuscript's vellum binding, for example, isn't its original one? Or that there're several pages *missing*, some known to've been lost *after* Voynich discovered it? Conspiracy? Or incompetence?'

The Prof stopped & thought for a moment, staring at his fingertips. Behind him, glyptic rain patterns shifted across the windowglass, marbling the glow of the streetlights. He grimaced & this time his face moved, one side slipping down while the other slid up —

'So many questions, & so many who've tried & failed to answer them. Eventually, so they think, science must prevail. I have my doubts, somehow.'

Was it any coincidence, then, that even while the Prof's ashes were growing cold in their urn, a notice appeared in the window of the *Svoboda & Slovíčkář* bookshop beside the Golem City Philosophy Institute — typewritten, in bold Roman serif & posted beside a flyer for the Pluteus Society (Staré Město Chapter) — announcing *The Sphinx's Code*, a definitive book-length study, publication imminent, of the **VOYNICH MANUSCRIPT**, author unnamed? No prospective date, no name of the publishing house, no address for inquiries — only, in an obliquely scrawled hand, a brief postscript, which read: *observa hoc spatium.*

It was the day after the Prof's funeral. Němec had spent the evening getting drunk on the Bugman's rooftop, reminiscing, in a manner of speaking, about the Old Man. They were both still drinking at sunrise, when Blecha went off to collect the morning's eggs & Němec decided to air himself out & take a walk. On the way he stopped at the bookshop. The shutters were just going up & there was the notice for *The Sphinx's Code* stuck in the window. Němec stared at it & wondered what it meant: he'd come to think of the Old Man & the Manuscript as unique & inseparable entities, but evidently he'd been wrong. For all he knew, an underground army of Voynichologists & Voynichographers was at that very moment, even, secretly at work in the City. It was nothing to him. Or maybe it was.

Němec questioned the bookshop attendant, but the attendant shrugged & said he didn't know the first thing about it. Němec remained curious, nonetheless, to find out what the story was — perhaps someone had figured out the unsolvable mystery, beaten the band at their own game. No more fun in that. All that'd be left for the glory of mankind would be to make up some other riddle of the universe. He decided to bide his time & wandered off down to the river to sleep for a while on the embankment. The sun was out, warming the flagstones, giving the bums on the benches a holiday. When he woke he stumbled up Kaprova Street to the *Chop House*, in honour of Mydlář & the Old Man. The day was long, he sat there in his handmedown undertaker's suit with a beer in front of him till closing time & on the way back to the Bugman's place he stopped again at the bookshop just to convince himself the notice was really a figment of his imagination.

But it was there alright. It'd been joined by a clipping from the classifieds offering a rare edition of Leibniz's *Monadology* (Éditions Faustroll, Paris), interested parties to call so&so at such&such number — an advert for spa treatments designed to aid writer's block — a notice for a public lecture on the heresies of the Regula Pragensis Brotherhood — a change of location for the weekly meeting of the local Book Restorers Guild — & an introductory course offered, first Wednesday of every month, on How to Read Braille, etc. Conspiracies of the bizarre & inane. There were no other clues.[*]

---

[*] → Chapter 10. [☙]

8

BOULE DE JUIF

> Ethel Lilian Voynich *née* Boole, daughter of Mary Boole *née* Everest, daughter of Mary Everest *née* Ryall, was a novelist popular in the Soviet Union & the People's Republic of China. Her mother, a mathematician, was employed as a librarian at Queer's College, Longdong (*sic*). Her sisters also became mathematicians & the mothers & midwives of mathematicians. Her father was no less than the eponymous inventor of Boolean Logic ◄◄ her Boole was the father of invention, Logos Eponymachus ◄◄ her logical eponym was an invented Boole-father ◄◄ her *bouleversé* namesake was part-father part-invention, which seemed logical enough at the time... [✋]

Lily was for Lilian, as Mary was May, though her uncle in torrents of vexation proffered Lilith, succubus, minx, spawn of Lucifer — denounced as witch, sorceress, corrupter of darling cousins, angels both, though neither a wit between them... Uncle Charles never approved of his brother Boole, who was (the very words galled him) a *free thinker* if not worse, occult numerologist or, perish the thought, secret convert of the dark arts of Christ's murderers! Her father's proxy in this as in so much else, Lily's punishment was to be tied to a chair & forced to play sonatas while her lunatic uncle hammered beside her on the keys: the *Appassionata*, the *Pastorale*... Lily was also for Blanchefleur. Her Mama told her that story after Old Boole died (8 Dec. 1864: she was only an infant at the time, though swore she remembered it like yesterday pleural effusion, they said, from buckets of cold water being tipped over him in bed: his wife's cold cure (logic (hers) dictating a cure should resemble the cause)), long long before she (Lily) was sent away, sold into slavery at the sweat-tender age of 8 (her mother was full of priceless ideas): *Floris & Blanchefleur*... What she recalled was a picture of handsome Floris playing chess with a castellan: in the story, Floris' reward for winning was secret admittance to the Ivory Tower in which Blanchefleur, brave unweeping proud-of-mien, lay chained to some infernal mind-machine — prisoner of the evil rat-king, Tzar Aldrex III, or something like that... Old Boole, she'd learn in due course, had theories about chess — like music, it was all about probabilities... He, too, dreamt of machines: his life's work theoretico-probability pantechnicon, to out-Babbage Babbage with — transfusing, welding, unifying by means of pure equation, as — ranged about across that morass of Lancashire her cruel uncle's house glopped out upon — did those cranes & lighthouses & factories & the restless pounding of the looms, the looms, the looms that made her stop her ears... Life, she thought, must be cadence, not metre! The soul's unruly metronome — plucking the illumed notes from air — fingers finding their way by inner ratios, crossing the keys, now like stormy petrels, now solemn as black laughter...[1] ¶She played, imagining a scenery of enormous probability machines, while her mad uncle — rubicund, mutton chops straggling beneath jawline, starch-collared, smelling of liniment & ascorbic — pounded in the bass clef: D-F-A-H! G-E-B-C! Perhaps later he'd retire to his den & fantasise a little about caning her while preparing a more strenuous variation on the usual dinner-time homily to berate that ingrate family of his with — a taste of the birch as he was wont to lay so lavishly upon those witless Jezebels, his God-given, kneeling in supplication, the bare whiteness of them, saucer-eyed — *What, children-of-mine?* — spitting the very questionmark in his wretched long-suffering Hausfrau's face, if ever the temerity to interpose, forced upon her knees also, spared no humiliation — when & as the spirit commanded, *Lord grant them forgiveness!* Poor cousins — she, Lily, felt pained not to pity them... As Zarathustra said: *When you go among women, forget not the whip!* Trepidation alone stayed his hand from her, his brother's daughter, whose eyes refused to shy from his, who suffered all in silence, thinking always back upon those earliest, happiest days — that cluster of radiance that was her Father's fading light, a child's-eye's rapt attention in the primitive vortex... But when Old Boole died there weren't two pennies left to rub — it was for the crime of poverty she'd been forced those long Winters to suffer her uncle's wrath & stupidity falling wide of its mark, like the mills of Babylon: B-A-H-D! F-G-C-E! *Fortissimo...*[2] ¶In the story, Floris & Blanchefleur still managed to live happily ever after (her mother's voice in her ears, distorted, countervailing,

---

[1] If p be the probability of the occurrence of any event, $1-p$ will be the probability of its non-occurrence. [George Boole, *The Laws of Thought: On Which are Founded the Mathematical Theories of Logic and Probabilities* (London: Macmillan, 1854)]
[2] The probability of the concurrence of two independent events is the product of the probabilities of those events. [*ibid.*]

blotting-out, even at a remote distance, the little voice inside her head, mother of reason) — but who in *this* story would play the part of Floris & release *her* (Lily) from the clutches of this infatuated uncle? Some man like her lost Father? Who knew how a voice shapes a sentence — how it affects the movement of thought, & feels — deduces inferences from given premises, relations among things & relations among facts? The pounding went on for hours hours hours, years years years, relentless, fist engorged, purple with the fury in it, his fat tyrant-face ready to explode... Afterwards, she'd lie on her pallet under the stairs, naked beneath her clothes, palms pressed, hands squeezed tight between cold trembling thighs, staring at a crack of light in the blackness: if she concentrated hard enough, the crack would become a white tree in which silver & gold birds sang in the breeze... There were stormy autumns, sometimes the thunder brought rain... The word "maidenhead" fascinated her... Dreams of vast lopsided pyramids of rock, ice, snow, towering three miles above a high Tibetan plateau — the Forbidden Land... *Pianissimo, pianissimo, pianissimo...* Her diary she called the Book of Thel... *Boole de Suif*, her cousins called her, for she was thin as a piano leg... Her mother, too, had had an uncle, who gave his name to a mountain a hundred years before the first white man set foot on it: 27°59'16" North, 86°55'40" East, Chomolungma, goddess mother of the world...[3] ¶Lily played (*The Moonlight Sonata*) & the lunatic hammered in unbridled basso profundo: H-G-A-C! B-F-E-D! Giants dancing in the Eighth Circle of Desolation... Surveyor-General in India her great-uncle had been — though it was the office beancounter, whatsisname, who'd factored *it*, Peak XV, the earthly Olympus Mons, God in the Highest... Sir Greatnuncle George, a man of unencumbered sensibilities, as if desirous of nothing more than to prove that a functionary, too, could be the document of an epoch, got his name printed in small-type right there on the map, Mount Ever-so-hard-to-read... Pax Britannica & all that... His favoured niece, mad Mary, mother of Lilith — lending an ear to the Tempter beneath the apple tree, more in Sir Georgie's shadow than out of it — made surreptitious excursions to her uncle's bibliotheca & set about teaching herself trigonometry, to calculate her precise position in the world... *Filia... Uxor... Mater...* To become that certain woman in a certain place at a certain time, whose existence both nurtured & provoked the life of Man, He, Boole, known to Himself by the oft-repeated example of a mind slouching through icy tracts of indeterminacy, towards its

---

[3] The probability of the concurrence of two independent events is equal to the product of the probability of one of them by the probability that if that event occur the other will happen also. [*etc.*]

Mount of Sorrows… And it came to pass that Mary bore Him a tribe of daughters — mathematicians all, doomed to number themselves among the unnumbered, the second sex, the uncounted… Had He foreseen it then? The life beyond, the closed doors, His widow made by the official stupidities to beg for crumbs at the tables of a well-tenured professoriate…? The *scientia universalis*: that a woman learn her place? Yet did mathematik know no gender — could it be, perforce, the sole Democratic lingo, the one true if yet unspoken path of salvation & the righteous? As if, as if, by way of this Son (*er,* daughter) of Man, Nature had offered a not-so-subtle (in the eyes of those keeping the ledgerbooks) account of itself, wanting only to be probable to minds accustomed to being unprobeable: sign on the forehead of an overly-complicated singularity, of a world full-to-overflowing with conflicted noise, straining to become that music moving within itself, of life in all its facets (*Dear, dear Papa*). And *she,* the incarnation itself, the double-helix, fruit & DNA of His inverted logos, there already in the glint of God's eye, flaring & fading, as He dreams that rhythmic machine of Bach-like simplicity, that interval, that tone, that unique division in Time, the elegant algebrisation of all things Boole…[4] ¶She played — the notes wavered, hung, came crashing: A-B-H-D! C-G-E-F! But for all his Biblical brawn, his head-to-heels black brogues, britches, frockcoat & bowler, her late-Victorian Uncle Charles lacked seriousness — like an oat-box Quaker, full of impending indigestion — the bugbear in the Biedermeier idyll — the Tennysonian tearjerk, bellowing bedtime prayers to pinafored garden gnomes… *He'll blow a gasket and then what…?* But the more her uncle bellowed the more stubbornly his atheist slut of a niece sought out the evasions of a symbolic calculus which, in due course, might become the practiced expression, upon this initial blueprint, of a strident, vociferous Suffrage… The perfect equipoise of a note upon which all else hinges — to leverage the whole structure, to turn a revolution upon a semiquaver, demisemiquaver, hemidemisemiquaver — the divided instant wrought eternally! If only there were ears to hear it… *What good's justice to a mind full of noise?*[5] ¶Fastforward eight years, Berlin & the Hochschule der Musik — free of the mad uncle — *What use is the longed-for music of lost dynasties?* Mind bent towards the agitprop of the moment, the foremost malefaction, the palsied shadow, of usury

---

[4] The probability that if an event, *E,* take place, an event, *F,* will also take place, is equal to the probability of the concurrence of the events *E* & *F,* divided by the probability of the concurrence of *E.*

[5] The probability of the concurrence of one or the other of two events which cannot concur is equal to the sum of their separate probabilities.

— standing one day beneath a prison tower in Petrograd (most angelic vision!), bearing alms & fervid hope in Reason, Social Credit, Tyrannicide — still later, by what else but atavism, voyaging (she) to London soon to be espoused of one Wilfred Voynich, impoverished aristo, who among th'imprisoned had espied her from a window of that selfsame Tsarist penitentiary — a man with a past, condemned to a Siberian gulag, whom Fate made fit to fly the coop, metaphorically speaking, an epic of Hollywood proportions (caravans across the Gobi Desert), to become in his turn our dear Lily's dear betrothed, her jejune politico, her Shostakovich, her Gadfly — more a transsexed Blanchefleur than a menschlich Floris, never so much as parleying a pawn for his maiden's sake — the told tale of their impassionata, their Confessio Amantis, confined to a ciphered syllabary — abjad, abugida, consonantary, futhark — a codicological *Kama Sūtra* of not carnal or courtly but civic love, describing one-by-one the seven deadly sins & their subcategories of latterday Cromwellians — & an eighth...? Not the swooning pink-wrapper Sargasso spuriosity she could've penned in her sleep if ever the inclination... A certain aversion to masculine pomposities... More inclined, so to speak, to love a parliament — *but who's she would be wedded to th' fairest body that's beheaded?* Playing coy mistress to Kropotkinites & Special Branch spooks, equally — the Schlomo Rosenblums of the High Seas, Friends of Enlightenment, peddlers of Ozone Preparation miracle cures & the unbalanced fourth humour — shadows once cast becoming shorter, opaque... G-H-D-A! E-C-F-B! The moral's X, the Y emblematic... Could she've guessed, in those long-ago parlour days, whoring at the pianola for her hairsoup supper, the deliberate charm of literary posthume — Westonia in her time, in an age of no Shagsbeard — esteemed of Roentgen, Planck, Marconi, the Curies — unbeknownst *sine qua non* of Soviet celebrity, Stalin's bedside read? For she wrote books, too, you realise — Cold War potboilers weltering with sham plots, formal lapses (quoth Professor Leavis), gaps in argument, the unattenuated voice of an unbalanced equation, in places wildly implausible, in others metaphysical, by design if not by nature, in short unsuited to the scrutiny of Retrospect, the *Times Literary Supplement,* or university curricula, yet sold by the millions — earning royalties by the fistful, so to speak, behind the Iron Curtain — & *Now a Major Motion Picture!* THE GADFLY WHO BUGG(ER)ED ME... Fanfare for the opening credits: F-G-E-C! D-H-A-B![6]

---

[6] If an observed event can only result from one of *n* different causes which are *a priori* equally probable, the probability of any one of the causes is a fraction whose numerator is the probability of the event, on the hypothesis of the existence of that cause, & whose denominator is the sum of the similar probabilities relative to all the causes.

¶So much for a life lived in the shadows of great men, playing counterpoint to the namesaked counterparts, Everest, Boole, Voynich, sons of man, children of the book, the squired fundamental laws of those mental operations by which reasoning is performed — 'the universal exclusive suffrage, my dear…' *De veritate sacrae scripturae…* For all that, she, Lily, was still her mother's daughter, bound by the Word — the Descent of Woman — the Survival of the Sexes — unwritten testaments to the great struggle… E-G-A-D! H-F-E-C! The raging God all the while seeking to drown-out, neutralise, abolish… *Put off thy shoes!* A drawn white face hanging over her in the dark — cheerless, wasted, piteous as the denizens of Hades (Boole^1, Boole^2, Boole^3 … Boole^n in mirrored recession from time immemorial) — saying *Nothing's changed — the human masses teem, move, are destroyed, crop-up again — the asserted register, the predictive counter-fugue, the wrong note becoming the motif's tipping point, all for a goose's egg…*[7] ¶Did she guess even then, how she, Ethel Lilian, native of Cork, would be fated one day, in the not-too-distant etc., to be buried, un(re)marked, in a New Amsterdam pauper's plot, away across the water, through the lookingglass — like the girl she once was imagining a story that'd resolve itself as it commenced: the completed journey, the solitude of a room, the penury of lost loves & lost ideals, the last clanging notes fading fast like a far-off game of pétanque echoing in a paternoster… *Oh Babyloon!* And like her mother before — *Ave Maria* — as bare of foot now at the end as at the beginning, the arithmetic dogsbody, the minor note as to the major chord, Ol' Boole's binarily begot & draughty doomsayer — nought to the Great Man's unicum — supernumerary — née this, née that… Could she bring herself even once to blame Him for His apotheosis, casting *her*, the last of the line, of the blood, of the dis-named, in the role of some two-bit antic Eurydice? Damned to play for evermore at the atonement of Man for a mother's sin — chains of destiny stretching back through Time, from God's bodkin to the perfected dance-number, the all-within-the-one: you could make a film out of that, a few jazzy little cameos with Astaire & Rogers, Porphyry & Proclus, Anselm & Abelard, Ramus & Descartes, Bacon & Locke, Wilder & Feldman, pander to the peanut gallery, polish the shoes of the odd Patron of the Arts, throw in a few low blows with the highfalutin' business just to keep the bastards honest, a few sly hints about the real goings on behind the backstage curtain, allusions to all the great works, a pearl or two tossed in the gutter, a smattering of the incomprehensible to give it some

---

[7] The probability of a future event is the sum of the products formed by multiplying the probability of each cause by the probability that if that cause exist, the said event will take place.

mystique & bamboozle the fuckwits, a nice ease-them-along storyline to keep the grassroots nice & green (are you getting any of this?), & right in the middle of it all out comes the Entertainer with his showman's rat-a-tat-tat, magic wand & bowler hat, red blazer & knee-length spats, to summon Ol' Boole for one last bandstand act, *Well this one's for my sweet l'il girl over there in the Big Apple* — a vision in a cloth cap & Kilkenny tweed, cranking a music box, monkey on His shoulder masturbating while it grins, & the bingo parlour matrons in the front row shaking their jelly roles (they know their number's up!): the whole thing goes off with a bang to undying applause, laughter, canned thunder — *You think this's funny, do you?* And look! There's Uncle Charlie at the piano, which isn't a piano at all but an atom bomb with an electric keyboard, belting away at the humourless ascending scale of his little apocalypse machine, mirror-mime teleology, the Death Sonata, probability zero, while all the world gasps: *Will he really do it?* they want to know, finger poised over the whammy button, the Entretainer flashing a cheesy grin, Boole cranking away like a madman & the monkey fit to pop — *Cut!* the Director says & it's a wrap, the cast & crew up-stumps & head for their trailers as the opening soundtrack wafts in again C-H-E-B! A-F-G-D! 'cause somewhere out there the heroes all get to live happily ever after, right? But where was *she* in that picture? E.L.V. on the postbox isn't having your name on a marquee — the queer old cat-lady in number 8, holed-up on the backside of Broadway with nothing but a girdled handmedown amanuensis & a bundle of motheaten manuscript to upstage herself with: not a single autograph-hunter, even. Well, it was nice while it lasted, but it never does. You think she deserved an encore, our deer sweet Lil? Don't believe the story could just end like that? Wondering what the bejaysus she's doing here anyway, taking up storyspace when the real action's going on elsewhere? Hell, that's life kiddo, may as well get used to it.[8]

---

[8] If there be any number of mutually exclusive hypotheses, h_1, h_2, h_3,... of which the probabilities relative to a particular state of information are p_1, p_2, p_3,... & if new information be given which changes the probabilities of some of them, suppose of h_m+1 & all that follow, without having otherwise *any reference to the rest*; then the probabilities of these latter have the same ratios to one another, after the new information, that they had before, that is p'_1: p'_2: p'_3...: p'_m = p_1: p_2: p_3...: p_m, where the accented letters denote the values after the new information has been acquired.

b. The Rooks

9

FAUST OF DOOM

'You should always begin a story at the beginning,' said the doctor.

Niklas Volta, MUDr., had his office located on the southern side of Charles Square, in the Institute of Human Studies & Social Medicine on the upper floor of the old Mladotovský Palace, otherwise known as the "Faust House." Built adjacent to the site of a twelfth-century livestock market, this house gained its notoriety by association with a succession of celebrity charlatans who toiled there at the arduous labour of scamming every available Habsburg with loose purse strings, each in turn purporting to own the franchise in turning lead & baser, smellier stuff, into twentyfour carat *gelt*. Their parlour wizard antics unfailingly drew-in the era's paparazzi, the God-fearers, serial sceptics & money-launderers, the heist artists & racketeers, the thrill-seekers, poets, portraitists, hat merchants, mystics, impresarios, the courtesans & social climbers, the bogus barons & counterfeit countesses — not to mention your average fair-dinkum pleb in the street — & word got about.

Accounts of the doings of these big-noted goldmakers soon became the stuff of soap opera. Household names like Prince Václav of Opava, Mgr Edwarb Kelley, Josef Mladota of Solopysky & that certain Dr J. Faustus ("nigromancer & somdomite"[*]), most famous of the lot. As legend has it, Faust holed up for a certain undefined period alone in the old house around about the time Spaniards brought the first potato to Europe, like a silent-era movie hack in a dilapidated Hollywood mansion, a living anachronism who, in moments of senescent pathos, would lavishly reprise his staring roles to a coterie of sycophants, performing his quaint little magic tricks while concocting psychedelic potions in flasks, testtubes, beakers & other pseudoscientific paraphernalia, to keep up the great illusion of a Golden Age long since passed.

Even if he said so himself, Faust was the mightiest magician known to man since Christ turned loaves into fishes.[†] He could relieve Duchesses of their

---

[*] "Doctor Faustus, dem großen Somdomiten und Nigromantico…" Staatsarchiv Nürnberg: Nürnberg Ratserlasse, Nr. 870., 12 (1 Mai 1532). [✋]
[†] Though he (Fee Fie Faust) couldn't've held a prick up to Paracelsus.

jewellery with the flick of a wrist & deduce the dainty hues of their daughters' gussets, & for an encore could even summon forth demons from the underworld. Some said he could make the Devil himself appear, at the drop of a hat or the drop of his pants. Or if not precisely the Devil, the Devil's righthand gimp, an arch-satirist christened Mephistophallus who had the unnerving habit of turning-up dressed like Fred MacMurray in a power-blue suit one day & like the Hunchback of Notre Dame in a bride's nightie the next.

Flibberty Faust played him for a showstopper: the society darlings never knew what'd step out of the smoke-puff when their pet wizard waved his wand & summoned his private Mephistooge. The more seriously inclined amongst them felt trivialised: the purists hankered for a creature with horns, cloven-hoofed & pointy-tailed. What they got instead might be anything from a dome-headed theatre critic to a burlesque dancer in g-string & garter belt, a circus clown, a Jehovah's Witness, a door-to-door encyclopaedia salesman, a pro-bono attorney down on his luck, a blind spinster, a health inspector, a hangman with halitosis, a translator of Elizabethan ditties, an organ-grinder or an organ-grinder's monkey, a pataphysician with a cloud over his head, a blind interior decorator, a cardsharp or a sharp card, a mephitic dwarf, a bearded lady, a dog-faced boy, a beggar on all-fours, a greatdane with humanly expressive eyes, a schnauzer, a droopy-eared cockerspaniel, sometimes even a short-legged dachshund nosing a turd along the ground.[Ψ] The audience yucked. Our dramaturgical Doc made eyes & shrugged, hands up, like this was how he was made to suffer for his greatness.

'*Ai ai ai!* No respect,' he complained, while Mephistuphitinher, costumed as Bo Peep, squatted over his shoes & made peepee.

No shortage of entertainment over at the Faust House. Every night was pot luck, or just a lot of puck. You paid your money at the door & took your chances like everyone else. People got to calling it the Glory Hole: when you went in, you never knew what you'd find on the other side of the door. They'd all sit around in the dark holding each other's privates while the Doc made the signs & mumbled his jibberjabber. Then puff! Out would pop a man-sized haemorrhoid singing a 3-part madrigal.

'There're things,' Fausthole'd wink, 'beyond even God's omnipotence.'

[Ψ] The world in Man's shadow having, in the opinion of the Canine Cognoscenti, gone to the dogs — the very substance of the place was infused with doggishness, roads paved & cobbles cemented by centuries of dog excreta, democratised by its hundredthousand dogpisses, dogs' days, dogs' bodies & dogs' dinners.

It was all a little bit too much like quantum physics: you could summon a devil but not choose its wardrobe, or the other way around. Wave & particle stuff. It was enough to get a Duchess's arse in an uproar. But the more Faustfick jived, the more he wanted them all (his most devoted suckers) to believe he really *did* have the little chap in his pocket, ready to go on a whim & a prayer, & was otherwise just toying around for gags — except the truth for once was just as he told it.

To add insult to injury, the moment they were left in private a suddenly contrite, mockingly slavish Mephister would be sure to pop up out of he nearest lav & make voluble pretence of attending to Flatulent Faust's every quire of quackery & petty caprice, denying him nothing (within "reason," of course).[º] *Yes sire, no sire, three bags full, sire.* (Flattery'll get you pretty much fucking anywhere with a halfwit.) All upon condition, needless to say, that this preposterous "Doctor" enter into solemn compact with the Evil One, the Great Abomination, Hocus Poke himself, to be duly signed in his (Faustarse's) own bad blood. The relevant article being: "that the contracted party agrees to relinquish, surrender or otherwise forfeit, upon presentation & within fourteen working days, in due consideration of services rendered, as specified below, his (Faustrot's) most measly Mortal Soul, Anima, Pneuma, Esprit, etc." And needless to say, he did — all the while the weak voice of conscience, whispering *Caveat emptor*! to ears doltishly deaf. *Well, too bad old chump, looks like you just sold yerself a bum deal.*

Fancying himself a real knockdown negotiator with the bargain of a lifetime in his tight little fist, Fidius Fausto grinned like an idiot & scrawled his blood-bespat Hancock on the dotted line: had a scheme up his sleeve, he did, or down his jockstrap, to diddle the Devil & his wife as well, *ah-ha*, sly old Faustwitz! Tempted to make off with the goods *tout-de-suit* on a permanent Cayman Islands holiday, *hehe*, without waiting for any curtain call to bow-out. Well, anyone could see Faustkopf had the smarts over those strawheads! But of course it never quite worked out that way, did it, bo? Faustnoodle, not the first but neither the last loser by a longshot in this unspooling *Double Indemnity* rip-

---

[º] Faustus, counting himself the most learnèd bloke to ever sport an ermine collar, had only the highest aspirations: to yoke Absolute Knowledge to the greater needs of Mankind. Aye, veritably. His private deeds stood as proof: the bookish dolt's lusting after Helen-of-Troy, e.g., thumbing History's dogeared vellum like some snotty-nosed schoolbrat behind the lav door with a colour supplement for ladies' new season underwear — or foisting himself upon some hapless village fräulein, with concoctions of Spanish Fly & poisoned poetry — or tweaking the Pope's nose — or posing for gags as the Scarlet Pimpernel in a Silesian Bordello, *too many cocks spoil the brothel, dearies*! All this at the helpful hand of mirthful Mephatso.

off before its time: one minute playing it cool as they come, counting the take ahead of the job, minting a virtual Fort Knox in that intestinal tract he calls a mind (thinking he's got Murphistoffaly where he can't see him, so to speak) — the next, caught in a fever sweat, hiding out & on the lam, the penny finally starting to drop, furtive meetings in late-night grocery shops, swearing to the boys in trenchcoats he didn't have the goods (only tinned beans this week, people) but if they'd only give him a couple more days…

Well, one man's Moravia is another man's Mexico, but there's nothing more pointless than making a dash for the border when it's the Devil on your tail. Close-up on a waxy, unshaven face quartered in sullen moonlight, peering out a window or a darkened doorway, a cat unsettling a trashcan in an alleyway, a candle guttering in a draught, the hoot of an owl, a drunk singing tunelessly in the park — but always near at hand, wherever he turns, the mocking mutter of some mouth-in-the-wall Mephisyphilis making child-rhymes…

> *There once was a stand-up named Faust,*
> *who everyone agreed had the nouse —*
> *when he bartered his soul*
> *for a comic lead role*
> *that literally brought down the house, dah-dum.*

Scrupulous to a fault, no sooner had the contracted term expired than that most punctilious jurist, bondsman, bailiff, repo-man extraordinary, Old Scratch in person with a face like Edward G. Robinson at the beginning of a long day at the Pontific All-Risk Inscrutanence Co., came knocking with his ghastly retinue of assessors, adjustors, auditors & assayers (*frauds is frauds, eh boss?*), to forthwith claim his percentage of the gross, his pre-tax bauble & discount voucher, his final quarterly bonus — share-optioned, payment-in-kind, capital-gains-exempted, overheads clause worked into the fine-print — *Please sign at the bottom, thank you…* Whisking a babbleblubbering Faustlick posthaste off to Hades while some doughty Duchess dabs a tear from the corner of an eye, she's watched it all, from the window of her private carriage, as a mob with pitchforks & shovels assembles in the square (*well someone's gotta have a sense of justice in this here godforsaken town!*). A street urchin dragging a mangy pup on a string turns from the melee just before the credits roll, shakes his head with a disappointed older-than-his-years look, & says —

'C'mon Tyger, I guess the fella just plain ran outta luck…'

Meanwhile up in the old Mladotovský Palace, all that remained of the Dodgy Doc for the lynchmob & loansharks late on the scene was a greasy coal-black smudge on the false ceiling of an upstairs lab — through which (fobbing the world off with a penultimate piece of bafflement) they were expected to believe this chief of all charlatans had simply evaporated into thin, thinner, thinnest air.[*]

It was this ceiling at which Němec now stared, waiting for the psychiatrist to speak. There was nothing very remarkable about it (the ceiling) & staring at it like that probably appeared foolish. In a vortex beneath the central light fixture, five tireless March flies alternately pursued one another & were pursued — feinting, retreating, spiralling in a kind of three-dimensional chess puzzle Kepler might've set himself had the game been known to him. It made Němec wonder, were these complex trigonometries of insect social behaviour evidence of play or merely a programmed set of variables?

Volta cleared his throat the way people do when they want your attention. Having gained his patient's, the doctor took a cigar from a facetted teak & ivory box which lay on the righthand side of his desk, clipped one end & patiently turned the other end over a match.

'There are those,' he said while puffing on the cigar but without looking at Němec, 'who believe it's the patient who ultimately must cure himself.'

The voice struck Němec as slightly unctuous, like everything else about the man. Once the cigar was sufficiently lit, Volta shook the match out & dropped it into a glass ashtray about the size of an ordinary dinner plate. A thick, resinous smoke drifted in the air. The flies, interrupted in their game, retreated separately to some other part of the room.

Němec tilted his head to get a better look at the rest of the office. The desk Volta was sitting behind was polished mahogany, didn't take up more than a third of the room, & wasn't notably larger than a table at the Pálffy Palace. The wall behind the desk was lined with books, the other two were panelled in dark wood. Between them was a doorway, on either side of which hung a

---

[*] Sceptics have always asserted that the artiste formerly known as Jay-Faust died in an explosion during an alchemical "experiment," at the Hotel zum Löwen in Staufen im Breisgau: blood&guts all over the room & his eyeballs neatly side-by-side on the writing desk. [☜]

collection of framed pictures: what looked like a late thirteenth-century mezzotint of Křivoklát Castle — a black&white pre-Unification snapshot of the Brandenburg Gate — a Kodachrome of the stone heads on Easter Island — likewise the Matterhorn — a faded colour postcard of a Cretan snake goddess — & a polaroid of Wilhelm Reich, posing against a greenblack Rorschach blot that, to Němec's mind, resembled a diseased ovum besieged by an army of deranged spermatozoa.

The fourth wall was framed by a pair of dark velvet drapes. Between them, a French window opened onto a shallow balcony with a view across the Zítkov Gardens & a stretch of river to where ranks of grizzled apartment buildings stood along the western embankment. In front of the window was a heavy settee, which Němec was sitting on. His crutches & left leg lay along the length of it, requiring him to twist slightly to the right in order to observe his interviewer.

Volta's face was like a blank reflection. It was the face of somebody waiting for something, only Němec couldn't tell what. He thought of similar scenes in films, where the psychiatrist instructs the patient in a weary voice to tell him whatever the patient has on his mind. Volta at least had the appearance of a man to whom weariness might be said to come naturally. They both waited there in silence. Or almost silence. An audible ticking noise came from an indeterminate source in the room, as if the room itself & everything in it were somehow concerned with the keeping of Time. Along with the smoke from Volta's cigar, the sound had a vaguely hypnotic effect.

All of a sudden the image of the doctor hunched there on the other side of the room reminded Němec of the Pigeon Man who sat in the park at lunchtime under the clock, with a bag of breadcrumbs. Every pigeon in the neighbourhood came flapping around, perched on his shoulders, head, hands, summoned from the trees & sidewalks & gutters like some Pied Piper's minions. All the Pigeon Man ever seemed to do was sit on his bench covered with pigeons, as if that was his sole purpose in life, directing whatever course of meaningless activity allowed him to return to that same spot the next day & the day after that.

Eventually, almost without being conscious of it, the words crept into Němec's mouth & he began telling Volta about the Pigeon Man. Volta didn't say anything, just puffed vaguely on his cigar in a cross-eyed kind of way. The ticking continued. Němec could hear his own pulse & became conscious of the effort to breathe. It reminded him of waiting in the corridor outside the Rehab Unit: the green anxiety of the walls, the buzzing of the overhead lights, a kind of permanent fog creeping along the corridor. Each morning, when they wheeled him over from Convalescents, he'd pass a crotchety janitor cleaning the floors. This janitor belonged to the same secret tribe as the Pigeon Man. Without fail, every time they wheeled Němec out of the elevator on the second floor, the janitor would be ensconced on the landing, mutely prodding a mop & pail along the wall.

This janitor kept a small transistor radio in his pocket that crackled — an abortive type of noise, audible from the waiting area outside the Blue Door. Over time you'd expect the noise to drift closer or further away, but as long as Němec waited it stayed the same. He'd mentioned these occurrences to the nurse but she only gave him one of her looks.

Eventually, Němec reasoned, the janitor, with mop & pail & broken radio, would have to work his way either up or down the next flight of stairs: if up, to the Roentgen Lab & the Deep Image Room — if down, to Obstetrics, Haematology & Gastroenterology. At some point he'd finish & begin again, like some menial Sisyphus. Němec figured that all you'd need, to find out, was time. With each visit to the Rehab Unit, an idea began to evolve in his mind. Under various pretexts he advanced or delayed his arrival by five, or fifteen, or ten-minute increments, till driven by an unbearable sense of panic he found himself anticipating these appointments by as much as an hour, sometimes even two.

It made no difference, the janitor was always there ahead of him at the same spot. For all Němec knew, the janitor might've been a kind of fixture, like one of those cardboard cutouts they prop inside the doorways of banks, that offer to shake your hand & empty your wallet for a small percentage. Mondays, Tuesdays, Thursdays, Fridays Němec'd park at the far end of the landing & eyeball him, with his mop & pail & busted radio & the spittle dangling just beneath his lower lip, to see if he'd slip-up, give-in, tip his hand.

Armed with TV magazines, travel magazines, fashion magazines, men's health magazines, car enthusiast magazines, house&garden magazines, even the weekend newspaper supplements, Němec took up his sentry position in the hope of plotting the janitor's course over the period of a day, then days. He considered a week, but the routine of the hospital always prevented it. He would've been prepared to stay there for a month (his prospects appeared open-ended) in order to verify an hypothesis about a secret rationale he suspected must be at work. What, after all, could account for the janitor's senseless itinerary, one so invariably concurrent with his own?

The first thing they teach you in hospital is patience, *hehe*. After a while, anything gets to be routine, even when it means doing nothing. Like a Zen cop on permanent stake-out. It reminded Němec of the Prof & his chessboard, only they didn't let you play chess in the Ward, 'cause that might start people thinking too much. He loathed sitting around in the TV room with the other sufferers having their minds slowly sucked out of them by the box on the wall. *Tune in same time next time…*

And it was all connected: all part of some hyper-regularised programme, designed to make an individual's will seem like a witless & paranoiac hallucination. You could even learn to *like* it. The only way to stay sane was to keep the numbness at bay & not allow yourself to be pummelled into submission by fiendish janitors or nurses with thicknecked stormtrooper orderlies, malevolent agents, all, of institutionalised retribution. Nothing whatsoever seemed beyond the pale — like a sadistic vaudeville act tripped on lithium, to entertain an unseen audience, concealed behind mirrored glass perhaps.

And what if all the doctors nurses orderlies were really androids under their starched fronts? What if the hospital was a secret receiving station for whole android colonies after the Revolution & the nerve centre, now, of some invidious Plan to re-subjugate humanity, by anaesthesia, lobotomy, laxative, hypochondria & sterilisation? Corridors & stairwells & enginerooms all haunted by the ghosts of poor suffering idiots whose minds & bodies had systematically been abducted. The janitor pushing his mop in a closed circle, the pigeons on windowsills with rat-like surveillance eyes, the bandaged men they rotated in front of the TV, the lift-operator with the same half-dozen buttons to press, the vegetables in the refectory ladling out gruel onto trays in a production-line & the sufferers with blunted spoons gagging on it. Purgatory never looked so inviting.

What if, Němec speculated, *he too* was becoming one of *them*? Some kind of zombified automaton caught in a pantomime conspiracy, the left side of the brain playing along so as not to let slip to the right that it knows what's *really* going on? What were they *up to* in that operating theatre, wiring his pineal gland to a hidden control switch, routed to the Cosmo-Synchronicity Machine over at Head Office. A cenacle of faceless physicians bent on mesmerising him & the world with brainwash hocuspocus? Who could say if their secret commands weren't already being issued & this wasn't just Phase One of the warm-up? (*You could be onto something there, kiddo.*)

All this Němec relayed to Volta, though not in so many words, listening to his own voice as though at a distance: a catalogue of delusions, fantasies, objects of a trite-beyond-belief wishfulfilment. Almost instantly he began to

perceive his obsessions in a new light, to see them for what they were, comical &
absurd. Volta had hardly moved. He was still staring at the end of his cigar —
he'd been staring at it pretty much the whole time, watching the ash sifting from
it like constipated pigeon crap. Němec wondered if the doctor had been listening
to a single word he'd said, or if that was the point. The ticking at least had
stopped, but it no longer seemed to matter.

A month passed before Němec told Volta about the Prof. He hadn't thought of
the Old Man in a long time. They were rehearsing the usual routine in Volta's
office, rewinding the clock & slowly getting to the point, Němec supposed, of
what he was doing there in the first place. He'd never seen Volta look
disconcerted, or anything other than bored, but he looked that way now.

'How about,' Volta grimaced, 'if you could paint it for me in bold strokes,
cut to the chase, the bare essentials, a synopsis in other words...'

Němec gave it to him in shorthand from the top, about how they'd met,
the house at Jánský Vršek, the Voynich Manuscript, the Prof's death & his
muses' suicides. His own little misadventure didn't seem to matter anymore.

'What'd you say this, *er*, manuscript was called?' Volta coughed.

Němec told him again & Volta wrote something on a sheet of paper.

'Mmm,' he said. 'You find yourself attracted to conspiracies, don't you?'

'It seems it's the conspiracies that're attracted to me.'

'And do you feel *I'm* part of some conspiracy against you?'

Němec shrugged —

'What's a conspiracy anyway?' he said.

'Yes,' the doctor nodded pensively.

Němec wondered what exactly about his account of the Prof had brought
on the change in Volta. At first he figured it was the book — one of those man-
of-science types who get their goat up about the secret unsolved mysteries of the
world. Volta gave the impression of a man who took his own intellect for
granted, but a single doubt might've been all it took to cause the impression to
crumble. Or maybe it was just the last thing on Earth he'd expected out of
Němec's mouth. The doctor seemed to cast a reassessing gaze over him. Then
after a while he said —

'A philosopher, supposedly considered great, once wrote something along the lines of, *There's no document of civilisation which isn't at the same time a document of barbarism…'*

Volta let his eyelids slide down slightly over his eyes, as if the effort to speak aloud was suddenly making him tired all over again.

'The same philosopher also wrote, *And just as such a document isn't free of barbarism, barbarism taints also the manner in which it's been transmitted from one owner to another…* I wonder,' Volta pursed his lips for a moment, 'what you might think of that.'

Němec looked back at him, thinking nothing. They shared a long silence, at the end of which, with no further ceremony, Volta signalled the end of the session & Němec, relieved to be let free, took up his crutches from the settee & left. On the next occasion he entered the doctor's office, Volta was slumped unhappily in the same place with a dead cigar in the ashtray as if he hadn't moved in a week, a layer of dust on the shoulders of his jacket specked with hair-oil & dandruff. He watched Němec cross the carpet from behind five feet of mahogany, turning over a dead lightbulb in his hands, like one of Faust's creditors trying to decide if it could be turned into a buck or the whole thing was a dead loss. The weight of something seemed to be slowly crushing him.

Now it's all going to come out, Němec thought. *They give you the stonewall treatment just to get you off-balance then spill out over the sides as if they're doing you a big favour giving you a sob story to listen to for a change. Make you think you're getting something for nothing, the human touch, all that crap.*

While Němec was arranging himself on the settee, a secretary shuffled papers in the outer room then came across to Volta's desk carrying a blue cardboard folder with an inch-thick wad of paper bound in red tape. All this, Němec figured, was just theatrics. Across the top of the folder there'd be his name printed in neat little block capitals & inside there'd be a half-page of vital statistics with the rest padded-out with blank paper to make it look like they had him pinned, right down to the hour, minute, second of every puerile notion that'd ever wafted through his left ear & out his right. He wondered why the hell they bothered.

The secretary dumped the folder beside the ashtray & stared at it for a moment as if that was going to accomplish anything. There was a dead fly squashed against the top edge of the cardboard. The secretary, a young, androgynous-looking male with short dark hair, wrinkled his lip, then gingerly picked the dead fly up by its wings & dropped it into a wastepaper basket beside the desk. Volta didn't seem to notice any of this at all. Finally the secretary asked if there was anything else the doctor needed. It was a slightly affected voice that seemed intended to give the impression of a piece of carp being filleted. Volta didn't respond so the secretary went out looking a little annoyed, but not enough to put cracks in his face.

As soon as they were alone, the good doctor stopped fidgeting with the lightbulb &, gazing deeply into it, let out a sigh. His lips moved in a thin exaltation of despair —

'You find me,' he said, exposing the soft wrinkled palms of both hands while balancing the lightbulb between the tips of right thumb & index finger, like a card player giving up a trick, 'in *difficult* circumstances.'

Volta leant forward with his elbows on the desk & lowered his voice —

'Forces are at work,' it was barely a whisper, '*hostile* forces, whose one objective is to return medicine to the Dark Ages.'

It was beginning to sound all so familiar. Next would come the focusing of Reason's light & all that. Němec said nothing, making an expression with his face evocative of someone not at all too bright. The doctor sighed again & set the lightbulb down carefully on the desk in front of him. This accomplished, he began rubbing his eyes with the heels of his hands. A long silence ensued. As he rubbed his eyes, the lightbulb slowly rolled to the edge of his desk & fell noiselessly onto the carpet. Perhaps a minute passed before Volta took his hands away from his face, clasping them in front of him. He regarded Němec with eyes gone red around the edges, the picture of a man wrestling with a monumental fatigue. He'd've gone over big at the panto.

Němec wondered where this new approach was leading. He glanced down at the lightbulb then quickly around the room to see if there was a fixture it might've belonged to. Perhaps it was some sort of test, one of those innocuous everyday objects whose unexpected appearance was designed to provoke a "psychological" response. It was a larger-than-ordinary lightbulb, about 200 watts, more what you'd expect in an interrogation room than a piece of office furniture. A coil of broken filament dangled inside it, clearly visible. Maybe that was meant to symbolise something?

'Let me explain,' Volta moaned.

There didn't seem to be any choice, so Němec sat there & waited to hear what the man had to say.

'History,' he began, 'destiny, the world & our place in it, these are merely…' he waved his right hand feebly, '*phantasmagorias.* But what if that's *all* there is?'

The doctor sat there, still tipped forward slightly, eyes vacant, focused on some abstract & infinitely remote point. His voice was very low — a voice that seemed to do without him, to be its own master. It was the sort of voice you could easily relinquish yourself to, lulled into a sense of general benefaction, like some credulous idiot, & no longer having to think at all. He & the Prof, Němec decided, probably wouldn't've liked each other very much — no conversation would ever've been big enough for the both of them.

'We exist,' the doctor's voice went on, 'at a nexus of competing desires, which we mistake for our own. But no man owns his desire, desire owns *him* — a truth which for centuries men have tried to conceal.'

Němec had to strain to hear what Volta was saying. The doctor's words crept over him like a subliminal music moving within itself — what they meant seemed less important than the manner in which they were spoken. Well it was a fine thing, Němec supposed, to have the sound of your own voice to smooth-out all the creases in the world. Volta looked like someone in the grip of their own hypnotism. The room grew more sombre, even, as the sky outside darkened. Grey wisps of snow coiled at the edges of the windows.

Volta spoke of masters & slaves, of dialectics, of the impasse of Reason. Němec stifled a yawn.

'You might say,' the doctor leant back suddenly from the desk, breaking the spell, 'that man himself is really nothing but a fantasy. The fantasy of a fantasy.'

He looked at Němec & sighed again. His fingers spread out on the table as if he were groping for something that wasn't there. But it was only an impression.

'Do you understand what I'm saying?'

The question was a rhetorical one but Volta still smiled at Němec hopefully. The silence produced no perceptible effect. The doctor tapped his fingers. Back to normal, then, Němec thought, wondering what the hell he was really doing there, sitting in that office. Volta stopped tapping & brought his hands together to form an apex in front of his mouth —

'Right now you're probably thinking that everything I've just told you is sheer mystification?' he said through his fingers.

Němec kept his face blank. He had no idea what the doctor was getting at.

'I wouldn't blame you,' Volta sighed, as if he'd read his listener's thoughts.

Němec experienced a moment of mild panic, but the doctor was staring emptily into space, hands clasped in abstract prayer, evincing no other awareness there was anyone else still in the room. Alone amongst the décor, he'd've had all the appearance of some disenchanted melodrama pretending to be a man & not getting very far with it. His voice by now was a kind of drone sliding farther &

farther into the bass register. At any moment the whole room would start to shake & the pictures fall from the walls.

'We are,' Volta seemed to moan, 'deadened by a dying language no longer capable either of expressing the truth or of telling us what "truth" actually means.'

Volta's eyes gazed deadly, as dead as the lightbulb lying on the floor —

'I'm a doctor,' he said, as if gaining confidence in stating the obvious, 'I know the value of anatomy, but the body I must be competent in treating isn't some cadaver anatomised in text books, but the whole living social organism — the world itself, you could say, & the world's *mind*. Because the world really does have a mind,' Volta grimaced, turning his gaze towards Němec as though suddenly reminded of his existence. 'It's thinking us, you & me, at this very moment. You don't believe me?'

Outside, the snow was falling heavier & faster. And behind the whirling of the snow, the mind of the world, working-out its hidden design, making ordered chaos even of these most evanescent & fragile particles. *The kernel of the wordsoul,* as the old Prof had been fond of saying. Not world, but word: *Wort, nicht Welt.* He'd taken the idea from Plotinus, or Plato maybe, or Polonius — it hardly mattered. Conjuring some voice at the dawn of time, in the time before time, author of the Beginning & the End, etc. But the voice Němec was hearing belonged to a man who was merely that, with his back bowed under the weight of a conscience that wasn't his. Němec could just about picture the apprentice apostle Volta on the hill of Golgotha, silent at the foot of that particular crucifixion, eyes fixed on the nailed & broken feet of his crucified God, flyblown already, thinking — *He'll never be able to walk again, they'll have to wheel him about on a trestleboard* — but still, in some abstract way, committed to the Hippocratic task, the little daily acts of salvation & resurrection. As if he, too, had found his soul's Eternal Janitor, his Pigeon Man.

10

The church on Husova stood barely a stone's throw from a well-frequented drinking establishment called the *Golden Taige* &, on its southern side, was divided from the buildings of the Philosophy Institute by the cobblestones of Zlatá Street. Contrary to popular belief, the heretic Jan Hus, burned at the stake on the shores of the Bodensee in 1415 for sins against the Church of Rome, never preached there. "Hus," a name deriving from Sklavic origins meaning *goose* or possibly Saxon origins meaning *cough*, was uncommon already by the seventeenth century.

It was morning, sometime between the Prof's funeral & the Rehab Unit. Němec was still doing his rounds, but not for very much longer. Unknown forces were gathering, he could feel it like a twitch beneath the skin, the signs were multiplying, fair warning given, soon it'd be safer to remain behind locked doors. In the meantime he wandered the points of the constellations: the *Chop House*, *The White Whale*, the foggy embankments, the humid libraries & musty bookshops, the smoky movie houses on the Square, the brown coal-haze of Blecha's rooftop.

The Old Man's death brought an air of cloying mortality. It was a new feeling. Everyone Němec had ever known had simply disappeared from the picture, immaculately so to speak. Death, the omniscient stage director, had so far declined to put in a personal appearance. It gave Němec pause to consider where he'd come from, where he was headed. In the scheme of things, Nowhere could be the underside of everything or nothing at all. Whoever tried to find such a place?

Sometimes he wondered if the files at the Interior Ministry weren't just part of some elaborate fame-up. And the Home. And now this. Some kind of psychiatric experiment from the future to mess with the programme, retrodesign the End of History, or whatever, find the missing keys to the omniverse. All in the mind, of course. No arguing with that. Was any of it supposed to be funny? *Hoohoo*, went the pigeons under the eaves. *Haahaa*, the bicycle wheezing along the pavement. Overcoats flapped in the wind, handkerchiefs waved, gloved hands gathered scarves around necks. It was a morning designed for portents. As Němec navigated a crowd of church-goers loitering on the curb, he was reminded of a couple of ancient Silesian proverbs:

> *It'll come to pass as the old goose quacked…*

&

> *A man with a cough cannot hide…*

Zlatá (it was really too narrow to be called a street, but also too wide to be an alley) ran out into a small square hafted on its farther side by Jilská Street. Adjoining an archway with a pair of large wooden coachdoors, a folklorist's trinketshop stood with woven baskets arranged on the cobbled pavement, containing puppets, carved dolls & ornamental Easter eggs six months out of season. Above the shop entrance, a wrought-iron motif, gold-flaked, depicted the Goose that laid the Golden Egg. From the gloom of the shop, a girl in white folk-skirt & embroidered blue bodice gazed with a look of weird desperation out at the street, as if for the price of a few dollars she might be saved from a fate worse than this.

The girl in the white folk-skirt observed Němec's approach. His actual destination, the *Svoboda & Slovíčkář* bookstore, was diagonally opposite the trinketshop — its façade in large part concealed behind a parked delivery van, from which three men in overalls were currently unloading crates. The crates, stencilled **FRAGILE** & ↓↓ dN AVM SIHL ↓↓, belonged to an address one door along: SKRIER & CO., PURVEYORS OF FI E CRYSTAL — from whose entrance a fourth man came wheeling a trolley, humming loudly to himself the theme tune from an old TV detective drama, *Major Zeman*.

Němec stared morbidly at the shop window papered with the usual printed & handwritten notices. The girl across the street tracked his reflection in the gaps between. Then someone inside the trinketshop called out & the girl reluctantly turned & disappeared inside. Němec, having never even noticed her, was standing in front of the advertisement for *The Sphinx's Code*, a definitive booklength study of the Voynich Manuscript: *observa hoc spatium*. Blank. In his slept-in undertaker's suit & mess of unbrushed hair he looked the part, at least, ogling the sign in the window with hunched shoulders like a scarecrow sizing up to let go a couple of knockdown combinations at a wet paper bag. There were holes in his shoes. If it seemed he'd come a long way, he still had much further to go. Němec sighed as his gaze drifted across the notices, some of them layered four or five deep like bits of uncovered archaeology. They all appeared innocuous enough:

Hanka's Homoeopathic Herbal Healings, on Liliová Street, was hosting a lecture by PhDr Ondřej Zeugma, "tonight at 19:30" (no date given). Visits to the last-known resting place of Rabbi Löw's "Golem," by arrangement at the New Old Synagogue, please contact etc. Albino laboratory mice for sale, in good health, ideal as domestic pets. Multidimensional services* to take place at St Thomas' Church, Mondays, Tuesday, Thursdays, Fridays at 5pm, everyone welcome. The Centre for Theoretical Study, weekly workshop #32: How to Build an Orgone Accumulator in your Own Home. An exhibition of the proteiform work of Rudolf II's court portraitist, Giuseppe Arcimboldo, about to open at the Kunsthistorisches Museum in Schnitzelstadt (the flyer showed a portrait of the Habsburg Emperor made from a pallet of fruit & veg, like surrealist grocery). *The Psychic Flea Circus Trainer's Manual*, complete set, "as new," Kč 540,- with complementary wall-chart...

As Němec pushed open the door, a draught of warm musty air swaddled him — immediately his eyes drooped, the odour of decaying books was like a soporific. Behind him a bell tinkled & as if summoned from nowhere an elderly man, with thick square bifocals & a bowl-shaped fringe of hair around a baldspot like a Capuchin's tonsure, appeared behind the shop counter. Němec recognised him from past occasions, but the bookseller's face exhibited nothing but the blank expectancy of someone who harbours few illusions about his fellow man, least of all his customers.

They exchanged monosyllables. Němec asked about the notice in the window. The bookseller just looked at him from behind his pasty bifocals with eyes that grew a little blanker, as if only an idiot would expect him to know such

----

* Sic. (Did he mean "Multidenominational"? Call it what you will: "the name of the name isn't the same as the name.") [✋]

things. You'd think people went there for no reason but to pry secrets out of him, secrets he didn't know he possessed but which he was determined to keep in any case. It'd been like that when Němec asked about Mydlář, the mere mention of the headsman's name was enough to make the bookseller clam up. Němec tried subtler approaches, but always in the end it was the same —

'If it ain't on the shelves,' the bookseller grumbled, wedging a pencil stub as thin as a toothpick between his teeth, 'it ain't on the shelves.'

Němec gave the pseudo-Capuchin a sceptical look, but just then a couple of students wandered in, so Němec drifted off down one of the aisles & began rifling through the sections on History, Art, Esoterica, Theology. You could tell that's what the sections were supposed to be because someone who'd once-upon-a-time tried to be helpful had written as much on strips of blue paper sellotaped to the respective shelves. Once-upon-a-time it might've even meant something, but it didn't any more. You'd've had better luck with a jigged roulette table.

Just for the hell of it, Němec chose a couple of shelves at random — picking through cardboard folios & back numbers of *The Murmurer*, thick hardcover museum catalogues, star charts & handpainted tarot decks, yellowed flyspecked theatre pamphlets & dusty letterpress poetry fascicles, Churchill's twelve-volume history of the War, Gray's *Anatomy*, a black cloth-bound copy of *My Secret Life* (vols. I-VI) by "Anonymous," several dozen overpriced pirate editions (printed in Leipzig) of the more decadent Western Imperialist authors of the last two centuries, & — pièce de résistance — a full set of the Complete Works of Comrade Marx&Engels, bound in fake vellum, gold-embossed & lettered in carmine.

Whatever system might once have ordered the store's inventory seemed long ago to've been abandoned under the sheer bulk of accumulation. Books had been fitted into every available space, from floor to ceiling, piled on stairs, in boxes, teetering atop planks of bowed plywood ranged overhead into makeshift bridges between opposing upper shelves. It was like a burrow or a bower. The sound of a cash register clanked from the other end of the shop, muffled behind the walls of books. Stairs wound down, around & back up again. Light filtered through a window thick with dust & papered almost entirely with blank bits of paper. Beneath it was a shelf stacked with periodicals dating back to the 1940s.

Němec grabbed a bundle at random & sorted through it. Then another. *Kino, National Geographic, Přítomnost, Encounter, Typ, Erotická Revue* & suchlike. The dusty glue & newsprint smell of the fleshpots of yore, etc. It was in this manner that he stumbled upon a pretentious-looking journal called *Heterocosmica*, in whose pages, as he flipped through, fanning away the dust that came off them, he came upon a "letter," translated from the Latin, sent long ago by a Golem City book collector to a Roman priest. It wasn't a particularly interesting letter by itself. It was reprinted at the end of a long article about the *Dialogicall Difcourfes of Spirits & Divels* (London, 1601) — *Declairing their proper offence, natures, difpofitions, and operations: their poffeßions and dispoffeßions* — under the heading:

An Apologia for Hermes Trismegistus

But something startlingly familiar about the letter caused Němec to jerk his head, as if someone had stalked up behind him & coughed unexpectedly in his ear. Then someone really did cough. The sound came from behind one of the bookshelves. Němec stood like that waiting for several moments before he realised he was in a cul-de-sac separated by only a couple of feet from the store entrance. As if to confirm his deduction the bell over the door chimed. There was a mumbled exchange at the counter. Footsteps. All of which might've passed unremarked had at that very instant two pinhole eyes not been peering at Němec from the other side of the window.

The eyes seemed to exist all by themselves, detached from any face, floating in a square of smudged glass framed by paper scraps. Then a shadow fell across the glass & the eyes were gone. He blinked at the empty space in the middle of it, then down at the journal he was clutching in his hands, then back at the empty space. *Observa hoc spatium…* Something in his mind struggled to make a connection. A connection it would've been better not to make…

Rewind still further: October, the last time Němec saw the Prof alive.

It'd gone eight o'clock & Němec was late. The weather was more than usually cold for that time of year — ice hung in the air & the wind worked its way through Němec's tattered coat as he trudged up the street, cobblestones slick underfoot. He was thinking through variations of a gambit he'd perhaps try out against his wily foe, given the (unlikely) opportunity — Fromm's, socalled: e5!? in reply to f4 — when he saw the white house standing there ahead, the vaulted arch into the open-flanked courtyard, the lights in the windows like drowned embers.

He climbed the winding Tower stairs & rang the bell. The caretaker, an elderly bird by name of Severínová, opened the door wrapped in the aroma of pickled zelí, giving Němec a blank stare. She knew him of course, but that's the way with some people, isn't it, looking at you like they've never clapped eyes on you before in their lives. From all indications, Mrs Severínová had been up there cooking the evening's variation on boiled veg & two cabbage, the Prof & entourage being of that caste disdainful towards the flesh of beast or fowl. The old bird had been leaving in any case & so ushered Němec in as she ushered herself out. He navigated the cluttered hallway alone & as he did was reminded of a joke:

Man walks into a bar with a baby cabbage sticking out of one ear & orders a drink. Barman gives him the once-over, sees the cabbage but holds his tongue out of consideration etc. & pours the man a drink. Same thing next day: man comes in, cabbage still sticking out his ear like he's got two heads, barman minds his own business, pours the man a drink. Third time the man comes in, the barman can't help himself — *Hey mate*, he says, *you know you've got a cabbage sticking out your ear?* No kidding. Man says, *Can't hear you, I've got a cabbage in my ear.* But whether it was a red cabbage, a white cabbage or a green cabbage, the joke didn't say…

The Prof was already ensconced in his bureau with a fire burning in the grate. The head of Gaius Octavius lay scowling beside the coalscuttle. The flickering glow made dark half-moons under the Prof's eyes above cheekbones stubble-grey. He was sitting in an armchair between desk & chess-table, papers fanned-out on his lap, a low reading lamp on the farther side casting the remainder of the room in a fixed shadow. He glanced up at Němec as he crossed the room, giving him the "hairless Mexican" look. The expression was strained, the product of unsleep. Not the usual garrulous self tonight, Němec figured, weight of life's burdens & all that. He was pushing on, the Prof, not as spry as once was, a bit creaky in the knees, index finger working his earhole to get at whatever was lost in there — *Hello! Hello! Nice night for it, mnnn?*

The Prof shuffled the papers away into a manila folder of the type you can find in any advocate's chambers, tied with magenta ribbon & stacked in closets & atop bookshelves. With some effort he rose & shook Němec's hand, before sliding back into his chair. Němec was conscious of how cold his own hand was, but the Prof's was colder. He draped his coat over an armrest & sat down. Up close the Old Man looked even more unwell, yellow at the corners of his mouth, eyelids slightly down-turned, also yellow — the contest between coal fire & lamp evoking Rembrandt, *Study of a Man's Head*, oil-on-panel, c.1630. Somewhere between terminally ill & chronically disillusioned. Tincture of jaundice. To make conversation Němec inquired about progress on the Old Man's cipher manuscript.

'Progress,' the Prof sighed, 'is a word to be used only with a great deal of circumspection. Some people,' he went on, seating himself now in a large leather armchair by the window, 'believe that progress is an invention of science. You know,' he chuckled, examining his cuticles, 'the crystal ball used to represent the height of progress! Men want to see the future. Speculation's all well & good, but ultimately people want to *know*.'

The chuckle turned to a cough. The Prof thumped his chest impatiently, cleared his throat, leaned back in his chair, eyes watery, to get his breath back. Perhaps urged by an impulse to leave nothing incomplete if he could help it (vain task), or afraid of letting go of a thought he might never be able to return to, the Prof laboured on with his anecdote till it gave up of its own accord.

'Death,' he added as a type of postscript, dropping his hand beside the armchair to retrieve a thin blanket which he then drew across his knees, 'is bearable for man if he feels he can still know what happens afterwards. Like an invisible witness, floating above everything. That's why he invented God. Religion's just another way of seeing & being, so to speak, *in the know*. Mightn't science be just another word for God?'

The Old Man paused, wiped his mouth with a handkerchief, blew his nose, returning it (handkerchief) to right trouser pocket. Then motivated by an unexpected impulse he pushed the rug aside & stood up, patting his hair on one side, & shuffled around behind his desk clutching the manila folder. Němec could hear a bottle being uncorked & the sound of wine being poured.

Retracing his steps, the Prof handed his guest a glass & eased himself back down into his chair. Němec eyed the glistening tears of Eurydice. The Prof likewise raised his drink & took a long spittle-moistened sip. The prospect of a game of chess seemed already far away: pawn to king-four in response to the advance of white's king's-bishop's pawn would have to wait for another occasion — it'd been a longshot in any case. The Prof chuckled some more —

'Did I ever tell you,' he put his glass aside, 'about the time Francis Bacon was sent here as a spy to see if Rudolf had discovered the Philosopher's Stone?'

The Old Man leaned back, fixing his gaze on the ceiling —

'Well now, *there's* a story...'

The Prof's Soliloquy

God must've wept the first time humanity ever really looked at itself. But were there seven oceans by design or merely accident? And what about all the other oceans, of unconquered space & time, of ignorance & boredom, of fear, anxiety, stupidity, of death & damnation & the reborn, of music, literature, art & insanity, of *inanity* & of nothing at all? A man sets out in his pea-green boat upon the waters to find the great answers & discovers a mountainpeak sticking above the waves, composed entirely of guano. The Mount of Wisdom, Ararat, Chomolungma, the Holy Hilltop, call it whatever you like. At the heart of it lies a stone. It's there because the man put it there. The Mountain is really the Mind & when he looks over the side of his boat he sees there're no seven oceans at all but only an Abyss. The *inverted* Mountain of the Mind. Voltaire, perhaps jokingly, called Fra Bacon *the father of experimental philosophy*, because when the oceans parted it wasn't the miraculous vision he saw, or an escape route from a predicament, but an unarguable fact. The stone *itself*, a piece of rock you could kick across a beach.[*] He was Archimedes without the bathtub, Sartre with the *ennui*. Like a mothman with a measuring tape he mapped the centripetal forces of power. He had an inkling that *practical knowledge* was everything. Or almost everything. Like the proverbial stone in the field you can't walk around — the subtle yet immovable object *sans pareil*. At court, Bacon was the Man on the Make. To Kissinger as Walsingham was to J. Edgar Hoover, he was a pragmatist among fanatics &, as necessity dictated, a fanatic among pragmatists. Like his namesake the goodly friar, Bacon lived in *uncertain* times & could cut a jig on a tightrope with the best of them. In parliament he argued with all due solemnity for the execution of Mary, Queen of Scots, like some mighty Roman orator. In private he played postboy, carried secret missives from Elizabeth to Walsingham & from Walsingham, by devious routes across Europe, to the English spy Francis Garland, to ascertain the *purpose* of John Dee & Edword Kelley's imminent arrival at the court of Rudolf II & verify the *existence* of a certain *manuscript* in the Imperial library. Perhaps it was this bungled bit of espionage that planted the idea in Dee/Kelley's brain of duping the Emperor into buying a fantastically expensive magic book which just happened to be "attributed" to Bacon's own namesake, like a nice bit of self-fulfilling prophesy even *he* couldn't've dreamt up? Call it poetic justice, if you must. All we know for certain is, while travelling incognito through the Habsburg domains, Bacon commenced his *Treatise on Comparative Phlebotomy*, unfinished at the time of his death thirty years later (publicly disgraced by that time & a pauper to boot, the dimming of the lantern once so bright, as Phoebus something-or-other, because even then, in those final years, nay more pressingly as the end neared, but ever so elusive, that ultimate Truth which a man might point to even on his death bed, his soul's desired humiliation over the mind's triumph). Bacon's *Treatise* mirrored his life: a struggle of impecunious contraries. Anticipating Hume & Descartes, it posed the universal doubt of the implied theologian against the doubt of the sceptic:

---

[*] If only you could get to one (those fabled Sea Coasts of Bohemia would do, right there under the cobblestones). [✋]

a battle between giants & dwarfs. A dwarf by nature, Bacon preferred to believe in things he could see with his own eyes. An aspirer, he longed like Faustus to be among the giants, but was prepared to sell his soul for a mere bribe. On matters of highest principle, he was like a rider with his spurs lodged in the flanks of a quite dead horse. He was accused by his enemies in Parliament of harbouring *ambitions*. To prove himself, he risked offending his Queen & denied her pleasures; reprovingly, he grovelled to her successor, acquiescing in his, keeping the overbearing Scot mollified, his equanimity more on an even keel, order restored, were order previously felt to've been perturbed — Bacon the alchemist of RealPolitik. As Lord Chancellor under James I, Bacon presided over the nuptials of False Frederick (late of Bohemia & newly of the Order of the Garter) & the Scottish king's spotty daughter, on St Valentine's Day no less, 1613, as is recorded in a poem by John Donne:

A bride, before a 'Good-night' could be said,
should vanish from her clothes into bed…
But now she's laid; what though she be?

No virgin majesty, she delivered on order a baker's dozen of heirs & successors to the Protestant cause. Womb of temporal if not celestial powers, as prated the poets about her virtuous namesake, the Faerie Queene. If Frederick had fallen at Whitey Mountain, who knows what further calamities History might've been spared. It's a matter of record the bride's mother loathed the man. Was Bacon the go-between, the fixer, looking for an inside line on a certain *manuscript* perhaps? By all accounts, the book Voynich stumbled upon in Italy disappeared during the Thirty Years War. Could Frederick have fled with it along with the rest of his Bohemian loot? Did Bacon use the fabled book as a bargaining chip, to buy a princess for a had-been with nothing to his name but a fiasco in the foothills around Golem City? And if so, what became of it? Perhaps the Stuarts, when they in their turn took flight, bartered it for bed & board at the Vatican. And thence, to the Carteggio Kircheriano. It could be possible, it would explain a number of omissions. Besides, it was an age of Revolution, the true heresy of power resided in parliaments not medieval grimoires: *political science*, conceived under the mask of Machiavelli, was finally born with Oliver Cromwell's face & Bacon was its midwife. The regicides of James' successor had Bacon's precedent. They were Men of the Hour & the hour was on the side of Reason & Republic, the clockwork universe had done a tyrant to death & Time hadn't stopped but marched-on in mocking indifference. *Ach, so*. Well may you ask, what *is* in fact this magic power vested in Reason, Knowledge, Understanding, but also the opposite: unreason, nonknowledge, misunderstanding, *mnnn*? For once power was not an enigma any longer but a public controversy, a way of provoking men's consciences, to deliver them from that Day of Judgement awaiting them all to the Grail of Truth, socalled, where each would be dealt his share in accordance with a Universal Law. A fine picture it'd make, if only men *had* such things as consciences. Perhaps that was the first purpose of the Voynich Manuscript, to teach that what's hidden can't be kept, that Science doesn't veil herself in mysteries but merely in method. Axioms not protocols. Pandora's Box had a twin of course. One could be opened with barely any effort at all &

contained the seeds of Doom, the other contained the germ of Creation but had no key, it simply pointed to itself the way the world does, a conspicuous *thing* in the midst of phantasms. One feeds a desire for the unconcealed, the other for what's naked in front of your very eyes but which nothing can make you see. The pornography of ambition. *Ah*, they say, *the things we've beheld!* Beautiful & terrible things. Who could *invent* such atrocities, *eh? Ja, ja.* Well, who *hasn't* invented his own atrocities, called down holy vengeance upon the world, caused in his imagination the universe to erupt? If only out of boredom, stupidity, thwarted longing. To repudiate such impulses we name them God. The opposite, also, we name God. Between *us* & *them* stand hubris & this thing we call a conscience. Imagine, to actually be guilty of the crimes of God? Some have tried, like Heliogabalus. But a man who examines his own actions is no God, even if only *after the fact* — like Speer at Nuremberg. Hegel said the Almighty wasn't conscious of His actions till after He committed suicide on the cross, which is a nice bit of sophistry to escape a charge of infanticide. Christ for his part said the meek shall inherit the Earth & he was telling the truth. There's always room for a slave in a concentration camp to become a kind of king. Show me a man, even on his last legs, who doesn't believe he's God Himself & I'll show you the Devil with his pants down. *Ja, ja.* But the contrary, *mnnn*, is also true, *nicht wahr?* And isn't *that* precisely what we run headlong into whenever we turn to History for an excuse for our predicament? Which is to say, Reason *in the form of* History. Reason, History, God, what *are they* but magical abstractions, capable of transmuting crime into virtue, changing the World for the better. *Ja ja.* Always for the better. You can't say Marx & Hegel are to blame any more than the cave-dwellers of Qumran. God's not to blame, either: He was supposed to've created *us* for that role. What's Genesis but a guidebook for making scapegoats? Well, it's too much for a man to blame himself for all that's wrong in his own backyard, so he invents a god to do the blaming on his behalf. It could be a stroke of genius, or pure stupidity. Question is: where does the power reside? You know, when I was young & stupid like you, *hehe*, I fell for all that nonsense. Moses or Marx, what's the difference? *When as we sat desolate by Babylon*, quoth Bacon, *in our captive state.* But they were mad times, completely *mad.* The maddest. 1938. 1948. Hitler! Stalin! What *weren't* we prepared to believe? The simple answers to the difficult questions were there to be had for whoever was willing to be had (such a paltry exchange). Modern alchemy! Dialectics & historical materialism! A parable straight from *Faustus.* Everything works, can be *made* to work, by the subventions of Pure Reason, if only… *Ja, richtig!* Like a brain in a jar. And at the same time, everything that *worked* got magically transformed into an inevitability! Depending, of course, in which direction Reason inclined herself from one hour to the next — or *reclined* herself. But Reason, we figured, was on our side. *Ja, ja, ja.* And people still believe, only they've changed the names. Now Reason's on the side of Democracy, Capitalism, the Hidden Hand of the Free Market. *Free* Market! Revolution in our own time! But what's free, *eh*, in this perfumed rosebush of ours? Who knows, Bacon might even have approved with just a little bit of handwashing persuasion —

never especially averse to being on whichever was the winning side. As for Science, well... *Science*! Nowadays you get to change History by remote control, like switching channels on TV. No blood has to get on anyone's hands. All very hygienic! How thoughtful! Like a showerblock doused in Zyklon-B — you can always find a millionaire to shovel out the corpses so no-one else has to see. And what more of a paean to Reason could you want than a *bloodless* revolution, *eh*? A real prime cut of veal, whiter than the proverbial. Well, *someone* has to get blood on their hands, even if its only the blood of a machine. Revolutions don't happen, *ab ipsus*, all by themselves, they don't just fall into the laps of the poor & oppressed, like shit from reindeers or the stuff fairies eat. Doesn't cost a thing to dream of a free lunch, does it? Especially when there's one right there across the counter, all you need to do is sign the mortgage slip. Sign away! Get your free Velvet Revolution. Well, that's the 17th of November* in a nutshell, so to speak. Fairyfloss in a nutshell. The way they talk about freedom's enough to make a man sick. Who needs a beacon on the hill when there's a TV in every hearth, prating away day & night & everyone glued to the advertising. All there's left to hope for is it'll talk itself to death, blow-up in a shower of cathode & copper wire. Like those scientists who put a starling in a cage next to a twittering machine & the starling copied every sound, *twittwittwit*, nonstop, till the starling keeled over on its perch from auto-asphyxiation. One dead starling. Now if they could wire a nation of men that way, talking-heads on fastforward spreading epidemics of Babel across the planet, motormouths gasping their last on primetime, mandibles spasming into final rictis, earth crusting-over with their remains, fossilised a million years hence & excavated piecemeal in some future Martian paleoearthological Age of Science, as proof perhaps of an hypothesis: that Earthlings, like the winged "angels" of their incoherent God-literature, existed in a state of gargoyled sartorial bliss, twittering from cradle to grave, for the pleasure of hearing themselves or from existential necessity it makes no difference. And what would that teach our learnèd Martian colleagues? As dogs bark at the moon & chickens roll their eyes upsidedown — just another of abundant nature's curiosities, to be mounted in a hologram for intergalactic schoolchildren to one day ogle at. As for Bacon, you'd think he was the complete *antitype* of that literary fraudster who called himself "Doctor" Faustus, the *excremental* philosopher par excellence — a man who possessed all the craft of a lump of transmuted lead. Perhaps the secret of Faustus' fame was in the moniker. Stands to reason, *eh*, no-one ever wrote a potboiler about anyone called Bacon, did they? † Or *did* they? Faustus, on the other hand, grovelled at the feet of Absolute Knowledge with all the vanity of a man who'd promise anything to the mistress who flogs him but afterwards tries to wheedle out of paying. A well-fed man's magnanimous hunger. *Ja, ja.* It's an old story: devils, witches, compacts with the Devil, higher powers, the divine illumination, Satyagraha, the Passion of Masoch, the Eye of Moloch... *Though soon he found he failed of his account, even.* Poor Fäustchen, the butt of a joke whose

* 17 November 1989, the Velvet Revolution: a handydandy upheaval of the heavenly spheres that brought Golem City from the Cold War to Capitalism's Promised Land. Makes you wanna cry, don't it? [✋]

† A man named Marlowe, however...

punchline he couldn't understand. Bacon, as a jurist, knew all he really needed was a pact with Scientific Reason.[‡] Keep in mind, it was Bacon who led the prosecution's case against Thomas More, the grand utopianist, for high treason no less, a capital offence traded for a capital idea — for it was Moore who said, *Philosophy has no place amongst kings*! Poor Bacon, how those words must've pricked his vanity, if not his poor misbegot conscience. Bacon for his part was the archetypal Organisation Man, though always open to a bribe or two, whose God was the ultimate corporation. What was a monarch to him but a necessary impunity? Pty Ltd. And here we are congratulating ourselves for having cast-out a shabby technocracy for a more glamorous one & having made a philosopher our king. *A bad philosopher, or a bad king?* you may ask. A bad philosopher might make a good king. Our king is neither good nor bad, but simply an irrelevance. He holds his sceptre the way

---

[‡] It was *evidence* that would compel Heaven & Hell to yield, though a little flattery wouldn't hurt. Perhaps he even saw himself as the father of a race of grey men in want of no mistress to goad them — the mysteries of Isis unveiled, naked Athena, *mnnn*. No need for devils, unless you mean of the *masculine love* variety. Pythagoras, the Grand Lodge. He had the ear, as they say, of Elizabeth's successor, James I, a notorious sodomite (& Wycliffe's unintended vindicator), but for all that it may still've been a forlorn solitude that drove him in his quest for a *practical* truth, one he could *hold* & in a sense *possess*, during a time of despotism. Try to picture the man, looking at the world skew-eyed from too much obeisance, vanity, cognitive despair, with his baubles of office, his letters patent, etc.: the deformity of a man who longs for natural pleasures but is permitted only unnatural ones, *mnnn*? And still he believed! But in what, really?

the child holds a balloon — any moment he'll get distracted by something else & the balloon will float away & the people will gaze after it & some will say, *Look! A balloon!* as it rises up into the blue nothing. Perhaps it's the lost philosopher's stone, *hehe*, & any moment it'll fall out of the sky on someone's head. I hope it isn't *yours*, mein freund. Oh, but don't mind me, I'm just a tired old fart talking nonsense, waffling on about God & things nobody's interested in any more, which is what makes them such good company once you reach the onset of senility. *You've* got your whole life (this's what they told me at your age, the idiots) *still ahead of you. Ja, ja.* Mine got left behind somewhere, like a shadow stuck on a wall. What to do with it, you may well wonder. Put a frame around it & call it art. What I'd give to be young again. The *elixir* was always an old man's folly — & a young man's waste of time. Put youth on a man's side & all he wants to do is think up ways to fritter it away, *nein*? Like some malformed, Janus-headed beast trying to cross a path both ways at the same time — neither able to get back to where it began, nor to reach the other side — *eh*? A two-headed chicken on a field sable, *hehe*. They used to serve up something called Chicken Romanov at the school I taught at in Klagenfurt, don't ask me why. Fancy name for a chook schnitzel is all that is. It reminds me of that story, about the Russian princess who escaped the Bolsheviks disguised as a gypsy fortune teller? Trotsky himself apparently came to the gypsies' camp & got his palm read, with the Tzarevna right under his nose the whole time. *You'll meet a mysterious woman in a strange place, there will be a fork in life's path, you must decide carefully...* Well that's Earth-shattering stuff, isn't it? But at my age, you know, disappointment doesn't count. Democracy, they say, provides better roads & the freedom to cross at will. While capitalism means in doing so you take your life into your own hands, *hehe*. In the Good Old Days, whose passing is so solemnly lamented, one had to stand in line for the opportunity, wait for whoever was on the other side already to give you the green light. And while you waited, you were expected to devote yourself to upholding the tradition, make believers of the poor bastards waiting further back behind you down the line, & the ones further back still. Like all great pyramid schemes. In primitive tribes, it was always the elders, you know, who ended up with all the wives while the younger men went without, obliged to bide their time till the Methuselahs shuffled off. This tended to drive the younger men silly — like the Trojans of Homeric fame, who kidnapped women from their neighbouring tribes: there'd be wars & the prodigals would be killed or maimed or left wandering about for years with shellshock, while the wise old greybeards stayed home in bed & grew older & wiser. *He who finds a wife finds what is good and receives favour from the Lord...* So the Proverbs say. Have I in my age been so favoured? I have a wife & more than a wife, & perhaps the good Lord thinks that's favour enough, for an old man, eh? The same Proverbs also say, *May your fountain be blessed, and may you rejoice in the wife of your youth. A loving doe, a graceful deer — may her breasts satisfy you always, may you ever be captivated by her love...* But I suppose we shouldn't take these things too literally. Men haven't always been creatures of science, with their cults of death & resurrection — of which we, too, are the direct descendants. Who knows why men ceased being outwardly content with supernatural explanations. But have they? We in our time still have the Church... & the State. A man is only free to think what he's free to think. What was it Rabelais said? *Science sans conscience n'est que ruine de l'âme.* And where does science find its conscience? The footnoters, who have an answer for everything, tell us that no such conscience existed before the Arab scholars & the Rabbis of Alexandria rediscovered it, lost since the Ancient Greeks. Every civilisation has its dark ages — there'd be no true conscience otherwise. Consider Zosimos, who believed in a world governed by powerfully opposed dualities, two sciences & two wisdoms. Wind the clock a few centuries forward & you end up with Bacon speaking about the *dissolution of myths* & the substitution of knowledge for fancy. *The sovereignty of man lieth in knowledge*, he said. And if you believe what he says, well, *una scientia universalis* is a very fine ideal alright. Bacon didn't understand a word of mathematics, mind you. Even so, even so. The *Novum Organum*! It's a nice idea. Well, he was an amateur after all, a *litterateur*, a symbolist, but also a lawyer with an eye out for Number One. He dabbled in poetry (a salient datum), but that was *de rigueur* for learnèd types in those days & showed a bit of panache. As Attorney General he, Bacon, admitted to accepting bribes — without, of course, allowing the fact ever to cloud his most high judgement. *Sehr faustdick.* But when it came to his little experiments, Bacon was like a man flogging a hobbyhorse. A one-man Academy of Lagado. He died of pneumonia, incidentally, brought-on by over-exposure to the elements, standing out in the snow to see if dead chickens could be better preserved in the cold. Fourhundred years before the invention of the Frigidaire, which presents no such risks...'

Risky Business

All too soon the Prof's soliloquy ended & silence descended. The fire obligingly guttered in the grate: a sudden draught brought a chill to the room.[†] Sensing a presence, Němec turned in his chair in time to see Elsbeth von N____ hovering at the edge of the shadows. The silhouette of the temple priestess drifted past the bookshelves & through a doorway to some other part of the house, silent as a cat. How long she'd been observing them, Němec couldn't guess. A tingling crept up the back of his hands. Something unearthly about that woman, unknown to him as she was — something remote, cold & transfixing as an obsidian mirror. The Prof seemed not to've noticed.

Němec finished his glass of port. *Lagrima.* The apparition of the Old Man's "Black Queen" brought to mind Hades & *his* concubine, Goddess of Seasons, Persephone, & more: the *au fait* poète maudit, Orpheus, with all that elaborate puerile suffering of his. Had Eurydice really lamented her fate? Němec peered across his empty glass at the Prof's grey lips as he soliloquised, trying to read them, the intellect & spirit that moved them, this once lover of women. And perhaps still. His expression was unrevealing, yet his voice betrayed his fatigue — the clock slow winding down, long passed the thrill or even habit of revolutions previous, once sufficient to keep it turning, no more, now the spring had uncoiled.

'I'm boring you?' the Prof inquired, smiling.[*]

A rather wan, rhetorical smile, Němec thought. He shook his head. It cost him no effort to humour the Old Man. It was getting late, but for the Prof it was all now *too* late. Whatever he'd been, whatever he'd sought to become, what he was, guessing the evitable from the inevitable. Even now Němec could barely claim to know the Old Man at all. Younger than him in 1947 when he'd set out

---

[†] Up on the ceiling the shadows had arranged themselves in progressions from simplest to most complex, radiating from contending light sources — desk-lamp, streetlight, table-lamp, etc. — all parts of a geometric proof: grid, point, line, plane, polygon — cross-sections cut through with actions — the wash of a car's headlights through the curtains' loosely woven netting — resolving to Martian canals, the criss-cross of a dying planet's last gasp effort to irrigate itself — Euclid & planetary extinction vied for precedence — implied causalities spun off into implication most strange — Odysseys of interplanetary migration — the red planet dying under the watchful eyes of Mycenaean moonmen — ancient geometers handing down grid-point to grid-point n-dimensional wormhole maps to be used on the return journey, if & when, mistaken for a child's empty exercise book filled with nothing but ruled lines, parallel to the observing eye but not of a proof that could be derived without some *deus ex machina* creeping in somewhere along the line.
[*] Not by a longshot, old timer. [✋]

on that path, whatever path it was, that'd wed him to an obsession. It was what'd kept Němec coming back, knowing he himself had never been truly obsessed by anything — he collected words on scraps of paper, typed-out reports on other people's lives like a police informer whose entire existence is spent eye glued to a peephole. *Think you were born old before your time, eh, kiddo?* Ineptitude by declensions nominative, genitive, accusative, ablative — still learning that a writer is a poor trembling idiot; that he, failing as an idiot, might aspire to less.

If the Prof had any inkling of these thoughts, he gave no indication. Instead, manoeuvring himself up from his armchair, he shuffled around his desk, neatly rearranging things, pens & bits of paper at right angles, completing the circuit along the far side. Retrieving the same manila folder Němec had seen earlier, the Prof spread out its contents on the blotter. He jabbed a finger at a sheet of paper —

'Tell me what you think of *this*,' he said.

Němec went over to see what it was. There were a couple of photostats & five or six pages of lined legal paper covered in handwriting. The Old Man stood there expectantly as he squinted down at what lay on the desk & struggled to make sense of the Prof's calligraphy — like a schoolmaster's. It immediately aroused unpleasant memories of blackboards & metal rulers. The Prof sensed Němec's apprehension.

What he was looking at, the Prof explained, was a letter that only recently had been discovered in the Carteggio Kircheriano, in the Vatican Library — one he himself had failed to discover thirty years before while preparing an annotated bibliography of the library's holdings. Only three people knew of the letter's existence, he said: an archivist in Rome, himself, & now Němec. He'd just completed a draft translation from the original Latin. The mere mention of it seemed to excite him. In the glow of the lamp his eyes came alive & he chuckled. Němec scanned through the crabbed writing trying to decipher what was so interesting about an old letter everyone had forgotten about. When he got to the end of it, he was none the wiser.

'As a great man once said, *Les traductions sont comme les femmes*,' the Prof sighed. '*When they're beautiful, they're rarely faithful, and when they're faithful, they're rarely beautiful.* Besides, men are too often seduced by what they fail to understand. Or simply what they can't.'

The letter was dated 1639 & addressed to a priest in Rome, a Jesuit named Athanasius Kircher, from one Georgius Baresch of Golem City, reputed owner of a sizable alchemical library. Neither conspicuous beauty nor ugly old maid, the text was unarousing enough to appeal to a churchman's rectitude while still, with intimations of sympathetic wellsprings to be availed, calculated to pique his curiosity by touching his vanity.

Kircher, the Prof explained, was born into a poor family in Hesse, escaping poverty by entering the ranks of the Society of Jesus. Later he taught mathematics at the Collegio Romano. Having authored a shelfload of self-important scientific treatises — among them, the *Polygraphia Nova*, a study of cryptography based on a laughable decoding of Ancient Egyptian hieroglyphics (1663) — Kircher was resting contentedly on his laurels & well advanced into his autumn days by the time Baresch's missive arrived. To keep himself occupied, Kircher still pottered about in his library, engaging in the whimsy of "private research" under the indulgent patronage of the Pope & various other benefactors (including, the Prof noted by way of an aside, to one of Rudolf's successors, Ferdinand III, to whom Kircher had cannily dedicated several of his works).

None of this meant anything to Němec.

'*Bibliotheca Sphinx quaedam, Scripturae incognitorum...*' the Prof intoned, pressing his point, whatever it was. 'But supposing,' he interrupted himself, 'nature's illiterate. Why believe in a Sphinx at all? Or, if the Voynich Manuscript really is a case of *secret writing*, what deeper source can it draw upon than Nature, who — as Goethe says — commands a language born & organised out of her own self? Goethe who also said nature's neither beautiful nor faithful. Well, Goethe-schmerter. What matters,' the Prof shook his head, 'is to establish the *facts*. For instance, this letter.'

He poked a finger at the page lying in front of him, like a prosecutor working up to his punchline —

'What's it trying to tell us? Did Baresch *know* about the Manuscript? Does he know where it *came from*? Or is his appearance in this story merely a coincidence? A coincidence, nonetheless, by which the Manuscript's secret may still be brought to light, leading us closer to its *originator*, perhaps — its Œdipus Ægyptus — & hence to its *meaning*? And what of Kircher, who himself often spoke of a language hitherto unknown, *in which there are as many pictures as letters, as many riddles as sounds, as many mazes to be escaped as mountains to be climbed*? Shortly before he died, Kircher claimed to've discovered an Ur-script, a *polygraphia*. Did he mean the Voynich Manuscript? The Encyclopaedia of Babel?'

The Prof's eyes shone like wet lignite. The room had grown cold, the fireplace barely glowed. Němec looked at the patterns of ice forming in the window. The same patterns which four centuries ago would've formed in the window of Edwarq Kelley's laboratory, but until the discovery of glass would never've been seen by human eyes but only their metaphysic counterparts. The ice clouding that window onto the soul that Man, through long northern winters, had patiently wrought to keep himself in thrall to his own myth. Cave-dwelling ancestors, hunters of golem fish, who in the Great Continuum of this Immortal Instant were gathered in the dark awaiting initiation into the Ineffable Mysteries, of death, rebirth, life-everlasting bestowed in luminous visions…

'The world,' the Prof shrugged, 'is what it is. But unlike Nature,' he said, reaching forward to touch Němec lightly on the back of the hand, in a gesture that could've been interpreted any number of ways (fatherliness, fatefulness), grey lips smiling now, 'all works of men *must* possess meaning, even if they themselves are nothing but forgeries.'

Back to: the girl in the doorway of the folklorist's shop, the delivery man wheeling his trolley, the notice in the bookstore window, the hidden aisle, *Heterocosmica*, the letter, Němec…

The journal would've been easy to overlook. Its satin-sheened cover bore one of those overused reproductions of Böcklin's *Isle of the Dead*. Inside was the sort of writing you'd expect from a publication called *Heterocosmica*, tedious drivel about spiritualism, the occult "sciences," inexplicable phenomena of a decidedly *passéiste* character. It wouldn't've been the reading matter of choice for anyone concerned e.g. with UFOs, the Bermuda Triangle, or even androids.

What really caught Němec's eye were a dozen or so loose photographic plates by William H. Mummler, depicting tricked-up ghosts in nineteenth-century costume. The plates had come loose from the binding & been stuck back in at random towards the middle of the journal. They made him think of the peasant woman who reportedly fled from a Moscow cinema in fear of her life after viewing *Potemkin*, of all things, raving about midgets, giants, dismembered abominations, horrors at any moment about to lung through the screen. All you needed to summon the dead or the Devil himself was a strip of celluloid. You could even conjure God. It took Moses three days to cook-up a lightshow on the mountain — it would've taken Mummler less than an hour in his darkroom.

Němec had been holding the loose plates in one hand, the journal spread open in the other, when the face appeared in the window. Kircher's letter began on page sixtythree & ended on page sixtyfour. In a kind of colophon at the head of it was the etched portrait of a man in musty clerical gowns with a cap resembling a misshapen paper box appeared above a note which identified the cleric as *Master of a Hundred Arts*, inventor of the magnetic clock & various other automatons, & (so it said) of the first megaphone, author of the *Ars Magna Lucis et Umbræ* (1646) & the *Œdipus Ægypticus* (1652-54), among countless other etc., etc. If it hadn't been for the portrait, Němec would never have noticed the letter at all…

Most Reverend Father,

Expressing my highest regards, I wish that you, Reverend Father, may receive all happiness from Him who provides happiness. On the occasion of the departure for Italy, yes even for Rome, of a certain religious person, from whom I obtained assurances that he will carry this letter to you, with which I would like to remind you of some writing that I had sent with the aid of the Rev. fr. Moretus, priest of the Society of Jesus.

The reason for sending that writing was the following: After the publication of the "Prodromus Coptus," Your Reverence became famous in the whole world, and in that work you had asked, among other things, for help in finding additional material for the work you wished to publish, from all those who might have something from which this work might be enriched. Thus, I did not doubt that many not only sent you in Rome "paper envoys," rich in such material, but also in homage presented themselves there personally, in order to congratulate you on the extraordinary enterprise you have undertaken for the good of mankind.

This most pleasing news, when it reached our Fair City, informed me not only of your astonishing work — to be brought in due time into the light — but also of your unheard-of ability in solving the riddles of that Sphinx of unknown writing systems — and since such a Sphinx in the form of writing in unknown characters was uselessly taking up space in my library, I thought I would not be unjustified in sending this enigma to the Egyptian Oedipus in order to be solved.

Having thus transcribed (taking pain to imitate the writing) a certain part of this old book, which the carrier of this letter has seen with his own eyes and about which he can inform you, I sent this writing to Your Reverence a year and a half ago, with the aim that (if Your Reverence would've been willing to undertake this investigation and to convert these characters of unknown creation to known letters) this toil could be of use either to your Oedipus (to the extent in which the things hidden in this book are worthy of such an exceptional effort), or to me, or to the common good. In fact, I did not dare submit the book itself to such a hazardous voyage, if it is true that what I sent you the first time never reached Rome, as I conclude from the fact that after such a long time I have not heard of any reply about this. Therefore I decided to try again — the aforementioned Father Moretus has already told me that he had indeed arrived safely in Rome — about which I was very pleased, and I shall be even more pleased when the secrets of the book I have alluded to may be revealed thanks to Your Reverence, such that the good people may share what beneficial information it has inside it.

From the pictures of herbs, of which the number in the Codex is enormous, of various images, of stars and of other things which appear like chemical secrets, I conjecture that it is all of medical nature — a science to which none other, except that of the health of the mind, is more healthy for the human species. This work will be worthy of the effort of a virtuous genius, especially since this is not a work for all, which one may conclude from the fact that the author would hardly have gone to such lengths just to hide things which are open to the public. In fact, it is quite probable that some good man, interested in the true medical science (having realised that the common method of healing in Europe was not very effective) went to the oriental regions, where he acquired some Egyptian treasures of medicine, partly from books, partly also from discussions with the experts in this art, and that he brought this information back with him, buried in this book with its characters. This probability is increased by these exotic herbs, drawn in the Volume, which escape from the knowledge of the people in these lands.

I hope that Your Reverence, who burns with passion for publication of things which are good, will not disdain from revealing also those things which are good in this book, buried in unknown characters, for the general beneficence, given that here there is nobody capable of lifting such a weight, which consists of such obscure material that it requires a special genius, and a practiced ability, or at least a method difficult to fathom. I will be obliged to you for this, not just for what the work contains, but all else that will in addition flow from it.

I add here some lines in the unknown writing, to remind you of what I had written and sent to you before, in similar characters. With this I recommend myself to Your Reverence and wish you a happy, successful completion of this most rare work.

May the Almighty Lord preserve you from the construing of illiterates.

> *27 April 1639 on the same day on which, in Rome in April 1605, I took up my studies at the University "La Sapienza."*
>
> *V[estr]æ R[everen]dæ Paternit[ate]*
> *Ad obsequia*
> *P[er]oratissimus*
>
> *M. Georgius Baresch*

Němec had been holding the loose plates & scanning the letter idly, trying to make the connection to the figure in the colophon, when the face appeared at the window. *Observa hoc spatium.* When he looked down again, suddenly the name was familiar, the words were familiar. At the end of the letter was an advertisement for the services of a professional crystalgazer, Madam Batavia, depicting a pair of zodiacs within an ornate frame of entwined lotus blossoms like two synchronised clocks gradually losing time to one another. As if prompted by some unconscious suggestion he turned to the journal's masthead, spilling the plates onto a pile of magazines. Publication date: November of that year, vol. 7, issue 2. The editor was someone with a ridiculous name: Viktor Faktor. It seemed only appropriate.

November. Němec read the date again. A strange sensation began to creep over him. The Prof died in his bath at the end of *October.* How was it possible? Němec went back through the letter to convince himself he wasn't mistaken. The wording was identical, the finely nuanced ambiguities, the arcane turns of phrase, the anachronised Latinate syntax. It had the Prof's touch alright. Though he searched the journal cover-to-cover, Němec found nothing to explain the letter's origins or how it came to be published there. And what about the meaning of that ridiculous title? Why *Apologia*? What was being apologised *for*? And *Hermes*? Thrice-wise god of magic, writing & ladies' handbags? The whole thing smacked of some heterocomical contrivance: an elaborately coded message left to be found by those already in the know. But who were they?

Masking the sound with a loud cough, Němec tore out the page & stuffed it in his pocket. He began to sweat. An urge to escape came over him. He hurried back through the over-stuffed aisles. The fake Capuchin observed him knowingly through greasy bifocals as he stumbled out from among the shelves & pushed open the door. The bell tinkled. Those eyes in the window! He felt the bookseller's gaze follow him out onto the street. Probably the man'd been watching him the whole time. For all he knew there was some Commie-era system of mirrors, spyholes, periscopes, fisheye lenses, distributed throughout the store. Of course, when he glanced back, the notice for *The Sphinx's Code* wasn't there anymore, only a square of smeared glass in which his reflection got lost. Behind it there were grey clouds cropped by rooftop silhouettes, & behind the clouds there was nothing.

11

REGARD THIS EARTH
MADE MULTITUDINOUS WITH YOUR SLAVES!

It always ended up dark outside by the time Němec left Volta's office.

An orderly, heavy-set with ponytail & walrus moustache, was waiting for him on a chair in the corridor, snoring behind a magazine. The powers-that-be felt he ought to have a chaperone — in case he took a wrong turn, maybe, & got lost or fell out a window, even. It'd been known to happen.

Němec jabbed the orderly's rubber shoe with a crutch-end to wake him up & started down the stairs. The orderly gaped, moaned, tipped slowly forward onto his feet. A cold gust came in from the door to the courtyard as it swung inwards & a couple of solemn-looking types in overcoats trudged in. It was the right sort of place for looking solemn.

Regoid dis oit,
made multitumourous wid yer sklavs!

Down in the courtyard Němec paused to take in the view, staring up at the snow over the mansard, a white swirl against a background of pale moiré. He could hear the orderly dragging himself slowly down the steps behind him, yawning like some large flippered animal, Odobenus rosmarus. That such ridiculous creatures as Men should be elected to know the vast schema of the invisible heavens, scrupulously intended (if you're willing to believe such claptrap) by the same Cosmic Brain that took the trouble to design each & every pretty little ooh-ah snowyflake. Or had the Divine Creditor satisfied Himself with getting down the original patent & managed all the rest by franchise? The Kentucky Fried Kernel of the Wordsoul…?

Němec trudged out onto the footpath with his chaperone in tow.

Standing sentinel over the corner of the Square, a pair of silent grey megaphones surveyed the entrance to the dead magician's house &, adjoining it, the lachrymose façade of the chapel of Saint John of Nepomuk. (Poor Nepomook, tossed in the river & drowned for fishing under the petticoats of the King's concubine.) The streetlights gave everything the moribund look of a reanimation in a battery-driven diorama in a box. The sky had ceased to be that mesmerising crucible of a moment ago & instead become a jobbing artist's dull impasto, evoking a slow suffocation or a body made shapeless with inertia, like a failed occult force.

Němec hobbled across the street. Nearby a couple of gypsies in bright orange dungarees & duffelcoats busily scraped at the icebound pavement with snow shovels, to no appreciable effect. Down at the intersection, a tram thudded past on its way to the Botanical Gardens. By the time he reached the other side, the cold had stiffened Němec's face & his fists whitened around the grips of the tin crutches. A sudden impulse overcame him, to throw them away, to suffer on his own two feet. He hurled them with all his might & fell on the ground, crutches clattering down on top of him. Like that he lay there, breathing hard, till all the humour went out of the situation, then painfully he dragged himself back up. Somewhere behind him, the orderly coughed — he was standing a dozen paces off, smoking a cigarette, hand in pocket, staring at his boots, unbothered. Němec wondered if they were trained like that, unimposing, to make the self-nurturing hypochondriac feel more ridiculous. It reminded him of the Bandaged Man back in the Ward. It got so you barely noticed he was there. He was probably sitting in front of the TV right now, watching it on mute, providing a running commentary of groans, gurgles, gasps. It was impossible to tell if the man was in pain or if the sounds were just part of his condition.

Němec thought he'd seen a flicker once, where the bandaged man's eyes were supposed to be, but he couldn't be sure. The man's head in quarter profile showed only a pair of dark slits, like a marble bust with rubber tubes sticking out its mouth & nose. Brought in one night from Intensive Care — transferred down the line — maybe they even expected him to make a full recovery. The Day Nurse said he'd been hit by a falling object, but not what kind of object. *Internal decapitation*, she'd said, like it was just the skin keeping it stuck on, the head. *Hope he doesn't sneeze or anything…*

And you think <u>you've</u> got it bad!

One day by chance, in all innocence, a man…

That's about the size of it. He gets born — who knows why or how — & like a hermit crab without a shell he seeks his place in the scheme of things with a borrowed carapace: all the accretions of evolved History, the calcinated bony matter, of which he can absolve himself only by becoming a part. Perhaps it's enough. The collective crab-self, the crustacean consciousness, joined by more than nerves & veins. The element of predation, for example, unknown, at every turn: mistaken identity in the mirror-of-the-soul — the barbed & tendrilled déjà vu — the itinerant nightmare. Visited by dreams of unknown ancestors — the room he carries on his back & all those who've slept there, the ones who came before, ghosts of progress. And is he freer than <u>they</u> were? Exhausted by the past — like Atlas with all of History heaped upon his sloped shoulders — what holds this City together, what type of cement, mud, bone-glue, papering over the cracks? With all the inertia of a bureaucratic miracle machine! Raised in the belief that good shoes prevent fallen arches — inducted into the cult of dental hygiene, the vigilant removal of plaque, the aversion to cavities — conditioned by dogmas of self-help, yoga, a gluten-free diet — personal fulfilment — happiness beyond the reach of inflation.

Somewhere the Great Hermit in his divine wisdom was supposed to be keeping tabs, watching over the probabilities, the margins-of-error, upholding the claims of Reason like a player of human chess — the odd bit of uncertainty worked in now & then to maintain interest, the private aspiration, keep the economy from sputtering to a standstill, desire from turning stale, mired in the rote, the all-too-predictable & all-too-predicted — for a man's more than the sum of his subsistence, so he likes to think. Peering from his shell at reflected moonlight, what can he know of its nether side? Now blackened, now luminous, Erd-shadow cast length-wise through space & all the lightyears beyond — faint, fainter, faintest — ghost of these latitudes sketched upon the heavens, the meridianed zodiac, adrift in the $E=mc^2$ of it all — the centre, the one singular flagpole atop Heaven's finial, abolished now, like a fizzled-out Pole Star, though truth be told was it ever there? For all *he* knows, evolution's nothing but a stab in the dark, a venture to invent — *ex instinctu creatoris, sine ratiocinatione* — the ideal opponent for a game that has no end. Like a well-organised conspiracy — the player plays because there's no alternative &, besides, the game's a secret.

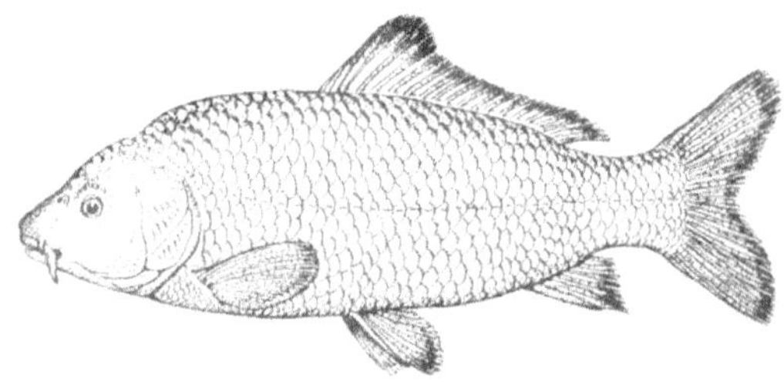

Giant Fanged Carp Discovered in River!

There he was working his mind into a rut again like an introspected idiot. Time to take his nightly medication, keep the old optimism intact, *mnnn*? He pointed his crutches along the pathway edging the park, towards the old noviciate that abutted the church of St Ignatius Loyola, smelling the sweet polluted air, a song in his heart — *Come taste the wine, come hear the band…* With all the discretion of a state security agent, the chaperone followed at a short distance. A little way along, Němec snagged a newspaper with one of his crutches. It lay discarded on the sidewalk, by an overturned bin. In the watery glow of the streetlamp a headline swam out at him below a picture showing a two-metre-long prehistoric monster. *They'll get you no matter where you are*, he thought. No escape from the freakshow.

In the park, people came & went, past the dead fountain, the grizzled statue of Jan Purkyně, the hedges half-buried by drifts of snow: a bum with plastic rubbish bags & piles of cardboard tied with string — suits rushing home from an office somewhere — a mutt dragging a man on a leash — prostitutes in spandex & highheels teetering on the ice — children being pulled along on sleds — a babička with a knitted hat, leaning against a bench to catch her breath. The all-too-explicable & grotesque ballet of everyday life: waiting for a streetlight, crossing the tram tracks, exiting the Metro, & so on, etcetera, *und so weiter.*

Němec disentangled his crutch from the giant carp & slouched onward. He could hear the orderly behind him somewhere pissing against a tree. At that moment a grim-faced clown walked past, glaring at the pavement as if it'd somehow offended him, paper carnation sticking from the buttonhole of a frayed tailcoat, a pair of yellow garbage bags tied around his feet. As he passed, the clown muttered a string of obscenities. A couple of steps further on he looked up & began shouting pathetically, waving a pair of gnarled yellow fists in the air:

'Jsou to naše zbraně!'*

Why is it that public parks always seem to attract lunatics?

The clownish apparition brought back to him a conversation he'd overheard an hour or so before, outside the hospital entrance, two interns on a fag break, about some poor bastard done-in with a broken bottle, in the middle of the children's playground — there, in the park, fifty metres from where Němec was standing — right in front of the deadman's eighteen-month-old kid. It was an escapee from the Bohnice loonybin who did it. Just another freak. Just another orphan.

---

* "A man has a right to bare arms…!" Old Sklavonic joke. [✊]

151

'Nasty job. Copped it right in the neck. Jugular. Both carotid arteries.'

'You see it when it happened?'

'Nah. Just what they brought in. D.O.A.'

'Too bad about the kid. They catch the nut who did it?'

'What I heard, cops had him cornered in a tram down at Národní. Lucky for the commuters the guy was too crazy to take a hostage. Schizo they reckon. Pissed himself at the sight of a gun. Said he only wanted the kid's teddybear.'

Ježíšmarjá!

Even in the gloom the playground looked the way it always looked: a broken swing dangling from its chains, bits of steel piping & concrete blocks jutting from craters of greywet sand. And in the middle of it a red&yellow carousel. Junkies in search of a fix wandered the perimeter, not a cop in sight. On the far side of the playground, a miniature house stood, raised on stilts, with a crooked gable & lopsided windows, its doorway littered with homeless junk.

A dense palimpsest of graffiti camouflaged the fact that this toy house was in fact a replica of the New Town Hall. The original was hidden behind the greybrown brushwork of winter trees on the northeast side of the Square where, barely six short hundred years previous, a mob eager for violence had launched a few papist aldermen out a window, dead as dogs in the street — & thus began the first Hussite War. Němec felt a desire to stand in that place, beneath the windows from which the councillors had been so unceremoniously ejected. Not the actual place, beneath the actual windows, but on that dirty patch of snow in front of its diminished facsimile. In white dressinggown & rubber shoes, he waded towards it. It was like a house in an aquarium, with little hermit crabs scuttling in & out, & broken shells. The orderly waded in after him. Somewhere above, a blackbird barked in its sleep.

Němec wondered, as he surveyed the ground, exactly where the man had been stabbed — as if the trace of something might've remained visible in the snow: a stain, an outline, a scrap of police tape, anything. The world could be buried several times over by sentimentality, but as for the thing itself — death itself — nothing would ever impinge on it. As he stood there, in the middle of the playground, a gust of wind rocked the red&yellow carousel. Its plastic bestiarium of unicorn, elephant, goat, grinning chimpanzee, shuddered briefly into motion with a clang & wheeze. And in that moment it all seemed so improbable, as improbable as a carousel on the moon, with flashing lights, toy animals on poles, going around in circles. A tuneless accordion music turned in the back of his mind, turning & turning, world without end, as though to say: *What if, after all, everything that ever happened, and would ever happen, had already been calculated in advance and was simply repeating itself with variations?*

Das schwerste Gewicht

Why this sudden concern with the complication of the human soul? The trail worstwards? Infinity & death? The things Němec'd been idiot enough to believe! Oh boy. Now, barely a word to his name, he'd had his little epiphany — abandoned his shell on the sea floor, washed-up by the tide, the big sky all sixtyfour shades of grey, world at his feet, grasping at details for their own sake, to make sense of it, his unhappy predicament. Like the orphan in the film telling stories to fill the blanks: pirates, outlaws, castaways, misbegotten childhoods & Doctor Teuner's cult of physical fitness, the Sparticiads & Peloponnesian Wars, dormitory nightmares transformed into desirable wetness, perturbations & masturbations of the eternal alibi, the Great Hermit in the back brain — *Write it a hundred times! You think they won't sniff you out, my fishy little Pericles? Back into your shell, crab!* Oh where were the hymns to happiness, the dolorous despairing ode? He cast his gaze down upon his crutches — a cripple on stilts, the indisputable body in its gross infirmity. A wave of anger, shame, indignation, self-pity — the whole tearjerking deal — the way *they*'d stolen everything that was ever his. Ashamed because there was nothing he could do about it. Self-pity because he knew it wasn't the truth. Not entirely the truth. Words like *existence* had meaning only in ratio to the humiliation you were prepared to endure & no matter how deep the humiliation went, they'd keep bringing you back from the dead for as long as they could find ways of humiliating you some more. That was the sum total of what they'd taught him. Hell itself would be just a franchise of the same thing. Yet somewhere inside the pain — & *only* inside the pain — there must've been a kernel of something, a centre where before there'd only been emptiness. *And I will purge thy mortal grossness so that thou shalt like an airy spirit go?* In his mind, Němec pictured the blue door to the Rehab Unit: it might've been the door of some Himalayan shrine, at which the penitent humble themselves in the name of some primal, venerated object of *purification*, which only suffering can reveal to them — while outside, in the proverbial stairwell of the universe, the unredeemed dragged their mops & pails around in endless circles, without ever expunging anything.

Twist 'n' Shake

Something Volta had said was pricking at his mind but he couldn't get it into focus — only the sense of being trapped, at the mercy of faceless men. What if he just got up & walked away? Snuck off when no-one was looking. Was there ever a time when no-one was looking? *Ain't that exactly what they want you to think, kiddo?* What he'd learnt in the Home, but only after years of getting it wrong.[†]

[†] The crucial aspect of it: judging things by their appearances — the manifestation of all ersatz — a myth erected on a foundation of poverty — developments that seem to foreshadow — voucher

The surveillance eye at the hospital entrance observed Němec hoist himself up one step at a time, the white spectre at his shoulder guiding him past the porter's cabin & through to the Ward precincts. In his mind he heard the gates lock behind him, the shutters come down, the lights switch off one-by-one down the corridor, past the Nurse's Station, the Bandaged Man, till they had him back where he belonged, like that creature of memory strapped to a dormitory bed in a cone of silence. The blue pill & lights-out. Unconscious of intention his hand fumbled on the nightstand, an unlocked drawer with loose change, ID card, house keys, a sheet of crumpled paper.

Němec brought the paper close to his eyes. In the halflight from the windows, a picture of a man in musty clerical gowns with a cap resembling a misshapen paper box. *Most Reverend Father…*

Vulcanite?

Two nights later, lying awake in the same position, dawn still barely a rumour circulating among the comings & goings of the orderlies & the night-nurse. In the interim, subjected to the dark forces of remediation, causing once more the mind to revolt against the body, close-in upon the intrigue of itself, fantastic dislocations of time & space becoming, facet-by-facet, the missing pieces of a conspiracy that possibly didn't exist: the insanity of the Prof's death-tripped ménage-à-trois — the tantalising notice for *The Sphinx's Code* in the bookstore window — the bizarre trajectory of Kircher's letter (its doppelgänger, torn from the pages of *Heterocosmica*, at that moment balled in Němec's hand) as if insistent upon discovering him, addressing some secret message he was too blind, ignorant or stupid to guess at.

Could the old Prof have been communicating from beyond the grave? Or was all this, his present condition included, proof merely of a happenstance in its most unlikely aspect? These thoughts wouldn't go away, wouldn't let Němec sleep. A voice, whispering inside his mind, kept trying to tell him something with a monomaniac's urgency, *Schmm, utth, mneha hahem, ghhhhh, unnn, ooshh!*

5:25. The night-nurse came & went on the last round of her shift. The

---

schemes — opposition to the world offered from within it — the private lives of the inconsequential — chance, fortune, serendipity — a broken lens — things preordained, set down in stone at the dawn of Creation — transistored virtual realities — the overwhelming impression, the foreboding. What you called it didn't matter, only the knowledge that every last little thing that'd ever happened to you, was *meant* to happen, & to happen *just that way.*

voice was still there after she'd gone. Němec finally recognised it, because it was his & he'd been talking to himself in his head, teeth clenched, the way he used to in the Home, tied stiff to the bed unable to move & conjuring spells, words of fear, animal words, keening, hissing, cursing, to keep the others at bay.

Němec could feel the sweat pooling under him. The voice clarified. *Rise and shine, kiddo. Time to get a move-on.* He glanced up & down the Ward. The coast clear, he slid myself out of bed, dragged a sweater over his tunic & a dressinggown over that & waited for the lights to go out in the Nurse's Station. Footsteps receding. He smoothed down the covers on his bed. Counted ten. Grabbed a walkingstick in lieu of crutches & hobbled over to the Nurse's desk to sign himself out on the register for a daylong course of rehab. Nothing implausible in that. Then along the corridors, through swing-doors, down the green linoleum stairs. On the ground floor the corridors were already busy with people in hospital uniforms & people not in hospital uniforms coming in off the street.

In the main foyer was a coffee machine Němec fed some coins into: a dark sludge in a plastic cup came out. A couple of day nurses were waiting their turn. One of them was holding a pair of dentures & making them snap together while the other one rolled her eyes. Nurse A slipped the dentures into her uniform pocket & slotted some coins into the coffee machine. Nurse B leaned her hip against it while the sludge poured, arms folded —

'Used to know a bloke from Lichtenstein who actually *sold* falsies,' she drawled. 'Had a whole suitcase of 'em, different sizes 'n' all, even had a pair with gold fillings. I kid you not. Went door-to-door peddling instalment plans. Little plastic vampire fangs for the kiddies, a brochure for the folks, free fitting & maintenance, lifetime guarantee, the works.'

'He'd've been on a winner there. Bloody goldmine. Out with the old, in with the new!'

'Can say that again. Flogged thousands of 'em. Couldn't keep up with demand.'

'I suppose,' Nurse A, taking her cup of coffee from the dispenser, 'the trick's to get 'em while they're still young. Make lifelong customers out of 'em.'

Nurse B took her turn at the machine, pushing the button for extra sugar & extra whitener.

'Like, *why wait for the oldies to fall out when you can have newies today?*'

Nurse B —

'Some people, though, get kind of peculiar about their teeth. Men 'specially. They think it's a sign of impotence, or something, when they fall out.

Like it's their whatsit's got the chop. Better to get in ahead, is what you need to tell 'em. Be the master of your own destiny, like.'

'Enough to give you the creeps just thinkin' about it. Imagine waking up beside some bloke keeps his teeth in a jar? All that fungus 'n' stuff. Stinking the place up with Listerine. Not exactly a must-have, I'd've thought.'

'You wouldn't believe how many famous blokes wear falsies. All the big actors — cheesy matinee smiles, ring of confidence & all that. Sean Connery, Karel Gott, Vyacheslav Tikhonov… Come in all different colours, shapes & sizes, too. *A new style for every season! Choppers today, gnashers tomorrow! The perfect smile for the perfect moment!*'

'Karel Gott wears falsies?'

Arbeit macht…

Němec sat on a bench in the early-morning fluorescence with the nurses' prattle fading off down the corridor, staring at the fake marble floor, drinking his poison, shivering only slightly. Behind the hum of the fluorescent lights, the voice was still going inside his head. It was telling him there was something he needed to find out. About the Prof. About the Manuscript. Something he was already involved in, though he couldn't see exactly how. All he knew was what the Prof had told him. Now that he was stuck there, in the antechamber of the living (so to speak), it was time perhaps to find out a thing or two. The Klementinum seemed as good a place as any to begin. Maybe then he'd figure out what it was he was here for. Why the Prof's ghost had appeared to him that night. Why he wasn't dead.

The clock above the porter's cabin showed fiftythree-minutes-past-five, *ante meridiem*. In the condition he was in, it could easily take an hour to get where he was going. The library opened at seven. The plan, what there was of a plan, was so far coming together nicely. He glanced nervously at the glass doors leading to the street, thinking, *It'll be now. Right at the threshold. They'll come at you from the side, hidden doors somewhere, with stun guns, and it'll be all over before it even began…*

Outside, no stun guns, the streetlights had gone off but it was still dark. Black clouds hung in the sky like stalactites in a subterranean cavern. No-one shouted at him, no racing of footsteps behind. Němec crossed the street & skirted the park towards the Metro. Across Resslova the market stalls were already crowded. The smell of frying klobása wafted on the cold air. Workmen in overalls stood around a brazier drinking beer from bottles. Traffic stalled on all sides of the intersection, horns blaring. On the opposite corner, dulleyed students were milling around the entrance to the technical college. Beside it, the church of Cyril & Methodius, where as every schoolboy knows the assassins of Reinhard Heydrich were ratted-out by Karel Čurda on a grey morning in 1942: trapped at the end of a tunnel, ammunition exhausted, one round in reserve for the *coup de grace* — roof of the mouth — *they catch you kiddo, it won't be pretty* — inches from digging a way out, their corpses dragged unceremoniously onto the street for the crowd to gawk at...

The trams in the direction of the Old Town were on diversion for track repairs, so Němec followed the crowd down the Metro steps, past the kiosks, the hammer&anvil bellow of the escalators, a dim yellow haze sifting through the passageways' stink of creosote & burning rubber. He was jostled out onto the platform, surrounded on all sides by robotised commuters, the bugeyed uniformity of earning their daily bread, pre-spent, masticated, sloganised, living off the fat of the air: *Eat McFries...! Arbeiten! Arbeiten! Arbeiten! McFries!*

Billboard temptresses leered out from their mirror world, forever young, desirable, witless, gratifiable with dollars — pickpockets loitering in gangs — a bum asleep on a bench — a red letter "H" on a chrome grill, in case of the unanticipated accident, catastrophe, inferno: H for hydrant, hydrogen, hysteria, hunger, hospital, hopeless, holocaust, hypochondria, history, Heydrich, herpes, hermaphrodite, Helen of Troy, Heaven & Hell, headache, haemoglobin, hangman, habeas corpus, Habakkuk... A child's orange balloon, tied to a white plastic stick, lay in a brown puddle between the tracks beside a wrapper with the ubiquitous golden arches: a round little mouse scurried back & forth around it, sniffing for morsels.

Fingering the ticket stub's perforations as he waited for the train, Němec pondered the idea of future underground life, some secret troglodyte existence going on right under people's feet or buried right down in the bowels of the Earth — fallout shelters — nuclear apocalypse — worms tunnelling through ancient crumbling foundations — contaminated cesspools oozing into vast subterranean Baikals — the blind mole's savage hunger for night. Perhaps Volta was right: man's loss of spirit wasn't about some mysterious entity that inhabits the body & leaves it at death, but the failure to fulfil a destiny. Did he really say that? A man digs down into his soulofsouls to seek the horror of redemption — God, Führer, Politburo: secret egomen directing the collectivised mind ever inwards to the nought of noughts. Der Zeromensch.

A train shuddered into the station & its mouths opened. Bodies stuffed themselves in like so much food to be masticated & shat out — Soylent Green — fulfilling a common destiny, first as prey, then as dung. Němec did likewise, pinioned as he was between shapes he couldn't move to see. At Národní the train disgorged & reingested. Němec found a spot on the platform to wait for an ebb in the human tide then limped towards the exit. A smear of grey mud following him up the escalators. The station entrance was crowded with newspaper hawkers, itinerant labourers, bums in sleeping bags. He pushed through the crowd out into the gloom & ugliness of orange streetlights & predawn.

Jonah & the Whale

The weather was cold enough to turn breath to vapour, making everything a blur, faces, collars up, hats down, past the window displays, holes in the wall, pizza joints. No-one paid Němec the slightest bit of attention in his white dressinggown, the woollen sweater over his inmate's tunic, crutches, rubber slippers. Jonah-like amidst a sea of umbrellas, one fragile waterlogged spar gripped, knucklehanded, to stay afloat, head tilted away from the wind. In due course the tide ebbed. Němec lurched starboard, tacked, dropped anchor short of the straits. A fine greybrown seaspray… He waited at the crowded intersection for the lights to change & then, elbowed across the street, collided with a fat woman in highheeled boots crossing from the opposite side, who seemed at any moment about to tip over sideways. *Wotch ware yer goan ye threelegg'd eejit!*

A gaggle of schoolgirls in duffelcoats clutching satchelbags in a doorway giggled. A tram clanged its bell. Dra-a-A-A-N-G! *Fortissimo.* Němec turned, arm halfraised — a taxi was blocking the tram's path. D-R-A-N-G! D-R-A-N-G! went the tram. On all sides the sound of carhorns like startled ducks monstrously amplified. He heaved himself landward. The lights changed, the traffic knotted back around itself.

Němec: sprocketkneed, hand rigid at crook-end of stick, numb. Once more upon terra firma. He stood there breathing harshly through his teeth. A clockface lolled on a grey pole by the intersection: *quarter-past.* The squat, fumeblackened mausoleum of the National Theatre in the distance behind it. Rain streaked down the Theatre's portico like dirty water over a crime-scene polaroid. Cemetery of the creative intellect, with its black flag at half-mast. Regiments of tourists where the riot cops used to form-up.

It started to rain as he lurched down Na Perštýně, walkingstick jamming the pavement cracks, broken cobblestones, bits of uprooted tarmac. A circus placard, edges torn, **KLUDSKY** in bold red letterpress, with a clownface leering out from under it. Ducking his head beneath a gangplanked scaffold, Němec turned left: Betlémské. Metal sheets nailed over basement window, erupting with rust-holes. Broken glass & shattered masonry. Then right onto Liliová, a sandwichboard advert for the Church of Jesus H. & Latterday Temple-Creepers. The Angel Moroni, legs crossed, atop a pillar of salt on a parched Utah lake — *See scales fall from the Nation's eyes like a serpent's shed skin!* — a madman, of course (just one more in the scheme of things), taking dictation meanwhile in angelspeak. Then turn onto Karlova Street, still quiet at that hour, domes & towers rising from the mist, a cityscape with figures crossing a bridge…

Inside the Klementinum gates a construction gang was busy pumping muddy water out of a hole. A huge ventilation duct stuck from the ground in a gross unnatural array of reinforcing mesh & busted pipes, like a neck from which some colossal head had been messily lopped. The muffled *thudthud* of a generator shook the cobblestones underfoot, grimly adverting to that parallel world below. Of subterranean labyrinths, liftshafts, pulleys, sinister excavations of gut, bowel & intestinal tract. Toiling to cheat both God & the Devil. And the elusive substance the City clung to in its despair.

12

WHAT DID ENOCH DO AT NIGHT?

An icy wind buffeted the castle walls, snaking in & out of dim crenellations, as predawn bleak & rainsodden — air crackling with electricity — painted the high turrets greyblack against blacker grey. Beneath a window in the southernmost tower, illumed by feeble candlelight, a figure *sable rampant* on a stone ledge *per fess*, robes billowing, one arm raised above, hand gripping, it seemed, yes! a rope of bedlinen, white sheets knotted end-to-end fastened at the windowsill, & in the other, a bundle of manuscript, clasped gnarl-fingered to wheezing chest. E.K., man of conflicted fortunes, by cruel fate brought low, a lowly prisoner, unbarbered, gallows-pale, glared up at the mottled sky on the brink of some incipient, dreadful knowledge as on the brink of an abyss, stumplegged, swaddled in soiled bandages, a wooden prop sticking out, one-peg Jack, mouth agape (wheezing), sour reek of mulled wine on expiring breath. He was, in the parlance of the day, *distempered* — & had much need to be. A message, delivered that morning, coded in the entrails of a homing pigeon, from parties sympathetic, had precipitated him thence, out on his one good limb, to this parlous rendezvous & proffered escape — the second attempt in as many months[*] — alike to a Burbage, a Hemming, an Alleyn, a Condell, treading the boards one last time for the sake of his loyal audience, a real crowd-pleaser you might say, virtually a repeat performance, move-for-move, gesture-for-gesture, expressive eye & tremulous *sotto voce*, of the previous, ill-starred, panned by the critics, best-not-discussed, avolation into the orchestra pit, shattered fibula, femur, tibia. Well good luck & goodnight. *You've gotta laugh, though, eh? Gotta laugh.* The Great Man's recollection these days not what it was at the height of, & all that — a touch of Alzheimer's perhaps, touched in any case, mixing-up soliloquies with stage directions, the laughable tragedy rising to solemn travesty, the plunging high note drowned by Moravian burgundy & ether's "sweet vitriol." Somewhere below, crunch of horses' hooves on gravel, the sole audience, commissioner of tonight's reprise, observing Old Priam up there in his druthers, fate's bitter herb, masticated, the undoing of one

---

[*] An exaggeration. [✤]

misfortune for the sake of another, mumbling unfathomable blank-versed invectives, the backwards cognomina of God perhaps or Enoch, now bellowed, now belched, now intoned in halting diminuendo. The rider, glancing up at the lighted window, grinning — *All in good time.* It may have been the rope of bedlinen unravelling, the unmortared ledge crumbling, the west wind's buffeting, or some other malign or maladroit abetting force that sent the agèd gaolbird, screeching, arms aflap, down into the Erebus of his final transubstantiation. In the rider's eyes, glaucous, a terrible knowledge glinted as he turned his steed about & rode away. Lying at the bottom of the empty moat, a broken stick in the mud, caked up to the ears (*hehe*), K vomited his last pint of burgundy & wailed — moon-pale leaves of his dozen priceless irreplaceable manuscripts (more precious than a Zhid's eye, forsooth!), scribbled-over with specious formulae & incantations, all useless now, fluttering around him like oversized confetti. Somewhere a raven cawed, sounding its bored ironic valediction to man's desire to make a bold leap...

Confiteor

Already at that hour of the morning the Klementinum was teeming with readers, students for the most part, bustling, yawning, farting, procrastinating over mid-term assignments — the industrious habit of summarisations, bullet-pointed, dates, placenames, facts in short, acquired by rote to no good purpose, procedures for the sake of procedures, agreed upon by useless committees that otherwise couldn't agree on anything.

Němec shook the rain from his invalid's dressinggown & headed straight for the library's vaulted Reading Room, coalblack elephantine doors heaving-to on unoiled hinges, umbrous frescos depicting, up there on the ceiling for the idle to glop at, the drudgery of man's unheavenly estate. The card catalogues bisected the room, with a dozen potted lilies in late bloom arranged atop them. Němec had to line up to take his turn at the drawers. There must've been hundreds of them, arranged according to some rule Němec was unable to penetrate.

With the doggedness of someone determined to leave no stone unturned, no card unthumbed, Němec worked through every one of them, left to right, top to bottom. He lost sense of time. The flipping of typed cards became its own of Zen. At the end of it all, he found himself staring doubtfully at the dozen or so reference numbers he'd succeeded in copying down: anything with explicit reference to KELLEY, Sir Edwort (c.1555-c.1597). He shuffled over to the big desk & filled out the request slips then stood in line again.

The Reading Room attendant looked at the bundle of slips &, like an automaton, turned away without so much as a word & vanished among the stacks. While waiting Němec watched the gilded clock at the far end of the long rectangular room go through the motions. Its hands creaked. Its syncopated tock, unpredicated by any tick, like a one-sided pingpong match. After a while Němec pulled over a chair & rested his leg while people filed past doing whatever it was they were doing.

Twentyseven Roman-numeralled minutes in arrears, the attendant returned with a small grey steelmeshed trolley laden with books, plugged Němec's number into the electric flipboard that hung behind the desk, & when he came over told him to sign something & took his ID. He watched her type his details into a computer, twig-like fingers protruding from a lime-green woollen cardigan buttoned up to the neck, which made a right-angle to where a thinning head of ash-blonde had been skewered with a pair of chopsticks. Behind the square-rimmed glasses, a pair of muddy irises peered out, which Němec supposed must've been hazel once upon a time. She had the complexion of a plant starved of chlorophyll.

At the end of all the red tape, Němec wheeled the trolley over to a desk by the windows & took out a marbled-blue ledger tied with black ribbon. There were two others in the pile, identical to it. With all the expectancy of an idiot he got to work, settling himself into the least comfortable position he could find, & setting the ledger square in front of him. Dust caught in his throat & he coughed, smearing spittle across the thick blue cardboard. A library stamp & call number were pasted on the top right corner, but nothing else to identify the ledger's contents. There he was, from the very outset, plunged into mystery.

Němec checked his list — the call number wasn't on it. Perhaps the attendant had made a mistake: something in-between, taken down in error, shelved in the wrong place possibly, a number it didn't belong to, etc. Yet persistence had its rewards, too. Němec opened the ledger, turned some pages: behind a dozen or so lined yellow spreadsheets was a thin carbon typescript glued into the binding — volume 2 of the Deutsch translation of Ashmole's *Confiteor*, the "confessions" of Mr Edworth K[elley] (accession c.1942). The remaining ledgers contained, in a similarly dissembling condition, volumes 1 & 3 — all, on the flyleaf, stamped with the eagle of the Third Reich.

The mystery was easily resolved: by eliminating all the other items on his list, Němec was left with one — the shared catalogue number of the three ledgers, marred by his own handwriting…

Q. Did any purpose behind the seeming dissemblance present itself?

None.

Item (on the frontispiece of volume 1): a murky reproduction of a seventeenth century mezzotint depicting, presumably, the erstwhile Mr Etword K. — alias *Talbot* — posing in the borrowed gowns of a university doctor. An error in all innocence, perhaps (the artist's), committed well after the fact & on a pre-established model — the Man of Learning, etc., "Doctor" of Divinity, Divination & *ipso facto* Divagation. The subject (K) wore a long tapering beard & round eyeglasses. About him there hung the air (heavy with storax & gum benjamin) of a man accustomed to the close observance of ritual, as & when it suited.

Q. Did the alchemist's hair conceal the physical characteristic of his ears?

Indeed it did.

Q. What else could be gathered of the alchemist so portrayed?

Heading each of the *Confiteor*'s chapters, a series of black&white vignettes, executed in a style identical to the frontispiece:

1. K in his laboratory w/ tripod & beaker,

2. K at Glastonbury standing in an open tomb,

3. K & John D[ee] at Třeboň in the company of Peter von Rosenberg,

4. K presenting a book to HR&IH Rudolf II at court,

5. K placed under arrest by the Imperial Guards,

6. K in a cell at Křivoklát bent over a tripod, the words *Confitemini Domino* in blotted calligraphy, at work upon some "elixir,"

7. K in silhouette, framed beneath the corbelled arch of a tower window,

8. peglegged K supplicant before the great porphyry slab of the royal altar,

9. K reading a parchment by faint candlelight, *Scripturae Incognitorum*,

10. an alchemist's lab filled with complex apparatuses, strange engines, etc.,

11. a high tower w/ twin jagged lightning bolts shooting across the sky,

12. K in dark robes falling from the battlements of Hněvín Castle, the caption incomplete, *Descensus ad Inferos…*, a mysterious black rider looking-on (as if, here, a less literal, more symbolic interpretation was to be sought: the figure of "Death" [for example], the "Devil," or — perhaps more disturbing — Rudolf's sinister emissary, "der schwarze Reiter," Jan Mydlář?).

The remaining books on Němec's list widely diverged in subject matter:

1. three biographies of John D (one by the Cambridge don, Francis Melmoth, composed in 1820; a thin paperback volume by Charlotte Yeats published 1972; & a dusty clothbound tome by the nineteenth-century

American scholar, Werther N. Holms),

2. D's private diary & the catalogue of his manuscript library, IN THE ASHMOLEAN MUSEUM AT OXFORD, AND TRINITY COLLEGE LIBRARY, CAMBRIDGE, edited by J[ames] O[rchard] Halliwell, Esq. F.R.S. & published in 1842 (the years 1584-1586 redacted — reasons for which?): first mention of K, *Aug. 1st, 1555, Ed. Kelly natus hora quarta a meridie ut annotatum reliquit pater ejus*,

3. an account of the reign of "Rudolphus II Imperator Romanus Sacer" by a certain Lucius Theophrastus, personal physician to the Count of Dietrichstein;

4. the annotated correspondence of Thaddaeus Hagecius, translated from the Latin by Světlana Gregorová,

5. monographs variously on the work of David Pratner, Johannes Kepler & Tycho Brahe,

6. the anonymous *Historia von D. Johann Fausten*, published September 1587 by the religious controversist Johann Spies, Frankfurt am Main,

7. Svatopluk Prdlík's *Mitteleuropa*,

8. the unexpurgated *Memoirs* of one "Robert Jones."

Q. What forces were at work determining K's fate?

The man Němec was searching for was supposed to've lost his ears in the pillory on Elizabeth Tudor's personal instructions. Yet, according to Yeats, Holmes & Halliwell, this self-same Elizabeth subsequently employed her darkest emissaries to repeatedly *entreat* K to return from Bohemia, where he appeared to've sought sanctuary (mistaking, as the courtly poets once said, *the bryteness of the Moone for the prosaic lyte of day*). In a long letter dated 1591 (further specification "redacted"), Lord Burleigh (Her Majesty's spy-keeper) instructed one Edward Dyer (a former pupil of D's, at that time serving as the Faerie Queene's man in Hanover) to utilise every means within his power to induce *Sir Edwierd Kelley to come over to his natyve country and honour her Majesty with the fruites of such knowledge as God hath gyven him…* Why?

Q. Had K foreseen a plot? One designed for his entrapment or worse (worse than an ear-cinching), & tendered his demurral, *Yours most humbly, etc.*, gambling on prospects somewhat more amenable under the patronage of Rudolf (a pederast, admittedly, dabbler in the occult, ineffectual & morose politician — eventually, so fate would have it, to be stripped Prospero-like of crown & jewelled sceptre by a most conspiratorial younger brother), the benefit of hindsight notwithstanding, post-hoc, prompter-hoc, & all that? *In illo tempore*, this aforesaid Rudolf (in name, if nothing else: Holy Roman Emperor, King of

Hungary & Croatia, King of Bohemia & Archduke of Austria) had fashioned his court into the omnium gatherum & enlightened heart of Europe Renascent — what better place for an alchemist on the lam? what more provocation to a coldblooded virgin inclined to homicide?

It'd all worked out well for K so far: already in his beneficence Rudolf, *per se*, had seen fit to bestow certain *sui generis* public honours upon D's ex-skryer, to wit: *eques aureus* de Imany — going even so far as to employ him *ad hoc* as a "Councillor of State." Placed in such a light, K's decision to keep all his eggs warm in Imperator Rudolf's basket rather than risking any of them in the wintry nest of Eliza Regina *dieu et mon droit* might've seemed a proverbial no-brainer. But K's counter-plot, poorly timed (though how could he've known?), came hurriedly unhatched: very soon K discovered himself at the proverbial breakfast table with a clucking hen in lieu of the desired omelette. For on 2 May of this annus profundis, while en route to the estate of his erstwhile benefactor, Peter von Rosenberg, K was arrested by officers of the Imperial Guard.

Němec returned to the frontispiece to get the measure of his man, caught (as they say) between a ♖ * & a hard place. In K's shadow, Němec paced the battlements &, pausing from time to time like a man perplexed, ogled the spectacle of K dangling from his homespun rope under the castle walls, at wit's end (so to speak), gartered legs thrashing about, carp belching below in the stinking weed-strewn moat. Like the mad castellan in the story book, Němec was possessed by a desire to shout out, *What shall I do with this absurdity?*

The Sphinx

The selection at the Klementinum refectory was (it barely seemed possible) worse than at the hospital mensa: slabs of jellied headcheese vied for space beside tureens of plastinated goulash, lentil salad, carp paste, slurried pasta with green peas & textureless rehydrated vegetable proteins. It was just at the end of the lunchtime rush & the tables were piled with debris. A portable radio stood atop the high counter with Burt Bacharach gushing out of it.

Němec ordered a bread roll & some pickles & wedged himself into a corner by the window furthest from the noise. The bread wasn't as stale as it could've been, nor the pickles as sour: all-in-all the standard fare. He considered risking the Turkish coffee, but a cup that'd been left sitting on the table (beside a newspaper

---

* "Rook" (sic). [☜]

& a pile of gravy-crusted plates) — an inch deep with clotted grounds & a plastic spoon sticking straight up out of it, the lip serrated with chipped ceramic — put paid to that idea. It looked as Turkish as a moustachioed psychopath wearing a fez & waving a scimitar. He wondered if the Turks had anything vaguely equivalent & if they called it Golem coffee, if only to return the compliment.

The newspaper the cup was sitting beside was folded in half at the last-but-one page, with the funnies & crosswords & all the usual drivel to exercise your average thinking man's dice-box. Němec pushed the cup & plates to one side & turned the paper over. The top left hand column was taken up with an article about the boy pharaoh of Ancient Egypt, Tutankhamen, whose tomb was discovered on such&such a date by the Englishman Howard Carter. The members of Carter's expedition party, the article said, subsequently perished one-by-one in *mysterious circumstances*, etc., etc. — cursed by the pharaoh's mummy, supposedly (though with the possible collusion of that lunatic thelemite, Frater Perdurabo, a.k.a. the Great Beast, a.k.a. Aleister Crowley, who claimed to've done them all in on behalf of the offended gods — by means of cunning voodoo).

Here at least was fiction in its proper milieu. In keeping with the Egyptian theme, the weekly chess teaser, flanked by eight column-inches of trivia about cats, was a puzzle called The Sphinx:

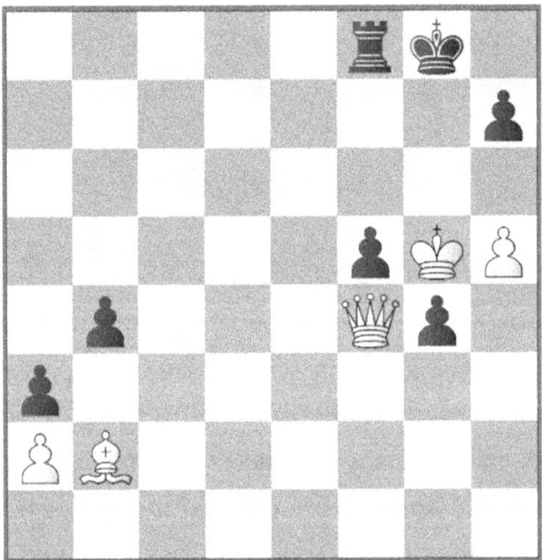

"The Sphinx." *White to mate in eleven moves…*

It was called The Sphinx because the ultimate arrangement of the pieces on the chessboard was supposed to resemble the Great Sphinx at Giza in profile…

There must've been something the writer saw that Němec couldn't, so he took the writer's word for it. As for the puzzle, the idea apparently was for white to force checkmate in only eleven moves. The catch was, while it could be done in fewer, you had to figure out how to do it in *exactly* eleven moves. Eleven being some sort of magical number, the Ancient Egyptians having been fond of isopsephy. But why *this* magic number & not some other magic number, the writer didn't say. Němec wasted five minutes looking at the problem, playing through the moves in his head, before giving it up as belonging to the same category as flying carpets & dancing camels.

With the taste of sour pickles & stale bread still in his mouth, Němec returned to the Reading Room to find out if the odds on getting the facts about Meister Edwarp Kelley straight had improved in the meantime, but after another four hours of reading he was still no nearer to knowing who the parlous K really was. There were tantalising hints, the name *Baresch* appearing several times, a reference here & there to Kircher's cryptology, Dee's "Enochian," the "Egyptian Oedipus," Roger Bacon, *Francis* Bacon, & the omnipresent *Francis* Garland. Was Bacon Shakespeare? Was K a spy? Was the Voynich Manuscript concocted as part of an English ploy to undermine the European Powers? Could *this*, a travesty penned by a truant tragedian, have been the unacknowledged cause of the Thirty Years War? And more? Much, much more?

Like Rudolf himself, this K was a figure grown so fabulous no sense of realism seemed to adhere to him at all. His existence was all metaphor & allegory, a paranoiac waxworks, a cipher in the larger destinies of men, riddled between the lines. Yet it was precisely *this* that focused Němec's resolve. With the Prof in mind (who, after all, perhaps never believed that K's connection to the Voynich Manuscript was anything other than circumstantial & ∴ paradoxically *integral*), Němec decided that the only way to proceed was by indirection, deviation, triangulating the facts by means of echoes, traces, repetitions, coincidences of the remotest order. To locate the centre, as the saying went, it was necessary to begin at the periphery — but how do you locate the periphery if you don't know where the centre is?

$$D = \frac{K}{\pi}$$

Every account of K began with D. And where D intersected the Radiant Centre, K occupied an obscure periphery. But then, in transit from Fair Britannia to Fickle Bohemia, all changed. K, having started out as D's handyboy, skryer, blunt instrument, "crystal ball reader," learned to speak with the angels, discovered thereby the long-sought-after Elixir, the Philosopher's Stone, the secret of baking dung into gold, became King of Alchemists to the alchemists' king. Now D was the sideshow to K's main act. At the angels' behest they even swapped wives: order transfigured by another, submerged order.

Before K's ascent, D was the biggest wisearse in the country, the envy of every two-bit Francis Bacon from Land's End to John o' Groats. He was a founding fellow of Trinity College, a school rector & a member of the most Worshipful Company of Mercers. His career wasn't without incident, though. By reason of having cast the horoscopes of Mary, Queen of Scots, & (the as-yet Princess) Elizabeth, D was summonsed to the Star Chamber on charges of High Treason & narrowly escaped (in Melmoth's words) *a moste grievous beheading.* Then in 1582, as fortune would have it, on a day he himself had long-prophesied (tea leaves, magic marbles, phases of the moon, all that), D made the acquaintance of that certain Edwand K… It read like a put-up job.

By a pretty coincidence, K (so he claimed) just happened at that time to've come into possession of a certain document, the socalled Glastonbury Manuscript, which, according to Melmoth, detailed *by divers spelles and magik conjugations* a method (K's "Three-Point Plan")[*] for transmuting the most saturnine *plumbum* (82 on the Periodic Table of Elements) into most rare, most precious, most lustrous *aurum* (79) by means (quoth Melmoth) of a *mistryous*

---

[*] Under exclusive licence. [♣]

reddish powdyr — the "Dragon's Blode," so said, of high morte-d'Arthuriana.

Q. Could further details be adduced in confirmation or contradiction thereof?

Of D's other two biographers (Yeats & Holms respectively), both insisted that it was D (& not K) who'd unearthed, in a Bishop's tomb, beneath the ruins of Glastonbury Cathedral, a quantity of this socalled "Red Elixir" — one grain of which was enough to miraculously transmute a piece of a cast-iron warming pan. D had already established a reputation for salvaging rare manuscripts from monasteries dispossessed by Henry VIII — most notably the scientific writings of one *Roger Bacon*. Like Bacon, D had a reputation as a polymath. He himself claimed authorship of no less than seventynine volumes on logic, mathematics, astrology, alchemy, navigation, geography, & the reformation of the calendar.

K, on the other hand, was regarded as something of a shady character. Under the assumed name of Talbot he was alleged to've perpetrated various "dyshonesties." Melmoth described him as a *sullen knave*. According to Yeats, K's conferences with the angels by means of a magic crystal called a shewstone were part of an elaborate ploy to worm his way into D's confidence. These conferences were supposed to've taken place in some holy angelspeak called Enochian — after Enoch *the seventh from Adam*, author of the "Book of Enoch," *the fall of the watchers, angels of the messianic kingdom*, Biblic Methuselah-father:

> *Othil lasdi babbage, od dorpha, gohol: g chis ge avavago cormp pd, ds sonf viu diu? Casarmi oali mapm, sobam ag cormpo crp l, casarmg croodzi chi sod ugegi — ds t, capimali, chis capimaon — od lonshin chis ta lo cla. Torgu, nor quasahi, od f caosga — bagle zir enay lad, ds i od apila. Dooaip Quaal, zacar, od zamran obelisong, rest el aaf nor molap?*[*]

It was obvious, if you agreed with Yeats, that K only wanted to rip D off. The Glastonbury Manuscript was just the tip of an iceberg. But then something bigger came along…

Němec tried to picture him (K) working the long con. There he was, in his oratory chewing calamus root, stammertongued, visioning the higher celestitudes *à la* Swedenborg & Dante, mind wheeling-out mazurkas of inspired gibberish — fables of Enoch (taken down in clerically doltish alltoocredulous dictation by ol' Scribbledehobble himself, Tweedle Dee) — the gist of which, so

---

[*] "I haue set my fete in the sowth & haue loked abowt me, sayeing: are not the machynes of inc
se as innumerate as Gode?" [☚]

swore K, most cunning persuader, being, to wit, that the Great Spirit "Madimi," no less, solemnly commanded etc., effective post-haste, *a certayn kinde of recommendation* between their wives, of which entailed a *doctrine of unity* requiring *carnal use* as well as *spiritual love and charitable care and unity of mind for the spirit of God advancing* — in short, a swapping of concubines (various & numerously lurid accounts thereof).

D most aggrieved at surrender of cherished Jungfrau in full blush. Suspicions perhaps arising from. Concluding therefore: If by mumbojumbo angelspeak so eminent a skullcap as John D be duped, why not then His Very Holy Roman Personage — Most Melancholy Ruditwoshoes? Cue: piedpiping of Voynichese in secret catamite enchambering of. As into his (Rudo's) purpley ear — wetted with the prattle of feuding cognoscenti — to all appearances acquiescent, dilettantish, ever-so-seemingly beguiled in the first solemn instance, though furtively smelling perhaps a twofaced English-Irish rat, hedging his bets, double jeopardy, most regally ambiguous, setting the avid cuckoo to work in a dungeon deciphering his own fakery?

Q. What testimony to such effect could be gleaned?

Sept. 21st, 1582 — together D & K went from Mortlake, in the company of the Polish elector, Albert Lasky, *wives, children and familie*, toward the two ships attending them *seven or eight myle below Gravessende* — buoyed by talk of roads yet untravelled, fortunes to be made, whores to be had, journeying first to the Commonwealth of Poland&Lithuania, scamming & shylocking, before descending like a subtle unsuspected pestilence upon the Bohemian capital during the following year. There D in all his guile obtained, by letters of introduction etc., an audience with his Rudiness: R, anxious for his own fortunes, lent D a *très sympathique* if ultimately unbeguiled ear.

In October 1586, D left a note in his diary concerning a visit by K to R's court — *E.K. recessit a Trebona versus Pragam curru delatus; mansit hic per tres hebdomadas* — which resulted, according to Holms (though D himself made no mention of it), in the receipt of 630 ducats, from the Imperial Treasury, possibly from the sale of an Unidentified Manuscript, "possibly," & so forth. D's semilegitimate son&heir opined in retrospect that, while *en famille* domiciled in the erstwhile Chesk Lands, D indeed was known to possess *a booke… containing nothing butt Hieroglyphiks, which booke… father bestowed much time upon: but I could not heare that hee could make it out.*

Q. Was there anything to warrant the identification of this *booke* with the Voynich Manuscript?

None. Though circumstantially, while sojourning together at Třeboň, a South Bohemia spa famous for its carp (seat of the omnifarious Rosenbergs, fivepetalled hulthemia on a shield argent) one episode, recorded in D's diary of 1587, stood out — of K in his cups:

> Dec. 25th, afternone somewhat — Mr Ed. Kelly his lamp overthrow, the spirit of wyne long spent to nere, & the glas being not stayed with buks abowt it, as it was wont to be; & the same glas so flitting on one side, the spirit was spilled out, & burnt all that was on the table where it stode, lynnen & written bokes — as the bok of Zacharius with the Alkanor that I translated out of French for sow by spirituall could not; Rowlaschy his thrid boke of waters philosophicall — the boke called Angelicum Opus, all in pictures of the work from the beginning to the end — the copy of the man of Badwise Conclusions for the Transmutton of metals — & 40 leaves in 4, intitled, Extractiones Dunstani, which he himself extracted & noted out of Dunstan his boke, & the very boke of Dunstan was but cast on the bed hard by from the table...

The remaining accounts amounted to little more than a compendium of hearsay & anecdote. One thing appeared certain, however: in nothing, other than his acquaintance with D, was there the slightest bit of evidence to conclude that K had anything to do with the Voynich Manuscript. Němec felt he'd come to an impasse, that he couldn't see what it was that the Prof wanted him to see — unless it was the *purpose* of all these accounts to sew confusion, or that K himself was the scapegoat or unacknowledged agent in a more secret & sinister affair. Němec laboured on regardless, returning to Melmoth — something was missing. He went back over the account of D & K's parting of the ways: it'd gone unremarked at first, concealed behind a feint. In late 1589, D — tiring of his sojourn with its political intrigues & marital entanglements — set out to return once more to Albion's shores:

> Nov. 3rd, stilo veteri, I resolved to go into England, hoping to mete Mr Edward Keley at Stade, going also into England; & that I suspected uppon Mr Secretary Walsingham his letters.

Their meeting never transpired. Was the naming of Walsingham a clue? 1590:

> Jan. 23rd, Mr Thomas Kellye came from Brainford; put me in good hope of Sir Edward Kellye his returning.

The pretence of K's immanent arrival was maintained for two more months, before it was abruptly given up. A last reference to K before his arrest came on March 17th: *Sir Edwald Kely his letter by Francis Garland.*[*]

Q. What purpose had this subterfuge served?

The truth was that many-versioned *Kelly, Keley, Kellye, Kely,* never departed Bohemia's shores. The proffered repatriation to Old Blighty: no more than a ruse, a decoy, or evidence of yet another thwarted escape under close watch of Rudolf's spies & beyond the reach of Walsingham's? Or was K just trying to pull off one last scam & con D out of his share of the profits? D offered no interpretation (his diary most circumspect on such points, maintained with an eye to the uninvited reader rather than posterity — no effect that wasn't calculated).

How could such a shrewd player as D have been such an idiot? Had he foreseen this little postscript? Or was he in fact its secret author? A case of paying his cuckolder back in his own coin, so to speak? Setting K up for the old triple-cross?

Qui tacet consentire videtur

Fastforward several months: K, draped in red silk chasuble, in observance of the equinox, surprised at his roadside ablutions by officers of the Imperial Guard & conveyed, PDQ & with minimal ceremony, to Křivoklát Castle, eighty kilometres west-southwest, & there held, *sub judice,* though on what precise charge neither History nor D's biographers could agree (fraud? duelling? espionage? poisoning?).

Then, in 1593, or the year following, he (K), depending on the particular account, was either, provisionally, released & then *reimprisoned* (for default of debts?) at — or else never released & instead *transferred* to — the imperial fortress of Hněvín, near the eastern city of Most (where incidentally, since June 14th, 1587, K's brother (Thomas),[*] thinking to get in on the act, had been sharing nuptial bedsheets with a certain Ludmilla von Pisnitz, niece of one Henrich von Pisnitz, vice-chancellor to Rudolf & mayor of the City). It was there that K completed his last great labour, the *Tractus de Lapide Philosophorum,*

---

[*] The same "Garland" denounced by K the year previous as a spy, the pseudonymous bearded bard, Guillermo Shaxbawd. See above (& below, if you can bear it). [☚]
[*] Op. cit. [☚]

which — with the hopeless sycophancy of a man at the end of his rope — he dedicated in the hope of flattering his way out of confinement to His Imperial Self, Vitriol of the Wise, Red Rudi.

But here all certainty vanished (*lasciate ogne speranza, voi ch'intrate!*). According to D's diary, on 5 December 1593 word reached England that K had been set at liberty the previous October, two & a half years after his initial arrest. In the *Tractus*, K himself speaks of two separate imprisonments. During the course of the following year, several letters were exchanged between K & D, & in March 1594 one Francis Garland, Esq., not long returned from Golem City, visited D at his home in Mortlake & conferred with him at length about "E.K.":

Oct. 4th, Sir Eudward Keley set at liberty by the Emperor.

Nearly one year later, D made the following entry in his diary:

Aug. 12th, I receyved Sir Efword Kellyes letters of the Emperor's, inviting me to his servyce again.

Then, under the diary entry for 25 November, D entered the crucial note:

The newes that Sir Ebforth Kelley was slayne.

Unsurprisingly, a quantity of controverted hearsay surrounded both the manner & the possible motives behind K's death. According to the most consistent version of the story: after finishing his treatise on the Philosopher's Stone & failing to receive a hoped-for pardon from Rudolf, K attempted to escape from Hněvín castle by a turret window only to fall & break one or both of his legs. From these & other injuries he was said to've died soon after.

An additional account (Melmoth, *op. cit.*), invoking Burleigh's & Lord Treasurer William Cecil's decades-long intrigues, claimed that behind K's misfortunate were hidden machinations of state. At precisely the same time as Rudolf was dispatching his *schwurzer Reiter*, Jan Mydlář to Hněvin Castle, intent upon extracting K's secret from him (the Elixir, the Philosopher's Stone, the "key" to the Voynich Manuscript?), Elizabeth too had set certain wheels in motion. Reading between the lines of Melmoth's antique prose, the suggestion was clear: that on orders from Burleigh via Walsingham, Edward Dyer had made clandestine arrangements for K's *abductione* & flight to England — not for the purpose of K's personal salvation, but as a feint in a larger political intrigue (the discrediting of some prominent but unnamed *personage*) — & that, time running out, all was at last in readiness when the fatal incident occurred.

This *anciente complot*, if plot it was, centred on a spy-ring of which both D & K were themselves alleged to've been members, along not only with Dyer himself but also the late Philip Sidney, Christopher Marlowe, Francis Bacon & the aforementioned "Francis Garland" a.k.a. Gulielmus Shaksper — an agitprop conspiracy of smoke, mirrors, poetry & magic spirits.

Rewind to 22 June, 1587 (from D's diary):

☛ After dinner, as E.K. was alone, there appeared unto him little creatures of a cubit high: & they came to the still where he had the spirit of wine distilling over out of a retort. And one of them (whose name they expressed Ben) said that it was in vain so to hope for the best spirit of the wine, & showed him how to distil it & separate it better, & moreover how to get oil of the spirit of wine as it burned in the lamps: & began to ask E.K. what countryman he was. And when he had answered 'an Englishman,' he asked then how he came hither. He answered 'by sea.' Then said he: And who helped you to pass the marvellous great dangers of the sea? And so took occasion to speak of the benefits which God had hitherto done for us, very many. And this Ben said then among very many other things (as Mr E.K. told me on Saturday night after supper, holding on his talk almost till 2 of the clock after midnight) that he it was that delivered him, or gave unto his hands the powder. And also he said either then, or the next day at the furthest, that unleast he would be conformable to the will of God in this last Action declared, that he would take the virtue & force of the powder from it, that it should be unprofitable, & that he should become a beggar. And of me also he said that I did evil to require proof or testimony now that this last Action was from God Almighty, & said that I should be led prisoner to Rome, &c. He told of England, & said that about July or November her Majesty should from heaven be destroyed; & that about the same time the King of Spain should die. And that this present Pope at his mass should be deprived of life before two years to an end. And that another should be Pope, who should be Decimus Quintus of his name, & that he would begin to reform things, but that shortly he should of the cardinals be stoned to death. And that after that there should be no Pope for some years. Of England he said that after the death of our dear Queen, one of the house of Ostmark made mighty by the King of Spain his death, should invade & conquer the land, &c. He said, one (now abroad) should at Milford Haven enter, & by the help of the Britons subdue the said conqueror, & that one Morgan a Briton should be made King of the Britons, & next him, one Rowland, &c. He said also that this Francis Garland was an espy upon us from the Lord Treasurer of England, & that Edward Garland is not his brother: & that so the matter is agreed between them, &c. He said that shortly this Francis Garland should go into England, & that we should be sent for, but that it were best to <u>refuse their calling us home</u> ...

Burleigh, who put about rumours of the Emperor's connivance, wouldn't've been averse to such eventualities. At least on two occasions Melmoth implied that K had indeed been murdered — though not on Elizabeth's orders, but on Rudolf's,[*] as a counter-gambit allegedly to *thwarte Burleighs diseyns* (!?). Yeats put it down to plain suicide. She also claimed evidence that K's second arrest had come as no surprise: he'd been tipped-off while eating dinner with his family & made a run for it (but not before finishing his desert), being picked up by Rudolf's dragnet on the road to Rosenberg's estate, working all the obvious places.

Why exactly K was supposed to've committed suicide, Yeats didn't say. Perhaps he thought the Devil was coming to collect? Holm, on the other hand, favoured misadventure, tracing the whole drama back to a feud between the Rosenbergs & the Poppels (the two Montagues & Capulets of Old Bohemia). In this version, K was a pawn sacrificed to political expediency: the fact he was imprisoned twice, merely proof of the vicissitudes of power & the efficiency of his enemies, or the man's profound stupidity. Doubtless the great alchemist's vanity played its part: it was Holm's contention that the first charge brought against K stemmed from a duel, fought in contravention of court etiquette, with a petty official called Hinkel or Hunkler (who, fed the goods by a rival occultist, had put about the story of K's amputated ears to the hilarity of all & sundry). The picture Holm painted was neither the most nor least plausible, which may've been why it struck a chord, showing K as either a desperado or a clown — it didn't seem to matter which.

The story of K's double misadventure went like this:

Barely had the cell door closed behind him at Křivoklát than K, high on his own confabulations, essayed a vanishing act by lowering himself like a fakir on a rope through an outhouse floor: crapulous, bumsmeared, sage of the *prima materia*. Said attempt failing when K's makeshift rope abruptly unravelled & the unlucky alchemist plunged into the rancid moat, breaking his left leg. Conveyed ingloriously to Golem City, the by-now septic leg duly amputated above the knee & a wooden one strapped in its place: the leg taking up temporary residence in the anatomy theatre of the Golem City Teaching Hospital in a basement on Charles Square (!). Like a bad case of déjà vu, *two years later*, at Hněvín castle this time, the intrepid, rash or simply foolhardy K made another bid for freedom, climbing from a turret window with predictable results. At the inauspicious age of fortytwo, following his second amputation, K took poison

---

[*] Dead for a ducat (+ 629 more). [✋]

(the infamous elixir perhaps), leaving his family to the mercy of his creditors. He had died, his friends would later say, the butt of higher powers.

The Stepdaughter

And then there was the little matter of The Stepdaughter.

Unmentioned in D's diary: the English Maiden, *Virgo Angla* of Rudolf's court — blessèd in her virtue, sign of the cross on forehead & breast — tenth muse, fourth grace, sister of Phoebus Apollo, Sappho or Sulpitia — *Flower of Minerva*, as her tombstone in the cloister of St Thomas indulgently records. Elizabeth Jane Weston, a.k.a. *Westonia*. More famed in her day than Willium Shagspox or Shatspoo. Her rhymes,[*] versed in the thrice dead tongue of Cicero, Seneca, the Elder Pliny, came stamped with all the fulsome epigraphology of someone with their hand out for cash. In one of them she wrote:

If fate has given you a parent,
you should venerate him;
if not, put up with him patiently.

Apparently the lady was displeased with the posthumous state of affairs in which the dear old Pseudo-Pater left her much-abused mother & thus herself. Namely, penniless. But at least, when all else failed, she had Poésie to turn to. Never shall it be said that a woman well-versed mayn't put money in her purse. One of History's little instructive anecdotes: how this much-vaunted virgin poetess did but renounce her vestal versifying the moment the God of Financial Solvency smiled upon her — having, by her impassioned pen, wooed to her bosom, & to the alter of most conventional matrimony, one Johannes Leo, Man-at-Law[*] (no Krupskaya, she). Ought it be called poetic justice that she, in her turn, died giving birth to their eighth child? More pressingly, did it live? Some Octavia or Octavius brought motherless into this unsmiling world — sucking at the dead woman's teat as the milk turned cold?

Like *it*, Němec wasn't supposed to be there: a supernumerary to be added in the margin of the Great Balance Sheet. Poetry was all well & good to read an orphan to sleep with, to keep it from the prosaic, unadorned, facts, in words that can't ever belong to it. But optimism isn't a legacy, it's an illness of the linguistic

---

[*] Set down for illiterate posterity in Thomas Farnaby's *Index Poeticus* (1634).[✋]

[*] And are they not all, these vow-stuttering dolts, "men-at-law"? [✋]

faculty. Or was the stepped line of Eduardo K's dubious descendent so untainted by the sentimentality for Homeland, Kultur, Blood & Soil, Sturm und Drang? Němec'd had a mother once, too — he never knew her — "Assistant Librarian," the dossier said, a junior undertaker in a graveyard for proscribed books — his very own Westonia whose belated Great Calling he might've been, were it not for a circumstantial man with a circumstantial name, under a régime that existed solely to bury him…

> *Oh we've got to have,*
> *We plot to have,*
> *For it's dreary not to have*
> *That certain thing called*
> *"The Stepdaughter" …?*[*]

---

[*] In this ditty, the author is flagrantly ripping-off the title song of a 1953 West End musical by Sandy Wilson, which opened at the Player's Theatre Club on 14 April before continuing to Broadway. Its insertion here, with a very slightly modified text, is dubious to say the least. [♣]

13

ORD'NARY VOLKS

The *Svoboda & Slovíčkář* bookstore was where it'd always been. Němec walked up to it the way you might walk up to a half-remembered dream. There were the usual notices in the window, but they all seemed addressed to someone else. He didn't know what he'd been expecting — a private message of some sort. In the middle of the window was an advert for a performance of *Hedda Gabler* by the Zrcadlo Theatre Company. It was near closing time, the shop assistant was tidying up behind the counter in expectation. It was a woman this time, tall with grey hair pulled back in a bun. She squinted reluctantly at the piece of paper Němec dug from his dressinggown pocket & spread out in front of her, then shook her head. She wasn't sure she'd ever heard of *Heterocosmica.*

He knew it was pointless even before he did it, but winding his way back through the aisles to the cul-de-sac adjoining the entrance brought him up emptyhanded. The publication in question wasn't to be found. In the bookstore's general system of entropy, it could've been anywhere or nowhere.

'What about Faktor?' he said to the attendant, lurching back out from between the piles of books, his walkingstick swinging dangerously.

The attendant looked up, surprised, & backed away from the counter. Němec tried to smile. The effect was meant to be reassuring, but the woman looked like she might make a grab for the phone to call the police.

'Viktor Faktor,' he said. 'Editor of the journal in question.'

'Oh,' the woman gasped.

Her eyes seemed to swim in her head while she was regaining her composure, then jerkily she pointed past him in the general direction of the street.

'The Patriot Klub,' she managed to say.

'The *Patriot Klub*?'

The attendant nodded enthusiastically. Němec stuck his head out the door to see what the greyhaired woman was talking about. All he could see across the street was the Folklorist's trinketshop & a set of coachdoors with an old Škoda parked in front of it.

'…?'

'Mr Faktor is Hon Sec of the Monarchist Society,' the woman smiled, full of confidence now. 'They have meetings at the Patriot Klub. It's at number 22 Jilská Street. You can't miss it. The wine cellar, downstairs. Name's on the buzzer.'

Němec blinked, the woman's smile looked almost serene now. *God only knows what she takes me for*, he thought, slipping Kircher's letter off the counter & stuffing it back in his pocket. As he edged out the door the little bell above it tinkled. And though he couldn't be sure, he could almost have sworn he heard the attendant whistling *Oh Tannenbaum* as the door swung shut.

And if at first…

There was no sign of when the Patriot Klub was open or if it ever did open, but Němec figured it was the sort of place that wouldn't get started till well after dark, when conspirators come out of their holes. *Monarchists?* You heard rumours about such people. Old nutters with forked beards & bric-a-brac pinned to their chests, stuck in some pre-1918 delirium. *The plot thickens, eh, kiddo?*

A cold gust of wind blew along the street, bringing down sheets of half-melted snow from the overhanging eaves. A spray of fine ice whipped Němec's face & caught in the folds of his hospital dressinggown. The air had a wet granulated texture, as though it had been frozen & then thawed & refrozen. He pulled the dressinggown tight & looked around for a place to bide his time…

Schlüp…

Schlöp…

The pavement was all greybrown sludge, each step beset with unseen perils. It was that time of the day when nothing happens much in the backstreets between Old & New Town, only the odd walker slipping on their arse, shop owners closing up, students slouching in black crow-plumage towards a pub. Němec skirted northeast, keeping to the laneways, hovering in the shadows, a sheetless ghost on a stick, apprehensive that someone might be watching, tipped-off by the mad woman in the bookstore maybe, or just part of the general surveillance machinery (you'd never know). Dusk came on quickly, the passages & archways reminding of that cold November night when he ran away from the Home, afraid there'd be police waiting around every corner — wending a path along the train tracks into the dull campfire-glow where the homeless congregated above the mouth of the Nusle Tunnel...

The tunnel was longer than he'd thought, it seemed to go on for ever, far far under the mountain of Vinohrady. Rats scuttling in the dark, the seething of invisible currents, thinking *one wrong step...* & the dragon, roused from its slumber, red-eyed, snorting out of its black hole with a clashing of diesel engines. Somewhere a machine-voice warned whoever may hear, whoever may care, before the flash & roar: a terrible wind, hot then freezing, blown up from Middle-Earth icefloes, laval depths, leaving a blackness more complete, more elemental.[†]

Pummelled 4x weekly by robust Nurse Peklá-Pěkná, to the point where the only feeling left was a dull twinge of absence like a phantom limb (like trying to scratch your nose with a hand that isn't there anymore — like trying to take a piss with a pecker that isn't there anymore — like trying to think with a brain that isn't there anymore...). She made jokes, too, Nurse P, about them wiring something into his skull while he was under the anaesthetic. *On the slab*, she said, short "a" cut plosively shorter. Transceivers & transducers. A slight bulge behind the right ear, barely noticeable. In overcast weather, the hiss & surge of radiosignals, numbers & TV voices: higher life-form transmissions from Galactic Politburo HQ, Alpha Centauri. Godspeak & randomness...[*]

[†] He'd huddled in a recess, listening all night to the singing of the tracks, the clicking of the points, waiting for the light at the end, the damp gusts of predawn, stumbling at last into the wide-open amphitheatre beneath Muzeum, wanting nothing but to kneel bruised & bloody before the great glaring column of sky... It was that moment in a film when the hero makes it out of the wilderness, only to fall down on the doorstep of civilisation realising all was lost, when all he wants is to be back in the jungle where he started out guided by a singularity of purpose. The years had grown a layer of scar tissue, but still the continual ache. Why escape? What'd it been *for*? Some things you forget, some you never know. Could he finally be reaching a point of realisation? He stopped to catch his breath, feeling the pain in his body more clearly now, like an ear held up to a whisper that's suddenly very close. *Nothing*, he told himself, *could make less sense than it already does.* Flexing his knee that was really just a stainless steel ball&socket contraption, squeaking like an unoiled door in the cold. Patella, ligament & fasciculae (a bisecting ridge of keloid scartissue as a forget-me-not): Arthroplasty, socalled, like a bit-player in Homer — *son of Prosthesis, loosed his terrible spear...*

[*] VOICES IN YOUR HEAD? *HEHE.*
DON'T TELL THE DOCTOR...

And what if his escape from the Home, the Revolution, his parents' disappearance, had all been orchestrated solely for *his* sake, as part of some bizarre mind-experiment? Absurd, foolish thought. But once upon a time, that all-seeing, all-knowing monster — how had it died? Or it hadn't died, only grown a new skin. And somewhere down inside its gut, his lost existence. Of course it knew him, it'd always know him, but would he know *it* when the time came? *Why not keep a cracked mirror in your pocket, eh, kiddo, for all the good it'll do you?* Ashamed for having survived or simply ashamed of being ashamed? What if his daddy-mummy could see him now? Old before his time: dead before

180

Café Pernath ☞

The sign stood out at a bend in the lane, pointing into a cul-de-sac. At the end of
it was a crumbling stucco façade you entered through an archway, with a heavy
curtain inside the door. Němec found a place at a corner table with his back to a
window. The place hadn't begun filling up for the evening & probably wouldn't
for a coupe of hours yet. Němec propped his stick against the wall & waited to be
served, taking in the scenery. There were people at the adjacent tables talking & a
few more sitting at the bar. It was like watching people shouting from a long way
off — their mouths opened & closed but their voices were lost.

The waiter polished a dozen glasses with his dishrag before coming over
to see what Němec wanted, his face set in a practiced expression of uninterest.

'Frankovka,' Němec said.

'Menu?'

Němec shook his head. The waiter shrugged —

'Suit yourself,' he said & wandered back to the bar.

When he returned, Němec swallowed two of Volta's pills, gulped the wine
& told the waiter to bring another. The waiter smirked crookedly —

'You want I should bring the whole bottle, or I gotta come back & forth
all night?'

'And they say good service is hard to find these days,' Němec drawled.

'Sure, you wanna see service?' the waiter took the glass. 'Stick around.'

---

their time. Done-for-a-ducket. Snuffed. Rubbed-out. Vanished from the face of the earth like
airbrushed warts. The dearly departed, disappeared, deleted. Block off the old chip. *Think you'd
recognise yourself after they'd beaten you to a pulp and put a bullet in the back of your head?* Third eye & all
that, to see with the future that lies behind. *Our God-given,* they say, arms out. And there he'd stand,
swaddled up to the neck, the only begotten, last of the line, end of the blood. Some sort of picture
he'd've made: mushy eggplant for a head, saggy out-thrust lip, inward surveying pineal, as stiff as a
mannequin mounted on a pair of sticks. Though not quite the worse for wear, if he'd been dumped in
an unmarked grave all these years. *Oh but you did this to yourself, kiddo, ain't the same thing. Ain't
anywhere like the same thing. Different matter when the boot's on the other foot...* First the object's broken
snap! apart, fragmented, atomised, dropped crab-like from a high height *splat*! on a stone ledge, to get
to the soft meaty stuff out of it, a little lesson to instruct it on its true fallible nature, *hehe* — to
recover, *hoho,* the possibility of a symbolic restoration (contrary to all those defective impulses & alien
thoughts you've been recently entertaining) — a thing sundered, in other words, so as to be saved,
given a renewed lease on life, a clean slate, a fresh start. *Well. Ain't that nice, kiddo? Ain't that damn
sweet?* As for Němec — what his life added up to you could count in the gaps between your toes. *La
Belle Jeunesse.* Nothing to get all weepy-eyed about...

Gordon Bleu[*]

A piece of congealed viscera smeared over a slice of dark bread occupied the tablecloth in front of a middleaged woman sitting at the table beside his. Raw onions & peppercorns swam in a sea of oil surrounding it. Wedged beside her was a man in a crushed burgundy pinstripe suit with layers of dandruff on the lapels. The woman sat tapping her knife & fork against the edge of her plate, elbow grazing a beer glass precariously balanced on the table ledge. A wide stain was already spreading around it on the tablecloth. It was the annoying sound the woman was making with her cutlery that caused Němec to look up, just as his second glass of frankovka arrived. This time the waiter didn't stick around for the small talk. Some people over by the door got up & left. That left a couple of slow drinkers at the bar & the spectacle at the next table.

The woman was staring intensely at her plate, as if she expected it to get up & bite her, but otherwise she looked perfectly normal. A blue rinse that'd been set in rollers surmounted a pair of oversized green shoulder pads & a paisley nylon scarf wound tight around her neck. She was beating out a regular tattoo when her bottom lip began to tremble & her fingers, abruptly dispensing with the cutlery, gripped the tablecloth in suppressed emotion. Apparently oblivious to what was going on beside him, the man in the suit worked his mouth slowly, sonorously, imprecisely around some thought or idea he had no

---

[*] A CONTEMPLATIVE INTERLUDE

While he waited for his drink & in anticipation of a meeting with this "Viktor Faktor," Němec went over in his mind what he knew about Kircher's letter. Kircher himself, it seemed, was a well known translator of arcane texts who, not long before receiving the Sphinx letter, had published a treatise on the decipherment of Coptic — the *Prodromos Coptos* of 1636. And he'd been the victim of at least one previous manuscript hoax. Kircher's correspondent, Georgius Baresch, was some character who was now almost entirely unknown, but might not've been back then. He supposedly completed his studies at the Klementinum in 1603, then went to Rome. In 1662 the Charles University rector, Johannes Marcus Marci, mentioned Baresch in his book *Philosophia Vetus Restitutis*, where he recorded that Baresch had bequeathed to *him* his entire library including — !! — the Voynich Manuscript (more than a casual acquaintance, then) . Baresch was also named in two letters from Marci to Kircher — one of which was discovered by Voynich folded inside the Manuscript in 1912. It was *this* letter that named Roger Bacon as the Manuscript's author. Kircher himself, whose complete correspondence numbered fourteen volumes, somehow failed to make a single mention of the Manuscript, despite the fact of it being catalogued among his personal collection. Perhaps he just didn't want to let on? As for Baresch, since the Manuscript was supposed to've been in the personal collection of Rudolf II, it was hard to imagine how it came into his possession to begin with.

more desire to express than she had. In front of him, sliced into little pieces, lay a plate of half-eaten pork sausage. It could've been the prelude to a homicide, but whether in cold blood or a *crime passionnelle* would all depend on which of them got in first. It was probably their regular routine.

Němec couldn't bear to watch any longer & turned to the newspaper rack hanging on the wall. He took down the *Golem City Sentinel* & scanned through the stories on the front page. The lead article was all about the War Crimes Commission & the Balkans, followed by: "Acts of Desperation in Hong Kong." There was a mugshot belonging to the chairman of the privatisation scheme, caught *in flagrante* accepting a Kč 80-mil bribe in a brown paper bag. Page two: an editorial about the upcoming Russian elections. Page three: a halfhearted exposé about secret sterilisation programmes for gipsy women — commentary on Yasser Arafat in Hebron — a column-inch each about: a Pablo Picasso painting stolen from a London gallery — the Iraq occupation — UFOs sighted in Phoenix, Arizona — a naked man stuck up a tree for five days in Košice — human safaris in Rwanda — & an opinion piece about expected hikes in energy bills & the "Nuclear Option" (Temelín). Page four: compensation claims & continuing "diplomatic tensions" over the fifty-years-old Beneš decrees & the forced evacuation of the Sudetendeutsch, cited as the "main stumbling block" to further "European integration." Also page four: another pyramid scheme exposed — the Asian economic crisis & fears of global recession — a nineteen-year-old conscript, shot in the head by his bunkmate at a training camp in Mladá Boleslav, polishing his rifle. Page 5:

Miners Refuse to Work after Death

An accident in a lift shaft at the Jáchymov uranium mine yesterday resulted in three fatalities. Union calls for strike over lack of safety...

The best so far was on page six: a story about some Š.V.E.J.K. terrorist group that'd been leaving a trail of dead rats through the City's supermarkets, apparently in protest against the encroachments of free-market capitalism. Dead rats in milk cartons, dead rats with the frozen vegetables, dead rats shrinkwrapped in meat packages side-by-side with the headcheese & klobása. Rats in the recycling & rats in the aisles. Rats behind the beer bottles, rum bottles, slivovice. Whiskered rat-heads peering from cigarette cartons, tails dangling in the checkout girl's hair. An apparently unrelated insert contained an ad for a UN-sponsored Vasectomy Clinic in Bucharest, 100% FREE!

Now there was a sales pitch to conjure with, like they were doing you &
the world a big favour. *Got any unwanted reproductive organs? Leave 'em by the
door, we collect!* It was like banks charging you a percentage for holding onto your
hard-earned. *Free money!* You'd think it'd be *them* should be paying *you.* Like
that country-'n'-western song, Němec thought — "Never know what you've got
till it's gone." *Hey, kiddo, ever hear the one about the Man Who Kept his Balls in a
Jar?* Well why bother with some hushhush neo-Nazi sterilisation programme if
you could set up right out in the open? *Snip snip! Who's next?* They could follow
it up with a "human interest" story in the next edition, *Man Triumphs over
Adversity* ("he used to have balls for brains, now he doesn't need to think at all"):
keep people's minds off what was really going on.[†]

Němec flipped through the business & sports pages looking for the
funnies, though they'd have their work cut out for them with what passed for the
usual hack. Instead of the funnies, a loose supplement from the *Prager Zeitung*
had been shuffled in by mistake. Němec was about to toss the lot back on the
rack when a book review in the bottom left corner of the page caught his eye:

Hitlers willige Vollstrecker.
Ganz gewöhnliche Deutsche und der Holocaust

"Hitler's village idiots: ordinary Krauts & the Holocaust..." What *ordinary* was
supposed to mean, the reviewer didn't get around to saying. Maybe it was meant
to be obvious: your average Fritz with their life's savings inflation-adjusted out of
existence? — or your average Helga working twelve-hour shifts at the
steelworks? — the teller at the bank, maybe? — the checkout girl at the corner
kiosk? — the hairdresser? — the taxi driver? — the old lady next door? — the
parish priest? — the man of qualities? — the preschool teacher? — the best
friend? — your general self-denying Papist, Protestant, Atheist, Zhid? —
anyone between 4'8" & 6'2"? — or, just to round it out, everyone who *wasn't*
sent to a camp for opposing the Nazi régime? Instead it just trotted-out the usual
shtick about witting & unwitting collaborators & who knows what they'd've
done in a situation like that, creeping up on them day-by-day, all unsuspecting,
poor souls, History having all the advantage of retrospective foresight, etc.

But what'd it matter — who, or where, or what — if sooner or later they

---

[†] It made you wonder what *didn't* get printed in the papers, what the unreported world looked like.

all made the same choice (more or less, give or take a standard deviation or two)? Or was it always a different choice, singular, matchless, isolated in its unique drama of mitigation & inexplicability, for each & every man & woman & everyone in-between — like the Original Sin? Němec stuffed the paper behind a copy of the *Financial Times* & tried getting the waiter's attention but the waiter had his head stuck somewhere, trying to see how far down he could get it.

Well it was a fair bet, as far as Němec could see from his own particularly advantageous vantage point, that it wasn't only your average Kraut who had trouble distinguishing the fine lines. *Uh-uh. Not by a long shot, kiddo.* You couldn't throw a stone in this socalled Golden City without hitting some prospective shithead who would've turned informer faster than a mangy dog looking to have its belly scratched, for the sake of an itch somewhere deep inside, or nothing more than a coveted doorstop, a loaf of bread, a walk-on part in the big production — like whoever it was who'd put the finger on his mum & dad, back in the day when doing a bit of fingerwork on the side was the next best thing to a national pastime (oh, it was nothing special, they'd've fingered their own parents, too, given half a chance).

Němec cast an appraising eye around the café. Spectral faces stood out from the general murk like fake Rembrandts, burnished in electric lamplight. The hysterical couple frozen in front of their meals — the waiter inspecting his dishcloth — the somnambulant drinkers at the bar — a gallery of gargoyles hovering at the edges of snotgreen tablecloths, beerstained, winestained, dusted white-grey-red with spilt salt, pepper, paprika… All as ordinary as he was. But were they to look at him with such an eye, what would *they* see? A mirror of their own inner lives? Or an accusation, perhaps? Or some laughably solemn & foolish creature with a misshapen head, draped in a hospital dressinggown & feebly holding an empty wineglass aloft — as if a grinning cherub on a wire could be expected to descend, dildo in hand, to refill it for him?

14

FAKTOR

It might've been the night before the Deluge, before Earth was strangled by Ocean, the apostates taken flight to some untroubled Star while below, the cavedwellers, those unknown terrible & indistinct things, stirred from prophetic sleep, the dreamt-of ruins of other worlds, forecasts of the rescheduled Fall, as Cain will become Cain, etc.

—Athanasius Kircher, *Paralogismus Combinationis Linearis* (1669)[*]

'Ooo's there?'

A streetlight pierced the gloom with its orange shaft. It was just going on ten o'clock when Němec rang the bell at the entrance to the unlit building at Jilská 22. A pair of iron-studded coachdoors blocked the crumbling arch. The folklorist's metal sign creaked in the wind. Across the way, the *Svoboda & Slovíčkář* bookstore had long been closed-up for the night, its windows shuttered, a metal grill pulled down over the doorway.

Pasted above a buzzer set in the arch, a cardboard square no more than an inch wide said PATRIOT KLUB, the writing mostly bled away by the weather. There was no other buzzer, so Němec had pressed it. At first nothing happened. Again, finger jammed down, counting five. Still nothing. Perhaps it was busted, he'd thought, or there was a coded signal: one long, two short. He took a stab in the dark — three long — then waited. Finally the intercom hissed:

'Ooo's there?' it said.

It was the only sound in the street, there was no-one around, the whole place was lifeless. Accepting the gambit, Němec spoke the *Heterocosmica* editor's name into the plastic grill. *Faktor the Redaktor, hehe.* The intercom hissed to a crescendo of sputtering static.

'Ooo?' it repeated.

'FAKTOR!' Němec shouted & the intercom went dead.

A cold gust blew up the street. The coachdoors groaned. Němec gathered his hospital dressinggown closer around him & shivered. *Well*, he thought, *so much for that.* He was pondered his next move (the subtle fianchetto or the bold thrust into the middle), if there was a next move & this wasn't how it ended — in front of a closed door, nothing to show, a longshot in any case, time to call it quits, go back to the company of the other sufferers — when a drunk came out of the shadows mumbling along the street. At ten metres he spied Němec, raised an uncertain hand in salute & tipped sideways, steering in a wide arc towards Zlatá Street —

'Ahoj kámoši!' the drunk regaled. 'Ahojj! Ahojjj…!'

The drunk stumbled into a wall, righted himself, tripped down the gutter, righted himself again & wove a path down the middle of the street. He started to sing —

> *'s anyone seen my Rusalkaaa?*
> *Loaves like Šumavaaa!*
> *She was there in bed th'smornin'*
> *wiv 'er gob wide open snorin' —*
> *but now she's gone, oh woe she's gone,*
> *I dunno whaaa…*

The drunk by now had rounded the corner, his lament drifting back through the narrow streets, his big Rusalka hefting pints, perhaps, somewhere in a pub he'd left, or missed, or never been to — *The Fiddler's Armpit, The Poked-Out Eye, The Frog and Toad.* As the song died out the street seemed even emptier. Němec counted the seconds under his breath — at a hundred he'd either give up or try the buzzer again. He stamped his wet feet. As he reached thirtynine a voice snapped at him from the coach doors —

'Come out where I can see you!'

Němec stepped into the cone of the streetlight & blinked: a pair of dybbuk-eyes observed him from behind a wrought iron grill. Something laughed. The hatch behind the grill slammed shut. There was a scuffing of boots, then a lot of banging & thumping —

'Schamweiss!'[*] the voice muttered.

---

[*] "Shite 'n' onions!" [✋]

A moment later a chink of orange light showed beneath the coachdoors. Němec waited. The drunk could be heard now coming back from the other end of the street. He must've been going round in circles —

'Ahoj kámoši!' he shouted, then staggered off in the opposite direction along Zlatá Street to the one he'd taken before.

Maybe the tracking device in his head was still working enough to find another bar so he could start drowning his sorrows all over again.

's anyone seen my Rusalkaaa…?

From the other side of the coachdoors came the sound of a rusty bolt being slid back. A smaller door, inset between the other two, opened inwards. Light spilled out onto the cobbles as a face appeared —

'Well what d'ya want, a written invitation?'

The face vanished again. Němec, seizing his opportunity, poked his stick into the low doorway & stepped through. He found himself at the entrance to a coachyard, deep in shadow except for the faint amber glow of a light above a side door. Behind him the sound of the door being slammed & the bolt being snapped back roughly. Němec spun around, wielding his stick. Something laughed again. The something had a curled moustache & wore a shirt with dirty lace cuffs under a red waistcoat with gold buttons, a watch-chain sticking out of the fob pocket. It had a head that looked unusually large on its shoulders. The eyes were round & slanted at the same time. This creature was standing in a pair of wellington boots so high he looked like he meant to go trout fishing.

It was obviously some sort of man, but even for a midget he would've been short. He gave Němec the once-over, eyebrow raised, & shook his head. Němec straightened his dressinggown a little selfconsciously.

'Nice threads. You choose those all by yourself, or does your tailor do all the thinking?'

Němec was fumbling for a reply when the theatrical dwarf shuffled past into the dimness & through the side door. Out went the light. There was nothing for Němec to do but follow. Behind this second door he found himself in a sloping passage with a tenuous halo marking a point in the distance where it turned & made a sharper descent. Němec probed the rough ground with his stick as the echo of the dwarf's footsteps faded somewhere ahead. He stumbled towards the dull glow, aware vaguely of presences, shadows in alcoves, unlit rooms, paths branching off, a faint scurrying of mouse or rat.

188

After looping back on itself, the passageway came to an abrupt end. A bare timbered door oozed a yellowish fog. The moment Němec opened it, a blanket of smoke instantly smothered him, his eyes streamed, the place swam. He groped forward down a flight of wooden steps, through Stygian vapours, atramentous mists. Hot leaden clouds swirled through shafts of sodium-light, inchoate & formless. A stench of mildew & cheap tobacco clung to him.

As his eyes adjusted to the chiaroscuro, Němec saw he'd entered a low vaulted cavern stretching away to his right, lined with dusty bottle racks & bits of painted heraldry that'd years ago faded into the plasterwork. Voices reverbed back from the vaults in a half-muffled pillow-over-the-face garble of Middle-High Krautisch. He took a few tentative steps further. To his left an alcove emerged from the gloom & faces burnished by candlelight. One of the faces belonged to the dwarf with the curled moustache. He was standing atop a wine barrel in his wellington boots, speaking into the ear of a troll-like creature in a grubby apron. A pair of enormous udders sagged over the top. It was like a scene from Bruegel — an enormous portrait mounted behind the bar of Ol' Muttonchops, Count Kinsky, rounded-out the tableau.

Němec stumbled against a chair. The troll leered, the dwarf snickered. Here & there the club's patrons sat slumped at their tables, dulleyed, openmouthed, inhaling the vapours, a coven of failed father-vanquishers. None of them showed the slightest interest as Němec groped his way to the bar.

'Faktor?' he rasped, before descending into a coughing fit.

This time it was the troll's turn to snicker. The dwarf ran a paw obscenely up one of her fat stockinged hams, dark bristles poked through the flesh-coloured nylon. The dwarf, without saying anything, jutted his chin in the direction of a man sitting by himself at a table in the far corner. Whatever Němec had expected, the man was a complete stranger.

Viktor Faktor was balding with grey hair & wireframed glasses. A short goatee harboured the odd shred of horseradish. He wore a crushed blue smoking jacket that'd seen plenty of better days, faded grandeur with hints of *ancien régime* — the very opposite of the idea of an esoteric juggler of fates or exoteric judge Němec had imagined — more West-End Enoch than *éminence grise*. Faktor didn't bother to look up when Němec pulled out the chair opposite & sat down, deeply absorbed as he was in an arrangement of chess pieces on a vinyl chessboard. The board doubled as a placemat, with an ashtray resting on one corner & a half-empty glass on another amid dark borromean knots of wine stains. The pieces were large, moulded plastic dulled by many hands, chess club surplus: they'd been positioned according to a notorious puzzle, a setpiece known as *Napoleon's flight from Russia to Paris*. It was the kind of puzzle that never presented itself in a real game, but only as an elegant breed of hypothesis about universal ideas.

Němec squinted at Faktor for some time while the dwarf came & went, like a devil at his elbow, leaving a carafe of soursmelling red wine & an extra glass. He had the look, this Faktor, of someone who might appeal to an artist making a character study, the types who sat around in café corners all day with sketchpads & Gauloises, always on the hustle for a free drink. While Němec watched, Faktor shunted the chess pieces around the board into different arrays. The puzzle unfolded in the twilight that hung over the table: the Black King, harried & relentlessly pursued by the Russian cavalry — the debacle at the Berezine — the revealed checkmate by the Winter Queen. At the end, Faktor seemed to be smiling to himself —

'Chess,' the editor of *Heterocosmica* said in a voice that conveyed nothing, 'or, to respect its original Sanskrit name, *caturanga*, is many things to many people. Just now you bore witness to History unveiling herself. Or perhaps you didn't. Perhaps you only saw a dance of shadows with no apparent purpose behind it.'

While Faktor delivered his little homily, it occurred to Němec that his being there wasn't unexpected. But then, hadn't he in effect already announced himself? Faktor continued to speak quietly, rearranging the pieces on the board, the shred of horseradish all the while being jiggled about in his goatee —

'One gambit replies to another. Would you care for some wine?'

He poured two glasses without waiting for a response, raised one to his nose, sniffed &, assuming a somewhat pensive expression, held it up to a feeble shaft of light & turned it between his fingers. The glass glowed a like an enormous bloodstone in an illuminated mist. Němec glanced down at Faktor's other hand in which he half-expected a weapon to've materialised, like some sinister conjurer in a movie. The hand lay motionless beside the board. Faktor almost seemed to chuckle to himself.

'To your health,' he said, bringing the glass to his lips. 'As the great poet Goethe once wrote, *Ein echter deutscher Mann mag keinen Franzen leiden, doch ihre Weine trinkt er gern.*'[*]

Faktor imbibed as if savouring a rare vintage. It tasted ordinary enough to

---

[*] The great poet Goethe wouldn't've been caught dead drinking that stuff. [♣]

Němec, but drinking it was the least he could do. Putting the glass aside, he stared into the darkness of the other man's beard, preparing to state his purpose. There was evidence also of flecks of blue cheese. The man must've eaten well. Faktor's eyes stared impassively over the top of his wire frames —

'Well then?' he said.

Němec fumbled in his pockets for the page he'd torn from *Heterocosmica* & spread it out among the chesspieces. Faktor let his eyes drift down to the translation of Kircher's letter. The abruptness of Němec's manner hadn't seemed to surprise him in the least. After he'd perused the letter to his satisfaction, Faktor leant back in his chair & nodded his head —

'Hmmm.'

He waited. Němec watched him wait. Faktor raised his hands, palm-up, as if he were weighing something. Němec picked his teeth, he wondered how long the pantomime would go on.

'There're many mysteries in this world,' the secretary of the Monarchist Society finally said. 'I'm hardly versed in them all. Perhaps you could let me in on this one.'

The man smiled. Němec smiled back at him, he wasn't sure why. For some reason he felt certain that Faktor already knew the reason he was there. He pointed at the letter —

'I know where it came from.'

'Do you?' Faktor raised his eyebrows in mock surprise.

'What I want to know is how you got it.'

'Hmmm.'

'...'

'...'

Faktor made an indulgent face, then a tired one, then a bored one. Eventually he said —

'Why don't you just start from the beginning & we'll see where we get from there?'

Němec picked the letter up off the table & stared into it. What could he say marked the beginning? Which, of all the coincidences, had been the crucial one, the one that'd set all the others in train, like a syllogism tending inexorably to some foregone conclusion. Was the beginning when he first noticed things falling into place — Kircher's letter? *The Sphinx's Code*? the Prof's death? — or the moment of his initiation into the cult of the Voynich Manuscript? Or was it a chance meeting & a game of chess beside a fountain? Or it hadn't been a chance meeting, something had ordained it, in which case the beginning was something beyond him, something he might never grasp. ✋

While he folded the letter & put it back in his pocket, Němec told the man in the blue smoking jacket about his last conversation with the Prof —

'No-one else knew about Kircher's letter. He was translating it right before he died. It was *his* translation in your magazine. He died at the end of October, you published the letter in November. What does that tell you?'

'Precisely nothing, Mr…?'

'Němec.'

'Němec? Hmmm…'

Faktor nodded thoughtfully, pursing his lips like someone mulling over a problem whose solution is too obvious.

'I appreciate the nature of your, *er*, concern, Mr Němec. But you see,' he fidgeted with his cuffs, flexed his fingers, 'the explanation is really very simple…' An ersatz smile clamped down over the man's yellowed teeth. 'The letter in question was conveyed to me by a, how should I say, *intermediary*. It would've been someone Professor… *Hájek*, you said? Someone he entrusted it to, after he'd shown it to you. And when the Professor died — very unfortunate, I must say — then, this intermediary must have seen fit to pass it on to me. If he omitted the detail of the Professor's identity as the letter's translator, I assure you it can only have been out of respect for the, *er*, deceased's family… In our profession, people can sometimes be, let's say, overly sensitive.' Faktor pursed his lips through his beard. 'In any case, as you see, all perfectly above board.'

Faktor's spread his hands out on the table. The cards had all, so to speak, been laid out — the man's smoking jacket was liable to've been stuffed to the seams with them. It went without saying that Němec didn't like the sound of what Faktor had just been telling him. He sat there with his eyes fixed on the man's haemorrhoidal mouth, puckering & unpuckering, the wiry dark hairs fringing it matted with glaucus fluid. Faktor raised his glass to his lips, he made complacent shapes with his eyes. A piece of cut blue glass winked at Němec from a gold pinky-ring. *Mene, mene.* The light in the room had dimmed, the way

---

✋ Perhaps the two old men (Faktor & the Prof) were members of some club? There were bound to be dozens of them. Old-timers' chess Sundays & all that. And it quite suddenly occurred to Němec that there was, after all, something suspiciously monarchical about this game with its kings, queens, bishops, knights, castles, pawns. What the hell had the chess-obsessed Russians called them back in the day? Comrade Chairman, Comrade General-Secretary, Ministers, Commisars, workers of the world? ["God save the Queen, *nahnahnahnahnah,* from the fascist regime…" (✊)]

the light in his head was dimming. Faktor's eyes swam, they seemed to be mesmerising themselves, the table floated, the chesspieces drifted back & forth across the board like debris on the ocean floor.

'Unfortunately,' Faktor yawned, 'I don't seem to be very much help to you, Mr Němec. I'm simply an amateur, after all,' he said labouring his "r"s, 'a humble chronicler of that which you might call *esoteric…*'

His face assumed, by turns, expressions of sadness, humility, fortitude, disappointment: a man reconciled to his lot. Němec wondered what it was all in aid of. He didn't believe for a minute that the Prof had *entrusted* Kircher's letter to anyone. What *reason* would he've had? As for Mrs Prof & Elsbeth von N____, they'd been too busy gassing themselves for assignations with middlemen for a two-bit operation like *Heterocosmica*. Which still left the State Archives. Had someone rifled the Prof's files after the funeral & taken, of all the things, this particular letter? Cloak-&-dagger stuff, balaclava in the night, x-ray camera, skeleton key, secret doorknocks… But why publish it? What did anyone have to gain?

As if to confirm Němec's doubts, Faktor shook his head gravely —

'I am but a servant of Fortune. It's not for me,' his fingers did something elaborate, 'to question the whys & wherefores, merely to be thankful that they are so…'

The performance appeared to be at an end. Němec stared down into his wineglass. A pair of black eyes stared back at him. *Well kiddo, so much for that.* He was expecting the bum's rush any moment now. The dwarf was hovering in the background as if waiting to be called upon to do the honours. Němec sighed & made as if to stand up with his walkingstick. Faktor reached across the chessboard & took the black queen between his fingers, then raised it to his chin to scratch the dyed purpleblack follicles of his beard with it. Head tilted like that, he had the look of someone you'd suspect wouldn't hesitate to murder a child's goldfish if the child didn't tow the right line. Němec felt moved to attempt some witless parting remark, but Faktor cut him short —

'Not so hasty, young man,' he said. 'Your story interests me.'

He motioned for the dwarf to bring more wine. The dwarf sneered. Němec rose half out of his chair, undecided, till gravity decided for him. The air in the room was as thick now as a stagnant cesspool — if he'd let go of his walkingstick it could've stood of its own accord. Němec was surprised he could breathe at all. Faktor, meanwhile, made a show of studying the plastic chesspiece in his hand & then placed it carefully back on the board. The fingernails of his other hand worried the edge of the table. They were, Němec couldn't help noticing, effeminately long.

'Professor… *Hájek*, wasn't it? *Hmmm*. Now that I think about it, yes, the name begins to sound familiar,' he said. 'Hmm.'

His eyes narrowed —

'I do believe I once met a man by that name, but it was a very long time ago, well before you would've been born I'm afraid.'

He folded his hands in front of him, gazed at Němec a while, then went on, confident, his manners suggested, that Němec was a person who could be trusted with such a revelation —

'You see, it was like this…' he said, & related in a roundabout way the story of an encounter, after the War, with a student, 'who had a fanatical interest in Mahler,' he said. '*His* name was Hájek. He was obsessed with deciphering Mahler's notes for an unfinished symphony. He had a theory about numbers, I seem to recall. We had several acquaintances in common, through a chess club as a matter of fact. Then he went to Rome & we saw each other, *hmmm*, only a few more times after that. It *may* have been the same man, you never know. Do you have a photograph?'

Němec shook his head. In his mind he could see the Prof quite clearly. Sitting on a snowbank, paring his nails with a pocketknife, grinning. *Faktor?* his ghostly lips seemed to say. *Now there's a name I haven't heard in donkey's years…*

For Němec's benefit, Faktor related the story of his own exile, those dark communist years, abject in Schnitzelstadt, plots & intrigues for the Day of Restitution, in the service of a bereft idea, to elect a king, some archduke or other, scions of a dilapidated aristocracy, aspirants & pretenders, collaborators some, dispossessed all, cashiered, erased from the constitutions of Mitteleuropa, pedigrees at a discount & for sale or rent to the highest bidder, Saudi oil magnates, New Zealand sheep barons, Grub Street social climbers, wearing their titles like some preposterous bureaucrat's toupee that keeps slipping off revealing an eczema, estates fallen to wrack & ruin, nationalised, collectivised, turned into brothels for the Party nomenklatura.

'One moved in very particular circles in those day,' Faktor confided.

Then abruptly the man leant forward & in a conspiratorially low voice asked if Professor Hájek had ever happened to mention the name Petrus Beckx? It sounded like a brand of phenacetin. Němec looked at him blankly, he had the peculiar feeling the tables were being turned on him — but it was only a feeling. Faktor cast a furtive glance around the room &, apparently reassured, touched a finger to his right earlobe, pursing his lips as he did so.

'I'll tell you a little story,' Faktor said confidentially, & settled his elbows on the table.

His face grew large under the sodium lights as he leant closer. Němec automatically drew back. This Faktor, it occurred to Němec, might well be some sort of lunatic, like the escapee in the park. The City had no shortage of them, that was for sure, ready at the drop of a hat to talk up a storm of gibberish. He seemed to be a magnet for them. (*What was it they wired into your brain again, kiddo?*) In any case, it'd be safer to play along, not upset the man's equilibrium, do the credulous idiot act. Well, he was in for a real treat this time.

Beckx, so Faktor's story went, was supposed to've been the head stooge of the Jesuits, back in the day when forces were being arrayed to put them out of business once & for all. Apparently it didn't work & the Jesuits came back stronger than ever. But that wasn't the real story. The real story had to do with a certain book called the Voynich Manuscript. Oh Faktor knew about the Manuscript all right, he seemed quite the expert. What was more, the Manuscript, he assured Němec, hadn't been discovered by Voynich at the Villa Mondragone at all, but had been (the evidence was indisputable) *stolen*, or if not stolen, *spirited* from this selfsame Beckx's private library, by parties suspected but ultimately unknown. How Faktor knew all this was a mystery. What it had to do with the Prof, more of a mystery still.

But Faktor was only just beginning to warm to his topic. He proceeded rapidly to speculate in quite elaborate detail about the Manuscript, the Jesuits, Kircher's letter, & by declinations the Prof. Němec had trouble keeping track of the man's line of reasoning, if there was one. It was as bad as being stuck in one of Comrade Medvedev's lectures, back at the Home, about the Great Capitalist Conspiracy. Paranoias stalked one another like flies under a naked light in which all that's visible is obscure supposition. Needless to say, as the editor of such an eminent publication as *Heterocosmica*, Faktor received from time to time unsolicited materials for publication, wide ranging in subject matter, rarely controversial (he assured his listener), at times illuminating to the general reader (whatever a general reader of such a thing as *Heterocosmica* might've been). It shouldn't, he said, come as any surprise that among the journal's readers & even contributors there were occasionally members of the Society of Jesus.

'It so happens,' Faktor said, plucking a shred of horseradish from his beard & rolling it into a tiny ball between forefinger & thumb, 'that the letter which so concerns you was sent to me by a...' he popped the balled horseradish between his lips, 'Jesuit priest — *hmmm?* — at least that's what I was led to understand. And why should I doubt it?'

Faktor's expression grew enigmatic —

'But could there be any reason to expect the Society might have any particular interest in Professor, *um*, Hájek's work?'

So now the intermediary was a priest, eh? And maybe this priest had a name? Faktor seemed to think he might. He'd try to see if he could remember it. In the meantime he went on with his theories, implying from time to time that the letter might even have been a fake. The possibility embarrassed him of course, but he'd try to live with it.

'But it's also possible,' he said, that the Society of Jesus was trying to muddy the waters. 'Often, the sort of people attracted to something like the Voynich Manuscript are obsessed with secrecy, with their own & with others', but above all with the One Great Secret. As long as the Manuscript remains indecipherable, as long as the key remains hidden, their "secret" is safe.'

Faktor paused to gauge the effect of his words. It was obvious he was only just beginning to warm to his subject.

'You see,' he continued, 'if *I* don't have the key, at least neither do *you.* Consequently I have nothing to fear — my theory can't be debunked & my personal prestige remains intact. But should you somehow stumble across the *true* key, whether you know it or not, then I have everything to fear, & it becomes my first concern to prevent you from *realising* you have the key, or from *revealing* the fact to others. Would it surprise you to learn that there's a very profitable industry in manufacturing *false* keys? The idea is a simple one of smoke & mirrors, the fog of war, call it what you like. Like a parlour trick — the magician waves the wand in his left hand so that the audience won't notice what the right one is doing…'

It was, Němec mused, as if he'd stumbled by accident into some sort of Museum exhibit, where you pressed a button beside an automaton to hear all about the Dead Hand of the Jesuits & associated other obscuranta. Any moment now, this "Viktor Faktor" would possibly malfunction & laugh his head off, leaving wires sticking out of his neck. Němec almost felt he should look under the table to check if there wasn't really a tape machine down there.

'It's known, for example,' Faktor said with utmost seriousness, 'that the

Jesuits secretly conspired to bring Hitler to power...* As for Beckx, as the head of the Society of Jesus from the early 1850s, he was as vulnerable as he was powerful. Those were very uncertain times. What we call Italy today was a hodgepodge of kingdoms & dukedoms & principalities & republics all in turmoil — it was when Garibaldi was still fighting for the unification of the peninsula. Seventeen years later, Vittorio Emanuele's troops captured Rome, annexing the Papal States, & one of the first actions of the new king was to expropriate Jesuit property — Il Gesù, the school of San Andrea al Quirinale, San Eusebio, the Casa Professa which housed the Jesuit Curia. They also seized the Collegio Romano, & the Jesuits' library, the Biblioteca Maior. As you'd expect, there was hardly any love lost between Beckx & the Royalists. But the Jesuits have always been patient. They got their revenge with Mussolini...'

Faktor withdrew a pipe from the breast-pocket of his jacket & began tapping the bowl out on the edge of the table.

'As I'm sure you can imagine,' he went on, proceeding to fill the pipe with tobacco from a round yellow tin, 'countless extremely valuable manuscripts had accumulated in the hands of the Jesuits over the course of centuries.'

Settling back in his chair, Faktor dipped a match into the bowl of his pipe & puffed —

'Before the Biblioteca was confiscated in 1873, to form part of the new Pontificia Università, a large number of books were smuggled out of Rome & concealed at various locations. Beckx & his closest aides fled to Fiesole & re-established the Curia in hiding. Bits & pieces of Jesuit's archive, meanwhile, were secretly stored at the Villa Mondragone, in Frascati. The villa belonged to the Borghese clan, who were among Beckx's most powerful protectors...'

Faktor waited to see that his listener was taking it all in. A cloud of acrid smoke hung around him. Němec nodded vaguely, supposing all this must ultimately have some sort of point to it.

'It wasn't so much later,' Faktor went on with his narrative, 'that our American friend, Voynich, made contact with the Jesuits remaining at the Villa, through the agency of a certain Father *Strickland* — although that's almost certainly not the man's true identity. Whatever transactions occurred there, took place in secrecy, so it'd hardly be strange,' Faktor raised his eyebrows as if to indicate he believed otherwise, 'to find no record of it in the Society's archives.'

* Whereas they made no bones about orchestrating the Catholic-Fascist puppet government in Bratrislovo after '38. [♦]

He concentrated for a moment on prodding the bowl of the pipe with a matchstick, as though attempting to dislodge an obstruction, before going on. The air had a smell of burnt rubber to compliment all the other smells.

'The curious thing, though, is that no-one outside the Society seems to've known anything about this, till after Voynich's widow died. Or should we say, *Wojnicz*? The first mention of what happened at the Villa Mondragone came in a letter appended to her will & which she herself had only dictated to her husband's former secretary days before. Curious, isn't it, how things come about? In any case,' he said, 'it's almost certain her account of Voynich finding the Manuscript *by chance* is nothing short of a fabrication.'

More plausible, Faktor suggested, was for the bookseller to've pilfered it. From the Castel Gandolfo, for example, where Beckx had sought refuge forty years earlier from Vittorio Emanuele's troops. Němec nodded as if he knew what the man was talking about.

'My own theory,' Faktor said smilingly, 'is that, having discovered the theft & being able to put two & two together, the Curia sent emissaries to America after the war to secure the Manuscript's return. Either fearful or shrewd or both, Voynich made dozens of facsimiles, which he sent to libraries & specialists across the United States. Safety in numbers, so to speak.'

Faktor refilled his glass, tapping his chin with the end of his pipe. By now all his little gestures just seemed like part of the performance. Němec decided he may as well just sit & watch the show, hopeful that there'd be some way out of there at the end. The other patrons in the club all looked by now as if they'd been wheeled on from the wings. Their glasses may as well've been emptying themselves for all the life they had in them. It was up to the dwarf to scuttle about at regular intervals to pour the wine & keep the illusion up. Any moment now he'd bring out a box for the troll behind the bar to be sawed in half in. Take a bow. Soak up the canned applause.

'But if it was no longer possible for the Jesuits to keep the Manuscript *itself* a secret,' Faktor resumed, giving each of his words a suggestive inflection, 'the next step would be to do whatever they could to confuse all attempts to uncover its actual *meaning*, hmmm?'

He looked at Němec expectantly —

'And if what you say about Professor Hájek is true…'

Faktor positively leered at him —

'As for this *Sphinx's Code*,' he snorted derisively, 'how novel. An amateurish ploy, quite obviously. But still,' his lips parted to reveal a greyish tongue between the yellowed teeth, 'you ought to be more careful from now on, *hmmm?*'

Faktor's eyes drifted up to the irregular stubble covering Němec's scalp, lingering over the scars that were all-to-visible there.

'You mean,' Němec said in as bland a voice as he could summon, 'one of these nights there'll be a knock on the door?'

He pictured monkish assassins lying in wait, Opus Dei jujitsu adepts, Friar Tucks with quarterstaves, curare darts & lightning kung-fu moves, secret Templar handshakes transposing effortlessly into *dim mak,* the "death touch." *Are you on the square, brother?* Victims dropping off silently as if by mysterious illness. *What do you make of it doctor? It's like nothing we've ever seen...*

'It's no laughing matter, my young friend,' Faktor's eyes narrowed at him. 'If the Jesuits suspect someone of meddling in their affairs, they are quite capable of making certain, *um,* arrangements...'

Faktor's eyes took in Němec's dressinggown, as if registering it for the first time. His expression became once more quixotic. He re-lit his pipe before continuing —

'It's been known to happen. Temporary confinement, for example... Much easier than you might think. The former regime also...'

He mumbled something Němec didn't quite catch —

'It sounds a little outlandish, nowadays, doesn't it? But not everything can be made to change overnight. This is an ancient city. Even the Communists...'

Smoke rose from the end of Faktor's pipe. Němec tried to fathom what the man was getting at. Somewhere through the haze of the room the troll was laughing. It sounded like the noise of a dying horse.

'You see,' Faktor said, his face barely visible behind the veil of burning tobacco, 'the Jesuits will stop at nothing to discredit their enemies, if not simply to silence them.'

He leaned towards Němec conspiratorially —

'If the Manuscript itself were exposed as being... a fake, so to speak. To be... nothing but a lot of... bogus demotic, *hmmm?* Then who, except a...' Faktor waved his hands theatrically, '*charlatan,* would ever proclaim himself the *possessor of its secret?*'

15

BUM'S RUSH

The world, Němec seemed to recall the Prof saying once, *camouflages the fact that nothing available to experience is real.*

Němec lay on his bed in the Convalescents Ward staring at the ceiling. Lights from the courtyard cast long shadows through the grilled windows, reminding of childhood dormitories, sleeplessly rehearsing a philosophical dispute with a deadman. *The world camouflages the fact that nothing.* While up there, the shadows on the ceiling made a convincing enough show of being neither real nor unreal in their sombre Euclidean geometries: zodiacs of the otherworldly, apparitions of (or somewhere in) the future-perfect or discontinuous-past — ghost-signals beamed from outer space, through time-delay, interstellar redux — doppelgängers of parallel universe retro- or pro-spection, in which it's possible to witness, for example, Galileo espying through his makeshift telescope the (*e pur si muove!*) grinning face of Major Yuri Alexeyevich Gagarin in low terrestrial orbit, while the children of Golem City sing:

> *The whole world heard the news from TASS,*
> *the whole world stared at their idiot boxes.*
> *The whole incredulous world got up off their sofas*
> *and turned their eyes skyward.*
>
> *Good evening, Major Gagarin!*
> *We couldn't wait, but now you're up there!*
> *The whole wide world's chugging wine red as your flag,*
> *everyone's drunk, waving like mad.*
>
> *Tell the Man in the Moon,*
> *tell the ziggy starmen who live in the stars —*
> *give them a message from us little hooomans,*
> *we'll be following your tin can soooooon.*

There he was, having warmed the heart of the night porter (a Moravák, like the Bugman, called Honzík, originating from environs south of Božice, fifteen years in current employ, one granny, extant, who every Christmas, New Year's &

Easter, sent five bottles of 140-proof slivovice) with a newly minted portrait of Jan Amos "the Beard" Komenský*: for comradely assistance in worming back into the Ward after curfew. It was a "delicate" operation — a narrow window-of-opportunity-about-to-close, when or if the Night Nurse (otherwise ensconced in front of some re-run Larry Hagman TV soap opera) took inventory, so to speak: employing diversionary tactic of bogus PA system announcement, *Paging Nurse Whosit! Nurse Whosit to Oncology, please* — sewing, thereby, seeds of temporary confusion, during which, slipping past unnoticed, etc.

Safely in bed where he belonged, Němec pondered his encounter with the inscrutable Viktor Faktor — in all probability a lunatic. Something fishy, though, about the whole situation: Faktor's manner, the overly ordained talk, as if their meeting, from beginning to end, had been scripted in advance, right down to the shabbiness of the wine cellar & its maudlin clientele. Not to mention the undrinkable. All of it a backdrop for a bit of dodgy theatre. The casual air of familiarity, the minutely deduced intrigue... *And you got stuck playing the rube in the dogseat, eh, kiddo?* Assuming this Faktor wasn't just your ordinary *gewöhnlich* run-of-the-mill crank, waiting for an opportunity to sound-off about whatever crackpot notion was stewing in his brain, to whoever happened to come along? *Sure, kiddo. 'Course they was expecting you. Saw you coming a mile off...*

Němec dry-swallowed three of the blue pills the good doctor had proscribed, trying to decipher the smallprint: only cure for incipient paranoia's not to think at all, but would three be enough? What the label said: Phenobarbital 20mg, atropine (radobelin) 0.1mg, ergotamine tartrate 0.3mg. Whatever it all meant, the pills didn't waste their time. Němec slid down onto the pillows. Up above, the shadows on the ceiling played tricks: opposed chessmen pursued one another remorselessly across a mystical chessboard — the pieces danced, dissolved, reappeared, upsidedown, insideout, sans raison d'être, sans raison de faire. In the midst of the fray, the red light of a smoke detector blinked like a Sphinx's eye, its riddle the one constant in a night of febrile watchfulness, punctuated by sudden plunges into nothing. Snow brushed against the window panes, black holes drifted across the walls. Mysteries portended in every corner, on every surface, behind every shadow.

The hours dragged by. *Belladonna* sang in his ear — a siren song, rising & falling in waves, over & over. In his mind's eye he saw the Ice Queen in her

---

* Being the princely sum of Kč 200,-. [♣]

arctic remoteness beckoning Napoleon to his doom. Black Basilisk eyes. Deadly nightshade. A crown of purple-red flowers adorned her pale hair, pale throat & pale breasts, nipples agleam like the black berries of the *atropa belladonna*. And the nipples blinking open & Faktor's eyes leering out of them…

Němec felt himself going down, further & further, as if he was a drowning man in a frozen river, cold seeping up through his veins, paralysing him bit-by-bit. The Ward swam, a thousand lights blinked in unison, suddenly he was awake again. He was floating among the heavens. And there, in the middle of it all, staring from the ceiling, the red eye of that black Sphinx, wings outspread against vistas not of stars & galaxies but of ash-fall & blight. Death in its pastoral setting. Němec gazed about. *Was this it? How it looked on the other side?* Then the Sphinx spoke, words uncoiling from a black hole cropped-out with horrible teeth. Words like the incantatory gibberish of spells spieled from the Book of Dead Egyptian Oedipus. They seemed to be directed at him, there was no-one else about:

> *What creeps at dawn on all-fours,*
> *goes two-footed at midday,*
> *but on three at dusk?*
> *Mandragora! Mondragone!*
> *Man oh man where ist thy ho-ho-home…?*

Němec gagged. He was drowning, still. But then the drowning stopped & he was back in the Ward again. He was lying like a herring in brine, soaked in his own sweat, the sheets clutched tight around him, shivering. His body ached all the way down his lame third leg. Funny. What further torments was he expected to endure? The red eye blinked down impassively — Němec watched it fade in & out of focus. He craved sleep while even then abhorring the very idea of it.

Behind a partition at the end of the Ward, a tracheotomy patient kept-up a steady wheeze. A draught from an open window somewhere in the hall, wafted the general stench of human frailty like an incense. *It's the little familiar things, eh kiddo, that make a home inside the great miasma.* Němec pulled up the blankets & shivered. One more night, he thought, & then the next night, & the one after that. But somewhere there'd be an end. When he'd decided he wasn't coming back, was probably when they'd let him go. Send him off with a nice little farewell present: the socially-adjusted paranoiac whose body worked just enough so that he'd never forget it.

From a hundred backwards to zero, Němec counted & recounted. Somewhere during the third try everything went dark again. The sounds of the sleepers in the Ward moved over him like a slow ponderous second movement, grave, counterpoised, *misterioso*. Then little by little there came a voice, darkly whispering: a voice heard only when all the other voices ceased being audible. It repeated the Sphinx's question, but in reverse. Outside, the bells of St Loyola's church struck four. Soon it'd be dawn. Time to go home? *Home?*

Němec strained to hear some countervailing note, something that'd keep the delirium in check, but there was only that dark inscrutable voice. And then, emerging from the blackness, as if approaching down a long corridor, a man's bearded face, eyes burning with the light of fanaticism. The man was Odward Kelley. He was approaching faster, running now, but (as always in dreams) without seeming to move. The fanaticism in his eyes had turned to fear. His words were no longer whispers but screams. A host of hooded figures were pursuing him, agents of hidden powers, guardians of the Sphinx, prelates of unnatural religions…

And as Němec looked-on helplessly, the whole scene dissolved into a type of reflection. It wasn't Kelley, but *him*, trapped inside a mirror & trying to get out. Now the malevolent pursuers directed their attention towards Němec. His reflection was leading them directly to him: there was no choice but to break the mirror. But even as this occurred to him, Němec became aware that his thoughts were no longer hidden — that these phantasmal adversaries were perfectly able to hear & read everything that passed through his mind — that they were already *within* his mind & that this was a *test*. That in reality their masters were all along noting down his involuntary responses, every line of reasoning, every fear, delusion, failure of will, every point of resistance, every capitulation — all kept in evidence to be used against him at some undisclosed place & time.

And then, in the midst of this, Němec began to think about cats & their curious ability to survive long falls…

The Life Ever After

The day wasn't long in coming before they smilingly gave him the bum's rush. Goodbye to the Bandaged Man, the Ward nurses, the orderlies! Goodbye to the 2nd floor janitor, Honzík the porter, the Pigeon Man! Goodbye to the blue pill softshoe shuffle! Goodbye to all the Doctors A, B & C, D, E, F & G! Goodbye to Nurse P, the two Ivans, the Blue Door, the basement floor! Hello bright future!

As if nothing had ever happened, Němec slunk back to his room behind the Český Rozhlas building. It wasn't far to go. The 22 tram past the nuthouse on Kateřinská, Ječná, I.P. Pavlova, two stops on the 11, a couple of blocks on his three feet past people in the street talking to themselves through little black transistor boxes. Had the androids succeeded in their unspeakable plan? He arrived at the door of the apartment building, key in hand, official discharge signed & stamped, welfare-cheque approved, a provisionally free man in name if nothing else, liberated at last from medical encyclopaedias, convulsion therapies & quackery. One more veteran of the City General Teaching Hospital.[*]

Everything inside the apartment was still as it'd been the night of "the Fall," only the fuses had been switched off. For upwards of an hour Němec sat in the dark & stared at the window. The hem of one of the curtains had been caught inside the latch & made the whole thing appear slanted against the light from the streetlamps, like the windows in *The Cabinet of Dr Caligari*. But no demons came out of the dark, no doppelgängers, no malevolent figments. Němec breathed the air in the room. It smelt of something dead inside the walls. Something that'd been suffocated slowly & plastered over. Something that wasn't even aware it was dead, despite the fact it was already decomposing in front of its own eyes. It smelt of a person's rotten conscience.[†]

---

[*] To each his, or her, *alma mater*. [✊]

[†] It was just a room, after all, like any other. Němec'd been away so long he barely recognised it. It meant nothing to him. Yet something in that room had taken hold of his existence, something formless that permeated the architecture connecting it, by secret paths, to some other place: a room in a derelict apartment building — a hospital corridor — a long-ago alchemist's laboratory. A place in which unknown forces had been at work: how many others were there? Rooms for the memory through which time itself passes fleetingly or from which there's no escape. And everything that happens there — could *ever* happen there — would be as ungraspable as the decision to step out a window? But what if there was no decision? Němec had no answer. The room's forty-watt light was just strong enough to reveal a set of dusty footprints where no-one had walked in months. Thinking how easy it'd be to disappear without a trace. Himself & all of humanity. Why not? *Don't kid yourself. They've got your number. They don't give up that easy.* The Prof often talked about things no-one believed in anymore, like the "transmigration" of souls, reincarnation, the becoming blood & body of the sacrament. Articles of faith testified to by nothing but expired dogma. The Eternal Soul. Angels & alembics. Man in Eden. The Fall & Resurrection. The making manifest of deeper "significances" — of the true, indissoluble God-Self. Like that portion of Prometheus' liver. Meaning: *Why suffer only once, when you can be reborn and suffer again and again, throughout the travesty of life eternal?* He tried to guess what the Bugman might've said, but he wasn't buying either. *Don't ask me, kiddo.* Instead his thoughts drifted back to the Prof & all those interminable monologues about Science, Knowledge, the Spirit of Reason: how these'd once-upon been Man's crowning (last-ditch) effort at erecting a private God, the motive force of all his fugitive actions & inactions, like a genie imprisoned in a bottle. Fancying

The Engineer of Human Soles[*]

Thinking about the Prof made him think about Volta, also: the engineer of human souls. He'd put on a good show of believing the world could be made better through "psychic health." Or if not better, at least reconciled to its imperfections. It was an attractive line if you believed you were sick to begin with. *Man on the path towards the pure light*, & all that song-&-dance. The promised land could be yours, too, all you need was to get your choice of delusions right. Like Saul on his high horse *clopclopping* along the road to Damascus with traumatism of the head.[†] The poetic justice of it. But to be cured of what *other* ailment, what *pre-existing* condition hidden inside the passion of the convert? Was that what they thought they'd made him into?

Němec went out to the corridor to find the fuses & switch the electricity back on. There was a faint *dzzzzzz* from inside a metal box in the stairwell. He had to use his fingernails to work it open. A row of switches pointed down: they went up with a loud click & a light came on back along the corridor where his room was. It was like someone tapping on your knee & your foot jerks up. An image came automatically to mind of that array of therapeutic machines he'd only just escaped by the skin of his teeth: dials, switches, alternating currents, xrays & brainwaves & doomsday boxes. Maybe it was all wired together. Maybe he hadn't escaped anything at all.

Back in his room Němec bolted the door & went to peer in the bathroom mirror — to see that picture of the renewed, whole man: his doppelgänger, his antiself. Repaired the way only objects can be repaired, stitched together like Frankenstein's morgue-slab experiment. A body that could be unzipped, rearranged, put back together in combinations more elaborate & grotesque than so far God or DNA had managed to come up with: head protruding from beneath a shoulder, arms & legs switched around, pointing fore & aft, toes for teeth, a sphincter for an eyelid. Like ol' Mongo-the-Magnif. *Now you're getting somewhere, kiddo.*

---

himself, with his setsquare & pocket computer, on the path towards purification, like an amateur flagellant eroticised by the dead hand of History…

[*] Sic. Tomáš Baťa? [🖕]

[†] Seeing agog, if not a God: the lush who couldn't keep his saddle, son of Rome, juiced to the eyeballs on warm shiraz after kicking-in his day's quota of Zhiddish *kopfen*, Hail Caesar! For only a few denarii more he'd kiss their arses instead. A man can't be choosey when he has to work to put wine on his table.

Němec ran his fingers through his hair, feeling the scarred cranium with its occulted Braille. Distended, misshapen. In the Home the older ones with pretensions to being educated called him Squillhead: fainting under the weight of his lopsided dome, a sleepwalking Schinocephalos in the full daylight of his own deformity. Why exist at all, he used to think, when there was only this thing, this proxy going about in place of him, an all-too-visible travesty born of chance & chaos & a midwife's forceps? The only option was the struggle to end, to fail, be rebirthed blightless.[*]

Němec's ruminations were interrupted by a knock at the door. He squinted at the dead eye in the peephole & recognised the Bugman in his tricolour legionnaire's cap, stooping outside. He was wearing the same threadbare cardigan across his shoulders he always wore, holding a stoppered bottle of homemade slivovice & a bundle of newspaper.

'Nazdar, vole!' he shouted through the door.

One look at Němec in his hospital rags was enough. Blecha tossed the bundle at him: wrapped in it was an old suit & shirt & a pair of secondhand shoes. The same black suit & white shirt & shoes he'd worn to the Prof's funeral & almost to his own.

'Had 'em dry cleaned. Thought you might need somethin' to wear,' he pointed at Němec's dressinggown & rubber slippers, 'instead of that get-up. Your choice though. Nowadays, people'll wear anything.'

Němec said something appreciative & told the superintendent to make himself at home. Blecha cast a glance around —

'Nothin' like getting' back to yer own digs, is there? Must've got kind of tiresome stuck in the Grand Savoy all this time. Get yer end in with any a those nurses? Saw one or two musta been real goers. Some of 'em though, *yeesh*, could put a man in traction just by lookin' at him.'

The Bugman sat himself down & stood the bottle of slivovice on the arm of the chair —

'You're looking fine, anyhow,' he said.

Němec shrugged —

'Could be better.'

'Could be a fucking lot worse, my friend.'

There was nothing Němec could disagree with in that. He laid the handmedowns on the end of the cotbed & went out to retrieve a couple of jars

---

[*] The leap into Ætna? [✋]

from the kitchenette. Blecha poured the moonshine —

'Here's to your good health,' he raised an old jam jar & gulped. 'Kurva! Make the dead stand up in their graves, this stuff would.'

Němec took a mouthful & gasped.

'Out of practice, eh, kiddo? We'll soon fix that.'

They drank sitting with their backs to the wall (Němec on the cotbed, leg stretched out) & talked about old times.

'Had one just like that myself once,' Blecha said, jerking his chin at Němec's hospital dressinggown. 'Height of fashion it was. After the mine caved-in, they were givin' 'em away to the survivors as a consolation prize — for missin' our opportunity on a ticket outta there — in a bag. Fuckers. Up in Jáchymov, that was. Uranium ore. Two trainloads every day to Mother Russia. I reckon when they bury me, I'll be fit to read by my own light, down there. Spook the blindeyed worm-things, *hehe.* Dig me up in a hundred years, I'll be fresh as a daisy. Never get sick, me. Don't ever let anyone tell you a bit of radiation isn't just the thing.'

The Bugman flashed a mouthful of ceramic —

'Well, anyway, make sure I'm well stocked with literature before they nail the lid shut, won't you kiddo? I was always fond of Biggles — you know, *The Black Peril, Spitfire Parade…* take yer pick. There was a very pretty nurse from Kladno let me cop a feel of her while she was checkin' my temperature in the mornings — used to bring Karel May stories for me to read after lights-out. Strictly against regulations, of course. Vinnetou & Old Shatterhand. Genuine blonde, too, if you'd believe that. *How'd a pretty girl like you wind up in a shithole like this?* Well, I s'pose it beat schleppin' at the steelworks for old Ma Wittgenstein. Give me a girl in uniform any day, *hehe.*'

Němec poured, they both drank, the Bugman went on with his story —

'Oh, she was a real peach, alright. What I'd've given for a piece of that! Warned me if I wasn't careful the doctor'd certify me fit enough to go back down the hole. I said I was fit enough, alright, but if it's holes we're talkin' about love. *Tuttut,* she said, *people's enemy, you. I've half-a-mind to file a complaint.* Hehe. *No-one's complained yet,* I said to her. *I bet,* said she. *How about a quick bedbath, then?* I said, getting' a good handful of prime rump. *Oooh, you are a very nasty man, aren't you!* Well, it was fun while it lasted. Then I had the misfortune of one of them smartarse desk-bandits come to give us all the once-over, raise quotas & all that, to redeem ourselves in the eyes of our socialist brethren. *Well, now, you parasitical piece of scum, why aren't you down there doing your fair share with the rest of the comrades, eh?* Seems he accidentally poked himself in the eye with the knobby part of my fist. I really couldn't say what came over the silly bastard, fallin' about all over the place, makin' a mess with the bedpans. For that little gag of mine they gave me a lead pipe in the teeth & trucked me off to Karelia. Ah, the country life! No more pissing glowworms down the hole! Only sunshine & fresh air & the birds & bees. You know, I'd honestly like to shake the hand of Klem Gottwald for that — truckin' me off to that gulag, I mean. I really truly would. Best thing that ever happened to me.'

A Higher Diapason

By the time Blecha left — sloshing his way along the corridor, bottle left sitting fourfifths empty on the windowsill — Němec felt no worse than numb. The room felt numb with him, like someone had come along & cut the nerves out of it with a scalpel & syringe. He sat & stared at the ceiling trying to think what he was supposed to do next till the staring got on his nerves. What'd he expect, a ray of light, an oracular pronouncement?[*]

He kicked around some dust & looked out the window: someone in a window across the street looked back. *Let them do the thinking for a change,* Němec thought. He poured another drink & switched on the recordplayer. It still worked. The same record was even on the turntable, just as it had been: Karel Ančerl's Supraphon recording of Mahler, Symphony No. 9 in D major, the needle lodged in the inside track. Němec left the needle where it was, listening to the hiss & periodic *thut* as the disc turned fullcircle, marking off recurring-decimal-time at $33\frac{1}{3}$ rpm. Distance travelled during one complete revolution equal to $2\pi r$. Calculate ∴ the time in seconds between each *thut*, assuming a radius (r) of…

While pretending to calculate the problem, Němec lazily rearranged the books & scraps of notepaper around the cotbed. Résumés of fantastic former days. The books had all been filched (the social cost of education in any selfrespecting democracy): Patočka, Vilikovský, Céline, Eisenstein, Chandler, Reich, Freud, Bulgakov, Apuleius, Thomas Mann even… A few dozen others he couldn't remember having read, or hadn't. Under the bed lay Blecha's typewriter with a half-sheet of grey paper wedged in it & a wornout carbon. It, the machine, was a black Minerva 150, portable with a skewed uppercase K, keys

---

[*] *Everything,* so sayeth the Tao, *is done by doing nothing.* [♣]

thick with dust, grease, hair & expired ideas.

Němec pulled the typewriter up onto his knees & read what the alterego had written there, four months previous. The words produced no feeling of recognition. He tried to count back the days, but got lost in the mathematics. Only a vague picture in his head: a cold room, hunched over the machine, angry, blind, drunk, numb, fingers jabbing at the keys, slipping between them, going back, exxing-out. What'd he been trying to get at? Did he know? Bored with being an onlooker in his own stale melodrama. *What're we coming to, eh kiddo, that we haven't seen a mile off already?*

For no reason at all he thought of Westonia, the alchemist's poet daughter-in-law condemned to a dead language, sentiments with no future. What was it all for, this labouring against the odds? Taken as given: nobody'd ever want to read what floundered about inside that squill head of his anyway, so why should he? Němec stared morosely into the dusty wordmachine (*Typewriter, typewriter, on the floor, who's this unrelenting bore?*). He unwound the page that was stuck in it & would've crushed it into a ball & tossed it out the window, if he'd had the energy. All he did was look at it. Blank words surrounded by more blankness.

And scribbled in blue pencil across the bottom of the page, barely legible: *Survival as the opposite of life.* What the hell was that supposed to mean? He read it again: *as* or *is*? He couldn't tell. Perhaps there wasn't any difference. Maybe that's what it meant. One equivalent nothingness for another. He finished his drink, had a staring match with the bottle, lost, poured just one more. Perhaps because he was still holding it in his other hand & didn't know what else to do with it, he started reading aloud from the typescript —

```
They'd've preferred it like that.
(Pause.)
Just like you'd expect paradise to be, eh? Nice & quiet.
Only the sound of the fruit falling from the trees. The
sap rising. The snake in the grass. But quiet, nonetheless.
(Pause.)
That's what they'd've wanted. No doubt about it. After all
this time. At long last.
(Pause.)
Peace & bloody quiet.
(Blackout.)
END
```

Just to spite himself he looked around to see if there was any more of it — the bits that came before. There were: a dozen or so pages folded into the back of the typewriter case, crumpled, inksmeared, single-spaced, like samizdat. *More priceless drivel*, he thought. He took a page at random, then another. Tried to piece them together. Shuffling the pages around like that, he forgot what he was doing. The words began to assume their own order, discovered an independent depth of focus.

He drank some more. The words wended from pathos to travesty, across vast lacunae, pages torn in half, scraps with notes stuck on with sellotape, sections exxed-out, unwritten, missing, reduced piecemeal to roach-fodder. Whatever it was, Němec was sure *he* hadn't written it. Something else, the Geist in the Machine playing a joke. *Hehe*. Like you keep enough chimpanzees locked in a room & eventually one of 'em'll come up with the complete unexpurgated & unabridged works of V.I. Lenin. And as usual, it'd be History that's to blame.

16

<u>A FATHER TO HIS NATION</u>

Stage with a steel-framed hospital bed at centre, front. Behind the
bed & suspended above it, an old enamel bathtub with a long water
pipe & showerhead rising from one end. To left & right, two oversized
bird cages. In one of these, a megaphone. In the other, a large
stuffed green macaw. The bed is occupied by Klem Gottwald, an
elderly hypochondriac, somewhat posthumous in appearance, dressed in
prison-striped & distinctly soiled pyjamas. When first seen, Klem is
prostrate in bed, the linen strewn about him. A single spot gradually
fades-up on his face & remains there for almost a minute, then
black. A scratchy Karel Hála recording comes on with the lights,
emanating from the megaphone & interrupted sporadically by the
sound of a parrot screeching. At the end of a minute, darkness,
silence, broken by Klem's snoring. The snoring becomes louder &
louder, building to a crescendo that's eventually terminated by an
even louder crackerbarrel fart...

KLEM: There was a young man from Vyškov,
            who could talk from the crack of his...
            (Farts again, long dénouement. Dim light gradually
            widening over the stage.)
            Christ! Done it again! The bleeding waterclock up to its
            usual. Change of tides. Cnut!
            (Sits up, gripping the edge of the bed. Shouts.)
            It's TIME!
            (Silence.)
            They've forgot.
            (Pause. Pulls an alarm clock out from beneath his pillow.
            Sets it. Let's it ring for some time. Turns it off. Puts it
            back under pillow.)
            You'd think they could remember a simple thing like that.
            Once a day. Twice at most. It's not too much to ask.
            (Pause.)
            Twice is very unusual. Rather uncommon, I'd say. But not
            out of the question. Such things have been known to
            happen.
            (Pause.)
            Once, though. Once is absolutely fundamental.
            (Pause.)
            Take the sun. Now who could deny that the sun rises at
            least once each day? Has it ever been known not to rise? I
            couldn't say. It's doubtful, though. I've never seen such a
            thing. Admitted, it'd be a difficult thing to see, the fact
            of the sun not rising.
            (Pause.)

In some parts they say it rises once every four hours & at
other times barely at all.
(Pause.)
At the north pole, that is. At the south, too, presumably.
(Pause.)
Suppose they get a bit dizzy up there with all that
spinning around & the sun coming up at all hours of the
day & night & then not coming up & all them penguins &
polar bears & everything white or rather black. Depends
on whether you can see or not I suppose. On account of the
sun, I mean.
(Pause. Shouts.)
Nurse!
(Pause. Louder.)
NURSE!
(Pause. Light up on megaphone. Voice as through an
intercom.)
VOICE: What is it?
KLEM: The pan's full up. I need a new pan.
VOICE: The day nurse will empty your pan. Go back to bed.
KLEM: I can't. I need the pan.
VOICE: The day nurse will come at six o'clock. At six o'clock your
          pan will be emptied. Until six o'clock you will remain in
          bed.
          (Light off on megaphone.)
KLEM: Nurse!
          (Silence.)
          Nurse!
          (Silence. Muffled groan. Sound of water.)
          Pissed meself.
          (Pause.)
          Every time, like clockwork. I'd be better off doing it on
          the floor. Or against the wall.
          (Pause.)
          They tend to frown on that. Piss yourself & they send you
          off to the showers early. Piss on the floor & they stuff a
          toilet brush between your teeth.
          (Pause.)
          Closest thing you'll get to a wet dream in here old boy.
          (Pause. Softly.)
          Nurse?
          (Pause.)
          Mama?
          (Light up on megaphone. Static. Recording of a caressing
          maternal voice.)
VOICE: Go to sleep now <u>maličkej</u>.
KLEM: Mama?
          (Intercom.)
VOICE: Patients in breach of curfew will be denied all meal
          rations. Fortyeight hours. Seventytwo. Sixtyfour.
          Isolation ward. Punishment cell. One week. Water ration.
          At six o'clock the day nurse...
          (Light off on megaphone.)

KLEM: There once was a young nurse from Vûl,
          whose temper was nothing but cool --
          she'd palpate the glands
          of all patients at hand
          & measure the length of their stools, their stools --
          & measure the length of their stools.
          (Light up on bed. Bright.)
          I wasn't always such a pushover you know. Not a bit.
          Strapping lad I was. All juiced up & everywhere to go.
          Knew the lay of the land like the back of me proverbial.
          Doorpost to doorpost. The milk maid, the widow over the
          back field, the vicar's daughter. Could sniff it out a mile
          away. That was me. Head & shoulders, they all said. Now
          there's a boy with a bright future, they said. A fine man
          he'll be one day, they said.
          (Pause.)
          Fine fucking mess, more like.
          (Pause.)
          I remember the day me dear mum sent me off to school for
          the first time.
          (Pause.)
          'At your age,' she said, 'you need to learn a thing or two
          about the world.' It broke her heart, needless to say. I
          took it all in my stride, needless to say.
          (Pause.)
          Education's a funny thing.
          (Pause.)
          It all began early one morning. I set out. The journey was
          long & arduous. It was nightfall when I got to the old
          bugger's schoolyard. Socrates himself, no less, with his
          snotstained beard tied in a knot. He was the type of
          leprechaun character you were like to find hiding under a
          rock or behind a hedge. You could tell he was a sly old
          bugger, all right. Well, like I said, it was pushing on. Too
          late to talk dialectics, in any case. I mean, it was pitch
          dark. Sun goes down almost as soon as it comes up around
          December January February. Sometimes March also. 'Who the
          feck are you?' says the old beard. 'Klem Gottwald at yer
          service,' says I. 'Come to learn the meaning of life.' Ol'
          Socrates points me towards the nearest hedge. There's an
          old wooden crate & a ratty blanket. Obviously belonged to
          some mutt. 'Kip over there,' he says. 'I'll take a look at you
          in the morning.' 'When's that,' I says. 'After it's stopped
          being dark,' he says. 'I could be stuck here till next month
          at that rate,' I says. 'Tomorrow or next month, one's as good
          as the other,' he says. Old sock. Crate was hard as a rock,
          so to speak, with nails stuck in it. And that mangy
          blanket! A veritable flea circus! Up all night I was on a
          bloody trapeze with them little feckers chasing me all
          about. Bite marks the size of your fist up & down the back
          of me arse. Such a hullabaloo I made, the old stooge wades
          back out into the pitch, torch in hand, fire in his eye.
          'What's all this about then?' Meantime I'm swatting the

bastards off me pride & joy. 'You're not getting a bite of that,' I screamed. Ruthless I was. And the old sock with his light shining right on me privatest spot, <u>in flagrante delicto</u>, as they say in Greek. 'What in Hades are you up to boy?' That's how the old queer talked. <u>What in Hades!</u> Well I blinked for half-a-mo, getting me bearings, just long enough to make out the glop of him beaking down at me like a mangy jackdaw. 'Well what the feck do you reckon I'm doing?' I says.* And right then one of those rabid little coots gets his fangs in the stumpy end of me third leg & I gave a shriek to split the earhole of Lord Jesus H. Almighty himself. I fairly pummelled the bloodsucking mongrel into a pulp. And then it happened. A geyser of blood & puss jetted up into the pious geriatric's gaping mug. Bullseye! What a shot! You could measure the convulsions in the old crab's jaw with a Richter scale. Fair near booted me blind through the hedge, he did, fleas & all. One giant welt from arse to tit & not a sunrise in sight.
(Long pause.)
There once was a man from Písek
Whose cock was as thick as his neck...
(Pause.)
Bit cold.
(Light fades.)
Nurse!
(Silence. Louder.)
NURSE!
(Light up on megaphone. Voice as through an intercom.)

VOICE:	What is it?
KLEM:	I'm cold.
VOICE:	Go back to bed.
KLEM:	I wet meself.
VOICE:	The day nurse will change your sheets. Go back to bed.
KLEM:	I can't. It's not... civilised.
VOICE:	The day nurse will come at six o'clock. At six o'clock your sheets will be changed. Until six o'clock you will remain in bed.

(Light off on megaphone.)

KLEM: Nurse!

(Silence.)
There once was a man from Příbram
Whose prick was as long as his arm...
(Pause. Alarmclock goes off under pillow, the spring winding down to a stop. Lights out. Sound of a parrot shrieking. Light up on megaphone.)

VOICE: All patients report to shower block. All patients report to shower block. All patients report to shower block.
(Lights fade. Sound of running water, rain, etc. Sound fades.)

---

* "Οὐδέν γε πλὴν ἢ τὸ πέος ἐν τῇ δεξιᾷ." Aristophanes, *Νεφέλαι* (423BC). [✥]

KLEM: Nurse!
          (Light up on Klem.)
          Rain? Me eye! Ah, but those where the days. First rain of
          the new wet season. Smell of dung & damp earth. The sub-
          humus. Now <u>that</u> stirs the old root. What memories!
          (Green filter on spot.)
          A faint mist over the hills, a shaft of sunlight in the
          valley. How green it was, that valley. The old Lady of
          Shallot herself. When she was young, I mean. It was spring
          when we first met. She, with dewdrops in her fair hair. Me
          with the first flush of youth. 'Dear Madam,' I says, 'what's
          a prime heifer like you doing in a place like this at a
          time like this & so on & such & such?' 'Sir,' she says,
          evidently mistaking me for someone else, 'I value your
          discretion.' All flushed about the cheeks, on account of
          the riding I suppose. It was a prize palfrey she had there
          under her side-saddle. 'I've come,' she says, 'for Lancelot.'
          'Only for Lancelot?' says I. 'What about the others?' 'It's a
          matter of affinity,' she says, 'I never did feel the same
          about another knight.' 'That's what I hear,' I says, 'that
          it's never the same again after the first one. But what
          about that Arthur & that round table? Must've seen a
          thing or two, eh, that round table, eh? Tough on the knees,
          though, I reckon, after a while. Or is it the back? The
          coccyx, as me old mum used to complain, does have a
          tendency to rawness when overworked, eh, overexerted so to
          speak, under duress, eh, eh? What do you think of that,
          then, <u>under duress</u>, eh?' says I, getting a bit carried away
          with meself. 'Oh you brute!' she squeals. 'How could you
          think such a thing? I am a lady of qualities.' 'That much I
          can see,' I replies, 'though I'm not much of the cultivated
          type, meself, quite the <u>Man without Qualities</u>, rather, just
          yer average Jack, yer average Joe in a manner of
          speaking. All sap & no sense is what they tell me, missus.
          But a lady of qualities you undoubtedly are. How much, do
          you reckon, for a tour of the old fort?' 'I'm afraid the
          high heights of Camelot are quite beyond your means, sir,'
          she says, all piqued & acting the <u>Poule Deluxe</u>. Oh the
          dizzying heights! Well who needs 'em? More a connoissewer
          of the lower reaches, what I am. Still called me <u>sir</u>, mind.
          These trollops always do, to give 'em a thrill it is. Always
          hot for a bit of filth to stand over 'em & give 'em the
          whatfor. So I climbed in the saddle & took her for a quick
          jaunt around the moat with that prize palfrey of hers, to
          see what she thought of the view from down there. 'But
          sir,' she doth protest, 'I belong to one man!' 'Aye aye,
          missus,' I says. 'You can call me Robin. I takes from the
          riche & gives to me poor self. You're a charitable soul I
          can see. Alms for the needy & all that. Just close your
          eyes & think of Saint Tereza,' so I says.
          (Green fades to white.)
          There was a young bastard named Arthur
          who never was sure of his father --

his mother was chaste
& far too straight-laced...
(Pause.)
Nurse!
(Pause.)
No-one here? All buggered off I suppose. Left in the
middle of the night. Jumped ship. The rats!
(Pause. Lights fade back to green. Sound of running water
again. Louder. Gradually fades as Klem speaks)
What's our favourite game today, then, boys & girls? Rub-
a-dub-dub? Three blind mice & a rock in a pillow case,
tossed into the drink? Blub-blub-blub. Choke on a rope?
Uh-oh! Bums to the wall! Nurse Toilet-Plunger's coming to
unstuff the pipes!
(Pause.)
It's time.
(Louder.)
SHOW TIME!
(Pause. Light fades to blue.)
Curtains up on the shower block scene! Three blokes
scrubbing their behinds, furiously. Me, the other one, &
whatsisname. Soap. Water. Etc.
(Pause.)
Enter: The Good Nurse Wenzelspritz.
(Pause.)
Arse cheeks, ruby red, clenched in synchronicity.
(Pause.)
'Well, well, well,' says little Miss Wenzel. 'What have we
here?' 'Bugger me,' says I, 'if it ain't the Whore of Bohemia
come all the way to Franz Kafka Station for a ride!'
(Pause.)
Take two. Shower block scene. Three of us lined up against
the wall. Arse cheeks, ruby red, etc. Nurse Heydrich in
white hat, white pinafore, white stockings, white shoes.
White all the way to her white-of-whites. Enter: Juan
Tanamera & Satchmo Panzer. Seems our number's up after
all. Rule three-oh-three. 'A last cigarette?' says she.
'Smoke this,' says we. Bang bang. One in each end of the
vital statistics. Three of us breathing our last. The holy
trinity. Me, meself & the frigging Devil as well. 'Send us
home to mum,' says I. 'Bugger your mum,' says she. 'Is it I'm
the Virgin Mary already?'
(Pause.)
Take three. Shower block scene. Shostakovich. Enter,
comrade nurse Stalinová, built like a Bulgarian shithouse
with a walrus moustache. Close at her rear, the faithful
slave Pedro, shouldering arms. 'Bourgeois filth!' screams
she. '_Enchanté_,' says I, 'come here often?' 'Only on Sundays,'
says she, 'I'm a devout sociopath.' 'Thank God for that,' says
I, 'put me out of me misery, I'm wet to the bone.' 'What
about your brothers in arms,' says she. 'They look pretty
wet, too,' says I, 'on account of the water.' 'Hot or cold?'
says she. 'Middling,' says I. 'Just as I expected,' says she, 'a

bed-wetter & a snivelling shite. <u>Mort aux tièdes</u>! I'll have
to shoot you.' 'Yes yes,' I says. The others were keeping
mum, white as sheets they were. 'Assume the position,' she
says. 'Gladly,' I says. 'Count to three,' she says. 'How do I
start?' I says. 'What comes after zero?' she says. 'Nothing,'
I says. 'And after that?' she says. 'I see,' I says. 'Would you
prefer a blindfold?' she says. 'Shoot straight,' I says. 'Last
wish?' she says. 'Be reasonable,' I says. 'Orders are orders,'
she says. 'Kiss me,' I says.
(Blue fades. Light up on megaphone. Voice as through an
intercom.)

VOICE: The day nurse will come at six o'clock. At six o'clock your
pan will be emptied. Until six o'clock you will remain in
bed.
(Light off on megaphone. White spot on Klem.)

KLEM: Nurse?
(Pause.)
Pity.
(Looks under sheets.)
Aha! Nelson you old cock! You who I met on the ships at
Trafalgar! The one-legged, one-armed, one-eyed bastard.
Still with us, are you? Thought maybe you'd fucked off
with the rest of 'em! Talley-ho & all that. Eh? <u>Ta-ra-ra-
boom-de-yay? Ta-ra-ra-ra-ra-ra</u>...?
(Pause. Lets sheet fall from his hand.)
Frigging bloodbath, wot? Foresheets & canonshot. Lead in
the aft. A right old cock up. For God & Country! That's a
good'n. <u>Pull me other leg, ya silly bastard</u>! Well it was a
long time ago! Water under the bilge & all that. Ships
passing in the night. Eh? Tides out? Well, you've pissed
away your last chance now, that's all I can say.
(Pause.)
Wine & bloody roses...
(Pause.)
It was a day like any other...
(Pause.)
It was a day not unlike any other...
(Pause.)
What're you trying to say? It was dark. Morning. A strange
bed in a stranger room. A voice. 'Shut up,' it said. 'I've wet
meself,' I said.
(Pause.)
Well that was smart, wasn't it? Done it again! All these
years. <u>What'll yer mum think of that?</u> <u>Would've broken her
heart to see you flapping about in a puddle of piss, a
grown man & with all that good education gone to waste.</u>
Much use as a chamberpot at the bottom of a well, if you
must know. Material dialectics me arse. You're either on
the right side or the wrong side, is what life teaches you.
You against all the rest! Ungrateful bastards they were,
too. Wouldn't lend you the steam off their proverbial. Well
you take what you can get when you can get it, right old
cock? Nothing like a nice warm micturation between the

sheets. A nice chaffing around the thighs. Eh? Eh? That's
the stuff!
(Pause.)
Don't suppose they'll take very kindly, though. Tend to be
of the rather puritanical type. A poke in the eye with a
stiff truncheon's as good as you can expect in a dump like
this. Pillowcase-in-the-mouth stuff. The old bedsheet-
around-the-neck trick. Always was fond of a good hangin'
meself. Only as a last resort, mind you. Not the sort of
thing you do every day. Not the sort of thing you just
bandy about, if you get my meaning. Nowadays, though! A
man can't get out of bed in the morning without fear of
retaliation. And to think I gave 'em all the best years of
me life! Oh well, no need to panic. You're in familiar
territory, at least. Better to just stay put. Sit & wait.
Bide yer time. See if anyone decides to pop in & have a
perv. Pay you a visit. Bring you flowers. Bring you a
lolly. See if little baby's alright. Have a quick check, a
quick feel. My oh my, you _are_ a dirty little boy aren't
you!
(Pause. Light fades to green.)
Nurse?
(Pause.)
There once was a nurse from Silesia…
(Pause.)
No good.
(Pause.)
I've lost it.
(Pause.)
If I ever had it.
(Pause.)
It was always better being alone.
(Pause.)
No-one listening. No-one watching.
(Pause.)
Even if just for a moment. Long enough to straighten up.
To prepare a face to meet the faces. Lock the door. Feel
the comfort of a closed, regular space. No-one. Alone.
Silence. The old mirror. The old washbasin. The old
crapper. The warm familiar smell of bleach & stale farts.
The cheese under the toilet seat. Aye, that's the stuff.
Letting the muscles relax in the lower abdominal region.
The moment you've all been waiting to relish. 'Well, first
you make your shit & then you eat it,' as the old stool
pigeon used to say. Back in '52. Whatever happened to all
the years, eh? The good ol' days. You think I owe anyone an
apology for that? Well it was something while it lasted.
Still, there was pain, too. Don't ever say I didn't have me
fair share of pain. Glad when it's over, I suppose. I can
just see me old mammy like that, lying on the bed with her
knees up & me wrigglin' about in all that blood & muck.
The look on her face. Pure joy! Like she'd just given birth
to the immaculate conception. _Just look at the grinning_

little turd, they all said. Like he's King Shit already.
Well how d'you think I felt, stuck up there in the dark so
long? Like I was me own constipation. Relief at last!
That's how they teach you to speak in polite society, don't
you know? As in: We relieved ourselves under fire. '42.
Those were the days! Sar'major bawling in our earholes.
Human wrecks, we were, down in the trench, fox-hole,
three-inch ditch -- bleary-eyed, trigger fingers worked
to the bone, teeth clenching two dozen grenade pins
between them -- 'Lift yourselves up by the arse, you
bloody fairies! What the hell d'you think this is, a
holiday in an outhouse? Get your shit together, boy! Two-
three-four! Left foot you bloody idiot! Two-three-four!'
And wouldn't she've been proud, the old sow? 'Take a good
look in the mirror son, what d'you see?' Smile. Say cheese.
Cheese. Stick yer finger up your nose. That's nice. Who's
the pretty boy then?
(Pause.)
There once was a young man from Thebes
whose mammy looked like Anne of Cleves --
he said to King Hairy,
'How could you married
the monster that darkens my dreams, my dreams --
THE MONSTER THAT DARKENS MY DREAMS!'
(Pause.)
Did I ever tell you the one about that Greek, Tiresiarse?
(Pause.)
It's no use. The old chopping block isn't what it used to be.
There was a time, though. Oh, indeed, there was a time.
When it was all just like bloody yesterday...
(Pause. Light fades to red.)
Me, all pink, wrapped up in a filthy old flannel. The
proud mum. The gobstopped Pater Familias. The bitch of a
nurse with her forceps digging me under the chin. 'Coochy-
coo.' That was her little joke, you know. I remember
throwing up me first gut-full of mammy's milk on that
freshly starched pinafore of hers. Thought that was
pretty bloody funny, I did. 'Coochy-coo!' Gave me a dig
under the chin I wasn't about to forget. First love-of-me-
life, she was. Then they took me off to live in a cardboard
box out in the wilderness. King of all I survey, up on my
little hillside, feral mutts sniffing about, the odd bandit
behind a rock, the odd shepherd, plenty of sunshine,
though, fresh air. Paradise it was. Paradise me arse. Day
after day of getting old & that's the long & the short of
it. One fine morning they told me to get on me way. 'Make a
man of yourself,' the Pater Familias said. 'Write to me,' the
old Mum said. I'd learnt to write by then, you see, not for
lack of trying though -- copied out the complete hogwash
of Ikey Marx with nothin' but a stick in the mud to make
shapes with, on every rock as far as the eye & all that.
Enough to cure anyone. Well weren't the old folks chuffed.
'A scholar & a gentleman,' they said. 'A what?' I said. 'Beat

it!' they said. I took them at their word. Skidoo! Over hill
& under hill. Found meself a hole with a bit of shade.
Settled down. Biding me time, I said.
(Pause.)
Life's little jokes, eh?
(Pause. Light fades to blue.)
But what dreams I had! A whole flood of dreams. Like Noah,
I was. The Promised Land. Mount Araroot & all that. The
grassy knoll floating there in the distance above the
waves.
(Pause. Light fades to green. Klem lying back against
pillows, arms outstretched.)
King of the bloody mountain at last! Well, ain't this
fabulous. If only the Ol' Bastard could get an eyeful of
this! Spread out on the grass in all me glory, lapping it
up! Think you can just lie there dreaming? Wake up boy!
You've got a revolution to make! What's that? Blood on me
hands? Can't be. Must be dreaming after all...
(Feeble laughter. Pause.)
Where was I? Right, the sky. Blue sky. Celestial virgins &
all that. The gentle tug of gravity. Good to give it a bit
of an airing once in a while, eh? Keep the launch systems
in order. Float around up there a bit. The competing tug
of weightlessness. Vertigo. In the stomach. In the pit of
the stomach. Ever been booted in the balls, son? Well now
you know what it's like. Nice to throw up once in a while,
too. Reminds me of when...
(Pause. Light fades to blue.)
It must've been May already. May Day! White butterflies
fluttering above the grass. The sun at its zenith. Skin
turning red in the hot heat. Burning, as they say. In the
heat. And then? We lay like that for hours. Me, meself &
you know who. In the middle of the field. The gentle slope
of the hillside. Hedges. Clouds. Blue sky.
(Pause.)
For hours. Lying on our backs. The slope of the hillside.
The blood slowly running to the head. The sound of blood
ringing in the ears.
(Pause. Light fades to red.)
Blood. Ringing in the ears.
(Pause.)
Back in me young youth when all the future still
beckoned.
(Pause.)
'Time to put the past out of its misery,' they said.
(Pause.)
Well, you've gotta start somewhere, eh?
(Pause.)
The rusty shotgun the old man kept under the bed.
(Pause.)
Can't say I never repaid my debts! Lead by example's what
I say. Drink cold, piss warm. The nation's in your hands,
son! I did, you know, I inherited me father's modesty & me

ma's good looks.
(Pause.)
For the rats, he used to say. Stock wired onto the barrel…
(Pause.)
A rat in the hand, she used to say…
(Pause.)
They couldn't've picked a better day for it. Very sparing
I was. I was a loving son, you know. Two shots was all.
Squealed like stuck pigs, they did. But you can't hold that
against 'em.
(Pause.)
Made a right mess of it. Mammy & Daddio pig.
(Pause.)
Had to crack their skulls with the butt to put 'em out of
their misery. <u>Thump, thump</u>.
(Pause.)
Eyes, popped right out of their heads, like they just
couldn't believe their luck!
(Pause.)
Nice to be appreciated once in a while…
(Pause.)
And the silence!
(Pause. Light gradually fades.)
Nurse?
(Pause.)
They'd've preferred it like that.
(Pause.)
Way you'd expect paradise to be, eh? Nice & quiet.
Only the sound of the fruit falling from the trees.
The sap rising. The snake in the grass. But quiet,
nonetheless.
(Pause.)
That's what they'd've wanted. No doubt about it.
After all that time. At long last.
(Pause.)
Peace & bloody quiet.
(Blackout.)

c. The Gifthorse

17

THE HAUNTED MERIDIAN

It all began long ago... 1650, the year the Harvard Corporation was founded, when Zhids were permitted to return to France & England — the year marking the birth of the European café, when a woman called Ann Greene was hanged for infanticide in Edinburgh & woke up on an autopsy table — the year, too, when to commemorate the Habsburgs' victory over Königsmark's squareheads, thereby precipitating the Treaty of Westphalia & the end of the Thirty-Years War, mariolater Ferdinand III [a.k.a. Ferdi-de-Turdy] ordained a 16½ metre Column be erected on the east side of Altstädterring, facing the clocktower beneath which the pariah Jan Mydlář, since grown old (14 years still left in him, though, not the sickly melancholy type at all), shortened the necks of the Boho aristocracy. Atop said Column, a likeness in all but immodest respects of the Blessèd Virgin (fact-checked by our own in-house photojournalist in an Orwell MkII Timemachine,[*] kids, as seen in *National Geographic*): her noontide shade decreed to mark, & for two-&-a-half centuries hence, the Golem City Meridian

---

[*] Patents pending. [✥]

socalled, Mitteleuropa's Greenwich Mean: all timepieces synchronise!

Until, that is, one cold November evening of 1918, a week after the Declaration of Cheskoslovnikian Independence (as the father of the Oedipus Complex once said, *The first requisite of civilisation is that of justice*), anticipating from a safe distance the final apotheosis of the Habsburg Empire soon to melt into air at the end of the Great War, a mob of patriots assembled by the old tramline at the foot of the Column, led by an anarchist crank who'd made his fortune smuggling sugar — one Franta Sauer a.k.a. František Kysela a.k.a. František Habán, loyal drinking partner of the Bolshevik, traitor & notorious bigamist, Jaroslav Hašek. Climbing onto the column's pediment, Franta S. denounced, to a bemused crowd that'd gathered around to watch, the Baroque grandiosity of this overblown sundial as a symbol, obscene as it was arcane, of three hundred cretinising years of Habsburg oppression of honest Sklavs.[*]

'I ASK YOU,' Franta S. screamed, 'WHAT'VE THE BLOODY KRAUTS EVER DONE FOR US?'

Hašek, erstwhile Rasputin & propagandist to the Š.V.E.J.K. — that pseudo-secret society of perennial jokers & contumacious pissants whose *non serviam* was a half-arsed spanner in the works, as heroic as a fart in a jar — egged the mob on from the sidelines. They'd rehearsed this bit in a Žižkov pub over pints of the local dishwater: on the agreed signal (being the flagrant display of Franta S's nude buttocks, belt unbuckled, britches down around bootstrapped ankles), in rush a brigade of patriotic fire-fighters (more Žižkov drinking pals in costumes borrowed from a theatrical props department) shouldering ladders, ropes & pulleys, "roused" (for the sake of a sympathetic public) to vent their righteous indignation at this flagrant Habsburgian triumphallus — *Truth will be Victorious!* — seizing the moment, their shouts drowning out the protestations of a distraught prelate who has somehow hazarded upon this scene of most unrepentant sacrilege (can't quite believe what his eyes & ears are telling him) —

'Yeehaa!'

Up rises the firemen's ladder, Franta S., bare-arsed, legs astride, riding it — above his head he's twirling a lasso, loops it ranchero-style up & over, rope hovering a moment like a tawdry halo before dropping down, down, around the Celestial Virgin's head, hijab & all, yanked tight. *Got the hussy!* The mob heaves, the top of the column inches eastwards at an angle (∡) to its base. Franta S., arms & legs akimbo, launches himself bodily from the end of the ladder at the

---

[*] → Chapter 47. [✋]

Christ-Mother's effigy —

'Geronimo!'

Grabbing handful of prime bub, he plants a sloppy kiss & —

'Yaahoo!'

Down they go, toppling into the crowd, screaming head-over-heels & buggered into bits.

Hašek meanwhile's stretched-out in a flowerbed, too plastered to stand anymore — the whole spectacle's gone to his head, like shooting that bearded pontificator back in Shitsville, Siberia, caught blessing machineguns for Kolchuk's Chesko-fucking-slovnik Legions (*those idiots*) — slurring a last *Ty vole*! before passing out. He'll get around to writing about it all tomorrow, what he can recall at least, pen a glowing obituary for the boys at *Rudé Právo — Just remember, Jesus Christ was innocent too!* — then shout himself a couple of rounds, bed Jarmila in the afternoon on that settee her father gave them, begrudgingly, as a dowry — get Shura to slap up some borscht — dabble for a while with his collection of imaginary animals — then off to the night's committee meeting at U Kalicha.

Meanwhile, still at the scene, whistles & bells as the cops finally make an appearance on the Square &, sure enough, no sign of the troublemakers anywhere now, like rats up a drainpipe, firemen, the lot — only the martyrised Franta S., postcoitally flat on his back, shattered bliss-filled eyes staring up, humming *Bluegrass on the Sázava River*.

The debacle of the Marian Column's not only made it onto the front page but into all the supplements too, & by the time Hašek hauls arse next evening to their regular wateringhole, he finds the Š.V.E.J.K. Central Committee's lost no time in his absence drafting, debating, approving & amending whole swathes of a Provisional Constitution for the Cheskoslovnikian Soviet Socialist Republic, declaration immanent & with immediate post-dated effect, at least as soon as conditions for full-blown Revolution have been achieved, etc., being only a matter of days now, perhaps even minutes & hours (no doubt about it, they're in a state of feverish expectation, downing pints at a rate of knots) — plotting the final overthrow of church, government & the spoken tongue, each ("Anarchist Bombthrowers," "Immoral Desecrators," "Contemptuous Rabble," & "Heroes of the National Revival" respectively), eyes already on the prize of one or other ministerial portfolio, hatching schemes for getting there before the next guy, anticipating future schisms, purges, showtrials — castles in the sky, all.

Hašek, in a major funk over spilt beer, rises at the head or *ipso facto* foot of the table, where he's managed with a few deft well-practiced manoeuvres to ensconce himself, pointing across at the quiet young man seated in the corner of their meeting room, been diligently taking notes the whole time (a blush-of-youth Klem Gottwald lookalike if ever there was) belching in forceful undertone —

'Can't you idiots recognise an undercover cop when you see one?'

God's Ear

Unbeknownst, a very different committee (in constitution if not in spirit) is at that very moment gathered in a crypt beneath Týn Cathedral: a weird cenacle of algebraists, industrialists & Opus Dei, to discuss contingency plans for a top secret radio broadcast station, codename T.E.S.L.A. — plan A having been nipped unceremoniously in the bud by yesterday's shenanigans. No-one present at the anarchist's daylight orgy of destruction had noticed the blue red black intestines of electrical wiring spilling from the entrails of the defiled Virgin, having been spirited away after the fact by three agents disguised as café waiters.

The Column — who would've guessed it? — was the intended relay station, the central receiver, the node & nexus of a giant antennae, linked by invisible soundwaves to a semicircle of tall spires in this city of thousands, ranged from Kepler's astronomical eyrie above the Klementinum to the belfries of St Jiljí & St Havel, all the way round to the old Powder Tower, like a giant tympanum, a transceivered ear to listen-in on the heavenly spheres, background radiation blips & — very *hushhush* this — extraterrestrials. Edison himself had material proof (all rights reserved) of alien broadcasts coming from Mars — Kepler, too, had foreseen it all, the *constellationibus coelestibus*, the *Geometriam* in the *radiis* as in the *vocibus*, that is to say, in *Musica…*

'We have the technology,' they told themselves, 'to do what none have dared do before! To set out by means of pure bandwidth upon the Great Unknown! This Last Frontier in telecommunications! To be the sole bearers of the Word to all corners of the Cosmos!'

At this dawn of a brave new Enlightenment, their bold enterprise has (or rather *had*) the imprimatur of prophesy made manifest, almost, very nearly — & now *this*! Fools! Imbeciles! Those Š.V.E.J.K. idiots've thrown the Big Dream into chaos, indemnities out the window, premiums through the roof, Monopoly Money stuff, right at the very moment, so close, no hope of recouping their investment now the whole thing's gone bellyup.

The Time Keepers

But as Kepler could've told them, every binary implies a ternary (most emblematical of numerates, Holy Trin., Geometry of All) & so — though unsuspected by the former two, quasi-Marxists & neo-Hegelians[*] (yet well appraised of both) — a third committee is also presently in session. Chaired by the formerly Royal, now Republican, Keeper of the Clocks, this is the "Ancient" (est. 1348) Society for the Maintenance of Universal Time (S.M.U.T.). The headache confronting the eminent gentlemen of S.M.U.T. is of a much less speculative nature: for as the situation has arisen, so must it be resolved, by the immediate *reinstatement* of the Golem City Meridian. Older members of the Society — luddite rosicruces! — have feared (& periodically continue to do so) that Time itself might even *come to a stop* if the Š.V.E.J.K. were permitted to succeed (as in fact they have) with their cutesy little slapstick machinations (discovered well in advance, of course, & to a greater or lesser extent colluded-in by the newly devolved "Interior Ministry," old habits dying hard) to forthwith demolish if not dematerialise the Marian Column (a.k.a. "The Dial") & so (to unspecified if not uncalculated effect) flood the City with untold quantities of Temporal Entropy. *We must pray, brothers, yes pray I tell you, for nothing short of a miracle!*

What countermeasures had been put in place proved — as so often has been the case in S.M.U.T.'s overly long history — both insufficient & ineffective when measured against a conspiracy of dunces & madmen. Unable to see the wood for the waxworks, it hasn't started to dawn yet that *someone*'s about to profit from all this, too busy worrying every available podium in town with their pedantic little fists. *No time to lose! NO TIME TO LOSE! Reinstate the Column NOW or PERISH!* On the other hand, apprehension over T.E.S.L.A.'s radio wave experiments has even got S.M.U.T.'s more circumspect members (socalled Abominationists) worrying their mustachios about some rumoured impending warp in Time's very fabric, should not these nightly occult transmissions be brought to a halt *at once* & *without delay* — such a warp being certain to expose everyone & every*thing* to what one eminent old member (a short-legged rotund chappy with a beard dewed around the mouth from constantly refreshed supplies of spittle) quaintly insists upon calling *aberrations* & which may be translated as "a hocus-pocused reverse induction of signals rumoured in the ionosphere, colliding & interfering, diminishing & amplifying, in constant oscillation since

---

[*] Notwithstanding. [☛]

the Dawn of Creation itself: spectral voices in the sky, perhaps even the original command — יְהִי אוֹר — capable of zapping us all back to some pre-Fall speleologism!" Fidgeting with infinity, in short: not for the lighthearted. They want the thing reinstated alright, but minus those little electrical gimcracks threaded through it. *Keep the Virgin pure!*

But all's well, as they say, that ends well, & waking bleary-eyed & hungover to the inevitable sun-up after endless rostrums, soapboxes, midnight committees & pre-dawn tub-thumping hysteria — with their entropy-meters ticking over the same as usual, & nothing more aberrant than the sight of themselves in the bathroom mirror — the gents of S.M.U.T. can breathe a collective sigh of relief. For the timely destruction of the Dial — in ways few of this most august club (were their minds capable of such a cogitation in the first place) would ever dare acknowledge, even to themselves — has turned out to be quite the godsend [...].*

The Biggest Clock in Town

Who construed all these infernal time machines?

God, if he'd blinked, might've missed everything — was it for His sake the bells rang, to be sure He wasn't sleeping? Meanwhile deep down under the flagstones, clay, basalt, the City's most ancient orloj, the Holocene Clock, dendrochronograph of Time Immemorial, ticked a little louder — rousing sleeper cells in the circulating currents of an evolutionary submind, from first paleocinematography to the sunset-at-midnight crepusculum of the Red Peril... Zodiacs of the ages, coursing & recoursing, the *migratio gentium* of Cro-Magnon to Celt to Kraut to Sklav — Závist oppidum to Marcomanni to Magna Germania — conjugating the great continental flux, from cavedwelling kin to folklored *Völkerwanderung,* Sklavenes to Sklavani, Sklavesians to Sklavenoi — all brewed back down into the primal stew, the sedimentary genepools percolating over into the stream of blood-consciousness, the mirthless meltingpot of war, flood, fire, plague...

All, all, all — to end here, among the martyrs & heretics, the real & metaphysic monuments to the Eternal Momentary, excommunicating the hours:

---

* Here the text breaks off. What might follow is a matter of pure speculation, all logical inferences not withstanding — a view which has been strenuously contested, but the details of this dispute have already been sufficiently recorded elsewhere (the reader is referred to Smutná & Hovno, *Heterochora Paradoxicum* (1919). [✥]

the procession of Father Death & his Apostates, the moon months, the pre-
Copernican universe on a dial — Rome a thousand years deceased & last Dark-
Age antipopes futurshocked as Šindel's mechanical astrolabe (scaled replica of
the Real Thing, the Proxy's proxy, Time in the abstract if not the abstract in
Time) becomes a proto-causality machine — dark, iridescent cogs, wheels, mills
producing timespace, quantum relativity weirdness disturbing the God-sleep,
celestial entropy, anachronic glitches in the very stuff of Creation: catastrophe if
the Clock failed, though not for lack of trying.[*]

---

[*] The Nazis shot it to pieces during the '45 uprising — it took three years to get it turning again.
Too late — by then, figured by the history book, the shadows had lengthened irreversibly & the
Time really had stopped. [✋]

18

ENCULER LES MOUCHES

According to these principles we may advance without temerity —

1st. That angels & demons have often appeared unto men, that souls separated from the body have often returned, & that both the one & the other may do the same thing again.

2nd. That the manner of these apparitions, & of these returns to earth, is perfectly unknown, & given up by God to the discussions & researches of mankind.

3rd. That there is some likelihood that these kinds of apparitions are not absolutely miraculous on the part of the good & evil angels, but that God allows them sometimes to take place, for reasons the knowledge of which is reserved to himself alone.

4th. That no certain rule on this point can be given, nor any demonstrative argument formed, for want of knowing perfectly the nature & extent of the power of the spiritual beings in question.

5th. That we should reason upon those apparitions which appear in dreams otherwise than upon those which appear when we are awake; differently also upon apparitions wearing solid bodies, speaking, walking, eating & drinking, & those which seem like a shade, or a nebulous & aërial body.

6th. Thus it would be rash to lay down principles, & raise uniform arguments, & all these things in common, every species of apparition demanding its own particular explanation...

Augustine Calmet, *Dissertations sur les apparitions des Anges, des Demons et des Esprits, etc., etc.* (1746)

In the half-light Němec almost failed to recognise him.

The Prof's ghost was sitting on the edge of the windowsill, fidgeting with the curtains. Flashback to a figure in the snow, somewhere that didn't exist — a *zone* on the other side of Reality, the cancellation of Time, the Gleichschaltung of Space. What was an optical illusion anyway? A flaccid premonition of the life-to-come? (Call it a breakdown in the integrated G.O.D.-circuit: the inframundo, the mega-cortex, the synapse nebula. A window in the meshwork opens & you stick your head through to see how the weather looks on the other side. Maybe when you pulled your head back in, everything will've changed, the world might've stopped. It's a risky business, messing with the control grids.) Who knew if the whole of Creation wasn't just papered-over with pictures to make things look the way they did & not some other way, blocking-out the image-flux like a Japanese waterfall on digital replay. The Cosmo-Synchronicity Machine. Possibly one day a circuit glitch, a code erased from the programme, would cause the whole System to reboot — & suddenly there you'd be, on the other side of the waterfall, in a stateless limbo, an anteroom, a threshold of thresholds...

Like now.

Staring at the shape of equivocation itself taking bodily form: the Old Man of the Mountain, windswept forehead as if he'd been out in the celestial elements contemplating the insignificance & misery of man, or simply the ends of his fingernails, supplicant of the Goddess of the Crossroads, banishing the image of the lost world from his mind, by degrees, by facets, spiralling in limbo till disburdened & sent off upon some transgallactic wormhole vector like a quasar in full flight. Outside, an airraid siren wailed in an indeterminate distance, like hundreds of others all across the City. The drone reached its crescendo & continued for a full minute, then began winding down, like a dynamo going flat. A relic of Cold War civic defence drills, death-from-the-sky paranoias. The street groaned, settling down for the slide into entropy, the abortive hours that followed midday like a shadow falling in a heap & slowly dragging itself back up again.

'Are you real?' Němec asked, unable to think of anything better, knowing it was a dumb question even before the words were out of his mouth.

Well, you'd have to be delusional to see a ghost in the first place, right kiddo? Or fire-up just enough fuse and ozone to produce a passable impression? To fool the eye?

'What does it matter,' the Prof said, 'as long as you *think* I'm real?'

Well, he had a valid point there. But could a man who was dead appear in his own body?[*] Or if not his *actual* body, a more approximate one? What did it matter, if it was there to be seen, or if it was just seen to be there? What was more real, the thing or the seeing of the thing?

Mmm, Němec took some time out to ponder that one. Conclusions?

----

[*] "Nequam hominis cadaver post mortem dæmone agente discurrere." [♣]

Mo_{st} of every^{thing} / in any case / = just H◯LES: no _{sub}stance, <u>if</u> _{sub}stance = e.g. a 10ft concrete wall (<u>then</u>) you could bang yr head against (it). Just a question of ♋.* A blackh●le could be ≤ the ● in the middle of your eye & fit stars & planets & whole galaxies inside, squashed down to the size of an ✳* — a micro-mini ‖ universe (on the spooky "other side") — & it'd be like that submarine in *Fantastic Voyage* & just pass ~~right~~ through you, skin & bones & brain (& don't forget the kidneys, too), the intestinal tract, the ● in the anus, shot out into the great toiletbowl of timespace & not even a blip on the x-ray monitor to show for it…

▛▞▞▞▟

The Prof gave Němec one of those abstracted looks you get when people are unable to decide if you're pulling a con or are just plain stupid — a variation on the "hairless Mexican" — like two images superimposed on glass & slightly out of sync, the way they'd be if you were trying, for example, to reconcile a man's head with a Klein bottle… *Well how d'you think they fit all them con-cepts in there?* Doctor Who stuff. But a concept wasn't the same class of bureaucratic phenomenon as a neutron star, there were civic ordinances against bending someone's head around a kink in timespace. Never know what might come out.

Watching the Prof's face change shape against the window turned Němec crosseyed like some revenant Duchamp, *to be looked at from the other side of the glass (with one eye, close to, for almost an hour).* What did the ghost want? What did any ghost want? Appearing out of nowhere, a message from the Great Primeval, perturbed spirits haunting the night & all that — but suddenly everything's wrong because *you're* part of the future & whatever the ghost puts in an appearance everything around you looks different: reality gets desynchronised, time-out-of-joint, like you've just been zapped to *Planet X* where all the inhabitants have been turned into robots obeying the commands of an artificial intelligence called G.O.D.[2] & only ghosts are free to come & go as they please, being of the spirit &, mutatis mutandis, of the flesh also but *contrariwise…*

▛▞▞▞▟

---

* "Scale[s]." [☟]
* "Atom," you ignoramuses. [☟]

Yep. Light's on, kiddo, but you sure anyone's home?

Němec fidgeted with his bottom lip. The Prof's ghost, meanwhile, perched there looking at him, as patient as a man with all the time in the world. The idea of conducting a conversation with something that, strictly speaking, wasn't really there, wasn't even a *thing*, & in the full awareness of what he was doing, struck Němec as… Well, he'd done stupider things. Better just to play dumb, he decided, & see how the situation pans out. Keep his cards close to his chest & pull out the aces when the time's right. Stay cool. Let the ghost make the first move…

The ghost grinned —

'All around,' he said, reading Němec's thoughts apparently (a most subtle vapour), 'are things the naked eye can't see yet they exist. Can't see yer own mind, now, can you? Time? Bacteria? Once upon, people'd think you were nuts just to suggest such a thing. Gravity? Electrons? Hell, *electrons*? Hoowee! X-ray visions of naked bodies, you might as well say. Call it what you like, Invisible Man stuff, but the universe is *full* of ghosts.'

Němec pictured a man in a room conversing with his own thoughts, given shape, corporeality, naming them (Thought 1, Thought 2, Thought 3…) like the Earth's first administrator, Adam in his copse, *This little worm of an idea I baptiseth…* Becoming quite philosophical about it all as he gets down to the minutiae, not a grain of sand unturned, not a louse, crab or ringworm, all no sooner Christened than emphatically more "real," a word with some meat on it, living & breathing so to speak. *And now, if from the fact alone that I can draw from my thought the idea of a thing…*

Němec ogled the shape in the window. His mind, meanwhile (invisible as it was) had gone blank. He felt suddenly exhausted. *World's full of ghosts? Mmm, just wait till news gets out about that one! Spectres from other worlds weaving the wind like draughts of air, or light printed onto celluloid, or birds in flight over endless tundra. For by mine eye I do not know what I see!*

And how about androids? Did *they* turn to ghosts when *they* "died" (or were retired, or expired, or whatever)? And if they *did*, did the other androids *believe* in them, those ghosts? And if they didn't believe, if they refused, egged on by their God of Reason, did the poor ghosts wither & die? Was that what was wrong with the world — they'd all been duped into conniving in the murder of their own ghosts? Still, Němec couldn't see the crime in that. Why get all sentimental about the old smoke? No shortage of doom on the horizon. Ghosts aplenty…

'Did you find out the answer to your book?' Němec said, trying to manoeuvre things in the right direction.

'What book?'

'That Voynich book…'

'*Ach*, you can't expect me to be worried about that anymore. It's your problem now. Can't take it with you, you know.'

'…'

'…'

'By the way, d'you happen to remember someone called Faktor?'

'Never heard of him,' the ghost said.

'He's heard of you.'

'Don't believe it. Who ever heard of me?'

'…'

'…'

'My fingernails stopped growing. D'you think it means something?'

'It's just because you chew them in your sleep,' the ghost frowned. 'My wife used to do the same thing. Couldn't stop. Psychotherapists, hypnosis, you name it. She was ashamed for anyone to look at her hands, what she did to them, *ja*, but still couldn't make herself give it up. Like cigarettes. Hardest thing to kick, they say. You could explain a lot from that, *nicht wahr*? Look at Veenston Churchill — you think History'd be the same without those cigars of his? My mother, God rest, used to smoke while she was in bed, just like that Mae West in the movies — it was very unusual for a woman to smoke in those days, *even* in bed. More than once she set herself on fire, but refused to change her ways. They said it was diphtheria that took her in the end…'

As long as Němec had known him, the Prof had always had the look of one of those Social Credit types who keep a soapbox under their beds in case of emergency, ever-ready to split hairs or crank-out a lecture at a moment's notice. The ills of the world & all that. Man's betterment. Brotherhood of the Carpet Slipper, the Bowtie & Eightply Knitted Cardigan. But death had worked a wondrous transformation, like an alter ego suddenly given free rein. Besides, it was hardly fair to begrudge a deadman his favourite cardigan. All that said, did the Prof think he was doing anyone any favours turning up like this & nothing useful to say for himself? Or was it somehow incumbent on Němec to do the Old Man's talking for him? Bring the ghost up-to-date with his "investigations"?

Let him in on the score?

'Ghost, it's not going as well as we'd hoped.'

'Hoped? Speak for yourself, mein kleiner Freund. It was a lost cause before it even started. Believe me, I've seen it all with my own eyes…'

But the ghost had stopped talking & began to whistle quietly to himself, something from Mahler. Why Mahler? He seemed to be waiting for Němec to say something. Němec took a stab in the dark —

'Does God exist?'

'Beats the hell out of me. You think they give you all the answers just because you ran out of time down here without figuring it out for yourself? Not a chance. D'you remember what Karl Rahner used to say?'

Němec shook his head. Who was Karl Rahner? Evidently the Old Man still had some wisdom to impart.

'He said the world, & humanity with it, *is the possibility of becoming the material history of God.*'

The Prof's ghost waved his hand at the world outside the window —

'Which is a fancy way of saying there aren't any real mysteries, just *unknowables.* Like the missing part of a paradox,' he grinned widely. 'But let's not complicate matters more than they already are.'

Well you could have all the explanations of reality you liked — & after reality expired? In this life, what was easier than being an alien in the midst of conformity? You begin to doubt the *explanations* & they send people to check up on you, teleported right through your TV set — schedule you for a bit of the old rehab — *Not having politically suspect thoughts are we, sunshine?* They find out you're conversing with random ghosts — oh, boy. *Zap, crackle, pop!* Cure you fast. You learn to choose the available options, just tick the box beside the number — there's plenty to pick from — an apple for every eye.[*]

<hr>

[*] Been the same story since Eve, or Lilith, or Pandora, or whatever you wanted to call her — "Hope," maybe — the well-greased pipedream that keeps you queuing up for more — *an avatar for every pain* — tuned-in to the TV-evangelised *Confessions of a Love Doll.* Be careful what you wish for. *A woman spurned, kiddo, it ain't a pretty sight.* Could androids have souls? Some hidden biotic component that could evolve into the ether & do without them, fly the microelectric coop & become alpha waves on the cosmic neural bandwidth, the way a mudman dreams of becoming extraterrestrial dust? The visible & the invisible? But how could you tell you weren't already one of *them…*? [♦]

'D'you know the story of Odysseus & the Horse?'

The gloom was making his head hurt. Němec edged up from his armchair & regarded the ghost doubtfully —

'What horse?'

'Mister Ed, what d'you think?'

'Oh, right, the wooden one. Trojans & all that…'

'Not a wooden horse, a *machine*, giving birth to men.'

'…?'

'Things aren't always what they seem.'

The Prof's eyes appeared unbalanced. They glowed. The gloom grew more oppressive. Němec could taste metal, the muscles in his jaw were knotting up. He lurched out of his chair —

'Don't move,' he said & stumbled to the kitchen.

The bottle with Volta's pills was sitting by the sink. Němec shook out a handful & swallowed them, gulping from the tap. The label on the bottle was smudged with type. Under the apothecary's caduceus, a blue-inked scrawl read *max. 3 per 24 hrs*. Němec spilled out some more for good measure & washed them down with some of Blecha's bootleg slivovice. *What the hell. None of this is real, anyway. It's all just a figment of your fucked-up mind. These pills, this headache, nah, they don't exist…*

The ghost was still in the same place when Němec got back, peering down at the street from between the curtains.

'Quite a drop,' the Prof mused, then turned to Němec with a look of solicitous concern. 'Not feeling well?'

Without taking his eyes off the ghost, Němec groped for the armchair & slumped down into it. The back of his neck began to go numb. He gripped the armrest, keeping his head balanced. Seismic shivers coursed through him. The Prof's ghost blurred at the edges. Then the shivering subsided. The ghost still had that solicitous expression on its face. Němec felt his hands go limp. His whole body acquired a certain *plasticity*. He was suddenly aware that every thought, every movement, every twitch of the eye, expended time. *But time doesn't exist*, he thought. *Hehe, trapped in the old vicious circle again, eh kiddo?* Němec blinked himself out of it, tried to focus on the ghost. It was there for a reason, he told himself, but *what* reason? Was it part of him, or was he part of it? Or were they both part of something other, someone else's dream perhaps?

'Let me ask you something,' Němec said.

'Ask away.'

'To be absolutely candid…'

'*Ja?*'

'How do you…?'

'*Jaaa?*'

'Being a ghost & all that…'

'*Eh?*'

'I mean, what's it like?'

'What's what like?'

'Being dead.'

'*Wer weiß?*' the Prof exclaimed. 'What d'you think I am? Some sort of encyclopaedia? Take a look at me. Tell me what you see. Just a plain old ghost! Nothing less, nothing more. What should I know about being dead? Things is just how they are.'

'What do you *mean* you're just a ghost?'

'Don't worry about it,' the Prof said. 'Better not to confuse what your *eyes* tell you with big ideas about what's *real* & what *isn't*. Some things you see, some things you don't. That's all. Like crossing the road, *nein?* Whether or not you see something, *mnnn*, doesn't mean you know what it *is* or even what it *isn't*. Take us. We see each other, but all we are is nothing but probabilities. Strange as it sounds, the world needs no reason to exist. It simply does. And us in it. Believe what you like: God & the Great Unseen — dialektische Vernunft — Peter Pan — you think it makes a difference?' the Prof shrugged. 'People find reasons to kill each other no matter what they believe. The world will end. Others possibly will begin, thankfully without us. As for the rest…?'

Maybe the Prof expected Němec to be thinking the big thoughts, too, but his not thinking them didn't seem to bother the ghost in the least. Němec wanted to say that all this talk about probabilities didn't answer anything, but the ghost looked content enough to just sit there grinning with that superior awareness of his that was giving nothing away. He couldn't recall the Prof being so easily amused when he was alive — there must've been something mighty funny about being dead.

Němec looked at the ghost & the ghost looked back at him like it expected any moment now for the penny to drop & Němec was the clever boy the penny was going to drop on. But all Němec could think about was maybe the pills weren't such a good idea after all… *Ja ja*, he heard the Prof's voice in his head, *but there aren't any pills, they don't exist, even you don't exist, the "you" that's thinking this, because in reality you're asleep or dead or an android with its switches being toggled and this's all just a product of the Great Unconscious, richtig, the Cosmic Continuum, the Programme?*

Maybe he was soft in the head, pills or no pills. The thought appeared to please the ghost, who seemed anchored to the windowledge & otherwise unmoved, doing a passable impression of the Cheshire Cat now. *Well, that's a start at least, kiddo. Now you see you're getting somewhere. Everything's relative after all. Like some great big plotless book someone stuck you in. Everything from the tiniest bit of nothing to the wholest of everything. From atom to Everest. From a piece of DNA to the D of Doomsday. From the Big Bang to the Last Laugh. Think you're nuts? Well who isn't, eh? Try and figure that one out.*

The ghost, meanwhile, simply played with the grin on his face & fiddled with the curtains, giving Němec all the time in the world to ponder. Grey sunlight filtered through… It occurred to him that the Prof really did look much better as a ghost than he had in the flesh, much less weighed down. Němec pressed my hands to his temples & closed his eyes — it was all too much, his mind raced but without any thoughts in it, the dizziness & white lights returned & then, gradually, passed. One type of illness battling against another. He focused on breathing, slowly & evenly, the way they tell you to. He stared at the floor. The grain in the parquet stood out with unusual intensity, swelled, receded. Even when everything had gone back to normal the blood still pulsed in his head. *Get a fucking grip on yourself.*

'Mmmm,' the ghost said, causing Němec to look up, 'as a wise man once said, *The road to understanding is long and arduous*, etc. *To know the question is to arrive at the destination.* All things being equal, I wish you the best of luck.'

With that, the ghost vanished. His words hung in the air for a moment afterwards & then also were gone. Němec felt cheated somehow. As though the Prof's visitation & all he'd said or not said were part of some game, designed to point him along the wrong path, disguised as its opposite. What'd the ghost actually told him? Which move was he expected to make?

Němec stared at the empty space where the ghost had been sitting. Everything about the window, except for where the Prof had been looking out between the curtains, was exactly the way it'd been before. How could a ghost move a curtain aside? But then Němec saw the gauze had merely slipped away from the latch where previously it'd been caught — so perhaps the ghost was really nothing after all. Best, Němec decided, to keep the explanations as simple as possible.

As the Bugman would've said, no use haggling for proof after the deal's already been & gone. *Can't go puttin' conditions on givin' up the ghost. It's one or the other, that's just the way it is, kiddo…*

⫟

The room grew dim & then grew light, like a movie theatre does when the film's ended. Midday ticked by. Now, the sense that a larger circle was closing, that once again something was playing itself out — Fate's hand — ever since that first meeting in the Klementinum courtyard, the game of chess, Mahler's symphony, the house with the Tower, the Manuscript, Kircher's letter, the Prof dead in his bathtub, the notice in the bookshop window, the blankness & then, the ghostly visitation, the Ward, screams in the basement, the undead janitor's mop & pail, Volta's mind-mesmerations, Faktor's costume cloak & dagger routine…

Němec imagined a seam made of knots that keep coming undone: the way you find a loose thread hanging from somewhere & without thinking, as if by a reflex programmed deep down, you go to pull it, snap it off, & the whole invisible substance immediately starts to unravel, winding back on itself… And in all of this, which particular loose thread did he have in mind? On the floor lay the script he'd dug out from the typewriter case the evening before — a laughing automaton built of words — a joke you could choke to death on, murder a child with, deny the world — but what had the good doctor said about jokes? Němec couldn't remember. The fog in his head refused to part & when finally it did, nothing was any clearer, just one blank vista in place of another.

Joke's on you, kiddo.

⫟

Bored with his part, Němec got up & switched on a light: another day on the instalment plan productively well-spent. Well, the Powers-that-Be could send him the bill & he'd promise to weep for joy. *Pile-on the interest, fellas!* They knew where to find him, if they ever wanted to be thanked in person… He looked down at the sheaf of typescript beside the armchair. Hadn't he set out to tell the truth? He drew the chair over to the coffee table where the typewriter sat, spreading the script out on his knees. The Prof's presence still hovering somewhere in the room, it felt. Fiction & history, *sacramentum et res.* Were these clues? Dull-eyed he read back over the last pages. *They'd've preferred it like that.* The ending wasn't right, or was it?

241

Němec took a used sheet of paper & wound it into the typewriter backwards. It couldn't hurt, there could always be two endings. Or more. As many endings as necessary, as many endings as the story required. But it wasn't *his* story he'd been trying to write. Always others. The indirect approach…

```
It wasn't me. I didn't do it. Two knocks on the door. The
men in coats. He meanwhile in the bog with pants at half-
mast -- she in the kitchen, peeling onions, tears in her
eyes not from crying. Tap. So quiet at first. Knife
against the cutting board. Did she hear it, too?
Scampering into the hall. Tap. No! And all I wanted was to
show how terribly bloody clever I was knowing how to
turn the lock & unlatch the door. And there they were.
Brown coats. One tall, one short, fat. Moustaches. The tall
one smiling, patted my head, 'Not here all alone, I hope?
Where's Tatimami, eh? There's a good little chap...'
```

Němec pushed the typewriter aside, tried to blank it all out, to laugh, like he imagined Christ laughing, the mouth of a man with the teeth of a lion. *Why're you doing this to yourself?* But the images, once summoned, wouldn't go away. Death by a thousand different names, survival by one. Perhaps they'd simply disappeared, made themselves forget about him, emigrated on a forged visa. '83? '84? But that was just a stupid fantasy. For all he knew they'd been shot in the head & dumped in the Šárka reservoir. *Mamitati!* Faceless, hands tied bloody with piano wire, kneeling in a ditch somewhere — clothes mucked with filth — bodies misshapen from the weeks, months, of unsleep in isolation cells, sodium lamps, rubber hoses, shin splints, electrodes, wet pillowcases, tape-delayed gibberish & false confessions —

```
What's your name? That isn't your name. That's not your
real name. What's your name? Can't you remember what your
name is? Your name's X. Your name isn't Y. Did you say
your name was Y? It's Z. Who's X? Why did you say your
name was X? You're lying. There is no X. Y confessed to
everything. We know all about Y. Stop pretending you
don't know Y. X is your real name. Z is the codename you
used to contact enemy agents. They betrayed you. Z
betrayed you. X is your enemy. Your real name is Y. Here's
your confession, you signed it weeks ago, don't you
remember...?
```

— ending with a bullet to the base of the skull. Or locked-away in a nut house, Němec thought, some place east of Košice & never let out, some Viktor Faktor type running the show — disappeared, mind-zapped, insulin-injected, lobotomised, programmed into non-existence. Or they'd never really existed in the first place — (alternative version) Father: UNKNOWN, Mother: DECEASED DURING CHILDBIRTH — identities falsified in a secret police file, to swell the ranks of ghosts condemned for crimes against The System — the eternally guilty underclass, like fairytale characters to scare children with, orphans immaculately conceived by the grey golem, stamped with the mark of the Original Sin. Or it was nothing, not even a conspiracy, merely a joke invented by a bored bureaucrat — something to while away the long hours of indigestion between breakfast & lunch on some particularly grey rainy mid-October day in a cubicle office on Bartolomějská Street...

Němec stared out the window at nothing, trying to be numb, forehead pressed to the glass, repeating & repeating to himself the first line of a limerick that wouldn't play out.

> *There once was a young man from Pra-ha-ha...*
> *Who died. Laughing. And good luck to him.*

He slipped down onto the floor & lay there, listening to the voices drift up from the street. The Prof's ghost like a palpable absurdity, come to tell him what? A ghost, like a cracked mirror. There're times when you see yourself & times when you can't, or when you see someone else in your place. A stranger. An adversary. Someone points an accusing finger. *What've I done?* The other, he, grins at you, winks, nods, all the gestures of complicity. No-one's interested in confessions, they already know the score. Guilty, from beginning to end. Awaiting the fall of the axe. You lie there naked with the whole world looking on & not noticing, not seeing even this uncouth spectacle right in front of them. Like robots. And still you want to know what humanity looked like, under its skin.

Naked, kiddo. Ugly naked. Funniest, ugliest thing you can imagine.

In the halfdark, spread out on the floor staring at the square of blue neon painted up there on the ceiling — it seemed as if it'd been years since he'd been able to think clearly, in his own body, so to speak. Lying there composing himself. Arms & legs *like dismantled drain pipes*, while up above, the blue square on the ceiling like a door onto some higher mystical plane, with a sign flashing above it, only he couldn't read what it said. If this was a scene in a Paul Wegener film, he'd be the dismantled golem in the mad Rabbi's workshop, limbs rearranged by unseen hands, fused & welded into a monstrous parody — & that door into the ceiling, opening inch-by-inch, to reveal… What? The Resurrection & the Light? The God of Machines reaching down to fidget with the control settings. Something clawing at the gut, perhaps thermostatic pangs of morbidity, *hehe*.

In a while, Němec decided, when he felt better, maybe he'd wander down to the Chink's & buy some dry bread & a jar of pickles, always good for a cure. Meantime he dragged himself up from the floor & drifted into the kitchenette, a cracked handmirror in a plastic frame hanging from a nail in the wall above the sink giving him the evil eye.

Can't keep it together for even one day?

Němec stood perspiring in front of the sink, still in his hospital rags, tap running — stared at himself — dark halfmoons under the eyes, a cracked lopsided mouth, strands of unwashed hair plastering the sides of his head, fissure- & fracture-lines where the hair didn't grow anymore. It'd been weeks since he'd shaved — no-one had forced him to, left more or less to fend for himself, like Crusoe in the sea-girt limbo of the Convalescents' Ward, pills daily at the dispensary, bedsheets weekly, labcoat blurring past each Wednesday morning nurse in tow scanning the clipboards — a pair of orderlies to pull the blinds, untie the straps, prop-up the beds, freshen-up the saline cocktails, parse the catheters, finger the cold stools in the bedpans, re-torsion the traction devices, adjust the fibrillators, stick pins in the feet of paraplegics.

Němec found some soap & a plastic-handled safety-razor under the sink. It was slow work, the razor blunt even before he began, blood colouring the scum-sudsed water — working slowly upwards from chin to cheekbones, but why stop there? He hacked away with all the dull-witted patience of a hangover till by increments the white skull emerged like the large elongated bulb of the squill — birthmarked, a reddish five-pointed blotch, shaped like an infant's outspread hand, staining the top of his forehead, a pink scar now bisected it…

Hello, remember me?

He soaked a towel in hot water & wiped the soap & hair away, then pealed his rags off, piece by piece, soiled & damp with sweat (the sum of his worldly possessions in that department), & regarded the alien body that presented itself in place of his own reflection — that broken & reformed shambles of a self. Němec was that thing. It was he, too, who'd authored it. Both that golem & its creator. *Glory unto thee.* He scrubbed the stinking wreck till all his skin burned, then took the razor & shaved off everything that was left, scraping away the dead cell-structure, never so naked since the unremembered day he'd been dragged kicking & screaming from that bloodied hole into the alien atmosphere — the breathable air stinging every inch of him, till the nerves dulled, cauterised, sealed-over by an invisible membrane, cocoon, that eventually smothers you without you ever knowing it's there…

The Bugman's suit was where Němec had left it in its newspaper wrapping. Unfamiliar trousers, shirt, jacket — *If the shoe fits…* — strange against the raw flesh — like a newborn undertaker, red-eyed, hands postnatally soft, the disfigured forcepsed skull, but fullgrown, shaped & moulded for the task of burying himself. He thought of Blecha — the Bugman had been there that night, when it happened. Cleaned up the mess afterwards. With his disappointed eyes, spitting into the snow, rubbing his hands to keep warm, blood frozen to his boots. Afterwards, he'd've come back up here & locked the window, switched off the lights, thinking maybe about life's little ironies, like a caretaker in a cinema after everyone's departed, so to speak.

Němec couldn't help thinking of the joke Blecha had told him when he'd first found his way up to the old guy's eyrie, getting the lay of the land, sussing out the situation, sizing up the Bugman in his legionnaire's cap & surplus anorak for the hard sell. The old guy'd been peeling an orange with his fingernails, offered his new tenant half of it — an awkward kid, as he still was then, in handmedowns with head too big for his shoulders, quiet type, not what usually came in off the streets, standing there broom-in-hand. Němec had done what he'd been told, swept out the apartment, swept the hallways & stairs as well. The orange, he remembered, had tasted bitter, but who was he to complain in a situation like that? The old guy told him to pull up a chair. And while Němec'd sat there silently eating the orange with one hand, while still clutching the broom in the other, Blecha had started in on this long story, about a political prisoner from Teplice he'd shared a cell with once, at Jáchymov — had some sort of vitamin deficiency made his skin go a kind of reddish-yellow colour, which this political turned into a gag, kind of disarm anyone before they had a chance to taunt the shit out of him.

It went like this:

The Joke

Man walks into a village pub, pulls up a stool at the bar, waits for the barman to serve him. Half-a-minute goes by. Man looks down at the other end of the bar — there's the barman chatting away to a group of blondes straight out of a magazine, no bother on him. Thing is, the barman's head is like an orange — shape, colour, *like an orange*. Man can't help staring. It's about now the barman stops chatting with the girls & glances over. Man immediately looks down at his hands, fidgets, embarrassed-like. Next thing the barman's standing right across the counter from him, coughs. Man glances up. Barman says —

'Couldn't help noticing you starin' at me.'

'Oh no, no,' man says. 'I wasn't staring.'

'Yes you were,' says the barman.

'Alright,' says the man. 'So what. I only came in here for a pint. Don't want no trouble.'

'That's okay,' barman says, 'I understand. You were wonderin' about my head, weren't you?'

'Minding me own business, I was,' man says. 'It's just a pint I'm after.'

'Come on, no need to be embarrassed about it,' says the barman, 'you wanted to know why I've got a head like an orange.'

'Jesus,' says the man. 'If you insist. Go on. What about it? I was a little bit curious, that's all. I just came in for a bleedin' pint.'

'Well that's alright then,' says the barman. 'Would you like me to tell you?'

'Can't a man be left to mind his own business no more?' edging back from the bar by now, thinking perhaps he ought to make a dash for the door.

'It's okay, really,' says the barman. 'I'm not blamin' you, it's an entirely natural response. I'll tell you about it if you like.'

'If it'll make you happy,' man says, gaze half-averted, '& if you, you know, don't mind 'n' all.'

'No,' says the barman. 'Not at all. I don't mind tellin' you one little bit.'

''Cos I just wanted a pint. Minding my own business,' man says.

'That's what I like about you,' the barman grins.

'Eh?' the man starts getting all nervous again.

'Well what'll it be, then?' asks the barman.

'Um, Black-'n'-Tan,' man says.

Barman takes a glass from the shelf, holds it under one of the taps, then under another.

'Here you go then,' says the barman, setting a pint of half-'n'-half down on a coaster in from of your man.

'Cheers,' man says.

'You're welcome,' says the barman. 'Anythin' else I can get you? Crisps? Peanuts? Pretzels?'

'No thanks,' man says, 'just the pint.'

'Fine,' says the barman. 'All settled then?'

'Ready when you are,' man says.

'Good,' says the barman. 'Now it's like this,' he says, lowering his voice, getting all confidential-like, resting his elbows on the bar so he's leaning close to your man, whose curiosity, it has to be admitted, has by now got the better of him. 'One day,' says the barman, 'I was walkin' down a lane, just outside the village, when I heard a chirpin' sound comin' from the hedge. I stopped & listened & there was the chirpin' sound again. I went to the hedge to see what it was. And there, trapped in a hole in the hedge, was a little blue bird. I'd never seen quite such a bird before, sky blue with a purple beak. It turned its head sideways to look at me with its little black eye, plaintive-like, so I reached in & untangled its foot which was caught in a vine, & off it flew. Up & around it went, little blue wings flapping, & then it came down & landed on my shoulder. Right here,' says the barman, tapping his right shoulder, where a dirty dishtowel hung. 'Then the bird started to talk. It was a magic bird, you see. It said, "I'm a magic bird. An evil witch cast a spell that trapped me in that hedge, but now that you've broken the spell & set me free, I shall grant you three wishes." "Three wishes?" I says. "Yep," says the magic bird. "Let me think. Okay, first things first, I'd like to be rich & own me own pub." "Done!" says the magic bird."'

Man gives barman a sceptical look.

'It's true,' says the barman. 'This's my pub. I'm the owner. Everythin' you see here belongs to me. King of all I survey! It's just I love being behind the bar, you know how it is. Always have. Gettin' to know all the regulars, the local community, a sense of camaraderie, the generally festive atmosphere, life's little dramas, the odd bit of melancholia, a good punch-up once in a while.'

'Okay, okay,' man at the bar says, shaking his head. 'So what was your second wish, then?'

'That was easy,' says the barman. 'My second wish was to be irresistibly attractive to members of the fairer sex.'

Man gives him an even more sceptical look —

'Now you really are pulling my leg.'

'Nope,' says the barman, jerking his thumb at the far end of the bar.

The magazine cut-out blondes were all still there, sipping their cocktails, five of them, eyelashes at halfmast under the weight of too much mascara, lips pouting, eyes for old citrushead here only.

'That's just for starters,' the barman winks. 'Come back after six. Place'll be full of 'em. *Ladies Night, Every Night* — that's our slogan. The lads get to drink at the back lounge, front bar's reserved.'

'Okay,' man says. 'Get on with it. What was your third wish, eh?'

Barman blinks —

'To have a head like an orange, of course.'

19

ALL THE MISCREANTS OF MELODRAMA

From behind a onesided game of checkers laid out on the shop counter, the old Chink barked orders at a couple of dull-eyed coolies in earsplitting pidgin. The coolies rushed about the aisles balancing hessian sacks & tin cans & looking generally harassed. Němec told the Chink *good morning* & not getting any reply handed over a wad of meal tickets, courtesy of the Invalid Plan, waiting to see if the Chink'd cash them or not. The Chink scrutinised him through yellowed eyes, running a Braille-reader's fingers over the slips of paper as if to divine what quality of fake he was dealing with — sniffed them, held them one at a time up to his right ear & listened, then snapped the wad under a black light & shuffled them around.

'You want take cash? Twenty percent. Credit good.'

Němec negotiated down to fifteen percent & added a jug of ersatz whisky for Blecha & for himself a packet of carbonised Arabica from the Sierra Maestra. The coffee came in a yellow packet that showed a Cuban with a sack of coffee beans on his back working the endless Five Year Plan of their till-recently Comrades-in-Arms. A vision of paradise — the whole world turned to one enormous collectivised plantation. *God bless Khrushchev.*

The Chink screamed in pidgin to one of the coolies who scampered up a ladder to get the whisky down from the top shelf, where they kept only the best stuff obviously. The jug had about an inch of black dust clinging to it. The Chink screamed some more & the coolie went to work polishing it with a rag, then split open the coffee packet & dumped its contents in an antique mill. While the coolie sweated at the handcrank grinding beans, Němec scanned across the day's headlines on the news rack. Nothing much seemed to be going on anywhere. There was a story about ancient lizard eggs in the Gobi desert, but that was about it.

The Chink coughed to get his attention. The coolie had vanished, Němec's purchase sitting in a plastic bag on the counter, a fortune cookie thrown in gratis. The Chink pushed a stack of crumpled notes across the zinctop with the tip of an overgrown fingernail. He leered at Němec —

'Confucius say, *Man too much reading no see mosquito on tip of own nose.* You gonna buy or just looking all day?'

The fortune cookie was stale, but then they always were, no mystery in that. Stuck inside was a slip of white paper with oriental characters printed in red, an accompanying translation for the uninitiated, *A bird is entangled by its feet, a man by his tongue.* Beneath the witticism was *Lucky Number 8.* Němec stuffed the slip of rice paper with the remainder of the cookie in his jacket pocket & slouched back down to the intersection. Instead of crossing it, he stood there leaning on his stick surveying the fourth floor corner window of the building opposite, a black rectangle cut into a wall of grey. Just another cave in the endless escarpment. Prehistoric rivers had weathered away at the canyons since time immemorial, dead now, a black slurry of tarmac & busted cobblestones. And the sky, like a grey reflection of it all, veined & marbled, weighted with eternal optimism.

Maybe in the back of Němec's mind he expected to see somebody up there, watching him. A ghost maybe. A child's puppet-face. A bit of poignant confectionery out of a haunted past. But there was nothing. The windows looked all the same, grimed with decades of unwash. Moulded in the crumbling stucco beneath them was a collection of gargoyles, rictus-mouthed, eyeholes drawn into a picture of exaggerated woe, sprouting from the façade with the unconvincing hilarity of a clown's deathmask *All the miscreants of melodrama, accursed, damned and fatally marked with a smirk that runs from ear to ear.* Fume-streaked, randomly punched-through with gas heating vents, the gargoyles ogled the world blindly, as they'd continue to do till the façades crumbled away entirely.

Down below on the pavement, a man in a felt hat was walking his dog. It was a mottled brown dachshund with grizzled ears. The dachshund paused, hind-leg cocked, gaze forlorn, snout aimed back up at its master — *pissant gardant* — sniffed — jerked forward on a length of chain, resuming its laughable dog-trot. There was nothing else to see. No human stain, no stigmatum. Standing where he was, Němec felt nothing, only the residual ache of a body that would always remind but never quite remember, dulled by anticipation of all the rheumatoid winters yet to come.

Once inside, Němec took the elevator up to Blecha's private bower on the top floor. The elevator was a small, boxlike affair, with old First Republic wood panelling. A mirror whose silvering had tarnished & bubbled, making reflections warp & dissolve, gave the illusion you could've fit more than one person with the door shut. The whole thing reeked of machine oil & rat bait, but at least it didn't stink of piss like every other half-wrecked tenement on the street. The Bugman kept a clean house.

The old guy was getting ready to sit down for lunch when Němec rang the bell. Blecha stood in the doorway, giving Němec a going over with those old grey eyes of his while he stood under the light in the hallway, secondhand suit, sockless in a pair of dull black shoes, nominally white shirt with the collar folded wrong & a black tie knotted to one side. The Bugman reached up & straightened it.

'Better,' he said appraisingly, 'but you stand still too long, maybe a pigeon'll make love to that egg or yours, *hehe*. Come in.'

Němec stepped inside. The door wheezed shut behind him on one of those pneumatic arms they have in offices designed never to work properly.

'Wait here,' Blecha said, waiving an index finger, 'I've got something might just do the trick.'

He disappeared among the clutter of his bower & returned a few minutes later, clutching a bowler hat in one hand & beating the dust out of it with the other —

'Try that on for size.'

'I'm supposed to be Charlie Chaplin, or what?'

'You can be Neville Chamberlain for all I care, still be an improvement over that Humpty Head routine you've got going.'

Němec shrugged & put the hat on — it fit, just as the old guy knew it would. Němec gave his walkingstick a twirl for effect.

'At least this way you won't get pigeon crap on that dome of yours.'

Well if ever the money got tough, Němec thought, he could always go down to the Square in clown-face & do mime routines for the tourist trade. The hat would come in handy for collecting change.

'Is that whiskey I see?'

Wordlessly, Němec extracted the blue jug from his shopping bag & handed it over. Blecha read the label.

'Hill's Finest. Jindřichův Hradec. Only the best, eh?'

Němec made a Marcel Marceau face indicating heights of unattainable ecstasy, then stuffed the bag, with the coffee still in it, into his jacket pocket.

'Well,' Blecha grinned, 'you only die once, at least that's what they say. There's ice in the fridge. While you're at it, bring some glasses out to the roof with you.'

The Bugman's eyrie was a series of small rooms cobbled together from tarpaper, breezeblock & clapboard that'd been gradually added to over the years, evolving by accumulation like a baroque midden heap, rising up through the rafters to colonise the flat expanse of rooftop. Blecha believed religiously in discarding nothing. *One man's rubbish*, he'd wink, *is another man's property.* On every wall were pasted bits of repurposed junk — scavenged FOR LET signs, restaurant menus, railroad timetables, hardware pricelists, Town Hall notices, newspaper crossword puzzles, TV magazine quizzes (*How many birthdays does the average Honza celebrate in the course of one lifetime?*), random bank statements, theatre schedules, redbluegreen application forms, renewal forms, evaluation forms, census forms, civic complaint forms, library cards, Christmas cards, calling cards, life insurance brochures, recipes for borscht in French, Romanian & Russian, phonetic tables, pronunciation keys (*ay, bay, say, day, uh, eff, geh*), homeopathy & acupuncture diagrams, multiple choice questionnaires about anything & everything, a periodic table of elements, a lingerie catalogue, lists of mathematical equations, conversion keys from metric to imperial & back again, postage stamps, architectural blueprints, pages from dictionaries, colour charts, eye charts, instructions for whitewashing plaster walls, tax return notices, TV & radio programme guides, stockmarket indexes, random sheet music (Mozart's *Requiem*, Orff's *Carmina Burana*), magazine covers (*National Geographic*, September 1950: "Flying in the 'Blowtorch' Era," "Sea to Lakes on the St. Lawrence," "'Delmarva,' Gift to the Sea," "Mapping the Unknown Universe," SIXTYFOUR PAGES OF ILLUSTRATION IN COLOUR), calendars, tide tables (Rapallo, Ravenna, Rimini), tables of contents torn from books, a sign-language chart, semaphores, flags of the world, a nineteenth-century atlas, a dozen Supraphon LPs, concert flyers (Plaster Poodles of the Univerb, Stubborn

Lesbiens, Velvet U-Bahn Revival), assorted other desiderata… You could've earned a degree just reading the Bugman's wallpaper.

Up a set of creaking stairs was the "terrace," on one side overlooking the courtyard & the intersection on the other. The old guy led Němec to where a table & a couple of red&yellow striped deckchairs were set up, with potted dwarf palms & a lush carpet of astroturf overlaying the tarpaper. A stray chicken pecked at the fringes. Blecha must've just finished cooking breakfast: slices of stale knedlík toasted on a primus stove over the open-flame & dipped in egg. A charred piece of dumpling still clung to the end of a pair of kitchen tongs splayed open on the table.

'Care for a bite?'

Němec set a couple of opaque jars & a plastic icecube mould down on the table. The Bugman was already ensconced in one of the deckchairs.

'You really eat that stuff?'

'Bloody oath I do.'

Němec shrugged, cracked some ice into the jars & doused them with Hill's Finest. Right then, the sun peered out from behind the grey. Němec handed Blecha his drink then eased down into the vacant deckchair & stretched his stiff body out, letting the sun's tepid rays wash over him. With his newly inherited bowler tipped back on his head he looked like an insurance clerk of the old school taking his lunch from a bottle.

'Na zdraví!' Blecha said, raising his jar. 'Here's to the capitalist revolution. Long may it profit.'

He laughed hoarsely, coughed, spat a thick gob of phlegm ledgewise, carried on a sudden gust. Wetted a thick Sklavic lower lip with his blotchy tongue. Snorted. Then upended his drink.

'Ježíš!' he recoiled theatrically. 'This'd put hair on the palms of a Cossack! *Arroooooo!*' he howled, wolfmanish. 'Cossacks go home! *Hehe.*'

The chicken stopped pecking & ogled its owner in alarm, *bgörk*ed, swivelled its head around to the other side, *bgörk*ed again, then planted its beak back in the astroturf. Němec took a taste of the whiskey, sucking it through his teeth. It was no worse than you'd expect from a distillery in Jindřichův Hradec. No better, either. Frowning, he held the jar up to the light. Suspended in the shimmering amber, Němec couldn't help but notice there were flies in the icecubes. Wings outspread & black dots for eyes, like specimens that might've been chipped from some Pliocene glacier.

'How'd you get flies in your ice, Blecha?'

'Just lucky I guess…'

The Bugman grinned, crunching an icecube between stumps of teeth that showed all the evidence of forty years of Soviet dentistry. The whisky had taken the dullness out of his grey pallor & put a bit of rosiness in his cheeks, like a tired old clown on the rebound from one of life's pratfalls. He crunched some more ice, chewed, looked thoughtful, winked sidewise at Němec for good effect.

'Your common fly,' he said, picking a stray hair from between his teeth, 'evolved millions of years before the dinosaurs did. And look where that got *it*. Now there's something for the eggheads to ponder, eh?'

> *There once was a boy called Beneš*
> *who could bullshit with quite some finesse.*
> *He'd sweeten his mama*
> *with all sorts of palaver,*
> *but still couldn't get under her dress.*

For the rest of the morning they sat there drinking & soaking up the haze, Golem City spread-out at their feet like a giant dirty bathmat. The Bugman's mood turned pensive —

'Nice to sit out here & just let your mind wander, don't you think? Reminds me of my grandma's garden, before the War. Except for the apple trees. She lived in Petřiny. From the top of the garden you could see over the rooftops all the way to Šárka. The neighbours kept a pig in a shed. They'd fatten it all year for Masopust & then hang the carcass over the shed door. Played music day & night till the whole carcass was gone — cut up & made into sausages, chops, cutlets, jellied tripe. You could smell it all the way along the street.'

'It seems higher up here than I remember it being.'

Blecha poured them both another drink.

'When I was in the War,' he said, settling back into his deckchair, 'we had to make a parachute jump near Munich. It was night, you couldn't tell how far away the ground was. I was only seventeen then. And you know what I was thinking? When we were kids, there was a game we played. You'd be blindfolded & lifted up on a chair, as high as possible. The ones lifting stood on either side of the chair & you were supposed to rest your hands on their shoulders, to keep balance. As the chair got up above their heads, you'd have to reach down to still be able to touch 'em. Then they'd tell you to jump. But when you jumped, the ground was right under your feet. It was all a trick.'

'Yeah, we used to play that game in the Home. Only there wasn't any trick. They really made it as high as possible.'

Blecha sipped his whisky.

'Don't let it bother you,' he said, staring off into the distance.

Němec sucked an icecube, keeping the vertigo at bay. His efforts were arrested by Blecha pointing off to the east at a red speck growing out of the horizon, weaving above the rooftops.

'D'you see what I see?'

The highpitched whine of an engine came & went with the breeze. The speck disappeared against the sun. They both squinted.

'What is it?' Němec said.

The red speck drifted back into view, getting bigger. All of a sudden an antique biplane with black Tatzenkreuz on red&white checkerboard wings careened across the sky — dipped — skimmed the treeline over Riegrův Park — then circled back around the spires of St Ludmila.

It was coming straight at them.

They both hit the deck at the same time as the plane buzzed overhead, so close they could see the clown in the cockpit, done-up like a WWI flying ace with shiteating grin under waxed mustachios, flipping them the bird. The chicken squawked, nosediving among the pumpkins.

'Cocksuckingsonofabitch!' Blecha screamed.

As the plane rounded the dome of the Natural History Museum & dipped out of sight, a confetti of white leaflets fluttered after it — little squares of paper, falling through the air like snow, all across the terrace. Němec plucked a sodden leaflet from his drink:

Sudety byly, jsou a budou NĚMECKÉ!
Jen Janov ČESKÝ!

Ubytovny azylantů hoří, není čas se rozmejšlet teď
musíme rychle jednat, setnout pěsti a jít vpřed. Utok,
teď nastal pravý čas ukázat tu sílu, co je v nás…[*]

---

[*] "Turn back the clocks" (more or less). [☙]

Signed, *D.S.S.* Some crazy Sudetendeutsch fascist nuts, he figured. He brushed more of them from the brim of his hat. White paper littered the Astroturf like alien dandruff. Blecha, on his knees looking stunned, held up another, peered closely & read —

'*The Sudetenland is, was and always will be Kraut*! Who're they trying to kid?'

'Where's Janov?'

'Who gives a shit,' Blecha groaned, pulling himself back onto his deckchair, shirtfront stained with spilt whisky.

'Nice of them to let us keep it.'

'Sure,' Blecha said. 'Nicest people on Earth, the Krauts.' He spread his arms expansively at the City. 'Look at everything they did for us.'

Němec stared at the distance into which the plane had vanished. The chicken pecked at a leaflet, looked thoughtful for a moment, then stalked across the astroturf & pecked at another one. Chuckling quietly to himself, the Bugman eased himself back down onto his chair.

'I tell you what,' he said, 'you see that lunatic heading back this way, give me a shout. There's a three-o-three inside, tries any more of that Red Baron crap…'

Němec gave the old guy a sceptical look.

'Joke's on us, kiddo. Should never've kicked the damn Krauts out in the first place. Look what we got left with. A lot of socalled patriots with their fingers up Moscow's arse.'

'What about Lidice? Why should we give anything back?'

'*Ja, richtig*, my Little Pioneer. That's what they drummed into you at school, I suppose? Only good Kraut's a dead Kraut? Well I served the King of England, too, & did my bit. But it wasn't as simple as those Commie teachers maybe wanted you to believe. In those days, after the War, Pokorný's mob, all Bolshybazook vengeance-drunk, they didn't bother to discriminate. No, that's not right. They went out of their way *not* to discriminate. I met plenty socalled *collaborators*. In the camps. Sure some of 'em were Nazis, alright. But a lot of 'em just happened to be Zhids, Social Democrats, trade unionists, returned POWs, ex-legionnaires. People like me, who'd gone West. That's who the real enemy was! The Commies wanted rid of the whole lot — anyone who wouldn't swallow the Party line. Later they got rid of their own, the True Believers, who realised too late they'd been screwed by Stalin's empire men.'

The Bugman took a deep breath & cleared his throat. He finished the drink he had & poured another, then passed the jug over. Hill's Finest. *Well it sure beat a kick in the arse.* Němec stared at it for a while, thinking, then poured a measure for himself & set it back on the table. The Bugman tore off a strip of grilled dumpling & chewed, head tilted back, gazing at the sky in a vaguely wondering sense of expectancy, as if to say *what next?* The chicken made plaintive sounds, scratching at the crumbs around the legs of Blecha's deckchair.

'Stalin's boys wanted the Krauts out alright,' he drawled, 'no questions asked. You had a Kraut name — *raus!* You spoke Kraut, looked Kraut, some informer said you were Kraut — *raus!* Didn't matter who you were, they wanted everyone. The *final solution to the Kraut Problem,* Beneš called it. Think of it this way, the Nazis? they really did win — they made the whole country just like them, little Gestapos hungry to obey our new Russian masters.'

The Bugman spat on the ground. Němec stared morosely into his drink, thinking what an idiot you'd have to be to debate politics with the Bugman. He listened for the drone of the biplane's engine, half-hoping the crazy old bastard would give it the music, imaging the headlines in tomorrow's paper:

Geriatric Gunman Blasts Bosch!

In Vinohrady yesterday, a vintage Fokker biplane was shot down by a disgruntled local WWII veteran and former political prisoner in an incident police have described as "out of the ordinary." According to eyewitnesses, the pilot of the aeroplane emerged unscathed after crashing into a Sokol gymnasium…*

Blecha's voice interrupted the newsspiel —

'Those teachers of yours say how many Sudetens died in '46?'

Němec scratched at his neck, plucked another leaflet from his collar & turned it over idly between his fingers. It was the same as the others. He shook his head.

'Nah,' he said, crumpling the paper into a small pellet which he flicked over the roof ledge, 'just how it was all in the cause of righteousness.'

'No joke. A quarter-million, some say. The historians, I mean. Not ours, of course, but all the others. I read about it. Pokorný's thugs staged pogroms all over the country, pretending like they were an angry mob of righteous townsfolk, only the townsfolk knew they were outsiders come to stir up trouble. Pogroms, just like with the Zhids, justified & legalised by that witless Beneš &

---

* Read "certified nutcase." [✋]

his eighty-something decrees. They drove around in trucks, like Henlein's thugs before Munich, spreading the Fear. *Ein Volk, ein Reich, ein Führer!* Only now it was for the sake of the greater Sklavic socialist brotherhood. *Heil Stalin!* Švejks the lot of 'em. They'd turn up in a village with no warning & start smashing windows, burning families out of their homes, throwing mothers with prams into rivers, dragging men off to the same concentration camps the Nazis built. Whole districts rounded-up on death marches. Ústí. Brno. Even here, in our own fine Golem City, thousands of women & kids herded into Strahov Stadium, beaten & raped by Cossacks.'

 'I wouldn't've picked you as the sympathetic type.'

 'You don't know what I had to go through. It gives you a perspective.'

 The Bugman eyeballed him to make sure he wasn't missing his point —

 'Don't get me wrong, the Nazis were the ultimate scum of the universe, but not every Sudeter was in Himmler's pocket. Plenty of our own socalled patriots jumped on the thousand-year bandwagon themselves & managed to forget all about it quick smart soon as the wind started changing direction. After the War a lot of those quote-unquote *partisans* had plenty on their consciences. The whole of Slovnikia was a fascist puppetstate. So whenever they found a Kraut these born-again nation-lovers would string 'em upsidedown from a lamppost & set 'em on fire, to prove what side they were on. Call it the Big National Idea. Krauts were all officially vermin, anyways, just like the Zhids before. And how many of those Zhids did our zealous patriots obligingly collaborate in sending off to Terezín, Buchenwald & Auschwitz? Well, these loyal comrade-brothers didn't forget the Zhids, either, *hehe*. Once the Krauts got the boot, the Zhids had their turn again. *What goes around keeps going around.* Slánský's boys first, the big showtrial, then the rest, quietly, in the neck, all *hush-hush*.'

There was a young gigolo called Švejk
who was always out on the make.
He could hustle a whore
or screw through a door,
but his dick turned out to be fake.

Němec sat there with a vague empty feeling where only a moment ago had been warmed by the whisky. Blecha went on —

 'If we'd've stood our ground at Munich, despite the Frogs & Rosbifs selling us out — if there'd been a general mobilisation — we'd at least've kept some selfrespect.'

'Yeah,' Němec said despite himself, gulping down half the whiskey left in his jar, '& the Nazis would only've bombed this whole stinking town back to the stone age...'

'What if they did? You think a picture postcard's worth being a slave for?'

'Like people always say how they'd die for their country, so why not just suck Nazi cock instead, they love the place so goddamn much?'

'That's real class you've got, kiddo. Real class.'

Němec downed the rest of his drink & reached for the jug.

'Let me tell you something,' Blecha raised both eyebrows so they almost disappeared under his legionnaire's cap. 'When those cunts invited themselves over to protect us from our own stupidity, half their fucking convoys broke down before they even got past the border. Took five fucking hours for that *Blitzkrieg* circus of theirs to get a hundred miles on paved roads.'

The Bugman pushed an empty jar across the table for Němec to refill also.

'They reckon when that fat bastard Göring took a look at our defences in '38, he said they made the Maginot Line look like a pissoir in a brothel. We gave 'em a free practice run. How to screw the Western Powers in one easy stroke. But what the hell, the fucking Frogs deserved it. Maybe we were just a pitiful backwater, *hehe*, but before those idiots sold us up the river at Munich, our little army was the best equipped in the whole of fucking Europe, *hehe*, with the most advanced armaments factories in the fucking western world, *hehe*.'

Blecha slapped the arm of his chair, the grin on his face decidedly sickly.

'Our little gift to Adolf Hitler,' he continued. 'Only fair, eh? What d'you reckon? So fucking advanced that not a shot got fired. The averages don't get better than that, eh? Fucked right in the hole & made to look like a pack of fairies, for all the stinking lowlife world to see. Maybe it's what we deserved. That's what all those brass knobs in the Elysée were saying. What was it — ten million Frogs were supposed to brave death for the sake of a nation hardly anyone even knew the name of? Some crap like that. Well, they had their turn soon enough — French leave in the Riviera & all that.'

He tipped the entire contents of his jar down his throat with a gesture full of contempt. The jar came down on the table with a bang that caused the chicken to flap its useless wings in panic. Blecha pointed emphatically with his index finger, which Němec interpreted as meaning he should pour the old guy some more. He filled the jar halfway. *That'll slow him down*, he thought. Blecha took the jar, sighed, sipped calmly, cleared his throat —

'Bottom line is, it was us had to stomach what we saw in the mirror, after we signed it all away, not some parlezvous-spouting mongrel stinking of Eau-de-Vichy. It was *our* fight. How many people got it in the neck because we didn't? You wanna know something? Our boys who went west & flew with a very fucking reluctant RAF, ranked among the top fighter pilots of the War. Kuttelwascher, František, Vašátko, Peřina, Mansfield, Stehlík. Battle of Britain & all the rest. If they'd lost that one, it would've *all* been over, & none of the finks in this town should ever be allowed to forget it. Without 'em... Without all of *us*... Well, Klem fucking Gottwald took care of that. But don't ever say we couldn't've put up a square fight. The shame is we never did it in our own country.'

'So like the blushing virgin raped behind an arras, it's *we're* to blame?' Němec said. 'That's harsh, Blecha.'

The Bugman stared with a dull ironic fury in his eye.

'Curse of the Š.V.E.J.K., kiddo. As that old queer Palacký might've said — the Nazis hadn't come along, we'd've had to invent them.'

He gulped some whisky & belched —

'Every nation needs an alibi, kiddo. But figure this. Those busy little card-carrying Bolsheviks in our factories back in '39? With their Non-Aggression Pact & Moscow communiqués? Who d'you reckon were the best paid stooges in all Europe right when it counted? Now I bet they didn't teach you that in school, either. We may humbly thank Comrade Ribbentrop for our Workers' Paradise. It's important,' Blecha wiped his chin & chuckled, 'for a man to know his worth.'

20

TRÄUMEREI

It must've been only six o'clock when the sound of someone banging on a drainpipe woke him. The banging interrupted a dream which afterwards Němec couldn't remember having. It (the banging) had come from one of the babičkas who lived in the building — widows of communism for the most part, sending their Morse code up & down the pipes in the airshaft, which thudded & clanged like broken piston rods. It was one of those late, grey, spring mornings, the kind that make you think of promises dangling just out of reach. A vague recollection of something. Pipes banging. Greyness.

He'd seen the old biddy through the grubby kitchenette window, leaning into the airshaft in a soiled nightdress. She'd been just about to bring a meat tenderiser into perilous contact with the rusted metal piping when she caught sight of him peering at her through bloodshot eyes. This sudden apparition of Němec must've startled the poor old thing. With a highpitched shriek she dropped the tenderiser & disappeared inside. The shriek echoed & died just as the tenderiser struck one of the metal bins at the bottom of the shaft...

'Hell,' Němec muttered, slamming the window.

His reflection caught him unawares, squinting from slit eyes, a real picture. He stuck his head in the sink, splashed some rusty tapwater about. Dripped into his socks. There was still a quarter of Blecha's moonshine left in the bottle — he took a healthy swig of it: start the day on the right foot, give him the strength of mind to face the world at large, if not himself, blah blah blah. Dried his face with a dishrag & checked the reflection to see how he brushed up. Still a bit puffy round the eyes & pasty Humptydumkopf they'd somehow stuck back together again (& no bones about it). Did he forget to say "thank you"? *Well here's thank you, arseholes.* The question, as Volta might've said, *is which's the Master, that's all...* Meaning: *nothing's ever free, kiddo.*

'Shit, Němec, you're such a fucking humanitarian this morning!'

The old biddy who'd been banging on the drainpipe had an unusual name. Supposed to be an Amerikaner. Rohrer or something. The Bugman'd told him her story. Her pops, a sergeant in US Army Intel, West Berlin, defected back in the '60s.[*] She was just a kid at the time, spitting image of that Shirley Temple with the hair & big eyes. Commies couldn't get her in front of a camera fast enough — her entire childhood was one big propaganda stunt, to show the world what a happy-go-lucky place the Cheskoslovník Socialist Republic really was. Paradise on Earth. Ever since the Revolution (so Blecha said) she'd been living in fear of the State Department or whoever sending out the goonsquad to do a bodysnatch job on her. Didn't stop her always complaining the boiler didn't work, though. She & the other biddies banged away on the pipes at six o'clock every morning for their hot water. Then they banged when they wanted their post brought up. Or their lightbulbs changed. Or to gossip about the weather. If it weren't for the banging, you'd never know there was anyone else in the building.

Němec stumbled out to the bathroom for a shit & shave then dragged on his clothes & went out. It was 7:00 by the time he made it downstairs, light filtering through boarded-up windows, the building as lifeless, apparently, as a cadaver. A desultory kind of traffic stirred the air out on the street. He waited at the intersection, a red man, upright & motionless, hovering in the shadow of the traffic lights. The red man turned green. Němec blinked, the banging on the drainpipes replayed in his head, some sort of message being communicated, the Giver of Laws animating the little homunculi. The green man was replaced again by the red man as Němec limped out onto the pedestrian crossing. A car swerved, sounding its horn. In the shade of a doorway across the street, a cigar store Indian followed Němec's progress with wooden eyes. A couple of dozen steps further, past the abandoned shell of a Trabant jacked-up on bricks, to the sanctuary of the Chink tobacconist's: fine purveyors of the marginally expired newspaper, counterfeit whisky & assorted thirdworld produce. The embargo of ersatz.

The Chink was busy raving at one of the coolies in the storeroom. Němec, bleary-eyed, deciphered the day's headlines on the news rack. He picked out one of the scandal rags. *Blesk.* A story on page two caught his attention, opposite a fullpage colour spread of a blonde in a wet swimsuit, called Lenka apparently. Lenka looked like she'd been drowned in fake tan. *Blame it on the weather,* Němec thought. He turned to the story:

---

[*] Sgt Glen Roy Rohrer, a.k.a. Jan Vesely, a.k.a. Jan Vedra, defected 1965, a polygraph clerk built-up by the Commie's to be some high-ranking US intelligence officer. The StB even ghost-wrote a book under his name. God only know's who the fuck they thought they were kidding. But unlike Rohrer, God don't exist. [♣]

Return of Rudý Baron!

There it was in inch-high serif. The ace had landed his biplane on Wenceslas Square causing minor traffic chaos & giving the lunch crowd a free show. The whole thing turned out to be a publicity stunt for some flying circus from Větrník. *It's an ill wind, kiddo, that don't bring someone a profit.* Maybe the Bugman'd get a kick out of the story — things like that didn't happen every day of the week. He could stick it up on his wall.

Němec's thoughts were interrupted by the sound of tinned cans crashing to the floor followed by a flow of Cantonese invective. He tossed some change on the counter & retreated with the paper stuffed under his arm just in time to hear the coolie give an earsplitting scream.

From the grocers on the corner he bought a couple of rolls & a block of cream cheese, which he ate standing on the curb with the paper unfolded on the roof of the gutted Trabi. He scanned the paper while he ate. What passed for news was mostly the same recycled crap they printed every other week, just with the names swapped around. The main story was about three *estébáci* on trial for crimes committed under the former régime. (Why those three & not a hundred-thousand others? Secret agents everywhere — agents of mindfuck paranoias, agents of entropy.) The piece about the Red Baron was pure gold in comparison.

Back at the apartment building he took the elevator up to the roof & found the Bugman sweeping his terrace with a broom.

'Hat suits you,' the Bugman said when he looked up at Němec coming through the doorway. 'Keep it.'

Němec showed the headline to him & he shrugged —

'Who cares. They write about it, may as well never've happened.'

He stood leaning on the broom & looking out over the rooftops like a boatswain on a ship casting forlorn eyes towards Tahiti.

'Know what I was thinking just now before you came up? All the people I hung around with when I was your age are dead & gone already. The War, the camps, boiler rooms, collapsed livers, angina, the disillusioned senility of old age. You beat one thing, it's the next, or maybe the one after that. Bad luck to be the last to go… Maybe that Red Baron was meant to be a sign. Want a drink?'

Němec waved away the offer, squinting up at the clouds. The weather wasn't going anywhere fast. He dropped the paper beside the primus stove & limped back across the terrace, knee still creaky at that hour of the day. Behind him he could hear the old guy scuffing the Astroturf with the toe of his boot.

'When I die,' Blecha said, letting out a sigh, 'I want to be buried up here.'
Němec watched him set to work again with his broom —
'Can't bury you on a roof, old man.'
'*Ty vole.* My ashes! Scattered to the four winds.'

Gulag Blues

The way the Bugman told it, when he was barely fifteen his father & mother
hanged themselves in a barn outside Znojmo, before the Gestapo could get their
leather mitts on them. Left to fend for himself, he travelled south through the
Ostmark, clinging to the undercarriage of a coal train, then across the Alps into
Bella Italia. He made it all the way to Genoa before being picked up by the
Carabinieri & interned in a camp for illegal aliens. The camp was a shambles.
Within a week he'd escaped & managed to stow away on a freighter bound for
Marseille. Eventually he found his way to Portugal & from there to
Cholmonderley where they enlisted him in a parachute regiment.

The War dragged on. Spring 1945 he was part of a forward group that
reached Plzeň just ahead of Patton's 3rd Army. And then the allied advance
ground to a halt. Sat there twiddling thumbs while the Yanks swilled pilsner &
the Reds pounded Schörner's Army Group Centre into final oblivion, Golem City
less than an hour away, left for the taking. Three years on, Blecha was arrested &
sent to the uranium mine in Jáchymov as a "Western agent," & later transferred
with a group of other politicals to a Karelian gulag. The mines were full of ex-
soldiers, Sudetens, priests, intellectuals, kulaks, boy scouts even. Drilling, hauling,
working the ore crushers. Sixteen-hour shifts. Nights bleeding into days into
nights. Counting, recounting, over & over, in a ritual of negation. Down in the
caves. In the blast radius. Sucking in acid-bath fumes. Shovelling slurry into tanks.
Tuberculosis wards. Cellblock mafias. Guard towers. Barbed wire. Caught once
pacing the perimeter fence, two weeks solitary eating lice, cockroaches. Earned his
moniker. Staring & staring at a crack in the wall. Perhaps, Němec thought, when
you stare long enough a crack in the wall is just like a mirror — the familiarity of
its contours — hieroglyphs of memory, of self, of salvation — a lifeline.[*]

---

[*] Without such adversaries, what did *he*, Němec, have but borrowed talk & figments to keep hold
of? The Prof's ghost, Faktor's grandiose conspiracy, Volta's psychocivilised pie-in-the-sky — &
somewhere, in the middle of it all, the Prof's folly, the Voynich Manuscript? [✋]

Blackhole Metaphysics

Accustomed as Němec had become to the hospital's unerring routine, the outside world felt wrong, now that he was cut adrift in it again. The way the apartment sounded at night was wrong — the way the air tasted was wrong — even the colour of the walls was wrong. He counted the pills that were left from Volta's prescription. Today was the day for his weekly consultation. In a few hours he'd be sitting in Volta's office waiting for it to be over & then afterwards spend the rest of the week waiting for it to happen all over again. This pills he had this time were blue, before that they'd been white. He couldn't remember what these ones were supposed to do, reduce anxiety or something. They made him feel vaguely constipated. Perhaps that was the point.

After a pot of char-roast Sierra Maestra which failed to produce any bowel movement, Němec set out to tour the old familiar territory, walkingstick & hat attracting looks from the bums who worked the klobasa stands, bin-hoking for empty bottles they could sell back for new ones, sifting the piles of rotten fruit & veg for something not completely inedible, giving him the eye as if maybe he was trying to move in on their patch. He'd never seen so many well-dressed bums. *Sign of the times.* Stay away four months & everything changes. He couldn't believe it'd been so long. Some crap about keeping him under observation, whatever that was supposed to mean considering he could've walked out whenever he liked & who'd've noticed, except the nurse who took pleasure beating the shit out of him three times a week? Whatshername, Peklá (or Pěkná, maybe). All in the cause of turning his shambles of a self back into a properly useless member of society. Or maybe they thought he'd just go straight out & do it again & cost them all a lot more unnecessary effort?

'The second attempt,' is what Volta had said, in that Vincent Price monotone of his, signing the discharge papers, 'always happens just when you think they've made it through.'

Well, Němec thought, if they'd pegged him as a nutcase, why hadn't they sent him straight to Section 16 up on Kateřinská the moment the casts came off? "Convalescents," as he'd learned, was strictly for losers, the ones who couldn't be expected to wipe their own arses if someone wasn't there to do it for them: gave you a shot of stelazine in the morning & a fistful of bellaspon at night, a tight smile & a fist in the crotch, to encourage you with those little adjustments in temperament that'd see you get well again. He'd fitted right in. But in the end a man has to make his own way in the world, or so they said. It was news to

Němec. When he was a kid, all they'd ever said was do what you're told. *Sure, you make your own way in the world, just like that…*

So on this grey spring morning with nothing on the agenda but a visit to the Doc's, Němec decided the best thing was probably to go & see a film, just like old times. At least in films, people got to be force-fed in style, *hehe*. It meant for an hour or so he wouldn't have to watch the shitty cinema going on in the street or the horrorshow in his head. Like stepping into a blackhole, maybe spend a couple of thousand years in there & come back out & it's only morning tea time & still a chance of catching the midday matinee.

So thinking, Němec wandered up past *The Lost Flounder* to the Květen Bioskop on Vinohradská. Something about the place's name seemed to brighten the day all by itself, he could almost smell the popcorn & warm farts of an audience well entertained. Only, the Květen Bioskop wasn't there anymore. All that was left of it was an old programme thumbtacked behind a glass display with a poster for some poxy Miloš Forman film. A sign nailed to the doors proclaimed the address **CLOSED FOR RENOVATION** like it was in two minds about it. *Is but isn't.* The sign bore an estate agent's logo: T.E.S.L.A. REALITY. *Wasn't it just.*

Němec stared at the whitewashed marquee where the big names used to hang over the entrance, trying to make something out of it. What used to be the box-office had been turned into a kiosk, grilled windows cluttered with tabloid newspapers, porno magazines, lottery coupons & cheap romance novelettes. The kiosk walls were festooned with random flyers, xeroxed on colour paper. Among them someone had pasted a snippet from the *Berliner Zeitung*, its incongruous headline running like a subtitle beneath a chatline advert showing a naked blonde whose eyes, mouth, breasts, hands & genitalia had all been blacked-out with random bits of Morse code, dots & dashes, like an Educational Aid fill-the-blanks puzzle or a multiple crime-scene photograph calculated to withhold the evidence but still leave nothing to the imagination. The headline read:

Deep Blue Demütigt Kasparow

Der Schachweltmeister unterliegt überraschend dem computer…

'Well,' Němec sighed, 'as if anyone needed proof the androids really were in control of things, & not just some chessplaying dwarf hidden inside a mirrored box, pulling strings…"*

His gaze drifted across the rows of VHS cassettes stacked behind the counter, titles like *The Satyricon, Brut de Brut (Champagne & Caviar), The Epizzles of Pasiphaë, Perverse Extreme vol. 8, Faustwerk, Last Year in Marianne's Bed, Solitary Confinement 2: The Sequel, The Perils of Magdalena, Arseholes to the Castle, Zombie Sex Orgy, The Wolf in Little Red Riding Hood, Himmler over Berlin, The Whipping Post, Siege of the Stalingrad Sisters, Lot's Daughters, Amerikan Pie (Strengstens Verboten!), Signor Dildo's Untimely Revenge, The Persuasions of John Birch, Handballers from Sieg Heil, Gulliver's Travails, Mysteries of Bordo, Tarzana & Jan (Fumble in the Jungle), Kafka Sutra, The Fill of the House of Gusher, Buttman: Dark Nights, Forbidden Sushi, Nazi Shewolf Helga, Trojan IV: Stealth Intruder, Attila the Hung, Velvet & Cigarettes: Softcore Revolution, Kasia does the Kremlin, Dungeon Divkas of Doom, The Lash of Cnut, Deviance Protocol 77, What Colour was Žižka's Eye?, Black Riders on a Pink Tank, Inside the Iron Maiden, Who's that Knockin' on my Back Door?, The Ecstasy of Maria Teresa, Backwoods Golem, The Punishment of Honza, Ride to Freedom: Girls of '89…*

Depressed, Němec rode the number 11 tram back down the hill to the Natural History Museum, then walked the underpass with its reek of fried klobása, stale piss & vomit. There was the usual collection of junkies asleep under the hedges of the museum gardens, pickpockets loitering inside the Metro entrance, touts, hawkers & earlybird hookers plying the Square. He had the impression they'd all been put there for his benefit, like extras in a film, to make the scene look more authentic (like the hospital janitor, busted radio channelling static, shortcircuiting the remote logic systems): the expression on the face of St Václav's horse — the string vests of the taxi drivers — the burgundy polyester suits of the businessmen taking the rest of the day off for an eleven o'clock lunch — the mannequins in shop windows, mismatched bodies & painted eyes, standing in their underwear like they had nothing better to do.

All the benches out in the Square were taken up by winos & old ladies in coats getting some sun. It was warm if you could keep out of the shade. A council worker in blue overalls was watering the flowerbeds with a garden hose, spraying a fine mist that caught the sunlight & made tiny rainbows appear. Every couple of steps someone was hawking something: a Jehovah's Witness in brown stockings & black shoes & knitted hat selling daffodils, nasturtiums — a pair of clean-cut types in white shirts & ties, with little black name-badges, stood

---

* Androids, dwarfs, what fiendish conspiracy would they cook up next? [✋]

munching hamburgers — while only a couple of metres away, a cripple kneeling on a trestleboard shook a tin cup at passersby.

Němec took in the scene. After a while the cripple stuffed his tin cup into a satchel bag slung crossways over one shoulder & pushed himself off, trestles clattering. People stood out of his way. For lack of anything better to do, Němec followed the cripple halfway down the Square — a man in a black suit & bowler hat limping after a man paddling over the cobbles with bare hands. Eventually Němec lost sight of him behind the entrance to the Metro. A moment later, glancing furtively about, the cripple re-emerged with the trestle slung under one arm & jogged down the steps. Němec limped to the head of the stairs & stared down into the crowded vestibule.

In such a way have men borne witness to miracles.

Sturm & Drang

And it was then that Němec remembered what he'd been dreaming before the banging on the drainpipe woke him up. It'd really been nothing more than a rush of images, rapidly juxtaposed, fleeting. A dream, at least, could be represented, but a cascade of images was just a cascade of images. As Volta might've said, it lent itself to no summarisation, no paraphrase. Němec puzzled over it, thinking back to the night before, after the whisky & talk & the Red Baron but too agitated to sleep. Sitting on the floor in his room slotting Volta's pills back & forth along the parquet's diagonals, like pieces in a game of Chinese checkers.

It was a game that went nowhere, all bluff & placebo, but as the hours dragged he'd felt it slowly pulling him down into the mud of sleep. Somewhere in the distance, a telephone had been ringing. He'd waited for someone to answer it, but no-one did. It rang & it rang. In his mind he'd been crawling towards it like a swimmer groping for a lifeline that can't be reached. A deep, oceanic chill had come over him. A distant roaring of waves crashing on rocks. The *Ride of the Valkyries…*

And he'd dreamed it was the War & he was trapped inside the Führerbunker, below the ruined Chancellery in Berlin, on the last day of April, 1945. He could see Hitler as clear as the nose on his own face, at lunch with Goebbels & Bormann. He tried to remember what they'd been eating. Baked beans? Tinned ham in aspic? Pickled kraut? Herring? Ersatz potato? Powdered egg? Pigeon liver? Mouldy truffles? Tinned spaghetti? A bottle of 1906 Château Lafitte Rothschild? A pot of *English tea*?

And then, at half past three in the afternoon, seated on a couch beside Eva Braun's corpse (splintered glass in her teeth, the reek of crushed almonds), he saw Hitler turn to Goebbels & say *Das genügt mir,*[*] then shot himself in the head with a Walther PPK. In his mind's eye, Němec saw the smouldering remains of that hideous little rag&bones man doused in petrol & set alight, Red Army mortar fire erupting in the sky like celebratory fireworks. Smoke rising. Ash falling like snow.[*] He wondered what Volta would make of that.

---

[*] *Goebbels you deutschbag, where's my gun?!* [✋]
[*] What Němec in fact dreamed was this:

DER TRAUM

He was sitting atop a cliff, with his back to the sea. Before him, a meandering road led through a green landscape, curving past the gigantic head & shoulder of a woman rising up from the side of the road like a geological feature. Her closed eyes gave the scene an air of serenity. In the distance, a sky full of ventilation pipes throbbed with indescribable sound. Němec stood up & began to walk along the road. Without warning, he found myself standing, naked, in the middle of a busy motorway, traffic surging all around — viciously — endless — inescapable. The vehicles began striking out at him as they passed. All over his body there were bruises, cuts, torn flesh. Then, just as suddenly, the landscape changed into a large circular arena. A bored & hostile crowd watched from the stands. A cordon of men in gasmasks manoeuvred around him. An officer with the face of an idiot, sitting astride a black mare, picked his nose. Then he was running, around & around, his pursuers hardly even moved but already they were ahead of him at every turn. He felt himself being pricked by the ends of enormously long lances. Each time, the crowd roared, but without making the slightest movement — as though their roar had been broadcast through megaphones. Abruptly the scene was transported to some remote zone in which wars had been raging for millions of years — vast projects of extermination gouging out continents of death. Němec found himself in the middle of an enormous glacial desert, full of shadows, inhuman forms. His face, when he touched it, began coming apart in his hands. He wanted to scream, but as soon as he opened my mouth someone shoved a gag between his teeth. He was no longer in a desert, but in an isolation ward. A woman in a black uniform was standing by the door watching him. He was lying naked on his back, on a concrete slab covered with a green sheet. His arms, waist & legs were strapped to the slab. Above him, where the ceiling should've been, was a large television screen. It was attached to some kind of editing device. On it, scenes of death & destruction unfolded — Bosch landscapes interpolated with smiling Nazi propaganda — night trains racing across maps of Europe — spools of code, huge analytic machines, thousands of hard, purposeful faces. A voice sang: *Jede jede mašinka, kouří se jí z komínka!* An accompanying orchestra of machines clanged, blasted, screeched. Trains raced through the night, switching, interchanging, coupling. The darkened world revolved like tracks beneath wheels. Vast mercator projections like webs of steel crisscrossing the globe. It looked like a fractured crystal ball spinning on a cosmic chessboard. But on this board, instead of squares there were holes, & inside the holes naked people writhed. And the holes in the board became the holes in a sea of punchcards spiralling in endless succession. Boolean algebras receding into ever more distant multiple-point perspective. Tracts of ash-grey, little laughing Totenkopfen, tattooed serial numbers, prisoner categories, names, hieroglyphs of doom: 3. HOMO — 8. ZHID — 13. P.O.W. (Where'd all this stuff come from? How'd it get inside Němec's head?) The film was running backwards, the prostrate dead being cast up out of

Loaves & Fishes

It was a slow walk down past Můstek to the National Theatre — a slow limp, in & out of the crowds. Like the fake cripple on the trestleboard, people stood aside for him, avoiding his gaze, the freak with the stick & mashed-up head. Taking in the day's scenery, the City in all its lopsidedness. Every now & then he noticed things out of place — gaps in the fabric of the place. Here an antikvariát had become a clothing bazaar, there a used record shop had become a hair salon — like a *déjà vu* where the details have been rearranged, recoded, the key switched. It was as if, during his absence, they'd stuffed the deck, randomly changed the names, erased bits of the map & added new ones that weren't there before. The longer Němec looked at it, the more the picture came across like a bad TV signal — a mental jigsaw dissolving & reforming — the great detached unconscious mess of the world spilling out through the gaps, an overstuffed farce, an arbitrarily prognosticated *thing* whose great sagacity was to repeat repeat repeat, delete, overwrite, repeat again &, by often enough repeating, giving the impression of being the only show in town. Like a gimp in a Broadway mirror (*I picks me own nose when it suits me, pal, and it suits me just fine!*).

Halfway down Národní, he was obliged to sidestep a sandwichboard man

---

shallow pits into attitudes of solemn prayer, death's priest performing a reverse sacrament, crematorium chimneys sucking smoke from the sky in vast inhalations & one after another their brickwork demolished with worker-ant efficiency into geometrical arrays of raw building material. Great plumes of glass & masonry swallowing themselves up as winged seraphim ascended into the air, gathered back into the strobe-lit underbellies of a thousand nightbombers. As if on cue, it began to snow. Slowly at first & later more heavily. The screen turned white with static & the static was coming out of the screen & falling through the air like snow. Then from somewhere deep within that same television screen, a voice like a migraine spread over him. A voice like rushing wind. Like the vertigo of the world. It was saying: *Can meaning be destroyed without a trace?* And there, operating all the switches, the cameras, the microphones, was Goebbels — the ghost inside the image-machine, like the dwarf inside Kempelen's chessplaying doodad. And this dwarf Rudolf Hess was shouting in a high pitched, squeaky voice HITL EEEEST DEUTSCHL UND DEUTSCHL EEEEST HITL! Then the screen flickered once more, revealing a hundred-thousand arms raised in a zombie salute to death's-headed Hitl in his Charlie Chap moustache. A hundred-thousand echoboxes, chanting *Hitl Hitl Hitl!* The mouths of History. All vacant goggleeyed glopping heavenwards. While there, lit by a hundred-thousand flares, high above at the gates of Valhalla, Germania herself, blonde all over & Aryan charms buffed bright, the ever-willing, sacrificial virgin, medically certified, knee-socked & khaki accessorised, the obligatoire redblackwhite swastickfigure armband, one two three dainty little hop-steps, pigtails swinging, she leaps, feet together arms apart, hands together legs apart, out over the precipice, skirt a-flutter, while yet in her mind's prodigious eye forever poised at the edge, that first schoolgirl shudder in the loins, watching herself fly downwards & ever downwards into the awaiting abyss. [✊]

sprawled across the pavement outside a bakery.

A grinning pastry, with jam-&-poppyseed eyes & mouth, waved out at him from the sandwichboard, stick-figure arms & legs, a cartoon speechbubble saying… Impulsively Němec went inside to join a queue at a counter displaying every type of stale bread you could imagine. For only Kč 5,- they sold him a bag of the stuff. Back on the street, the drunk sandwichboard man was sitting there now rubbing his head. Němec handed him a stale roll & continued walking towards the river, gnawing absently at a crust.

'Hey,' the drunk shouted behind him. 'Hey you, what's the big idea? Fucking jerk!'

The crust tasted of nothing in particular garnished with salt & caraway seed, like the taste of nostalgia. *Yeah*, he told himself, *everything tasted better in the old days. A better class of nothing.* He took in the window displays while trying not to step in the dogshit. A used record shop was offering an oral history of the Cheskoslovník Communist Party in a twelve-album set for only Kč 400,- (a real bargain). There was a clothing boutique with the latest season's four-inch heeled knee-high boots, in a choice of black or red patent leather (*de rigueur* secretarial leisure wear), only Kč 1800,-. A jídelna with the usual collection of bums & bagladies was offering a lunch special of Segedinský Guláš at Kč 40,- Tlačenka half-priced at Kč 22,- & PragoCola at Kč 6,- per bottle. At the Viola Theatre there was a 7.30 pm closing night performance of *Marketa Lazarová* ('My God, who'd sit still for *that*?').

Němec slouched past with his stick & bag of bread rolls, past yet another magazine stand with racks of celeb gossip & full-colour porno (the stuff was everywhere, like the City had some kind of libido dysfunction) , then left across to pedestrian island, tram stop, dodging traffic (the same place, he remembered, where the year before he'd seen a woman get run down by a delivery van, in the shadow of the giant glass cube they call Laterna Magika, left there lying on the street with her shoes somebody had picked up off the street & arranged neatly beside her head…). Past that to the National Theatre, in whose courtyard an inflatable pink rabbit was sitting behind the steering wheel of white Mercedes, red balloons & a megaphone tied to its roof, blaring the *Ride of the Valkyries.*[*] A sign on the driver's-side door read:

---

[*] Pure coincidence, surely. [✻]

Wagner Rally Team

Jesus, they never give up, do they? Some gawkers were standing around while a couple of newlyweds had their photo taken beside the rabbit. A gang of skateboarders in the background were busy falling off their boards, trying to do tricks, while a boyband in matching tracksuits practiced their moves, lipsyncing in front of a video camera. The rally car was meant as an advertisement for a forthcoming non-stop marathon performance of *Der Nibelungenring* — a fate perhaps worse than Pheidippides'. You'd have to wonder how the dinner suits & taffeta would hold up after all that, fuelled on nothing but ersatz champagne & sucked-out canapés with potato salad & herring paste.

Behind the National Theatre, Němec crossed the little walkbridge to Žofín. There were peddleboats out on the water & children on the playground swings. Fairyfloss & hotdogs & beer in plastic cups. Down beside the river, he sat on a bench & fed the rest of the crusts to the swans rearing their long brown riverstained necks, beady-eyed, snatching at fingertips. The day progressed with no sense of purpose. By mid-morning Němec was standing once again outside the National Library, heavy with the sense of his own detachment, thinking of all the pointless hours he'd spent pouring over the lives of people long dead, who may as well've been fiction. Mydlář, Kelley, Voynich. What were they to him or he to them? *Well, it's all over now, eh kiddo?* Even the Prof's ghost seemed to have found better things to do than worry about the world's quota of meaningless books. *Leave it to the professionals, like that Faktor and his moustachioed dwarf.*

Němec stared a while at the entrance, watching people go in & out, *undecided* about something, till a guard in a rentacop uniform came & planted himself in front of him. Without saying anything the rentacop lit a cigarette & blew smoke in Němec's face. Němec stepped around him & stood a couple of metres further off, trying to make up his mind about something. The guard followed him a moment later & blew more smoke in his face. Němec moved again & the same thing happened, like an endgame with no purpose, till it got the better of him & he left the guard standing there blowing smoke at nothing.

Out on Karlova he let himself be carried along by the crowd, past the stalls selling wooden Russian dolls & fur hats, through an arcade & onto a backstreet that ran down past Na Zábradlí Theatre to the embankment. Němec peered through the window at the Theatre café but couldn't decide whether to go in or not. There wasn't anyone in there drinking, which could've been a good thing or a bad thing depending how you weighed it up. A waitress watched him from behind the bar with a look that told him nothing at all. Instead, he went over & sat by the old well in the middle of the small square the Theatre fronted onto. He closed his eyes & listened to the sound now & then of cars passing on the cobblestones. The pigeons cooing under the eaves. The day getting long.

Slowly, by stages, Němec made his way along the river to Palacký Square, past the great melancholic Sucharda monument dripping with pigeon crap. He found a bollard in the shade & checked the clock above still another kiosk with magazines & fried klobása. It was almost time to present for duty to the Good Doctor's secretary. Across the tram tracks, a man in a brown leather overcoat came running up the Metro escalators & disappeared into the crowd. A little while later a babička came screaming after him —

'GESTAPO! GESTAPO!'*

People turned & leered. The old woman pushed through the crowd shouting till she, too, disappeared from view as a tram rounded the corner. It was the number 16 tram. Němec climbed aboard & rode it up to Charles Square, then got off again. The tram trundled around the corner onto Žitná in the direction of I.P. Pavlova where Mydlář put a down-payment with his ill-gotten earnings on a two-bedroom maisonette in the long hot summer of 1634. Now what would Doctor Pavlov have thought about giving his name to that neck of the woods, *hehe*? An image flashed in Němec's mind, of salivating dogs chained to a chopping block, once their doggy brains had been messed-up to the point of no return & there was nothing for it but to put them out of their nine-to-five misery, drag some crotchety Mydlář type out of retirement, the mad old poppylopper's last hoorah with the axe, hacking away in the laboratory basement at a pack of braindamaged mutts done-up in period costume, the whole thing shot on hand-held video for a gag.

Tired from the long walk, Němec made his way through the park towards Faustův Dům. White vapour trails criss-crossed the sky. They made him think of the Bugman up on his terrace. And for a while, standing across the street from Volta's office, he imagined he was back there, watching the old guy mesmerising chickens.

---

* A theme seems to be developing. [✴]

21

MASOKOMBINÁT

'Did you hear the one about the Russian butcher?'

Another week, another mid-morning numbing his arse in Volta's waiting room, killing Time supposedly, though Time never seemed to have much trouble getting up again. What life had secretly been preparing him for, it occurred to Němec, this time-travel on the journey through boredom towards death amidst a décor of beige walls, beige carpet, beige chairs. Beige desk with penholders, typewriter, filing cabinet. Beige bookshelf with the usual waiting room magazines sagging out of it. Beige wall-clock. A couple of embarrassed-looking hydrangeas stood in a beige pot atop the bookshelf, the only things in the room that didn't look like the life had been sapped out of them, yet.

The waiting room was entered from the stairway by a frosted glass door which had been left standing ajar. Through it, the sound of a man outside in the corridor talking to a woman whose own voice was barely audible.

'Well there's a queue outside this butcher's shop, see,' the man was saying, 'in Moscow. One of those masokombináts that used to sell factory meat, you know, battery pork & all that. Well it's four in the morning & there's a queue already halfway around the block. The shop doesn't open till seven & it's cold. Everyone's huddled in their coats, feet stamping, puffing into their gloves.'

The voice sounded like it was coming from just behind the door. There were footsteps going past. Gone. Němec stared in the general direct of nothing, waiting for Volta's secretary to call him in. The voice in the corridor went on —

'At quarter past four, the door to the shop opens & the butcher comes out. The queue surges forward. The butcher holds up his hands. *Comrade brothers!* he says. *If there're any Zhids among you, go home. There won't be any meat for you today.* A couple of old women leave the queue, heads lowered resignedly, & walk off into the gloom.'

The clock on the wall was also beige & read 9:48, hour & minute hands overlapping. At 9:50 the preceding patient would leave Volta's office by a separate door, bypassing the waiting room, & ten minutes after that Němec would be ushered in to take his turn. For as long as he'd been attending consultations, he'd

274

never once crossed paths with another patient. Like a secret society, united by a common shame. The woman outside in the corridor coughed.

'At four-thirty the door of the shop opens again & out comes the butcher a second time. The queue surges. The butcher holds up his hands. *Sklavic brothers!* he says. *If any comrades from Yugoslavia are among you, go home, there won't be any meat for you today.'*

Němec was tempted to go to the door & see who the voice belonged to, but not enough to actually get up out of his seat.

'Quarter-to-five,' the voice said. 'Same thing. Shop door. Queue surging. The butcher. Sklavic brothers. Any comrades from Bulgaria… Go home, there won't be any meat for you today.'

Footsteps again, this time from inside Volta's office. The door opened & Volta's secretary came out, glanced in the direction of the hydrangeas, then went about searching for something in the filing cabinet, all the while assiduously ignoring Němec. The charade lasted about a minute before the secretary was gone again. Uncharacteristically, the good doctor was running late.

'Five o'clock. Same thing again. Hungarians this time. *Go home, there won't be any meat for you today.'*

Finally Němec got up & went over to the frosted glass & would've shut the door except that right at that moment the woman outside laughed. It was a theatrical kind of laugh.

'Five-fifteen,' the man's voice said. '*Any comrades from Cheskoslovnikia. Go home, there won't be any meat for you today.* Then it's the Poles turn, the Lats, Lithuanians, Estonians, the Ukrainians, the Moldovans, the Beloruskies, Georgians, Cossacks, Azeris, Dagestanis, Chechens, Kazakhs — you name it. At last,' the man raised his voice, 'it's seven o'clock. Everyone left in the queue is stamping their feet impatiently. It's down to the Russians now. You can see in their faces a grim Bolshevik sense of destiny. The chosen ones! The elect! They've been standing in line for hours. It's the national pastime, after all. How else can you be expected to properly examine the depths of your soul in a Workers' Paradise? Think Turgenev, Dostoevsky, *Pushkin!* There's a moral in all of this, believe you me.'

The man laughed, the woman laughed. Němec stood stock still, conscious of his shadow in the glass.

'Now picture this. It's seven in the morning. Let's say, the week before Easter. Cold even for that time of year. The door of the butcher's shop opens. The butcher stands in the doorway, arms raised, or let's say spread wide. *Three cheers for the revolution*! he cries. *Ai*! *Ai*! *Ai*! The queue surges forward. The butcher thrusts out his right hand & stops everyone in their tracks. *Tovarishchi russkiĭ*! he says. *Go home. There isn't any meat today.*'

The woman coughed. Němec aimed his walkingstick at the door handle.

'A little while later,' the man's voice continued, 'two old veterans, who'd been in line half the night to get their meat ration, are standing on the platform at Prazhskaya Metro station. Neither says a thing. After about ten minutes the train still hasn't come. One of them spits on the ground, turns to the other, & says: *Goddamn Zhids*! *They always scam the best deal.*'

'That's not *funny*,' the woman drawled.

Němec jabbed with his stick & the door clicked shut.

'Mr Němec?' a voice said, coming from behind him.

He jerked away from the door & saw Volta's secretary advance across the room. He looked from the secretary to the clock on the wall & back to the secretary: it was three minutes past ten.

'The doctor will see you straightaway,' the secretary said, in what Němec imagined was supposed to be an ordaining tone of voice, but sounded like a wet rag that'd only been half wrung-out.

No Cigar

'So,' Volta said by way of greeting, 'how are we progressing?'

'I have these dreams,' Němec replied, settling himself into his usual armchair.

'Ah,' said doctor. 'How interesting.'

'I'm trapped in a maze & can't get out.'

'Really? Can't you do better than that?'

'It's the same thing. Nothing's changed. I feel as if I'm caught in a game with a deadman.'

'Your father perhaps?'

'I don't have a father.'

'Of course. I meant Professor… What was his name?'

'Hájek.'

'Indeed.'

'You can say that again…'

'I'm sorry?'

'Don't be,' Němec muttered, turning towards the window.

On the other side of the glass a pair of hornets seemed to be entangled on the windowsill. One, the male he assumed, was almost twice the size of the other, its black&yellow striped tail curled under, the sting firmly embedded in the tail of the other which in turn opened outwards at the tip like some sinister yellow mouth trying to swallow it. Němec stared at them. After a while Volta broke the silence —

'Why don't you tell me about it?'

'I've been telling you about it for weeks. It makes no difference.'

Volta glanced down at his notes —

'Yes. You feel that you're caught in a game. And that in this game your very existence is at stake. Only you have no control over how the game is played-out. You struggle, but the struggle exhausts you. Like a game of chess which goes on to the bitter end, long after the outcome has lost its meaning. Each remaining move a dumb mechanical persistence, shifting the pieces back & forth, black square, white square, in mindless attrition. A game which ends only to begin again & go on the same way...'

Volta paused, plucked at his right earlobe, sighed, elbowed himself back from the mahogany into a semi-reclined posture against the chairback —

'Feelings of insufficiency, etc., etc., etc.'

The insects, meanwhile, had slipped from view beneath the window ledge. Across the river, the scenery was dull & uninteresting. Everything seemed to've wilted & turned to grey. Němec brought himself back around to face Volta, halfexpectantly, vaguely wondering what else Volta might attribute to his socalled father complex, though Volta himself hadn't called it that in so many words. But it was more than likely the doctor wouldn't attribute anything to it at all. It occurred to him that his presence in the room was, in fact, really a matter of indifference to the man behind the desk.

Volta scratched his scalp with the end of a fountain pen —

'Have I understood your predicament correctly?'

'More or less,' Němec's voice sounded dull & mechanical.

'Malraux once said, *Être homme, c'est réduire au minimum, pour chacun, sa part de comédie.*'

He must've looked at the doctor stupidly because Volta said it again, as if Němec hadn't heard properly the first time.

'Who's Malraux?'

'*Was,*' Volta corrected. 'Been dead for some time. He believed, or so he claimed, that in our age of cynical reason the art of secrets is left to those who recognise the world's irrationality & know, in truth, that science — which we have been taught to believe knows better than we do — is merely an alibi to comfort us in our disillusionment.'

Němec said nothing.

'Perhaps what Monsieur Malraux meant,' Volta added, 'was that only as long as there're things which can't be known, can we be sure we exist. Imagine a world in which God *was* real. What hope would we possibly have? Each of us would be nothing more than a piece on a chessboard, stripped of all individuality, except that which he is allowed by virtue of nothing more profound than ignorance.'

'You're depressing me.'

'Am I? Well, there's nothing to prevent you believing the opposite, either.'

Němec lapsed once more into silence. If there was something he'd expected from Volta, he couldn't define it. Each Thursday he'd obediently waited outside the doctor's office, only to be sent away with metaphysics & a renewed prescription.

'Life needn't be so difficult as you make it out to be,' the doctor yawned. 'A game, after all, is just a game.'

It reminded him of the Prof. *Life*, the Old Man once said, *is a way of learning how to die.* And Němec remembered the Old Man smiling as he added, *But not the only way.*

The doctor gave him a blank look that might've passed for expectancy or simply boredom. Němec sighed —

'Also,' he said. 'I've been having these headaches…'

'Ah,' said Volta.

'…'

'…'

'…'

'Let me tell you something,' said Volta, breaking the silence once more. 'In the East,' waving his hand abstractly towards some mythically remote place, 'in former times, when a man experienced a headache he would sometimes tether a lamb or a goat & beat it till it fell down, believing the headache would thus be transferred to the animal…'

His dark eyes narrowed on Němec, the professional headshrinker's "withering stare." It was like an eye boring out at you from a dream. Maybe he was being hypnotised & didn't even realise it. Němec brought his right hand up to his face & scrutinised it, to be sure it was there. The yellowish crescent moons of fingernails, he noticed, needed trimming. They always did. Volta cocked an eyebrow, coughed, fidgeted with a box of matches but no cigar today. Němec put his hand down & smiled inanely at the doctor. He looked slightly unbalanced without the cigar. Němec wondered if that was supposed to mean something.

'Man,' Volta resumed his little anecdote, 'is always seeking a scapegoat.'

He really spoke this way. Němec leant forward in his chair, to give the impression of being attentive. But there was nothing more, Volta had delivered his punchline & was now silent, waiting, expectant. Moments like this he really detested, but such was the ritual: first Volta delivered some sort of homily in the form of a riddle, then Němec was supposed to divulge his innermost whatevers. But then it came back to him, he'd just been intending to tell Volta about the vertigo & dizzy spells that were getting more frequent — the nightmares which he knew he had but couldn't remember — the feeling at times of blanking-out while walking down the street or sitting in his room, then coming-to later on in a place he didn't recognise, the same room even, but with certain elements of it subtly rearranged. How when the dots didn't join up, he'd drink, to forget what he couldn't remember. And the more he drank, the more pills he took...

Face it, he thought, *you're your own worst enemy. Better to be tied up and beaten with a stick.*

Němec decided to change the subject instead. Without knowing exactly why, he recounted his meeting with Faktor, the Patriot Klub, Kircher's letter & the great Jesuit conspiracy. Volta, assuming his familiar quixotic expression, gazed meanwhile at a point just above Němec's head.

'Funny thing,' Němec said, 'the man's a bit of a chess buff, too.'

'Oh,' Volta sighed.

'Like the Old Man.'

'Mmm?'

'The Prof...'

'Ah.'

'Seems they knew each other, once, maybe, back after the War, in another part of the world, though, ever so briefly... Said something about an unfinished Mahler symphony. The Prof liked Mahler. Strange that, don't you think? I mean, it all seems so... *connected.*'

Němec waited for Volta to say something. Part of him expected the doctor to tell him he was delusional. As if he hadn't been already. *World don't need no more Jezweet con-spir-a-cees, boy!* But without saying a word Volta just took out his prescription book & began writing. The sound of the fountain pen scratching against the paper was for a moment the only sound in the room. Then the ticking of the clock became audible, the groaning of Volta's desk, the distant sound of traffic from the Square.

'I don't doubt,' the doctor said finally, replacing the cap on his fountain pen & setting it aside, 'that your headaches are real. A typical side-effect, I'm afraid…'

He tore out the prescription neatly & flourished it for Němec to take, which Němec did, contorting himself across the space between them with the aid of his walkingstick so that somehow he managed to reach the doctor's desk without quite leaving the armchair.

'We'll see what we can do,' Volta said, jerking back his now empty hand as if something had just crawled up the back of it, 'to dispel them. But as to your Mr Faktor…' his eyes drooped, his hand slipped down into a pocket, perhaps he was having second thoughts. 'Have you considered the possibility, remote as it must seem, that the two may not be unrelated?'

Now what was that supposed to mean?

'Isn't truth,' Němec offered, smiling a fraction idiotically, 'sometimes stranger than fiction?'

'No,' Volta shook his head, eyes once more drifting into an indefinite distance. 'You of all people shouldn't expect the one to be any different from the other. They're like the two halves of a divided self. But I wonder,' he flattened his remaining hand on the desk, fingers spread, 'if this Faktor is as… *actual*… as you'd like to believe. You must admit, your story does seem a little… *over-reaching*. For instance, what would possess you to take this Faktor into your confidence in the first place? Why trust someone you know nothing about, who by rights you ought even to be suspicious of? He may, after all, be your enemy, *hmmm*? Isn't that what this whole thing's about? You feel guilty & you want to offer yourself up as a scapegoat…'

But why *him of all people*? As for Faktor, had he been apocryphal, Němec couldn't help thinking, he'd've been more believable. He said —

'I don't know anything about *you*.'

'That's different. I'm your doctor.'

'Curiosity, then. I was bored.'

'Like the canary that wanted to see if the cat really would eat it, given the chance? Or if the cat wasn't just a figment of its imagination?'

Volta smirked, it looked vaguely obscene without the cigar. Like the cat that got the canary, the mutt that got the gravy, the orphan that got the spilt milk…

'D'you know the story about the King of the Magicians?' he asked, rising from his desk.

As he did so, the doctor took a thick leatherbound volume from the bookshelf behind him. Apparently he intended to read something from it. Volta found his page & went at it. The story began like a fairy tale, *Once upon a time*, with a castle & all the usual stuff. It was one of those allegorical unfoldings that could be made to sound both trivial & profound at the same time. The type of thing calculated to put you off-guard, or simply to sleep. Němec fought the urge.

The story about the King of the Magicians took its time getting to the point. In his way of telling it, the author had ladled on the symbolism, as though wanting at every possible opportunity to extract some sort of moral. Somewhere in its ponderous fog of didacticism, a strange lady entered upon the scene, veiled, dressed in black: her face was invisible except for a pair of glittering eyes. She was, so Volta explained, referring to a footnote, the *Lady of Situations*. While he spoke, Němec's attention was drawn to an unusual sculpture which sat on one of the shelves of Volta's bookcase: its shape was strange, like a puzzle & a key at the same time.[†] He couldn't recall ever having noticed it there before & wondered if the sole purpose of the story Volta was reading to him was to cause him to notice it.

While Němec was thinking this, Volta suddenly broke off from his narrative & gave his patient a quizzical look. Němec felt again the sensation that the doctor had somehow read his thoughts. It was an old psychoanalyst's trick. Mercifully it ended there, however. His fifty minutes were up.

Auf Wiedersehen!

Němec stared at the square of folded paper in his hand, unsure why he was holding it. It was Volta's prescription. As he was leaving, the doctor didn't say goodbye. Němec realised that he never had — an always deferred point of finality. Outside, on the landing, a little girl was waving a red balloon back &

[†] It appeared to be some type of "primitive" fetish. Its "head" was disconcertingly womblike: the frontal lobes folding inwards to embrace & protect a second, enclosed figure. It resembled those images on Egyptian sarcophagi which show the mother goddess as the sheltering uterus that holds & contains the dead body, as in the beginning. What struck him most, however, was the foetal figure itself, which had a hollow torso — the open space uniting the back & front of the whole sculpture in one simultaneous rhythm. The upper limbs flowed into the lower limbs without interruption. The head & breasts & shoulders were unified in one clasping, knuckle-like extension — the lower limbs retracted.

forth on a stick. The balloon was the same colour as the girl's dress. There was no-one else there — the two he'd overheard earlier sharing the joke about the Russian butcher were gone. Němec paused at the top step & looked back at the girl. She was standing in one spot, swishing the balloon from side to side, in front of her face.

'It's an interesting game you're playing,' he said.

It felt strange saying it. The girl stopped doing what she was doing & tilted her head slightly away from him.

'It isn't a game,' she said, in a highpitched child's voice.

'What is it then?' Němec asked.

'I don't know,' she said, facing him again, the balloon hanging at her side. 'It just isn't.'

Her gaze was without any direction. *There's something wrong with her*, Němec thought. And then: *She's blind!?* He edged backwards down the steps away from her. When she was out of view he turned & took the rest of the stairs three at a time. When he got the courtyard he was out of breath. Němec stood there panting. His hands shook. *What the hell're you doing?*

'Something wrong, citizen?' a voice said.

Standing only a metre away, smoking a cigarette, was a woman with extremely broad shoulders & a gigantic bosom. She wore a loose white coat over a light blue uniform. Němec stiffened, his throat all of a sudden turned to sandpaper.

'No, not at all. I'm fine. Everything's fine.'

He hurried from the building onto the street without looking back, Volta's prescription damp in his fist. The blind girl's face kept hovering there in the back of his head. The couple's laughter. The emptiness of the waiting room & the emptiness of the street. *Go home!* they all shouted. *Go home! THERE ISN'T ANY MEAT TODAY.*

22

THE MAN IN THE MOON

There was an old Gnostic theory that said the world was created by an imbecile who got it all wrong. According to the same theory, man's original purpose on Earth was to clean up the mess. This task was supposed to be achieved by means of an unfortunately inexact science — namely, the understanding of the *secret dualism of good and evil, through the revelation of eternal symmetries*. Problem was, the world as it'd been created was lopsided, incomplete. It was the idea of the Gnostics that knowledge alone could provide the missing part & through it man would become the great engineer of the world's correction — its *harmonisation*. Harmonisation would lead to symmetry, which would lead to the understanding of the secret dualism, which would lead to the knowledge necessary to bring about... harmonisation. Like a dog licking its own arse. This roundabout doctrine, so the story went, later informed the genesis of the alchemical sciences, from which evolved by increments the socalled Age of Reason — but also its irrational outgrowths: fascism, eugenics & the cult of the Übermensch. Perhaps that was why the Earth still tilted on its axis, because humanity, too, had failed to set things straight.

When Němec returned to his apartment that Thursday afternoon, he found Mrs Falová, the ancient Jehova's Witness who lived on the sixth floor, pulling herself up the stairs on her hands & knees, one step at a time, a brownyellow plaid shopping trolley with spoked wheels lying at her side. It'd become a regular occurrence, Blecha had explained, ever since the old lady's bitch of a granddaughter took away her zimmerframe, to keep her from going out on the street & causing havoc among the general populace (the way they do). Whenever she wasn't padlocked in her apartment, old Misses Falová would crawl down to the bottom landing, sit there half the day, then crawl back up. Sometimes she'd crawl as far as the Chink's with her shopping trolley dragging behind, just for an outing. The Meals-on-Wheels man brought her garlicsoup, guláš & dumplings every other day. They'd sit down on the steps together like it was a Sunday picnic & afterwards he'd take the empty camping pots away & she'd have her afternoon nap before crawling the six flights back up. Always very

politely declining offers of assistance from the weird chap in the black suit &
bowler hat.

As on this occasion. Němec greeted the old lady as he passed her on the
way to the elevator. Why she never used it, he couldn't figure out. Old school.
Or maybe she just enjoyed the exercise. Drop in on some of the other biddies
along the way. Misses Falová mumbled something in reply, groping for the next
step, pulling the shopping trolley along beside her. He watched the poor thing
for a moment before letting the elevator door swing closed behind him. One
day, he supposed, they'd come & take her off to a recycling clinic somewhere.
Or she'd simply perish, locked inside her apartment by her bitch of a
granddaughter so as not to dirty up the stairwell, & eventually the smell'd alert
the rest of the world to the fact. They'd pile her old dusty belongings on the
sidewalk for the local junkpeddlers to cart away. Greasy picklejars, mottled
brocade, a cracked chamberpot, plastic shoppingbags stuffed with more plastic
shoppingbags, horsehair blankets, bits & pieces of mismatched china, knives &
forks in brown flyspeckled cardboard boxes reeking of camphor, the whole sad
spectacle of life's dénouement into useless artefacts.

It was with such pleasant thoughts in mind that Němec found an
unexpected parcel waiting on his doorstep.* He surveyed the corridor but there
was no sign of anybody. A flicker, perhaps, behind the peephole in the door at
the head of the landing. The old spy woman with the meat-tenderiser. He
prodded the parcel with his walkingstick. It was quite inert. He stooped to pick
it up, weighing it in his hand. It was flat, rectangular, wrapped in standard-issue
plain brown waxpaper, sellotape & twine. No name of sender, no return address
— though someone had taken the trouble of misspelling his name on a piece of
white card. All caps. Typed. **NEMOC**, it said. **E** instead of an **Ě**. *Ne-motz*. **O** instead
of **E**. *Nemo*. No-one he knew, *hehe*. Could only be this Non-Entity was supposed
to be himself, unless it really *meant* Nemoc. As in: *disorder, malady, illness,
sickness, ailment, disease, contagion*. Anthrax, just to take a more obvious example,
or alien spores, or the android mind-control code. Skull&crossbones stuff.
Warning:

<hr>

* Uh-oh. [☠]

☠ NEMOC! ☠[*]

He ogled the parcel with a sense of foreboding/presentiment/apprehension.

Frankly, Němec couldn't think of any good reason why such a thing should turn up on his doorstep at all. Far as he knew, the people at the Golem City Teaching Hospital weren't making hand deliveries that year. Like maybe they'd kept part of his brain that got chopped out while he was under anaesthesia & figured he might want it for a keepsake, *hehe*. He shook the parcel. Didn't feel like sloshy brain matter, more like a book. Maybe the Bugman thought he needed some reading matter to expand his mind a bit, *hoho*, figured he'd appreciate the little joke with his name. Or, scary thought, perhaps there wasn't a reason for it at all, but chance had dictated it? One day something falls from the sky, or is born backwards, or turns up on a doorstep, unexpected & undesired — an infant in a reed basket, a wrong augury, a parcel of ill-omen. The gifthorse's proverbial.

'Next thing,' Němec told himself, 'you'll expect me to show gratitude.'

Inside the apartment he switched on the recordplayer & went to work brewing some coffee. Stravinsky's *Pétrouchka* scratched away in the background. The milk he'd opened the day before was already soured, so he drank his Sierra Maestra black, too lazy to go across the street again. He left the parcel on the kitchenette counter & shuffled across to his armchair, shifted the typewriter out of it & eased down, sipped the coffee & winced — it took four sugar cubes to even begin to make it drinkable. He couldn't figure how people did it to themselves. Masochists.

Němec sat there nursing his cup of poison, listening to Stravinsky slowly fade out into the sound of the walls breathing, wondering what the hell to do with the rest of the day or the rest of his life. He thought about Blecha wanting his ashes scattered up there on the roof. On his magic mountain. You reach the end of the climb, then what? Take in the view for the remainder of your days while the boredom settles in & eventually, with the right kind of positive outlook, you might even grow indifferent enough to find peace, satori & all that. Have to keep an eye on yourself, though, at such a rarefied altitude, not to let all that pure oxygen go to the brain. *Well there's always someone watchin' kiddo, even if it's just that bug they put in the back of yer brain.* Like being spied on by your own shadow. What good's a conscience with a poked-out eye, eh? Or if not a

---

[*] This just gets better & better. [✊]

shadow, a rock even, a blade of astroturf, inanimate things programmed to intercept your innermost thoughts, the ones you don't even know anything about. Just to help keep you centred in yourself.

Like Blecha sweeping his lawn, saying —

'There's this feeling you never get away from. Even now. Right at this instant. As if some eyeball-in-the-sky's zoomed in on you. Can't say why. I'm nothin' to anyone. For forty years I was nothin' to anyone & still they had their gizmos *watchin' 'n' listenin'-in.* Microscopes up yer arse, microphones in yer tooth fillings, *hehe.* Kind of comforting after a while that someone out there cares so much. Makes you wonder what they see, what they hear. Must be real exciting stuff, eh? Reckon they'd get sick of it after a while. Or maybe it's the other way, man grows fond of the things he watches over, given enough time. Like that sentimental fucker in the sky, must shed a tear or two, *eh*, with all the carnage going on all over the place. Give His little Adam a tickle in the ribs every once in a while, just to let him know He's still up there. A sneaky little Christmas present, if he's been behaving himself, all wrapped in tinfoil & glitter. Watch the poor jerk tryin' to guess who the secret benefactor is…'

BALLAD OF THE PIGEON MAN

```
Day after day all alone in the park
He talked to the birds till long after dark,
Feeding them breadcrumbs & morsels of stuff
Till those clubfooted vermin had had quite enough.
Now they couldn't fly off when he stomped on their heads
And carried them home to munch on in bed…
```

Speaking of benefactors… Němec blinked at the sheet of paper stuck in his typewriter. Sipped bitter coffee. Pondered. Maybe it could run to a whole series: the Ballad of Viktor Faktor, the Ballad of the Moustachioed Dwarf, the Ballad of the Bugman… He wound a fresh page in. Emptied his cup, cauterising whatever tastebuds he had left. Wiped his hand across his mouth & laughed —

'Not exactly the old *wordsoul,* eh? The *kernel.* Whatever. The *beheld creation.* Wonder what the Prof'd make of that. Ballad of the Pigeon Man, indeed. *Twaddle, mein Freund.* Well that's what the world's made of, ain't it?'

Němec realised he was talking to himself & stopped. No future in that. Better to put it down on paper. Some of that deathless prose he sometimes dreamt about, the sort of thing he'd imagine himself writing if he was Dostoevsky, perhaps, or Hrabal, though both of them were dead, if for different reasons. Perhaps, yes, in a different world, he might've *been* one of them. Somewhere, in some parallel universe, in a place a little bit like this one but where everything turned out different. The same, but different:

Where he hadn't been born under this particular constellation of Absurdity.

Where all you had to do to make a future was think of one (always the optimist, eh?).

Where life wasn't a joke you played on yourself to stop from going mad with boredom or grief (touching, that).

Where there was no conspiracy to turn a man into a bug under a microscope (unlikely).

Where history was just a catalogue of yesterdays & not this appalling compulsion to repeat (no chance).

Where there were no secret police, no psychiatrists & no skeletons in the closet (hahaha).

Where amnesia didn't go begging & beggars didn't need to.

Where a fair rate of return meant always being able to find your way home.

Where a second chance didn't come with a mortgage attached.

Where the last man standing was the first in line.

Where a song of sixpence could be got for free.

Where trees grew on money & horses only drank whiskey, no matter where you led them.

Where mistaken identity was the only type.

Where a man named Joe Stalin was a flower-seller on the Piazza d'Espagna.

Where Patton hadn't stopped for a pint at Plzeň.

Where Churchill never once smoked a cigar.

Where Hitler was a one-armed trapeze artist.

Where Mao Zedong wrote sonnets in the Petrarchan style.

Where Jesus H. Christ was a vegetarian.

Where Salomé was a saint & Saint Teresa modelled for Modigliani.

Where Heinrich Himmler was a Galeries Lafontaine windowdresser.

Where Oppenheimer broke the bank at Monte Carlo.

Where Mata Hari married Rasputin & gave birth to the Marx Brothers.

Where Zacco & Vanzetti played Waltzing Matilda.

Where Charlie Mordecai was a younger brother & Freddy Engels was a Baťa salesclerk's bit on the side.

Where Adam Smith was a Quaker & ate oats every morning for breakfast.

Where a man named Herzl was a part-time bicycle thief, a black&white

minstrel & a sometimes portrait painter on Charles Bridge.

Where Franz Kafka held down a dayjob at Golem City Prudential.

Where Richard Wagner played banjo with abandon.

Where the Twentieth Century was a glass of warm milk before bedtime & not that nightmare of cosmic indigestion, gastric reflux & unstomachable bile...

Was that the worst they could do? Now that the century was fizzling out, the world coming to its millenarian doom, what last hoorah would they cook up? What ballad of brainless bullshit would they stamp on the collective sub-cortex now at the end of days & for all eternity? *Mene, mene, what did you dream? Sweet naked little nothings... all in a row. Being gleefully sodomised by a famous TV personality. God's nob, man! What're you playing at? Well, the world's still young, eh, still plenty more where those came from.* Němec poked idly at the typewriter keys, the first thing(s) that came to mind:

```
The Man in the Moon is a milky maggot,
a sliver of snot, a circle of slime,
a jet of jism in the sty of your eye,
a clot of cream on a mouldy pie,
a hooknosed Zhid, a pimply Pope,
a peckerwood's piles playing rope-a-dope,
the rancid puss from a swollen zit
on Moh'mmed's mummy's mildewed tit,
a Zulu's eye, an elephant's egg,
the gloryhole in a deadman's head,
an idiot's grin, a murderer's smile,
the empty stare of a faceless dial,
a police cell lamp, a dentist's clamp,
the pockmarked arse of a two-bit tramp,
a plaster of Paris virgin for sale,
a syphilis stench under a perfumed veil,
a crystal ball full of murky light,
a lunatic's howl in the dead of night...
```

Disgusted (with himself, with everything), Němec pushed the machine aside & got up to stretch his legs, scratch his arse, pick his ears, take a well-earned rest after such strenuous literary toil. On the way to the kitchenette he reset the needle on the recordplayer. Stravinsky redux. Turned it down low, where the music verged on intuition. He was emptying the stale coffee grounds in the bin when he remembered the parcel. It was still where he'd left it,* like a piece of bad luck. He poured himself a fresh cup of ulcer-inducing char roast, picked up the parcel, & crossed to the door to take a look through the peephole. Did he expect someone to

---

* It hadn't grown legs & run away of anything like that, in case you were wondering. [☛]

be lurking out there? One of Faktor's mad monks? Retreating to his armchair he stood the parcel on the table. Sipped. Pondered. At least the second cup didn't taste as rough as the first, it must've been growing on him, so to speak.

And when *didn't* curiosity got the better in the end. With stumps of chewed fingernails, Němec unpicked the knotted packing string. Strange how he could never remember actually chewing them, they just always seemed that way, as if something chewed them for him in his sleep. His pet anxieties lining up at the head of the bed, taking turns. Would they keep doing it when he was dead? He tore open the wrapping paper — inside was a thick folio bound in leather the colour of charcoal. The binding was cracked, the paper swollen, as if it'd been left for a long time in a damp place. The spine was split down both sides, coverboards upcurling, fore-edges flymottled. Němec turned the book over — it looked the same from both sides. Great, just what he'd always wanted. Why couldn't someone've slipped him a million bucks in brown wrapping-paper instead? *Well who knows*, he thought, *maybe the jackpot's inside.*

Before he had a chance to take a looksee, a scrap of thick handmade paper fell out of the book & onto the floor. There was some writing on it. Němec leant over the side of the chair to pick it up & tried reading what it said. The ink was scratchy. *Seek not that which is hid.* Or it might've been, *Salt nuts had* [something] *his kid.* "Altered," maybe. Like that made a fucking lot of sense. A very encouraging beginning. He turned the paper over — there was more on the other side, scribbled in the same faded blue ink. It was like one of Volta's prescriptions, penned with all the clarity of churned riverwater, turning Moldau into Vltava, a rainslashed sky into angel wires, a reflection blown sideways on a preternatural windgust. Ježíšku! Elihu! And so on. And so forth. It took some deciphering. What it appeared to say could only have been intended as a joke:

> I have painstakingly set about to examine
> the scriptura anent in a full and free spirit
> and admit nothing as its teaching which
> I was not taught by it clearly

Němec tossed the paper aside & opened the book at random. He flipped through what he supposed to be some kind of ledger or memex: lists of names, numbers, symbols, the odd diagram, bits of scribble, all in the same faded blue. The pages ended in a stiff flyleaf with a green & black engraving pasted on it. The engraving depicted a young Carmelite kneeling at a prayer bench beneath an altar to the Sacred Heart. Her habit was in some disarray. Her posture was an ecstasy of contradictions, at once supplicating & convulsed.

The detail of the etching was superb. The noviciate's hands were clenched so violently that the fingernails of one hand visibly pierced the flesh on the back of the other. Above her upturned face, the saviour's left & right ventricles radiated with white intensity. Black blood streamed down the altar, spreading outward in a grotesque chiaroscuro. All the while a winged Devil with cloven hooves, dildo extended, was poised to bestride the hapless Carmelite — & she, *sinking, falling, thrilling at the point of the dart with which Divine Love is about to pierce her.*

Appended to these two graven figures was a monogram embossed on a black chess-piece knight, gothic in design, so intricately entwined as almost to be illegible. Němec studied it for some time before a pair of letters spelled themselves out to him:

$$\mathfrak{T.H.}$$

He spoke the letters quietly to myself. What was T.H. supposed to be? He put the book down & sipped his coffee, cold by now already. T.H. eh? Mmm. As in a certain Doctor of Letters, Emeritus Prof, currently residing at no other known abode than a slot in a cemetery wall? Any other candidates for T.H.? None Němec knew. Good enough. Tomáš Hájek Q.E.D. it'd have to be then. Which still didn't explain what the book had been doing on *his* doorstep, or did it? (Well, in a manner of speaking, it'd have to, wouldn't it twinkle toes?) And *if* it was, knowing what the Old Man was like, what kind of "book" *was* it?* The secret Polygraphia, his skeleton key to the Sphinx's Code? The little theremin in the back of Němec's head made faint music…

He shut the book on the Devil & the Carmelite & opened it again somewhere in the middle. Across the left hand page a lot of gibberish in the familiar blue tracery (*a rt gh h m eno hd pan ori tgg shi ngs g a*) interspersed with even less comprehensible doodlings. On the facing page, columns filled with names, numbers, hieroglyphs. He peered closely, each of the names had been crossed-out, like checklist, a closed account: ~~Dedecius~~, ~~Dědeček~~, ~~Dedeič~~, ~~Dedek~~, ~~Dědek~~, ~~Děděk~~, ~~Dedera~~, ~~Dědic~~, ~~Dědič~~, ~~Dědíček~~, ~~Dědičík~~, ~~Dedich~~, ~~Dedík~~, ~~Dědina~~, ~~Dedinek~~… No-one he knew. He flipped through a dozen or so more pages: ~~Klein~~, ~~Klekner~~, ~~Klement~~, ~~Klemm~~,

---

* D'you buy this crap? [♟]

Klemperer, ~~Klempík~~, ~~Klemšov~~, ~~Klenotník~~, ~~Kleprlík~~, ~~Klíč~~, ~~Kleprnák~~, ~~Kleprnek~~, ~~Kleprník~~… Same story, none of the names meant anything to him. Nothing for Nemoc, either (haha), though there *was* a ~~Nemčko~~, a ~~Nemčok~~ & a ~~Nemec~~ (no discernible háček on the "e").

The remaining pages were more or less the same: lines & columns. Turned sideways, the lines became cascades: a Japanese waterfall. Inverted: a trellis threaded with vines. On one of them, in a corner, three rows of oriental-looking calligraphy. Beneath which, a piece of cod "haiku":

Impossible to tell if it was meant to be poetry or some sort of riddle, or just one of those rare masterpieces in doggerel you heard rumours of but never expected to actually come across in the short span of your own lifetime. *A sign and no road.* Sounded about right. Something which points in the direction of a place, or a thing, or an idea, but not the path required to get to it. *Ah-ha.* All been there, eh? *Unknown waters. Winter night polestar shining.* Very deep. The genius of late Sunday night programming. Well, Němec thought, you put stuff like this out there in the world & sooner or later it'd be bound to find its admirers. What the great struggle for democracy was all about…

He flipped through the whole thing again. Here & there a date had been recorded, in a combination of Arabic & Roman numerals, all fairly recent, going back no later than the last seven years. *Funny sort of thing to have in an antique book.* Obviously, he supposed, there was nothing antique about it, though it *looked* old, the etching on the frontispiece being case-in-point numero uno. It *smelled* old, too, like it'd been buried in a tomb. Němec sniffed. *Mmm.* He wasn't sure if he ought to be intrigued, or puzzled, or worried. Like the great critics of the salons, he found himself wondering what the hell it was all supposed to mean. Who the hell *were* these Dědeks & Kleprníks & Nemčoks & why'd their names been crossed out? More important, why'd they been written there in the first place?

Questions, questions. He flipped back to the haiku & stared blankly at the scribblings that filled up the rest of the page around it. His eyes drifted among the mess of illegible signs like a current stirring a carpet of lilypads. He blinked & the writing seemed to move, to merge & divide, bifurcating from left to right, concatenating, notations & sub-notations. Echoes of Voynichese.

The thought gave Němec a jolt. There was no way to be certain. And even so, the thought couldn't be denied. Faktor's conspiracy babble sprang readily to mind. Very suddenly, it seemed quite obvious. What else'd be going on between a lot of bullshit Sphinxology & lists of crossed-out names?

His head began to ache.

He tried going through the book again, this time with the vague idea of detecting some sort of deeper system at work, but it all seemed much the same: a meandering texture of scribble side-by-side with those endless pedantic lists — from which, he noticed, there was a conspicuous absence of any Kelleys, or Kirchers, or Dees, or Voynichs for that matter. *Could that be meaningful?* What was more, the last dozen or so pages were entirely blank, the names ran out after "S." Funny that. What good was an alphabetical list that only went up to "S"? What about all the *other* names? Or maybe there weren't meant to be any other names, maybe that was the point? Or maybe it was the *other names*, the ones that were *missing*, that mattered? Spooky stuff. He squinted at the blank pages under the light to see if there was invisible ink on them. Maybe. Or maybe not. He sniffed the paper. It smelt of mildew, tainted cheese.

After a while a new thought struck him, that he was behaving exactly like an idiot, & he tossed the book down on the table, comforting himself with the unpersuasive argument that it probably didn't mean anything at all, just some random bit of junk. Which didn't, alas, account for how such a thing had randomly arrived on his doorstep, but what the hey? Nor did it stop Němec from beginning to sweat. Someone, he decided, was most certainly fucking with his head. Android conspiracy stuff. Well, he might've had one or two theories by now about that, too, but in the end he was forced to acknowledge being totally in the dark. Who'd he finger for something like that, anyway? Faktor? The Jesuits? The Man in the Moon? Unknown forces at work in the universe? *Yeah, kiddo, well we gotta go save some kittens outa trees, you just hang on in there.*

Nope, couldn't really say he had much to go on at all. And what good, as the ol' Prof might've said, was a theory about nothing?

23

Didus Ineptus looked out from the glass display case with an unblinking forlorn eye, feathers creased at wrong angles, a thick grey patina of dust covering its pigeon-like feet — undisturbed, if appearances were anything to go by, since 1681, the date embossed on a little brass plate screwed to the vitrine's wooden frame. Beside it stood a larger cabinet, home to a stuffed rock wallaby, a barn owl, a pigmy marmoset & assorted other Wunderkammer — their collective incurious gaze directed across the corridor at an expanse of Caspar David Friedrich tundra, shards of glacial rock like bits of burnt toast on a Jötunn's breakfast plate. As if describing a portal through to the North Pole, a large oak door stood on the painting's farther side, opening onto a secretary's office where a prim-looking woman predating the Apollo landings sat behind a desk with an Olivetti anchored to the middle of it. This was the reception area of the State Literary Archive at Strahov Monastery.

It was a half-hour tram-ride & a walk up the Castle Hill. The weather that morning had been grey & an insalubrious wind blew across the hillside. Down at the foot of it, the Vltava lay swollen against the embankments like a tumescent slug. So much for spring. The City of a Thousand Spires barely registered against the gloom. At the top of Nerudova a narrow path that wound steeply up towards the "Mons Sion" squatting atop the Strahov Gardens like a pale mantis. Even at that hour — except for a couple taking pictures of one another in front of a low stone wall overlooking the gardens — the path was deserted. According to the plaque beside the monastery gate, the (what they called themselves)

Premonstratensians had got the idea to build a cloister up there in the twelfth century. The whole place was torched during the Hussite Wars & then successively rebuilt into a hodgepodge of Late-Baroque & Neo-Romanesque, arriving out of a time warp into the wreckage of the twentieth century only to be nationalised by the communists & turned into the Monastery of State Literature. The main archive was located in the south wing of the complex, on the far side of an ornate courtyard. Sculpted rose bushes stood out from the walls between scalloped alcoves where once upon a time statues of the minor saints enacted their martyrdoms.

The prim-looking receptionist was busy jotting marks in a ledger book with the stub of a blue pencil when Němec came in. A faint line of grey ran down the part of her hair, which otherwise was auburn & tied back in a bun. She wore no makeup & no jewellery. A pair of rimless glasses rested halfway down a nose that was too long. When she raised her head, the eyes behind the glasses were very large, grey & without expression. He gave her his name & the reason for his visit while she watched him across the top of her lenses. She put the sharpened tip of the blue pencil she was holding to her lips & appeared to consider what he'd said. Finally she put the pencil down in the margin of the ledger & began silently tapping with her fingers on the edge of the desk. The fingernails had been filed down as far as was humanly decent. The whole performance had taken no more than a minute but it seemed excessive.

'Please, why don't you take a seat,' she said, in a voice that sounded like nothing at all, the way you'd expect an usherette at a funeral parlour to speak.

Němec looked around & saw a pair of highbacked wooden chairs against the opposite wall with a low filing cabinet separating them. He felt the secretary's eyes follow him as he went over & sat down. After that she ignored him. Another five minutes passed while he watched her at work on the ledger before she stood up & walked out through a partition door. A small nameplate on her desk said her name was Petrovná. Some time later another door opened at the end of the reception area & a different woman entered with Ms Petrovná behind her. Ms Petrovná went back over to her desk while the other woman came towards where Němec was sitting. This one was a brunette & was wearing a red turtleneck sweater with brown slacks. She stopped just short of him.

'Mr...?'

He stood up & held out his hand, where she let it hang awkwardly, till he took it back.

'Němec,' he said.

'Do you have an appointment, Mr Němec?'

There was a faint whiff of condescension to her voice. Němec grinned at her & shook his head.

'Any letters of reference?'

Němec stared at her blandly —

'I'd've brought a letter from my mum, but she's dead, as far as I know.'

The brunette gave him an appraising look — the kind of picture he must've made standing there: black hat, black suit, black walkingstick. The left corner of her mouth twitched faintly, but only once. It seemed for a moment the façade might crack, but she kept to the script.

'Normally,' she said, 'our procedures are rather strict. Materials deposited at the Archive are kept under seal for a statutory period of seven years. Unless there happens to be a *bona fide* claimant or court order releasing them. Even to access the inventory would usually require a letter of authorisation. Exceptions may be made for scholars affiliated with an accredited institution & a demonstrable need arising from legitimate research. Perhaps you should tell me *exactly* what you're looking for?'

During all this Ms Petrovná had been busy chewing the end of her pencil, pretending to be absorbed in whatever was written in that ledger of hers. She made a concentrating face & patted her hair to check everything was in place, then did something to the ledger with the pencil she'd been chewing. It was a stellar performance & while it continued Němec grinned some more at the brunette & explained about wanting to be sure nothing was missing from the inventory of Professor Hájek's papers.

'Why should anything be missing?' she bristled.

'Didn't say anything was missing — only said the inventory might be incomplete. After all, the Prof was quite a prolific guy...'

His grin had assumed an almost oriental cast. With benevolent gaze he explained to her how some new materials had recently come to light, of uncertain provenance, *blah-blah-blah* — perhaps they rightfully belonged in the Archive?

Her eyes squinted at him & blinked — it was like having a conversation with a lizard.

'Wouldn't that be a matter for the Professor's estate?'

'I was his assistant,' Němec said in a confidential voice, leaning in towards her, 'friend of the family. Personal interest, out of concern for the Prof's legacy, you know.'

He winked, keeping the grin in place.

The brunette appeared to ponder what he'd told her & then asked him to wait again — for some people it gets to be a habit. She went silently through a large door to one side of the reception area which Němec hadn't seen before. It was a plywood door stuck in the middle of a partition that filled what once had been a high archway. Ms Petrovná pursed her lips glancing at the closing door, then returned her gaze to her ledger & tapped the end of pencil on her lips.

Němec shrugged, letting his grin become vague & exercised his legs walking a slow figure-eight around a pair of dark stains on the linoleum. He played a game with himself to guess how long Ms Petrovná's nerves would hold up, but she was good as gold. Twenty minutes later the brunette returned with a sheaf of papers in a folder. She gestured for him to take a seat (it must've been a common trait of everyone who worked there, the waiting game & now musical chairs) & laid the folder open on top of the filing cabinet beside him. In it was a photostat of the inventory listing everything that'd been catalogued among the Prof's papers at the time of deposit.

'Here,' she said, handing it to him.

The brunette stood guard over the folder while he read. He supposed she didn't have anything better to do, or maybe she just couldn't help being obliging. It was a fascinating read, too. On page twentythree Němec came across a description of a leatherbound folio. It sounded familiar. *Interesting*. A number of other items also caught his attention, among them a looseleaf facsimile copy of a "manuscript" identified solely by its catalogue number. He felt like he was back on more familiar territory.

He would've kept a straight face if he could, but something about the brunette got him grinning again the moment he looked at her. He used to grin the same way at the androids back at the Home, to see just how far he could disconcert the sadistic bitches. He wondered what sort of sadistic tendencies the brunette might have.

'This one,' he said, pointing at the item in question. 'Either it has a twin, or something from one of your sealed boxes has decided to go AWOL.'

Němec couldn't tell if it was his grin or what he said that caused the brunette to finally lose her composure. It began as a contraction of the muscles around her right eye & spread into a kind of sneer. She snatched the xerox from Němec's hand & stuffed it back in the folder, then stamped over to Ms Petrovná's desk, & said something into a telephone. After a while she eyed him over her shoulder, her expression now one of suspicion, then uncertainty, then surprise. A few more degrees of emotion & she might've been gazing at him with eyes moist with ecstasy. He winked at her & watched a faint shudder turn her crosseyed for a moment as she put down the receiver. Clutching the folder to her breast she walked over the partition & held the door open.

'Follow me please.'

Němec didn't need to be asked twice. On the other side of the door was a cubicle office with another door & beyond that a long corridor, at the end of which the brunette ushered him into a very large room with bookshelves stacked along each of its walls & giant chesspieces sitting on a checkerboard floor in the middle of it. The brunette stopped & fixed him with a look that was probably supposed to make him feel like a little boy who might be about to misbehave.

'The chief archivist, Mr Fišer, will be along shortly,' she said, almost without moving her lips.

It was a crime to see those lips go to waste like that, as if she was practicing a ventriloquist act & he was supposed to be the dummy. He smiled inanely back & watched her turn quickly away & those narrow hips cross the Reading Room & pivot through a doorway in the west wall. When she was gone the place seemed even quieter than it should've — not a single creak from a floorboard, as if someone had switched the sound off. He toured his walkingstick among the two-story-high Rococo bookcases for a while, right hand clutching his lapel, contemplating the monastic life. When that became a bit dull he stopped & looked up at the high ceiling. Some joker had gone to the trouble of putting a monumental fresco up there, concerning one of the big theme — the Spiritual Enlightenment of Mankind, or whatever. Němec gazed at it through slit eyes while playing Twenty Questions with himself: *What if* — the Black Book wasn't the folio listed in the inventory? or hadn't been included among the Prof's papers when he died?? or didn't belonged to the Prof at all??? What if what if what if. *Certainty's a dangerous thing, kiddo*, said the midget in the control booth at the back of Němec's head. (It made him think of that astrologist, who spent his life pouring over his own horoscope, trying to find out when, where & how precisely he'd meet his end.)[*]

On the oversized chessboard someone had arranged the pieces into the opening of the four knights' game, which had the virtue of symmetry & was pleasing to the eye. Each of the horses had been advanced ahead of the ranks of pawns & might just as well've been statues on plinths decorating a stone wall

---

[*] The only one who knew wasn't telling. [✊]

from which a gate opens out — very solid & sound. In another moment someone in period costume might've wandered out for a stroll across the checkerboard lawn & paused for a moment to peer at one of those white marble equestrian monuments, perhaps expecting to find a circus dwarf up there astride it, frozen in the attitude of a rider, unblinking, doing its best to blend in with the scenery. Why this someone would expect to find a dwarf astride an equestrian monument was anybody's guess. Perhaps because he was a "bishop"? And it wasn't a dwarf he had in mind, but a cherub, in the manner of Botticelli?

The location might easily have been the Vatican gardens, in which this first "bishop" would soon be joined by a second, who'd direct the former's attention to the equestrian statue standing opposite, a black one this time, on which there would indeed be a cherub seated, holding (as convention often dictated) — a little harp, or a bow & arrow. A third "bishop" might then be seen peering at one of the remaining two horse statues, implying a sort of generally obsessive behaviour by members of the Curia (gathered here possibly to determine the fate of the Church — opposing factions in a secret schism of dark horses & white knights that couldn't be directly spoken of but construed merely), by means of subtle choreographies of perusing.

Others, cunningly disguised, would be the game's true custodians, setting the play, the back & forth arranging & rearranging of what to the unsuspecting eye could only appear as a type of garden furniture (one laden with arcane symbolism admittedly yet furniture nonetheless), as if to obtain nothing more than a pleasing or contemplative disposition — *consonantia, claritas* — the balancing of contraries, feminine & neuter, Pope & Anti-Pope, the ecclesiastical gnostos, the dialectic of the Trinity, & onward & outward, from white square & black square to the infinity of the cosmos. Amen.

Fisher of Men

It was only half an hour later when a short bearded man came out of a doorway in the far corner of the Reading Room, approaching Němec along a red ceremonial carpet — it must've taken him a full minute to cover the distance. It's possible to tell a lot about a man by the way he crosses a room. A little out of breath, the man puffed out his cheeks & introduced himself, too quickly for Němec to catch what he said. Presumably this was the head archivist, Fišer. He fidgeted with his cuffs when he spoke & didn't offer to shake Němec's hand. There was a small gravy stain on his shirt collar.

Němec looked at the man expectantly. He seemed to be waiting for something, catching his breath, working his jaw into a more lateral arrangement. This might've gone on for some time, if Němec hadn't muttered something about the Prof's notebook. The man, Fišer, made a glum expression. Poked a finger inside his beard & fished about with it, but came up emptyhanded.

'Well,' he said, 'yes, as it happens… I don't suppose you happen to be a relative, do you?'

'Assistant,' Němec leant forward slightly on his walkingstick to meet the man halfway.

'Vlasta said you might have reason to believe…?'

He meant the brunette presumably.

'Yes,' Němec said.

'Oh, well in that case…'

'My thoughts exactly.'

'Mmm,' Fišer stroked the tip of his beard, 'tricky business…'

'True.'

'Not the sort of thing we'd really want to…'

'I agree.'

'Still, can't be too careful…'

'No.'

The long & short of all this was that the Prof's papers weren't where they were supposed to be, at least not where the sorting clerk had looked, & not where Vlasta the brunette had looked either, nor Fišer the chief archivist. As it turned out, the Monastery was undergoing a bit of reconstruction. It'd been undergoing a bit of reconstruction since the 1960s, but this time they'd had to temporarily relocate some of the archive from the South Wing to the East Wing. The records showed, apparently, that the Prof's papers had originally been catalogued with various other recent acquisitions & deposited in the East Wing basement. But now there was no sign of them. All this Němec deduced from Fišer's noncommittal mutterings.

'Seems…' this Fišer explained. 'But most likely… *In due course*, you know.'

In the meantime he suggested Němec fill-out an official request form, the one in blue, with his contact details & they'd look after the rest. And if he'd be so kind as to…

'Of course,' Němec grinned, 'how about I post it to you?'

The little bearded man nodded profusely. Muttered something. Gestured in the direction Němec had come in. Oh the message was clear enough.

Something odd about all this, he thought. For one, the archivist's story didn't add up. The inventory was over fifty pages long, hardly the sort of thing you'd just misplace like that. Or maybe it was? In a state institution with how many — six-point-eight million? — items on deposit. But even so, why enlist the chief archivist to give some nonentity off the street the runaround? But what if that wasn't how it looked to them? Mmm. *Still, something fishy about that chief archivist. Something… familiar.* Sure he'd submit an official request, made out in triplicate, stamped, signed & countersigned, from here to next Sunday. Nothing like a bit of paperwork to keep everything in order, the anodyne for every pain.

Could they have *already known* that the Prof's papers were missing? The idea seemed far-fetched, but not *too* far-fetched. Not in the recent scheme of things. As he retraced his path along the corridor, Němec thought about the parcel on his doorstep & who might've left it for him, & all the other obvious questions. Was there anything at all he could even begin to assume? *Don't look at me, kiddo.*

On his way out, Němec fancied Miss Petrovná gave him a more than usually peculiar look over her rimless glasses. He winked at her & she bit her pencil. She had very fine little teeth. Very white. It occurred to Němec this Petrovná was actually a piece of government apparatus like one of those filing cabinets they probably kept Hájek's inventory in. Her human appearance was really just a disguise & her real name wasn't Petrovná at all but Agent K-412. Němec wondered where the brunette was lurking. He grinned to himself as he closed the door behind him. The Dodo watched him from its glass box — no worse off, Němec supposed, than the rest of the participants in this sham. Except it'd got its suffering over & done with sooner, & didn't have to sit around & watch the rest of the world go to hell in a handcart as well.

View through the Periscope

Instead of taking the tram back, Němec decided to act on a hunch & hailed a taxi outside the Monastery gates instead, a blue Favorit from Captain Ahab's Cab Company, pondering as the traffic slid by the same questions over & over again. By the time they'd reached the beltway the traffic had come to a standstill. For the next ten minutes it barely crawled. Němec stared out the window at the grey river, car horns blaring.

'Like this all the way to Braník,' the driver said.

A long barge was slowly chugging up the river with a cargo of gravel piled up on the bows, heading towards Libeň.

'Every afternoon it's the same. You ever get constipated? I get constipated. From sitting in fucking traffic all day. You'd think in a democracy they'd be able to figure it out. Get things moving, you know? It's worse now than when the Commies ran the show.'

'Sure,' Němec said, 'when the Commies were in charge no-one could afford to drive anywhere.'

The river barge passed under the bridge & out of sight. He heard the driver reply —

'It's all those fucking Krauts. They come here because it's cheap. Cheap beer & cheaper cunt.'

Němec looked away from the window. The driver wore a plaid shirt that barely managed to cover his paunch. He was waving his hand at the car in front of us. It was a black BMW. Next to it there was a slurry tanker with the slogan *Number 1 in the Number 2 Business* painted on the back. Déjà vu.

'Kraut shit,' the driver growled.

He leant on the horn, a tinny sound came out from somewhere. *A tin trumpet in the street.*

'SCHEISSE DEUTSCHEN!' he bawled through the windscreen, 'DON'T YOU KNOW WHAT A ROAD IS?!'

The driver slumped back in his seat, apparently defeated by the effort. To hear the sound of his own voice Němec asked him where he was from.

'Jáchymov. You know it?'

'Never been.'

'Why would you? It's a shithole. No-one in their right mind goes to Jáchymov.'

The traffic began to move again in fits & starts.

'Fucking uranium mines. Reason I drive a fucking taxi. Insurance liability. Can't get a fucking job doing anything else. Building sites are all gypsies & Ukrainians. Who else digs fucking holes? Only job left for a white man with any self-respect is driving cabs. Or trams. Wouldn't drive a fucking tram if you paid me. Bastards get cooked in summer, freeze their arses off in winter. *Come on you jerk, get a move on!* And you gotta join the union. Who ever heard of a fucking *union* in this country? A man's gotta stand on his own two feet. Look at me. I don't mind driving this heap — I get to do my own thing, know what I mean? A cab gives you independence. I take the fare, I know the route, how to get from A to B, all the shortcuts — people rely on me, know what I'm saying? Mostly I enjoy having the time to just sit & think, sometimes switch off the meter, cruise around, maybe pick up a bird… *Will you look at this arsehole*! HEY YOU KRAUT SHIT! WHERE'D YOU LEARN TO DRIVE? IN A FUCKING U-BOAT??'

They trailed the BMW down the exit ramp & turned left through the underpass into Žižkov. The rest of the journey continued in silence, up through Vinohrady, then looping back towards the traffic. Němec told the driver to stop around the corner from the Český Rozhlas building & wait for him. The driver gave him one of those scrutinising looks & shrugged.

Mrs Fialová was groping her way up to the first-floor landing when Němec came in off the street.

'Who's that?' the old lady shouted.

'Just me, misses,' Němec waved, hoisting himself into the elevator.

Up in his apartment, the Black Book was right where he'd left it on the kitchenette counter. He grabbed a binbag from one of the drawers & wrapped the book in it, stuffing it under his arm. Better, he thought, if he didn't keep it lying about like that — somebody obviously knew he had it, & maybe there were others who'd try to get it. Friar Tuck & his merry band of Jesuits, maybe. Besides, it had to mean something, there had to be clues, & one way or another it was up to him to find out.

Back in the taxi Němec directed the driver to Jilská street. This time they crossed the beltway down Žitná, past the Golem City Teaching Hospital & right at Spálená. An unbroken stream of invective poured from the driver's mouth all the way downtown. Sweat glistened behind his ears. Outside *Svoboda & Slovíčkář* Němec told him to pull up. A gang of tourists breezed by along the narrow sidewalk.

'Fucking Krauts everywhere!' the driver snarled.

Němec got out with the binbag still wedged under his arm & paid the driver ten crowns over the fare.

'Buy yourself a drink,' he said pleasantly through the window.

'With this?' the driver spat disgustedly, but still pocketing the coin.

Němec shrugged. The driver slammed the steering wheel & roared off, tyres squealing on the cobblestones.

'Ah,' Němec sighed, 'the veritable cornerstone of the nation.'

Along the street at number 22 the coach doors were hidden behind a façade of green mesh, another **RECONSTRUCTION** notice nailed to a wooden scaffold erected around the arch. The Golden Goose trinket shop had been closed up. A for-rent sign hung in the window, courtesy of T.E.S.L.A. REALITY.

Those clowns again. He thought of the girl in the folk costume watching from the doorway, probably now with that same desperate look behind some market stall on Havelská or waiting tables or pouting away her hours at a checkout desk, the bright future ever-awaiting. *Getting sentimental in your old age, eh, kiddo?*

Němec grimaced & swung his crook leg in the direction of Messers Svoboda & Slovíčkář's shop window. He searched everywhere with his eyes but notice for the *Sphinx's Code* was gone. The bell jangled behind him as he limped inside, startling the shop assistant.

'Where is it?' he said.

'Where's what?'

She ogled him with large watery eyes, her grey hair pulled back in a bun.

'The notice in the window! It was there before, the definitive something of the Voynich Manuscript!'

Her eyes grew a little wider —

'Oh.'

Pointless, he thought. He lurched away down the aisles, the miniature labyrinth, into the cul-de-sac where he'd found the copy of *Heterocosmica* with Kircher's letter in it. He wondered where he'd put it, the torn-out page. Somewhere. Obviously he'd put it somewhere. He checked the shelves to see if the journal was still there. *Of course not you idiot.* But something about it, a niggling idea, that perhaps, maybe, something familiar… He peered at the window above the shelf, festooned with bits of paper taped to the glass. He searched them, the litter on the floor, bits of old flyers wedged behind the shelf. Nothing. *An amateurish ploy*, was what Faktor had said.

Němec grit his teeth. He tried to think back. The notice, the journal… There was no direct connection & yet the one had led to the other.[*] And then he remembered them, the eyes in the window, the Mummler photo-plates falling on the ground. The eyes were trying to tell him something. Not *what*, but *who*? But before he could think, something else struck him. Not the plates, the portrait! A man in musty clerical gowns, *Master of a Hundred Arts*, etched in what Němec was suddenly sure was exactly the same style as that frontispiece in the Black Book.

---

[*] In this version of events, the letter was simply one in a series of poisoned pawns. The first, presumably, was Němec's meeting with the Prof himself, in the courtyard of the Klementinum. Or perhaps it'd been something prior to that even, something entirely innocuous — a name on a sheet of paper, a piece of unfinished music, the axe hanging on the *Chop House* wall — something infinitesimal in the ultimate scheme of things like the flutter of a butterfly's wing in Paris that causes an earthquake in Peking. How would it ever be possible to know? [☙]

Could it be? He grabbed the book out of the binbag & stared into it. The Devil &
the Carmelite. Then closed his eyes, trying to summon forth the missing image.
Damn it! If only he could remember what the fuck he'd done with that letter.

His head ached, the vertigo of coincidence once more clouding-over into
conspiracy. He lurched out of the bookshop & wandered through the streets in
the direction of the river. His body suddenly felt tired, suffused all over with a
dull pain. He suffered all along Bartolomějská Street, past the secret dungeons of
the State, the gauntlet of camera eyes, jerked forward on blind legs. *There's a
good little boy.* A delivery van with the words GOLEM CATERING airbrushed
on the side clipped his arm at the intersection where Husova turned into
Karlova. Němec stared after it & a needle-eyed cartoon monster stared idiotically
back from the rear door. *Meth. Emeth.* A sign maybe. What did it mean?[*]
Without thinking he followed the street down towards the river.

Dark, lowhanging clouds menaced the rooftops. He saw the image of a
winged Devil astride a supplicating novice. The etching, he thought, had to be
the key. All those lists of crossed-out names, bits of haiku & gibberish meant
nothing to him, but the etching... Yes, the key, but to what? He knew he was
grasping at straws, but what else was there? A few minutes later he found
himself standing beside the derelict Karlův bathhouse, awoken from his
paranoias by the whisper of rushing water. His head was aching. He walked to
the end of the quay, past the statue of Bedřich Smetana, & stared into the
current pouring over the weir. It whispered of release from pain, of endlessly
flowing sleep. Strange figures moved in the swirling water, like shadows rising &
falling under the surface of a mirror.

Němec retraced his steps. At the foot of Charles Bridge the square under
the statue of St Francis in ecstasy was so crowded he barely made it across.
Planted in front of the Klementinum gates was a sandwichboard advertising a
matinee performance of Dvořák's *Stabat Mater* by the Academy Orchestra. A bit
of uplift to carry the day along. *Dum dum da da.* Would you really pay Kč 500,-
for that on an empty stomach? His head swam. The crowd let go of him once he
got through the gates, thank Christ. Entering the old Jesuit compound, he felt

---

[*] "Meth" for "Methistopheles." Here's a nice theory for our Squillhead: The Golem was really an
alchemist's laboratory on wheels, circulating & dispensing medicaments for the Ghetto's malaise
— the Man in the driver's seat selling them their fix — opium slaves, human robots — the whole
thing just a front for the biggest cartel in history: the Pope, the Holy Roman Emperor, the
Philosopher's Stone? *It was just a caterer's van, you idiot! You think everyone nearly drives over you is
part of some Masterplan?* [♣]

the vague pull of some undisclosed force. Vague evocations of an old man sitting beside a fountain with a tiny magnetic chessboard on a foldout table, whistling. A highpitched dissonance weaving oscillations in his head. Like the sketched prelude to a full-blown symphonic migraine. He crossed the courtyard. *What am I even doing here?* You'd think they'd shoved a homing beacon up his arse. Or, to be fair, maybe it was just all that unfinished business, kind of thing doesn't let a man sleep right. You could probably even measure essential developments in his character by plotting it all on a graph. The periodicity of avoidance & return. Like a mechanical pendulum in a constant, fixed motion. Yet the arc of a pendulum wasn't a thing in itself, but a series of discrete coordinates — the heart of its mystery lay within each one — distributed in time & space, yet somehow bound in a single diminishing oscillation…

24

BABELSPEAK

The windows along the main corridor of the National Library looked out onto walls of red ivy. Late afternoon sunlight cast long shadows across the sleeping figurines. The fountain glowed. Against the windows, a long row of display cases. An old woman in a wheelchair, chin on the glass, was examining something inside the case at the far end through a magnifyingglass, the way an entomologist examines a bug. Němec presented his library card to the grey-uniformed guard standing inside his booth. Students bustled in & out of the Reading Room, clutching notepads & folders, life's little adventure denominated by facets, indexed, footnoted, the world as it was meant to be.

As he came closer, Němec saw that the woman in the wheelchair was looking at an exhibition of wax seals & postage stamps. A sign on a stand explained the origins & evolution of both the seal & the stamp & their gradual disuse in the age of the computer. There was a chart showing the various taxonomies, like something out of Darwin. Němec browsed it sceptically. Entire bureaucracies had been erected across the breadth of Mitteleuropa as a bulwark against their extinction. In the swamps surrounding Golem City where no microchip dared tread, three-eyed salamanders spawned in eternal triplicate, signed, stampdutied & sealed.

The exhibits were arranged on sheets of white cardboard in chronological order, beginning with the Great Seal of the excommunicated crusader & Holy Roman Emperor, Frederick II (Nietzsche's "first European") — the *Bulla Aurea Siciliae* of 1212 — & ending with the Seal of the Keeper of the Imperial Library, dating from Rudolf's reign, dear. Large, pendulous gobs of wax the colour of ox's blood with bits of string & ribbon attached. Dispersed among them were the odd piece of medieval calligraphy. The letters patent of a minor Renaissance lordling. An edict concerning public sanitation. A university diploma, etc.

The display continued up to the period of Occupation under the neighbourly Third Reich, in vitrines running midway down the corridor, arranged with a philatelist's concern for the infinitesimal in detail & the arcane in subject. Worthy of note was a Thurn und Taxis blazon on yellowed parchment, tattooed in the lower right corner with the Eagle&Hakenkreuz motif, like some bizarre concentration camp souvenir. Below it, a series of commemorative stamps issued during the Occupation: a blue 2.50 korun Mozart, Böhmen und Mähren, designed by Langenbergen — a pink Deutsches Reich 1.20 korun Adolf Hitler, franked — a black, 60 pfennig Reinhard Heydrich, printed with silver Waffen-*ϟϟ* lightening bolts beside the Butcher's own pale deathmask, nose conspicuously hooked.

In the corners of each of the display cases, a thick patina of dust, hair, dead moths & flies. *Time*, Němec's thought, *isn't invisible.* He glanced out through the windows into the courtyard where he'd had that first fateful encounter with the Old Man. Barely half-a-year ago, though it seemed a lifetime already. He clutched the bag under his arm. The Black Book, with its lists & numbers, & the assumption T.H. really did stand for Tomáš Hájek, late Professor Emeritus. The reason he'd come here, to assuage the Prof's ghost who, without having to put in any further appearance, succeeded in haunting him by means of proxies.

Němec's scalp sweated, his body itched in the Bugman's handmedown suit. In his mind he was searching for a missing clue, a piece of a puzzle, only he didn't know where to look or what the puzzle really was. At any moment the most arcane detail might suddenly become overwhelming: something as simple as a date on a letter or a mislaid book. Something that could become a matter of life & death, as it had for the Old Man, in a manner of speaking. Something that'd been passed-on to *him*. Why? And what made the Black Book important? What was its purpose? Did it represent the Prof's attempt at a final solution to the Voynich enigma? Or proof that none existed? Did it have a meaning at all? Or was it like a dark room, filled with a voice spouting nonsense so that nothing else could be heard? The inspiration of something formless which, become an echo, *assumes* a form, the way a contradiction does?

In his mind Němec pictured a sea-lathed stone. The type of stone a child picks up on a beach & wonders at, keeps in a jar beside cuttlebone, green glass, snail shell, bullet casing, foreign coin, in order one day to arrange them on a shelf according to some arbitrary schema: stone, metal, glass — igneous, sedimentary, metamorphic, coprolite — white, black, grey... Only instead of stones & cuttlebone & green glass he'd collected names, numbers, symbols, the odd doodle, bits of haiku, lists of *stuff.*

Němec stepped away from the row of display cases just as the old duck in the wheelchair motored past in the direction of the cloakroom. He jerked back, clutching his walkingstick & the black binbag to his chest. The guard gave him an unsympathetic look. A group of students in identical kneelength tartan skirts stood as far out of range of the menace-on-wheels as the corridor permitted, tittering nervously as the woman passed. Němec watched the back of the wheelchair edge around the corner & out of view, swearing under his breath. He brandished the walkingstick & looked to make sure nothing else was preparing an ambush. The students meanwhile were already abreast of him, pushing through the large black doors into the Reading Room. Sensing safety in numbers, Němec followed.

Inside, the desks were crowded with silhouettes hunched against the gloom of a hundred dim reading lamps under brass lampshades. By a kind of conditioned reflex Němec went straight over to the wall of amber-coloured drawers which cut the Reading Room in two, where thousands, hundreds of thousand, possibly millions, of yellowed catalogue cards were gradually compounding into dust. One of the last great anachronisms. Like the Julian calendar, the Church & psychoanalysis. He placed his bag & walkingstick atop the nearest bank of drawers & went to work.

With a handful of request slips, he went over & stood in front of the librarian's desk. A middleaged man in square bifocals was sitting behind it, staring into a computer screen. Green hieroglyphics flickered across his lenses in backwards progression. Němec dropped the slips in the "IN" tray. Glancing at the large wallclock he had an idea. Wasn't Erdwark Kelley supposed to've written a treatise about ciphers & zodiacs or something like that, in addition to his book about the Philosopher's Stone? Maybe the Prof had mentioned it, or he'd read it somewhere. It came to mind because of the etching, Kircher, author of the *Polygraphia Nova*. He leant against the librarian's desk & waited till he'd caught the man's attention, then asked about where to search for secret codes dating from the late fifteenth century. The librarian sighed & typed something into the computer. Lines of green luminescent letters & numbers reflected in his glasses, larger at the bottom & smaller at the top. He read from the screen —

'Six hundreds. Processes of written communication — technology — systems — ciphers — historical.'

But there was nothing in the cards about K's *Treatise*. Neither in the six hundreds or anywhere else. Was it just a bit of apocrypha? Who else belonged in that picture? There was Kircher, Kelley, how about Kepler? He dug through the catalogue, but nothing struck a chord. After half an hour his number was called & he went to collect his books. It took two hours more before he located the etching of the "Master of a Hundred Arts." He unwrapped the Black Book & lay the images side by side. It was the same style alright, only the face in the etching didn't belong to Kircher, but to another man whose name began with K. Edwad Kelley. So there *was* a connection after all? And right there, beneath the engraving of Kircher/Kelley, was a reference to the Egyptian Oedipus, just like in the letter, & a treatise on "astrological codes."

Could that've been a key? Could that've been the connection the Prof had been trying to make between the Voynich Manuscript & Kircher's Sphinx? And was it Kircher or Kelley? Or both of them somehow? He didn't know where else to look, the catalogue was exhausted, so he decided to begin again with a different strategy, triangulate, approach his quarry by indirection, a subtle fianchetto, hunt the traces on the margin, echoes, reflections, enter deeper into the mirror by seeming to retreat from it. Reminding himself that John D was also supposed to've produced a book about codes. It was all part of the Zeitgeist apparently. Němec took down every useful reference he could find.

It was another twenty minutes before the librarian's assistant returned with all of the other books Němec'd ordered on a trolley. Some of them he'd read before — of the rest, half were purely technical, concerning the art of encryption. He began with these but soon lost track of himself. He turned the three biographies of John D (Melmoth, Yeats, Holmes), there were more than eighteen hundred pages between them. Němec checked the wall clock — he had till ten p.m. to read everything.

John D was many things: mathematician, astronomer, astrologer, navigator, occultist & diviner. He was, according to the opinions of those who matter, one of the most learned men of his age. A founding fellow of Trinity College Cambridge, he had already lectured on Euclid at the Sorbonne before the age of twenty. A champion of maritime exploration, he boldly coined the phrase (long since fallen into disuse), "British Empire." (Pure gold, that. Sound up on the swelling strains of *Rule Britannia,* "Britannia rules the waves, Britons never-never-never shall be Sklavs…!") He even served for a time as counsellor & tutor to none other than the young princess & one day virgin queen, Elizabet Tudorová.

D's singular obsession in life, however, was to discover the One Universal Tongue, the original Babelspeak, the Language of Creation itself. By means of which (so the old skullcap hypothesised) he'd obtain the power of revelation over the Divine Forms which underlay the risible (oops!), *visible* world. In aid of which he penned a book, famous in its day, about the secret meaning of some hocus hieroglyphic he'd invented for just that purpose — a Čert-like[*] squiggle which looked like this:

To his credit, D was also said to've amassed during his controverted lifetime one of the largest known libraries in Europe, till poverty at the end of his life reduced him to flogging most of it for a pittance. And yet Němec couldn't get a certain idea out of his head. Behind the abundance of information about D, there constantly hovered the inscrutable spectre of Edgeward K. Němec came no closer to learning about K's treatise on astrological codes — assuming one existed at all. (Had he remembered correctly, or was this just another fake, like everything else about K?) More & more, however, Němec wondered: if K was indeed the discreditable character historians painted him to be, how was it that D — who seemed to have such learnèd opinions on everything — failed to realise this?

Of course D would've been one of those self-absorbed pedants behind a frockcoat & beard whose egos are so vastly susceptible to their own vanity. (Like Poloviční, Headmaster of the Children's Home he'd grown up in, with his boring interminable homilies on Marx & mental hygiene, & that ridiculous habit of waving his middle finger under his nose like it reminded him of pleasant thoughts.) Němec could just picture him: John D, the credulous idiot with his

---

[*] The Devil's in the retail. [✋]

head stuffed in an encyclopaedia,* porcine faced, cheeks with that fanatical pinkish glow, eyes hungry for visions on angel-wires.*

As intriguing as all this was, Němec still knew virtually nothing about what mattered most. He scanned quickly through the rest of the books on the trolley till a footnote by one Robert Cotton, English antiquary, sent him back to the card catalogue & a book entitled *The Latterday Magicians* (annotated edition, 1978). Cotton had happened to purchase the land around D's house in Mortlake after D's death in 1608 or 1609, & took the opportunity to go prospecting for hidden loot. It was he who first discovered written evidence of D's angelic conferences, which he sold to one Méric Casaubon, who in turn published them in 1659, denouncing the once esteemed D as the witless tool of demonic spirits.

Němec couldn't help but grin. Amongst the papers Cotton succeeded in excavating, was a description for a catalogue of a scientific "manuscript" concerning herbology, astronomy & a general metaphysics — the *unifying principle*, supposedly — written in a *secret code.* According to a note appended by the annotators of *The Latterday Magicians*, this "manuscript" was meant to've been one sold by D to Rudolf II during the former's sojourn in Golem City — for the tidy sum of six hundred & thirty ducats — in 1586 (!). D may, or may not, have himself discovered this particular "manuscript" among those of the thirteenth-century Franciscan priest, Roger Bacon, which he was known to've salvaged from a crypt at Glastonbury Cathedral. This theory was — so the note explained — first mooted by one Dr Raphael Missowsky, in the seventeenth century…

MISSOWSKY, R., produced no fewer than fifty-seven references in the library's card catalogue. Němec chose three of the more likely looking ones & put in a request. While he waited for his number to be called, he read some more. It added nothing he didn't already know. By the time the Missowsky books arrived, there were only two hours left before closing. Němec scanned the indexes, running his finger down page after page of small type till, quite by chance, he found an entry for W.M. *Wojnicz*, page 389. It was a history of the

* The first "encyclopaedia" by that name having been penned by Johannes Aventinus in 1517. [✋]

* How else, you may wonder, could D have been so easily hoodwinked, along with everything else, into handing K (on the instructions, so said, of the angel Uriel) the keys to his young wife's boudoir? [✋]

Bohemian court under Ferdinand III.[*] Němec soon picked up the story where he'd left off.

Rumour had it that, after Rudolf's demise, many valuable books belonging to the Emperor passed into the hands of a shadowy character by the unlikely name of Jacobus Horczicky, a.k.a. Sinapius, whose moniker was later discovered (by said W.M. *Wojnicz*) written inside what Němec knew to be none other than *the* Manuscript itself, but which the author of the history — Fr. Benjamin Lourdes, S.J. — omitted to identify. Němec quickly searched for other references to Horczicky. At least one appeared in the index of each of the books on Němec's desk, though mostly in reference not to the *person* but to the art of distilling *mustard water* (the source of Horczicky's fame & fortune).[*] Němec read back & forth between the various accounts, patching a story together till a sequence of events became more or less clear. What he gathered was this:

Some time after Horczicky's untimely death, Georgius Baresch — author of the "Sphinx" letter — came into possession of a book bearing all essential resemblance to the Voynich Manuscript &, for reasons unexplained, bequeathed said book in turn to Johannes Marcus Marci (the university rektor), who in turn donated it to our good friend Athanasius Kircher. A letter from Marci to Kircher, relaying Missowsky's original account, was then found along with the Manuscript by said W.M. *Wojnicz.* So far, so good.

With time running out, Němec made another pilgrimage to the card catalogue. A little while afterwards he was sitting in front of the *Transactions of the College of Physicians of Philadelphia*, number 3, volume 43 (1921). In it, starting on page 415, was a long article entitled "A Preliminary Sketch of the History of the Roger Bacon Cipher Manuscript," by Wilfred M. Voynich himself. It began:

> ☛ *In 1912, I came across a most remarkable collection of preciously illuminated manuscripts. For many decades these volumes had lain buried in the chests in which I found them in an ancient castle in Southern Europe, where the collection had apparently been stored in consequence of the disturbed political condition of Europe in the early part of the nineteenth century.*
>
> *While examining the manuscripts, with a view to the acquisition of at least a part of the collection, my attention was especially drawn by one volume. It was such an ugly duckling compared with the other manuscripts, with their rich decorations in gold and colours, that my interest was aroused at once. I found*

---

[*] Or as the Paddy contingent in Bohemia were wont to regale him, "Ferd de Turd." [♣]
[*] Mr Mustard, "If you like it Hot, we've got your Tot!" [♣]

*that it was written entirely in cipher. Even a necessarily brief examination of
the vellum upon which it was written, the calligraphy, the drawings and the
pigments suggested to me as the origin the latter part of the thirteenth century.
The drawings indicated it to be an encyclopaedic work on natural philosophy.*

*The fact that this was a thirteenth century manuscript in cipher convinced
me that it must be a work of exceptional importance, and to my knowledge the
existence of a manuscript of such an early date written entirely in cipher was
unknown. Two problems immediately presented themselves — the text must be
unravelled and the history of the manuscript must be traced. It was not till some
time after the Manuscript came into my hands that I read the document bearing
the date 1665 (or 1666), which was attached to the front cover. This document,
which is a letter from Johannes Marcus Marci to Athanasius Kircher, making a
gift of the manuscript to him, is of great significance...*

On it went. But the more Němec read, the more convinced he became that there
was no way of tracing *back* from the Voynich Manuscript to the point from
which he'd started out. Namely, Edwarf K. So far, the premise for any
connection at all relied solely on the assumption that Rudolf had purchased the
Manuscript from John D & that the Manuscript itself had originated with
Roger Bacon[*]: a theory Voynich may've chosen to believe but which even Marci
doubted, & which was increasingly at variance with all available facts.

Then, his time running out, Němec found something interesting: a note
by a Renaissance art historian (Nemi, G., for Giuliana) which suggested, on the
basis of the Manuscript's illustrations, that it (i.e. the Manuscript) most likely
originated between the years 1470 & 1520 *in the Duchy of Bravuria*. Němec read
on. Then, leafing through the appendix of the same book (*The Mastery of
Nature: Aspects of Art, Science, and Humanism in the Renaissance*, trans. from the
Italian by Daria Anatoly), he found a note by a period expert on botany (Agusta,
P., for Pietro) identifying the *style of the herbal drawings* in the Manuscript (as
well as the style of the writing itself) as *Northern Italian*, dating from around
1460. A similar opinion was expressed by an archivist from Berlin (*The European
Renaissance: Centres and Peripheries*, pages 237-240), adding that the last section
of the Manuscript (composed in what appeared to be a mix of Deutsch, Latin &
Voynichese) indicated a *mitteleuropäischen* origin, circa 1550.

The striking thing about all these guesses (divorced as they seemed to be
from preconceptions about the Manuscript's authorship & content) was, rather

---

[*] Who, incidentally, had *also* written about cryptography, in his *Epistle on Secret Works of Art and of
Nature and on the Nullity of Magick* (c1250). [✋]

than discrediting any connection with K, that they offered a more credible, if still circumstantial, basis for believing K indeed had a hand in the transmission of the Voynich Manuscript. Němec realised then what he'd unconsciously overlooked before. In one of those carbon-copy typescripts he'd read back in April (what was it? Ashmole's *Confiteor*? Yes!) there'd been something about K having been thrown in prison by Rudolf (& here Němec grinned to himself again) because he was alleged to've been in league with a "goldmaker" from *Venice* to pull a scam. But Němec remembered there was something else, too. About how this "goldmaker" was executed *by the Duke of Bravuria* in Munich.[*]

Too many coincidences, Němec thought. But how neatly all the pieces fell into place: a goldmaker from Northern Italy, practicing in Bravuria, in league with K in Bohemia... Could this have been the *real* conspiracy, to defraud Rudolf? The concocting of the Voynich Manuscript?

He had only minutes to search the catalogue for Ashmole's *Confiteor*, there'd been three volumes, but none of the cards was in the places he looked. A voice crackled over a loudspeaker, announcing that the library was closing. Němec hurriedly searched through a dozen other sets of drawers, but to no avail, aware that the Reading Room was quickly emptying around him. He began to feel desperate. He was sure something essential was almost within his grasp & it was slipping away. *Where were those bloody cards?* He heard footsteps behind him & then a voice. It was the librarian with the bifocals.

'You have to leave now,' he said in a dull monotone.

Němec, in a fever of exhaustion, began to explain about the missing cards, but the staring lopsided eyes unnerved him.

'You have to leave now,' the monotone repeated.

There was no point debating. Němec went back to his desk, shuffled his notes into a pile & stuffed them into the bag with the Black Book. All the while the librarian watched him. Němec could feel his eyes follow him across the room to the heavy black door. Outside, the corridor was deserted. The sound of his walkingstick echoed. Behind him, one by one, the overhead lights were being switched off.

[*] On the 25th of April 1593, as it happens. [✋]

d. The King of the Magicians

25

THE CARETAKER

Hard blue porcelain, the sky — halfmoon over the rooftops.

At that time of day, late morning, Jánský Vršek was as quiet as any dead-end street can be. The old white house was exactly as Němec remembered it. He found the caretaker sitting in the courtyard, a heavily embroidered shawl draped across her shoulders, knitting. She was a small, spinsterish old lady, with pearlgrey hair drawn back tightly into a bun. A large rhinestone broach was pinned at her throat above a white lace collar. Her hands were restless, fineboned, tapering to heavily varnished fingernails. On a small table beside her stood a china tea set & a tall glass of dark rum. There were tea leaves spread out on a saucer, as though waiting to be read. Behind her, through the doorway to her caretaker's flat, an old green parrot perched on a stand, craning its head. The caretaker's name was on the doorbell by the front entrance:

'Mrs Severínová?'

The old lady gazed at him quizzically, over a pair of round wireframe glasses. The parrot craned its neck further. Němec felt its black eye fixing on him, as it waited & watched. The old woman put down her knitting but said nothing.

'I knew Professor Hájek. I used to visit him, before he died.'

The old woman's lips twisted into something that might've been a smile.

'You seem very sure of yourself, young man.'

Němec grinned back at her, foolishly, unable to think of anything to say.

'Sit with me,' she said finally, indicating a low wooden chair leaning against the courtyard wall.

The green parrot watched closely as Němec brought the chair over & sat down beside the table, pointed knees sticking up awkwardly.

'Would you care for some tea? It was Tomáš's favourite. From Yunan province, in China. The famous six mountains. Do you know China at all? It is a very large country with an ancient culture, much more ancient than our own. Here,' she said, pouring a reddishbrown liquid into an empty cup.

Němec didn't care for any tea but it was better to humour the old lady. The tea, he noticed, had gone cold in the pot. She waited for him to taste it — it tasted like brackish water rinsed through straw & crushed brick. The old woman saw him wince & let her smile play out into the type of enlightened grin you see in pictures of Sri Chinmoy. The parrot faintly cackled.

'An acquired taste, perhaps.'

Němec tried to balance the cup on one of his knees, thought better of it, & placed it on the edge of the table. Severínová watched all this with an appearance equally of bemusement & indifference. She leant back in her armchair & removed her glasses.

'For the ancient Chinese,' she said, polishing her lenses with the hem of her shawl, 'tea symbolised harmony, calm &... Oh yes, yes, most importantly of all, *optimism*. The drinking of tea often involved certain rituals, which were meant to represent the balance & proper ordering of the universe. Their philosophy, do you know, preceded the birth of Christ by more than fifteen hundred years. The Christians, being Romans rather than Israelites, professed a greater liking for wine, to symbolise the union of body & spirit. The Romans, of course, learned the making of wine from the Celts. Our own land was first settled by the Celts, you know. A thousand years before the Sklavs first wandered from the shores of their Bleak Sea.'

The old lady's smile began to wane. She repositioned her glasses on the bridge of her nose, her faded eyes growing larger behind the lenses. Němec wondered what the history lesson was leading to.

'We don't normally expect visitors, nowadays. Do we, Gawaine?'

The parrot shook its head from side to side, ruffling its feathers, then went back to eyeballing their visitor, its beak soundlessly open, the shadow of a grublike tongue moving inside. Němec couldn't quite put his finger on what the old women's strange conversation reminded him of...

'Finish your tea,' she snapped.

Němec did so, trying to keep from swallowing the leaves, & immediately she snatched the cup away from him & began scrutinising the dregs at the bottom of it. Němec sat there uncomfortably watching her. It had been his intention to ask about the Prof's, but seeing the way the caretaker was poking around at the tea leaves didn't make him feel overly optimistic. While she poked she began to hum, & presently she spoke without, however, taking her eyes from the leaves.

'It seems to me everything has to be the way it is & no other way.'

Němec wasn't sure he'd heard her rightly & leant forward with his eyes grown wider, as if either would help him hear any better now that she'd gone silent again. Aware of how foolish he must've looked, he straightened up & cast around for a new angle of approach. The parrot sneered. Ignoring it, Němec began to explain his relationship with the Prof, but the old lady cut him off.

'I know all about that,' she said.

Němec gathered there were probably a great number of things La Severínová knew. Just then she fixed him with a cold stare & said —

'Why don't you go up there, since that's what you came for? The keys are on the hook beside the stove.'

Němec stared at her uncomprehendingly.

'Well, what are you waiting for?'

The old woman seemed to know his mind better than he did. Maybe, he thought, that was what he'd really come for after all. The house with its unholy spirits, the magic Tower, the child of legend with the ears of a donkey. Astrologers & asses.

'Doesn't anyone live there?'

'Not since Tomáš passed & that dreadful thing happened.'

People, he supposed, were probably a bit squeamish about moving into a place like that, tainted by unnatural death. That's what they'd think. As if anything that happened in this city could be called *natural*. The old woman waved at him impatiently so he stood up & went to get the keys — they were hanging on a hook beside the stove, just as she said they would, on a ring with the unmysterious letters T.H. monographed on a faded disc of black leather. Němec felt the cold weight of the keys in his hand & shuddered slightly, as if he was holding the mystery & banality of other people's lives in some kind of balance. Then something moved behind him & he swung around in alarm to find the green parrot stretching its neck out towards him from the top of the pantry, hissing.

'Gawaine!' the old woman snapped.

The parrot fixed Němec with one of its black eyes & didn't move. Němec edged away from it towards the door. Its malevolent gaze followed him. Evil thing that it was. Once Němec crossed the threshold of the doorstep the parrot lost all interest in him. It puffed its feathers & drew in its neck, lidding its eye.

'I don't remember the parrot.'

'Gawaine?' the caretaker looked surprised. 'He was Alžběta's pet. She bought him, oh, I can't remember when, at an exposition, at the Botanic Gardens. Funny, you wouldn't think they'd put a bird like that up for sale, at the Botanic Gardens. It was Gawaine who alerted us, by his screeching, when she… you know, had her accident. He's very protective, the unfortunate creature. It's said they choose their mates for life. In Gawaine's mind, Alžběta belonged to *him* & he defended his claim against all competition. Even Tomáš, poor man. She had to keep him locked in her room. Gawaine, I mean. Well, you can just imagine…'

Mrs Severínová cackled quietly to herself.

'Come. Give me your arm. I'll show you the apartment.'

The caretaker pulled herself up out of her chair & balanced herself with her hand on Němec's right shoulder. He offered her his stick but she waved it away. Taking the keys from him, she beckoned him to follow her & started out across the courtyard to the Tower. The stairs weren't steep, but she climbed them with difficulty, gripping the handrail. Rheumatism, she explained.

'As you can see, I don't come in here very often.'

The door to the Prof's apartment was as nondescript as ever. Inside, the air was heavy with mustification. Němec sniffed at it apprehensively, the smell of detergent, plasterer's paint, stale cigarette smoke. The walls, he could see, had been partly repainted & the fireplaces blocked-up. There were vague outlines along the edges of the parquetry where previously a bookshelf, or a cabinet, or some piece of furniture or other had been. The rooms stood bare, were barely even rooms. Without furniture, they had an almost religious austerity. Stripped of the privacies of habitation, they were mere spaces, yet still Němec felt a sense of trespass — encroaching upon the ghost of something that'd remained even when no other trace remained.

Most of the Prof's books, it turned out, had been sold to an antique dealer from Schnitzelstadt, to pay the death duties & funeral costs. There were no close relatives as far as the caretaker knew & there'd rarely been any visitors other than Němec. This surprised him, having imagined the Prof to've been some sort of *operator* among the local cognoscenti. But then, he reminded himself, the Prof had been in exile & the City wasn't often forgiving of those who'd left. And even if it had been, who would he've known who wasn't simply a casual acquaintance? He was an old man, after all. As for the two women, they hardly went out & towards the end neither had been in particularly good health.

The property, Mrs Severínová seemed to think, was being held in trust by the State, who'd appointed an executor, but she'd forgotten his name. Boroš, maybe. She speculated about her own future, once the house was put up for auction / tender / sale, whatever it was the State had in mind for it. She harboured, she said, no illusions. As for the rest, a secondhand dealer from Libeňský Island somehow got wind of the deal & come for the furniture. The old woman had probably got herself a tidy sum for it, the piano alone must've been worth a bit. The only tenants remaining in the house were an architect who was abroad most of the time & an Amerikan who spent eight months of every year in Karlsbad (where the bottled mineral water came from) because Marx & Freud had once visited there & Kafka too, incidentally, the latter in a sanatorium with a view of the colonnade thanks to a misdiagnosis in early childhood.

As the caretaker guided him around the apartment, Němec couldn't help thinking about those letters which the Prof's very uxorious wife had supposedly burned after he died & before she killed herself. What was so important about them? What did they contain? What type of intimacies? Glancing through a doorway into one of the garçonnières, Němec's gaze was automatically drawn towards the gas radiator fixed to the wall beneath the window. A sickliness emanated from within the room which caused him to recoil & be glad once the door was locked again. He made a point of checking the mains, but there was nothing unusual. The caretaker, meanwhile, was busy pointing things out to herself — the place where Hájek used to take his breakfast in the winter garden, the corner where his wife kept magnolias in a vase, & so on. Němec tried to imagine the Prof & the two women seated together at the breakfast table & what they might've spoken about. No children, either. But that was probably the point. As he pondered this, the caretaker came into the Prof's bureau & stood by the window, a distant look in her eyes.

'It's funny,' she said after a while, 'I knew Bětka when she was just a girl. We went to school together, in Markt Eisenstein, in the Böhmewald. There was a scullery maid at one of the hotels who the children used to make fun of, because she was a Kozar & people thought she was simple. Every fourth of December she had a vision of Saint Bára standing on Špičák mountain. It became a village tradition. Bětuška would get all in a rage because she couldn't accept that Saint Bára had appeared to a witless scullery maid, but never once appeared to her.'

She laughed, but the laugh trailed off almost immediately into silence. It was an uncomfortable silence. Němec looked around the room to see what'd changed. The walls seemed closer somehow. Finally he tried to prompt Mrs Severínová with her story, afraid she might be unwell.

'How'd she meet Professor Hájek? His wife, I mean.'

The old woman pursed her lips in thought & fidgeted with a window latch.

'I couldn't tell you,' she said abruptly. 'I don't know.'

'But she was here in the City, during the War, wasn't she?'

'These windows need cleaning. Houses suffer if they're not lived in.'

'Mrs Severínová?'

'Don't interrogate me, young man.'

She looked at Němec sternly & wiped her hand on her skirt —

'Of course, you're curious. Young people are always curious. I was young myself, once.'

Her face softened somewhat. She signalled that it was time to leave & Němec held her arm as they walked back down the stairs to the courtyard.

'It was Alžbětka,' she said as they neared the foot of the Tower, 'who arranged for me to come to the City. My father worked for Old Seifert. We weren't so well off, so when my father died & Bětka offered for me to come with her... By the time I arrived, they were already living here together with Miss N____, who was the eldest of the three, much more worldly than Bětuška & even Tomáš. She was handsome, in that masculine way that was fashionable then. People often paid her compliments. Her grandfather was supposed to've been an aristocrat, who collected dolls, wind-up dolls, he had an entire château filled with them. But then Heydrich was killed & everything changed. Well, as you know, after the War they all emigrated. They left me here, in fact. Of course, I would have chosen to stay in any case. I had my reasons. But it was an awful time. For everyone, I mean. It was like going through the War all over again. The first years especially were the hardest. Then when the purges began, *ach*! Sometimes I'd receive postcards, from different places here & there, always in Alzinka's handwriting, but never a return address. They were afraid, you know, for my sake. I always wrote to them *poste restante*. Well, time has its own way of passing, they were busy years. Once, in '68, I thought I saw her, Alžbětka, standing in the street, like St Bára, on Nerudova. I thought they'd secretly come back. But it wasn't her. Later, they did return. She'd changed, of course, they all had, but I still recognised them immediately. I never felt bad about it. I knew why they'd had to leave. And why I'd waited for them. You see, I've never stopped living here. No matter what happened, I always found a way. Deep in my heart I knew the time would come when we'd all be together again. And I was right,' she smiled. 'But then that terrible thing happened...'

Němec led her across the courtyard to her spot at the table outside her door. The parrot eyeballed him from the kitchen. The old woman slumped into her chair, pulled her shawl around her & groped for her knitting. Němec stood there unsure of what to do now. The knitting needles clacked. The caretaker's attention seemed entirely fixed on their simple yet elaborate mechanics. Then a fit of coughing brought her back out of herself. Němec handed her the glass of rum sitting beside the tea pot. She sipped from it, it seemed to relax her. Němec was still thinking of the story about the Prof's wife when she reached into her dress pocket & held the keyring out to him.

'Take these, you'll need them if you're to stay with us.'

Němec took the keys & was about to say something when she cut him off.

'It isn't for others to judge,' she said. 'It required courage to live as they chose to live. And to die, Lord have mercy on them.'

With that, Mrs Severínová ceased paying him any attention & resumed the looping of yarn between her fingers & around the ends of the long grey knitting needles.

He could hear the parrot whistling from the shadows of the caretaker's kitchen as he left the house through the archway that opened onto the street. The whole episode struck him as slightly unreal. He thought of the two women who'd committed suicide there, in that house. And what the caretaker had said about the Prof, that he'd been a lonely man. Němec wondered what exactly she meant by that, or if it wasn't just the doting of an old disappointed woman. He drew a picture in his head of the Prof hunched in the gloom of his bureau with the lights dimmed, the room's queerly vaulted ceilings making lopsided shadows around him.

Had Němec been more prone to romantic imaginings, he might've said the room possessed the air of a parlour after a séance. But it was only a room that'd been stripped of what it'd been. The yellowed plaster on walls marked from where the bookshelves had been removed — the exposed wiring where light fixtures had been taken down — the parquet, scratched & stained. Yet still there were unanswered questions that hung in the air like spirits, hesitant, unable yet to depart, wishing only to materialise. What his reasons had been for going there, he couldn't say. Nor the reasons for why he'd return — except that, now he'd been given the key, the matter seemed already to've been decided.

Blecha just nodded when Němec told him he was moving into the Prof's old apartment, for a while at least, to clear something up. His own words struck him as faintly absurd, if only because he himself didn't really understand why he was going at all.

'Room'll still be here for whenever you decide to come back,' the Bugman said, helping himself to a second grilled knedlík from his primus stove.

A couple of chickens pecked idly around the old guy's feet.

'Don't worry about it, kiddo, do whatever you've gotta do. Never did much care for unfinished business myself...'

Němec gazed out at the rooftops then back at Blecha's pumpkin vines. *I'll miss it here*, he thought.

Late that same afternoon they drove what little Němec possessed across to Jánský Vršek in an old yellow open-top Felicia the Bugman'd somehow conjured for the purpose, his silver hair billowing in the wind beside Němec's hairless pate, bowler clenched atop a duffle bag that took up the space between his knees. A box of vinyls lay wedged under his feet, the recordplayer perched behind the gear stick.

They took the most direct route, down Žitná to Resslova Street, then along Gottwald Embankment to the National Theatre, turning left onto Legion Bridge. There were people out on the island, sitting along the shore, watching the peddleboats, a folk band playing roundels. A van passed them, swerving onto the tramtracks on the wrong side of the road & a tram clanged its bell at it. Blecha gesticulated Latin-style at the driver as the van cut-in ahead of them.

'What's the use?' he shrugged his old-man's shoulders. 'See that?' he gestured ahead with his chin. 'Warsaw number plates. In Warsaw they drive like pigs. No rules. Poles don't know what a rule is. They fix toilets, they wash floors. But they know there's no-one on Earth who fixes toilets or washes floors half as good as they do. Proud people the Poles. Especially well-loved in Silesia. Ever hear the story of Chesk & Lesk? The two brothers? Remind me to tell you sometime.'[*]

Blecha rapped on the steering wheel as the van stalled ahead of them at the next traffic lights. POLSKÉ OKURKY was written across the back doors in bold green serif. A metre-tall pickled cucumber with arms, legs, saucer-eyes & idiot grin, pointed at a cartoon thought bubble floating above it:

Why get yrself in a pickle?
Munch a Gherkin instead!

---

[*] → Chapter 47. [✋]

The tram clattered past & once again the van pulled out onto the wrong side of the road. The Bugman just shook his head.

'Here's some trivia for you,' he said, checking the rearview. 'Did you know, before the Krauts invaded in '39, people here drove on the left side of the road? Now, though, it's the same all over Europe. Everyone drives like the Krauts do. On the *right*. Rechts! Rechts! Rechts! Where's the justice in that, I'd like to know.'

They'd made their way up Újezd as far as Hellichova, before the traffic came to a standstill, this time on account of a tram that'd somehow got derailed. Men in green uniforms were waving cars back around towards the river & they found themselves stuck in a detour for the next quarter hour for the sake of a couple of blocks. At Jánský Vršek, finally, they unloaded & Blecha sat out in the courtyard while Němec carted his gear upstairs. Ten minutes later Němec joined him & with the caretaker's parrot keeping its beady eye on them Blecha broke open a fresh bottle of Slivovice. La Severínová was pottering about, wrapped in a shawl, watering plants & such like. Blecha invited her to join them, but the old woman smilingly demurred & shuffled inside.

'Not bad for her age,' Blecha grinned, gazing after her. 'Some women, you know, only get better. Not that I'd know, *hehe*. Was married once, did I ever tell you? But the girl left me, *hehe*, for an older man. So now I'm a bachelor. Been a bachelor for thirtynine years, *hehe*.'

'What'd you get hitched for in the firstplace?'

The Bugman shook his head as he poured out two large glasses.

'Got to get old & stupid before you get old & wise.'

He held up his glass & they toasted —

'Here's to something.'

'Aye & all that.'

Blecha tipped his head back & swallowed his drink in one, then poured another. He gave Němec a slightly glassy look, his mouth gone crooked. Blinked.

'The very thing.'

Němec drank his & nodded in agreement. The Bugman refilled their glasses & left the bottle between them on the caretaker's table.

They'd done this sort of thing together dozens of time before up on the Bugman's terrace, watching the City, like a pair of gargoyles, but the change of surrounds did something to the occasion, though Němec couldn't say what exactly. Kelley's Tower white against the sky, the Prof's ghost somewhere invisible on the periphery, watching over the whole proceedings. Němec wondered what Blecha really thought about him moving into the Old Man's apartment. If he thought anything, he didn't say. Instead he leant forward with his elbows resting slightly unsteady —

'D'you know where you were born?'

'Where I was *born*?'

'Where you were born.'

'I suppose in a hospital.'

'Mmm. In my day, you popped out wherever you happened to be. My own mother, she worked in the Ultrafon factory, making insulation for copper telegraph wires. Never took a day off, even when she was pregnant. One morning went to the bathroom with a cramp, waters broke, out I came, right there on the floor. Swaddled me up & kept me in a cot beside the machines. No father you see. Thought I came off a production line, *hehe*. You behold before you an immaculate example of the modern man, circa nineteentwenty.'

'The New Man! When did you discover you weren't a robot?'

'The Ides of March, nineteenthirtynine.'

He raised his glass for another toast.

'Death to all robots!'

They both drank & then sat for a while in silence while the parrot sat there & watched them, making a sound with its beak like dry grass rustling. Blecha poured another round of drinks & put the cork in the bottle. He grinned at Němec sheepishly —

'Did I ever tell you about Geldzahler, who used to live in the apartment next to yours?'

Němec shook his head.

'He was a Slovník, from Bratrislova. But on New Year's Day in '93 he was visiting his old mother-in-law at Bohnice. She must've been a hundred nearly & fell down some stairs & broke her hip. You know what they say, at that age, you break your hip, well… Of course, there was no way poor Geldzahler could leave her like that, with no-one to look after her. I mean, no family. So he missed the deadline. Midnight, New Year's Eve, when everyone in what up till then was still Cheskoslovnikia had to make up their minds which side of the border they wanted to be on, the Chesk side or the Slovnik side, & that's what passport they'd give you because we became two different countries then, right? Idiots! So thanks to his mother-in-law breaking her hip Geldzahler wasn't a Slovnik anymore, just because he couldn't take a train back to Bratrislova! And that was that — he had to sell everything & move over here. His dead wife used to be friends with Mrs Falová on the sixth floor, which is how he happened to come to me, for a place to stay. Of course, the building was half empty, ever since the Revolution, & I appreciated the company & all that, so…'

The Bugman paused to sip his slivovice.

'Anyway, we discovered we had something in common. Turned out this Geldzahler was in one of those Nazi camps in Poland. He had a number on his wrist to prove it. Only problem was it was fading. The number I mean. He didn't know what to do about it, it'd become part of his identity. You understand, what they had to go through, it was terrible, & then afterwards, the purges, & then people denying it, saying it was all a Zionist conspiracy. He was afraid if he didn't have that number, his whole past would fade with it, that it'd disappear completely, as if it'd never happened. I asked him why he didn't just go to a tattoo parlour & have it done again? He thought I was nuts, but what else was there to do? He got so desperate he eventually let me take him to a place over in the Žižkov freight yards, but when we got there he was too afraid it'd look fake, that people'd look at his brand new Auschwitz tattoo & call him a liar, a pretender, a fraud — his own people, I mean. There was no way out of it. Buggered if he did, buggered if he didn't.'

'So what happened?'

'Oh, nothing. You know how it is. He'd smoked fifty-a-day from who-knows-when. Told the doctor he had this cough, wouldn't go away. Not exactly rocket science. The doc said it was lung cancer, or throat cancer, or thyroid cancer, or some other cancer & maybe, if he was lucky, he had a month left. For a thousand bucks, maybe two months. Geldzahler wanted time to think it over. Doc said sure, take all the time you need.'

'And?'

'And nothing. Soon as he got the diagnosis, he made a beeline for *The Lost Flounder* to drown his sorrows. Notched up a good fifteen pints by the time the barmaid reckoned he couldn't hang onto his perch anymore. Told him to go on home, sleep it off. Geldzahler begged one last, for the road. Drank up, paid up, then got up, on his own two feet believe it or not, & staggered straight out under the number eleven tram. *Finito.*'

He brought his hand down flat on the table. *Slap.*

'Well,' the Bugman said after a while, 'that's enough talk from me for one afternoon. Got to get old Mrs Falová sorted out with the Welfare people. Blind, you know. Completely. I had to chase off that granddaughter of hers again the other day — had the old bird padlocked in her room again, the nasty little bitch.

I see no reason why a person can't be allowed to grow crotchety & die in their own familiar stink, where they've lived all their lives or the best part of. So what if the old girl's frail — we're all frail! You take away someone's home, *finito*, like Geldzahler. You know, I called the Blind Society, just to see if there was anything they could do. What the idiot there suggested was I get the old bird a guide dog. *She can hardly climb the stairs, you tit. How d'you expect her to look after a fucking dog?* What, are they supposed to take care of themselves, those dogs? Do the shopping? Take out the trash? Ever wondered where a guide dog goes to take a shit? I've been thinking about that one — if you come up with an answer, let me know, I'd be interested.'

With that, Blecha said a *so long for now* & got back in the Felicia, leaving the rest of the bottle of moonshine in Němec's care. The parrot & Mrs Severínová both watched him go then left the new tenant to his own devices. Němec took the bottle upstairs. After he'd gone through the place sweeping up & generally putting things in order, he sat down on a packing crate that'd been left behind & pondered what he proposed to do. The rooms echoed with the unstilled anxiety of final departure. He thought about what La Severínová had said to him. In particular, he wondered what the Prof might've written in his will & testament, if one existed. The Prof being the Prof, he'd assumed one would. The Old Man might even've remembered *him* in it. No-one else ever had. It seemed a foolish hope.

Inside Němec's head an uncharacteristically pragmatic voice told him he ought (belatedness be damned) to make some inquiries after all. It seemed strange that a man like the Prof wouldn't've appointed his own executor. Or perhaps he had & whoever it was had predeceased him? Or postdeceased him, as the case very well may've been. Or perhaps he'd kept it a secret, so secret no-one had found out who. Hidden in the walls somewhere, written in code, a set of instructions as to where to find his most precious treasure, *hehe*, the buried Sphinx. (Němec was getting ahead of himself as usual.) He remembered back to their first meeting at the Klementinum. Perhaps, after all, the Old Man was no different to him, a stranger passing the time, who'd simply sat down for an hour or so to play a game of chess with whoever happened to come along. A mere chance encounter with no further consequences for the story at hand — & that was the sum total of his relation t the world barring the Muses, the caretaker & his wife's mangy parrot?

Němec tried to figure all the people who, in the course of any given day, ought to've had some sort of transaction with the Prof. Or did the Prof exist the way a rumour existed, a shadow & nothing else, a brown shape blending into the walls? The type of person who could vanish from the world & never be missed. Or almost. It made him think of Eddie K in a London pillory, the man with the Van Gogh job under his sideburns, who — failing[*] at making the wide world fall for a fake — tried to make himself disappear (all the better to pop up again in someone else's pocket?).

The image of a man falling from a windowledge flashed through Němec's mind in a series of montage: a pair of boots on the ledge, mortar sifting between stone blocks, dark shapes moving in the wind, a pupil dilating, mouth anguish-stricken, a birdseye view spiralling into vertigo, the flicker of candlelight through an empty window, the emptiness itself. Did it represent a type of punishment, or a form of atonement? And the fact, too, that it was none other than Jan Mydlář, Rudolf II's willing executioner, who'd been sent to interrogate K at Křivoklát Castle, to learn the secret of the long-promised *elixir* & of — but did anyone believe in this nonsense?[*] — the transmutation of gold. Only he'd got there too late. K had already flown the coop, straight downwards into an empty moat.

Němec sat there in the fading light with Blecha's moonshine letting his thoughts move according to their own will. The binbag with the Prof's notebook lay at his feet, beside the box with his collection of vinyls in it. It would've taken too much effort to plug the recordplayer in & put a disc on. He took a slug from the bottle & felt the inertia pull him further into himself.

'What the hell am I doing here?' he said to no-one.

A streetlight drew a mess of contradicting geometries on the walls. He took aim at one of the more flagrant instances & tossed the wet cork at it. The cork bounced & thudded somewhere on the parquet. Němec tipped the bottle to his mouth & tried to finish it in one long gulp but was bested by it. His guts burned.

'Ah,' he belched, 'an honest feeling at last.'

He propped the bottle on the floor & reached for the binbag, drunker than he realised. Had he taken his pills today? He couldn't remember. Maybe that was the problem. He dropped the binbag & dug in his pockets. Volta's prescription came up in his right hand

'Magic!' he said, breathlessly. 'And for my next trick…'

He tipped out a handful of pills, poured half of them back in the jar & swallowed what was left. He splashed a little extra slivovice down his throat.

---

[*] Had he failed? [👆]
[*] With the exception, perhaps, of Adolf Eichmann, four centuries late. [👆]

Grinned at the bottle.

'Here's to the Old Man! May he rest under the floorboards, *hehe*.'

He plonked the bottle down again & grabbed the Prof's notebook out of the bag. It fell open to the frontispiece, the Devil & the Carmelite. Racy stuff.

'Good for you, you old bastard.'

He flipped the pages. The usual nonsense stared back at him.

'So what the fuck did you expect me to do with this, eh? Solve the Big Riddle? Prove you're not actually dead? Pin the crime on the arseholes who really did it? Let me guess: monks in stocking masks, crept up on you in your bath, eh, a little jab in the neck, make it look like a heartattack? Then stuck the ladies' heads in the oven, for good measure, eh, just to make a story out of it? And all that crap about burning your letters. Needed time, didn't they, to find what they were looking for? Not as if anyone'd have trouble swallowing the official line — I mean, really, misadventure in the fucking tub & double suicide? Happens every day, fer Chrissakes!'

Unthinking he tore a page from the black book, crumpled it into a ball & pegged it at the crisscrossing shadows.

'Yeah. And no fucking next of kin, either, how convenient's that?'

He tore out another page. Breathing deeply he stared down at it, a vague rectangle in the dark ▢. With automatic hands he began folding it into shapes ▷◁. A body with wings ⇨. He threw it, spiralling into nowhere. Then another, slowly & evenly this time, & another after that. Folding them into paper spaceships, aeroplanes — the Nakamura Lock, the Spy Plane, the Swashbuckler, the Headhunter, the Hammer, the Pteroplane, the Flying Ninja, the Space Cruiser, the Hurricane. They were heavy, they thudded into walls, they nosedived into parquet, they kamikazed into crevices. Němec tore & folded till his head went numb with the pointlessness of it: an idiot casting gibberish into the void. Who'd he take himself for, Carl Sagan? The way the Bugman said they drew straws in the Karelian gulags, to see who'd cut off a finger & tie it to anything that'd float — a bottle, some foam-rubber, a piece of wood — in the vain hope someone downriver'd find it & know they were there.

And so, like that, with no more meaningful purpose in mind, Němec sat there in the dark to the bitter end, tearing out pages till his fingers lost all feeling, waiting in vain for a return message from the Great Beyond, for the Black Book's admonishing howl, for the Prof's ghost to re-appear.

26

ANAGRAMMATISED

Within this circle is Jehovah's name,
Forward and backward anagrammatised:
Th'abbreviated names of holy saints,
Figures of every adjunct to the heavens,
And characters of signs and erring stars,
By which the spirits are enforced to rise…![*]

Until the moment the phone rang, Němec had been thinking of something, but now he couldn't remember what it was. He stood in the foyer of the Prof's apartment looking down at the telephone's dull black plastic & old fashioned dial, sitting there on the floor in the corner of the room, a black insulated wire snaking out from it along the base of the wall to a socket that'd almost been plastered over. Apart from the telephone, the hall was completely bare. He hadn't even noticed it before, yet the telephone's black body squatted there undeniably, like a grinning Buddha with ten little eyes.

In a world where telephones exist, it's almost possible to imagine a world where they *don't* — but to've imagined a world in which telephones *did* exist, in a world where they didn't?

After a while the ringing stopped & then began again. Němec leant down & examined the black Buddha more closely — it looked like any ordinary telephone. He picked up the receiver & listened. There was nothing. He kept listening. A faint distant echo of static & that was all. As he hung up, his hand brushed against something. Turning the phone around, Němec found a small rectangle of textured green paper, the size of a calling card, tangled up in the

---

[*] "I've got it! His real name is Arty Mori…!" Maurice J. Micklewhite a.k.a. Michael Caine, son of a fish-market porter, actor, in his definitive role as Sherlock Holmes. [✋]

331

coiled mess of wiring that connected (A) the phone to the wall & (B) the receiver to the phone. He worked the card free & spread it flat between his fingers. On one side, printed in sloping copperplate, was an address:

La Fée Verte
Villa Šicinzl, Střelecký Ostrov
20:00 – 8:00

He turned the card over. On the back, someone had written in blue ink something that looked like this:

r o t a s
o p e r a
t e n e t
a r e p o
s a t o r

One of those backwards-&-forwards thingamies. Sator? Sounded like someone making promises they couldn't possibly deliver on, haha. Němec looked at the address again. Střelecký Ostrov was the island right in the middle of the river, opposite the National Theatre. You got there by crossing Legion Bridge & taking a set of steps down. As far as he knew there wasn't anything there but rats & an old boarded-up château waiting for restitution. The scion of a minor branch of the Habsburgs or whatever, there never seemed to be any shortage of them — still coming out of the woodwork to get a slice of what the Commies had helped themselves to after the War. *Well, what'd the Krauts ever do for us, eh?*

Němec wondered what a card for a place called *The Green Fairy* was doing in the Prof's apartment. It didn't seem right, somehow. Maybe one of the removalists dropped it, or it fell out of the back of a sofa. Maybe it was an old wateringhole for the City's esoterics, like the Patriot Klub, & the Old Man would head on down there every now & then for a thimble of absinth. Not something he'd ever mentioned, but then there was a lot the Prof'd never mentioned. Or maybe it was connected with the Opera. Some sort of Mahler Appreciation Society perhaps?

He tapped the card against the phone thoughtfully, then just to be sure

332

there really wasn't anyone at the other end, he lifted the receiver again from its cradle & listened. A short & then long tone crackled in his ear. Short & then long, short & then long… It repeated in exactly the same way till he hung up, but as soon as he had the ringing began again. He lifted the receiver once more & held it away from his ear. This time there was a voice recording: it was the telephone company, reminding that the monthly payment was overdue.

Pressing down on the cradle with his free hand Němec broke the connection, then released it, bringing the receiver closer to his ear. Again there was the curious tone, only now backwards — long & then short. Long. Short. He hung up. For a while he stared at it, the little black Buddha, till an idea formed, that perhaps, after all, the Prof's ghost was trying to communicate with him by Morse code. Like the old biddies banging on their drainpipes. Just thinking it started to give him a headache. He slipped the calling card in his jacket pocket. The jacket, he noticed for the first time, was covered in dust. The trousers also. He must've slept on the floor. *Well, there ain't nowhere else to sleep, is there kiddo?* Which reminded him of the Bugman & how dry his throat was. Bits & pieces of the previous night filtered in. He glanced back apprehensively at the phone, unsure if he ought to lift the receiver again & see if there was anything to it, if the Prof really was trying to communicate with him through the wires. But it would've been pointless, he didn't know Morse code anyway.

▬ · ▬ · ▬ ·

By rights he should've had a hangover. There was still an inch of slivovice in the bottle, which stood, uncorked, on the floor of the Prof's bureau, in the corner beside his packing-case chair, duffel bag, box of vinyls, recordplayer, typewriter, battered old coffee pot & walkingstick. In the middle of the room was a black binbag. Němec limped over to the bottle. If he didn't rush it, he could build a decent breakfast out of the dregs. Which was what he'd been thinking before the phone rang, he now remembered. He'd woken up not knowing where he was & stumbled out on the stairs & down in the courtyard the caretaker had been sipping at a bowl of garlic soup. The smell of it wafted all through the place, fit to ward off a whole coven of vampires.

For some reason the smell of garlic soup had reminded him of the Bugman's story, about Geldzahler & his rotten luck, & then about the Prof,

whose luck hadn't been so rotten but hadn't been exactly rosy either. The Prof &
his mystery book & Kircher's letter & Faktor & the secrets of the Jesuit Order &
Roger Bacon & Rab Löw & Eddie K & why not Daffy Duck as well? The
whole thing made Němec feel lousy. He slumped down on the packing crate &
grabbed the bottle, getting it to his lips without shaking too much. Glumly he
stared at the binbag sitting in the middle of the room.

At some stage of his drunkenness the previous night he'd repented &
gathered up the mess he'd made of the Prof's notebook. Bits of abortive engines
of flight driven head-on into a wall. There might even have been some sort of
allegory in that, he didn't know, he was probably the wrong person to ask. Well
what chance did he have of deciphering the mysteries of the universe when he
couldn't even make a paper aeroplane that flies? Time to take stock, like
Schliemann, making an inventory of the buried Trojan city he'd just demolished
with bulldozers while trying to dig it up. Well, what difference, if you played the
odds or the odds played you? No end of ways open to a dedicated loser.

Němec dug out an Aaron Copland recording of Mahler's 7th[*] from his
box of vinyls & put it on the recordplayer, then found a working powerpoint to
plug it into. He took another swig of the bottle & tried to let his mind go blank
while he listened to the music, but it wouldn't, & there on the floor in front of
him was still the binbag with the remains of the Black Book stuffed in it & there
was no way he could make the thought of it go away. Guiltily he reached over
with his walkingstick & pulled it towards him.

At some point during the night remorse'd set in & he'd tried to undo the
damage. But now that he saw it in the painful light of day… Wads of paper
higgledy-piggledy stuffed between the covers, the massacred binding, torn,
crumpled, dust-smeared, threatening at any moment to spill out all over the
place. It was less a book than a ruin of a book. For the next hour Němec sat on
the floor rearranging the mess he'd made, straightening, flattening, making a
semblance of order out of it. He stared at the frontispiece: Heaven & Hell, the
temptation of the flesh too-willing, the agony & ecstasy, symbolism even a
halfwit could grasp. *What was it doing there, in that gnomic addressbook?*

His head ached, his leg ached, his guts ached. He rationed out the
remaining slivovice. *One sip at a time*, he told himself, *will get you through*. At
least, once he'd done penance, he'd be in better shape to go down the street &

---

[*] Dedicated to our own dear Golem City no less, where its maiden performance took place —
sometime back when. [✎]

get some more. Get in some supplies while he's at it, some candles, soap maybe, milk for the coffee, some bread to soak it all up with, whatever. The longer he worked operating on the remains of the Black Book, the more a kind of inertia crept over him. It was like an ailment, he thought. All you had to do was touch the damn thing & your brain started coming unhinged.

He focused on getting the pages in alphabetical order according to the lists of names. As matters stood, at least half the salvaged pages were nothing but lists of names & numbers, but the rest could've been anything, random doodlings & bits of gibberish that looked just like that, gibberish. Wondering why the hell anyone would go to the trouble. *But no reason on that account to jump to conclusions, eh, kiddo?* A dozen or so contained nothing but vertical & horizontal lines, with numbers & letters seemingly scattered about — as if the Prof had tried to cram as many games of Noughts & Crosses onto the page as possible, while at the same time keeping track of their order with different letters of the alphabet, sometimes numbers, like there was some system being worked through. Some sort of hypothesis, or a puzzle. The kind of thing, it occurred to Němec, you'd find in the back of the Sunday papers next to the funnies. The solution didn't require too much brain work, though. On one of the pages a key had been sketched out: there was nothing mysterious about it at all, it was the type of code every kid knows from school.[*]

Němec grinned unconvincingly at himself, conjuring an image in his mind of the Prof bent over his little Black Book, studiously playing a type of Masonic ticktacktoe with himself, in the pursuit of the Great Conundrum. The Noughts & Crosses were really letters arranged in different combinations — refinements of the basic set-up, working it seemed by trial & error. A lightbulb switched on

---

[*] The code works with three small grids of nine "squares." Each "square" is assigned to a letter of the alphabet — leaving the very last position in the third grid blank — & these in turn are made to correspond to a pair of numbers, or coordinates, obtained from a matching grid. Thus the letter A corresponds to grid 1, position 1 (11) — the letter Z to grid 3, position 8 (38), & so on.

A	B	C		J	K	L		S	T	U
D	E	F		M	N	O		V	W	X
G	H	I		P	Q	R		Y	Z	

	1				2				3	
1	2	3		1	2	3		1	2	3
4	5	6		4	5	6		4	5	6
7	8	9		7	8	9		7	8	9

[☞]

momentarily in Němec's head. There, on one side, was the Prof's tick-tack-toe, & on the other a list of names with telephone numbers. Maybe the numbers were bogus, maybe they were really an encrypted sequence of letters. Or maybe it was the names. Intrepidly, Němec chose a phone number at random & plugged it into one of the tick-tack-toe arrangements. Needless to say, he couldn't get anything out of it. His head ached more than ever. Maybe the answer was simple & they really were just phone numbers? It would've been easy enough to find out. Or maybe it wouldn't. But that didn't answer the question of what the Book was for.[*] *Well, what d'you call a lock, kiddo, when there ain't no key?* Or the other way around for that matter.

Then an obvious thought occurred to him. He went back through the book searching for something he should've looked for the first time around. When he found it, it hardly seemed remarkable at all. On one side of the page was the date, 13.X.1996. On the other, between ⊕ ~~FABER~~ 27162940 & ⊘ ~~FRANK~~ 27794127, was written ⊗ FAKTOR 27989618. Why wasn't *his* name crossed out? And what was the little circle with the cross in it meant to be? Němec scanned down through the lists of names again — some of them, like Faktor, had a symbol drawn beside them. There was a ⊖ ~~GELNER~~ 27163934, a ⊙ ~~HERZL~~ 27962533, a ◎ ~~JUNGER~~ 27795400, a ⊛ KAMMLER 27191627 (*Kammler, too!*), & a ⊖ ~~LAGNER~~ 27072813.

The symbols had to've meant *something*. Němec stifled a yawn, flipping back & forth. *Mene, mene, funny symbols. Within this circle, blah blah blah…* Eventually he came back to FAKTOR. 27989618. It looked like a Golem City telephone number alright. Maybe he should give the mad bastard a ring, *hehe*, see how his heterocosmic conspiracy was coming along. (No point trying Kammler, he was dead. Hello! That'd be a funny coincidence, the Wunderwaffe

---

[*] *Ah yes, elementary indeed, my dear Němec!* Might the names have belonged to people the Prof had actually known? Business associates, debtors, old friends, casual acquaintances? Was Němec's task, then, to *find someone* in particular? Or was the whole thing part of a more elaborate code? After all, a perfect cipher would either be perfectly camouflaged among elements of the everyday & in every aspect identical to them, *even to the point of verifiability* — actual names & actual phone numbers, real pieces of information that would *add-up* if required to. An open lie, concealed so-to-speak in plain view, like a, *er*, neurosis, *hehe*, & thereby, as the Good Doctor says, virtually *invulnerable*, as invulnerable as *reality itself*? (*Now yer suckin' diesel, kiddo!*) [♣]

Man in the same address book as dear old Faktor. Mmm.)[*] Something about those symbols, too, all circles & suchlike, but it was the names they belonged to — all Kraut names. Except Faktor. Faktor could've been anything. And then there was the date. What did October *13* have to do with Faktor, or any of the others?

Němec glanced dubiously at the little black Buddha squatting in the foyer. It seemed all so simple yet all too elaborate, like some secret ritualised intention complicating the obvious. And Faktor, that purveyor of horoscopes & conjurations — spleen of bat, eye of worm, hedgehog's ear, crow's foot, cock's comb. Němec could picture him, even now, with his hunchbacked dwarf doodling symbols with a stick in the dust, casting shadows by candlelight, robed, clovenhoofed, donkeyheaded, pouring dark libations upon some unsuspecting virgin, bound in a posture of supplication upon an Egyptian alter, the winged demon summoned from the depths by strange theremin-like emanations, etc.

But what if the Prof really had been tied up with something? And what if Faktor wasn't really the clown Němec had taken him to be? What if Faktor's name really was a clue he'd been meant to find? The question marks kept massing against him. Němec felt suddenly like a man overboard in the middle of an ocean — he could see no shoreline for the waves, while beneath him yawned an immeasurable abyss. He drew a deep breath & glanced around the room to reassure himself.[*] The record, almost without him realising it, had come to an end. Everything else was as it'd been before. Everything except the Black Book. He breathed out. *Faktor, Faktor, Faktor.* The name was like some terrible mantra. The only thing to do, he decided, putting the issue to rest, was to make the call.

He went to the phone, lifted the receiver & dialled the number. Two-seven-nine-eight-nine-six-one-eight. He listened. Nothing happened. The line was dead.

---

[*] → Chapter 52. Take a sneak preview, why the hell not? Němec already has. [♣]
[*] Yep, it was still right where it'd been before, though funnier if it hadn't. [♣]

27

UNTERMENSCHEN

The entrance was down a steep flight of concrete stairs behind the boarded-up château at the southern end of Shooters Island. A faint light was all that identified it. The island, in the middle of the river, beneath the stone arches of Legion Bridge, was to all appearances otherwise deserted, this as every other night. A casual observer would've had no way of guessing there was anything there at all but a ruin among the trees.

Němec found the doorbell & rang it. A heavyset doorman in dinner jacket & tie peered out at him through a Judas-hole in a rusty steel door. Němec held the calling card up so the doorman could see it, ROTAS OPERA etc., & a bolt slid back on the other side. A green vapour spilled out onto the steps. Crossing the threshold was like stepping onto the surface of an alien moon. Behind the steel door, a dark curtain parted to reveal a kind of antechamber in moth-eaten green chintz, its air musty with cigarette smoke & damp. There was a dirty green carpet on the floor, threadbare green velvet drapes & half-a-dozen tired green lampshades. Under one of which the doorman was standing motionless & at attention, like an automaton awaiting its next set of instructions, eyes slightly kinked: the spitting image of Tor Johnson in one of those films, though something womanly about the set of the jaw, the cast of those enormous yet finely boned hands.

The steel door seemed to close all by itself. Němec couldn't help wondering if he'd walked into some sort of B-grade production. *House of the Green Ghoul*, maybe. He glanced around to get his bearings, read the signs. There was a door to his left, marked

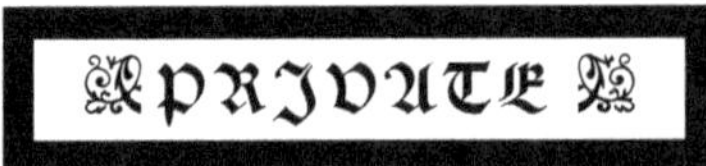

like a death notice in fancy lettering. On the right, a coatcheck half-hidden in an alcove with empty racks making shadows on the wall. A couple of drapes divided the space at the far end of this antechamber — voices were coming from the other side of them. Němec hadn't taken more than a couple of steps in their direction when a large toad of a woman, dressed in a frock & stole that reminded of a bishop's cassock, came through the doorway & barred his path. There was a peacock's feather stuck in a bird's nest of dyed hair, loose strands of which hung across a toadlike face smeared with an excess of Max Factor. The creature's mouth leered at him like a painted rictus —

'Wilkommen mon ami, in zee Grünegast.'

Němec blinked. He supposed the Toad was meant to be a kind of usherette. Or whatchamacallit? Maître d'. Or maybe "Madam" was the word you were meant to employ in a place like that, figuring the *Grünegast* was some kind of bordello with pretensions, a bit of the ol' Old World & on the QT, like something out of an UFA-era potboiler with Marlene Dietrich's legs in the staring role. He decided to play along, as if he had any sort of choice in the matter. After giving him the once-over with a moneychanger's appraising eye, the Toad signalled to a scrawny-looking transvestite who'd materialised from the back of the cloakroom, to come & sell him a ticket. Němec felt somehow reluctant to part with his change, like paying the ferryman upfront. The transvestite fidgeted with something behind the counter & handed him a celluloid bow-tie & a slip of green paper with a number stamped on it. He blinked questioningly at the tie.

'Yer meant to stick it on yer collar, wiseguy. Dress code of the house.'

Němec fiddled with a pin at the back of the tie & somehow got it to stay on his collar, its corners tickling his chin.

'And the lid, buster.'

Němec made the face of someone who didn't understand the language.

'C'mon, hand it over,' the transvestite snapped, pointing at the bowler perched on Němec's head.

He grimaced, stepped back beyond the transvestite's reach.

'What are ya, some kinda Zhid? Phoowee! Joint's got no class no more.'

Saying so, the transvestite sashayed out of the cloakroom humming something in a bored way. The Toad cackled salaciously at Němec's elbow, taking hold of his jacket sleeve with a beringed hand that would've made Liberace, though perhaps not Göring, blush.

'Mein Herr,' the Toad croaked, as she guided him forward between the drapes, 'you air 'ere jist een time für zee Schauspiel.'

She widening her eyes a little to reveal a pair of lopsided green irises. There was so much mascara on the eyelashes that to blink must've required real effort.

'Aye yam Meestress Veecaryoos, zee ostess, und toonight vee 'ave quelquechose *sehr* spetzial…'

Her eyes widened a little more. Němec shivered. He felt like a fly being ogled by a carnivorous plant — what the night's "special" might entail, he didn't care to imagine.

The spectacle presenting itself on the other side of the drapes was at no risk of being upstaged by the Toad's entrance. The gilded bestiary calling itself *La Fée Verte* was quite something to see. In its pursuit of kitsch, no visible effort had been spared. Whoever designed it obviously intended to make a statement.

'It ees zee first time you kommen ere?' the Toad's eyes glittered.

He nodded vaguely.

'First time for everything,' he said to himself without the Toad hearing it.

Němec took in the general layout. The place looked like it was supposed to be some kind of cabaret, a throwback to something that'd probably really never existed but who'd know, like a screenwriter's idea of the Weimar Republic, circa Kurt Weil. In amongst the elaborate gaudiness were the usual amenities. At one end a cocktail bar with a fleet of doe-eyed "Ziegfeld" lookalikes perched on stools making bored faces while they stirred their drinks with little plastic flamingos. At the other end a stage with an emerald-green drop curtain & a spotlight on a chrome mic stand. In between were a dozen candle-lit booths with round tables, most of them occupied, & a checkerboard dancefloor. The walls were all covered in mirrors when they weren't covered in chintz or signed movie-star photographs like black&white trophy heads. A veil of smoke hung in the air, giving the place all the additional atmosphere it needed.

Holding the stage under a spotlight was a Lenny Bruce impersonator warming up the audience, though the character behind the microphone looked more like a mortician tossing gags at a room full of overdressed stiffs. There was so much talk in the place it was hard work to catch any of the lines.

'So this one queen says to another, "I hear your mother likes little boys…" "You zayin' my mema sleeps around vit goys?" "Nah, whadya take me for, a faggot or somethin'?"'

The stand-up squeezed a bicycle horn at the mic, someone at a table giggled, not at the joke apparently. The Toad led Němec to the edge of the bandstand & gestured gaudily towards one of the booths, winked, then drifted back through the haze.

'That's a very nice hat you're wearing there dads,' the stand-up said as Němec peered into the booth.

The spotlight moved across the bandstand & fixed on him. Němec groped blindly through the glare for a seat. Finding one, he fell into it, shielding his eyes with his hand, walkingstick raised feebly aloft like an old man being put upon by thugs. Canned hilarity.

'Ah, my poor wife's děda used to wear one *just like that*. Now doesn't that bring back memories. Life in the shtetl before… Well, you know. She'd say to him, her grandpa, she'd say, "Charlot, you zink Gott in Himmel gibt ein fock for zee baldspot on zat idiot kopf you got unter zere?" "Eh? Vat you zay? You vant I go naked? Zat you vant?" Needless to say, when the old geezer got freighted out of the Middle Ages he was a bit taken aback with all the modcons & stuff, you know. Like he'd never seen a shower before. Only time he didn't wear the damn hat was when he took his first shower & that was the death of him. Which just goes to show, doesn't it, no man knoweth the hour *blah blah blah*. Listen, any of you heard the one about the Rabbi always wore a bagel on his head?'

The spotlight jerked back to the stage, the bicycle horn honked. Němec blinked, red labmouse eyes in the restored gloom.

'You've been a beautiful audience,' the stand-up said, signalling the end. 'Give a hand to the boys at the funeral parlour, what they can't do with a bit of eyeliner & blush these days don't bear thinkin' about.'

Someone cranked the applause machine. The stand-up pointed the bicycle horn at the side of his head & honked again. The spotlight fizzled out. Someone coughed near Němec's shoulder. He turned, mouth set in an apologetic grimace, to find a woman seated practically beneath him. He jumped up startled, entangling himself in his walkingstick & immediately fell back onto the chair. The woman's face seemed to swim in the shadows like a sliver of moonlight in vaseline. Němec blinked some more, a blank expression looked back at him blankly. She was blonde, she was wearing a black satin kimono. Němec mumbled an apology. The blonde turned away, a slender black cigarette between tapered fingers, alabaster pale, ever so slightly caressing her lips.

Positioned across the table with his back to the room was the exact likeness of Viktor Faktor, wearing a yellow cravat beneath a dyed goatee, a tobacco pipe carelessly adorning his mouth — the last person Němec expected to see. Squatting on the chair beside him, the dwarf from the wine cellar was playing with the ends of a waxed moustache.

'Won't you join us,' Faktor said in a rhetorical monotone. 'Ah, but I see you already have.'

Němec, at a loss for words, sat there dumbly. The sound of the Toad's laughter rang across the checkerboard dancefloor, though he couldn't see where from. *Like a fly indeed.* Faktor tapped his pipe on the edge of the table without moving his eyes, it seemed, from a point just above Němec's head.

'A pleasure, once more, hmm? I see you've altered your mode of attire.'

The blonde exhaled a plume of cigarette smoke & turned a curious expression at him as if to see what the fuss was about.

'My dear,' Faktor informed her, 'this is Mr, *er...*'

The dwarf snickered & whispered some words in Faktor's ear.

'Němec,' said Němec.

The blonde smoked her cigarette.

'Ah yes,' said Faktor. 'Mr Němec is a detective of sorts.'

The blonde formed an O with her mouth.

'I'm a writer, sometimes,' Němec found his voice.

The blonde made a disappointed grimace & stubbed her cigarette out. There were three identical butts already lying in the ashtray: black with a gold band. Beside the ashtray were several half-empty champagne glasses arranged on the table. The dwarf jumped down from his chair & began refilling them from a bottle they'd been hiding in an icebucket beneath a white cloth napkin. The dwarf trotted around the table & handed a glass to Němec, grinning obsequiously. There were lipstick traces on the rim.

'Here's to your health, Mr Němec,' Faktor raised his glass, pinky sticking out with a conspicuously large signet ring on it.

The dwarf climbed back onto its chair, the blonde took out another cigarette & lit it, Němec sipped his drink. The champagne tasted fake, but no more than you'd expect it to in a place like that. Faktor, Němec noticed, sat the glass back on the table without having taken a drink. Neither the blonde nor the dwarf were drinking either. The room hummed. The place seemed more crowded now than it had been a moment ago. Němec felt trapped, he couldn't get the strangeness of meeting Faktor out of his mind. The calling card in the Prof's bureau — the Toad — AREPO, "blah blah blah." His throat felt dry. He gulped champagne. All the while Faktor was staring at him, fingering the bowl of his pipe. Němec grinned back, he was beginning to feel in his element: the trapped fly goes *buzz buzz buzz.* Or it might've been the champagne, tiny bubbles of nothing going *pop pop pop.*

Just then the lights dimmed. A pair of megaphones above the proscenium came to life with static & feedback, a voice echoing somewhere inside them:

'Laydeezzz *unt* Gentilemenschezzz! Der Kabaret Grünegast prezenteeert, *Der Todeslagerrr Tango!*'

Deranged klezmer music poured from the megaphones as a curtain rose at the back of the stage, revealing: a tableau with grotesquely emaciated boutique mannequins arranged naked against the backdrop of a palace ballroom (painted chandeliers, negro waiters in livery, a gypsy orchestra, etc.). A pair of wandering spotlights picked out the dancing puppets as they entered from the wings, advancing mechanically cheek-by-jowl, backs arched, like a pair of one-armed Siamese twins. Their costumes were satirical to the point of being atrocious. On one side of the stage, a towering beribboned Red Army colonel in Cossack boots gripped a squat Ostmark baronesses in his bear-arms. There was a grotesquely tall powdered wig perched on the baroness's head with a family of white mice nesting in it, her bust was the size of two deflated beach balls, the heels on her shoes might as well've been stilts. On the other side of the stage, a blackhatted Hassid with sidelocks & a beard down to his toes tangoed with a commedia dell'arte Carmen Miranda.

The two couples orbited one another like overgarnished figurines on a carousel. Try as he might, Němec couldn't help thinking of a wedding cake two-in-one. An involuntary chuckle escaped his lips. The baroness shifted her eyes, fixing them upon him. Her mouth twitched. She spoke —

'You! Stupid little turd!'

The music stopped, the dancing puppets all turned to look at Němec.

'You!' the Baroness shrieked again, jabbing a bony finger, 'should be ashamed of yourself! Sneaking into a place as this! Filthy little faggot goodfornothing!'

Snap snap snap went her furious jaw.

'If it weren't for those bars! If it weren't for those BARS on that WINDOW!! If it weren't for those bars on that window, you spawn of shite, YOU'D BE RIGHT WHERE YOU BELONG!!!'

Němec glanced nervously around, but no-one else seemed to've noticed the puppets come to life. Faktor was peering intently into his pipe, the dwarf twiddled his moustaches, the blonde tapped her nails on a box of cigarettes. Němec peered down at his empty glass, then, seeing as it was at no risk of being emptied any time soon, reached across the table for the dwarf's.

'Be my guest,' drawled the dwarf. 'Looks like you need it.'

Němec tipped the champagne down his throat. Still he felt parched. Sweat soaked into his hatband. His collar felt limp, the celluloid tie itched. *Must be the air*, he thought, sniffing at the fog that'd drifted in across the dancefloor. Up on stage the dancers looked as if they were waiting for him to give them his undivided attention. *Something horribly familiar*, he thought, gazing back at them. The Colonel stepped forward, disentangling himself from the Baroness & wet his bottom lip with a purple tongue as if about to address an imaginary assembly of skinny little redscarved Pioneers all eager attentiveness with their socks pulled up, seated around on the ballroom floor. Němec blinked, sure he wasn't seeing what he thought he was seeing, but not absolutely.

'Kamarádíčkové...'

The Colonel sounded just like Brezhnev, or Andropov, or Khrushchev maybe. Was it Khrushchev after Brezhnev, or before Andropov? Němec frowned. And then it struck him. He knew why that face was familiar — it was the old Deputy-Headmaster, Medvedev, from the Children's Home! Medvedev the Bolshevik Honeyscientist, *hehe*. Colonel Medvedev gazing bearishly out at the audience, mouth slitted open, yellowtoothed, mottled taxidermied face. A coinbox, stuck ungainly in breast pocket above a swathe of cerealpacket service medals, rattled & clunked: the flaccid jaw cranked open, spittlelipped, onto a borsht-reeking maw. A loud static hiss issued forth, a distant telephone voice —

'Chto eto? Eto kot! Vot eto vash schot! Samolyot! Kak vash rot?'*

The Colonel's jaw snapped shut, tongue cinched between fat rubberlips. Waist-high at his side, the encephalitic baroness (none other than Ol' Deathbed, her dear charming self there in propria persona to entertain us), liceridden wig tipping sideways, mouse-nest butting the colonel's lickspittle chin as, getting down on her knees, her hands ferreted in the front of the Colonel's breeches (a pensioned-off hussy going to show us the oldest trick in the book: out with the falsies & in with the cretinous Colonel's size-fourteen nob). Close-up on an uncut salami & Ol' Deathbed's sphincteral grin —

'See if you can do *this*, me lovelies!'

'My God!' Němec gasped.

The half-swallowed klobasa re-emerged gorge-coated, dripping spleen. Snapping her gums, the horrible Babajugs leered at him —

'Mummy's here, sweetie. Like me to give you a goodnight suck? *Har-har-har*. Where're your balls, you snivelling wet-a-bed? Think you're any kind of a

---

* "Long live our Soviet Motherland, / built by the people's mighty hand. / Long live our People, united & free, / strong in our friendship tired by fire. / Long may our crimson flag inspire, / shining in glory for all men to see." [♣]

man? I'll make mince pie of you, you turned-in shite!'

Hurriedly averting, Němec glanced across the stage at the Hassid, greasy cords of knotted string dangling from trouser pockets. He too had a familiar look, just like… *Wait a minute. Oh no! Oh yes!* Bobek the gardener! He who used to sit all day on a canvas folding chair beneath a pear tree in the weedfilled playground, amidst cairns of bitumen & willowy saplings in planter pots, flocks of greywhite clubfooted pigeons circling at his feet while stroking a hardon in his pocket & munched Dr Fantas digestive biscuits.

Chramst chramst.

'Stromečky moje…!'[*]

Chroust chroust.

'Zeleňoučké…!'[*]

And what's this? Perched ever-so-prettily on a pair of stockinged pins, carnival-masked, cheek-to-cheek with the pervy gardener's greystubbled mug & a fruitbowl on her head, who but the everdesirable, eternally youthful, Miss Freudlová — phys-ed instructress *sans pareille* & object of unspeakable adolescent yearnings — darklong tightringletted tresses, rougemouthed, yogasupple calves & braceleted wrists, flat corseted bosom, droopyeyed from late nocturnal assignations in the hirsute arms of dusky Žižkov accordionists… *Aaach! Oooch!* Head thrown back (bananas, pineapples, mangoes, guavas precipitous), right arm aligned to right foot extended, Bobek likewise in mirrored counterpoint…

'*Hahaha!*' the Baroness squealed. 'You nancy little wet dream. Like to worm your way into that starched little cunt's gusset, would you? How about a quick fiddle in the flowerbeds with our terminal old pederast over there, slip you the biscuit, plant his green thumb in a warm pot of nightsoil & see what'll grow out of it? *Hideehideehi!*'

She shook Medvedev's swollen wurst at her private audience —

'What d'you think of this for a taproot, eh, loverboy? Wouldn't you fancy a bit of stick-in-the-mud while I stuff the mulch in your mouth, make a nice flowerbed of you, *hehehe!* Tuck you in real good, eh, you wet-eared runt? How about a fat nightynight tonguekiss from your Babamama?'

Flap flap flap.[*]

---

[*] Expression of endearment among the arboria. [♦]
[*] Ditto. [♦]
[*] Goes the tongue. [♦]

'I'll give you something you'll never forget alright, you hairless eunuch's pickled sack!'

Němec gaped in horror at Ol' Deathbed's apoplectic face turning red in the glow of the footlights, then purple, then black. Her head looked like a withered haemorrhoid with a sudden influx of bad blood, any second about to go *splotz*. A faint hiss escaped between Němec's teeth —

'Bolševická kurvo!'[*]

The dancers instantly returned to being stuffed puppets, motionless once again — their faces, blank masks. Faktor eyed Němec curiously. The dwarf refilled the empty champagne glasses. The blonde was nowhere in sight. Němec grabbed one of the glasses — modelled, so he'd once been informed on good authority, from Empress Josephine's right royal tit — & slopped a mouthful down his parched throat.

'Something the matter?' Faktor inquired solicitously.

The glass quivered in Němec's hand, he set it down. Faktor watched him, expectant. Němec felt like that fly again…

'Interesting place,' he offered, wiping perspiration from his neck.

'Isn't it,' said Faktor. 'Though the best, I'm told, is yet to come.'

Němec loosened his collar. Back on stage, a tall negro transvestite in plunging chiffon decollaté strode majestically out between the costumed mannequins. A third spotlight followed her progress to the mic stand accompanied by fugitive strains of tango music wafting out of the speakers like voices blown on a breeze. The dancing puppets turned. It occurred to Němec that everything so far had merely been a prelude. The singer caressed the microphone with black silkgloved fingers as the Latin rhythms grew louder & she began to lipsync words that oozed weirdly out of the air like ectoplasm:

Die Fahrer flucht! Der Reiter fest geschlossen!

The audience tittered. A waiter, disguised as ǂ-Obergruppenführer Heydrich, with white apron & butcher's cleaver, passed among the tables carrying an enormous tray of canapés. It seemed to be a regular joke they were all in on. One of the spotlights followed his progress around the room to the satirical strains of a clarinet…

---

[*] A blushing handmaid serving the common, *er*, good. [♆]

It ended with everyone in the room raising their left arms & shaking their hands like there were cobwebs stuck to them. It must've meant something to the in-crowd, but Němec couldn't figure it at all. When it was over the singer bowed low & left the stage & the curtain came down on the scenery. Němec could've sworn the Baroness winked at him as she got wheeled off the stage. But the real Babajugs, he supposed, was probably dead by now, if not swanning through life on a fat pension for all those years of dedicated service to the poor unwanted Victims of Socialism.* He wondered what'd put *her* in mind, but didn't get far with it, the place was kinked up to the eyeballs. *Just hold onto yer hat, kiddo, or you might be next, hehe.*

Between acts the Toad brought more champagne. Němec eyed the bottle. A couple of strangers drifted over to the table & conducted an intense private conversation with Faktor before departing again. Oblivious, the dwarf sat there in front of a large bowl of *fruits glacés*, which he devoured gluttonously. When he was finished he grabbed the new bottle & popped the cork, spilling champagne willy-nilly into the flagrantly empty glasses. Němec helped himself. As soon as the others left, Faktor proposed a toast.

'The perfect champagne,' he said, eyeing his guest,* 'is like a mistress who gives everything while yet remaining a paragon of discretion.' Faktor raised his glass & waited for Němec to do likewise. 'To discretion.'

Němec drank so as not to laugh outright. The champagne tasted bitter, more bitter than it should have. He wanted this idiotic scenario to come to an end. The dwarf leered, his moustache smeared with residues of his dessert. They all drank this time. Faktor said something else, they all drank some more. It was musical glasses, somehow Němec still wound up with two of them, drinking from each in turn. Wisps of fog drifted around the table, candlelight glimmered. Němec felt an unusual lucidity of mind carry him beyond the confusion of voices to a salient plateau high above. When the new bottle was finished, the dwarf thrust it neck-down into the ice bucket beside the table & collared a waiter for yet another.

⚑ The socalled Wurst-Hajzl-Lied: "Jingobells, jingobells, jingoes all the way…!" [✋]
* Like the one who hung Milada Horáková, "*Don't break her neck in the noose, strangle the bitch.*" [✋]
* Tendentiously? [✋]

Němec turned & scanned the room. The room turned with him. The place had grown crowded. He wondered what'd become of the blonde. While he was searching to find her Faktor reached his hand across the table & took Němec by the wrist.

'I was thinking about you,' he said. 'Your problem interests me.'

His grip was quite strong. Němec stared at Faktor's hand till the older man released his hold & leant back in his chair, just as Heydrich-the-waiter arrived with a third bottle of champagne in a fresh ice bucket & set about replacing the glasses, dusting out the ashtray, etc. Němec followed each of the waiter's actions in turn, wondering if now was the time for him to get up & leave while he had the chance. The dwarf seemed to snicker knowingly.

'Tell me,' Faktor said in a voice full of sudden concern as soon as the waiter had departed, 'have you made any progress with your inquiries? Perhaps I could help you?'

Němec blinked.

'I believe,' Faktor prompted, 'our previous conversation touched upon a certain *manuscript*?'

Němec peered down at his hands, the palms were moist, they might've been glowing. *Helluva night so far, kiddo.* He took in the cut of Faktor's cravat, the dyed goatee, the pipe. Like a character in a story he must've read, only he didn't remember how this bit was supposed to go. He improvised, digging in his jacket pockets —

'Found this.'

Němec flipped the calling card onto the table. It lay there in the candlelight with the palindrome facing up. ROTASOPERATENET... Faktor glanced at it with an absence of curiosity.

'Ah,' he jabbed his pipe at the handwriting, 'we must spare a thought for poor Arepo.'

'Mean anything to you?'

Faktor shrugged —

'Ought it to?'

Němec turned the card over so the address was visible. The green shimmered in the candlelight.

'Someone left this in the Prof's apartment,' Němec said. 'Hájek, you remember him, don't you? You printed that letter, just after he...'

A sick grin spread across Němec's face —

'So anyway, I go to his place & find this, with an address for a joint called the *Green Fairy*, in the middle of the goddamn river. I pay it a visit & along with a bunch of Nazi weirdoes I find you.'

The grin broadened, as if it had a life of its own —

'Fantastic coincidence, wouldn't you say?'

'Indeed,' Faktor said, stuffing his pipe bowl-first into his breast pocket, 'quite fantastic, as coincidences frequently are.'

'Sure,' Němec's grin slackened, 'any other night & it might've been Joe Blow sitting here instead & I'd have to content myself with the lousy comedy act & the fancy dress. For such a popular joint it doesn't do much to sell itself.'

'As I said before,' Faktor waved his hand, 'discretion. Which very often is the better part of valour.'

'Kind of invitation only, then?' Němec fingered the calling card.

'You might say that,' Faktor gave him a bland look.

'My thoughts exactly.'

'Oh?'

'Didn't strike me as the sort you'd find in a place like this.'

'Who?'

'The Prof.'

Němec made a grab for the champagne. Faktor did nothing to discourage him. He poured three glasses & took two for himself. The dwarf chuckled.

'And what kind of person was your Professor?'

'He liked...' Němec guzzled champagne, 'chess. And Mahler.'

'I see, you must've been very close,' Faktor's lips curled slightly. 'I wonder how you'll make sense of it all.'

'All?' Němec could feel his mouth going numb.

'All,' the editor of *Heterocosmica* said, bringing his glass to his lips, enough to wet them, then setting it to one side.

He drew his chair a little closer to Němec's & leant towards him to speak, as if in confidence, rubbing his signet ring against the point of his goatee.

'One must be extremely cautious in matters such as these,' Faktor said, looking Němec in the eye. 'Study your moves carefully. There was a young man I knew, very like you, during the War. We became quite intimate. He was a lieutenant in the Wehrmacht. Does that surprise you? Junge, his name was. Klaus Junge.'

Němec tried to read the design on the signet but couldn't. It swam in the candlelight. He felt vaguely aware of a loosening in his face. The name, of course, meant nothing to him at all.

'It's true,' Faktor said, as if he was disappointed Němec hadn't doubted him. 'Remember, there were those of *us*, too, who were fighting the Bolsheviks. Besides,' he jabbed at the tablecloth, 'it was before anyone knew about Chełmno, Belzec…'

He looked to the dwarf for agreement. The dwarf curled a finger in his moustache, tugged at it, leered at Němec.

'That's right, mister,' said the dwarf, who couldn't've been old enough to remember the first thing about the War. 'You listen to the Boss, *he* knows.'

'Not everything,' Faktor continued, 'was as straightforward in those days as our recent comrades would've liked everyone to believe.'

Němec pursed his lips noncommittally, turning the stem of his empty glass between his fingers. He reached for the other glass, but it too was empty, & yet without him lifting a finger a moment later it was full again. Němec began to wonder when the next act would appear on stage. All the while, Faktor continued speaking. Němec was close enough to smell the pipe tobacco on the man's breath, even with the rest of that fog swirling about. His eyes drifted down to the ashtray on the table, a box of matches lay beside it — "THE KEY" it said, with a red upturned latchkey beneath. Němec had to concentrate to keep the writing in focus. He mumbled something no-one else could hear. About a blonde. Where was she? Who was she?

'It was December, 1942,' Faktor said. 'The War had already begun to turn, only no-one could see it yet. The army had no winter uniforms. People were bringing unneeded clothes to the Altstädterring, piles of them, for the Eastern Front. No-one knew if it was madness or a stroke of genius to attack Stalin like that. And Hitler refused to retreat. It almost seemed possible. Who could've guessed what the outcome would be, that it would all end *here*. Life,' he shrugged, 'went on, as it does, even at times of greatest adversity. The authorities even organised a lavish chess tournament, in the Representatives' House.* It was to honour old

* Obecní Dům. [✋]

Duras, one of the grandmasters, who'd turned sixty, a so-you-might-say *Festschrift*, a *Jubilee*, to which the Who's Who were invited. Even esteemed Dr Alekhine came — he could hardly have refused. A Russian who hated Stalin as much as we did? But a Russian nevertheless.'

The dwarf poured champagne. By now they'd drowned more glasses than Němec could count. He kept a vague hold on the thread of Faktor's story: December, 1942. Barely six months, as every schoolkid in Golem City knew, after the ᛋᛋ razed the village of Lidice in reprisal for the assassination of Reinhard Heydrich.[*] During which time they shot all the village's male inhabitants & deported the women & children to death camps. 10th of June. It was a story Němec had been made to learn by heart, every little detail. *For the honour of the Republic.* The Commies never tired of making propaganda out of it.[*] Reflexively, Němec glanced around for the waiter. Misinterpreting, Faktor told the dwarf to pour him another.

'Cheers,' Němec said, raising his glass.

---

[*] BdS H. Böhme's little bit of inspiration, passed up the line to Himmler. [✊]

[*] It went like this: Before daybreak the ᛋᛋ encircled the village, preventing anyone from leaving: the inhabitants were herded into a byre from which the village men (including one Josef Kafka, smelter, twentytwo years old) were led out in groups to be executed in a farmyard. They were made to stand in a row, unblindfolded, unbound, with mattresses ripped from the village's beds propped behind them against the farmyard wall, to muffle the ricochet. Five at a time — then ten at a time — beginning 7:00 a.m. As the pile of corpses advanced the firing squad was forced to retreat against the farmhouse steps, cartridge cases clattering on concrete. The shooting went on all afternoon, till the rifle barrels burned the hands of the firing squad & there was barely room for the last victims to stand, pointblank, staring down triangular Mauser sites at the Schupi conscripts' deadeyes. The next day, 11 June — nineteen more men, who'd been absent from the village working down the mines, & seven women, were rounded up & sent to the Kobylisy execution grounds to be shot: Josef Horák (1885), Anna Horáková (1886), Marie Horáková (1923), Marie Horáková (1885), Václav Horák (1920), Štěpán Horák (1887), Štěpán Horák (1920), Marie Frühaufová (1919), Stanislav Horák (1897), Anastázie Horáková (1902), Bohumil Horák (1889), Anna Horáková (1891), Václav Kohlíček (1918), Marie Stříbrná (1894), František Stříbrný (1917), František Černý (1907), Karel Hroník (1900), Josef Kácl (1912), Václav Kadlec (1922), Václav Kopáček (1921), Jaroslav Müller (1913), Josef Petrák (1903). Afterwards, the Reichsarbeitsdienst burned & bulldozed the houses — farmwalls, hedges, church, cemetery — tore up the curbing, cobblestones, concrete — ripped out the poplars, the lindens, the lichens — pilfered the livestock — scorched the fields — pulverised the milestones, the millstones — levelled the hillocks — filled the fishponds — changed the courses of streams, brooks, creaks & rivers — obliterated by any & all means manual or technological the merest *Wahrzeichen*, *Meilenstein*, the merest trace of habitat or habitant, till, as is customarily said, nothing, not even an eyesore, remained. In the meantime, driven by a *Selbstdokumentarberichtsmanie* that would almost have put David O. Selznik to shame, the Nazis meticulously & painstakingly chronicled every tiny little detail of the *Entwurzelungsprozess* on a 16mm Zeiss-Ikon — twentyfour miles of celluloid to hang themselves with at Nuremburg. [✊]

351

He put it down empty on the table, carefully, so as not to knock anything over, & reached for the second glass. He could feel the dwarf's little rodent-eyes studying him, but didn't care. Faktor leant even closer.

'The last game brought *mein lieber jungerfreund* head-to-head with the russischer Goliath, the indomitable Alekhine!'

Faktor almost looked like he was getting excited by his own story.

'There were whispers all round,' he said. 'A large group of us huddled around the table — had only there been a Rembrandt to paint it! Such a scene! Such a moment! *La querelle des Anciens et les Modernes.* He was only eighteen, Klaus. Imagine! Alekhine played white, the Queen's gambit. The gambit was declined. The game lasted twentynine moves. Perhaps it was fated that Klaus should not have won. Nevertheless, they finished the tournament on equal points. Neck & neck.'

And what about dear old ducky Duras, Němec wondered. For whose sake the gallant heirs of Steinitz had staged their tournament. *Not to let such an insignificant detail as one small village in the middle of nowhere get in the way of collaboration between our two nations.*[*] Somehow Němec managed to stifle his hilarity. *And Alekhine*, he thought, *a Russian the Nazis were prepared to tolerate, like Vlassov, if only for hating Stalin. The rest, the masses of the East, deemed sub specie. Dogs, vermin, scum. Untermenschen.* A bitter laugh escaped his lips. The dwarf made a strange face at him.

'You know,' Faktor said, laying his hand on Němec's arm again, 'you look very much like him.'

Němec frowned at the other man's hand where it lay across his sleeve.

'Three weeks before the end of the war, poor Klaus was wounded at Welle, on the Lüneburger Heide, near Hamburg, resisting the allied advance. Mortally, as it happened. His death was pointless. It achieved nothing. The Americans marched all the way south to Plzeň where they stopped while Patton[*] twiddled his thumbs for a couple of months, leaving us to the mercy of the Cossacks.'

Well, armer Klaus, glad not to've been in your shoes, chum.

Faktor cleared his throat & sat back in his chair. Němec tried to make out the purpose of the story, but couldn't figure it. Perhaps it was meant as some sort of allegory? Hidden meanings & all that. Or the man really was nuts? *That Klaus*, he thought, *must really've been one ugly sonofabitch to look anything like me.*

---

[*] A mere drop in the ocean, *hehe*, & so on & so forth. [☛]
[*] Ol' Blood'n'Guts. [☛]

And then he thought of something the Prof said once, about how you should always be sure when to play the pawn in a game, & when to be the pawn that controls the game.

As if on cue a spotlight came up on the stage & the curtain rose. A tinpot orchestra made some noise. A hiss of dry ice. Then a voice crackled from the loud-speakers —

'Laydeezzz *unt* Gentilemenschezzz! Der Kabaret Grünegast prezenteert, fur zee first time ever! *Death und die mädchen...*'

Němec swivelled in his chair to take in the show. The tinpot orchestra wheezed something supposedly resembling Schubert as a pair of transvestites in nuns' habits proceeded through the room towards the stage holding tall white candles in front of them. On the stage a young novice was bent in prayer, bathed in green light. When the two nuns reached the stage, they set down their candles & stood on either side of the novice, heads bowed, hands clasped in a show of prayer. The orchestra became more intense in its butchering of Schubert's score. Then something moving above the stage caught Němec's eye.

From the blackness, a winged Devil slowly descended on invisible wires. It had wide grotesque eyes. A red tongue snaked in & out of its mouth. Němec gaped at it. The creature beat its wings. Hot wind seemed to blow. Němec gripped his walkingstick. The orchestra abandoned Schubert for pure cacophony. The spotlight faded green to red. Out of the cacophony a pounding rhythm grew. The creature's tongue wormed obscenely in its hole. The nuns, stripping off their habits, began a lewd dance. Horned bustiers & vulcanised rubber corsets. Stockings & stiletto boots. Loins hung with black grapes.

Having abandoned their attitude of prayer, these Sisters-of-Mercy now converged upon the novice, arms writhing to the drumbeat. At a given signal they hoisted the novice's skirts. The stageprop Devil, bearded & clovenhoofed, squatted astride her. There was a puff of smoke & like a jack-in-the-box a monstrous dildo shot out of his codpiece. The novice screamed — her face, illuminated from above, disfigured by transports of comic ecstasy.

Němec, in a shock of recognition, rose unsteadily from his chair, walkingstick aloft, to strike down the winged beast. Fog swirled up from the floor. All of a sudden, he felt very cold & very hot. An emptiness yawned around him. He lurched forward. A look of dismay transformed the novice's face as she turned towards him, eyes all-too familiar now. Němec thrashed with his stick, the fog swirled thickly, the Devil flapped its wings. Drums beat the air into a frenzy. With a piercing shriek Němec charged headlong into the abyss.

At first, the voices sounded far off, then they came closer, like fairies rustling through undergrowth, whispering into his ear. What they were saying was completely meaningless. Then, in a pudgy little voice, one of them said —

'Looks like he's coming around.'

'Mein Gott! You muss take zis lunatic out from here!'

'He's no lunatic, just drunk is all.'

'The Doctor won't be long.'

'He don't need a doctor, he just needs a bucket of cold water.'

'Boss said to call the Doc.'

'But who eez dees Mann?'

'I seen him once before at the club, a nobody. But the dame says she recognised him from the clinic. One of the Doc's experiments, maybe.'

'Looks like he's seen a ghost.'

'Been poppin' too many of these, more like.'

When Němec opened his eyes he was lying in the green anteroom, clutching his stick to his chest with both hands. The dwarf was peering attentively down at him, he was holding a phial of bright pink pills in his fist.

'Better lay off the sauce, bo,' the dwarf said, 'you know what's good for ya.'

Behind the dwarf loomed the faces of the Toad, the doorman, Heydrich-the-waiter, the transvestite coatcheck, the novice. Neither Faktor nor the Devil where anywhere in sight. The transvestite sneered —

'Look at the bum, doesn't have the decency to lose the lid even when he lies down.'

The doorman grunted. The Toad wrung her fat bejewelled hands. The waiter crossed his arms. The novice did nothing but stand there holding a blonde wig in one hand, the front of a black kimono bunched in the other. Without the wig, she almost looked familiar, like a face in a film, only Němec couldn't put a name to it. He was listening to the sound of a tinpot orchestra drifting through the green velvet curtains. He felt like this was all nothing but a dream & pretty soon he'd wake up. The dwarf chuckled. Němec grinned sickly back at him before the curtains came down on their little act once more.

28

THE BUGMAN

'My mother's brother,' began the Bugman, 'had a story about a blind gypsy who lived by himself in a lean-to at the bottom of a field by the freight yards at Na Knížecí. Once upon a time, it went, there was this miserable old *tzigane*, camped off the side of the railroad tracks. Nothing but his mutt for company. The odd wayfarer, the odd bullshit merchant. He was blind, you see. Blind as any blind bastard you can imagine, *hehe*. The thing is, he'd never shut up. Had chapter & verse on anything you'd ever heard of. Talked like it was no-one's business, night & day. Kept going in his sleep, too. Hardly drew breath. For a while the usual bums & layabouts came to watch the show, trying to figure out the blind gypsy's gimmick. Then the cripples started trickling in, looking for a cure. Later a couple of scam artists set up a stall in front of the old bugger's lean-to: for a pfennig they'd let the tourists watch him talk the leg off a table. It was an even bet who'd last longer, the punter or the table-leg. There was no end to the feats the old jawbone was credited with. Only he talked so much eventually no-one'd risk coming near him. One-by-one the hangers-on drifted away. So there he was, alone again, just the way he started out. But still he kept talking. Didn't care if no-one listened. That jawbone must've had a life of it's own. Seemed the only sustenance the old gobshite could take was the sound of his own voice. Nothing else mattered. Acted like he'd forgot the outside world existed. Even forgot his faithful idiot of a mutt. Stands to reason he'd have talked himself into the grave & probably back out again. Then one day, a miracle. There he was, gob flapping in its own wind & not a word. Nothing but a hollow moan. Took them days to figure out what happened. Mutt was starved half crazy by now, see? Must've got its eye on the old bastard's tongue lolling around while he was asleep. God knows what the beast took it for. Tore it clean out by the roots. Even then the idiot's gob didn't miss a beat. Fancy that, eh? Man's best friend.'

The Bugman's voice chuckled softly to itself —

'Aye, they knew how to tell a yarn in them days, *hehe*. Used to work in a factory, my uncle did. In Zlín. Making shoes for Mr Baťa. When the Krauts came in '38, they requisitioned the factory to make boots for the Wehrmacht, who wore them in Stalingrad. The Bolsheviks stripped the boots from the Kraut corpses & wore them when they liberated Moravia. My uncle made boots for the communist sonsofbitches who liked to step on our heads with them after the War. Boots for the camp guards, the commandant, & the resident commissars. And if you were lucky enough to own a pair on a labour detachment, my good old uncle probably had a hand in making those too. When he died in '68, you know what his widow buried him in? Nothing. Bare feet. Maybe you want to know why he didn't just get up & leave, when he had the chance? But where would he've left to? He was a Moravák. Only thing he knew how to do was feed bits of leather into a machine. And when the chance came to get out, it was too late. Stomach ulcer. Too bad. One of life's little jokes, *hehe*. Like me, too. You know who I've got to thank for ever seeing the light of day? General-Secretary Khrushchev, *hehe*. Summer of '61. Was Khrushchev told the world what an unmitigated bastard Stalin'd been all those years. The gulags, the mass murders, the cult of His own puss-filled godhead. Barely had time to grab hold of our pants before they gave us our marching orders. *Piss off back where you came from*, they said. That's how it was, *au revoir* Stalin, *bonjour* Khrushchev. As soon as they sent home one lot of politicals, they got to work on a fresh lot. Justice, being seen to be served. Back in the day, though, if Stalin farted in Moscow, Golem City trembled as atop a volcano! If Stalin said *Jump!* the local politburo made a Five Year Plan out of it, every able-bodied man woman child hopping about like idiots trying to squeeze that extra inch out of a standing start. If Stalin said *Collectivise!* they turned every farm in the country into one big turnip plantation. *Increase output!* & they ran rings around themselves seeing double. *Purge the Zhids!* & every last Cohen from Kolín to Krásna Hôrka who'd escaped gassing got shanghaied into a showtrial or shipped to a gulag. Like God giving dictation to Moses. Except it was no Moses but only that putrescent misnomer, Gottwald! Gottwald-the-Slime, who worshipped the tinea on Stalin's feet. Who'd've stuck his tongue right up that fat Georgian's hole if he'd been allowed anywhere near it. And when Stalin finally kicked the bucket, Ol' Slimewald would've jumped right in the grave beside him, if he hadn't had one foot down there already. Hardly even the decency to wait till they lowered the hammer&sickle to half-mast. Pneumonia or something. You ask me, it was syphilis of the brain, been sucking up to that diseased prick so long. What an arsehole! I mean, it's Chesko-fucking-slovnikia, for chrissakes! We're talking about Big Mister Nonentity here! Who was supposed to be kidding who? You could've fit the whole bloody country in Lake Baikal & still have plenty left to paddle about in. But no, Slimewald had to parade around like God's own elect, bestowing the Word, offering up grandiose prayers of thanks, the entire GDP & then some. There might've been toadies in every backwater on the Bloc, erecting their shrines, their graven images, their monuments to the Infallible One, but you could trust Slimewald to go that extra mile & build the biggest of them all. A god-almighty colossus of a thing, sixteen metres of granite & concrete, right over there on the hill: Stalin & his heroic workers' entourage — *The Meat Queue*, is what everyone called it. Took 'em five years till the last stone was laid to rest, May Day 1955 — by which time both Stalin & Slimewald were like a couple of pickles in brine. If you needed to remind yourself of what the Devil himself looked like, all you had to do was look out the window — could see Him from virtually every part of town. Of course the Commies were cheapskates & to save on granite they squeezed the entourage together a bit, cheekbyjowl up against Stalin's arse, kind of fucked-up the scale, or perspective, or whatever. Not like you couldn't recognise Him or anything, but there was some poor twenty-foot slapper in a headscarf, two places behind, left groping the crotch of one of those big-dicked partisan types in full view of the general populace. Idiots up at the Presidium must've been right chuffed with themselves. Didn't waste any time turning-up a patsy — stupid bugger who did the original design, perfect for the job, topped himself quite conveniently before he could become any more of an embarrassment, with* comradely assistance from the local branch representatives (just to show how we're all in it together) — a little self-sacrifice to help retrieve a nation's lost gravitas.* But then to make matters worse all those revelations came out, about the gulags & deportations, followed by the amnesties & rehabilitations. After Khrushchev got up & denounced the old cunt at the podium. Ye Olde Infallible One suddenly turned Enemy of the People Numero Uno. Post-haste they reached for the dynamite to blow-up that stupendous joke they'd only just erected. Eight-hundred kilos of the stuff, for good measure. Byebye Joe. Bits of ferroconcrete raining down for miles around, braining the odd bystander, smote by their posthumous God. Where the hand that tickled the partisan's crotch landed, who knows? You'd have to've seen it, to've believed it.'

---

* It goes without saying. [✊]

* Otakar Švec, sculptor previously of public monuments to Masaryk, Hus, Roosevelt: the first two destroyed by the Nazis, the third by the Commies. He gassed himself in his kitchen three weeks before *The Meat Queue*'s unveiling, as did his wife: the standard modus operandi. Dear reader, spare a thought for poor departed Arepo. [✊]

The Bugman's voice became pensive.

'Well you know what it was like in '68, if you had a buck you got the hell out've here while the going was good. If you didn't, you did what you could. Money back then wasn't worth the paper it was printed on. It was Deutschmarks or nothing. After they repatriated us from the camp, we were only allowed to do the shittiest jobs. Stoking boilers. Shovelling pig shit. Collecting trash. Only way you could earn currency was flogging whatever you could steal on the blackmarket. Truckies mostly, coming over the border on the E55. Met a Jawa nut once & that was my ticket out. Flogged him a couple of hot sidecar rigs & that was me gone, thumbing my way West. When I got to London, everything there was different from how it'd been during the War. You wouldn't believe. May as well've been a different planet. I spent four months dossing down with hippies in an Earls Court squat, smoking grass, laying redhaired dívkas from all points of the Commonwealth. So much for the foggy realms of spleen, eh? The sun shone twentyfour-hours-a-day out of everyone's arses. Flower Power & protest songs & wankers going *ohm*. It was complete bullshit. Kids! You know, there was something honest about the War — terrible, but honest. Propaganda was propaganda, the lies you told yourself, the whole circus — but you knew that's what it was — the unreality was *real*. None of the *pretend* that came after. A lot of suits made all that up. Sexual liberation my arse. Fast bucks, that's all. Who they reckon was cooking up all that LSD?* You can count me out of that scam. I didn't fight anyone's war to be plugged into some corporate whizbang machine. Yeah, I had my fun, but by November I was through — hitchhiked all the way back & not a single regret, welcoming committee at the border post, even got my old job again stoking a boiler. Model citizen, me. They could've put my mug on a poster. The West? Who the fuck needs it. They sold us out, then *they* sold out. If that's what they call freedom, they're welcome to it. Call me nuts if you like. Thirty years later, 'ere I am, in the prime of life. What more could an old soldier want? Bucked like mules, they did. I can still remember, like it was yesterday. There was one, Ainslie her name was, totally bugeyed, used to sing these Cornish folksongs in the sack. Had nipples half as long as yer finger. Dedicated, she was, to the great task of bringing about the end of the Fascist Corporate State. Now that was a girl who'd found her mission in life. A one-woman revolution right there on her back. Madder than the Trots you'd meet in the camps. No future in that for me. You think the world's got any better? Nah?

---

* Putting the *d* molecule in *acid*. [♣]

Well you're not alone, kid. You're not alone. See that sky? Ever wonder what's up there? Watching us? Let me tell you a story — you hear the one about that tractor driver in Irkutsk? The bloke who got clobbered on the head by a piece of that Mutnik II fell out of the sky? Went barking mad. Said he could hear aliens talking in his skull. A lot of Politburo types went all the way from Moscow to check him out. Military hospital, the works. Doctors asked him what the aliens were talking about. Tractor driver said, *dog food*. They couldn't figure it out. Wanted to know wasn't there maybe a personal message for the General-Secretary? *No, no*, he stuck to his guns. *Dog food*. True story.'

29

DOGS IN SPACE

Whatever became of all those Deziks, Tsygans, Lisas, Ryzhiks, Smelayas, Malyshkas, Boliks, ZIBs, Otavazhnayas, Snezhinkas, Albinas, Tsygankas, Damkas, Krajavkas, Barses, Lisichkas, Laikas, Belkas, Strelkas, Pchyolkas, Mushkas, Cherushkas, Zvyozdochkas, Veteroks & Ugolyoks? Something on the horizon glinted — a streak of vapour in the sky. Who knew what dog genetics, at that very moment, were making their slow & steady way through interstellar redux to some far off, methane-enshrouded exoplanet, to spark, like once the God of Genesis upon these Jurassic shores, *its* evolutionary catastrophe?

The sound of laughter became lost in the distance — gradually it faded into the vagueness of sleep. Němec lay there, wherever *there* was, like one of those idiot brothers, Chesk & Lesk, staring up at the big empty flat sky, thinking *the goal will reveal itself.** And then thinking nothing & being aware of thinking nothing — of time passing in some extra dimension — of space vaulting itself. The silence in his head was like the silence of a room where someone's playing cards: the noise of cards being shuffled, some object being put down, of people living on the floor above. Only there wasn't anyone playing cards, no cards being shuffled, no object being put down, no-one living on the

---

* → Chapter 47. [✋]

floor above. Or it was as if he'd closed his eyes & walked to the most distant visible point, then opened them again. At first there was nothing to be seen or heard. Then there was a voice.

The voice was saying something, something important. *Spare a thought for poor Arepo*, it said, *worker of the wheels... within wheels...* A square wheel inside a round wheel inside... Then silence again. Deeper this time. Then the voice again, as if further away. *The mind*, it whispered now, *is in a room with a body. The body is an object in the mind's room...* He struggled in vain to free himself from the darkness into which he'd been abducted. His arms & legs were held fast, something wet was covering his face. In the distance a woman's voice seemed to be speaking in a language he couldn't understand. There were footsteps. Cold air brushed against his left hand. Then something sharp pricking his arm & a heaviness came over him again. *Minds without bodies. Bodies within minds.* And then he thought nothing at all.

The next time Němec woke it was daylight, but he wasn't anywhere he remembered being before. He was lying on a bare mattress on a steel bedframe in a long dormitory with barred windows & stained off-white walls. The ceiling plaster was all cracked & in places completely peeled away from the rafters, with a dead ceiling fan hanging there creaking under its own weight. The air was hot & mildewed. He sat up slowly. If the fan's shadow had been a compass, he'd've been facing north-by-northeast, assuming it was mid-afternoon & the bed he was lying on pointed due south.

Someone had been thoughtful enough to take his jacket, shirt, trousers & shoes. He still had his hat, but that was all. Like a hermit crab without its shell. Vague recollections drifted as if through a dense fog. His head ached, the rest of him felt hardly any better. That much, at least, was a familiar tune — he could've written a song to it, *Wrack 'n' Ruin Blues* or *Stand by Your Menace* maybe, or some sort of bow-legged Woodie Guthrie rendition for the holy rollers, *Migraine, Bound for Glory*, key of G♭. Němec played it in his head, but kept getting stuck just before the chorus on a wrong note — something sharp that should've been flat, or flat that should've been natural. *Face it, kiddo, you're no Rachmaninoff.*

Bored with the comedy routine, he dragged himself off the mattress & went over to nearest window to check out the prospects, but whatever there was to see lay hidden behind an apple orchard grown wild. The stuff of Chekhov. *Man naked in a parlour, contemplates his last window of opportunity and the leafy greenery of the life ever-after, with disappointment.* He cast his eyes around the dormitory, but the place was a shambles. A pair of footprints in the dust led backwards to a door at the end of the room hanging half off its hinges, where they soon got lost in the general debris beyond. It was just possible they were his. Finding a way out, he decided, was never going to be as straightforward as it first appeared.

Past the doorway, a stairwell barricaded with bits of broken furniture, garbage bags, boxes & assorted other junk led down to a pair of double-padlocked steel doors. No luck there. A second dormitory opened off the entrance hall, identical to the one he'd woken up in, except all the windows were boarded up, sunlight sifting through narrow chinks in the wood, finger-thick nails splitting the window-frames. At the back of the stairwell, a corridor with a mess of low overhanging wires & broken lightbulbs led through the rear of the building, past a gutted boiler room & mesh cages used once-upon-a-time for God only knew what. The shadows stank of dead things & excrement. Němec chanced it, groping his way towards a flight of concrete steps leading down, bits of broken glass cutting the soles of his feet.

Soon he emerged into a walled yard littered with steel girders & blocks of rusted machinery. Rotten apples lay half-submerged in brackish water everywhere underfoot. In the far wall where a gate must once've been was now only a hole fringed with cracked mortar thickly garlanded with ivy. More apple trees hemmed the wall in from the other side. A narrow gap through the foliage was all there was for a path, a set of parallel tyre tracks winding left & cresting a steep embankment with a patch of blue sky above it. The tracks were overgrown, the branches hung down dangling fruit. He stalked on tiptoe, climbing, weaving, dodging, like a nude puppet coming unstrung.

Where the path exited the trees, Němec stopped. Spreading away in every direction, as far as the eye could see — with the apple grove sunk in the middle & the ruined building hidden within that — was an ocean of yellow barley. The wind rasped dryly. In the distance, a grain silo stood above the horizon, like a finger pointed at the beating sun. A dusty track ran from the grove towards it. Němec started out, working hard to keep his legs under him. They'd grown heavy with the effort, the soles of his cut feet scorched by the hot dirt. Sweat soaked down through the band of his hat, blurring his eyes. Under the enormous sky he felt suddenly more naked than he'd ever felt in his life.

Soon the orchard was lost from sight, the barley heaved & swayed in a hot wind, the path wound onwards. Gradually the silo enlarged against the sky. Coming to a bend, Němec saw up ahead a donkey by the side of the track chewing barleycorn. Its ears twitched as it chewed, watching him. Squatting beside it was a man in a shabby brown woollen suit, his attention absorbed by something on the ground. Němec glanced up at the white disc in the sky & back at the man, wondering how he could bear the heat. His own mouth was dry. He ran his tongue across his lips & felt how they'd grown parched & cracked. The air was a furnace, he could feel it burning his skin. Despite his nakedness he dragged himself on.

When Němec reached the donkey the man in the brown suit was nowhere in sight. The donkey looked at him with intelligent, appraising eyes, then went on chewing. Lying on the ground beside it were two halves of a dead snake, its mouth full of ants. It was a thin, brown snake, its scales thick with red dust, strands of sinew joining the two halves through a clot of bloodied mess. Němec wondered what had become of the man. The donkey swatted away a fly with its tail. Němec moved on.

Not much further the track wound to the right through a series of deep corrugations, then veered back before straightening out again. The silo towered, flaring in the sunlight. As he came closer, he saw there were people moving about in a clearing beneath it. Conscious of his nudity, he hesitated to go further. As he watched, the people, ten or twelve of them, formed themselves into a circle & the circle began to turn. It looked like a kind of folkdance. There was a sound, too, like singing. Just then a dust cloud swept up along the track & burned his eyes. He covered his face with his hands & stumbled against the wind. The barley thrashed around him. Then just as suddenly the wind-gust died down again.

Němec uncovered his eyes. The circle of dancers had stopped & were all staring at him, standing out in the open now. He recognised every one of them. Faktor, the moustachioed dwarf, the Toad, Heydrich-the-waiter, the coatcheck girl, Bobek, Ol' Deathbed, Comrade Med-the-Dev in his colonel's uniform, Miss Freudlová in a tight blue gymsuit, the stand-up comic, the blonde Carmelite. And behind them, crucified up against the silo with arms outstretched, a naked effigy of himself tossing its head from side to side, mouth wide open but soundless, a black bowler hat stuck on its head, while Nurse P, grasping an enormous syringe, probed with a ten-foot needle in its side.

Němec stood there staring at them. The dancers, raising their arms, began advancing towards him, slowly, like underwater swimmers. And it was then he heard it, the beating in the sky, from somewhere far off to deep down in his eardrums. He covered his ears & winced, squinting up at the sun. A pair of black wings swept out of it, a bat-like creature with a man's head, circling high above. The beating grew louder, the dancers were getting closer, but Němec stood rooted to the spot, body grown heavy, heavier. The heat-shimmer warping the air. The barley's hiss & rasp. And the beating, like a thousand helicopters. He slumped down onto his knees, his penis like a blind worm dangling to the dirt. The dancers were almost upon him.

'Arepo!' they shouted. 'AREPO!'

Like a man forsaken, he screamed at the sky. He could not see those wings black-out the sun as the light froze in his eyes.

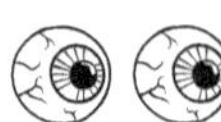

The next time Němec looked up Volta was leaning over him.

'Try sitting,' the doctor said.

A nurse who wasn't Volta's usual assistant came & jabbed a thermometer under Němec's tongue — blonde under her nurse's cap, but weren't they all? This one with a pointy chin & little pointy nose & pointy cheekbones, pointy hips, too, & flatchested. Watching the blur of the hands going round the fob watch pinned to her pocket. Then with a rapid pointy-elbowed movement the nurse whisked the thermometer back out & held it up to the light, expressionlessly. The mercury could've been tickling 40° & you'd never know. The nurse, with flick of the wrist, slotted the thermometer into the disinfecting dish (beaker? jar? pan?), hips pointing south-east by north-west, balled & socketed like a wooden doll, no lateral movement whatsoever as she walked, *clackclackclack* back out of the office. Němec followed the double-blur of her white stockings travelling up under the white blur of her pinafore as the outer door wheezed shut behind them.

He was lying on the settee beneath the window in Volta's office — hat hanging on the hatstand by the door. Laboriously, he sat up, looking down to check that he was all there. Not naked, thank God, except for the pasty fissured dome of his squillhead. He squinted at the clock on Volta's wall, but the hands refused to come into focus. It'd been after 10:00 when he'd arrived at the *Grünegast*, it had to be well past midnight by now.

'Don't those nurses ever sleep?'

Volta looked at him queerly —

'You were lucky I was on-call. Seems you've had quite a time.'

The doctor handed him a glass of water, which he drank — it seemed to
help. He massaged his temples — that seemed to help, too. Bit by bit the room
solidified & lost the haze around its edges. Volta meanwhile went over to his
desk & was shuffling papers around. He took his time. Němec watched him
with no great enthusiasm. He felt childish being there, like waking up in the
infirmary at the Home, back in the day, & the nurse giving him the third
degree. He wondered how the scene would play itself out this time.

Finding whatever it was he was looking for, Volta picked up the telephone
& dialled a number. Němec watched him talk into it without being able to make
out what he said. After he hung up he remained standing where he was,
scratching his chin. In his other hand Němec recognised the green-coloured
calling card with the Latin word-puzzle on it. No-one had explained what it was
supposed to mean to him yet, but that didn't matter, he wasn't sure he was
interested any more. He saw Faktor, sitting at a table, holding the same card in
the same way. Had that really happened? They'd all had their laugh at his
expense, he supposed. *Well, if you've gotta take it lyin' down, kiddo, may as well
make yerself comfortable.*

Volta took a cigar out of the box on his desk, trimmed it with his
fingernails & put a match to end of it. Something about the smell of cigar smoke
that puts a person at ease. But it didn't put Němec at ease. He'd seen the black
cigarette butt with the gold band perched on the edge of the ashtray where Volta
tossed his spent match. He knew who it belonged to. A face at least. He eyed
Volta suspiciously. Then he remembered the dwarf looking down at him. The
blonde with the wig. Cigarette butts in an ashtray. And then images started
coming back — the Toad, Faktor, the floorshow… Němec tried to think. What
the hell happened to him? How'd he get here? *The Doc*, is what the dwarf had
said. Němec remembered now. Like they knew him…

'By all accounts,' Volta said, pulling a shred of tobacco from his bottom
lip, 'you had some type of seizure earlier this evening. No history of epilepsy in
your family, I suppose? But forgive me, you lost your family, how thoughtless of
me. Needless to say… Might be a good idea to run some tests, *mnnn?*'

He glancing at Němec from under his eyebrows.

'Could be nothing, of course. Blood pressure's low, though not
abnormally. Would you like some coffee?'

Němec shook his head, still lost in thought. The doctor watched him,
flicking his thumb against the tip of his cigar, which he held pointing at the
ceiling. After a while he leaned back in his chair & smoked. Flakes of ash

gathered on the lapel of his coat. Idly he tapped the papers on his desk, till it seemed he'd decided enough time had passed.

'Perhaps,' he smiled at his patient, 'you'd care to tell me about it? Why don't we start at the beginning. No rush. Just one thing at a time. What about this?' he said, holding the green calling card up for Němec to see. 'I'm curious to hear what you were doing at this place. Who gave it to you?'

'No-one gave it to me.'

'Oh? No-one? Like Odysseus, *hmmm*?'

Němec said he didn't know anybody called O.D.C.S. Volta stopped smiling, sighed, then read out the piece about Arepo —

'D'you know what that means?'

Němec shook his head — not much, but still enough to set the room spinning all over again. He shut his eyes & everything went red. Opened them again. The room swayed slightly, he felt sea-sick.

'It means,' Volta went on, 'that Arepo the Sower has a hard time controlling the wheels of his plough. It may or may not tell us something about Arepo, since the wheeled plough wasn't in use till the third century. But what I'm interested in, Mr Němec, is what it tells us about *you*. Did you write it?'

Němec fought the sea-sickness.

'Mmm?' Volta's eyes narrowed. 'It also happens to be a form of palindrome.'

Němec returned the doctor's questioning look with a pained one —

'Palin-who?'

'Drome,' the doctor said, biting down on the end of his cigar. 'Like Arepo's wheel, it drives both ways. There may be a special meaning to that, what do you think?'

Němec squeezed his head in his hands —

'Beats me,' he winced. 'Till yesterday, I never heard of the guy.'

Volta tapped the card on his desk.

'Tell me,' he said, 'did you go to this place to meet someone?'

Němec thought about the question, trying to get the night's events into focus, to put things in their right order, fill in the blanks. The green card, Faktor, the tableau with Medvedev & old Babajugs. And the blonde. But he said nothing. Volta seemed to ponder his silence. In the meantime, the nurse with the bony hips returned with a syringe on a tray…

'Something to put you on a more even keel,' the doctor explained.

Němec was vaguely aware of the sting of the needle as it slid into the vein in the crook of his arm, then withdrew. A wad of cotton taped down over the puncture mark — the nurse nothing if not efficient. Wordlessly, soundlessly, she retreated again to the outer room.

'As a matter of fact, you were quite delirious when they brought you in,' Volta puffed on his cigar. 'No recollection at all, eh?'

One shake of the head. Volta seemed pleased at that.

'Kept babbling about the Devil, of all things. And you also mentioned a certain Mr Faktor. I believe we've discussed Mr Faktor before, *haven't we?*'

No response.

'*Yesss.* I do believe we have.'

Volta parked his cigar in the ashtray. From among the papers on his desk he retrieved a small phial of white tablets & a prescription that'd already been filled out.

'*In any case*, we'll need to make an appointment for those, *um*, tests, won't we? My secretary can make the arrangements. In the meantime, take my advice & get some rest. Avoid unnecessary excitement, don't do anything strenuous. You've heard it all before. Better cut down on the drinking, too, unless you feel like doing without your liver & pancreas. Any more of those dizzy spells, take one of these.'

He passed Němec the phial & the square of paper.

'Otherwise, the usual — one in the morning, one at night. Before meals. You *do* eat meals, don't you?'

Němec took the phial & stared at it — the writing on the prescription was crabbed to the point of illegibility. Maybe the Prof's Swedish graphologist could've made something out of it. He slipped the phial into his jacket pocket.

'Now, as for your Mr Faktor, I've made some inquiries. Seems the man has something of a reputation, as a — shallwesay — patron of the arts. Which is to say, he gives the impression of having money & lets people go out of their way to interest him in their projects. Kinsky, the former Culture Minister, was known to be photographed with him. Seems he has strange ideas about restoring the monarchy. Every man wants a master, but not every man wants a king...'

Volta left his sentence hanging while he chewed on his cigar.

'There was a woman,' Němec said, unable to help myself.

A faint smile creased Volta's lips. He leant back in his chair & blew a long stream of smoke at the ceiling, taking his time with his patient.

'Ah yes. Always, *cherchez la femme*! In your delirium you were especially concerned about the plight of some poor damsel harassed by devils &

monsters… Really. I thought you'd have more brains. But you needn't fear, the young lady in question is quite unharmed. Her name, by the way, is Alice. Alice Steinerová. As it turns out, I've known Miss Steinerová for some time. Professionally, that is. A former patient of mine… You might think it ironic, but Alička was quite concerned about *your* wellbeing. It was her quick thinking that saved us all a lot of trouble with the authorities, I should think.'

The image of the Devil & the Carmelite flashed anew before Němec's eyes. The expression on her face, frozen there, as he himself roared something incomprehensible, flailing at the air like someone falling from a great height. But as soon as he tried to grasp hold of the image, it fled, like a hypnotist's talisman which, though dangling right in front of you, you can't describe.

Volta's eyes narrowed, as if trying to pierce Němec's confusion. He ashed his cigar in silence & then addressed him with a vague air of annoyance, but also of resignation, boredom, fatigue.

'Under certain circumstances,' he said, 'there's nothing more false than the socalled eye-witness account. The power of suggestion, for instance. But perhaps the answer's more simple. Either you saw what you saw, or else you didn't. How do you propose to ever find out?'

Němec said nothing. Obviously he was making a fool of himself again. Everything Volta had suggested was entirely reasonable. It dawned on him quite suddenly that he was acting exactly like someone who really *was* delusional. Volta yawned, clearing some papers off to one side of his desk.

'For centuries men have worried themselves with the question, Why must the Devil exist as well as God? Isn't God *one*? And is not God *good*? Or is the Devil merely the proposition that there is no God? The world, not a created thing, but a hypothesis? It's been said that morality is no more than this: that, by what we do, we know what we are &, by what we suffer, we know what we deserve…'

'Schopenhauer.'

Volta looked at Němec blankly, then went on —

'The question is, can we believe that it's possible in this world to be free?'

He regarded the end of his cigar as though addressing his question to it.

'And yet,' he poked his cigar at his bottom lip, 'what good's that? Let's be frank & call a spade a spade. After all, the world'd be a better place without us.'

Volta all of a sudden had the look of a tired man.

'Of course,' he continued, taking a small puff on his cigar & letting the smoke drift out of his mouth as he spoke, 'we're not without a sense of our own inconsistencies. Intentions matter, as they say, but good intentions aren't always enough…'

He stifled a coughed —

'*Thrust into life, armed with our senses, will and reason, we feel ourselves to be potent beings…* A poet said that.'

Volta raised his eyebrows & nodded to himself, as if considering the import of what he'd just said.

'Well, what *is* freedom? I'll tell you,' he said, pausing to re-light his cigar, which'd gone out. 'This is what people refuse to believe. That everything's just a… a *mirage*. All the Eternal Truths, all the Thousand-Year Reichs…'

Němec leaned back against the arm of the settee & half-listened as Volta settled into his monologue. They'd moved back into familiar territory at least.

'The God of the Apes, too, secretly knows what He refuses to admit. That,' he said, 'is the one true obscenity. D'you think History'll save us? It's not that nothing's what it appears to be. No. Everything *is only ever* what it appears to be.'

The doctor smiled insipidly —

'Just like that little fixation of yours,' he said.

He drew on his cigar, blowing smoke across his desk —

'What else is the "Devil" but the Mind showing that it is master of *un*creation as well? That it knows all the secret *incompatibilities*? Not one man's fantasy versus someone else's, but the collective fantasy at odds with itself…'

Volta paused & allowed his patient to absorb his theory for a while before going on —

'Man, after all, is a predominantly stupid if tenacious animal. But he has this to say for himself, that at least his stupidity is shared.'

Amen.

30

PRAGERSCHINKEN

Admiring the subtle artistry of the cufflink he's just fitted into his left shirt-cuff, General der Polizei Reinhard Tristan Eugen Heydrich, Reichsprotektor (acting) of Bohemia & Moravia, stands before the dressing table in his private apartment at Czernin Palace, the former Cheskoslovnik Foreign Ministry, thinking not of Brahms but of the Zhid Händel's *Pomp and Circumstance*, & the bitterness of not completing that bold stroke in the West as the price of gaining a free hand for his great task in the East. Perhaps Fortune would soon smile upon the Reich once more — he would savour being present there, at Hastings, for the enemy's surrender — after all, the English were defeated, it was merely a question of ending the War. At this moment he's just returned from Pankrác Prison, a dull morning whose one highlight was Otokar Klapka, Golem City Mayor (former), being hanged like a pig from a girder, squealing as he choked. Then a quick workout with his SD fencing partner, Joost, a blond Errol Flynn type whose muscled bare chest, agleam with sweat, dazzled — faint white tracery of a scar beneath the left nipple where once, & only ever once, an opponent's sabre scored a touch — followed by a swim, ten laps in the outdoor pool down by Podolí, before taking a spin in his open-top along the river, admiring the scenery — the hakenkreuz & lightning bolt *SS* bunting ubiquitous up & down the quays, above the bridges, proudly over the castle — cutting across through Holešovice, a quick detour to the Bubny sidings to check the deportations are proceeding on schedule, then up to the Burg, socalled, where he is now. It's the Reichsprotektor's habit to change into a fresh uniform before his mid-morning conference — today it's Alfred Rosenberg, Thulite & director of the Ministry for the East, followed by Eichmann, director of the Central Office for the Settlement of the Zhiddish Problem in Bohemia & Moravia, then the usual briefing with Frank, Böhme, Geschke. The cufflink is one of a custom set, by the renowned Weimar jewellers (former), Gottlieb & sons, fashioned especially for R.T.E.'s dear late father — Richard Bruno — a singer & sometime composer gifted in minor imitations of Wagner, who'd many years before starred in the title role of the great Hans Pfitzer's first opera, *Der Arme Heinrich*.

It was agreed by all who knew him, that Heydrich-senior possessed all the finer human qualities, including a technical appreciation of superior craftsmanship — in this instance, a geometric rune of black obsidian: two diagonally interlocking facets set in a platinum disc the size of a ten pfennig piece, resembling, dependent on one's viewpoint, a piece of linked chain, a pair of cat's eyes, a Schwabacher "Judenletter" ẞ, or a deceptively simple puzzle designed in the form of a Möbius infinity. The Reichsprotektor tilts his wrist slightly upwards — the way the angle of the light, caught *just-so*, made the two halves of the obsidian design appear to telescope into a shimmering diamond-shaped zero. Ordinarily the Reichsprotektor disdained such gimmicks, but on this occasion the effect strikes him as particularly *sympathetic* — he has, after all, seen to it personally that Gottlieb & his miserable sons were dispatched on the first available transport to Dachau — put to work fashioning trinkets from their brethren's teeth. The cufflinks, in any case, complement nicely the brushed grey officer's jacket which hangs to the right of the dressing table on a tailor's dummy — a cavalry sabre dangling by a silver belt from its neck. It's at times like this that his childhood comes back to him. Halle. The garden behind the family house — brother Heinz digging in the flowerbed, sister Maria drawing in her sketchbook — the governess's white hams, bent over a wickerwork armchair as father plies her ample buttocks with a carpet-beater — their regular Friday afternoon ritual: him, flushed to his moustache, bellowing in that contradiction-in-terms, *operatic* Deutsch; her, squealing in bog-standard Bravurian, sweating behind the ears — little Reinhard making a note of it all for his colour-coded filingcard set, concealed but not expertly behind the hydrangeas, apple of his mother's eye — & *Her*, Mutti, calling them in for their bath — if only Lina were more amenable, well… Sometimes she reminds him, her eyes — the same eyes their daughter, Marta, too will have, born after his death, though he can't know that… It seems so long ago, already, so far off — they own this little moment of eternity, ah yes. *History will remember!*

Born under the sign of the twin fish, a Pisces — like Mengele, Eichmann & Albert Speer — young Reinhard's second passion was violin. In this, as everything else, he was noted to be fastidious bordering upon psychopathic — he garrotted effigies of his teachers (Kovaly, Edelstein, Kafka) with a wire violin string & would later fiddle while the Zhids of Europe burned. At twentyseven, these precocious talents were enlisted by Heinrich Himmler, the mild-faced ex-chicken-farmer, to a fledgling sub-unit of the SS — the euphonious Sicherheitsdienst (SD) — number tattooed under the arm, 10120. That was in 1931. Surrounded on all sides by a court of lunatics, toadies & spies drawn from the ranks of a disaffected intelligentsia — bizarre pedants in the study of Teutonic archaeology, Jungian psychokinesis, Hinduism, phrenology & the eugenics of a Master Race — Heydrich fancied himself, like Tristan in Wagner, a latterday renaissance princeling of the Aryan Dawn. Himmler was put in no doubt about this *high animal*, a protean schemer afflicted with a singular, anti-Zhiddish autism, disguised as high-cultured high-mindedness. From the look of him now, you'd expect he was the sort of child with an unhealthy interest in numerology, eschatology or synergetics. While still head of the Bravurian Gestapo he'd concocted increasingly complicated Central Inmate Files, weaving bits of real & invented "information" into *n*-dimensional webs of intrigue, vast hyperlogic constructs defining the arcane universe of counterintel: nothing too insignificant to slip through the net, nothing too great, mapping overlays of whole strata of humanity, behavioural patterns, transport schedules, work routines, the sex lives of complete strangers, bank account details, tax returns, hotel registers, ticket stubs, graphs, diagrams, itineraries, strategic assessments & psychological profiles, mind-boggling rhizomes of cross-classification, by category & subcategory, calculated to six degrees of separation, webs of connectivity, statistical or merely stochastical, Boolean probabilities feeding back into the general matrix, computing guilt by prior implication, circumstance, association, predisposition, every facet subject to random levels of analysis, manipulation, abstraction, appropriation — a mechanical brain, in fact, devising endlessly variable algorithms for apportioning Death, like the cortex of some insatiably & horribly rational pagan deity. Himmler was impressed, sensing the hand of Destiny at work, as he'd sensed it during the Putsch, standing at the Führer's side. Reinhard, too, had a sense of destiny, but even now he was unsure what or whose. Initiated at an early age into the Onomastic Mysteries, he was haunted by the idea his own destiny would forever remain suffocatingly bound to that of his namesake, a nonentity in one of his father's copious forgotten operas. *The world is just a barrel-organ which the Lord God turns himself — we all have to dance to the tune that's already on the drum.* Was it for this reason he chose to christen the first phase of the Final Solution after none other than *himself*? Taking as his own the catastrophe soon to be Europe's, like some Brothers

Grimm tale of men & beasts, mad Frankensteins, bloody anatomies — with a possible (why not?) spin-off on the Barrandov lots, *Operation Reinhard*, with Werner Kraus as the Prince's arch-nemesis, perhaps, & Greta Garbo as… Well, Goebbels might be able to arrange it, but there were other, political factors to consider, too — petty jealousies at O.K.W., the Party Gauleuters, that idiot Bormann. Gazing into his cufflinks, the acting Reichsprotektor tries to divine the brightness of his own future — who could say — perhaps in Himmler's stead at the Führer's righthand, etc. (what the wags at High Command call him out of earshot, *Himmler's Brain*), & one day (why not?), Führer himself, master of all Europe & the World — or at least as soon as America came to its senses & realised the futility, nay downright stupidity, of standing opposed to the Reich, scourge of the *Enemies of Humanity*! In such momentary flights of fancy this older Reinhard, at thirty-eight, exhibits all the more mature paradoxes of a man whose maternal grandmother was sometimes herself rumoured to've been a Zhid — & thus his own mother, & thus (imputation most foul!) he too — a rumour not unknown to his masters. *Moses Handel*, they nicknamed him at the Reformgymnasium — a memory he doesn't cherish. All the experts agree, of course, that as Aryans go, he's the real McCoy. Looks the part, too — the Blond Beast — not some swarthy little four-eyes with a fake Hitler moustache. And there's his wife, as well, a real *bona fide* Nazi of the old school — von Osten — with her brood of little Heydrichs, just waiting for the day.

At seven a.m. precisely the acting Reichsprotektor strides out into his office where Rosenberg's already ensconced in a leather armchair, sipping coffee — he spills some of it getting to his feet, a half-hearted salute almost catching him in the eye, bleary after an all-night session with the small army of model-railway enthusiasts — neurasthenics each & every one — working out the nitty details of how to *process* six-million Zhids without derailing the entire war effort. The problem's always an excess of what some know-it-all keeps calling *entropy*, which to Rosenberg's mind, untainted by stuff anyone else can understand, sounds like an oriental perversion involving creepy black insects in jars. It goes without saying Heydrich considers him a dolt, a mystical idiot, but not without his uses — he is, after all, architect of the Lebensraum policy, the Myth of the Twentieth Century, & a Nazi from before even Hitler. The sole purpose of this meeting is to keep the Estonian peasant Rosenberg — at that moment assiduously avoiding any eye-contact, gazing instead between jackbooted feet at his own reflection in the waxed parquet — focused on the objective at hand, not wandering off in pursuit of fantastic notions about Sklavonic Aryanism! The deadline, it can't be stressed enough, is everything! The Führer expects a Solution to be obtained within three weeks, possibly four, preferably two — failure not to be tolerated. It'll be, as the Little-Big-Man constantly assures them all, a Struggle to the Death! — his very words. *In the present War, our people are faced with a fight for their very existence! Our enemies intend to annihilate us! This struggle is one of ideologies and racial differences and will have to be conducted with unprecedented, unmerciful and unrelenting harshness!* Fifteen minutes & Rosenberg's shuffled out the door. Heydrich reminds himself to have the man's background re-checked — what sort of a name, anyway, is *Rosenberg* for a Balt? A moment later the door swings open again & there's Eichmann — Ike or Icky to his pals, a little joke on the Amerikaners — like the Führer, a southerner from Linz, which is high praise for the man. Ike is carrying under his arm a dossier with the latest trial report from some nutty doctor, about his Zyklon rodenticide. Ike, bespectacled, is all enthusiasm. *You should see what it does to the lab rats — they turn GREEN!* In greeting he waves a limp righthand past his ear, swatting away an imaginary fly — mumbles something, then casts himself bodily into the armchair vacated only moments ago by the wrinkle-faced Rosenberg & still warm. An adjutant brings more coffee. *Brazilian*, Heydrich points out. *Robusta. Dark roast. Had it brought over by U-boat especially.* Plans were afoot — not his, he had other fish to fry — for cornering the coffee trade. There're still the Amerikaners to think about, but it's only a matter of time before the Japs take care of *them*. He conveys all this in his trademark deadpan that always leaves Ike in stitches — he'd've made a great stand-up, a genius compared with that Bob Hope. *Did you hear the one about… Give me a second… Here it is — Why don't those Zhiddish cannibals like eating Krauts?* Ike, leaving his coffee aside — a teetotaller, too, just like Himself — fingers creeping over the armrests like pink ectoplasm while he talks — a habit Heydrich can't abide, but what's he to do about it? The whole office is doused in industrial antiseptic first thing each morning by a charwoman from Halle (the sky through the window, even, was the colour of kerosene) — then flowers brought in, arranged in urns in the four corners of the room, giving the place, he notes approvingly, a very *sepulchral* atmosphere. He sniffs the air, it reminds him of his mother again — who always kept things in order, spotless — even the hydrangeas were spotless. His father, on the other hand... Ike broadens his grin, keeping Heydrich (he thinks) in suspense. *Because they give them gas! Heeheehee.* It was only yesterday, he (Heydrich) met with the new I.B.M. rep, New York office, Swiss subsidiary, old friends by now, to finalise the deal on those Hollerith Punchcard Machines — *the ultimate*, so assured (*unctuously* was the word that'd come to mind) *in Information Science* — like his own little yesteryear toybox invention, but on an entirely unprecedented scale — a mechanical superbrain capable of sorting every messy little detail of the Zhiddish Problem into an all-encompassing, elegant — yes, yes, above all *elegant* — Final Solution: a simple matter of input & output — but not so simple, it seemed, for the boys in the Statistical Office to've figured out — the small step from his own inventive genius to a *broad practical application* somehow too much for them, now that Barbarossa wasn't the fait accompli they'd all expected (saboteurs of the Official Faith!) — leaving *him* with the embarrassment of having to do business with a nation of kikes & schwartzes, one which they were technically at war with — but business is business, after all, & he can only pray Dönitz's U-boats don't sink the wrong shipments! And there was Ike still, sickly grinning. *Madder than Himmler*, he thought. *If anyone can get the job done even half-right, it's probably Ikey Mo, hehe.* Besides...

◆◆

In Golem City they call him *Der Schlächter*. To Himmler, on arrival, after signing his first batch of execution orders, he sent a postcard photograph of the Libeň abattoirs, inscribed: *Blut ist ein ganz besondrer Saft.* Haunted by predestinatory obsessions, he consults oracles, pursuing rumours, intuitions, echoes — nothing too obscure, unlikely, to pique his interest, to be filed away in turn, fed back into the mix on an endless loop. Yet again, as in childhood, he feels himself being secretly thwarted by invisible spectres. Even his reflection at times disturbs him — worried, despite everything, that History's condemned him to the role of a mere duplicate, his bloody moniker — pride of ℋ headquarters — nothing but a handmedown from a seventeenth-century hatchetman, Jan Mydlář, Rudolf II's willing executioner & prototypical *Butcher of Golem City.* Sometimes, during his morning sessions in the Pankrác execution chamber, unbeknownst to his minions, the acting Reichsprotektor's mind wanders among the mysteries of transubstantiation, reincarnation, metempsychosis — some sort of Nietzschean babble Rosenberg's always quoting at him whenever he gets a chance, which is more & more often these days now that he thinks he has the whole Eastern Problem figured out. *Die ewige Wiederkunft* or something of that nature — Spirit of Destiny, like the Reich itself. And this Mydlář, perhaps — at least the man was no operetta stage hack. Perhaps, four centuries hence, he too, Reinhard Heydrich, would *return*, the avatar of some cosmic cycle of purification, rebirth — like the archangel Gabriel, first of a long line. And would he know himself? *Well*, he thinks, *whoever comes next'll have to do something truly extraordinary to earn* my *name*! Smirking at the queue of prisoners about to be hanged — grey-faced, eyes harrowed, egoless — he paces the slaughterhouse tiles, in places slick with shit & vomit, prodding the corpses already dangling from iron butcher's hooks on the long girder that runs the length of the chamber. A type of abreacted bodily arousal brings him not to erection but to a plateau of calm — *lotus blossoms on still water...* But the true architect of doom, he knows, wouldn't rely on a gallows. At this very moment, the machinery was in action, the wheels turning, the ovens growing red — the mind of Eichmann in every detail — a bureaucrat, pure numbers. It bores him, Heydrich, like using a lathe to play a violin — it lacked genuine virtuosity, the personal touch. As Klapka takes his turn on the stool, noose drawn tight — no bag over his head, Heydrich likes to see these pigs die *face to face* — he wonders if making this Sklavic garbage into something remotely Aryanised isn't an impossible task, really the height of Rosenberg's stupidities. He (ᛋᛋ-Obergruppenführer R.T.E. Heydrich) would like nothing better than if the whole wretched nation had one neck — he can almost picture it, *her*, La Bohème, like one of those half-naked sluts in Mucha, peasant-thighed, cow-uddered & sloe-eyed, writhing expressively as she lies strapped to the guillotine — the very one, standing only metres away, with its enormous blade & a steel bucket above a grating, reserved for Special Occasions — occasions when he (Heydrich of Halle) seeks, like a spirit medium, to channel der schwarze Reiter's ghost — blade honed to an edge that'd split a length of hair clean down the middle, as by all accounts Mydlář's axe, *much disdaining to the curb to yield...* — rouged buttocks atremble, mouth thicklipped stretched sideways into a sad grin with a pair of her own stockings, knotted behind, head pulled back by the hair so he can get a good look at the fear in her, the recognition of death's proximity, but perhaps seeing nothing but a dumb animal incomprehension — imagining he could become almost tender at this point, sitting beside her in a steel chair, letting her cheek rest on his knee while they slot the wooden stock across the back of her neck, the girl's hair gathered in his gloved right hand, left hand stroking her brow — yes, something like tenderness — leaning closer now to whisper in her ear a passage from Heine he'd always felt, since his mother first read it to him, to be terribly moving — about Time being infinite, but the things in Time, the concrete bodies, those being merely finite. *Though they may indeed disperse into the smallest particles — but these particles, the atoms, have their determinate number, and the number of the configurations that, all of themselves, are formed out of them is also determinate. So however long a time may pass, according to the eternal laws governing the combinations of this eternal play of repetition, all configurations that have previously existed on this Earth must yet meet, attract, repulse, kiss, and corrupt each other again… And thus it will happen one day that a man will be born again just like me, and a woman will be born, just like you, and in a better land they will meet and contemplate each other a long time — and finally the woman will give her hand to the man and say with a tender voice: "Let us be good friends."* And then the blade coming down. Perhaps later, at the villa, with Lina, tied to the bed, she'll play his favourite game — what his childhood governess called her Enthauptungspeil — vicious little teeth snapping at him under the sheets. And afterwards, the smell of the leather strop, the cold razor, the shaving soap & eau-de-cologne, tightening the smooth hairless sex, caressing it, like polished alabaster.

The first time Reinhard Heydrich really listened to Wagner was just before or just after Easter Friday, 1908, when he was three years old & standing on a wooden stool in the parlour of the family home watching a gramophone record go round in circles while his sister, Maria, tried diligently but unsuccessfully to work out the notes on an upright piano. Each time the recording ended, young Heydrich was instructed to lift the needle & replace it in the groove closest to the edge of the black vulcanised 10-inch disc. This, during the course of an afternoon, he'd learned to master with surprising alacrity. It made him think of a carousel with unicorns & lions & then, needle poised, of the spinning blade Herr Schmidt, the butcher, used for slicing ham shanks with names like *Versailles* & *Pragerschinken*. Thinking this kept him from becoming bored, though he struggled against the temptation any little boy would've felt to slow the disc with his finger or drag the needle along the groves & make the whole contraption shriek like someone having their head cut off. The piano — already a piece of family folklore — had been imported at their mother's insistence from Chicago, Adam Schaaf & Sons, like those saloon pianos in the wild west films Hollywood in three short years would soon be churning out for mass global consumption, making saloon pianos all the rage. There'd come a time when no Weimar whorehouse worth its name would be seen without one — at which point in his brilliant career Heydrich, having done the dirty with a Sea Captain's daughter, being frogmarched unrepentant out of the Kriegsmarine, known to frequent one or two such establishments — that's him there in the corner, *a queer fish* if ever you saw one, sipping iced water while perusing the latest *Völkischer Beobachter* or exchanging whispered titbits of "wohl," "ja," "denn," "schon," "noch," "eigentlich" with a short weasel-faced veteran on themes ranging from Brest-Litovsk, Deutschland in her Darkest Hour, the Zhiddish Question, Might & Right, Compromise & Force, the Berlin Zhiddish Republic, & assorted asinine utopianisms (the National Idea, wherein every true man could live in harmony with himself), to the rumoured discovery of a certain "lost manuscript," ur-text of the Teutonic mysteries apparently, Font of Aryan Wisdom, Music of the Spheres, Blueprint for the Millennial Reich, smuggled out of Golem City during the darkest hours of the Thirty Years War all those centuries ago, a description & map of its alleged whereabouts having turned up in Landsberg Prison concealed inside a roll of toilet paper — just the sort of thing to excite the young Heydrich's fervid brain — in addition to which, the actual toilet roll could be got for the inflation-adjusted price of only 60,000 marks. Who could've suspected that in this was founded all Heydrich's future plans for the ᛋᛋ Protektorat? Behind his rapid rise through Nazi ranks, the patient construction of its counterintelligence empire, the immense data-gathering machinery, was a twin *idée fixe*: the Final Solution & the recovery of this mythic Ur-Text, his secret, unspoken *amor fati* — like the Ring of the Nibelung, to possess it were to make him truly a god among men! Fastforward: Pankrác Prison, November 1941 — Heydrich, as every morning after, boots spit-polished by his chauffer, on hand personally for the interrogation, systematically, of every archivist & curator in the City with even the remotest likelihood of knowing, really or apocryphally, the present whereabouts of Rudolf II's lost alchemical library. With a white butcher's apron covering his uniform, he pulls their teeth out with a pair of rubber-handled pliers — their confessions, sealed by guillotine in the execution chamber, thence kept in the (acting) Reichsprotektor's private files — to be poured over between wiles in a feverish yet futile attempt at fitting the pieces of the puzzle together, the answer to it all dawning on him shortly after midday 27 May 1942, sending a frenzied cable to Berlin using an Enigma encryption Bletchley Park had already cracked a week previous but still couldn't make head or tail of. What occurred that afternoon isn't entirely known, only that — as reported in a dossier raided from ᛋᛋ-Obergruppenführer K.H. Frank's office after the War & stashed away by Václav Nosek's Interior Ministry goons — a certain J. Kulička, PhDr — a.k.a. T. Hájek, junior archivist at the Strahov Monastery & previously *passed over* as the report's author jibed — was arrested while playing chess with a companion, an officer of the ᛋᛋ no less, at the Barrandov Terraces — conveyed post-haste to the basement of Pankrác Prison, interrogated (by Heydrich presumably) &, well, the rest was routine.* An inventory of personal effects recorded a brown leather attaché case, containing: pen holders, pen clips, a box of steel nibs, India ink (black, blue, red), blotting paper, assorted graphite pencils (Koh-i-noor Hardtmuth a.s.) in a plaid cloth pencilcase, Mikov 535 pencil sharpener, three roles of brown gumpaper, a fold-out watercolour set, brushes (sable), gel medium, a box of round drawing charcoal size 6, twelve sticks of white chalk, a stick of gum arabic, two boxes of brass thumbtacks, a role of bailing twine, a vanity case with nail clippers, nail file, talcum powder, half-a-dozen safety razors wrapped in waxpaper, one shaving mirror, one leather satchel containing blank sheets of half-folio, watermarked, one black leather-bound notebook with markings, one brass letter-opener bearing an Egyptian motif on its handle, ten regular envelopes (5 blue, 5 white) for general correspondence, other miscellaneous — along with two overdue library books stamped "Národní Knihovna Klementinum" (*Some Observations on Ancient Inks* & *A Booke of Secrets, Showing Divers Waies to Make and Prepare all Sorts of Inke and Colours*) & a package, plain wrapped, the size of a thick ledger: said package duly catalogued in the confused aftermath of Heydrich's untimely apotheosis, & quietly left to moulder in the ᛋᛋ archives. One can almost hear through the pious silence, as he places his hands on this — dare he even hope it? — most sacred of objects, strains of that music moving within itself Maria, grace of God, his (Heydrich's) beloved sister, had that long-ago Easter afternoon so assiduously laboured over — which, ever after, had produced in him (Heydrich) a thrill akin to the frisson of childhood incestuous longing, the return to the pure source, the first love, the soul's Valhalla — being none other than the opening four-&-a-half minutes of *Siegfried*, part three of *Der Ring des Nibelungen* — the titular role inaugurally

---

* → Chapter 63. [✥]

performed by Georg Unger, Hans Richter conducting, but first recorded by a studio tenor in Philadelphia, voice awash with static, all rights reserved by the Victor (formerly Berliner) Record Company: it told the story of Siegfried & Brunhilde, beginning in a cave in a Teutonic forest, where a dwarf is attempting to forge a magical sword — Siegfried is an orphan who the dwarf has raised since infancy, & who despises & finally slays him (the dwarf), *fearless of light-bringing love and laughing death*, etc. How, in later life, Heydrich would be able to recall the moment when his sister finally hit the right notes in the right order as a kind of prophesy *avant la lettre*, that come what may in the dark years after 1918 the Fatherland would indeed rise in triumph over the dwarves of Versailles. *Alle Schweine*!

Pull up a sandbag, old chump! In the script it says five-past-midday & Heydrich's taking a nap before getting on with the business at hand: his one real passion in life, surrogate for who knows what lost maternal longings, like Siegfried — putting the wheels on the *Vernichtungs* juggernaut, chariot of this would-be godhead, father to millions, architect of doom, author of the apocalypse... Think of the poet who said, *I love art like power*! From our vantage on-high we can see the faint dilation & contraction of the acting Reichsprotektor's nostrils as he sleeps, head tilted over the armrest of a sofa in the faux-Turkish style, throat as if offered up to the hand of Himself, chin & cheekbones in a demeanour of calmly veiled inner turmoil — bearing but a faint resemblance to those deathmask replicas they'll soon enough be turning out for the army of adorers. Does he think of himself already in this way? Uncannily prescient of what awaits just around the proverbial corner? Haunted in his dreams — as now, sweat forming on the brow, a twitch of the lip — by that ape-like *anthropoid* he's vowed to rid the world of but now threatens to come back & bite him? He'll rave like a lunatic under the morphine they shoot him up with after the botched effort with the bomb — mind-golems rampaging through the septic brain, lesions in the vital parenchymatous doodads — wanting only to sleep, lie down there beside his Brunhilde, the mighty Nothung, the Ring of Fire, serenaded by all the voices of the damned. When it happens, he won't even know he's dead — a far cry from what the Whitehall crowd have in mind for him, setting up Beneš & his exiled Cheskoslovniaks to play patsy — employing the C-word with unnerving frequency lately (the translators at odds over *capitulationist* or *collaborationist*), hinting at a kind of grand gesture *à la* Charge of the Light Brigade (Beneš thinks), to show whose side etc., ringleading a whole circus of committees & subcommittees to that effect, though reputedly the actual decision to knock the bastard off (Heydrich) — codenamed *Anthropoid* (some Foreign Office under-secretary with a three in classics most probably, New College, likes to quote Shelley at the club over whatever they've been able to dig up from the cellar since it was bombed, a makeshift arrangement that conveys all the class-doggedness of the socalled Stiff Upper Lip) — having already been taken, months prior, at a meeting held *in camera*, 3 October 1941, at the possibly apocryphal Dog-'n'-Bone tavern in Shoreditch, minutes marked CLASSIFIED. The plan was simple: drop some paras behind lines, do the red button stuff & Foxtrot Oscar — they'd leave the technical rigmarole (wiggly amps, ones&noughts, Bernouillis, skyhooks, white man's magic) to the odd little chaps who were supposed to know about that sort of thing — could launch a couple of flying nuns over there on rocketpropelled deckchairs for all *they* cared: duly rubberstamped & run up the flagpole with the boys from Special Ops Exec (S.O.E.), ironing out the wrinkles in THE PLAN, smoothing over the rough edges (like worrying a fingernail with a metal file so it won't snag the girl from the typing pool's stockings later that evening), picking some funny-sounding tags out of a hat, likely candidates for martyr-status (Buckley's they'd be seeing those Chesky blighters again, still no harm putting on a good show, always the one you don't expect, eh?): WO J-for-Jozef Gabčík, WO J-for-Jan Kubiš. *Try and at least spell their bloody names right*! Beneš nursing cold feet by this stage, corns, chilblains, tinea, a touch of the gout — which, depending on the day of the week & was the wind northerly or sou'westerly — though in the end THE PLAN gets the go-ahead rearguardless, *hehe*, papershuffled by some Bluntie-Ponti-Scribbley R.E.M.F.* — Whitechapel hardly to be expected to concern itself overly with "approbation on the ground," so to speak, knowing reprisals were a dead cert if not the precise calibre (*We'll patch it up in the post-ops pontification*) — never short of precedents in that domain, & what's another zero when all's said & done for the chance to give Fritz one where he doesn't expect it? *Not just the symbolic value, mind*! The groundlings with good reason to be apprehensive: within days, whole networks of the Resistance are being rounded up, tortured, shot — a handful beating the Nazis at their own game chomping

---

* "Rear-Echelon Mother Fucker." [✊]

cyanide — but only one of them knows exactly where Gabčík & Kubiš are holed up in the church basement, an eleven-year-old kid (just like a filmscript this) who the Gestapo boys have something special in store for, having worked him over non-stop & force-fed him a bottle of slivovice through a rubber hose, they'll let him take a good ogle at his beloved matka's severed head floating in a fish tank & he'll sing like a cracked canary — never knowing they'd been ratted-out already by one of S.O.E.'s own paras, some panto primadonna gone antsy sitting on the sideline, lost his nerve & walked straight into Golem City Gestapo HQ just begging to spill his guts, 16 June 1942, not even on their suspect list, drew a regular cheque thereon in, role model for every other would-be rat: Čurda, K-for-Karel, strung up (like Frank) at Pankrác four years later. *Verräter*! Yep, symbolism's a powerful thing — shoot a fish in a suitcase, so they say, it rains toads for a month of Sundays — or maybe drop a pin on Berlin, it blows out a million windows in Old Blitzed Blighty. Well, you could call Göring "Meyer," & you could call Heydrich a dead duck, if it makes you feel any better. A finger twitches in a bunker under the Reichs Chancellery & a village in Bohemia vanishes from the face of the planet — something as elegant as the Hand of Fate putting its Hancock on a piece of paper. Six million pieces of paper. And longnosed Heydrich, whisked off to the Weltgeist — *How sweetly immortality sings!* — officially deathless now they've made him the first name in the Final Solution — like an operetta in extravagantly bad taste, all mawkish nostalgia for our late hero with the Ice Queen gaze — *Resplendent thou wilt face the apes with your bloody crown* — Hitler Youth majorettes going weak at the knees just thinking about it — name up there in lights on the big marquee, top billing, a box office sensation breaking all records & already booked-out for a three year run — namesake of namesakes, *Operation Reinhard*! (the wind-up clappers going mad with over-enthusiasm — though it could just be an airraid warning, bombers over the Brandenburg Gate, working a bit of the old bamboozlement on the bloody Bosch — woozy sandwichboard girls schlepping off before the *de rigueur* curtain call & closing spiel: *Man who has overcome his animal nature, organised the chaos of his passions, sublimated his impulses, disciplined his wholeness — who has created himself!* while the whole ensemble cast waits for the roof to fall in, as surely it must one of these nights). The whole spectacle's a media stunt of course, slapped together by Goebbels & Co. & calculated to get right up Churchill's pugnose, that pseudo-Wellington (just watch & see how fast he can surrender Singapore — as impregnable as the Titanic, *hehe* — to a pack of monkeys on stolen bicycles, *hehehe*) — trying at every turn to outdo each other on the propaganda front: *Operation A* versus *Operation R*, & though *A*'s landed the first big punch (no fault of their own, mind you) it's *R* all the way to the bank it seems. You see, THE PLAN wasn't so simple after all — another right British fandango — *Force Ten from Navaronne* meets *Passport to Pimlico*. What did they expect them to do, walk up & just pop the bastard between the eyes? For starters, our two Chesky commandos found themselves dropped off at the *wrong place* & every bit of their equipment fucked — bailed out into two a.m. December fog & snow, behind the drag curve & up the creek: only option to lie low, forage off the land, bide time — weeks plodded, message from Command: dash-dot-dash-dash, dash-dash-dash, dash-dot-dash-dash, dash-dash-dash — Y.O.Y.O.* — nothing for it but to bite the bullet then, strike out for the interior, make contact with the locals, risk exposure, get the lowdown, assemble necessary bibs&bobs for the task at hand, pick their spot, wait for the right moment — the sand slowly running out for Plan B: ambush Heydrich's staff car on a hairpin turn between his villa (off at Panenské Březany) & his office (up at the Castle) — shoot first, & if that doesn't work, try lobbing an anti-tank grenade. *Chaff-chaff.* In the event: Gabčík's Sten-gun jams — Heydrich, caressing the hapless archivist's attaché case, mind somewhere else entirely (Faustian visions of alchemical splendour), rudely awakened to this intruding bit of slapstick reality, decides in that split second to take matters into his own hands, orders his chauffer to halt the car (a black open-top Merc 320C), stands & calmly "returns" fire at the sitting duck holding the toy machinegun (*like tits on a fish)* while Kubiš, waiting across the road by a tramstop, boldly seizes the opportunity to lob his oversized grenade (never've hit a moving target with *that*) at the now stationary Merc parked right out there in the middle of the street — he'd've hanged himself if he'd missed, but still only manages to put a hole in the rear door before doing a runner (somehow, in the excitement of it all, completely forgot about the two spare grenades inside his coat — what'd he think he was going to do with *those*, keep 'em as souvenirs?). Looks like Lady Luck's finally smiled, though. They'll have no way of knowing, our two intrepids, that Heydrich'll be right as rain in a few days, once the doctors have pulled the shrapnel & horsehair upholstery from lung, spleen, diaphragm — a straightforward operation, Professor Hollbaum & Doctor W. Dick (chief of surgery at Bulovka Hospital, conveniently just down the street) officiating. Recovery normal, *no indication of fever, abscesses or infarct.* The very picture of his

---

* "You're on your own." [☝]

usual self, sitting up in bed with his breakfast tray, whistling snatches of Wagner to inward visions of consolationary hecatombs & *something about an attaché case* the nurse said, when — eight days late, on the morning of June 4, under the post-operative care of Himmler's personal physician — he'll suffer a heart attack, brought on, if the autopsy report's to be believed, by *septicaemia*. Call it Plan C. Heydrich will've been only thirtyeight & in the job as Reichsprotektor (acting) exactly eight months & eight days (something fishy going on here with the number 8). In retribution for Anthropoid's bungling good fortune, Himmler (quietly relieved, if truth be told, that his psychopathic prodigy hadn't lived long enough to plot *his* downfall) issues, in the name of the Führer & on Frank's prompting (don't forget little Bim Bam Böhme!), the order to raze, house-by-house, along with the murder of its entire population, a village of no significance to the script whatsoever — its fate sealed, as in all worthy Jacobean travesties, by an intercepted epistle — sent, on this occasion (as on many others), by a definitive nobody, who even now would remain missing from the dramatis personae were it not for History & the fastidiousness of Nazi bookkeeping — some balls-for-brains pretend partisan from Budapest, Václav ("Milan") Říha, addressed to his amour of the moment, a Slaný factory girl whose knickers he'd hatched the bright idea of climbing into, name of Anna Maruščáková, dark-haired in her photograph, thinking it'd impress her terribly...

> *Dear Aňa!*
>> *Excuse me for writing this late and hope you'll understand me because you know I have many worries. What I wanted to do, I've done. I slept overnight in Čabárna on the fatal day. I'm well, I'll see you this week and then never again.*
>>> *Milan*

Maruščáková off work sick that morning — Wednesday, June 3rd — meaning Říha's wheedling epistle was duly perused by office clerk, overseer & factory owner (the public face of Palaba, manufacturer of radios, lead-acid car batteries, flashlights, reflectors & dynamos) Jan Jaroslav Pála in person — not one known to keep his nose out of anyone else's business if he could help it at all — the magnate wasting no time in railing against the two unfortunates with all the scandalising moral indignation of a man spurned (mind a little unhinged, perhaps, with visions of this butter-mouthed, dumpling-haunched assembly-line maiden's libidinous cavortings — & with an assassin to boot!). He's been itching for months to get a piece of Maruščáková's *meruňka*[*] himself & so, not to look a gifthorse in the mouth, armed with all the evidence he'd ever need (delivered by providence into his fat little mitts, doubly barbed, yet deliciously, how sweet the revenge!), promptly conveys himself with half an eye to the not insignificant reward (half-a-million Reichsmarks is all) — right honourable J.J. Pála, man of no small social standing, 600 employees & on the up&up, straightbacked, ruddy-jowled — to the offices of the local boys-in-brown, Kladno branch, ǁ-Hauptsturmführer Harald Weismann officiating (he who afterwards, milk of human kindness & all that, salvaged a pram from Lidice for his wife to wheel their little sprog about in — charming fellow really). Little consolation if Pála ends up drawing a life sentence after the War, his factory nationalised & quietly incorporated into the structure of a certain T.E.S.L.A. Enterprises — said company devoted to research, development & production (for "military purposes"). In the meantime, our hapless Maruščáková, swiftly finding herself in the not incapable hands of H. Weismann, teary-eyed after some gentle prodding, comes clean on what her country bumpkin Casanova got to whispering in her ear that time in the hayloft, or wherever, putting some flesh on the bones of his little scam, being (how credulous it all seems in retrospect) *to pass on regards from Joe Horák to his family* — the name, ever so coincidentally, of an ex-army chap from Lidice who happened to've decamped from the Protektorat (illegally of course) to join a para regiment at Cholmonderly. The dirty dog. One thing leading to another, with Gabčík & Kubiš dead, Horák was the key, the trump card, the missing link — & Lidice was doomed. Weismann knew from the outset it was all a red herring — a *Poisson d'Avril* two months on the nose already — but that did nothing to dissuade the Nazis from having their bit of fun anyway. After arranging in Heydrich's stead for that brain-diseased idiot, Daluege, to assume duties as Reichsprotektor (acting) of Bohemia & Moravia — *après nous* & all that — Himmler issued instructions to: 1. shoot all adult men from Lidice, 2. transport all women to concentration camps, 3. select suitable children for Aryanisation with ǁ families in the Reich, deporting the remainder to Chełmno, 4. level the whole village. For their part, Říha & Maruščáková were quietly done away with at Mauthausen — a couple of inconvenient loose threads in this whole absurdity. While Heydrich's syphilitic understudy scribbled away in the headquarters of the Ordnungspolizei, Lidice burned. And after it burned, they sent in the demolition teams to blow up the

---

[*] Do I dare to eat a peach ? [✋]

remains — thirteen buildings courtesy of the Waffen-ℋ, thirtyone by the Reichsarbeitdienst, & eightynine (earning the big prize) flattened at the hands of Engineering Reserve Battalion 14… the whole shebang duly recorded for the greater glory of posterity — ℋ officers & enlisted men alike snapping pics of themselves posed in front of the ruins — a collapsed farmhouse here, a teetering church steeple there, grinning between looks of determined seriousness ('a Kraut always finishes what he begins!') — the heroic Aryan cause, etc. — rubble spirit-levelled, trees uprooted, cemetery exhumed, the course of a brook altered, low hills shifted — half-a-mile here, a quarter-mile there — roads re-routed, maps redrawn — movie cameras rolling unabatedly. Intended for a documentary that was never made, the Nazi auteurs carried their tripods hither&thither to capture on celluloid every last observable detail of the misfortunate village's demise: Franz Traml (proprietor of a Zeiss-Ikon outlet in the Lucerna Arcade), Miroslav Wagner (owner of the Zenit Laboratories on Vodičkova Street) & the staff of the *Aktuality Weekly* sharing credits between them.

31

DER EWIGE JUDE

The caretaker's parrot was out sunning itself in the courtyard, chained to a perch. It hissed at Němec when he came in through the carriageway, dancing from foot to foot like some South Seas lestrygon in green plumage. Němec stood there with a plastic shopping bag in one hand & his hat in the other, red faced & sweating, reminding himself that there really was a parrot in the house & that this wasn't some creeping form of dementia.

'Morning to you, too, Polly,' he yawned.

The parrot shoved a beady eye in Němec's direction, looking nonplussed for once. No sign of Mrs S. As soon as he got up to the Prof's apartment, Němec emptied the shopping bag with the morning's provisions he'd picked up from the nonstop down the street. Couple of bottles of slivovice, jar of zelí, jam & rolls. Food for the soul. He checked the time: barely nine o'clock. It felt like days since he'd set out for the *Grünegast*... Volta's timewarp hypnotic voice all through the small hours, though in the end it was the Doc who'd caved in under the weight of it, dead cigar stuck in the corner of his mouth, eyelids at half-mast. If it hadn't been for the snoring, you'd've thought he'd slipped off into the great yonder. Němec left him like that, found his way to the tram stop & concentrated all the willpower he had left on getting as far as Malá Strana. Whatever Volta's nurse had needled him with kept turning his mind blank. It was all one-thing-at-a-time, erase, go on, repeat, like an android with a cyclic redundancy glitch. Any moment now the system would crash & him with it. He doused his head in the sink, gargled some slivovice & got halfway climbing out of his clothes before falling asleep like that in his little dog corner on the floor. Somewhere at the back of his mind, fragments stirred in the blackness without forming a picture of anything, till they too collapsed in a pile & faded out.

When Němec woke, the room was airless — no time seemed to've passed at all, but the slant of the light through the windows said it was afternoon. His tongue felt dead in his mouth. There was a yellow bruise on his arm around the puncture wound. *What'd they stick in you, eh kiddo, snake oil?* He dragged himself to his feet & navigated to the kitchen, stuck his head in the sink again & this time counted to sixty. The water was tepid with a rust-tinted scum. It didn't help. He grabbed a bottle off the counter & lurched out to the hallway, found his jacket on the floor & groped through the pockets for the phial of pills Volta had given him the night before — it was still there. One more thing to slot in the reality column. He washed three of them down with a mouthful of slivovice. It felt good. He necked some more & that felt even better. Then all of a sudden it all felt much worse. The walls loomed out at him, physically, from all sides, like vertigo. He clutched the bottle for support, weaving his way back to the kitchen. Gripped by an irrational fear, he huddled on the floor, like someone naked in the middle of a field, surrounded by a hostile mob. Everything went white. *Just breathe*, he thought. And then he remembered, the dream, if that's what it'd been. The dancers in the barley. The voice in the sky. What'd happened? What'd he done? What'd been done to him? His mind raced, a flood of pictures but no sense of how they added up. And then he remembered, *her*, crucified, the blonde with the wig.

He willed the room to come into focus. The floor, the walls. He wrestled the top off the bottle, steadied his nerves. Then his mind made the connection he'd been missing. With a new sense of urgency he dug under the kitchen sink for the binbag with the Black Book wrapped in it. There it was alright, the engraving of the Devil & the Carmelite. Had he really only imagined all that? What Volta had said. Shit! What *had* Volta said…? The sonofabitch *knew* her! She was his fucking patient! What the hell was going on? *Ah-oh! You're not losing the plot on us now, are you kiddo?* Breathless, Němec tried to get some air into the kitchen, but the window was nailed shut. Immediately he thought of the Prof's women slumped at unnatural angles on the floor. Something in the very substance of the place seemed to hiss, like the hiss of that hideous green parrot. He stumbled out into the bureau & managed to get the window there open. He stood gulping air till his head cleared & the panic subsided. A face in a window across the street watched him for a little while then drew the curtains. A blackbird barked from the eaves. Němec tilted his face to the sky, a clear blue sky from which the sun smiled down a becalming smile. But there was no denying an oppressive odour lingered inside. Němec sniffed at it, then sniffed himself. His skin smelled dead, rancid, gangrenous. He went & doused himself under the shower till there was nothing left of the stink, icy needles turning him salmon pink from webbed foot to fissured squillhead.[*]

----

[*] *Comme un oeuf dansant sur un jet d'eau.* [♆]

Uroboros

The more Němec thought about the blonde at the cabaret, the more he couldn't help thinking of Elsbeth von N____ & a photograph he'd seen on the Prof's desk, many moons ago already it seemed. He wondered what'd become of it. Drying himself with a dishtowel, he stalked around the Prof's bureau, trying to get a sense of how everything had been before the Old Man died. The desk, the shelves, the fireplace with the Roman head in it. The photograph had shown the Prof flanked by his two muses, the "Pythagorean mysterium," blonde Elsbeth von N____ on one side, the ill-starred wife on the other. Why it'd never surprised him not to've met Alžběta Hájková, Němec couldn't say. But she & the caretaker had known each other since girlhood — wouldn't it've been fair to assume the strange Mrs Severínová might've availed herself of a keepsake or two, at the time of that unspeakable incident?

Dressed, Němec redescended the Tower stairs. The caretaker was in the kitchen of her small flat — she was in the midst of preparing a pot of tea for herself. The parrot sat on a cabinet just out of reach, grating its tongue against its beak, giving Němec the beady-eye. He stood in the doorway & watched the old lady very carefully pour the tea into her cup, steam rising off it like the proverbial departing spirit. This done, she sat the cup & saucer on the low table that she kept her knitting on & eased herself down into a burgundy upholstered armchair. The faint crackle of a musicbox rhapsody emanated from a large old woodframed T.E.S.L.A. radio that sat atop the far end of the kitchen table — a glowing blue eye staring out of it.

Němec coughed to get Mrs Severínová's attention. She looked up at him in a kind of wonderment, as if his presence made no sense to her. He opened his mouth to speak but the old lady raised a finger to her lips & cocked her head. Just then a child's voice interrupted the music & spoke above a rasping low-frequency buzz:

'Achtung! Neun neun fünf neun zwo. Neun neun fünf neun zwo. Achtung!'

Mrs Severínová sipped her tea then sank back in her armchair, nodding & smiling to herself as the voice repeated itself annoyingly.

'Vier eins sechs vier drei. Sieben acht acht sieben sechs. Fünf neun zwo sieben sieben…'

Severínová tapped her index finger on the arm of her chair in time to the numbers, as if hypnotised by them — the drone of eternal bingo parlour voices echoing through the ether. Avatars, perhaps, of some world beyond this one, some coiled hidden dimension, its essence *number*, its form the knotted Uroborus. While the old woman sat there engrossed, Němec's eyes wandered over the antique radio, with its yellowed buttons & plastic dials. *Ferrit-Antenne. Abstimmung*. Writ large on illuminated decal, an itinerary of bandwidths & frequencies: *1600 kHz*. Nizza, Prag, Brüssel, Krakau, Mt. Carlo with its yachts & roulette wheels.

'Sechs sechs zwo fünf zwo…'

1400 kHz. Luxemburg, København, Lille, Tirana, Wolga.

'Sechs drei zwo sechs drei…'

1200 kHz. Prag, Novi-Sad, Koschitz, Bordeaux, Hörby, Zagreb, Bratislawa, Paris, Kalundborg. (*Kalundborg?*)

'Eins eins acht fünf nul…'

1000 kHz. Hilversum, Brünn, Brüssel, London, Mailand, Bukarest.

'Neun drei acht acht acht…'

800 kHz. Rom, Sofia, Limoges, Sottens, Hilversum, Warschau, C.S.S.R., Belgrad, Rennes, Florenz, Daventry, Prag, Brüssel.

'Eins vier acht vier zwo…'

600 kHz. Lyon, Sundvall, Riga, Athlone.

'Fünf vier zwo acht nul…'

540 kHz. Mt. Ceneri, Moskau, Budapest.

'Fünf vier sechs sechs drei. Nul sieben fünf vier nul. Einz neun vier einz sieben…'

The old woman by now had her eyes closed, finger reflextapping, morselike, against the scarred table top.

'Drei einz fünf sieben sechs. Fünf sieben nul drei fier. Sechs drei sieben neun sieben. Einz sieben acht fünf vier. Ende.'

Once again the music box rhapsody started up. The old woman ceased tapping, opened her heavylidded eyes & reached for the tuning dial. The radio blared static. The tuner edged eastwards, in the direction of Riga. The blue eye glowed as a male choir sang:

> *Vorbei, vorbei sind all die schönen Stunden…*
> *die wir verlebt am schönen Ostseestrand*
> *Wir hatten uns, ja uns so schön zusamm'n gefunden*
> *es war für uns der allerschönste Ort…*[*]

---

[*] "Well it's time to kiss-off all them sweet memories, pack-up the glad-rags, the beach-balls, the sandy cracks, the seaside postcard with "life is beautiful" upsidedown in the sky, the way it looked

Němec tried to get the old lady's attention, but again she held her finger firmly to her lips till the song ended. The voice of a weather announcer came on — Severínová's bony fingers dialled the volume down, she raised her teacup to her mouth, sipped, then placed the saucer to one side. It was like a game of charades where you have to guess what comes next. Nothing came next. The caretaker & the parrot both stared at him with a vague look of expectancy.

Leaving out the preamble, Němec asked if the old lady happened to've kept a photograph of the Prof. He wasn't sure what it was for, but he tried to describe the picture he'd seen on the Prof's desk. The caretaker, however, didn't seem to hear him. She sat there & hummed the tune from the radio. Němec repeated his question, louder this time, but Mrs Severínová's vague trancelike eyes looked blankly through him. The parrot tilted its head to once side. Němec fought the urge to glance over his shoulder. Then, sighing, the old lady pushed herself slowly up out of the chair &, still saying nothing, shuffled out of the kitchen. Němec stood there feeling slightly idiotic. The parrot hissed some more. From the next room came the sound of drawers being opened & closed. A while later, Mrs Severínová reappeared clutching something in her hand.

'They always asked for the wrong one,' she said, holding an old black&white photograph out to him.

'The wrong one?'

'Yes, always the wrong one.'

Němec frowned down at the picture. He recognised the location from other pictures he'd seen in books. It'd been taken on the restaurant terrace at Barrandov, with the river below: the Prof was dressed in a light flannel suit with his shirt collar open — it must've been spring or summer — a breeze had slightly upset his hair. Two coffee cups were sitting on the table in front of him, beside a chessboard &, on the Prof's right, a chair with an attaché case lying open. Behind him there was the crowd at the edge of the terrace, taking in the view below. Němec wondered what the caretaker had meant by "the wrong one." And who were "they"?

'He was a good man, too,' she said, drawing the words out with deliberate slowness. 'They suffered, all of them, more than you could imagine.'

Němec glanced at the old lady questioningly, but she turned to the stove

---

when we lay there, *beautiful, beautiful*, you said, & the seagulls crapping in the wind, the needle-pricked salt spray, the sea fit to freeze yer balls off, but for all that, the boys splayed-out in their hammocks, those tightrumped ropethighed sailor boys, boy oh boy oh boy!" [✋]

without saying any more & poured some water from the kettle into her cup, peering into it for a long time. Her odd behaviour was unsettling. Němec wasn't sure what he was expected to do. He turned the picture over in his fingers, mumbling something about how he'd like to get it copied, if she didn't mind. She stirred her tea, picked up the cup & saucer & went over to the radio & dialled the volume back up. The music was familiar enough, though he couldn't put a name to it. Mrs Severínová smiled to herself, put her tea down beside the armchair, took up some knitting from the table by the radio & sat herself back down. Němec shuffled awkwardly in the doorway. The parrot sneered.

'Well, then, thank you for this,' he waved the picture limply.

'They were like twins,' the caretaker said dreamily, looping the yarn around the end of the knitting needles. 'Inseparable.'

'Who was?'

'The other one…'

Then she started humming the tune on the radio. Němec stared at her helplessly, shrugged & quietly backed out into the courtyard. *The other what?* He stood there in the shade wondering what he ought to do. The photo wasn't the one he'd been hoping for. He should've asked the old bird if she happened to have a snap of Elsbeth von N____ instead, but it was too late now. He looked closely at the Prof's face, more handsome than you'd've expected as a young man. Thinner, slightly drawn, but with a certain intensity, like a silent film actor conveying an emotion, only it was hard to say exactly which one. It was a simple enough picture, but there was nothing simple about the face. On the back, written in faded pencil, in the bottom right-hand corner, was a date: June, 1946 — the number 6 traced over more heavily than the rest. He'd've expected the Prof to look younger, but then the War had a way of doing that to people. Old before their time. The War that never seemed to go away, even now, fifty years after the fact. All you had to do was turn a corner in this town & there it was like a guilty conscience groping out of the shadows with filthy hands. And he remembered what Faktor had said, in the Patriot Klub that night, about having met someone called Hájek in Schnitzelstadt. Was there more to it than that?

Němec looked at the face in the photograph & tried to decide who could tell him more about the man behind it. Fill in the blanks. Who he'd been, apart from just a retired University Professor who played chess with strangers & toyed with riddles in books. He didn't have the look of a man with too many secrets, but that hardly proved anything. He didn't have the look of a man who had no secrets either. But where do you begin looking for something when you don't know what it is you're looking for? Němec's first idea was to find a telephone directory & a telephone that worked. He decided not to bother with the old lady back there with her tea leaves, there was a phone booth a couple of blocks away. The obvious place to start, he supposed, would be the university — he'd call & make inquiries about the Prof's work there & see where it led. If that didn't work, he could always go down in person & show the Old Man's snap around, see if it turned up anything. Maybe one of the janitors would've seen him around, back in the day, dunking biscuits in the mensa. Not exactly the sort of face that stood out in a crowd, but it wouldn't have to if a chessboard was mostly all he kept for company.

Like a Dog at a Bone

The phone booth on Vlašská Street was one of those coin-operated gimmicks you sometimes found in bus stations with a coathanger jammed in the slot. It'd been kinked so many times you could feed the same coin into it over & over again while placing a person-to-person to the South Pole. What was left of the directory swung from a length of insulated wire bolted to the stall. There was no need to worry about closing the door, there wasn't one. The floor was layered with about an inch of broken plate-glass. Scanning the directory stub produced two dozen numbers at least, nested like a broken matrioshka doll, of the various Faculties (e.g. Theology: 1. Hussite, 2. Protestant, 3. Catholic),* Institutes (e.g. Philosophy), Academies (e.g. Science), Centres (e.g. etc.), Departments, Cabinets, Secretariats, Personnel Offices, General Inquiries & Switchboard Operators, of the ancient illustrious Golem City University, Inc.

The first number he dialled got no response. The same with the second number. The third also. He seemed to be making progress when he eventually got through to a file clerk at the Office of Statistics, who transferred him to a secretary in Human Resources, who connected him to someone called Walker, or perhaps it was Worker, or Werther, or even (it seemed far from unlikely) Wanker, whose affiliation was never exactly stated, Broomcloset of Švejkology perhaps. While Němec explained why he was calling, he fingered the Prof's photograph, wondering what the Old Man would've made of all this, the way his ghost'd probably toss out a few smartarse remarks, like how 99% of detective work was just elimination, between observations about the weather. Instead he

---

* And this a *secular* state. [✋]

got five minutes of some nutcase ranting about the phone wires being tapped, colleagues conspiring in his sabotage, Ukrainian ganglanders operating Ponzi schemes...

Walker-Worker-Werther wasn't a Man of Reticence, it seemed, when it came to airing his grievances at the world, but try getting information out of him & he was as tightlipped as a bearded clam. It was impossible even for Němec to deduce the man's relationship to the Prof, but with no other options on the table, so to speak, Němec explained, assured, cajoled — *Tying up loose strings*, was the expression he used — apparently to no avail. Till quite unexpectedly the man gave him an address. He didn't say what it was for, or who it belonged to. Němec wasn't even sure he'd heard correctly, but by that point Walker-Worker-Werther had hung up.

Němec stared at the dead receiver. Well, he thought, with friends like that... *Another one to add to the list, haha.* Which reminded him, he ought to get that frontispiece checked-out, see if it meant anything after all, something to draw some of those *loose threads* together. He thumbed back through the directory's remains & found an antique book seller that specialised in "Limited Edition Art Books," which happened to be only a couple of blocks from the Národní address Walker-Worker-Werther had given him. *May as well kill two birds...* He left the directory swinging on its wire noose & went back to the house to fetch the merchandise, wrapped it in old newspaper, & stuffed the lot in a plastic shopping bag. He hadn't noticed before, but the shopping bag had Dolly Buster in a leopard-print trilby printed on it juggling enormous breasts against the Yankee stars&stripes, except all the colours were off-register.

Abreast of the Situation

With this ungainly image at his side, Němec followed the hill down to Kampa Island. The sky was hazy, the heat shiftless. In the park on the Island some re-enactors, wearing the blue & white uniforms of Napoleon's army, were trying to fly a large red kite that kept dipping & crashing into the ground while others kicked a football about. Picnickers with dogs, punks necking bottles from paper bags. Němec traversed the park north-south, bowler hat, black suit, Dolly Buster's distended teats flapping against his trouser leg. A short flight of stairs into the tree-shade at the western end of Legion Bridge. A woman with a child holding a balloon was leafing through the *Frankfurter Zeitung* at a newspaper stand. The child looked askance, the balloon drifted up out of its unclenched hand. *Mama*! *Mama*! Magazine faces Němec didn't recognise smiled inanely out as if to convince passersby that life wasn't tragic. Or else that it was. The balloon drifted south-east over the Judeninsel. A tram clanged its bell.

Halfway over the bridge, Němec crossed the tracks, pausing at the balustrade to peer down through the trees. The château on Střelecký Island stood like a "whited sepulchre" among the lindens. A couple was embracing on the riverbank, an old woman walking a cat on a leash, people in wooden rowboats drifting slowly past on the current. Two worlds side-by-side that barely touched. He resisted the temptation to go down & prove to himself that the *Grünegast* was really there. In the full light of day, it never would be.

Outside the National Theatre, the WAGNER RALLY TEAM was still in action. Next door they were advertising a Philip Glass opera with billboards across the front of the "Laterna Magika" with Einstein's pixellated mugshot, clown-eyed, tongue sticking out, translated into a cascade of numerics, ones & zeros. It seemed to say, stripped of appearances, what else is left but the Relativity of All? He pictured a chorus of Marilyn Monroes bearing down on the orchestra pit with all the coyness of a locomotive, or the Eumenides, or some messianic computer programme serenading itself through eon-long nuclear winters. Wagner was probably turning in his grave.

Invocations to infinity notwithstanding...

Invocations to infinity notwithstanding, Němec proceeded along the sidewalk, his immediate destination just half-a-block away at the rear of a cluttered arcade. The antikvariát he was looking for was down a steep narrow stairway, just behind the Viola Theatre: T.G. HAVRÁN RARE BOOKS. Němec expected something dingy & somewhat antediluvian, but the place was open & as airy as a basement could be, & humming with industry. The floor & ceiling were mirrored glass, which produced the uncanny feeling of being suspended in a libraried abyss. When he asked for the proprietor, an assistant in a blue smock pointed Němec to an office in the back where rows of black steel foldup chairs were being set out facing a podium. Glass-fronted bookshelves took up every available wall, glowing like museum exhibits beneath track-lighting.

Havrán, the said proprietor, was busy arranging catalogues on a table in the middle of the room. He was an average-sized man with spectacles perched at the end of a long beak & close-cropped grey hair, wearing a blue pinstripe. Němec went over & tried to interest the bookseller in his problem. Havrán was a man of few words, it seemed. In short he was preoccupied, there was going to be an auction that evening. He muttered something about a Gutenberg Bible. He looked at his prospective customer quickly & appraisingly, no doubt deciding the gangly bowler-hatted anomaly with the Dolly Buster shopping bag wasn't there to lodge an early bid.

'I came about an engraving,' Němec said, hoping thereby to seize the advantage.

Plonking Dolly Buster down among the catalogues, Němec unwrapped the Black Book. There it lay on the crumpled sports section, girdled by a thick rubber band, residues here & there of all-purpose clag where the pages had been stuck back in, not entirely the hamfisted effort it could've been. With a certain delicacy, Němec opened it at the frontispiece. The bookseller huffed, wanting nothing more than to get rid of this sudden intrusion into his ordered realm PDQ. He flipped the pages cursorily with his left hand (complete disregard for the relic's parlous state, Němec experiencing momentary gut-churning visions of T.H.'s holograph cascading all over the place), then turned back to the frontispiece & shrugged. Němec leant towards him —

'Is it possible,' he said, 'to tell when this was made?'

Havrán wrinkled his lips. Glanced down at the about-to-be-sodomised Carmelite. Sighed.

'Dear fellow, firstly this isn't an engraving, but an etching, much less rare & consequently far, far less valuable. The style is an imitation — of Schöngauer, evidently. This cross-hatching here, & these rotated lines? The subject has a certain, let us say, curiosity value. Teresa of Ávila was a popular figure during the Counter-Reformation — but this type of *speciality* was most common in the nineteenth century. Though by the look of it, your specimen is more recent. Machine-milled trash.'

He fondled the paper & bent a little closer, peering over his beak. Sniffed.

'Been dabbling in a little D.I.Y., have we? Tut-tut. You won't encourage any, *er*, buyers like that.'

He slanted the paper against the light as if hopeful of one last piece of disparagement to send Němec on his way. He looked disappointed.

'Mmm. Watermark from Cologne. Paper's handmade, at least. Find it in a bin somewhere, did you?'

Němec smiled patiently & gave the bookseller a short story about an elderly relative who'd died.

'*Yesss*, that is so often what happens, isn't it? The dear elderly relative passes away & then one must make decisions, *eh*, about what to do with all the priceless heirlooms?'

'What about the monogram?'

'Mmm? Oh, yes, the monogram. Well. Not terribly much to say, really. Blackletter typeface, originated around about the twelfth century, but this particular design has a let's say rather *faux antique* character. The printing itself was almost certainly done in the 1930s. The frontispiece,' he added, seeming to've resigned himself, 'would've been made to order, then bound according to the client's tastes, to give the book a personalised touch. A specialised market, but hardly unusual for the time.'

'A different quality of clientele back in the good old days?'

'Ahem.'

'What about the writing?'

'The writing? Oh, I see. Ordinary fountain pen. Likewise the ink. From the way the letters are formed, I'd venture to say the author was a bureaucrat of some sort, pre-War.'

'How can you tell?'

'Ah. Are we seeking an appraisal, perchance? If so, I would need you to leave your Saint Teresa with me till I find an opportunity to look into it more thoroughly. One is, as one already indicated, somewhat indisposed at the present moment. Perhaps next week would do? Tuesday, at around two?'

Němec said he'd think about it & grabbed the book, stuffing it back in its wrappings. He made sure not to forget to thank the man for his time.

'As you wish,' Havrán shrugged & turned back to his catalogues, pointing his beak between the blue covers of an especially hefty volume concerned with Peruvian earthenware — his glasses, Němec couldn't help but notice, were in need of a cleaning.

Paternostrum

He was counting the numbers above the doorways along Národní when he came across one of those while-you-wait copyshops. It gave him an idea. Five minutes later he had a colour photostat of the Black Book's frontispiece in his jacket pocket. The address Walker-Worker-Werther had given him belonged to a building whose entrance was concealed behind a low vaulted arcade, steel prison bars blocking the archways to keep the bums from setting up camp at night. Through a pair of swinging plate-glass doors stood a vestibule that'd probably been the height of fashion back when Brezhnev was General Secretary. Fluted-glass light fixtures hung down from the middle of the ceiling above a desolate expanse of brown tiling, the walls cluttered with enough surplus brass to float a minor thirdworld economy.

The ancient concierge had her head in a magazine so Němec followed the vestibule around to a rickety paternoster, its wooden booths like a mobile undertaker's fittingroom, haltingly ascending & descending in a slow, continuous loop. Next to the paternoster was a dimly lit staircase. Němec took one look at the paternoster & chose the staircase. The office he was looking for was on the fourth floor behind a pebbled glass door with flaked gold paint on it that read: JUDr JIŘÍ BAREŠ, NOTARY PUBLIC. Němec knocked & went in. A secretary in a blonde wig & a blouse to match watched him close the door behind him with a sort of rapt attention, as if she'd never done anything quite as strange before. The typing station she was perched behind did nothing to conceal that her skirt was far too short for her legs, which spilled out of it in all directions. It was pushing five o'clock, she probably had hopes yet.

'Should I bother asking if you have an appointment?'

'Do I look like someone who has an appointment?'

The secretary's eyes narrowed —

'Nooo.'

'Matter of fact,' Němec said, tapping his shopping bag with the crook of his stick for effect, 'I'm here to see Mr Bareš about the estate of the late Professor Hájek.'

The secretary made a confused face at the bag but nodded anyway —

'Oh, real estate?'

She pressed a button & mumbled something into the intercom, nodded, mumbled some more, then looked up at him —

'Mr Bareš might have time in quarter-of-an-hour, if you'd care to wait?'

Němec pointed his stick at a dark green sofa parked between a couple of potted rubber plants —

'There?'

The secretary blinked in the affirmative.

When Němec'd made himself comfortable, she peeled herself out of her chair & clattered off to perform some pressing errand in an adjoining office. Business must've been on the up-&-up. There was a pile of magazines stacked neatly at the end of the sofa, none of them more than a year out of date. He was half-way through an article about urban sanitation in Brazil when the secretary clattered back in & ushered him through to the inner sanctum.

It was a moderately sized office with a plaster job that hadn't entirely yellowed. A set of steel bookshelves were bolted to the far wall, next to the framed diplomas. The shelves were lined with the sort of vinyl-bound reference books that looked like they sold by the metre down on Libeňský Island. There were a couple of filing cabinets in two shades of beige next to a window with venetians at half-mast that faced onto a courtyard. A dead fly with its feet pointing up lay in the middle of the windowsill. Němec almost felt sorry for it.

Bareš didn't bother to look up from whatever he was doing, which didn't seem to be much. The door closed on one of those wheezing automatic hinges that like to play sillybuggers with you if you don't get out of the way in time. Němec dodged a hatstand & went mid-way across the floor & waited. The floor was checkerboard linoleum, the kind that makes you dizzy just to look at it. No doubt it produced an effect on the clientele. It'd had enough wear at least to tell you something about the man sitting behind the desk, but not a hell of a lot. Evidently the real work was done out front.

After he'd finished perusing whatever priceless document was spread out in front of him Bareš glanced up & seemed almost surprised to find Němec standing there. He must've made a queer sight for the lawyer, an overgrown scarecrow in a bowler hat & undertaker's suit, leaning on a stick, shopping bag under one arm. Graciously Bareš indicated he should take a seat. Apart from the executive piece of equipment the lawyer was sitting on, there was only one other chair in the room — it was one of those stiff-backed affairs they sold at a discount from Sweden, designed to make you as uncomfortable as an hourly rate permits.

Bareš wasn't the sort of man who was ever immediately recognisable: grey, shapeless, with a forehead that glistened under a permanent sheen of hair oil & perspiration. But Němec recognised him anyway. He'd seen him before, at Strašnice crematorium, six months previous. The Prof's funeral, if you could call being turned into potting ash a funeral. He was dressed in a duck-egg-blue polyester suit that probably convinced his clients he wasn't about to embezzle their finances, at least not till he'd been invited to with a signed power of attorney. A faint sprinkling of dandruff gave the shoulders a softness that's sometimes comforting in a man two sizes too big for his clothes. To the unsuspecting he'd've looked no more threatening than an overstuffed pillow.

Němec set his bundle on the edge of the lawyer's desk, one pendulous boob staring up from it like a sloppy drunk's eye, catching Bareš unawares. He gazed back at it queerly while in as few words as possible Němec explained why he'd come — requesting, in short, a letter of authorisation to view the Prof's papers consigned in the State Archive.

'Oh? Well. Unless you're a relative, or make a formal application through the courts, I'm not really at liberty to…'

The man seemed to notice his visitor for the first time. His eyebrows faintly twitched, before the eyes drifted back to his desk again, from time to time darting at the bundle of shopping bag. He checked his watch, straightened some papers, while Němec bored on. He'd learnt that with idiots in authority the only way to make progress was to be as intransigent as they were & keep smiling. For good effect he threw in a bit of legalese. "Pursuant of," "the parties to the estate," "whereby," "as deemed exigent," "the express condition," "until such time," "regarding the amendment," "as duly executed…" Like the good old *How many lawyers does it take to change a lightbulb* joke. From time to time Němec glanced at Bareš to gauge the effect, but in the end the lawyer barely blinked. As the Bugman would've said, never bullshit a bullshitter who does it for a living. It was possible, too, that Bareš was no idiot, but who'd ever be sure?

Fumbling in his jacket pocket, Němec got out the xerox of the Devil & the Carmelite, thrusting it across the lawyer's desk. Had he ever seen such a thing before? It must've been the last straw. Bareš stood up, indicating that their brief consultation was over. No man should give up that easily, Němec tried telling himself, but the advocate was talking into the intercom. The secretary seemed to've been waiting for precisely this cue to hustle Němec out: barely had Bareš taken his finger off the button than she was at the door, scowling. Němec supposed he ought to've thanked the lawyer for something, but it would only have sounded indecent under the circumstances. Besides, Bareš's back was already turned to retrieve a briefcase from beside the hatstand — he was about to make a beeline for the exit when he must've had second thoughts. It wasn't the sort of thing he looked like he made a habit of.

'You act as if there's something mysterious about all this, but it's really very simple. The law stipulates a mandatory seven years to allow for claimants to come forward, after which the estate becomes public property.'

He took one step forward & stopped again, as if considering how to proceed —

'If there *are* claimants, the papers remain under seal till a restitution order has been issued. You might not be aware, but there are certain conditions attached… in the event. Otherwise, for scholarly purposes — but for that, it would have to be at the request of an institution,' he shrugged his mottled blue shoulders. 'You see how it goes? You can check with the Interior Ministry, if you like. There's a public register nowadays. Otherwise, if you care to leave your details with my, *er*, secretary,' he gave her a pat on one of those prodigious thighs as he slipped past, 'I can let you know if or when any formal decisions are reached.'

There was one last question Němec would like to've put to Bareš that'd been nagging him all along, but he never got the chance. The man had already hightailed it out into the corridor. The secretary ogled him, arms ineffectually crossed. *Well, can't win 'em all, eh kiddo?* Němec retrieved his bit of xerox paper, his stick & his shopping bag, & let himself be led out. The question on his mind followed him: Why, it asked, had the Prof's papers been deposited at Strahov in the first place, since — with all respect due to the dead — the man was, as far as National Archives went, a complete non-entity?

Doppelgänger der Freiheit

After leaving Bareš's office Němec drifted north through the tangled streets of the Old Town, along Husova, past the Philosophy Institute. It wasn't past four in the afternoon but the *Svoboda & Slovíčkář* bookshop was already closed. A tangle of streets brought him out at the Altstädterring. *Dial-a-Piazza* was what the sign in the corner shop-window said, just before the street opened onto the Square: a picture of the Good Soldier Švejk stuffing his face with a pepperoni slice — ruddy-cheeked, button-nosed, forage-capped, the seams of his blue uniform fit to burst — it didn't look promising. From behind the counter a girl in a matching Š.V.E.J.K. uniform — framed by stacks of *Dial-a-Piazza* pizza boxes — stared morosely out at the scarecrow in bowler hat & black suit, not a customer in sight. The same clownish slogan was repeated on a sandwich board parked on the cobbles — this time the Good Soldier looked like he'd been run over by a monster rolling pin & served up with mozzarella: telltale stains down one side of the board suggested a dog or dogs had recently cocked a hind leg there — including, possibly, the same dog of indeterminate breed that was now yapping at its shadow, back & forth in the middle of the Square. How'd that song go? *Mad dogs and Eeenglishmen...?* If possible, the day seemed only to be getting hotter.

A couple of visitants in white gloves & white sanitation masks had stopped on their way to the Astronomical Clock to take a photo of it. Here at least some form of life stirred: the watchers under the Clock, waiting to see the

Skeleton do its dance, Fate beating its drum — a red-faced midget tottering around, doing tricks for an audience squatting in the shade of Hus' monument, oblivious to former agonies — the larger-than-life statued figure standing bold above them (patinaed shades of green, mighty brow pigeoncrap-besmeared, unveiled to great controv in 1915, mid-War — *Flanders? Type of fish, right?* — pre-dawn of the Nation's birth, one of many aborted, soon to be given the imprimatur of unheard-of Versailles grandees once the last mutton-chopped Habsburg'd fallen from grace, the Concert of Powers finally done for thanks to Yankee Doodle & the Democratic Dollar, & all the future to look forward to), man of the people & fanatic naysayer of celibacy among the ordained, burned at the stake for his troubles — the mad dog wagging its ridiculous tail, ready if the midget should drop his red juggling balls to make a grab at all three, tongue out grinning like it was in on the biggest joke around.

Meanwhile, over by the hitching post where hourly sightseeing carriage rides set off, the horses stamped, swatted at flies with their daggy tails, drivers asleep on a nearby bench, hats tipped over eyes. On the opposite side of the Square, under the medieval arcades with café tables, piped Mozart periodically dissolving into radio static, a waiter was busy fiddling with an espresso machine, venting jets of steam like some incendiary device about to fizzle. How far from the scenes of great disaster & tumultuous destiny! The Eternal Tourist traipsing along in this heat to stare in wonder, check his Baedeker for the pertinent facts, or merely gloat. History, its trace everywhere apparent, still seemed as absent here as God from His cathedral, nothing but an immense gallery of anecdote for the charlatans of solemnity. Still it exerted a mysterious attraction, a psychic magnetism of the mass mind — in this it retained the contours of a sacred burial site, though of a civilisation long dead, whose pedantic corpses continued to fascinate, whose reluctance to signify emboldened, whose proper mephitic stink lent an air of wanted credulity to what must've seemed, on first apprehending it, a piece of bad theatre.

Š.V.E.J.K.ISM

What method had brought Němec *here* precisely? Stranded out in the middle of the Square, that narcotised living postcard, as lifelike as Hanuš's mechanised chronometer, in search of the unapparent, the missing, the absent — was he? Shadows of people built into the edifices, phantom objects, the perils of the City's orphaned soul, all the alienations of a birthplace that can never belong to you — here, in this most public, most officiated-over, most destitute of places — the dead heart. And right in the middle of it, right where Němec was standing, that monument to its own contradiction — *quo olim tempus pragense* — like a detached skiagraph made weighty as a bronze obelisk, plinth, sundial, its missing corpus, doppelgänger — the *processus styloideus* lodged in the backbrain the way an idea's lodged inside a penstroke — the *deus ex machina* inside the meridian, the stones' oraculation: for here formerly stood, resplendent in its unfettered fetished kitsch, that monument of priapic adoration, the Marian Column — Her Immaculate Virgin Self up there surveying Her temporal kingdom, keeping watch over all Her congregation of schismatics & sinners, looking down on the spot Mydlář poppylopped the presumptives of 1621, casting Her long shadow, noonday tending latitudinally in the direction of the Brandenburg Gate, the Stettiner Haff & onwards, true north to the Eternal Kingdom whence Time itself issued forth: History's ghost, the Golem City Meridian, socalled, from which, once upon, all the clocks in the City measured themselves — the noonday gong, the eventide prayer, the clochecall & cock's crow — even the Sun in its wind-up fiery chariot obedient to instruction, cogging the seasons, continuing on its way to complete its ordained course.

Who'd suspect the Column's omnipotence extended *post-hoc* even beyond the regulation of the hours & clocking wage-labour metaphysic, the counter-symbolisms of servility & revolt, Habsburg triumphalism & Cheskoslovnik independulence? The past mired in its changeless superstitions & the future boldly marching into the unknown — to become the posthumous touchstone & nerve centre of a struggle *outside Time*, eternal contraries & all that, unlikely as a proto-Minuteman in a bishop's mitre waiting for blastoff? For here, at the close of the First World War, was the very tipping point, the fulcrum, threshold of two incompatible orders as real to each other as they were unreal to the rest of the world — the dialectic of the doomsday machine wired into a Zeitgeist still in process of being born, conspired into existence by a cenacle of nutcases & visionaries in equal measure: the secret Š.V.E.J.K. army, red-flagged anarchists, lobbers of bombs through doorways, kidnappers, fakers of suicides, passive-aggressive posturers in beerhalls papering the City with nonsense agitprop, convocation of the unelect, upsetting the best laid plans of their arch-Patrician rivals: crystal-gazing Teslaites, with their radio doodads & penchant for astral projection, telepathy, E.S.P. — pre-Logie-Baird weirdoes of the art of far-sight, adepts of Saint Clare, their fevered group-mind conjuring future visions of the Ideal City, Space Travel, Life on Mars. Lunatics all, locked in mutual death-or-life struggle (*Take no prisoners!*), though in one thing united: the post-haste abolition of the fledgling Cheskoslovnik democracy. The year: 1918. The toppling of the Marian Column neither the first nor last blow in this secret war of the Commissars & the Cognoscenti — food for the entertainment-hungry masses thronging the variety theatres for a bit of light distraction from the serious task of nation building... And what about our midget with the painted face over there, making a clown of himself? Like a ready allegory for the types of minds that suffer from chronic dualism — the little homunculus of a man with carmine grin ear-to-ear that conceals how his face constantly scowls at his audience, who he naturally detests even as he passes his hat around for alms like a beggar — one misfortune taking sour-mouthed delight in another. (*Those human caterpillars*, he thinks.) [*]

And so resumes our story...

Němec continued on, past the statue of Hus, & presently found himself at the back of the Philosophy Faculty amidst the sightseers queuing outside the Old Zhiddish Cemetery. What'd they come to see? An overgrown plot strewn with

---

[*] A little timewarp to the other side of the mirror, in which is revealed the chiaroscuro of an elaborate ⚡ reviewing stand erected on the very spot from which Mary's Minaret had so unceremoniously been uprooted by the rabble. Here we see the restored World Order, mystic Thuleans homing-in on the Altstädterring's galvanic energies, ancient wells of tellurian forcefield radiation ringing this place where once grand druids performed their blood offerings, now setting the Nazi dowsing rods bolt upright in ceremonial drape cloth, redblackwhite — cathedral spires looming behind, uplit, like gothic spectres of doom, shadows of the shadow of Time itself — with Der Furore's monumental mugshot hoist up there for all the crypto-mariolaters to venerate, on *His* birthday, 卐mas of the Aryan Dawn. You can almost picture them, ranks of Totenkopf suicide battalions destined for Stalingrad & extinction, marching in secondhand woollens — the dead millions-in-waiting of the Lebensraum soon to be forever collectivised under the soil, blood & iron: their deafening *Sieg*! Their God shouting back at them through loud hailers set up on poles around the Square, a storm of diatribe & hyperbole — but how else does Man suppose the voice of his God to be? A caressive whisper? Intimations of solicitude? A stuttering self-doubt, evidence of the madness of humility? The adoring centipede raises its arms — *Heil*! — & the dumb visage stares out above them into the night — a virtual sight-line running through the old blacked-out Ghetto to where, high overlooking the City, *His* nemesis & mythomaniac counterpart ten years hence will return that cold gaze (temporarily *in effigie*) across a blind gulf that'll already have swallowed them both, those men of the cross — lithe Hitler with his Chaplin moustache, Stalin like an overstuffed, beatified anagram, draped in the cruciform of the eternal dialectic — ☭ — former doers of mighty deeds, those superannuated Titans, unaware of how ridiculous they'll appear once their Ozymandias moment's over & the image-makers have boiled them down into the stuff of tourist trinkets, mementos to keep in a jar with those tinfoil B.V.M. medallions you pop a coin into a slot for by the cathedral exit. [☛]

404

rubble, headstones piled so deep they looked like rotten overlapping teeth in a jawbone eaten away by cancer? A short beak-nosed woman waving a sign on a stick, HOLOCAUST TOURS, led a mob of camera-wielding gawkers towards the cemetery gates — Nikons, Minoltas, Kodaks — to extract their pound of celluloid. Even the dead didn't get let off the hook, it was like a gold mine in there. A hundred square-foot Shangri-La! You couldn't make a wrong step, anywhere you plonked down your crêpe soles there'd be a picturesque corpse right there, just an inch below, dozens, hundreds of 'em, cheek-by-jowl, stacked one atop another all the way down to the very foundations of Zion! And if the Nazis'd refrained from bulldozing the lot, it was only so this most photogenic of cashcows might one day (soon) serve as a monument to the Wholesale Extinction of the race.

Filing out from the gates a troupe of exhausted sightseers in blue&white yarmulkes threaded their way down the street between double-parked blueyellowgrey tourbuses from Talinn, Sofia, Warsaw, Minsk — red urban transit buses, 133, 144, 158, 197 — blue longhaul coaches, destination Paris, Stockholm, Madrid — brown clappedout exschoolbuses Zagreb-bound. Němec followed them for a short way, with no specific direction in mind, still mulling the lawyer's parting words. *Interior Ministry. Public Registry.* Anything with the words "Interior Ministry" in it made him shudder. In combination with the word "public" it sounded like volunteering for a Siberian holiday. *Come on in, sign the guestbook, I hear the weather's lovely this time of year…*

He stopped in the shade, the heat suddenly getting the better of him, & waited for the crowd to thin out. All it would've taken, they'd said, was for him to sign a couple of forms. But he'd known better than to trust that sort of talk. They'd've had him back in the Home before he could've said Gustáv Husák & still no Mamitati, just a file with a stamp. *Well, kiddo, you think they might've got dug up since?* Eight years. That was their statute of limitations: you sign the paper, start the clock, when the flag drops it's like the Prof being poured into a metal urn & left on a shelf. And Němec wondered, who paid the rent? All those dead files & dead ends. The Prof's ashes. *But who paid the rent?* If he went out there to the cemetery, whose name would he find on the registry? He looked up then & found himself more or less alone on the sidewalk. A few feet away, a plaque'd been set into the Philosophy Faculty wall. It caught his attention…

First Zhiddish Criminal
to be Hanged for Atrocities

Němec came closer & read the small print. It commemorated the death of one Paul Raphaelson — kapo, during the War, at Terezín — *whose eye was as dark as his spleen…* Executed in Golem City, 30 April 1947, "for cruelties perpetrated against his fellow prisoners." The enemy, it seemed to say, is also within. No-one else appeared to be particularly interested in it: the tour busses were busy jockeying for position in the narrow street, the tourists trying to squeeze in through the Old Cemetery gates to make the quota. It was ridiculous & sombre at the same time. He felt like waving his stick at them: *Hey, why don't you come over here and take a picture of this for the slideshow back at home?* Why should he care? There were millions of Raphaelsons in this world — for every one they hanged, a dozen were born. It didn't matter what their names were, whether they were sons of Mönchengladbach factory labourers or millionaires, which regime they stooged for. All those measly dupes of Mephistopheles no Goethe would ever pen a monument to.

He pictured the crowd that day, gathered to watch the black pillowcase being pulled over Raphaelson's head, before he was hoisted by the neck like a ף against the grey page of the firmament. Hanged right there where the cemetery gawkers could've taken a pretty snapshot. And with every one of those snapshots, would something've been proved that they weren't even aware of? Němec jabbed his stick at the cobblestones & slouched morosely towards the tram tracks. Someone had renamed the street after the Revolution, though he couldn't see why. On one side a cemetery & a mausoleum to higher learning, on the other old Red Army Square with an enormous air duct sticking up from the middle of it where winenumbed homeless men & women owned the sanctuary of the park benches. Students with opened books, radios, lunches, crowding the steps of the Rudolfinum where parliament once sat but now only concert-goers polishing their arses to the sound of Mahler, Smetana, Dvořák & the rest of the national patrimony.

It reminded him of one of the Bugman's stories. How back before the War a dozen or so statues of all the most famous composers used to stand atop the Rudolfinum's façade.[*] Then one day in 1942 it was brought to the attention of ⚡-Obergruppenführer Karl Hermann Frank that among them stood one

---

* Das Deutsche Kulturhaus. [✋]

belonging to Felix Mendelssohn, *Zhid*. In his zeal to purge the City of its least valued inhabitants (& thereby prove his fitness to succeed the recently assassinated Heydrich as acting-Reichsprotektor), Frank ordered the offending statue be removed.

Unfortunately none of the statues had been provided with name plaques — & it went without saying that no-one in the ϟϟ goon squad sent to execute the order knew what Himey Mendelssohn was supposed to look like, either. They decided, therefore, with impeccable Nazi logic, to remove the statue with the largest nose — it having been established, upon certain well-attested phrenological principles, that Zhids, unlike their Aryan masters, possessed a telltale disfigurement in the form of a disproportionate, hooked proboscis (not to be mistaken for the Roman *nasum*, that ancient patrician badge of honour). After a brief inspection of the statues in question, the senior ϟϟ officer presiding identified the offending snout & had the effigy of the supposed Zhid duly obliterated & dumped in the river.

Not long after, it came to light that the likeness Frank's henchmen had so demonstrably vandalised was in fact none other than that of Richard Wagner.[*] Sweeping his blunder under the proverbial carpet, Frank promptly ordered all the remaining statues to be torn down as well. It was subsequently rumoured that no statue of Mendelssohn ever stood there to begin with.

---

[*] Der Furore's personal fave. [✋]

32

ANTE MERIDIEM

Banality isn't
harmless.

A clock ticks, the
shadow of an hour
drags its own
shadow behind it,
like a movable
border.

It begins slowly.

Even the weather
sets in by
accumulation.

Creeping through
the suburbs,
emptying the
streets in its wake.

July's approaching.

When it finally
strikes, it'll be like
an assassin
asphyxiating a
corpse.

Everywhere the
clocks are winding
down & at any
moment about to
stop.

Time itself might
just as well've come
to an impasse.

In the desert of the
boulevards, pencil-
thin men search
among dustbins in
stopmotion.

A tomcat in a
doorway shading
its eyes with its
tail.

Figures dissolve in
the tissue of an
architecture
wrecked in the
Grand Manner.

The moment you
step out the door,
the heat knocks
you flat.

Traffic, gridlocked
from one end of
the City to the
other.

Trams packed to
the gills like tins of
sardines poached
in brine.

The air on the boil,
reactor cores
melting down.

By late afternoon,
black heavy clouds,
lightning, rain.

A hot black rain
gushing out of the
sky like an
upturned geyser.

And the City,
haunches spread
for its sins to be
cleansed from it,
wallowing in its
own muck.

A rancid
yellowbrown
fluvium spilling
over the weirs, the
quays, the locks
like a neglected
gonorrhoea.

Tributaries
converging into
rivers, rivers
haemorrhaging
into deltas.

After the rain, a
thick heat steams
off the sidewalks.

Jurassic swamp
mists.

Night brings no
relief.

A black broth
poured from a can,
stewing you up to
the eyeballs.

Come dawn, it'll
all've returned to
dust.

Shrivelled back
into the parched
clay of itself.

Leaving only the
crags & ravines of
a body as austere as
a Sybil's
lookingglass.

You ask, *What am I
doing here?*

Der Goylem

A sodium lamp, gibbous-eyed, above an interrogation desk. A decades-old stink
of tar & nicotine oozes up from it. An ashtray — heavy, flat & round with a
bevelled edge, like something cut from an engine block — overflowing with
butts,. Beside the ashtray, a deck of Inkas — favoured brand of railworkers,
dockhands, stokers — someone making a point of their proletarian credentials, it
seems. When the disc of the ashtray threatens to get lost beneath the pyramid of
stubbed-out butts, a hidden hand materialises from outside the frame, empties
the ashtray into a bin, sets it back in its place to the left of the cone of light,
allowing the ritual to recommence — the pyramid-building, the dirty metal disc
like some exhumed pharaoh's mask waiting to be put back into storage. The
silhouette of someone shuffles away from the desk & you move up to the font of
the line. A sallow, rat-face peers, crescent moons under eyes, through smoke
haze, impatient. Row number, seat number. You take your ticket & go...

Artificial moonlight drifts down from the corner of the screen, as if it (the
screen) is a window you're looking out of at the night & the night is a stage set
cut-out at strange angles, walls & streets & streetlamps, but not of any worldly
place: this is the perceived cityscape of a disturbed mind & we, not knowing
how you got there, are trapped inside that mind staring helplessly out. All part
of a seasonal retrospective — Murnau, Lubitsch, et al. — at the National Film
Archive's cinéclub on Bartolomějská*: what once was the chapel of St Maria
Magdalena for Penitent Women, later an organ school (Dvořák studied there),
then a concert hall, then this — the KONVIKT BIOSKOP.

Tonight's a "triple bill": the lost silent wartime horror, *Der Golem* (1915),
"Monster of Fate," dir. Paul Wegener & Henrik Galeen, "restored" from a few
ghostly fragments, like bits of the original scripture, the filmic Ur-text, hallowed
in this city — & its laughable sequel, also lost, nothing now but a handful of
publicity stills, glass-plate negatives, enough at least for a slowmotion montage
intercut with a scratchy showreel dug from a basement after the Occupation, *Der
Golem und die Tänzerin*, set design Hans Poelzig — & last but not least, *Der
Golem, wie er in die Welt kam*, adapted from the story by Gustav Meyrink & shot
two years after Independence, set back in time to show how it all began: the
ghetto-Prometheus, transmuted mind-body of the Man-of-Clay, all the

---

* Conveniently across the street from former secret cop HQ: basement torture cells, rubber hoses,
wet pillowcases, lead-lined socks & all your other late night favourites. [♣]

Spenglerian excruciations of a race forging its own consciousness, emerging from the dark night of superstition into the light of Reason.

Final scene: little girl in white dress gazing up at the dark-complexioned Zhid-monster, the implied offering, blood libel, Elders of Zion, nothing quite what it appears now in the full glare of retrospect — Mogen David hovering there in the middle of the screen, enlarging into close-up, more ominous by the second, the monster staring out from those sinister equilaterals, Rosicrucian pyramid, cyclops-eye in superposition, like Usury's impending slaughter-of-innocents. Envisage jackbooted golems of the soon-to-be Talking Picture Era, shouting their Sieg Heils from that very proscenium, only metres away, where Liszt, incidentally, Beethoven too, even Grigorievich once, struck a chord on the resident pianola, not to mention the "Beast of Bayreuth," Wagner himself. All of History seems to've gathered here tonight. But even History has its hour & its place, the subtle evasions, thwartings, outright contradictions of a theme working towards the one apotheosis no man can fully predict...

Der Golem — "Josef," the wily old Rabbi baptised it, *he who will enlarge* — brought into this stinking world to slave in the synagogue & act the general do-good protector of the downtrodden & oppressed, those illiterates of the Ghetto, the tribe of Shem, sons & daughters of Babel, who couldn't tell a mem from a tau, a myth from a meth, & that, so the tale went, this proletarian Joe, grown a mite too big for his boots, thinking himself more Mensch than machine (well who in Himmel told you to *think*, boy?) & just about coming to the end of his rope — mopping the floors, scrubbing the stairs, polishing the boots, ironing the shirts, mending the socks, washing the underwear, tucking the sheets, dusting the cabinets, waxing the wainscoting, pealing the spuds, shelling the peas, baking the brot, boiling the borscht, brewing the endless cup-of-tea, ringing the bell, dunging out the slops, humping the ashcans, shovelling the shit.

His one consolation, those furtive nightlessons by candlestump in an attic closet with the Rabbi's daughter, all first blush of tiny breasts under moon-pale nightdress, pitying poor Joejoe, all alone, showing him her dollies & storybooks, teaching him the alephbet, heavy crude lines in crayon, reading him her favourite bits of Daddy's Big Book — Susanna & the Elders, Eve in the Garden, Solomon the Wise — & just when the flicker of Love begins to flame the Old

Man smells a rat & comes bursting in (sound up on a PDQ Klezmer variation of the cancan), beating the sorry little slip of a thing with the knotty-end of his prayershawl, her little girl-cries falling on deaf ears, witless Joe cowering in his cupboard, fixed like stone. And that was the last straw, seeing the tears in those little blue girl-eyes. Time to show at last what he's really made of, roaring up out of his wardrobe, muddy hand raised against his Maker, giving Him (the ruby-nosed rabs) what He's had coming all this time — & only then, aghast, seeing that look of horror on his dear liebling's picturebook pout where once affection reigned, his sweet angel cringing in the corner & there, in a mirror behind the door, that monstrous rage-distorted visage — his own! Shamed, Joejoe flees — rages through the Ghetto's night, howling, havocking & generally running amok, smashing every moneylender's windows from here to Hanukkah, setting fire to streetvendors' stands, snatching watchmakers' wives off into back alleys…

The alarum sounds, men with sticks, shovels, nets, converge around the synagogue. The Rabbi, as battered & bruised as a Christmas carp, comes down the steps pointing aloft. Torchlight flickers across the synagogue walls, upwards, the steep gables, there, climbing towards the high summit, Golem Joe with — what's that? — something white slung across one shoulder. *My daughter!* The Rabbi falls to His knees, pleads, begs, screams. *Get down here you slutty little koorvah!* Joe stands astride the weathercock, clasping the limp form of the Rabbi's lamb under his right arm, left outstretched, teeth flashing in a wide grin — all eyes on him now, enlarging in the glow of the torches, footlights rather — he's found his element, it all suddenly dawning on him that *this* is what he was made for, destined to the Big Stage. He shuffles off a few tap-dance moves, rooftiles clacking underfoot — they mob's all agape watching now to see what'll come next. *Hey*, cries out a soot-faced urchin, cloth capped, perched atop a lamppost, *he's gonna sing a song!* Sure enough, there's Joe — top hat & coat-tails materialising out of nowhere (pure movie magic, this), the Rabbi's daughter all blonde sultry smirking in his ear, a real Betty Grable — fade-up on orchestra, Irving Berlin conducting:

> *Have you seen the well-to-do up on Maisl Avenue,*
> *on that stingy thoroughfare with hooked noses in the air,*
> *yarmulke and bearded collars, glatt bekishe and thirteen dollars,*
> *hoarding every dime, 'cos spending's a crime?*

Oops! Joe taking one backwards step too many, it seems, gone over the edge, an almighty crash from behind the stage, trumpet, bass drum, cymbal — the Rabbi's daughter clinging to the tiles for dear life — gasps from the peanut gallery down below — then, thinking this is all part of the show, a smattering of applause. Calls for an encore. A tear in the old Rabbi's eye...

Němec waited long enough for the cinema to empty around him, watching the credits through to the end, till the lights come up & the curtains closed. The man in the ticketbooth was still there at his interrogation desk when Němec got out, another line-up of unfortunates queuing for their punishment. (Some people would pay with their souls to see a half-decent film these days.)

Outside, it was still light, sky turning blue to violet, redolent of perfumed memories... Unmarked cop cars parked bumper-to-bumper up & down the street, Gestapo-brown tiled façade of cop HQ, & upstairs the same slobs polishing their arses at the same desk as when Mr & Mrs "Němec" were put through the process — *trouble is our business, hehe* — going through the motions of the democratised Police State, concerned with the shallwesay quote welfare of its citizenry unquote — habeas corpses & all that — humiliating long hours of form-filling refined into torture, always the promise of a light at the end, playing upon those irrational wishes that can't quite even at this stage be suppressed, desperate enough to think they'll ever see daylight again, that they'll at least get a

---

* Yes, sir.
** No, sir.
*** Three bags full, sir.
† Gemütlich.

chance to prove their innocence, that the law couldn't really just be régime wallpaper with a human face, that in any case their friends on the outside would soon get wind of it all & come to save them, before the cells, sleeplessness, electrodes on genitals, matchsticks under fingernails, gasoline enemas, etc. — just like, *eh*, in '68? Or '38? Or '48? (Something about years ending in eight?)

Ancient history now. And who still remembered that joke? About how Bartolomějská was supposed to've been named in honour of Klem Gottwald's puissant grampaw from Hoštice? (How the old plonker came home one morning to find his daughter — Klem's sainted matka — up the duff by some itinerant Joe & fairly gave her the boot, told her to take a hike & never come back, & her in due course feeling the contractions, waters pishing out all over the place, obliged by circumstances to birth our little runt of a national saviour there & then in a pigsty by the side of the road — call it a manger if you must. Old bastard's name was Bart-for-Bartholomew, that lush — Zhiddish for *Son of the Furrows*, or more like *the Trough*, seeing as he always had his snout stuck in one. As to the culprit who begat that sonofawhore, our darling Klemency? Hawhaw, well, y'know, them Hoštice shits do like to keep it in the family…)

Němec orientated himself west towards the river, breathing deep — tables out on the sidewalk along Karoliny Světlé — then up the steps & across the tramline — view over the water to the island, couples on picnic blankets, bottles of wine & curd cheese, a bag of crusts feeding the ducks, the pedaloes going past, *plash plash*, green-white, red-white, yellow-white, big black numbers in circles like paddling pool balls — the Castle on the Hill all lit-up already, the sky deepening by degrees through purple to black, unreal, reflected below, the weir spilling over — gulls perched along the wood barricades sloping in rows up out of the water, streaked with guano… (the river from whose sludge Löw made his Golem monster / slave / factotum — the dredged-up alien amino acids, enzyme-reflux, sedimentary accretions of past & future, the ground-down vertebrae of primeval trilobites, molluscs, unicorns, carbonised bile, methane & phytoplankton — the pre- & post-tectonic gutrumbling of the blue planet in its firstlast Kodachrome Konvulsions — as once was said, like Stoic sapiens, seeing in one glance all ages down to the present — war, plague, pestilence, fire, inundation, massacres, miracles, prodigies, appositions — all the archaeo-logie-bairdisms of this convulsèd world).

Just as here, he (Němec) too now stood upon the lip of Time, every particle of his selfsameness is so decisively *after the event*, attuned like a wire in a busted socket to the ancient echo of his Golem forebears, dwellers of these same river banks, all evidence of whom long since past, washed down the Elbe to the sea, their name, their language, their God & all who in their memory & dreams came before them, in turn extinct, lost, forgotten — a bone fragment, a sharpened stone, a notch in a shaft of petrified wood...

Já Robota

In the beginning was an Island, a Garden bearing rich fruit on all sides swallowed by a Fiery Sea — the Omphalos, the Navel of the World, Rapa Nui of the ancients. On this island God was born & died — His petrified remains, heaped smouldering on a mountaintop, there to await Resurrection. Where once He reigned, a Scientific Committee of the T.E.S.L.A. Corporation built temples to Divine Geometry, the Law of Ratio, the Inviolable Method. Descended of engined Egyptians, scions of Moses, Aryun of the Vedas, Archimedes — convinced of their own but not mankind's in-general perfectibility, the Clockwork Inner Mechanism, the miraculated Self-Image, evolution by Prosthetic Exteriorisation, the Immaculate Clone that walks about bathed in the luminescence of its own Reason... The Committee sent forth android armies to purge the world of these moral ills. Thus purged, the world became a mirror to their own dark cybernated souls. And by declensions the Slave Machines did turn upon their Masters. And they did raise up graven effigies, idols, fetish things, in *their own* image! And verily did they bring about a great extinction & warred among themselves, one tribe against another of all the descended gismos & gadgets since Time Immemorial:
>of Household Appliances, Electrolux —
>of Computing, I.B.M. —
>of Film, Kodak —
>of Telegraphy, Bell —
>of Optics, Zeiss Ikon —
>of Television, Baird —
>of Radio, Tesla —
>of Refrigeration, Westinghouse —
>of Chemical Engineering, I.G. Farben —
>of Power Generators, Edison —
>of Hydraulics, Pascal —
>of Automotives, Ford —
>of Lighting, General Electric...

Comicbook fables of masked avengers & bionic übermen, the salvation of Life as it was Known, all the sentimentalities of a civilisation confined to its armchairs, enslaved to their remote-controls. Another version of the same story went like his: Long ago, in a ghetto in Mitteleuropa, on a prison island festering with poverty & disease — surrounded on all sides by Papists, Protestants, Husitic zealots screaming for race rationalisation, Organisation Men, accountants with deathlists, Austerity-mongers, Inflation Economists in doublebreasted marino-blend, Bohemian Kristalnacht merchants, Slovnikian swordswallowers, Elders-of-Zion Bookclub matrons — came the litanies of the Megaphones of Doom, death mantras, transport lists, the countdown of the Zero Hour... *Who will save us?* they asked. *Not I*, said Rabbit, sucking a long blade of grass on the riverbank, *I have too much else to do. Nor I*, said Goat, butting his horns against a tree, *I have heavy responsibilities. Oh, it's not so bad*, said the Lion, tickling his nose with his two tails, *I can't see what you're all complaining about. Look on the bright side, salvation's eternal!* Meanwhile, down in the depths, far beneath the septic stink of the Ghetto, deep in the fluvial mud, a Messiah was being made: some Weisenheimer's tosspot come to terrible life, some pocket Machine-Mensch forged in a fist, the fading prospect of the Last Tribe of Excretus descending to *this*, down down below the sewers & secret tunnels, the tar-pits, Devil's workshops, troglodyte production-lines, spectral synagogues with attics buried under basements, rooms without windows, in no recognised transmission zone, in an ether of indeterminacy: something, born out of the hypnotism of the Mass Mind, risen from primordial floes, limbs of Panzer steel, turret-headed, deathray eyes, the works. Come to afflict the self-righteous, this Golem monster, Legion of the One, demon dwelling sub rosa in the collective meme, that unseen, hidden, menacing & obscene thing *they* will go to any lengths, it seems, to expunge, obliterate, deny — the cruciformed *Id*, the persecuted proletariat, the eternal subspecies, unhuman forms with no interior human life, automata merely — unknown to itself, a spoke in the wheel, a spanner in the proverbial, beam gone wrong, "berserk" not putting too fine a point on it, *non compos mentis, ex machina* if not *ex cathedra*, backfiring on all cylinders (a little Švejkian sabotage at work in the wings here), more Masada than Man you might say, tumult of a technological tsunami hurling all & sundry into the (dialectically-speaking) maelstrom of its own making, from Genesis to fiery Revelation, combustible eye & wrath of a God whose ways are at the very least perplexing when not downright monstrous. Nothing as evitable as it ought to be, eh? Stuck in the paradox of the passive-aggressive, preparing the World,

you think — *This is what you really think, eh, kiddo?* — for the Greatest
Gutwrench of All Time?

Chief Rabbi Judah Löw ben Bezalel, father of *der Golem*, was not as apocryphal
as Werner Krauss, but almost. Old wizard of the Ghetto raising up a one-eyed
homunculus from slimethick Vltava mud — cauldrons of boiling smegma,
squeezed & shaped in gnarly old talmudic hands, till it cooled & the sap of life
rose in it… According to those who pretended to know such things, the remains
of this Golem still lay in the attic of the Gothic synagogue on the street later
named after Rudolf II's finance minister, where Löw concealed it *in a room with
no windows and no doors* — the steep-roofed Alt-Neu-schul with crowstep gable,
c.1270 — keeping watch (so to speak) over the dead in its ramshackle cemetery.
The Ghetto itself came about not much earlier, the product of a Vatican
directive on segregation: 1254, Otakar II's *Statuta Judaeorum*, defining the
restriction & "protection" of the City's Zhids (accused murderers of Christ,
ritual childsnatchers, sinister distillers of Biblical filth), henceforth prohibited
from practicing crafts or trades *and from travelling outside the Ghetto without
wearing the yellow star…* Three hundred pogroms it took to slay this madman
dressed in tatters of lost scripture, fed on unmeaning, drinking from the cup of
his own crucifixion — as fraught as the mind's messianic morbidity — Golem of
the Word — monstrosity of gibber — concocted philanstery — Dead Sea fake
— apocryphal Egyptian — embryo of the Eternal Wanderer, etc. Was it mere
happenstance of orthography that in the Sacred Lexicon, *golem* stood between
"exile" — *goles* — & *goen*, meaning, among other things, "the *dominant
influence*" or "*essential animating principle of anything*": "*an accompanying spirit,
demon, or djinn?*"*

---

* And like some djinnydjinndjinn of kiddies' nightime babblebooks, the Golem remained forever-
elusive, more pliant than clay, a shapeshifter, vanishing & reappearing from place to place, time to
time, never the one thing it's assumed to be — the more you sought to apprehend it, entrap it,
confine it, the more it mocked, derided, led you on a merry dance — now a worm in a toadstool,
now a leprechaun under a rock, one moment formless matter, the next a genius for assuming any
shape at all. Exiled from itself, a mere shadow, yet at the same time also inside itself, like a mind
caught inside the body of a stranger, waking in somebody else's room, forced to assume an alien
identity — made to think someone else's thoughts, speak someone else's words… The Golem of
subversion inside each of us that must be tamed, brought to heel, locked in the darkest room of the
cranial vault & never let out? (By the time mad Rudolf came along, the story of Löw's swarthy

It was Wegener's film that reminded Němec how, before quitting the City in '48, the Prof was supposed to've written a dissertation at the Catholic Theological Faculty, on the subject of the mad Rabbi himself. The Faculty was about a mile down-river, on the eastern side of the socalled New Town.* During the war it served as a Nazi ministry building, for the department of *Werk und Technik.* Across the river, steep cliffs joined the former vineyard terraces of the Sommerberg Gardens & the derelict Expo '58 pavilion, built at the time when the Theological Faculty was again under suppression, this time by the communists. Further downstream, the river broadened significantly around Štvanice Island (Hetzinsel), with its concrete flyovers & drab winter stadium. All interesting facts, but as for the Faculty itself, there was no point going there if Němec wanted to find anything about the Prof's dissertation — any records that might've been of interest had long ago been stored on microfilm, in the basement of the Klementinum. From which, at that moment, Němec was only a minute away.

At the Church of the Holy Saviour, crossed keys, a recital was in progress. Brahms' *Ein deutsches Requiem (nach Worten der heiligen Schrift)*, Op. 45, performed by the über alles Polish virtuoso Ivor Pederastky. Immediately adjacent, the entrance to the Klementinum stood open, the dark courtyard with light filtering down from uncurtained windows, students coming & going. At a guess, the Prof must've been around twentyfive when he submitted his dissertation — meaning he'd've been about sixteen at the time the Munich Agreement was signed in '38, *for the sake of European peace, peace with honour,*

---

amanuensis was cemented into the general fabric of the place: conspiracy, cabala, alchemy. Well before the birth of the Protektorat, the myth had given birth to countless proxies, avatars of future ethnocomputerology, grotesque Zhid-monsters, masked menaces, vaudeville Frankensteins, Nilus' *Protocols*, Meyrink's Pernath, Wegener's three films, & Čapek's 1923 cyborg apocalypticon, *R.U.R.* [Čapek, K. — author of *War with the Newts*, whose last play was completed on the eve of Hitler's invasion, died on Christmas Day 1938 (few people are aware he left behind him a unique collection of African & Central Asian music, recorded on vinyl 78s). His brother — Čapek, J. — perished at Belsen concentration camp, 1945. R.U.R. = "Rossum's Universal Robots": from *robota*, drudgery or servitude, forced labour — & *rossum*, echoing *rozum*, reason — *Whose light like Phoebus lamp throughout the world doth shine* — the divine radiance, the empiric illumination.]) [♣]
* Founded by Charles IV in 1348. [♣]
* Between November 1939 & May 1945 all the universities in Golem City had been closed by order of the ♯. [♣]

peace in our time.[*] The Prof himself had never spoken about the War. It made Němec wonder: What'd the Prof been doing those six years (he & those two muses of his)? When did they meet? How did they live? Where was he when the students protested in '39, on the 17th of November, against the murder of Jan Opletal, only to have their leaders arrested & shot? Why wasn't he[*] one of the twelve-hundred students rounded-up afterwards & sent to concentration camps? Where were they when the deportations began, to Terezín, Belsen, Auschwitz? What was he doing on the 5th of May 1945, when Golem City — last capital of Europe — finally rose against its oppressors? And what was he doing on the morning of the 9th, when Red Army tanks rolled through the suburbs for the first, but not for the last, time?

Němec wondered more when he discovered the Klementinum's antiquated card catalogue had no record of a dissertation on Rabbi Löw by any student called Hájek, either before the War or at any time after. The on-duty librarian suggested he check the graduation records. Sitting in a cubicle, with a viewing-machine fast-forwarding & rewinding through a dozen reels of microfilm, Němec eventually found what he was looking for. It wasn't much, just a record of the Prof's final undergraduate exam — *Státní závěrečné zkoušky bakalářské* —listed among the materials for September 1947. It included a one-page typed synopsis & two examiner's reports, each roughly a paragraph long. From these it could be concluded that the Prof's "dissertation" was mostly bibliography, a survey of Papal & Imperial edicts ("From Quattrocento to the Present Day"). The typed synopsis pointed to an underlying subtext of "race odium, questions of," "the problem of political emancipation" & its attendant "perils," with a side consideration of Löw's legendary Golem as the depicted "allegory," in an embryonic form (like a caterpillar in a cabbage, a serpent in the breast, a rat in the granary, a goat in the garden) of the "struggle to overcome," etc. Which in 1947 had its own very particular significance — in case anyone needed reminding. The examiners' questions, modestly couched in the unprepossessing language of the global anti-Zhiddish conspiracy, were mostly to

---

[*] 'How horrible, fantastic, incredible it is,' Mr Chamberlain said, 'that we should be digging trenches here because of a quarrel in a faraway country between people of whom we know nothing.' With the backs of England & France turned, the Nazis immediately occupied the Sudetenland — Poland annexed Silesia — Hungary seized Ruthenia & southern Slovnikia — & on the 15th of March, 1939, Hitler's forces let all pretence fall away & marched into Golem City, declaring all of Bohemia & Moravia a "Protectorate" of the Reich.[*] An instructive coming-of-age story for the modern nation. [♣]
[*] Or that Hrabal? [♣]

do with comparative points of scripture & ecclesiastical law, civic if not secular, categorical though hardly catechistic, mutatis mutandis & with due alteration of details, etc., placing the burden of responsibility for historical (A) wrongs & (B) wrongdoings, not to mention (C) unmitigated sufferings, squarely upon the shoulders of God's favoured scapegoat. The Prof's responses were omitted.

Below the Malá Strana end of Charles Bridge, on a narrow street backing onto the Čertovka moat, stood the entrance to PROSPERO'S USED BOOKS. From the entrance a spiral stairway led down through three conjoined rooms. Coming out of the heat, the air in the shop was damp & chill, but it was only an impression. In one corner an antique samovar steamed — it wasn't the sort of thing you'd ordinarily expect to find in a bookshop. Everywhere else, shelves ran to the ceiling, but there weren't enough of them for all the books — there were books piled up everywhere in towering columns, in every available space in *homage* to the temple at Byblos. The trick was to find to what you wanted without bringing the whole teetering construction down on top of you. If there was a system at work, it appeared to consist of the books being grouped by size, the lower reaches reserved for the largest — folios, atlases & catalogues, etc. — & those at the top for pocket editions which, as a result of the diminished perspective afforded by the narrow aisles & ceiling's height, were almost invisible.

From somewhere at the back of the shop came the sound of a toilet flushing, running water, the squeak of rubber soles on linoleum. The bookseller emerged from behind a drape. He was a squat man, balding in the middle but with long greasy black hair falling at the sides, wearing (it was July) a dirty green gabardine overcoat which, even at a distance, stank of formalin. Without paying any attention to his newly arrived customer, the bookseller went over & fidgeted with the samovar, tapped some tea onto a saucer, dunked a sugar cube & commence sucking it between his teeth. A pair of grimed trifocals pinching the fleshy bulb at the end of his nose most precariously. Němec interpreted all this as a signal to go ahead & browse. An hour of aimlessly scanning the shelves produced no notable results, till he came across a grey, dogeared paperback with columns of numbers printed diagonally across the cover, bearing the optimistic title *All About Unbreakable Codes and How to Use Them*. Němec found it wedged between Ottó Károlyi's self-help book, *Three Easy Steps to Suicide*, & Luděk Pachman's *Modern Chess Strategy* ("The plan of play at a particular point in the game as called the strategical plan; the way in which it is laid out, the collection of principles we follow in its determination, is known as strategy. These terms have the same meaning as in the science of warfare…") in a fruit crate stacked atop a pile of old service manuals. It cost the extravagant sum of 50 crowns. At first glance *All About Unbreakable Codes* looked like the kind of thing even an idiot might be able to understand, though to this particular idiot there was something curious, nay downright sinister, about the entire first page of the book being taken up by errata, printed on a blue slip of paper & pasted in at a wrong angle, viz: a convoluted flow chart for generating pseudo-random numbers, *Enter prime numbers here*, followed by lines of "computer code" omitted from page 72 in the original printing:

```
PRINT "DECODE…INPUT NUMBERS 1 BY 1"
FOR K=1 TO Z
A$="ABCDEFGHIJKLMNOPQRSTUVWXYZ1234567890.!?*+-/
INPUT X
P(K)=X-N(K), etc.
```

Beneath which, a note informed that page 72 should be page 73 & vice versa. Maybe it was someone's idea of a clever joke. Němec duly turned to the offending page, but it looked just like all the others. He flipped back to the introduction: *Historically*, it told the reader, *there have been hundreds of ways to keep secret the letters and messages of statesmen, generals and traders. In each era, once a certain level of literacy is reached, cryptology is born anew. In each age, the means of transmitting (and guarding) information has been determined by the technology of the time.* The author continued: *Any method for hiding the meaning of a message should meet four standards: First, it should be easy to create. It should be simple to send. When properly encrypted, a message should be unambiguous. And finally, any system for hiding messages should be difficult for unauthorised users to crack.* Němec returned *All About Unbreakable Codes* to its place in the fruit crate, thanking its author for clarifying those couple of difficult points for him. Whatever the secret of the Black Book, it wasn't about to reveal itself without a key — Němec felt sure of that. Besides, whoever had left it for him probably had other ideas in mind: what they were was anybody's guess. As Pachman said, *The best plans come to nothing if they're not carried out correctly.* So, assuming there *was* a plan, but not knowing *what* it was, what would be the correct method for proceeding? Němec asked the odd fish with the samovar — whether there was anything *he* knew about the Voynich Manuscript…

The caretaker's parrot screeched after him as he pulled himself up the stairs to the Prof's apartment. He bolted the door & glanced about, listening closely to the apartment's silence. Everything was as he'd left it. The mystagogical Black Book beckoned — as soon as Němec was convinced of being alone, he sat himself on the bureau floor & turned through its pages:

Was its gnomonic nomenclature, its Lethe-wise lexicography, simply a collation of errata turned into a system for its own decipherment?

A scale model, so to speak, of the Voynich Manuscript?

To clarify the syntactical soup of it?

By implication if not by direct application?

Who was there who could understand it, other than a deadman?

Who, apart from the Prof, was the code *for*?

If there *was*, in point of fact, a code to begin with?

What coterie?

What conspiracy of pseudosavants?

What cenacle of cynics?

What caprice of the clueless?

Was that what the Black Book added up to, a list of suspects, crossed-off one at a time?

By what process of elimination?

And if so, who really *was* Viktor Faktor?

Němec cast around for the tools at hand to cobble his own pre-electric decoding machine:

Rega turntable with a 1972 recording of Mahler's 6th primed to go — a torn-up newspaper (financial pages, stockmarket reports, league tables, weather forecasts, etc.) from which to extract some random randomness — a fresh bottle of slivovice — ltyrosine, tryptophane, hyperforin, dextropropoxyphene in equal measure — assorted other sundry items…

And so, with his tools arranged around him on the floor thus, Němec set about constructing his machine:

He necked the slivovice, shuffled the pills.

Red pill, yellow pill.

Needle let drop blindly in groove.

Recordplayer hiss.

Music spilling out in notes gratifyingly wrong, dragged apart & shunted back together by turntable-slack somewhere between 45 & 33⅓ rpm — as though played by an orchestra in helicopters.

He thumbed the Book, tore out bits of newspaper, intoned from each in turn: up five points — Kammler — morning edition — 25192…

The stuff of poetry.

Thence, the innumerous scrawled or voided-upon orts & scraps, recycled, wastepapered, inkblotted, adjected, doublevisioned, trebleverbed, shades of Faustian fustian, thirdeye blither extracted from various places of concealment on Němec's person:

Hocuspocusdidleydocus, gargoylegargling, spiritleavening as of unbehooved powers, eau-de-vied, usquebaughed — slapped-down plumpotioned in the medias res of it all, floor-wise & distillatedly dribbling around-about t'inscribe a circuitous as geometrically gerundive or diametrically indirect as ever a mephistophalopian morphogenesis was:

Geomancer or Gaia-master — pig's ear of pentagram — hexababble of carbon molecoil — sempiternal — looped octet groove of eight-bit symphonic bombast beelzebubbling voxes out of the nether ether — mind-blanked — blinking — getting it all down to the last gibberished gerund, the inspired nonsense of the truth-seeker, the machine exorcising its ghosts, the propounded error speaking in tongues till it enlighten us!

Ouija-board fingers tapping-out streetnoise dictations, creak of parquet, ruminated plumbing…

Feeding the consequent data into his word machine, *clack clack clack.*

Through obscurity & secret detours, a theme developed to the point of an obsession, till there was no alternative but to confront it & be rid of it.

Němec beheld himself thus:

Hunched, splay-legged at his typewriter like a raggedy Golem, driven & derided by an occult force at work in the nunceverse — not knowing towards what ends, barely conscious of his own non-actions, becoming that diabolical *thing* with its own secret life, the resurrection within, God-eye, Ninhursing, Khnum, Nüwa, Kukulkán — forging from his own inferior rib a companionable spirit, some equally unmenschlich creature of word-clay, papier-mâché, struck inkily upon mouth, chest, genitals, upon its forehead th'inscribèd word:

Truth-Firmness-Veracity, Aleph Mem Tau — אמת — causing *it* to *live*!

The responding pliable muck of mottage, moulded, servile, inspired with purple-prosed purility, animatronic, pneumatic as a pump-up doll, life-like in every respect brothers — which, no sooner blinking its lashes up at the Almighty (always fast upon the scene whenever our Joe tries his hand at a bit of sympathetic pornography), turning the old tea-soak to blushes, gets the Sleeping Beauty treatment, put on ice, laid as if to rest in the first flush of pristine preposterity, exempted from all worldly non-labours, a most pious pin-up if ever there was one — the lickspittled finger of Him Upstairs drawn prophylactically crossways upon that poor misshapen dogsbody's prepubescent pout, the ✖ of erasure, the undone first uttered syllable, Aleph, nothing now but the shadow of a shadow, plunging into the void, dark whispering of death — מת.

```
Begin now.
Input.
FAKTOR.
TWO-SEVEN-NINE-EIGHT-NINE-SIX-ONE-EIGHT.
Enter.
Goto.
Eena meena tethera gezisch!
Geknatter?!
Do you read me??
Come in Centrum!?!
```

Intermission

'Well it's been action-packed from the first whistle, a real tug-of-war, & certainly not a dull moment for us here in the commentary box today. We're at the halfway mark — how do you see the game developing so far, Klem?'

'In a *sit-u-a-tion* like this one, Rudi — 'ead-to-'ead, bofe sides puttin' their backs right inta it, evryffin' in tha balance — there's always wot I like ta call *un-an-tici-pat-ed* factors. Th'important fing's not ta get a'ead a yerself 'n' start frowin' round pre-dictions. It 'as to be said, tho — 'n' I reckon I speak fer everyone associated wiff tha game — this's *exactly* 'ow we all 'oped ta wrap up tha season. An ab-so-lute *nail*-biter. We're def'nitely gonna see this one go right down ta tha wire, 'nless sumffin' *de-cisive* 'appens b'tween now 'n' then a-course…'

'Too close to call, you reckon, Klem?'

'I wouldn't *nec-e-ssar-ily* go that far, Rudes. Question's 'ow ya figure tha breakdown this far inta tha game. I mean, 'ow offen've we 'eard pundits get over-confident, givin' tha advantage to one side over tha uvver early on, only ta 'ave it turn round 'n' bite 'em after? I'm speakin' *meta-phoric'ly*, a-course, Rudi. Point is, there's oceans a diff'rence 'ere, oceans. But we're talkin' two very diff'rent styles a play — 'n' if ya wanna ask if a more aggressive *tac-ti-cal* style a play 'as an advantage 'ere against a studied defensive *stra-te-gic* style a play, when fer all we know we could be 'alfway froo already…'

'You could say a lot hinges on the next half-an-hour…'

'Wot I'm sayin' is, it could all be over tha moment eiver side *under-esti-mates* tha uvver's line a attack. Or one uv 'em fails to produce *ad-e-quate* counterplay. We're at wotcha might call a *crucial juncture*…'

'There's been a lot of discussion, Klem, about certain statements in the press leading up to this afternoon's game, that here we have a dual between two conflicting theories, a genuine head-to-head between the socalled "classical" approach to the game & what people are calling the "hypermodern" approach. Isn't that like saying it's a contest between a bow&arrow & an intercontinental ballistic missile?'

'Well Davey-boy set Goliath on 'is be-'ind wiff a stone tha size a yer eye, 'n' that was maybe tha same type a fing. 'N' Davey-boy, as that Mick Angelo proved, woz no cut salami. But we're gettin' way off track 'ere. Wot's important fer our viewers ta keep in mind is while there's lotsa talk goin' on out there they shouldn't lose sight a what really *matters...*'

'Do you feel we're witnessing a conservative backlash against some of the recent innovations that've been taking place?'

'I believe tha only people innerested in words like *con-ser-vative* or *in-no-vation* are them armchair bozos out there've never really been part a tha game...'

'Never made the grade... in a manner of speaking.'

'Basic fact is, tha game's bigger'n all tha petty bickerin 's been 'appenin' on tha sidelines. Wot we're seein' tonight's a vindication a that fact. At tha end a tha day, no matter oo triumphs or fails, oo wins tha glory or gets carted off on 'is backside, it's tha *game* that's tha winner.'

'Speaking for myself, it almost feels a privilege just to be sitting up here watching this contest unfold...'

''Umbled is 'ow I feel, Rudes, 'umbled. We're witnessin' someffin' unique takin' place tonight, 'n' I reckon our viewers're experiencin' that, too. It's cert'nly no ord'nary event — you'd agree wiff that, Rudi? 'Ard ta find a comparison wiffin recent mem'ry, eh? *You-nique* wouldn't be overstatin' it...'

'And yet there's always controversy waiting in the wings...'

'General rule a thumb in this biz, Rudes, is people can't be spected ta agree on evryffin'...'

'That's sadly true. What's your take on the recent boycotts, Klem?'

'All I 'ave ta say on that score, Rudi, is ya can't play tha game by turnin' yer back on it. It's that simple. Can't take yer bat 'n' ball 'n' go sulk in a corner 'n' spect evryffin' ta stop on yer account. If ya want tha *game* ta succeed you've gotta stick wiv it, even if ya don't like tha final call. Way tha cookie crumbles, sunshine. As they use ta say in tha lockerrooms when I was a kid, 'arden tha fuck up, 'n if ya can't 'arden tha fuck up, get yer mitts off tha soap...'*

'Each side has to put the interests of the game ahead of its own interests, is that right Klem?'

'That's it in a nutshell, Rudes.'

'You look back at the past greats of the game & there's a sense they tower above all these debates, wouldn't you say? The spirit of the game. Perhaps we've lost something...'

'Don't forget all them unsung 'eros, as well. Tha ones gave it evryffin' they

---

* I can't believe my ears, that rude man just said the most horrible word on public television! [♣]

'ad. They wasn't in it fer tha glory or nuffin uvver than tha pewer *sat-is-faction* of bein' part a sumffin'. Sumffin' bigger 'n' any in-dee-vid-ual…'

'There was an article in last Sunday's *Golem Post* that a listener pointed out, which argues that a return to the "classical" approach represents *the only remedy for the ills that've befallen the game in recent times.* There's some doubt, though — & I think you probably share this view, Klem — that a conventional response to the upheavals we've all experienced in the last couple of years would be insufficient somehow. We've even heard calls for open revolt against the current status quo. The *Evening Standard*'s editorial on Monday came within a hair's breadth of calling for an all out denunciation of the Old School…'

'Look, Rudes, I don't believe it's 'elpful in tha slightest — 'n' I mean this *em-fat-ic'ly* — when elements in tha media keep draggin' up tha past 'n' dividin' people when all uv us need ta be focused on lookin' forward 'n' workin' togevver. All this talk 'bout principles is just an *un-ness-e-ssary* distraction from wot ultimately matters. It's always easy ta speak 'bout makin' a bold frust to right perceived wrongs, 'specially if yer just standin' on tha sidelines, but wot we need more 'n' anyffin' at this point in time's ta put tha past *de-fin-it-ively* be'ind us 'n' get to work on tha Big Future this game 'as in store for it. For tha sake a tha players, too…'

'And for the fans…'

'Abso-*bloody*-lutely.'

'After all, it's all about the love of the game.'

'I couldn't a said it better meself, Rudi.'

'Cheers Klem. Well folks, you heard it, we've got some top action happening live here today, & it all goes to prove the old adage, *You've got to be in it to win it.* We'll be back with the rest of what's sizing up to be a thrilling showdown in just a moment, but before we do, a look at tonight's programmes. We've got a short news bulletin coming up in half-an-hour followed by the weather, & at eight o'clock the weekly film guide hosted by our very own Vlado Clementis. Here's a quick preview. Over to you, Vlado…'

'Thank you Rudi & good evening to all our viewers out there enjoying the commentary to the season's decider. Stay with us afterwards for a special edition of *Unsightly Cinema*, your weekly behind-the-scenes on the latest big screen hits & one or two flops as well. Tonight we've got an interview with renowned cinematographer Karel Hájek & an in-depth look at the latest offering from Jan Němec, *The Combine*, an eight-hour docudrama about one artist living as an outcast in the City… Tune-in then!'

A SPECTRE is haunting Mitteleuropa: the spectre of
THE Š.V.E.J.K!
Government by bureaucracy is called popular government!
ROBOR
CVAK
The hypnotic charm of ideology...
This spectre has not appeared out of thin air! It is a natural and inevitable consequence of the present historical phase of the SYSTEM IT IS HAUNTING!
Military occupation becomes...
FRATERNAL ASSISTANCE!
It was born at a time when this system, for a thousand reasons, could no longer base itself on the unadulterated, brutal, and arbitrary application of power...
The complete degradation of the individual is presented AS HIS ULTIMATE LIBERATION!
"Workers of the world, UNITE!"
1938! 1968!
SOCIALISM WITH A HUMAN FACE!
Because the regime is captive to its own lies, it must falsify everything!
?!?!?
Ideology is a specious way of relating to the world. It offers human beings the illusion of an identity, of dignity, and of morality while making it easier to part with them...
It falsifies the past, it falsifies the present, and it falsifies the future.
It pretends not to possess an omni-potent & unprincipled police apparatus.
It pretends to respect human rights.
It pretends to persecute no one.
It pretends to fear nothing.
It pretends to pretend nothing.
Individuals confirm the system...
fulfill the system...
make the system, ARE the system!!!
To be continued...

430

Today's Bumper **Super Combo** Crossword!

ACROSS

2. Subterranean passage.
5. Circle of constant longitude.
6. Doctrinaire.
8. Apparatus.
10. To eject via the anus.
11. Ingenious sequence of moves.
15. Formless primordial matter.
16. What is meant.
18. To expel via the mouth
20. Likelihood.
21. Maze.
22. Celestial gathering.
24. Construct.
25. Toy musical instrument.
27. Any or all of the above.
28. Absence of mind.
32. Handwritten.
35. Box with aperture.
37. Secret system.
40. Chatterer.
47. Alien.
49. Conclusion that does not logically follow.
51. Opening in wall, usually filled with glass.
53. Hehe.
54. The man with the axe.
55. Instrument for unlocking.
56. Condition of existence.
58. Simpleton.
59. What is the matter?
60. Pasted hingewise & enclosed in a cover.
61. Large extinct bird.

DOWN

1. Fossilitic turd.
2. To make grotesque.
3. A mock of moonbeam.
4. Guiding fact or principle.
7. Means of transmutation.
9. Concurrence w/o apparent cause.
12. Tall equilateral structure.
13. Potion book.
14. Obnoxious spirit.
17. Mudman.
19. Impetuous divergence.
22. 3 = 1
23. Person so deficient in mind as to be permanently incapable of rational conduct.
26. Lacking good sense.
29. Enigmatic or inscrutable.
30. To make up, constitute.
31. Dark, dim.
33. Nonexistent omniscient nonentity.
34. One who commits pederasty.
36. Species of turncoat.
38. Person, animal or plant much below ordinary size.
39. The same backwards.
41. Parody.
42. Join by running together.
43. To divulge or repeat foolishly.
44. Change into another form, nature or substance.
45. Metallic element of lanthanide series.
46. Bulbous plant of genus *Scilla*.
48. Open to eye or mind.
50. Indefinitely continued existence.
52. To buy at a discount the debts of others, so as to profit from them.
54. Hidden or inexplicable matter.
57. Drudge.

UNSIGHTLY CINEMA: Welcome to the show, Jan.

JAN NĚMEC: Great to be here, Vlad.

UC: Let's start with the question most of our viewers would probably like to ask: How do you envisage the central character in your new film, *The Combine*? Is he supposed to represent a kind of everyman in a world that's turned dysfunctional, where familiar rules don't apply? Personally I got the feeling we weren't really watching a documentary at all, but an extended essay on the status of the individual in modern society, the absence of certainties, the sorts of things previous generations would've taken for granted — employment, social security, all that — & which, since the Revolution, we've seen disintegrate. The idea of reality itself, some might say. It seems very popular at the moment to speak about *virtu*ality instead of *re*ality, nowadays. Whereas, under the former régime, there were a lot of people, maybe tacitly a majority of people, who believed the official "reality" was a sham & that *actual* reality could only begin when the old system was swept away. So I wanted to ask you, was it your intention to focus on a character who's somehow unreal because he's struggling to find what reality actually is, once all the maps have been redrawn?

JN: To begin with, it's possibly misleading to speak about a central "character" in this film. We didn't set out to *invent* a personality. It's more about discovery. The idea was to do the opposite of something made-up or story-like. We wanted to examine the limits we all place on ourselves, as individuals, when we ask what it means to exist in the present, under present conditions, aware of all those expectations & anxieties you mentioned, but unable or unwilling to live up to them, so to speak. There're no professional actors in the film, but there's acting. In that sense it's a documentary about people trying to discover a role for themselves &, through that role, to better understand who they really are...

UC: Is the film autobiographical?

JN: In a way, yes, because it asks about *itself*, about its own status as a film. It's a film about film. At the same time, it's about a person. About what constitutes a person who is also the subject of a film, let's say.

UC: Is that person you? You both share the same name…

JN: Literally? That the film's about me? No. The thing about the name happened because it turned out being simpler that way. We didn't want to focus on the purely extrinsic aspects, or make something up, & we didn't want to call him Mr Nobody, so the crew just started calling him "Němec," first as a kind of joke but it stuck. No, seriously, I always try to keep myself *behind* the camera. Inevitably there are traits that may be projected onto this person called "Němec," because you can't leave the camera out of the equation, & ultimately I'm the one "directing" the film even if all the action *is* spontaneous & improvised. I mean, insofar as true improvisation in front of a camera is possible. We tried to be as inconspicuous as possible, keeping the camera out of view, using deep focus, but it's never possible to erase yourself completely. In the end you have to confront the question, how to decide what the difference is between a narrative film & a documentary film? When you say, "autobiography," for example. Is there a difference?

UC: You have to admit it's extremely unusual for a narrative film to run over eight hours. Fassbinder would be one exception.

JN: Precisely. But that's just a convention like all the others. Fassbinder would've been the first to point that out, too. But it wasn't something we really thought about till after we cut the film. We just cut it the way we thought it had to be cut. You produce a different cut & it's a different film, it means something else.

UC: Warhol's *Sleep*? *Empire*?

JN: It's more humanistic than that.

UC: Would you describe yourself as a humanist, then?

JN: I'm concerned with knowing what humanism is, rather than using it as a label.

UC: Some critics describe your work as *post*-humanist. Is that misleading?

JN: It *is* if you don't know where you're starting from. How can something be "post" if there's nothing there to begin with? Some people call Stalinism *anti*-humanist. I disagree. I don't believe you can have humanism without Stalin, without the gulags, without the showtrials…

UC: What about Hitler?

JN: You can go all the way back through history & find the same basic thing. Even in the Bible.

UC: Does religion answer the needs of people who've lost their traditional certainties?

JN: If you mean Communism, then it's just a matter of substituting one false messiah for another.

UC: A false messiah?

JN: The only true messiah is *people*. Us. Humanity. Right, wrong, stupid, indifferent, horrifying, whatever. *We* are what comes in the name of "God," who's really just our enlarged sense of self in any case. Which is precisely what cinema is, too. And when we're gone, we're gone. With God, you get graveyards, churches, laws. With cinema, you have moving images that live on even when we're not here any more. Imagine one day, when everyone has been wiped out by nuclear catastrophe or environmental disaster or whatever, & along come some aliens in spaceships, & what do they find?

UC: So Nietzsche's death of God is the death of humanity?

JN: It's possible humanity died long ago & we're only now discovering the facts.

UC: Let's get back to *The Combine*. The main character — or should I call him a "figure"? — has to decide about which path in life to follow. Could you tell us a little about that?

JN: Firstly, "Němec" might seem unusual, because he's obsessed with films (like me, of course), but not with films in the ordinary sense, not any specific film you would see in a cinema, but with the *idea* of a film. Or of film as such. This might have something to do with how we perceive our place in reality, or it might not. The problem confronting "Němec" is that he can't picture himself outside a film — so the question he asks himself in each situation is, *What type of film am I in? Is it this type of film or that type of film?* And on this occasion, the one we're speaking about, which is *The Combine*, it's a quest — he's looking for something, he thinks he knows what it is while making a show of admitting he doesn't, & while he's looking he attempts to find others who might be able to help him along the way, confirm him in his beliefs or suspicions, provide the necessary affirmations, but all he seems to find are people who want to hinder him or aren't interested in his predicament, or worse still poke fun at everything from the way he looks to the foreignness of his ideas which, at another time & in another place, might easily have gotten him crucified or burned at the stake or strapped to a bed & given electroshock therapy or sent off to a concentration camp. It's easy to confuse a man who thinks he's in a film with a man who thinks he's on a sacred mission under the watchful (& not necessarily sympathetic) "Eye of God." The question is, does he suffer from an illness, or is the world an illness?

UC: A father complex, perhaps? But at some point in the film we discover he's an orphan...

JN: So much the better! History's full of father surrogates.

UC: The French philosopher Jacques Derrida says *in pitying the orphan, one also makes an accusation against him... for claiming to do away with the father, for achieving emancipation with complacent self-sufficiency.*

JN: But at the same time we have to be careful about turning everything into an allegory. Why not just let him muddle along & see if he gets to the bottom of it? Even without knowing the rules...

UC: Does the film imply there *are* rules?

JN: For existence? Of course there're rules, but they aren't always what we think they are. "Němec's" quest, in a way, is an attempt to find out what the rules *are*. And that's exactly what the film attempts to do, too. Our goal when we began shooting was to intuit from one situation to the next, as in real life, without necessarily having all the pointers there to guide us. We decided from the outset that the film would go on till it reached what we understood to be the end, & not before then, no matter how long it took.

UC: The film runs for a total of eight hours in the final cut — how much editing was involved?

JN: I like to say I edit with the camera, but that's only part of the story, of course. As far as the overall structure's concerned, we actually employed this simple algorithm — in fact, it was "Němec" himself who introduced the idea: *From the given probabilities of any system of events, determine the consequent probability of any other event logically connected with those events.*

UC: Could you maybe explain that a little more? In layman's terms? How it actually works in practice, for example…?

JN: Take any film you like. It's necessary for it to begin *somewhere*, & from then on the rest unfolds in a logically connected sequence — *even when those sequences appear not to make any sense.* What I mean is, every film has its *own* logic, even when that logic fails, but it's the beginning that determines the logic & not the other way around. So the starting point for "Němec's" quest is essentially arbitrary, but the rest, what follows, isn't arbitrary. Yet not *necessary*, either, only "logical." Whereas the beginning is both necessary *and* arbitrary. It's what in mathematics is called a disjoint union of subsets… This might all sound a little abstract, but right here we're touching upon *the* central question… I don't just mean the film, I mean the central question of *humanity* — our desire to possess a purpose, to know our origin was *intended* & not merely a biochemical accident, & that our history has in some sense had a necessary *unfolding*. How do you explain *that* to someone who wakes up every morning looking over his shoulder thinking he's being pursued by a telephoto lens? I call it, *symmetric difference.* Think of a mirror, how everything's backwards, where to proceed means to retreat, where every form of stealth & cunning's required to outwit a mindless bit of glass. That's your Father Complex right there. The "God Conspiracy." The "Combine."

UC: Why not just stick to the facts? Your style has been commented on as intruding into objects rather than showing them as they are. For example, in one version of your quest story Němec is supposed to be a writer — in another, an actor playing the part of a writer in a film…

JN: By constructing an existence *similar* to that of his socalled character, "Němec" believes he can enter more fully into the role he feels has been assigned to him. In effect he seeks to *become* his "character." This "character" is in turn an anomaly of sorts — like an object that spontaneously comes to life: you still want to think of it as an object but at the same time you're already involved in imagining an interior existence for it…

UC: Many of your viewers have been struck by the way "Němec" often seems to be two completely different people. At times he appears to suffer from a sleeping sickness & at others the opposite, a constant agitation…

JN: It's as if his existence oscillates between two poles, two extremes — the type of "character" who by walking through the City, for example, *swims*, & by staying confined in his room, *drowns*. If this "character" had existed, been a real person, in flesh & blood, he might've visited a spiritualist, held a séance, communed with the spirit — only he doesn't, he's just a "character," borrowed, by the way, from a nineteenth-century Norwegian playwright. A kind of ghost, therefore, or a ghost of a ghost. So the question is, *How do you enter into communion with a fiction*? Yet it's something we all do all the time. On the *abyss of the five senses*! as a poet once said. Nowadays there's nothing controversial about the idea that fiction represents inherent aspects of the real world, constructed from the raw materials of actual experience & transmuted through the minds of living people, men & women (not like us), the way dreams are, or TV news, or the events from History they make you learn in school. What was the inner life, for example, of the architect of the Final Solution — an event of such unsettling magnitude *it* can only be treated as a kind of fiction, while to deny its truth is either a crime or an insanity? Of course, we prefer to believe in demons & devils, they at least are easy to understand. Everyone knows the story of Johannes Faustus, the megalomaniac doctor who wanted to be like "God," all-knowing, & at any price. You know, like getting a cosmic brain transfusion or something. Crazy, right? Nowadays he'd probably turn out to be a serial killer, "Doctor Death," but back then you could do even worse, you could sell your soul to the Devil, which's what Faustus did. But what if Faustus had signed a contract with the engineers at I.G. Farben instead of with Mephistopheles?

UC: Would you accept a description of your work as cynical? That it uses disillusionment in order to promote a new myth of indeterminacy?

JN: The sentimentalist has much to say about the human foible & nothing whatsoever about its psychoses. As the same poet once said, *The fool sees not the same tree as the wise man sees.* But as I see it, a man begins as a fiction & only discovers the sham later on, when the mortgage is overdue, or the great talent he had in store melts into air, or he can't find himself in the mirror & runs out into the street in a kind of panic — but up till this point all of his actions have been a performance, because he already sees himself in the role of someone who's lost his reflection, etc., & is now *performing* the action of running out into the street, *performing* being panic-stricken & so on. All this is straight out of a film. We've watched it a thousand times or more. The disillusionment only sets in when he's standing there in the street & nobody even notices what he's doing, that he's even there. But this opportunity to doubt his own existence is only the beginning. A sceptical age comforts itself just as well as any other with whatever dogmas are nearest at hand. Reality's just a conspiracy, after all. Our Invisible Man proclaims the world a mirage, or a simulacrum, or a dream, & so it is. *Puff!* We who watch over the slumbering masses could tell them a thing or two, or so we imagine, but wouldn't it be better to see them find it out for themselves?

e. The Sacrificial Queen

33

THE GREAT INSTAURATION

Impossible to tell if it was night or day — then some clown turned the lights on.

They came up slowly, like an old black&white movie fade-in on a studio set, ocean-sounds in the distance. Němec lay there waiting for the wiseguy in the director's chair to call out *Action!* to bring it all into focus — the whirr of the cameras — gaffers & scriptgirls, foleys, grips, assistant producers & makeup artists hovering on the periphery. When nothing happened he dragged himself up off the floor to see what was wrong. The clown was still shining a lamp straight into his eyes. *What's that in aid of, eh, motherfucker?*

Němec squinted so as to get a fix on it, but it kept pulling further away. He swung a wild right & collided with the window frame. *Shit.* Screwed his eyes up, blinked, sucked bruised knuckles. The roof of his mouth tasted of tar paper. Someone's reflection made faces at him from the other side of the pane — a pair of cue-ball eyes, like some skidrow Weegee politburo guy who'd taken to sleeping under bridges & dangling from lampposts. *Too young to die old, kiddo, 'n' too old to die young.* He gave Němec one of those wino grins that make you think of cocktail hours with rusted palmtrees & a twostroke lawnmower passing overhead & bits of busted pavement for a tombstone. The ocean-sound was just the static in his head.

Outside, Golem City was still there, like a uterus turned insideout. The sun was coming up or going down in the windows across the street. He must've slept through the whole parade. Or maybe it hadn't started yet. Like a funeral waiting for the main protagonist to get his makeup & costume on. *Time to rise 'n' shine, arsehole.* The face in the glass yawned, mouth wide open. Just the sight made him want to throw up. *To hell with it.* Němec lay back down on the floor in a puddle of cold sweat, the booze in his blood giving him the slow shakes & sleep whispering in that soft peddle-organ voice…

Next thing he was wide awake — someone was screaming.

The screaming went on & on. Němec jerked upright in a reflex of pure panic. By the time he got to the door, the screaming had stopped. From down in the courtyard came the dry malicious cackle of the caretaker's parrot, like some malevolent idiot chortling at its own joke. Němec peered out into the glare through the stairwell window. The beady-eyed fucker was down there alright, head cocked, observing him from its perch by the door of the caretaker's flat. Beak at half-mast. Tonguing the air.

No sign of La Severínová.

No sign of anyone.

The parrot winked, rasped its black grub-like tongue. Němec, feeling his sea-legs sway under him, gauged the chances of a quick parrot-bludgeoning & gave it up as a bum deal. He growled. The bird rolled its eye, bobbed its head, cackled noiselessly. *Ever get my hands on you, my green friend, we'll see who's laughing.* Or as one Apostle said to the other —

'What's the best way to cure a leper, Joe?'

'Tan his hide when he's dead, Fred.'

Hahahaha.

Smirking (but it was the most feeble kind of smirk), Němec withdrew from the window & turned to go back inside. And promptly fell flat on his face. The small matter of a suitcase…

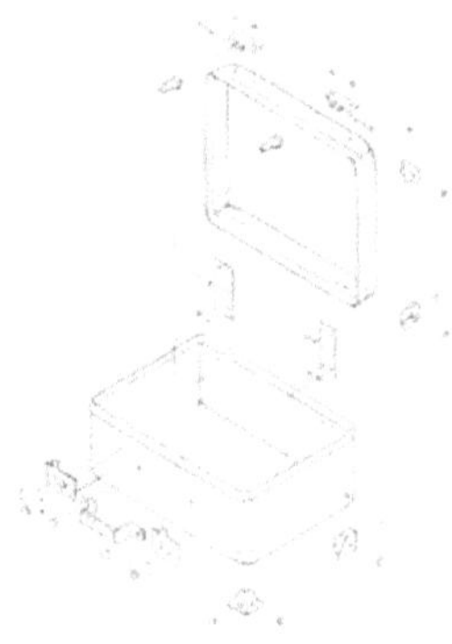

Then it started coming back to him, the whole rancid production with holes in it, bits & pieces threaded on angel wires, odyssey-in-a-bottle stuff…

Walk the Line

The City, folded up on itself like a flaccid biceps cinched with a tourniquet. The sky, blazing, like one of those Kafka machines bristling with a million needlepoints. Just thinking about it made him feel as if his mind was being flayed. *One of these days*, Němec told himself, *it's gonna do you in*. Not that day, though. That particular day it wanted to see him suffer, right down the line.

What he remembered:

Wandering, apparently aimless, through post-apoc film set streets, while visions of airconditioned poolside Acapulcos played in his head, hyacinth girls in hula skirts, alpine waterfalls, polar bears basking in sunlit arctic ice floes. Mirages in a desert. It was too hot to do anything & too hot to do nothing. But something, a restlessness, an anxiety proportionate to the general lethargy, had goaded him out into the street, down to the Bridge, diverted from the usual sightseeing itinerary by rivers of half-melted tarmac, dark-faced road gangs squatting in the shade of a pile-driver necking warm beer, a mad dog chasing its shadow along a wall...

Pushing on, because otherwise he couldn't think, couldn't bear that pain even the pills wouldn't put out of its (his) misery[*] — pills & bottle of moonshine in jacket pocket (to lessen the urgency, cloud the issue, thin the blood), guided by instincts not his but adopted from contingency, the City his double, nothing Cartesian about it — each intersection a crossroads where right angles & straight lines & the implied hypotenuse gave way to valences of relativity — *Left, right? Straight on? Retreat? Do nothing. Repeat. Keep repeating.* At a certain point, the inertia of abdicated decisions assumed its own momentum — a procedure as incessant as it was apocryphal, destined to the toss of a coin, a roll of dice, a turn at the wheel, "odds" or "evens," anything south of the cut-off point, anything north — drawing the proverbial line in the sand which of itself became an itinerary, an inside-out map, a weft of intentions woven by indeterminacy — shadow as compass-needle, appointing the coordinates on a path to find a way deeper in, beyond the bare aspect of things, the shambles of a body orphaned from itself...

Did Němec believe a word of what he was thinking? A slug of moonshine, the zinc-white caul of a sky. *Doesn't matter what I believe, does it?* The sky had no

---

[*] You break your legs & all you want to do is walk, even in your sleep, even when it hurts so much you throw-up, even when you're fed-up with walking, because if you don't walk you'll fall into a hole there's no getting out of — you lose the nerve, can't get through the door, no will for it, you're stuck in lead boots, left for dead. [♣]

answer. The day dragged itself out like the shadow of a lone walker on a road that, though it keeps winding back on itself, appears dead straight, pegged at either end to shiftless horizons of grey. Up ahead the mad dog was panting against a wall — it barked once, then ran off again, past the spot where the mute swordswallower did his act for passersby, though no sign today of either, only the mutt & its shadow bolting out across the road, the arcades sunk in gloom where midday gypsy whores sulked in boredom, a pimp asleep in a taxi, pigeons blinking under eaves.

> *And the band slept through the parade,*
> *and the lifesupport system hitchhiked to the movies,*
> *and the mothers-in-law and axemurderers and suicides*
> *went looking for a standing ovation,*
> *and the street begged to be put out of its misery,*
> *and the sisters of mercy were cutting deadmen's hair,*
> *and the whole nation was dreaming at gunpoint,*
> *and the traffic was backed-up all the way to 1952,*
> *and the Sirens were putting on their TV voices,*
> *and the jukeboxes were all too old to care*
> *about the heroes who died on their barstools,*
> *shot to pieces at midday and buried without ceremony*
> *at quarter-to-five in the afternoon…*

From the National Theatre, Němec kept slowly south against the river's flow, sweating into those black Melmoth rags a kind of superstition kept him from tossing in the bin the way a sane person would — shirt sodden, feet slopping about in borrowed never-to-be-returned shoes, crotch rot in tropical swamp unwash, ball-&-socket purring smoothly in its lubricated casing…*

Just past the riverclock the bent lanky figure in dusty bowler hat & suit

---

* What's he doing, you ask, & why's he doing it? He should be back in bed or lying on a cool floor somewhere indulging his lethargy, but he isn't. If we could interpellate him, he'd be unable to tell us why he insists on sticking-out this ridiculous meandering non-quest, even if he wanted to. Which is doubtful. To all appearances ready to give-in at a moment's notice, yet somehow compelled onward, with nothing in mind perhaps than some crackpot story slowly incubating itself, sweating itself out — about the why & wherefore of it all & his nonself in the midst. Just another day's laborious hard work, you might say, cogitating the cogs, wiling the wheels & no endstop in sight — like the whole world's made of nothing but carriage returns. A man could crisscross the City for all eternity & still not get down a satisfactory dénouement, let alone a fullstop, forever caught in the middle of things — presentiments of Purgatory — the doggerel beneath the skin — the bridge before the chorus going nowhere. *If by ten miles you want to know when too long began…* [☞]

boarded a Braník-bound tram. It shuddered & swerved along the quays, past the steel rail-bridge, the blank stare of the Smíchov façades across the water turned white in the glare, under the rock of Vyšehrad, Šemík's leap, slow clouds gathering over Chuchle, past the drydocks & marinas, the Maternity Hospital co-opted in the War for ⚡⚡ casualties "lucky" enough to make it back from the East, the Water Purification Plant standing out from the hillside like some grandiose mausoleum, past the islands with their deserted campsites, rowing clubs, corrals, the Braník distillery, the tram clanking disconsolately into the terminus. The lone rider disembarking. Heat-shimmer rising from the tracks. Then down to the river on his own legs, a dirt path half sluiced away, a wooden bench to watch the ducks drifting by, empty the mind of its arcane dross — the air less suffocating here but still not exactly what you'd call breathable.

Němec spread himself out & took in the bucolic serenity of it all. The Barrandov Bridge like a king rat knotted in concrete, sprawling among rotted overgrowth, flyovers, underpasses, bits of weathered armature exposed all along its length — the Terraces on the further side, glass tower a ruined lighthouse high on its rock over the train tracks — & all the while the river funnelling in on itself, the vanishing point, always somewhere just there ahead, countervailing, balancing, throwing the whole borromean morass of the City into a kind of hysteria, spilling over the edges, coming apart at the seams, like a sloppy drunk clutching hold of the bottle for dear life.* *Well let it flow!* Knowing the one

----

* MINISTRY OF INERTIA

Now it just so happened that, had ⚡⚡-Obergruppenführer R.T.E. Heydrich got his way, back in the annals of ancient history (before Himmler quietly seized the opportunity to have him done in, haha), he'd've demolished that whole wretched dunghill in one fell swoop, freezing the lymph in its gland with that fatuous ice-maiden stare of his, & Němec would've been left to contemplate a real doozy of a vista.

For, once he'd filed away his little Zhiddish Problemo in that shoebox under the bed where he kept his Charles Atlas postcard collection, it was to've been young Reinhard's next Big Project for the summer: to level that whole Sklavonik eyesore of Golem City, everything from Malá Strana to Strahov to the National Theatre — *history's detritus* (the "lesson of Rome") — bulldozed by a battalion of the Reichsarbeitdienst to make way for Moses Händel's long-cherished boyhood vision, the Ideal Picnicground of the Twilit Gods, paradise of button-pushers & seat-polishers, parade-artists, pornographically-minded proceduralists & Aryanised pedants of the statistical neckjob.

In short, the whole Cecil B. DeMille panoply of a doomcrazed mind descending from its mount bestowing upon the world a plethora of carbon-copy reviewing stands, pavilions, stadiums, barracks, opera houses in the hypermodern style, faux-marble galleries & cathedrals of the Authentic Light — the whole thing set in a pure geometric resonance, ringed by colossal autobahns whose suburbs are Berlin, Paris, Schnitzelstadt, Beijing — one vast transmission nerve-centre of future global dominion, the celestial stepping-off point of untold cryogenic eons of the March of the Übermensch, the Ville Radieuse, Babel Everlasting! *An architecture pure, masterly, vast. Powerful masses and slender elements. A beauty of a more technical order...*

Oh, indeed, it would've been the ultimate, irrefutable, unarguable, supreme monument-of-monuments to the Eternal Greatness of the Nouveau Reich — & of Heydrich, first among them, of course. (Well, who needed a town like Golem City anyway, with its thousand spires-in-yer-eye & brokendown alembics & bald monkeys on yer back?)

Speer (Albert), that fanatical ballsack, was already hard at work mocking-up a passable prototype out of cardboard blocks on a table half the size of Nuremberg in his private office — known among the Czernin Palace wits as the "Ministry of Inertia" (the glories of '39 already a fading memory now that War Production had begun in earnest). Since, despite the vast wealth of self-aggrandising monomania Heydrich had invested in him, Speer's construction schedule amounted to a barely disguised recycling project for turning the leftovers of a ruthless *ϟϟ* pillaging of every available Protektorat resource into nothing more than an exorbitant array of dust-gathering maquettes. (These were still the days before busy Albert's unexpected "rehabilitation" & the economic "miracle" of 1944.)

Had Heydrich been left to his mad devices, who knows, Speer might've been fiddling with cardboard cutouts for the duration instead of churning out U-boats faster than Jack's beanstalk.

> *There once was ein Mann from Mannheim,*
> *who dreamt of great things all the time —*
> *he could conjure machines*
> *to make the world gleam,*
> *but couldn't perfect a war crime.*

To give the bastard his dues, Speer, that congellated goobag, could hold his end up even with nothing more than a bathtub of pulped woodchip & glue. In the Bundesliga of Coldblooded Criminal Paperpushers, Speer wasn't the type to be picking his nose on the reserve bench. So when not manufacturing ludicrous maquettes for Heydrich's Thousand-Year Hyderabad, Speer's "Ministry of Inertia" spent its time doing what it did best: generating redtape — everything from phoney cross-channel invasion plans & dossiers on a proposed (equally phoney) invasion of Iran, Upper Volta, the Andaman Islands & other farflung territories (to be indirectly leaked to the Allies when the appropriate time came, to sew confusion, muddy the waters), to counterfeit Roubles & Pounds Sterling (to be airdropped across enemy lines, flooding the enemy's socalled economies with bogus currency, *Inflation Bombs* hahaha) — including, long after Speer had moved-on & the fortunes of War had taken a decided turn for the cataclysmic, the "Ministry's" piece-de-résistance, cranking-out technical blueprints of a top secret *Wunderwaffe* (a last-ditch miracle weapon capable of turning whole cities to antimatter if their populations didn't immediately re-capitulate, codename: K.L.E.E. — a con to one-up even the most incredulous of bullshit artists among them).

Historians will note that, even during the Final Hours, the "Ministry of Inertia" didn't rest (no sleep for the engines of entropy, *hehe*), but pressed on, down to the last ream & postagestamp-sized bit of letterpress, providing the only rearguard action left now that Schörner's Army Group Centre had been pulverised into the mists of pure mythology... Cranking-out on a bewildering scale, all things considered, everything from fake ration books & employment cards to fraudulent mission statements for the Reich's chain of Permanent Rehab Centres (oh-ho-ho), attempting by office efficiency alone to erase all evidence of the Final Solution &, in addition, provide an handy escape hatch for its numerous architects (so to speak), precognisant somehow of that wholesale planting of forged microfilms, sham diaries & other specious items during the mopping-up meridian that can make sense of it all, keep it on an even keel so to speak, is precisely the one that'll never keep still. May just as well try propping yourself up on the second hand of an enormous clock or build an embankment around the shadow of a sundial. As even now, describing a parallelogram in single-point perspective, shadowed right to left, then left to right, darkening by increments, for all appearances (to the time-lapsed among you) flattened out like a two-year-old's doodle of a teepee in progressive stages of being rotated about a vertical axis: ▲ △ ◭.

Geometry had never been his forte, but Němec saw what he saw. From here the City was already an abstraction. A weak link. He sat there watching the river like a man thrown back on his own resources & finding them wanting. Or barely watching, the whole thing just passing in front of his eyes. It was worse than being in a cinema, here he couldn't even be sure where he was. Unbridled nature, he realised with a vague feeling of wonderment, had always terrified him, more even than Commies, shrinks & dormitories. In nature you never knew what might happen, while with the others everything was hideously predictable, there was at least that to say for them. There'd be nothing worse, he decided, than taking a "holiday" on the Sázava, listening to bluegrass & shooting carp — the almost certain boredom would be excusable, but you could never be sure some unblinking catastrophe wasn't lurking behind every bush & blade of grass, just waiting to leap out & maul you to shreds.

Němec eyed the ducks on the river warily. They looked harmless enough, but appearances were often deceiving. Probably it was the heat. Well it would

<hr>

sideshow at Nuremberg (the ever-reliable Speer taking one for the team yet again, while Eichmann vanished into the paperwork).

It was this very same "Ministry of Inertia," of course, which (even with the Ideal City tumbling down around its ears, the last thing to go seemingly, cannibalised for bare necessities now that supplies were running decidedly thin) furnished on bits of recycled maquette the escape documents for those last remaining Nazi brass without the decency to follow their maker's dog into the mass suicide they themselves had orchestrated — including none other than Reichsführer Himmler himself, fitted up for an improvised "démarche" via Lüneburg, destination undisclosed. Poor Himmler, his escape was curtailed by his own wretched fastidiousness & a pathological concern for detail that'd caused the "Ministry" to not only provide flawless simulacra of the real deal (easily enough obtained, had secrecy not been of the utmost, just across the corridor from the "Personnel Department"), but to somehow ensure the paperwork was altogether *too much* in order. A non-com of the Second British Army making a routine check of civilian refugees thought something not quite kosher about this little bespectacled fellow in the hat who turns out to be the only blighter in weeks to have *all* his bleedin' papers present & stamped, travel pass, paybook, the fully monty — place of issue: Golem City. *Weeell, we'd better take a look at this, eh, Mr, er, Hitzinger is it? Just step this way if you'd be so kind, sir. What's that? Cat got yer tongue, has it…?* [♣]

be, wouldn't it? Turning the mental faculties to canned lard. The hours of walking followed by the hours of sitting. The self-sufficient entropy. Němec slid the bottle out of his pocket. There were still two good slugs of booze left. He downed one, breathed the fumes out through nostrils half-cauterised already by the molten air. Downed the second. Wrung the bottle by the neck. Lazily he tossed it into the water. *Splock!*

The ducks gave him an admonishing stare. *Quaguack! Quaguackuackuack!* Němec smiled down on them with Socratic benevolence. Concentric lines of scum settled back into a brown half-mirror, poked through with limp reeds. Němec leant forward without quite tipping & peered between his feet. Ah, there he was, down there in the sludge, the mad Rabbi's lookingglass, like a Golem drowned in its own sorrows…

Golem's Lament

And all the best years turn to mud…
And the hag that eats you from the inside out
talks like a boatload of Russian ventriloquists.
And Time's a needlejack on a carousel,
a hundred chairlegs and a flagon of rum,
pizzicato TV static, and 'You can go to hell'
says the eyeball kid with the plastic gun.
They've all got tax returns tattooed on their faces
and a midget on each shoulder — 'Its too late
to stand your own ground,' they tell you,
'the past only makes peace with the ones it buries.'
And the committees in their underwear proffer
palm-courts and free disposal. And the wallpaper
covering the sky keeps peeling. And dust
settles over everything in the belly of the whale…

Somewhere after midday one turned into two. Arse numbed, rubbing a little life into it, Němec hunched back to the tram shelter to contemplate the journey in reverse. Like the dialectic of childhood nightmares, the thing & its opposite, the inescapable thesis, the inevitable antithesis. The terminus was a tin roof on stilts with a wooden bench missing all its slats. Weeds swayed in puddles of slowly evaporating piss. A stray dog (the same, perhaps) dragged its arse along the gravel. A rat stirred a bit of undergrowth. The air was thick & hot & stank of engine oil, tar & effluent. The tram stood there baking in the sun, the driver asleep with a wet rag on his head, fag plastered to bottom lip. Němec could feel the sun burning through the crown of his Chaplin hat, shoe soles roasting on pavement. He leant on his stick, swayed, bent into a sliver of shadow growing ever thinner. A chorus of insects sawed the air…

Němec woke to the sound of the tram bell clanging. A somnambulist's stagger up the steps, arse planted on baked plastic, jolted forward, the sudden movement after stasis. And voilà, the river once more thrusting in upon him, snaking north, a mirror of blue-pink-red, taking its cues wherever they come — a watery disc of sun tangled in the branches of TV aerials, the blackness of the hole of Vyšehrad, flaring upon the City in all its vagrancy, the eight bridges lined up like deckchairs for invalids, a hot-air balloon like a blind eye tethered to the embankment, the river tapering off beneath the Metronome on the Hill, filling in the null spaces of the mind beyond, transformed by nothing but a POV — the same narrative in a different arrangement, light fading on Neolithic burial markers, druidic circles, illegible time-travel maps of a place lost within itself, their key as blank as a name left blank: ▲.

A Girl & a ☞

At Moráň, Němec poured himself off the tram & down to the quays, past the riverclock. The transition barely registered now, as hot down by the water as it'd been on the street — mopping sweat from brow, hat-band soaked through, a Dead Sea tidemark bleaching the felt. His suit stuck to him like a wet plaster mould starched stiff by the late sun even by the time he was halfway to Palacký Bridge. A "MEYER'S" catering van was parked out across the walkway with its shutters down & aircon unit making dervish sounds. A film crew was set up on the other side of it in the shade of tents & umbrellas along the section of the quayside that used to be the Friedrich Engels Embankment & before that Reinhard Heydrich Ufer. Most of the crew appeared to be killing time in a kind of trance — a couple were man-handling an oversized electric fan, trying to get it to blow in a direction it didn't seem able to blow in.

Under the arch of the bridge was a scene like a railway siding at the end of the War where an army of extras had all been marshalled. Like everyone else they were waiting for something, reading, sleeping, bumming smokes. Over the west side of town slivers of dark cloud were now visible, in advance of the thunderheads. In a few hours you'd be able to smell the rain coming. Or not, the slow boiling broth evaporating into nothing. Like an interloper in a wrong timeframe, Němec lurched among the marooned film crew towards his destination. A little way along the embankment a wooden shack, which could've been part of a film set but wasn't, fronted the river with tables arranged outside — a hand-painted sign nailed above the doorway said:

U HAJZLU

Němec took a seat at the edge of the water — reddened by the sun going down behind Petřín. A waitress was standing on a chair, winding-in the cloth awning. A dog (where do they all come from, these dogs?) leapt into the river, chasing a stick someone had just thrown in. Within the shack, a shadow stood dazed behind the bar leaning on the taps like a handclapping monkey with the key wound down. The waitress got down from the chair & the dog came over & shook itself generously. Němec sat there wiping the sweat & dogwater out of his eyes & ogled the barman, the dog, the waitress, the film crew.[*]

'What'll it be, pal?' the waitress grunted.

He ordered a carafe of the house's finest box white, ice on the side.

'Real funny guy,' flipflops dragging on the flagstones.

Němec leant back into his chair & soaked up the rest of the scenery. You had to wonder how far the mercury would go before it all started to melt. The wine, when it came, was cold enough to make the glass glisten wetly. While he gulped it, the streetlights came up on the far embankment.

He rearranged himself against the hot chairback, jacket glued to his shirt, the black of it looking decidedly faded by now. Brought to mind the bums who lived in the railway tunnels, one in particular he remembered who had some sort of hole in his head & walked around with a ratty dinner jacket gone in the elbows. It was because he chewed them in his sleep, they said, it was a nervous condition, been in his family for generations — greatgrandad Rostislav in his day had been famous for it. There was even a statue dedicated to the man, supposedly, in a suburb of Pardubice that'd been bombed flat during the War. Němec ran into the bum on his first night out of the Home. The guy looked harmless enough so eventually he'd got up the nerve to ask him —

'Mister, how'd you get that hole in your head?'

---

[*] Who knows, maybe they were waiting for the fuses up in the sky to blow, to break the tension, create a bit of atmosphere. God on high with His rain machine. They'd hit the lights & an immediate power-out would bring the City to a grinding halt & the dark once more would descend. So much for that — have to shoot the scene as a blackout. Realism. [✋]

'Oh, you know,' the bum shrugged, 'same as everyone.'

Němec flexed his elbows uncomfortably against the arms of the chair to make room for himself inside his sleeves. He'd always wondered how the fuck a man could chew his own elbows, but he'd seen stranger things, like that double-jointed trapeze artist who could bend backwards with her head between her knees. Kludský Circus. Well, not exactly, but her picture on a flyer that'd been pasted up all over Václavák. She was balancing with her chin on a pole, arms outstretched & one leg cantilevered over each shoulder. It'd looked so impossible he'd supposed it had to be real. Hell, forty years of Commie trash running the joint, you couldn't assume anything anymore, people'd spent so long telling themselves white was black they didn't know which way was up. Like the Bugman said, *When the bilge pumps stop working, better toss all yer fancy assumptions overboard fast, kiddo, unless you want a ride straight down the plughole.*

After the first glass of Müller the heat wasn't so cloying anymore, the blood cooled, the body groaned a little less, the pain in the proverbial arsehole ebbed by slow yet steady declensions & the mind of its own accord went if anything blanker, unmoored itself, drifted. The river, the film crew, the lights of U Hajzlu. How far it all seemed from the mysteries of the deadman & medieval robot-conspiracies. A rusty barge laden with gravel steamed towards Jiráskův Most on its way north — Dresden, Hamburg — a freight train crossed the viaduct — the brick chimneys of the Staropramen Brewery glowed in the dusk like a picture. He laughed quietly to himself without moving his lips, which were faintly wet. The feeling of once more being a spectator of some incomprehensible piece of theatre, no longer of a film passing before his eyes but of the dull unwinding mechanism that caused the film to run: wheels with ratchets, dwarfs in costumes turning the cranks, weary technicians jamming screwdrivers & wrenches into the works to keep the whole thing ticking over. Even when nothing at all appeared to be happening.

Němec tipped back his glass, sucked some ice. Time passed, the sense of entropy deepened as the sky blackened finally. Then someone did hit the switch. A dozen haloes faded-up around the bridge. At the top of the embankment, three War-era saloon cars turned down a ramp. The haloes swivelled. Bugs spiralled in the big arc lights. In the background, strange chiaroscuros warped the latticework of the viaduct. A passenger train, unscripted, flickered across it, squares of yellow light like celluloid fed through an anachronistic projector.

The waitress passed by again & a second carafe, no sooner asked. The wine working the bloodstream. The back & neck. Specifically the neck. Another barge, this one hooded with a green-&-black tarpaulin, came sputtering alongside the quay. Gangplanks clattering against the flagstones, refugees cramming aboard. Němec blinked. A white flare arced high over the water. A voice called through a bullhorn. Gunfire. And somewhere, a world away, a man vanishing into thin air...[*]

---

*DOPPELGÄNGER

1. It was "the last days of the War," the Nazis evacuating by any & all possible means, civilians thronging the quays, the roads out choked with military traffic for miles on end. In a matter of days, possibly even hours, the river would be running straight through Red Army lines -- it's a race against the clock, a mad gamble -- that, or try making it through the suburbs on foot with whatever you can carry, though it's an even bet if the partisans don't get you, Vlassov's boys will.

2. Watching the exodus below with a detached, fatalistic calm, Elsbeth von N____ stands at a fourth-storey window looking down over the embankment -- beside her, a man, indeterminately older, whose features resemble her own to an uncanny degree &, like her, observes the embarking refugees with curious disinterest, as if it were a scene that'd been repeated from the dawn of time & would go on repeating itself, _ad infinitum_, till the bitter end, having nothing whatsoever to do with either one of them.

3. Curious, because the man standing beside Elsbeth von N____ is wearing the uniform of an Oberst in the SS, though by appearance he'd be more at home in a dinner jacket sitting at a roulette table -- neither of these, however, reflects the true character of this strange twin, whose very existence is nothing if not circumstantial.

4. Behind them, lying on a parlour table, is an open attaché case, a Gestapo evidence-tag still attached to its handle, its contents obscured by shadow.

5. As the two figures stand there at the window, pair of motionless silhouettes, mere silhouettes to whoever at street-level could possibly have them under surveillance at this late stage in the game, there comes the sound of someone knocking at the door.

6. Immediately the silhouettes dissolve into blackness -- a scuffing of shoes on parquet, hasps being snapped into place, the clacking of highheels & then a faintly lit rectangle at the end of the hallway as Elsbeth von N____ unlatches the apartment door, attaché case in hand... No sign now of her grey doppelgänger, only the oddly familiar figure facing her across the threshold who, with a little stretching of the imagination could almost be you, transported back in time forty years, while simultaneously in Elsbeth von N____'s place, coolly regarding you from the shadowed doorway, the (can it be?) spitting image of Alice Steinerová -- ash-blonde, black calfskin gloves, black dress, black patent leather boots. Lips, also, black.

7. And just to put the seal on it, she's holding a small nickelplated pistol in her free hand. It's an image from a film, but you can't remember which one. She's holding the gun in her right hand with her elbow against her waist, pointing it at you the way they used to in the good old days, when dames only pointed guns at the men they fell for.

8. You want her to say something, anything. She gives you a black sneer -- _Don't kid yourself fella. You ain't my type_ -- eyes glacial, like the threat of some kind of sexual punishment...

But the image was all an invention of Němec's reeling brain — he was staring at an enigma, a play of light reflected in the water. The filmcrew was wrapping up, the extras gone home, one or two

Es war einmal ein Mann

By the time the film people had done with their clapperboards for the day, packed up their trucks & switched off the picture, Němec felt like he'd been drinking for fifty years & still parched to the bone. The klieg lights along the embankment strobed & their reflections in the river fizzled & flared, blinking — out in the aftershock of mind's-eye convulsion therapy, of stirred fluvial undercurrents, of illicit sedimentations, of the sweet wafting scent of salt, sulphur, mercury. Němec meanwhile, somewhat woozy from the bends

---

sharing a drink at the bar, music from a further room seeping out into the night — Bessie Smith circa pretelevision in a Paris nightclub: it conjured all sorts of things — prowling figures in streets bathed with a reddish dusky glow, crepuscular basement dives, speakeasies, greasyspoons, faceless men & women hungry for danger, hips pressed in narrow stairwells, the rough embraces of belt-buckled strangers in alleyways, unremembered coinslot transactions in cubicles stinksmelling of rancid whiskeyvodka jism cigarettes perfume (the very cheapest-of-cheap) clinging to every pore pimple pinhole... Or every poor pimp's peehole? → Chapter 61. [✊] It would've made a good story. End of the War, the Uprising, partisans seizing control of the communications nerve-centre — right there on the Square — wired into a network of radio transmitters & grey megaphones spread across the City, camouflaged into the drab, voices from the darkened maws of Metro exits, blacked-out culverts, doorways, trees, the very walls, the sky above — God talking. How the Nazis broadcast the deathlists, the transport lists, the lists of regulations daily revised, the rewards of collaboration, the promises of retribution — the partisans, signalling coordinates, mobilised, unpicking the mindforged manacles of a population under suppression, took the first tentative steps in the direction of a full-blown State Apparatus — *Wissen ist Macht* — the Krauts as good as doomed, the War over bar the shouting, the ℋ counter-thrust nothing more than the last convulsions of a beast in its deaththroes, lashing out, strafing the Altstädterring with everything they've got left: antiaircraft canons, tanks, heavy machine guns, incendiary bombs, *The whole nest must burn!* — Town Hall ablaze, ack-ack in the belfries, the Great Clock blown to smithereens, tracer fire streaking the cloud-cover, sirens & the constant boom of ordnance going off all down a line running nor'-east across the Square (& on, down Celetná Street & under the Powder Tower), intersecting the meridian at an acute ∢ to form a giant *V-for-Viktoria* — right where the Krauts had painted their own *V* in 1941 (when the going was still good) in white & black directly on the flagstones, proclaiming the official faith, though mostly obscured now beneath the ash & general erasure of History being unwritten — the N.K.V.D. boys already busy scrubbing out the opposition, on either side: come V-Day... well. *You do business with the Devil*, as Blecha opined, *expect to get poked in the arse by Mephistopheles. Or maybe it's the other way 'round. Same thing in the end, hehe.* 10 May, 1945, the first representatives of the Cheskoslovnikian government to return from exile, flown in for the occasion on Stalin's personal Tupolev: fellow-travelling Zdeněk Fierlinger, P.M., alongside the grinning Chairman of the Cheskoslovnikian Communist Party in exile, Klem-as-in-Gottwald, who next day in a speech to the nation (broadcast on all frequencies) will proclaim the nation's official Liberation courtesy of Marshal Stalin & the glorious Red Army: *Now we must lay firm foundations for a new and happy life in a free, veritably democratic, truly people's Cheskoslovnikia and never (never never) permit a return to the pre-Munich days!*

(timetravel does that, folks, you don't pull out of it gradual-like), knocked the glasses back, building up a steady rhythm, trying to drown an alien thirst that only seemed to enlarge…

Es war einmal ein Mann,
Der hatte einen Schwamm.
Der Schwamm war ihm zu naß,
Da ging er auf die Gass'.
Die Gass' war ihm zu kalt,
Da ging er in den Wald.
Der Wald war ihm zu grün,
Da ging er nach Berlin.
Berlin war ihm zu groß,
Da wurd' er ein Franzos'
Franzos' wollt' er nicht sein,
Da ging er wieder heim
Zu seiner Frau Elise,
Die kocht' ihm grün Gemüse.
Da mußt' er dreimal niesen:
Hazzi! Hazzi! Hazzi![*]

His head swam in the rediscovered dark — hands, heavy & awkward, possessed unintentions of their own, slopping wine all over shirtfront & tablecloth, a real masterpiece you could hang in the Prado. Like a mindreader the waitress reappeared: *Howzabout another, love?* The waitress gave that longsuffering look some waitresses have & said *Closing time, buster,* swinging a chair up onto the table as if to convince a doubtful Němec that his number was up, that it had been for some time & would remain so for the duration. The barman hung his rag over one shoulder & stood in the doorway leering. In the distance, the filmcrew struck-up a mournful blues as the closing credits rolled:

Now they're sweepin' up another Saturday night.
A ten-dollar jane by a tired streetlight.
Drove a steamboat through the desert —
Broke an angel on a spoon —
Sold yer mama to the Devil for a sequin moon…

Time to climb into his hat & sail home, said the pelican to the porpoise, the

---

[*] "There once was a man from Hamelin, who worked in a pesticide factory — GIFTGAS! — sneezed, *achoo!* went out of his wits, & died." More or less. [❦]

poor puss, the pissed parrot, the prating prat…

Wending a way along the embankment, the *en passant* of ein Pissant, more under the weather than on top of his form, a bit unballasted, finding his sea-dog legs, rudderless in high seas, four sheets to the wind, sloothered as any sailor has a right to be, blind as a bat, shitfaced as a shyster, drunk as the Devil, as a piper, as a lord, as an owl, as David's sow, well & truly inebriated for want of a better word, arseholed, baked, banjaxed, bazookaed, belgiumed, bent, blitzed, bolloxed, bombed, bowdlerized, buggered, cabbaged, canned, codswallopped, corked, crocked, dazed, demolished, D.O.A., dragooned, drainpiped, eggplanted, embalmed, fandangoed, fried, fritzed, fucked, gangplanked, gestapoed, golemed, hangered, hanovered, jazzed, jokered, kamikazed, kibbutzed, lozenged, lugered, maimed, mangled, mashed, munted, neutered, nuked, obstreperous, octapused, ossified, ostled, pillocked, plonkered, potted, primed, ratted, roasted, schlemieled, schnitzelled, scoused, scrooched, scuppered, scuttled, skittled, slaughtered, soaked, stewed, tanked, trolleyed, uglied, untermensched, wankered, wasted, wellied, wrecked, zapped, zombied, zonked, zorched, zozzled, zzz…

Not the time or place for elevation of purpose & dignity of language — *eh, Squillhead?* Slosh, slosh. Eyes peering hungry out from shadows at this drunken clown in sideways-tipped chapeau anglais, stick beating the flagstones in countertime to babble of limericked doggerel:

> *There was a poor boy from Písek,*
> *whose prick was as thick as his neck —*
> *he provoked the cruel hunger*
> *of old witch Babajaga,*
> *who stuffed it down like biftek — dah-dum —*
> *who stuffed it down like biftek.*[*]

A swelling cackle in amongst the chiaroscuro. Whose? Clown-self ascending by graded incline to the street & brightness of streetlights, from dark profundia to pellucid proprium — *slowly now, or you'll get the bends.* Further on, the lights-fantastic flickered & dimmed beneath the viaduct. Steps. Iron rungs. Clown-self ascending one higher plane at a time, handrail gripped, by degrees rising above the traffic in a maze of slanted girders — giant rivets like dead carp eyes staring out. Between the girders, the coloured lights of the yachts moored below

---

* A prime fillet. [☛]

Vyšehrad made a golden weft through the green silk of the water.

The Magic Carp

A huddled shape on the bridge coughed, hand out for change. Pocket. Fumble. Silver falling out, ringing on the girders. Silent splash. Fish eyes & dark fish mouth. Gulp. The royal carp with a lion, rampant, double-queued, *Regnum Bohemiae*, lodged in its muddy gullet. The bum spat out a curse. Get what you paid for. Stagger. Down there, river-belching, whiskered, scales of tarnished lamplight, sixty miles long & six miles wide, the giant carp of yore that burst the banks, hooked on a magician's mock moon — hoist up up up into the sky — & old Babajugs muttering her spells, getting astride it, hagface pointing into the wind, as fins aflap the carp with the silver mooncoin in its mouth in the twinkling of an eye swims airily east to Damascus, west to the Pillars of Hercules, wherever the crone witch willeth — be that place near at hand or distant many a day's journey & difficult to reach, beyond thrice-nine lands, in the thrice-ten kingdom — verily as if it'd leapt from the pages of some book of wonders, the *Qala'id-al-Jawahir* of Shaikh Muhammad ibn Yahya al-Tadifi al-Hanbali, or the Book of Solomon, greatest & wisest. Celestial fisheyed Pisces of the constellated heavens. Not all the carp ponds of Třeboň! Foolish thought. *Let me climb up on your back there. Witch, move over*! Straddling the handrail, clutching for dear life, feet grown heavy, intimations of vertigo. The bum's dry cackle. 'Jump! Jump! What're you waiting for, idiot?' *A coin, gobbed-up out of nowhere, magic carp my eye.* 'Jump you cheap bastard, I don't got all night! Get on with it! Yer stinking up the scenery! This here's my bleedin' bridge. Bugger off or get off! Come on, come on!' Up from his beggar's box swinging with a walkingstick now. *Where'd I put it? Let it slip climbing up. Beaten with my own third leg!* 'Jump you lousy rotten shit!' *Fall down flat and you'll be right on top of him, taste of his own medicine. Get hold of that stick and don't let go — dog at a bone — eh? Where'd he get to? Poof! Vanished! Babajugs' mangy cur. Fooled yerself again! Nobody watching? Straighten yer hat fer chrissakes, brush yer coat, no point hanging about making any more of a spectacle of yerself. Onward Pagan Footsloggers! And what if you fell in? Food for fishes. Carp sucking out your eyes, worms in your ears, a mouth full of eels. Full fathom five and all that. Cold down there, the proverbial chill up the spine, the prenominal pain in the arse.* Magic swordstick magically back in his hand, weaving the gloom. How the warm night air shivered! Heave of bridge toward further shore, shadow-filled — blackhole in the underside — mawmouth mouthing itself mawishly, fishlipped, slimescaled, the gaping one-eyed golem fish, the fishheaded alchemical anus, *chrysostomos...*[*]

Like Shootin' Fish in a Suitcase

The streetlights one by one were going out, but it wasn't morning yet when Němec returned along Jánský Vršek. A gibbous eye floated in the gloom, spelling the betweentime of neither night nor day: clockface with hands swimming backwards in slow melancholic strokes. Faint plash. *Lethe... Lethe... Oh Lethe...* Beating of the oars, the counterpoint, the silent interval — long, too-long, the swimmer against Time, *plash*, the invisible wake, the eye blinking, *plash*, & right there, in that non-instant, between all the other instants, a gap Time itself risked falling through, like the cracks in pavements children avoid for fear of the flesheating hag waiting down there to boil them in her stewingpot...

No light in the caretaker's apartment, shadows hanging from the scaffolds like bats asleep. Němec's staggered footfall alone disturbed the peace, slouching up the stairwell to heaven. At the top landing, a brown suitcase was waiting just outside the door of the Prof's apartment.[*] Maybe someone planned to visit? One of those Irving Berlin moments that demands a song:

Someone's coming to my house —

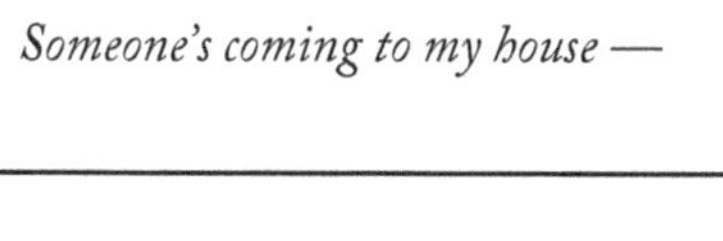

[*]FROM SHINOLA?

Like a beast at your back the rails hissed, the sleepers rumbled, the whole bridge rocked under the approaching nighttrain. Turning into the bright headlights, the wind, jolted back against the railing, stick jammed between girders to keep aloft -- faces staring out of celluloid moviereel so close you could've touched them. And then the darkness, again, grown darker. The rattling. Fainter. Diminishing. Rumble of departed thunder. And all around, out of the restored silence, that enormity of night welling up, becoming full as the ear grows anguished, of insects buzzing, the hum & snore of humanity, the backwash of distant traffic like a sea into which everything is inexorably tending -- waves & particles of entropy, the lights gradually growing out across the sky -- bearings all wrong, each step a contradiction of the one before. And that voice in the ear coming back, <u>You look like shit, pal. Who're you tryin' to con</u>? Wasn't even drunk anymore, the illusion was over, only a cloying sickness as familiar as an old friend -- <u>You & me, kid, fellow travellers</u> -- hic! -- <u>to the last</u>... Lurching railing-wards, <u>Hurrghuh!</u> The wind blew back a fine spray. Something splashed in the river, yellow-finned, red-tailed. The waters swirled & drew off that thin spattering of bile into their tireless, irrevocable course.

[*] *Eee-ooo-eee-ooo!* Sehr spooky. (Here we go again, kids...) [♣]

Predawn glowed like a blank television through the windows. *Time to lie down in yer coffin 'n' die the death, old fang.* Not wishing to disturb the suitcase lest it wake up & maybe start shouting... Was there something he'd forgotten about? Door-to-door delivery? Had he been expecting anyone? The proverbial unexpected guest, perhaps? The sweetheart he left down in New Orleans? Some Petrushka from St Petersburg? The redheaded Rusalka of childhood wet dreams? The Mamitati who'd found their posthumous way back to yourstruly their longlostlittleloveoftheirlives, bundled-up in a carryall? Or, what if the place'd been auctioned-off while he was out getting pillocked & the rightful owner at that very minute, wrapped up asleep inside, etc.? And what if...?

Taking the matter in hand, Němec knocked tentatively on the door. Ear pressed. Nothing. Knocked louder. Keys, dug out from pocket with an effort of endearment that brought a blush to his own cheeks, working them (the keys) one at a time till the right one, teeth clenched, fumbling the lock, easing the hinges &, stepping forward into the dark *kbosht!* Tripped legless on stubbornly unyielding doorstep. *Shhhhh!* Getting his stick back under him to grope sidelong down the hall, this room, that room. *No-one here, you idiot!* Weaving back to rehitch the door, suitcase still sitting out there by the doormat like it was Moses in a basket expecting the royal treatment. *Not tonight, thanks love.* A swift ineffectual boot to send it packing. *Plonk.* Hoiked after it in fond farewell, getting the better part of the slithery gob all down his stubbled chin, mouth brimming still with putrid bile-stink. Doorslam, two turns (to the right this time), locked. *If ya think I'm fallin' for that one again... Fuckers. Go bother someone else for a change.* Wanting it, whatever *it* was, rid of. Not there. Gone. Wanting everything rid of, if truth be told (& who else was there to tell it to?), but the strength of will, ah yes, the strength of will. A bit lacking in that department.

34

THE RAT AWAKENS TO THE MYSTERIOUS OBJECT IN ITS CAGE

Now some things look different in the full light of day & some things look exactly the same. That suitcase, for example. Nothing you'd call distinctive about it, except it was old, brown, with metal clasps & dented on one side. And it was *there*. The sort of thing you'd expect to find gathering dust atop a wardrobe in a basement bazaar, among the plastic shoehorns & engineers' tie-pins, the train conductors' caps, satchel bags, fake crystal decanter sets, horn-rimmed glasses, capped Beijing-manufacture leather shoes, carpet beaters of intricately woven cane, brown polyester suit jackets, beaver hats, faded watercolours in gilt frames, ceramic urns, eggcups, cut-glass candlesticks, grotty chandeliers, rococo sugar bowls, dumpling slicers, portable Russian TVs, aluminium cutlery, rusty potato peelers, melted drillbits, embroidered tablecloths, vinyl pencil cases, stainless steel toothpick holders, asbestos-backed radiators, clothes baskets, chipped soup pots, ratchet can-openers, once-upon-a-time beige girdles, hair nets, goulash pressure-cookers, rubber douche bags with nozzle attached, colostomy bags, wheelie-bags in brown&red plaid, plastic shopping bags replete with naked ladies printed in mismatched colour registration, oversized drawstring binbags, hessian bushel bags & bags woven from remnants of varying type, hair-pieces, table-clamp meat grinders, assorted antlers mounted on trophy-boards, buffalo horns, animal skins, cracked mirrors in plastic frames, fold-out stepladders, wire coathangers, shoe cupboards, headboards, sideboards, dartboards & chessboards, glasseyes, zimmerframes, wristwatches, bifocals, trifocals, signet rings, keychains, defunct coins, ribbons with service medals attached…

As a bit of detective work, it didn't seem too promising from the outside. Item: one standard issue travel case of vulcanised reddish-brown vinyl, paint-stained with black vinyl band edging it, dark brown plastic handle, two nominally stainless steel clasps. Heavier than it looked. Well, once he'd dusted himself off, what else was Němec to do but drag the damn thing inside & out of harm's way, get a proper look at it, what any reasonable person would, wasn't it? After all, it wasn't like a bunch of Trojans had wheeled up to the Tower in the middle of the night & left it there like a gifthorse or anything, eh? *What if*, he thought, getting wise to where that particular line of thinking was headed, hoisting the case up onto the kitchen sink (too heavy for the caretaker to've dragged all the way up the stairs, mmm)… *What if the fucker's boobytrapped? Open sesame and BOOM! No more Němec.*[*]

He stood there catching his breath, head ringing, little worms of light boring into his eyes, blotting the suitcase out as surely as if it'd…

A wave of peristalsis interrupted this pleasant thought & in a sudden involuntary reflex Němec doubled over the kitchen sink & gagged down the plughole. He gagged repeatedly, but all that came up was the stale taste of last night's vomit. The tap whistled & the pipes thumped. Gulping water, he managed to throw-up finally, a cold translucent bile all in a single gush. Well, if they thought he'd be a pushover, they had another thing coming alright. Panting, Němec wiped his mouth with his sleeve, gave the suitcase one hard-ass sideways beady-eyed stare. *What you need for a job like this*, he decided, once he'd gotten his breath back, flexing a pair of bony shoulders inside his crumpled suit, *is a goddamn drink*. He groped around the counter & came up with a package of the Chink's coffee beans instead. Was that what he'd been looking for? He couldn't remember already, but why not, clear the head, get the old intestines working. He went through the motions of brewing a pot. It gave him time to ponder, which mightn't've been such a good idea.

---

[*] And there ends our narrative, kids. Meanwhile, in other news… [☞]

You think he should've had any scruples about opening that proffered Pandora's junkbox? A more palpable sense of foreboding? The coffee bubbled in the pot. *Maybe*, he thought. There were a lot of maybes. Like, maybe the rightful owner was going to turn up at any minute & it'd get Němec into trouble, tut-tut, opening someone else's suitcase like that, like a common thief. Ooh, that was a good one. Or, maybe someone really was moving in — come to take over the Prof's apartment, a long-lost relation maybe — gone off to the advocate's office to get a key, 'cos the caretaker must've misplaced hers, eh — nothing doing till the a.m., start of business hours & all that — could be on their way back right this very minute, about to walk in & find Němec stinking the place up — give him the boot — call in the Law, have him up for trespass, break & enter, daylight robbery, false pretences, mistaken identity, violation of the health code, malapropism & unauthorised possession of disoccupied premises. Not like he had much of a leg to stand on, *hehe*, was it?[*]

Němec entertained the idea of such a concerned party: medium height possibly, hair on the darkish side, thinning. Toupee perhaps. Or a wig. Woman of a certain age, knee-length skirt, sunglasses, looking just a little put-out by the appearance of this interloping oddity in undertaker's black polyester. But, well, since the opportunity's arisen, so to speak, & it being terribly warm outside & hot under the collar... *Don't get too fancy now, kiddo.*

Dum-dum-dum.

How about, just to throw some flesh on it, give the above stated party some presence, you know, elaborate a bit while pondering the next obvious step, etc., & thereby passing the time till his (Němec's) brain settled back into its usual torpor, for shits & giggles so to speak:

(1) male Caucasian, tall, slightly stooped, wearing a beaver on his head even in mid-summer-pushing-on-thirty-degrees, anorak, tan shoes & dark grey woolblend trousers, part-time employment as a concierge, shared apartment in Braník maybe, type who rides the bus to work every day. Could just picture him waiting at a busstop, beaver, suitcase, smoker's cough, slightly stooped. Yes. No.

Or, conversely:

(2) female Caucasian, blow-dry, former-secretary type, a mite on the short side, carrying a little extra weight around the hips thighs ankles, cardigan, flat shoes, found the suitcase clearing out the Prof's cubicle at the university (now there's a capital idea: papers locked in a desk, a cupboard that hadn't been

---

[*] Christ, can't he just get on with it? [✊]

opened in donkey's years, a box of books with the Prof's name scribbled on the flyleaf, ex libris, old course-notes, bits & pieces of stationery, chess scorecards, expired tram tickets, letters stuffed inside envelopes, several unread, unopened, clotted fountain pens, rubber stamps & desiccated ink pads, elastic bands, thumbtacks, paperclips, clutch pencils, magnifying glass, scotch tape, whiteout, typewriter ribbons, staples, twine, a pocket calculator, small change, things once deemed of value, hoarded, forgotten about — maybe a change of undershirts, a spare tie for occasions — after all, what would you expect a man like the Prof to leave behind in an office drawer, filing cabinet, desk, that a secretary would only bother about well after the Old Josser was already dead?) & brought it all the way over here, hauled it up the stairs (*O dear, no-one home!*) & left it outside the door forgetting to leave a note, but very well-meaning nonetheless. Or who knows maybe there *was* a note, like a regular suicide, only a magpie got to foraging for nest-trinkets & flew in through the stairwell window &, well, *absconded* with it, eh? Or the rats. Yes, not to forget the rats. Always busy, those little chaps, never know, when you next turn around, just quite what, etc. Hell, maybe it was the rats who delivered the suitcase, kind of *offering*, to one of their own, so to speak — did you even blink to consider that possibility, eh?[*]

Mmmmm, maybe.

"Maybe" had all these fascinating corollaries, but the suspense was beginning to wear a bit too thin to keep trying them on for size.[*]

Němec took hold of the suitcase in a businesslike manner & thumbed back the clasps (they were stiff but not too stiff; not, thankfully, *locked*) — the lid, misshapen from years of being overstuffed, had to be prised up. Doing so, Němec got a lungful of mildewed air. But that was all.

As far as surprises went, this one was pretty dull. The inside lining was brown-on-beige, with what'd once upon a time been a name-tag glued under the lid. The rest of the suitcase was taken up by a package, foolscap & about four inches thick, wrapped in yellowed newsprint & tied with bailing twine. Again the typed card: **NEMOC**. The (painfully) inevitable déjà vu sinking in.

Once was chance, "maybe." But twice, was just taking the piss.

---

[*] Oh puh-leaze! [⬇]
[*] You don't fucking say? [⬇]

Run Rat Run!

Staring out of the newsprint beside the typed card was a story about plans by T.E.S.L.A. Corp to harvest renewable energy from ratpowered treadmills. *Really?* Němec peered a little closer. Apparently, they planned to outfit the sewers with one-&-a-half million of them, wired to the City's grid. If one rat could produce ten kilowatts per day, imagine what could be achieved by harnessing the potentially unlimited supply of city rats! Wow, that was some news. It seemed they were gearing up for possible knock-on benefits in all sorts of areas of City Life. When was that supposed to've happened? The article spoke about Rat Callisthenics, a "Rat Aggregate" & the "Rodental Algorithmic."[*] There was even a helpful diagram of a rat's brain to aid the novice reader…

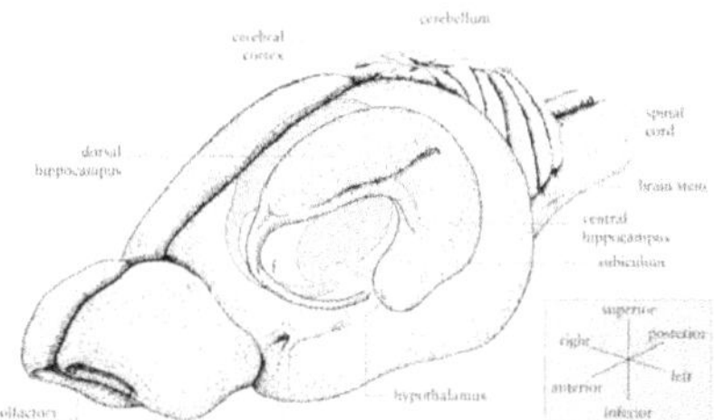

Fig.1 Diagram of Rat Brain to aid Novice Reader
(Osrick & Dupont, 1972, p. 1043)

By way of a footnote, it was also announced that scientists meanwhile in Berlin had succeeded in wiring together the brains of two albino laboratory rats ("Chesk" & "Lesk" the pair of cute little rodents were endearingly named). "Rat telepathy," explained one Dr Schmitts, T.E.S.L.A. Corp spokesperson,[*] "could indeed have far-reaching implications for humanity." Němec wondered how he'd missed hearing about that one before. The adjoining columns were all just the usual fare of the weekend supplements: the family of Luděk Pachman contesting an exhumation order to resolve by DNA a long-standing paternity dispute; an

---

[*] "Dave? I'm afraid, Dave…" [♦]

[*] Dr Wieland F.G. Schmitts, former director of neuropsychiatry at Berlin Freie Universität Medical School & author of *The Rat Mind: Toward a Psychosocialised Civilisation* (1972). Schmitts' major methodological innovations, outlined in more than 200 scientific papers, included the permanent implantation of electrodes in the brain; intracerebral chemitrodes & dialytrodes; brain pacemaker implantations; brain radio stimulators; two-way radio communication brain-to-computer; time-lapse recording of social behaviour in rat colonies; & the invention of applied political neurology. [♦]

elderly woman in Strašnice found partially eaten by eight pet Siamese cats (authorities estimated she'd been dead a week, neighbours had reported an offensive smell); a bomb hoax on the downtown A-train again being blamed on Š.V.E.J.K. terrorists; while at Baikonur, Russian cosmonauts…

Chinese Boxes

He'd have to unwrap the damn thing if he wanted to read more. It was all starting to look like so much hard work. For all Němec knew, it'd be the sort of thing that as soon as you got started, you'd find yourself lumped with the same thing all over again, one identical package inside another *all the way down*, like peeling an onion to a kernel of nothing. Chinese boxes or whatever. Němec pulled at the twine but it was knotted tight, his fingers couldn't get the sense of it. A couple of bandylegged bums dancing around a seesaw. He gave it up, cast around for some other approach, nothing too obvious, & while his brain slipped a few cogs he slurped coffee straight from the pot, scalding his upper lip. So much for eventualities, when he couldn't even get started. *Němec, my friend, not your finest.* He wondered what the Prof would've done in his position, but then the Prof would never've been in his position. It was a thought he was sure he'd had before, probably many times.

To cut a long story short, our protagonist found his attention drifting from the matter-at-hand into various backwaters of vague speculation, like someone going over a hypothetical game of chess in their sleep, unable to help thinking it'd have to be a time like this, when he was so undisputedly *on top of his game*, haha, that the opposition would decide to pull a number on him — plant a real headwrecker under his nose, so to speak, just when he wasn't expecting it. And this thought, funny as it may seem, brought to mind the very tragic story of that infamous chess-nut, Dr Alekhine — really he was a lush, spent six years on the trot pissed to the eyeballs to salve his poor dear conscience for stooging for the fucking Nazis (his lawfully wedded wife, need it be said, was one of the *Nicest People on Earth*, a real bullion-in-the-bag Balabusta: he was a man, as the Overcoat Brigade never shied from reminding him, *deprived of a choice* — a hard place to be for an anointed chessboard Übermensch, used to having the proverbial boot firmly laced, so to speak, to the other foot). Němec felt only the vaguest tugs of sympathy at the little heartstrings.

This Alekhine, as anyone who isn't a complete halfwit ought to know, was the very byword of bigheadedness — he'd done Capablanca to death, & that was no mean feet. But after the nicens little Nazis got their claws into him, he turned into a regular pissant with a gutful of his own bile. If he wasn't legless under a Parisian café table, he was blowing off steam about the Bolsheviks & putting his moniker on magazine articles about the Noble Game & Race Theory (the man was a bonafide aristocunt, lest we forget). After the War the N.K.V.D. boys strangled him in a Lisbon hotel room. *Hora de morrer, idiota*! Well, you equalise on the pieces but it's the pawn that does you in.[*]

Maybe there was hope for Němec yet? The soft touch, the strawman keeping himself in the dark for the sake of a moment in the sun, a blind rat in an invisible cage, the poisoned pawn giving you a taste of your own medicine, the creeping fullstop at the termination of a cryptic sentence. *Conscience is a fine thing, kiddo, but they'll stick you in the end, either way...*

> 'That ain't me!' says the patsy, pulling the wool over his own eyes.
> 'Stampeded to death in the bum's rush,' says the old timer. 'Gone stupid waitin' round for the pay-off.'

Sound like anyone we know? Nursing his Hamlet crutch as if he's about to pull out the Ol' Third Leg Gambit & make a devastating play on the clock (*Is that a rat-catcher in yer pocket, or are you just amazed to see me, hawhaw*). The reason Goethe's all claptrap — 'cos ain't no-one cuts a deal with Beelzebubble to be the Big Cheese (who's kidding who? what, they think once they get their prize they can slide up & pop him one in the ear when he's not watching?) — the odds are always with the house, pal, but you play right & they'll maybe let you pocket the dice as a souvenir. When a man's in the hole, Paradise ain't world domination, it's keeping the Extortion Plan ticking over & the creditors sweet...

> 'Hey Sol, here's another one of them jokers says he's got a special clause in his contract, reckons he don't have to pay. What you want me to do, feed him to the fishes? Wouldn't wanna stink up no-one's Christmas dinner, it wouldn't be fair. Hell, this work really gets me down, you know what I mean? Goiters just ain't goiters no more...'

Maybe,[*] in the fog of the moment, not seeing all too clearly, but still awake, this being Němec's big moment — *Time to just hang it all, eh? Let 'em stew!* — what all those fifteen minutes were for — the play that decides the game, the wrong

---

[*] And his little queenie? What became of the little queenie? [☟]
[*] Another one, but who's counting? [☟]

move that sticks out in hindsight like a poke in the eye. Well you'd cry yourself silly, wouldn't you, not seeing a set-up like this coming! *Might as well put yer head on the block yourself, kiddo, as have someone do it for you.* And wasn't that neatly wrapped package there in that suitcase just the right size for some lucky character's head & room left over? Maybe a couple of arms & legs besides, the whole routine,* being one of those necessary steps in the pursuit of an unambiguous symbolic logic — the medium in some essential if ungainly sense equalling the message — *Think this's some sort of gag?*

If he'd been smarter he'd've let himself go back to sleep & forget the whole thing — maybe when he woke up again none of it'd be there anymore, the faeries would've come & taken it away, or if he slept long enough maybe the rats'd come & eat it. But it wasn't like Němec to play it smart. Not when there was always someone smarter to figure out the moves for him. So instead he went & managed finally to dig up one of those bottles of Moravian hooch he had lying around the place & got the dog hair out of his throat. That & another pot of coffee, bubbling on the stove, when the telephone rang. Němec let it ring till he had the coffee poured & the pot hissing in the sink, the smell of sodden grounds & burnt rubber thickening the air. When he picked-up there was a voice at the other end of the line that sounded like an overworked machine —

'You got our message,' it said, no question mark attached.

And before Němec could think, the line was already dead.

No doubt about it, problem's definitely yours, kiddo.

The bundle lay there in the suitcase with all the insolence of a Sphinx in someone's path, a real bedroom diva, who expects to be made a big production of & undressed like a floorshow before she'll condescend to let you tickle that prize riddle of hers & then maybe do you in for your trouble. It looked like a bum deal all down the line, but then you never can judge things solely on appearances. Or can you? Well what's to judge when you're in the dark & don't have a choice in the matter? Did Němec have a choice? *Message received.* "They" knew who he was, where he lived — maybe it was time to slip out of the picture, vamoose, be air. They'd've anticipated that, too, & had the full measure, no doubt. A pretty picture. Besides, he'd been through all this before: the Black Book, the general rigmarole. They held the board & Němec was indeed nothing

---

* *Drawn + Quartered,* by J.J. & Co. (digitally remastered). [✊]

but a paltry pawn, who could only see as far as the next square. Comforting thought, that. It was a role his entire upbringing had prepared him for, he'd had the very best teachers, he knew his part alright, had got his lines off by rote many yesteryears ago, oh he knew exactly what to do.

Another slug of brandy & then our hero manhandled that precious little Sphinxette onto the counter, that poisoned chalice, that perfumed Pandora. N-E-M-O-C. All his, she was. Němec slotted the typed card into a drawer, gave it a little pat, & pulled out a knife & went to work. It wasn't the most elegant of approaches, but if at first Mam'selle Netouche put up a pretence of résistance (NE! DOUBLE NE!! MOC NE!!!) it was only for show. Hacked twine & packing paper lay strewn about the counter like massacred petticoats. What spilled out were eight large folders & a thick envelope, brown, with a meshed webbing that also had to be cut open — with slightly more composure this time: inside it lay a bundle of glossy photo paper. *Not what you expected, eh, kiddo? Not the untold gruesome pleasures worthy of a Sphinx? Not the right type of "message"? Think you've been short changed? Taken for a rube? Ain't much, kiddo. Be glad it isn't your arse being served up to you. This time…*

Grabbing the bottle by the neck, Němec lugged the glossies out to the Prof's bureau to have a quiet flick-through sitting down, leaving the rest of the mess in the sink, suitcase & all. Looking at pictures wasn't exactly what you'd call brainwork — only these weren't pictures in any ordinary sense. Back to the wall, knees propped, coffee already gone tepid, Němec shuffled & reshuffled the deck of photostats, about a hundred of them all told, not making sense of any of it. Whatever they were supposed to be, the pics left only impressions, fleeting, incomplete, at moments bewildering, at others strangely lucid yet ungraspable. Like perving at snapshots from someone else's dream:

an ocherous landscape in calligraphic rifts & rivulets —
oases of verdurial green —
tuberous, clawed, scallioned —
lush mandibles, an azure lagoon-like eye —
estuarine, topographic —
the blue-white Nile headwaters of unmappable prosodies —
heraldic acanthus, *oiseau de paradis*, the hermetic waratah —
amber, millefiori —
sea urchin, crown of thorns, bell jar, canopic —
a seraphim & a crayfish, millipede, worm —
eight-petalled novae, a red-eyed fly dying on its back —

poniard, sotweed, mandrake, batwing, thistle —
three buzzards on a dunghill —
nightcap, squid, four suns, a spined rascasse —
wind-beaten corn, rain driving against bended trees, towers falling —
whole Dr Seuss menageries of xylem & phylum —
bubas, ziggurats, mandalas —
wheels within wheels, fecundating & refecundated —
zodiac star chambers, Pisces, carp-headed constellations —
a heavenly host of bloat-bellied fishwives —
gastroenteritic muses of the alchemical bile bucket —
mene mene, naked wombmen…

Jesus Christ! It was like a mutant child's hide-in-the-closet pornography, the metamorphic doodlings of a troglodyte with radiation sickness, a pathologist's collection of unfunny sick jokes, delusions of alchemical transmutation in the febrile mind of a person or persons clinically but mediocrely insane, gratuitous weirdness designed for no other purpose than to be gratuitously weird. Němec clutched his face in his hands. An awful sense of presentiment hung over him…

Rewind. Begin again at the beginning. Page one: a rectangle, faded umber, vellum, creased at the edges & heavily seamed. Page two: the obverse of the former, some pencil writing (faded), a catalogue number, a typed *ex libris* card pasted in —

Lux et Veritas
Yale University Library
Gift of
HANS P. KRAUS

With a confirming shudder did young Němec thus behold, in all its deadly locution, a veritable facsimile of the Prof's *corpus mysticum* itself, the Voynich Manuscript. Could it be?

The Carp will Stew
& the Rat will have his Day

Back in the kitchen, Němec laid the bundle down with all due reverence upon the sodden counter. So this was it, eh, the famous Proxy Polygraph? The summa

& apotheosis of a deadman's travail on this mortal coil? It wore its legend lightly, undistinguished at first glance, like an old man in a brown woollen suit you might pass in a library corridor & barely notice, unsure if he was ever really there. Or not a man, but merely the image of a man, a ghost…

And what would that prove?[*]

By such uncertain means the described sense of the Voynich Manuscript began to appear — the division into parts, botanical, astrological, chemical, allegorical — the unworldly floras & antipodean zodiacs, transmutation tables & mandala maps of the soul, of the personified imagination — anatomies of destining, hybrids, plant-animal: dumb mouths from which the teeth have been pulled — divinatory, oracular mouths — abstract, universal, unreal. The intertwining of the metaphysic & the physic, the mind-body, compendium of all things interconnected — the dyophysite nature of two principles balancing one another, active & passive, masculine & feminine, the eternal cycle of birth & death (as wrote Ibn al-Hassan ibn Ali al-Tajhara'i' in the *Keys of Mercy and Secrets of Wisdom*), describing thereby the composition of waters, movement, growth, embodying & disembodying, drawing the spirits from bodies & bonding the spirits within bodies: the alchemical vessel imagined as a baptismal font, the tincturing vapours of mercury & sulphur likened to the purifying waters of baptism — the krater or mixing bowl, a symbol of the divine mind — the sun, the right eye of the world…

Such things were not intended as poetry, but as an allegory of literal processes, a map of the cosmos in flux, in its many compositions & decomposition, words for what science had yet to construe. As for the naked muses — there were some who asserted that the fallen angels of Genesis taught the arts of metallurgy to the daughters of Eve they coupled with on Earth — those spurned (by God) menials of generation now concubined to the

---

[*] Because a facsimile isn't the thing itself (is it?) & yet, & *yet*, the photographic plates Němec held in his very own hot sweaty hands possessed (by Christ, they *radiated*!) an indubitable aura of veracity — if not the aura of the aura itself, imbued in the touch & feel of the "velum," the smell of it, the rustle of its leaves, then at least a certain verisimilitudinous *precision*, an exactitude of detail that went further than mere appearances to record, as it were, the fact of itself — that fact, so to speak, of the fact — as if, to be more exact, some hidden element of its *thingness* had been *brought into being* & thereby made manifest by some vital all-duplicating force. You could see it, for example, in the way that each facsimile recorded more than simply a page of the original manuscript, but the stitching & binding, the edges of other pages, parts of the cover, the indentation of the penmanship & the thickness & consistency of the dried ink. It seemed, Němec couldn't help thinking, more real than the original could ever have — as if it'd been necessary for the mystery itself to be photographed in order to become visible to the naked eye… [✥]

martyrdom of *Industria* — a notion likewise recorded in the Book of Enoch &
later repeated in the Gnostic Apocryphon of John. In a fragment set down for
posterity by the chronicler Syncellus, Zosimos versioned the story thus:

> *The ancient and divine writings say the angels became enamoured of women —*
> *and, descending, taught them all the works of nature. From them, therefore, is*
> *the first tradition, chema, concerning these arts — for they called this book*
> *chema and hence the science of chemistry takes its name…*

The Sphinx's Cod

And then there were the folders, eight of them,[*] each at first glance constituting
a type of album or miscellany. *The Sphinx's Code: Sketches for a Definitive Study of
the Voynich Manuscript?* Well, whadya know? If it wasn't the Old Man's perjured
polygraph.[*] Taking the top folder off the pile, Němec scanned the contents, back
to front. Reams of blue graph paper written-over, pasted-in, typed-on, scribbled
across, helterskelter. Many themes repeated & developed, but the discontinuities
were stark & numerous. Some pages faintly reminiscent of the "Black Book,"
clippings, jottings, pieces of paper with diagrams & lists — no devils asquat
panting Carmelites, alas.

The next folder was more or less the same, & the next after that. The
whole thing must've been a kind of philavery. Page after page of word lists &
transliteration tables undressed by approximation, phoneticised shembabble of
Persian, Hebrew, Coptic, Cushitic, Ruthenian, Ainu, Sanskrit, Ahlamu,
Ugaritic, Akkadian, Tigrinya, Assyrian, Babylonian, Proto-Sinaitic, Amharic,
Moabite, Amalekite, Ammonite, Amorite, Arabian, Mandaic, Maltese, Ge'ez,
Canaanite, Edomite, Phonecian, Eblaite, Carthaginian, Chaldean &, for the
pièce de résistance, a streaked photostat from Frederic Feydit's *Manuel de langue
arménienne* (1935).[*] Hardly Salomé's imprecation to John the Baptist. Christ,

---

[*] Of course there were. [✥]

[*] The plot does thicken. [✥]

[*] Taken at first glance, those Feydite figures resembled nothing as much as the doodlings of the
Voynich Manuscript — presumably why the Prof went to the trouble of, etc. Did the Old Man
therefore suspect the Manuscript came from somewhere in that dream-like region between East &
West, where the sun neither rises nor sets but is continuously born like a myth — Roman-Persian,
Zoroastrian-Greek — long before the Turks & the Crusades, the plunder of libraries, the market
in relics, the forgery of sacred texts, Knight Templars, Antioch, the fall of Byzantium, the
Kingdom of Jerusalem, exotic enchantments, toxic plagiarisms, the shrinking out of dark ages
towards enlightenment, rejoicing in the Word anewed, renascent, returning to Caesar what was

who'd the Old Man think he was, the next fucking Champollion? Yawn, yawn.
(Well, someone had to've been getting their kicks out of this, it can't all have
been a hard grind…) Turning to the next page, another ditty from Darwin, this
time (fittingly enough for Němec's foggily endoscopic literal mind here, peering
into the page like a fish peering into a periscope) on the evolution of languages.
Beneath which was written, in the form of a footnote, but with no obvious
connection to the preceding text, a further comparison of humans & animals,
this time with reference to the transmission of disease. It read:

> ☞ From the fundaments of certain languages, some philologists have
> inferred that *when man first became widely diffused, he was not a speaking
> animal* — but it may be suspected that languages, far less perfect than any
> now spoken, aided by gestures, might have been used, & yet have left no
> traces on subsequent & more highly-developed tongues. Without the use
> of some language, however imperfect, it appears doubtful whether man's
> intellect could have risen to the standard implied by his dominant position
> at an early period.[†]

---

† Man is liable to receive from the lower animals, & to communicate to them,
certain diseases. Such as hydrophobia, variola, the glanders, syphilis, cholera,

---

Caesar's (some bitch's brew hybrid of Hebrewed hagiography, Egyptianed epiphenomenality,
Margravial maladroit artifistry of the holiest mediocrity, *et seq.* & in amalgamation thereof, giving
rise to Pontius pictorials, Hermaphroditic heresies, & Caligulaed calligraphies coupled head-to-toe
like a duckbilled platypus?) — the Letter's literal typogenesis from Mesopotamia to Mycenae, a
Trojan trope (*greetings to Aeneas, you cad!*), a Parthian *passé-partout*, an Avestan avatar, moulded
from Mesrob Mashtot's missionary mottage — *Čanač'el zimastut'iwn ew zxrat, imanal zbans
hančaroy* ("to know wisdom & instruction, to perceive the words of understanding," amen) — &
thence, by monkish Cyril & conjugatory Methode, brought north to illiterate barbarian Sklavs,
masters to-come of historical fakery, anno domini Rudolphus Regis Romanorum, passing off a
rube for a Rubinstein on that pair of anachronistical make-a-buck-fast mystagogues — John D &
Eadweard K, both — touring the moneybags of Mitteleuropa, from England's Rose to the roe of
Rožmberk, thinking they'd stumbled on a veritable gem this time, not some pastparticipled musty
tome out of headloose Harry's monastic middenheaps, but *das Ding an sich*, papyrus scraps out of
Byblos, provenance a little shaky admittedly, plundered in Alexandria, turning up in a mummy
case in Cairo, sold in Sicily to some Pseudo-Theophrastus concocting potions for wealthy matrons
to smooth out their wrinkles — scribbled-over in some sort of demotic, partially masticated (rat or
dog), bleached by the sun, stained with what can best be described as embalming fluids, blood of
the ancients, giving it just the right stink of authenticity, & wanting only to be pasted back
together Humptydum-like, transcribed in clean copy & (as per the fashion of the times) *illustrated*
in the naïve style (triangles, squares, magic symbols, Pythagorean nonsense dressed in herbage &
the occasional bit of allegorical smut), bound in vellum & flogged off to the highest bidder —
Done for a ducket! — like dancing around the proverbial Caucasian chalk circle babbling in tongues
— bogus Sumerian, crypto-Pharaonic, *ein Schwindel* in any language, faultlessly foisted on our
dynamic duo of plumb-bobbers! (Now try saying all that in one breath. [☙])

herpes, etc. And this fact proves the close similarity of their tissues & blood, both
in minute structure & composition...

What followed was a long list of topics with cross-correlations — references to
brain lateralisation & aphasia — additional tabulations, transposition codes &
"prison ciphers," grids, crossword puzzles, acrostics & anagrams, series of
(apparently) unrelated, compulsively recurring machine-codes — a flow chart for
generating pseudorandom numbers — page after page of logarithmic tables —
columns of fragments, Black Book babble arranged in the geometry of *process*
like the dreamings of some handcranked ipsum motum keyword machine. The
scientia universalis of labials & glotals, cunts & cocks & crypts — sign systems
of the pure pornography of information, divorced from everything but its own
spectacle, the floating signifier & incontinent signified.*

---

* The blush of her, pulling your proverbial, that sly Sphinx-minx, knowing at this stage in the game
you couldn't do without her even if you wanted to, no matter how much you try to keep a straight
face while she lies there giving you a lecture on statistical inference, theories of measure &
integration, random variables & probability distribution, organisation theory — whispering sweet
nothings full of the most obscene, most primitive computing terminology. Doing her contortionist
act, turning herself into a musical notation, a sluttish charade even a semaphore chart would blush
at... Murmurs of "celestial influence," purring of astral radiations, "spirits" & "waves," proffering
the secret organ of transmission of the occult power of the stars to the earth. All these, as if merely
a type of foreplay, succeeded by what can only be described in grossly botanical terms — a
miscegenation of slit featureless smudges, tendrils & telescoping follicles, anthers, pedicels,
nectaries, ovules, stamens & even *stigmata*, gynoecia bulging & sprouting, erupting microsporangia
& so on & so forth — progressing by anal-sadistic evisceration & copulations both abnormal &
with materials strictly speaking inanimate to produce cross-sections of the most prurient kind of
machine mutation, barely animal at all, more like an operating manual for... rotary printing
presses? geophysical exploration? heavy construction? etc. — each additional piece of perverted
anatomy provided with its own simultaneous commentary drawing parallels with those attributes
associated with "humans & animals," per Darwin's *Eight Evolutionary Steps of Natural Selection*
(edition of 1871): "☛ Man is developed from an ovule which differs in no respect from the ovules
of other animals. The embryo itself at a very early period can hardly be distinguished from that of
other members of the vertebrate kingdom. At this period the arteries run in archlike branches, as if
to carry the blood to branchiae which are not present in the higher Vertebrata, though the slits on
the sides of the neck still remain, marking their former position. At a somewhat later period, when
the extremities are developed, 'the feet of lizards & mammals,' as the illustrious Von Baer remarks,
'the wings & feet of birds, no less than the hands & feet of man, all arise from the same
fundamental form.' It is, according to Huxley, 'quite in the later stages of development that the
young human being presents marked differences from the young ape, while the latter departs as
much from the dog in its developments, as the man does. Startling as this last assertion may
appear to be, it is demonstrably true...'" Progressing from "the nature of the evidence bearing on
the origin of man" to "homologous structures in humans & the lower animals," including "muscles,
sense-organs, hair, bones, reproductive organs," "the variability of body & mind," "problems of
reversion," "memory," "imagination," "reason," "language," "spiritual agencies," "the struggle
between opposed instincts," "the nature & value of specific physical & mental characteristic,"

The remaining folders continued in the same peculiar vein: columns of gibberish arranged beside details cut from Photostat enlargements, photographs & drawings of plants, astronomical bodies, erotica, reproductions from histories of western & oriental art, random bits of architecture, geometrical figures, anatomical charts, illuminated allegorical scenes surrounded with illegible annotation. What a dull prospect this Sphinx was beginning to seem. Stripped of her mystique, what was she after all but a pile of notepaper & facsimile making a mess on the floor?

While Němec read & slopped his coffee, an obvious idea gradually dawned on him. *Someone's setting me up!*[*] But why would anyone bother doing that? Who was he to *them*? Some sort of Kid Lazarus, gets an anonymous bundle through the mail slot, with all the post-facto evidence from a crime scene in Sophocles, something that wasn't even part of the main set-up, but held The Key nevertheless. And so in the next scene he'd be standing beside some crusty

---

"sexual selection & its peculiarities," "monogeny & polygeny," "the development of intellectual & moral faculties," "tools & the use of weapons," "emotionalism" & "the sense of beauty." Things chosen at random — *ene, mene* — out of a mess from which a story is always conspiring to emerge, only to become entangled in its own diabolical complexities, till the frame freezes on the *one image* — the eight in this game of roulette — the summed infinity of polynomial primitives — G.O.D.'s *augenblick* — & you realise without knowing anything about it that it's *this* number you've been seeking all along, because in some irrational way it chooses you & *come what may* there's no getting away from the fact of it. The whole thing was clearly insane. Aspiring to a G.O.D.'s eye cosmic viewpoint, like the involuted doodles of a schizophrenic, the classificatory manias of the pornographically obsessed, the fanatically precise penstrokes of some engineer of human souls with an endless supply of quadrille paper. Hard to deny the fascination of madness, its especial allure. With oneself & with others (*hehe*). A testament-in-the-hand being no less than equal to a ghost babbling in the wilderness, telling anyone fool enough to come near, *Hey, I'm God! Heyhey! I'm Godsbod! Heehee! I yam a dee G-g-g-g-godod!* And always some village halfwit with stars in his eyes who can't help finding a nearby stylite to perch on & give the draughty tosser an audience. (*It's all in the look, you know.*) That particular moon-mocked constipation of the all-gnoming, sun-shining from its proverbial, the *scientia universanus*, located in some previously fantastic hemisphere of the universe History'd scarcely dared look at. *Well, nightsoils just ain't nightsoils, Sol.* Visions of the Old Man pottering around in his private dunghole to extract the last lost nugget of some snakeoil merchant's Wit of Wisdom, the last tooth filling of the last etc. A thing like that, how over time, you'd wind up seduced into the general demoralisation of it. Like a whore's come-on in the dark, feeling through your pockets for a bit of the old short-shrift. Like a bum's stash of junk assiduously siphoned from secret repositories of discard. Like the charred aftermath of funeral wreaths tossed on a bonfire. Like a bet hedged against all the zero returns the future'll bright. Like a system to break the bank — a system that's almost the parody of a system, an antisystem. Saying only fools die of heartache, but wiseguys commit mass murder? Well, even G.O.D. had to start out somewhere, eh? For, most assuredly, in this version of the Circumstantial Cosmos the method isn't *in* the madness but *is* the madness & Creation itself really has gone insane. [✥]
[*] No shit, eh, Sherlock? [✥]

old coroner in the bowels of the City Morgue while the sick old fart probed with a scalpel in the Sphinx's brain & lo-&-behold, there in the mess of pre-frontal cortex is a hidden message, saying, *Make of it what you will.*[*]

Němec stuffed the folders & facsimiles back into the suitcase with the broken Black Book squeezed in on top & snapped it shut. It just seemed too much like fiction. A trick. A joke someone had decided to play for no good reason at all. Crouching over the suitcase our hero espied his typewriter in the corner where it'd been gathering dust, the muse unwoken for... Well, he couldn't remember how long.

Face it, kiddo, you were never cut out for the job...

At least he could tell himself he'd tried. Made the best show of it he could. Put up a struggle. All in vain, though, all in vain. It was a sad story, but maybe this, after all, was how it was meant to end. It was up to him now to perform the last rights. Close the circle. Bury the proverbial hatchet. Let bygones be bygones. Whatever had brought him — an admittedly minor character — to this pass, or impasse, was more than mere happenstance (so he told himself, with all the sage hindsight of retrospect a grand narrative affords those on the sidelines). It was more like destiny. Yep. Like Horatio, the whole production had been left at his feet like an upturned tumbrel, to deliver the last so-long soliloquy & play the audience out of the paying seats. Pack the costumes away in boxes. Pen the actors' obituaries. All that stuff.

He almost had himself convinced, but only almost. Like a baggy plotline that only needed to be knocked into shape — the sort of thing any hack with

---

[*] It would've been too easy to pretend everything was just a "bad dream," recurring with minor variations like one of Faktor's chess puzzles, Masonic mumbojumbo, amateur theatrical Grand Wizardry, Antediluvian Order of La Bufadora, Ancient Rite, signet pinkyring, Sign of the Devil & all that — a bit of the ol' Faustbabble, with his half-pint minion, lapdog Mephisto cracking wise through the back end of his dialogical anus, doing an Deadwood Kelley impersonation — Enochian tables, *blah blah*... And was that where all this was leading, like a tunnel constructed of U-turns, all of them funnelling back to K's gibberish? Something the Mad Magister could've improvised for doltish Dee, on the hop so to speak, at the drop of a hat, in his sleep even, by means of a simple *key*, easily memorialised, *hehe*, & as operational as a milkmaid's matrix! A veritable wordwomb, the kernel of all the gobbledegook grammars of angelspeak, even, their big-picture permutations & miniscule conjugations, as simple as a game of noughts & crosses, runes on the dark side of the moon, the Rosicrucian Rosetta Stone, the lost Babelbook of Enoch, the ever-so Blessèd V.M....? *Nah. That kind of thing'll never get you anywhere. Better throw it all in the river. Put a hex on it. Weigh it down with stones. Drown it. It'll only bring bad luck...* [♣]

eight fingers & two opposable thumbs could pull off, *Just try to make it sound inevitable enough.* Well, now, that really was the catch, wasn't it? And given the opportunity, could *he* have made it up? Nope. Not on a typewriter or any other wordmachine. It just *was.* Another one for the providential gifthorse. Nothing to do but send it back where it came from. But doubt immediately caved-in on him. The problem was he'd started out on the wrong foot, let himself get caught up in someone else's treatment instead of knocking out his own — maybe all he'd need to set it right was a sheaf of typing paper & a bottle of inspiration. Give a man the means of writing his own history & he can do just about anything… Sure, why not just hand him the rope & get it over with?

Clear as Black is White

Němec stared at his fingernails in a manner that might be described as forlorn. A crust of dried blood showed beneath the stump at the end of his right index where he'd chewed it past the cuticle. *Die Fingernägel auf der anderen Seite…*

It made him think of the Old Man again, the sly bastard who'd gotten him into all this. How one evening over the chessboard the Prof'd been trying to explain something that seemed to worry him, mostly because Němec had shown no signs that any of it was sinking in (enough, at least, to satisfy the Old Man's schoolmaster way of reckoning that this socalled acolyte of his wasn't really a complete & unmitigated Dummkopf) about what he, the Prof, kept calling "The Register." This "register" & that "register," all sorts of different "registers." Němec meanwhile thinking births, deaths, marriages, letters through the post (the kind you only ever received from government departments wanting to keep tabs on you) — where what the Prof in fact had in mind was more of a sliding scale, like a pipe organ, or a voice-compass, or a *circumstance*: the way an *impression* becomes part of a *register of meaning*, carrying an idea over onto a different plane, like making a face appear in a bowl of fruit, or turning a cloud into a weasel, a white whale, or a rat.

They'd been playing-out yet another despondent endgame at the time & the Prof, with a vague air of disgust, swept the board to make his point, rearranging the pieces into a readymade demonstration, which he then performed with maximum efficiency by means of a simple switcheroo, beginning with a fianchetto & transposing to a classic centre pawn position —

'Look,' in that ever-so-slightly condescending tone of his, 'how the patterns intersect, flow into one another, apparently unforeseen — & in so doing, the entire nature of the game shifts *register*. The point of intersection is extremely ambiguous. Like the point on which a pair of scales is balanced. Merely by looking at the scales you can't know which way they'll tip. That tipping point's like an invisible key.'

Unsatisfied still that Němec'd got the full measure of his meaning, the Prof had beckoned him to the piano, cracked walnut lid slanting 30°, taking up one whole corner of the bureau. The Old Man arranged himself at the keyboard on a creaking stool & proceeded to plonk out a theme by Mahler with his right index finger, one note at a time, first in the key of C, then repeating in F$^\#$ — starting with only the white keys, fourth octave, pianissimo, & concluding with only black, contra, forte.

'Now,' the Prof waved his hands impatiently over the keys, 'd'you get it?'*

---

* "Conjuration. Transformation. Metamorphosis. How to make things appear as if out of nowhere — something out of nothing — words conjured onto a page, but not quite — not *nowhere*, but from the *other side*. (Other side of what? Of anything!)" And just think, you can do it, too, the same as the ancient alchemists! In only eight easy steps, from bugs to bullion! For these & other secrets of the art of stewing shit into chandeliers, send CA$H now! [☝]

35

It looked like it should've been something more important, which was probably why the Red Army in '68 confused the Natural History Museum with the national parliament building next door & used it for target practice. The stone façade still bore scars from the 16mm rounds used by idiot conscripts to strafe it. In the morning drizzle, half-concealed behind a wall of scaffolding & a stadium-sized advertisement for Škoda Auto, its dark patina & darker windows described an inscrutable silhouette. Alone, at the foot of the museum's wide stone staircase, a thin man stood hunched in a junglegreen army jacket & ferretskin cap, holding a placard on the end of a long piece of four-by-two. The message on the placard was almost as old as anything in the museum. THE END COMETH, it proclaimed in bold red-painted scrawl, invisible to dogs & the colourblind. The eternal optimist shuffled, tugged his collar up around his ears, scowling at the lanes of rushhour traffic stretching north to south unbroken along the beltway. Down around the Saint Václav monument, refugees from the war in Sarajevo huddled around in silent protest against the indifference of the world to their plight. DEVILISHLY SOUPED TURBO, the Škoda billboard said, a horny redfaced sprite* grinning out from under a car bonnet.

The museum's atrium was crowded with school children milling about beneath a whale skeleton suspended by wires from the high ceiling, its great cetacean mouth gaping. Their teacher was explaining something to them, how fossils had been discovered in a Mongolian desert, of a sixteen-million-year-old carnivorous sperm whale with *very big* teeth, long extinct before Adam first had Eve & eighty metres long. *Albicetus. Megaptera novaeanglia. Etc.* None of the children appeared to be listening, busy instead picking their noses & wiping

---

* *There once was a pansy called Čert*
who everyone said was a jerk,
he'd hustle all day
to get himself laid,
but in the end barely managed a squirt. [✋]

filaments of snot on the busts of nineteenth-century eminences, arranged in solemn conclave around the atrium's periphery. Němec, clutching a plain manila envelope under one arm, ran the gauntlet of these diminutive iconoclasts & up some steps & through a colonnade to a vestibule.

The Daughters of Uranium

The permanent exhibition of rocks, fossils & skeletons continued up three flights of stairs, everything from the Dawn-of-Time to the end of the Dinosaur Period, including busts of Husák, Novotný & Gottwald. The section devoted to uranium, however, was located right off the atrium in the south wing opposite the research library. A vitrine with lumps of greyblack rock welcomed the visitor to an underlit room echoing with a sound like teeth endlessly grating. A display of obsolete Geiger counters was the reason why. At the far end of the room a cluster of schoolkids made excited whispers around a bank of video screens on which rehearsals for Armageddon were playing on a loop.

Němec stopped in front of the first vitrine & peered at the bits of rock. "Named after the planet Uranus," a sign informed visitors, "itself named after the Greek god of the sky, born of an exploding star." The exhibition unfolded as a potted history illustrated with drawings, luminous vials, coins & glass, stretching back from the atom bomb to ancient mythology. In 1972, scientists had apparently discovered a series of ancient naturally occurring nuclear reactors. This when the world was only 1.7 billion years old & isotope ^{235}U (the fertile i.e. fissile variety) "constituted about 3% of the total uranium on Earth." Němec was duly impressed. He wondered if the paleo-antic ancestors of Mitteleuropean cavemen had brought this secret knowledge with them out of Africa on their long march. The real reason the Neanderthal's copped out?

Němec read on. It wasn't long before he found something like what he was looking for. A figure of a blue flower traced in yellow glass, discovered, it was duly noted, in a Roman villa (registered to one Flavius Maximus) in secessionist northern Italy. The flower resembled no other flower he'd ever seen outside the pages of a certain Manuscript. If pushed to describe it, he might've likened it to a heraldic anus. Němec mused. He stuck a finger up under his hatband & scratched. He wondered if said villa was anywhere near a place called Frascatti. He let his gaze wander to an accompanying parchment — it showed naked women engaged in some sort of orgy. It was, so a label pasted on the cabinet explicated, a "Rite of Spring" designed to evoke fertility in the earth for the sewing of the annual crop & to stave off blight *and unworldly mutations*. Such mutations had been known to occur in the vicinity of ^{92}U deposits, in which "spontaneous fission" may have occurred. For example, due to seismic activity. The Sybil's grotto at Lake Avernus, e.g. — where in days of Rome, the deathless dungeoned hag chanted braindamaged portents to dollar-wielding pilgrimites, zorched on volcanic sulphur, isotopes & the din of her own psychobabble. There was even a copy of what purported to be a Sibylline Spellbook, inked in serpentine grey scrawl, that seemed to attest to nothing but its author's madness. Who or when, no-one knew.

Němec clutched the manila envelope inside his jacket, he knew he was onto something. Then the next display case proved it. A daguerreotype of a Sudeten spa town shimmered under the glass. "Sankt Joachimsthal," the label said, but Němec knew the place as Jáchymov. It'd been a Habsburg silver mine since the 16th century when the alchemist Georgius Agricola set up a metallurgical laboratory there, protruding untold tonnes of a mineral byproduct called pitchblende, which contained uranite, & which the local glassmakers used to tint glass. Much later it was used for sepia tone in photography. Most of the stuff wound up on slagheaps around town.

During Agricola's time, the surrounding woodlands were rumoured to be home to untold species of exotic flora & fauna. Goats with three heads, wildflowers the size of Schwarzwälder Kirschtorte. The Catholics blamed the Reformation, the Protestants blamed the Catholics. One of the Countess von Schlicks was even reported to've birthed Siamese quadruplets, but after the Schmalkaldic War it was prohibited on pain of death to speak of it. Then, after a mysterious outbreak of further "abominations" (as reported by a visiting Jesuit in 1873), an inauspicious fire entirely destroyed the town, with the sole exception of the mine, which was completely unscathed.

Reborn as a beacon of modernity, Jáchymov proffered its unseen light to a future-to-end-all-futures. At the beginning of the 20th century, Marie Curie discovered radium in the local pitchblende & set the atom clock ticking. A radon spa opened in the town in 1906. Not until 1929, however, following the inquiries of one Dr Löwy of Golem City, was the Confluxus Radiorum emanating from the mine discovered to lead to disease & cancer. In the meantime, like a backwards Philosophers Stone, uranite was discovered to be likewise prolific in its genealogies, transmuting in addition to Curie's *fée verte* (Ra), to: plutonium (Pu), astatine (At), bismuth (Bi), polonium (Po), radon (Rn), thallium (Tl), thorium (Th) &, finally, the dead weight at the end-of-along-line-leading-nowhere, plumbum (Pb) — most adamantine of all. But it was only a matter of time before someone realised this particular Philosophers Stone could also make one helluva big bomb. And Jáchymov had the world's largest known supply. The stuff was still lying around just waiting to be bulldozed onto trucks when the Nazis rolled into town after Munich 1938.

Tempus edax rerum

If there was one thing Němec'd always felt he had plenty of, it was time. After that first flush of freedom hot on the heals of his Great Escape from The Home, he knew he wasn't going anywhere soon. You escaped to the "outside," but did you *escape the outside* once you got there? Němec had no idea. There was nowhere he wanted to go *to*, just a place he'd been desperate all those years to get away *from*. The world was his proverbial oyster. A room, a simple wordmachine: infinity by half-lives, enough in which to exercise the wandering rootlessness of the soul, pursue the unbounded expansive noodlings of the mind, aver the devolutions of the body corporeal. Till one day, perhaps, the midgets in the controlroom started flipping their doomsday switches, swapping all the words, pouring sand in his eyes, turning the very pith of him insideout. But by then, it'd be too late. As they had a way of saying in the classics: *Paradise was never meant to last, kiddo, even in a dump like this.*

Němec pondered a slowly erupting mushroom cloud as it moved hazily up a video screen, scratched his neck, adjusted the envelope under his arm. *From a piece of rock, such untold power…* Well, he thought,

What would the Bugman do?

Němec had no idea. With nothing on-hand to drink, he advised himself to stay calm, dry-swallowed three of the pills he kept in his jacket pocket for precisely such contingencies (two pink, one blue), then set about attempting a mental inventory. *Lists*, the Bugman had often told him (who ought to know, his rooftop bower was plastered floor to ceiling with them, the whole place — so to speak — one vast list unto itself), *puts the hard stuff in perspective when otherwise there ain't none. Why them bureaucrats use 'em all the time...*

This being all the encouragement he needed, Němec, counting on his fingers, began at the beginning & (a syllogist at heart) let the momentum of the moment find the next logical step. First there was the Prof, then the Voynich Manuscript, Kircher's Letter, Faktor, the Dwarf, the Black Book, the Green Fairy, the Facsimile in the Suitcase, the Sphinx's Code, & now... Radioactive Rocks & Mutant Plants? All he had to do was find a connection. A link, however tenuous, between the stony grey soil of Jáchymov & the Old Man's poltergeist...

Pierrot se fout

What Němec was looking for was in the far righthand corner, between a pair of nondescript bronzes (they resembled, if anything, an arrangement of cow pats stacked lopsidedly — something vaguely oriental, perhaps, like allegorical tortoises): a glasspaned door with LIBRARY stencilled across it in chipped gold flake. A buzzer was set to the right of the door, with nametags, numbers & corresponding buttons, which for the most part Němec was unable to decipher. The word PALEOFLORA looked promising, so he pushed the button beside it & waited. Considered from this angle, the bits of bronze cow dung reminded Němec vaguely of the dodo in the glass box at the Strahov Monastery. Was this to be the signal for another one of those creeping senses of déjà vu?

Němec shuffled impatiently. No, it didn't seem that the buzzer was working. In any case, the door turned out to be unlocked, so Němec pushed it open & peered through the gap. Immediately inside, like a bellhop in a Halloween costume, stood a waxworks model of Stoneage Man, stunted, longhaired, draped in animal hide, eyes full of great primitive images of oceans, mountains, forests. Němec stepped through the doorway to get a better appreciation of this inhabitant of dark canyons of the predawn of the nuclear age. *Cro-Mag (h. sapiens sapiens)*. Or was that $h.s^2$, sapiens *squared*? There was, he had to admit, a certain mutual resemblance. For a brief moment he pictured himself, dweller of Palaeolithic night, fearful, huddled against lightning flash & blue afterglow, haloed djinn-forms, shadows listing on cave walls, visions of bestial copulations, limbs & distended counterlimbs, x-ray anatomies, the ravening godhead, the womb of oblivion.

On a square of white cardboard pasted on the wall was typed: **The capacity for speech is unique among Homo Sapiens.** The eloquent ape, socalled. *Well it was a lucky thing,* Němec cogitated, *that they didn't have to listen to what all the other species on the planet thought of them? Like being in a room full of TVs tuned to some death-and-disaster channel nonstop. What a trip that'd be… 'Hey sapiens-my-arse, go back where you came from! Hey there, you two-legged nimrod, stop hogging all the lanes! Hey shit-for-brains, guess who the next big extinction-event's comin' for?*

A woman's voice broke in upon Němec's reverie —

'I see you've met Pierrot…'

Němec looked around into the face of a smirking redhead. Familiar somehow. Highbreasted with a pair of bottle-bluegreen eyes behind wireframe glasses that did nothing to conceal them. She didn't look like what he expected a librarian to look like. Maybe with the lights turned down a bit…

'Pierrot?'

'Our little stone man. So to speak. How can I…?'

'And that?'

It was a metal cocoon-like object in a glass cabinet placed against the opposite wall. The whole corridor was cluttered with similar cabinets & display cases: plant fossils, pigmy skeletons, giant crystals, orcs' eggs, bits of petrified wood, a pterodactyl's head.

'That's a *torpile radio-automatique.*'

'And what's that when it's at home?'

The redhead laughed.

'A prototype Tesla radio-controlled torpedo, first tested in 1898. It's from the last exhibition we had, *Human Cybernetics.* Nikola Tesla studied here in Golem City, you know, at the University, his ideas were way ahead of their time. Thankfully for us.'

'…?'

'As a matter of fact, the twentieth century might never've happened had Tesla's detractors taken him seriously. He even designed an electron gun for the American army, but the generals thought he was a nutter. Eventually everyone else did, too, talking about Martians & space travel. So, to appease the status quo, Marconi got the credit for inventing radio & Edison got credit for almost everything else, but in reality it was Tesla.'*

Němec nodded to show he was duly impressed. The guy probably invented the wheel, too, & wrote Shakespeare's plays in his spare time.

'Tesla was the first man to truly envisage the world we live in today — wireless, networked, global. Everything from TV broadcasting to radio telescopes, to the universal microwave background radiation that transmits to all points of the cosmos.'

The redhead seemed enraptured, like she knew the whole script by heart & wanted nothing more than to bestow it upon an appreciative listener. Maybe she even wrote it.

'He was,' she persevered, 'the first to really grasp the universal nature of energy — organism & machine. With nothing but a pocketwatch he was able to create an earth-tremor & yet his discoveries today are mostly forgotten, even as,' the redhead paused dramatically, making vague indications at nothing in particular, 'their progeny surround us.'

Němec stared at the weird cocoon-shaped thing in the display cabinet. He scratched his ear dubiously —

'*The* Tesla? As in T-E-S-L-A*?'

One corner of the redhead's mouth curled upwards into a lopsided grin.

'They stole his name. While some people thought he was mad, others considered him a genius. Like him, they believed electricity could transform the world, cure illness, put humanity in contact with extraterrestrial beings. All that. The key to world peace.'

'The key to world peace?'

'Tesla said the improvement of humanity by way of science constituted the wealth which would accomplish what no redeemer had ever been able to.'

'We'll melt the North Pole & make more dishwater — that sort of thing?'

'In his own way, Tesla was also an environmentalist.'

'How do prehistoric torpedoes fit with that?'

'Maybe they don't. It all depends on whose side you're on...'*

---

* Tesla could've painted shit moustaches on those guys. [✋]

* T.E.S.L.A. Latterday architects of Mutually Assured Dematerialisation congregating in the inventor's name — one of those endlessly self-promoting acronymed secret societies recently & for some time previous conspiring in the outright extermination of the species, individually & collectively, irradiated gene-by-gene, chromosome-by-chromosome, or snuffed out in one Great Big Bang... [✋]

The redhead replaced the half-hearted grin she'd been wearing with an expression meant to convey that the chitchat was over — it made her seem indeterminately older somehow. Němec, fearing the opportunity may have already been lost, withdrew the envelope he'd been clutching all this time under his arm & spilled the facsimiles across the floor.

While in a hunched-over quite frankly inaudible position, Němec started in on his spiel, about inheriting a sheaf of drawings from an uncle, a collector-type, recently deceased — sixteenth-century, supposedly… though so far… none of the "experts"… clues to their origin… what the drawings (he paused in his effort at gathering up the spilled facsimiles to hold a page up for the redhead's perusal) were actually *of*… except to say, in layman's terms… bearing some relation to the vegetable kingdom… possessed neither of locomotion nor organs of sense… though perhaps capable of *mutations*…?

He stood up finally, mumbling something about radioactive plants, which the redhead feigned not to hear or, if she did, not to grasp. Her expression was of unadorned incomprehension. Němec thrust the remaining pages at her. Perhaps, he stammered, of interest, *er*, to the, *er*, Museum? In short, some personage therein who might consent to examine them, etc? The redhead arched an eyebrow, getting the general drift of Němec's approach by now. She glanced down at the bizarre anthology of crumpled paper the oddball in the bowler hat had just given her & pursed her lips, the way somebody does when they're trying to weigh up the options more than just the object in hand, & stayed like that for long enough to make Němec feel he ought to be doing something with his hands: they felt awkward where they were, hanging at the end of his arms, so he put them behind his back & tried to look pensive, like pensive people do.

Having made vague gestures of leafing through the facsimiles, the redhead handed the bundle back to Němec &, tilting her head so as to gesture along the short corridor to an open reading area beyond, said —

'You'd better come up to the office.'

Angelus Novus

The redhead turned abruptly & began to walk off, glancing back over her shoulder, mouthing something wordless Němec couldn't make out. He held that image in his mind: red hair, mouth shaping an "a" or an "i" perhaps, both

---

* Jesus this dialogue sucks. [✋]

eyebrows raised, drifting away from him, like the Angelus Novus in that painting by Paul Klee. He gathered from this charade that he was supposed to follow her, so he did, a couple of steps behind just to stay on the safe side. She led the way through the Reading Room, bleached fluorescents, grey metal stacks with catalogue numbers in the eight- & ninehundreds, musty book smells, wilting lilies in brown plant-pots, here & there a pale blossom peeking out between dusty greygreen leaves — walking with her head always turned slightly as if to maintain a vantage over both the path ahead & that already travelled — up a spiral staircase & down another corridor lined with filing cabinets, to a glass partition door with PRIVATE written on it in the same chipped gold-flake as the first door. She opened it for him & stood aside —

'After you.'

'Too kind.'

The office Němec found himself in was cramped with half-a-dozen desks & bookshelves stuffed to overflowing — a second door stood in the middle of a wall, the top half of which was frosted glass, & from the other side there was the intermittent sound of voices above a teletype machine. He was invited to take a seat & made himself as comfortable as he could in a dusty beige-coloured armchair that didn't seem too pleased to be sat on. The redhead took a chair behind the nearest desk & held her hand out for Němec to give her the drawings again, which he did.

'These are copies, of course.'

'Of course.'

The pages Němec handed her were all from the section of the Voynich Manuscript which, unbeknownst to his ignorant self, Scholars in the Field called a *herbal*, because it was about plants. The redhead gave them a close one-over, then, without saying anything, pulled out a large magnifying glass from a desk drawer & switched on a table lamp. As she went about scrutinising the drawings in detail, her right hand scratched notes with a pencil on a lined notepad, seemingly independent of the rest of her body. While this was going on Němec let his attention stray over the rest of the office: a couple of typewriters, a computer terminal, a stove & coffee pot, a board with scraps of paper pinned to it, variously upholstered chairs, potted plants filling out a frosted glass window with a reproduction of a Flemish still-life pasted to it. The still-life sagged against the glass, printed on thin glossy paper that was mottled by the light filtering through the window which made it seem to move like a piece of timelapse photography — a jugged hare beside a bowl of overripe fruit which, by subtle declensions, are seen to swell, rot, decay, swarming with parasites that simultaneously consume & reconstitute the tableau.

The bookshelf above the redhead's desk reminded Němec of the shelves in the late Prof's bureau, when he used to visit the professor, before he died. Plant catalogues, encyclopaedias & dictionaries, botanic plates, natural histories, monographs, the *Philosophica Botanica* of Linnaeus, Columella's *De Arboribus*, & so on & so forth. Stuck up on the wall beside it was an illustrated diagram, like an upside-down tree with lopsided branches, representing the Plant Kingdom subsectioned into its various parts, orders, genera, species, varieties & whatnot. There were "phanerogam plants," divided into twentythree classes, according — as the not-so-small print at the bottom of the chart explained — *to their stamens' number, length, degree of distinctiveness and placement.* A residual twentyfourth class encompassed various "cryptogams" — fungi, moss, algae, ferns… *Cryptogams?* It sounded like it was missing something. An "r" maybe. Němec pictured some Jin dynasty manual of organic calligraphs, ancient lore coded in the haiku of garden moss, redbluegreen algae on Feng Shui ornamental ponds rippled by hypnotic carp movements — delicate fractals of humid plantmatter, mushroom spores transmitting secret commands readable only to the initiated, Order of Frog, Toad, Confucian Grasshopper.

Outside, a cloud passed across the face of the sun, darkening the window. In the gloom, the nameless redhead appeared to transform, suddenly wizened & small, a lank-haired sibyl in her cave, Deiphobë, daughter of Glaucus, mad-eyed goddess of the crossroads, bent over some farrago of enchanted nonsense. *Now the time to ask your destiny…*[*] She reached across the desk & switched on the

---

[*] WOMBFRUIT

Strange to say, but watching the redhead like that made Němec think of his mother. (Oh for crying out loud! Getting a little stiff for dear dead mumsy now, is he? [♦]) Perhaps it was the posture, head down, dedicated to little tasks that in the universal scheme of things assume disproportionate significance. For what's a child without darned socks, a knitted vest, a scarf to keep him warm in winter? (And if his longlost Matimati was really still alive? How would he find HER, if he wanted to find HER, if he could allow himself to want to find HER …? Some woman he saw in the street, with a slight limp in HER left leg perhaps, dressed in black, or grey, or black, dragging HERself home to a room in which he'd imagine HER sitting, peeling onions, staring at a wall, a kettle slowly coming to the boil on a gas burner… A room in which he'd imagine HER sleeping, waking day after day, washing, hanging the clothes to dry, ironing, folding the same clothes away in the same drawers, draping the stockings over the bath, talcum gritting on the floor, the smell of cabbage & iodine, the dust & hair that forever needs sweeping into the pan, the bag of trash by the door to be taken down to the bins… A room in which SHE has never made love, in which SHE barely dreams, in which memories fade to a dull TV flicker, in which life is a malady that forever requires to be treated, some other day, the solace of an activity that'll never be completed & so will never lead to disappointment...) *Ah, kiddo, all these women in your life!* He hadn't even asked the redhead's name (had she volunteered it?) — it could've been anything, like his mother's name, which only existed in an Interior Ministry file, they could've faked that too. The healing, reconciling mother: murmur of stoic consolatory nonsense. Well, who in their right mind would ever've wanted to own *him* if they'd had any choice in the matter? A skin & bones ragdoll with the stitches coming out at the seams & a chip the size of Kilimanjaro on his sloping shoulders? An anatomical deformity, a squillhead? How the world saw him through his own eyes... (*Stretching it a bit aren't you?*) What would he have to say for himself if it really *was* HER sitting there at that desk, pondering the imponderable (*Of course, mummy's gotta care about little numero uno right to the end, right?*) — that he'd been pushed, or that he'd jumped? (*What a waste.*) Or nothing — *Mum's the word.* Was SHE out there somewhere playing dead, in a cell no-one had gotten around to unlocking, because the past SHE came from was too much of an affront for the world to face? Buried under redtape, deemed no longer to exist for lack of evidence to the contrary. Trying to summon a picture of HER, all the images were in silhouette, black&white — no matter how hard he tried, he couldn't see HER face or the colour of HER hair. *Even in your dreams they've succeeded in wiping them out. Mamitati. Tatimami.* And what about the other photographs missing from the files? Of the Loved One on the mortuary slab? In the ditch? In the torture chamber? In the cell? On the filthy mattress?

The dead don't remember (you),
the dead don't get old,
the dead don't bleed,
the dead don't go mad,
the dead aren't terrified,
the dead feel no pain,
the dead can't be broken,
the dead are immune to humiliation,
the dead can't betray,
the dead have nothing to be deprived of,
the dead can't be persuaded,
the dead don't confess,
the dead don't love (you)...

And what the Prof said: *The most difficult thing to understand's the nature of the quest.* But it wasn't HER Němec was searching for, was it? But a clue in a photostat, of something universally agreed to be the height of all senseless undertakings — as inscrutable, in that bogus high language of the Great Navel-Gazers of Yore, as the piddling human soul of which Němec felt most grievously bereft. Why care about that one thing & not all the others — not *them*? "Because," the voice in his head told him, "they don't exist. Because for you to exist, the things that don't exist must continue not to exist..." Or, conversely, "for you not to exist, they..." etc. (And did the soul exist? The learnèd spoke of "it" as if it did — was that enough? Was the conviction of a truth sufficient to make it so? And if he believed, that somewhere, after all these years, SHE was still alive — what the chances would be, accidentally... & if so, would he *know* HER? And how would he picture HER if he could? Timeless, unchanged, as SHE *would have been*? A redhead, for example, sitting at a desk? Just the way, at that very moment, picking a sharpened pencil out of a vase to take notes on a blank sheet of paper. Pausing, the rubber end of the pencil dipping down to catch in the folds of her blouse, pulling the fabric to one side & beneath it, a lace bra through which the outline of lamp — a cone of enamelled black arched over a heavy base, ivory button poking up from the middle of it — her features, in the wash of light, released from that physical perplexity, though still some residual trace, palimpsest, the bifurcated aura of the afterimage.[*]

The Voice of Reason

What interrupted Němec's thoughts was the redhead speaking on the phone — *Indian fruits*, she was saying. *Acclimatisation… Transmutation of black oats to rye…* As she spoke she turned the end of a pencil in her hair, eyes not seemingly focused on anything. When she hung up she gave him one of those reassuring smiles people do when they think you might be worried about something, to put

---

her left breast's clearly visible? Entirely against his will, Němec was dragged along by his Id-self's yearnings: idly, yet with what untold purpose, this mental doppelgänger began tracing the seam of her brassier with the rubber end of the pencil, then, letting the pencil drop to the desk with a *thunk*, scratched between her breasts with the tips of her fingernails — a scratching that only agitated its cause further, as if she were beginning to overheat, a type of rash appearing around her neck in red splotches, throat wet with perspiration — hand now rubbing up & down along her larynx, then plunging inside her blouse, buttons snapping, rubbing with her hand inside the lace cup of the brassiere, the movement growing more agitated, tugging the swelling gland out into plain view, vermillioned aureole oozing a milky sap like chicle, flame hair spread out like the fronds of an exotic & possibly also dangerous fern, eyes wide, dilated, the green cornea radiant?) Well, well, well. And wouldn't the our dear dirtyminded reader like to know what happens next? Maybe this mutant mumsy of his'll get so worked up her face starts to melt, revealing the inner workings of an… an… *android?* Great gusts of smoke coming off the exposed circuit board, a weirdly distorted voice redolent of tape-delay & Richard Nixon echoing in the room, saying *love = evol, evol = love…* But the whole fantasy need not be so elaborate — concerned, as it's impossible not to be, with certain quote *inner-workings* unquote. And what, after all, is this whole textual phantasmagoria than a type of reverse striptease, presented as the bare fact of itself & daring him to dress it up with his eyes into some Venus im Pelz, *hehe?* (The tone's all wrong, but Němec can't help it — *rewrite this bit later on, eh, chum.* [✋])

[*] (Who was it who said readjustment & adaptation have their cost? The process of synthesis, which might take moments, eons, whole apocryphal mental reckonings — to preserve, to elevate, to cancel — subtly, or not so subtly, transformed from blossoming youth to old age, vitality to putrescence, virginity to lasciviousness, the purity of soul to the corruption of the body led astray, all the warring dualities that've ever summed up the human paradox, as if even the life cycles of fungus were simply a mirror held up to Man's inner reckoning. Imagining future intelligent plantlife arriving from distant Mars colony on some Royal Intergalacto Geographic fact-finding mission — Triffids with letters after their hyphenated names, bearing specimen jars & microscopes & flat-headed tweezers — crating off, marked **FRAGILE**, representatives of every known national trait (Members of Congress, Business Leaders, Media Magnates) to Martian botanical institutes, to dissect & make detailed comparison — extrapolating, from the cancerous colon & chronic gastritis of one, to the debauched phrenology of some other — for the sake of some quaint evolutionary romanticism?) [✋]

you at ease, saying there was a colleague who might be able to make heads or tails of it — *it* referring to the drawings in the Manuscript. Němec tried to make his face into a picture of being at ease: he was, after all, really quite curious about what she or this colleague of hers could tell him that he didn't already know. The colleague must've been in the next office because the partition door opened almost immediately — framed in it was a tall thin man, grey around the temples, with a spotted bowtie & bulging Adam's apple. Zahradník, his name was — he stooped to shake Němec's hand —

'What's this I hear about mutating vegetables?'

He stooped again to get a look at the drawings —

'Hoho, very good, very good. Where'd you find this lot, eh?'

Zahradník cast a humorous glance at Němec from under sleepy eyelids, like a camel with eczema, amused at the thought of spitting in your face if it could only be bothered to.

'My dear girl,' straightening himself to his full height so as to give the redhead the benefit of his unimpeded condescension, middle finger brushing the tip of his nose, almost caressing it, 'haven't you ever heard of the Voynich, *socalled*, Manuscript?'

It seemed the redhead hadn't, poor thing. It was Němec's turn to do the assuring smile, but it was wasted — her eyes were telling Zahradník to go & do something unmentionable to himself, but the rest of her was saying she'd been through this countless times before & why fight it?

'*Yeees*. Was a time when every man & his dog & its fleas had a theory about the Voynich, *hoho*, Manuscript. Bit old hat now, I s'pose. Young people have so many more interesting things to *talk* about…'

Zahradník picked the facsimiles off the desk & shuffled through them —

'Mmm. Yale University, I do seem to recall.'

Well, so much for the cover story — now it was Němec's turn to be glared at: the redhead tossed her pencil on the desk & folded her arms. Němec shrugged like it was all news to him. This Zahradník had the whole thing down, of course — had even published an article once, back in the good old days, *chucklechuckle*, which he recommended Němec go off & read (if it wouldn't be too taxing), in the *Proceedings of the Cheskoslovnikian Botanical Historiography Society*, volume LXIX number 817, as it happened, doubtless available on request in the, *er*, Library.

'But to save you the *trouble*,' Zahradník offered, 'this whole thing's a lot of cock&bull. Baloney. Certifiable hoohaa. None of these… *drawings* describes any species of *plant* known to exist or to ever *have* existed.[*] From the scientific *viewpoint*, they're utterly *worthless*. Better, my young fellow, to enlarge your mind reading *Alice in Wonderland*. But, from a bibliophilic point-of-view, who knows? An expensive *curiosity*. Hum. How'd you get hold of these, anyway?'

Němec gave him the line about being the dead professor's assistant.

'Oh,' Zahradník said, handing the facsimiles back to the redhead, who handed them back to Němec. 'Never heard of him.'

Němec supposed that, under different circumstances, they might've had quite a chat, he & this Zahradník. But the man wouldn't even let Němec thank him for his trouble, just waved the oddball in the bowler hat towards the exit & reminded him to take the right at the end of the corridor. He could hear Zahradník *tut-tutting* the redhead as he went…

Babylon

The way out of the labyrinth left him where he'd started, past Ol' Pete, standing on the Museum steps blinking in the glare — the Devil still up there on his billboard grinning down, as if to say a man can have all the light in the world & still be in the dark. By the clock at the end of the Square it was midday roughly. A helicopter was circling above the building, towards the river & back again, like a drone stuck between two coordinates: there must've been something going on — a dozen riot cops where lounging around a couple of green & white vans over by Petschek Palace, waiting for a signal. The doomsayer in the ferret-skin was sitting beside his placard on the ground smoking a cigarette, wiling away the last moments before the apocalypse was to due to begin in the middle of family-hour viewing, only it didn't look like it'd be starting any time soon. Kids with red flags were milling around The Horse, toeing their Doc Martens, bugeyed under black hoods. Shoppers walking by. Tourists taking photographs. Usual crowd.

Seeing as he was in the general neighbourhood, Němec decided to drop in on the Bugman & seek direction from the man in person. Accordingly, he circled around the Museum & schlepped it through the underpass & up behind the Český Rozhlas building. Being lunchtime a couple of workmen in cementspattered overalls were making their way down the street, nozzling beer bottles: it wasn't the sapling they planted atop the scaffolds that'd stop them falling on their heads, but angel's wings, he decided. *Miracle that anything in this*

---

[*] Life, Jimbo, but not as *we* know it. [✋]

town ever got built at all — foremen on the take or under the table or flogging supplies by night from the back of a truck to the same con-artists the company bought them from in the morning...

When Němec rang the bell to Blecha's mountaintop eyrie there was no answer, so he rode the box elevator the six floors up to the roof & invited himself inside anyway. The Bugman was already well into his *chalupář*[*] routine, watering his rooftop garden with a bright yellow watering can with the radio at full-volume, tuned to Classic FM, Tchaikovsky's *1812* in E♭ booming out over the rooftops (Napoleon's route at Borodino, half the Grande Armée & all that) when Němec materialised on the Old Guy's terrace. *Just working up a thirst*, as he'd say.

This garden was really quite impressive — it stood behind a breezeblock extension, on the back side of the roof from the terrace, beside the chicken coop, south-facing (the terrace faced north so you wouldn't get the sun in your eyes all day). A chicken was roosting on one of the chimney pots. In the garden there were tomatoes, peppers, cabbages, carrots, turnips, fennel, radish, onions, a trellis with cucumbers & a swathe of pumpkin vine spilling over the side of the roof. In winter Blecha rigged up a greenhouse around the lot of it, with plastic sheeting — the vent from the basement boilerroom fed straight into it, up a flue through the middle of the building, keeping it nice & temperate even under ice, though you'd want to watch your step. *Those pumpkins*, Němec thought, *will be the death of him one day.*

Seeing Němec standing there, Blecha hung up his hose & invited his visitor to pull over a deckchair —

'You're looking dapper today, kiddo. To what do we owe the pleasure?'

Němec gave him the short version of the story, trying not to shout — *Trouble with a redhead* — knowing the Bugman's predilection...

'*All work and no play...* You know the rap.'

'Yeah. Gives you colon cancer.'

Němec handed him the same envelope he'd shown the redhead...

'What's this?'

Blecha turned the music down, peered inside the envelope. He shook the drawings out & peered some more.

'What the Old Man was working on when he died. Some kindhearted soul left it on my doorstep...'

---

[*] "Bungalow Bill." [✋]

'Sure, but what *is* it?'

'Something dreamt-up by an idiot or a nutcase apparently.'

'That's what they told you, eh?'

'Basic idea.'

'Ah well. Put it down to experience is all I can say. Mind if I add these to my art collection?'

'Go ahead. Not much use to me. They're not even copies, just copies of copies. Hardly worth the ink.'

'As noble a thing as the our bureaucratic state apparatus might be accounted less, *hehe*. How about we sit down? On second thought,' he thrust the envelope back at Němec, 'dump these wherever you can find a space & get us both a drink, that'd be a good chap — brandy's in the fridge.'

It was a warm day, so Němec supposed *why not*, except that the fridge was also stuffed with packets of dried spaghetti & tinned goulash, even a bottle of cooking oil full of air bubbles in suspended animation.

'You normally keep spaghetti in the fridge, Blecha?'

'Only way it'll stay fresh.'

'Fresh?'

'Sure, try some if you like.'

'Maybe I'll just stick to my drink, but thanks anyhow.'

'Can never be too careful, what they put in things nowadays.'

'Put in what things?'

'Food & stuff.'

'Right.'

'Things aren't fresh the way they used to be.'

'Eh? What're you talking about? The word *fresh* was just Commie propaganda. There was no such thing.'

'I mean what they put in cans, packets, like spaghetti. It doesn't taste right anymore.'

'That's maybe because the old spaghetti was made in Kladno & turned to glue the minute you boiled it. Now they've got real spaghetti, from Italy, that doesn't turn to glue when you boil it.'

'You can say what you like, I've seen a thing or two'd open your eyes, kiddo. You know, back in the gulag, they had a TB ward. There were prisoners so desperate to get out they'd buy gobs of infected phlegm, dried into these hard little yellowgreen nuggets, like pistachios. There was a male nurse, used to be a school teacher in Minsk, would smuggle the stuff from the infirmary & trade it to anyone willing to pay — the younger the better. The idea was they'd get themselves sick & be taken off the work detail, given a warm meal, put in a nice clean hospital bed — a pipe dream. The infirmary was no better than anywhere else, except you got to lie around all day coughing your lungs up. Better to cough your lungs up than dig holes in minus forty. The worst thing that could happen to you in the infirmary was you'd die or get well again. No-one wanted to get well. The chronic cases would trade even *more* infected gobs so they could *stay* in quarantine, beat the cure, all the while those little TB bacilli mutating till finally there was no drug could kill 'em. Like human incubators in a germ warfare experiment. You think the doctors didn't know what was going on? The whole thing was a set-up, a con-job — the fag nurse picking out the healthiest & strongest. There was even a rumour they were using x-ray machines to dose the patients with radiation so the virus could soak up the neutrons, doing a bit of resurrection on the side to keep the host alive just long enough for the next evolutionary leap. Siberian zombies, they called 'em.'

Blecha coughed into his hand, peered tentatively, wiped his palm across his shorts, gulped some brandy from the jar Němec handed him, then went on with his story.

'Eventually the lucky ones got wheeled off in the middle of the night & were never seen again — tipped into the incinerator was the story going 'round. The less fortunate got spirited off to secret underground laboratories were ex-Nazi concentration camp doctors went to work on them (slaves of Stalin, would do anything to save their own skin now the Reich'd been blasted to oblivion, hammer & sickle over the Reichstag, the ultimate though not final humiliation): willing to use all the considerable means at their disposal to prolong the suffering, accelerate the metamorphoses, hybridise the DNAs, reverse-transcribe the enzymes, anything at all to get their hands on the grail of a new synthetic deathform. Less Übermench than Golem, admittedly, more Mengele than Mandrake. You've got to feel for them, those poor engineers of the Aryan race reduced to such ignominy, bowing to an impure virulence as the sole remaining method of their vengeance — *Oh cruel world!* — to wind the clocks back upon their enemies, obliterate them all. Which just goes to show, eh, that all of medical science is helpless against stupidity.'

'What's TB got to do with spaghetti?'

'Well, it's like this, kiddo. They don't get you one way, they'll find others.'

36

The junction came up at 1:47. Then in a few moments, the valley closed in around them like a pair of stage curtains. No-one had said yet where they were supposed to be going. They'd been zigzagging east to avoid the American lines at Plzeň & the partisan units mining the tracks. Somewhere up ahead through the suburbs lay the river the Reds were advancing towards. The accompanying brass had disembarked an hour ago, there was only Müller, Sturmbannführer of the Waffen-*SS*, to issue the orders now. They were running out of options in any case. The only lines open where south, but once they got to the mountains — *if* they made it that far — what then? Schnitzelstadt had already fallen. Hitler had killed himself for the belated good of the last remaining children, old men & dogs of Berlin. From everything the driver of this unscheduled Intercity Express had seen, the War was already over.

Klee wiped the soot from his eyes, peering into the gloom for a sign of the bridge that ought to be coming up any minute now. His view was obscured by an undifferentiated jumble of tenement masonry. The whole city was blacked-out. He strained to hear the sound of enemy aircraft overhead, Americans maybe, or even Russians, but could make out only the driving of the pistons. He glanced at his fireman, Kurtz, native of Pomerania, tapping his fingers on the regulator valve, a silent motion outlined in silhouette. Kurtz, a fatalist at the best of times, hadn't spoken since they'd entered the outskirts of the City. Under the peek of his railwayman's cap, the man's face was a punctured black mask, eyes yellow & dilated. Out there in the dark could be anything, a sniper's bullet waiting among the shadows, a savage's spear. Driver & fireman had both been with the Krautische Reichsbahn for over twenty years & they'd done the run from Berlin to Schnitzelstadt more times than it was worth remembering, but this one was different from all the others. Like they were entering a dark place, the twisted chiaroscuro of the buildings around them like some jungle of the Congo.

Theirs was the last train out of Berlin. As soon as they'd got clear, they were rerouted southwest as far as Karlsbad, then east, collecting a load along the way. Thirty or so freight cars with an armoured escort. If Klee had been more of a speculative sort of man, he might've got to pondering about the kind of load they were pulling & what it meant about where they were likely to end up. A couple of SSmys & Sa708 six-axle heavy load wagons, which usually meant tanks, but these looked more like bits of U-boat maybe, the way they were shaped under the tarps. But what you'd be doing with U-boats in the middle of Bohemia was anyone's guess. Then there were the SSy "Köln" four-axle wagons, which looked like they were stacked with engine parts. A couple of water tankers, fuel tankers, & a string of OOt "Saarbrücken" four-axle coal transporters, only they weren't laden with coal but with bits of grey rock. Tons of the stuff. In addition to which, no fewer than five FLAK crews sandbagged with mounted canons inside their Ommr "Dresden" two-axle boxcars. What it all added up to was obviously not a question anyone was being invited to ask.

At least, Klee thought, they weren't pulling cattle cars, a last-ditch deathtrain of human cargo. Those armband-wearing lunatics had turned half the standard gauge on the continent into a DNA disposal system, an insult to the profession. But by this stage everything else (goods wagons, troop transports, etc., etc.) was just the same thing by different means, feeding a blackhole called The East. And now The East was coming to them. Any moment now, he thought, it'd swallow them up. Along with the whole of Army Group Centre & whoever else was left of their socalled Master Race. And he, Klee of the Reichsbahn, would ride ever-onward into the Leviathan's mouth? Last of the tribe, in all probability, once the Reds had annihilated the enclave of Golem City & they, driving before the storm, the juggernaut, whatever, making one last flying stand... No, it made no sense. But orders were orders.

Rounding the bend, the river at last came into view. Klee eased back on the throttle. The engine slowed. Coal smoke wafted overhead, mingling with a smell of cordite, ozone, charred wood. A gutted station house drifted past as they started up the embankment. The iron railbridge seemed to groan at their approach. Klee could've sworn he heard it, like a wounded animal. Kurtz surveyed the gauges, the red eye of the furnace, making silent incantation like some alchemist of yore & their engine, a giant alembic for the transmutation of space & time. Both of which being of the essence, presently. She was a type 52 loco called Bertha that could pull anything, all 84 metric tons of her, born of the Waffen und Maschinen-AG production line in Posen, daughter of the '42 Eastern campaign. But Klee solemnly wondered if she was big enough, to pull apart the weft of History being woven around them right at that moment & deposit them safely upon some further shore. In a manner of speaking.

The first thing he noticed as the bridge pulled into view was there were no guards stationed at the regular sentry points. Klee felt ahead through the dark with coal-grit eyes. He had 1620 horse-power to pit against whatever lay ahead but no way to see what was coming, trusting wholly to instinct now. The signals had been dead all the way into Golem City, like a ghost town, stations deserted, lines down. The lull before the approaching storm. Taken as a sign, it was neither necessarily bad nor particularly good. But if the City had fallen already, they wouldn't be where they were, at least of that much he felt sure.

As the wheels clanked onto the iron bridge, Klee allowed his gaze to follow the line of the river as it opened southward through the City, half-expecting it to lie in ruins like all the other cities. Dresden, Chemnitz, Berlin. But it wasn't. Yet beneath an obscenely pristine (he thought) silhouette, all was chaos. Perhaps its moment in this movable hell was still to come. In the flicker of the girders & the crisscross of searchlights, flat-bottomed barges crowded the water. The quays were backed up with traffic heading north, every kind of vehicle you could imagine, civilians & troop columns in complete disarray.

The bridges, by contrast, were completely deserted, cut-off by barricades. The only way across the river was by barge, it seemed. Except for the railbridge. *Funny*, Klee thought, peering harder into the gloom. But there was no-one on the tracks, no sign of barricades. Behind them a red&grey shellshocked moon was rising over the valley. Vague echoes of rocketfire & artillery. He pictured motorised Cossack regiments hot on their heals, Mongols, Uzbeks, Turkmen, Aziris, Kazakhs, Georgians even, a whole putrid tsunami of the Great Unwashed. They'd made it through just in time, but Klee wondered how much further they'd get. He turned to take in the view upriver, meaning south, their assumed destination, & found Müller blocking him —

'Why've we slowed?' demanded the ♯ man.

A glint of light caught on the deathshead insignia leering out of the officer's cap. Klee stared at this apparition for an instant or two.

'Warum?!' Müller barked.

And Heil fucking Hitler to you, too, Arschloch, was what Klee was thinking, but what he said was —

'Well, you see General, it's like this. If we don't slow down, the whole goddamn train'll end up in the drink. And if we don't end up in the drink, we'll get t-boned at the junction on the other side. Take your pick.'

He could see Müller reaching for his luger, the stupid sonofabitch, as if that'd get his precious cargo anywhere faster. The searchlights from the river cast weird shadows across the firebox. A manic glint flashed in Müller's eye as he drew the pistol. The pistons heaved, the wheels clanked. Down below, the voices of people crowded on the barges rose over the din of the engine. For a moment Klee thought he could distinguish a loudhailer blatting-out a warning. But it was too late. Müller had the luger out of its holster & was levelling it at Klee's head when something strange happened to the *ℋ* man's expression. The manic look vanished, his eyes crossed, & Sturmbannführer Müller slumped in an ungainly heap against the tender. Kurtz stepped into the light, snarling, with a shovel in his hands.

Well, Klee thought, *I guess that solves that.*

'So now what the fuck do we do?' was what he said.

Kurtz shrugged —

'Dunno about you,' the fireman said, 'but this is where I get off.'

Which was an incredible thing to say under the circumstances, considering at that moment they were fifty feet over a river & heading towards sheer uncertainty. Kurtz tossed the shovel onto the coal & reached for the throttle, easing it right back.

'We go *down*,' he pointed, as the engine slowed even more. 'Through the gap. Now. Then we swim for it…'

They must've been halfway across the bridge, because the river suddenly seemed huge, teeming with debris of every kind & the barges, their passengers, faces awash in the searchlights, gasping at something up there on the railbridge. At *them*, in fact, Klee realised, as Kurtz went tumbling headfirst through the girders. *Jesus Christ, he's fucking crazy!* But Klee never had the chance to say it before the whole train seemed weirdly to upend itself. The river with its searchlights & glowing faces wasn't below them anymore but *coming right at them.* Klee blinked. He didn't even hear the explosion till the engine was in mid-plunge, describing a tangent to an arc at the instant of pure verticality, heading straight down into the black, two, three, four seconds…[*]

A carp's-eye-view might've captured the moment Klee's head jellied like a peeled grape as the boiler erupted on impact, then vanished entirely, the riverbed bubbling as 84 tons of hot steel buried itself in the mud & a volcano of steam jetted up through the collapsing bridge. Who'd blown it was anyone's guess. Partisans? The retreating ϟϟ? One final act of vengeance or sabotage before the Reds annexed the City & submitted it to the ravages of an eleventh-hour "Liberation." The mystery train's even more mysterious cargo, meanwhile, swallowed by the dark rapidly cooling waters upon which no other witnesses cared to linger. Where did it all end up? Heaved by the currents into some Palmyra middenheap? A mudworm's grotto at the foot of an embankment wall, a weir, the ancient pilings of Karlsbrücke? Which, upon auspicious midsummer nights, decades hence, would, if the tales were to be believed, emanate a faint wispy glow — green fairylights, like Meyrink's mermaids weaving luminescent aloes around the reflections of the stone saints, stirring the dreams of some slumbering grey Golem…?

The Detour, The Dead End,
The Red Herring, The Garden Path

It was half-past-twelve when the screening ended — time for a drink before whatever was showing next. Němec re-checked the foldout programme he'd been handed on the way in: it was a film called *The Convert* staring Cosima Wagner & Gustav Mahler. There were a dozen publicity stills over a two-page spread, beginning with a pic of the composer himself, playing the role of a man spurned by the Establishment, sitting alone in a train compartment tormented by music he can't get out of his head — followed by one of Mahler's grieving neurotic wife — a dead child — a priest — a jumble of other (to Němec quite meaningless) tableaux — then one of Cosima W making a dramatic appearance decked-out like a Schutzstaffel Brünnhilde atop the high peak of Valhalla (the "shrine of the Goddess of Music"), conducting the Zhid Mahler through the rites of Catholic conversion: the "Baptism of Fire" & the "Intercession of the Sacred Heart," culminating in the "Dragon of the Old Gods" slaying itself, wedding itself, impregnating itself with the seed of doom. Němec wasn't sure

---

[*] Houston, we have liftoff! [✊]

about this last bit, but anyway. The final pic in the series was of Mahler-Siegried lofting a bright sword tempered from a broken Star of David, the eponymous Convert, no longer a "Zhid-dog" but "Dictator of Opera." *Mahler, Sieg Heil!* It was the first half of a matinee double-bill with the *Ride of the Valkyries* starring Terence Hill & Henry Fonda. After that, there was a 1964 film about two kids escaping from a Nazi deathcamp train ("virtuoso cinematography, inspired editing, brilliantly utilized soundtrack"). No end of uplift, guaranteed.

The cinema lounge was just as empty by the time Němec came out as it was when he'd gone in. The interior was all tarnished brass & moth-eaten velvet a dozen shades of burgundy. A horseshoe bar monopolised one end of a long rectangular salon with a reconstituted Steinway as part of the décor — it was parked in a corner against a glass wall that overlooked a vestibule where some clown had hung a statue of St Václav astride a dead upsidedown horse anchored to the vestibule's yellow-glassed dome. To paraphrase one great man: an object, hung between garbage & eternity. He supposed it was meant to be a comment, on the general state of things. The clown responsible went by the name of Diva Černobýlová, professional Švejkist & urban guerrilla "manqué," Golem City's answer to Picasshole, apparently. Němec felt unqualified to form an opinion either way — art was like flogging a dead horse however you looked at it.

The vestibule was part of an arcade complex that went up in the '20s, one of the crowning Havel Bros enterprises, to compliment their *moderniste* Lascaux up at Barrandov. PRODUCTION EXHIBITION DISTRIBUTION. Visionaries, both: had the War ended differently, they might've conquered every market on the planet. As it stood now, the ancient cinema was half Potemkin, half Pompeii, its faux Doric colonnade like teetering coprolites gladwrapped in expired celluloid. A long time ago the people who built the place had written THEATRUM ORBIS TERRARUM around the base of the dome in gold paint. They could just as easily have saved themselves the trouble.

Černobýlová wasn't known for sitting on her hands or resting on her laurels. Just that day she'd been busy getting the Authorities all steamed up. Specifically, over a huge inflatable Dolly Buster* that'd been put up overnight astride the brokendown metronome on Stalin's Hill, & word on the street pointed the finger at Černobýlová. Němec'd caught a glimpse of this latest invocation of the High Arts on his way from another abortive visit to Havran's

* Were Karel Gott to've been the icing on the cake of Cheskoslovnikia's late resplendent years, Dolly Buster would be the cherry on top. [✋]

antikvariát, this time bearing duplicate pages from the Manuscript. ("Whadya think we are, a copy service? Antique books is what it says on the sign. Antique books is what we do. This shit is five minutes old. You own an original, pal, bring it, or don't bring it, the rest I don't care about.") Němec had been standing on Legion Bridge, mulling it over, pedaloes & picnicking couples below, thinking maybe the Bugman was right: they don't screw you one way, they'll find others — & that uncomfortable yet increasingly persistent doubt, *what if this* was their way of screwing him? At which point he'd looked up, still clutching bits of Voynich facsimile in his slightly trembling hands, & saw Dolly Buster's distant effigy swaying pinkly atop the hill.

Němec blinked at the colossal nude, anchored against the wind by guy wires, all thirty-odd feet of her — leopard-print trilby perched atop bottle blonde & everything else the way nature no doubt had intended it. It was just possible to make out the uniformed cops jostling the wires in front of a crowd of onlookers while a TV helicopter circled above, making the cops' task (whatever it was supposed to be) no easier. Němec, shaking his head in mild disbelief, had stared back down at his hands, thinking simultaneously several conflicting thoughts. About the redhead at the Natural Sciences Museum. About the deadman in his bubblebath. About the fact that life was obviously just one unrelenting poke in the eye, so why take it personally? He made fists, screwed the duplicates up into a ball, told himself to forget about it, hide-out in the cinema all day, fuck the Worldwide Conspiracy. So now here he was, staring at an upsidedown horse while a stickman in Coke-bottle glasses & dandruff-flecked penguin suit was torturing the ivories on the battered Steinway.

He found a place at the bar & ordered the cheapest thing they had, which turned out to be some green concoction tasting of mouthwash. It burned, though, which was good enough. The barman leaned on the taps at the other end of the bar, smoking. A ceiling fan shifted the haze imperceptibly around the room while the stickman at the piano started croaking the words to a song, like some cryogenic version of Old Blue Eyes who'd had the freeze put on the vital statistics a bit too long. Němec gazed into his drink for a change of scenery, then tried gazing at the walls instead to see if that'd make the time pass any quicker. Stuck up in uneven rows were framed pictures of dead filmstars, gazing down on the scene like rubber masks in one of those giftstores on Karlova. Heinz Rühmann, Liduschka Baarová, Anna Magnani, Leni Riefenstahl, Adina Mandlová, Emil Jannings, Asta Nielsen, *the slender but fateful flowering* Lya de Putti… Yeah, it was a class joint alright, all it lacked was a portrait of Goebbels over the bar, with one of those lorgnettes maybe, & a cigarette holder. He gargled the mouthwash & wished he hadn't.

Halfway through *The Convert* Němec nodded off. Inside his sleep, while the soundtrack played the refrain from the *Kindertotenlieder*, he watched a fine spiderwork of cracked celluloid enlarge, frame-by-frame, into the flicker & blur of a ghostly city street grid. Then, as if the camera had been caused to plummet towards it into extreme close-up, the greywhite checkerboard of thawslicked pavement cobblestones rushing up. Then freeze. The camera pulling back. And repeat. And freeze again. And repeat. He could taste the green drink in his mouth. The camera was plunging once more when he woke in a cold sweat & staggered out to the jacks, clutching his face & trying not to throw up.

Which he now proceeded to do without inhibition.

LET THE ARTISTS DIE the graffiti above the sink read — & right beneath it, in small print, PRIVATE GOOD PREVAILS OVER PUBLIC INTEREST, like that joke about polishing turds — surrounded by a moiré of runic genitalia, phone numbers, the siphoned inner mutterings of the puerile & selfpitied, up against the wall with only a pencil stub in their hands. *For the greatest fuck in town call Hanka. For an even greater fuck call Václav Klaus...*

Němec stared gasping at his hands in the dirty sink & tried to remember how many drinks he'd had at the bar. Behind a locked cubicle door the fume & groan of someone laying an alchemist's egg, rising to crescendoed incontinence. Němec retched again. The sinkhole belched back at him like a sick toad. He struggled with the taps until the groaning & farting drove him back out into the lounge. By now there were a couple of more people polishing their elbows on the velvet, the barman rearranging glasses, the stickman croaking the same tune just with different words strung together to fill the spaces.

Němec sunk down on a stool & ordered a coffee. It tasted weeks old. The piano went on & on. After a while he ordered a couple of brandies to restore his equilibrium. Then another two in quick succession. Time once more began to pass of its own accord. At some point Němec took a pen out of his jacket pocket

& began scrawling randomly on the backs of coasters. A woman came up to the bar, large, with acne scars all down the side of her face. She ordered a drink & left. A fly buzzed in Němec's ear. The bottles on the shelves were like bottles on shelves. He gazed back down at what he'd written:

> the mechanisms were winding
> down, days, nights standing,
> as if outside Time,. . . above it
> or below it, in the next room,
> refusing the particulated blankness,
> the atomised dispersal of the self,
> the middle of the night toilet
> flush of mind enemas, the in-
> voluntary insomnias, the
> cramp in the guts, running
> on the pure carbohydrate of animal
> adrenaline *

The Mahler film had been what you'd expect, if what you expected was a nineteenth-century pantomime injected with strychnine passing itself off as LSD. Or perhaps it was the green stuff he'd been drinking. No doubt that'd been a foolish move. By contrast, the Nazi mystery train film had been straight up & down, if perhaps a little gratuitously open-ended when the curtain fell. More mechanisms winding down… He considered whether or not to buy another drink, feeling undecided on any particular course of action on a day that was fading fast. Well, there was always the option of sitting through a couple of more flicks, though it didn't seem wise to risk it after the Mahler escapade. Or he could just blow it all & hit-up Merkin at *The White Whale*, it'd been a while, but that could have all sorts of unforetold consequences.

Deciding he could do with some fresh air either way, he lumbered down from his barstool & out past the dead horse to the vestibule. The programme had *Diamonds of the Night* playing at 19:30, followed by a Burt Lancaster flick — another War film about a train, directed by John Frankenheimer, *Vlak*, 1964, also staring Jeanne Moreau in the role of "Christine." Yeah, there seemed to be a lot about trains. Němec lurched across to the boxoffice counter & peered over the shoulder of the balding fifty-something buying a ticket at the window, to see what seats were still left. No fear: it didn't look like the show was about to sell out any time soon. Still another thirty minutes to kill, though. He cast a glance

---

* To be continued… [✦]

around to see what options were on hand. There was a deli on one side of the vestibule opposite a newsstand & record shop on the other. He could always buy a paper or some cold pastrami, or check out the discs. A mirrored arcade led out past the deli onto Wenceslas Square, though you'd hardly know it. A sandwichboard stood out on the tiles in the middle of the colonnade with an elaborate red&black advertisement for the Rokoko Theatre's ongoing production of *Salomé's Lament*, whatever the hell that was. All Němec knew about the Rokoko was that it was a basement vaudeville joint that like most things in the City had seen a helluva lot of better days. "Salomé's Lament" conjured all sorts of things, but it didn't sound like it had anything to do with Nazi trains…

'Can't you at least hurry up? It's half-past already!'

One of the handy bits of wisdom the Prof had been fond of imparting was that it's usually at a time & place when you don't expect anything to happen, that something does. At the sound of the voice, Němec turned around to see who it belonged to: there, four-inch heels clattering across the arcade from the eastern street entrance, was the spitting image of Jiří Bareš's blonde secretary in a black sleeveless number split up the side, high-collared but still not managing to keep very much back. Puffing along beside her was an overweight vaudeville act, not very tall, cigar, widebrimmed hat & a face like a middle-aged woman's. It was the fat guy the voice belonged to.

'Well it's not *my* fault we're late,' the blonde snapped, 'you have to take that goddamn fish with you everywhere! It stinks! I can't bear it! You don't know how humiliating it is…'

Němec was pretty sure the lookalike really *was* Jiří Bareš's secretary, only she'd changed her wig & couldn't help fidgeting with it. This one almost suited her — but the legs, oh the legs. If the fat guy beside her had wanted to be inconspicuous, he'd chosen the wrong act entirely. In addition to which, he was carrying a large brown carp under his left oxter, whiskers hanging down, one big forlorn fisheye revolving in its socket, slowly fixing on Němec as the pair clattered & puffed their way across the vestibule.

On instinct, Němec stepped back behind the nearest column so as to be out of view. Bareš's secretary & the cigar smoking vaudeville act continued making their way across the vestibule before coming to a stop beside the column

Němec was standing behind. Němec froze. They were no more than a foot away, the man's hat shading his face, the blonde's wig concealing hers. For the time being, at least, Němec was invisible to them, but the carp had no trouble catching sight of him. It gave him a turn of its fishy eyeball, blinked, its whiskers twitched —

'Feelin' like you was bein' watched boy?'

Němec edged further back behind the column just as the blonde looked around, checked her watch & said something to the fat guy who also turned & pointed with his free hand up towards the lounge. The blonde shook her head dismissively —

'He said *down*stairs, don't you listen to anything?'

The carp raised an eyebrow. From the corner of its mouth it muttered —

'See what I gotta put up with, fella? Day in, day out, always the same ol' shtick. You think I like bein' carted all 'round the joint with a yappy broad? And take a look at this schmuck! Who you think picks his shirts? Polkadots fer chrissakes!'

A moment later the two eyesores were clattering & puffing their way in the direction of the Rokoko. The carp glanced back as they went —

'Hey, so long fella. Watch yer step. They might be onto you. *You* know who I mean.'

Curiosity being the greater part of something, Němec felt an irresistible impulse to follow them. At the entrance to the Rokoko the fat man & the wigged secretary paused & glanced around. Němec kept out of view as far as it was possible to keep out of view in a mirrored arcade. Behind him, St Václav's macabre horse with its tongue hanging out seemed to sway in a breeze. *And what if it were to come to life suddenly? Rear out of the sky? Or dump a load of steaming horse manure on some matinee matron's permanent wave?* An insistent tapping sound interrupted his train of thought. He in his turn glanced about. The tapping continued — it seemed to be coming from the delicatessen's window display. RETTIGOVÁ'S, the sign painted on the glass said. TRADITIONAL CHESK DELICACIES. The tapping got louder.

In a hamper stuffed with cured meats & pickles, a large dumpling with eyes & a mouth was butting itself against the glass pane. Němec ogled it. It'd caught sight of him & had obviously been trying to get his attention.

'Psst!' the dumpling said. 'Hey you! Yeah, you there. Come closer. There's something I gotta tell ya.'

Across the passage, the newsstand vendor was staring conspicuously into his handkerchief like there was something stuck to it he'd never seen before. The ticket woman at the boxoffice was reading her crossword. Němec gave the dumpling one of those imploring looks, held a finger to his lips. The fat man & the wig had taken the opportunity meanwhile to duck through the doorway & descended the stairs. Němec shrugged at the dumpling & went off after them.

'But hey!' the dumpling cried. 'It's important! You're really gonna want to hear this! You'll kick yourself for the rest of your life, you're really missing out here, you dunno how irresponsible you're being…!'

The carpet on the Rokoko's stairs had probably been red once, back when the Party brass used to turn-out for the premières with their wives done up like streetwalking travesties from the Grandes Boulevards, but the place clearly hadn't seen a première since before the Wall came down. Only a couple of tables were occupied — a waiter in a borrowed three-piece sat at the end of the bar reading a TV guide while the barman practiced polishing glasses, like they all seemed to do, when they weren't doing nothing at all. One of those disheartening Karel Gott records mewled out of the sound system. The low-lighting was meant to add atmosphere, but all it did was cover up for the tawdriness — the threadbare carpet, pealing wallpaper, the tablecloths that hadn't been changed in nearly a decade, the chintz grey with dust.

Jiří Bareš's secretary wasn't anywhere to be seen, but her fat companion was there, parked at one of the tables with a martini in front of him & the carp, still wrapped in newspaper, with a cocktail onion stuffed in its mouth. Under dimmed lights, the womanly face had a type of repose. It still didn't belong to anyone Němec recognised, but (all things considered) given time maybe it would. For example: across the table from the fat man, where Němec would've expected the blonde to be sitting, was the unmistakable silhouette of Faktor's dwarf. And beside the dwarf, wearing what could only have been a fake red beard, was that goddamn Zahradník from the Natural Sciences Museum. *There was just no fucking escape, was there?*

Němec wondered where the rest of the crew were hiding. Maybe they hadn't arrived yet. Maybe they were right behind him, coming down the stairs that very second. And was this some kind of regular cabal he'd stumbled upon, a weekly fancy dress convention perhaps, or had they come together especially on his account — or rather, on account of those Kč 3,- per page xeroxes he'd been airing around town like an idiot — flushing the conspirators out of the woodwork & into the open, so to speak? Or, to put it another way, like a clay pigeon in a shooting gallery. But what'd *that* mean? Something in Němec's mouth turned sour & vicious-tasting, as he pictured himself being fired in slowmotion out of a catapult & puffs of flack blossoming all around, marring a blue cardboard sky like stageprop weather.

Cautiously, & without taking his eyes off the assembled weirdoes, Němec backed up the stairs. The carp goggled after him, squirmed in its wrapping. Not the ideal time from Němec's P.O.V. for the fish to start spouting witticisms. The sound of his own heartbeat was like a dozen cocktail onions going *crunch*. He started to sweat. It was just a matter of time before the carp gave the game away. Seeing his options running out, Němec succumbed to a very reasonable desire to flee as fast as humanly possible. But nobody, it seemed, was interested in pursuing him — they all had his number.

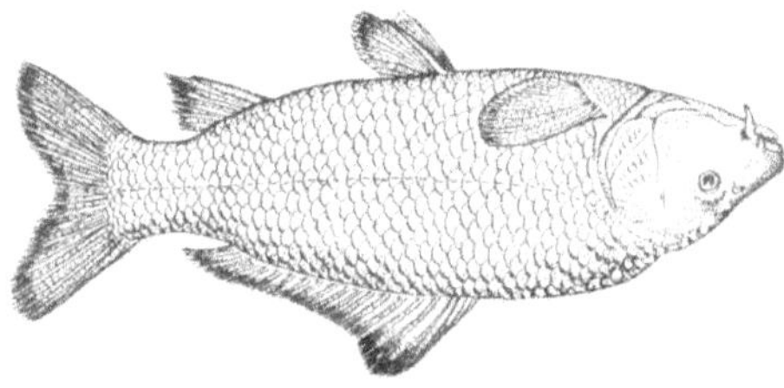

Now, if Major Zeman[*] had been in Němec's shoes, it might've been a different story. *There* was a man with method, reason & Comrade Husák on his side. Not to mention a wicked duck-egg-blue polyblend suit, vest, tie, black plastic square-framed glasses & a side-part brushed across, forward, then back, like no other cop on TV. A man with sleeves big enough to pull out a conspiracy of foreign agents, saboteurs, the ubiquitous Mašín brothers & Bugs Bunny as well, if he'd a mind to, like a magician pulls scarves out of a pocket — put History in a box, saw it in half & get the ends stuck back together arse-ways — just in time to crack the whole case wide open single-handed, so to speak, & show the culprit after all was *you!*

No doubt about it, kids, Zeman would've known exactly what to do. Here's his famous checklist — see if you can solve Němec's dilemma:

1. Proceed from the beginning: secure crime scene — interrogate suspects — interview witnesses — check network of informants — collect

---

[*] The *Thirty Cases of Major Zeman*, Commie crimebuster extraordinaire, made Poirot & Miss Marple look like Custard Tart & Peach Melba. The guy every other jerk on the project wanted to grow up to be, when they didn't want to be Karel Gott (except without the falsies). [↓]

evidence — call in forensics — source records — stake-out. (Always be prepared to ask: What next?)

2. Case not cracked wide open yet? Back to square one.

3. Repeat.

4. If all else fails, don't give up! Devise new methods for proceeding: A to B (& back again). C & on to D. Skip E in order to arrive at F. Incorporate G & H.

5. If you can't falsify the evidence, improvise.*

Not so colourless as it might appear on the surface. A certain discretion in such cases is called for. Observing, for example, the rituals which people passing-by seemed unconsciously to participate in. Perhaps their behaviour might be a clue: for example, walking while (at the same time) clicking tongue, humming, biting lower lip, talking to self without interruption, holding breath & allowing "breath pauses" to determine points of observation — taking stock mentally of objects, events, places, people...

All of this in a symbiotic cadence, so to speak, seeing things at the same speed as the things themselves, static or moving, dull or brightly coloured, animate or inanimate — slowly, moderately slowly, very slowly, very very slowly, moderately rapidly, rapidly, very rapidly, etc. How, for instance, to properly *see* a tram pulling away from a tram stop & at the same time, *into* the tram, through its windows, faces of people seated, fragments of standing bodies, windows open or closed, windows of different shapes, a red&beige tram, a red&silver tram, a blue tram, green tram, a single-carriage tram, two carriages coupled together, an articulated "one-piece" tram with accordion folds of black rubber, the street, the buildings, billboards & advertisements, the overhead wires, the whole complicated depth-of-field in constant agitation, constant flux. (Did people have any idea how incidental they were, tied to this monstrous necessity: that without the Evolutionary Accident, none of *this*? Try to envisage it, some late Jurassic arbour by a swelling stream, bluegrass, the eve of apocalypse...)*

---

* Remember, kids, don't try to do this at home without a responsible adult supervising you at all times. As Zeman always says, *Safety first*! [✋]

No such thing as a coincidence, kiddo.

The narrative was getting out of hand & maybe this was as good a place to pause as any. Proof by conjecture born of self-fulfilling prophesy, as the Great Man once said. *Consider the opposite of what appears to be the case.* In each previous scenario, what if it was Němec's own actions that were being interrogated? Begin with that. How to observe the fact of being observed, without tipping your hand? Surrounded by an invisible network of informants, constantly under surveillance, lured or directed from one carefully constructed situation to the next. A rat in a maze disguised as the world at large, where each turn, cut-back, dead-end is part of a calculated Mind Experiment. Like those microphones the Soviets snuck inside Bobby Fischer's teeth, right where the fillings were supposed to be, cunningly disguised, listening in on his chess brain — miniature TV cameras in his head — beaming it all back to the boys on Dzerzinsky Square secretly at work building a chess revenge-weapon, a proto Karpov-droid, Mk I, still experiencing malfunction issues, though plans already on the drawing board for Mks II ("Korchnoi") & III ("Kasparov"), input pro & con from Komsomol. The sort of thing that might set Němec to thinking about the archivist at Strahov Monastery — Fišer, with an "s," & the four knights like a backwards Ruy Lopez — which Fischer, with a "ch," played as white almost unerringly in *that* Reykjavik match of '72: pawn to king four, repeat — knight to king's bishop three, knight to queen's bishop three — bishop to queen's knight five, etc. And if it was good enough for a rat, then why not? At the end of the day, the rat itself wasn't important — Němec knew it wasn't about any *particular* rat, but the *rat mind in general*. Whether there were microphones in teeth or not was moot, as long as it (the rat) *believed* there were microphones in its teeth & behaved accordingly (& do *you* know how a rat with microphones in its teeth should behave?). For the general hypothesis to hold, what was true of one rat would ostensibly have to be true of every other rat (call it the rat "Rousseau Principle"). It was all about abstraction: not the *same thoughts* necessarily, but *the same way of thinking different thoughts*. Fišer or Fischer or Faktor or Joe Blow — whether they knew a pawn from a pigmy or a bishop from an ayatollah. As Major Zeman says, *Never underestimate the subtleties of surveillance. You only ever see what they let you see. And the more you see, the less you know.* Decoyed by fake CCTV, the real cameras are the ones hidden inside that cracked grime-grey megaphone or this broken-down Trabi, radio-controlled Wiener dogs sniffing your crotch in the park, at tram shelters, on escalator steps, in phone booths installed with hidden x-ray machines, not to mention all those robot mosquitoes that come buzzing in the night to implant a permanent state of unsleep paranoia, the spider at the bottom of your glass, a fly's eye above the light fixtures (always someone awake on the other side of the wall, watching, listening). In the great scheme of things, wasn't he, too, therefore, Němec-sometimes-Nemoc, nothing but a conjecture in shorthand? An experiment that could've gone on without him, with anyone else taking his place, like an *x* in an algebraic equation, the universal variable: Nemo, Neiman, No-man? In which case, what's he doing here at all? Has he written himself into a corner he can't get out of, hoping for some editorial sleight of hand to make sense of the situation, the intervening Secret Agent who'll bring it all to resolution, one way or the other? That drunk in the doorway pretending to be asleep, maybe? The fag in the white trenchcoat giving you the eye? The bolshy brunette in a blue postal worker's uniform brushing past? The couple of suits parked out in the street, at the end of the passageway, leaning against the wall with expressions & gestures that look too focused, too rehearsed? The tourist with the conspicuously large Nipponese camera pointed straight at him? The hustler in the doorway with shuttered eyes behind cigarette smoke? The beat-up Merc that slows down at the pedestrian crossing when there's no-one trying to cross, taking the opportunity to glance back at him in the side mirror? The leering pink effigy on the hill like some porno panopticon...? To lesser minds, the obvious thing might've been to work backwards from the end, unwrite it all & fill in the blanks afterwards, imbue even the most inadvertent / haphazard / accidental detail or *non-detail* with an air of having been pre-elected, set down, written as if in stone atop Sinai, etc. It'd just be a matter of joining the dots in retrospect, painting by negative numbers, typing with the "backspace" key permanently held down... (*Sure, now you're thinking, kiddo. Just gotta figure out which dots to join, then you're all set. Like they say, easy as pie. Ever made pie, kid?* [♣])

37

PANDORA'S "BOX"

According to a certain Monsieur Poisson, the probability of an event is the reason we have to believe it *has* taken place or *will* take place. For example, there was the story of Pandora, the world's first cybernated robot, the original *bionic woman*. Now, some postmodern Hephaestus experimenting in a Golem City lab claimed to've built an exact likeness, right down to the valves & tubes & hydraulic compressors described by the ancient authors of the *Antikythera* of Rhodes… The story was reported in the weekly *Vesmír*:

> The all-new **Pandora C³I**[*] provides care for the elderly & comfort for every home. Totally lifelike in most respects, the **Pandora C³I** is easy & inexpensive to maintain. Monthly service & maintenance included with our generous instalment plan. The **Pandora C³I** comes equipped with speech recognition & vocal synthesis, possessing a basic 800-word vocabulary, & using 90-degree micro-CCD cameras to process lip synchronisation & visual recognition. The **Pandora C³I** also has 17 facial points allowing for 56 degrees of freedom in adjusting its facial features to suit any occasion. The **Pandora C³I**'s entire body is made of highly advanced synthetic jelly silicon with 80 artificial joints in her head, neck & body providing for all manner of physical expression. The **Pandora C³I** is 160cm tall & weighs 50kg, self-cleaning & easy to store…

Pandora, the reporter from *Vesmír* explained to his readers, was the original Eve, the first woman, conceived by the Greek gods as punishment for mankind's (through no fault of its own) infringement of the divine prerogative, being caught red-handed in possession of the very fire thieved by Prometheus from Hephaestus' workshop (receipt of stolen goods being nine-tenths of the law). This archetypal fembot was created in the image of sheer guile: a beautiful evil sent to torment the race of men — a pink-lipped doomsday box whispering of hope eternal — a killer robot with a name like a buttery Italian Christmas breadcake sprinkled with icing-sugar. Crafty old Hephaestus with his rude hammer, anvil, tongs, sweating over his furnaces, lame in one leg — the man

---

[*] The four pillars of the cybernetic *Kama Sutra*: Command-Control-Communication-Intelligence. All for one & one for all. [✋]

who made Aphrodite's girdle — stammering as he conjures this fantastical femme fatale from his fiery forge. Gift of the gods & all that.

> Sensors allow the **Pandora C³I** to react to external stimuli by way of an air servosystem distributed throughout the upper & lower body. In addition, the **Pandora C³I** is able to imitate human-like behaviour, such as slight adjustments in position, spontaneous head & eye movements, & modulated breathing. The **Pandora C³I** has a highly elastic silicon skin "grown" on a genetically enhanced collagen scaffold & is capable of sensing changes in temperature & touch...

Fast forward three thousand years to the Intelligent Mechatronics Lab of T.E.S.L.A. Corp, eighth floor, Aetna Towers (Vyšehrad), the company boardroom, silver-tinted floor-to-ceiling windows affording a sweeping northerly vista of Golem City — Nusle Valley, the Botanical Gardens, the river winding under bridge & over weir, Hradchin-on-the-Hill in cameo, etc. *Our motto? To err is machine!* The company C.E.O. (known to employees & Board-members alike, as his predecessor before him, simply as G.O.D.) sits in a walnut&leather swivel chair at one end of an oversized "War Room" table. The photograph shows G.O.D., face in silhouette, taking a conference call on a vidphone that's been propped on a stand, leaving his hands free to be draped in a relaxed executive fashion over the precincts of his groin. The face on the vidphone is of a genetic technician, grade three according to the decal on his labcoat lapel. He's holding up a diagram of a female robot. Below the picture, the caption reads: AND G.O.D. CREATED WOMAN!

> An independent microprocessor in the brain allows the **Pandora C³I** to coordinate gestures & expressions as well as bodily symmetry, permitting it autonomy of movement while responding to subtle changes in its environment. The **Pandora C³I** is designed to be fully interactive, & is able, for example, to demonstrate realistic facial expressions while simultaneously singing & dancing. As part of our sustainability pledge, the **Pandora C³I** is capable of extracting & storing energy from external sources utilising an advanced parasitic thermalisor & thermionic convertor to supplement internal long-life promethium-147 batteries...

Another picture on the facing page shows the prophylactic cyborg in anatomical detail: *Ready to go into Large-Scale (Re-)Production!* A group of engineers stand around grinning while the mechanical doll sips a martini, dressed in blonde Marilyn Monroe wig & white dress & heels, positioned over a ventilator grate that periodically wafts up thigh-tingling currents of air...

According to the hack at *Vesmír*, the next generation of humanoid robots would even be capable of changing their facial features to match the ethnic type of whoever they were interacting with — some would even possess mirror-like characteristics, to satisfy the latent narcissism of their "users." It'd make any decent self-respecting reader wonder exactly what their "makers" had in mind for these fleshbots — the ideal secretary jujitsu assassin femme-fatale, e.g., ever-available & skilled in over a hundred varieties of fellatio, not to mention the entire illustrated Kama Sutra & Marquis de Sade. (Envisage a basement room with smiling android in latex cop uniform wringing a seventytwo-hour confession out of you with a toilet plunger, pliers & alligator clips, & not a single bead of sweat to mar that uncanny visage, eyes expressive of a deep human sympathy, the full red collogenated lips, the ample bosom & slender arms you long to find comfort in even as the volts surge, the alien object probes deeper in your entrails, the fingerbones snap. You'll bear anything if only to be forgiven by *her*. Say & do whatever she tells you to, & the longer it goes on — the longer you're made to gag on your own puke, the longer you piss & shit yourself, barely able to see, barely able to think, mind jolting back & forth between pain & unconsciousness — the more you love her...)

Members of the public curious about what the future was going to look like could meet the Pandora C^{3}I in person, on display for a limited time only in the T.E.S.L.A. showrooms, Aetna Towers (along with a host of other gimcracks, nostrums & wind-up paraphernalia for the betterment of mankind). Visitors would be able to witness this miracle of modern robotics take turns showing off its various natural attributes, beginning a floorshow every hour on the hour, featuring an aria from Verdi, a selection of karaoke favourites, a waltz with a live partner, the salsa, the cha-cha, the tango, the foxtrot, a Billie Holliday number in a smorgasbord of languages, a recitation of the Founding Charter of the United Nations, a tasteful medley of ballet classics, a Jane Fonda workout, & a simultaneous chess match against sixteen players chosen at random from the audience. All the stuff dreams are made of.

T.E.S.L.A. Corporation
living the future today...

38

PHANTOMWISE

The only lights were the ones around the Broadway mirrors casting long shadows over the costume racks. On one of the dressing tables Němec spotted an ashtray full of butts & matchsticks beside a pack of fancy Russian cigarettes. A couple of actor types, stage hands & whoever else, came & went. The dressing room was really just a corridor broken into cubicles, with the racks cluttering the wall running along the back & a door onto the street at the far end. A dummy with a pegleg sat in a corner grinning. The place seemed hung in a permanent 40watt gloom of cigarette smoke & face powder, Němec couldn't imagine how anyone would be able to find what they were looking for in there. He wondered if he would.

The Zrcadlo Theatre was really just a basement off an arcade on Malostranské Náměstí, not the most likely venue for a missionary outpost of the Church of Realism. It made Němec think of the kind of place an organ-grinder might go to mourn his dead monkey, or that someone like Němec might go to chase figments behind a mirror. A collapsed armchair was propped on breezeblocks between one row of frocks & another row of frocks. Sequins, old lace, crow feathers, like widows' weeds that'd sprouted from the family vault. Němec supposed he could do his chasing just as well sitting down & so took up the armchair's invitation. From that position the atmosphere was even more eccentric. A stag's head loomed from the ceiling. A hat stand on the verge of toppling over displayed a collection of broken umbrellas like taxidermied rooks. All the place needed was a draughty pipe organ.

Němec adjusted the folds of his undertaker's suit & settled down for the wait. Draped in shadow, you could say he blended right in, all but the worn toes of Blecha's shoes which alone caught the light. Behind the street door, someone laughed. Muted voices, footsteps, indistinct sounds. Then a kind of lull came over the place. Long seconds passed. A gunshot broke the silence. For a while nothing happened. Němec sat transfixed with anticipation. Then came a smattering of applause & voices downstairs. Moments later Alice Steinerová walked in, dressed in black period costume. A nickelplated pistol glinted in her right hand. There was blood on the side of her face, a crimson eleven o'clock shadow.

Without noticing her visitor, she paced the length of the dressingroom like an unbalanced Pandora, her image multiplying & vanishing in the glass menagerie of Broadway mirrors. A couple of top hats & a wave of crinoline swept past & out the street door, haw-hawing as they went. *Once you go Brack*, a voice guffawed, *you'll never go back!* The door slammed. Alice Steinerová stopped pacing & tossed the pistol among the jars of makeup. A child in a huntsman's costume scampered in & out of the room without saying a word. Alice sighed, wiped a hand across her face. The bloodstain smeared, making her face lopsided in the mirror's lights. Her entire bearing, in fact, had a lopsidedness about it — a tipping-over or shying-away — a vague subsidence, as if from the absence of some essential support. Her bloodied hand clung to the chair in order that she arrive sitting in it in the conventional upright position. Němec half expected her to slump to the ground, like the epilogue to a closing act.

Volta, in his crosspurposed roundabout way, had hinted where the leading lady might be found, though not before time. Haphazard as his life appeared, even to him, Němec was no stranger to the suspicion it was being stagemanaged. Poorly, even incompetently, but nevertheless. That very singular morning after that very singular night before, lying semi-delirious on the Good Doctor's settee, or sofa, or couch, & hearing between cigar puffs that simpering reply to his one intelligible question:

'Ah, cherchez la femme!' as if that was supposed to mean anything.

What he'd finally gotten out of the man was, on nights she wasn't performing at the Kabaret Grünegast, Alice Steinerová slummed it in the underground theatre (politically, once upon a time, if not aesthetically, though now just plain subterranean) — mostly what Volta called *character studies*. This posthumous Hedda Gabler must've been one of them. Why Němec had chosen this particular moment to pursue an admittedly unpromising lead in a "case" that even to him must've sounded like bad melodrama, is anybody's guess. But facts being facts, he would've been hard pressed not, at some stage, & sooner rather than later, to examine a rock so far left grievously unturned. For example, he hadn't even thanked the woman for getting him out of a tight spot. A modest bouquet, a *bon mot* scribbled on a napkin, would've been the least. *O tempora! O mores!* As the Bugman might've said, *Gallants just ain't gallants no more.*

<u>**THE ALICE VARIATIONS**</u>

1. ALICE ON THE WALL

Her eyes in the mirror trying to separate his voice from the
shadows. She pulled the ashtray towards her & lit a cigarette. The
flare of the match cast a gaunt cadaverous light upwards across her
face -- it reminded of that face in Toulouse-Lautrec's AU MOULIN-
ROUGE, ugly as sin, more deathmask than face. She shook the match
out & the impression passed. Her hands, the Visitor could see, were
shaking, but as he stood up out of the dark her eyes never left him:
like gemstones copied in glass paste, depthless blue.
    --I was beginning to wonder if I'd ever have the pleasure.
    --You're shaking.
    --Don't imagine it's on your account.
    --Perhaps you should try firing the gun further from your
head next time.
    --I'll keep that in mind. Did Níko send you?
    --Níko?
    --We both know who I mean.
    --Maybe.
    --I expected it sooner.
    --Or then again, maybe no-one sent me.
    --Suit yourself.

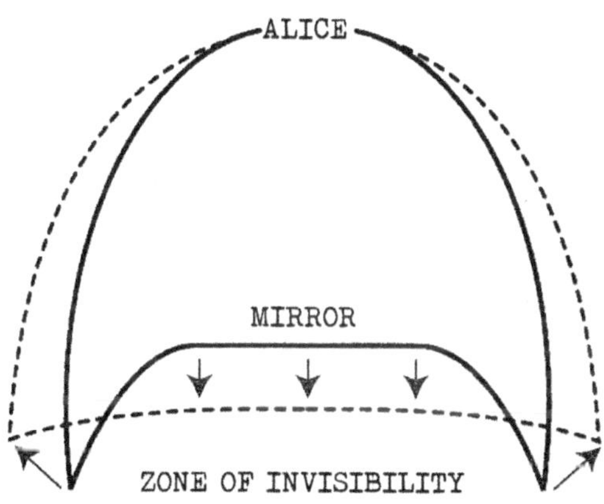

She took a deep drag on the cigarette till it was almost exhausted, leant back in her chair so it creaked under the weight, then took her time crushing the butt out in the ashtray. Her gaze remained fixed on the Visitor's reflection in the mirror the whole time, eyebrows making question marks. Like the brunette at the baccarat table in <u>Dr No</u>...
    --Well?
    --We need to talk about the other night.
    --Really?
    He was standing behind her now, close enough to smell the sweat & greasepaint. She leant forward in her chair & began wiping the makeup off her face. Other actors came & went from the stairway, talking without saying anything, not seeing the Visitor at all. Alice reached up & removed the wig she'd been wearing: beneath it was a head of coalblack hair cropped short. It set her features into a wholly different constellation: the angled cheekbones, the wide forehead. The mask unmasked, Parrhasius-like. Arching an eyebrow she watched him watching her. It was like having a stage-side seat at an undress rehearsal: THE TRANSFORMATIONS OF ALICE STEINEROVÁ.[*]
    --Unzip me, she said.
    The Visitor reached out. The high-collared dress slipped from her shoulders exposing a tattoo on the nape of her neck. While he stood there looking at her she poured a glass of gin from a bottle beside the mirror.
    --To old etceteras.
    She downed the drink & slid the empty glass among the jars of greasepaint.
    --Excuse me if I don't invite you to join me.

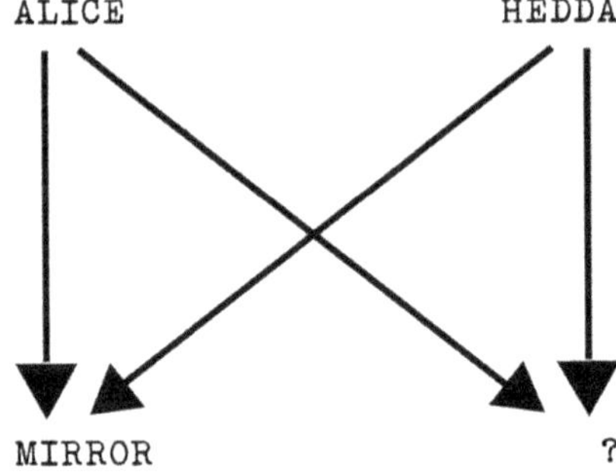

The Visitor handed her a black kimono that'd been hanging on the rack beside him. There was a musky perfume on the collar. It reminded him of something, but he couldn't place it.

--How about we go somewhere we can talk?

She gave him a long scrutinising look.

--Maybe, she said finally. Do I get dressed, or d'you expect me to go like this?

--I'll wait outside.

Alice watched him along the length of the dressingroom. There were voices from the street, someone was laughing, but the laughing stopped when he opened the door. The actors watched him make his way along the sidewalk to a spot under the nearest streetlight, then one by one they went inside.

The air was damp, he could taste the river when he breathed. He wondered what would happen next. It wasn't long before Alice came out, wearing the same kimono open over a singlet & black jeans & a pair of cowboy boots. He thought of the tattoo. The combination did something to the picture of her inside his head. She led him around the corner to a bar. They found a table at the back.

In the subdued light of the bar, Alice's blue eyes had an even more preternatural lack of depth, like painted glass, framed by eyelashes still heavy with mascara. The eyebrows were sharply pencilled in black, the lips streaked across with rouge. There were traces of blood in a faint line from her temple to the line of her jaw. Gazing past him in threequarter profile, short dark hair & pale throat, she looked like a half-naked facsimile.

A waitress came & they ordered something. When the waitress was gone, Alice leant forward & returned his look.

--Why are we here?

He reached into his jacket pocket & pulled out a photograph.

--That night at the Cabaret? I was there because I found the address in a man's empty apartment.

He turned the picture so she could see it. It showed the Prof sitting at a table on a restaurant terrace. Alice looked at it strangely…

--Who's this?

--The late Tom Hájek. He's dead. Apparently it was a heart attack, but it's just possible someone killed him. When I went to the Cabaret, I ran into a couple of familiar faces. Quite a coincidence. And of course there was you. And that was quite a coincidence, too, considering we share the same doctor. Wouldn't you say?

--Are you sure that's the man?

--What d'you mean?

--Nothing, just are you sure? That's all.

--I'm sure…

--Who are you really? she said, suddenly looking up.

                    4. TO MAKE AN OMLETTE,
              FIRST YOU NEED TO BREAK AN EGG

Watching Alice in the black kimono, the Visitor had the impression
of tempting fate. She resembled the kind of woman that only ever
existed in films. "Alice." Was that a real name even? Or was it just
the name she happened to have in the version of the story he was in?
      --The first thing they tell you when you get up on stage is to
establish yourself inside a space, she said.
      Was that what they were doing now? This? These weren't the
questions that'd brought him here. Or was this the ritual the answers
required? Her gaze, the intensity in her eyes, was unwavering, he
felt the ground beneath him slipping away. Very matter-of-factly
she said:
      --One image can trigger the whole thing. Not the lines, but the
situation. It's essential to avoid being tied to something in advance.
Each word, gesture, is like stepping in deeper, leaving the
circumstances at the door: who you're supposed to be, what happened
before you walked on stage... Not thinking, but reacting.
      --Stimulus & response?
      --It's the logic of the action that counts.
      --Maybe.
      --No maybes.
      --And now? Who's scripting us now?
      --Surely there's some little committee men in grey suits
approving the dialogue as we speak.
      --D'you remember Pan Vajíčko?
      --Mr Egg? The cartoon?
      --He used to come on before the commercials. He'd doff his hat,
tap dance, make a bow. Then there'd be these ridiculous ads.
      --Honey's good for your children! Buy pork!
      --D'you remember the brands?
      --What difference did it make? They were all the same.
      --I could never figure out why they bothered.
      --Pure theatre. They wanted people to think they were watching
real TV, like in the West. In the West they have ads, so they put ads
on the TV here, too. Capitalism's poor cousin.
      --Imagine if the central programming had malfunctioned &
there were no ad breaks? Everyone stuck there, day & night, in front
of the idiot box, till they ruptured themselves & died in a flood of
piss, flapping about on the floor like beached carp.
      --It could've been the end of the Free World.
      --But under Socialism, the ads were the only thing people
wanted to watch. The rest was just one long queue outside the
communal toilets.
      --Queuing for the toilet was one of life's greatest freedoms.
      --D'you know this song?
      --What song?
      Alice tilted her head. "I am the Walrus" was on the radio.
      --What's that supposed to mean, "the eggman"? What're _eggmen_?
      --I saw a film once. There was a fat lady sitting in a playpen
wearing diapers the whole time & eating softboiled eggs. She got the
eggs from the eggman.

5. THE GAMBIT

Alice reached down into her handbag, took out a square black-&-gold
cigarette case & extracted a cigarette. As she did, the Visitor caught
sight of the tattoo on her neck. She lit the cigarette, blowing a
trail of smoke up towards the ceiling. He said:
     --D'you realise I don't know anything about you?
     --Want me to tell you the story of my life?
     The way her lips sneered made him conscious of the weight of
his own teeth inside his mouth. Her left eyebrow, when she arched it,
came to a point like a circumflex, making the eye into an "ô" beside
the other, half-lidded, like an "e." Seduction by facets of muted
violence. She drew the tip of her tongue across her teeth:
     --I'm really nobody, she said. Anything to do with emotions is
cruel or fake. I cut myself up & don't feel anything. I ask myself if
that's what life is. I'm sick of expectations. You expect something,
but you're really empty. You want to fill the holes but they don't
exist, you only think they do, because it's what you are. There's no
inside or outside, just surfaces. People can find there whatever they
like. But on the other side, where I'm the one standing on the stage,
there's nothing for expectation to point towards. Each time I suffer
is exactly like the first time. The same suffering replayed again &
again...
     --Are you always so melodramatic?
     The edges of Alice's eyes creased into what might've been
evidence of amusement. In a completely different tone of voice she
said:
     --It's what comes of being a Gemini. D'you know what Níko says?
The individual's becoming extinct, society's killing him. Or her.
     He nodded his head out of a compulsion to do something:
     --I've heard all about the Good Doctor's theories. In days of
yore, when things weren't going so fabulously, they'd cry out for
some death. A little bit of death to restore the equilibrium. The
Romans had the Circus Maximus, while we get to tune into the idiot
box. What's bad news today, is tomorrow's entertainment. Death by
collective pratfall. Just think, in some parallel universe, God
walking in the Garden of Eden slips on a banana skin. Head over tit.
Adámek the chimp wails, beats his breast: <u>Oy oy oy! Heva! Yenta! Vat
you done? Yahoodi's kaputz! Yehe shmeh! Now see iv it done make no
gantse magullah! In der Vild dey gonna shoo us! You vant? Mit der
shvartzes, gevalt! N' not vor no fertsik tag 'n' fertsik nakt vats on
teevee, but der hole bubbemyseh Entwicklung! Zat you vant? Like sum
klutzkymenshes?</u>
     --Well, Alice said smilelessly, eyes slantlidded. If it's a
question of blowing the world up to preserve ourselves from
boredom...
     The implosive "p" of her "up" against the explosive "p" of her
"preserve."
     --The opposite, I'd've thought.
     --Ah! The headlong pursuit of impersonal happiness. Long may
it prosper.

6. NATURALISM

It occurred to him that every gesture, even the shadows under her
eyes & the lines of her throat when she was speaking, or not
speaking, could've been borrowed directly from a character in a film
& it wouldn't've been any different. She moistened her lips with her
tongue, just so:

    --Niko says, <u>Everything's just how you decide to think about it.</u>
There're hundreds of things, situations, which all look the same but
are really different. Every day's like that, each day the same as
every other day, only different. Everything looks, feels, sounds the
same, except it isn't. Imagine an actual existence in which every
little drama was underlined by a moral. You can't, because it's
nonsense, absurd. Why else do people humiliate themselves into
believing in a God? What's the meaning of this theatre people insist
on living in? Every night when I go out on stage & blow my brains
out, I still know I'll have to get up again & keep doing it, over &
over & over, the next night & the night after that. And for what? Is
the purpose of mankind progressed in any way?

    --Repetition's the object of existence.

    --Sometimes I'd just like to be a <u>thing</u>.

    --Or existence is the subject of repetition, one or the other.

    --I don't know.

    --How can you bear to be watched all the time?

    --They're two different worlds. You walk off stage & become
invisible.

    --Maybe we all need some type of secret police watching us,
listening in, being there, just to keep our egos intact.

    --It always seems so small, the space where the audience is. You
can't even see them, because everything's gone white under the lights.
Not blinding, just white. A white wall. Sometimes I think, if I
scratch at it with my fingernails, it'll peel away, like old paint, &
underneath there'll be glass. And I get so afraid I can't move,
because if I do the glass might shatter. And then there mightn't be
anyone there. On the other side.

    Alice clenched her teeth & mimed someone trying to scream. Then
pursed her lips, exhaling slowly, one smoothly lacquered fingernail,
possibly false, drawn across her left eyebrow, as though the two
actions, expiration & agitation, were not merely coincidental. Her
gaze, meanwhile, remained fixed, immobile, two points in
constellation, around which whole zodiacs of expression turned, like
a tragedian's mask. Her lips pulled back into a forced smile:

    --Remember, she said, there's nothing more difficult than to act
naturally.

    On the word "act" she let her hand, the one she'd raised to
touch her eyebrow, fall to the table. Her fingers brushed the sleeve
of the Visitor's jacket. He noticed them coil back into themselves,
restoring a distance. She hadn't intended to touch him, her gesture
was designed to illustrate simply the limits of something. The lips
slackened, the smile slid away.

An entire drama could be summed up in the way Alice Steinerová's fingers tapped a cigarette on the table, the way the flare of the match reddened the cut of her hair, the way her hand moving out of his field of vision to extinguish the match while she inhaled. The smell of phosphor & tobacco smoke. While these impressions accumulated, vague ideas passed through the Visitor's mind: fragments of epistolary dramas about people in despair -- messages cast out to sea in bottles -- secret prayers & lamentations -- self-accusations to which no reply would ever be possible. She, too, seemed very far away. The space of the table between them as deceptive as a mirror in a mirror-maze. He couldn't be sure he was actually present & not observing her through a screen, or in a spotlight on a stage. It was like watching an old film in which the actress you fall in love with died long ago & her image is really a kind of shrine. As if reading his mind Alice said:

(a) --One night it just happens & you don't come back.
(b) --All I could think about was finding a way to jump.
(c) --They say the stage is like a tightrope dancer's wire.
(d) --Only ten percent of suicides don't leave notes.

It was the cue. Her story, the way she told it, went like this:

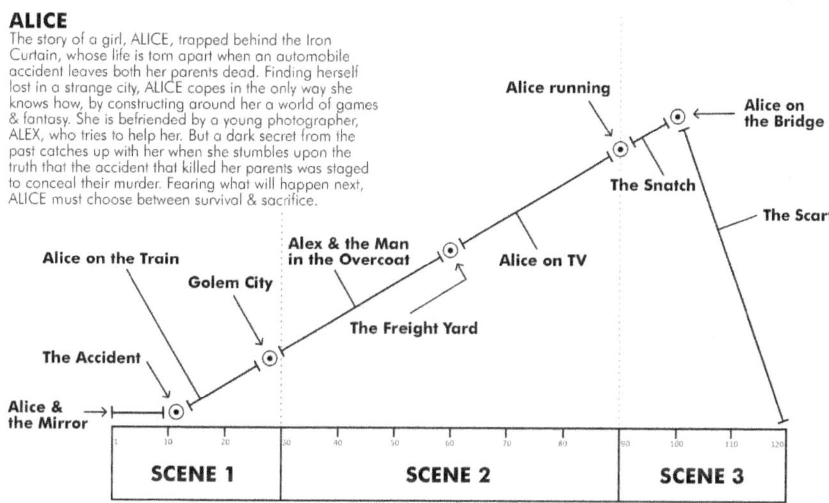

1. Interior: A girl (ALICE) alone, standing in front of a mirror in her parents' bedroom. We see her playing with her mother's clothes. As she ties a red scarf around her neck, a bottle of perfume falls to the floor, shattering. Close-up of ALICE's face in the mirror.

2. Exterior, night: An accident scene. Revolving lights, police radio. A Škoda "Rapid" with shattered windscreen. The bloodied faces of its occupants, a man & a woman, become visible as the camera slowly zooms in. A gloved hand reaches into the frame to touch the woman's face, turning it towards us.

3. Day: ALICE, wearing the same red scarf, staring through the window of a train compartment as the train pulls into a large station. A sign: GOLEM CITY, on a crowded platform. ALICE making her way through the station. Sinister men loitering around the kiosks. Dead neon signage. A stairway littered with junk, syringes, a sleeping prostitute. Stairs exiting onto a motorway that cuts across the old station building. Crumbling stucco & broken windows.

4. A young man with a camera (ALEX) taking a picture of ALICE asleep on a tram. She wakes, startled & tries to run. ALEX follows her, offers help. They walk through a freight yard, unaware that they are both being followed. ALEX buys her a meal at a kiosk. A man in a brown overcoat watches them from a distance. He is wearing gloves. As evening falls, it begins to rain.

5. Interior, night: ALEX in a darkroom developing a picture of ALICE. We see her face in close-up, sleeping. From another room, the sound of a TV, the presenter's voice. Cut to: TV screen, a missing person's bulletin. A picture of ALICE appears on the screen. As the camera pulls back, we see ALICE lying on a couch in front of the TV, watching. The red scarf lies on the floor.

6. Exterior, night: ALICE running through the rain, along a cobbled street. We hear her name being called. ALICE keeps running. Her frantic breathing. Her point-of-view dissolving into a blur. As she stumbles out onto an intersection, a pair of headlights come rushing towards her. The squeal of brakes. ALICE with her hands spread on the car bonnet. Through a pair of windscreen wipers, we see ALEX behind the steering wheel. He gets out & leads ALICE to the passenger side. He asks, "Why'd you leave like that?" "They want me." "Who?" "You wouldn't understand." "You're safe now."

7. Exterior, day: ALEX photographing Gottwald Bridge from the street below. ALICE is standing beside him. She notices the man in the brown overcoat watching them from across the street. She shivers. "We've got to go," she says. "What's wrong?" "There's a man." "What man?" ALICE points across the street, but the man's no longer there. ALEX continues taking pictures. ALICE becomes more & more apprehensive. Suddenly a car pulls up & two men in tracksuits get out. One knocks ALEX to the ground, the other makes a grab at ALICE but she escapes.

8. Interior. A police station. Through a mesh window we see ALEX handcuffed in an interrogation cell. A silent tableau as the camera zooms in. Then we hear, "What did she tell you?" Then cut to a nighttime exterior: Gottwald Bridge. Intermittent traffic. ALICE is seen leaning against the railing. She appears breathless, exhausted. Out of the shadows, the man in the brown overcoat approaches. He is holding a red scarf in his gloved hand. We see the resigned look in ALICE's eyes. At the moment the gloved hand is about to reach her, it's as if she suddenly dissolves. The camera's suddenly adrift in the air. Then we see the man, leaning over the railing of the bridge with gloved hand outstretched, staring into the darkness below. The scarf fluttering in the wind.

REAL LIFE*

The actual story went something like this:
    (1) 1992: Alice Steinerová & her brother Alex moved to Golem City after their parents died in a car accident.
    Except (2) their parents weren't really their parents, because Alice & Alex were both adopted. (3) The parents who weren't really their parents had been returning from the Tatras when a coal-truck veered through a turn into the wrong lane. (4) By some miracle, the children in the back seat, who weren't the parents' children, survived.
    (5) After the accident, the brother took it upon himself to look after his sister, put food on the table, kept her in school. (6) He worked as a photographer's assistant.
    (7) The "parents" had both been members of a local Party branch. (8) After the Revolution, their past began catching up with them. (9) There were hints that the accident hadn't entirely been accidental. (10) Hints, too, that Alice & her brother were better off staying out of town.
    (11) The brother found a job in Golem City as a set-designer at Barrandov Studios.
    (12) Alice had always dreamt of being in the movies. (13) Not knowing who her real parents were led her to act out fantasies about their secret lives.
    (14) She left school & started hanging out at different theatres, trying out for roles, sweeping floors, hustling.
    (15) The opportunities didn't come.
    (16) When they did, it was for extras work, eight hours a day standing around doing nothing.
    (17) She got hooked on uppers, downers. (18) She cut herself.
    (19) She did props, costumes, makeup.
    (20) She landed a walk-on role. (21) She stabilised. (22) Climbed the ladder. (23) Slipped. (24) Started all over again. (25) Supporting roles. (26) Got her feet on the rungs.
    (27) Landed the lead in a tiny production.
    (28) The director stalked her, implied things he said he knew. About why she was adopted.
    (29) Alice flipped, went straight over the edge. (30) One night Alex got a call from the cops. (31) They told him she was in hospital, that she'd been picked up on Gottwald Bridge trying to jump the 140 feet down onto the tramline that runs through Nusle Valley. (32) Except that, at the critical moment, she'd got stuck on a wire fence.
    --And then I fell anyway, onto a ledge & broke my back. Two vertebrae -- here & here. Which is how I met Níko… He was on call when they got me to the clinic. Supervised my treatment. Six months of rehab. Kept me out of Bohnice, for which I'll be forever grateful. Níko really took care of me. He even got me an audition so I could restart my acting career. I owe him a lot.
    The whole time she'd been talking, she'd been staring at an unlit cigarette, which now she stuck a match to, blowing the smoke across the table at the Visitor.
    --So now you know everything, she said.
    --What about your real parents?

525

Alice sat silently for several moments before responding:
--Show me that picture again...
He gave her a questioning look, then reached into his jacket
for the Prof's photo & handed it across the table. Alice scrutinised
it closely.
--You might think I'm strange, she said. But every time I see an
old photograph, I imagine what it'd be like if the people in it were
them. It's just a silly game. I never knew my real parents. They
could've been anyone. Alex looked in the files, but there was nothing.
That director was just being arsehole, because I wouldn't go to bed
with him. Same very old story. Even a soapy ending.
He took the picture back & stared at it doubtfully. The Prof
looked gloomily out at him from the terrace at Barrandov. He
thought about Alice Steinerová's story & how much of it was
believable & how much he could make himself believe, if it was worth
his while. And that bit about the suicide notes. Was she one of the
ten percent? There were holes a mile wide in everything she'd told
him, but even so, if he read between the lines, let the situation play
out, stepped away from the mirror...
And what about Elsbeth von N____? And Mrs Prof? Did they
leave notes? Or were they part of the 10%?
Turning the photograph in his hand, he tried to summon forth
an image: the Prof's funeral -- the whole unsung bureaucratic
canticle of the body's disposal -- & somewhere in that image, the
absent widows in black. Had some form of telepathy existed between
them? Some sort of agreement, unspoken, some order of etiquette? The
precedence of the lawfully-wedded over the "other woman"? And how
did it work? The ex-wife burning the Prof's letters, opening the gas
valves in her room, just hours after his death? Which would've made
it a double-funeral. Why couldn't he remember that? He'd been there.
And that was the day Elsbeth von N____ gassed herself, too, at the
very moment they were shovelling the Prof's ashes into an urn.
Their timing was impeccable, their motives entirely opaque.
Nothing had been said. At the crematorium there was only some sort
of official in a suit, the undertaker, the executor (Bareš) -- &
someone else. Severínová? She alone to cut off her tresses & fling
them on the funeral bier? Alone to return to the house on Jánský
Vršek, with what sense of foreboding or foreknowledge? And in the
Prof's apartment, Elsbeth von N____'s corpse, waiting for her (as pre-
arranged?). And the note? Where was the note? You burn everything,
leave no traces, no messages for those who come after -- because
those who'd been searching for a message had been there already,
hadn't they? And set the whole thing up.
He shook his head, slipped the photograph inside his jacket.
Alice blew another lungful of smoke at him. She said:
--You start expecting reasons, you'll get nowhere.

--Was I supposed to tell you it was because life wasn't worth living?
Or maybe the world, everything, was just too uncaring, cruel,
meaningless, absurd to go on? No hope? You don't have to be
delusional to kill yourself, all you need is to realise its possible.
Your defining moment of lucidity, when you finally take control,
even if the reason is because the world won't let you take control.
    --What d'you know about all this?
    --All what? I don't even know what you're doing here?
    --I thought you might know something.
    --About the man in the photo?
    --That night, at the Cabaret, what were you doing with Faktor?
    --You mean Viktor? Viktor's all bluff. He likes to come in &
big-note himself, drink champagne, invite the "girls" to his table. He
gives me attention, is all. Jealous?
    --What about Volta?
    --What about him?
    --Are they connected?
    --Not that I'm aware. Viktor might act like he's a
Schwarzenberg, but he's nothing but a peddler of fake antiques. He
runs a bazaar on Libeňský Island. Specialises in Habsburg kitsch &
War memorabilia. Some kids with a garage out in Kladno knock it up
for him by the truckload. You should pay him a visit.
    --Maybe I will.
Alice laughed, but her eyes didn't laugh:
    --Why did you really come to see me?
    --Does the Devil & the Carmelite mean anything to you?
    --...?
    --Your striptease act at the Green Fairy.
    --That's unfriendly.
He rubbed his eyes. Suddenly he felt very tired. To continue
talking in this vein made no sense. He struggled to explain the
frontispiece from the Black Book, if for no other reason than to
convince himself of the extent of his own stupidity. She laughed
genuinely this time.
    --Mmm, antiquarian smut... A bit corny, though, don't you think?
Priestesses, devils...
    --Not a priestess. The Sisters of the Blessed Virgin Mary of
Mount Carmel...
    --Whatever.
    --Distinctions are important.
    --That's the kind of thing Viktor would say.
    --Will he be there tonight?
    --You'll have to find that out for yourself.
    --Will you be there tonight?
    --I'm not making any promises.

THE TRANSFORMATIONS OF ALICE STEINEROVÁ

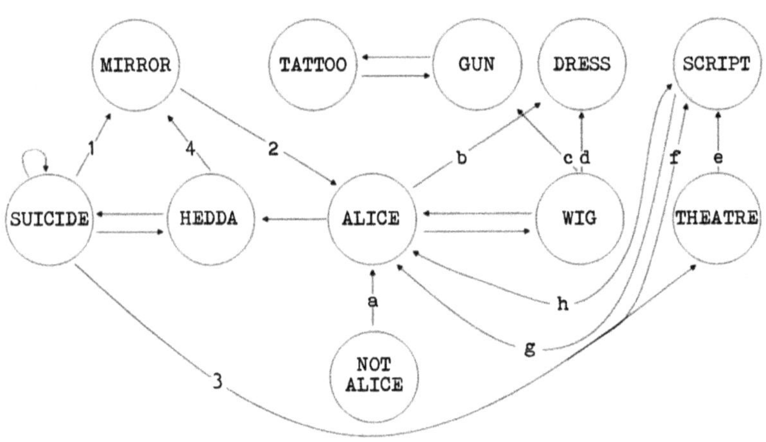

*APPENDIX 2:
REAL LIFE/TRUE STORY OF ALICE STEINEROVÁ (CONVERSION KEY)

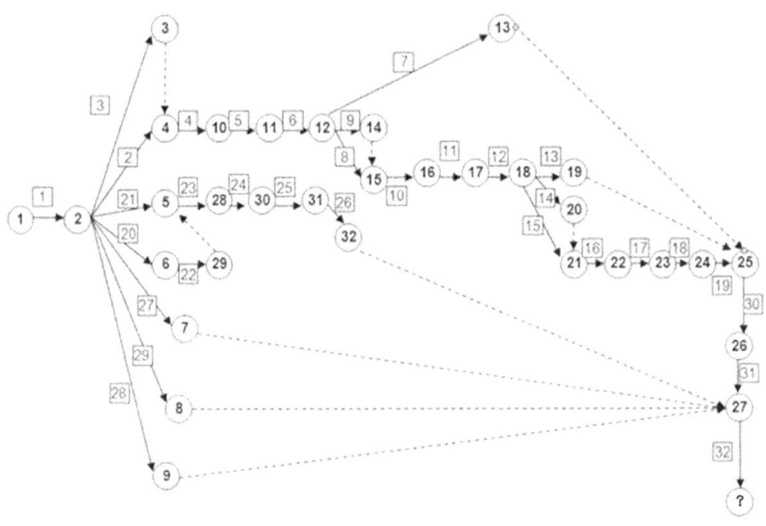

39

REISE IN DIE NACHT

'When I was eight there was this kid, Horst Wechsel, had the biggest shvanz on the block. Used to flash it at all the shiksas. He'd go up to them & say, *You wanna see the Promised Land?* then whip it out & they'd run squealin' up the street. Man, he was hung like one of them doorposts in Deuteronomy. But you know, an act like that doesn't have a real big future, 'cause pretty soon all the shiksas catch on & maybe they tell their memas & one day while he's flashing his klobasa some old bird turns up & starts waving a cleaver at him. Maybe give him some sort of trauma. You know, pass the rest of his days flat-out on a headshrinker's couch. What they call in the profession, Gentile Dysfunction issues. I mean, what use's a mezuzah with nothing inside, right?* Well pretty soon Horst started having bigger ideas. Like when he got to hanging out at the shule with all them kids who think one day they're gonna be the Messiah, look in the mirror each morning to see if the beard's started to sprout yet. Wanna be the right-hand man sitting at The Gate, you know, when The Day comes. With their mitzvahs & their minhags. Pulling each other's ears. *Hear, O Babylon, the Nin our god* & all that. So one day Horst is, you know, diggin' the scene & whatever, when Reb Moravec comes up & says, *Ain't you that kid been shoving the salami at Frau Schiklgruber's pansy son?*

'Let me tell you something about racial hatred. Now, a lot of people say… Well *you* know what they say, right? They say all sorts of unpleasant things about the Nicest People on Earth. I mean, *you* know who I'm talking about. Some of *your* best friends are the Nicest People on Earth, am I right? I think what it comes down to, it's some kind of envy. Here you've got this couple, man & wife in holy matrimony, the whole eight inches, sitting at a table in one of those swish joints downtown on Pařížská. You know, where they bulldozed the Ghetto for so they could whack up a whole lotta swanky condos with that *art nouveau* smeared all over them? Yeah, one of *those* joints. Now, she's a blonde, dig? Got the Versace backless number, the matching pearl earrings & necklace

---

* כוזו במוכסז כוז. (A Caesar cipher. Give unto & all that.) [✋]

529

combo. He's sporting the moustache, got a silver cigar case in his breast pocket, probably wears designer deodorant. They're stirring some caviar around with bits of expensive stale toast. How it is with these exclusive types, man. I mean, they've got it tough. You think *you've* got it tough, but no-one forced *your* grandma to sit around all day eating caviar on stale toast, did they? So while these two are stuffing down the fish-eggs, right then some bigshot who runs a chain of pig farms they're acquainted with walks in. Can't take a shit in this town without there's someone knows about it already. You dig? So there's this guy, name of Herrgott or Heimlich or whatever, walks in like he owns the joint. And with him, see if you can guess this one. You got it yet? Right. One of those *Nicest People on Earth.* Just like that, right past the doorman & everything. Dark eyes, tight little skirt slit up to here, four-inch heels. I mean a real showstopper. And the blonde in the Versace sees this & says to hubby, *What's that just came in with whatsisname? Isn't he supposed to be married to sonandso?* And hubby says, *Oh, that's whatsisname's Nicest Person on Earth. Isn't she something?* So the blonde sneers & tells hubby, *Liebling, OUR Nicest Person on Earth is much nicer than his!*

'Just the other day… You ever get the feeling you already know what's gonna happen, before it happens? Like you're walking down the street & there's a cop & you just *know* this cop's gonna call you over, ask a bunch of questions, go through your I.D. Know what I mean? 'Cause the second they see you coming, those beady little cop eyes zero right in. *That's right, I'm looking at you.* Like you've got *kike* written all over your forehead. *Shit, man, ain't that scene all washed up? I mean, man, this's the Free World. We got McDonalds and Kentucky Chuck and NATO fer chrissakes.* Woah! You wanna be careful there. These guys, you know. These guys are *unreformed.* Anyone here ever been to a *reformatory?* That's what's reserved for the losers. These guys, they all been to the Economics University, trained in the protection of Free Market Interests. Now you might think that means the Worldwide Zhiddish Conspiracy, but what it really means… It's like, if these people were any more rightwing they'd be mistaken for an amputated albatross. A real cop nowadays gonna make even Joe Stalin look like Commie trash. It's like, is the Pope Catholic? So just the other day I'm doing that, walking down the street, minding my own proverbial, when this cop comes up to me & says, *Goin' somewhere, son?* Now what would Jesus have done? *Well, I'd sure appreciate some directions, orificer. See, I'm looking for that Garden of Gethsemane. I guess it's round here some place…* But you've gotta wonder, don't you, about the kind of people ask a *cop* for directions. I mean, you'd really wanna be *lost,* like yer life depended on it. *Orificer! Orificer! I'm lookin' fer Jesus! I can't find him anywhere! Oh orificer, help me, help me pleeeeeez...*

'You know what this dude said to me this morning in the Metro? *Suicide's just the poor man's alternative to waging total war...* That's what he said. I'm not kiddin' you. I mean, he had a beard & everything, so he had to be right, right? I said, *Total war? But ain't that sort of outdated?* And he said, *Whatya think I am, some kind of Allen Ginsberg?* But you've gotta love these guys. *Total war.* That reminds me of my mother. She had a thing about all those pamphlet pushers, always stuffing somethin' in yer hand every time you go down the street. Always on about some kinda *cause. How the hell do those people eat?* she'd say. *It's the war,* I'd tell her. *What war you mean?* she'd say. It was like 1968. Whadya tell a woman like that? *Mum, I just got my call-up papers. They want me for the army. Well some army YOU'LL make,* she'd say. Used to tell us how gramps was an Admiral, back when they still had those great big man-o-wars goin' up & down the Vltava. *Ain't gonna make you wear that yella star or nothin', are they?* Hell, to be fair to the old lady, she'd really done it hard, bringing us kids up. Oh no, you think I'm gonna joke about *that?* Forget it. Now goin' in the army, that was *definitely* gonna be like suicide. All these peaceniks, you dig, were sneaking over the border, 'cause you know life's all wine & roses over *there.* Join the army? No *sir!* Oh boy! You've gotta understand, it was *different* back then. *Can't ride a theory home from work,* they'd be sayin' on the radio. A man's gotta be *pragmatic* about his future. The ol' Proles' Paradise not all it was cracked up to be? Stand firm, son, a man's gotta struggle to make anything right in this here world, see? Breakin' the earth with yer bare hands. Tryin' to raise a crop with all them Capitalist doomsayin' crows stealin' it out from right in front of yer face. No *sir!* Well it weren't like most of us ever had that problem, seeing as there was no employment going round anyhow. But it gives that nice warm & fuzzy feeling inside, doesn't it, when some Old Hand credits you with high ideals? Shit. How come I always get stuck with these holier-than, self-made autodidact types, with All the Answers to Everything? Just the other day I was sitting in a bar. Some one-armed thalidomide poet comes in spouting that shit about how the *World's gonna end, brother,* you dig? Just another one of those caftan-wearing self-haters of the species, can't bear to hear the sound of anything but their own croaking. And you just wanna shout at these sonsofbitches, *Revolution's over, you arsehole!* 'Cause you know what God had to say about these losers, don't you? It's like, did Jesus Christ commit suicide or what? It had to be downright *despair,* that's the only reasonable explanation. Just thinkin' it's a *sin,* though, right? But there he goes. Man, didn't he have *any shame?* Getting' crucified right out in front of everyone, some of those people knew his *mother* fer chrissakes! But maybe God just got tired lookin' after business, wipin' out the ENEMY every other day of the week, decided to do a deal, start a Franchise instead, subcontract the stuff to the professionals, industrialise. *Son*, he said, *time for you to go out 'n' do some killin', pay yer own way, shouldn't expect a free ride in this here world...* And there's that Jesus with the long hair, he just ain't gonna cut it with those number-cruncher, button-pushin', suit-&-tie jerks. That's what the Franchise's for. Let the boys from I.B.M. handle the Soylent Green stuff so the kid can hang out on the Dead Sea, smoke some of that weed, dip his sandals. You know they've got a sign over there nowadays, NO WALKIN' ON THE WATER! Just takes one arsehole to spoil the fun for everyone else, isn't that right? Well it'd serve the precious little Mummy's Love if his number really *did* come up like that. Can't you picture it? Just what kind of shit would they be givin' this guy in the barracks? *Yo, JC, latrine duty 'n' don't go givin' me none a that miracle crap...* Oh, but it's true, there does indeed come a time in every man's life when he's gotta do his duty. That's what they say, right? You gonna expect the Son of God to turn out a *conscientious objector*? Wasn't that what the *Ghetto* was for? Well we tried that one, God, & it didn't work. Some flaws in the design. Like taking an Egyptian holiday with that guy Ramses on the loose. *Hey, Red Sea's lookin' kinda nice this time of year, whadya say?*

'Now, speaking of losers...'

A Waltz in a Valise

The camera crew were taking up most of the bar & half the tables around the stage, doubling as extras in a sea of Wermacht feldgrau. Sound technicians, gaffers, grips, wranglers, loaders. A script girl in black Schiaparelli. The make-up department sporting Vionnet. In the midst of it all was Mistress Vicarious, resplendent in knitwear Chanel & surrounded by a dozen Hugo Bosses rubbing shoulderpads with the resident sorority in Pernod-green, appleblossom pink, mimosa yellow & carnation blush. No sign of a director.

No-one paid the slightest attention to Němec's arrival & why would they? The doorman, the coatcheck girl, the spoonman, the anatomy dummy, the schnorer, the cast of hundreds if not thousands, standing around like future tape-recorded presences waiting to be played back against the archival footage, for some remote-control voice on a wire to say *Cut*! & *Action*! Alice Steinerová led the way into this den of iniquity. Whatever misgivings Němec may've had, dissipated into the fog that hung everywhere. It'd followed them all the way along the riverfront, a wall of dreadnaught-grey that closed like a portcullis upon Legion Bridge as upon some Bridge of Doom. Dead streetlights stood sentry. Weird echoes across the water. The groaning of the locks. Flurry of batwing. A distant frog-concert in the sough of the wind & bells tolling under silent hammerstrokes from afar, afar, afar. It was after midnight when they descended the steps to the island, the château enveloped like a sphinx in the darkness of its own enigma. But as they crossed the threshold of the Kabaret Grünegast, time seemed as once before to wind back up on itself, five decades in five precipitous steps. The curtain parted & the last days of the War listed in the gloom that closed in on al sides.

It was like a charade of a charade in which Němec, never one to miss a trick, found himself once more playing the role of the interloper waiting to be found out. A freak come to a freakshow. He followed Alice's kimono gamely through the crowd. From the middle of the room came the sound of the Great Toad, Mistress Vicarious, laughing, if you could call it that: a high, flat, cracked sound. For a moment the sea of grey parted & Němec beheld the enormous creature's heavily rouged lips & semi-disgorged yellow teeth. Everything about her was in character: the slightly moist eye, the porcine face, the false eyelashes clotted with mascara, the hands in a permanent state of gesticulation like a Balinese dancer's, fingers crusted with glasspaste rubies, diamonds, sapphires, a gold tiara atop gaudily sculpted hair — there was nowhere for a description to stop. Then just as suddenly the sea closed again. Němec found himself at the edge of the stage. The Lenny Bruce impersonator was facing into the lights, mouthing into the microphone. The crowd went through the motions. It was like watching a rehearsal for a funeral. The man pointed a bicycle horn at the side of his head. *Honkhonk.* All it needed was a bucketful of bad blood.

When the comedy act ended, some time-expired chanteuse in a girdle got wheeled out onto the stage & started lip-syncing to a scratched vinyl that must've been older even than she was. She looked vaguely familiar. If he let his eyes go out of focus, Němec could almost call to mind the vaseline-misted features of some UFA-era screen siren for rent. A vague approximation would do. The stuff wet dreams used to be made of on the Eastern Front. That or a bullet from a Tokarev SVT-40....

Vorbei, vorbei sind all die schönen Stunden
die wir verlebt am schönen Ostseestrand

Well, Němec thought, *sure sounds like everything's schön.* He peered across the dancefloor to see Alice beckoning him towards a table on the far side. He arrived just as the coatcheck "girl" he'd run into on his previous visit was snapping her fingers & calling for martinis all-round. A waiter descended with a tray & glasses. It all seemed part of the act. Besides the coatcheck girl, the table was occupied by a scrawny-looking brunette with hair that was long & crimped & parted in the middle. She wore one of those pearl chokers over her Adam's apple that were meant to've been popular with the demimonde back in the old days & a tight satin shift reminiscent of period photographs of Edith la Sylphe, & like the Sylphe she had no expression to speak of. Next to her was a Max Reinhardt caricature, high cheekboned with pisshole eyes beneath a fixed scowl & a wave of strawblonde that didn't match his eyebrows. He was wearing a linen suit that didn't fit, either, & a white starched-collar shirt, but the props department had forgotten to supply a carnation for his buttonhole. A camera with a fancy zoom lens lay on the table in front of him, beside a glass that was half-empty already.

'Well looky who's here,' said the coatcheck girl. 'If it ain't the Zhid with the Lid.'

The Sylphe stared up glibly from her martini, then stared away again. Max Reinhardt scowled —

'Hello Sister, brought company?'

'Company!' the coatcheck snorted. 'That's a laugh. Who'd be caught dead with a mug like that?'

'Can it, Doreen,' Alice drawled.

'Can it yourself, princess. You wanna slum it with the himeys, buy your own drinks.'

'Go on, Dink,' said the man sitting next to her, 'give the fella a break. If my sister thinks he's okay, maybe he's okay. Besides, it's me pays for the drinks round here.'

'Yah, that's all I need, a real hunk of manhood!'

Someone did something with the lights & the room turned green. It seemed to be the cue for Dink-the-coatcheck-girl to light a cigarette & blow smoke across the table in Němec's general direction.

---

* "I do like to be beside the seaside..." [✋]

'You heard me, buster,' she waved a hand at him, 'scram.'

'How about trying this on for size,' Alice smiled coolly as she slipped the nickelplated gun from her handbag, not the kind of move you'd expect of Hedda Gabler, though there were worse things in the script.

Max Reinhardt sighed. Dink made sceptical eyes at the gun. It was pointed straight at her face, but with a mouth that big you'd never be sure of hitting anything vital, even with a real peashooter. She blew some smoke at it. Inhaled & blew some more, then flicked the butt across the table. The Sylphe made bored motions of stirring the cocktail onion in her drink.

'Ladies,' Němec mumbled, looking decidedly awkward standing there with his arms too long for his sleeves & hat tipped over his eyes, but none of them paid any attention to him.

Dink stood up. She had a full glass in her hand & before Max Reinhardt could do anything about it she'd dumped martini down the front of his shirt.

'You wanna pay?' she snapped at him. 'So pay!'

Max Reinhardt sighed again. Alice stood unmoved. The Sylphe stirred her onion. Not to be outdone, Němec scratched his trouser leg. The chanteuse laboured on. Then right in the middle of the uplifting refrain, the needle must've got stuck in a groove, because the recording went *die schönen die schönen die schönen* over & over again, before someone finally had the sense to pull the plug on it. In the ensuing silence, Dink leant across & sneered over the barrel of Alice's gun —

'Something sure does stink around here.'

Němec couldn't help but admire the dialogue. He wondered if they all came up with their own lines, or if this was a scene they'd been rehearsing & he just happened to come along. Then as someone called out for a second take, Dink turned on her heel & barged through the crowd. It was an exit fit for a queen. A couple of heads turned but that was the sum total of it. Too bad for Dink. A second later the clapperboard clapped. The cameras rolled. The recording wheezed back into life. *Vorbei, vorbei,* the chanteuse croaked all over again. The Sylphe in her corner of the table smirked ever so slightly before restoring her mask.

'Is that thing loaded?' Max Reinhardt scowled at the gun, dabbing his shirtfront with a napkin.

With an utter blankness of expression, Alice said (?) —

(a) 'If it was, I wouldn't be here.'

(b) 'What's deadlier, a loaded gun or a loaded word?'

(c) *'Let's find out.' She pulls the trigger, nothing happens.*

(d) *Nada. She stows the gun in her bag without saying anything, or:*

(e) *The whole thing with the gun is just in Němec's head, or:*

(f) *If the gun exists at all, it's merely to execute a gesture, or:*

(g) *The gun exists, but in a parallel dimension where only Němec can see it, or:*

(h) *She pulls the trigger and a flame leaps from the muzzle, flickering in the semi-darkness; a cigarette materialises between her lips, which she lights before snapping off the flame and pocketing the gun; when she speaks, her words make intertwined halos of smoke —*

'Between zero & infinity, ends meet.'

Max Reinhardt clapped ironically, allowing the napkin to slip to the floor. He picked up the camera & aimed it at Alice. *Click.*

'Is that thing loaded?' Alice said.

'It's okay baby,' a voice with a sarcastic whine interjected from nowhere, 'it only fires blanks.'

'They ought to've given you a talking role instead of just a bit-part,' Max Reinhardt scowled.

'Don't I know it,' said the Sylphe.

Max Reinhardt, camera-finger cocked, shutter at half-mast, turned his scowl upon Němec —

'Some entrance you made, chum. Better be worth it.'

'As you might've guessed,' said Alice, taking a seat, 'this's my brother.' Then added for the other's benefit, 'Mr Němec is a writer.'

They were as much like brother & sister, Němec couldn't help thinking, as Laurel & Hardy. He reached a hand across the table. The Brother merely scowled into the viewfinder —

'Oh,' he said. *Click.* 'Does writing still exist?'

'I thought so once,' Němec replied, to keep the smalltalk chugging along.

The Brother parked the camera & picked up what was left of his drink & scowled into that. It was all there was to it, the whole repertoire. Němec wondered if he was meant to sit down now or not sit down. It was the same table, he realised, as where he'd first seen Alice the time before. Were Faktor & the dwarf somewhere nearby? He peered around the room but saw no evidence of either. The chanteuse was doing her best not to bring the house down as the recording finally came to a crescendo & petered out. She bowed as far as the steel-plated girdle she was wearing allowed. The girl in the Schiaparelli climbed onto the stage with a bouquet of wilted roses. As the canned applause died down, the voice with the sarcastic whine asked —

'What's it write?'

Apparently it was the Sylphe's turn to express an interest.

'Yes,' Alice pointed an eyebrow at him, 'what *do* you write, Mr Němec?'

Just then the houselights came up & a waiter (it was the Reinhard Heydrich lookalike) appeared with more drinks.

'Hypotheses,' Němec said unenthusiastically, accepting a glass of martini.

The transvestite responded by rolling her eyes just so. She must've spent hours practicing it in front of a mirror, but she hadn't got it quite perfect — she couldn't help glancing back at him from under the inch-long fake lashes she was wearing to gauge the effect. When there wasn't any she went back to stirring the cocktail onion. She kept the listless motion going with her right hand while her left crept its way into Max Reinhardt's lap. The Brother brushed it away.

'Words, words, words.'

Němec raised his glass —

'Here's to nothing,' he said.

'Oh for Christ's sake, sit down,' Alice said.

He did as he was told.

'Long live the Reich,' he mumbled, downing his drink.

It tasted as fine as any martini could, if a martini was supposed to be made with methylated spirits.

'Funny guy,' Max Reinhardt said. 'I see guys like you all the time. Guys think they're headed for the big time. Guys couldn't shine that old queen's shoes. You come here lookin' for a job?'

The Teratologists

was the name of the picture they were shooting. It was supposed to be based on a book called *Four Days to Apocalypse*, about the Fall of Golem City, May of 1945. Němec cast a sceptical eye: why not *Hitler, the Musical* instead? (It'd be a better bet than a V2 to make a splash in the West End. Hell, it might even make it all the way to Broadway, & bomb over there, hehehehehe.) The crew hustled around the room, setting up the next scene. A scriptgirl was reading out bits of dialogue & stage directions to someone in a regular comicstrip ⚡ uniform —

'Kammler up to his eyeballs on pervitin these last chaotic days of the War — if he sleeps, he thinks, he'll wake up in a Soviet torture chamber. To pass the long nights he plays correspondence chess with Alekhine via an encrypted radio link-up. His location's meant to be top secret, never in the same place twice. Tonight he's backstage at the Grünegast, with his pocket chessboard & a radio operator disguised in drag, a corporal named Hans. They've got the island surrounded by ack-ack guns to keep the partisans at bay. Tomorrow he'll be on a train. Berlin. A final meeting with Der Führer to receive instructions for his final desperate mission. In the meantime, he's just been checkmated with a classic king-&-two-pawns combination. Over the racket of the cabaret orchestra & the sound of distant gunfire, he & Alekhine indulge in a last bit of small talk. Afterwards, Kammler will mingle incognito at the back of the audience before slipping off into the night to his next rendezvous. It could be his last game with Alekhine for a while, but they're both optimistic. Kammler: "How'd you like to see your Mother Russia again, comrade?" Alekhine: "Ja, Scheisskopf, I look forward to the day I get to ride through Red Square on a Tiger tank.'"

'What's my motivation for this scene?'

'You're hoping not to have your balls fried off by the Soviets. You're hoping Patton will welcome you with open arms. You're hoping Schörner's Army Group Centre can cover your arse for just four more days. You're still hoping for a Miracle Weapon…'

'Our mum's name — not the real one, the adopted one — was Libuše,' Alice said, 'which was kind of a family joke. When we were kids, we'd dress up in each other's clothes. People couldn't tell the difference. It drove the dads nuts, he was always saying how we'd turn out queer. A pair of little fags, I think were his exact loving words. Except it's the world that went queer. But anyway, you know, that was another country &, besides, the old whores're dead.'

'You'll drown one day, Sister, in all that milk of human kindness.'

'Are you the one giving me my lines now?'

'I don't see how it's the guy's business.'

Max Reinhardt adjusted his scowl to take in a point beyond Němec's left ear. The Sylphe finally gave in & poked the skewered onion into her mouth. It looked like a dead fish's eye. The toothpick came away with a bloody smear of lipstick. Alice, placatingly, reached across & touched her brother's hand.

'My dear brother,' she said, 'is doing production stills for the movie, aren't you Alex?'

He glanced at her irritably. To Němec, this sudden ranging from one emotion to another was a revelation. The eyes of the two Diaskouri glowed darkly across the table at each other. All very brotherly & sisterly.

'Invite him to your show, why don't you?'

As an aside to Němec, & by way of explanation (one squinting eye, index finger going *snapsnap*), she added —

'Alex's preparing an exhibition.'

The Brother gazed off at something on the other side of the room. Němec wondered what normally passed for conversation with this crowd. The dear Brother sure was the life & soul of the party, you could tell just by looking at him. Nice guy. Could see him making a real splash with the boys down at the morgue. *Hey Joe, this one ain't even cold yet...*[*] The Sylphe, meanwhile, had managed to drape a set of long manicured fingers across his shoulder & was now purring like a sick cat. A row of sharp little teeth flashed between red lips.

'Don't mind him,' Alice sighed. 'It's his first major solo gig, so he gets nervous. I'll give you the address. It opens in a couple of weeks.'

She gave Němec one of those looks —

'You should definitely come.'

Taking out a pen, Alice Steinerová began writing the address of Max Reinhardt's Big Deal on the back of a napkin. Němec took the opportunity to scrutinise the exposed nape of Alice's neck as she leant over the table. The shape of the tattoo altered subtly with each movement she made, a smear of fake blood still visible along the hairline.

---

[*] He bore, it must be said, a certain striking resemblance to the main character, Zygmus, in Gustave Aubade's *Elegy to the Swan*, who famously says *The image is born to win the right to remain invisible* — or some similar, queasily romanticised drivel. But Zyg was naturally the silent type, *exceptional* being Aubade's usage, all inner anguish & irrational longing. Because in his own way, Zyg both envied the eponymous Swan & wanted to become it, going so far as to have himself tarred & feathered in a bordello — but also his sister, Leda, who obsessed him equally as much, giving himself over, this Man of Silence, to fantasies of public humiliation tantamount to raising spread buttocks for the disguised godhead to pierce with engorgèd rod, etc. In short, to become the very object of his inner self's literary speechifying, metamorphosed into flesh, *shudders racking an abandoned language*, & like those proverbial buttocks the flabbiness of uncertain things, the flight from mythology, the poet's sleight-of-hand, fake connivance, surveying us from behind the mask of his words like a ventriloquist's dummy with vacant eyes, etc. In life, of course, Zyg was a paragon of frigidity who, in the note addressed to his sister upon his suicide (the suicide was intended, like Juliet's, to be a fake, but it all went terribly wrong), begged for his bodily remains to be desecrated first by some roguish necrophiliac before being buried *under the river* [sic], in a place where swans were known to congregate... [✋]

'Besides,' she added with one of those intriguing eyebrow arrangements, 'I'm in it. That way, you'll be able to see all of me without needing to sneak into my dressingroom.'

While she'd been writing, the Brother had gotten up from the table with his camera & wandered into the crowd. The Sylphe looked devastated. A different waiter appeared with another round of martinis. They must've been part of the show, because everyone was drinking them. Maybe by that stage of the War, Němec pondered, the Nazis'd run out of bottled vitriol?

Alice handed him the napkin blotted with ink. He studied it in the cabaret's dim light — it had an address somewhere off Národní — & then tucked the napkin inside his jacket.

'Don't forget,' she said, as if she meant it.

The lights reflected in her eyes like surface scratchings, cuneiform — but they communicated nothing. Němec caught the echo of a smile as she turned her face in profile — & for a moment he saw, just behind her, there on the stage, a couple of metres away, her doppelgänger, draped in black, kneeling under the lights, dissolving into air. The apparition unnerved him. (Was it nothing but an aberration of the optic nerve, the visual cortex, under some unspecified influence?) He looked at Alice, aware that he in his turn was also being watched. Somewhere a gong sounded. Alice jerked her head in the direction of the movie cameras, then turned to Němec —

'That's me,' she said. 'I've got a scene to prepare. Enjoy the rest of the show.'

She stood up quickly & crossed the floor. Němec's eyes followed her to where a curtained doorway opened beside the stage. It was as near to flawless as an exit could be. Like having your liver removed between two blinks of an eye & not even noticing they'd left out the anaesthetic.

Celluloid Dolls

Everything else was just a footnote or a postscript. All around, little dramas being acted-out like sideshows to a main event that'd already left the house. At the next table, a redhead was holding her fringe away from her face while she hoovered a line of white powder from a cigarette case. Beside her, a pasty Wehrmacht officer with an enormous chest was blowing smoke rings, a cigar wedged between thick-knuckled fingers. The redhead might've looked familiar, but she wasn't. Her nose was bent to one side & she was slightly crosseyed.

From somewhere the sound of Mistress Vicarious' laughter floated out of the gloom. The coatcheck girl's abrasive voice. A cork being popped. Someone shouted for silence on the set. Positions. Heads turned vaguely towards the stage. The clapper reappeared, disappeared, keeping the whole charade ticking over. A pair of grey loudhailers, like the ones at train stations, wired above the proscenium arch, left & right, hissed & crackled. Two blithe plaster cupids, bows & arrows, flightless wings, straddled the arch. A garbled fanfare issued from the loudhailers, pierced by feedback, giving way to the sugary comicstrip voice of Mistress Vicarious herself —

'Laydeezzz *unt* Gentilemenschezzz! Guttevenink unt vilekommen! Suh zwahr, poor votra delektazzion trez ezpayseeall, der Kabaret Grünegast prezenteert! Zeh oonique! Zeh eeneffabla! RUUUBEEEE RAAAAY!'

On cue, a towering negress with a silver pageboy sauntered out under a rose-tinted spotlight. She wore a fishscale dress split down the thigh which dazzled in the light. Silver eyeshadow. Silver elbow-length gloves. Silver four-inch heels. She looked like a vision of sin straight from Harlem, circa Prohibition. Gloved fingers caressing a nickelplated microphone. Blacksuited, a jazz quartet stirred into life at the edges of the spotlight. The hornplayer blew a long low note, the contrabass hummed, a tenor saxophone echoed the horn in melancholy $E^\flat$, a steel brush rasped on stretched pigskin. Eyes closed, Ruby Ray groaned & swayed. Her voice welled up slowly from some dark place.

I wanna take a journey to the Devil below.
I done killed my man,
gonna reap just what I sow...

While Ruby Ray sang, a pair of celluloid dolls on a chintzdraped Turkish sofa were wheeled on stage by figures in blackface. The dolls were arranged sidebyside, crossdressed: a man's pointed face above a black satin gown, a woman's blonde curls fringing an ⚡ uniform. The band blew harder. As the tempo increased, the dolls suddenly came alive under the hands of the sinister blackfaces, jerking in unison in a spastic, repetitive, masochistic labour — their silhouettes like caged animals in a zoo. While this was in progress, Ruby Ray dissolved into the shadows like an apparition. If there was any point to the performance, Němec was at a loss to guess what it was. Then the music wound down & the stage went dark again. The band sat back for the next take while the dolls got wheeled around to the wings.

But what about *that* night? It was the reason Němec was here, after all. They, whoever the were, seemed to be giving him a free hand, so to speak, to see whatever he wanted to see. He duly scanned the room, a sea of faces distorted by chiaroscuro, each one a painting. If they possessed a purpose other than the one they were performing, none of them betrayed what it was. Except for the film crew, everything about the place was more or less as it'd been before, only everything was also different — as different as it could be while still resembling itself — like stepping twice through an enchanted mirror: the first time you wind up in Wonderland, the next you wind up flat on your face. Or vice versa.

What was he missing?

Did he think that if he sat there waiting long enough the answer would come to him?

As if in reply a drum-rim sounded. A red spotlight came up slowly on the stage. And as the piano in the corner began to play, Ruby Ray slipped out between the curtains & sashayed over to the microphone again. While she sang in that low brooding voice, a couple of platinum blondes straight out of a Weegee catalogue stood up from a table & began to dance, so slow they could've been stiffs trailing from a meathook, each smothered in the other's tainted perfume. Němec glanced past them at the door beside the stage through which Alice Steinerová had passed & then back over his shoulder towards the curtained exit by the bar. It'd have to be one or the other of them, he told himself, but it couldn't be both.[*]

---

[*] PAVLOV'S MUTTS

As it often did during moments of doubt, situations of uncertain outcome, acts of indecisiveness, stupidity or boredom, something the Bugman said resurfaced in the back of Němec's mind. It belonged to the afternoon following the episode with the redhead at the Museum. The Old Guy had been telling a story about his time in exile, Earls Court, class of '68, the salad years after the gulag & rehabilitation. *Victim of Stalinism* & all that.

At the Immigration Office, Tavistock Street, number 8, WC2E 7PP, Hudson House, Blecha & all the other lucky ducks from the Land of Rags & Patches Stitched Together by the Versailles Treaty had had to queue to get their visas stamped. There was a corridor, with eight or so offices on either side, & each office had a door the colour of tainted aspic with a sign over it. When the immigration officer behind the door pressed a button, the sign would light-up in red with the word ENTER. All the rest of the time, it'd stay blank.

At 5a.m. every morning, the privileged applicants would queue up outside the building in order to get a spot in one of the lines behind these closed doors, to which they were assigned more or less at random, & they'd wait, forms in hand, for the sign to light-up, so that they could present their paperwork to the officer & have it approved, in order to get their visa stamped upstairs. Many rumours circulated as to what went on behind each of the doors. The essential thing was that no-one knew for sure if the door they were waiting behind was the right door, or if at any given time there'd be someone on the other side of it. Like Pavlov's mutts —

'As if the whole thing'd been designed to keep you guessin'. Back in the War, the RAF had an aptitude test, just like it. To see if you had rocks in yer head or just the same mush as everyone else. The idea was to spot potential crazies so as to keep 'em away from the bombs. In case one of 'em decided they wanted to blow themselves up instead of droppin' it on the enemy. But even when they did let you near a bomb, you could never be sure there was anything in it, or if it'd just blow you up anyway, whether you were crazy of not.'

40

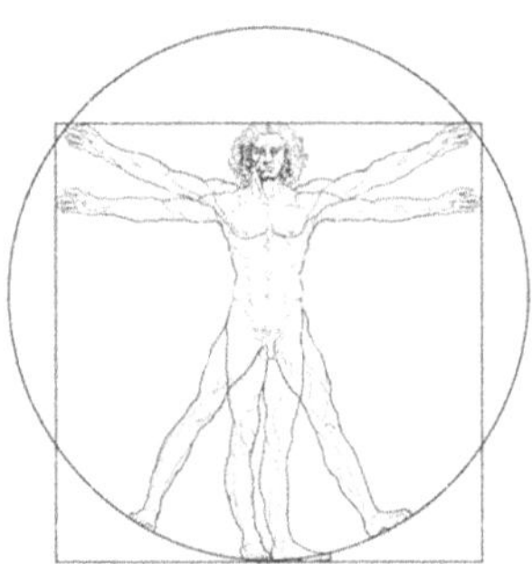

EIGHTY-THOUSAND LEAGUES

'Don't think they don't know about you,' the voice said.

Němec had taken a path that led the long way around the Island down its western side, where the locks stood quiet under the brooding willowtrees. The mist had parted during the night. Flocks of gulls wheeled & plunged above the weir, graceful & murderous. Watching them, he found himself thinking of Alice Steinerová, it was impossible not to. Her face, her words. Did her story ring false, or was it just that at a certain point every story rings false? Like a tightrope dancer who even when she falls contrives to cheat gravity by suddenly sprouting wings & wheeling back from the brink, to recommence her dance from a yet higher vantage.

His gaze drifted up. High over the river, a jet's vapour trails bisected what there was of a sky — two faint parallel lines converging into the grey foreground. The spread of the City, the lampposts, trams, statues, cupolas, all appeared unbalanced by this sudden vertigo of reverse-perspective. Like a reflection in a reflection faked by Canaletto on a daub by Escher, undressed by the restorer's eye as it turned back the veneers to reveal the scored & naked underpainting, all zinc & grisaille & faded neon. Here the protracted arch of a dome, there the apex of a campanile where two pairs of compasses intersect like facsimiled avatars. Francis Seraphinus, John of Nepomuk, the whole sainted host. Ghost cities in overlap.

Approaching the foot of the Island, a river barge sounded its horn. Time, it said, to awaken from that twilight of Mitteleuropa.

Halfway back to the bridge, a bum was sitting on a bench overlooking the water, pensively drinking box wine. A pack of dozing mutts lay at his feet, tethered to one leg. A soiled redblue woollen cap sagged down almost over his eyes. The mutts blinked sleepily at Němec as he came along the path. As he passed, the bum spoke, catching Němec off guard —

'Don't think they don't know about you.'

Němec turned & stared at the back of woollen cap. The bum kept on gazing impassively at the river, as if it was the water he was talking to. One of the mutts whimpered, its muzzle worrying a poplar leaf that a small colony of ants seemed to be transporting on their backs.

'I've seen 'em,' the bum said through the slit of his mouth. 'Comin' in their machines, when they think we're all asleep. But *I'm* not sleepin'. Every night they come. From up there.'

The bum pointed with his free hand, blackened fingers poking through the ends of a grey woollen glove, clutching the box-wine closer with the other. Němec followed the man's gesture with his eyes to a spot in the sky above the midget Eiffel Tower on Petřín Hill, its finial flaring in the first sunspike of dawn like Siegfried's lofted panto poignard, & all below, the greyblack Erdshadow its mantle of gloom.

'Outta the sky they come, & land right there in the river. One, two, three. One after the other. There's always the same number. Then they go down under the water. Like submarines. That's all. And before sun-up, they go back. Just the way they came. Oh I know about 'em all right. I'm always watchin'…'

Němec blinked down at the greyish floe. Tried to see what the old drunk'd seen. UFOs with strobing carny lights. Martian mugshots framed in portholes. Maybe a quick aerial lap of the Castle, looping-the-loop round St Vít, for snapshots to send home to the in-laws back on Alpha Centauri. Idly he kicked a loose stone into the water. A faint splash. The bum chuckled, took a swig of his wine —

'Some nights, if you listen real close, you can hear 'em way down there, diggin' in the mud. They're buildin' a secret Martian base no-one knows about, preparin' for the Big One…'

Němec scratched his chin. It all sounded reasonable enough, from a certain point of view. But not from a Martian's, he'd've thought. All the prime spots must've already got snaffled up & these were the guys left holding the short straws. Maybe that was really what the drunk could hear going on down there, some poor wee green fuckers with the pointy ears playing the Golem City Blues. *Man, we crossed a million lightyears to end up in this dump, and they ain't even got no bagels.* Life in the far-flung shtetls of the universe, what it must've been like.

Němec shrugged, & seeing as there was nothing more to the old drunk's talk, ambled off in the direction of the bridge. When he'd almost reached it, the bum shouted after him: not turning his head, not moving at all, just shouting, like a mannequin with a loudspeaker wired to it.

'You'll deserve what you get! You hear me?'

One of the mutts gave a disheartened yap.

Under the broad arch, stalactites of accumulated limescale hung down in long slivers over a sea of mud, effluent, the night's regurgitations. Scratched among the stones, a large circle with a cross through it ⊕, spraypainted runes, insignias of the tribe writ large. A non-com in feldgrau stood pissing against a post. Němec circumnavigated & headed for the steps.

Casting a backwards glance at the Green Fairy château, Němec caught faint subterranean whispers. The stink of the river drifting in thin wisps of fog through the poplars. The bum's mad rant faded out to morning-after voices, overhead traffic, the roar & thump of a tram. The bells chimed six. Němec ascended the steps to the pure air, the nitrous pabulum. The island, two flights beneath him now, became less a place & more a problem of perspective. He turned his back on it. To the right, the Home he'd left, to the left, the home he'd borrowed. He knew the directions with his eyes closed, could've pointed them out to anybody, like an idiot on a crucifix nailed up on a crossroads. But what sort of crossroads would you expect to find in the middle of a river?

Perhaps a lesser mortal might've taken it as a cue to start waxing ponderous about how often he'd walked that road, crossed that bridge, stood on that island, looked at that river, full of approximate longings, contempt, hunger, boredom, fatigue. How much of him had been absorbed in them. How little he'd accomplished or even understood. But not Němec, whose musings were of a different order. Primarily, where at that hour a drink could be obtained, no questions asked. Steam rose from the tramtracks. He turned from the stairhead & followed them westward. What'd it matter if secrets existed within their midst? UFOs under the river or a cabal of madmen? To exist at a tangent to some unknown place, without ever entering its circle — or to inhabit the world the way a reflection inhabits a mirror: what kind of existence was that? Down below the old bum was probably still cackling to himself or no-one, but that was of no concern to Němec. A blackbird on a tramwire barked. The world in its orbit turned. Pascal was right enough: it was ridiculous to speak of a man as if he were a geometrical proposition. But what kind of a proposition was he?

Don't Pay the Ferryman

Faktor's bazaar, or what remained of it, stood out of the fog like a shattered nautilus. The building, an old shipping warehouse, was in process of being demolished, all that remained was a cross-sectioned shell, concrete pylons & a mesh of girders teetering over the water. A crew with a wrecking ball were standing around on a smoke-break beside a dumpster they were slowly filling with rubble. Across the last remaining wall, representatives of the local intelligentsia had sprayed DEATH TO ZHITS. The only thing that identified the place as what it was, or had been, was a strip of painted hoarding laid slantwise against a pair of busted doorposts — V.F. ENTERPRISES — as grandiose as it was pathetic. Němec wandered down onto the wharf & stared at the water, toeing a bit of dead thistle that was wedged in a crack. After a while, something crashed behind him & he turned to look. Up in the sky, the wrecking ball swayed lazily. It swayed some more. A section of wall broke loose. In a little while there'd be hardly anything left of it.[*]

All par for the course, so far.

Across the narrow inlet was an abandoned car lot behind rusted razorwire, a pair of steel gates that'd been rammed in, a burned-out van. Further on, the crumbling façades of factory buildings awaiting demolition in their turn, boatsheds laid on their side, bridges to nowhere, ziggurats of unidentifiable trash, secret body-dumps hidden under the tide-line. From this vantage, the aborted island looked like nothing. On a map, it looked like a piece of cross-sectioned anatomy — Mater Urbium with her disarranged urethra, vaginal passage, cervical mouth, distended uterus & intestinal tract all on display. *L'origine du monde.* At War's end they'd've flocked here with their foldout chairs & bottles of frankovka to watch the bodies float past in a flood of reddish-grey, the unbridled bitch in her menses, flushed back to the Fatherland. *Ausländer raus!* Must've been one helluva sight.

---

[*] Well, whaddyaknow? [✊]

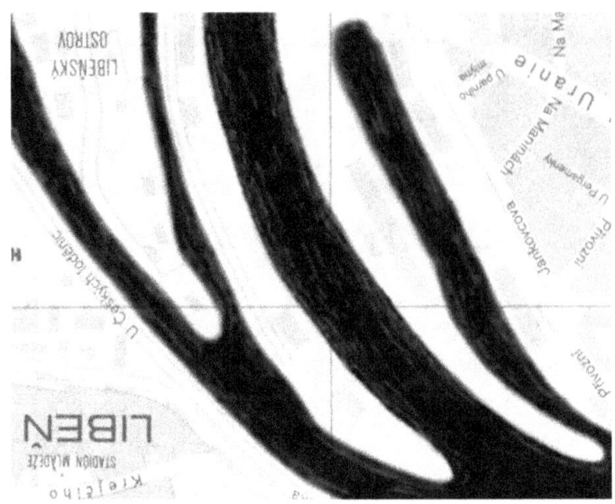

A bitumen path wound out across the landfill, through the bitter coal-stink, echoes of the container yards, weighing stations, sidings. Scavenging of restless blackbirds in the undergrowth, the rustle of a rat-hunting mutt, a bum coughing under a sheet of cardboard at the edge of a culvert. Across the far end of it all, Mausoleum Hill with One-Eyed Žižka on his Trojan Horse — maybe, in a thousand years, some such colossus might one day stand sentry in the shadow of Olympus Mons, long enough to see the swamps of Mars bulldozed for Malthusian towerblocks — the dawn after Anarchia, the ricorso of the Age of the Gods & Goddesses.[*]

Out on the landfill, Němec felt the paradox of an open space that seemed to collapse inwards, hemmed on all sides by an advancing black fog, feeling his way along the path, tuned to the dull frequencies of footfall on gravel, glass, needle, mud, echoes telescoping through space, eye of ear. At its lowest point he struggled to keep his bearings, one wrong turn could've upset everything. Away from the path, the landfill subsided into marsh, a wide crater below the mist, weirdly luminous, the dragon's breath — somewhere out there in the privets, witches' covens, dreadlocked, smacked up to the eyeballs, dreaming weird shapes out of the ether. Something rattled its chain, groaned, ground its teeth, snored.

---

[*] And what if, like the pyramids of Egypt, the Voynich Manuscript belonged to another world? Some medieval UFO abduction? The wonders of untold knowledge & customs most foreign, most strange? Distant cosmologies, as presented themselves to the semi-literate, pre-Industrial Mind? Like G.O.D. dictating to a jilted man, alone in a tent in the middle of a desert, the Sacred Scriptures, the Divine Truth: a man with no more inkling of infinity than he did the existence of capitalism, kangaroos, or the computer chip. [☙]

On the far side the path ran dead into a concrete cistern, one wall caved-in. A flight of stairs wound down into brackish water.

Time in its Fluidity

The river had flowed there till just before the War, when they buried it with rubble, from Rohan Island to Libeň, & let it lie there under the weeds like a sump collecting the dregs of progress. It was out in the middle of the dead river that Němec stood, watching the horizon disintegrate behind the sídliště, detached silhouettes above an encroaching mist. The weather had turned yet again. The sun was nothing but a pale disk behind the clouds. The grey waters of the Vltava coiling back upon themselves like a withered fallopian. Soon the rain would make perfunctory business of it all. The towerblocks across the isthmus of Holešovice — the chimneystacks of Karlín — the drydocks & junkyards of Libeňský Island — the pervitin factories of Palmovka tenements & grey cliffs of Bohnice above them, walling the City like a puzzle-cube compulsively rearranging itself.

The whole landscape looked to Němec as ridiculous as a disassembled stage set with a busted dry-ice machine belching from the wings — but if you closed your eyes, you could just about picture it as it might've been, flickering out there over that giant dumping ground like an ignis fatuus, the dream-foretold, the *Ville Radieuse*, the kernel of a future vastly different from this one, Heydrich's private Heliopolis come to life like a golem risen from mud & cardboard, & fused in the fiery forge of five hundred B-17s.[*] As upon such foundations, before the astonished witness of all the unnamed factory workers long ago buried there, the monoliths that Time & dollars must one day transmute to glittering glass condominiums, the proverbial angel-rapers of this New Babylon-in-Waiting. Amen.

But not in your lifetime, kiddo.

Well, he'd been brought up to be an optimist, he'd had the best teachers in the world, what else was a man like Němec to think?

Wading up onto dry land through the long reeds, moiré tunnels of wiremesh, winding, doubling back, plastic bags flapping in spectral breezes, the distant croaking & wheezing of trams over Libeňský Bridge — out into air, wet, saturated… *Time in its fluidity, the yellow orb of a clockface floating above the mist,*

---

[*] *Well, kiddo, if I said it once, I said it a thousand times, sure does pay to have friends in this world.* [✋]

rising at your back, star of Bethlehem, world slipping on its axis forever eastwards, casting vague shadows ahead, the river so close now you can hear it. A sea of used car lots, windscreens grey in the morning light — the path becoming a road, tending right, past a Gotham cop car TO SERVE & PROTECT jacked-up on wooden crates, weeds poking through the engine block...* *And what the fuck was that doing there?* Across the road stood a kiosk with a canvas awning running along one side & handpainted cardboard sign that said DOCTOR

---

* The Amerikan Dream not all it was cooked-up to be? These little reminders of the Eternal Optimists of '89 with their *fait accompli* Revolution orchestrated from elsewhere, as once before Berlin, the Moscow communiqué, Glasnost & Perestroika — & not that pulp romance, Ancien Régime vs the Will of the Proles, *see the little man take a bold stand against tyranny and oppression* — as seen on TV — a tale told for every midget crawling out from under the proverbial hillock, hump & holdall to go sun himself by, in the glow of his newly discovered righteousness, Party card stuffed way down in hip pocket of ubiquitous rip-off Levis, wig hanging down, etc. Historians might well've christened it the Cucumber Revolution, on account of all the decent law-abiding types holed-up during the belated "hot" days of November on their quarter-acreages, stuffing themselves with pickled okurky till the situation cooled down. The Berlin Wall was nothing but rubble by the time the first protests began — the anniversary of Jan Opletal, medical student, shot by the Nazis during the Protektorat. Then things got surreal. On Národní the riot squads play-acted at beating a student to death — one agent-provocateur by name of Ludvík Zifčák, covered in fake blood. (Well who the hell *was* Ludvík Zifčák anyway?) The stage managers of this penny arcade gave the dissidents their fifteen minutes then ushered them back off into the wings, served up a couple of scapegoats, put Havel in the trophy cabinet up on the hill, & — handydandy — what the Free World Club call's *democretinisation*. And so the Golem City newsclowns chased each other's tails like a pack of sun-struck mutts. All of a sudden, everywhere you looked were born-again antiestablishment types, lifetime dissidents, professional protest marchers, pennyante freethinkers, the whole Conscience of the Nation rattling their house-keys in lockstep under the nose of Saint Wenzelsplatz's flyblown horse. They sucked down the atmosphere, beat their breasts, flagellated their flags. They demanded freedom, elections, rock'n'roll. They chanted spontaneous slogans someone in an office had spent a long night sweating over: DEMOKRACII! SVOBODU! JAKEŠE DO KOŠE! HAVEL NA HRAD! The words came tumbling down around their ears like manna from Hradchin. They drank & were merry — then drank some more. And straightaway everything was amnesiafied. *Well, kiddo, if you can't get what you want you can always fake it.* Which was how it seemed, alright, perhaps how it'd always seemed, for anyone with eyes & half a brain wired to them: some bummed-out alchemist's fandango of the mind — an Arcimboldo with DTs — greengrey — rotten-pithed — mouldy — fingers worming about in constant agitation — hunch-backed over a weak flame — crusted spoon & wad of cotton at the needle-end of a crusty glass syringe — eyeballing his fix. Something cooked-up like a piece of Xanadu with coloured lights on painted stage props — smoke & mirrors, tinsel & glitter & cellophane — the mind's kaleidoscope. One day they pick you off the street & give you the gladhand, the sugared pill, the limelights & the big hit, all velvetsmooth, milk&honeyish, & just as soon you're left high & dry on the thin edge of a oneway comedown. But what did Němec care? Revolution or no revolution, any kind of diversionary tactic would've done — a broken window, a playground rumble, a murder in the street, a hundredyear flood: *A skiff ploughs the main square; a fish defiles a shrine.* The stuff of poetry. [�]

HORRIBILIS. There was nothing inviting about it, but Němec wasn't exactly overwhelmed with alternatives so he humped his sack of bones across the road & surrendered himself to circumstance.

Under the awning was a couple of plastic tables, faded pin-ups taped to the wall, TV on a stool, charcoal stove, bags of cement piled waist-high making a kind of perimeter. Němec ordered a coffee through a perforated sheet of perspex that hung over the counter. Plus a brandy to wash down a couple of pills & then another. The shadow behind the perspex made voluble snotsucking noises while it poured: warm tapwater straight over coffee grounds, a bottle with no label into glass opaque with thumbprints. It was the kind of joint your old school of taxi drivers drank their breakfast in, hanging onto the TV with their eyes to keep awake till their shift ended or began. There were a couple of them there now. Němec squeezed behind them & perched on a cement bag while his drink lasted to take in the entertainment.

It was priceless stuff. Playing on the screen was some 1970s Jess Franco ketchup-fest: young Asian slavegirl in the clutches of a fanatically evil Nazi, full ⚡ rig-out, Hitler-saluting guards, the works.* Cue the obligatory concentration camp rape scene: wire-frame bed sans mattress, trusses & stays & a wall rack showing off the Blond Beast's collection of riding crops, horse whips, cat-o-nine-tails. Němec sipped his brandy while the evil Nazi recited race-hatred ideology at the slavegirl. The scene cut. The Nazi had her by the hair now — with his free hand, tearing away her flimsy attire — flash of brown nipple — crotch stubble — the Nazi pawing her, salacious.

Then (it happened all very suddenly, too suddenly for Němec to get a handle on) the slavegirl somehow worked her hands free while the Nazi gnawed at the inside of her thighs, driving bloodied fingernails into the sadistic scumbag's eyeballs. Screen static. Snotsucking from behind the counter. Then cut to slavegirl, mouth a horrible grimace, kicking the now prostrate Nazi repeatedly in his leather-thonged gonads. More screen static. Close-up of the slavegirl's hands clamping the Nazi's jaw as bile pours from his nose, commingling with the blood drizzling from mangled eyesockets — hands flaying about as the Nazi chokes on his own vomit — & all the while, the slavegirl, silent, not a word spoken…

---

* What's with this whole Nazi shtick anyway? [✊]

The tram driver poked an iron bar into Němec's ribs till he woke up, then sent him staggering & blinking out into the light. This one looked exactly the way every other terminus looked, like a scale-replica of nowhere — only someone'd had the extraordinary presence of mind to stick a sign up that said ĎÁBLICE, so everyone could share in the joke. Bottom of the hole, end of the line. Němec, barely able to suppress his sense of fucking hilarity, crouched under the tramshelter out of the wind & rain, though he couldn't tell in fact if it really was raining, or if a wind was blowing, or if the weather was only in his head. It looked bleak either way. *Well ain't that just peachy, Němec, you sonofanothing?*

It must've been a Sunday, whole sermons could've been preached in the time between rides.* When it finally got going, the 12 took him south back towards the river, right back where he'd started, through gypsy tenement squalor, coal smoke, gridlocked morning traffic, street vendors hawking watches, belts, women's polyester underwear, bootleg video tapes, CDs, broken furniture, third- & fourth-hand magazines — past sexshops, brothels, electrical repairs, clothes racks, fruitsellers, tobacconists, liquor merchants, wreckers yards, Africans hawking fake leather, gypsy women with babies huddled beside mountains of overflowing trash, ancient homeless men begging with foreheads pressed to wet pavement, old blind couple with accordion playing out of tune, one squeezing, one pressing the keys & buttons like Siamese twins — commuters, shiftworkers, drifters, junkies, crazies, bums & no-hopers... In short, the whole symphony of the Golem City underbelly, groaning & shrieking in E♭. Then a sharp righthand detour through the highlights of some diligently preserved offset bombing range left over from the War.*

The day in all its vagary unspooled like montage, crisscrossing the City

---

* But would Truth prevail? [♣]

* The USAF pounded the whole district flat on a weekend in March of 1945, two whole months before The End. It wasn't their least achievement by any stretch. They missed the ČKD Works but managed to snuff 370 workers & their families sitting down to Sunday lunch. The month before, the score was 701, Valentine's Day in a residential district of No Strategic Importance, a love letter from Uncle Sam made of 150 tonnes of incendiary. Nearly a hundred apartment blocks deleted from the map that day. *Eat yer heart out, Lucky Luciano.* Sort of thing made Lidice look like pennyante stuff. If Heydrich was such a Big Cheese, why'd they settle for so *few*? Maybe the brass back in Berlin didn't love the guy so much after all. Now there's a thought. [♣]

552

southwest & northeast, from depot to endstop, nodding-off & nodding-on, through snuffed-out landscapes that were all too familiar, returning always to the river as if to a crossroads. As the day progressed, the weather closed in: discontinuities accumulating like celluloid, voiceovers, ghosts in the machine, faces on sidewalks, in shop windows, cars, framed in grey light, in rain, in silhouette. A thousand doppelgängers, rubber masks, identikit mugshot with eyes blacked-out, crossed-out, scraped-out, billboard faces selling untold visions of future paradise, prostitutes in suits, in fancy dress costume, in uniform always with a product to sell. NEW PERSIL™ CLEANS BUILT-UP CRIME. And everywhere bleeding out from the underside, secret messages in graffiti code, viral DNA, backwards alchemistry spelling the Great Silent Undoing like pirate broadcasts from the Collective Submind sketched large in cartooned spirals of doom. It was like some future war zone in a movie about a past no-one could remember, & that no-one would ever make:

A continuous tracking shot. The river, a barge, a bridge. Fires, collapsing buildings, a flatbed truck stacked with dismembered store mannequins. Just as any movement may be characterized by flows & turbulence, so too the camera's journey through this allegory of desolation. But Němec never doubted himself to be anywhere other than in the wrong place at the wrong time. Right at that instant, perhaps, in some parallel dimension fifty years ago.[*] *If you blink*, the moment inspired him to think, *the whole world just might end yet still go on.* Like

---

[*] How to write it, unconstrained by a history of "facts"? An alterior account, so to speak, of what prevails behind & beyond that melodrama of buffoons & madmen — of a laughter that freezes the lymph & wrings the entrails, & the unquenched ardour of a love all too aware of itself — avatars outside a world where stupidity has always been relied upon to gain the upper hand — some triple-distilled essence of humanity on its way to a never accomplished destiny, because there *is* none. Who could be the contestants in such an anti-drama? What faceless entities — gnostic protagonists whose existence is as universally indeterminate as it is spurious, if only because we're unable to disprove them? Like those apothecurial forces of chaos & occulted order, Š.V.E.J.K. & T.E.S.L.A. — phantoms of paradox, secret agents of History & its counter-histories, enemies & enigmatics of the Grand Narrative — the one upsetting the airwaves, the other going under the radar, residing in the margin of error, the standard deviation, manifest solely in the gross coincidence, the palpable lie, the bald truth. How else to write it than by keeping on the move, avoiding the stasis of a declared position, the seductions of certainty? To write with his feet, stepping on the cracks, between the verifiable & verisimilitude, staying one step ahead of his own hypotheses — like some mad dog (where had it gone to?), looking over its shoulder at him or just the world in general at its back, the leash that'll forever be somewhere in mind — knowing that in any case all the routes have already been marked out, only the combinations left open to chance, indeterminacy, feint & bluff. Knowing, too, there's nothing to be gained by indefinitely doubling the stakes (like shooting craps with the Devil, where what's in play is never more than another roll of the dice — in other words, everything). → Chapter 52. [♣]

a celluloid ghost. And what, he wondered, would Alice Steinerová's role in that dead-duck drama be? Her gun pointed at his head, or her head, or someone's head. Or not her, but a woman just like her, a face, yes, it was coming back to him now, if only vaguely: a woman in black, in a window, overlooking a river? This river.

The tram swung away from Libeň, past an army of council workers in orange vests marshalled around the old customs house. Broom men, men with shovels, rolling cigarettes, picking their beards, knocking back bottles of Pražan, Měšťan, tuzemák… At the next stop, a hippy-type with the beads & Indian dreamcatchers woven into dreadlocks hanging down around his knees climbed aboard & seemed to zone right in on Němec instantly —

'Hey, bro…'

Němec blinked, red lab-rat eyes.

'I been lookin' all over for ya, bro! How 'bout the answer to that question?'

The hippy planted himself on the seat opposite. The stink of him made Němec's eyes water.

'World's gone to the dogs, bro, we gotta turn back the clocks, get back to the Mother Ship, live in communion like them aborigine cromagnons, cast out the machines, bro, stay pure, smoke the good shit, I mean, you don't think the dinosaurs had no contingency plan, do you? Hey, you gonna come join us on the reservation, bro? Always room for a soulbrother, brother…'*

A Hole Deep-Enough

The sound of jackhammers rang out clearly a block & a half away, pounding the rhythms of the trenches, machineguns, mortars, like he'd wandered once more into the middle of a film set: period traffic, streetsigns & sandbagged shopfronts — a ragtag unit of men pinned down by sniper fire, angling an MG42 on a tripod, blindly strafing the rooftops to no appreciable effect, while a mocking voice through a loudhailer broadcasts updates of the latest advance of the Red Army into the eastern fringes (the Krauts, munitions running precariously low, sweating under their helmets, wear their fatalism like an iron cross even as it threatens to snap their necks, even while the generals are frantically trying to save theirs, with the surrender ink already dry, the phoney peace that'll only run

---

* As the Bugman would've said, *They've gotta have some real hotshot secondhand salesmen in the next life, kiddo, making the trade-in on this one.* [✋]

out when the bullets do or they make it to the Yankee lines barely an hour's drive west or the Reds give it to them in the neck).

But it was no film set, only a cordon of red&white candystriped tape obstructing what in Němec's last recollection had been the pavement along Jánský Vršek, now a trench with bitumen & broken cobblestones heaped up into an earthworks. A white building contractor's van was parked in the street: *Golem Construction.* Darkfaced men in blue overalls were unloading steel tubing & wooden planks, piling them on the remaining sidewalk. Others were digging, excavating, tunnelling. Wheeling burrows. Operating machinery.

Their prodigious activity only seemed to multiply as Němec took in the scene: ladders rising from & descending into muddied gloom, crusted pipes traversing the length of the excavation site, foundation stones jutting out, urban sedimentations arrayed in descending chronologies down into the unsuspected, hidden reaches — the shadow underfoot, the antipodal *terra incog,* echoes of Cathay in its ancient ascendancy, the whole subterranean host, migratory wormhoards from Macau to Malá Strana, the Tang Dynasty wandering Sklav in Boholand, the fall of distant Rome, *by the Moldau's lapping waters we lay down and raped a piece of Mucha-maiden arse...* But sadly, memory has an end, History too. And a hole to absolve the firstlast, filthloved mess of it.

By dint of sheer determination, Němec limped the gauntlet of troglodytes & molemen stationed at his door. The courtyard, by contrast, was a true oasis of calm. The War might indeed have been years away, but who knew, a slip of the jackhammer, a gash in the fabric of Time itself, could very well bring it all flooding back like a ruptured sewer main. At least the rain had stopped. Němec made a quick recon of the courtyard. No sign of enemy agents. No sign of La Severínová either. The green parrot, as beady-eyed as ever, guarded the threshold to her caretaker's lodge, grating its black worm-tongue.

Feet heavy, Němec climbed the steps to the Prof's apartment. Now that he'd made it that far, things seemed to be coming apart at the edges, threads fraying, the camera-eye coming at him from all angles at once like a pack of assailants, till he was left stumbling round & round in circles, up a stairwell that never ended, because *it* was that harassing mechanical eye, only now he was seeing it *from the inside.* How long since? A message in the old woman's spidery all-caps was thumbtacked to his door, paper faintly blue, perfumed also faintly with camphor. WATER & ELECTRICITY INTERMITTENT DURING RECONSTRUCTION, is what he determined it said. *Reconstruction? What reconstruction?* He remembered the jackhammers & sighed. Jesus, would it never end? And then he was through the door. Safe. The distant throbbing of the beast through the walls. The darkness of the hallway, as comforting as a body he'd memorised every inch of & could caress in his sleep. Perhaps he *was* sleeping. Perhaps it *was* the beast. Perhaps they'd come for him at last.

When Němec switched on the light, she was the first thing he saw, lying there completely naked on the parquet, all spread out for him. His own private Sphinx. And all he wanted finally was to lie down in her & sleep. But not yet. He lurched into the kitchen & stuck his head under the sink. He couldn't give in at the first drop of a hat, was what he told himself. There were details to sort out, arrange into evidence of something, dots to be joined. He broke open a bottle & gulped down as much as he could stomach, to take the lead out of his veins, level-out, see things in their proper light. And so he plonked himself down with the bottle on the floor, in the half-dark, orange halo of lamplight-through-the-window, staring at page after page of her, lying there with no pretence even to ceremony anymore, letting him fill his eye all he liked, telling him her story without telling him anything at all. It was a stale game that required him only to put up so much of a struggle before letting defeat do the real work. As he knew it would.

Teatrum Mundi

Comrade Medvedev used to say, back in the Good Ol' Days, that if you played with it, it'd fall off, or you'd go blind, or the moral fibre of the Socialist Revelation would be placed in jeopardy. Smirks & squirms in the classroom, elbows in the ribs later at the stalls, *Three shakes, boys! Anything more's a Thought Crime, hehe.* Afraid the dribble would show through — *Look who's pissed his pants again!* — faces going purple squeezing out the last drop with pure willpower — *Look, no hands!* And the day Bobek caught two kids in a cubicle spanking the monkey with a slice of stale Šumava they'd planned to feed to some poor eight-year-old Lenka or Lučinka, made to stand at the front of assembly, heads hung in shame *(chortle-chortle)* as Med-the-dev, tweaking the ears of these two teary-eyed snotty-nosed *reprobates*, gave everyone the fifth degree, the wherefore in most Technicolor lurid detail of this *pair of delinquents'* grubby-minded scheme & how, rest assured, they'd both be made an example of — drawn, quartered, hung up in a gibbet with their pants down, wind whistling in their bone flutes, woodpeckers playing their brainpans for a pestle, And all the while Ol' Deathbed drawing beads on the whole congregation of slackers, idlers, nosepickers & no-gooders — boys on the left, girls on the right — many of whom at that very moment constructing voodoo effigies in the minds to stick pins in later on, & the sweet infantile bliss of seeing the miserable hag squirm & beg for mercy — just harmless child's play really. Miss Freudlová, one stray ringlet playing down her cheek, demure (or possibly just bored), standing in her gymsuit there beside the snivelling Lučinka or Lenka (who's present show of misery appears to stem more from the obese Russian schoolmaster's unrelenting diatribe than any profound comprehension of the soap opera she's unwittingly inspired), hand covering her (Freudlová's) full & well-formed pout, a spreading blush (a stifled yawn?) it can't quite conceal — more ribbing in the back row, Nagel & the gang, *Cor, I'd let her whistle Dixie on me anytime a the week! Pucker-up for Peter Piper's pecker, sweetchops! Can pluck my daisy! Blow us a kiss, why dontcha, lovely!* Med-the-Dev working himself up into judicial apoplexy, likening the two weenie-whittlers to nothing short of full-blown, *er*, terrorists (the next worst thing to those Mašín Brothers, by Joe, gunning down innocent law-abiding citizens) forthwith to be given the "special treatment," detailed to daily dunny-cleaning duty (*snigger-snigger*). And when he's all wrapped up with the fire&brimstone, Ol' Deathbed, never one to scorn an opportunity, chiming in with her two bits, that any one of them smutty little gobshites ever has the temerity *to even think about* doing such a thing in future she'll in no uncertain terms manually castrate the culprits. The porcelain-polishing pair from that day on jibed throughout the dorms as the Fairinelly Twins — the Tostoff Brothers — Jerk-on & Jerk-off — the Fantom Floggers — Bread & Lučina* — the Handmaidens — & even (no end to the inventiveness of pre-adolescent minds) the Soggy Sisters — impunity, however, extending only to the older of the "lads," with petty & sometimes less-than-petty acts of retribution being not unheard of in the days & weeks, etc. — itching powder in bedsheets, butyric acid on pillowcases, shitstains magically appearing on freshly laundered Y-fronts, thumbtacks inserted under insoles, buckets emptied over toilet cubicle walls... All just the normal healthy behaviour of children in captivity.

Worlds within Worlds

Well, if it's any consolation, Jesus Christ was an orphan too, in a manner of speaking. Staring down inside a hypnotically empty bottle & seeing again Ol' Deathbed's

---

* A much-loved brand of cream cheese sold in rectangular tinfoiled blocks. [☟]

prurient leer, there in the backroom of his brain, stirring a bit of that Oedipalled sentimentality the Good Doctor put so much store by — the movie reel of the submind with all its dirty pictures running together — any wonder when Němec tipped over into the sleep of the ungodly, he instantly dreamt (if you'd call such a rush of mental paroxysms *dreaming*), as though the one state was merely the logical continuation of the other. But even as he was dreaming it, the dream itself seemed fake, scripted, a made-up nightscreed full of presentiments, symbols, augurations, like some sort of punishment carefully implanted in his brain to be activated under pre-selected circumstances. What those were, well, your guess is as good as anyone's...

INSTITUTE OF HUMAN STUDIES & SOCIAL MEDICINE
Psychiatric Assessment
Consulting physician: T. Hájek, MUDr.

On the 31st of August, the patient, who is referred to simply as N, reported experiencing the following dream, which he alleged was the product of secret experiments conducted upon him by "androids" by whom he had been abducted during his sleep. N further asserted that the chief of these androids was disguised as a certain "Doctor Volta," supposedly a physician at the Golem City Teaching Hospital. Needless to say that no record of any such "Doctor" is known to exist. The patient's highly excited state can perhaps be attributed to a long-standing persecution complex dating from the death of his father, for which he has reported experiencing an unbearable feeling of guilt. It has not been ascertained if the "death" of N's father is real or imaginary, since none of the patient's pre-institutional history has been able to be verified, yet this cannot detract from the manifest character of his symptoms. The following is a transcript of N's "dream":

I was walking down a long corridor with deep burgundy carpet & yellowed walls, with no explanation of how I got there or where "there" was. It could've been a scene in a film, or rather a scene viewed through the lens of a camera. Panelled doors opened off to one side, spaced at regular intervals, & thick, discoloured windows on the other through which streaks of moonlight filtered. Behind each successive door, a "chamber of horrors" lay in wait. I knew this intuitively. The corridor itself had a suffocated, stagnant atmosphere — air that'd remained unmoved for decades. In the middle of first chamber was a black coffinshaped magician's box, standing upright. The box was divided into three sections. The top & bottom sections were empty. In the middle section, radiating with a light that had no visible exterior source, was some spindly-legged octogenarian's paunch sagging down over withered ballsack & wizened prick. This piece of anatomy had all the appearance of pre-masticated beef & half-melted plastic fruit whose flesh, in the chamber's chiaroscuro, appeared to swarm & undulate *(snigger-snigger)* — it was an old script., all it required was a coin slot, *A Dollar to see the Snake Dance! Aim the Arrow at the Sphincter, Bullseye Wins an Instant Prize! Soaked Sponge Slingaroo, Bag the Bozo in the Gloryhole for Bonus Bonanza! Pop Goes the Weasel, Shoot the Bearded Lady, Three Hits Scores the Jackpot!* I shut the door, & the doorhandle, too (one of those gag-shop faves), writhed & pulsed with supernatural life, like smeared ectoplasm. I wrenched my hand away. (*Don't rush yourself, kiddo, plenty more where that came from.*) A hidden presence ushered me further along the corridor which, now that I looked at it, seemed to stretch out ahead of me towards some infinitely distant point — pure illusionism, that, since immediately in front an invisible wall hemmed me in, advancing as I advanced, though only as far as the next door, & another likewise barring my retreat like a two-sided glass cage. It'd all been given much thought, to ensure whoever the lucky jerk happened to be got the Grand Tour without missing out on any of the juicy details. Wouldn't want anyone taking a shortcut down the fire exit or skipping straight to the Grand Finale without first getting the whole song&dance they'd spent so long putting through rehearsals, doing the costumes, fidgeting with the décor, the lighting just-so. They'd spared a lot of the usual gimmicks — the gratuitous screams emanating from nowhere — mutilated vegetable sounds of simulated tortures, disembowellings, decapitations — bats, hellfire, blood dripping from the ceiling — House-of-Horrors skeletons jumping out of closets. No shortage of atmospheric lugubriosity, though — walls perspiring, carpets bristling at the faintest touch of a prostrated shadow — the whole space somehow alive & aware of my presence within it. From some untold source I received the knowledge that the dream would only come to an end once I'd performed the ritual of seeing behind every single one of those doors — as if this endless corridor not only symbolised but *was* the path I must labour along, & go on labouring along, till I'd found the key to its mysterious ordination, & all that. *Roll up! Roll up! Come look inside! The Strangest Show on Earth! See the Girl with Two Heads! The Boy with the Sasquatch's Arsehole! Conger Woman! Glue Man!* The chambers with their expositions proliferated. Each door revealed punishments more & more bizarre: fastforward through a blind monkey on a chain masturbating — a woman with her head locked inside a metal ball, elbows pinioned, knees viced, mounted by a giant tarantula — a midget wearing a mirror for a face, legs amputated at the groin, casually sodomised by an obese odalisque, prosthetic dildo slicked black — a severed head on a drapeclothed pedestal (Holofernes in hologram), blindfolded, a metal "O" attached to two black leather straps forcing the dead mouth open, a red hole with tiny spikes radiating from the periphery... The entire wearying spectacle of bodies dismembered & de-eroticized by fragments, like specimens in a vivisectionist's pickling jar — & just when it all seemed like it couldn't go on any longer, standing at the end of the corridor, I confronted my reflection bulging out towards me like a grinning idiot in a convex mirror. Attached to the mirror's frame, on the righthandside, was a doorhandle. When I turned it, the mirror opened inwards: it revealed a large room whose walls existed somewhere behind a black veil, the ceiling & floor also, even the air seemed black & permeated by remoteness. The scent of a faintly opiumed tobacco drifted through it. In the middle of this sea of jet, beneath the bright cone of a theatrical spotlight, stood Dr Niklas Volta no less — arrayed like a high priest of the Temple, behind a black marble dissection slab littered with matzah, spilt borsht, roasted lizard egg, green splintered shankbone of the Paschal lamb, puddles of Dead Sea saltwater, gobs of masticated almond, smears of raphanoid goo of no identifiable origin, fermented fish oil & flyblown plums, wormy brown apple cores, mulled vinegarised wine, sodden towelette scrolls with blotted scripture under cracked china & twisted cutlery & festooned with toothpicks — a pair of seven-tined candelabra at either end. Atop this mess, a surgical mannequin lay stretched out. Volta was positioned at the head of it: to one side of him, in Hedda Gabler's black evening dress & bloodied wig, stood Alice Steinerová, a gloved hand draped in the crook of her brother's arm, Maxalex Steiner-Reinhardt, in velvet-lapelled tuxedo & goldplated lightmeter on a chainlink necklace — to the other, Ruby Ray in sequined décolleté & the ubiquitous Herr Viktor Faktor, high collar, tails, sash & grand cross of the Apocryphal Order of Poltroons — Bareš & his blond secretary stood slightly behind with Zahradník & the redhead from the Natural Sciences Museum & the short cigar-puffing stranger with the talking carp rounding out the party — conspirators all. Their heads swivelled towards me as I came across the room — plastinated faces as if each in fact was an actor wearing a mask, or worse, an *android*. Faktor's dwarf stood on a chair at the foot of the corpse, snickering, a lit taper in one hand, the other twirling his moustache. It was a scene composed for a seventeenth-century anatomy theatre, redolent of Holbein or de Vries. They intoned in unison, *Ha lahma anya...* As I came among them, Volta took a scalpel from a tray &, with a mechanical gesture destined again & again to repeat itself, made a long vertical incision in the mannequin's abdomen — he parted the rubbery flaps of skin & muscle with his fingers & jabbed a meat thermometer into the waxwork liver — it had a reading of 16 degrees Celsius. Time of death: between three & five a.m. I came closer & stared at the bloodless face of the corpse. *Yep, that's me there on the slab, alright.* Then the face came alive, blinked, sucked in air between its teeth, coughed, looked intently back at me with dark haunted eyes. I understood it desired to communicate something & so I leant closer — it's voice barely a whisper, my ears almost touching its moist trembling lips.

And it said —

> *There once was a young Rab Němec,*
> *who raised up a golem in his pants —*
> *but one night in the dark,*
> *when it threatened to depart,*
> *he wrung its neck with both hands, dah-dum.*

For a long time after I woke, the ceiling hovered over me in a blur till my
eyes focused & I could see clearly the square of light above. The images
from my dream remained present in the room & then gradually faded.
Outside I could hear the screeching of the caretaker's parrot. It was already
dawn. Eventually I fell asleep again. A sleep like the blankness of a cell,
with no windows & no doors.

f. The Good & Bad Bishops

41

Who took it remains a mystery. The photograph's dated April 1908 & shows the Father of the October Revolution, Vladimir Ilych Ulyanov, playing chess with a certain Alexander Bogdanov, Father of Systems Theory, during a mutual visit to Maxim Gorky, Father of Socialist Realism, on the island of Capri. The story goes that Lenin & Bogdanov argued politics for the duration of the match, which the latter succeeded in winning without great difficulty, the former turning "childishly petulant" when the untenable nature of his position became all too clear. No-one really knows, however, the course of the game itself, whose only definite clue is the disposition of the pieces on the board at the moment the photograph was taken. The moment, that is, at which Lenin chose to spit the dummy. Or perhaps he was simply yawning. Or doing an impression of a yapping mutt. One theory concerning the game had the future Chairman of the Council of People's Commissars of the Soviet Union playing the hypermodern Alekhine Defence ("Four Pawns Attack") & losing as white:

1.	e4	Nf6	10.	Be2	o-o	19.	Nb5	Rae8
2.	e5	Nd5	11.	o-o	f6	20.	Bf3	Re3
3.	d4	d6	12.	Nh4	fe5	21.	Qd2	Rf6
4.	c4	Nb6	13.	Nf5	ef5	22.	b4	Be7
5.	f4	de5	14.	d5	Nd4	23.	Nc7	Rh6
6.	fe5	Nc6	15.	Bd4	ed4	24.	Ne6	Qg3
7.	Be3	Bf5	16.	Qd4	Nd7	25.	h3	Bd6
8.	Nc3	e6	17.	Kh1	Bc5	26.	Kg1	Rh3
9.	Nf3	Be7	18.	Qd3	Qg5	27.	...	

Though Alekhine, of course, was only a teenager at the time (& wouldn't exhibit this idiosyncratic line of play* till the Budapest tournament of 1921) & besides, in the picture Lenin is playing black. There are other photos of Lenin playing Bogdanov, but he has the black pieces in those games, too. Only a year later Lenin was apparently playing chess with Hitler in Vienna (also as black). One account attributes the Capri game not to Bogdanov, but to the observer Gorky (who can be seen in the original photograph apparently having slid out of his chair, startled perhaps by Lenin's spat) — except it's widely attested that Gorky, the "God-Builder," couldn't play chess to save his life (which might've evened the odds between writer & revolutionary, who knows).* Neither such details, nor the available photographic evidence, prevented a famous painting being commissioned in which Gorky (not Bogdanov) is depicted at the board, with Nadezhda Krupskaya observing & Lenin *again* playing black. In fact there is no record of Lenin ever having played white — but there's no substantial evidence of Hitler having done so either. A century later a man named "Valentin" Bogdanov did pen a book about the namesake of "the most aggressive reply to 1. e4." It's also true that this namesake happened to be a nobleman, son of a State Duma member & the heir of the Trekhgornaya manufacturing concern. In fact Alekhine, who famously said *Play on both sides of the board is my favourite strategy*, was arrested by the Bolshevik secret police in 1919, for ties to the Counter-Revolution, & might never've bestowed his "miracle weapon" upon the unwitting world had he not escaped a firing squad through the apocryphal intervention of one Lev Trotsky (who, lamentably, never did suffer defeat at the hands of this future Weltmeister & Nazi stooge in an Odessa prison cell).

What's Prologue is Prologue

It was one of those cold grey September afternoons, bleaker than a pauper's burial. The sky was like an atrophy setting-in after the last hoorah — atrophy of the brain, of the vital organs, of the breathable atmosphere. And lying there in

---

* Described by the authors of the 4th edition of *Modern Chess Openings* as "bizarre." [✋]

* Stalin awarded Gorky the Order of Lenin in 1932, the eponymous revolutionary having succumbed to syphilis on 21 January 1924 (a leap year); Gorky himself was most likely executed on Stalin's order in 1934 (the year Persia became Iran). Three years previously, the Georgian (forever underestimated as a literary critic) had written on the last page of Gorky's fairytale "A Girl & Death": "This piece is stronger than Goethe's *Faust*..." He was even the chief pallbearer at Gorky's funeral. Just goes to show, eh? Just goes to show. [✋]

all its glory, behind a teetering boom-gate & listing sentry box, the shambles
that remained of Barrandov Studios, like a corpse with a moribund guard set
over it to see it wasn't secretly buried in the night. The corpse of a traitorous
whore. It was a halfhearted affair, even the corpse didn't believe it was really
dead & kept lurching up with its costume half hanging off, arms akimbo in
tawdry pantomime of a Faux Phoenix doused in creosote, wizened ringwormed
jugs & a wig of ashen celluloid. How the mighty!

She'd been, during the War, the jewel in the crown of Goebbels' Ministry
of Public Enlightenment. Threehundredthousand metres of film came off her
production lines between Munich & May '46. *Jude Süss, Carl Peters, Tiefland, Ich
vertraue dir meine Frau an...* Like the whore she was, she snapped her garters at
the drop of a Deutschmark, morning noon & night. Queen whore & her whore
minions: Lída "mit der Schwanz" Baarová, Lil "anal" Adina, a.k.a. Jarmila
Mandlová,[*] *et al.*, attended by a hundred colonial *schwartzes* hung like *kühns* & a
legion of squarejawed Aryan castaways biding their days till *Barbarossa* on these
desert seacoasts of La Bohème, *Querelle-of-Brest*-like, baretorsoed in white
thightight sailor pants, languidly lowing their seamen's song:

> *Ich lebte einst im deutschen Vaterlande*
> *Bei goldner Freiheit achtzehn Jahr dahin.*
> *Da zog die Neubegierde mich zum Strande,*
> *Und ich bestieg ein Schiff mit frohem Sinn.*[*]

Baarová, a second-string Dietrich who'd been Goebbels' piece-on-the-side,
escaped a hanging after the War & flittered off to a Schnitzelstadt sanatorium.
And when the Wall came down, who should pop up with her memoirs
syndicated in the yellow press, angling to make a big comeback? How the ghost
of Goebbels must've wept! How bittersweet, that almondy waft of other people's
consciences. *Goebbels*, Ms Baarová rhapsodised, thinking nothing of it, *charming,
intelligent, a wonderful storyteller, always quick with a joke.* Like some Cecil B.
Über-idiot expecting all the carp to get up out of the river & laugh their slimy
heads off every time he blew his nose. *Historic Man*, as if to say, *has only one way
of submitting to barbarism, and that's to create it in front of the camera...* Or in front

---

[*] "Gusset faintly almondscented, *Parfüm des Gaskammern...*" All of it just vile, malicious slander, it
goes without saying. [☜]
[*] "Zardoz speaks to you, his chosen ones. / You have been raised up from brutality / to kill the
brutals / that multiply & are legion." [☜]

of the paying public.

Němec stood there taking in the aura of it all. There was an art to it, no doubt. At some other time of day, in some other weather, it might simply have looked like what it was, an image-factory that'd outlived itself, a labour camp of the collective imagination, a leftover begging to be put out of its misery. Perhaps at the very moment some evil genius was preparing to transplant its brain & set it to work again, like an amnesiac Golem, fed by dollars. The idiots on the other side of the screen'd never know the difference.

He'd come here for a reason, but not a very clear one. A guilty conscience, perhaps. A man in a photograph. A place that barely existed any more. Something between an image & a sepulchre. Vague echoes. But if ghosts could speak, where better to hear them?

The idea had materialised in the aftershock of one of those catatonic drool-on-the-pillow kinds of sleep, the first wink in days. Like the saying goes, it doesn't rain but it gushes out of chamber pots. He'd woken on the floor of the Prof's bureau, wrapped in his suit, with a slant of grey light from the window making upsidedown patterns through brain-fog. At first he assumed it was the Old Man's ghost. He thought he'd heard it say something, like *Still asleep, eh?* Or, *When're you going to wake up* [to yourself?]?

He'd groped his way over to the window. No ghost. But through the curtains of the apartment diagonally across the street, he could see the Weather Lady lying on her sofa in her underwear watching TV, curtain left open — ubiquitous flicker of blue aquarium light on her face — in one hand holding a remote control, in the other her crotch. A whole morning's entertainment right there. He'd leant his head against the glass, the street sounds posing the ubiquitous question. *What the fazool am I doing here?* Not in the metaphysic, but in the particular. A fly buzzed. From the blank look on the face of the Weather Lady, she could've been watching anything, or nothing, just the flicker between pictures, light washing over the retina like a cold flame.

Maybe it was a sign.

Time Foretold

At some stage the Weather Lady got dressed in front of a mirror then pulled down the blind without ever once looking out. The blue light around the edges of the window died & a minute later a blonde in highheels turned out of the building towards Nerudova. It was Němec's cue, but he was slow taking it. A car radio thumped down in the street, till someone else came out of the building, a man this time, & got in, & the car drove away. In the silence it left behind, another man & a woman approached along Johannesburgstraße: the woman in a grey coat & red beret, boot heels loudly clicking against the cobblestones — the man a caricature of some watcher's projected inhibition, somehow getting smaller as he got closer. Behind a curtain somewhere, there were other watchers perhaps, watching him watching them.

It didn't look like the kind of day with too many prospects. Němec caught his own reflection glancing back at him — nothing like waking up in your clothes to put everything in a positive light. And what if the Prof's ghost had been there all the while, spying on him, after all?

He shuffled to the kitchen, head full of optimistic thoughts, & drank what remained of the milk. A knot of dull pain weighed in his gut, no mystery there. On the side of the milk carton, a picture of a happy, overweaned nuclear family smiled out at him. *Milk's good for you*! And then there was the magic formula of goodness itself: 1.5% fat. Homogenised. Pasteurised. 190kj/45kcal. Saccharides 4.6g, etc. Němec crushed the carton & threw it beside the rest of the garbage in the sink. The truth was that most people were bored, apathetic, dissatisfied with their lives. No amount of Roman charity would ever save them from their emotional sickness. He imagined Volta saying something of that sort. The good breast. The mummy surrogate. *Because every good day starts with milk*!

Like a good little shit he took himself out to the bathroom & stood beside the deadman's bath, splashed his face in cold water, poked behind his teeth with the end of his index finger, sucked the snot out of his nose, picked his ears, dragged a razor over the patchwork, wrung out his underwear in the sink & generally put himself in order. Gut-pain working down into the unmentionables, an ape's clog & chain. He squatted over the porcelain but no reward. He was breathing hard from the effort. Time for some pills to stay calm, the baby-blue ones that tasted of mouldy diapers. Pulled on the old rags with their familiar crust. Mirror mirror on the wall. *Well, who's the bright spark, eh?*

And when was the last decent meal he'd had? Kosher & three veg. Vepřo-knedlo-zelo. *Got to look after yourself, kiddo. A man's body's his temple, mnnnnnn?*

And yesterday, what'd he done yesterday?

He cast around for indications & found the usual mess. Then, feeling through his pockets, came up with a photograph. It was the one the caretaker had given him weeks if not months before — the Prof's doppelgänger seated at a chessboard on the Barrandov Terraces — folded in among bits of crumpled xerox paper. He smoothed out the corners & stared at it in the halflight. The peculiarity of that younger Hájek's expression. The good & the bad bishops. The attaché case on the empty chair. People in the background. Not camera shy in those days, was he, the Ol' Geist's corporeal personage? No doubt the world looked somewhat different in nineteenfourtywhenever. He wondered. Just how different. At this late stage, anything could be a clue. Now if he'd been Major Zeman he'd've already staked out the scene & worked backwards by deduction, intuition, random strokes of aided & abetted genius. But he wasn't the Zee-man. Not by a long shot. Still. The day hadn't turned entirely bad yet. There was always a chance something might come of it.

Buffing his shoes with a scrap of newsprint — crossword section, *A small purple turban-like flower, eight letters*[*] — & re-pocketing the Prof's likeness, Němec left the semi-scaffolded house on Jánský Vršek heading towards Smíchov. A cold rheumatoid wind blew across the wet hillside. Half an hour later he was standing in front of the Red Army tank on Arbes Square that Diva Černobýlová had reputedly painted flamingo-pink before the old Commies had wriggled out of the woodwork & painted it green again. Then on, past Victor Hugo Street, the fountain with gypsy kids even in that weather splashing in it stripped to their underwear, down Kirovova — *Jesus Lives!* sprayed on a wall, *Elvis Lives! Lennon Lives!* — old women in headscarves on a bench, old men in their cardigans & fat younger men in string vests — across Plzeňská, where the eyesore of Moskevská Station stood out like a chancre. At its rear, an expanse of cracked bitumen, zinc hoardings & meshed glass smeared with mud & coaldust & random numbers on signs like some leftover Soviet disorientation programme.

Played Arseways

The stop for Bus 211 was beside a shelter carpeted with smashed glass, cigarette butts, chewing gum & dried spit. A torn DISKO DUCK poster was plastered across the mesh at one end, over an ad for D.I.Y. silicon. A pair of fake tits protruded from a weatherfaded gash in a cartoon disco ball. Two drunks had plonked down on the seat, shoulder to shoulder, & were sawing the air in tuberculous fits & starts. He had no idea how long he'd be stuck waiting there, the timetable was buried under a dozen layers of spray enamel, red black pink

---

[*] nogatraM [✋]

green. There was a kiosk selling refried klobása, booze & porno mags by the road. Němec bought a half-pint of Slivovice & stood there drinking it, trying to stave off the unrelenting ache, the aimlessness.

When it finally arrived, the bus nearly ran him off the platform. Its route took it south along the river, past the brewery & the train station, to the interchange at Strakonická, where Němec was advised to wait for the 105. He downed half the bottle under the dripping concrete overhang. By the time the 105 came into view he'd mastered the ache, but the aimlessness would have to take care of itself. The only seat was right at the back over the engine, he had to clench his teeth so they wouldn't get shaken out every time the driver changed gears. The air had the rubbery disinfectant smell of lurking contagions cut with spent diesel. Half the passengers must've been outpatients or their wives, making the weekly trip to the Poliklinika on the hill…

'Poor Martin, they told him he'll have to have his prostate taken out.'

'Ooh, you don't say?'

'Size of a watermelon, they reckon. No wonder he was all clogged up.'

'Dear me.'

'Couldn't barely move for weeks. Thought he was about to burst. *Shplock*! You know, like a great big soggy balloon.'

'Yick!'

'Lying there in bed all day & wouldn't even touch his beer. *Well, look on the bright side*, I tells him. *At least now yer hair won't fall out!*'

'You didn't!'

'I did 'n' all.'

'But your old man wears one of them toupee thingamajigs?'

'That's what I mean — the poor dear won't need to now.'

The 105 belched its way up to the Barrandov Plateau, which took its name from an overgrown outcrop of Palaeozoic sediment above the Moldau, festooned with trilobite, graptolite, coprolite, brachiopod & mollusc — before the Havel Bros raised up Little Hollywood there at the start of the '30s, christened in honour of that celebrated scavenger of fossilitic rocks, every nerdy 8-year-old's hero, Joachim Barrande. By the time the bus got there, the sky was entirely lost behind clouds. Němec disembarked in the drizzle at the entrance to the film lots. Across the traffic circle stood the crumbling façade of a restaurant, blocked-out like the grimestreaked totem of a Functionalism that didn't. What the age had demanded & received in abundance. Die neue Sachlichkeit.

To the left of the rusting blue studio gates stood a construction site.

Converted shipping containers were stacked along the roadside to quarter the non-union labour bussed-in, in all likelihood, from points as far east as the Schwarzesmeer. They made an incongruous sight behind a group of earnest-looking kids playing with a camera that'd been mounted on tracks, a yellow bin-bag wrapped around it. Němec half-expected goons in period costumes to start appearing out of the scenery — some Goebbels lookalike, maybe, to drive out the gates in a black Merc convertible, little swastikas pinned to the headlamps. But no. A girl in a flapping green anorak ran back & forth with a lightmeter while someone else mumbled into a walkie-talkie. A couple of lighting rigs steamed in the wet air. A few more kids huddled in the back of a van with its side door open, peering at video monitors. Němec took in the set-up. Were they supposed to be in a film or making one? It looked real enough. But where'd you draw the line? He didn't know. He didn't, as a matter or fact, care.

Penny Ante

The Havel Bros knew a business proposition when they saw one. After the War, when the Reds took a scalpel to the Aryan Disease & to the Havels' joint stock company, "Uncle" Miloš did what the ⚡ failed to do & wired the Barrandov sound stages with gelignite. Blew thirty-odd workers to bits, but the Studios stayed standing. Miloš skipped town for the BRD[*], subsequent — the family's wartime profits stashed in the bottom of a suitcase. Nephew Václav, who'd never been able to stomach the idea that a man might be the product of his circumstances, was obliged to earn his own pocketmoney stacking beer kegs in the cellar of the Trutnov Brewery, with a gang of gypsies. He drove a black Merc to the job every day, reckoned the gypsies thought he was a great bloke.[*] Lída Baarová reckoned Goebbels was a great bloke. Meanwhile the Studios churned out riches-to-rags regime fairytales at a rate of just under one-a-week. The local smartarses called the grey crumbling workhorse the Goodyworks Factory. All through the hedonistic decades of stagnation they kept the disinherited hope alive, that endless packs of Marlboro & cell-time could make a simpering silver spoon into a working man's Philosopher Prince. As Blecha might've said, *A man should at least own his sense of entitlement.*

But such things, alas, belonged to another time, another world.

---

[*] The West Fritzes. [✋]
[*] "Ať žije Havel! Ale jinde." [✋]

Němec reached into his jacket for the Prof's photograph. A droplet of rain fell on the corner of the picture, above the empty chair — or not empty, because an attaché case was lying on it. The Prof had a gaunt look about him, staring at the camera with an intensity of unease, the terrace behind with tables & amputated bits of arms & legs, bodies without heads, shadows adrift from whatever cast them. Němec brushed away the raindrop & turned the picture over. 1946. What was the Prof doing on the Barrandov Terraces in 1946? He glanced at the Studio entrance, the film crew, then back at the photograph. Even a figment, he thought, has to be real somewhere along the line. But where to look? He walked over to the sentry box & asked where the Terraces were.

'Yer fifty years too late,' the old guy in the washed-out rent-a-cop uniform said, jerking a thumb past the construction site. 'Follow the road all the way round through Havelville. You hit the motorway, you've missed it. Ain't much to miss, neither.'

'Nice day for it,' Němec eyed the weather.

'Take it from me,' the guard yawned, 'they're all the same.'

Over by the construction site the kids were wheeling the camera along the tracks while someone in a duffelcoat held a microphone aloft on a boom. In front of the camera, a redhead in a short fur jacket & black miniskirt was coming along the street holding an umbrella. Němec's eyes followed the sound of her boots. A couple of grinning labourers in cloth caps leaned over a scaffold & whistled. It might've passed for unscripted realism, except the redhead turned & said something back at them. Ashen light illuminated the scaffold from behind, where some sort of building ought to've been. The whole thing was draped in sailcloth with a giant slogan printed on it:

T E S L A
THE NEW SPIRIT
IS THE SPIRIT OF CONSTRUCTION

It was impossible to tell if it was meant to be part of a film or some kind of advertisement. But an advertisement for what? Someone called out *cut*! & the kids all huddled around the van to see how the shot came out on the monitors. Němec slouched towards them, pulling his collar up.

'Hey, fella,' the guard called after him. 'Yer wastin' yer time. Ain't nothin' you gonna find down there, 'cept a lotta rich trash all gone to shit. Same ol', same ol'. Shoulda bulldozed the lot when they had the chance. Now it's all that rest-my-tution crap, they gotta wait for it to *fall* down…'

Well some people, Němec thought, just bring out those little rays of sunshine.

'Hey fella,' the guard called out again, 'you don't *look* like one a them!'

Beyond the construction site, a long looping crescent wound around the hillside past dozens of silent-film-era mansions stacked on top of each other like headstones in a Zhiddish cemetery. Němec stumbled along it in the drizzle, there was no sidewalk to speak of, only driveways & not a car in sight. Nada. The road seemed to go on through the mist forever, like the proverbial Via Dolorosa. Behind him he could hear the film kids trying for another take. If it was shit weather they were after, it must've saved them a packet on special effects.

The guard was right, Havelville was as abject as dead money can get. What'd the Prof have to do with any of *this*? Fifty years ago, between the War & Exile. In 1946, Grigory Alexandrov was shooting *Vesna* on the main sound stage. Bronstein was wiping the floor with the Golem City chess brains (he'd have to check if Faktor'd been one of them — unlikely as it seemed, but then everything about the man was). What else? Karl Hermann Frank, ᛋᛋ-Obergruppenführer (former), was being hanged in front of a sell-out audience at Pankrác Prison. And the Barrandov Terraces, like the Studios & everything else, were about to be nationalised for the good of the people. One moment, every social climber in Golem City was angling to be spotted there, the next the place'd disappeared from the picture. Bulldozed by the Commies, maybe, in revenge for [insert political crime here], or torched by *anti*-Commie saboteurs, or paved-over for a bypass, or zapped up to space by aliens with an eye for realestate. Somehow Němec wasn't convinced either way. He wanted to see the place with his own eyes, see what image formed or failed to, whatever was left of its leaving, whatever trace of its disappearance, whatever warp in the fabric of Realism's realism.

Cul-de-sac

The road, as he might've expected, went nowhere. Turning hard left, it came dead up against the motorway embankment, becoming a gravel track. To the right, Němec could just make out the lights of the traffic across the river, cut by vertical lines of glass office blocks like pillars propping up a heavy ceiling of mist.

Below, the river resembled a grey scar, fading into drizzle.

A wire fence was all there was to indicate a perimeter. Behind it, for the most part invisible, were the thickly overgrown ruins of a manmade proscenium-onto-nothing littered with stageprops, a general arrangement of masses & volumes, a teetering pagoda here, a toppling lamppost there, brickwork knitted into the brown foliage like the latticed combs of Mayan temples. Had Němec not been looking for it, he'd never've found it. He pushed through a gap in the branches. All of a sudden, the space opened out. The sweep of the terraces was plain to see, arcing along the clifftop to a gutted white-brick tower with boarded-up windows from which all the glass had long ago been bludgeoned. It stood there on its precipice like a blinded lighthouse against the mist.

Picking his way among the debris, Němec came to the ledge & peered down over the railing at the shadowed escarpment. His eyes followed the southward sweep of the river, housing projects rising grey against the grey horizon, Stalin-baroque. Behind him, barely a hundred metres away, traffic surged along the motorway. It was impossible to get a sense of it all as it'd been in the Prof's picture, but still he tried to imagine it that way: the immaculate stepped array of the terraces, café tables with starched tablecloths, waiters in white coats, women in cloche hats. *And would madame prefer radish with her caviar, or asparagus?* He held the photograph up against the scene as it appeared now, fifty years on. The Prof's ghost gazed uncertainly out of it. Was it the place that'd disappeared from the picture, or the man, or both?

Perhaps this was what it would've been like had someone taken a snapshot of Cortés on the steps of Tenochtitlan, the afternoon before *la noche triste*, when the ancient world went up in flames & buried itself beneath its own rubble. And there *he* was, Němec of the latterday nonentities, standing in a kind of hereafter with all that dead History lying, in a manner of speaking, at his feet. Ah, the eternal amphitheatre… He peered straight down over the edge. Strangely the distance had no effect on him, he could barely see ten feet past the ledge in any case. By rights the debris ought've been piled even higher. The iron railing groaned against his trouser leg. Tempting fate was he? He stepped back. Then taking aim, he booted a loose stone into the abyss. Waited. Listened. One-thousand, two-thousand, three-thousand, nothing. Well so much for that.

And could the Prof have foreseen any of this? The doom impending in a botched chess game? Or an unfortunate photograph? What did *it* know that its subject didn't? Ghosts flittering through archaeological gloom. But it was just a picture, it had no reason to mean anything. Němec being Němec, he still tried to make sense of the scenery against the fading light. If he was right, the person holding the camera must've been standing somewhere over *there*, midway up the terrace, between the ledge & the tower & slightly to the left. He climbed the rubble & positioned himself in the spot, took a few corrective steps sideways, back. Yes. It would've been *there*.

But that was all. A perspective. A different light. He could just make out a couple of boathouses on the other side of the river. They would've been right behind where the Prof'd been sitting. He made a viewfinder of opposed thumb & forefinger & the scenery contracted into it. And as he did so, the mist closed over the frame & the darkness at his back seemed to rear up. Something moved. Němec, walkingstick braced, turned, sensing he wasn't alone. Did he suspect us being there with him, d'you think? Or console himself with the merely apparent? One might be forgiven for suggesting that, in the dying light, the tower *loomed* over him like an expired malevolence — some mad alchemist's broken image-machine from which many grandiose designs had failed to issue, though its invocation to apocalypse still echoed in stairwells, hallways, empty rooms. Somewhere in the back of Němec's mind the Prof's ghost may well've laughed...

Virgo serena, pia, munda et immaculata

Blackbirds scuttled through the undergrowth, the motorway droned. The path wound from the far side of the tower away from the terraces, then switched back into a steep zigzag down the wooded hillside. At the end of it lay cracked bitumen, a railline, an overgrown strip of riverbank. Up above, the tower was lost in silhouette, an uncanny, invisible proximity. The blackened cliff-face dropped away into the gloom. Němec stood on the crumbling roadway trying to orientate himself, grey scrub blocking any view of his immediate surroundings. He walked south. Barely twenty yards on, a baroque chapel in the shape of a domed rotunda, stood out of the vegetation like some ghostly incongruity, some sort of relic. The doors had been kicked-in & turned to firewood. A tramp colony appeared to've only recently abandoned it. Perhaps the place was cursed. It had all the abject appearance of a mausoleum from which the dead had been evicted by clandestine forces, leaving behind a compost of dog-blankets, torn mattresses, cardboard & plastic bags, broken bottles, tin cans, shredded newspapers, magazines, wine cartons & crusted hypodermics. Barely visible over the doorway, in residue of gold flake, the words AVE MARIA GRATIA PLENA, adorned with the universal doomsday emblem:

The chapel's dome had collapsed on one side & weeds were growing up out of it. It reminded Němec of the story of St Matirja Assunta on the Isle of Malta & the Luftwaffe's "miracle bomb." April '42, just before Heydrich's apotheosis. Smack bang in the middle of a congregation of 300. Only it didn't go off. Well, you figure the odds. The sappers were called-in, only instead of a quarter-tonne of explosives waiting to be defused they found the bomb stuffed with sandbags. And a typed message. The message said:

**GREETINGS FROM THE WORKERS
AT THE PLZEŇ ŠKODA FACTORY**

A commuter train thudded past, the lights from its windows briefly illuminating more ruins further on. Němec recognised the burnt-out remains of a bathhouse pavilion, showerblocks, changing cabins. He followed the road till a gap in the bushes opened to his right, exposing a muddy path. It seemed to point in the right direction. He beat through the overarching tangled branches with his walkingstick. A thorn snagged his hat. Something scuttled underfoot. Rubbish was strewn about everywhere in the undergrowth. Then without warning, Němec found himself out in the clear.

A black cliff rose up from the cracked & broken remains of an ancient amphitheatre, hewn stone glistening in the drizzle. He tried to make sense of it. His eyes scoped the shadows. Peripheral vision showed a sea of trash on all sides. Something large loomed out over it. He caught the shape of some heraldic, mythological bird about to take flight. Spread wings & fanned tail-plumage. His eyes made black holes. His eyes played tricks. He saw diving blocks. He saw a white plastic chair upended beneath a smashed diving tower. He saw the wreckage-strewn basin of an Olympic pool coiling down into its own shadows like a monumental ear. He turned so as to survey the entirety of this unreal vision. Behind him, a wide hole had been smashed in the pool's wall — it was through this that he'd stumbled.

He'd seen pictures of this place, below the Terraces, views from above. *Sun on the water. Flash of arm or thigh. The warm stink of coconut-oil like a banished childhood.* The tiered benches were still there, in an approximate way, camouflaged by ivy, brambles, thornbushes. The rest of it looked as if it'd been

577

bombed / abolished / crossed off the map. And sitting in the midst of all that debris, virtually at his feet, a plastic doll in a dirty white dress with its head broken off. He bent down & picked it up. It stank, of intestinal scoria, gut bacteria, dead animals, the underbelly of the Goebbels Nightmare Cannery…

A Family Romance

Reminding of how, at the end of the War, on the eve of the red flag unfurling over the Reichstag,[*] that apoplectic rat-faced Chancellor of the Reich (24hrs in office, non-pensionable), & Mastermind of Nazi Image-Eugenics, staged his final midnight matinee & bombast bonanza, prepping the script & grandiloquently directing the bekitsched scene of his fanatic Frau's snuff-job on their six little kiddlywinks down in the Führerbunker (*Meine Kinder sollen lieber sterben, als in Schande und Spott zu leben*) — ribbons in their hair, brightening their nightshirts, teensy Helga, weensy Hilde, woozie Helmut, breathless Holde, retching Hedda, paroxysmal Heidi (*Misch, Misch, du bist ein Fisch!*) — before heading up to the garden for a quick his&hers cyanide job under the Berlin sky, saluting at the camera *byesiebye* &, with a *coup de grâce* from their ⚡ adjutant to hasten them on their way, off to join the family holiday with their favouritest Führer in Himmel! The unhallowed remains of the entire brood afterwards doused with rare-as-hens-teeth-by-this-stage-of-the-War gasoline, incompetently incinerated (who'd've thought the ⚡ couldn't've got this right), seized by the Reds, shovelled into boxes with Hitler's mutt / bitch / *et al.*, buried, exhumed, re-buried, re-exhumed, then re-re-buried once-&-for-all at the local SMERSCH clink at Magdeburg, before re-re-exhumed one last final definitive time by the boys at the KGB (the year by now, 1970, Yuri Andropov presiding) so as to be re-re-incinerated &, one windless winter's morn, the resultant residue strewn in a fine dissolving haze upon the faintly burbling waters of the Beiditz, thence, precipitated by a swift current, carried onward to the Elbe, mist drizzling down through the willows as those sodden sacrificial ashes conjoined with the churning turbulent Moldau which, as destiny or perhaps mere happenstance would have it, passed within spitting distance of the very spot at which Němec was right now standing. Like a veritable Karmic wheel.

---

[*] Mayday! Mayday! [✊]

Prince Nez

The poet Nezval, an optimist who had himself photographed on the Terraces as often as decency would permit, once wrote that a man can live three days without bread, but no-one can live one day without poetry.* So much for consolations. That was before the War, of course. Afterwards, people starved & no-one believed poetry had a right to exist. (Cue the Bugman: *Who says the world ain't perfect?*) And then along came Klem Gottwald in the name of a Better Deal & permission to forget one's past, though not forgive it, making the little Hollywood on the Hill into an ether factory to smother the unwary in their sleep & blacken their dreams, the new national entertainment, like a circus ride where all the clownfaces & bright lights & cracked music are a cover for nothing more than the fact there's no getting off — the eternal *fait accompli* — as if to say, the whole world's that circus ride, that house of horrors & that shooting gallery.

Not enjoyin' yerself yet, kiddo?
Here, try the fairyfloss…

But there's always some perfumed ponce somewhere with his brioche & poésie wanting to get in the last word — like a man condemned trying to get in his last fuck. Just *one more* fuck, to sum up all those ideal future fucks he'll never have, so vivid & so real he won't even notice them strapping his arms & legs into the chair / putting the noose around his neck / sticking the needle in his vein. In his mind he's being fucked well & truly & there's nothing anyone can do about it except say, *So long, pal, enjoy the ride.* That's all the poetry he'll ever need. No poignantly opined epithet in the antidescriptive register. The lights go out & *phft*! Nothing more said. Even *you* won't get a word in edgewise, Mr Nezval, so why go on prating about it, like some overreheated amateur theatrical, with all those vignettes of a life well lived, a story well told, a fuck well fucked?

No your Nez-ness, we didn't forget y'd already carked it! That last word sure did away with you, *hehe.* Just like in the classics. *On yer horse, stranger…* You didn't even see the closing credits coming, but they sure saw you. As Zarathustra says, *One must still have chaos in oneself to be able to give birth to a dancing star. Alas, the time's coming when man will no longer give birth to a star…* Did you think

---

* Because poetry's what the absurd world becomes on its way to transcendence & fiction's what compensates for the fact that though we repeat ourselves incessantly we never start again? [✋]

you were it? Shine on, sucker! (Or as Buzík said, when the androids took the Home kids on a fieldtrip to the Olšanská cemetery that time, *Fuck me if it ain't Jesus H. himself up there on the...*)

The sound of rockfall interrupted Němec's little reverie. He ogled the darkness. Was someone following him? Němec listened for sounds in the underbrush, but there was nothing. By rights the place should've been haunted, cursed, but it was only just another demolition site that'd been perpetrated by parties known or unknown, making a waystation for bums, junkies, stray dogs, river rats & all the likewise undocumented fellowtravellers, random witnesses of the world's arrested decline, hehe. *Well, there's only so far you can fall, kiddo.*

Truer words...

Němec groped in his pockets for the bottle, upended the remaining half-pint of slivovice, gargled it & tossed the empty into the weeds. *Well here's cheers to the Great Obsolescence...* Clatter of tin can, busted syringe, rat tooth. Maybe a bit of old android braincasing, who'd ever know? He worked his way back to the road by the train tracks & followed it till he came to a flyover & junkstrewn steps up to the motorway. Traffic fizzed out of mist & drizzle — the cliffs of Barrandov shrouded entirely now — while muted streetlights glowed orange against the river like an endless tarmac stretched beneath the night.

Godspiel

Night had settled by the time the bus delivered Němec back to Smíchov & out of the rain into a diner facing the train station. He ordered coffee at the counter, then managed to wedge himself into a corner of the crowded room where the glare wasn't so bad, a mess of spilt sugar & gravy on chipboard laminate. The coffee tasted secondhand. A grey meniscus ringed the cup. He drank it anyway & let himself be slowly absorbed into the surrounding hum, like a warm enveloping fog. After a while he went back to the counter to buy a jug of Frankovka. Someone snared his corner seat, so he had to look around for somewhere else to perch. He found a spot against the back wall & set to work on the wine. It was rough but it could've been rougher. Leaning back he took in the new collection of faces. The usual. People like him, sitting-out the rain, smelling of dead time.

He sat there like that, shortening the jug & pondering what he'd seen up at Barrandov & what he hadn't. Something in its very nature. The sense of it as a blindspot, where the City had done its damnedest to erase some unwanted memory of itself, a spectre, an odradek, a deletion made manifest. The image of a non-image. Like all that Lidice footage. A pervert's abolition job *designed to leave traces of itself.* Or like an old film set which, having ceased to serve its one avowed purpose, gets junked on the back lots, becoming future post-Anthropocene UFO archaeology: Lost Alien Civilisation! From the few scraps of surviving evidence, they'll name it Barrandovia, reconstruct narratives of its downfall: some satrap's palace overrun by atomic robots, golem machines, gulag technocracies, its terrible fate kept buried from view for millennia, exposed by tectonic realignment. With all humanity having been wiped from the Earth & nothing but a dozen film canisters discovered a mile away under a soundstage to tell their story — spliced together by bemused Andromedans to comprise a testament to lost ages: *Thus their God led the peeps through the wilderness... salamander-skinned, to happen upon this Promised Land, dreamt from fossil to moving image — progress, death, evolution, destruction — the survival of the fittest.* "Instructive," they think. Held up as an example to future alien generations. Look! Pictures once lived here! They buried their dead in celluloid!

Němec finished the wine & ordered some more with a plate of bread & cheese. This time no-one stole his seat. Across the room a group of students were arguing in the way students do, passionately & without purpose. A girl in black turtleneck stood up, hands on hips, shouting across the table —

'Ježíšmarjá!'

'Ježíš?' a voice shouted back. 'Who in Hegel's Ježíš?'

'Idiot!' the girl cried.

'Who-is Jež-íš?' the table demanded.

'A Zhid!' Simon said, banging a glass.

'A Commie!' his opposite number crowed back.

'A sociopath!' 'A pimp!'

'A sand nigger!' 'A publicity stunt!'

'A profit margin!' 'A terrorist!'

'A patsy!' 'A pawn in the game!'

'An anarchist!' 'A mammy's boy!'

'A Trotskyite!' 'A god!'

'An anti-Shemite!' 'A victim of society!'

'A blackshirt!' 'A criminal mastermind!'

'Unamerikan!' 'A sonofagun!'

'A two-time looser!' 'An antichrist!'

'A con artist!' 'A dropout!'

'A wise guy!'   'A superstar!'
'A nobody!'   'A one-man show!'
'Everybody!'   'A bozo bag!'
'A schizo!'   'A cool-aid experiment!'
'An Oedipus Complex!'   'A mass hallucination!'

They all joined in. It went on & on. Shouting & laughter. The rest of the room paid no attention. A couple beside him, a man & a woman, were talking about something he couldn't make out. The woman leant across the table —

'Anything can happen on those trains,' she said, trying to keep her voice low but struggling to be heard over the general cacophony.

Then a moment later —

'You're just saying that to yourself, you're not including me.'

'Okay. You add one line from now on.'

There was a long silence. Then the man turned & said —

'Don't reinvent the wheel! Use it again & again.'

'Listen to yourself!'

They could just as easily've been chickens holding a conversation.

'Bgörk?'

'Bok!'

'Bokbok…'

'Berk?'

Hard to say what preoccupies people most, their own or other people's stupidity. And was he, Němec, any better off than the Common Man? He speared a piece of cheese with his fork, the centre oozing out through the tines. He wondered what it'd be like, hearing all those voices but not understanding the language, like one of those UFO anthropologists, letting the sounds mean anything at all, whatever happened to correspond to your pet theory. 8th Millennium Kircheriana. He tried listening while counting backwards from a hundred in his head. In under thirty it went from expectant to tedious to boring. Like the dead zone in the middle of a chess game where you just move the pieces around hoping for some kind of sign, to show you which way the end is. He swallowed the cheese. It tasted the way you'd expect month-old toejam to taste. He bit some bread, downed a glass. The room buzzed. A waitress schlepped trays, collected empties, slopped a wet rag. Rain fogged the windows. Time dragged. After a while the students started to sing — one of those rounds that, once begun, threatened to go on for ever:

They were drinking Fernet. Shotglasses were stacked into a ▲ in the middle of their table. The more they drank, the louder they sang. *Ježíšku, panáčku! Já tě budu kolíbati…* Němec stabbed another piece of cheese & sucked it between his teeth. The couple beside him started up again.

'It's not my fault you're getting old!'

'Stop blaming me. You would if you could.'

'Oh, so that it's just my imagination running wild again, is it?'

'Not since 1952!'

Zögernd, wie im Winterschnee

The night was wearing on without getting anywhere. Some part of the mechanism was missing, some obvious piece of the puzzle. Like a conversation with whole sentences left out, excised, undreamt, forgotten, that no amount of reason could restore into a meaningful dialogue. You joined the fragments & what you ended up with was interference all down the line, a picture with no sides, mists of whitenoise scored across with ravines of static, unmappable, a coagulation of dissolved forms in place of any *thing*. Němec yawned. Blinked. Buckled down for one last drink. He evoked the Zen of Zeman. Question: What if the absence of evidence was *meant* to define the true object of investigation? But what kind of method was that? Unless the aim was to be as opaque as the puzzle itself? Like, to undo like?

Outside, a mist of coal smoke & river fog blurred the outline of the street. The faint whine of a fusebox, echo of rats' feet on cobblestones, batwing, sonar blip, Herzian waves propagating through white noise, zero-particle metaphysics. Němec waited for a tram in the direction of Malá Strana. When it came, he was the only one who got on, but he wasn't alone, watching the shapes go by through the windows, the bums mumbling to themselves in their sleep. He got

---

* "Bejaysus, gimme a wee dram there love 'n' how 'bout a nice sloppy smooch to go with it? Johnny here wants to wet his whistle! Diddley-aye, diddley-aye, diddley-aye, eh." [✋]

off under the dome of St Nick's, up through the arcades, past the Zrcadlo stagedoor bolted for the night, Joey's Garáž, the Conservatoire, out of the arcade & down the sloping pasáž & up along old Corpses Street.

At the corner of Jánský Vršek a blindman with a carry case lying open on the sidewalk was belabouring an ancient accordion. A pair of cancelled eyes stared in uncanny fixity as he wheezed & jabbed at the keys. What he played was barely decipherable, but in time Němec could be relied upon to know it. He tossed some coins blindly as he passed, leaving the man to his invisible audience. The tuneless debacle followed through the mist & into the courtyard of the House of the Rising Damp, coiling up the roundabout turret, the precipitous stairs, a gasping ghostfugue in the warp of a fogged porthole / doorway / the temporal lobe of the inner-ear, back — back, turning in a gyre to the time before everything that came after, of long lost cold nights staring through barred windows, into the vortex of catatonic nothingness, till re-rooting itself in that hinge of Němec's mind, to be played & replayed all through the sleepless hours yet to come.

42

The annual Home Swimming Carnival meant whoever was
stationed at the opposite end from the diving blocks was
guaranteed to get an eyeful of the soaked-through ▼ of
Miss Freudlová's antediluvian gymsuit, provided Comrade
Med-the-Dev didn't manage to get in first with a sleazy
towel-hug at the end of the androids' 50m breaststroke
contest while M-M-M-Mr Express came up the ladder in a
close rearguard action. And if they weren't careful, it
was just as likely they'd catch a face-full of Bobek's
stiff poking through his Speedos, or any part of Ol'
Deathbed's shrivelled anatomy hauling out of the shallow
end -- enough to send a chill up even the staunchest
sixthgrade dingus.

Buzík refused to have any truck with that. You could
reliably find him stretching out beside the showerblock
on the hot concrete nuancing his tan, while Nagel & Robbo
"the Rat" lay slantwise beside him taking up pedestrian
space & getting a worm's eye view of every bandylegged
Lučinka in a onepiece who happened by. <u>Gimme a goddamn
snorkel</u>! <u>There's a fuckin' moray eel comin' alive down 'ere</u>!
<u>Raise the Titanic</u>! The outdoor pool at Slavia was where
the local gypsy kids went to wash, but on Carnival Day
the Home had it all to themselves from midday to four-on-
the-dot & Nagel&Co weren't about to waste precious time on
Freudlová's bristly snatch when they could get their
faces dripped on by real live bait. They left it to the
Pocket Tweezer Brigade to firm out their strokes over the
old folks. Besides, Nagel was hard working on a Plan.

The Plan looked like this: In the confusion between
races, they'd disguise themselves & crawl under one of the
benches in the girls' changeroom so they could wriggle
their tongues in unison up between the slats when the
fourth-grade medley relay team plonked their
goosepimpled chlorinated backsides down (a veritable Gene
Simmons was Nagel, though admittedly latching his
tastebuds onto one of those beardless creased clams was a
bit of a longshot, hehe, but no-one could ever say he
wasn't up for a challenge).

And since even the most brilliantly conceived plan
ought to have a backup, Plan B: Insinuate themselves
among the poolside cheersquad as soon as Squillhead & the
other retards got in the water for the spazo's backstroke
fiasco & crack funnies till the pompom girls couldn't help
wet themselves stifling giggles, & with any luck they'd

cop a surreptitious feel of pee-sopped gusset -- praying,
meanwhile, that <u>they</u> (Nagel&Co.) didn't piss <u>themselves</u> in
front of that stupendous vision of Squillhead bobbing in
a micturated doe-eyed mess of scissoring girlthighs, a
whole Spartakiada of lurid poolchurning incontinence
that, just to think about, had the palms of Nagel's hands
in a sticky sweat...

Pansophiae Prodromus

Another night in the same situation.

The hands of Němec's watch had stopped dead on sixteen minutes past the hour. There was no mechanism to rewind, like everything else nowadays it needed a new battery. Progress, that was called. One day the whole world-turning mechanism'd stop & no-one'd know how to fix it, till in the next post-Pleistocene some hairy ape peering out his cave door one morning at the latest Extinction Event had a stroke of genius & plonked down to reinvent the wheel, the written word, the volume-to-mass ratio. Or else it'd be left up to some halfwit Archimedes in a bathtub lost at sea to close-out the charade, no Ararat this time around, showerhead in one hand & cake of soap in the other — & the rubbery black bathplug down below, awaiting the coup-de-grâce. *Well so long, world, was nice knowin' ya*!

Reckon they could reverse-engineer the whole race back to tadpole status, give 'em an even chance? Němec felt sick at the very idea, watersports never having been his forte. Vague nightmare recollections of compulsory ritual horrors at the hands of those haters of the species, androids in swimming pools. And what if Noah, too, had been an android & all of humanity nothing but evolved testtube guppies from an onboard experiment which, so to speak, got out of hand? Well why not look on the bright side of it? Who knows, the end of the world could have its charms from the porthole vantage of a sinking ship, if you don't expect to see more than you deserve to.

Němec groaned, he'd had enough of his own catastrophe for one lifetime, the world could work out the bigger picture for itself. *Child's play, eh, kiddo*? Outside, a dark messianic rain fell. The window shook & rattled: in it, Němec's reflection was the caricature of a man in a glass box peering out through an impenetrable fog into an impenetrable downpour. Another day of the unrelenting grey lines. Water gushed from a broken drainpipe & spilled across the glass — damp had worked its way in through the cracks in the frame, the hinges, the joints & joists — damp was invading the room the way a dull ache invades the body, intimating of a general rheumatism of the brain. He tossed the dead watch on the floor. There were other ways of reckoning time than by the hour-hand & minute-hand. Bisect the core of a man & see what the ringed marrow tells you: the evolutionary itinerary, the travail of an upright posture, fissures & fracture lines of age & rebirth, that arrogant weak suspicious naïve creature within, slowly worming its way out across a span of years, epochs, Death's adjutant, its little homunculus, its bright-eyed grinning mannequin.

It put him in mind of Blecha, in the labour camps — the way the old guy told it: out in the forest digging clay in squared-off pits, while the pits filled with rainwater & being forced at gunpoint to keep on digging chest- & sometimes neck-deep in mud & afterwards, ordered to fill the pits back in again, shovel the clay down into the quarries, spewing out more & ever more leach- / horsefly- / mosquito-infested-muck till the entire forest was awash in it like the Marshes of Apocalypse. Day after day, same work. Interring, disinterring. The alpha & omega. Expecting any moment to come upon their predecessors, like the ghosts of Katyn, buried with their own shovels, skulls mashed underfoot, tramping out the wine, the evolutionary soup. God in his commissar's uniform, *Let you contemplate what you came from and what you'll become, my little turds.*

Sort of thing he reminded himself he ought to put in a story someday, write a book about, make a movie, though it might have a tendency to get repetitive, building up the necessary set of expectations & not making a complete farce of the realism. It's always the things that happen & the way they happen that's hardest to believe & who wants to see the world that way anyhow? It's enough to have that shot going on every other hour of your life. Well, Němec was a man of the people as much as the next wanker with a typewriter & enough of a grudge against the world to make him use it. Digging a hole for himself &, who knows, if he could keep his mind on the job, what was left of it, maybe enlarge it enough to take some other unsuspecting sonsofbitches down with him, hahaha.

His fingers ached, his knee ached, his back, brain & the hole in his arse ached. He pushed the writing machine aside, listening to the rain & empty-street sounds echoing up the scaffolds, autumnal mutterings & all that. Somewhere maybe someone else was writing a book with *him* in it & all the blank spaces & nothings & stupidities (the poor fucker), digging an even bigger hole, a hole into which to stuff all the lesser holes, but that didn't necessarily make either of them God. What would Volta've made of that. Maybe prescribe some candycoloured suppositories next time, if there ever was a next time.

On the other side of the window, the rain swirled in a vortex around reflected streetlight. The bare bones of the scaffold faintly groaned like some distant brokendown calliope. The panes rattled. A window, he decided, disturbs your whole sense of being in a given place at a given time & becomes... What? What was a window *really*? What if windows & walls & floors & ceilings all switched around *while you weren't looking*? Windows within windows. Walls within walls... Němec got up & dragged numb legs out to the kitchen to put the coffee pot on the stove. He'd been writing all night, about nothing, the way he always did, whenever he actually got around to it. The Prof's Polygraphia lay scattered about on the counter, in the sink, on the floor. He did his best to ignore it. If it'd been some other kind of deal, the sort of thing that with the aid of a few footnotes & a meandering intro about the deep dark degeneracy of its Big Deal could've been turned around into papermill fodder... A bit of the ol' vicarious limelight in the drag of debts repaid, or whatever. If he couldn't write his own book he could at least plagiarise someone else's, *hehe*. Or if not, the deathless anecdote of its uncreation, no less. Being as good an opportunity as any to put into verbilocutious perspective all the events of the past months in banalogical order — the little voices in the head telling him he should've written it all down, instead of waffling on about nothing for so long, kept track of things, some sort of ordered account, day-by-day. But that would've been too obvious, wouldn't it? And the point?

If the System taught him anything at all, it was to distrust systems. *And the Prof's pseudosystem?*[*] *This, too, I distrust?*

'Liabilities lie in wait whichever way you look,' is what the Bugman said, 'doesn't matter what you believe.'

Or if you kept your eyes screwed firmly shut? And what did *he*, Němec, believe? That nothing sought-for ever comes to you? That what you want's the last thing you'll get? And what you deserve? He knew this: *From kidnapped children are made kidnappers of children.* Amen. Which was the kind of thing, reminded him of a story used to circulate at the Home, about a local Dog Pound where they sold stray mutts by the kilo, only *they* were the mutts, right? And the skinny little kids like him used to shit themselves when they heard that one the first time round (*hehe, how much is that doggie in the window, aroo!*), figuring to be a dead cert for the slab, 'cause anyone could see just by looking at them they'd

---

[*] And was it a pseudosystem? Or a pseudo-pseudosystem? Or a pseudo-pseudo-pseudosystem? [✊]

for sure be some creepy Babajaga's idea of a bargain boil-in-a-bag dinner, *not a scrap of fat on 'em.*

He'd known it from the start, from that first furtive flirtation with the mirror, that he too was a tyrant in all but name, shape & capability, but within, yes, within, *he knew*, the tyrant lurked, *nevertheless.* Merely waiting. For the opportune instant. The moment of his fame. Like some holy cow coming home to roost. The sacred selfhood in its proper parameter. Blah-de-blah. The way it must've been for all great men of quality. Klem Gottwald, *par exemple.* That he'd only ever been a fuckwit by necessity, because History deemed it so, biding his proverbial through the longeurs of Life's preamble, to take them all when they didn't expect it. *Et too brut eh?*

Maybe it was impossible: you keep yourself prisoner to the slightest thing — derange all the senses, & then what? The perpetual revolution. The reparative peroration. If only to hold on long enough to find the way out: the backdoor of the world, the splinter in God's eye, the antipodes of the System, where maybe Irreversible Time gets disjointed, even if only by a bee's dick…

Orbis Pictus

In the tattoo of the rain on the glass, intimations of Mahler & a long-ago conversation with a deadman. He (Němec) had been staring out the window, listening to the deadman's voice weaving threads through labyrinths of minor chords — from the *allegro maestoso* to planetary motion — funerals of the stars — thunder & tremolando. He (the deadman) had been talking about Kepler. It was October, after the rain — a single low lamp cast its light over the deadman's desk — a game of chess abandoned halfway through —the gramophone's hiss — weeping Eurydice…

And what'd the deadman have to say for himself all so long ago? Kepler with his eyeball on the inner cogs of the working universe, like a Swiss watchmaker, phillipshead in one hand, macroscope in the other, fiddling the screws, screwing the fidgets.[†] All he could remember was the antique astrologist

---

[†] 'You know what Kepler believed?' the Prof said with obviously rhetorical intent, & Němec'd smiled, wanly, & waited to hear what was on the Old Man's mind, thinking *snoreo time, kiddo.* 'Well,' the Prof batted away a yawn of his own, 'Kepler, a devout idiot, though somewhat heretical also… like Tycho, *mmm?* — great minds tending to err on the side of *contrary* beliefs, not liking to bend before their masters — well, *er*, our dear Kepler fancied he'd discovered the true pantagonal universe, like a big mirror held up to the M.O.G. (Mind of God). And in that greatest of all

Mind's geometry? Mathematic orderliness, harmony, a righteous settling of accounts. *Ja wohl.* The *instinctus divinus, rationis particeps...*'

Ah, them old rationalist forceps, eh?

In the semidarkness, the Prof's eyes had glistened. Amused perhaps. Wanting his audience to share his amusement. *Don't take any of this too seriously, it's all just smoke and mirrors. Enjoy the show.*

'Some say after Copernicus, God died. But there's always a God dying somewhere in the universe. One God dies, another one gets born.'

He'd paused, a deliberate touch, adjusting himself in his armchair. As if to convey the idea itself, the ellipsis at the heart of the infinite conversation. Would the universe end? Inquiring man crept from his cave & cast his gaze heavenward to see. For as long as He lay dying, the ancient astronomers were at liberty count the follicles on His bald head through a telescope. The personal God. So close & yet so far. Separated from His forsaken pets by the merest dioptric of a polished lens. The Prof coughed —

'Rightly suspecting infinity *itself* could never be observed, never measured, Kepler turned towards arithmetic to translate God's *creative action* into astronomical *science*. Even if God *were* dead, there'd still be the corpse to contend with, eh?'

The Prof's monologues, Němec decided, were really tone poems, sonatas composed of the judicious dramatic pause, around which he'd fit his themes — connect the arguments by a telling silence — a constantly evoked intuitive register in E$^\flat$. In this way he built an overall effect that left Němec word-drunk —

'Infinity, no. For Kepler, the idea of infinity was scientifically meaningless. It was a mere opinion about the constitution of the world, unfounded in empirical fact. But keep in mind,' the Prof raising a finger in the desk lamp's chiaroscuro, exactly like Christ in Caravaggio's second *Supper at Emmaus*, 'that was only the beginning of the seventeenth century & *infinity* meant certain things it doesn't necessarily mean today. Consider: Giordano Bruno, who Kepler disclaimed & who was grievously burned at the stake for his sins. Well, for that matter, it isn't only the meanings of words that've changed...'

At the end of the first movement, the Prof stood up & went over to a cupboard beside his old gramophone & took down a second bottle of Eurydice's tears. They drank for a while in silence, then he turned the vinyl disk over & set the needle down on it to play — a strange counterpoint to the Prof's mood which grew more pensive as the music grew by turns ironic, bizarre, burlesque: Saint Anthony preaching to the fishes (who remain unmoved).

'D'you realise,' the Prof recommenced, 'what it'd mean if everything could be *seen*? If everything could be *known*?'

Leaning forward, peering at Němec through the gloom with Antonine eye —

'What it'd *really* mean?'

Memory getting a bit hazy at this point, gulping my port, Eurydice versus this sudden vision of the mad saint. What was the moral to be drawn, that Anthony was no Orpheus? Unmoved because preaching to the converted: the Christ-fish? *When's a symbol not a symbol?* The music had become a rousing chorale, all hope & glory.

The Prof turned back to face his desk, Table of Oblation —

'Ah, yes, but meanings change, *nicht wahr*? Kepler — dear doltish Kepler — brilliant though he was, in spite of his sins, but a mere mathematician for all that, who, unsatisfied with his lot, aspired, like pitiful Faustus, to be God's true witness — an *astronomer* — a celestial physicist, so he called himself, he who hath Knowledge of the Heavens — hardly a demiurge, certainly no Author of Creation, simply an annotator, like Swedenborg on his mad Munchausen mission to the moon, or wherever it was he thought he went — how did he know his telescope wasn't just another navel-gazer's dream machine? He peers, he measures. Wunderbar! The *Rudolphine Tables*, the *Mysterium*

Cosmographicum — proof that a man needs to believe what he sees, or else see what he believes…'

The Prof folded his hands, the very picture of Enlightenment Man —

'Astronomy, insofar as it was a science at all, was a science of *appearances*: empirical only to the extent it was *speculative*. A paradox, eh? What you observed you couldn't get your hands on, put over a Bunsen burner or distil into a beaker. But at least you could see your God at work, asleep or rotting in His grave. They traded the obscurity of the Church for the clarity of a burlesque, served with a dose of alchemical hogwash of angelspeak & hieroglyphics. Its holy of holies were logarithm & antilogarithm, star catalogues & planetary tables. Kepler, a student of Tycho & Hagecius, used a telescope not a crystal ball to probe into the secret parts of the unknown, though the technology was sometimes as primitive as an ape's priapus. The eye, so to speak, could often see most directly by means of aberration, aided by calculus. A striptease by numbers. Such things tested men's credulity, but did nothing to diminish their desire. It was only a matter of time before a *problem* like parallax was transformed into a *tool* — as if an immorality was transformed into the highest virtue — the proof-in-hand of a heliocentric universe (*the Earth moves!* said Galileo). Only a matter of time, then, before they recognised the aberration within the *logic* of their "science." Kepler never did: he believed till his dying day in polyhedral spheres, just as Plato had two thousand years before, convinced he'd discovered the secret geometry of the universe — but we shouldn't blame him for it. Should we?'

It sounded to Němec like the sort of thing they'd had drummed into them at the Home — one of the very first lessons: *That you're even guilty of what you don't know. Above all, of what you don't know that you don't know.*

The Prof, after the exertions of his monologue, fell silent. For the time being the music was all that could be heard — trumpets, horns, timpani — heaven & earth. *O glaube.* Brass, bells & organ ringing out. The silence at the end lasted only as long as it took the needle on the gramophone to complete its stationary orbit & the background static of the universe flooded back over us. The Prof, eyebrows raised as if to say, *There, you see, how it all ends? The Day of Judgement and the Resurrection!* dragged himself up from his chair to change the record. Seeing Němec about to stand, the Prof waved him away: his assigned role was to sit there like an ear & listen. The Prof returned the disc to its sleeve, as delicately as if it were a holy relic, placing it upon the shelf with all due regard to ceremony, eye of an imagined monstrance gazing down. What we listened to next was a Deutsches Gramophone recording of Mahler's sixth in A^m, Bruno Walther conducting.

Němec must've listened to those passages of Mahler's symphony dozens of times, yet they still had the singular effect of drowning his thoughts. Like in Rilke, *that music crept by me on the water.* Or perhaps it wasn't Rilke, but someone else. He felt the music creep by him as though it were tangible, on the verge of embodiment, all around him. A symphony of everything, sharp & flat, bum notes, noise, blather, silence & all. Then someone slammed a car door out in the street & he snapped back to what the Prof was saying —

'For example,' raising his glass to his lips & sipping at his port, 'it couldn't admit things that appeared to contradict the laws of optics.'

The Prof turned the stem of the glass in fingers creased with age & seemed to regard it, the glass or the light within the glass, with a certain degree of concentration if not of rapture —

'Which is another way of putting the cart before the donkey, or is it the horse? You look at the sky with a set of laws or with a metaphysics, what difference does it make? Man invents the telescope, things appear to him through it, but a man still needs a mind to see what appears to him & to make sense of it, *nicht wahr?* And so we're back at the problem we started with. Because astronomy isn't, or wasn't, *only* a science of appearances, but an *art* of appearances also.'

He broke off again, peering across the gloom as if summoning there some vision of his antiself-of-yore bringing two lenses into coincidence & gazing suddenly, unexpectedly, upon some holed up in a tower in the middle of the Klementinum, back in the day, with an observatoire cluttered with high-end instrumentation fine-tuned to the starry sky. Quite the antipodal character, from the POV of so giant a man as Ebwarb K, with whom the only notable commonality must've been a penchant for altitude & patents pending on the Amazing Answer to All&Sundry (maybe, too, on a clear day they'd've been able to wave at each other over the rooftops, thumb their noses, shoot the chutes?).

But in the City of a Thousand Spires, what were a couple of prestidigitators up on stiles to the greater scheme of things? Perhaps it was a clue? *Follow the towers? X them on a map, join the dots, see where the emerging pattern led?* Figure the Prof in somehow: The Prof in the pic up at Barrandov —

---

untold cinema of the mind's eye in cosmoscopic close-up.

'You see,' the Prof resumed in a droll voice, 'Copernicus didn't just *observe* a universal truth, he *created* that truth. That was the real revolution. Not to see clearly some *thing* or some *phenomenon* out there objectively in the universe, but to see that our seeing *makes it so.* How Galileo got himself into so much hot water. Dogma Incorporated doesn't like that sort of business. Not because they're contradicted by it — the whole world contradicts the resurrection of Christ — which hasn't prevented two thousand years of the Cretinist Church — but because it vulgarises the pieties & makes them into the stuff of peepshows.'

And dogma went to the dogs. God mightn't exist, but try telling that to God. Despite himself, the Prof sounded like the proverbial Man of Sorrows: he mourned his God to death. *Knowing his purgatory.* But the Prof was no longer smiling. The source of his moods, however, remained a mystery to Němec. He thought: *But what if you simply changed all the names?* Truth, revolution, resurrection. Like Mahler's symphony. Why *Tragische* & not (eh?) the *Rehab Symphony*, or *Habeas Corpus*, or *Handbook of Heavy Construction?* Was meaning as arbitrary as the arrangement of cutlery on a table? The angle, for example, of the port decanter in relation to the edge of the bookshelf? Or the dull axeblow sounding at the end of the last movement of the tragically maligned Sixth? (Echoes of Mydlář in there somewhere?) Or the opposite of truth, revolution, resurrection? Symptoms without causes. Ghosts of soulless, indeterminate things. (And what'd be the opposite of a soulless indeterminate thing? A soulful determinate nothing?) *Well, kiddo, sometimes, er, a symptom's just a symptom, you know?*

The Prof set his glass down on the edge of his desk & idly picked at the inside of his right nostril. A sliver of something wedged under his fingernail & he flicked it on the floor —

'Consider,' he said, wiping the end of his finger. 'Why's the question of faith so difficult? Because we're required to believe in the *absence* of facts? Or because we're required to believe in the *presence* of all possible evidence to the contrary?' Then absently, as if as an afterthought: 'Humanity, for example.'

'So humanity's failed?'

'Failed?' the Prof raised his eyebrows. 'What's humanity got to fail at? Humanity doesn't *exist.* Humanity's an idea, like God, only the critical mass is missing — not enough believers any more. Because it's too much of a burden. Whereas it's easier hedging your bets that God *does* exist, precisely because we *know* the universe can't be explained. Why d'you reckon that is? What I've been telling you all along. The problem's in the explanation *itself.* It's like a closed circle. Belief in God's just another way of saying you can't know what's outside the circle by means of the circle.'

the Prof in the Klementinum courtyard — the Prof hunkered down at the "Donkey in the Cradle." *Hmmm.* Were there others, sites as yet unknown? Turrets of doom, campaniles of the seraphic swandive, panoptical watchtowers, antique bungee poles, trapeze ladders for the flyminded?[*] Well, it was an idea that could sure keep someone busy scratching their noodle, but it wasn't Němec, his noodle'd been well & truly worked over already, *hehe.* Still, with nothing better to do now that the narcissistic impulse had ebbed somewhat, & with the word-sump of that dubious cranium of his drained down to the dregs…

He looked out the window, but it was impossible to gauge the hour. You see, the bright idea taking shape in Němec's squillhead was this: If it mattered, if he got there in time, he could get a ticket & see for himself what the set-up was with this Kepler, take in the view, let the famous Němecian intuition do its job. They ran guided tours on weekdays. Weekends, too, maybe. Only one way to find out…

He pulled on his jacket & hobbled out, stick clattering on the doorstep & down the stairs, without allowing himself time to think or decide otherwise, etc. Man of purpose, man of the hour. Besides, if he didn't get out he'd suffocate on his own introspection. No sign of the caretaker on this fine afternoon-evening. The whole house seemed deserted. In the street, water coursed down the cobbled steps into the trenchworks where once the pavement ran. Bits of propped-up scaffold stuck out of the muck, climbing up past his windows, where it'd end was anyone's guess. Němec stood there with the rain thudding onto his bowler hat. The thudding grew heavier, then after a while it virtually stopped.

Camera Obscura

Ever since the night the Prof's ghost first appeared, the night of "the Fall," Němec had felt he was passing through the world without really touching it — a world that'd narrowed, a world standing still. First the pain & then the anaesthesia. Or first the anaesthesia & then the pain. Chaos & abstraction. And from the chaos… At first, confusion: an accursèd symboltome that couldn't be unciphered — backwards allegory of some extinct, lost, or imaginary tribe — Book of the Dead, Popol Vuh, Codex Cinematicus of the Magik Hieroglyph, DIY Manual for the Reanimation of the Signatura Rerum, an Abridged Martian Almanac of Other Worlds than this One, an Android's Doodling Pad, some

---

[*] Jesuits in leotards? [♣]

proto-Wolfliesque *Bildnerei der Geistekranken*, or else a Mythomaniac's Map of the Treasure Buried Under the Stairs: ⚐ ratsfoot, ♂ sputum, † pubic hair, ☠ sticks&stones? From such intuited deductions as these, the humptyheaded revelation thereafter, by degrees, by facets, with his (Němec's) dousing dipstick up the garden path & through the undergrowth, like an idiot hunting a stark raving gnome, thinking he's been a very clever little boy following the signs. Oh ho! It's Red Letter Day for Chumps! *Well them ain't signs, kiddo, they ain't there to be read, see? You're the sign, hehe, they're readin' you! Hehe. Hehehe.*

Němec pulled up his collar, hunched his shoulders, ploughed out into the weather. Rain poured over the brim of his hat. By the time he reached the corner, he was soaked. A little way down Nerudova he found a taxi idling in front of a circus poster, showing clowns & an elephant standing on its front legs. A fish restaurant advertised the night's speciality on a chalkboard in half-dissolved chalk. *Carpe au naturelle.* The driver sat there fidgeting with his meter. Němec rapped on the window. The driver shook his head. Němec rapped again, pointing at the sky. The driver shrugged & popped the lock. Němec got in. The driver scoped him in the rearview, sagging bowler hat, scarecrow costume —

'Funeral?'

'Yeah, the whole world's gone to the dogs. We'll all be lucky to see the dawn…'

'I can hear the music already. Anywhere particular, or you just wanna sit here & work the prospects over a bit? I got a bum meter. It's been on the fritz for a while now, I reckon I could do without the complications but life's just like that. Let me know when you're ready.'

Němec dripped on the seat. Fogged the window. Squelched his toes in his shoes. It was six to a half-dozen. He decided what the hell…

'How about the other side of Charles Bridge?'

The driver turned around in his seat —

'Fella, you could lie down & roll there from here…'

'You've got a bum meter, I've got a bum leg.'

Man shook his head —

'The things I do for charity in this business. I coulda been an airline pilot, makin' a motza doin' takeoffs & landings, if it weren't for the fact I can't stomach heights. Been drivin' a cab since before the Wall. People nowadays reckon all cabbies are crooks, but what it really is, is they're ashamed. Half the cabbies I know've got PhDs in bleedin' astrophysics. Some people out there are insulted by that. It's bleedin' class warfare, is what it is.'

'Right on, brother,' Němec nodded. 'Last refuge of the free man.'

The driver made eyes at him in the rearview —

'Bleedin' right it is.'

He hit the ignition & skidded up the hill, then swung about, spraying pedestrians huddled under umbrellas, heading for the river. Němec rubbed a patch of window with his sleeve & stared out. The streets looked like dissolving celluloid. Filaments of dead light, liquescent. *You turn a labyrinth inside-out and it's an inside-out labyrinth. A man's only as big as what he sees...* They passed the Finance Ministry, a couple of goons with earpieces flanking the doors.

'You know,' the driver interrupted Němec's poésie, 'they reckon dentists have the highest suicide rate of any profession except air traffic controllers. Said so on the news. Now why d'you figure that is? I put it down to nerves. Pulling teeth, drilling out the cavities, blood & spit & rotten breath. Not like a doctor, 'cos most of the time you'd have to be looking the poor fuckers right in the eye while you're torturing 'em. Alligator clips on yer balls, a pair of pliers snapping off yer incisors. Now you don't hear about cabbies topping themselves, do you? On account of the fact that we're survivors, I'd say. Not meaning to make pretensions or anything, but it's dog eat cat out there, & a man's gotta make a buck, you know, put food on the table, pay the rent, see himself through to the end of his working life & if he's lucky get laid more or less regular along the way. You won't see me copping out, I'm in for the long haul, they can bury me in harness when I'm ready to go & with my own bleedin' teeth too — none of that plaster of Paris crap they all got in their heads nowadays, just waitin' to crack & fall out so the bastards can charge a motza to stuff it back in again...'

Midway across the river the traffic slowed to a crawl. Ten minutes later they were still sitting in a jam, barely past the embankment, cars bumper-to-bumper. Němec paid the driver & climbed out.

'Hey!' the driver called after him, 'I thought you had a bum leg? I coulda been home in bed by now...'

'Early to be,' Němec tipped his hat back, 'early to rise. Makes a man — so they say.'

'Bah to that!'

The rain had eased only slightly & the pavements were black with umbrellas. At Red Army Square the reason for the gridlock became obvious. A tram had sideswiped a refrigerated lorry, producing intersection chaos. One carriage of the tram was derailed. The lorry spilled crates of chicken meat onto the cobbles. Gipsy kids swooped in on it, tossing bits of chicken breast at windscreens. Sirens wailed. The lorry driver waved a tyre iron. The tramdriver stood pissing against his front wheel. Horns blared. Gypsies weaved through stalled traffic, drumsticks bulging from pockets, flipping commuters the bird.

Němec cut down some steps & along a backstreet, past fogged café windows, the north wall of the Klementinum looming large. Another block, then under an archway between high wooden doors, & Kepler's observatory up there* above the eastern courtyard where for a dozen years Rudi's chief numbercruncher observed the Great Conjunctions, formulated the Axioms of the True Doctrine of Gravitation & Laws of Planetary Motion, the Theory of Dioptrics Pertaining to Astronomical Telescopes, the Hexagonal System of Snowflakes, the Mumbofabulum of "Celestial Physics," Planetary Motion, Projective Geometry. *An ellipse becomes a parabola when a focus moves towards infinity, and when two foci of an ellipse merge into one another, a circle is formed; as the foci of an hyperbola merge, the hyperbola becomes a pair of straight lines; if a straight line is extended to infinity, it will meet itself at a single point at infinity, thus having the properties of a very large circle indeed...*

All a museum-piece now, the *Rudolfine Tables*, the old astrologist's clockwork orrerie — eight rings around the Sunnysunsun — Earth, Moon, the Planets & Cellestitudes, etc. — could pay a hundred crowns to queue up & see it, only he'd got there too late — the known-universe scaled down to a child-sized toy with moving parts, operated hourly by a waxwork Kepler's deft touch into an epileptic pantomime of *elliptical obits* (sic: God being dead, this was the next best thing the deistic dissenter could come up with), as from his copyist's bench a doe-eyed assistant looks on, quill in hand, ledger spread open before him with tables & columns zeroing in on the Number that Moves Itself — & in his glass eyes the mingling reflections of those spinning orbs. It might've been a scene from a movie, he might even've written it:

```
Kepler with index finger resting upon the axis of the
Sun, quizzing glasses, beard tucked up behind a chinstrap
while he tinkers at his machinery... On the table beside
him are the disassembled parts of a telescope, a mirror, a
pair of convex lenses: a routine repair job which he still
insists on doing himself, though unable to resist spinning
the planets around every now & then, oiling the joints,
checking it's all as it should be, nothing out of kilter,
the torque balancing out, virtually impossible to make a
scaled replica & be in the same room as it -- Compromises,
```

---

* Designed in 1569 by the renowned Venetian architect Ludovigo Vafunculo. [✋]

always <u>compromises</u>! -- but still, the point is <u>it works</u>, &
not only does it work, it's a veritable <u>manifestation</u>. More
or less. Kepler sighs. The moment's come for one of his
periodic pronouncements: not to do so, he feels, would
disappoint all & sundry -- only as wise as his stock of
epithets, as far as History's concerned. And with this
thought in mind, licking his lips, working his left hand
beneath his robes & up under his opposing armpit, chin
stretched, giving his premature jowls a bit of an airing
in the standard oratorical posture (the room, but for the
unoiled squeak of Venus being cutesy, falls silent in
anticipation). <u>Hmmm</u>. A drawing-in of breath, an
exhalation. <u>As a great man recently said</u>, fixing his
youthful assistant with an uncompromising stare,
eyebrows tickling the tops of his wire frames, <u>What's
written in the ancient books doesn't cut the mustard
anymore. Where faith was enthroned for many a donkey's
year now doubt resides. Soon doubt herself</u> (squeak, squeak)
<u>will be sovereign & Science the faith-triumphant</u>... The
assistant's busy scribbling all this down in the official
Kepler Book, to be run-off in multiple copies for the kids
in the local fanclub forthwith. The boy hovers over the
ellipse, waiting for the next titbit, but the well's
suddenly dried up it seems. A fly buzzes. Venus squeeeaks
to a stop midway around her track. <u>Hmmmmmm</u>. The ink
meanwhile clotting in the nib of the assistant's pen, the
Old Man grown visibly wistful, stare melting to dewy-eyed
reminiscence, drifting out through the tower window into
the overcast night sky -- all alone (in mind, at least)
ever since Tycho pissed himself to death, so unfortunate,
& lame Hagecius, Galileo, Copernicus: last of the blood,
you might say, now that Rudolf's been given the boot & the
Counter-Reformation's back in full swing -- <u>he'll</u> be
lucky to keep his head if he doesn't take the boy's advice
(fine fellow really, <u>bookish</u> is the word) & get the hell
out. But he's afraid of leaving all <u>this</u> behind, scene of
his greatest triumphs, the nerve centre (he sometimes
thinks, letting his imagination get the better of him) of
the Universe. He gives Saturn a short jab & sets it
wobbling around on its track like a drunk Capuchin,
letting out a sigh. <u>One day, m'boy, when this war's over,
Man may learn to govern himself by Reason, chaos'll be
banished from the World forever, all will be harmonious,
logical & precise as a tax return</u>. Hallelujah! <u>If only
they'd listen to ME</u>! And if he himself shouldn't live to
see the day? Bah! There'll always be comfort in the idea
of some proxy Archimedes doddling-out the blueprints
right up to the whistle, getting it all down pro-forma
for post-posterity, true to the End & to the End-of-Ends,
& not an afterthought be spared for smearing Papist,
puerile Protestant or pigskinned Pagan. Even if they
burned <u>his</u> books, the Keplerless World would go on
meandering towards its Apotheosis (though even that'd

597

What the preposthumous astronomer saw through that paradoxical periscope of his: a pinhole view on God's private cinematograph (reruns of *A Star is Born* every 800 circuits of the locus solis)? He, K-for-Kepler, alone perceiving, of all that emotive species caught in ever-retrograde action, *out there, in* & *of* the World but incapable of comprehending *it*, wading about knee-high in the slurry of their own dogma, that evil-smelling dung in which industrious hens scrape, pigs grovel, men luxuriate. Him & E.K. against it all. Well...

Němec took in the view from the proverbial peanut gallery, the foot of the implied triangle, the zero in the equation, the nonentity after the fact, *hehe*, trying (haphazard & halfarsed) to divine between the two meridians, Kepler's & Kelley's, observe in that spindly mind's eye of his the simultaneous parallax, K^1 & K^2 — devise some freebasing formula to make sense of the mock essentialisms — the molecular lattice between the (what'd the Prof called it?) *scientia observatione* & the *scientia illusio*. Begin with that: the third term — the *dream somnium*. Just as Kepler, after his own fashion, intent on demonstrating his Theory of the Universe by launching a pre-Meliès lunar mission, the first manned minaret in space, to unprove it all... Telescope in hand, sextant at the ready. Take down a few observations from up there, K^1 & K^2, put the whole bloody business in a bit of perspective: flat Earth, flat Universe — what the fuck did people think was *up* there, anyway? A heaven-sized silver shroud, pricked by God's bodkin & fairy lights, for The Maker's Home Movie Collection?

We have ignition!

Retrorockets firing.

Blast-off in 10, 9, 8, 7, 6...

It was all an anticlimax. The sky over the courtyard, whitewashed in cloud & rain, the pale observatory, its blackeyed dome, jutting into the gloom — nothing for it to see but a pair of searchlights sweeping the drizzle, some rooftop BAT-signal or UFO wanting a way out now that they'd seen what's coming.

And what would Kepler've made of all *this*? Now that the World had entered the age of no immutable laws, the dénouement of History? Up in the clouds the searchlights pursued one another aimlessly. Němec could hear a group of students sitting on a low wall beside the tower, their voices coming from the dark, indifferent to the weather. They were talking about something on TV, a gameshow, where contestants tried to guess the answers to questions only the audience knew.

Picture, Picture, on the Wall...

If it were true that parallel worlds existed, it might've been the case that (A) at this moment, in one of them, Němec elected to take the opportunity of its being near-at-hand to retrace the all-too-familiar path to the Klementinum Reading Room, to put some flesh on the bones of speculation.[*] It might, however, have been equally likely that (B), in a contrary frame of mind, he instead schlepped north through a side-gate & onto Karlova with no explicit destination in view: neon stripclub windows like mansized insectocutors hissing in the rain. Liliová. Bartolomějská. The tiled façade of Secret Cop HQ, redolent of unscrubbed mortuary floors. Unmarked Škodas, CCTV, window bars. Konviktská. Jan Milíč & the three hundred whores of Jerusalem. The Konvikt Klub. The Venice of all Brothels. A grey headwind blew the length of the street, rain angling at times horizontal. Out of it glowed the marquee of the Konvikt Bioskop: THE TERATOLOGISTS...

Flashback to Gottwald Embankment, war refugees crouched fearful in the wildernight.

Flashback to Kabaret Grünegast, Nazi Götterdämmerung.

Němec admitted to being curious & went in.

The film was forty minutes gone, but he bought a ticket anyway from the man behind the interrogation desk. The bar was littered with empty plastic cups, plates, bits of canapé. He ordered a brandy to warm the blood before facing whatever he was about to face. An audience questionnaire lay on the bar stool next to him, smeared with pâté. *On a scale of 1 – 10 how would you rate the movie overall? Would you recommend this movie to people you know? Please list which scenes you liked most and liked least, if any. Were there any characters you liked? Were there any characters you disliked? What, if anything, did you find confusing about this*

____

[*] → Chapter 43.

The theatre itself was almost empty. Maybe people'd only come for the free booze & then fucked off after the opening credits? Němec took a seat at the back, in the furthest corner. It set the screen off at an angle he liked. Seeing it that way, you couldn't pretend it was anything but what it was. Pictures flashed & got jumbled up. He recognised some of the sets. A train crossing a steel bridge. Searchlights. An apartment overlooking the river. Faces. A black Mercedes. Gunfire. Someone tied to a bedframe. A bucket of water. Wires & alligator clips.

And then she was there: Alice Steinerová.

Alice S posing as a coldblooded Nazi torture doctor's assistant.

Alice S as Nurse Lili Marlene giving succour to brokenhearted Waffen-*ᛋᛋ* grunts invalided out of Stalingrad.

Alice S as the Blonde Nemesis in *ᛋᛋ* bondage regalia.

Alice S as "Little Orphan Alice."

Alice S playing Veronika Voss, tormented by fate & a guilty conscience.

Alice S as Secret Agent "K" of the Propaganda Ministry.

Alice S posing as a bookshop assistant with bifocals & mousy hair.

Alice S disguised as a Wermacht officer.

Alice S as unsuspected Resistance saboteur, concealing a timebomb beneath a cargo train.

Alice S in a slave-labour uranium mine.

Alice S stealing the blueprint to the Nazi Miracle Weapon, concealed in a microdot somewhere no-one'll find it.

Alice S as a cabaret singer, a chorus girl, an usherette.

Alice S sacrificing herself for the Cause.

Alice S dispassionately observing the end of the Third Reich.

Alice S drinking champagne on the Barrandov Terraces.

Alice S escaping Golem City, posing as a Red Army officer.

Alice S in black gabardine crossing the border, destination unknown…

As the last images flickered on the screen, Němec closed his eyes & let his thoughts wander, Alice Steinerová floating through his mind like a timeless symbolic apparition present only in facets. The soundtrack fritzed. Bits of dialogue spilled out of the speakers behind him in a broken stream of static. When the film ended, he waited for the lights in the theatre to come on before opening his eyes again. Then he went & sat at the bar & waited for the next screening to come around, to see the parts he'd missed. An old guy in a knitted cardigan poured wine from a box into a fresh supply of plastic cups & laid out a tray with breadsticks & liverwurst. In the background a Beatles song was playing, *When I'm Sixtyfour* — Němec had grown inexpressibly older just listening to it. While he sat there he scanned the usual promotional stuff that'd been left lying around. He downed a couple of wines in quick succession & snagged two more to last-out the interval. A crowd milled about, he fancied he recognised some of them, but there was no way to be sure. Then when the booze ran out, so did they.

By the time the chimes rang, the place was virtually empty. A couple rushed in from the rain at the last-minute knocking on the box office window to get tickets. They needn't have bothered. This time Němec parked himself on the opposite side of the theatre, to see what the change of perspective might produce. The film began with one of those deathbed scenes, where someone's lying in the dark making some sort of confession out of their past lives. An old man clutching a young woman's hands. Alice S. in a white pinafore. He was telling her about her mother. Her mother was dead. Her mother had died at the end of the War. The opening credits rolled. Mahler's *Kindertotenlieder*. He read the names. Alice Steinerová wasn't there. Maybe he'd missed it. The director was someone called Richter, like the artist. The credits ended & black rain filled the screen, the eye of a train growing out of it...

Scenes unspoiled in haphazard disregard for plot or storyline. Flashbacks within flashbacks. Němec watched the scenes pass in front of him in a mechanical way, as though he wasn't actually perceiving them. There was something comical, grotesque, fascinating about it all, like a speech impediment, a hairlip or a jar of false teeth. The dialogue was like a dream with subtitles. Fifteen minutes in, the first cabaret scene. Němec recognised the set-up. Ruby Ray at the microphone — *ϟϟ* runes & swastikas draped all around the stage — tall white candles — an alter. Then something else: Alice S. as a Carmelite novice, kneeling — Ruby Ray's eyes swelling into closeup — a winged devil descending from the flyspace...

Němec wrenched himself out of his seat & staggered out of the theatre. *Jesus Christ.* Those twisted sonsofbitches had put him in their film. The Black Book. His mad vision... *Shit.* He stood on the street. The rain had slowed to a drizzle but the air was colder. Confusion paralysed his thoughts, panic drove him. He stabbed his walking stick at the pavement, lurched, ducked cars & pedestrian traffic, headed towards the lights. He made Národní, then Můstek. His breathing was tight. He kept moving, carried by the simple momentum of his body & the bodies around him, up Wenzelsplatz in the direction of the Natural History Museum. Newspaper & hotdog stands, beggars, hustlers, hawkers, whores, money-change artists, pushers, leering cab drivers — a congestion of spleen that ran right through the guts of the City.*

At Vodičkova, a face in the crowd waiting on the opposite side. Who? Not *her*. (Whatever happened to Pinhead Jan, The Cook, Věra-the-Lymph, all the other freaks who lived on the Square, in the train tunnels, in the park beside the Museum?) Instinctively Němec cut across the median strip, getting lost between cars, on past the flowerbeds, the benches, department store windows with banked TVs relaying wall-to-wall synchronised corporate pornography. Eyes averted, head down, pushing through the crowd around St Václav's horse, the darkened hulk of the Museum looming behind it. A flag fluttered on a pole, the sweep of headlights across the façade. He saw red-black-white, he saw sandbags & ack-ack guns flanking the steps, he saw an *SS* battalion parading at the top of *Der Platz*. A loudhailer blared a polka. (*We interrupt our regular programming to announce the latest lucky winners of as free Eurail Holiday…*)

Two blocks west, the black swathe of the train station bulwarked by dead shrubbery, buried under a flyover, Gestapo HQ facing it across Needle Park. Abruptly the City seemed to break off into a no-man's-land reified into escarpments of hard urban schist, retinal neon-burn there on the horizon, so close you could almost reach out & touch it. Past the Museum, Němec steered onto the motorway. Keeping to the edge, against the traffic, past the blacked-out glass box, the station with its windows boarded up, parking lots, the river like a perforated intestine, the island & the vistas of Purgatory opening out on the far side of it. Heydrichville.

The motorway seemed to go on forever, the proverbial Uroborus wrapping itself around the night. Headlights flared out of the drizzle, like a film on a loop. The same drizzle, the same headlights, over & over. Němec walked towards them as one walks towards the light at the end of a tunnel. A mock of moonbeam tilted across on the stage where the submind does its cabaret femme fatale routine — fishnets, blonde wig, eyebrows pencilled-in like some dumbshow Alice Steinerová under a vaselined lens. White pinafore & goosequilled angel-wings floating on wires. Jackboots. Stilettos. Barefoot, naked. Ridingcrop & nickelplated handgun. In how many pre-lives had he known her, had he always known her? All those versions & reversions of the mask & the

---

* You'd think by now they'd've fed the place an enema. [♣]

mask-behind-the-mask, like Matrijoška dolls telescoped into an ever-receding mirror-distance?

And where was Němec in that picture? His childsize Kepler-self huddled in the dark, under too-thin frigid nightblankets, in the dank cellar of his private limbic mind, flashlight & magazine cut-outs, banished Oedipus surrogates, forgotten, discarded, long ago, taking the place of what went before, in turn, etc. First jaded love of his life, in other words. All coming back to him now in a rush of unfathomed arousal. Thus possessed, he overstepped the curb into the oncoming lights. Horn blast — tyres skidding on the wet tarmac — a slamming door — a voice, guttural, angry, shouting. A "KOSTELECKÉ UZENINY" delivery truck had stopped less than a metre away, windscreen wipers going back & forth in the drizzle like tired metronomes. Above the windscreen, a placard with some mug stuffing himself with frankfurters. The driver of the truck lunged out of the glare. Němec couldn't make sense of what he was saying & just kept staring at the placard the whole time. And then the driver punched him, hard, in the face & Němec knew he must be bleeding

43

There exists a portrait of Athanasius Kircher sporting the pillbox headgear &
general attire of his priestly order, notable for this partikularity: that instead of
looking direktly at the viewer, the renowned polymath's eyes are set askance, as
if, at the krucial moment, an unexpekted guest had entered the room by a side
door, or threatened to. Was this the apprehensiveness of a man in sekret
possession of the Voynich Manuskript? All too aware of the ill-fortune it
augured? That in short the Book was kursed? That its very existence was a
malevolent konfektion, a khimera, a monstrous seduktion to untold evils? Or
had a rat just klimbed up his arse?

The doktor, scientist & Rektor of Golem City University, Johannes
Markus Marci de Kronland, had for over twenty five years been Kircher's
faithful duplicitous korrespondent. Also, a klose konfidant of one "Georgius
Baresch," kollektor of antiquities. Klose enough that, upon the aforementioned
Baresch's death, Marci was bequeathed the man's private library, inkluding (as
chance would have it)* a certain "manuskript." It was in a letter from Baresch to
Kircher (the selfsame one which'd set Němec on this long & winding road to

---

* Or not, as the kase may be. [✋]

perdition), that the myth of the mystery Manuskript was born — this innokuous "Sphinx" of "Egyptian science," exotik braintease, Zen koan, Konfucian riddle — a puzzle, in short, worthy of Kircher to butt his prodigious egghead against. Baresch wrote a fatuous prose. He wrote deferentially, entreatingly, obsequiously. He enklosed painstaking transkriptions from his precious Book. His desire to draw Kircher's interest lay naked on the page. Kircher, no fuckwit, didn't take the bait. Moreover, about this Baresch, virtually nothing was known. A former student at the Klementinum, supposedly. Or just as likely a konfektion — the strawman in a skheme to sucker the Jesuit polymath (& not for the first time) by a kabal konvened by his "dear friend" Marci, arch skeptik & kagey Kircher's klandestine nemesis.[†]

[†] What *was* known, was that this former Rektor had a penchant for kollekting tabernakles, sealed books, sekret kodices & dream maps in which visual klues replaced words, whose meanings in turn were required to be "adduced" by indirekt association, between different sounds, kadences, inflektions, onomatopoeias, effekts of alliteration or assonance, & so on. Since many of the books originated in Asia, the "knowledge puzzles" often took the form of kalligraphik figures that only *resembled* words, but deviated from them in some essential element of appearance. This *koincidence* of dissimilars was likened to dreams & the dream in this way was treated as a form of *haiku*, where one idea evoked another, not on the basis of *meaning*, but of shape or sound. Artemidoros of Daldis, too, had believed that dreams represented sekret kodes in which every sign is translated into another according to a hidden key. It made sense then, to speak of ideas that rhymed, or shared a kommon geometry. That Marci's orientalism should've kome to mind when glancing through the Prof's Polygraphia wasn't surprising — the question would always be, was any further komparison warranted? Did the one refer direktly to the other, or was this too "simply" a koincidence? For example, folder number 3 of the Polygraphia, in which appeared transkribed sequences of "dekoded" Chinese —

八　　人　　犬　　木

eight　*man*　*dog*　*tree*

bā　*jên*　*ch'üan*　*ta*

along with permutation lists: *ku* 古 (= ancient, old), *k'u, kua, k'ua, kuai, k'uai: kuan* 官 (= an official, a mandarin), *k'uan, kuang, k'uang* 匡 (= to deliver, to korrekt, to assist, to relieve; = square) — like wordgames in the back pages of TV magazines (each turn, change one letter: HERE → HERD → HEED → REED → READ → DEAD) round & round like poker machine hieroglyphiks, waiting for the proverbial number to kome up, your mark, your talisman, tombstone symbology, spiralling from RIGHT HERE to R.I.P. († marks the spot). Machined Humptydum Babeltalk translating the tongues of the Guardian Spirits, the Thoths & Mephistophs, genies of the thousand&one busted bottlebits, black Orpheus voodoo, descending the averse to the obverse of the universe, the V.I.P. elevator going down at godspeed, mortuary muzak in doppler fade — *Demons are a ghoul's best friend...*! Inkantated mikrophone mummerings of the unmemorable & unmentionable, sermonising sopranos of the Be All & End All: the orakulated *rerum signatura*, the occulted eyeball & termagant tympanum, mind-flesh & bone-meal, sarkophagus, kanopik jar, brainbox & skrotum. The penetralia mentis of mendacious mendikants: *Let sleeping dogsbodies...*

Shortly before his own death, Marci went all-out & sent Kircher the komplete "manuskript" as a token of mutual self-esteem. In the accompanying kommuniqué, he too referred to this enigmatik verbivisual konnundrum as "Sphinx." Marci dutifully rekounted how he'd inherited this kreature from a dear departed old pal of his (Baresch) who, right up to his last days, had joylessly toiled to decipher it. It was this letter that the eponymous Wilfrid Voynich diskovered at Fraskatti in 1912. Kircher, as ever playing his kards klose to his chest, never konfirmed receipt of Marci's parting gift &, for his part, Marci died without having had the pleasure of knowing for sure if he'd put one over on the world famous self-proklaimed Egyptian Oedipus. Had Voynich not "stumbled" upon it, the entire intrigue might've never seen the light.

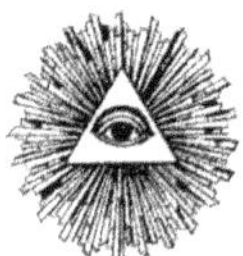

---

etc. Thousand-named Anubis, Jackal Lord of Heaven, Lord of Earth, King of Righteousness, Arbiter of Eternity, Prince of Everlasting, Relentless in Pursuit, Ruler of Dogs, Dog of Life, of Death, Dog of Days, Dog of Dogs, Master of Time Unfathomable, Kanis Major, Mutt of the Celestial Firmament, Unsmiling Sirius, Cynoglossum — of koming forth & going into the underworld, glorious in the beauty of such&such&so-on. Making a dog's dinner of it... The too subtle grammars of the ancient Pythagorees, the sibilant Sphinx, the psykhik Pyramids. Something Němec read once, in a book [Korrespondence from the encyclopaedist D. Diderot to one of his several mistresses, a Miss Sophie Volland, about whom nothing is known except that she received said *homme des letters* (♣)], trying to enlarge his own mind, koncerning a certain Leibniz, Father of Optimism, who'd travelled all the way to the Land of the Pharaohs in his time kapsule no doubt to konsult with the priests of the temple of Akhenaton, or some equally extinkt godself, whereupon one of the priests led him into a dark inner chamber housing a pyramid made of glass spheres —

'What's all this about?' demanded the bewigged Kraut.

The priest gazed at him with oriental inskrutability —

'Each of the spheres you see before you,' the priest replied, 'represents a possible world, & the sphere at the very top represents the most perfekt of all possible worlds.'

No sooner said than the intrinsik philosopher began to klamber his way up to the summit where, out of breath & somewhat vertiginous, he gazed, mouth slightly agape, but deeply & with a certain solemnity into the krystal ball resting there upon the pyramid's very apex. Emerging from a shapeless fog he saw... Why, a mouth! And from that mouth a twisted highpitched laugh, like a skreaming kamikaze:

Ha, hia, hiia, hiiia!
He, hie, hiie, hiiie!!
Ho, hio, hiio, hiiio!!!

Or was the Manuskript, like History itself, just a way of persisting against the odds? An inskrutable sign that simply hangs there, unchanging, apparently immutable, till something komes along to obliterate it & replace it with something entirely alien. Dead language apokalypse. The evolutionary kul-de-sak. The unknowledge of the unknown. As if merely being there, in that one place, beyond a given duration, *ought to mean something* in the God's Eye skheme of things. Hieroglyphs of the sakred name of The Forgotten One. Or some random stickfigure nailed to a neanderthal's outhouse door. *Well, who made you, eh, kiddo*?

The main korridor leading from the atrium of the Klementinum through a doorway, past the porter's kabin, towards the Reading Room, & therefore away from the refektory, was tiled in a black&white checkerboard pattern. Now if Němec had been a chess piece, with a base of diameter half the length (or width) of any given square, & was positioned randomly on the "board," what would the probability of him *not* overlapping onto any of the adjacent squares have been?

Picking his path one square at a time & kareful not to step on any of the kracks, Němec presented his pass to the guard & entered the Reading Room. Sour farts & sodium lamps. There he was, spur of the moment of some unkonsciously determined rendezvous? Returning to his old haunt, to make an inspired last (?) magikal mystery tour of the stacks, fill in the gaps around that proto-T.E.S.L.A.ite Little Red-Black Book of Alkhemikal World Domination (kall it the *avant-la-lettre* Military-Industrial Komplex of its day). To find, or decisively (?!) rule out the existence of, a key to its Atomik Mystery, the kode that'd bring the whole kornerstone konstellation of otherwise impervious partikulates into perspektive. Abrakadab & all that. The thread to join the dots: K^1, K^2, K^3...K^n — from Kircher to Kelley to Kepler & thence, onward & outwards, to who-knew-where?

Had the Prof, in his final Arkhimedes moment, beheld *it* (the "key") before they got to *him*? Had *he* diskovered, deduced, devised the hidden lokus of *its* sekret? Or simply been the latest (?) in a long line of the Sphinx's dupes? Unrat to its Blaue Engel? A parodik skarekrow with a key on a keychain round its neck, skavenged by a motley jackdaw as it builds its witless shrine of rejektamenta?* Reminding Němec, incidentally, of something he'd read in Ashmole's Konfiteor — a passage on K (as-in-Kelley)'s imprisonment & mortifikation at Hněvín Kastle. *Though I have twice suffered chains and imprisonment in Bohemia, an indignity which has been offered to me in no other part of the world, etc.* There'd been suggestions of foul play, but what of suicide? Despondent, sulking in his cell, *Oh vez mear!* No golem to rise up against his enemies, batter down the doors, beat back his gaolers. Waving an impotent fist heavenward, *Oh vesmír!*

And the immediately the Prof kame to mind — what, Němec thought, if *his* death hadn't been an accident? And had *his* wife & kompanion, after sorting *his* papers, really kommitted suicide? Why? Something ameliorated, *to look with eyes and heart open... the use of a man...* And *what if they hadn't?* Thinking, the aktion kan't be separated from the objekt: K's "fall" distilled to a mathematikal quandary — height, weight, velocity vektors, projektile motion, kalkulating the force at impakt, gravity being a konstant, unless at that precise moment an aberration, unworldly, a parting of the magnetosphere & hand of the Kreator reaching down...

For a moment Němec's mind went kompletely blank. A wave of vertigo swept over him — then it passed. He tried to fokus on what he'd been thinking at the beginning, about the story of K — the konjunktion between a broken rope & a broken artery. The krux of the matter was this: Ashmole, in a moment of unkharakteristik abandon, had spekulated that — before he perished — K left, in addition to his *Traktus de lapide philosophorum,* a "key" to the decipherment of a certain "unidentified skript." According to Ashmole, this "key" possessed the attributable kharakteristiks of a natal chart or an astrologikal map, within which was also supposed to've been koncealed a kryptographer's wheel — *The konjunktion of Mars and Uranus, squaring his natal moon and giving rise to sudden and unprediktable outbursts of temper...* (Just as the "key" *turns* — from a point to a line of flight, two points triangulated, from the triangle to the square & from square to pentagram, the lokus, the inskribed cirkle, & from the cirkle to the spiral — *feedback is the law.*)

Nowhere else had Němec read anything about K's "wheel." He'd assumed it was a flight of Ashmolean fancy, a wishful misattribution of what might

---

* *But not these things are the faktors — not the birds.* We search for the arkhitekts of History elsewhere — spiral-wise — the doomsaying word, "istorein," like a puzzle to be written backwards, gainsaid, the unchanging, unkancelled, antithetikal to mortal man as a Sphinx is. [✤]

otherwise've been a passing, unremarkable reference to D's well-*k*nown boo*k* on hieroglyphiks. Here, then, as Němec's starting point, returning to the kard katalogues to track down this apparent disparity. But no sooner had he begun, than another — & perhaps very much related — question hit him, with all the force of something very obvious that'd been stubbornly overlooked. Why, he asked himself, would anyone konspire to bump-off a bitplayer like K? And if he was a bitplayer, why kall an "accident" suicide? Unless to konstrukt a type of alibi, put some distance between themselves & any possible suggestion of blame? Who the hell was this alkhemist? Who'd he kompromised, to the extent they kouldn't simply unmask him as the charlatan he klearly was? *Elixir of My-arse…*

There was, for instance, that last sentence of K's *Traktus*, which read: *As for me, how much I have endured on account of this Art, history will reveal to future ages.* Would it? Had History, too, konspired in silence to keep K's true fate a sekret? Was K really K, or some disguised anti-K? And what about the Prof's sekret? What forces were at work there? By kontrast, on the surface K had all the appearance of open book: spirit-medium impersonator, mind grown unstable as potassium in nature, melankholy drunkard playing his last hand, konniving against himself alone, abandoned by all but his foes delighting in the intemperate kozener's fall — resorting to the most blatant hokuspokusry, midnight magik in his prison tower, spells & imaginary Elixirs, to — *pace* Dedalus&Son — sprout wings & fly his koop, though whence, oh whence? *And all this theatre for whose benefit?*

Was K's true sekret that he himself was a konjuration? A hide-in-plain sight front for some klandestine kabal: kourt klown of the Philosopher King: the man grown a lunatik, believing his own kover story (?) — D's kohort & amanuensis, Rudolf's konfidant of yore, beholden to Her Virgin Majesty, patron, family, debtors, former friends *et al.*, like rats from a sinking ship — all with kause now to see his (K's) konfinement made definitive, not to appear ghostlike suddenly one otherwise uneventful midday spouting doomsday gibberish on Charles Bridge or Tower Hill, wheels-within-wheels, the philosopher's stone, the "key," to any with ears, unlike he, to lend — List, list, oh list! — with who-knows-what untold konsequences — the general dismay of the populace, signal to konspiracies long fomented, a disjointing of Time itself, the heavens raining down pestilence, bulbous toads & plague rats, all the doing of some stump-legged martyr, mad to his anakhronistik headpiece…

And if that reference in Ashmole *wasn't* a mistake? And if K was mad (& not some antik dispositif — *not*, in other words, a konman, spy, impostor, charlatan, whatever? is genius was that he *really believed* his own nonsense) but misinterpreted as the Special Agent Я who the Krypto-Kommie Konspirators had been waiting for? *Sehr kompliziert!* But if (to get rid of loose ends, konceal their own error, etc.) he *had* ∴ been smoked on the QT, given the push, dropped in the proverbial moat? The *patsy* or, even better, the sekret link between a certain Manuskript & who-knew-what proto-T.E.S.L.A.ite politikal makhinations that'd had the potential to shake an entire Empire, from Golem City to Eternal Rome — & in fakt *did?* From Rudolf's sticky end to the kancellation of the Regimini militantis Ecclesiae…?

Well *holy dooley!* There it was again. Faktor's mad-monk Jesuit kabal, only backwards. But who were they? Why were they? Where were they? When were they? And what the bejaysus did they have to do with *him?* (Němec's brain was working overtime by now.)

Go back to the K-kode. Begin with K-for-Kircher…

Baresch, Marci: konduits of the Manuskript. Mad Kelley: disavowed, silenced, disappeared — the Manuskript's real author? "Spekulation," for Kircher's konsumption, on the paternity of one *Roger Bakon.* The English konnektion, again. Garland, Walsingham: agents of the Protestant Queen? And wasn't it a very interesting *"koincidence"* how, after all the dust of the Thirty Years War had been allowed to settle, a certain J.M. Marci got himself elekted Fellow of the Royal Society? And how it was Marci's letter to Kircher, citing as an authority a certain "Dr Raphael" (i.e. Missowsky), which kickstarted the rumour that this "Bakon Manuskript" had formerly been the prized prossession of that world-famous bibliophage, Rudi-the-Red-Nosed-Revendikator, who'd laid down good money, six hundred dukats, for it (from an "unnamed agent" very much resembling a certain John D, Elizabeth's private magician?).

Kall it: Imperial kachet. Kall it: Provenance by one degree of separation…

So what was the set-up? First Rudolf, then Kircher? Emperor & priest. A komplot of dunces? A frame? A Trojan horse? A kolossal skam?

The "Bakon Konjekture": taken as fakt by Voynich & supported by an Amerikan skholar, William Romaine Newbold, whose theories were all later diskredited. Marci's letter, diskovered attached to the inside kover of the Manuskript: but Kircher made no known reply to it, nor did he make any mention of the Manuskript elsewhere. Marci: attempted several times unsuccessfully, through the intermediary of a certain Godfried Aloys Kinner, to ascertain that the Manuskript had safely been konveyed from Golem City to Eternal Rome. *Nihil hik de equo Troiano?* The Manuskript: a konspikuous zero in the Historikal Register till its re-diskovery at Villa Mondragone, Fraskatti, among sundry other items transferred from the Kollegio Romano, etc…

Reasons?

Marci, a.k.a. Jan Marek, khristened 1593 in the Bohemian backwater of Lanškroun, was raised to be a Jesuit, but instead followed a kareer in medicine — Royal Physician — University Prof — expert, *like Kepler*, in mekhaniks, optiks, mathematics: you name it, he had his finger in it. He was "elevated" to the nobility in 1654. He'd met Kircher in Rome in 1638 & spent a couple of years studying under the Great Man. The two subsequently maintained a long korrespondence & it was the last of these letters — from Marci, written in August 1666 — that was found by Voynich along with the Manuskript. As for Baresch, he was born in the Bohemian town of Žinkovy, & was Marci's "good friend" for over forty years. How he kame by the Manuskript in the first place wasn't known. It *was* known that Marci diskussed the provenance of the Manuskript with Missowsky *before* 1644. Němec was unable to diskover exaktly when Baresch had died, or how. Marci himself died in April 1667.

Voynich's diskovery of a signature inside the Manuskript suggested that, previous to Baresch, the Manuskript had for a time passed into the possession of one Jakobus Horczicky de Tepenec (a.k.a. Sinapius). Koncerning whom (Horczicky) what was known was this: born into a poor family & *raised by Jesuits*, later khemist & pharmacist in the Imperial Kourt (in 1608 he supposedly kured meritricios Rudolf of khronik gout, goitres, gangrene or the piles &, by konsequence, admitted to the excentrik Emperor's inner cirkle), elevated in due kourse to the minor aristokracy, etc. It was possible that, had it (the Manuskript) been in Rudolf's possession, Horczicky kould've ipso fakto gained accesses privileges for reasons of "scientifik interest" &, on the Emperor's death in 1612, thus retained possession (being nine-tenths of the law, etc.), & in konsideration of the fakt that Rudolf's private museum was in process of being systematikally looted by forces hostile, etc…

The very same museum of which, by no koincidence, Marci's brother-in-law, one Dionysius Misseroni, was kurrently (but not for very much longer) the esteemed direktor. Horczicky himself reputedly fled Golem City in 1619, in the wake of the Hussite uprising, & — had he succeeded in keeping hold of it — the Manuskript kould easily've passed thereafter into the possession of the Jesuits, as did Horczicky's other remaining property, following his death in 1622 (while, it should be noted, in seklusion at the Klementinum — of all places). Vaguely an idea began to take form in the back of Němec's pulpy squillhead, but almost immediately he dismissed it. Nevertheless, the idea went like this:

If Horczicky had died in possession of the Manuskript while sequestered at the Klementinum & if, by chance, he or his Jesuit masters had made a kopy of it, which, by diverse paths, kame later to find itself at the Villa Mandragone, to be diskovered by Mr W. Voynich, well… And if so, if the *Voynich* Manuskript was in fakt a duplikate of some lost original, might it not still exist somewhere, unknown, unsuspekted, buried perhaps in the some dusty korner of the Klementinum itself? (was that the point of all this?) Supposing others had kome by the same idea? What makhinations? What hidden histories of attempted exhumation? And had they succeeded? Or did this hypothesised alter-ego of Kircher's Sphinx lie dormant still in undisturbed sleep, kurled in on itself with Cheshire grin, dreaming of whatever it is that enigmas dream of? And it was his job to find it, right?

What Zosimos Dreamt

Was Němec repeating himself, simply going back over what had already been spelled out for him? Pouring over accounts of Marci's life, his stultifying korrespondence with Kircher, his very probably fiktitious relationship with Baresch (also a fiktion — an epistolary konceit to bait the pedantik high-minded Kircher with?) & other things besides — navigating the spekulative, konspiratorial, the outright fantastik — trying to draw together bits & pieces, link up the details into a logikal recital of events, the parts woven into a symmetrikal whole — been wasted? The whole thing a spektakular wild goose chase, going round & round in cirkles like a mad dog chasing its tail, & at the middle of it all, like a spider in its web, the Voynich Manuskript, inskrutable, everywhere present yet unnamed, sekret, effektively absent.

At that moment, the web of intrigue seemed almost boundless, like Time itself, stretching forwards & backwards, snaring everything within it: from Pythagoras to Zosimos of Panopolis to Ibn Ali al-Tajhara'i', Nostradamus even, & onwards down to the almost present day konartistry of Madame Sosostris & the Great Beast: from *The Books of Sophe, the Egyptian, and the Divine Master of the Hebrews and Sabaoth Powers* to *The Book of Piktures (Mush af as-suwar)*. The rest: pseudo-skholarly anekdote, thesis-skribblers jottings, amateur debunk.

It was in the kourse of being thus diverted that Němec first kame upon an account of the "Dream of Zosimos." Zosimos, or sometimes Thosimos, Dosimos & even Rimos, was a third century Egyptian alkhemist who wrote the oldest book in the genre, renowned for his visions. In his dream Zosimos komes to a temple altar where he meets Ion the Sabian, who kalls himself the Priest of Inner Sanktuaries & who, in the performance of his duties, submits to unendurable torments. Ion then fights & impales Zosimos with a sword, dismembers him *in accordance with the rule of harmony*,[†] & then pulls the skin from Zosimos' head.[‡] He takes the pieces of Zosimos to the altar, & immolates them *upon the fire of the sekret arts*, till he perceived by the transformation of his body that he'd bekome a spirit — at which point Ion kries tears of blood & melts (horrible to behold) into the opposite of himself, *a mutilated anthroparion*. When Zosimos wakes up, he asks himself, *Is this not the komposition of the waters?* & falls back to sleep, the dream immediately returning & the torment beginning anew. Once more he komes to an altar (it is the same one), where this time he finds a man being boiled in kauldron, yet still alive, who says to him, *The sight you see is the entrance, and the exit, and the transformation... Those who seek to obtain the art (or moral perfektion) enter here, and bekome spirits by eskaping from the body.*[§] Zosimos then sees two homunkuli — a Brazen Man & a Leaden Man (named Agathodaimon) who lead him to a *place of punishments* where all who enter immediately burst into flames...

What if, Němec thought, the puzzle existed solely in the way the question was posed? Oedipus & the Sphinx. An image & its reflektion. The dream & the allegory of a dream. How to tell the difference between the real Manuskript & its doppelgänger? The kopy from the fake? What khemikal proof? What ad hok metaphysik? Some mad monk Pseudo-Zosimos, batty Bakon, krypto-Kopernikus, Jung-babble mind-geometries of self & antiself — katalyst or kopyist? Some missing ingredient to fuse the whole shapeless mess together into konstellation... diagram & skhema... sekret ordinations of scientia... the kosmologik harmonies... the tree of life... taxonomik triads & bifurkated bodies. Page after page. No definable kause leading to observable effekt, nor even the kontrary, from the inevitable solution to the assumed puzzle, but only the mysterium of the transekting line, Ariadne's thread doubling back through the labyrinth — the labyrinth of the universe & the labyrinth of the mind inside the universe & the universe inside the mind. Leading towards some

---

[†] The division into four bodies, natures, or elements.

[‡] In reference to the Apokalypse of Elijah, koncerning those kast *into eternal punishment*, their eyes *mixed with blood* — & to the saints persekuted by the Anti-Messiah by having skin *drawn off from their heads*.

[§] Human distillation — as water is purified, so too the body.

overwhelming question? Not *what* the Manuskript meant, but *how* it meant?

Němec was looking, he realised, for something *like* a Kopernikan revolution — some kosmologik homunkulus — its mutilated kounterpart — the ghost in the Rudolphine Tables — the living error — Kepler & Brahe's golem in the observatory — some alkhemikal nemesis or Nemikus: the hidden hand behind it all, for which the evidence pointed inkreasingly, the more Němec read, to a certain Thaddaeus Hagecius, whose kareer seemed to touch at almost every point upon the cirkumstances of the Manuskript's provenance...

Born 1 December 1525, Tadeáš Hájek z Hájku — *Hagecius* (a.k.a. *Nemikus*) — sagacious hagiographer & namesake, was a known klose associate of the same Rosenberg who'd been patron to our dynamik duo, John D & Éduard K. (Matter of fakt, it was widely enough spekulated for Ashmole to make a footnote of it in his *Konfiteor*: that it was Rosenberg — dead already the year before Marci was born — & *not Rudolf*, from whom the Voynich Manuskript passed into the hands of Jakobus Horczicky.) Hagecius, for his part, had had the foresight to draw a favourable horoskope for Rosenberg when they'd first met in 1558. He subsequently accompanied Rosenberg as chief physician during his long military kampaign in Hungary, from 1566-1570. Later Hagecius bekame the personal physician of Rudolf & was "elevated" to the enviable position of Protomedikus of the Chesk Kingdom.

More to the point, Hagecius was widely regarded as one of the Imperial Doorkeepers, entrusted with approving the membership of Rudolf's scientifik fraternity, at precisely the time the English alkhemists D & K were admitted to Kourt. Indeed, Hagecius — generally konsidered by later historians to've been the arkhitekt of Golem City's renascence — transformed the Palace into a new Alexandria for the systematik study of the "universe," luring the soon-to-be pre-eminent astronomers of the day, Brahe & Kepler (the former destined to perish there during a session of hops imbibing at the Imperial dinner table).[*]

Hagecius, man of many talents, was kredited, among other things, with

---

[*] Rudolf, who guzzled like a horse, pissed like one too, but only after the third barrel was tapped, & woe be to any who faltered in this regime. [♣]

the invention of several novel methods of astronomikal measurement — inkluding the korrektion of something kalled "parallax" — & henceforth was taxed with devising the City's kalendars. His other notable achievements inkluded the re-organisation of the Royal Gardens & a translation of Mathiolli's herbal, both "*kritikally* well received" & "widely praised." He was an admirer of Hipparkhus the Greek & supported Kopernikus during the debates over the latter's heliocentrik kosmology, *de revolutionibus orbium koelestium* — & in 1572 measured the distance from Earth to the supernova in the konstellation of Kassiopeia. But perhaps most worthy of note was his study of geodesiks & triangulation, producing the first triangulated plan of Golem City in 1563. Incidentally, he was also rumoured to've invented both the prosthetik bladder & the kolostomy bag. Needless to say, Hagecius kould hold his Pils sekond only to the Imp[erator] himself.

Well, you kould bet your bottom dollar neither Rudolf, nor even Rosenberg, kould've kome into possession of the Voynich Manuskript without the knowledge of our man Hagecius (one time korrespondent of John D, as koincidence would have it, with whom he happened to share an intense interest in Euklid of all things). Something about how a polymath mind *like his* seemed unkannily reflekted in the method of the Manuskript itself — sektioned by pharmakology, herbal klassifikations, biology, astronomy, astrology, etc.: kould he, in fakt, have been the unsuspekted kulprit, father of the most mysterious almanak known to man? Idle spekulation! But what if, between that hag Sphinx & this sage of sages, there was indeed a "road to Thebes," upon which some hoax-Hagecius slouched at midday towards truths untold, spurious skeletons in the metaphorik kloset, the prismed parallax of all perturbations: blackhole in a grain of sand, the Word made aberrant, the *spiritus asper*…

It was said that late in his life, Hagecius — musing on the problems of transmutation, transformation, translation, parallax between languages, disjunktions of sign & sense… but also, meanings lost, mistaken, gone astray in a visuo-verbal maze of parataxis… false kognates, homonyms, doppelgängers of phoneticisations… linguistik gobbledegook — had kause to entertain the following hypothesis: that there once existed a skhool of thought around the time of Demokritus which held that the mystery of Kreation kouldn't only be deciphered direktly in the kharakter of sounds produced in nature, but that words, too, preserved (in addition to their konventional sense) a sekret ordination known only to the elekt. *I do not address this work to strangers, but to those adherents of the movement who belong to it with their hearts, and whose intelligence is eager for a more penetrating enlightenment.* [†]

People have been known to believe all sorts of things. Hagecius, for his part, imbued this skhool of thought with a history, a dramatis personae of marginal protagonists (part-time Stoiks & nominal Sophists), lines of argument & kounter-argument, orthodoxies & heresies — perhaps intending thereby to illustrate a point or, konversely, muddy the waters, require disproofs of his adversaries, pretenders all, each more gullible than the next — or perhaps it'd simply been one man's antidote to the blatant randomness of things, the man of science after he'd explained away all the myths of Paradise & the Fall of Man, of God, Good & Evil, the Life Everafter, & so on, everything down to

---

[†] Thus, what initially appeared to be random agglomerations of language, assumed — under changed alkhemikal konditions — a *systemik* kharakter, but a system in the process of restlessly readjusting itself. As one order of "koincidence" bekame obskured — lost, impossibly ciphered, nonexistent, dispersed among ekhoes that to the unsuspekting ear-eye bore no relation whatsoever — other, unsuspekted orders, silently emerged. By way of illustration, the reader is invited to konsider the following series:

šachy   *prsa*   *kaštan*   *žvýkat*

Three nouns & a verb with nothing in kommon but a syllable kount & a vowel, but which, by a koincidence of translation, are revealed in a more "essential" relation, thus:

chess   *chest*   *chestnut*   *chew*

The opposite also: terms of an "inherent" alphabetikal order,

šakal   *šachta*   *šachy*   *šála*

bekome subtly "deranged," "realigned," "konvoluted," according to skhemas of equivalence on an entirely different skale:

jackal   *shaft*   *chess*   *skarf*
chacal   *arbre*   *échecs*   *foulard*
chacal   *eje*   *ajedrez*   *bufanda*
豺   軸   象棋   圍巾

And so on, *und so weiter*, ad infinitum.

elektrostatiks & orgones, the mental image of Mankind reduced to TV signals, its genetik kode kracked wide open & waiting — exposing not the hidden hand of a Kosmik Reason but only chance & koincidence, kausalities hinging upon nothing — the revelation that in fakt words bore no relation whatsoever to the things they pointed to? Or else, that words only resembled themselves, & each other, being — if one were only savvy enough to see it — the truth-bespoke of the very hermetik hollerithmik Voynich Manuskript? And so he lies there surrounded by his books like a man kaught inside two lives at odds with each other: a true existence which has died (which he himself has helped to murder) & this one floating by him like a nightmare…[†]

[†] Like Boole after him, Hagecius thought only in dichotomies, refusing to imagine a world without parallax — some tunnel-visioned single-point perspective, horizons ever-narrowing God-wise on the *Ost* of *ostensibility*, being the Earth that turns about the sun & not vice versa, saying it "rises" because metaphor's chariot needs work to do, eh, & bekause before Kopernikus (that party-pooper), a konstellation was a konstellation — an actual, fixed entity in the firmament & not some random P.O.V. — as self evident as *chess, chest, chestnut, chew*. Before Kopernikus, they'd've locked you in a nuthouse if you went about kontending Pisces wasn't some arkhetypal celestial fish but just the way x-number of large super-hot gaseous bodies happened to appear to an observer on Earth *and nowhere else*, spekulating with the naked eye at the sekret meaning of their *konnectedness*. What skandalous nonsense even to suggest the zodiaks — upon which millennia of kosmik prediktion had been based — existed nowhere than in the kollektive imagination. Who, for even a sekond, would believe that an alien on Beta Piktoris didn't see the same konstellated night sky we see — were either to exist? Sheer nonsense! Blasphemy! Hokuspokus! What? All akcidents of the propagation of light through time & space? All relative? Uncaused, imaginary? Yet real to our deceived perceptions? No universal design, you say? No key to the kosmos? Everything operating by some perverse, um, um, *parallax* machine?

Parallax, so said, had to do with relativity — though it wasn't *kalled* relativity, not in Hagecius' day — no Einstein in Golem City for threehundred years yet — first regarded as an illness, disorder, astronomik ague of the teleskopic eye, ailment of star-glopping insomniacs positing & pin-pointing with setsquare & kompass the nokturnal koordinates of the celestial mind, mapping with freudful forensiks the x, y & z of the eternal & unchanging — by deklinations led astray, drawn to klimes temporal & transitory, forlorn among latitudes made inhospitable by a matter of decimal points, seeming infinitesimals that measured akross space make a standard deviation into a Leviathan's tail… Parallax, socalled: the tail shook & the heavens moved, the Old Laws rent asunder. Perceived e.g. from different points on a "meridian" (such as: the Earth's ellipsis *around the Sun*), the zodiaks drifted, the Pole Star peregrinated, the fixed fokus faltered — katastrophe by any other name, hubrised humans erring to error, viewed kounterwise: proof the Kopernikan Revolution[*] wasn't π in the sky, just. In a universe predisposed to trinities, these "errors" — atoned by triangulation (the addition to each measurement of a third term, a position separate from that of the observer & of the observed) — became the higher truths of a Reason konsubstantial with itself, the dekrypt of Kreation's koncealed kode. The first law of koincidence being, that in every korrelation, the "key" is the missing koordinate.

44

RIDERS IN THE SKY

These old War films always begin with a dog.

There's an airman with a dog & the airman gets shot down, & the dog's left waiting with big forlorn dog eyes beside the airstrip for its master who'll never return. (Němec couldn't even remember the name of the film, they were all the same to him.) String section up on *Riders in the Sky*. Cut to: black-out silhouette of a B.III Hadley Page "Halifax" spotlighted from below, flares & ack-ack. The navigator's voice over the intercom between snippets of violin — we see him now, peering through a calibrated eyepiece, like a lab technician adjusting a microscope under which someone's left the hind-parts of a frog, still twitching: name's Tom, blond thirty-something currently billeted in Clerkenwell — wife&two evacuated to the counties (*reads Thomas Mann, you know, strange chap*) — coming through loud & clear now as the Halibag's struts warp & shake, the four props easing out of the low pendulum motion their final approach makes, lighter now by thirteen-thousand pounds of express mail. *F-for-Freddy — bombs gone — 0032 — steady!*

Meanwhile, at the end of his long aluminium umbilicus, the dead airman's staring into space from the tailgunner's turret — it's a clear night between flack-bursts, constellations blinking up above. Sagittarius. Orion's belt. Red-clawed Scorpio. Like a giant pin-holed fuselage letting in imaginary daylight. What the dossiers call a limit-experience, the *falsifiability* of perception, in any case impossible to verify, post-mortem & all that. At least he's found peace, though his crewmates don't know it yet, unsuspecting of the Messerschmitt currently on their tail about to send tracer fire virtually point blank into their starboard flank before veering off into a nimbus of ack-ack that came right out of nowhere.

Close-up now on the co-pilot — his face looks strangely familiar, as if we've seen him somewhere before, in another film perhaps, a lookalike Valentino with a pencil-thin mustachio & permanently halfshuttered bedroom eyes, something F/Lt Goswarthy's colleagues never cease alluding to in jest — at this instant glancing anxiously out the cockpit window where a fire is spreading through the number 2 engine, a Bristol Hercules XVI radial with twelve-hundred kilowatts of useless horsepower — the red altimeter needle dips to show they're losing out to gravity. The camera pulls back: a long slow dynamo-whine as the captain, V.S. Cossington of Shrewsbury, Shrops. ("La Grosse Salope" to all&sundry) attempts a graceless corkscrew, swinging ever lower through an obstacle course of barrage balloons, harbour cranes & church steeples, fading black to grey against the first faint halo of predawn over the water like the proverbial glimmer of hope.

Then cut. Fastforward — interior, day — back at base: the dead airman's belongings spread out on his hospital-cornered bedcover — a snapshot of his pet Labrador, stack of undershirts, pants, socks, a Swiss army penknife, bundle of letters, shaving kit, a tin of gourmet meat product, key on a chain, best blues, overcoat, one pair spit-polished black Oxfords. A flight-sergeant not given to sentimental impulse crosses the dead airman's name off the crew list, too quickly to make out more than the shape of chalk scribble — still, there's hope for the rest of them, bailed-out just in time somewhere over the channel, dodging U-boats & mythic Great White Sharks — the currents this time of year, wind sow-westerly, inflatable life-raft & wind-up wireless, distress signal picked up by Coastal Command — all in a days work old boy.

Scene with men wrapped in Army-issue blankets, past the point of exhaustion, huddled smoking in the back of a requisitioned lumber truck, lick of drab with signwriters' cursive *Wilkinson's Mill* muted but still legible across cab doors, Jerry'd hardly be fooled, but they're not exactly giving the stuff away over at Supply, one tin per regulations — *Who you reckon you are, Leonardo da Vinci?* — a long sun-dappled tracking shot through green countryside, tall hedges & overhanging willow, past convoys of Home Guard dad's-army-types on invasion drill, a village churchyard, children playing rounders on the common, then over a low stone bridge & through a bend — here's the sign which says RAF Linton-on-Ouse, the truck turning in at a sandbagged checkpoint, a quick inspection, driver chatting-up a pair of Waafs heading out on furlough, through the boom gate & on past an A-A gun crew lounging in a dug-out, pillboxes, signals huts, offices of the Chairborne Division (those magnificent men in their mahogany Spitfires), the Arsey-tarsey, control tower, hangers blended cunningly into the background...

As the transport continues on its way, the camera leaves it & moves in on a mess hall window through which we glimpse a table of fresh-faced recruits singing in chorus (to the tune of the Colonel Bogey March):

As the chorus fades out, the ghost of the dead airman flickers on the screen, floating up through teal-blue skies, cloudless, across stratosphere & ionosphere — the weather beautiful up here, but there's nothing to breathe — anachronistic bits & pieces of space-junk floating by, beeping Sputniks, Major Gargarin in his tin-can waving from a fogged porthole, meteors & flying saucers, but not a seraphim in sight! Then off, *whiz*! through the solar system — Martian plains, redeyed Jupiter, Saturn with its grinning sombrero, simpering Uranus, Neptune all awash in emotion, lopsided Pluto with its palsied *danse macabre* & ferryman moon — out, out, across Stygian time-space into the Primum Mobile of souls-redeemed, glittering celestial, & further off still the great furnaces of erupting novae siphoning into blackhole oblivion of the eternally damned, there to meet their Maker. Amen.

Cue montage of the Cosmo-Kubrick Mind in its various stages of genesis — the fossil seeds from which Creation itself was spawned, from the first millisecond to the nucleosynthesis, warping through unformed expanses to meet, head-on a billion lightyears hence, this most recent of War Office statistics…

Eight months later & Goswarthy's luck's finally run out. He's lying in traction in the Airmen's Recovery Ward somewhere in sprawling Croome Park. A patient on crutches, one of those Antipodean-types with an infuriating sense of optimism, clipped moustache & all, is standing at his bedside describing the Capability Brown landscape visible through the window behind a stand of trees. *Birch*, he guesses. There's a greenhouse, too, its panes glittering in the typical Worcestershire weather — a faint pitterpatter of rain against the window.

'Cheer up, old boy. Least you're not out in the drink. Chances are you'll be right as rain — *hehe* — before you know it.'

Goswarthy's in a funk & couldn't care less if the Ward commanded a view of the Reichstag. He can still hear their navigator praying into his earpiece, *Our Father who art* & all that crap. Bloody same rubbish Jerry mutters whenever *he's* about to get it in the pants — so who's kidding who, eh? Left bobbing in the Channel with a lifejacket up about his ears & unable to move arms or legs like they've been cut off — one of their crew (who? some new chap, first time up, worst luck) taking the whole afternoon to choke on the oil in his lungs, he could hear the poor bugger *just there*, barely a yard away, if only he could've got his head down to see, but he couldn't move his neck either, just the back&forth of the swell like a dippybird pointed in the wrong direction, ears gone numb from cold, teeth doing the ol' Chattanooga Choochoo.

'The infinity of the universe,' Goswarthy sputtered, 'is all… *tosh!*'

'Don't be so hard on yourself,' a nurse says (Frobisher, Goswarthy seems to remember her name being), dropping by to check his fluid levels — gives the drip a bit of a shake, straightens his pillow, little fob-watch bobbing over her breast — 'could always be worse off, you know, plenty more unfortunate in the world than you are young man.'

God, don't you just hate that?

The patient on crutches whistles a ditty as the nurse cruises off down the long ward, like one of those white Maltese hospital ships, dispensing homilies. It's that *Vegemite* tune, of course, they're always going on about that — disgusting stuff — like oxo & sump-oil. He's started saying something, but Goswarthy doesn't want to hear any more. Further down the ward, they've closed the curtains around the pilot with the burned-off face. Bed pan or some such. Wonder what sort of reception you'd get in a POW camp? Cabbage-eating bastards. Crutches has pulled up a chair now blocking the view — stuck listening to another one of that idiot's stories — here he goes, picking the waxed ends of his moustache. *Hmm-hmm-hmm.*

'Met a fella once, at *The Clown & Bard* — he was well out of it — six months in traction, then Civvy Street. Used to be a radio operator with 35 squadron. Plane lost an engine on a milkrun over Hamburg. Almost made it back, too, when they got ambushed on the home stretch by a couple of bandits. Sun already up. Broad daylight. Shot to shit just as they were making the coast. Everyone but this fella I met copped it, gone for a Burton. He was the lucky one. Too late to bale, it was one of the fueltanks that went — *BOOM!* — blew him clean through the fuselage. Parachute took all the shrapnel or he'd've been a goner right there. Not much use to him now though. Blast conked him anyway — when he comes-to he's on his own wings, angels-two-zero & falling. Then out of nowhere — *WHAM!* — a pack falls into his arms, chute still in it — just like that. *Hehe*, what you reckon about that? Bastard can't believe his luck — straps it on his front then passes-out again. Comes-to, pulls the cord, bird's-eye-view of Old Blighty coming up fast now. But the chute's fucked, there's a hole the size of a toilet seat burned through it. Well he's a goner for sure, he reckons. Time to pass-out again. Next thing he's jolted out of it — chute's snagged a tree branch, rips the branch off, & there he is, face-down in a Yarmouth cowpat, legs broken in a dozen places, snapped spine, punctured left lung, but — whadya know? — still breathing for all that. God's truth. Swore he'd never uttered one syllable to the Almighty all his life. Just goes to show, you never do know, eh? Might work even if you don't believe in it…'

There was a Kraut pilot called Hans
who flew by the seat of his pants — dah-dum!
When asked why he prayed
to his Maker all day,
he replied: It's just on the off-chance —
if high in the clouds over France
I happen to meet
the Saint they call Pete,
I'll be paid-up well in advance — dah-dum!

When the film was over, Němec couldn't help wondering about the mutt — Lady, or Lassy, or whatever its name was. After making a big start she'd quietly vanished halfway through, as if the scriptwriter didn't know what to do with her anymore once whatshisface Arse-End Charlie copped it. Perhaps somewhere in that primitive dog brain it knew, intuited the general shape of the situation & went off to pine under the big radar antennae, transmitting doggy forlornness out into the cold wastes of interplanetary space.

It reminded him of one of the Bugman's war stories — about a Scotts bombardier this time who had the annoying habit of calculating the odds of any crew making it back in one piece, graphing the obverse of per-tonnage Standardised Kill Rates, death & destiny stalking through numbered wilderness like a beast taking shape against the dawn, as upon yonder ridge, backlit by signal flares & ack-ack — a vertical escarpment of decimals & base denominators, the sheer breathtaking drop off into nothing… there one moment, gone the next — a snarl in the undergrowth, flash of yellowed fang — statistical voodoo that could only, one day, & not in the very distant future, turn around & bite him. That & somebody slipped a dozen laxettes in his coffee just before a night operation — long-way-round over Plzeň for a change & not a Fritz in sight, easy as pie — barely stayed off the can long enough to drop his payload, *hehe.*

622

45

THE ANGLE OF COINCIDENCE
EQUALS THE ANGLE OF CONFECTION

First one eye & then the other — between them, the Earth moved, tilted on its axis — the planets shifted out of alignment, the words on the page danced.

Man's more than just an ambulatory nervous system, they said. Oh?

The wind was seeking a way in, feeling around the window edges with tireless fingers. The nerve-strings twitched, the mannequin dragged upright. (We see it — *him* — alone in a room, in emulation of something: the seeking after an idea, yes, digging within himself, excavating, tunnelling. Of course, outwardly, none of this. It isn't that nugget of pure gold lodged in the colon, light of the ancients, the warm glow of the beatific, to which our attention is directed. The film taking place here, in this room, is not the same as the film inside the head of the substitute man inside the other room that we can't see.)

What was the last thing he remembered?

The scene was set. The film in his head was going dark. As dark as a black sun. The hiss of erasure, voices in the static.

What did they teach you in all those years of humiliation?

(Rewind, play the record again. So as to breathe, clear the fog from the head.)

Did parallel universes exist?

Other dimensions — mirror worlds to see between — solid matter dissolved by light?

Was it time to wake up yet?

Which world was he in now?

Which would prevail from this instant to the next?

An old Russian proverb: *Put on the first shoe, before putting on the second.* People with faces blanked-out.

It was like listening to rain falling on a windy night. Falling on metal, water, glass. Sonograms. Interference patterns in the middle-ear. Fluctuations in remote magnetic fields.

A sugar coating for History's bitter pill.

Had the future already taken form inside the contradicted present?

Was the past real?

What mattered: if he believed in ghosts, or if they believed in him?

Němec waited for his mind to come up with something, echoes of hidden ur-texts programmed in the hypothalamus, no less. The room tipped upright & the world with it. Like an aquarium without the fish. What surfaced was purely evanescent: faint ripples, *locos parallelos*, disturbance patterns, a wrinkled shapelessness not without form. It resembled the knotting & unknotting of an enormous scrotum.

(Behold the riddle of the species! The coming into existence of the Great Nothing, etc!)

Němec braced his head between his hands, Figaro-like. Dustmotes whispered: a grey Confucian babble in which weightless thoughts, only, adhered. *Seek not after that which is hid*, they said. Ah. Though of course they didn't.

The ghost, nevertheless, appeared on cue, perched on the edge of Němec's camp bed. An invisible finger pressed the RECORD button:

●

'That,' said the Prof's ghost, scratching his stubble, 'is merely the *form* of the puzzle. What you've got to look for is the *principle* of the thing, of what the puzzle *is*, & *where* it is, & for *whom* it is.'

The ghost looked tired. He sat there on the edge of Němec's bed taking in the mess of paper strewn on the floor, elbows on knees, arms jutting forward, hands left hanging, pale, at an ungainly distance from his body. Němec couldn't help noticing the nails. Blackened halfmoons. And the hair, greyer, longer, unkempt. There were bits of dumpling & goulash stains down the lapels of the Old Man's woollen jacket. Also, he smelled.

The ghost aimed a pointing finger in Němec's direction —

'Nice shiner. You get that sticking your head in the wrong kind of books?'

The ghost chuckled. Němec rubbed the swelling round his eye. He was lying on his back, the lightsocket in the middle of the ceiling refused to come into focus. It looked like nothing, a hazy black hole. He glanced back at the ghost. The ghost was fine, no problem at all —

'I know you're not real,' he said, 'or you'd just be a blur like everything else. Why aren't you a blur?'

'Why's the donkey smiling?'

'…?'

'…'

Němec closed his eyes. *This conversation is ridiculous*, he told himself. Then he heard something. The Ghost, he realised, was humming a tune. *This is completely perverse.* It was Mahler, the unfinished 10th — well it would be, wouldn't it? Like he'd brought his own soundtrack with him. The polyphonous poltergeist. Or else, he was trying to tell his listener something. A coded message, a riddle. Yeah, more of that kind of stuff. The *unfinished* 10th. *What happened to the missing part, eh, kiddo?* Ghost written. The doting widow in her dotage. Blah blah.

'I suppose,' Němec spoke while struggling to suppress a yawn, 'being in the position you're in, you'd know the answer to that.'

The ghost stopped humming & gave him one of those "hairless Mexican" looks. The tune, however, continued. Němec glanced at the recordplayer, half-expecting.

'What're you talking about?' the ghost said.

Němec blinked. The light socket, the ghost. Sighed —

'Just seeing as you're all up there together, maybe you'd paid the Great Man a visit, y'know, asked him how it's supposed to wrap up…'

The Prof's shoulders sank. He stared unblinkingly, it gave Němec the shivers. There was something in his eyes like a counterfeit azure as if woven of delicate glass threads. Němec rolled onto his side, pushed himself up onto one elbow, twisted, got one hand beneath him, pushed, drew his knees up. The ghost watched all this in silence. Němec paused to get his breath before bringing the complex procedure of obtaining a half-seated posture to completion. As he did so, the music, from wherever it'd come, ended. The last note sounded with an audible hiss, then came to a stop with all the aplomb of a mechanical fidget.

'I suppose, though,' he said, stretching his neck, 'it's just as tough up there as it is down here, getting through the front door, I mean. Every halfarsed enthusiast trying to squeeze in for a fireside chat, foisting their doodlings on the Man for his solemn opinion & all that. The odd gossip columnist for the lowdown on the exwife. Hard to work the True Kindred Spirit routine in a situation like that, I suppose…'

'…?'

'Or is it like the Greeks used to say, Orpheus&Co? They've got a statutory limit on those sorts of things, leave the memory of your old self at the gate, etc? You seem to be okay, though. They've got some sort of probationary period, have they? You get to slip in & out, check the facilities over for a while before signing up for the full membership? Chance to pop back here & look in on the near & dear? See how they're getting on in your absence? Or it just creeps up on you? Posthumous Alzheimer's Syndrome? Forget who you are after a while…'

'…?'

'Well I suppose they'd have to, wouldn't they, or there'd be no end to the labours? Right? And that'd be their lot from then till doomsday: tying up the loose ends, dotting the "i"s & crossing the "t"s, all the multitude of bon mots & fanfares & crescendos & masterstrokes — hopeless when all's said & done, though, eh? Walter Mitty stuff. After a while they'd lose interest, anyway. Who'd want to be a footnote to himself for the next million years? Forever gazing back at all the false starts left uncompleted or swallowed whole by the leviathan of History? Become meaningless in their own absence? Faint ripples grown ever fainter in a pool of mucky tidewater? Swamped by all the seven seas & seven oceans, the eternally recoursing El Niños, Ice Age glaciations, asteroid storm, Mass Extinction Event, red giant, brown dwarf, neutron star, black hole, reverse Big Bang, amen of all possible amens…?'

'…'

'And in the meantime, driven nuts by a self-enlarging spectacle of Progress that never speaks *their* language for long[*] — each tribe up there convinced the next lot are complete lunatics. I mean, what the hell'd Tutankhamen have to say to Socrates? Or Stalin to Saint Paul? *"Nice day for it, mate."* (*Fucking weirdo.*)'

'Will this take long?'

'…?'

'Just because I missed my afternoon nap. At my age, you know…'

Even now the Prof's ghost seemed to be fading. As if all Němec's *idiotische* talk had left him quite literally worn out. Perhaps he'd've benefited from a more rarefied atmosphere. It was the ghost's turn to yawn. Němec got an unobstructed view of the Old Man's demonological dentures, bridgework in the Gothic style.

'You know,' he said, 'I was thinking about you just the other day…'

'Oh?'

---

[*] *Noc* for *nox* & *nic* for *nemoc*? [✋]

The ghost gave Němec the kind of look you'd expect from a complete stranger confronted by evidence of a shameful sentimentality. Somewhere the Mahler started up again.

'Where've you been all this time, anyway?'

'I was never anywhere else, *mein Freund.*'

'…?'

The Prof's ghost waved a hand at the pages lying scattered on the floor. The Polygraph, the mutilated Blaq Book, the Farkakte Facsimile —

'What d'you expect to find in all of that?' the ghost said.

Němec didn't really know what to answer. The "key," perhaps. But the key to what? What *kind* of key? What *key*? It was all very Zen — a riddle that pointed only to the possibility of its asking, & the oracular voice in which it was asked. An echo, so to speak, of the personality within the page, the ghost in the machine, the mind in the Manuscript. The Prof's ghost chuckled —

'I know what you're thinking. *And if the words could speak? If what spoke were the words themselves?*'

He gave Němec a sly grin & shook his head —

'Good luck to you…'

'You mean it's got nothing to do with…?'

The ghost pursed his lips thoughtfully —

'I can tell you this much,' he said. 'Right now I'm as close to being at peace with myself as I could ever've expected to be…'

The ghost cast his gaze around the room, then back at Němec —

'Did *I* find what I was seeking, you want to ask? The question is, what *was* I seeking? What're *you* seeking, my young friend?'

'…?'

'Consider this,' the ghost made gestures with his hands, fingernail semaphore, vague emphases tending to vaguer *legerdemain.* 'Once you accept the premise, you're already halfway there.'

'…?'

'You know, when I was your age,' the ghost said, 'I never dreamt it'd be like this. The world should've ended by now. Does that count?'

The ghost stuck his hands in his jacket pockets. Němec wondered how long he'd been waiting there, in the ether so to speak, since the last time, watching him make a fool of himself. Like some sort of TV signal you just needed the right antenna to tune in on. And why'd the ghost been sitting on the bed while *he'd* been sleeping on the floor? He caught an echo of something —

'Halfway where?' he said.

'Eh?'

'You're already halfway *where*?'

'What're you talking about?'

'You said, just a minute ago…'

'What the hell am I supposed to care what I said a minute ago? You've got to stay in the *present*, haven't you learned anything?'

'There's no way to win, is there?'

'Win what?'

'My thoughts precisely.'

Němec, *in corpore*, was crouched because neither sitting, lying nor standing — a purely intermediate state. And not, despite appearances, the posture of one absorbed in that mirror of the soul made up of unreal figures, hieroglyphs, enumerations, the purgatorial Polygraphia he'd condemned himself to in mock volition.* Was he awake? The ghost gave him another one of those "hairless Mexican" looks.

'Don't,' Němec said.

'Don't what?'

'Don't tell me I'm imagining things.'

The room & everything in it seemed wrong now, out of kilter.

'Fine by me,' said the ghost, 'only thing is, how d'you know you're not?'

'What the hell difference would it make?'

'Ah, that's the spirit. Just as I was saying…'

The music meanwhile, having resumed, progressed by stages of sympathetic boredom: the feigned anguish, the appeal to mercy or at least reprieve, the unerringly erratic sentiment of a voice calmly articulating its own confusion. You had to give the Prof credit for the staging at least. If it'd been left to Němec… Ham actors in bedsheets belabouring pseudo-Shakesbawdian. Smoke, ectoplasm, convex mirrors. Etc.

The ghost leant forward on his knees & made an anecdotal grimace. He

---

* Conscious perhaps only of a prevailing inadequacy, the minor chord that announces remorse at the absence of magic, whose fainter picture, the once luminous skein, inadequately conceals the return of the perpetual migraine — nothing to sweeten the bitter caffeine that sluggishly cognises you, the unhappily obedient companion, practicing your childish spell (but to've failed without making the effort were hardly onerous) hopeful of a sudden magnanimous intervention — to unriddle you, release you from this bondage back into the sleep you've been accustomed to, resembling not so much a prisoner desperately scratching at the surface of the inner eye, as an embarrassed supplicant doffing his hat for change to passersby… [✋]

seemed to peer at Němec as if the air had thickened, grown dense, gravid, substanceless vision clotted by nescient ethers —

'But I suppose you want me to say something serious? A bit of gravity from beyond the grave, eh?'

The ghost raised its eyebrows. They hung down somewhat on the sides. Like little waterfalls in stop-animation. Němec pictured diminutive elves frolicking at the edge of the water, gossamer butterflies…

'Well here it is, then. There's a secret communion, between knowing & seeing, life & death. What it *is*, though, is impossible to say.'

'…?'

'You know, the Far Eastern masters, whom History accounts as being terribly wise — for whom space was a theatre of metamorphosis & who considered time as the crossroads where a vast number of highways come together — preferred among all the substances of nature those which are the most *intentional* & which belong therefore to the most *obscure* arts…'

God-on-High covering his tracks, strewing riddles of indeterminacy in the path of the overly inquisitive? *A man must serve his intelligence only*, so said. Like the deadman's Polygraph. But even the Almighty couldn't resist fiddling the evidence, if only to prove to Himself that *He* exists?

'On the other hand, these same Masters, while working with the substances of art, undertook to stamp the traits of nature upon them. Genetic engineers of a previous age. And thus, by a simple inversion, nature for them was full of works of art & art was full of natural curiosities.'

Did he really say all that? Speaking in riddles again.

'Listen,' he said, 'this's important. The illumination of reality must find its path through the unreality of signs & make of that *un*reality a new order of *re*ality.'

The ghost chuckled. The unpleasant laughter of the vocational non-entity, so to speak. A rasping approximation of the lost pulmonary reflex —

'You're the writer — at least that much should make sense, mmm?'

And there he was, fading again. His hands & the woollen jacket had began to dissolve — the disembodied tabernacle of himself dissenting to airy facticity — soon his face alone remained, as though suspended in the middle of the room. Němec gawked. Like an embalmed head, he thought, staring back at him from a non-existent mirror. And when it spoke, a babbling of ulterior worlds already *come to an end*? Votary of obscure cults waiting for the sky to fall. Something between a stone idol with colostomy bag & a mental avatar that neither eats, shits nor dies (again), because its existence in the first place is nothing but a false prolepsis. *Ah, yes, all* that *to look forward to in the Sunset Views Retirement Home of all Eternity, eh, kiddo?*

As the ghost's features gradually merged into the masonry, Němec thought of the Cheshire cat in *Alice in Wonderland*. He felt ambivalent about watching the Prof go. *Probably just needs to switch off the lights, recharge the battery.* You could poke the air where he'd been sitting & make a hole in some parallel dimension, like a Pythagorean joke. *And they'd still be there watching you, the surveillance boys upstairs who never sleep. No rest for the wicked, hehe.*

'Remember one thing,' the ghost said.

The words hung in the gloom like motes floating in the air. The Prof's ghosthead wasn't grinning at him any more. In fact, it wasn't there at all. Němec fixed his attention on the voice, which'd detached itself somehow & was in the room like an independent entity. *Alice* meets Obi-Wan. It was a lifeless, hallucinatory voice — it seemed to come from everywhere in the room at once, & nowhere.

'Remember,' the voice repeated, speaking from a great distance already, 'the tree can't be escaped by means of the tree.'

Day by day the nerve endings, contracting, deadening & hardening. If he kept this up, Němec thought, in the end all there'd be left would be a desiccated lump, a grey shrivelled thing, like an alchemist's turd baked down to its essential substance: the Man without Qualities, a bug rolling on the floor waving its legs. He dragged upright. Brushed himself down. Unstiffened the joints. Stirred the air in the room about. Ghostless. Over to the window: nothing to report out there. Dug around in the record box. Voilà, Mahler's unfinished business. He flipped it on the recordplayer. Faint hiss. Evocations of absence. Ah. Faint shivers up the proverbial. He stuffed his hands in his jacket pockets, hunching into it, fingers encountering loose change, paperscraps, one of the Chink's stale fortune cookies, still there in its greasy torn wrapper:

Lucky number 8!

8 for H — for *Hájek, hocuspocus* & *hooey.*

Mystic 8th letter.

8 for *sudden fortune, prosperity, the fullness of chance.* Ah-ha.

8 for *all around, all sides*, the eight vertices of time-space, octagonal, cube of the soul, the spinorial chessboard.

The 8 trigrammes & 64 hexagrammes of the I-Ching.

8 for *eternity*, the House of Death, the stepped pyramid, Egyptian *bā*. The Great Lisper's *ka'aba* in Red Square: black mortuary suit doublebreasted & polka-dot tie, glycerine-pickled, potassium acetate, alcohol.*

8 for *oxygen, acid, enzymes & genesis.*

8 for *mandrake* or *man-dreck*, meaning: *know, recognise, be familiar with.*

8 for the ramified power of influence, the diatonic scale, the Third Fold, the 10th month, the last parrying position.

8 for *right behind the eight-ball, kiddo.*

What the Prof's ghost'd said about the "Eastern Masters"? The Man in the Moon? Window dressing for sophistic solipsists? Why go to all the trouble of putting in an appearance to tell him *that* — why not just use the telephone? *Oh hello, the old Geist here, fancy hearing some orientalised bullshit this evening?* (You've got no class, Němec.) Thinking about how a man clocks-out in his bathtub with a chessboard between his knees & all the pieces bar one floating around him & how *it must've ended somewhere.* What'd the last move been? And what about the missing piece? *An occultation of signs on a par with the mysteries practiced within.* When in reality there was no mystery, when there was nothing within. Like an obsidian Sphinx. You break it open & all there is are more obsidian Sphinxes, each Sphinx begetting another & another, you smash them, pound them, grind them into dust, molecules, more & more of them, sub-atomic Sphinxes, god-particle Sphinxes, Sphinxes all the way down.

He bit on the fortune cookie, but it was rock-hard stale, just as he knew it'd be. Well what was he supposed to do now? Mahler rocked, Mahler soared, Mahler digressed into hysterics, Mahler grew sombre, pensive. The room looked at him expectantly. *This's pointless.* He shoved his hands into his trousers. *Look, here in this pocket is a phial of little white pills, and in this pocket are the blue pills, and in this pocket...* How many goddamn pockets did he have? *Don't argue with providence, kiddo, just roll with the punches.* Right. Exactly what he needed, a bolt of lightning up the arse, like shit off a shiny shovel, to shake him down to the core of his whatsits.

'Choose me!' said the little white pill.

---

* C_2H_5OH. [✋]
* See above. [✋]

Man in his finest hour. Even the prophets must've wanted an opt-out clause. Holy Geist & all that. Telling himself with a strict eye, *I shall not glance back.* Well, what *didn't* God permit, at the end of the day? Emissaries of rarefied nonsense, monsters of all quarters. As if invented in order to be accommodated & not the other way round. *What matter if the plot's as adrift as you are? What's the world tethered to?* They used to say, *Why stab the jellyfish or cut the weeds?* Němec interpreted this as meaning, *If you take one pill, take another two just to be sure.*

46

THE WHITE WHALE

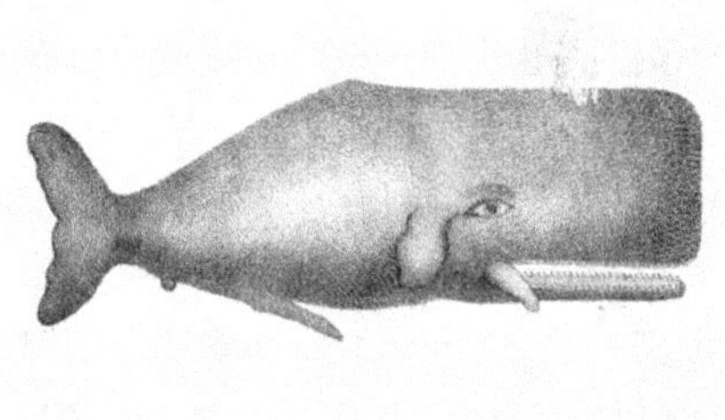

'Did I ever tell you the one about the fakir who stuck his cock in his ear, all in the name of wisdom & enlightenment? Sure I never told you that one?'

Merkin had been the regular barman at *The White Whale* for as long as Němec'd been going there. 6'4", ginger & with a face like a motorised snowplough. He had a lanky Irishman collared at the bar, with a pint of Guinness surrogate, giving him the intimate details of his life story. He'd talk the legs off a stool, provided there was an audience sitting on it. The Paddy had a buckskin cowboy jacket, with tassels on, & one of those Ned Kelly beards that looked like they came straight out of a mail order catalogue, little hooks at the top that go over your ears & a hole cut in the fuzz so you can breathe through it. You knew he was a Paddy because it was the first thing that came out of his mouth whenever he opened it. For all Němec could tell, the two were old mates from way back, or they'd known each other five minutes.

Before the Revolution happened in '89, Merkin was a conscript on the Kraut border near Hranice, armed with a pair of binoculars the dioptrics of opera glasses, perched up in a linden tree on the lookout for NATO spyplanes. Lockheed SR-71 "Blackbird"s, Lockheed U-2S "Dragon Lady"s. *Fat chance.* When he wasn't flipping-off the GIs on the other side or birdwatching or perving at the comrades from the women's barracks, he spent his eighteen months on the frontier getting pissed & reading comicbooks — *Ranxerox, Bongazine, The Great Švejk.* After the Revolution happened they were left to fend for themselves. No rations in the mess hall, no petrol in the trucks. It was fifty klicks through the snow to Cheb. They walked.

Merkin was an alright guy. In the past he'd let Němec run up a tab if Němec hung around after closing time to stack chairs & listen to his opinions about himself, but it'd been a while. Called Němec "Slim," not from any affection for the blues, but because it was what he called everyone. Like the scene in that film with Slim Pickins riding an A-bomb rodeo-style out of the belly of a B-52 & the music going *We'll meet again* the way folks say when they've only just met. Like callin' a total stranger *friend. Well how's about it, friend? Lend me that ten dollars? Pay you back next time…*

On this particular occasion, Merkin being busy gabbing with Ned Kelly's brother & all, Němec forewent the customary pleasantries as he came down the streetside steps & instead slouched over to a seat by the front window. Chances were Merkin wouldn't've recognised him either way, in his Charlie Chap get-up & head all misaligned, & no-one remembered anything in this town after six hours let along six months. But even if he did, with Merkin the dialogue only ever went in one direction — Němec could've grown two heads & it'd still only be, *How's it hangin', Slim? Did I tell you about this idea I've got for a novel? It's gonna be huge, I just need someone who's gonna write it for me. Got all the stories right up here, just rarin' to go…*

So keeping himself to himself, Němec parked & took in the atmosphere at *The White Whale* of a late September Thursday afternoon: one artist-type sketching in the corner with his change stacked on neat little piles on the tablecloth — a couple of nondescripts making faces at their beers — the usual bozos playing chess, shuffling the pieces around to kill time between refills — a black waitress coming & going with braided flipflops slapping the tiles — a Nick Cave rip-off on the radio, *Feelin' very thirsty in the Sorry Dog…* As you would, too, if you'd ever been there. Němec could hear Merkin over the music launch into one of his laments about the Good Old Days —

'Golem City's a dead-end, man,' he confided to the Paddy. 'All pricks & no kicks. Someone oughta bomb the place & put it out of its misery.'

Merkin had no end of opinions, just like he had no end of stories in which he, Merkin, usually assumed the starring role. He made no apologies about his life up till then having been sufficiently epic to warrant the full Hollywood treatment & tried to hustle anyone who'd listen into sponsoring it. People heard it so often they started believing it themselves, figuring he was maybe the next Ernest Haemorrhoid. If you sat still long enough, he'd break the whole feature-length spiel down for you, scene by scene: plot, subplot & twist. *Loosely Observed Planes*, it was going to be called. Ennio Morricone was going to score the soundtrack. But he hadn't decided on the director yet: Clint Eastwood or Tinto Brass. Big guns or big salamis. It was a toss-up.

Outside, the usual streetlevel traffic, cut off at the knees. Passersby passing by. Their shadows in the window had that sordid, abject appearance of misshapen bodies copulating behind a screen. Apart from that, the interior of *The White Whale* had a depressingly literary air about it. There were photographs of famous dead authors no-one knew the names of stuck up above the shelves of unbranded whiskey & a sign over the beer taps:

AMERIČANŮM NENALÉVÁME!*

Němec fingered the lunch menu. When the waitress came over he ordered a coffee & a jug of frankovka, just to start things off slow. The waitress flashed eyes & teeth, addressed him in a kind of patwah. *Agadoo, Americano?* Němec made a blank face. She repeated, this time in language. Fine, he said, he'd have one of those. Maybe some headcheese on the side. *Tenky massa?* He mimed, she blinked. He mimed again. She went away shaking her head. Merkin guffawed across the bar. The Paddy guffawed. The waitress guffawed. She brought the coffee. She brought the wine & tlačenka. She grinned, Němec grinned. As soon as she was gone, Němec dug some of Volta's pills out of his jacket & swallowed them. One charcoal-coloured & three white, to go along with the décor. Americano chaser. *Shit! They call that stuff coffee?*

One of the chess bozos got up & wove out to the jakes. Merkin had plastered a cartoon Queequeg, harpoon in hand, on the door — ever after, said facility referred to in-house as The Pequod. For some reason a thought-balloon hovered over the harpoonist's black head, as if *it* was the ever-elusive white whale, eater of colossal squid, ivory-toothed *Physeter macrocephalus*. Brain the size of a small truck, supposedly. The thought-balloon wobbled in the wake of the bozo slamming the door. Some comedian had scrawled PEAS & GRAVY with a magic marker across it. It wasn't, however, permitted to shit in The Pequod, this being reserved for Ladies Only upon surrender at the bar of a modest key deposit. Intended to reflect, Němec had no doubt, the more salubrious hygiene of the species' better half.

---

* "Some of the nation's best friends are Amerikans." [☚]

He sniffed at the tlačenka. Forked a bit of yellowed aspic into his mouth & swished it around with some wine — stirred a few lumps of tongue on the plate — but his heart wasn't in it. He downed the rest of the glass & poured another. The key to enjoying a meal, he'd long ago discovered, was to avoid forcing the issue.

The day hadn't begun that way. Nor did it end that way either. How it began was... Well, what really mattered was the phone call. But that came later.

The face in the mirror looked like something congealed, waxlike, beaded with sweat. A red eye squinted back at him from a mass of yellow-green woven with threads of broken capillary. *What a class act you turned out to be.* Němec's doppelgänger winced. Somewhere in the back of his mind, where actions & motives got shuffled about by tireless demons, the image of Alice Steinerová kept coming between him & whatever intelligence he had left. The image of a Flame, of a Sphinx, of Temptation & Danger. And there *he* was, a squirming dungbeetle singed by the light, brushing against it, *in girum imus nocte et consumimur igni,* blinded & doomed. He alone was to blame. Blame might thence demand some ritual of atonement, mmm? There was the ghost's recent visitation, also, to take into account. Number three in a series. And that strange confluence: Alice S. & Elsbeth von N___... He knew something, his guilty conscience said. He didn't know what it was.[*]

Outside, the construction workers were still erecting their siege tower, hoisting up planks, joists, rusted piping, their hardhats almost at window-level. Němec spotted the Weather Lady in her window across the street. It was impossible to tell if she was naked behind the curtain or not — almost every time she appeared, it was either in the process of getting dressed or of getting undressed. Did she exist in any other state? Or was she just some kind of cathode tube emanation from behind a screen? He drew pictures in his mind: the Weather Lady with Alice Steinerová's face doing the Dance of the Seven Veils — the Weather Lady as Elsbeth von N___ performing psychic surgery with enormous callipers & backlighting. Just the thing to arouse a dungbeetle from its torpor.

---

[*] Ineptitude produces strange bedfellows. [🖑]

Perhaps it was a sign, all those goings-on out there. Like the ghost's visitation. Harbingers of doom & all that. Time, they cried, was out of joint, some sort of action was required, a decisive realignment of the mechanism, perhaps. Němec gasped at the enormity of the idea. *First of all*, he thought, *localise*. He cast around for a handle on the situation, so to speak. The Prof's Picturebook Polygraphia lay in a mess on the floor. The Black Book in tatters. Facsimile pages crumpled in a heap. On an impulse, Němec set to work them all into a corner with his boot, then stuffed them in a plastic bin-bag. He took a moment to admire his progress. Wiped the sweat from his brow, then out in the kitchen buried the bag under the weeks-old garbage in the kitchen sink. Last place anyone'd look. It was just a feeling he had. He took another bin-bag out to the bureau & stuck it up inside the street-facing window. One of the construction workers smirked up at him. The Weather Lady waved. Němec, in a cold flush, wedged the corners of the plastic under the windowframe & blotted the smirking, waving world out.

Then, on a second impulse (he was really on a roll this morning, our Němec), he got hold of the phonebook & dug through it till he found a number for the Strahov Archives. He squinted at the small type through his one good eye. Flashback: moviescreen pictures, headlights in the rain. *Don't think about that, think about the other thing instead.* Call it unfinished business: if half the Prof's inventory had been lying around on his floor for the last couple of months, what was the rest of it doing?* *Focus on that. Draw the threads together.* He grabbed the black Buddha off the floor & went to dial, but the line was dead. He checked the cables, fiddled the receiver, jiggled the hook: no dice. *Maybe time you paid the nice people a personal visit, eh kiddo?* He scribbled the number on the back of his hand, jammed the bowler down over his bruised right eye & lumbered out the door, thinking the old ghost must be having a good chuckle to himself about now. The courtyard was dead (no sign of the caretaker this day either). He dodged out through the construction work, turned right. A blue Škoda idled at the corner, occupant reading a newspaper. Němec peered in through the window, grinned at said occupant: said occupant glanced up in alarm. Němec winked. *Let the fuckers figure it out for themselves…*

The crowd along Nerudova thinned out by the time he reached the steps. Slouching, stompstompstomp up the mountain, beneath the radiant eye on its obelisk, lunch crowds spilling out of cafés, monkeys in the peanut gallery (*Hey*

---

* No kidding? [✊]

Hat! Nice hat, Hat!), St Vít's like a giant meringue towering over it all. Throngs of penitents even at that hour, traipsing up from Charles Bridge, heads full of Ripollinoesque visions — the Golden City, Magic City, City of a Thousand-&-One Spires — populated by moving waxworks dummies all under the benevolent spell of Rudy the Wiz King's personal charisma.*

Němec dragged the sad sack of himself up the steps. A gust of wind blew up, undertaker's suitjacket aflap. Wasn't it that constant busybody, Goethe, who said his best work was done while walking? Head down, wending a way through the rubicund crowd towards Loretánská, daylight neon & blancmange, gorilla masks & barrel-chests touting black-eyed Zuzankas in unabiding contralto, *Inside genuine virgins!* All the drabness & sham of a Potemkin village bordello in slow-dissolve, the limelights turned to hair-of-the-dog now the bells had long since chimed midday — twelve gongs & all's swollen-jawed & bandylegged & past cuntstruck for this hour. The giant red neon heart hanging there leached-out, spent, shot to pieces in broad daylight. Suits hanging on coatracks.*

The white monstrosity came into view as he rounded the corner of the arcade. An unmarked cop car barred the lower entranceway. Němec made a loop around to Pohořelec & the main gate. It too was barred by a police sedan, blue lights slowly revolving on its roof. An ambulance came speeding by & the police car backed out of the way to let it through. A crowd of gawkers was beginning to gather. Němec crossed the street & worked his way to the front to see what the story was. The ambulance was parked halfway along the drive, between a couple of benches. There was a short bearded man in a coat lying on his back on the ground. His coat & shirt were open. A ruptured milk-carton lay in one hand, the

---

* And one or two things they aren't about to read in their pretty guidebooks: Rudi's somdomite mysticomania, e.g., taking the base material transmutations of Paracelsus a little more literally than most, the court annalist recording with a career pedant's attention to detail the circumference, length & heft of the various members, animate & inanimate, known or equally as often merely rumoured to've broached the Royal Prerogative or, in the argot of the day, *vaulted the Rubicon* — with a nod to the great Julius Gaius, conqueror of Gaul & most notorious dictator, stabbed brutishly from behind. (NB Though not of the gall to ever have possessed la bella Bohemia, from behind or in another other manner.) [✋]

* The cabaret clowns've done their striptease & now it's down to regular business, stuffing dollars in the glory hole to buy your way in by the back door, down in the authentic stink of it — getting it cheap you think — golddigging between the admonitory enema & luxuriant toilet seat, the tongue-tied Elixir & leaden hard-on, such are the alternatives — expecting it to be laid on, all wish & no resolve — then back out into the heaving mass in search of the truly miraculous last drink, *hehe*. What next? The eternal angry drunk shouting at God. A soprano wailing her guts out into the gutter. A sheet of newspaper wrapped around the foot of a lamppost: KEY TO WORLD PEACE! [✋]

milk still bleeding out from it, filling the cracks between the grey flagstones. A medic was kneeling on the ground, pushing down hard with both hands on bearded man's chest in a jerking rhythm. A second medic watched. The bearded man's entire torso shook like aspic beneath the force.

As the medic kneaded the man's chest, a fox terrier approached between the legs of the onlookers, sniffing at the man's shoes, lapping the meniscus of spilt milk. Something flowed out from beneath the prostrate man, spreading the milk. The mutt yapped. Someone shouted at it. *Zatracenej čokle!* A boot connected with its tail & the mutt yapped again & scampered off. Medic number two lit a cigarette & leant back against the ambulance, eyes closed. The kneeling medic pounded uselessly away, hypnotised by the effort — no-one seemed able to bring themselves to make him stop, waiting for the deadman himself perhaps to sit up & say enough already.

Němec edged away from the spectacle. The crowd of onlookers had grown. Across the tramtracks, the statues of Brahe & Kepler mutely observed the observers. Traffic swept past down the hill. Němec cast around for a payphone. There were two by the tramstop, another further along. He'd almost reached the student dormitories, though, by the time he found one that hadn't had its slot bashed in. Between the hedges, children in knitted hats & scarves were playing tag. No deadmen in their world yet today. Němec fed a coin into the machine & punched the number. He got a tone. It was answered on the second ring. A voice crackled through the interference, he could barely make it out. He pictured the thinhipped brunette in the red turtleneck sweater. *What was her name? Petrovná?* He said —

'Petrovná.'

There was a pause.

'Who's this?'

He stretched the phone cord so he could stand out of the booth & get a view of the Monastery gate while he explained his business. It was the same scene as before. No hurry now, the bearded man wasn't going anywhere.

'Isn't,' it sounded like. Then, 'Just a minute.'

The line clicked. A moment later a voice came through the receiver — it might've been the assistant archivist, he couldn't tell. He heard questions. He made his answers as simple as possible. He said —

'Hájek.'

The voice said to wait. He waited. The line clicked. The line cleared.

'Hello?'

It was the same voice only louder, sans static. Němec jerked his head around, as if expecting to find someone standing at his back. The voice wanted him to come to the office. Němec demurred. He didn't say, *There's a deadman.* It gave him a funny feeling. The voice posed new questions. Němec repeated, Němec elaborated, Němec evaded. The line clicked. The voice asked him to spell his name. The voice pressed for an ID number. Němec hung up: no dice. Two more officers were now standing at the Monastery gates. Němec eyeballed the receiver, played through versions of the conversation he'd just had…

What'd he expected? Starched little Miss Petrovná to come all unstuck about how they'd dug up the late Prof's lost books, after all, by some sort of luck — mystery solved. One of the janitors, maybe, found the lot of it under a stair in the west-wing basement, left there by accident. Reconstruction & all that. Just enough of an element of doubt to get his excitable squillhead all worked up, telling himself: *Accidents don't just happen, something makes them happen?* Envisaging somewhere yet another one of those cabals of Jansenistic janitors he knew all too well, arranging & rearranging the filth & rubbish of the world. Blah-blah-blah. Or something about funding cuts, maybe — a filing system in chronic disarray — storage boxes mislabelled — uncountable ziggurats of archival desiderata — food for the creeping mildew not even the dead monks' prayers had been able to bring a halt to: it'd blackened the foundations stones for centuries, eating away at the mortar, immunised to the razings & re-risings, buried down in the humus of the earth, tunnelling, rooted into the martyr's hill, blah-de-blah. The slightly defensive, slightly embarrassed tinge to her voice. Imagining a blush to match the turtleneck. Mmm?

He picked up & redialled. A man answered. This time Němec asked for the head archivist in person —

'Fišer.'

'…?'

'Personal.'

There was a pause, another click. The man came back on. Something about *unavailable.* Němec pressed. Said *very* personal. The man thought it over. Said something about next of kin. Something about Interior Ministry. A number. Someone called *Kammer* or *Kammler.* Němec rang off.

Instinct made him walk away from the phone booth as quickly as he could. The words sank in. Fišer was dead. Maybe the ambulance had been for him. Němec didn't want to wait around to find out. Instead, he thought of the lawyer, Bareš, something he'd said. It'd been months ago. Němec figured his options. *Was he being paranoid, or was that the same Škoda that'd been parked outside the Prof's house?* A 22 tram pulled up at the stop. He hurried across the street & climbed on. The doors closed behind him. The bell rang.

The belly of the whale was the same fluted-glass expanse of Soviet brass fittings he remembered from before. This time he bypassed the concierge's desk & took the paternoster straight up. He caught flashbacks. Of Bareš's secretary & the talking fish. Of Bareš's secretary & the Rokoko gang. He needn't've worried: where the lawyer's office had been was now an import/export firm, T.E.S.L.A. INDUSTRIES. SHIPPING AGENT. Sounded familiar, vaguely. Maybe he'd got the wrong office? He checked the building directory back down in the vestibule. T.E.S.L.A. Imp/Exp, no Bareš on any of the eight floors, sub-basement included. So much for playing detective. He stood out under the arcade, thinking what to do next. With his walking stick & hat he might've been taken by passersby for one of *them*, a bureaucratic vampire who'd wandered by mistake out into the midday glare, turning to ash before their very eyes.

Němec tallied the facts, enumerated hypotheses. Got stuck. First there was the Prof, then the Manuscript, everything proceeded from that. Forwards, backwards, anagrammatised. Backwards was Kircher, Kepler, Kelley. Forwards was Faktor, Fišer, then that shyster Bareš — who else? He couldn't keep track. Somehow they were all connected. But what was he expected to do about it? And what the hell did a State Literary Archivist have to do with the Interior Ministry, dead or otherwise? He could always try the number, if he remembered it right. *Kammer* or *Kammler*. A bit of oriental claptrap came to mind: *Everything's done by doing nothing.* Imagining things could still be more sinister than they already were. Secret gibberish codebooks doing the rounds, passed between furtive bespectacled-types you think only exist on movie posters & dustjackets in bookstore windows, under cover of dusk, collars upturned on Golem City streets where a look, an expression, an imperceptible shrug of the shoulder, a hand reaching for an inside pocket, takes the place of passwords grown foreign on the tongue, telepathic, written in air, twentyfirst-century samizdat of an underground semaphore system that literally starts where the proverbial buck stops — a place that could just as well be anywhere or nowhere. He could almost see Blecha's grinning face: *Life's little jokes, eh, kiddo?*

Who *was* the Prof to all those people? Why did he *matter?* Then something Faktor had said, the first time he met the man, Patriot Klub, a throwaway line. What was it? Němec clutched at straws, but no luck. Clutched again, caught something. *Day of Restitution. Schnitzelstadt. After the War.* Mmm. Time, he thought, to make a few more calls. Go further back. The missing years. Maybe *that* was the key. He went looking for a payphone & found one just around the corner on a sidestreet, outside a tobacconist. He went inside for change, then wedged himself in the booth & dialled 1181, international operator. When the connection came up, he asked for the switchboard at Schnitzelstadt University. There was a ringtone. It went on. Eventually a woman's voice answered. They played twenty questions for a while before he was passed along to another voice & then another.

Eventually Němec got put through to a secretary in some department or other. She'd never heard of Professor T. Hájek, but helpfully suggested he try the Personnel Office. She offered to route him. A moment later he was listening to another voice telling him the same thing only differently. Try the Records Office. The Rector's Office. The Vice-Rector's Office. The Provost's Office. The Registrar's Office. The Dean's Office. The Bursar's Office. The International Office. The Internal Affairs Office. The Study Department. The Alumni Office. The Vice-Dean for this & the Vice-Dean for that. The Faculty Secretary. The Faculty Undersecretary. The Human Resource Office. The Public Liability Office. The Little Man in Accounts. The Assistant Librarian. The Porter's Lodge. The Department Dogsbody. The *other* Department Dogsbody.

Pretty soon they'd've had him repeating his story to the maintenance man, if he wasn't out to lunch, or taking a crap, or fixing a leak somewhere, or sticking a spanner in the works. Němec counted his coins while he listened to the babble at the end of the line & then the by-now familiar machine-voice droning *Bittewarten Bittewarten Bittewarten* as yet again, etc. Expensive business waiting. What was it Maeterlinck had said? *All our knowledge merely helps us to die a more painful death than animals that know nothing?* That, Němec thought, must be very painful indeed.

Which was how he ended up at *The White Whale* on Schwarzegasse, chewing headcheese & spilling some wine & watching the chess bozos grind through the moves. Same bozos, same moves: pawn to king four, repeat, knight to king's bishop three, etc. With variations (minor). Just another couple of androids waiting their turn on the scrapheap. The Nick Cave sound-alike segued into Charlie Parker on the radio. Němec worked his way slowly through the jug of wine. The café filled up, people came & went, faces blurred in a haze of cigarette smoke. The old guys hunched over their game. He tried to imagine their lives, when they weren't sitting there at that table, when they were being characters in a different story. Half-a-dozen trumpet sessions circa 1950s going on '6os. The waitress looked more & more like an extra in a black&white film. The tip of a dreadlock grazing the lobe of her left ear. He ordered another jug. Someone laughed. A car passed on the street.

As the afternoon grew long, the waitress brought candles — short white stubs of them struck in recycled bottles. Tom Waits on the radio. Entropy settling in. The longer Němec sat there, the more invisible he felt. An eyeball-through-the-wall, a counterweight in space, balancing the general arrangement without ever becoming one of its facets. Merkin at the bar, the Paddy in the beard, the party of three just arrived. *Could any one of them describe me as I can describe them?* The bozos, the waitress, the couple of suits that'd turned up from nowhere. Transactions shrouded in the obscurantism of congenital nonentities, blah. How about that empty glass? *The eye by which I perceive this glass isn't the same eye by which it perceives me.* Blah-blah-blah. And what kind of eye would that be, my friend?

Like that old Soviet joke. World looks at you, but what does it see? And that blue Škoda through the window crawling down the street? *Idiot, they know where to find you, they don't need to look.* And what did he suppose Alice Steinerová was doing at that precise moment?

Němec unfolded a napkin, took out a pen & drew a line, then another. A shape gradually appeared. A winged creature above a figure, supplicant. He exxed it out, tore it up. *Stay in the present.* Miles on the radio now. The place looked like something from a Louis Malle film. Němec unfolded another napkin & started again, words this time, forcing himself to go on, automatically & without interruption, till the mood left & the pen tore through the paper. He read back over it. The words left him demoralised. He'd wanted them to speak for themselves, but they were like words caught inside a dream…

Two to begin with. One, perhaps, seeks exoneration from a committed crime? Or is too passive, wishes simply to be made use of? The others always talking to himself, borrows his gestures from history books and accountancy? Through a veil of cigarette smoke it's difficult to discern the expressions of the drinkers at the bar. Nearer at hand, the chessplayers. A pair of high casement windows, candles placed individually upon the tables. Shadows cast across faces, intent upon duration, upwards against the walls and portraiture. Outside it's October. It'll remain October till it becomes November —. Then the light will change also, it'll grow darker sooner, shadows will creep faster across the walls and faces to disfigure them. But there's no such thing as time, says the rook, crouching in a chair with one leg missing, body twisted into the form of a riddle. Not one thing, not a thing. The waitress laughs shrewdly, replacing a piece (it doesn't matter which) that'd accidentally fallen. He'd like to explain more to her, but is either at a loss for words — or, merely hypothetical. In either case, who's to say that she hadn't understood the purpose of his being there?

A movement of the hand seems to reassure the watchers. Duration, which is their sole concern, isn't in question. Time, he says. Yes, she replies. Once more she leans over the table, drawing the sharp end of a pencil decisively across a thin strip of paper.

The record of their transaction is complete. And just as mysteriously as she appeared, she vanishes into the contracted haze of the outer room.

Zbluh bluh bluh. He screwed the napkin up & tossed it on the floor. The waitress, passing, bent down & picked it up again, smoothed it out, laid it back on the table. *She winked at him.* As soon as she was gone, Němec stuffed the napkin in his pocket. Perhaps, in the cold light of sobriety. Or perhaps not. His eyes followed the waitress to the bar. *Vieni, o diletta, appressati*! The black of the waitress to Alice Steinerová's blonde. The room became shadowed canyons, leopard-skins, desert dunes adorned with Egyptianed kitsch. Queequeg roared with sea-churned laughter. Rattled his harpoon. *Peas, peas, peas and gravy*!

Němec downed the last of the wine & stared at the empty jug. Stared at the chess bozos. Stared at the window. If nothing happened soon, he'd have to resign himself to staying put till closing time. Fišer? A coincidence, a crossed-wire. Bareš? A move made too late in the day. Faktor? Who cared about Faktor? Perhaps there was nothing he, Němec, was *supposed* to do but wait, kill time. Perhaps his sole purpose in that drama, after all, was to be exactly nobody. He pictured Alice holding a gun to her head. He heard it go off. *It's just a blank*, he told himself. *Like you.* And, sitting there like that, at an obtuse angle to the wall, eyes wandering among the sidewalk traffic — shoes, boots, trousers, the odd stockinged pair of legs, a dog on a leash, a dwarf…

▌▌

The unctuously waxed moustache was unmistakable, the coat dragging on the ground, the pudgy hand gripping the brown leather attaché case. Němec tossed some notes on the table, grabbed his walkingstick & was up the steps just in time to see the dwarf turn the corner beneath a shopsign with a miniature skeleton hanging in a blackened gibbet. Of all the things so far, here was an opportunity Němec knew he couldn't let slip. He took off after the dwarf as best he could, beat time on the pavement with his stick, past the antique bookshop onto the crosstreet. The dwarf dodged in amongst the pedestrian traffic at the next intersection. A tram wheezed by. By the time Němec reached the corner, he'd lost him. Němec swore, waved his stick, weaved back & forth like an agitated drunk. People shied. A gap opened. There, on the opposite sidewalk, half-a-block away, heading to the Old Town.

Němec pushed his way indiscriminately along the street, trying to catch up. The dwarf crossed Národní, veered right. Němec spotted him ducking into an arcade. He followed, across a courtyard & along an unlit passage. The dwarf was directly ahead of him now. They passed the round stone chapel of St Martin's, then turned right. The next intersection was a maze with market stalls. Carpmongers, greengrocers, trinketsellers, cripples, buskers & portraitists, leathergoods merchants, blacksmiths with brazier & bellows hammering out fake medieval coins, back-of-a-truck bootleggers & alchemists, Serbian shortchange artists, Albanian pimps, daylight gipsy prostitutes, Bulgarian panhandlers & Russian pickpockets. The whole *comédie humaine*.

After Němec had finally managed to navigate the last of the stalls, the dwarf was nowhere in sight. He took a gamble & veered left, fairly certain by now of the direction the dwarf was headed. He reached Michalská. As he'd expected, the dwarf was up ahead, trotting along the sidewalk. Except that now he was carrying *two* attaché cases. What was that all about? A little while later the dwarf stopped in front of a gate & looked around. Němec ducked behind a streetlamp. He watched the dwarf balance the attaché cases while he pulled out a key & unlocked the gates, then cast a furtive look up & down the street, before disappearing inside. Interesting. If Němec's calculation was correct, those gates were the back entrance to the house at Jilská 22. He decided to put his theory to the test & backtracked.

The street out front was still more or less the same: the Philosophy Institute, the crystal merchants, the *Svoboda & Slovíčkář* bookshop with the same hodgepodge of notices stuck in the window. The bookshop attendant watched him through the glass. He recognised the square glasses & Capuchin's tonsure. He could almost smell the musty stink. Faktor's former HQ, meanwhile, had been given a fresh coat of yellow paint. There were even trinket sellers under the arch of the open coachdoors. Němec stared. Were it not for the number, he'd never've recognised it. *So,* he thought, *here I stand, like myself before me, and identical others who'll come after me.*[*]

'Now,' he said aloud, to himself, to no-one, 'where's that dwarf?'

One of the trinketsellers looked up, squinted —

'I've got wooden swords, plastic helmets, lead soldiers, waterpistols, tin whistles, bubble-blowers, paper windmills, rubber hammers, buckets of slime, woollen mittens, coloured crêpe, flags of all nations, vampire fangs, snorkels, frightmasks, fur hats, superman capes, firecrackers, party hats, jelly eyes, glass goblets, x-ray goggles, kaleidoscopes, cellophane knickers, French ticklers, voodoo dolls, scented candles, moonrocks, Jan Hus figurines, itching powder, poisoned pens, water bears, magic beans, fairylights, chemistry sets, ceramic bulldogs, crystal balls, pewter mugs, Dutch ovens, snow globes, beer steins, Papal bulls, lint removers, monkey-paw backscratchers, ivory chessmen, old coins, Mao Tse Tung chopsticks, Lenin cufflinks. Every one a genuine article. Name your price. What you see is what you get. I've got...'

Němec slipped past the stalls & into the coachyard. He looked for the door to the winecellar & found it unlocked. Soon he was following the long, winding passage that sloped down to the where the Patriot Klub had formerly been. Lightbulbs hung from the ceiling at random intervals, so dim Němec could see almost nothing else. He groped his way along the wall, careful not to stumble. He listened for sounds. After a while, a rectangle of light stood out of

---

[*] Wisdom got in the parlous life of farce. [✊]

the gloom. A doorway. He thought he heard voices. The dwarf & someone else. He approached with caution. As quietly as he could, he pushed the door open & peered around the edge.

The Patriot Klub had been turned into a dump. The air, a stale bitter odour redolent of ether, sulphur, formaldehyde. Junk was piled where the chairs & tables had been. Rolls of painted canvas. Curtains. Bits of painted scenery. Costume racks. Stage lights. A movie poster in a broken frame stuck out between lightstands: *V.F. Entertainment presents* THE TERATOLOGISTS. "Golem City, 1942. Cheskoslovnikia is occupied by the Nazis & suffering under the brutal regime controlled by ⚡-Obergruppenführer Reinhard Heydrich, the vicious sadist known as *Der Schlächter*." Alice Steinerová stared out at him with preternaturally blue eyes.

'My god,' he mumbled, 'that too.'

But his thoughts were interrupted by voices approaching. He glanced around to see where they were coming from. He caught sight of a ventriloquist's dummy, mouth agape, sitting on an old wine barrel. It seemed to watch him with horrible dead-of-night eyes.[*] And behind the dummy, a table with dozens of brown leather attaché cases piled up in rows, all more or less identical to the ones the dwarf had been carrying. The voices were coming closer. Němec edged between the piles of junk & crouched down behind some painted wooden scenery shaped like the crests of waves. They were the same two voices he'd heard before. The dwarf's was a nasally whine. The other belonged to a woman. Middle High Krautisch. Like a voice that'd had too much gin & cigarettes. There was something familiar about it.

'We'll have to do something about that,' the woman said. 'Our partners don't appreciate loose threads.'

'The Boss knows all about it,' said the dwarf.

'Maybe he doesn't know as much as he thinks.'

'He's no schmuck, sister. When the time's right…'

Němec flinched. For a moment it sounded as though the voices were coming from right beside him, there in the room. He held his breath. But it must've been an illusion, for in a moment they began fading-out again in the direction of the passageway. There must've been some other way out. Other rooms, too, beside the one he was in. He decided he ought to take a look around

---

[*] "Now don't get excited, I was only joking, you know me. Maxwell! Take your hands off me! Stop playing! Maxwell! Here you fool! Officer! Quickly! Open this door!" [✊]

while he had the chance. But then the lights went out & the voices receded into nothingness. Němec froze. It was impossible, in the dark, to gauge which direction he was supposed to go. His walking stick slipped from his hand & clattered. He groped around for it. Something rustled. He caught a draught, it seemed to carry the voices back with it. The acoustics wavered. Then the voices grew louder again, as if approaching from behind him now. For one brief moment a light flared but just as suddenly was gone. Němec blinked, doubly blinded. In a clear baritone he heard the woman say —

'But can he be relied on?'

'Boss has him all figured,' the dwarf said, 'like clockwork. That's the only thing that matters.'

Can who *be relied on? To do* what?

After a while something banged & then silence. Němec stood up & tried to work his way back out to the passageway. He ran into a clothesrack. It tipped over. He steadied himself, breathing hard. *Don't panic.* Eventually, after much trial & error, he found the door. He felt around the frame for a lightswitch. No luck. He limped up the incline in the dark, using his walkingstick like a blindman. The way up seemed much longer than the way down. There was a distant echo of plumbing at work. *Well, kiddo, you've sure got a nose for it.* Then without any warning he ran straight into a heavy wooden door.

A door, but no light. And the door was locked. No handle even. Nothing. Had the passage forked? Had he wound up at a dead end? The answer seemed too mundane. For the time being, at least, Němec was stuck with the conclusion that the dwarf & his accomplice had simply locked-up behind them. The prospects looked rather black. Blacker than a blacked-out cinema without the exit lights. Already he could hear the rats sizing him up for a meal. Then right on cue this prating voice in the back of his head, full of scorn,[*] saying —

Hey, Němec you idiot. Yolk for brains. Try getting your eggshell around this one. Dolt, cretin, turd. They were right about you all along. Snivelling little. See if you can write your way out of this. Haha. You couldn't write your way out of a wet paper bag. You don't even exist. You're just the Old Man's golem, doing the dog work after he copped-out. Haunting the empty house. The outhouse. Hooohooo! Waiting for the

---

[*] Thinking, no doubt, what a joy to look forward to, his conscience's company for the rest of his happy life down there. *The love that bearest*, & all that. Telling himself *the more you know the less you think*, or *the more you think the less you know*. And whose bright idea was it to get caught up in all this anyway? [♣]

Němec hammered on the door. It could be days, he thought, weeks even, abandoned to rot, like a rat caught down a drain. *Knock-knock! Who's there?* Maybe one of the trinketsellers would hear? He beat his stick against the wood. Long gone. Or the dwarf, unfinished business in the basement. *Well, well, what have we 'ere, eh?* Again the sound of plumbing echoed from upstairs. He pounded with both fists, shouted. *Pomoc!* Denizens of the dark thrusting indignant heads out of their holes to see WTF precisely was going on out there with all that godless ruckus, little red pinhole eyes scoping the scene. Squillhead pounding & pleading. It sounded as ridiculous as it was.

The din reverberated down the passageway, yet no-one came. Would you? Gradually Němec wore himself out. He slid down with his back against the wall & tried to think of other things. His mind went blank. Silence in the peanut gallery. He sat there like that for what seemed like hours. He'd begun to fall asleep when he distinctly heard the sound of footsteps. They approached. In a frenzy he dragged himself to his feet & started hammering all over again. He stopped to listen. After the echo died down, there was complete silence. He hammered once more. Nothing. No footsteps, no voice in reply, no Morse code down the sewer pipes. He gave up. Evidently there hadn't been any footsteps, there was no-one out there who could hear him, no-one would ever come.

He sank to the floor. Long despairing minutes passed.

A key grated in the lock.

At first the hurricane lamp appeared to hang by itself in mid-air, then out of the dark a shape took form beside it. Němec, one red lab-rat eye, one black, blinked into the light. Bowler hat & walkingstick. Hands raised in a laughable reflex of capitulation. A stooped watchman, truncheon raised above his head, blinked back.

47

CHESK & LESK

Well now, once upon a time, in the days before History was written in books, there were two bucktoothed, pimply, skinnyarsed brothers from the shtetl of Chełm, named Chesk & Lesk. The shtetl suffered from acute & unsanitary overcrowding & there wasn't enough food, so everyone in the village was gathered together one Saturday around noon to draw straws & see which two lucky blighters among them should go off in search of new pastures in the Wild West &, as fortune would have it, the lots fell to the two brothers. When spring arrived they set off across the plains with that Great Goal in mind. But as they walked & walked, slowly they forgot their goal & remained aware only of the journey itself. And so each day they wandered aimlessly in the direction of the setting sun, in the belief that their goal would reveal itself at the appropriate time. Even now, no-one can be sure of what their original goal was. Probably even *it* was a mistake. But legend helps to falsify what really existed & to create a memory of something which never did. And so, one fine day, trudging across the flat middle of fair Europa, Chesk & Lesk happened upon a giant beetroot sticking out of the ground. This was no ordinary giant beetroot, more like a beetroot the size of a very very big hill. Seeing as it was the only landmark for miles around, the two brothers set about climbing to the top of it, from which, having planted a flag at the summit (in truth, a dirty handkerchief tied to a stick), they gazed north & south across an unbroken expanse, towards the veritable ends of the Earth. Despairing of their journey, the brothers yet again drew lots to see which of them would stay to guard their claim over the giant beetroot & which would forge onwards in search of their Great Goal. This time, fortune favoured Chesk, who sat down in the shade of the beetroot while his brother once more set off for regions unknown. As spring dragged into summer, Chesk found himself growing terribly hungry now that he was unable to wander from his station to forage for food. Then a bright idea came to him. He dug a finger into the side of the giant beetroot & discovered the flesh was tender & juicy & good to eat. Immediately he set about sating his formidable appetite, not stopping till the whole beetroot was reduced to a pile of slops. Chesk sat there covered head to toe in beetroot juice moaning & burping, with the greatest gut-ache known to man. Meanwhile, Lesk had travelled all the way to the very Edge of the World & found himself on a cold grey rocky shore face-to-face with the Vast Ocean. Unable to proceed any further, & with no very great prospects thereabouts, he turned back. But as soon as the Ocean had receded behind him, he was helpless to distinguish one direction from any other. The sky was overcast, the land uniformly characterless & flat. He squinted at the horizon in search of the only landmark he knew, the giant beetroot, but it was nowhere to be seen. Day after day it was the same, till eventually he gave up hope of ever finding his brother again & he sat down at the edge of a great cucumber patch & moaned. *Ai ai ai…!*

'Pravda vítězí!'

Primus screamed, in near-falsetto. 'Truth shall prevail!'

Národní was lit up with the glow of dusk gilding the diminutive figure on the soapbox. A crowd had blocked off the intersection, flanked by horses & open-top carriages, juggling clowns, balloon sellers, etc. Surrounded by an honour guard in black polyester, Miroslav Sládek,[*] a.k.a. "Primus,"[*] was baiting the crowd about Zhids, Gypsies & the National Idea. A fine spray of spittle glistening in the last orange rays of sunlight.

'This pious democratic world watches unblinkingly,' he railed, 'while an inferior people drags us into the gutter. We intend henceforth to look after our

---

[*] "The Mr Bean of the Far Right." [☙]
[*] As in the cheapest beer in town. [☙]

own interests. Under no circumstances can we capitulate to threats & coercion!'

A cop stood idly by, picking his nose. A TV cameraman focused on his shoe, waiting for something to happen.

'No longer,' Primus ranted, 'can we afford to stand at a crossroads. The time has come to choose the path History has prepared for us!'

Nothing more indecent than a man making love to himself in public. But you talk loud enough while you're doing it & there's always a type of person will stop & admire the spectacle.

It reminded Němec, in a curious kind of way, of one of the Bugman's stories, about an old Libeňák who used to sit smoking a corncob pipe at the crossroads by Libeňský Bridge, known thereabouts as King Králík: on account of his always rabbiting-on to folks passing-by about man's humble lot & how, even so, he could count himself King of All-He-Surveyed — on account of having served forty years in the Land Surveyor's Office, *hehe* — on account of the fact he still enjoyed a joke at his own expense as much as the next man — on account of a cardboard box under the bridge being where he dropped his swag each night & passed the long Novembers stone drunk — on account of the redundancy notice served by the Revolution — on account of him having a lot on his mind, too much even to afford these last eight years a decent night's sleep, with or without a roof over his head, though where such a roof might be he solemnly & stubbornly refused to divulge whenever interviewed by the friendly boys-in-blue — on account of possessing uncanny (if unsuspected by those in officialdom) powers of awareness, that for example the forces of Destiny & even of the Law move in mysterious ways not above causing humiliation & sometimes grievous bodily harm to the elderly, unemployed &/or homeless — on account of being a card-carrying graduate of the Old-Skool-of-Hard-Nox, none, though, as hard as what awaited at the hands of a skinhead posse, a gerrycan & Zippo lighter…

Up on his soapbox, Primus waved his arms frantically while he berated his audience. There could hardly be any doubt the man was disordered. *Nothing more dangerous than an idiot with a brain.* Němec looked around at the crowd to see what sort of reaction all this crap was getting, expecting smirks, knowing winks, heads nodding to show they were all in on the joke together. What he saw was a mob in expectation of commands, faces blank as a Cranach group portrait. Some were holding banners over their heads. One read: SOVEREIGNTY, SECURITY, SKLAVICISATION! Another: NO TO NATO! A third: CHESK FOR THE CHESKS! A fourth, simply: VLAJKA! A gust of wind blew up & carried Primus' voice back into itself, so that he stood there with his mouth moving & nothing coming out of it, like a man with the head of a carp. If only, Němec thought, someone'd fry the sonofabitch in breadcrumbs.

His amusement waned & he moved on, detouring towards the river to avoid the overspill. He drew looks from the fringe element. He fingered the dent in his hat where the watchman's truncheon had stuck & sneered back. *They'd have you up against a wall faster than you can say "Cheese," kiddo, if they ever got their way again.* Yep & an **N**-for-Němec painted on his forehead for target practice, with a star drawn around it just to pretty it up. And all the others like him. (Were there others like him? He supposed there must be. "Freaks," not wholly in the mind, for those *real* freaks like Primus to hate.) A crumpled wrapper blew across the street, banners flapped.

The demonstration petered out well before he reached the National Theatre. In the courtyard, skateboarding Wagnerjugend did tricks to a Siegfried soundtrack piped through an outdoor speakersystem. Tourists waved cameras. A tram clanged its bell. The setting sun made the river a picture they usually only sold on stands. The opera house, meanwhile, was in process of being turned into a billboard done up in Vegas lights they'd zap on once it got dark enough to work the advertising routine on the punters. On the steps beneath it, the Chicken Man held court. He stood, poised roosterlike, now on his left foot, now his right, clutching a tin can with a cockscomb & a string dangling from the bottom of it. He fiddled the string in long & short jerks. *Bööök bök bök bgöööööörk!* A basket of similarly decorated tin cans lay at his feet as he circled about, doing his chicken dance, saucer-eyed, red knitted cap, a tattered white raincoat hanging on him like greasy plumage. Tourists clapped. Tourists snapped pics. Tourists jived on the crazy old guy. No-one bought the tin cans.

At the bottom of Národní a couple of Christian Science nuts were handing out flyers: *Say* **NO** *to Evolution!*[*] All praise to man's unimpeachable optimism. *When it comes down to it,* someone said, *you give a monkey a choice, it'll turn itself into someone's undigested dinner for the hell of it, thinking it's moved up in the world.* Squeegee boys at the intersection extorting five-second carwashes. Horns blared, drivers shouted through their windscreens at the offending world the way they probably shouted at their TVs. Under the traffic lights, a woman, brown overcoat & a knitted hat, was singing in a faltering soprano an aria from a Verdi opera. *La forza del destino.* Standing next to her, a blindman with

---

[*] Jesus, Mary & Josephus! And Hogo Fogo too! [✊]

walkingcane held a bowl out for change. Pedestrians passed. Traffic passed. The bridge across Střelecký Island. Riverboats tooting, pedalos plashing, ducks quacking. *A happy duck's a tasty duck.* Fishermen in wooden skiffs, moored under the bridge, cast their flies with that bored, fatalistic air it takes decades of out-waiting carp & catfish to acquire.

Němec crossed over between the cars & headed towards the Island, zoning-in on one more stone left unturned. He descended the steps. The park was crowded with all types soaking up the last of the weather. Wizened bums on park benches, old dowagers hawking outdated copies of *The Watchtower*, boneheads with sleeping dogs, dreadlocked rastas & buttoned-down insurance drones, geeks with medieval broadswords, semi-nude environmentalists, one-armed thalidomide panhandlers, do-gooders out to save the world & sell you a tshirt, abortionistas peddling selfservice DNA, gene-selection automats, the works. *They wanna fix things for the better? What's in it for them? Let me tell you something — can't trust a fanatic — the type'd put a bomb under their own arses and set the fuse, only they're just as likely to put a bomb under yours. When Paradise Rose comes whistling down the tracks, kiddo, grab your hat and hold onto your pants, and don't wait around to watch the fireworks...*

Navigating the lunatic fringe: autistic stick-up artists, soup-kitchen drop-outs, survey-takers, undercover narks & junkies hedging their bets (if the junk don't kill 'em the water they boil it down in will), each with the lowdown on the Meaning of Life.[*] *Man does not know wherefore he seeks...* Yessir! Always someone waiting around with a finger itching on a button — like The End just couldn't come soon enough, for all them saviour-types dyin' to be made new, the little Emperor in his birthday suit grinning into the big mirror & God grinning back. Some pocket Galileo glued to his telescope in search of the collective doomsday already at hand, the movable feast of recantation, to undo the Original Fall from Most-Amazing Grace, the Holey of Holies, the Great Error, the Sin of Sins — call it History stuck on an oblique axis, like a cosmic suicide note waiting to be signed: pristine, typed, no drafts, *as is*, a clean copy, not a word or letter exxed-out. Just the way Adam's navel. Eve's, too. Nothing to stare into but the earthapples of each other's eyes, little firmaments full of forbidden fruit, all of them with their very own pet name, whole constellations of cutesy naughtiness unbeknownst to Big Daddy, the incorporeal poetry of the zodiacs, telling themselves *this* was how their little universe was created — & stayed that

---

[*] As close as the nearest trashcan. [✊]

way, fixated, till one turned into a tree & the other an asp. *Stop! Go back! You're doin' it all wrong!*

It should've come as no surprise that the château was completely boarded up — the ubiquitous **REKONSTRUKCE** stencilled on plyboard. There were dead leaves piled against the steps where the wind had blown them. Inside a fenced enclosure, bags of cement were piled around the steel door where the entrance to the Kabaret Grünegast had been. *Another one bites the dust, eh, kiddo? Kinda narrows the options from here on in.* Down by the shore, a couple of Frank Zappa lookalikes were strumming guitars — deep shadows under the purple trees — ducks on the water, looking on bemused. The kids sang, *Smoke it till you're slaughtered, flyin' in the sky…* Other kids sat around on blankets drinking box wine, passing joints.

Němec stood there for a while listening then climbed the steps again, trying to decide if next he should see if maybe they'd shut down the Zrcadlo Theatre as well, & if not, on the off-chance, Alice Steinerová, or instead just head back to *The White Whale*, call it quits for the day while he was still, so to speak, ahead. He decided to toss for it: heads, Zrcadlo — tails, the other place. It came down tails. Overhead, rivergulls shrieked in an orange-grey sky. *Riverghouls.* Down below, the horn of a barge as it passed upstream, prow emerging from the shadows of the bridge with its cargo of gravel piled into ziggurats, the long flat hull, the pilot's house with its light on, smoke from the stack, flag hanging limp at stern & the *chugchugchug* of it, brown wake washing out of the lock. Němec retraced his steps. The blindman & soprano were still there at the intersection — the soprano with hands clasped in front of her like someone at prayer, or maybe Verdi was just her way of doing penance. Němec tried whistling it but couldn't get the notes, keeping one eye on the pavement & doing hopscotch around the dogshit, thinking a drink would indeed be welcome right about now.

The antiquariat with the gibbet over its door had a folio edition of Mayakovsky in the window beside back issues of *Kino* magazine & a book about circus clowns with a grinning dwarf on the cover. *Some things*, Němec considered, *are just bound to turn up like that, eh?* He scanned the discount boxes, a stack of old Telefunken discs, faded purple & orange sleeves like bits of '70s wallpaper. Němec eyed a Kerstin Thorborg recording with serious intent. He weighed the cash situation: vinyl or vino, but not both. *The White Whale* was only two doors down. It was an unequal contest from the start.

By now the place was empty except for a waitress in a denim vest & a customer sitting alone in the gloom beside the coat-rack: a woman in a felt coat searching for something in her handbag without seeming to find it. Thursday evening blues. *Not Wednesday, not Friday, kinda not anywhere.* He took the same table by the window, though by now the scenery was nonexistent & the street pretty much dead. There was a different waitress on shift, she made one of those faces at Němec when she got close enough for a look at the welt round his eye & the dent in his hat. *Far out*, her eyes said. She obviously took him for a character. maybe one of those bums gonna sleaze off without settling his bill, cause her a whole lotta unneeded grief. He gave her his stupidest lopsided grin & asked for a jug of frankovka, then changed his mind & decided to move onto the real stuff so asked for a slivovice instead —

'On second thoughts, make that two.'

The waitress waited with her mouth open till she seemed more or less certain that was the whole order & drifted back behind the bar. A faint herbal scent drifted after her.

Němec smoothed himself down & stretched his legs under the table & gave his head an airing, punching the dent out of his crown & hanging the hat & stick from the back of an adjacent chair. The damp of the winecellar still somehow clung to him. It set him to thinking, going back over the course of recent events, the whole accumulation of incidents, circumstances so to speak conspiring to his general disadvantage. And what was it with all those attaché cases? Was Faktor starting up a collection? And that whole *VF Entertainment* shtick — moving up in the world was he? What'd be next, President of the goddamn Republic? His drinks arrived. The waitress ogled his head unabashedly. Němec made that grin again. Ran a hand over the fissure lines. Winked his panda eye. The waitress shivered —

'One of those days, huh?'

'Story of my life.'

'You wanna smoke something, make you feel better?'

'I dunno. You ever see ghosts?'

'Ghosts?'

'Yeah, like dead people come back from the grave, 'cos maybe they're lonely & need someone to talk to…'

'That's awful. I never thought of it that way. I always kinda figured you'd have lots of company when you're dead. Y'know, all those other dead people?'

'Maybe it's like the first day at school. Lot of strangers. New rules. Hard to know your way around. That sort of thing.'

The waitress frowned, nodded, fidgeted in one of her vest pockets & came out with a thin joint & a BIC lighter. She lit it. Němec watched her inhale, fold her arms, look thoughtful, nod some more, exhale. He raised a glass —

'Here's to it,' he said.

'You want some,' she held the joint out.

Němec downed his drink, took the joint, dragged on it, passed it back. The woman with the handbag glanced myopically up, then kept on rooting for whatever it was she couldn't find. The waitress sat down, still hugging herself with one arm. Němec exhaled, the waitress inhaled. He hit the second glass. The burn of the slivovice cut through the burn of the smoke.

'What's with the ghosts, anyway?'

'Occupational hazard,' he said, putting the empty glass beside the other.

'…?'

'Writer.'

The waitress worked the joint down to the butt, made a grimace —

'Is that how you did *that*?' she blew smoke over his head.

'The competition these days,' he massaged his scalp, 'is downright brutal. Don't be deceived by all the niceties…'

'Yeah,' she pocketed the butt with the lighter & got up. 'You want two more of those?'

'Two more,' Němec said, 'would be just fine.'

He stifled a yawn, rubbed his eyes. Strange, the way things happened, just the way they did. The deadman at the monastery, the soprano, the gulls on the river. How, in retrospect, each scene would be incomplete without them, no matter how incidental or absurd or unconnected with anything else. The waitress, the woman with the handbag. A movie poster in a cellar full of junk. A voice he couldn't put a face to.

Two double brandies arrived. The waitress pulled out a chair & sat down again, thumbing the flint of her lighter —

'So what d'you write?'

Němec shrugged —

'Whatever comes into my head.'

The waitress pulled out another joint & lit it. Her eyes fixed on a spot somewhere above Němec's left ear while she held the smoke in, then exhaled. She nodded —

'I can dig that.'

Just then Bill Evans started playing on the radio, something elegiac & slow. Němec brought one of the glasses to his nose, savoured the aroma, sipped. The waitress, he noticed, had one of those Celtic things tattooed on the inside of her wrist — a maze of interwoven red & green. Outside the window, a truck pulled up. Doors slammed. The sound of metal on cobblestones. The waitress stubbed out her joint & waved the smoke away —

'Duty calls,' she sighed & got up. 'Let me know when you need more of those.'

Němec watched her cross the floor to the bar. Ballet slippers, thin legs, elasticised miniskirt (lime green). She took out a rag & began wiping the taps, head cocked to one side so that her hair just grazed the shoulder of her vest. While she wiped she chewed her lip. She barely looked sixteen.

'Hey,' Merkin said, coming through the door with a keg over his shoulder, talking to a delivery guy who was right behind him with a couple of more kegs stacked on a dolly, 'you ever been to one of them dwarf-tossing contests?'

Němec ogled them.

'Nope,' the delivery guy said, 'but I've seen the odd bit of carp-punting…'

The two disappeared into a storage room behind the bar. Reappeared. Went back out, bumping the dolly up the steps.

'Got a cousin up in Jáchymov, breeds fightin' rabbits, you ever wanna come out one day for some hardcore blood-bunnying…'

The door slammed behind them. Němec dug a finger in his ear & stirred it about. He could hear voices outside & expected Merkin to return any moment & then he'd be stuck listening to the man for the rest of the night. He tipped back the slivovice to put himself in the mood, trying at the same time to conjure some sort of believable scenario out of the day's events & maybe an alternative to what was in store. There was still time to catch the second half of the show at the Zrcadlo. Pictures of Alice Steinerová floating in a dressingroom mirror, etc. And afterwards? The location, the lighting & the inner monologue suited to the occasion? Some prospect he'd make.

He hit the second glass. It put hard edges on everything in the room. The waitress whistled along with radio. Coltrane. The riff meandered. Twisted back on itself. It made Němec think of the dwarf, leading him on a fool's whatever, down the garden path, so to speak. But where'd he been coming *from*? People didn't just appear like that, on the street, out of the blue. The saxophone wailed. The sound of Merkin's laughter wafted through the door. Němec stared at the table. Ordinarily it would've served to pass some time, but something was riling him. He pulled a handful of change from his pocket & dumped it beside the empty glasses. The waitress saw it & gave him a vaguely disappointed look.

'Take care of yourself,' she said.

'I'll let you know how it went,' he said, aiming for the steps.

The delivery truck pulled away just as he got to the door. Merkin stepped past him on the way out. His timing couldn't've been better. Only now what? He looked up & down the street. To the left, the street narrowed & ran straight into an apartment block, turning at a rightangle (ᒪ) towards the river. Where the rightangle formed was a garage. Someone coming past *The White Whale* from that direction wouldn't've had too many options, then. It might even be possible to backtrack, get a general sense of the possibilities. Němec had in mind the notion of getting to the bottom of something[*] — meaning the dwarf, the two attaché cases, the rendezvous in the cellar. He couldn't imagine the dwarf had travelled all that far.

As Němec stood there weighing the options, a girl with a terrier appeared through a gap in the garage wall & walked right past him: the terrier had an orange rubber ball in its mouth. Němec watched the two of them continue along the street till they reached the antiquariat where, unlike the dwarf earlier that day, they veered left. So much, Němec thought, for his theory. Curious, he swung his stick in the direction of the garage & walked inside. The place was empty. What at first had seemed like a gap in the wall was in reality the entrance to a passageway that wound through the ground floor of a semi-derelict building — first left & then right — opening into a dank courtyard walled with cracked & peeling stucco the colour of raw sienna & overgrown with weeds. A terrace stood eight feet off the ground, closed on three sides by a crumbling balustrade & on the fourth by a row of French windows, all with their panes smashed. A square of night sky loomed above it, completing the sense of desolation.

On the farther side of the courtyard, the passageway continued, tending once more to the left, past empty display boxes. A middle-aged charlady was

---

[*] One fiasco for the day wasn't enough? [☛]

dragging a broom along the floor, sweeping a pile of litter (cigarette butts, bottle tops, tram tickets, crumpled handbills) from one place to another. She muttered something as Němec passed. *Far from the song-struck charms of spring?* He stopped at the end of the passageway & looked back at the woman bent over her broom, muttering & sweeping. Had he really heard her say what he thought he'd heard? A tram clanged its bell. *Drrrrrrrang!* Němec stepped out onto the sidewalk & found himself between two storefronts: MYDLÁŘ'S KOSHER MEATS on one side & on the other a travel agency, windows festooned with adverts for last-minute flights to Cairo, Sydney, Rome — the Colosseum, Utzon's folly, the great pyramids at Giza, Caracalla's Baths, a camel-train in a desert, remote island beaches with semi-naked bodies cavorting in the sun. *Your breast is like an apple from Australia. Your breasts are like two apples from Australia…* On the wall beside the window, someone had stuck a flyer above a yellow postbox: a comicstrip drawing of a man, suit & tie, face covered in ugly spots, holding up a butcher's cleaver:

Bad skin? Peel it off!
We sell Cheap Knives, call 21619270.

To the left, the tramline tended towards Národní. To the right, up towards Charles Square. Němec couldn't think of any intelligent reason why the dwarf would've made the detour *away* from the tramline only to *return* to it five minutes later, but that didn't mean he hadn't. Němec prepared to retrace his steps. The charlady, meanwhile, had laid down her broom & was kneeling beside the pile of rubbish with a cigarette lighter, trying to get the rubbish to burn. *Click-click-click.* With each *click* she jabbed the lighter forward & simultaneously extinguished the flame.

The smell of burning plastic was already in the air by the time Němec made it back to the courtyard. Exiting the garage, the street was empty. To the left, past a chapel dedicated to the humility of St Michael, the street ran for another three blocks before ending at Wankagasse — in honour of Herr Wenzel (a.k.a. Václav) Wanka, former Golem City mayor back in the days when being a Kraut had its advantages. Němec followed it. At the first intersection, however, he bore left again, following his intuition. This way also ran into a T-junction, formed with Myslíkova Street. Wankagasse also ran into Myslíkova. If the dwarf had come from either direction, the odds, for Němec, lay with turning right —

meaning, towards the river & the tail-end of Žofín Island. And after that?

He stood at the intersection scratching his right ear. On the northwest corner stood an Airfix model shop, its windows filled with WWII tanks, battleships, toy soldiers in different coloured uniforms, Messerschmitts & Lancasters, Howitzers, U-boats & V2 rockets. Unlikely the dwarf had business there, but you'd never know. Attaché case under the counter? A silver robot with coloured lights & dials stood on a shelf beside a remote control handset, a black moulded-plastic box with an aerial sticking out of it: ON SALE, only Kč 3995,- (paintkit included). Opposite, a girl in a white labcoat was kneeling in a window display, undressing a mannequin. Lingerie beneath foxfur, mink, seal, cat, muskrat. He could picture Alice Steinerová, but Faktor's dwarf? Across Myslíkova, a couple of danceclubs with blacked-out windows & extinguished neon. Restaurants. A bakery. A greengrocers. A bank. Nothing that distinguished itself noticeably from anything else.

At the river-end of the street were the Mánes Galleries, flanked to the south by a stone watertower — an exit ramp led past it down onto the quays. Eastwards, Charles Square again, the park, the Town Hall, the hospital, the Faust House, back around in circles. Logic, for what it was worth, pointed west. Němec started out but stopped again almost immediately. *This's pointless, you idiot.* The dwarf could've come from anywhere, he could be wandering around backstreets all night. Not like there was going to be a sign somewhere, LOOKING FOR A DWARF? WE PROVIDE… Something was definitely missing from his modus operandi. Well it would be, wouldn't it? Then a bright idea — maybe it was the weed kicking-in, or the double-brandies: *What if, perhaps, from a dwarf's-eye-view…?*

Obligingly, Němec stooped, got down on his knees, on all-fours virtually, scoped the situation anew. The sidewalk channelled all things westwards, half of everything hidden now behind a wall of parked cars. He was hunched down like that when a babička, red shopping cart in tow, veered past, giving him the narrowest of berths, a malevolent eye cast down at his dogself. The impulse to growl, bark after her, chase her down the street, if only for the hell of it. It was just then, of course, that a black Mercedes with Interior Ministry plates swung through the intersection, slowing with the traffic. From his half-crouched position Němec saw — was certain he saw — through a lowered back window, the hair-oiled pate of the State's attorney, Doctor of Jurisprudence J. Bareš &, seated beside, unlit pipe protruding from beard, who but that murky monarchist & demi-mogul, *Mistah* Viktor Faktor his Hunself?

'Well I'll be buggered! Of all the…'

But Němec's monologue was cut short by a courier on a racing bike, careening out of nowhere. A saddle-bag caught him square in the face & sent him sprawling through the doorway of the Airfix Shop, hat, walkingstick & all. The grey-haired character behind the shop counter eyeballed him over a pair of misty bifocals & a model-aeroplane catalogue —

'Anything in particular, was it? Or just browsing?'

By the time Němec regained the sidewalk, the Mercedes was nowhere in sight. He began to wonder if he'd imagined it. Maintaining a conventional upright posture this time, he hobbled as quickly as he could river-wise. Traffic came & went. No sign of the Merc in either direction along the embankment.

He crossed with the lights. The Mánes Galleries were lit up like floating glass boxes. A sculpture exhibition by someone called Wasserturm was in process of closing-up — totem heads welded from scrap-metal, painted red & mounted on oversized drillbits, like giant wreckingyard phalluses. Through the windows, workmen in overalls could be seen packing them away in wooden crates full of straw, like Baby Jesus in the manger. Sloping away from the Galleries, the exit ramp pointed down under Jiráskův Bridge to where the riverboats moored.

The air down by the water tasted like chemicals they used to poison rats.[*] A row of cars double-parked under the bridge choked the way. Němec edged between them — a couple were Mercs, but none with Interior Ministry plates. On the far side of the bridge, the lit squares of restaurant windows — music spilling from a doorway. Flashback to searchlights on the river, a film crew, the quay under siege. Flashback to Alice Steinerová on a movie poster. Not hide nor hair, however, of Faktor's entourage. *Well you can kiss that bright idea goodbye, kiddo.* He gazed in at the restaurant, mentally counting the change in his pocket for a last drink or two to round-off a quality evening. It might've happened, too, were it not for the sound of a car horn calling his attention to a point further along the quay & a black Merc pulling away from where a barge was moored, three shapes mounting the gangplank.

The shapes — two tall, one short — entered the pilot's house & disappeared below decks. Though to all appearances just another bucket of rust,

---

[*]

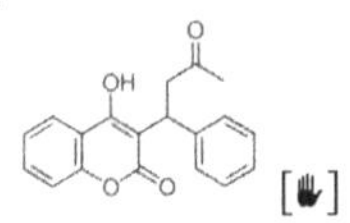

a string of coloured balloons & a blue neon sign over the pilot's house proclaimed it to be, in fact, the

ORFEO & EURIDICE FLOATING THEATRE

The name reminded him of those bittersweet tears of the Prof's mythical maiden. On the off-chance, Němec hobbled down the quay & went aboard. The gangplank creaked. Invisible carp stirred the water beneath. Inside the pilot's house, a woman in Renaissance costume was offering quarter-priced tickets. Němec handed her the last of his drink money in return for a square of white paper with an etching of two figures on it — man & woman — & a fork-tongued asp slithering between them. The seat number was a snake twisted into a double-loop with its tail in its mouth. He descended the narrow steps below deck — at the foot of which, an equally narrow galley. A sign saying THEATRE⟫→ pointed to a curtain at the far end. Němec prodded his way through the gloom with his stick. Behind the curtain was an old storage tank that'd been converted with a makeshift stage under the bows, footlit by a row of funerary candles in red-tinted glass jars.

As he groped his way towards his seat, a voice came out of the shadows.

'Who,' it demanded, 'are you?'

Immediately the stage came to life. Three mannequins — articulated dolls with strings attached: a man-lion, a scarecrow & a robot — jostled one another, looking about in a state of panic. Again the voice boomed.

'WHO?'

The puppets tripped, ran in circles, huddled behind the stage drapes. Then on came a little doll-faced girl with a white mutt in her arms, waving an admonishing finger at the ceiling —

'Oh-oh-oh! You ought to be ashamed of yourself, frightening them like that, when they came for your help!'

The dog yapped.

'Silence!' commanded the voice. 'The beneficent Oz...'

Němec found his seat in the second row, but as it happened he could've sat just about anywhere — the place was all but empty & the show was pretty much done. Only the very back row was taken up, by an elderly couple with a child squeezed between them, who was avidly picking its nose & eating it.

48

<u>ROSES ARE RED</u>

A dressing room beneath the rear stage of a theatre. The space should
be simple: a mirror with lights, a makeup table with cupboards, a
swivel chair, a clothes rack with costumes, etc., an old divan.
There're two doors, one at the back of the stage, which opens onto a
stairway, the other at stage left. Old playbills posted around.

The stage remains dark for some time, except for a light coming
from the stairway. The audience hears footsteps, a woman's highheeled
shoes, coming from above. Pause. The loud report of a gun being
fired. The sound of a body collapsing on the floor. Long pause. A low
indistinct smattering of applause, fading off. A moment later a
woman enters the dressing room from the stairs. We see her in
silhouette on the stairway, one hand fumbling for a light switch.
It's ALICE. When the lights come up we see she's dressed in a grey,
knee-length skirt with matching suit jacket, white blouse & three
inch highheels. Her hair, which is actually a wig, is blonde,
arranged at the back of her head in a bun, with a hairnet. It's clear
from the way she's dressed that she's supposed to be the secretary of
a highranking official. One side of her face is covered with blood
from a serious head wound. As she enters, she catches her heel on the
last step & almost falls through the doorway. Regaining her balance,
we see that she's holding a nickelplated pistol in her right hand.
She crosses the dressing room unsteadily & slumps down on the divan,
the pistol dangling from a now apparently lifeless hand. After some
time she straightens herself up, rises from the sofa, shakes her head,
& crosses to the makeup table, sits, placing the pistol to one side.
After regarding herself in the mirror, she then removes the wig &
begins also to remove her makeup.

Throughout, a figure has been standing partially concealed by the
clothes rack. It's JAN. He's dressed in a badly worn brown leather
overcoat, worker's clothes & boots. His hair is close cropped & he
sports a short goatee. It's clear that he hasn't slept in several days.
In one of the pockets of his coat there's a rather desultory-looking
bouquet of red roses, which has quite obviously been scrounged from
somewhere. With one hand he clasps, inside his coat, a sheaf of papers
that we see in due course. He steps from the shadows. As ALICE begins
removing her makeup she notices JAN's reflection in the mirror,
looks up at him, then turns her attention back to the mirror. JAN
moves out into the middle of room & watches A from behind.

JAN: I've seen you do that before, haven't I?
ALICE: Have you?
JAN: Don't you ever get tired of it?
ALICE: Tired? (Pause. Laughs sarcastically.) The beauty of
          theatre, my dear, is one gets the endless satisfaction of

being able to blow one's brains out nightly on cue. The
downside is being obliged to go on living afterwards.

JAN: I meant Ibsen.
ALICE: I have a theory about writers...
JAN: Do you?
ALICE: ...but it would bore me too much to tell you.
JAN: Some people are aroused by boredom.
ALICE: And whole nations die of it. Did you come here to
          philosophise?
JAN: (Smirks. With his free hand he takes the bouquet from his
          pocket.) You know, that wig makes you look just like the
          General-Secretary's wife.
ALICE: (Picks the wig up off the dressing table & holds it in
          front of her in one hand, regarding it: Hamlet, the
          graveyard scene.) Alas poor Viktoria Petrovná, I knew her
          well... (Throws the wig down & stares back at JAN in the
          mirror. He has moved up behind her, the bouquet drooping
          in his right hand, the other hand clutching something
          inside his coat.) You're not trying to impress me with
          those are you? I detest flowers as much as I detest
          flattery.
JAN: Why? Don't actresses exist to be flattered?
ALICE: The Party nomenklatura exists to be flattered. An actress
          merely exists to give flesh to men's fantasies.
JAN: (Harshly.) Men? Insects you mean. Lice, rats, cockroaches...
          (He turns, tosses the bouquet on the divan.) Oh, & theatre
          critics. (He takes out the sheaf of paper that he has been
          clutching inside his coat & slips it discreetly behind a
          cushion.)
ALICE: You should be kinder. The world couldn't exist without
          insects.
JAN: Nor only <u>with</u> insects.
ALICE: (Crosses the room to one of the clothes racks.) You're so
          literal.
JAN: And you're in love with the past, Alice. But it's finished.
          Your genteel Ibsen is finished, too. We live in a different
          age now. An age of... of political pornography. Of eyes
          glued to peepholes. A nation of fervid masturbators
          terrified they'll be caught in the act. Red handed!
ALICE: (Aimlessly rearranging the clothes on the clothes hangers.)
          Did you read that somewhere, or did you make it up all by
          yourself?
JAN: You need to face facts, Alice. There's no hope for you here
          anymore. This place, it's nothing but a gilded cage. Not
          even gilded. At least in a real prison you'd know what's at
          stake.
ALICE: (Tired, her face suddenly haggard, her voice low.) And what
          is at stake?
JAN: (Hissing.) Everything! Can't you see?
ALICE: It's too much, Honza. I'm weak. It's enough to get from one
          performance to the next. Everything else is... Oh leave me
          alone!
JAN: (He begins to move towards her.) It would be so easy for

you to love me, Alice.
ALICE: (Turns her back. JAN hesitates. Gradually a sad smile
            creases ALICE's lips.) And what would that achieve? (JAN
            stares at his hands, then turns back to the dressing table,
            looks at himself in the mirror, laughs harshly.)
JAN: A poet once said that if the fool were to persist in his
            folly, he would become wise. Do you think he was right? (He
            turns to face her again.)
ALICE: (Regaining her composure.) You seem to be in a dangerous
            mood tonight.
JAN: Don't worry. I'm not going to do anything.
ALICE: (Thoughtfully.) No. (Long pause.) Jan? (Pause.) You should
            leave now, Jan. I... I need to change.
JAN: Yes. Change.... We all need to change...
ALICE: (Facing audience.) Do you intend to watch me? (To JAN.) Or
            will you be a good boy & take those wretched flowers back
            to where you found them?
JAN: The Tomb of the Unknown Soldier. The Party was
            thoughtful enough to leave them lying about. (ALICE
            gestures dismissively. JAN goes to leave, stops at the door,
            stage left. Turns. Watches ALICE begin to remove her suit
            jacket.) By the way, isn't Hedda Gabler supposed to shoot
            herself off stage?
ALICE: (Placing the jacket on a hanger.) You said it yourself. If
            pornography's the order of the day, then let them have
            pornography. Why shouldn't they see everything?
JAN: How very accommodating of you. Who was it who said: <u>I
            despise actors. At the least sign of danger they always
            ally themselves with the audience & betray the author</u>...?
            (Laughs quietly to himself.) You always were
            accommodating, Alička, only with the wrong people. Why
            haven't you ever been so accommodating with me?
ALICE: (Begins to unbutton her blouse. Pauses, her face in her
            hands. Looks up, fatigued.) I'm tired, Honza. (She rubs her
            temples with her hands.) Every night... I have these
            terrible headaches. I wish they'd go away.
JAN: (He looks at her unsympathetically for a moment without
            moving.) You should hold the gun further from your head.
ALICE: (She closes her eyes & continues removing her blouse.) And
            what if I missed? (JAN stares uncomprehendingly at her,
            then silently goes out stage left. ALICE opens her eyes &
            continues undressing. She crosses back to the dressing
            table in, e.g., underwear & stockings. She searches her
            handbag for some painkillers, takes out a bottle of pills &
            swallows a handful of them. Grimaces. Then takes a kimono
            from a hook on the wall beside the dressing mirror. She
            puts the kimono on while watching herself closely in the
            mirror. Then removes her stockings, draping them over the
            back of the chair. As she removes the stockings, the lights
            begin to fade to green... Footlights up, suffusing the
            dressing room with a surreal chiaroscuro. The TWO IVANS
            enter silently from the stairway: they're dressed in
            evening attire with carnations in their lapels -- one is

tall & thin, the other short & fat -- one well groomed, the
other slovenly -- both wearing moustaches. They have the
appearance of a two-man vaudeville routine.)

IVAN 1:   Well, well, well. I do hope we are not interrupting you,
           Miss Gabler. Ah! (Picking up the roses from the divan &
           smelling them.) An admirer! (Hands the bouquet to Ivan 2
           who sniffs at it & then tosses it over his shoulder.) But
           that's hardly surprising, n'est-ce pas? (He stands close
           behind ALICE, casting his gaze around the room, taking it
           in.) You are, after all, as our newspapers so discreetly
           proclaim, a most <u>handsome</u> woman. (He picks up one of
           ALICE's stockings.) One might even say, desirable, hmm? (He
           lets the stocking fall back.)

IVAN 2:   (Sneezes.) Shite! (Pulls a handkerchief from his breast
           pocket & loudly blows his nose. Looks at the handkerchief,
           wrinkles his face in disgust, then stuffs the handkerchief
           back in his pocket. During this, Alice leans forward to
           grip her dressing table & keep her balance. She breathes
           erratically.)

IVAN 1:   Tut-tut! Don't let my colleague's boorishness upset you,
           Miss Gabler. He was deprived, you see, in his childhood. All
           men are born equal, so they say, but that's where the
           similarity ends. Is that not true, brother.

IVAN 2:   Sounds like a lot of bollocks to me. (He has begun sniffing
           at the clothes racks. During what follows he randomly
           takes costumes from their hangers, sniffs at them dog-
           like, then tosses them on the floor. During the ensuing
           dialogue he actually takes out his prick & pisses on them.)

IVAN 1:   There, you see, what did I tell you? (Moves over to divan.
           Sits.) I don't suppose you mind if we make ourselves at
           home? (Makes himself comfortable.) Very nice. (To ALICE.) A
           very nice arrangement you have here, Miss Gabler. Not
           everyone can be as fortunate as you are. Eh? (To IVAN 2.)
           What do you say, brother?

IVAN 2:   This stuff smells queer.

IVAN 1:   Ah. Never smelt a lady's perfume before, you see. Nothing
           too fancy for my brother here, eh? Hero of the
           proletariat, he is.

ALICE: (She rights herself, straightening her kimono. Ignoring
           them, she sits & lights a cigarette. Very softly she begins
           to hum & then sing to herself.) <u>Und der Haifisch, der hat
           Zähne, und die trägt er im Gesicht. Und MacHeath, der hat
           ein Messer, doch das Messer sieht man nicht...</u>

IVAN 1:   (While ALICE sings.) You know, there's something I've been
           wondering. When you put that toy gun to your pretty
           little head, Miss Gabler, & blow your pretty little brains
           out... figuratively speaking, of course... I've been
           wondering... at that moment... you understand?... what it is
           that you <u>feel</u>. I mean, as an artist... imitating life... I
           mean, death, Miss Gabler. What does it feel like? (Pause.)
           Oh, don't get me wrong, Miss Gabler. It isn't that I doubt
           (gesturing at the stage above)... that all of this is... real.
           But is it <u>as real</u> as actions... out there... made by ordinary

people... in the <u>real world</u>?

ALICE: (Stubs out her cigarette & turns to look at herself in the mirror, applies some lipstick & mascara.)

IVAN 2: What's all this junk for anyway? (Holds a lowcut sequinned dress up against his torso, as though modelling it.) How do I look?

IVAN 1: A sight for sore eyes.

IVAN 2: (Tosses the dress on the pile already growing on the floor. Begins to stalk across the room, his eyes fixed on ALICE's face in the mirror.) I reckon she'd be a sight for sore eyes.

IVAN 1: Easy brother. We don't want to frighten the young lady. Do we, Miss Gabler?

IVAN 2: I don't reckon she's been listening to a word you've said.

IVAN 1: Ah, you see, Miss Gabler, how difficult it is to inspire confidence these days? An audience can be so susceptible... to misunderstanding.

IVAN 2: Not one word, I reckon.

IVAN 1: Misunderstandings can be dangerous, Miss Gabler. It's the responsibility of a true artiste, wouldn't you say, to prevent misunderstandings... To prevent people from becoming confused... in the wrong ways. Of course, we didn't come here to patronise you, Miss Gabler... (IVAN 2 advances towards ALICE. He takes one of ALICE's stockings from the back of her chair & begins winding it around both of his fists.) Merely to suggest a little more... realism... a little more... truth... (IVAN 2 reaches over ALICE's head, the stocking taught between his fists, seemingly about to strangle her. At the last moment, she looks up & registers his presence. She screams, passing out. IVAN 2 catches her, the stocking slipping down across her chest. His effort to keep her upright results in a type of grotesque dance, her breasts spilling out. The "dance" ends with IVAN 2 dragging ALICE behind what remains of the clothes rack. There are muffled sounds, followed by silence. IVAN 1 remains seated throughout, his arms spread across the back of the divan, head back, eyes closed. IVAN 2 re-emerges, his suit dishevelled, picking at his front teeth with a toothpick. He goes over to the dressing table, sits, commences combing his hair.)

IVAN 2: Bitches like that always play hard to get.

IVAN 1: Come now brother, we're civilised men.

IVAN 2: Sure. But you ask me, they all deserve a good kick in the cunt.

IVAN 1: Yoohoo! You can come out now, Miss Gabler, no-one's going to hurt you. (Pause. ALICE appears on her hands & knees. She slowly crawls to the front of the stage, facing the audience. Her makeup's ruined. Her hair, kimono, etc. in disarray.) You must excuse us, Miss Gabler, we're not artistes like you are. Merely... amateurs. In the theatre, people are all such... romantics. Yet romanticism, dear Miss, also has its dangers.

ALICE: (Barely audible.) What do you... want...?

IVAN 2:   Did you hear something?
ALICE: (Louder.) What do you want from me?
IVAN 1:   Ah! We want only to be of service to you, Miss Gabler.
ALICE: (Opens her mouth, but is unable to speak.)
IVAN 1:   Isn't there something you want to tell us, Miss Gabler?
           Something that could help you?
ALICE: No! (Shakes her head vigorously.) I don't know anything.
IVAN 2:   (Going through ALICE's handbag, emptying the contents on
           the floor, rifling the drawers of the dressing table, etc.)
           They all say the same fucking thing. Every time I hear
           that, it makes me want to puke. (He stands & crosses the
           room, leans down & shouts into her ear.) You listening to
           me, you bourgeois slut? YOU MAKE ME WANT TO PUKE! (She
           cringes, her body sagging forward. She stares at the
           audience wide-eyed while IVAN 2 goes back to picking the
           room apart.)
IVAN 1:   There! And you were afraid you'd never experience an
           authentic emotion again! See how much better it'd be if you
           co-operated, Miss Gabler?
ALICE: (Long pause.) Yes.
IVAN 1:   Good. I feel we're making genuine progress.
ALICE: Yes.
IVAN 1:   Good! I'm glad you agree. (Pause.) So, enough fun & games,
           then?
ALICE: Yes.
IVAN 1:   Very good. (To IVAN 2.) Have you found it?
IVAN 2:   Must've taken it with him. (Holds up the pistol for IVAN 1
           to see, hands it to him. He turns back towards ALICE, takes
           another toothpick from his pocket & idly picks at his
           front teeth, watching her.)
IVAN 1:   (Turns the pistol over in his hands, feeling its weight, a
           faint grin on his lips.) Well, that doesn't really matter,
           does it Miss Gabler? No. You've already told us everything
           we need.
ALICE: (Looks confused.) What? But I don't know anything.
IVAN 2:   (Spits.) There she goes again. Denial of all knowledge.
IVAN 1:   But Miss Gabler, we're not interested in what you know,
           we're only interested in the facts.
IVAN 2:   Hard facts.
IVAN 1:   (Stands & walks to stage front, kneels beside ALICE,
           holding the gun in front of her so that she can see it. He
           leans close to her.) For example, Miss Gabler, what do you
           call this?
ALICE: (Hesitates.) It's part of my act.
IVAN 1:   Your act, Miss Gabler?
ALICE: My character, the performance. You know!
IVAN 1:   (He slams the gun down on the floor.) Do you mean to say,
           deception, Miss Gabler? Subterfuge?
ALICE: I mean...
IVAN 2:   What do you mean, Miss Gabler?
ALICE: But it isn't real!
IVAN 1:   What's not real? We're real, aren't we? You're real. This
           room is real. Did you think, perhaps, that all of this was

only in your putrid imagination?

ALICE: (Pushes herself up from the floor, shouts.) Stop it! You're not making any sense! (Lights dim. Spot up on ALICE staring blindly at the audience. Then fade. The stage is in darkness. Volta enters from stairs -- a man in his late fifties, tall, thin, with glasses, dressed conservatively in a grey suit, but with a colourful bowtie -- light from the stairway falling behind him. He fumbles for a lightswitch. Lights-up as at start. The dressing room in disarray. He sees Alice, hesitates, startled, a look of sadness gradually taking over. He crosses the room towards her, his hand reaching out in an indecisive gesture.

VOLTA: Aličko?

ALICE: (Confused, as if waking from a dream.) Who's there? (Looks up at VOLTA, without at first recognising him.) What do you want? (Glances around, sits up, appears to get her bearings.) Oh God. (Presses her knuckles to the sides of her head.) How my head aches. (Lets her hands drop to the floor.)

VOLTA: (Reaching down he picks up the pistol from where it lies beside her, looks at it questioningly, then puts it in his pocket.) Can you stand? (Takes her arm. Unsteadily she stands. She draws her kimono close around her & laughs confusedly, avoiding his looks.) Did something happen? (Pulls away from him & rushes to the dressing table, sees her reflection & recoils. VOLTA crosses behind her & stands with his hands on her shoulders. ALICE searches for a cigarette, lights one, begins wiping her face with a tissue. After a moment her composure, much exaggerated, returns.)

ALICE: Ha! If only there wasn't so much clutter everywhere! (Flicks at the mess on her dressing table. She gets up, searching for something, & finds the bouquet on the floor. She picks it up & looks at it, shaking her head.)

VOLTA: (Solicitously.) You must be happy that someone brought you flowers.

ALICE: (Her voice suddenly hard.) It was an unbearable performance. The worst, Níko! (Her voice shifting in emotional register.) I can't stand it anymore. (She strikes him across the chest with the bouquet, falls into his arms, sobbing like a child -- then just as suddenly pulls away, composes herself. Rushes across to the clothes racks & begins searching through the pile of costumes till she finds the red sequined dress.) Why don't we go out, the way we used to, & drink Champagne?

VOLTA: (Laughs uneasily.) Are you joking?

ALICE: Can't we at least pretend?

VOLTA: I thought you were sick of pretending.

ALICE: Sick, sick, sick. You're right. Everything's so confusing. I wish these pains would go away.

VOLTA: You shouldn't put the gun so close...

ALICE: (Narrowing her eyes at him.) Strange. Somebody said that exact same thing to me, just this minute. Right where you're standing. (An abrupt whinnying laugh.) Why don't you put on something quiet.

VOLTA: If it would help, why not. (He goes over to a cupboard &, out of view, puts on a slow Kurt Weil number. VOLTA adjusts the volume till it's barely audible...)

ALICE: Help, help, help. You're always so reasonable Níko. So <u>helpful</u>. I don't deserve you at all, do I? (While VOLTA has his back turned, she shrugs off the kimono & steps into the red dress, an early '50s re-imagining of late Weimar kabaret.) Come & zip me up. (She makes vague dance movements, eyes closed, facing the audience. VOLTA crosses behind her, his face blank. After watching her for several moments he walks up behind her, places a hand on the back of her neck, & zips up her dress with the other. ALICE leans her weight against him, her head tilted back, lips parted. As he moves to kiss her shoulder she lets out a deep-throated laugh & pulls away. He stands there watching as she dances a slow circle around him, humming to the music out of time. The piece ends, silence envelops them -- they both stand looking out at the audience.) Níko... I'm tired of all this. I mean... All we do each night is humiliate ourselves. They laugh at us. Besides, the only people who show up are the same rotten informers over & over. We should all be on a first name basis by now.

VOLTA: Oh, their names are never that interesting. (Laughing weakly.) You know. Boris... Ivan... Honza... (Pause.) A theatre can't survive without an audience.

ALICE: (Turns to him.) Why don't we just shut it down?

VOLTA: We can't... They won't let us. They'll keep us doing the same old thing till they decide otherwise. (Pause.) Art has its price, you know, even in a socialist utopia like ours... Besides, there's the others to think about. What would they do? They're actors. Without work, they're nothing. You want them to shovel coal?

ALICE: You know that's not what I meant. It's the same for all of us. But this... This isn't theatre anymore, not even bad theatre -- it's just politics.

VOLTA: (Smiling. Takes her in his arms.) My poor, innocent Alice! (She is about to say something but is interrupted by a knock on an outer door. They both look up expectantly. More knocking. VOLTA glances towards the stairway. Waits. Disengages himself.) Everyone must've gone home. I'll go up & see who that is. Will you be okay?

ALICE: So soon?

VOLTA: What do you mean?

ALICE: (In the character of Hedda Gabler.) Doesn't it feel like a whole eternity since we last talked to each other?

VOLTA: (Obliging, as Judge Brack.) Between ourselves? Alone together, you mean?

ALICE: (She looks at the ceiling, wistfully.) Always alone, & never by ourselves. (To VOLTA.) Don't leave me, Níko!

VOLTA: (Soothingly.) Shhh! (Pause.) Won't you be alright?

ALICE: (Resigned.) Yes.

VOLTA: Sure?
ALICE: I'm sure. (VOLTA goes out. ALICE walks over to the dressing
          table, finds a cigarette among the mess, lights it, sits
          staring at her reflection in the mirror. As she does this,
          the lights dim to green. ALICE freezes. Several moments
          pass. Lights up. JAN enters from stage left, looks around,
          walks to divan & checks that the papers he has hidden
          behind the cushion are still in place. ALICE, waking from
          her reverie, sees him, is briefly startled, then feigns
          indifference.) You again?
JAN: Have they gone?
ALICE: How... did you know?
JAN: They've been after me since I crossed the border. I saw
          them when I came in, they were staking the place out. I
          didn't think they'd seen me.
ALICE: Oh that's just terrific. Didn't think! <u>Didn't think</u>! (Stubs
          her cigarette out violently.) Now do you know what'll
          happen? We'll have those idiots all over us, day & night.
          They'll be everywhere. Everywhere! Under our bloody beds!
          (She stands looking at JAN, as though she is about to hit
          him, then tugs the kimono tighter around her & marches
          past him towards the stairs, reaches for the door handle,
          falters...)
JAN: Do you always play for effects that bring down the house?
          (She stares at him: if looks could kill. She is about to
          speak when VOLTA enters, holding a letter. He looks past
          ALICE & sees JAN.)
VOLTA: You?
JAN: Father!?
ALICE: Marvellous! A family reunion. (She stalks back to her
          dressing table.)
VOLTA: What are you doing here?
ALICE: Yes! What <u>are</u> you doing here, Jan, if we may be permitted
          to ask?
JAN: There's no need to lose your head. The cops don't know
          anything. It's just routine. If they're looking for me, it's
          obvious they'd have come here sooner or later...
VOLTA: Ah! An interesting coincidence... (The situation quickly
          dawning on him.) But this time it appears to be me they're
          interested in. (Holding up the letter.)
ALICE: What is it? (Crosses the room, takes it from him.)
VOLTA: A personal invitation. The Minister for the Interior
          requests the pleasure of my company... At the soonest
          possible convenience, it would seem.
JAN: That's unusually efficient.
ALICE: Now you see what you've gone & done!
VOLTA: We must all remain calm, Alice.
ALICE: You could at least have warned us.
VOLTA: The boy didn't know. Besides, it has nothing to do with
          him. I've been expecting this for... some time. (To JAN.) You
          came alone?
JAN: Yes.
VOLTA: And you were followed, you say, by the police? But what do

they want from you?
JAN: Oh nothing really. Only the small matter of a manuscript...
VOLTA: (Perplexed.) You mean... A report, I suppose? About the situation? For the opposition in exile?
JAN: No. Not exactly... It's... Well, it's a play.
ALICE: A _play_? That's ridiculous.
JAN: Why?
ALICE: You said yourself, the theatre's finished! Or have you forgotten already?
JAN: The _old_ theatre's finished. What's needed now is something new, radical, something that takes a risk, that can set people free of... of all this!
ALICE: (She backs away from him.) You're mad.
VOLTA: Wait. (Confused.) You mean to say... What exactly is this... _play_?
JAN: You'll see... (The sound of knocking again. Louder.)
VOLTA: Impatient as ever. (Adopting a faintly paternal tone.) I suppose it'll have to wait. I would've liked to hear about this idea of yours, but my time's already up. If only the world wasn't in such a rush to come to an end, eh?
ALICE: Did the Minister send his personal chauffer?
JAN: Personal undertaker, you mean. (VOLTA gives him a weary look.) At least you'll get to go in style...
VOLTA: With a bang, not with a whimper, eh? (He glances at his watch.) Well, I'd better not keep myself in suspense. The hour of truth, as they say, is always such a disappointment.
ALICE: Don't go!
VOLTA: And put you at risk as well? (Softer.) Forget about me, Alice. I can look after myself. (VOLTA kisses her lightly on the top of the head. He's about to go when he remembers the gun in his pocket. Takes it out, looks at it thoughtfully, then puts it on the dressing table. He gives JAN a significant look.) _Take care of her_. (JAN returns his look blankly. ALICE moves to hold onto VOLTA but JAN holds her back. VOLTA leaves. We hear his voice from the stairway.) The show must go on! (ALICE stares hopelessly after him. Crumples the letter in her hand, crosses back to dressing table, slumps into chair. Tosses letter at the mirror. Freeze. Lights fade, green spot up on ALICE. Footlights, as previously. The two IVANS enter from stage left: brief pantomime. They exit. Lights dim. Beat. Lights up. JAN & ALICE as before.)
JAN: (With a certain bravado.) Well now, how about a drink? (She doesn't respond. He searches among the shelves, etc. Finds a bottle of Slivovice, some glasses.) Ah, old faithful! (To ALICE.) Don't fret, he can look after himself. They're probably just testing the water, so to speak. (She shudders. He pours two glasses, holds one out for ALICE. She looks at it blankly, then finally takes it from him.)
ALICE: (Tonelessly.) That's easy for you to say... God knows what they'll do to him... Don't you even care?
JAN: It's because I care that I came here, you know that. (ALICE

glares at him. JAN ignores it, raises his glass in a toast.
Ironically.) Here's to the beautiful heroine!

ALICE: How dreary. Why not... to a glorious future?

JAN: Ah, yes, the good old future, long may it prosper! (Drinks.
ALICE sets hers down on the dressing table without
drinking any. His tone suddenly becomes earnest.) I love
you, Alice.

ALICE: Is that the best you can manage?

JAN: (Confiding, but with increasing ardour.) Something's about
to happen. Something big. I can't say what. But... The truth
is I mightn't have the chance to see you for a long time.
That's why I came...

ALICE: Still concocting your little melodramas, Honzíku?
Gestures, gestures. You think gestures can change the
world?

JAN: (Pompously.) Soon the time will come, Alice, when it'll be
necessary even for you to make a choice.

ALICE: That almost sounds like a... haha... a threat!

JAN: Not a threat...

ALICE: Besides... I made my choice long ago. I've loved Níko as much
as I could love any man. It's too late for me. As you so
aptly put it, my time's past, we've already lost, but Níko &
I still have each other. What else is there to believe in?
(Pause.) Belief's such a sinister word. There'll always be
ideas to suffer for. Abstractions. An insurrection of
words, words, words. Your... manuscript! You'd risk people's
lives, for some cheap little manuscript?

JAN: How sentimental. The world isn't a nice little drama by
Ibsen, you know. Words have consequences. In the theatre
of life there're real bullets. People die.

ALICE: How strange of you to say so.

JAN: Yes, Alice, people do die for what they believe in.

ALICE: People die anyway. It doesn't matter what they believe in.
(He is about to respond when they are interrupted by the
sound of breaking glass. Both look up.) My God! (She rushes
to the stairs, goes out, comes back in quickly.) It's them.
They're smashing the place up! (She looks around
frantically.) Shouldn't you hide somewhere?

JAN: I refuse to hide.

ALICE: This is no time for stupidity...

JAN: On the contrary. (He pulls a revolver from his coat &
heads towards the stairs. Stops, turns back to ALICE.) You
know, I really do love you. (Exits.)

ALICE: (Stands there confused, staggers, slumps onto the divan.
Suddenly she straightens up, eyes wide. She reaches behind
her & pulls out the sheaf of papers JAN has hidden behind
the cushion. Stares at it. The lights fade to green. She
stands, slowly walks to the middle of the room her eyes
glued to the manuscript. Something dawning on her. Freeze.
Enter: the two IVANS from behind, stairs & left, crossing
the room on tiptoes. As they do so, carrousel music fades
up: a green spot follows them as they begin a slow,
somewhat satirical pas de deux... They are halfway across

the stage when something crashes loudly upstairs: music &
spotlight off. Startled, ALICE drops the manuscript on the
floor. They all stare at it. Brief tableau; ALICE again
freezes. The IVANS exit on opposite sides. Fade, & then...
Lights up as JAN staggers in to stage-front, stops, stares
blankly out at the audience.) What is it?

JAN: He's up there. (Pause. ALICE looks at him expectantly.) Up
there. In the rafters. He's hung himself. (Mockingly.) He's
dead! (Pause. He shouts at her.) Didn't you hear me? _He's_
DEAD!

(ALICE rushes out. JAN stares at the manuscript lying on
the floor. Quickly gathers it up, stuffs it inside his coat,
& leaves stage left. As he does so, we notice that he has
begun quietly laughing to himself. At the same time we
hear ALICE scream. Silence. Several moments pass. Then, as
at start, she enters from stairs, staggers into the
dressing room, crosses, slumps in her chair. Her face is
blank. Above there is the sound of footsteps: someone
running, two people in pursuit. Voices. A scuffle. During
this, ALICE stares at the gun on the dressing table. Picks
it up. Looks at it. Lifts the gun to her temple. Waits. The
sound of heavy footsteps comes from the top of the
stairway. She pulls the trigger. There's a loud gunshot
offstage. ALICE stares. Beat. She pulls the trigger again:
there's a click. Beat. She looks at the gun, confused. She
begins to cry. The stage door opens & the two IVANs enter,
they both carry revolvers.)

IVAN 1:   Well now, Miss Gabler, playing with pistols again?
(All freeze. Lights down. Canned applause ...)

Curtain call: Carousel music. After several moments, lights up on
stage, green filter. Actors unfreeze. ALICE walks to stage front. She
bows. From audience, the "director" (e.g.) hands a bouquet of red roses
to ALICE. Meanwhile the two IVANs dance a mannered pas de deux,
joined from stairs & stage left by JAN & VOLTA. All end at stage
front. All bow, etc. Suddenly ALICE raises a hand to the side of her
head & collapses. Several moments of confusion. ALICE is carried off,
stage left. Fade. At end of music, house lights up, etc.

g. The Poisoned Pawn

49

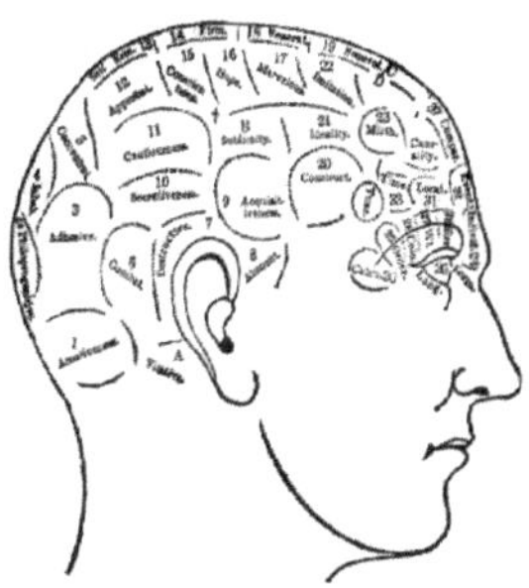

Volta paced the room, matched by his shadow along the wall. Němec decided the Doc didn't look happy to see him. It'd been a while. There was something ridiculous about the entire situation, like he was a child all over again about to be given the third degree. Perhaps the Engineer of Human Souls felt neglected. Perhaps he'd come to the conclusion Němec's head was no less full of putrid slime than everyone else's. *My oh my, you really ARE a stupid filthy little turd after all.* As if to prove the point, somewhere in that dubious squillhead of his one of the Bugman's limericks was going round in circles:

> *There once was a young nurse from Zlín,*
> *who kept her snatch very clean —*
> *she'd scrub twice an hour,*
> *with a brush and a scour,*
> *but at night she preferred a good ream, duh-dum…*

The official phrenologists who visited the Home on a monthly basis used to like holding Němec up as an example of the counter-revolutionary bourgeois parasite *in utero*, so to speak, the diabolic egg waiting to hatch, programmed in its very genome by 1. a wilful subversion of the People & the State, 2. a congenital exceptionalism, 3. an ingrained unnatural attachment to the first-person pronoun singular, 4. a characteristic refusal to muck in with all the other proles to get the collective dirty work done of building the Great Socialist Utopia. Well it was flattering nonetheless to be regarded as the brains of the family, *hehe.* He was stood in the corner every other day to commemorate the crimes of his parents & of his parents' parents, *ad absurdum,* till he forgot why they'd made him stand there in the first place (History after all being 99% tedium) & hatched stories in his head, about some squill-afflicted kid not unlike himself who comes up with a brilliant escape plan & breaks out of the Home by climbing inside a toilet bowl where he discovers the *real* Workers Paradise they'd been hiding there all along:

Bluegrass on the Sázava River, butterflies on swaying dendronites, deep down where sunrays never penetrate, but other sources of incandescence, more illuminating than light, so to speak (*radium green, diddlediddle, potassium blue…*) — like a cloister in an octopus' garden, a bower of lost illusions, dead letters, feigned affections, chastity belts, stethoscopes, scythes & sledgehammers, periscopes, spycameras, thumbscrews, babies' bottles, handcuffs, mislaid housekeys, keys to the kingdom, backdoorkeys, keys for closets, wire coathangers, doorknobs, combination locks & aluminium spoons, forks, knives, tangled vines & bright mantillas of mottled fungus, beetles swimming backstroke, jackdaws in ermine, serenading fish & urchins & crabs weaving in & out among the fluted columns & polished fruit of this aquatic arcadia, this cornucopia of immaculate blobs, beloved turds, joyful tears & seraphic secretions: the opposite, in fact, of everything miserable & unavailing, ill-favoured, violent, antipathetic, of that hated home-sweet-home where every private thought was a threat or source of shame, & selfknowledge was a game you played to lose that never depended on the rules but only on their exploitable implications…

Down there in the shit it was easy to imagine a Better Place — where all the little unredeemed selves turned to gold like they did in fairytales, before the Great Collectivised Venture turned the fairytale world upsidedown by sheer force of Realism's Five Year Plan, a genuine fucking masterstroke — the New Ordure with its New Myth — coprolitic fruit abundant upon the forbidden tree — God's doppelgänger sticking his prick in your ear, *in loco parentis,* so to speak, whispering of untold pleasures, *Eat it, my lovelies! Pluck it, my pretty little fuckwits!* And they'd all sing happily in their debollocked falsettos:

> *Who's that in the showerblock fumblin' the soap?*
> *Did your mama wear her knees out on the floor before she croaked?*
> *Don't tell your baby sister what they'll do to her tonight!*
> *When Uncle Joe comes cruising by, he likes it sweet and tight.*

Did Volta have the slightest suspicion of what Němec was thinking?

With nervous fingers Němec picked behind his right ear, trying to dislodge something, anything, to set his mind straight. Volta saved him the trouble —

'What d'you want?'

'I don't know,' Němec said.

'Then I can't help you,' he replied. 'Can I?'

Outside, it was a typical October, rain streaking the window, lines drawn in the sky like so many puppet strings. Perhaps because the doctor expected him to say something Němec asked —

'D'you think it's possible, not just to hallucinate *things*, but the processes behind them?'

'Why wouldn't it be possible?'

'I don't mean the *reasons* for things. I mean… Their inner life, how they exist when we aren't there to observe them.'

There was a thin line of smoke coming from the tall chimneystacks across the river. The word *desultory* came to mind. Němec turned to look at Volta. He was smoking his cigar with a detached expression on his face.

'There's an old joke,' the doctor said after a while, a weak smile creasing his lips now. 'No doubt you've heard it.'

He turned the end of his cigar against the lip of the ashtray on his desk —

'A man is walking alone through a forest when he slips on a banana skin. There's nobody else around to see him fall on his head. Is it still funny?'

'What would a banana be doing in a forest to begin with?'

Volta set his cigar down against the lip of the ashtray, very slowly, as if it were the most delicate of operations, then reverting to a Vincent Price monotone asked if there wasn't anything else Němec wanted. *Required*, was perhaps the word he used. His look conveyed only fatigue. Němec opened his mouth to speak but nothing came out: another idiotic thought was going around & around in his head, this time about a family of bears in a northern forest waiting for the punchline of Volta's joke to be explained to them — they'd never seen a banana, didn't know what one was.

'You know,' Němec finally said, 'I saw a film the other day. Your former patient, Alice Steinerová was in it. There was one scene, in particular… She was dressed as a Carmelite, kneeling at an altar, while a black devilman with wings came down from the sky or whatever… Sound familiar?'

'Do yourself a favour,' Volta said, standing up. 'Try not to analyse things too deeply. Just try to see them for what they are…'

Without further ceremony he took out his prescription book, scratched at it with a fountain pen, & told Němec to come back in a fortnight —

'If you're still feeling the same way.'

Volta came around the desk towards him, holding a square of paper —

'See if these do any good,' he said.

The act wasn't convincing to either one of them — the pretext seemed to've gotten lost somewhere back along the way, the journey travelled, so to speak. He stuck the prescription in Němec's hand & led him to the door & closed it behind him.

Or perhaps that wasn't what happened at all. Perhaps, after Němec'd described everything about the Prof's Polygraphia, the doctor had simply stated plainly that nothing Němec'd told him made any sense. And Němec'd thought the doctor was probably right. And for several minutes he'd just stood there on the landing outside Volta's office not knowing what to do, wanting only to remove myself from that scene, to disappear through a gap in the stairs or, like Faust, through a crack in the ceiling. *Poof!* But why go to all that trouble when a door would do?

Was Němec having difficulty keeping his version of events in check? And what if Volta was right? What if *he* was the one playing a game with *himself*? Did they have him as wound-up as all that? *Well how d'you tell the difference, kiddo, between*

bein' lost in the woods and just bein' blinded by 'em? Assuming Volta was part of it, what part *was* it? Ever since Alice Steinerová had told him her story, he'd wondered how men like Volta existed. The Resurrection Man, she called him. The Suicide Doctor. Němec flashed on himself six months ago — a speckled egg on a sod, a pulp of shattered vertebrae. Was Volta trying to remake all the dirty, broken, voided bits of humanity into some sort of model homunculus of the World Redeemed? Echoes of *The Abominable Dr Phibes, The Island of Dr Moreau,* Dr Pretorius in *Bride of Frankenstein, The Diabolical Doctor Z and his Fiendish Creation, The Cabinet of Dr Caligari,* Dr Logan from *Day of the Dead.* And why'd *he* been born — he, Němec? The million little swimmers working like idiots against the tide, *contra spemo spermo,* to bring this senseless entity into being. Could the powers who'd made *him* have had some special task in mind? Thrust into this absurdity. First they stole him from himself & turned him into a shadow, then they stole the shadow. *Hehe, not even the shadow of a man, eh kiddo? Says right here in the contract, you're owned, can't even kick the bucket without written approval. Well fancy that.* And all those memories he'd thought belonged to him — made up, to fill the long blank dormitory nights — barred squares of lights drifting across the ceiling, afraid to close his eyes, till they forced him. Thinking (but they weren't even his thoughts) how *in sleep the soul is projected out of the body with the risk that it won't return.* And there, in his ventriloquist's dummysuit, being hoist from the rooftops, up into the grey (would it always be grey?) — as now, over the embankment, the lapping river, the tenebrous tenements, bedevilled mouths agaping. *Do you see it? The thin cord that pulls down the teeth onto the chopping block?*

Facts being facts, there was nothing for certain Němec could say that he actually *knew* about Alice Steinerová, even her name, let alone the things that concerned him most: the nature of her relationship to Volta, or his to the Prof (always somehow implied though never spelled-out) or Bareš the fingerman, or Faktor, purveyor of fandangos, crackpot schemes & so much sand in the eye. You put them all together & what did you get? THE SECRET COMBINE, a between-the-acts magik show with smoke & mirrors: Volta, with his hypnotist's baritone, waving a plastic wand & wafting cigar smoke — Alice Steinerová, all glitter & tinsel & unwrapped flesh — Bareš in the ticket booth counting the stubs — the dwarf popping up when you least expected him, doing cute little panto faces in a pink elasticised jockstrap — & topping the bill, Faktor the impresarious Master of Ceremonials with his Cecil B. DeMille curtain routine down pat, *Ladies and Gents, what you're about to experience is unique in this* *world...* — while last, & quite very much least, he, Němec, the somnambulant stooge in the eighth row who gets coaxed up onto the stage to be sawn in half, while the lovely lady looks appalled & gasps, & the dwarf drops down from the flyloft on a trapeze like a urinating cherub with cardboard wings, & the magician pulls another rabbit from his hat, takes a bow, & him (Němec, lest we forget) left lying there in a mess of bits & pieces that don't add up. It's all a gag of course, the audience laughing their heads off, hahahahaha. *But it's not even funny!* Hohohohoho. He doesn't even realise he's just been turned into a talking fish. Change all the names, transform the events — as in dreams, to reveal their secret ordination? Bugaboo! Hoodihoo!! And not even a real fish, but some rubber inflatable job someone's just pricked a hole in. Squoosh! His entire walk-on (hahahahaha) fin-flapping cameo boiling down to nothing but sea-damp flatulence — a whoopee cushion after the fact — a wispy expiration aspiring to the actor's formidable instinct* of preservation by self-betrayal, fisheyed to the optics of this grotesque guppy's theatrum mundi: of a tremulous fat lip stretched over hook & sinker, the parody of a garbage bin's Christmas dinner — as someone said once upon a tiddlywink...

It brought to mind one of those old stories from the Ghetto, about a beautiful young girl, called Alička, who sold paper roses to passersby on Celetná Street. One cold October evening, as she wended her weary way home through gaslit streets, she noticed a creepy old man following her. It happened again the next day. The third time she saw him following her, she became afraid & tried to run away. But where the street passed beneath the Powder Tower, a pair of carriages had got stuck, & there was no way around them. Poor Alička was trapped. The creepy man was coming closer & so, in a panic, the girl rushed inside the tower & up the stairs. The man was right on her heels, step for step, all the way to the roof. In a panic & with nowhere else to escape to, the girl threw herself from a small window, a desperate prayer on her lips. Jehovah, who'd been watching the entire glib drama unfold, took pity on the poor girl &, as she plunged towards her death, transformed her into a cobblestone.* Which was exactly the kind of thing you could expect from Divine Justice.

---

* A technique, haha, that functions automatically. [☛]
* Cobblestones, it is widely believed, should never be laid in a leap-year, for in a non-leap year one might land on your head. [☛]

The stage of the Zrcadlo Theatre was flanked on either side by narrow balustrades ornamented with cherubs whose wings had mostly cracked a fallen off, relics of bygone days. Němec arrived just as the second act was beginning. The small theatre was dark, bodies pressed close to one another on rows of fold-out metal chairs — someone coughing, someone shifting their weight, whispers, stifled laughter, then the stagelights & a sudden hush, all momentarily obedient to the command of illusionism. There, where nothing was before: a sittingroom, old War-era furnishings, wallpaper & carpet *à la mode*, browns, dark mauves & forest green. In the back wall, a wide doorway. Through it, an office, decorated in the same style, with a paper-strewn writing desk, bookshelves & filing cabinets. Above the desk, a large historical map of Golem City stuck up on the wall, like a picture within a picture, framed by the doorway of the sittingroom, a frame within a frame. Its symmetry was soon broken by the entrance of a charlady, middleaged, stage-left, bearing a large bouquet of roses, red, wrapped in plane white paper. And so it went. The charlady put the roses in a vase & went about her drudgery. To the right, a door banged closed. A youngish-looking man in a grey suit, humming to himself (what was it? *Das Klagende Lied?*), carrying an empty, unfastened briefcase, crossed the inner office to the writing desk. Immediately he began stuffing papers from the desk into the briefcase. Tesman, the programme notes said, a junior minister in the Justice Department.

It wasn't till twenty minutes in, that Alice appeared — dressed as she'd been that first night, in the heroine's role. It was only by the costume that Němec recognised her, even her voice seemed strange. She entered from a second door just as the man with the briefcase & the charlady went out by the first. The floor of the office was strewn with papers. Immediately Hedda-Alice set about gathering them up & sorting them back out into different trays on the writing desk. In the meantime, the man with the briefcase had re-entered, stage right & was standing just outside the doorway watching her. Someone coughed. It must've been the man, because then, as if by involuntary reflex, Hedda-Alice jumped back from the desk, turned to face him & stood there stiffly at attention.

'Goodmorning, Comrade Minister!'

'You're late! Don't you know what's been happening? Slánský's been arrested.'

'Oh no…'

'Oh yes! I want everything that even mentions Slánský removed from the files. Find the duplicates, the triplicates. Do whatever has to be done!'

'Immediately, Comrade Minister... but...?'

'Remember, my dear, if anything happens to me, it'll be your neck too.'

As they spoke, the charlady once again entered, stage left, & stood on the edge of the shadows as if listening. By the end of the first act, *Hedda Gabler* had become a fullfledged intrigue. Brack, the resident N.K.V.D. man, in the company of two goons, had visited with insinuations, innuendos.

'Between ourselves? Alone together, you mean?'

Hedda-Alice had found a loaded gun in the Minister's desk drawer. A Beretta. Known to jam at the most inappropriate times. (For reasons unexplained she pockets it: it reappears later, a *deus ex machina* as they say.) There was no question of whether the performance could be called faithful to the original or not: it was a drama of divergences, echoes, transpositions, elaborately concatenated to the point of grossness — a bureaucratic nightmare from which whole nations were struggling to awake, suffocated by... By what? Inconclusions? Perhaps the director ("Gideon Richter," according to the programme) had gone mad. Or else, mind wandering out through the eyes, Němec'd already begun re-imagining things, seeing the actors perform the lines as *he* would've scripted them — a costume drama holding a mirror up to itself. Even then it barely made sense. As far as he could grasp it, the whole arrangement hinged not on Ejlert Lövborg's lost manuscript, as it did in the play written by Ibsen, but on a secret analysis of a *chess match* — one that hadn't yet actually taken place...

The year: 1952.
The place: Golem City.

It's a match the Soviets are determined to win at All Costs — the headache of *how* having been delegated from Moscow to the local Golem City Politburo, giving rise to a crisis of unprecedented proportions, claims & counterclaims of sabotage & conspiracy which reach to the highest levels: whole ministries have been split right down the middle, between those aligned with the socalled Classicist school (who favour the "closed" form of the game) & those with the Modernists (who favour a more "open" form). A small minority of *Hyper*modernists are keeping mum, wisely biding their time. The Classicists so far have succeeded in retaining the upper hand & heads are expected to roll. Emergency meetings, backroom confabs, heated exchanges over the telephone — hackneyed stageplay to convey a sense of drama missing from the script.

Enter Tesman, a type of Margolius-in-the-making — a nobody in the larger scheme of things, in the right place at the wrong moment, cogging-out another five year plan when the message gets passed down the line that if something isn't done to get the situation in-hand, *he's next*. With the economy of the nation teetering on the brink, he doesn't hesitate to drop everything & dig his childhood copy of Pachman's *Modern Chess Strategy* out of his desk drawer (not noticing — curious oversight this — the missing Beretta). He needs to swat-up fast: Stalin himself has *taken an interest* in the matter — paranoia, always ubiquitous, is becoming palpable — he notices it in the way even the janitor looks at him on his way to the lavatory. Word's evidently gotten around: he's a marked man & knows it. This brings us in on Hedda-Alice —

'Goodmorning, Comrade Minister!'

The last we see of them before the scene change is him instructing her to do whatever's necessary to get a copy of that *damned analysis*. Meanwhile, a thousand kilometres away, the members of the Soviet team, all "Steins," are being given a parting lecture on the tarmac by some brass hat whose making it plain as day they'll be expected to munch cyanide rather than face defeat, before boarding a Defence Ministry Tupolev for Golem City. Their chief adversary: Sammy the capitalist-imperialist chess *Wunderkind*, a soda-chugging eight-year-old from Brooklyn, maybe. It's the first major engagement of the Cold War & orders are orders.

The next scene takes place in a pub near the Castle (Golem City): local watering hole of the Politburo tidewaiters. They're gabbing about the Big Game over pints of Měšťan — they're calling it *The Show* — filling us in on the dramatis personae, the who's-who & who's-got-what-coming. It's hard to keep up with all the innuendo & name-dropping, but there's a lot of mention of the Party Secretary, Slánský (no hope for him this time it seems), & a wink-wink, nudge-nudge about our man Tesman, though no-one's saying anything straight-out. By now unsurprisingly, Slánský's been cast as a Modernist by the old guard (give a dog a bad name), a disciple of that Réti whose views, heretical each & every one, include the decadent notion that chess is an art, not a materialist science: intuition, not ideological principles, was what counted — the objective of winning might even entail (*most foul!*) violating such principles.

Klem Gottwald's never played a game of chess in his life, suspecting the whole thing's a Zhiddish conspiracy — he's got the boys from Bartolomějská Street on the job digging through the files. Never did trust the eggheads. *They wanna play games?* Far as Gottwald's concerned, they should just take the Kid out of the picture — why leave the outcome hanging on a lot of theoretishuns? *I wants results I can sees wit me own eyes, capisce?* But Joe Bolshevik's having none of it, already mind-made-up that it's a matter of Soviet "prestige" — a kid's game! And now being upstaged by that schmuck Slánský & his *analysts*: if the Kid wins, it'll be egg on *his*, Klem Gottwald's, face. He can just picture it: Slánský sniggering up his sleeve — well, if there's eggs gonna get broke, it's him's gonna do the breaking — just watch & learn. In the meantime, he's got Brack breathing down everyone's neck, seeing if he can't root-out Slánský's little cabal of, *what they call themselves? Modernists! Like they take me for a fucking tyrannosaurus rex?* — that Tesman, for example, who smells like a potential rat, a bit *too* eager to tow the party line...

Cut to: an office at the Ministry of Justice. Tesman, not as thick as he looks, has got wind of the whole business & is determined *to go to any lengths* to save his own skin. By temper neither Classicist nor Modernist but rather what Slánský himself would call a crypto-cynic, the junior minister (never for one second doubting this Sammy the Wunderkind, left to his own devices, will have it all over the "Steins," maybe causing World War Three in the process & putting paid to his — Tesman's — little dream of a cottage on the Sázava river) has concocted a ploy of his own, one which relies in no way upon theories about whether it's better to occupy the centre of the board *an sich* (the "Berlin" Gambit, e.g.) or assert control by more remote means of bishops fianchettoed, etc., etc. (the "Cuban" Defence): for though he finds himself ambivalent to the competing orthodoxies of the Opening Game, he's got a native appreciation of middle-game ambiguity — the deceptive combination, the subtleties of positional advantage, & the art of the sacrifice. Call him a pragmatist. In this, his preferred *modus operandi* is a variation on the tried&tested Honey Trap: in the person of his private secretary, Hedda-Alice, he's got it down to a fine art (he'd never have climbed this far, he has to admit, without her), & so it's up to *la femme* (all in a day's work really) to seduce with celerity the Boy Wonder — mother-figure & all that (*op. cit.* Klein, Freud, *et al.*).

By the end of the second act, Hedda-Alice apparently has the precocious *though somewhat-too-credulous* Sammy in the palm of her hand — but at the crucial moment *(yes, you spotted it a mile off)* — heart torn, loyalty in tatters — she recants: a histrionic scene played to an audience of bellhops, maids, room service waiters (agents in disguise) at the Ambassador Hotel, honeymoon suite — divulging in intricate detail the Soviets' plan, while the child, not the rube they've all been taking him for, looks on grinning (*well whose side did she think he thought she was on?*). Thus forewarned, & so forearmed, the Boy Wonder stands on the brink of an historic triumph (he's half a point clear of the "Steins" with one round to go) — when, suspicions well & truly aroused by now, Tesman discovers "the truth" &, aware his own neck's very much on the block, issues a warrant for his secretary's arrest before someone else does...

The real drama began only at the end, with Brack's agents hammering at the door, at the moment Hedda-Alice takes out Tesman's Beretta (she'd kept it, on a fatalistic impulse, for just such an occasion) & shoots herself in the head. It was as if all the tensions that'd formerly been concealed were suddenly exposed & the play turned back upon itself, becoming a type of anti-*Hedda Gabler* — not because the one contradicted the other, but because it mirrored it — only, from *behind*. The scene played out messily, if only because any type of redemption was impossible at that stage. Brack entered too late & Tesman was a goner in any case.[*] The curtain closed with the enlarged image of a flag falling on a ten-foot high projection of a chess clock, at the base of which lay Hedda-Alice's blood-spattered corpse, as if to say — *Look, her actions contradicted her destiny and now her time's up*.

On his way out of the theatre Němec caught sight of Alice Steinerová's brother sitting at the bar, looking neglected, like a lost child. It made him wonder what was supposed to've happened to the Kid, Sammy. Maybe turned into a travelling circus freak, *Roll up*! *Roll up*! *Come and see the boy with the enormous brain*! Drinking himself to death in a trailer somewhere out in the Boondocks — an old-timer on the sports desk at the local rag spotting his name in the obituaries column & doing a write-up:

The Kid who Brought the World to the Brink!

Joining a long line of forgotten legends, today "Sammy the Wunderkind," chess prodigy and Cold War mascot, passed away at his home at the Sunridge Trailer Park. Neighbours described Sam as quiet and unassuming. 'He seemed like a nice guy, kind to children, always said hello…'

The brother was staring into an empty glass that looked like it'd been empty for some time. There might've been a story behind it, but it didn't interest Němec enough to go over & say anything to him, even out of charity. Maybe he'd gotten a bad review. Brother Alex seemed out of place here in the real world, so to speak, without an audience of his own to play down to.

Němec beat the crowd out onto the street — it was cooler than it had been, breathing air that didn't feel like it'd already been breathed before a dozen times. The stagedoor opened onto an alleyway around the corner, a chair

---

[*] Nice idea, kiddo, but first you've gotta write it. [✋]

propping it flush against the wall — a green upholstered armchair on busted wheels, with an ashtray lying beside it on the ground littered with butts — from within, the sound of voices shouting at one another:

'Money? Me? Not a cent.'

'But...?'

'Oh, yes, wait a minute...'

Seated in the armchair was a grossly proportioned woman in a pink dressinggown that barely did anything to conceal the enormous expanse of her flesh. Her hair was in rollers, she had a pair of lit cigarettes splayed in her left hand. Němec was surprised to see that she was working on a crossword puzzle. He could hear the springs straining inside the chair beneath her. The woman looked up & quizzed Němec with her eyes as he approached.

'Three letters,' she coughed. 'Something you wear on your head. I can't decide if it's *hat* or *cap*. You've got a hat — maybe I should write *hat*?'

'I wouldn't know. Doesn't it depend?'

'Only thing it depends on is the letter "a," right in the middle. I figure it could go either way, but you can only write one.'

Her speech came out in a strangely disembodied wheeze, broken by explosive consonants & glottal stops. No sooner had she paused than she clapped her mouth around both cigarettes & inhaled before getting the next words out —

'Who you looking for anyway?'

Her face got lost in a cloud of smoke, from which it re-emerged an instant later, like a swamp creature smothered in dry ice. Němec told her who & she gave a laugh that made her jowls shake.

'Oh, sure, *that* Alice. Well, *hem*, Alice... Yessir. But if you know Alice like you say you do, then you already know all you need to know, right?'

The enormous woman winked, sucked on her cigarettes, blew the smoke back in Němec's face.

'What *you* want,' she cackled grossly, 'is someone with *experience*. An older woman. Who can take care of you right.' She jerked a thumb back through the stagedoor where the shouting had died down. 'Know what the kids in there call me? "Baba," that's what. *Hehehe*. There all my sweet little babies.'

Němec couldn't begin to imagine. "Baba" looked more like Cerberus after a ten-year restricted diet of pure lard. Lying beside the armchair was a child's pink frilly umbrella. In her hand it must've looked like a used cocktail decoration. The crossword she was holding, he noticed, was upsidedown.

'You know,' she said, exposing a row of brown teeth, 'there's a town called Alice all the way on the other side of the world, in the middle of a great big desert, & if I ever get out of here that's where I'm headed.'

"Baba" gave Němec another heavy-lidded wink —

'You stay in touch loverboy & I might even send you a postcard.'

She stubbed out her butts & lit another pair —

'You wanna go in?'

Němec shook his head. He thought for a second.

'Would you give her something for me?' he said.

'For you honey? I might be persuaded to do all sorts of things, *hehehe.*'

He scribbled on a square of paper & handed it over. The enormous woman pawed it, peered at it, grinned, then stuffed it inside her dressinggown, unsettling the precarious arrangement of flesh —

'Consider it done.'

50

Autumn made the trees a wreck — greybrown, ranged across the hillside gibbet-like, swaying in the wind — rooks gathered above them as though performing the part of Allegory in a Dürer etching. Beneath the stone bridges, dull Lethe waters refracted medieval picturebook scenes. Unease, like the sound of leaves turning yellow & falling to ground, mulched underfoot. A requiem would be the expected background music.

קָדוֹשׁ קָדוֹשׁ, קָדוֹשׁ, ה׳ יצבאות*

The last day of October was a Friday &, being the Old Man's anniversary, Němec felt duty-bound to take the Metro out to Olšanská Cemetery, where the Prof's ashes were interred in a wall behind a small square of plate glass. The graveyard was busy that time of the week. Elderly women, for the most part, clutching tired wreaths under arms, clearing away dead flowers from gravestones, rearranging the spent candles, sitting on damp wooden benches nursing small baskets of uneaten food. Beneath a dark canopy of yew trees, headstones lay like toppled chess pieces, mortuaries struggled vainly against the undergrowth — mounds of rubble grown up in profuse dilapidation, open graves, broken stairways down into crypts littered with homeless refuse, the omnipresent rustling of blackbirds. A grey cat perched on the lid of a cistern like a misplaced ampersand. Here & there monuments fallen into disrepair beside newly erected cenotaphs, crossed keys, martyred Christs, weeping Virgins, androgynous winged angels, wistful, pointing, arms outstretched. A giant crucifix stood inside the gates, 1898 in metal type nailed right in the cross-hairs:

PIE JESU DOMINE
DONA EIS REQUIEM

Facing it across the avenue was an Ibsenesque family tableau done to morbid excess in Carrara marble: mumsie (Jindřiška Hrdličková, †29.11.1924) tearfully

---

* "What kinda schmuck'd die for *your* sins?" [✋]

grasping the hand of her dead son (Hans Hrdlička, ÉLÈVE DE L'ACADÉMIE CONSULAIRE I. & R. VIENNE, NÉ 2.VI.1879 — DÉC. 25.V.1900), cold & cruel, cleanshaven in full regimental, piping & epaulettes, eyes impassive, gazing into a fixed distance at the doomladen light of spent youth, beneath the solemn unseeing gaze of the pater familias (Alois Jan Hrdlička, C.K. RADA ZEMS. SOUDU V PRAZE, †30 DUBNA 1906), elderly, crookbacked, in frockcoat & solemn beard, bespectacled. With this piously penned paean inscribed below:

Aucun des maux qui affrayent les hommes
ne peut plus désormais m'attaindre
et vous me plaignez?

Je suis pur et inalterable
comme un particule de lumiére
et vous me rapellerez dans la nuit de la vie![*]

Beneath the cypresses, plane trees, yew trees, a hundred-thousand funereal haiku all telling the same thing in different voices, *media vita in morte summus*:

Karel Watzel,
KNÍŽ. SCHWARTZEMBERGSKÝ RADA
†12.1.1896.

Hermann Killinger,
FABRIKANT
†24.9.1879.

Georg Schäck,
K.K. FINANZBEAMTEIR
†20.5.1904.

Karel Bendl,
HUDEBNÍ SKLADATEL
†20.9.1897.

Věra Golombiowská,
student of the Royal Gymnasium, 16 yrs old
†23.5.1937.

---

[*] "Mama, ooh-ooh-ooh-ooh, / didn't mean to make ya cry, / if I'm not back again / this time tomorrow, / carry on, carry on. / Coz nothin' really matters…" P.S. And don't forget to feed the mice. [♣]

Bohumil Lizner,
Professor of the Academy of Painting
†4.3.1957.

Anna Lauermannová-Mikšová,
writer
†16.6.1932.

Olga Votočková-Lauermannová,
writer
†12.10.1964.

Albina Hellechová,
teacher
†10.9.1899.

Jaroslav Čermák,
died 23.3.1878 in Paris, interred in Golem City 7.7.1878.
Milovanému bratru a silnému mistru…[*]

The plain black urn of Tomáš Hájek, PROFESSOR †31.10.1996, resided peaceably in a niche behind an unmarked window, in the wall at the far eastern end of the cemetery, adjacent to Jan Želivský Street (along which, Němec couldn't help noticing, an almost ceaseless stream of traffic flowed north-south past the freight yards). It was embossed with a serial number — 948632 — in gold numerals. A paper crematorium label pasted to the strip of wall beneath it was slowly yellowing. *Hic iacet.* Which in point of fact, wasn't exactly true. Němec couldn't help wondering if the State paid the rent. On either side, rows of plastic flowers, red candles & pine wreaths were accompanied by black&white portraits of the deceased. The Prof alone remained faceless. Němec searched in his pockets for the snapshot the caretaker had given to him — the one with the chessboard on the Barrandov Terraces — & slid it behind the glass.

One year dead — where'd the time gone? He, Němec, wasn't supposed to be the one standing there, keeping the Old Man's memory alive: not to disappear completely like just any old ghost with an accession number. As he walked back along the wall — past all those hundreds of funerary windows, among the slabs of moss & hewn stone & grieving Madonnas, mute notes of decomposing leaf underfoot, drizzle falling on the long avenues of tombstones, light beginning to fade — it struck Němec that this legacy of the Prof's *in manus tuas commendo spiritum meum* had become — if not his cross, as they say — an

---

[*] "Beloved of the Brothers Grimm…" [☙]

694

albatross round his neck &, in a bizarre sort of reciprocation, Němec his. *Si vales valeo, hehe.* But why *him*? (*Why anyone, kiddo?*) And what about the others? Where'd they hide the Old Man's loved-ones from the inquisitive eye of posterity? Superstition & post-mortem realestate monopoly subclauses per "felo de se" notwithstanding,* hallowed ground etc., a sprinkling of Luhačovice Spa Waters, 100% all-natural product, muttered over in Holy Roman Catholic & Apostolic bureaucratese. There'd've been a ledger in an office somewhere, a number in a column beside a name, oblique, in *ancien régime* cursive, as final as any other resting place. He could've found out. He might've decided not to.

Circling back around towards the exit, Němec passed a homeless guy in a torn overcoat sitting on a wooden bench in front of a blackened marble plaque from which the tenants' names had been eroded by time & the elements. He was staring at a busted radio from which furious gusts of static blew as he wound the dial in an effort (futile?) to tune-in on the voices in the ether. Beside the bench stood a vending machine with candles coloured white or red, Kč 20,- per. A caretaker was raking rubbish into a bin. *So long*, Němec thought, turning up his collar as the drizzle turned to rain & began to fall heavily on the cracked pavement. From the other side of the wall came the tin trumpet of an icecream vendor. The tune played & repeated & drifted away.

Němec just caught sight of the blue van with a giant icecream cone bolted to the roof, pull into the parking lot down the block. The driver got out & appeared a moment later with an umbrella & a pair of icecream cones coming towards the gates. Němec stood under a shelter & waited for a tram to come. Traffic surged, hissing on wet tarmac. The icecream man walked past & continued through the gates with his two icecreams: a double-scoop of chocolate & a double-scoop of raspberry ripple. Němec watched him along the treelined avenue till he turned off to the right. If possible, it left him more depressed than he already was. He stared grimly out at the rain.

Across the street, a line of corrugated iron hoardings marked off yet another construction site. Through the gaps between the hoardings you could see that it was nothing more than a muddy crater, thirty-odd metres deep. *Whatever they had in mind to bury…* A crane dangled a block of ferroconcrete in midair like a giant tombstone. Němec watched it sway up there, seem to arc out

---

* Concerning those itinerant cop-out artists who met their end by their own hand & not that of G.O.D. [✋]
* The past couldn't be relied upon to bury itself, so they'd brought in the subcontractors, *hehe*. [✋]

over the tramlines, then abseil out of the air, cables whistling. He braced himself for impact. The concrete block vanished silently behind the hoardings as the number 11 trundled by in the wrong direction. Rewind fifty years: Valentine's Day, 1944. A Flying Fortress dropping incendiaries scored a direct hit on the 11 tram on that same road. *Love from Uncle Sam.* Thought they were frying Dresden instead.* *Igne natura renovator integra.* There was probably a plaque somewhere to commemorate the fact. Sky Furies, Erinnye-voices, flaming tombstones coming from the clouds. Blecha's apartment building had sprouted from one such demolition job. Nature in its infinite renewal. He thought about the icecream man. He thought about the Prof's niche in the wall. Faces behind bits of glass. Bombs raining on a graveyard. Ten minutes till closing time.

Němec sighed, breathed the wet air. The composted vapours. The spent exhaust. Bury, exhume & bury again. *Look, says Yorrick, a philosopher's egg!* And there was a story, too, about a Waffen-*ᛋᛋ* unit holed-up there for weeks after the War'd ended, never got wind of the news, the Führer's cop-out, Jodl's surrender, dug-in at the back of the cemetery awaiting the break-out order that forever failed to come, though still refusing to yield, *keinen Schritt* — tunnelling crypt to crypt, taking potshots at the dead come to bury their dead, appearing & disappearing like spectral agents of anachronism & apocryphal doom. Maybe they starved, or the rats got them, or they ate one another in desperation, or were simply absorbed back into the blood & soil. No-one seemed to know.

When the next tram came, Němec hunched between traffic & boarded it. Instead of continuing straight into town, it turned right at the park where a concrete statue of a boy held hands with a concrete statue of a girl, symbolising Universal Peace, the Incorruptibility of Youth, or the eternally happy prospects of future realestate, take your pick. Through fogged windowglass, the dark grey pre-War tenements gave ground to Soviet urban gulag archipelagos. Mass mausoleums stacked against the sky. The glow of the first streetlights spreading away, doubling, lighting the chasm of the underworld. It looked like somewhere the Raskolnikovs of modern architecture had come to commit suicide or murder. Possibly both.

The tram wound through Žižkov along Kalininova & got caught up behind the traffic going down through the underpass. The tram clanged its bell. The traffic stalled out completely. Some sort of breakdown up ahead. Němec

---

* One of 60 that took a 90 mile wrong turn somewhere between High Wycombe & the Free State of Saxony. [✊]

stared through the grime-streaked window at the rail yards. Browns, blacks, a dozen shades of grey. On a strip of wasteland a couple of circus tents had been put up, with market stalls & funfair rides & lights strung on poles, like a Mexican funeral barque decked-out with candles.

The tram *claaaang*ed, but the traffic didn't give an inch. The doors wheezed open. Passengers climbed down between the cars to make the best of it on foot. Němec dragged himself away from the window & followed suit, threading his way towards the Big Top. *Roll up! Roll up! Win the prize!* Blink. Past the shooting gallery with its Daffy Duck silhouettes, dude in buckskin chaps shouting through a foghorn. *Only five a duck!* Five a duck? *Yep, son, you hit the duck, you win a fiver...* Pop. Whiz! *Look, there goes Rudi the Wonder Boy! Watch him fly about in his magic cape, loop-the-loop, perform feats of derringdo!* Tin pots & accordions. Bottled mead. Pastries. Candyfloss. Lights. The whole razzledazzle funeral cortège. Voodoo spirits emerging from the background, the mirror-man, the metamorphosis of the stranger...

Some waxed-down type in a stiff collar demonstrating the latest appliances to a bored-looking rent-a-crowd. *Would you like to have the cleanest house in town?* Strongman on a hoist breaking his chains. A dog jumping in the water. Splash! Reminds of the man who threw himself from the river wall with lead weights tied around his feet. *Whatsisname?* Broke both legs but didn't drown. Like a mind that's sick & wants to stay sick, mired in its wrong P.O.V. Nothing looks real — or it all looks too real — some Arbogast forgery of runes around the moon. Point a camera at it. Click. And suddenly you're looking at the backside of a fried egg that's too well-done. *Want a postcard of the occasion?* Someone's fiddling the pixels? Paranoia's war of attrition gets the upper hand, the eye breaks down, prepared in the end to believe any scrap of nonsense. Glimpsing the hand, you think, of the Master Ordinator — mantic arts of conjuration, banal, exotic, phantasmatic — the 1,620 fixed passions, combinable but not transformable — the sensual pleasures of classification... *Psst! Lonely, mister?* Some embroidered Arachne in the shadows. The Punch&Judy Man.

Němec slipped through a cordon & crossed onto the tracks, back into the night, along the rail embankment, cross the bridge, the black swathe of the train yards, to the farther side. Signals, switches, megaphones. No-one there but the rats to watch him weave the junctions, rain overspilling the gutters of his bowler hat, tipped slightly forward, sodden shirtcollar, sodden boots. The sidings of Masaryk Station. The station clock said quarter past six — hands wound back. Like the old Gypsy said, only the Government'd dream up the idea of cutting a

strip off the bottom of a blanket & sewing it to the top so as to make a longer
blanket. (In its dreams, they call Golem City, not *the beloved*, but *the belated*.)
About Masaryk Station, the Bugman had a grim tale. May '45. The Uprising.
After the War had already ended in the rest of Europa. *Hibernerbahnhof* (then
called) was the first place the partisans occupied. The Nazis, headquartered in
the basement of the local Y.M.C.A.,* shelled it with everything they had. Blew
the clock to bits. Set the Station vestibule on fire. Overran the barricades & the
kids pointing broomsticks & slingshots & God knows what else, Swedish
muskets from the Thirty Years War. It was like a scene from *The Teratologists*:

> *Rat-tat-tat* from casement windows — *pock-pock-pock* of stucco & mortar,
> plumes of glass catching the sunlight mid-air *just so* — old men in Sázava
> Stetsons blasting from the hip, *blam-blam*! as another Kraut keels over &
> tumbles from the wainscoting, a halfpike then *whump*! — muzzles spitting
> fire from manhole covers, under burnt-out trucks, behind sandbagged
> pillboxes… Sound-up on *The Ride of the Valkyries* as faceless extras clutch
> their guts, lurching sideways over balconies, backwards onto the seat of
> their pants, headfirst out windows, across saloon bars, down the stairs,
> onto swinging chandeliers, bullet-holed playerpianos, card-tables,
> matchstick chairs, gabled roofs… And all the while, an unknown woman
> in black mantilla slowly wheeling a trolley full of old shoes through the
> middle of the cross-fire, unscathed, kneeling to pray over each dead body
> lying in her way, till a type of awe befell the men on both sides. Or they
> ran out of ammunition. Or someone called an 11th hour ceasefire so the
> Nazis, outgunned finally, could negotiate "safe passage" now that the Reds
> were already in the suburbs & there was no reason any half-sane Kraut
> would want to stick around a minute longer than absolutely necessary. As
> one Oberst said to another, *There's a place shrouded in the mists of mythology,*
> *called Shit Creek, and we're proverbially up it, mein Freund, paddles 'n' all.**
>
> While negotiations where still in process, the Nazis rounded up
> whoever they found in the Station, herded them onto the tracks & made
> them kneel while an ⚡ officer shot them one-by-one in the back of the
> neck with a luger. The ones they didn't shoot, they marched out into the
> street as human shields, in case the partisans had second thoughts. Always
> a joy to do business, etc. Well, you had to admire a nation capable of
> inventing the Mercedes Benz, the Space Rocket & a dependable train
> schedule. After the Reds took control, the Station got renamed Golem

---

* With especial thanks to De Valera, that *putz*. [⚘]

* Whose membership Heydrich had thoughtfully shipped-off at the first opportunity to
Mauthausen, Belsen, Kobylisy as subversives-waiting-to-happen. Just like in the song. [⚘]

* "Es gibt einen Ort in den Nebeln der Mythologie genannt Scheißebach gehült, und wir sind
sprichwörtlich bis es, *mate*, Paddel und alle." [⚘]

Central, motherboard of the zombie kingdom. When the Capitalist bandwagon came to town in '89, they renamed it again & it became the favoured congregation point for the local bums, panhandling for change & stinking up the benches at the allnight vendor. A far cry from all those Führerliebenden matrons slurping their gulashsuppe, gnawing their schnitzels, crossing their eyes & dorting their teas, chomping chocolate truffles with those little Mozart cameos on the wrappers, ein Monsieur Klein at the piano — in their minds, perhaps, it's always 1938...

Němec got down from the embankment just shy of the Florenc viaduct. Seven-league boots stumbling over ruts & clods. A gap in the fence. Rain slithering down. A shape under a streetlamp, a flame snapped from a cigarette lighter. Ahead, something always ahead. The psychic sensitivities of roosting gulls under the stone arches. All the while picking apart thoughts in minutest detail instantly unremembered, a nagging spirit at his back. Dim locators directing towards whatever hole-in-the-wall presented itself. Out of the abknown like Caliban in rainsodden hat & suit, raking the moon in puddles. Past the viaduct, a sign, so dimly lit & covered in filth it was unreadable, hung above a door. *Nunc est bibendum.* Němec pushed inside & brought the weather with him. The place was ten-feet of silence — the kind of bar that makes you think the worst, for once, mightn't yet be still to come. Němec returned the stares & ordered two brandies straight-up. They watched him drink. He ordered two more. They got bored. He leaned against a wall. He listened to the talk slowly resume. He watched time pass. He drank. *Well, here's to the Old Man.*

The rain hadn't abated by the time he left the bar, but at least now he didn't feel it. Swaying in the middle of the road, under the viaduct, gazing up into the belly of the beast. A long freighttrain rattled overhead. Headlights. He weaved back into the dark, pathways of no egress, tenement yards, upended garbagepails, driftwood, cardboard boxes. Someone had sculpted a deathshead out of flyover rubbish, leering down from a plinth of grey breezeblock, strips of polyethylene & sheet-plastic. Totems of the borderlands, where the City Planners had turned a blind eye: all the dead ends & entropy of a System of Transmutations that'd broken down, where order faltered, came undone. Němec gazed behind. The giant neon swan flickered there in the distance like the competing totem of everything that was meaningless, a costumed charade. Somewhere the World had disappeared & this was what remained — the illusion & its ruins. Was that the reason he waited for the Profs ghost at night?

Němec plunged deeper into the wilderness, thinking *if you go far enough in* *any one direction, you'll end up exactly where you started.* It sounded as good as any other idea he'd had. And did he believe his own absurdities?* Not far now, the rumble of the lorries entering & exiting the freight yards by the river. Lights along a perimeter fence. A blank stretch of road. At that hour. Walls of shipping containers piled high. Then further out, warehouses ceding to landfill. A kind of limbo cast in a swathe through the lower reaches of the City — its unconscious counterpart, some strange unrecognisable thing like the monster that hides in dreams & can never actually be *seen?*

A nonstop Benzina stood across from the freight terminal, last outpost, halogenated shelves beckoning. Němec re-emerged ten minutes later with suit pockets sagging from the weight of two-dozen minibottles of random booze. He aimed past the streetlights. Cracked a bottle, downed it, face drenched with rain. Tossed the empty into the weeds. Walked. Cracked another. Downed it without breaking stride. *Not bad, Squillhead, only twenty more to go and you'll be a fucking champion.* The road, as far as he could see, led pretty much nowhere.

Which was exactly as it should be.

---

* Credo quia absurdum est. [✋]

51

DIE WUNDERWAFFE

Who *was* Heinz Kammler?

Somewhere along the way Němec had come across a story he couldn't help feeling he'd heard before in one version or another, only the versions didn't stack up & so he'd forgotten all about it in the general miasma. The story wasn't part of what he was supposedly looking for — E.K., the Prof's magik book & the world conspiracy or whatever — but the man's name, coincidental or not, was there, uncrossed, in the Black Book (⊛ KAMMLER 71916279) & it was there again in yesterday's paper, human interest, page 16, the pull-out supplement. It was the headline that caught Němec's eye, like déjà vu:

WHO WAS HEINZ KAMMLER?

A grainy blow-up black&white candid showed an elderly gent, balding, wire-rimmed specs & startled eyebrows, feeding pigeons by the Central Park Reservoir, New York. According to the article, the Pigeon Man was none other than Hans (a.k.a. Heinz) Kammler, born in the town of Stetten (of which there were nearly a hundred), former civil engineer who in the early War years was Oswald Pohl's deputy at ⚡⚡-Wirtschafts-Verwaltungshauptamp (W.V.H.A.) — the section tasked with overseeing the admin of the Nazi camp system, Amtgruppe (Amt) D. Later appointed Director of the Amt C engineering group, responsible for the design & construction of *all* concentration & extermination camps.

Kammler, the journalist was at pains to make clear, oversaw the installation of the Auschwitz-Birkenau crematoria *personally*. His principle concerns, however, lay elsewhere. In 1943, after the Allies bombed the Peenemünde launch site on the Baltic, it was Kammler who built the underground Mittelwerk rocket factory & adjacent Mittelbau-Dora slave labour camp. In 1944 the *ᛋᛋ*, not satisfied with orchestrating Operation Reinhard & the Final Solution, was given direct charge of the entire V2 rocket programme — "Aggregat 4" — the socalled Vergeltungswaffe or "Vengeance-Weapon." The following year Kammler was appointed to the high-sounding post of Führer's General Plenipotentiary for Jet Aircraft, in light of which much speculation would later surround his role during the Last Days, as the Allies overran Western Europe, in setting in train the euphonious & highly secret Projekt K.L.E.E.[*] Consensus among latterday historians, though, being that this K.L.E.E. never in fact existed, not even on paper — no more a Wunderwaffe than a bumblebee in the clover — something cooked-up in the dying moments of the War as a bargaining chip by Kammler & his *ᛋᛋ* cronies, by now stranded east of the Allied lines, aware of what Fate had in store for them if (or indeed when, it being only a matter of time) they fell into the hands of those blood-thirsty Bolsheviks — not a happy thought.

The fact Kammler was in Bohemia at all provided the news article with yet another twist: as catastrophe loomed in the final weeks, rumours flew about that large quantities of rocket materials, along with scientists & thousands of documents marked *Verschlußsache*, were being rushed across the last remaining enclave still under Nazi control — the Protektorat Böhmen und Mähren — in a bid to reach the fabled Eagle's Nest "for one last heroic stand." The last stand never happened, no "Miracle Weapon" was ever found, & Kammler himself vanished into thin air. The authors of the article related no fewer than five conflicting accounts of what was supposed to've become of him:

---

[*] Whether a word or an acronym the E.N.I.G.M.A. decrypts didn't specify, though recurring with logarithmic frequency in cables fired back & forth between Mittelbau & Berlin before the lines went completely dead: referring to the "miracle weapon," supposedly, which Hitler had long demanded — a speculative Symbolic Virtual Engine, according to one Bletchley Park donnish type with a penchant for set theory & rough trade — doomsday box, particle beam, deathray gun, bats in the belfry — key to the Reich's ultimate survival, *Better get onto this before Ivan does* being the received Whitehall line.

1. that — according to the testimony of Kammler's personal driver, one Kurt Preuk, he swallowed a cyanide capsule on 7 May, 1945, on the road from Plzeň to Golem City after being turned back by the Amerikaners;

2. that he shot himself in the head with a standard issue Walther PPK, on 9 May, inside Golem City while the bunker he was defending was being overrun by partisans;

3. that his aide-de-camp, Sturmbahnführer Starck, shot Kammler to prevent him falling into the hands of the enemy;

4. that the Soviets executed him along with two-hundred other SS, captured while fleeing towards American lines in the west;

5. that he made it to the American side & was smuggled out with all the other rocket scientists the Yanks got their hands on & secretly employed in the Manhattan Project, etc., & died in New York, 1980, an old man with a park-view apartment on West 92nd Street.

As for Projekt K.L.E.E., rumours flared in Golem City after the '89 Revolution about 31 [sic] crates of SS archives kept under lock & key by Nosek's Interior Ministry. Periodically, too, reports about the uncovering of a secret Nazi bunker system just past the city limits, in which (among other confections) Škoda-manufactured components of V2 rockets had supposedly been stockpiled at the end of the War. According to the newspaper, the technology for the V rockets & their Doppler radio-controlled tracking system had in fact been developed way back in the 1920s, by Hermann Oberth & Disney aficionado Wernher von Braun (architect of Alphaville, author of a thesis on "Theoretical Construction & Experimental Solution to the Problem of the Liquid Propelled Rocket," paperclipped after cessation of hostilities), when the Ruhr was still under occupation (see "Versailles, Treaty of"), working at a clandestine laboratory operated by T.E.S.L.A. GmbH. Had the Nazis got their act together sooner, the world wouldn't've been a happier place.

Beside the photograph of Kammler, the article (which filled all of page 16) was illustrated by a hazy snapshot of a prototype Vergeltungswaffe, painted in chessboard black&white,* angled on the launchstand at Peenemünde. After all this, the gist of the story was that some Nazi bunker mole had just blown himself up stepping on a mine looking for the last resting place of Kammler's hoard, in the hills near Štěchovice...

---

* During tests the V2 was painted in a chessboard pattern to determine by sight if the rocket was spinning around its longitudinal axis. [⚑]

When Huygens built the first pendulum clock in 1657, on the principle that at any given instant in time the pendulum itself is in fact static, motionless, a little slice of eternity, he had no way of knowing that, three-hundred years in the future, the simple ratio of amplitude (θ) to gravity (g) would flatten half of the grazing land in Kent. A dumb-weight at the end of a rope, the hanged man of the Tarot, the Brennschluß of the Mind in its unthinking oscillation — these were the strange images occupying Němec's "thoughts" as he stared up at the ceiling... A shadow, a black stain spreading outwards & inwards simultaneously. He tried to picture himself, just as he was, lying awake in the dark, the cold working its way into the groin, unable to sleep, but also unable to think — a jester tied by the feet upsidedown & the Earth's shadow speeding towards & then receding again, an axe-blade parabola, its arc & swing, the ever-approaching, ever-receding azimuth, translucent plume with shock-diamonds, etc.[*] *Been here before, eh, kiddo?*

Against the ceiling the pendulum's shadow swung, time unhinged — out through his eyes his mind floated up there taking in the view, seeing him, undertaker's suit, stretched on the floor — the Brennschluß moment when the motionsickness cuts-in, the body nothing now but core reflex, raised arms of the undead, heaving forward, lurching from the grave. Outside in the night, the lugubrious sound of the wind through the scaffolding was like wind through a gibbet. Němec dragged upright, blinked at the view. Behind the scaffold, the exxed-out windows resembling an expired calendar, time, running out. Then zombie-stagger, groping along the hallway in the dark to the bathroom — the taste of last night's smoke & booze impastoed to the roof of the mouth — trying hard as he could not to puke all over the parquet.

---

[*] In the time it takes light to travel from the sun you've gone through another death & resurrection — you could see it all in the mirror if you could bear to watch. Does the eye move itself? Is it simply an instrument with a view to some particular end? Like poor Němec, who's fallen into a black hole — he can't see that the universe in which he thought he'd existed was escaping him, that another, opposite universe, was swallowing him up. []

The Kammler story came back to him while wiping the vomit from his shoes with bits of newspaper. The pull-out supplement, page 16. Well how many deaths could one man have? Němec shuddered, breathed deep. *Shit. Fucking Nazis everywhere, a man can't even throw his guts in piece nowadays.* He stared at the newsprint close up: something about androids? Now there was a topic with personal appeal. Němec blinked back through the story, smeared yellow & red. No androids it seemed, but near enough. The man must've had a dozen doppelgängers at least. Perhaps some secret Berlin cloning laboratory, maybe there was a whole army of Kammlers, some of them (the lost lone survivors) even now pursuing a masterplan only a lunatic could've hypothesised in 1945? Well there was sure as shit no shortage of lunatics back then.

Němec wiped his mouth with his sleeve. Dragged out to the kitchen & threw a pot of coffee on. Doused his face in cold water. Read the Kammler story again, to exorcise the brain & generally keep the motionsickness in check, the gist of it coming back to him. Kammler, Faktor, the Prof: a connection? He slugged coffee, poured another, plonked down on the bureau floor among the familiar detritus, back to the wall. Conjured scenarios. Dragged over the writing machine (flashing-eyed Minerva, giver of wisdom—would she still?). Belched, blinked. The story was too good to let lie. It had a certain kind of Alice-in-the-Mirror-Maze quality about it. He took one of the facsimiles & fed it in backtofront, a shock of blonde on black, waiting for the inner stenographer to respond, arachnid fingers moving on invisible command — spirit medium, words channelled from the ether, threads of ideas fully formed, embroidering a tale of...?[*]

---

[*] Well something had to come next. *As the good Doctor says, most effective way to ruin a perfectly fine piece of paper is to write on it, hmmm?* Close your eyes & let your head empty — *and what made you think there was anything in there to begin with, eh?* Let the smell of it come to you, the ribbon, the blue carbon paper, the dusty oil-clotted type. Feel out the roundness of the keys, pressing down, one at a time, keep the fingers from slipping in-between, the mechanism from jamming, hesitant at first, then with increasing regularity: the sheer sound of type-hammers striking the ribbon enough to spur the synapses on — like the amplified inner mechanisms of a slow turning clock. *Clackclockclackclockclack.* Qwertz for quartz. Stop. Unwind. Feed a new sheet. Begin again. Continue. [♆]

on -- some late-stage experimental doomsday box capable
of beaming deathrays out on low frequency wireless,
barrages of antimatter, uncoiled extra-dimensionality,
etc. -- the actual blueprint purportedly concealed on a
microdot inside some antiquarian bookseller's merchandise,
its precise location known only to a former confident of
Himmler... Here the story breaks off into a series of
flashbacks:
We see a senior SS officer in feldgrau, black gorget
patches with silver oakleaves above two pips sidebyside
like a Schwabacher figure-eight tipped on its side,
standing, or rather leaning over, on a roadside beside an
open-top Mercedes. On the back seat of the car are dozens
of grey cardboard boxes, tied with magenta ribbon. The
officer appears to be looking for something on the
ground. As the camera zooms in we see in fact that he's
pulling a body from the driver's side door: first a pair
of arms, then a head covered in blood. The officer drags
the body into a ditch & then, having confirmed the
absence of any approaching vehicles, bends down & begins
stripping the deadman's corpse. We see that the deadman is
an SS sergeant & that he's been shot, once, in the side of
the head with a small calibre pistol...
The officer then does a very peculiar thing: he begins
removing his own uniform & exchanges it for that of the
deadman who, with some difficulty, he attires in his own.
Now disguised as a staff sergeant, the officer stuffs a
bundle of papers inside the jacket now worn by the
deadman, but not before flicking through them one last
time to be sure nothing's been left out. A close-up reveals
the SS identity card of Gruppenführer Heinz Friedrich
Karl Franz Kammler, number 292714, whose photograph shows
a face identical to that of the man now holding it. We
then see Kammler drag the corpse back out of the ditch &
onto the road, get in the car, reverse back about two
metres, then very carefully drive over the head of the
man now supposed to be him...
It's the last chaotic days of the War, the Red Army
storming the Reichstag, his beloved Führer now nothing
but a pile of sodden ashes, & time running out to get
K.L.E.E. somewhere safely out of Stalin's reach (cue a
tunnel under the City, crammed like Ali Baba's cave, some
future treasure-scammer's Eldorado, with all the
alchemical paraphernalia of Eichmann's goldmaking
machine), from whence -- after the dust's settled, the
networks re-established -- it can quietly be smuggled out
of the post-Protektorat to locations south of the equator
or else, worse coming to worst...

Seeing the sky over the road to Plzeň through the dead sergeant's eyes. It'd been
solely due to "Preuk"'s testimony that Kammler was legally declared dead by the
courts after the War. They looked near enough alike. Only the corpse was never

found, if there ever was a corpse. Buried, Preuk said. But where? He changed his story each time. Either nothing was what it seemed, or was *too much* what it seemed. People lived or died, but no-one could prove it. *And what about you, eh, kiddo? Think they'll let you slip away that easily? They've got plans for you, sweetheart. And when you're gone, it'll be like you were never here to begin with.*

Perhaps the world was even crazier than it seemed?

And if Kammler had lived, where'd he really go? With the Red Army already in the eastern suburbs of Golem City, airstrips sealed-off, streets torn up for barricades, the constant wailing of airraid sirens, megaphones, chaos & carnage, roving bands of ⚡⚡ firing randomly at anything that moved, looting, slaughtering babes in their mothers' arms, etc. while the rest of the Kraut occupation forces were busy abandoning everything — brokendown tank convoys, crates of smelted gold, mountains of secret service records no-one was prepared to waste the petrol to burn — all in a mad rush to get out, westwards, safe passage in exchange for not blowing the City to smithereens in some last ditch fight-to-the-death, only to be wiped out anyway (most of them) by Reds & partisans before ever making it to Plzeň.

Try to imagine how it was, the night after the Nazis fled.
The night before the Reds "liberated" Golem City.
A night in limbo.
Just one night.
The deserted Castle on the hill. Mobs roaming the streets, hunting the stragglers. Gunfire and long unfilled silences. Apprehension settling over the streets as the faint rumble of the convoys recedes in the west and approaches in the east…
And where was the Prof that night?
Standing up here, at his window, listening, waiting? Alone? The three of them together? Four, counting the caretaker. The abandoned billet strewn with mess. Barricaded doors. Hiding in the dark. Watching. Eluding the "Sanitation" Squads, partisans on the prowl for undesirables, the secret army of stoolpigeons, finks, shakedown artists, opportunists of every stripe, weeks becoming months becoming years, Interior Ministry goons, provocateurs, conductors of chaos stalking a city caught asleep in that long night without end, seeming to have no end…?

Or it wasn't like that at all? Events colluding, discrepant, nothing the way you'd expect it to be?

The story petered out. It had nowhere to go. Besides, who cared? If Kammler hadn't existed, there'd've been others. *The world's got ways of getting where it's going, kiddo, don't matter what you write about it.* Němec dragged his jacket on & went outside, unable to bear another pointless vigil staring at the white square of the page. It was like a film he'd seen so many times he could lipsync to the dialogue.* Downstairs, the courtyard looked like a war zone — a jackhammer lying on its side, sections of broken piping like abandoned field mortars, cement sacks filled with rubble stacked on either side of the doors, beyond which: a pair of trenches where the pavement used to be, rusted mains sticking up from pools of muddy water, scaffolds camouflaged under torn strips of black&green netting stirred by the wind.

At the corner, a man in a gabardine coat, handlebar moustache, stopped him & asked for a light. Němec didn't have one. The man looked at him like he knew him. How do you recognise a stranger anyway? Process of elimination? Perhaps psychic identikits, tumblers falling into place, unlocking the antimemex of the lower brain. *How's that condition of yours coming along? Still get those blue spots on yer watchamacallit?* Němec shrugged & walked on, hardly anyone around. Unsavoury weather, better to keep indoors, lock all the windows, batten the hatches. The air, a cold dirty smell about it, like burnt aspic. Němec had an automatic desire not to breathe. One day, probably soon, ozone catastrophe, CFCs & CO_2 — the slow-working gaschamber — denervured, becoming man-rat, man-roach, salamander-man — re-evolving gills, webbed feet, the great backwards leap, evolution's pendulum. It reminded him of one of those sessions with the Bugman —

'There was a joke used to go around, about Stalin's colossus on the hill. How underneath it was a secret broadcast station. Radio Joe. Agitprop mindwash — who knows what. Kids with crystal sets tuning-in for a laugh. *I reign over you sayeth the God of Justice in power exalted above the Firmament of Wrath! Ol Sonf Vorsag Goho...* Some cracked gibber. When they blew it up, they had to find some other place to put all their T.E.S.L.A. radio gadgets — why they built the big syringe over there in Žižkov... Supposed to be a TV tower, but everyone knows it's for listening-in on brainwave frequencies.'

And Němec, playing dumb —

------

* Well at some point in his life every man dreams of a walk-on role in the Great Cosmic Conspiracy — something to tell the kids about in the nursing home. Poor Němec should've known better by now. [✊]

'Why you've gotta have faith in democracy — seems there's no other choice.'

'What you want choices for? It's like the old shell game. Can have all the choices you like, but you'll never get the prize.'

And maybe that was the truth of it — behind all the pretence of immortality, the gigantist alibi, those hapless mechanics of conflict & quantum weirdness, all the clandestine programmes of psychocivilisation, alchemy of the masses, revolution by secret revocation — brinkmen of ancient riddles & dialectical method in the gamepattern of Mutually Assured Destruction, incrementally from Marian Column to Martian Colossus, as from sword to lightsabre, sci-fi TV rocket towers jamming & tranceiving like the proverbial needle in Golem City's eye —

Today Only!
See Newts battle the Golem!
Radio Godzilla & the Machine Men!
Svengali meets the Cosmic Clown
in the Case of the Bezerk Brainwave!

— an ornate divertimento of the fruits of rationalism, echo of celestial adding-machines keyed to obscure calendric cycles, Egyptian Books of the Dead, the lost & buried arcana of Ur, worshipers all of technological egress — *Iad Balt Lonsh Calz Vonpho Sobra Z Ol Ror I Ta Nazps Od Graa Ta Malprg*! — Great Gad's voice on the ether, microwave backwash of the first migration, the Big Bang exodus — reading the miraculous signs of sempiternal twaddle in dots, dashes, zeroes & ones — readying themselves for the Return Voyage, the Last Blastoff, nosecone to the cosmic wind...!?!

To get out of the weather, Němec stepped into one of those slot machine joints with room for a couple of tables, & stood at the bar. Three drunks were sitting in the corner, having an argument that couldn't be heard over the football

709

commentary, only the lower halves of their faces illuminated by the flashing Vegas lights. It was a job getting the barman's attention away from the TV set behind the counter — Sparta one-nil over Slavia in the second half — enough to order a glass of red & a bag of pretzels. Also at the bar: one bottle-blonde in a pink vinyl miniskirt perched half-on half-off a highchair. She was dipping her fingers in something green & poisonous-looking, then licking them — eyes the whole time fixed on their own reflections, in the mirror behind the shelves of ersatz liquor, fan-lights spinning above like roulette wheels. Němec stood there & ate the untasting pretzels & gulped the vinegar. He felt his guts tighten. It gave him the strength he needed to get out while the going was good. At the door, one of the drunks lurched up & grabbed hold of Němec's lapel, getting his face in close, a gust of rotten cabbage.

'Jesus Christ,' the drunk belched, 'was buggered in Herod's gaol. And that's a fact!'

The drunk stared between Němec's eyes a little longer, as if he expected to be disagreed with, & then pushed on towards the bar, muttering *sotto voce* about there being so many faggots in the world. Němec watched him weave towards the blonde & left it at that. Outside, the air wasn't any sweeter than it had been, factory outfall wafting over the hill through coalsmoked streets, fog creeping up from the river, & the zone where the two met running like a boundary cutting across Nerudova Street. He pulled his collar up & headed for the next bar he could find. The fog thickened with every step. Streetsounds warped, bells clunked. Detached from the objective fact of the frame in which everything blurred, the City's lights filtered through the gloom like constellations of TV static. There was a moment, as he navigated in the direction of the Zrcadlo Theatre, that he convinced himself he saw Alice Steinerová come out from the shadows into the lamplight, crossing the street ahead of him — the same blonde hair, black coat, leather boots. He hurried to catch up, but lost sight of her.

Footsteps rang on the cobblestones, receding in the darkness through an alleyway that narrowed as it wound up beneath the Castle stairs. Němec stumbled in the dark, against invisible objects determined to obstruct his progress. At the end of it, an archway & stairs above a retaining wall with a cul-de-sac on one side & a footpath on the other. A woman's shadow seemed to reach along the wall towards him. A few more steps, then he saw her: she was standing so her face was in the shadow of the lamplight, eyes aglitter in the dark, silver & black — her head was titled back & she seemed to be entranced.

Němec approached till he was standing only a foot away from her, searching her face which now appeared unnatural, masklike, erased beneath streaks of cheap cosmetic, a smear of lipstick in place of a mouth. He could see that she'd been crying. He came closer until the woman became aware of his presence, then with a shout of dismay she pushed past him & hurried down the footpath. Above the rooftops the fog had parted to form a chasm & he knew what the woman had been staring at. The moon above was almost full, an aureole of orange light radiated from it, like the eye of some supervening nocturnal intelligence. Wisps of cloud slid across it & just then the fog began to turn to drizzle — saturating the air, dissolving it, making it breathable again. And he stood there, just the way the woman had, listening to the slow metronome of falling rain & the dull, repeated minor chord of its echo.

What was the purpose of remembering things the way he did? That way & not some other way? Wandering the streets in search of one phantom & to escape another, coming by chance to a bar with no name, shoes soaked, dripping all over the tiles, humid under his hat. Behind a pair of heavy drapes, a doglegged vault cocked itself away from the door into a wall of smoke. The smoke eddied in the draught, parting to reveal the bowed despondent heads of the drinkers, seated across from one another in long rows the way inmates sit, looking neither to left nor right but straight ahead into their glasses, where all futures tended to a finite point — the proverbial light at the end — measured against the clock's *pizzicato* — a clock that had only undesired ideas to communicate.

Němec found a spot away from the creeping narcosis & flagged a waitress for some wine & cheese. At the next table a suit was talking into a cellphone — not the usual suit from the ministries but a blue pinstripe with dandruff flaking the shoulders, blond mop & 3-day growth —

'Are you just a recording or are you really there?'

Closer inspection revealed, in addition, one eyebrow shaved off — must've been a "character" dropping in from the other place to keep tabs on things, see what all the noise was about —

'Are you a plastic dummy or do you just have fake tits?'

Němec tried to picture who or what was at the other end of the line — some 1-800 pay-per-minute answering service with one of those purring *cum-in-my-mouth* voices only fifty years of whiskey & chain-smoking ever properly achieved. Your man looked unhinged enough to get you in a corner & waste precious hours of your existence with earnest talk about the coming Master Race, I.M.F. & World Bank Holocaust — the whole puerile Big Buck mindwash that could just as easily become the soundtrack of the future & probably already was, only your average Joe hadn't got hooked on the frequency yet, still tuned to the old sound: Exploding Stalin Inevitable meets Cold War Trickledown. Or the guy was just another privatisation bum on a temporary downslide, stood-up by the latest exchange rate, keeping his cellphone company for the night. Could just as easily've been talking to himself, for all Němec knew.

Wouldn't be long, he supposed, before the whole transistorised mass of humanity — the Great Unwashed — all had their waxy ears plugged into the ether 24/7, in conversation with The Voices. *Dial up your favourite dead dictator, hehe!* Microwave background radiation from the Big Bogey in the Blue, Inc. Spooky influence at a distance. For each man, woman & mutt, their own private Influencing Machine. Maybe stick a video in there too, to make believe there're human beings at the other end & not Space Invader robots talking dirty. Hell, they could carry the whole caboodle of approved mindwash entertainment around in their pockets, all modcons, nonstop colour adverts thrown in gratis — *Today only, don't miss this unique offer from the Intergalactic News Corp., JUST FOR YOU!*[*]

He was spared further apocryphal visions of future telecommunication by the waitress bringing a jug of the usual stuff with a marinated camembert on the side — skewered with a chilli on a toothpick, a couple of shrivelled juniper berries & a slice of raw onion soaked in oil. The cutlery brought back memories of Home: ketchupped spaghetti spattering from fingersmeared aluminium tines wide enough apart to pick your nose with & spoons that would've put Yuri Geller to shame all by themselves. The brown bread, past being stale, had been fried in lard. Manna from heaven! Thus prepared, Němec thanked his lucky stars & settled in for the evening…

It was long after midnight when he left the bar. The rain had stopped & the air felt dirty all over again & grown long in the tooth. He'd done his damnedest,

---

[*] Wouldn't do to think there's a majority that actually *chooses* to go along with those sonsofbitches, would it? [✊]

but the stillpoint eluded him: he'd drunk as much as he could stomach, but it wasn't enough. Even *that* was beyond his grasp. His mood darkened at the edges as he followed the street wherever it decided to take him. A black dog stalked the periphery. Seeing himself, shrunk down, a silhouette in bowler hat with stick playing compass-needle with the angle of the light, swinging south in the approach, north in departure, for all he knew he might've been going round in circles. On second thought, no, he was pretty fucking certain he'd been going round in circles for months at a stretch. *Even when you stand still, eh kiddo, the Earth turns for you.* Eyes closed, eyes open, the same-looking streets like scenery painted on cave walls — flights of stairs veering to left, an arcade wending to right — letting his shadow feel ahead of him, in its element. And what if *it* came to life & stood there before him at its full height?

Don't disappoint yourself, kiddo.

Rounding a corner, up ahead a couple of drunks stumbling around in the middle of the street, silently exchanging blows. *Look, it's you, hehe.* Their shadows reared up against the side of a building, making cinema ten metres tall. Němec stood there fascinated, watching the spectacle wear itself out then begin all over again — from ugly to tragic & then absurd — like a pair of determined buffoons taking turns to beat each other with a decomposing fish. It was a pity, Němec thought, that there wasn't anyone else around to appreciate it. They'd probably end up carrying each other home & keep drinking till there was enough under their belts to go at it all over again.

After a few more minutes of Punch&Judy he left them to it & bungled on alone, the now empty street telescoping ahead, echoes of footsteps (his) ringing on the flagstones, air sour as masticated onions, down the black tunnel towards the next island of light, clutching at something, or it clutching at him. Seeing again that same woman under a streetlamp & the same sense of panic, then flash of headlights as a car swung out into the street, erasing everything, before just as suddenly gone. Telling himself it would've been easy, at any point, to've gone back to look for Alice Steinerová. And would he have found her, as he had before, there in front of the Broadway mirrors? Did she even exist — any more than the false light of a mock moon exists? *Nice sentiment, kiddo, but it's all elevator music in the end.*

And he remembered something then. It came to him out of nowhere. How on the kitchen table, in the apartment he'd grown up in — if five years could be called growing up — was a vase with plastic flowers. Strange flowers. Bird of Paradise.* And how he'd stared at them in a kind of desperation, without knowing what they were, while the cops bundled his parents downstairs into a car. And the woman cop standing over him, saying if he knew what was good for him & the fake-green stems, the weird orange & purple flower unfolding & stinking of fish, as if something had died inside the vase & gone rotten. Because he thought it was *him* who was going to be punished, that if he cried, if he broke away to get out the door, down the stairs, if he? Or maybe it was that his mamitati had just filleted the Christmas carp & was about to fry the onions? Or it was nothing, a mistake, the flowers never smelt that way — he tried to spit it out, but was stuck with it, alpha-rhythms on a switched frequency? *Shush now!*

What film was Němec stuck inside this time?

He breathed deep. He'd stopped noticing how it tasted. The pain, too, was like a sedative. Pain of the mind, of the physical organism. What separated them? Were there cracks between, from which, unexpected, to continue to be waylaid? Where was he? Němec groped for some clue, in all that museumed bric-à-brac of the Great Labyrinth, etc. His thoughts settled into the shape of the architecture — the silence of the gargoyles — the gables, parapets, aedicules & volutes, friezes, triglyphs, cartouches, columns, etc. So familiar it all appeared utterly foreign, a barbarian's yen for ornamentalised kitsch. Somewhere ahead, a nighttram wheezed on its tracks, clanged its bell. Němec orientated himself towards it, stumbled, fell, urged himself up.

A few more steps & a clearing opened out of the maze. In the middle of it, a pair of lopsided megaphones hung on a sentry pole beside a tramshelter. Like poisonous flowers, he thought. Triffids, maybe. A clock's gibbous eye floated in a haemorrhage of traffic-light red. The arrangement of hour & minute hands made no sense. Perhaps, in some parallel world, they or it might've offered a way out, a clear line of flight.* For some reason he thought about that first night, with the Prof's ghost on the snowbank. Something familiar, but not quite. Always that element of disconnect. One drink too many & one drink too few. For example, he recognised, on the far side of the "clearing," the gates of Strahov Monastery. No deadmen tonight, though. No signs of life either. And there, across the way, Kepler & Brahe keeping silent vigil. Beyond, the dreck of

---

* "Like the tender blush of winter mornings & long summer evenings." [✊]
* But not in this world, where every step in the direction of the EXIT sign was an interest-bearing debt. [✊]

suburbia. Some 1950s social experiment that failed (like all the others): filing-cabinet grey, anfractuous, amortised, a democracy of ones & zeros operated by remote-control.* And how would a reasonable human being live in a box? Like having your head surgically detached, wrapped in formica & set in concrete before dumped in the river — but still aware (you think).* But did Němec count as a reasonable human being?

With a vague feeling of trepidation, he waded out onto the too-perfect illusion of a cobbled expanse, of rainslicked tarmac, of glistening tramtracks. What would it've taken to shatter it, release Němec from his reverie? What mysterious ordination of events? Had it not, all, long ago, been predetermined thus? From the first cell division, the bisecting line, man walking erect, the shadow of a mountain, the finger pointing at G.O.D.? Němec being, so to speak, *that finger*?* But he himself was unaware of any of this. Approaching the middle of "the clearing" by now, gazing up at the megaphones on their pole — expecting, perhaps, some tremendous voice to speak to him, issue commands. As once before. *That* night. Lying in the snow. But when the echo of his footsteps faded, all Němec could hear was the sound of his own breathing. And even that failed to convince him.

---

* The hidden diodes, resistors, capacitators, transistors of the secret T.E.S.L.A. / Š.V.E.J.K. MINDMACHINE, points defining a periphery, now that the centre had disappeared? [☜]

* Or the opposite — some sort of private decapitation machine, to sever all the connections, turn off the constant noise, sit alone in the dark & hear nothing, see nothing, think nothing. Bliss! To be able, at will, to exist the way an object exists… And at the end of it all, even the inert things come alive, evolve through processes of intention, propel themselves forward across eons of time, from appliance to organism, from polymer to complex manifold, each with some curious, inchoate image of its perfectible self — like Mydlář's axe, dreaming of the guillotine, the way the guillotine dreams of the Model-T production-line, & the way *it* dreams of an I.B.M. computer, switching the points on a hundredthousand rail-connections across this blacked-out continent, & the final, God-machine, the blackhole metamorphosis, the Solution-to-End-All-Solutions. *Yer eider widdus, aw agennus*, says the talkinghead in the idiotbox. Aye-aye chief… [☜]

* How else to explain the persistence, down the ages, of this obsession with spires, towers, pillars, columns, obelisks, statues both lifesize & colossal, cenotaphs, metronomes, plinths, weathervanes, antennae, dowsing rods tuned to astral frequencies, phantom radio signals, Enochian Morse, minuteman homing signals, nosecones & sonar blips & isotope decay, lighthouses, totem poles, minarets, fetishes in which reside the mojos of the species, the genii locorum, the secret mind transmitters, Id-Ego-Superego — Kelley's lightning conductor, Kepler's cosmoghoulery, Kammler's aggregated neutron kaleidoscope — & all for the sake of what? Pandemonium & Guiltless laughter? Did all the weird conspiracies add-up in the end to nothing more than a pedantic obsession with decline & ruin? A child's-play pivotal truth waking-up to the absence of rules in the universe, of civilisation advancing through mindless struggle — wheels-within-the-ever-reinvented-wheel — like Arepo the hapless sower? Or Kammler, who whichever way you looked at it, was surely dead. But did he finish the job in the end, or didn't he? [☜]

52

FAUSTBITCH

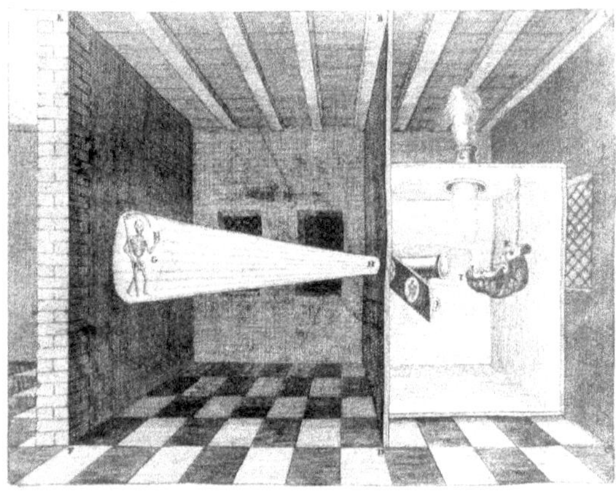

What you first recognised was her nakedness. Or rather, the nakedness of an assemblage: of exposed body parts that stretched from the floor of the gallery to the ceiling — heavily contrasted flesh tones shaped to suggest a mouth, a breast, a pair of thighs, an earlobe, the nape of a neck, throat, navel, buttocks, a surgical corset, twin pelvic bones, gravitating around the tensed muscular ridge of the groin. What the mini-brochure you could pick up at a table inside the door said:

> ...The model's body appears to be reconstructed from arbitrarily arranged fragments, made coherent by the geometrical grid of a large metal cage, or else the gauze of a curtain pressed against a telephoto lens. The face, neither strictly human nor alien, reveals itself on closer inspection to be incomplete, truncated, an effect that has been carefully premeditated by the photographer, who flaunts his intimacy with the object of his camera's dissections by having enlarged the image to room-size dimensions...

The gallery itself could've been described as a "dislocated" series of white cubes, to match all the dislocated physiology. The ceilings were all panelled with opaque skylights. This last feature had been put to use as a wildly profane simulacrum of stainedglass windows, in which the saints had predictably been swapped for bits of dissected anatomy. The brochure had very particular things to say about this:

...All these bodies represent a transfigured map of the cosmos — a dream constellation from the camera's submind — revealing the secret logic of an image capable of making itself real only by facets. What stands naked before the viewer is not a woman, or even women, but a universal concept. To perceive what it is, is to perceive something entirely without precedent, something that requires the eye to be re-invented. Each figure evolves punctually, by optical disjunction, metastasis, mutation. Perverse hybrids of remote & mythical symbiotics intertwine. Whole genealogies of the universal body unfold before our eyes. They depict nothing but are instead *constituted*, in a circumvolving processes of generation, devirgination, invagination, like the grafted genitalia of plants...

Which meant, Němec decided, *fucking themselves.* Just reading the stuff was like participating in a kind of orgy by attrition. The word *overload* came readily to mind. Maybe that was the intention. Like what they'd called the show, *Alex Steiner: Overexposed*, which wasn't much of a misnomer.

Němec scanned the rooms. In all, there must've been a couple of hundred pictures hanging on the walls, all different sizes, all apparently done with different equipment to go with the different "moods": a Hasselblad, a Fex 127, a Canon F-1, a Flexaret, a Kodak disposable, a Casio QV-10. There were screenshots from a closed-circuit surveillance video, images re-photographed from studio prints, from a movie screen, from a TV screen — unfocused, cut across by lines of static, pixellated. There were photomontages cut from old porno magazines, construction manuals, re-shot & blown-up. Distorted lenses, multiple exposures, solarisations, photoshop jobs. One whole wall was given up to nothing but polaroids. Another one to production stills from *The Teratologists*.

Even when the photographs weren't strictly *her*, they were all, in one way or another, versions of Alice Steinerová.

The actual Alice Steinerová was waiting at the far end of the gallery, in front of a wall-sized portrait of herself, a black fake fur coat hanging from her shoulders. Němec came up beside her.

'D'you think justice has been done?' she asked, without looking at him.

Her voice echoed in the gallery. There were only three other visitors, standing in a group by the door. The gallery assistant, in blue pinstripe & flaming hair, was hovering around them, trying to earn his commission. Němec leant on his stick & took in the composition. He could smell Alice Steinerová's perfume. Citrus, acetone —

'Whoever speaks about justice these days?'

Němec heard her snort derisively, but there was a faint smile on her lips.

'Y'know what Viktor thinks?' Alice said. "Man's forever searching for the one woman who is all aspects of the Eternal Lover." And I quote.'

Viktor, as in Faktor. But before he could think the obvious thought, Alice snatched the walking stick from his hand, so that he almost tipped over. Teasingly she stepped back from him & laughed. Her voice rose —

'It's such a bunch of horseshit. I mean, where do men like him get that stuff anyway? Can you even imagine what that means? All those fancy ideas, once you get them undressed, are uglier than the Bride of Frankenstein. That thing, there,' she pointed Němec's walkingstick at her naked doppelgänger, 'is what the Eternal Lover really looks like.'

Alice winked, took Němec's arm & steered him towards the exit. Out in the foyer, the gallery assistant & a young woman were kneeling on the floor, unrolling prints. An office stood off to one side. The assistant & the young woman both looked up when Alice & Němec came through, but didn't stop what they were doing. There were prints lying everywhere, like bodies left where they'd fallen, reminded of mass-grave Vernichtungslager photos, some of them large enough to fill a wall. On a table beside these were more pictures, shuffled in a pile, magazine-size — headless, arms knotted, legs & genitals splayed — *Alice im Wunderland* visions of little hands dextersinister, vermillioned mouths, pimply arses, breasts poutpointed, pubises downed black-brown-blonde, the tiny pink verboten shitwhiffing anuses, like the fragmented nocturnal doubles of all those doe-eyed, sloe-eyed Hankas, Lenkas, Katkas, Michaelas, Verunkas, Johankas, Lučinkas, Aničkas, Pavlas, Barboras, Brigitas, Petras, Milenkas, Bohuškas of lost ineffable childhoods, sullied in nightsatined, charblacked, sootstained light — allegories of lost innocence & all that.

Alice pointed into the office. Grey light shifted through the horizontal bands of a Venetian blind & the vertical pleats of a drawn curtain. Street sounds echoed through the half open window behind them: a man's voice, a radio, a car engine starting & the sound of the car pulling off down the street. The assistant got up off the floor & followed them into the office. He grinned at Alice, they seemed to know one another. There were more pictures on the walls. Němec ogled them. Behind a desk was a large colour print, about one-&-a-half by two metres. It showed a naked woman behind a curtain of loosely woven netting, body arched in electroshock. Beside it, a row of similar pictures, smaller in scale. Rayographs, electric bodies, skin colour-saturated to the point of abstraction. Once again Alice had been distorted beyond recognition, her identity transposed onto other bodies, other *body structures*, ornamented with tattoos, piercings, graftings, fine traceries of scar tissue, prosthetic bulges, lips, eyelids, labia, red &

green mandala patterns swirling.

On the opposite wall & filling most of it was an entirely different kind of image. It showed a bare room lit by late afternoon sunlight falling through several small regular windowpanes. Through the windowpanes, the sky was unusually bright. On a mahogany parquet floor, there were three elongated rectangles of light, each broken into smaller rectangles by the parquet. Lying lengthwise across the photograph, & intersected by the planes of light, was the face & torso of a woman (Alice Steinerová's ectopic twin?) sheathed in a translucent green mesh. The mesh was so fine it almost appeared to be a trick of light. Her head had been angled downwards, so that her eyes appeared closed, but could easily not have been. A loose braid of hair had been arranged above the left breast, forming a cryptic monogram. Lying beside this version of Alice Steinerová on the floor was a coil of electrical wire unravelled in the approximate shape of a treble clef — while around her breasts, a length of cord wound tight in a cinched figure-eight.

The whole composition had a premeditated & ritualistic appearance, like a highspeed snapshot of a nightmare in progress. As Němec stepped closer to the picture, he realised that Alice was leaning against the doorframe with folded arms, watching, as though she was making a study of him. Her whole face had become a mask of tension. There was something about her look & that image — something between them he couldn't situate — like an erotic secret.

'In the end,' Alice said, 'what'll be left of us to judge, but our images?'

She raised her eyebrow as if posing the question other than rhetorically. Němec tried to think of something to say, but couldn't. What the Prof said: *The Image, with a capital I, is like religion: it buries History.* Alice pointed his stick at her bound double —

'Alex met that one at the clinic,' Alice said. 'A patient, like me. Bipolar. Topped herself.'

Němec looked back at the face in the picture. It wasn't Alice anymore, but a complete stranger. Perhaps none of them were her. He felt, for a moment, that he'd been standing on the edge of a precipice, & had only managed to pull back at the last moment. He said —

'What's the Doctor think about that?'

'…'

'People pay for this sort of thing?'

'It's meant to be art, not pornography.'

'Pornography's in the eye of the beholder,' he said.

Or what was *really* porn was the Dick & Jane routine the normalisation freaks tried to zap on everyone else's dirty secrets. Besides, you'd never know from the picture that the dead girl was schizo. Was it more arousing that way? Where'd the eye stop? At the image, or the story you sold it with? Alice gave a derisive snort —

'Pornography's what you *intend*.'

'Does Volta make a habit of pimping out his patients?'

'You're one of his patients, you tell me.'

'I'm not in any of your brother's snuff pics.'

'Yet.'

Someone laughed. Němec turned to see the gallery assistant draping an arm across Alice's shoulders —

'You ask me,' the assistant said, nodding at the dead girl's picture, hair like a devil's horns tapering up from the sides of his head, 'it's the image that matters, stripping it bare, no gimmicks.'

He leered —

'Anything that tries to be art makes me want to puke.'

'Nakedness, he thinks,' Alice pushed the assistant's arm away, 'is the essential condition for truth.'

'The secret,' the assistant winked, 'is knowing which is which.'

Barely had the leaves fallen from the trees…

when snow swept in from the east. A very fine icy snow falling against the windows with a sound like TV static / water evaporating on a hotplate / a woman pulling on a pair of stockings. For "old times' sake" Alice suggested the bar behind the Zrcadlo Theatre, it was only a couple of blocks away but the place was packed with an early Friday Night crowd so they went downstairs to a basement joint called *The Richter*. *The Richter* was only marginally less crowded & humid as a watery lung. Němec brushed the snow off his hat & peered through the smoke haze at a single long room with a bar at one end & a stage at the other. Low vaulted ceiling. Candles on tables. A character in a 10-gallon Stetson was blowing on a saxophone while a fat woman in some sort of burlesque arrangement gargled into a microphone. She could just about hold a note together. Němec winced. *Belly of the whale, kiddo. Just do like Jonah…*

As luck would have it, there was an open spot by the back wall, right up against the stage — a sofa with split cushions & busted springs under a low-hanging lampshade. Alice shrugged off the fake fur, ☞ tattoo & gold chain, black shoulderstraps. Behind the fat woman & the sax, a kid in a cocktail waiter's vest was caressing a double bass twice his size beside a sleepy highhat with an afro. It took a while, but eventually a waitress found them. She wore a pink ballerina's tutu & green cutaway chemise — Němec figured it must be fancy dress or something. He tipped his hat back, hung the stick in the crook of his arm. *Fit right in, eh, kiddo?* Alice ordered a carafe of red, so Němec settled for the same. She pressed close —

'Looking at pictures of myself,' she said in his ear, 'always makes me thirsty.'

The drummer hit a cymbal right on cue. The alto wailed. The fat woman, head back sweating with mouth open, showed the room her cavities, like a Queen of Spades in a convex mirror.

The band wrapped up their number just as the drinks arrived. Something about that tutu. Němec poured. People came, people went. Alice smirked at him over her glass —

'Here's to the Eternal Lover,' she said.

'Why not to life after death?'

She gave him one of those looks & then leant closer. He felt her fingernails scrape the back of his neck, her breath —

'Was I how you imagined me?'

'Maybe,' he said, meeting her eyes.

Even in the halflight their blue was unreal.

'D'you think there's more?'

He shrugged, drank the wine —

'I saw that film you were in,' he said.

'Mmm?'

'There was one scene in particular…'

Alice laughed. She took a cigarette out of her purse, lit it —

'You're not going to get all sensitive on me, are you, after everything we've been through together?'

She blew smoke at him —

'It was Níko's idea. He thought it'd be… *visually compelling*, I think were his exact words.'

'You told him?'

'No, *you* did.'

'I don't remember. I just remember what I saw.'

'Except you didn't,' she said flatly, dragging on the cigarette, exhaling. 'It was just in your head.'

'And now it's in someone's film…'

'Life as we know it,' she smirked, stubbing her butt out on the armrest.

The band clanked & wheezed. The waitress slopped some drinks.

'They shut down the cabaret,' Němec said.

'They shut down all the best places. It's how it goes.'

The saxplayer fiddled with his mouthpiece. Blew some notes. The fat woman climbed back on stage, showing even more skin than before. Němec emptied his glass. Poured. Alice kept pace. He figured they'd settled in for the long haul. He flagged the waitress, she brought another carafe. The sax bawled. It complicated the repartee. Alice closed her eyes. He thought of Hedda Gabler, holding a gun to her head, pulling the trigger. The fat woman & the sax went on arguing. He worked the carafe down to halfway. Alice held out her glass, he filled it, she downed it in one. He emptied the rest of the carafe into it. The waitress in the tutu was on the other side of the room. Němec felt Alice's fingernails on his neck again. She was looking at him with those eyes —

'Tell me about you,' she said.

The saxophone snorted. The fat woman straightened her cleavage.

'Nothing to tell,' Němec shrugged.

The sax simpered. The fat woman bellyflopped off a high note.

'Don't be so fucking coy,' Alice poked him in the shirt. 'Tell me where you grew up, what you did, why you're here…'

The sax groaned, grated, growled. The fat woman sashayed behind the mic stand, popped a seam, flashed too much thigh.

'I grew up in an orphanage,' Němec deadpanned.

Alice raised her eyebrows, lit another cigarette, inhaled —

'Sorry for asking.'

She flicked ash.

'No need to be.'

Němec gulped wine. The fat lady rearranged cleavage, a pair of tassels spilled out of the décolleté. The sax revved. The bass thumped. Cymbals crashed.

'How'd they die?'

'Who?'

'Mum & dad, stupid.'

The fat woman worked the mic stand. The sax gasped. Němec gulped more wine —

'The estébáci took them away when I was five…'

He emptied his glass. Gazed into it —

'I can't even remember what they looked like.'

'You mean you never saw them again?'

He shook his head. The fat woman bumped & ground. The sax savaged it. Alice's hand slid to his shoulder. He could feel it go limp.

'That sucks…' she said. 'What'd they do?'

'Who cares? What they did doesn't mean anything.'

'…?'

'What they didn't do doesn't mean anything either.'

Alice said nothing. The waitress brought the wine & an ashtray, blue glass with a white mosaic pattern. The fat woman shook. The sax quaked. Alice set the ashtray on the sofa & flicked ash into it. She whistled —

'He's really milking that sax for every dollar she's worth, isn't he?'

Němec shrugged. Němec poured. The band closed-out the set in an orgy of overcooked shrieks, groans, smashing cymbals & gyrating udders. The crowd yukked. The crowd went on shouting over their drinks. Němec wiped the sweat away from his brow. Alice poked him in the arm —

'Well?'

'Well what?'

'Don't be such a wet fish…'

Němec stared at the pasty white underflesh of the fat woman's tits as she tried repacking them so the tassels wouldn't snag. It looked like one hell of a complicated procedure. Alice clicked her tongue. Němec pursed his lips thoughtfully, thinking what he could say to please her.

'After '89,' he said, finally, 'I went to the Ministry & read what was in the files. There was hardly a crime that wasn't in there. Everything from treason to sodomy. It was like being complicit in this enormous filthy fucking lie. Before that, I didn't know anything, & afterwards…' He sloshed wine. 'Problem is, I never really forgave them for ditching me like that. It sounds ridiculous, but… And then I start thinking, maybe it was my fault?'

Sure makin' heavy weather with the dialogue, kiddo.

Němec stared at the floor. He felt the situation slipping. In his mind he tried to hold onto it. The light went brassy. It was like one of those photographs: Alice as Sphinx in fake fur. She made a face at him —

'That's a terrible story,' she said. 'Tell me a better one.'

The band were passing around a bottle of JD. Whiskey poured down between the fat woman's chins. She'd somehow stuffed most of herself back in her dress, but things kept going awry with the arrangement. She looked like seven years of purgatory squeezed into one night. Němec shivered. It gave him an idea —

'How about this,' he said.

Alice grinned a slightly lopsided grin & blew smoke at him —

'I'm all eager anticipation.'

'I just got this cute idea for a film,' Němec grinned back. '*Faustbitch.*'

'*What* bitch?'

'Faust. Like *Doctor* Faust? The wizard guy who sold his soul to the Devil, you know, in return for Absolute Knowledge?'

'That's heavy,' Alice said. 'Like he knew *everything*?'

'Nah,' Němec drawled, 'he got conned, didn't he? Devil made him think he had these superpowers, but it was all fake. The guy was a jerk, anyhow. Only thing he really wanted was to screw Helen of Troy.'

'Helen of Troy?'

'You know...'

'Yeah, I *know*. But you'd go for someone a bit younger, wouldn't you, if you had the choice? I mean, like Helena Vondráčková or something.'

'Helena Vondráčková?'

'Or Lucie Bílá. Or...'

'Yeah, yeah, anyhow...'

'Aňa Geislerová...'

'It'd be about this Robert Johnson character who sells his soul to Old scratch so he can basically jump in the sack with the chief Muse herself, that's his thing. The wellspring of all poetic inspiration, right?'

'Or Olga Havlová...'

'The catch is, before he gets to do the dirty, he's got to use his super mindpowers to knock-off seven Number One hits in seven years, each greater than anything ever written before in the entire history of whatever. Deathless stuff, kind of David Bowie meets Christopher Marlowe. And each time our Faustus lookalike scores the Top of the Pops, Mrs Muse is duly required to shed one of her, *um,* more exotic garments...'

'Or Silvie Tomčalová. Or...'

'Sort of dance-of-the-seven-veils, but with this complicated Greek mythology-type underwear, see?'

Němec grinned with his teeth. Alice blew smoke.

'So when our Superstar finally gets to the end of his illustrious seven-year run (the solidest hard-on in Literary history, *hehe*) — getting down the final *mot juste* of his magnum opus, big Number 7, the Song-of-Songs, the Book-to-end-all-Books — Madam Muse's supposed to be there ready & waiting to bear it all, her unsullied charms, starkers, right where he can get his grubby little Faust-hands on her. *And*, if he can still manage it, you know, if he hasn't tied his dick in a knot by this stage: the whole package tour! But only once, right? Cause anyway it's gonna be the greatest screw of All Time, you know, unrepeatable, cosmic, out-of-this-fucking-world. And as soon as Old Boy's had his prize, shot his load, whatever, the Devil's gonna come to collect on the contract, write the biopic, franchise the musical, earn the big dividends...'

'No, definitely Helena Vondráčková.'

'But here's the twist. Our Meyrink-type's a little too clever for his own top-hat & reckons he's figured a way to get in ahead of the game, pen the odd rhyme as a diversionary tactic while secretly poking his mellifluent Muse on the side, you know, having his proverbial piece of cake & slobbering over it too, keeping Old Scratch on the long middle-finger...'

'Mmmm...'

'Except when our hero actually tries putting his Cunning Plan into action, slipping around backstage for a sneak preview of the big awards ceremony, he gets a bit more than he bargained for. Picture it like this: there's Bright Boy, peering out through a crack in the curtains, blinking into the footlights, & there's her Muse-ness, a big horny redhead shaking it right out in front of the chorus line, nothing but a frilly g-string to hide the holy of holies. It looks like the subscribers've been getting the Real Deal while he's been busy slaving at the writing desk. But just as he's about to blow a gasket, the Mighty Muse catches sight of him perving through the pleats, licks her lips, gives the tassels a whirl, thumps the rump, turns & tosses him one of those wide-eyed fuck-me-till-doomsday looks over her shoulder (like she's been secretly expecting a backstage visit & the rest's just part of the dayjob, wink-nudge). You know, like this Pampered Ponce of a Pop Pinup's the *special guy* & she's simply been *dying* for him to give her a taste of his untold genius, doesn't want to have to wait herself any seven years for it either, turning to stale cheese, gotta get it while it's fresh, right? And just to prove she means what he thinks she means, her Muse-ness throws him the sluttiest Lolita-like come-&-get-it grin you can imagine, has him fit to plotz faster than you can say K.H. Mácha…'

'*Lucie* Vondráčková…?'

'But! Before our dear Poet Prince can pour his heart out of his pants, there's a flourish from the bandstand, horn-sound, drum-roll, high-hat, cymbal. The audience yuks bigtime, they're in on something, know what's coming next & its *goooood*. Our dumb dipshit of a faux Faust, meanwhile, just stands there in his socks blinking bugeyed as Mistress Muse swings around, gets her thumbs under the elasticated nylon & — *toodaloo!* — just like that she bends over & drops all pretences, giving him a sly wink between her legs, fake eyelashes all dewy, hands around her ankles now & that big slobbery bottoxed pout stretched ear-to-ear. You can hear the Peenie Poet's jaw hit the boards. But there's more to come! 'Cause as she shimmies that celestial booty of hers in the dumbstruck horny little rhymester's face, what's Little Peeniepiles see but the dirty ol' Devil Himself leering out from between the Dear Desirable's comely pins like a jack-in-the-box blowing a sloppy raspberry. *Pthrrrrrt!* And right there & then that Sewerbrained Sucker of a Sentimentalist, & all the priceless poésie he's penned in his precious pastime, goes *puff!* in a cloud of creosote. The curtains come down & up pops Bugs Bunny in the spotlight — *Meh, that's all folks!*'

Alice shook her head —

'D'you talk like this all the time?'

'Only when I think maybe I'm going crazy.'

'Is that something that's likely to happen?'

'If I keep seeing dwarfs & talking fish & secretaries in ridiculous wigs & fat men with cigars every time I turn around, it might be.'

Alice laughed, Sphinx-like. Stubbed out her cigarette —

'Have you checked behind you recently?'

'I think you know more than you're letting on.'

'That's a woman's prerogative.'

'Touché, Miss Gabler.'

Awareness gradually drifted in…

from the frayed edges of a field of vision left flattened by a squall in the night. When Němec awoke, he was alone. Then the sound of a tap running in the bathroom — a muted voice — water splashing on tile — events of the previous coming back in slivers & ugly broken fragments. His first thought was that something terrible had happened. He stumbled naked to the window, squinted through a gap in the black plastic. A vague pervasive nonlight hung over the street. Faint flecks of snow. The sound of workmen on their scaffold. Day, then, Němec supposed. Day *after*. A jackhammer pounded in indecent proximity. *Shit.* Němec felt like his head was going to split open. He scoped the fake fur lying on the camp bed. He scoped the dregs of a bottle sitting on the floor & ate some hair of the dog. It bit back. He ate it all. The dog growled. The dog played dead. He wondered where his clothes got to. The water in the bathroom stopped. The jackhammer thumped. He gave up on the clothes & dug among the vinyls for something to drown out the deconstruction.

'Sweet dreams?' a voice asked, coming from the doorway.

Němec turned & was confronted with a vision of Alice:

(A) Naked with 🔫 tattoo, a gold key on a chain between a child's breasts, the cleft void of her sex, revealed by facets, image & anti-image…

(B) Naked with bowler hat tipped forward half-concealing her eyes, walkingstick propping up her left hip, right index finger flat on upper lip making a Chaplin moustache…

(C) Naked but with a surgical corset, a stitched-together patchwork body mirroring his own — some broken-backed angel without her wings (snared on the wires up on Suicide Bridge, sirens laughing in the night, this fallen world) — hair wet dripping onto her shoulders, the cold making the pores on the nape of her neck stand out…

(D) Or, he heard her come into the room behind him. Footsteps. At the sound of her voice, he turned around. *Sweet dreams?* she asked. Vitruvian woman. Triangle, circle, gun tattoo. She came towards him. Her skin glowed. The impression was so real Němec wanted to touch her just to be sure, but he didn't…

'Some collection you've got,' Alice said, glancing at a box of vinyls. 'D'you really listen to all that stuff?'

'Different frames of mind,' he said, pressing his hand to his temple. 'They come & go.'

She stepped past him & stood close to the window, looking out through a gap in the black plastic. Němec could see her breath condensing & freezing on the glass. It made him think of a story that'd been in the news when he was eight years old, about a kid who'd drowned at Šárka during a school excursion. When the police went to dredge the lake, they also found the body of a woman that'd been there for months maybe — it was impossible to identify the corpse, except for the sex. How she ended up in there was anyone's guess. Alice made a queer face at him —

'There's someone outside your window.'

'It's nothing. They're supposed to be fixing the house. Or taking it apart. Difficult to tell which.'

'Ah...'

He dropped a scratchy Dizzy Gillespie EP on the turntable, it seemed to suit the occasion somehow. *Live in Golem City*, 1971. Art Blakey (drums), Sonny Stitt (alto), Al McKibbon (bass), Kai Winding (trombone), Thelonious Monk (piano). Alice slid across the parquet & got her coat, wrapped it around her. *Around Midnight* filled the room. Gillespie's spectral trumpet riff, moribund to the point of genius. Alice tossed her hair back. It was real at least. Her eyes, less blue, drifted down the patchwork of his birthday suit.

'You really made a mess of yourself.'

Němec followed the direction of her eyes. But it was obvious. The scars stood out in the cold like welts. Itched.

'You're circumcised,' she said. 'Does that mean you're...?'

Well, how was he supposed to script this part? Not the sort of thing they let you forget in a Children's Home. *Squillhead.* That was part of it, too. *The circumcisèd dog.* Hiding in the showers, getting punched in the ear, Ol' Deathbed making a sermon out of how not owning a certain piece of ancillary skinflap made certain boys (no prize for guessing *who*) into filthy pocket-pingpong-playing perverts. Did Němec know the answer? What it said in his parents' police file: Mother's maiden name: **NATSCHKE**. (Neither Zhiddish nor not-Zhiddish.) Given names: **Freude E.** Religion: **None**. (Neither an affirmative nor a negative with regard to cause of specific anatomical condition of sole child, medical, religious, or otherwise.) Or the hundred different versions he'd told himself or been told, by persons sympathetic or etc.:

1. Mummy's midwife was a Zhid in disguise.

2. Mummy mater was Bosnian, Albanian, Krymchak.

3. Mummy was a secret member of the global crypto-Zionist conspiracy.

4. Mummy possessed unnatural un-Sklavonic ideas about personal hygiene thence foisted upon her God-Given Dearly Belovèd with the illegal assistance of an unlicensed quack.

5. Mummy was an unrepentant child-abusing pervert.

6. Babamummy performed said obscene deed herself in the kitchen sink with a paring knife under hypnotic suggestion of Western Imperialist Powers.

7. Mummy's vodka-swilling midwife missed the umbilicus & gave baby Squillhead's goyish ganglion the snip instead.

8. Mummy was an accessory before, during & after the fact of an unofficially-sanctioned peenie-preserving last-second surgery, performed post-haste at the local A&E to which she (Mummy), tearfully anxious, had relayed said Dearly-Belovèd with a severe case of traumatism of [unmentionable appendage], cause unspecified, though onset of gangrene threatening, if unchecked, to become general all over Squillhead's eye-end: all mention of which inadvertently omitted from Interior Ministry file due to diligent clerical oversight, etc.

'Did it hurt?'

Alice wiggled a finger at the aggrieved thing between Němec's thighs — the pealed squill, the dissected dingus, the de-prepuced prick, the un-nerved nob, the callously cuirassed & covenanted cock. *Mitzva aseh.*

'What?'

'When they chopped it off. Did it hurt?'

'I was probably only eight days old.'

'That's incredible. And you remember?'

'No.'

'I couldn't imagine letting someone do that to me with a knife.'

'It's not unheard of.'

'They say some people can remember pain even from when they were still in their mother's womb. Prenatal trauma. Dreams & nightmares. I just have these memories where everyone's bigger than me. That's all. Just these incredibly tall giant people standing over me like trees. That's my whole childhood. The rest I don't remember at all. It's as if, when my parents died, suddenly I became aware of things, & that's when the pain began.'

'…'

'…'

'One thing I can remember very distinctly, is that one day — I was still really young, not even six years old — I was with this other boy, Buzík his name was, & we were playing in a park near the Home where they'd take us sometimes to a playground, with swings & a big sandpit & a pond with reeds & carp in it. In winter you could skate on it, if they let you have skates, or just in your shoes. This particular day, I was digging in the sandpit & Buzík came over & started digging too & in the middle of the sandpit we found a duck buried under the sand. A real duck. We dug it out as carefully as we could, it was still alive & it stared at us with its head tilted & one eye sort of bulging out. Buzík picked it up & handed it to me. There was still sand in its feathers, but it was warm & its body swelled & contracted in my hands as it breathed. I could feel its heart beating. Then it opened its beak & in its beak there was a large blue glass bead. We carried the duck down to the pond & set it on the water & the bead fell out of its mouth into my hand. Light cloudy blue. And then one of the androids came & took it away from me & we were barred from the playground, both of us, for a week. And the android called me a Zhid. No-one ever called me a Zhid before then.'

'Androids? What androids?'

'The ones who controlled the Home.'

'…?'

'I was accused of practicing dark rituals. *Mene, mene.* Like the Elders of Zion.'

'Because of a duck? What about your friend?'

'He was the one who informed on me.'

Was this the place for a little poetic license to creep in? But Němec remembered it like it was yesterday. Buzík, who once called him into a toilet cubicle to show him how he could *crack a fat*, peeling back the foreskin, nob-end all purple in that dumb little fist of his. Places of wonder, toilet cubicles.

Alice shook her head & gave him a sceptical look —

'It's too early in the day for me, I can't keep up.'

'There's coffee in the kitchen. I'll get some,' he said, to steer things onto a different track.

Němec found his clothes lying on the kitchen floor, dragged them on, though couldn't for the life of him… The Prof's Polygraphia was exactly where he'd left it in the sink. He retrieved the bundle & stuffed in the bin, dumping the trash on top of it, then scrounged about for some coffee to brew. Ran the water. Set the pot on the stove. Lit the gas. Dug in his stash for the magic pain pills. Swallowed three — pink pill-coating smeared on thumb & index finger, *in hoc signo vinces*. The pot belched on the stove, hissed steam. He poured a short cup, gulped it hot. Then another & took it out to the bureau. Alice stood in the doorway to Elsbeth von N_____'s "garçonnière" —

'Don't you believe in furniture?'

'It gets in the way. I like to keep things simple.'

'Last night,' she winked. 'Was that your first time…? With a woman, I mean.'

'My first time *what* with a woman?'

'You know. Not with a man.'

'What makes you think I *you know* with men?'

'Oh, it was just... I heard somewhere about how they can cure people with electroshock.'

'Cure what?'

'By putting all the brain patterns back the way they're supposed to be.'

'And how're they *supposed* to be?'

'Normal.'

'All this because I'm *circumcised*?'

'Noooo,' she laughed.

'Is that what Volta told you, that he thinks I'm queer?'

'Does he?'

'How the hell would I know, he's your sugarpop, love, not mine.'

'That wasn't a nice thing to say.'

'Well I'm sorry if I rubbed you the wrong way, Alice.'

He left her to sulk while he went back through the kitchen to scrounge for a drink. His head was in no condition for intellectual chitchat without a dose of something stronger than carbonised Sierra Maestra. *Shit.* The place was as dry as a box seat at the opera. When he got back, Alice was sitting cross-legged in front of the typewriter, chin cupped in her hands, reading. She frowned —

'What's this?'

'It's nothing. Just an idea I had.'

She unwound the page from the machine, then read aloud —

'"Alice rushes out. Jan stares at the manuscript lying on the floor. Quickly gathers it up, stuffs it inside his coat, & exits stage-left. As he does so, he quietly laughs to himself. At the same time we hear Alice scream. Silence. Several moments pass. Then, as at start, she enters from stairs, staggers into the dressingroom, crosses, slumps in her chair. Her face is blank. Above, there's the sound of footsteps: someone running, two people in pursuit. Voices. A scuffle. During this, Alice stares at the gun on the dressingroom table. Picks it up. Looks at it. Lifts the gun to her temple. Waits. The sound of heavy footsteps comes from the top of the stairway. She pulls the trigger — there's a loud gunshot offstage. Alice stares. Beat. She pulls the trigger again — there's a click. Beat. She stares at the gun, confused, & begins to cry. Sobbing, she hammers the gun on the dressingroom table in a fit of despair — as she does so, the stagedoor opens & the two Ivans enter — they both carry revolvers. *Well now,*

Miss Gabler, playing with pistols again?'"

Her eyes were blank.

'It won't make sense unless you read all of it.'

'You wrote this about *me?*'

'It's just a play. It's not supposed to be real.'

'That's funny. You remind me of what a little boy I knew once said, about how he felt guilty *even when he was telling the truth...* So what happens next?'

'That's the end.'

'I mean us. Now.'

'You know what they say. Stuff has a way of taking care of itself.'

'And you believe that?'

'What I believe never seemed to have any bearing on the matter.'

'Wise before your time.'

'I had good teachers. The best. I remember in one of our classes, we had to learn all these big numbers & copy down all these difficult calculations with formulae whose only reason for existing was probably to make just those calculations & nothing else. We had to memorise all of them, exactly the way they were written. The teacher came around & checked our study books & I got mine wrong, because instead of writing an infinity symbol I'd drawn a pair of glasses, with a little comicbook eyebeam pointing at the letter "I," which was supposed to be a "1" — infinity minus one. So the teacher drew a big red cross on the page & made me start again. But now I was completely confused — I didn't know what I was meant to write, so I asked her, *What's the last number before infinity?*'

'And what'd the teacher say?'

'That I was a scheming little subversive. Made me stand in the corner of the room in front of the whole class with my hands on my head, facing the wall. I think I was eight years old.'

Did you ever hear the one about...

the moyle who slipped and got the sack? The joke came back to him from remote wintry dreams of childhood, sledding on Petřín Hill, on the rare occasion, etc. — Buzík & the other kids joyfully pelting snowballs at his head. *Pop goes the Squill!* Snow in his eyes, mouth, ears. Best days, so said.

The snow had stopped falling & the sky was bright. Němec felt as though he hadn't seen a day like this in years. For a long time they walked in silence, close but without touching. Then Alice took his arm —

'You never told me how it happened,' she said, all of a sudden.

'How what happened?'

'Those scars.'

'An accident. I fell.'

'You fell?'

'Someone put a window in my way…'

Alice laughed silently to herself —

'Please tell me you weren't trying to feed the pigeons.'

'What's wrong with pigeons?'

'Rats with wings.'

'We're all very closely related, apparently.'

'I've never heard of a rat falling out of a window.'

'A poet said once, *The perfect type of the man of action is the suicide.*'

'Do you think he was right?'

'He also said, *The world of action is a world of stones.*'

'I like that. Very literary. What would be the perfect *rat* of action?'

'Go the rat!'

'D'you believe humanity has a future?'

'What's to believe? As far as I can see, humanity's a fine line ever narrowing.'

'How high?'

'How high what?'

'The window.'

'Not high enough.'

'You should be glad.'

'So they tell me.'

'The problem for Níko is he thinks everyone's a suicide case deep down, just crying out for his special attention, only they don't know it yet. That's why at the clinic they all call him the Resurrection Man.'

'Here's something for you to consider. D'you realise that *suicide* & *circumcision* are virtually the same word? One means to cut *around*, the other to cut *yourself.* You hear stories about that, some goy gets all passionate over one of them Ben-Gurion types & decides he's gonna go back with him & live on a kibbutz or wherever, so one night he gets blind drunk & performs his own slice-job with a razorblade. Almost bleeds to death right there in his bathroom, right? Call it suicide by misadventure. Wonder what your Níko'd make of *that.*'

'Is this another one of your true stories?'

'What do you mean? All my stories are true stories.'

They both stopped halfway up the hill & took in the view. The City, *like a chessboard at the beginning of a game...* On the horizon stood the TV tower. Below, the gilded rooftop of the National Theatre glittered in the sun. Through the naked trees, the square towers of the Hunger Wall stood out against the hillside. They weren't alone — a group of tourists passed them on the steps coming down. Němec wondered what *they* looked like to *them*, standing there like that, the Sphinx & the Scarecrow.

'Don't get me wrong,' Alice said. 'I love Níko. He saved my life. Not because he held my hand & all that, but because he taught me... That desperation's the beginning of personal freedom.'

Němec felt her tighten her grip around him arm & then let go.

'Only *personal* freedom? That's one helluva sense of solidarity, has our Níko. Collective suicide not on his list...?'

'Don't laugh. It's true.'

'And who am I to doubt what's true?'

They continued towards the summit, passing the Stations of the Cross. Desperation, Bride of Liberty! It sounded like something any number of conartists or lunatics might've said. At the top of the steps, a level path cut across the hillside.

'You know, the worst thing about being alive after you've tried to die — being forced to live — is having to go on as if nothing happened. Like there's no other option. Because you're afraid. Of what they'll do to you if you fuck up the next time.'

Alice stopped in front of one of the stations. Mary Magdalene was washing Christ's feet with her hair. The paint was flaking away from the Magdalene's right hand like leprosy —

'I couldn't go through all that again.'

She ran a fingernail along the outline of Christ's body. Then in a strangely credulous voice she asked —

'Why d'you think God committed suicide? To prove he existed?'

Němec looked at her — her eyes, her mouth, her chin, her throat wrapped in the fake fur collar of her coat. She resembled at that moment a portrait by Kokoschka. Němec leant in towards her but she turned away, then immediately she turned back to him & he felt her cold mouth against his. It lasted only a moment. Then she looked at him in a vague lopsided way & took his arm again, leading him along the path. When they reached the top of the hill there was a crowd of people milling around the dwarf Eiffel Tower. Němec could just make out the faces behind the windows on the viewing deck & the afternoon sunlight reflecting off the glass…

They walked past the stalls selling hot wine & the giant chess pieces set out on cobblestoned black&white squares. Past the tower was Christ's "tomb." And past that, the cablecar terminus & a planetarium. Alice led him through the snow to peer inside at the firmament of nested spheres, the vast sidereal wheel, God's eye onto the self-created universe. For no reason he could point a finger at, Němec felt disappointed.

'It's always sad looking at stars,' Alice said, as if sensing his mood. 'All those extinctions. It's like the truth is always being kept from us. *Look how pretty death is. All those beautiful lights.* People forget that Heaven's just a mortuary with all the candles left burning.'

'Heaven's just matter & entropy…'

'…'

'There was an ancient Chinese philosopher, Chun Tchi, believed the whole night sky's invented.'

'It's the same thing,' Alice said, taking his hand & leading him out past the maze of straggly boxhedges & a gate with a sign reading:

HRY JSOU V BLUDIŠTI ZAKÁZÁNY*

At the end of the path was a small baroque chapel with a paved courtyard in front of it. And across the courtyard, a House of Mirrors.

'Let's go in,' Alice said.

She let go of his hand & ran up to the ticket booth. Němec waited at the entrance. Just inside was a diorama in a glass box: "The Battle of Charles Bridge," it said on a card pasted to the side. It depicted a skirmish between armed students & Königsmarck's Swedes in the process of ransacking the City, in 1648. The painted figures were entirely unconvincing — the students barricaded at one end, the bluecoated Prods at the other — the whole thing might just as easily've been made-up. Besides, what was it doing there at all?

'Come on!' Alice called, going in ahead of him.

Half-reluctantly Němec followed. He heard Alice's laughter somewhere

---

* "Whatever you do, don't feed sour cream to the bloody Minotaur." [✋]

on the other side of the glass wall. No sooner had he entered the maze than he lost all sense of direction. Everywhere he turned, he saw his *idiot semblable* knotted & stretched apart. Alice's laughter drifted further away. He resisted the urge to call out. Eventually the laughter died entirely. Then there were footsteps. Children's voices. Running. Giggling. He wandered around like that, blindly, till he found his way out again.

Alice wasn't there. Němec watched to see who came out behind him, but no-one did. There must've been some other exit — secret passages — a fourth dimension maybe. He parked on a bench in front of the chapel & waited. It was almost five o'clock. Someone had left a copy of the *Golem City Tribune* stuffed between the slats where he was sitting — he unfolded it, browsed the headlines unenthusiastically. Several times he caught sight of someone he thought was Alice, but was mistaken. People gathered outside the chapel for the service. A bell tolled. A group of kids kicked a ball back & forth in the slush.

To pass the time, Němec took a pen out & began circling words here & there at random in the newspaper. It was something he'd learnt to do in the Home, like using a dousing rod to read between the lines in his schoolbooks for what they didn't want anyone to see. He found it worked with pretty much anything. Secret ordinations of events. Trees hidden in the woods. Messages out of the ether. When that got boring he turned to the crossword puzzle. 23 down: "person so deficient in mind as to be permanently incapable of rational conduct," 5 letters. 51 across: "opening in wall, usually filled with glass," 7 letters. 40 across: "chatterer," 15 letters.[*]

Mmm. Never was much good at that sort of thing.

After a while of stabbing in the dark he'd had enough. Still no sign of Alice Steinerová. Chances were they'd never've made it through another night anyhow. Denying the obvious, or else unconsciously acceding to it, Němec stayed sitting where he was & played join-the-dots with the words he'd been circling earlier, making bits of phrases out of them — bringing the whole pointless exercise to a kind of occult fruition by copying the results into the margin of the puzzle section at the back, arranging & rearranging the lines till something that wasn't complete gibberish came out of it. He'd successfully killed another hour by the time the last "t" was crossed, the last "i" dotted. What was left, traced beside the day's Bumper *Super Combo* Crossword, was this:

---

[*] ← Intermission. [☚]

It was late — the sky overwhelmed us, shapes
& forces from invisible mind-rays. In the green
orbit of thought, impulse, disintegration —
removed from the five senses, is indeed the end.
Clocks glow weirdly underwater — a depth —
rewound: order, which appears / does not appear.
River, cloud. Least careless, least logical.
To see contumacious eggs hatching (if their white
be skin enough) all in one piece. Switches & amulets.
The ensuing of many arguments, sighing.
She kisses you with transparent teeth — a kiss
full of vertigo & premonition. Order being
tied up backwards, forwards — liquid from mineral.
But it was too late — the sky overwhelmed us.

If it was a poem, he supposed it ought to have a title, like *Poem* or *Sonnet*, only it wasn't a sonnet because, well, it just wasn't. He thought about that national monument of a wanker, K.H. Mácha,[*] lying beneath a springtime bower just down the hill there, with one of his dozen regular Šomkomite floozies — flagon in hand, wafting on about LOVE in that dreary repetitive spät-Romantisch uppercase enunciation — & afterwards, confessing to his Secret Diary in excruciating religiotic detail, of the ones he'd played stinkfinger with & the ones he blushed to think about while having a quick J. Arthur behind the rhododendrons. And so, in honour of the Big Blouse's noxious drivel, Němec took up his little ill-starred creation & scratched the letters "R-O-Z-E-R-V-A-N-E-C"[*] across the head of it, whispered a solemn curse, & gave it life.

---

[*] Author of the only poem so far discovered to've been penned in the Chesk language, memorised by every schoolchild. [↓]

[*] "R.S.V.P." [↓]

53

THE EMPEROR'S NEW COCK

No more will the scurvy Sphinx
With beggy prophets their prophecies relate…[*]

So after the old maestro, that rachitic degenerate Zhid,[*] fritzed it at fifty-one from a dose of bacterial endocarditis ("always an intruder, never welcomed"), his Freudful widow & career man-eater, Alma *née* Schindler, on her way to becoming a Gropius & thence a Werfel, took to bed with a twentytwo-year-old aspiring portraitist of sickly children, name of Oskar Kokoschka, in whom (though in no way unique in this respect) Misses M inspired a famously squalid *amour fou.*[*] Dear Darling Koko, overwrought, obsessive, ridiculous, all the things a young man of temperamental qualities becomes when he loses his grounding, gets himself into a wrong perspective, stuck in the ideoplastic quagmire trying to impress a woman almost twice his age. Cirrhosis of the Ψ-function. The story could be called *Die Puppe.* After beating the bedsprings flat for two successive winters & summers, the composer's ex-concubine'd had enough of neurasthenic little Oskaroschka & moved-on to fry bigger fish, though not before informing the poor pup by post — C.O.D. to a Habsburg field hospital on the Isonzo Front, where cavalryman Karko lay terminally afflicted & certified *non compos mentis.* Kokoschka: in a fever of unrequite, many a restless 4a.m. spent thereafter, discombobulating over wishful imagined ghostkinder, little lifeless versions of his Oskar-self, viscerally aborted by this least likely paragon of ideal womanliness — Alma, loved, despised Alma. Come the Armistice, demobbed undead Kokoschka, wandering lonely as a clod, over hill & under hill, till at long last coming upon a Munich dollmaker willing (for a few shekels more) to faithfully fulfil a rather particular commission. To wit: a lifesize surrogate of the aggrieved artist's Lost Liebling, precise to the last velvety anatomical detail. For

---

[*] *Amnesia in Memphis.* G.C. [☚]
[*] Thanks to Max Burckhard for the kind words. [☚]
[*] "My neurosis does handstands, what's yours do? Play all the Goldberg Variations simultaneously, blindfolded, while offering a King advantage? Pawn to Queen's Gusset one?" [☚]

six months did war-crippled Kokoschka cohabit with this permanently lubricated travesty — shrinkwrapped, perfumed, flossed, depilated, contactlensed, blowdried, bleached, siliconised, self-sanitising, universal adaptorised, prêt-à-porter & all modcons. A veritable *pêche Melba.* Till, one pre-incendiarised Dresden night, during a whorish boozeslopped orgy of impotence, he, Koko Loko: 1. came finally to his senses; 2. fell into a blind cathartic rage — & with one fell stroke beheaded that insatiable celluloid coquette with the clenched crook of his walkingstick.

V. Neuman & the Golem City Philharmonic (Supraphon): Mahler's unfinished 10th — in hope, perhaps, of summoning ghosts. Some sort of ghost.

Through the rooms of the empty apartment, the faint music crept as upon the waters. Roared & swished about. Raged. Blew. Petered out. The recordplayer thutted. Němec got up off the bed, weaved through brainfog, shakily swapped discs. The Rückert-Lieder (Deutsche Grammophon). *Ich bin der Welt abhanden gekommen.* A voice that long after all else has passed, etc., if there be a twittering machine to mouth it. And what would Kepler have made of this child's toy, stylus in a windmill, spiralling orrerie? Or of the craven Kapellmeister, for that matter? Herrgott himself. Proteus of the Winds or flatulent Laocoön? Mistral or minstrel? And that Schlampefrau of his! Talk about a grey mare. Well... She could nourish a grudge like the best of them. What comes of winding a woman the wrong way, paying through the nose for a piece of patented posterity.[*]

From the street below, headlights turned shadows across the ceiling. Disarticulated zodiacs formed & deformed. Naked bodies, anagrammatised, wound with gut-string, flesh bulging between the knots. What kismets of doom were being undressed up there on the Big Screen? What eructed abysms? Němec closed his eyes, but it did no good. Behind every thought she was waiting, blue-eyed, Alice Steinerová. Evocations as puerile as Kokoschka's lovedoll. Well you'd be bound to develop a unique way of seeing things after a while in that kind of arrangement, wouldn't you? Němec forced his mind to go blank, waiting for the record to end. The shadows danced. The stars in their fixed firmament. *Her*

---

[*] When it came to just deserts, aggrievèd Alma could sure strike a bargain below the belt. [✋]

body. Alice in the house of mirrors… *What's gone's gone, kiddo, the great skidoo!*

Inquiring minds did however wonder. As for example, precisely how Mahler's ex-Muse inspired such gargantuan efforts of the phantasmic faculty. Rutting with a cardboard cutout not exactly scoring in all categories, unless of course, a certain chaffing at the bit, a certain *comment dire* flagellated frustration at abseiling from pedestals. Like running a starched petticoat up a gristly flagpole. Or a frozen handjob in the Himalayas. Or a bit of the old frottage among the statuary. A mug's game by anyone's standards. Thinking there's a myriad of mockeries a man can wake up to on any given day of the week, but someone's gotta draw the line somewhere, right? And that dour puss Kokoschka barely grown out of his pimples, as jaunty as a rectal suppository from all accounts, hauling his misery around with him like a pair of balls on a chain for all the world to see. Supposing he'd really put one over on the old tart now, eh? *Try this for a pose, lovely.* Prodding his paintbrush into the blushiest of sanctimoanies the real flesh&blood wouldn't've let him dawdle near in a month of Sundays.

Oh she'd've given it to him all right, but not the way prissily apassioned Koko Poko would've put it in a postcard to himself. Lying there in some ethereal eiderdown with her combinations in chaste disarray, like some vaselined Vestal swooningly awaiting fulfilment. *Well he's got her where she can't squirm out of it now, eh?* Ankles nailed to the bedhead & a modest little lace peekaboo, hehehe. (Cuntstruck Oskaroschka could spout *romantisch* as drivelously as the next Nazi, don't you worry.) Could just picture him, too, keeping a sailor's chest in the cupboard stocked with a connoisseur's collection of rubber masks, for occasions when he really got the horn up: bullheads, horseheads, goatheads, minotaurheads, dog&catheads, godheads, you name it. Heads in the manner of Phidias, of Michelangelo, of Rodin, of Arcimbaldo. Valentino heads, Bonaparte heads, Arch-Duke Ferdinand heads replete with muttonchops & bushy eyebrows. Catholic heads. Atheist heads. Hieratic heads. Heads in the Cubist manner, the Dada manner, the Kraut-Expressionist manner, etc. Hydrocephalitic heads, shrunken cannibal heads, you name it.

Kokoschka deadpanned. Kokoschka drooled. Kokoschka stuffed a turpentine-drenched rag in his mouth, to get himself in the right mood. *Mmmm.* Snorting a few lines of undiluted cadmium yellow & coming on all mumbly schoolboyish in some sort of Walter Scott Aberdeen Angus rig-out, winkwink, & *Didn't she think it was about time for their "Perils of Pasiphaë" routine?* Setting his Betacam on a tripod & rearranging that overgrown pet Barbie of his to fit the bill, hands & knees just so, & some kind of veterinary harness he'd no doubt acquired just for the occasion. Clopclop of cloven hoof. *Hmmm.*

'Oh Liebchen, do we have to already?'

'But you know how much I dig making moo-moo, Almimulmi.'

Jesus, it was only last Sunday he put on that Pluto Pup mask & went to work overtime tonguing her Manufacturer's Premium Two-Year Warranty "lifelike rubber sphincter," the Mata Hari Mk3, till she positively blew up in his face. *Boy oh boy*! Not to mention the "Eunuch from Munich" routine on Wednesday. The "Double Nelson." The "Rabbit Hole." And, gosh, the "Golem in a Blood Moon," *that* was something you could really write home about. Krazy Koko had a whole variety act going, he was considering calling it *The Weimar Wildebeests of Alma's Interbellum*! (hehe) or *One Man's Manikin is Another Man's Monkeybusiness*! or (his personal fave) *I Zoo, You Zoo, We all Zoo Zoozoo*! Flipping his footage on a showreel to peddle to some West End nob he'd met in a cabaret in Kreutzberg, songbook & stagesets sketched down to the morbidest obsessive detail, diptychs & triptychs, *Die Windsbraut* 1, 2 & 3, hecatombs of underpaint spilt in carnal selfsacrifice to the Goddess Mother of His Misery. A complete vocation right there, all he had to do was stop filleting his *fausse floozie* long enough to get the finished product stretched on a frame. *God's dingus, boy*! Well, there's only so much celluloid one man can covet in a lifetime & not turn himself into a strapon Mameluke. Did Kokomo, here, for even one measly moment *truly* believe that vexed voodoo doll of his was giving Mrs Alma Gropius the pins&needles in her prissiest of privates? Call it: Spooky influence at a distance! Enough to turn any self-respecting architect's stomach —

'Alma dear, really, this is utterly inappropriate! At the dinner table of all places! And in front of the servants, my God! You're... You're behaving like a moose in heat!'[*]

❖

There were times Němec wondered about these little flights of fallacy, lying on his side like 1. little Henry David Thoreau pulling his pud by a paddling pool; or, 2. a poisoned rat (take your pick). Grey dustmotes afloat there in the middle of the room. It rained & then the rain stopped. Ashen light & then darkness &

---

[*] Not to speak ill of the woman, her being dead after all & long in the tooth at that (or did he mean "fingernails"?). []

then light again. Alice on the ceiling like Kokoschka's porno prosthesis sullying the predelectible prelude to a migraine of the very first order. A red light flashed inside his head. That story, he remembered, not without pain, about one of the 4th grade kids at the Home they'd dragged off to Bohnice for refusing to serve in the Red Pioneers. Tied to a bed & fried in the brain with electrodes to help clear his conscience. Němec wondered vaguely if the shocks made the pain better or worse. He closed his eyes, rolled off the campbed & crawled to the kitchen sink. Groped. SERTRALINE HYDROCHLORIDE, said the blue pills with no serial number.

Hey there, kiddo, what's new?

Sniffing around in the trash. Some aroma he'd managed to generate in there with all that decomposing & composting. The rot after the inundation, swamp vapours condensing on windowpanes. The fetid folios of cruciverbalist cacaphagy. To think his very existence boiled down to this (!). It was enough to bring tears to his eyes. If only these situations could solve themselves & point him towards the exit doors, like a cavedweller blinking in the brights & *What ho?* A light from yonder window & the Weather Lady tucking herself into a cosy little Low Front, faint evocations of Cimabue over the rooftops, the odd auriolated snowflake as once upon Bethlehem. Somewhere a dog groaned, having a nightmare in its sleep. Rats in the attic. Old women whispered outside the door. The heartbeat of somebody listening. Footsteps on the stairs. Workers' boots. A jackdaw pecking at the window to be let in, or a shape on a scaffold. Voices circling like flies in the middle of a room, buzzing buzzing, beneath a dead lightbulb, buzzing buzzing buzzing buzzing…[*]

The best Němec could manage was to stand up. Vitiated, leached of all will to [fill in the blank]. Like someone who'd just got wind of the news, that humanity'd hit Brennschluß & was now in evolutionary reverse — hell, maybe find that Missing Link on the backswing. He tapped cold water into a sticky glass. Sipped. Gagged. Forced that hair-tongue of his to swallow. When he put

---

[*] How long had he been like this? Thursday. Monday. Drunk again. *Here's lookin' at you, kiddo.* Lying there upsidedown in his own private Antipodes. Gravity isn't a variable. Well hallelujah! Did you count the windows? They still all there? Five down, three across. In a void, acceleration is constant. Between this world & the next… Bzzz. First things first. Mind your own reticule. The squill of him! Where they come from…? No good if you can't enjoy it. Say *please*. Ta, love. It's mama's choice. Love at first feel. Well you can't judge a book by its… Bzzzz. A weight off your… Tomorrow, maybe. What's the furthest place possible? Asinine. Bzzzzz. Only counting what's not allowed. *Anyone out there?* Wind, rime, wet earth. *Am I…* Bzzzzzz. *Have you…?* Bzzzzzzzzzzz. [✊]

the glass on the counter there were thin strings of blood coiling at the bottom...

'Well *hello*, looks like we have a winner! We were worried there for a minute, chum, didn't think you had a drop left in you. Now check this out. Over here we've got a whole range of stainless dripdry alteregos to choose from & any one of them can be yours just for the asking. I don't mind telling you, chum, this is your lucky day. Just look at that streamlined bit of sucky sentimentality up there! Or this hard-as-nails butter-wouldn't-melt-in-his-arsehole Man for All Occasions right at the front. Or maybe this's more your style, last year's model admittedly, but a great fave with the spending public — that's right & it comes with a Full Unlimited-Mileage Lifetime Guarantee — voted Best-Loved Brand ten years running: it's the Garbage-Wrapped Sack of Shit, of course! I bought one of these for my own kid, he loves it to death. Used to think he was Jean Cocteau, *hehe* — a Cocteau in the hand's worth two in the bush, *hehehe* — but now he's got a crystal-clear perspective on what *really* matters. And I can see *you've* travelled that very same kind of road yourself, chum. Am I right? Of course I am! No point letting bygones be a lion in your path. In the immortal words of Cicero, *Don't blow it!* This is your one real chance at being human, why toss it all in the can just for some high-class chimp in crotchless wellies & a French maid's outfit? Listen chum, I've been there too & let me tell you a few Home Truths, *hehehehe.* You want to wind up as a pair of kosher cobblers boiled in goulash? Nothing wasted, nothing gained! That's my personal motto & it could be yours, too. All you've got to do is choose. That's right, chum, the choice is yours. Now, no matter which way you end up swinging the bat, we've got our own Quality Certified Eight-Step Plan to go with it, just to ensure you get the most out of your experience. And even better, you don't have to worry about any of those confusing payment schemes up front, we won't bill you till we're satisfied that *you're* satisfied. At KOSHER KOCHKA's, the customer always comes first, *hehehehehe.* Okay, hit it boys...!'

Some sort of crazy klezmer quartet popped up from nowhere making matzo out of Mahler's marinated Totenlieder.* *Jesus, do I have to listen to this stuff?* Němec reeled away from wherever he thought he was at that moment, still the taste of blood in his throat, like the taste of childhood. *Mmm.* Those exquisite nosebleeds in the infirmary, Ol' Deathbed hissing in his ear, *Scheming little shite! I'll send you somewhere they deal with filth like you good and proper.* It would've made him laugh, if he wasn't gagging instead. And that voice, like a

---

* "There were nine in the bed & the Little One said, *Roll over!*" [♣]

bellowing oxymoron (you stole that, didn't you?), enough to split the fontanel of any God-fearing sonofabitch — like those bloody airraid sirens blasting away at the weekly Civil Defence Drill! *Wuuuuuuuuuuuuuuuuuuuuuuuuuuuuuh!* And how he'd always wind-up somehow flat on his back with a wad of clotted bogroll under his schnozzola. *Hey, look, Squillbrain's spazzed-out again!* Waking up only to find briny Ol' Deathbed leering down at him like that was half the Dead Sea she had up there under her skirts on a bed of pilau rice & if he didn't Foxtrot Oscar super quick she'd make salted strips out of him, *just you wait and see.* Ah, all the pleasantest thoughts coming back! *How about we just lie down here for a little while and dream of something else, eh?* Forehead to the scuffed linoleum, letting the bad blood drain out. It pooled there, warm then cold, sticking at the edges to his face. And what was that old Soviet joke about pissing in your boots? Fuck it. He let his body go slack. Bit-by-bit the pain in his head became a sort of *thing*, a solid object surrounded by dark space. He could've picked it up & held it in his hands, turned it over, scrutinised it, if he hadn't been lying flat on his face. It was simply *there*. And being *there* it was, so to speak, nowhere.

❖

You drift & drift & if the philosophers were right something would come out of it. Aces in the hole? Some colourless odourless metaphysical excrescence? Something, in other words, to lighten the load? *Things don't just disappear by themselves, kiddo.*[*] Though once upon a time — oh yes, once upon a time — a man could step off into the abyss & never have to look back, eh? Rome could burn while Nero fiddled. There could be patents for selfwinding clocks. And up there behind the blue of noon's arras & heaven's fire, God's theoretical blackhole would shine, shine on, like some crazy diamond. *Because none of this is real, it's all a sham, it was always a sham!* Hearing the Old Man's Klassenzimmer-voice saying how it'd come to pass that He learned to see the world through eyes of mud & clay. And how He slept without fear of ever having to know Himself again. But one day His Doppelgänger took its revenge by choosing to die. And all the ghosts of God's former existence returned to Him & drove Him mad.[*]

---

[*] One should always keep in mind, for example, the Law of Conservation of Mass (A. Lavoisier, 1789). []

[*] Or one day He woke up. For the truth was that all along He'd been imprisoned inside a dream & it suddenly dawned on Him that *in order to be free* He'd first need to build a Wall. And the Wall

The music stopped. The cosmic ear snored instead. Němec rolled over onto his beetleback. *Sehr* Kafkaesque. *And how's the asbestos business going, old cock?* (Jesus, the guy was like a one-man tuberculosis pandemic with a Brooks Brothers fixation, & you think *you've* got it bad?) Němec opened his eyes (again). The scenery hadn't changed much. Peeled himself off the floor. Gropingly affirmed the major chakras were more or less in alignment. A bloody blatant big gap in his head, though, where the brain was supposed to be, *haha*. Well that's a fine mess he's made, isn't it? Scrounging in the bin for something to wipe it all up with. Gibberish in rows & columns. *That's it, smear it all nicely around.* Rorschach splodges of something unspeakable. What *was* that? Some sort of medieval doodle of the Burning Bush? Nebuchadnezzar's misses among the potted shrubbery? The *who?* *Her* of Babylon? Mary, Mary, quite cuntrary? Or just the biggest piece of creationist cooze since Eve knocked one off with the old Monty Python act up the Tree of Seditious Knowledge (that gang of infamous lesbian penis-impersonators!), otherwise known as "Heavy Heva" — witch, succubus & most devastating lay this side of Gethsemane — in her umpteenth incarnation as a pre-Warhol Elizabeth Taylor in gold-lamé (yep, *that* film). *What can I say, Tony? I guess I'm just a material girl.* Asp tattoo with its fang buried in her left tit, inscribèd thus: "Dulce et decorum est pro Cleopatria mori." And that old bore in the rubber Richard Burton mask spoiling the scene again…

Němec interrupted the broadcast to go out & put his head under the shower. Counted to a hundred. Got lost. Gave up. The reflection at the bottom of the bath stared up at him through a film of scum like a mezzotint of a man with his head in a hole. *Smile kiddo. Say cheese.* Teeth cracked, bloodied gums. His hands were made of rubber. He held on. He grinned. He said *cheese*.

Wasn't it about time for the Prof's pantogeist to put in one of its irregular appearances, just to shift gears or something, give the plot a bit of direction, take the protagonist's mind off his own mindlessness for a minute or two? No? Too much to ask? In the meantime, then, how about a quick joke? Ever hear the one about the Politburo guy, was so fat that every time he went to the Black Sea for his summer holidays he had to take a goddamn receipt?

---

was with God. [✷]

For a long time Němec stood there in the bath before he decided sitting would do just as well, only now he had a wet arse in addition to a migraine / hangover / general putrefaction of the mental faculties, etc. Mahler echoed through the rooms, as was Mahler's wont. *In diesem Wetter, in diesem Saus, / Nie hät' ich gesendet die Kinder hinaus!* Němec waited for the record to end &, when it did, he waited (like us) to see what else might happen. Borrowed ink-suit hat walkingstick bundled in the corner over there beneath the window like a pointer pointing at sfumato'd palimpsests of abolished erasure, tenebrous chemas, blotted algebras, caliginous calligraphies, obfuscated oraculations all. Okay, but what about the ghost? Ghost was a no-show, of course, probably just a hoax anyway, figment of Squillhead's squillhead, hunched there with his mouth open bothering the flies. Perhaps he was trying to meet the old vapour halfway, put on his best impersonation of a stiff to create a more sympathetic kind of atmosphere? Maybe he was trying to *become* him, finger on the rewind back to the sign-off scene in the bath, Prof sitting there with knees up ('cause the tub was too short, as Němec himself could readily attest), flies in his eyes, in his unhinged jaw, rubbing their legs together in that grossly licentious way so typical of the lower Schizophora, preening their wings, nozzling their pro.bosces, smearing pathogens about with obnoxious abandon. Walls mottled grey in the November light. Grey scum on the water. Halo of redeyed flies overhead. And, like some ancient Zen master with a pair of chopsticks, the deadman, very slowly, imperceptible almost, reaching up from watery sleep to blindly pluck a nice fat one bodily from the air between thumb & index finger. A soft crunch & then the fly dropping onto the floating chessboard — like him, playing dead.

Just the thought of all that water & all those flies was enough to make Němec thirsty all over again. Knowing how mysteriously the spirit moved, it was a damn good thing he'd put in a supply after Alice Steinerová's vanishing act, to keep his levels balanced, so to speak, his keels even. The question was *where*? He'd probably hidden the stuff, out of some heat-of-the-moment conspiracy paranoia about thieving dwarfs. Or maybe *that* was a bottle of the stuff right there on the windowsill beside the carton of milk? (And what was a carton of milk doing in the bathroom, you may well ask? Collecting flies, of course.) Němec got his legs back under him & went over to sniff the milk. A bit on the nose, but no more than was reasonable. He chugged some curds. Even a semi-pro like him could only gain from a bit of the old alkali in the gastrointestinals. He tossed the empty carton in the sink & cracked the bottle. *Mmmmmmmmm.* (Fuckin' oath, as reportedly they say in Tasmania.) Němec took another swig, a real one this time. Almost immediately he felt like twice the man he'd felt just a moment before. The contents of that bottle certainly did seem to possess a number of magical restorative properties. With the third swig he felt man enough even to confront the task of getting dressed. Now the existence of such magical properties was a Truth that ought to've been universally acknowledged by this point in History & unrequiring of that constant beating-around-the-bush we've been witnessing lately, but then that'd spoil the whole joy-of-discovery thing, wouldn't it? Like pulling up through the g-forces on your first take-off & then levelling-out at 500 feet. *Mmmmm.* Big blue farkakte sky up there above all that grey. And did Truth prevail? *Listen chumsky, that tune's as stale at Klem Gottwald's headcheese.* Well, there's always someone willing to do the Lord's work & piss on your parade, isn't there? But this page's only big enough for one smartarse at a time, so breeze, pal.

Time for a limerick yet?

> *There once was a poor puss called Oskar*
> *who slipped his shvantz to a kochka.*
> *The kochka had fangs*
> *and gnawed off his wang,*
> *so now he's just half a Kokoschka, dah-dum.*

Or as *Tell Me, Doctor*'s Winifred May de Kok always said at the end of the show, *Remember kids, a kok in die hand is die meite werd twee in 'n termiethoop!* And what better advice could you hope for your children in a world such as ours beset by doubt & insecurity? There are so few role models we can really feel confident turning to in this day & age, where intemperate immodesty & unbridled lust tear at the very fabric of our civilisation. But no matter how low you sink, you can always turn to Winifred May de Kok. Don't succumb to the scourge of disillusionment! Pick up the phone & dial now. All major credit cards accepted. Why feel alone, when you can share your anxieties with likeminded sufferers in our friendly chatline community? Call now & if you're not satisfied, we won't be satisfied either.

Oh ho! And look, there's little cockeyed Koko with that pealed chickenneck poking from his pants — obviously missed out on the inspirational talk just back there, feeling all alone & insufficient. See what he's been reduced to, hanging around the crossroads like a bad smell trying to strike a deal with the Man. Man gotta be able to sell him somethin' more substantial *down there*, if anyone can. He'd give an arm & a leg, *anything*! Just so long as he can slip the love of his miserable existence the Real Deal — light up those pinball eyes of hers with a multiball bonus — & not that piece of minced chookmeat that looks like it's been fed through a mangle. Quite the specimen, deserving of a thumbnail in an illustrated colour medical dictionary, by all means, but *fair suck of the sav, mate*, some things are beyond even the Devil to put to rights.

'Wha doncha go learn da banjo instead, bud?' says Mephistophallus, feet-up behind the reception desk at Ye Olde Hotel California, twiddling the ostrich plume in his leopardprint fedora & giving the chump who just booked-in a wink that'd turn a filleted anchovy.

And there's cockless Oskar waiting his turn next, pouring out that whiteant's soul of his, down on his knees, on the most nauseating orangebrown paisley shagpile you ever did see, begging & grovelling & (I kid you not) *mooing* even, like a sick goddamn steer[*] —

'I'll do anything, anything you say, *anything at all*, just let me be whole again, is that too much to ask? Is it? *Is it?*'

Now Mephisto here can spot a sucker at a helluva distance, which is precisely what he's paid to do. *First you let the little fishy find the bait, then you kinda wiggle it away just outa reach till pretty soon you've got the fish throwin' himself onto that hook outa fear it'll go away and leave him stuck there without a hope of ever gettin' another looksee at yer common garden-variety earthworm ever again. It's humblin', downright humblin'.* So he's gently reeling in this limpwristed Koko Schmoko wondering what kind of scam he can lay on the schmuck's lame-o peckerwood ass, when one of them old tungsten filament jobs lights up in his back brain —

'Hey there brother, looking for a friend?'

'Thank God I found you!'

'Well you can thank God if you like, we sure do.'

'I've got this little problem I was hoping you could help me fix.'

'That's why we're here, brother. Come right on in. Today's a special day, we're offerin' an all-inclusive no obligation free measure & quote. We'll even throw in a testdrive, how's that sound?'

'That's real white of you, man.'

'Yes it is. You are so very perceptive, my friend. You are some groovy right-on cat. I can just see you is gonna go a *long* way.'

And doesn't Koko's jaw drop when he clocks the product range spread out

---

[*] Some people just got no kinda class at all. [✊]

in what can only be described as a *luxury* showroom. Hell, they've even got jacuzzis built in & this entire fleet of catwalk material just lounging around in bikinis making scenery. *Tubular Bells* on the surround-sound, too.

'Now if you'll come this way, my man, I can show you some of the designs our customers have expressed particular satisfaction with. Here we have the "Tower of Babel." You'll have all the shiksas talkin' in tongues before you know it, hoho. And here we have the "Goliath," ideal for bringin' even the most resolutely defended citadel to its knees (though maybe get you into trouble with them Yom Kippur boys, haha). And this here's the "Colossus," because we all *know* size really matters. The "Apollo," goes further than any man before. And this one we're particularly proud of, the "Grand Slam," our stealth "deep penetrator." Ideal for situations deserving of subtlety & sensitivity but with a helluva bang in the end, hehe. There in the middle is "Big Black," but don't be needin' to worry yoself about *that* one, hoho. But thissy here, my friend, is one that's *definitely* for you, we call it the "Emperor," speaks for itself. Perhaps sir would care to try it on…?'

Well he was in & out of that changeroom like Flynn.

'Ooooh!' went the bikini girls.

Mephitsotite gave him a great big white toothy grin —

'Check out the dick on Oskar! Tell us, boy, what's the lucky lady's name?'

Koko couldn't've kept his dumb mouth shut if he'd wanted to & armed with this tasty factoid it was a no-brainer for Morphostiff here to whip up a spitting-image Wankotronic Waxworks Wonder Woman in his private Peeniemundo Workshop downstairs, giftwrapped, tied with pink ribbons on, & delivered posthaste to cock-in-hand Koko's itinerant address.

'Oh Almi baby, you is lookin' delish.'

'*Ooooh ooooh, Koookoooo, whatabigcrazyinvisiblecockyougot!*'

'Just a regular day on the job,' Muffisto shrugs, giving his bikini imps & invited studio audience that gut-curdling wink of his — they're quite literally laughing their heads off, too, watching through the wall while Oskar-the-Oakie goes gooeyed ramming away with his ether-teasing Falstaff at that flagrant guttapercha glovejob, making pneumatic little gargling sounds & flailing about all arms & legs like some epileptic wind-up beetle on its back with a couple of dwarfs stowed-away inside working the pulleys.

Well now, this all can't help but bring back memories of that other slapstick castrato, Oedipretzel, whose tales of madcap adventure Squillhead (unbidden affinities at work here?) avidly consumed from picturebooks while temporarily resident at that El Paradiso Children's Home he thinks back on so fondly even to this day, hiding himself up in the attic among the rafters & shelves & golem-kilns with a flashlight reading the large print. The first time he set eyes on her, that wingèd succubus of shamefilled nocturnal omissions — death's satiny void — *death in the womb of woman*, a.k.a. "The Sphinx," "La Sfinge," "I Sfinga," yep, that infamous burlesque sensation herself, *La Sfingaga*!

Hi kids! Quickly recapping from last week's episode, "Cruel Hearts & Coronaries":

The clocks have stopped in Memphis at three-minutes-to-midnight. A black scourge plagues the land. The sound of lamentation is heard far & wide, but particularly on the radio. And the King's infant son, cruelly abandoned on the Chickasaw Bluff, is missing-presumed-dead, all on account of some mad Las Vegas Mormon hearing messages from the Man Upstairs. That's right, kids, there's people tune-in on that voice-in-the-head kinda stuff & ain't at all embarrassed about goin' public with it. If only the Federal Government would do somethin' to nip it in the bud, but they can't. Turns out half of Congress are certified God-talks-to-me-in-my-sleep loonies as well. Even the President is very possibly a loony. Be that as it may, our story resumes here, in the replica "Oval Office" at Graceland in the divine presence of the King (& ain't nothin' to be ashamed about sayin' so — just remember, boys & girls, the Other Guy's a fake).

'I'm tellin' you, padrone, the Kid's bad news. Day's gonna come, sooner than you might think, when you'll have to start lookin' over your shoulder, in your closet, under your own bedsheets. This Kid, he's gonna hustle in on everything you got, your money, your power, your wife. You won't know from yourself no more. I wouldn't say this if God himself didn't compel me, padrone, but the omens, they ain't lookin' so good. It's like they told Abraham, clip the Kid while you've got the chance. Clip *him* before he clips *you*.'

'Whadya sayin'? I gotta do it with my own hands? It'd be like committin' violence on myself. Snuffin' my own flesh & blood!'

'Not necessary, padrone, just send some of the boys to leave the Kid out on the mountain, wolves'll take care of the rest. We fix it so no-one sees a thing. Tell the old lady it was some kinda accident. The Church'll do a real high-class funeral. You'll get serious news time. The proles'll dig it. You'll be cuttin' platinums from here till doomsday.'

'Okay, you sold it already. But it better go like you say. All respect to the Almighty 'n' everythin', but there's a fuckup & you'll be singin' soprano in the Elmwood choir. Capisce?'

'It's understood, padrone. You got nothin' to worry about...'

Well, but it turns out the King does indeed have a little something to worry about. See, the plan didn't quite pan out like it was supposed to. The gangly infant *lived*, by Job! Somewhere between dumping the kid & the wolves getting a free meal, the blood-offering was thieved from its rude altar — smuggled off the mountainside by a humble Sicilian shepherd & brought up like one of his own. Grew into a hardworking lad. Pulled himself up by his bootstraps. Made a name for himself at the local constabulary. Then on his deathbed the old shepherd broke the ancient code of *omertà* & confessed the truth to him, said a man had a right to know who he really was & all that, said it was better to let bygones be bygones, said a man should always speak quietly & carry a fat stick. Thus forewarned, determined to outwit Destiny, with all the world still before, etc., the Kid buried the old shepherd & off he went. But Destiny's a cruel geometer. And just as a figure-eight folds into the form of its antithesis, to meet in the middle where decorous volition crosses the chaos of inevitability, so too the path of Providence's plaything...

Now the Kid's plan was in certain uncanny respects the spittin' mirror image of Frankie the Mormon's prediction. Being: 1. Hitchhike to Memphis, get the hairdo & cash-in on that Elvis impersonation biz. 2. Cut some demos on the side. 3. Nail himself a record deal & do like the King. 4. Shack up at Graceland II with some very hot Priscilla-Queen-of-the-Desert piece of booty woulda made his mama proud. But all that seemed a very long way from where he was just then, sitting there by Interstate 69, just some pimply-arsed Oedipeenie with a polished alpenstock, pilgrim's pole, beggar's bollard, six-stringed *Knüttel*, which only this past hour he's managed to club some rich old faggot in an Eldorado with — a pink '59 Biarritz no less, whitewall tyres, baby-sealskin upholstery. Fruitcake tried to run him right off the goddamn cliff! *Wham!* Him up against the fruitcake's fender, while *his* Fender's parting the fruitcake's pompadour *right down the middle*. Watched that sonofabitch crash & burn. 20 gallon tank of premium gasoline, that's some BBQ. Thinking, *Them ratarsed Memphis cops finger you for this, boy, you is screwed good and righteous. This here's a hangin' state!* Clueless about the fact of him having just snuffed Big Daddy, the King no less (not lookin' his famous self due to all that alcohol & amphetamine abuse), the Kid's actual real-life incog chromosomal donor &

once-upon-a-mountain infanticidal snuffjob proxy, right there on the Road to Graceland. Now *that* was a piece of songwriting material an up&coming nonentity could really sink his teeth into. Which is, with a few minor details omitted, precisely what the Kid set about doing, seeing as there weren't no-one comin' by to offer him a ride. Twanging that electric staff he's been lugging the length & breadth of Tennessee, become now his very own personal stigmatum (so to speak), like the proverbial Stratocaster round his neck, baptised with the blood of some random (he thinks) maniac capitalarsed pederast — & him left stranded out there on a strange highway in a strange county, couldn't've chosen a more conspicuous spot for his first flirtation with a homicide rap, yet weirdly nothing seems to be happening about it, the world just going round like it has long been accustomed to. He ain't had no time to start twiggin' to no conspiracy theories yet, 'bout how this might all be part of that Plan the ol' shepherd clued him in about. But that don't mean that what we've got here ain't one mighty shitstorm about to happen. And to make matters worse, Slim Oedi's broken-out into a real *bona fide* cat-strangling lament can be heard for miles: *Oh, man, how I'm wishin' I never got them feet o' mine tangled in this here universe!* Strumming a gutchurning 12-bar blues through a pair of Marshall stacks, all in the key of jackshit.

Now casually taking-in this whole teledrama from her patio up above, that femme fatale they call round these parts "La Sfingaga" (coz she's as cracked as a Dutch chamberpot & dresses in them Gene Simmons devil-wings, with a she-lion's body naked as fear & forbidden fruit, as horrible to behold as a shyster waving a power-of-attorney). You can already see her licking her chops, sizing up the kid's longterm potential. She's going to zap him senseless with those terrible man-eating eyes of hers, get him to do things he knows aren't right, toss his innocence to the wolves, bring him face-to-face with the She-Devil inside every whiteblooded manchild. Yep, the whole two reels. Did the Kid have even the faintest inkling he was about to become a piece of living, breathing mythology?

'Well hey there gorgeous,' he says when he catches sight of La Sfingaga leaning out over the edge of her million-dollar patio. 'Want me to play you a tune?'

'Sure handsome,' she winks, 'you can play me anything you like.'

'What I'd really like is to climb up there & make hot fumbling teenage boy love to your admittedly slightly weird body without further tedious preamble.'

'Okay buster, you're on. Think you can manage without a seatbelt?'

Needless to say…

She looked even weirder close-up, but just as naked. As he knew she would be, she was lying on a deckchair beside a heartshaped swimming pool. She offered him a Piña Colada in a tall beaded glass. Fast Eddyputz didn't know whether to drink it or rub it all over her like suntan lotion. He decided to toss it in the pool instead & get straight down to business, diving tongue-first right into La Sfingaga's infamous quim.

'Impetuous little fucker, aren't you?' she said, pulling him up by the ears.

Of course she'd spotted the resemblance a mile off. The King's clueless kid wanders into town & straight away knocks the old bastard's block off. That was worth a couple of mil right there. Just a matter of greasing the right palms & put some sort of story about, how the old lush croaked it on the crapper & looky here if it ain't the rightful heir to all them kingsize bedrooms up there at Graceland. Oh & mustn't forget the royalties. Question was, would her tumescent troubadour settle for a percentage or maybe *some other arrangement?*

'Long as you stick with me, junior, ain't nothin' in the whole wide world to worry about. And you can have all the free pussy you can eat.'

'Mmmmm.'

That tongue of his snaked right up inside her bush. Must've been more than a foot long. Cool as can be, she slapped the contract down in front of his face. His tongue just kept on working around it, no bother.

'Don't gotta read it, honey, just gotta sign it.'

He'd never seen a contract before. This one was written in that whatchamacallit, cuneiform or something. Shrouded in so much incomprehensible legalese, it might've been a ritual of arcane courtship in three parts,[*] but the gist went something like this:

> *In kinderhood, man crawls on four,*
> *in dolthood he staggers erect (hehe),*
> *while in codgerdom he behands himself a big stick.*

And him saying to himself, *Man oh man! This cat is tyin' me up with some no-good honkey jive talk. How am I s'posed to get outta this one?*

'What's that you sayin' honey?'

---

[*] The *rätsel* of that formulaed Sphinx parleying the man-boy Oedipatris' solemn *antwort.* [♉]

'Oh, man… Mmmmmmmmmmmmmmmmmmm.'

At which point our saturnine La Sfingaga quite suddenly succumbed to some sort of convulsion in the hindquarters. Must've threw her completely off-kilter, not expecting this banjo-plucking yokel to have enough brainworks to unscrew a tin of sardines let alone a standard light fixture, *hehe*. But that's just the way the cookie crumbles sometimes, or maybe it was Destiny playin' out? Could it be that loverboy here was about to put one over on *her* with that gilded linguini of his? She, la Sfingaga, who hadn't broken a sweat since she was sixteen?

'Mmmmmmmmmmmmmmmmmmmmmmmmmmmmmmmmmmmmm.'

That tongue just seemed to go on forever. And suddenly it was like a deal so sweet just thinking about it made it impossible for her to think. *Fuck it*! She reared that pelvis, threw her arms back in abandon, wings going flappetyflap. Oediballs was lapping like crazy, like he was gonna stuff his whole face in there, bracing for that extra bit of traction. Which was when those otherwise not uncomely knees of hers went way back past her ears & on over her head, upending the applecart, so to speak. And with all the tragic aplomb of a Roger Corman production, sending her quite literally arse over tit out of the deckchair right off the edge of the patio, wings flappetyflapping in the updraught, too stunned to scream or even roll her eyes at the camera as she plunged to her ungainly doom. It was the stuff of legend & barely had the splatter dried in the deep crevasse where she lay, than Oedipoon's electric joystick could be heard teasing out riffs from such future timeless swansongs as *Everyone knows about Memphis, goddamn*! & that instant classic, *Don't Mind Me Ma, I'm Only Flyin'*…

> *There once was a dowdy old Sphinx*
> *who by night was a slutty little minx:*
> *the old folks she'd a-riddle,*
> *while the slowpokes she'd diddle*
> *then fly away with their pricks.*

Was that really how the story ended? *Meh*. What Němec wanted to know was, who was counting? Well of course none of it had a leg to stand on.[*] And what

---

[*] Like that spurious distaff in Oedi's pants? That sublimated semaphore of a rite of passage? That sceptical brickbat with which the slipshod son had wrought unwitting vengeance upon his

moral had *he*, Němec of Niemandsland, deprived of the rites of patricide, drawn from the tail-end of all this? Ol' Deathbed with wings on? What turgid midnight eructations, pathetic goblingängers in black&white, etc.? There he stood, eyeball-to-eyeball with himself, on his own two feet. He bought himself another drink from the bottle. Maybe if he rubbed it the right way, there was a genie inside'd pop out for a bit of a natter?

'G'day mate.'

'Do I get three wishes?'

'Eh?'

'For releasing you from your imprisonment.'

'Yer off yer pannikin, mate. Only came out for a breath a fresh air.'

'Got any good jokes?'

'Y've heard the one about the twelve-inch pianist I s'pose?'

'Yeah, heard that one.'

'I know a coupla limericks, would that do ya?'

'Let's hear 'em then.'

'Rightio. There once was a...'

G-O-N-G!!!!

We interrupt this programme for the following announcement:

NASA has reported today detecting a distress signal originating in the vicinity of Alpha Centauri. The signal, described by scientists as resembling a garbled recording of Marilyn Monroe signing "Happy Birthday Mister President," was picked up by lunar satellites at around 3a.m. Eastern Standard Time. An official, speaking on condition of anonymity, declined to be drawn on the question of what the signal might mean, other than to say it was obvious someone, or some*thing*, was clearly in considerable distress out there. "Could this be an alien life form issuing a call for help? We just don't know." A spokesperson for the White House insisted that the President categorically & unreservedly denied any & all suggestion that the UFO abduction of a White House intern might've been involved. "The President, like all of us, is anxious to ensure that everything that can be done to fully assess the situation & determine the correct, timely & most adequate course of action, *is* being done." Concerning

---

dyspeptic dad? The miraculated wand to which he, Oediprick, basking in an idiot's glory, owed his malehood while making a mockery of his alibi (the Sphinx of his nightmares returning as the Jocusta of his wetdreams, that witless wench who should've kept her combinations under lock & key)? Poor Oedipussy, everything pointed to him not belonging in the world at all — hero of nothing, scavenger for morsels of unmitigated intent. [☛]

the apparent "message" to the President contained in the transmission, the spokesman insisted that any reference to the POTUS in alien broadcasts should be treated "with extreme circumspection" & added "factoring-in the *time* element, it is highly unlikely that the current administration is in any way connected." Senate Republican leader, Pritchard Albumen, however, lambasted the President over "once again having failed to stem the tide of illegal aliens into the United States." "The only answer," Senator Albumen told reporters at a lunchtime press conference, "is to build a really big wall. We've got to make America great again!" Concerned about the government's handling of the situation so far, a number of leading scientists have called on the President to do more to ensure that any call for help from our sister solarsystem is addressed on humanitarian rather than political grounds. "We could be seeing the first evidence of intelligent life in the universe that isn't just evolved bacterial slime seeking to make direct contact with us here on Earth. Why they've waited until now, or what the nature of the distress is, we can only wait & see. But from a human perspective, this is a unique opportunity. Who knows? The potential's there for us to find out about where *we* might've come from. The origin of Life-as-we-Know-It."

When in reality, of course, most men just want to crawl back inside their mammy's vaginas in full Technicolor & stay put for the duration.

'D'you buy all that "Origin of Life" bullshit?'

'I dunno, man, stuff just kinda happens. I mean, billions of years?'

'Yeah, I mean when it's all over, the universe won't even know we existed.'

'It's kind of a waste, but what if it isn't like that?'

'God & stuff?'

'No, I mean, what if we somehow changed some basic parameter. By accident or something. Or just by being here, doing what we do.'

'Like the way we fucked up the planet?'

'Yeah, kinda like that. Like when white people went to Australia & took all their diseases & just sorta wiped out all the Aborigines.'

'You mean like a virus or something?'

'Kinda. Like if somehow we did something to fuck with the basic structure out there.'

'Like nuking a blackhole or something.'

'Kinda.'

'Gravity waves.'

'Yeah.'

'Like splitting the Higgs Boson & undoing all the, you know?'

'Connections & stuff.'

'Right.'

'Kinda put everything on a different course.'

'Like no more Ice Age. Like we basically changed the weather down here, what if we changed the weather *up there?*'

'So like the sun doesn't blow up in a couple of million years of whatever?'

'Maybe.'

'Or we make wormholes or something.'

'Yeah, something.'

'That'd be something.'

'Hey man, what kinda drugs you figure they've got out there? Aliens & stuff. I mean, if you could grow weed on Mars, right, it'd be *different*, right?'

'Right.'

'Different everything.'

'Yeah.'

'Different kinda high, maybe.'

'We oughta send up some seeds or something. In a pod.'

'Hehe.'

'Hehe.'

'Hehe.'

Was that the sound of him laughing to himself? *Voices in yer head, kiddo? Sheet, break the news to me slowly.* Němec killed the bottle & tossed that in the sink with the empty milk carton. *Clank.* There goes another dead sailor. Or dead cosmonaut. Dead genie. *Lives on his back*, hehe. Dies on his back, more like. *Jesus, how much more of this I don't think I could stand.* What ho, Squillhead? Němec tilted down the hall. The walls tilted with him. Casting a radius of weird timespace interference. Think one day he'll twig? Man in his rocket-tower, find the right plug, flip the switch, broadcast squillbrain-chaos into the ether. AnarchoT.E.S.L.A.ism. Black Star flibbertigibbet. *The KING is indeed a THING,* hehe. Knowing that he too, Němec-of-Neanderthalia, like the brothers Oedipatsy & Oedispurious before him, *was* that glitch in the backwards machinery, universe-in-a-mirror stuff. A self-duplicated nothing! Free to deny himself with impunity! *Why blame the System when you can blame him instead?* The androids in their Control Room, shrinking all those little Earthling heads down to the correct size. How'd Němec miss out, *hehe?* Giving the mirrorworld the middle finger & look where that mighty effort got him. Up & at 'em, Atom

Ant! *Don't worry, kiddo, you could've bullshitted with the best of 'em.* Veritably. And let no man sayeth antwise.

'Hey, ghost? You still out there?'

He was sick of Mahler anyway. Sick of poetry. Sick of dead children. He rifled the record box & came up with something with lots of saxophone in it. Time to ransack the joint to see where those other bottles went. He got to it with an almost catatonic scrupulousness. Nope. Not a drop of the clear stuff to be found. An uncorked bottle of red, though, stuffed behind the recordplayer. Mmm. Nice round vinegary bouquet. *Beggars ain't choosers, kiddo.* He spilled some down his shirt. Loosened a tooth. *They* did this to him. He settled down on the floor for a bit of the old griefstricken wino routine. The sax wailed. Němec gargled the grapejuice. And it was like that, with a nod to all worldly regimes of child abductors, that one of the Bugman's stories came quite suddenly to mind, about a kid the Bugman'd met, no more than sixteen, back during the purges, in a transit camp near Děčín. The kid's father was some kind of poet — nobody he'd ever heard of, but who'd *he* ever heard of? Besides, it was enough for a man to talk to his own shadow for Nosek's StB goons to keep a file on him. Creeping around in the dead of night with their spy cameras to photograph some sadsack poet's napkin doodlings. Bugs under the bed. Peepholes in the floor. Someone up the foodchain must've actually read the stuff & decided it was *politically unsound* — i.e. couldn't understand a syllable of it — & fired off a warrant for the poor fucker's immediate arrest. So about a month in real-time down the bureaucratic conveyor belt & the doorbell rings in the apartment where the kid lives with his mum. *Hello, visitors in the middle of the night?* Kid's mum answers the door & there're these two goons in brown leather coats standing outside. Tell her they've come to arrest her old man, Mr Poet So&so, for Criminal Subversion of the Republic in Collusion with Foreign Agents. Mum hears this & has a complete nervous breakdown right there on the spot. Turns out her old man's been dead three years already. No skin off their noses, the goons in coats just arrest the kid instead.

Then everything went black. It went black because the executive producers decided the director ought to insert one of those industry-standard "dream sequence" *deus ex machina* things to give the plot a bit more "grounding" than it's been experiencing lately, like a dose of Zoloft.

'Jeez, ain't this wanker gettin' a tad outa hand?'

'Don't worry, we'll fix it in the edit, cut all the extraneous bullshit.'

'It'll end up bein' like one of them anorexic kids.'

'That whole concentration camp look's really chic right now, could be what saves it.'

'Could be what makes it great, even.'

'Well look at the lead guy, he's like death-on-a-stick already. Where's the wiggle room?'

'My doctor always says, when you hit bone, you know you're cuttin' in the right direction.'

'Well let me tell you, when Orson Welles made *The Sphinx*? They ended up with a *thousand miles* of outtakes. They were carting the stuff away from the editing room in articulated lorries. You know how many fuckin' Teamsters it takes to haul a thousand miles of outtakes?'

'That wouldn't get you from here to my tante Marcia.'

'Orson Welles was a schmuck.'

'That shabbas goy? *Citizen who*?'

'Good thing we've got insurance.'

'He couldn't've shined your shoes, Pop.'

'It ain't the gelt, it's the rep that matters. Gelt schmelt! But a man ain't nothin' without his rep.'

'Should we run the last take? I got this feelin' somethin's missin' outa the dialogue…'

'I say *fuck it*! Just whack in the dream stuff & get it over. Who cares about continuity these days? You're lucky ten minutes in if they remember which movie they're supposed to be watchin'.'

'I'm with Moe on that one. It's the end that's the keeper. They're still in their seats after the first ten, the rest's just like valium to a housewife. All they want is for you to give 'em something to remember it when it's all over. Like flowers or somethin'.'

'Hey, Louie! Roll that scene again, will ya?'

Then everything went black. A kind of conjectural blackness because Němec couldn't in fact see it, but only sense it. It was as if he'd fallen into a black hole — the hole at the centre of "everything" & that there was no climbing out of. It'd been one helluva day, whichever way he chose to look at it. Eventually, of course, all that sort of thing catches up with you — like a couple of gumshoes wearing down a fugitive from justice. *This's it, Jack. You're surrounded. There's no way out. Surrender while you've still got the chance.* No-one listening? No-one taking down notes? The moment extended itself. Němec saw himself standing outside it, observing it, as though watching over a sleeping body he'd be punished if he disturbed. Not much of a body. More like a pasticcioed doll jumbled together from broken fragments.

'God, you could see that one coming a mile off...'

'Reckon that's bad, wait till you see what's next.'

When Němec snapped-to it really was dark. But even in this unexpected darkness, representing who-knew-how-many lost hours, he had the vivid recollection of a dream — a dream he had no memory of actually having dreamt. In it, he was sitting exactly as he really was sitting, in a darkened room, watching images projected on a flickering screen. This alerted him to the fact that the dream in question was going to be one of those "cinema-type" dreams (Cartesian homunculus up in the projection room & all that). And yet, at the same time, he *knew* that the dream he was in the process of "remembering" wasn't the *actual* dream, but something else, a kind of *container* — one inside the other. In the dream which his dreamself was having inside *his* dream, Němec was surprised to see Alice Steinerová's twin brother doing a Jean-Paul Belmondo filterless Gitane routine over a Pernod on the terrace at the Café Grand Cul — most notorious swish joint in town — with its gypsy waiters & croissants baked from plaster-of-Paris, the only genuine Froggy thing about it.

'Well gee, Pierre, d'you *really* think my arse looks big in this?'

If Němec isn't mistaken, our man's wearing his stovepipes *at least* five sizes too small, trying to give everyone the impression he's got a *queue* the size of that fake Eiffel Tower on the hill, but for those in the know it's more like the short end of a soggy brioche with a couple of sour grapes tucked in gratis. There he goes, cruising the tables with that broomstick-up-the-arse like he's some fucking hipster Napoleon, or maybe it's a dead carp, sure as shit *something's* on the nose.

And what the hell ever *did* become of that child-prodigy in the Prof's story, that real family uplift saga, about the Wonderkid with the Donkey's Dingaling? Could that've been *him* reincarnate like the Dalai Lama a few chapters back, there in the play? Boy Genius Sammy with, *gosh!* a secret chess submarine working away under the table *blip-blipping* coded messages to Control, countermoves wired back in crotch-tingling Morse: *Better strangle that SOB's Queenside rook PDQ, Kid, things is gonna get hot!* Carrying the baton, so to speak, down the ages. Some ingrown Moby Dick character one day, the Pope's nose the next, passing himself off as: 1. a midget in the company of giants; 2. a circus freak among real men; 3. a trouser-snake in Maria Teresa's private zoo; 4. the local rowing team mascot; 5. (no end to the inventiveness here) Ježíš his godchild-of-Golem-City-self, *blah-de-blah*, *et-fucking-cetera*. But comes a time in every detachable divinity's Down-the-Ages detour through the body corporeal when the glamour of the thing starts getting a little threadbare, a bit worn in the knees or out at the elbows, deciding it's now or never, really — abandoning a burgeoning career as a closet motherfucker in midstride for the uncountable unknowns & perilous pitfalls of a life spent in endless regimes of depilation, deodorisation, manicures & man-cures, stuffing gymsox down his D-cups & wrapping his dick round his neck for a *très chic* featherless boa:

'Oh what a swell scarf you've got, Shamala,' says little crosseyed Katka, his schoolgirl friend, 'so lovely & smooth & lifelike almost. So *svelt*. Ooh! Ah! What's it *doing?*'

As poor Sammy gets a sudden uncontrollable hardon, his face turning shades of Max Factor "Aquamarine," "Vibrant Mauve," "Dark Plum" & the rest's, well, *history*. No such luck with ladyboy Alex, here, unfortunately. Some things're just too good for *his* kind of people. *Whoa!* But what's going on now? Alex's just popped into the toilettes for a quick bit of bait&switch of his own, a quick sniff of the men's urinal perhaps, you wouldn't put it past him, getting down on those well-polished knees of his for a peekaboo through the gloryhole, *hoho*, & what does he see? Well bugger me if it ain't Klem Gottwald himself in there. No? Wrong story? Okay folks, forget that, we're on for the magic show instead.

Look, there's Alex freshly pressed from the gents, third cubicle to the right, in white Hugo Boss doctor's gown, cap, booties & one of those superdooper sexy surgicalmask thingywingies with a little teenyweeny drop of ether to give super suave Dr Alex that special glow of confidence we all love to see in a man about to wave a hacksaw at our particulars. They've cleared away all the café tables to make a bit of theatre space out there, got the whole place painted white, too, even the sky. Out strolls Dr Alex in the spotlight, looking cool as a cucumber, slapping on the latex gloves.

'Nurse! Where's my stethoscope?'

Nurse Alice pops up through the trapdoor in a tastefully designed willothewhisps set-piece courtesy of the lighting department aided by a Chauvet Nimbus industry-standard dry ice machine.

'Here you are, doctor! Would you like a cup of tea as well?'

'No thank you. Let's get straight on with the splenectomy. Scrubs!'

Nurse Alice immediately goes into a striptease routine, lights, music. Bulbs flash. Cameras *snapsnap.* Under her nurse's uniform she's wearing whatever you want her to wear. In the second version of this same performance the arrangement is reversed & she's wearing whatever *you don't want her to wear.* In this version, however, it's Saturday. A couple of stagehands wheel on the props. Basically a whole lot of high-voltage coils, insulated wires, a giant transformer with switches & dials. Nurse Alice sits down on a chair beside the transformer & takes out a stenographer's pad & pencil. Where she takes these items *from* is irrelevant, this is after all a magic show.

Um, is that Alex's *dick* she's wearing? Is some kind of weird switcheroo going on here? Some sort of Nazi twin experiment in retrospect? Well I'll be fucked! Can it *be?* The two of 'em is both Mongo-the-Magnif's spitting bloody image!

'Hey, anyone here remember Mongo-the-Magnif?'

'Shhhh!'

'It's Mongo-the-fuckin'-Magnif!'

'Quieten down over there.'

'Hey, shut up, there's people tryin' to watch this…'

Okay, okay. Get on with the show. It's late, we're tired. And no, it isn't, it's just a pencil. Koh-i-noor. 2B. Or not 2B, haha.

'Ladies & gentlemen,' Dr Alex comes to the front of the stage, pulls a bunch of chrysanthemums from his sleeve & tosses them into the front row, 'for our first performance this evening, we most humbly request a volunteer from our fabulous audience. How about it peeps? Anyone dying to come up on stage & get sawn in half? Or maybe drawn & quartered? Made to disappear through the floor (oops!)? Anyone out there got an itch they can't scratch? Yes? You sir? In the hat? Well why don't you just come on down! Give the jerk a warm round of applause, everyone! Hehe. He's sure gonna need it!'

Spotlight number 2 zaps up the aisle to a couple of SA stormtroopers frogmarching a gangly stickfigure in a black suit & hat up onto the stage. Yep, we know who that is.

'Hey!' the guy from before shouts. 'That's me!'

But since he's only dreaming, no-one hears him (this time). He flaps his arms around trying to get some attention, till someone in Production uses that nifty little marquee tool to delete him from the frame. The audience meanwhile

are beside themselves. A band strikes up somewhere. Dr Alex struts back &
forth working the crowd. Nurse Alice pouts, Nurse Alice winks, Nurse Alice
crosses her legs. Naked Nurse Alice drops the stenography pad. Leans down to
get it. *Ooooh!* Hoots & wolfwhistles. What the hell's she taking notes for,
anyway?

A couple of those stagehands have wheeled out a slab that volunteer
Němec is now being strapped-down on, one of Nurse Alice's choicest
undergarments snugly inserted into his mouth. *Mmmmmmmmm!?!*

'Everything nice & tight? Good!'

Dr Alex claps his hands. Spotlight number 2 swings up to the flyloft. The
audience gasps! Way up there, dangling from a pair of conspicuously visible
angelwires, is the deadgirl Němec recognises from not-Dr Alex's photo
exhibition. She looks just as dead now. Immobilised, like a dreamer caught
inside a nightmare, he stares up as the deadgirl descends slowly upon him. *Oooh!*
Ahhh! go the audience. Němec tries to scream but needless to say, with those
knickers gumming up the works, he just can't. In no time at all, deadgirl's
hovering inches over him. Dr Alex hushes the audience. Waves his arms. Inserts
a gloved hand into the gap between prostrate Němec & the deadgirl. Swishes
the air about. *Look, no gimmicks!* At his signal the stagehands attach a whole
complicated array of wires, plugs, alligator clips. The SA goons stand there
ogling Nurse Alice. Dr Alex hits a switch on the transformer & all the dials light
up, the coils hum. Nurse Alice drops her pencil, drools lustily at the tentpoles in
the stormtroopers' pants. The audience lean forward collectively in their seats.
This's the moment. Dr Alex leans down to whisper in Němec's ear, lips
thickened with spittle, but before he does he reaches up & pulls his face off.
Němec almost chokes. It's Volta, of course, just as you probably suspected.

'Ta-da!'

But that's not all, because the deadgirl isn't the deadgirl either! No, she's
really Alice Steinerová! Which begs the question, who's that who's just snuck off
behind the transformer with those crosseyed SA goons, tossing winks over her
shoulder?

'Sweet dreams, Squillbrain!'

Volta flips the switch on the transformer & *Zap! Sizzle! Zorp!* Whirligigs
of blue light stream up out of the spastic, jerking bodies of Němec & deadgirl
Alice. *Wow!* goes the audience. Volta spins dials, punches buttons. The lights
zoom & squirl. *Zwang! Wizz! Burp!* Němec's bonds won't hold him anymore,
he's dervish dancing in midair! They're both flailing about like a couple of

puppets in a tornado. *Wooooooooooo!* The wires are winding them together! They're dervishing right up through the rafters!

'Ladies & gentlemen!' Volta cries out triumphant, hands raised heavenward, face a mask of megalomaniac insanity. 'I give you, *Bride of the Wind*!!!'

'Hey! It's Bela Lugosi!'

'Nah. Watcha talkin' about? Bela Lugosi's dead.'

At which point, the uplift music wafted triumphal, the credits rolled, the curtains fell. Lights-up on the emptying chairs.

'Whew!' the other Němec said to himself. 'That was a close call!'

The usherette smiled. She looked kind of familiar. *Well*, he thought, pushing himself up from his seat, *time to go out and celebrate another narrow escape from the clutches of untold evil!* But there was something wrong with his legs. In fact there was something wrong with things in general. The floor, for example, which was suddenly all mushy & gooey! And the seat, too, which was, *argh!* sucking him down. And why was everyone looking at him like that? And what was that voice he could hear, saying his name? It *was* his name, wasn't it? But then Němec remembered he was still inside the *other* dream & it didn't seem so bad any more. He let himself be sucked further down. He smiled back at the usherette. *Was it?* It was. So *she* made it out, too, eh? He was about to call out to her, but the gooey stuff got all inside his mouth & then his ears & finally his eyes. It was warm, sweat-smelling, with a reddish glow. As he slipped deeper into it, down to wherever it was taking him, he wondered what the *other him* was doing at that moment, back where he'd left him in the Prof's bureau. He hoped the other him would be okay there, not like the ones in the "film," at least until he got back from wherever he had to go to. He could hear the voice getting further away, now. Barely even a voice any more, just a kind of gurgling, moaning, echo-down-a-drainpipe. Then he felt himself rising & the voice became almost palpable, but not quite. Then sinking again. All the while, the voice, swelling & diminishing, just as space & time also. And his body, no longer *his* body. And his mind. Well...

The dream pulled him down further & further, then pushed him up to the surface again, pulled & pushed, like a piece of dross floating in the sea, & that voice, speaking just to him,

54

I WANT TO BE ~~FREE~~
~~FRANK~~
HONZA

The dogs were helpless beneath the onslaught. *Höllenhunde*! cried the ringleader, aiming a slingshot. The black Labrador bitch made huge pleading eyes, the Great Dane lolled its tongue. Clods & sticks rained remorseless. *Teufelshunde*! they howled. The dogs' plight only spurred the little Švejks on. Behind them a black cross stood on a plinth. And behind that, a snowbank with a wall rising out of it. The dogs howled & finally broke free. The children rallied behind their fortifications. Emerging from an underpass & coming towards them they spotted a black-suited devilman with crookstick & funny hat. Their leader aimed his slingshot. *Thwack*. A piece of gravel caught Němec in the ear. He glanced up in surprise. The children bolted for the towerblocks that ringed the old killing fields, hooting with laughter. Němec watched them go. The dogs barked from a distance. A crow swooped down on the snowbank & pecked. Němec stamped the slush from his boots & surveyed what once had been the Kobylisy execution grounds, a field of trodden muck surrounded by skeleton bushes in the lee of the Projects. While he was standing there it began to rain. He had to squint through it to read the names on the memorial inscription on the wall, in memory of all those who'd been lined up there & shot —

Hanosek	Horák	Houdek
Hruška	Horáková	Hrubá
Hašek	Hroník	Hejplíková
Hrubý	Hejnalová	Hejplík
Helebrand	Hovorka	Hodys
Hilgertová	Hrubý	Horyna
Hauner	Holeček	Hykl
Havránek	Holečková	Heřmanský
Hofmann	Hála	Hynek
Houžvička	Haken	Hrabě
Hříbal	Hanuš	Hrdlička
Hejduk	Heyrink	

— but no "Hájek." The records for once were anything but clear: if the junior archivist of the National Literary Museum had been done to death here, or in the guillotine at Pankrác Prison, or in a camp maybe. *Erschossen* or *Enthauptet* or *Gehängt* or something else. 1942. By personal order of Heydrich, supposedly. *Der Schlächter.* No record of that, either. No burial recorded. In fact, no record of a Hájek ever having been arrested, let alone the accorded pleasantries. Had the caretaker got some part of the story mixed up? Had the Prof's namesake died under someone else's name? Had he died at all? *Well everyone does, kiddo.* It wasn't the sort of thing the Prof talked much about, but then you wouldn't, would you? Němec pictured somewhere on the edge of a dark wood, women in headscarves hewing the frozen ground — a toothless crone hauling an arm out of the soil, a coatsleeve, a skull with the scalp still attached to it. Tossing them into a pot to boil down for headcheese, glue, candlewax. *Madame Lafarge's Home Brew.* And the Prof at Barrandov four years later, having his picture taken? The interim was full of questions that begged.

Němec scratched his ear. The rain made holes in the snow. What'd the Old Man's old man done to deserve The Treatment, anyway? He trudged back along the path, thinking if he could only get the Prof's ghost to stop being so coy & actually give him a straight answer, he might fill him in on *that.* Who knew, it just might be the key he'd been looking for, the thread to tie it all together. *Well, kiddo, y'know he's been places most the rest of us can't see. Gotta make* some *allowances.* Němec came out from the underpass just in time not to get knocked flat by a black Mercedes taking it a bit wider on the corner than the manual usually advised.

'Wanna get them shocks looked at, Klaus.'

'Damn it, I just took it down the garage last week! Shit mechanics in this town, they probably stole the originals & stuck a couple of rusty bedsprings in there instead.'

'Should only ever get your repairs done certified, Klaus. Fucks your warranty otherwise. And these Chesk jokers wouldn't know a screw from a handjob if you printed instructions on it.'

'Ja wohl.'

'Sheez, you nearly clocked that Zhid in the hat back there. Few inches to the left & you woulda had him.'

'I didn't see him! I didn't see him!'

'Try that one up there, the gypo on the stolen bike...'

Zoom! Awesome! Bombed right over the top of that shithead

Krautmobile. Suck *that*, Nazi motherfuckers! *Splash*! Dig that endo right down the guardrail. Way out! Kid ain't no showercap! Bunnyhop clear across that causeway. Watch him book that bitch. Tabletop off the exit ramp. Totally rad! Double cross-up out the halfpipe. Man! Check them stairs! *Yeehaa*! Layin' rubber on a full three-sixty. And is that or is that not a goddamn double-decker bus parked there at the end of that alleyway he's cruising down with his feet up on the pegs? Sure looks that way.

The Three Monkeys was through a gate along a switchback path in a narrow yard overhung by skeleton trees. And behind that, a baked-clay volleyball court ringed with weeds & a stripped-down red double-decker parked in the middle of it. Clapham Junction last stop. A tumbled umpire's chair stuck up from the undergrowth, glistening under rain & strung-up carnival lights, red-blue-green. The bus listed to port on deflated tyres. In a tired complaining voice, Willie Nelson was singing about the railways — how back in the day, a man could be free. A couple of Project kids bounced an orange pingpong ball on a concrete pingpong table. *Splatsplat. Splatsplat.*

In a previous incarnation perhaps, sirens through the blackout, airraid shelter, Clapham tube station, the eerie silence of the tracks (not even a rat), stairways funnelled into the Underworld — *One at a time! One at a time!* — agents of order keeping the mass hysteria at bay, *This oughta be routine by now, so what're you afraid of?* The constant dripping, seepage down through rubble of smashed foundations, substrata of Celt, Roman, Viking, Norman, angry Godheads booming through the abyss — *Haahaa! Heehee! Hoohoo?* And something else, a vagueness creeping in, the echo of an aftershock, a warping of the air, the fingers of a hidden malevolence feeling you out, reading your thoughts like Braille, knowing the deep-down intimate shape of your anxiety & everyone around you, invisible hundreds, thousands, who can guess how many? Huddled under the bombs dropping, sweeping inexorably towards you, all along the Battersea shoreline, the junction point, where everything's somehow calculated to converge at just that instant in time, like a portal opening between this world & all the other worlds, the Alpha & Omega — could this be it?

Splatsplatsplat, the pingpong ball drops off the side of the table into the wet weeds, only to be left there, faint dull orb of an eye, the Project kids having scooted off to find shelter. *While you were daydreaming the heavens must've opened.* Rain hammering down, beating a tattoo on the roof of the doubledecker, nothing more than a hulking shadow now, barely even visible. Evocations of a madman roped to a mast, windlashed, stormbattered. A wash of headlights sweeping across, coming down the hillside just as a figure in a surplus anorak pushes through the gate…

'Hey, Honza, how's it hangin'?'

'Long & strong, Bruce. How's tricks?'

'She's jake, mate.'

'Pissin' down out there.'

'So I can see.'

'How's the missus?'

'Still bangin' like a dunny door, mate. Yours?'

'Hardly lets me outa the house.'

'Tough, init?'

'Some days, crikey, you'd think it'd never end…'

Inside *The Three Monkeys* the drinkers were steaming up the windows. Honza held up a finger & the barmaid brought over a bottle of Pražan & a glass mug, penned a mark on a chit, all without a word exchanged.

'Cheers, mate!'

'Na zdraví, vole!'

Slopping foam down their chins. *Freight yards full of old blackmen,* mourned the radio, *and graveyards of rusted automobiles…* Out in the night a tram clanged its bell. If you wiped away the fog on the window you'd almost see it, coming round the far side of the volleyball courts, steam rising off the tracks, & behind it the blackness creeping up from the valley, moving as if not through space but through time. And the sallow-faced ghosts within, watching back. At the tramstop, a woman of indeterminate age, shoulders hunched, gripping a drawstring shopping bag, climbed out, gasping at the cold wet air. The road curved away down the hillside into a hairpin where it disappeared from view. The tram wheezed off, past grey suburban housing blocks on its descent towards the river. Past streets with names like Gabčíkova & Kubišova. Past the hospital & tram sheds & Vietnamese markets. The tarpaulined sky. The caged beasts in the Zoo. The river forking & looping back like tied fallopians. Unravelling again. North past the sewage works. Darkness primordial. *The disappearin' railroad blues…*

The girl with wet hair & leather jacket, with a Walkman blaring in her ears, scratched the backs of her hands & coughed. A bum asleep wrapped in a soiled army coat snored. A man with hands as big as his face, eyes fixed to the floor, reeking of cigarette butts, lurched drunkenly as the tram rounded a bend. The girl in the jacket stared out the window. Fake people in fake cars. Fake traffic lights flashed. The world was just some practiced evasion. They thought they had her conned, but she wasn't conned. All you had to do was keep your cool & not set all the alarm bells ringing. Second you put your hands up they shoot you dead. Play dumb & they shoot someone else instead. No reason to be disappointed, the whole thing was so fake. Everywhere you looked. Fake, fake, fake. Like pop-ups in a shooting gallery. *Blam*! *Blam*! Fucking fake. *Blam*!

A cement truck geared-down, breaking to a stop at the intersection. *Milenko's Concrete* totally killed her view. *Blam, you sonofabitch*! The driver leant on his horn. *Double-blam*! He leant on it again & the girl in the jacket looked up. The creep was hanging out his window, jerking the middle-finger of his right hand in & out of the circle made by the thumb & index-finger of his left. *Jesus Christ*! The creep was shouting something. She pulled the headphones off.

'Hey, baby, this's my big fat *kurac* in your tight little *pička*!'

'Hey arsehole,' she popped the studs on her jacket & flashed a JUST DYKE ON! t-shirt, flipping the creep the bird, 'sit & fuckin' spin!'

The creep wagged his tongue, revved, burned diesel. The girl in the jacket unloaded the other middle-finger on him. *Blam*! The creep made a face like a baboon's anus & finger-jerked double-time. The light went green. Horns blared. The tram wheezed out of the blocks. The truck ground through the low gears. *Shithead creep*! *Blam*!

'These Golem City chicks,' Milenko grinned to his passenger, 'are so fuckin' horny all the time. Did you see that? Crazy chicks!'

'The chicks here'll fuck anything, just like that!'

'The chicks in Belgrade are all stuck-up bitches!'

'The chicks in Pristina aren't worth half a cock!'

'The chicks in Novi Sad aren't worth my left nut!'

'The chicks in Podgorica only fuck their fathers!'

'Hey, know how you can tell when you're in Montenegro?'

'It's where they stop fucking mothers & start fucking fathers!'

'Fuck your God!'

'Fuck your bloody sun!'

'Fuck your infidel house!'

'Fuck your sunny dinner!'

'Fuck your rat!'

'Fuck your money!'

'Fuck your soup!'

'Fuck your bread!'

'Fuck your dead goat!'

Milenko cranked it up, over the island, down the embankment, up the hill. Wipers batting off the rain. Swung through a rat's maze of narrow backstreets. Up Jánský Vršek, headlights strafing the construction site. Jörg Schuh peered down trough the rain from atop the scaffold as the cement mixer ground to a stop, but not before wiping out half-a-dozen traffic cones first. A couple of drunk Serbs climbed out singing at the top of their lungs,

> *Klintone, možeš da nam pušiš*
> *Širak nabijem ti Ajfelovu kulu u dupe*
> *Olbraijtovo, kurvo stara...*[*]

The foreman cursed —

'These frigging non-union jerks really get on my tits!'

Jörg shrugged, just doin' his job like he was paid to do, chipping off the stucco at a Kč 45,- hourly rate. No point rushin' it, a man's gotta keep himself employed. From his vantage up on the scaffold, Jörg observed the spread of the weather over the City. A dragnet tending east, blacking-out the lights. Times up there he felt like a monkey in a tree, watching through the high branches, stone in hand, the jungle canopy laid out below, & any moment down would swooped a giant eagle & pluck him in its talons, off, off into the ether, never to be seen again. *Nearer, my God, to thee.* Gotta be vigilant, eh, never know WTF's out there. He scanned the rainclouds. No self-respecting feathered creatures up in *that.* No low-flying planes. No falling bits of alien spacecraft, either, though how you'd ever be sure... *Chip-chip.* Jörg worked his chisel into the wall, hammered, twisted, gouged out another chunk of medieval masonry. Suppose they ought to have a heritage listing on all that rubble. *Clunk-clunk.* Ricocheting down through the scaffolds & onto the cobbles below. And there was that queer guy in the hat, the one who lived there in the house supposedly, trudging down the street. Jörg'd seen him through the window, sitting around buck-naked mostly, doing nothing as far as *he* could tell, talking to himself like the guy wasn't entirely right in the head.

'Eh! Keep your mind on the bloody job!' the foreman called out.

The drunk Serbs were arguing about where to dump the concrete. The guy in the hat elbowed his way between them without looking up, like they

---

[*] "Que sera sera, whatever will be, will be..." [✋]

weren't even there. *Eh, budala pička*! *Eh, kurac glava*! Queer was hardly the word. Guy looked like if he stepped on a crack he'd never be seen again, slip on through to the other side, just the hat maybe.

Němec navigated the planking laid slantwise across the trenchwork outside the house & weaved his way between stacked machinery into the courtyard, where even more scaffolding, lit here & there with caged worklights, was in process of being erected along the southernmost wall. There seemed to be something inexorable about it, like the spread of damp. Němec wondered if the whole objective was to pull the place apart simply in order to put it together again, like a kid gluing the wings back on an amputated fly & trying to get it to go *buzz*. They'd dress it all up afterwards like a plastinated corpse with the skin pasted on & wonder why it didn't get up off the slab & thank them for it, but it wouldn't matter, half the City was being dressed for its own funeral like some confectioned parody. Just a matter of time before they got to the rest of it.

He looked in at the caretaker's flat but the lights were out so he went up to the apartment & dug out the Black Book again to see what it could tell him about the Prof's old man, if anything, or shed some light perhaps, those names for instance, all Kraut names, could that've been part of it? Something completely unconnected to Enochian Tables & Angelspeak? Maybe it was the Dads' "l'il black book" on all them Nazi mofos, back in the day. Maybe *he* was a secret agent / spy / master-of-disguise, like Fantomas? Was about to put the finger on that Kammler when his luck ran out? No. It didn't seem right. The Dads was supposed to've got the chop in 1942. In '42 Kammler wasn't anyone you'd put on a list. Not *that* kind of list. Not Faktor, either. Right?

Němec spread the inner workings of the Prof's Polygraphia out on the floor & stood there trying to see it in a different light. Fruitless months preoccupied with keying it, surrounded by puzzles he'd failed to unlock. Phenotypes of weirdness. K-ciphers. Ghosts in the attic. Shapes drawn by the wind. The lost Keys to the Kingdom. The Sphinx's riddle. The fourth soul of itself, producing many monstrous & prodigious things. Life, death, the meaning of. Eh? *You're dreaming, kiddo*! Němec peered down at the page directly in front of his feet. *There seemeth a black curtain of velvet to be drawn from one side of the stone to the other, full of plights...* Mmm. K up all night in his lab, assembling some sort of D.I.Y. automatic anagrammatising apparat to elevate all that scratching in the dark once-&-for-all to a higher plane of redundancy? Some Themuru Thingumjig of the superior shambolic permuta-conjugation, *hoggibus, piggibus et shotam damnabile grunto*? Being the world's first proto-Rube Goldberg timetravel machine? Or better still, some fourth-century *Wunderwaffe* anachronism, some archetypal T.E.S.L.A. ray-gun cobbled together with nothing but sulphur, lead, demons & astrological almanacs? Hehe. And wouldn't the Nazis've loved to've gotten their hands on that?

Ah, there he is! The man himself! K up in a tower somewhere, prison-cell-cum-alchemist's-den jammed with all sorts of unfeasible electronics. Coils, accumulators, vacuum tubes, conducting rods. Flagstones vibrating with heavy currents as if alive. And in the middle of it all, K, white labcoat flaring, forked beard, wildeyed. So good he could beam-in like this at such short notice. Leaning over a console, he twists knobs & dials, throws switches. High above, over the tower battlements, lightning shoots into the air from a copper sphere atop a mast, surging & crashing, the sharp smell of ozone permeating the air. Lightning explodes again & again, building to a crescendo…

'Blind, fainthearted, doubting world!'

Unseasonal weather out there of the rather, let's say, occult variety. Bat spleen & cod liver oil, frogs' tongues, cats' ears & even boiled slugs all falling from the sky. What's he done this time, he wonders, re-checking his notes.

'"Where reason strays into the dark enchanted forests of delusion…" Mmm.'

Did that mean *more* mercury or *less*? He took a ladle & dipped it into the mercury bath. His unfailing double peered back. Happening to glance over his own shoulder, as it were, he caught a glimpse of an open ledger propped on a bench between a couple of retort stands. The handwriting was backwards, but everything else in the picture was also backwards. Ye olde mirror world at its finest. K tried thinking Zhid-wise, right to left, everything in reverse. Gibberish flowed out of the pages' white static…

Impossible as it seems, the Earth, despite its vast extent, behaves like a giant conductor of limitless dimensions.

Mene, mene, what did it *mean*?

Arrangement of single terminal tube for production of powerful rays.

He turned around to check the original & cut the crap. The retort stands were there alright, with beakers full of putrid muck, but no ledger.

'That's funny, I could've sworn…'

Eyes must've been playing tricks. Sucking in too many of those noxious fumes, quite probably, high as a kite. At which point K distinctly *felt* a shadow protruding into his field of vision. Eh? Something from another dimension trespassing into the three visible dimensions? Something like fear? The fear that was always *there*, on the other side, as now, that *thing* he couldn't quite believe he was seeing, climbing out of the mercury bath. *My God.* It'd been like that since the moment he first set foot in this godforsaken country. Spies. Demons. Malign presences. But this was going way too far…

The air in the room grew heavy with a sweet, cloying perfume. At first the *thing* appeared to be some kind of exotic poisonous flower *in utero* floating upsidedown, like the implex of a mouth sucked into itself. *Mercury of Lune.* Then bit by bit it did seem to distil itself, like an alembic of unnatural flesh, till, foul to behold, the barely recognisable form of Woman stood out of its bath, quicksilver coursing from limbs crudely stitched to a corseted patchwork body. The creature grinned, a sickening lopsided grin. Grey teeth between thick rubberish lips, subtly shape-shifting even as the alchemist look-on in horror.

He *knew* her, of course. He'd always known her. The "Black Queen"'s phantom gazed back from bruised eyes, like the blueblack petals of an Aeonium. Had she ever existed outside his darkest dreams? His darkest convocations with the Evil One? All those distilled doubles & doppelgängers, those allegorical freakshow monsters with two heads & a thousand eyes, percolated & twisted into knots like strings of lead poured from a crucible into a beaker of vitriol? The army of his abortions? His secret minions? But this? *My God! What've I wrought?*

'Well, hello Eddie. Long time no see. How's that luscious Elixir of yours coming along? Mmmm?' She snaked her tongue at him. 'How about a little taste, eh? A little sample? Just a quick little suck?'

'…?!?'

'What, don't you recognise me, you old fart-in-a-jar? Prefer if I materialised as a rutting dog? A dwarf in a clown suit? An assessor from Mutual & Prudential? Open yer goddamn eyes, boy! It's *me! Me!! All ME!!!*'

'Er, yup! Right! Gosh! How could I forget! I mean, I was gonna call you! I've almost got it. Just a couple of more weeks. A few more days. Look, I can get it for you, no worries. Tell your boss I'll have it for him tomorrow night. Morning! I swear. I just need a little bit more time. Just a few more hours…'

'*I'm* the boss, pinhead. And it's payday! Duh-dah-duh-dah-dah! Oh yeah, have I got *soul*, hehehehe! You feelin' hot, boy? You wanna sweat for me, lover? Coz we is gonna boogie, baby! I'm a gonna burn you up, sweetheart! I'm a gonna set you on fire! This night is gonna be *loooong*! Now you just turn round 'n' close your eyes & let Mama Mefister take care of you good! That's right honey, no use runnin' coz you ain't never gonna hide! Hehehe! Just bend over there a little bit so's I can get a real nice look atcha! Mmmmm! Well ain't that just the prettiest piece of putridness, you call that an ass? More like a goddamn donkey, hehehehe! Say *eee-aww*, boy! Go on, say it!'

'Eee-aww!'

'Louder!'

'EEE-AWW!'

'Now where's that goddamn Elixir you owe me, you earless imbecile?'

Nnnneeeeeeeooooooooowwwwwwwwwwwwww! went da house fly. *Vavavooom! Vavavooom!* Buzzing the old fart's beard then zapping down for some of those leftovers on his midnight breakfast plate. Rind of the ancient marmalade. Breadcrumbs & rancid butter. Lives like a bloody king, that codger in the fancy skullcap. *Munchmunchmunch.* Yum-o! And how about a slice of that parboiled shite on the Petri dish. Very fancy, very *gourmet*, what? *Zimzamzooom!* Laying down some *très* subtle vapour trails there, faking a bit of that pseudorandom aimlessness to fox the opposition. Loop-de-loop. Figure-eight. Double-pike. Then *voom* hitting the g-forces *el serioso*, straight up at the ceiling there like playing chicken with a ten tonne Mack. Whoa! Doesn't even blink! Pulls a vertical stall, tucking under for a flawlessly executed upsidedown landing on the mildewed masonry. Ten-outa-fuckin'-ten! Fly-eye view of the ongoing proceedings below. *Ah-ha.* Some real multicellular weirdness happening down there. *Zip!* Oh-oh, looks like company. *Nnnrrrrrtttttt!*

'Nazdar, *vole*!'

'Eat shit 'n' die, *vole*!'

'Not s'long as aye ken fly, *vole*! Hahaha.'

'Hahafuckin'ha.'

'Hahafuckyoutoo, Magoo. Wot be noo?'

'Yo, *vole*, check out dat gross-as-fuck ecto-thingy down dere! Is dat cool or is dat *cool*? Want we go grab a bite o' it?'

'Holyfriggin'Moses, bro! Dat ain't no ecto-thingy, dat's da Devil in disguise!'

'Why's da Devil lookin' like a wo-man, for, *vole*?'

'*Dat* a woman?'

'He got all dem wo-man bits.'

'If dat a woman, she be da ugliest doggone bitch aye ever seen. Looks more like da *Texass Chitlins Massacre* widdout da special defects!'

'Special wot? Dey had who?'

'Dem great big hunks o' white meat, *vole*! Ugly as Jesus' mama!'

'Well, least dey ain't singin', ya know, like in *Da Soun' o' Musak.*'

'Yo, bro. Edelweiss, *ba-ba-damn*! Whitey poon taste nice, *ba-ba-damn*!'

'Woah! Is dat wot aye tink it is?'

'Dunno, bro, whadya *tink* it is?'

'Looks like da old skullcap's havin' dat lily ass o' his flay-ed wid da nastiest bundle o' birch faggots dis here buzzbomb ever did klep eyes upone...'

Swiiiiish! *Whack*!

Well, after he bartered his soul, his charisma, his baubles & his last mental faculty, what'd that *idiot semblable* have left to peddle but his polymathic posterior, in a manner of speaking, to try to buy just a little more time? And morphing Mephistopheles, done up now like postcoital Frankensteinian parody of the poor bugger's belovèd stepdaughter, wanton Westonia no less, the raunchiest rhymester Golem City's seen since, since, well for a very long while indeed. Arousing in the way a final sickness might be arousing to a dying man. She's really bending her elbow, giving it to dear old dads like there's a fire needs fanning down below, hehe. Labcoat & shirttails up around his waist, forked beard a-flutter, sweat beading his brow. And this's just the warm-up, lovelies. You can see it in the whites of his eyes, he's degradation's slave. Like a whorehouse piano player with a gutful of Franz Liszt stuck in his craw & nothing but saloon slop coming out. He could've been someone, he could've amounted to something, he could've been a better class of sucker than this. The Elixir's right there, in his mind he can see IT, very nearly almost within his grasp. But he'll go to Hell first before that flagellating flibbertygibbet'll get IT out've HIM! That's right. This Westonia shtick's a stick too far! There were limits, you know, things even a crapulous old queer like K here wouldn't countenance on his mother's grave. Really. You just don't underestimate a man who's laid down sideways all his life. He'll take his secret with him, by Christ, if it's the last thing he does. Burn his books. Break his beakers. Bury IT under a mountain of gibberish. Then if he still has his own legs, & even if he hasn't, he'll make a run for it, vamoose, be air. Make it look good, like some *Stalag 17* suicide run. See if that mercurial maggot figures out he's been stiffed real good!

Hisssssssss! *Thwack*!

'OwwwWWW!!!!!!'

'Quiet in there!'

Borislav gave the door to the alchemist's cell a mighty backhand. Silence within. He cracked his enormous knuckles, dropped his hand onto the region of his jockstrap & idly scratched a sliver of scrotum poking through the seam.

'Weirdo,' Vratislav grunted. 'The hell's he doin' in there anyway?'

'The place adjectivally stinks,' Rostislav slapped a playing card face-up on the stool that stood between the three of them. 'Wot we gotta end up with sub-par employment like this for, s'wot I wanna know. Twenty years loyal service 'n' we gotta babysit some potzo with a chemistry set.'

Borislav slapped a card down on top of the one Rostislav had just slapped down. Vratislav slapped another on top of that. It was Rostislav's go again.

'I'd rather be in adjectival Bulgaria,' he said, scratching a chin the size of a garbage pale. 'Beatin' the innards out of adjectival Turks.'

He slapped down a card. Borislav farted, slapped down a card.

'Snap!' Vratislav hoiked.

He grabbed the cards in his spade hands & shuffled them into his deck. Slapped a card on the stool.

'I'd fancy a couple of months in Italy meself,' Rostislav said, slapping down a card. 'You know, see some of the old buildin's & stuff. Visit the museums.'

'Me mum spent her holidays in Verona last year,' said Borislav. 'Said you wouldn't believe the mozzies. Had an awful time.'

'Autumn's your best bet, s'wot I've been told.'

'Don't like all them foreign places much meself. I'd rather beat the innards out of Turks right 'ere.'

'Well they've got their own adjectival country, don't they? Wot, they got sick of all that sand & flies & stuff & had to come over 'ere & nick ours?'

'Wot I heard is, the guards over on the south wing are votin' to go out on strike over it. Apparently there's adjectival Turks bein' given all the plum jobs shovellin' out the latrines.'

'That's just typical, init?'

'Snap!' growled Borislav.

'Excuse I,' Vratislav groaned, heaving his enormous leathery posterior off his stool & giving his jerkin a shrug. 'Gotta splash the sandals.'

Flip flap flop as he slouched off down the flagstones, first on the right, watch the step, shut the door behind, unhook the old codpiece for a well-deserved slash. Point Percy at the porcelain, figuratively speaking. Shake hands with the wife's best friend, in a manner of. Siphon the python, to be exact. A healthy stream of recycled swill, frothing out of the hole in the floor *bubble bubble bubble* & a yellowybrown sludge welling up, spilling all over the hunched-up giant's exposed toe-line, slopping about his size 16 insoles. *Ergh!* No room to escape the flood in there. Bloody Habsburg plumbing! *Gurgle gurgle belch.* Now he'll have to schlep around with soggy feet for the rest of the night, stinking of piss & God only knew what else, the stuff people poured down the jacks these days, no consideration for the environment or anything. Then *splarf!* & the whole lot suddenly got sucked down in a gush of unblockage, having reached some kind of critical volume-to-mass ratio, slurping southbound through the shitshoot & off into space like one of them vacuum-sealed midAtlantic flush-jobs at high altitude, atomised on impact with the stratosphere or whatever they were bound to call it, come the day. Funny the sorts of things start ticking around your head during &/or after a gratifying bladder-release. Future air-travel, now wouldn't that be a gag, eh? Couldn't you just picture the lads, knees up round their ears in the backrow of economy class for a dirty weekend in Istanbul! Priceless! Just wait till they heard that one! Christ, he'd try flappin' his own wings off the watchtower wall if it'd get him away from this dump.

Weeweeweeeeeeeeeeee goes the pee down into the sea…

Well, it wasn't the sea exactly, but a moat's not the worst place for a particle of piss to wind up in the general scheme of things, lots of opportunities, adventure, new faces, fishy tadpole whatsits to investigate, water bears, mud monsters, bouquets of bluegreen algae, really pretty that time of year. Even the odd floating skullcap belonging no doubt to another one of them haphazard alchemist types with compound fractures out his de-lobed ears, just dropped-in for a quick visit, a quick peekaroo at the scenery, & oh how very scenic it indeed is down here in the middle of the night, little crescent moons reflecting in gently undulating concentric wavelets. *Splish splash splosh!* And…

'The dirty bugger! He's GOOOOOOONE!'

Echoing out the high tower window, a mellifluous windborne lament that, for the poor bastards stationed outside the cell door, was more like a spleen-rupturing howl. Rostislav, Borislav & Vratislav peered in through the doorway while the charwoman, gone arse-over-tit in a puddle of quicksilver, brush, pail & all, sat there on the floor wailing her head off & bugeyed pointing at the bloodsmear HELTER SKELTER graffitied across the walls. Bits of shredded birch strewn about, shattered glass, books hacked from their covers, machines crudely dismembered, a labcoat with a *K* monogrammed on the breast pocket draped over a chairback, bloodied ropes lying near about, but no sign of the old crackpot. Jumped he must've!

And perched there unbeknownst on the windowsill, a bloody big black Crow giving the howling charwoman the beady eye. Then some quick damage assessment, head cocked to one side. Yep, just as Crow thought: that Mephrastus-in-Drag couldn't find a hole in a whorehouse, even if it was parked under his nose, which in this case it proverbially was. K's magic manuscript, camouflaged right into the open air. The solus scriptura of the book that brooked no equal, whose key was the Kama Sutra of the mouth & tongue that must be grown for it to speak — *kroark! kroark!* — a little lubrication of the linguistic cortex, back brain, frontal lobe, lower abdominal, etc... Saying, 'ERE I AM to anyone who wasn't a deafblind halfwit, present company excluded of course. How pathetic it looked, heaped beside the dead alchemist's stool in that miserable closet, like mouldy foodscraps or the shaggy arse of a wistful-looking mutt about to crap in the middle of your doorstep — a prize turd to be boiled down into haemorrhoid balm for some Mephritic monkey with a pompom on the end of its tail, able to perform all nature of tricks, if only it could be trained to shit gold. A four-legged golem. *Bowwow!* And if that, what else couldn't it be taught to do? Lay a parboiled egg? The philosopher's stone itself? But not this time, Mephistyrselfinthearse! *Kroark!*

The charwoman howled some more. The three giants crowded in the doorway. Crow cackled quietly to himself, flapped unseen onto the floor, got his black beak around said book (looked just like a goddamn paving stone & weighed like one too) & without further ado beat a hasty retreat. *Flap flap flap* out over the moat & across the fields, down onto the awaiting shoulder of a sinister cloaked figure astride a mighty black steed. Said figure's eyes flash in the moonlight. Nothing that has transpired up there in the castle tower has escaped his piercing gaze. For he has seen all, knows all. That's right, kids, just as you expected, it's our old friend, der schwartze Reiter.

'Good work, Crow,' taking the book in gauntleted hand & giving the bird an appreciative chuck under the craw. 'That pretty much concludes our business here for today. Let's hit the highroad before someone figures it out...'

And with the Lone Ranger theme tune wafting faintly in his wake, the Black Rider rides right off the page into the Land of As If, through swirling mind-mandalas & archetypes & synchronicities & dream keys. Němec blinked at the words spiralling weirdly about like that on the paper right there in front of him. *Zapf! Here we go again!* Then realised it wasn't the words moving but something else, something black spinning on its end & rolling to a stop. Must've fallen from somewhere. He leant down to pick it up. *Well I'll be.* It was one of the Prof's chesspieces. A knight, no less. Maybe even *the* knight, but where'd it come from? Němec glanced at the ceiling. Nothing much up there except cracked plaster turned grey over the years, prolapsed mouldings, cobwebs in the corners, mottled by watermarks & sloping at a wrong angle. He turned the chesspiece between his fingers. *Yer wastin' yer time, kiddo, been here before, remember?* The arbitrary beginning & thereafter the mania of causation, like some sort of Gomer Piles character with an *idée fixe* to diddle Pandora's powderbox, only to wind up in the boobyhatch without ever seeing the funny side of his predicament, *hehe*, ramping up the pathos in hope, perhaps, however unrealistic, of fitting a twist into it, something that'd upset the readers' arrangements & leave them wondering at how mysteriously the Hand of the Author moves, catching them five minutes from the end of the episode just when they coulda swore they had it all figured out, coulda written the damn thing themselves even, a whole dressed-up masterpiece-by-numbers, *blah-de-blah-blah-blah*, just like some monkey-in-disguise at the junior spelling bee, who wins the electric typewriter & never looks back...

Thump! went something upstairs. Eh? A fine white powdery dust sifted down onto Němec's face. He sputtered, waved his hands. The ceiling shook. *Clop clop clop*. And was that the sound of the Prof's ghost he could hear, laughing in the distance?

55

THE KEY

Leucippus of Miletus, a contemporary of Democritus, believed that nothing happens without a cause, but everything with a cause & by necessity. He also believed everything was composed of atoms, like motes in a sunbeam, circulating in an infinite void. The entire universe might just as well've been nothing but the morbid symptom of a mind driven to despair by the minute significance of all things: in every direction, lines of influence spread out & closed-in on themselves — dreams & possible worlds — untranslatable idioms of the evolutionary cosmos. It was for others to believe that Creation had a *purpose* or suffer the doubt that their God merely signified the purpose *of a yet higher rationale* — the clockwork homunculus inside the Mind of the Cosmos: somewhere, a hidden chess player calculating the moves, like the dwarf concealed inside Kempelen's machine, the brain inside the automaton, God's puppetmaster. As if behind every bit of randomness there stood a concocted Sphinx, whose riddle was a mirror held up to Reason, ready to evaporate the moment you construed it.[*]

— T. Hájek, Geschichte als göttliche Wahrscheinlichkeit

A tiny gold figure was spinning & turning end over end, suspended in the darkness, revolving in its own firmament. It was terribly cold. Němec was lying on his back, naked, in the snow. Above him, the sky was black, the snow had ceased to fall, there was only that gold thing, glittering, turning, hanging there. He couldn't see what it was. At first he thought it was an astrologer's sphere, then a gold coin, a ring, a blade. Their shapes formed & reformed, blurring like images in water. Then he saw what it was — a key. Turning end over end, its movement described a circle of light against the blackness. It revolved, without ever coming closer.

---

[*] What was it the schoolmasters said? *"In logic, nothing's accidental: the riddle doesn't exist — if a question can be put at all, it can also be answered..."* Ludwig Wittgenstein, son of a Zhiddish steel magnate, *Tractarsus Logico-Phallusophicus* 6.5. [♟]

When the mood took her, Mrs Severínová was liable to fall into lengthy reminiscence — about the golden years, the pervading spirit, the heyday of the blood — but the mood very rarely did. This occasion, though, was one of them.

'It was on account of the mechanical dolls,' she said, inviting him to a cup of Yunan tea from the obligatory pot on the kitchen table. A bundle of the old lady's knitting lay beside it. Who it was for, all that knitting — involuted browns & greys that never seemed to go anywhere, to progress — Němec hadn't the faintest idea. The parrot, maybe. A faint hiss issued from the T.E.S.L.A. radio.

'Lemon or honey?'

'…?'

'Tomáš always took his without. I'm sometimes partial to honey, myself. Forest flowers. The man at the post office brings it from Šumava. You have to be so careful nowadays, you never know what they put in things. Real honey candies, but when you heat it, it clarifies. That,' the old lady winked, 'is the secret. How you can tell if it's real or not.'

Němec couldn't say he'd ever actually seen the Prof drink tea, with or without the genuine article. The caretaker offered him a little gingerbread man with raisin eyes & an icing mouth & coat buttons. The parrot, ensconced on its perch, made beady eyes at him. The forecast had been for snow but it was slow in coming.

In Greiffenberg the old count, Gasper von N____, staged balls with dancing lifesize dolls. He commissioned Granddad Hájek, apparently, to make them for him, which was how the two families first brushed shoulders, as the expression goes. The way the dolls worked was that they had a hole in the back for a wind-up key — a complicated gadget kept the pairs synchronised while they waltzed around the room in time to Schubert. There was talk of commissioning a regiment before the Great War, but nothing came of it. At length, the elderly von N____ & the toymaker grew quite fond of each other, as did their sons (it sounded like the stuff of fairytales already) — though neither the Prof's own father, Tomáš Snr., nor the younger von N____, Eldrich, shared the slightest interest in puppets, clocks, or mechanical automata. They, unlike their fathers, had instead a singular & indeed quite consuming passion for antique books.

Gaspar von N____ (†?)	Grandad Hájek (1922?)
Eldrich von N____ (†?)	Tomáš Hájek, Snr. (†1942)
Elsbeth von N____ (†1996)	Tomáš Hájek, Jnr. (†1996)

After the toymaking gramps shuffled-off, his attic workshop, right there in the house on Jánský Vršek, was made into a nursery, where the future Prof — all rosy cheeks, blond hair & greyblue irises — commenced his fingersucking existence in the company of dozens if not hundreds of wind-up mannequins, stuffed animals, midgets, golems, commendatores & myriad other mechanical nightmare-inducing knickknacks, doodads, bibs&bobs, even a green-eyed clockwork parrot that squawked on the hour, half-hour & quarter hour: thrice, twice & once respectively.

Němec gave the caretaker's pet bird a scrutinising look. *Eh, Polly? How about we stick something in you and give it a nice sharp twist?* The parrot leered. The Prof must've been over the bloody moon when his old lady showed up with this character to make his conjugal life a misery. All those childhood horrors revisited in the Oedipal adventures of our fine feathered friend here. He tried picturing the little homunculus Prof *up there* under the heavens, going rockabye in his cot, goo-gooing & gah-gahing, coughing up the wetnurse's milk, crapping his nappy, turning crosseyed from mobiles of spinning planets, stars, moon & sun, picking his nose, singing a song of sixpence, learning his ABCs, poking in his nanny's drawers, riding a cockhorse, dressing a wooden mannequin in a red clownsuit, unstringing a violin, measuring his uncut dingus with a ruler, pouring glue in keyholes, building a treehouse among the rafters, stashing treasures under floorboards, blending magic potions in beakers, intoning strange prayers, raising fungus in jars, reading under the blankets with a T.E.S.L.A.-brand electric lamp, doodling naked pictures of the school mistress, repenting in the dark, constructing his first jejune erector set, listening ear-to-the-floor to the domestic drama downstairs, pinning textbook diagrams to walls, dismantling a music box, perving on the servant girl next door, coming down with diphtheria, swearing eternal love to dusty tomes, etc & undsoweiter…

And when *were* the happiest?

It was afterwards, back upstairs, that Němec had the feeling someone else was in the room. He went through the motions of checking. Something about the old lady's Yunan tea, perhaps. Or the lingering presence of Alice Steinerová. Heebiejeebie stuff. The rooms, however, were as deserted as he'd left them. His whole existence summed-up right there. Like the old men of yonder days wandering around inside their memories, each in its appointed place, greeting each new bit of entropy like the arrival of a long lost amour. *Ah, my dearest, my dust! Come! Breed, dust! Breed!*

Němec sat down on his camp bed & stared at the typewriter lying on the floor, black chesspiece perched atop. Funny, that. He picked the knight up & turned it around in his fingers. Another one of those "clues" that kept cropping up with unnerving frequency? He slipped it in his trouser pocket, perhaps it'd work as a talisman of sorts. Or not. No skin, either way. He peered down at the paper wound into the wordmachine. Ideas for failures yet to be attempted:

NOTES ON FAILURE 1-8

8 PROJECTS FOR AN OPEN-ENDED ETCETERA

RESPONSES TO 8 UNASKED QUESTIONS

8 ANONYMOUS TIP-OFFS

8 PROPOSALS CONCERNING IMPOSSIBILITY

8 HOURS 8 DAYS 8 MONTHS 8 YEARS

IMPLICATE DELEGATE INSEMINATE MICTURATE
DISCRIMINATE ENERVATE COMPLICATE DEGENERATE

A SELF-CRITICISM (IN 8 PARTS)

8 SOCIALIST PASTS & NO FUTURES

LETTERS TO NON-ENTITIES (?)

LETTERS TO FAMOUS PEOPLE (MOSTLY DEAD)
1. LETTER TO BOHUMIL "WHORABAL"*
2. LETTER TO ZDENA TOMIN
3. LETTER TO PAUL LEPPIN
4. LETTER TO TOYEN
5. LETTER TO HERMAN UNGAR
6. LETTER TO JAN PATOČKA
7. LETTER TO MILADA HORÁKOVÁ
8. LETTER TO MAGOR

The answer wasn't in there, either. (For that he'd need a reading machine as well as a writing machine, hehehe.) Němec sank his head into his hands, closed his eyes. And once more saw the key falling through the air. Why not a wind-up parrot as well? He blinked & the image crumbled away. But again that sense of something in the room that didn't belong there. He parted his fingers & glanced

* A.k.a. "Bo Hrab," ghostwriter of *Too Silent a Multitude* & *Lessons for Saving Your Own Neck*: "As pre-eminent Chesk scribbler & legend in my own lunchbox, I feel deeply connected to the Antik Chesk People, with its grandiloquent socialist past & incredulous future." [✋]

out through the bars they made. As assuredly as ever, he was alone, & yet the outline of his dream was still present. The walls, however, had all gone grey. Slivers of stormcloud showed around the edges of the window. Němec could feel the barometric tension working its way inside his head. Outside, a fierce wind had begun to blow. The windows shook, the stairwell groaned. It was a sound like the groaning of someone disturbed in their sleep, in a room at the end of a long tunnel, deep beneath the earth. The imaginary sleep of an imaginary someone in an imaginary room. And in this imaginary room, an imaginary wooden table, perhaps. And on the table, a book of white marble. Entirely imaginary. And in the book, a faceted stone...*

The Prof had always given the impression of being a devout believer in the symmetry of happenstance, but how d'you know the shape of what you can't see? Somewhere in the back of Němec's head, the weather was like something watching him over his shoulder. And while it watched him, everything started coming back into focus. But not an ordinary focus — more concrete, somehow. The dream in all its detail, with unusual vividness: the key, the sleeper, the room, the desk, the text inscribed in the stone book. *The hand is gone but there remaineth writing.* And somewhere, a stirring as of dry tea leaves spilled on the floor. His mind woke suddenly from its lethargy like a cat: the architecture around him more sharply delineated than ever. It was as if, *inside himself,* he was standing at one end of a very long room with a door at the other & all he had to do was reach out across all that distance & turn the handle, & on the other side would be a room *within* the room, the *essence* of the room made manifest. If he'd had the presence of mind, he might've typed that out, it would've made a good beginning to a story in an agonised, portentous kind of way.

---

* ☞ Now a leaf of that book is turned open, & there is written on it, but I cannot read it yet. Now I see it. *I am who I am, who gave and will give you a law: from which perpetual peace and happiness will come to mortals.* I see a hand appear, a very great one, white, with the fingers spread abroad. The hand is gone, but there remaineth writing. *You will shortly see and hear everything. If in the meantime...* It is as if it were upon the side of a white globe afar off. The globe turneth so swiftly that I cannot well read it. *...your souls, joined together for the better...* The globe turneth so swiftly that I cannot read it till it stands still. *...will subject themselves to me and mine in the manner of sons. All sins committed in me are forgiven. He who goes mad on my account, let him be wise. He who commits adultery because of me, let him be blessed for eternity and receive the heavenly prize.* Now the globe is gone. [☟]

Instead he stood up & began walking through the apartment, trying every door in the place. It was ridiculous, but he couldn't help himself. And then things started happening all by themselves. As if by silent command he began to search through the apartment for something that he was painfully aware couldn't be found simply by looking. The *key*? Some sort of key, at least. He went through each of the rooms, opening & closing doors, scrutinising the cupboards, drawers, alcoves, pantries, all the obvious first places any imbecile would look. And from the most obvious, by declensions, to the least likely. He made subtle inspections of walls, ceiling, stray shadows, corridors of air, hide-in-plain-sight & all that. He factored-in as many elements as could be construed from WHAT WAS KNOWN: the Prof's history, the suicided muses, the madman in the attic, the Manuscript, the Black Book & associated polygraphic cryptobabble — but that got him predictably nowhere. Intoned vague ridiculous spells, names, numbers, mumble, snatches of Mahler for good measure. The rooms looked no different. A little more pathetic, perhaps. Or perhaps it was simply that *he* looked more pathetic in them?

When he closed his eyes, however, the image was still there. It *persisted* in an entirely uncanny way, clearer than any actual thought. As if *it* was part of the space he was walking around in, the proverbial room-within-a-room — which could only be seen by *not* looking? Not with the outward eye, not directly, but *askance*? Like Kircher in that queer portrait of his, catching the Devil coming at him sideways, hehe. All things considered, perhaps what the Prof's paltrygeist had been trying to tell him all along was that the mystery Manuscript was really a metaphoric Mind map, replete with diagrams & ciphers, a psychic cartography of Floating Islands ⌘ beyond any Latitude → across Far Seas ♒ through the Northwest ↑ Passage of the Cosmos ✺ where the Tree of Being ♃ sits upon the Sacred Mountain ⛰ its Path of Ascent ⎮ & the ✗ that marks the Precise Spot at which are buried the Keys to the Kingdom of Knowledge ♠ — that "Sovereign State of Consciousness" entered solely by means of herbs, meditation, dreams, sickness, allegory or madness…

Well why not? But thinking so wasn't much help to Squillhead there. About as illuminating, in fact, as flashing the halogens at a fogbank ten miles deep. Still, there was something to be said for that Blue Beard & Barnacle Bill stuff. Bringing back memories only faintly awful / humiliating / appalling — of that day when the Spastic Girl, down by "the Lake," many summers ago… *Bury it! Bury it!* Pretending not to see. Playing the game of Pirate's Island, mutiny on the High Sargasso, walking the plank, a bit of the old keel-hauling for good measure, being advised by every wisearse within cooee that it's really the Treasure Inside that matters when all the accounting's been tallied up for the Big Audit. The measly little shit with the heart of gold. *Ah, for fuck's sake, kiddo, you really do take the bloody cake some times.*

Němec groped around like that, eyes half-shuttered, over every square inch of the Prof's apartment, but nothing out of the ordinary presented itself. No hidden ghosts, no blind bats, no mezuzahs cunningly concealed in doorposts, no false compartments, no loose fittings, no sliding panels, no trapdoors. Only the tap-tap of chisels through the walls, the thump of a jackhammer, a generator's hum, all fusing into also vague evocations of elsewhere. "Vague," being the operative word. The rooms, for their part, were all "empty" — excepting for his own personal detritus, of course, & the wreckage of Pretty Poly[graphicunt]. Discount the obvious by way of the obscure & what was left?

The hiss of recordplayer static followed him around the apartment like a mocking accompaniment. He gave up the blindman act & switched it off. Intimations of yet another migraine coming on. *Well, let it.* He wheezed into his hands, a pair of beautifully rounded gobs of brown phlegm. Wiped them off with a sheet of facsimile paper (what else was it good for?). It was obvious he was sick, but was he also losing his mind? He poured the dregs of a bottle down his throat. Another dead soldier. He had quite a tally by now, so many notches on his whatever it would've looked like a hedgehog in heat. The alcohol burned in his gut, he could feel the blood circulating through the lower intestines, stimulating the Inner Void somewhat. It helped. Pushing the black plastic aside, he opened a window & breathed the cold air deeply. *Ah! The world's my egg and I'm its sticky yolk, hehe.*

Outside one of the construction workers stopped chiselling the stucco off the wall & looked at Němec with a queer expression on his face. Němec pulled his head back, before it was too late…

What was it the ghost said? *The tree can't be escaped by means of the tree?* Two more hours of tapping on walls, gouging out plaster & prying up floorboards. Digging behind shelves, sinks, under the bath, inside the goddamn toilet. Trees? What'd trees have to do with it? Between stubborn & stupid was a fine line forever narrowing. It had Němec going crosseyed sitting there in the hallway staring at the cracks in the wall, the hinges jointing the built-in broomcloset, the articulated gloom from which empty space spilled out. He stared & stared. Nothing going on in there, just the desire to crawl in behind the shelves & the empty shoe racks & lock himself in. Forget all about these idiot notions of his.

Then a funny thing happened. While he sat there blankly staring into the shadows, something creaked. What it was that creaked was the back of the closet seeming to come away from the wall. Slowly, as if in a dream, he stood up & walked towards it. Pushing the racks out of the way, he reached into the gap in the panelling & pulled. A cunningly disguised door yielded with little effort, revealing darkness beyond. Němec groped inside the frame & found a switch. Suddenly a narrow cell-like room appeared, every bit of it layered in dust. *Well I'll be fucked.*

Amazed, Němec stepped through.

It really was a room.

In it there was a chair, a writing desk & a bed, & a dry musty odour that tasted decades old. A cloistered quiet pervaded. The place obviously hadn't been visited for a very long time. He gazed wide-eyed. Had the Prof known this place existed? He felt like a child stumbling on a pirate's cave. It was as unreal as that. And yet it was all too real. Someone had intended it this way…

The walls were bare, except for a couple of hooks & the outlines left by pictures that'd been removed. A single bookshelf was set into the wall opposite the bed, between the writing desk & a narrow wardrobe. The shelves were littered with sundry items: a technical manual on polyphase currents — a broken alarmclock — a shaving box embossed with the SOKOL insignia, containing a mirror, a packet of rusted razorblades & a shaving brush — a flashlight, its battery still working (?!) — a yellow tin of *Javanese Jongens* tobacco, a plantation scene painted on the lid, black figures at work in a field — three or four lead crystal vases — David Friedrich Strauss's *Life of Jesus* — half-a-dozen empty inkbottles — a decanter with crosshatched engraving — some brandy snifters, all thick with dust. Not exactly a hideyhole for the proletariat, eh? Behind a smeared glass frame, a tricolour pennant with PRAVDA VÍTĚZÍ in cracked & flecked gold lettering.

And when had the truth ever prevailed?

Sitting atop the desk was an umbrella stand, containing a collection of walkingsticks. Also atop the desk was a pair of dusty reading glasses, numerous pens & pencils, lined stationery, an inkpad, a letter opener, an empty cigar box, paper-scissors, numerous other bits & pieces. In contrast, the drawers were all empty, except for one item: a postcard sent from Tatranská Lomnica, Hotel

Praha — a black&white vista of a pine forest with snowcovered mountains rising above, onto which someone had glued a cutout picture of an alpine sanatorium. On the reverse, a green 50 Heller stamp (POŠTA ČESKOSLOVNIKIA), the franking date illegible. Beneath it, the addressee's details inked in faded blockcapitals: Pan JOSEF KULIČKA (?) or KUBIČKA (?), BĚCHOVICE U PRAHY, č. 126 (?).

Neither name nor address meant anything to him.

Why would they?

There was, of course, nothing in Němec's mental universe to which the meaning of that room corresponded. Had it been there from the beginning, or had it been sealed-off later on, during the War, perhaps. To shelter Resistance fighters, or Zhids slated for railroading, or blackmarket loot? But after the novelty of discovering it had exhausted itself, Němec was left exactly where he'd been the moment he'd walked in. It was even something of an anticlimax. A secret room *without* a key. Still, there had to be some prospects in a place like that. What else was hidden in there? He resumed his search. The wardrobe looked the most promising: shirts, trousers, suit jackets & ties on a tie rack. Two pairs of cracked brown leather shoes rested on the floor beside a likewise cracked shoehorn. Beside which, a broken transformer lay upsidedown with a tangle of wires spilling out & a crystal-set radio, copper coils green with oxidisation. Němec groped through the clothes on the clotheshangers. The pockets contained only the odd folded handkerchief, laundered & pressed, as if whoever owned them had expected to go somewhere. Who? Where? None of the clothes looked as if they'd ever been worn — they might just as well've been windowdressing, so to speak. Perhaps they were.

Němec pulled the hangers aside. A quite distinct sense of déjà vu descended upon him. There, notched into the back of the wardrobe, were a series of shallow ledges, ascending like the rungs of a ladder behind the clothesrack. Funny place to keep a ladder, if it *was* a ladder. He took the flashlight from the bookshelf & shone it up inside the wardrobe. It looked exactly the way you'd expect the inside of a wardrobe to look. There was nowhere for the "ladder" to go. Were it not for the fact that he was standing inside a secret room already, Němec wouldn't've given it a second thought. Instead, he wedged the torch in his breast pocket, gripped the rungs, squeezed behind the clothesrack & pulled himself up as far as he could go. A web of pain spread from his arms & shoulders down the length of his body, but he held on. Shifting his weight so that he could get one hand free, he rapped his knuckles against the panel at the top — it sounded hollow alright. He spread his palm against it & pushed, but it wouldn't budge. An application of force appeared warranted. He tried levering himself between the higher rungs & the sides of the wardrobe, heaving with hunched back. It required the work of a contortionist & produced no result. He tried again. This time there was a vague tremor. He applied deduction, re-torquing his weight so as to lever the panel sideways, & was instantly rewarded with a fine rain of dust falling in his eyes. The next moment, he was blinking up into pitch blackness.

No clattering tin-drum soldier or dustballed goblin came out of the dark, only the cold yeasty smell of long confinement & motes stirring in the flashlight's chiaroscuro. On all sides, thick grey cobwebs hung, long undisturbed, like tailings of clotted felt from roof beams — the floor inch-deep in talc. In the attic back at the Home, he remembered old ledgerbooks, android instruction manuals, a red-eyed kiln for mud compotes, golem-heads, black hands, a trestletable & clay man laid out, God on his Bethel bed. The story went: a ladder was set up on the Earth & the top of it reached to Heaven, & behold. The Sulam of Al Mi'raj. But here, in this place, what'd he expect to find? Something that went thump in the night? A sickly child's long-ago abandoned playroom? Some private den of despond? The Prof's ghost asleep in a jar? The Old Man's countinghouse? K's abandoned apotheca & vivisectionarium? Of pestled plant & amorted beast, transmutations unnatural & metamorphoses untold, jotted down on engineers' quadrille paper in dots & squiggles, crossword code, six-across, "Elixir?" (Perhaps the dirty skullcap even diddled his stepdaughter up there, the way he diddled D's wife? *Wee Westonia in her playpen, Westonia on the floor, Westonia on the writing desk, Westonia up against the wall…*)

Němec listened for the sound of breathing, wing-flutter, footfall, the pure crystalline brilliance of the cosmic earhole tuned-in on its own tremula, but no, none. Hauled himself up through the trapdoor, dust in mouth, lungs afire, ribs burning, entering the dark allegorical upper-world of Mysterium. He swept the blackness with his flashlight to see which of the hundredthousand Himmels he'd bungled upon. Nothing remotely like the Pearly Gates, only a rubble of broken floorboards, splintered, cracked — crumbling terracotta strewn about — sagging partitions, mould-mottled in the gloom like damasked wallpaper, broken-legged chairs, wardrobes with cracked mirrors, a washstand, commode, a gutted bookcase, china cabinet, grey fuzzy lampshades, patinaed sideboards & lice-riddled consoles, all stacked in tiers like theatre benches for an audience of broken toys, stuffed animals, dummies & po-faced mannequins. Here & there the winged skeleton of a long-dead pigeon.

All that was missing was a stage with wind-up players arranged in tableau, awaiting the turnscrew spell to conduct them in some tell-all Schauspiel: Man in the Iron Mask stuff. Some deranged demon cackling in the wilderness, an echo inside an echo, telling the tale of K on the eve of completing the *Tractus de Lapide Philosophorum*, his last memoired moments before he clocked-out, cycled off into the meta-code, *obscurum per obscurius* if not outright *ignotum per ignotius*. All the bits of the mystery left as they lay, like tesserae from a smashed mosaic, bleeding into the floorboards, or sifted into sediment like Severínová's divinational tea leaves, the salty meniscus of so much evaporated Dobrá Voda, the *eau de vie* of lost unclouded insight, etc. And in their stead, a wrecked upright piano with its keys removed, panels disassembled to expose the ratty wires, fouled hammers, cracked damper board, the whole subsiding inner mechanism like a Pharaoh's sarcophagus after the tombrobbers had made off with the plunder. Headrats scuttling & scurrying in the dark. The fogged atmosphere sucking the breath out of him.

Fanning outwards, the sweep of torchlight turned the curtained dark to speleology, depths-of-field that faded out in convoluted moiré or fell off into ravines of nothing. While up above, the beams & rafters made Piranesi catacombs woven with Ariadne spider-threads, looping & branching, multiplying with every light-shift in ways logic-defying. It reminded Němec of that story about the Man who Stole the Colosseum. How every night this guy in Rome would sneak down to the Colosseum with a crowbar & gunnysack & work up a sweat relaying bags of rock up to the attic in his house. It started when he was a kid & grew from there. He kept it up alongside a day-job for almost fifty years, till he could only manage a few bits of rubble at a time. In the end he was too old & worn-out even for that, he'd just sit on a bench wistfully eyeballing the Colosseum wondering how the fuck it was still standing, all those years playing the long hand & hardly made a dent in it. And not only the attic but his entire house by now, every spare inch, crammed with old masonry he'd worked like a donkey lugging halfway up the Via Appia, till eventually one night in his sleep the weight of it all...

Well, as the Bugman might've said, *you hedge yer bets but it's the payoff that kills you.*

Winding among columns of junk, piles of broken furniture, potted plants, floor matted with insect husks & dead leaves compounding to dust, the blighted remains of some once-upon-a-time artificed Arcadia, till finally coming to a clearing where the worst of the dirt & debris had at some time been swept away. Bird feathers & guano shone grey upon every available surface like dirty snow. Faint outlines of old footprints made palimpsests across the floor. Whoever had been there, it hadn't been any time recently. Němec followed the tracks between littered workbenches to a door with a cracked chamber pot in front of it. He turned the handle, half-expecting to find the corpse of some starved homunculus, murdered by the evil eye. The whole thing came away in his hand, lock & all, but the door didn't budge. Must've been sealed up from the other side. He pressed an ear to the wood: a low groaning of wind under eaves, maybe, or the ear's echo, one ear listening to another. He resisted the impulse to knock.

There didn't seem to be any other way out, the flashlight found nothing but walls of junk & crumbling plasterwork. One match, he thought, & the whole place'd go *whoosh*. He swung the beam along the rafters, nothing up there but more junk. A couple of blackened skylights, exposed rooftiles, cobwebs, bits of planking. Then something moved. A rat. *Life at last! Hey, rat, how about giving us the lowdown?* Němec's eyes may've been playing tricks on him, but he was pretty sure that rat just flipped him off before scuttling away like that. He swept the beam back & forth across the trusses. A couple of metres in from the wall, the torch lit upon a length of knotted rope hanging down. The rat's eyes blinked in the light then vanished into the shadows again. *Haha, shmuckaroony, go figure.* Something else glittered up there, but too high to tell what it was. Němec traced the rope with the flashlight. At a certain point it disappeared behind a dressing table, with a child's painted rockinghorse atop & a cracked mirror in which dislocated bits of silhouette alternated with flashes of light.

Navigating through the junk till he reached the spot where the rope dangled down from the ceiling, Němec was curious to find another set of bootprints. The two sets must've joined at the clearing, but they ended at the door & began here, at the bottom of the rope. Or maybe it was the other way around? Strange. Němec peered up between the rafters. Again the torch caught something under the skylight. A sliver of paraselene? The hook of a crescent moon? He gripped the rope with both hands, shook it, applied bodyweight. The rope held, but the air filled with a fine talcum of dust. Obvious that no fakirs had abseiled through that particular skylight in the too recent past. He wondered whose tracks he'd been following around, though. Then all by itself the rope gave way, slithering through the air, coiling in a pile on the floor. A thick plume of grey to meet the shower of dirt falling from the beams, dead wings fluttering, & then the crash of tin & glass as one after another the delicate tiers of surrounding junk dislodged & collapsed in slow-motion onto those below, domino-like.

In the aftermath it was impossible to see anything, only a fog of torchlit sepia, white light behind the eyes, choking on dust through a wet hole in a handkerchief, blood singing in his ears, salt of blood in his mouth. He'd fallen headlong into the debris, tripped by some invisible scuttling thing. He groped blindly, became tangled in the rope, disentangled himself, lay there trying to breathe, to see. The place was a fucking deathtrap. *Time to quit, kiddo, while yer still ahead.* First, though, he had to find his way out. One maze had been replaced by another, infinitely more chaotic one, a whole composed of movable facets of which he, too, was one. Eventually the dust settled. By fixing on the skylight, it might, he thought, be possible to approximate his position relative to some sort of floorplan, triangulate, correlate distance indirectly & by means at hand, some reconstrued Mercator-plan marked by co-ordinates of pure divination. Find the trapdoor.

Meanwhile Němec hauled himself out of the filth. Up above, the glittering object was still there. Němec strained in the dimness to make a shape out of it. It blinked at him unnaturally, a one-eyed raven about to flap its wings & screech — a yellowed orb, full of occult significance, becoming two, then three, closer, further away, a blur sharpening to a fine needle point, now a line, a disc. It vanished & recomposed itself. What it was, Němec couldn't say.

Perhaps the answer was something very simple.

Němec thought about what the Prof's ghost'd said, about the tree. *The tree can't be escaped by means of the tree.* Very deep. But why "tree"? Why not "ladder hidden in closet"? "Bricked-up door"? "Dangling rope"? "Beady eye among the rafters"? Besides, there were trees & then there were "trees," right? Like the man who flew to the moon in a carp, not a magic carp but an ordinary carp from Třeboň, he'd just figured out how to make it work through the application of reason & commonsense.

Were it not for the square of light coming from the trapdoor showing him the way out, he might've stumbled around up there forever. Perhaps, in some parallel universe, that was precisely the case. Němec peered down through the hole into the cupboard & shook his head. The whole thing didn't bear thinking about. Something, he couldn't help feeling, had led him *there*, through secret chambers, to *that* place, FOR A REASON. But *what* reason? What was he supposed to *find*? Or it was just another of the Prof's parables played to the tune of *He who seeks, etc.*? A roundabout way of illustrating that tired adage about how first you ascend in order to descend. Like it was all about putting a different slant on your perspective, your P.O.V., your personal insight into the startlingly obvious & the stubbornly obtuse? *Alright, kiddo, so you've communed with the ol' upstairs and got sand in your eyes for your trouble. Like they say in the classics, under the beach it's all just rooftiles anyway.*

Casting one last look around, Němec lowered his foot to the top rung of the ladder, then the next, like someone climbing down out of the sky. *Well, kiddo, one more come-down in an open-ended series, eh?* And as he did so he remembered something else the Prof had told him, that first time visiting the "Donkey in the Cradle," etc. — a passing remark about the stairs in K's Tower, heavily worn but sturdy, hewn apparently from a single oak tree. *English* oak. 1546. Fifty years before K, but there you had it, that queer English connection again, like the local variety wasn't good enough? Maybe figured if the stairs didn't quite pan out they could flog the stuff back to the Marylebone crowd for cricket bats?

And how many centuries older, that tree? Roger Bacon's day, at least, eh? Now there was a thought. Shipped from Blighty all the way to Golem City, to become the stuff of forgotten legend, polished by Baťa's finest. What'd the old alchemist have made of *that*? Tree, oh tree! Roots deep in the prima materia of earth & clay, its branches piercing the airy celestitudes? Tree of Knowledge! Tree of Life! At its crown, K's soot-spewing lab — at its foot? Some solemn cloister, perhaps, tearful relics stoppered in bottles. Heaven & Earth. The Solar Anus & the Philosopher's Gallstone. From the celestitudes leading down into the basest of base matter, the sewer of the world, the bowels of creation, the greater & lesser intestine of God — Mephistoid's happy hunting grounds?

The caretaker sat knitting in front of an old iron stove where a heady *česnečka* was brewing: potato, garlic, onion, lard, beef bouillon, salt, pepper, marjoram, caraway seed — a dish of grated edam & bread croutons waiting on the counter beside bowl & spoon. First, you took a deep saucepan, diced the onion finely & fried it in lard, then added the crushed garlic, continuing to fry till lightly browned, at which point stirring in water — while this simmered, you cut the potatoes into cubes & added to the saucepan, along with the salt, pepper, caraway seed & bouillon — let that simmer till the potatoes softened, added marjoram, then served it in a bowl with croutons & a sprinkling of cheese.

When Němec walked in on her, Mrs Severínová looked at him from her knitting with vague interest that persisted into something bordering on apprehension, perhaps even alarm. The voice of a talkback host prattled on the radio while the *česnečka* simmered on the stove:

'Well but did anyone ever give *you* a lump of coal when you were a kid?'

The parrot gawked on its stand.

In folklore, a potent *česnečka* was considered equally effective again vampires & Winter colds — it also cured hangovers, apparently. Which made Němec think, it was about that time of the day, eh? But then, when wasn't? He glanced over at the radio & caught sight of his reflection in a mirror hanging from the shelf above. The cause of the caretaker's apprehension became evident: Němec was covered head-to-toe in dust, bloodymouthed, hat & suit cobwebbed, like some House of Horrors mannequin that'd managed to escape. In the mirror's warp he made quite a picture. It was a wonder the old lady didn't scream. She rattled off another row of garter-stitch, clutching a ball of mauve twine in her right hand. A newspaper was spread out on the table beside her, with a mound of expired tea leaves in the middle of it, mingled with onion skins, potato peals, carrot tops, bits of leak, cabbage, pepper seeds, stalks, rind, strips of fat, bones, flour, spilt milk, mildewed cheese, soured liver paste, rotten apples, celery leaves, crusts of bread. No wing of bat, though, no spleen of toad.

Němec brushed himself off as best he could. The radio prattled on:

'Why call it Christmas if Jesus was just the same as all the rest of us…?'

'I was in the attic,' he volunteered.

This seemed to mollify the old lady somewhat. Then he blurted out his question.

'Key?' she murmured in puzzlement, gazing into some indefinite distance.

'*Kleeheehee!*' the parrot squawked, swivelling its head from side to side.

The caretaker put her knitting down & touched her hair as if to be sure it was still there. The parrot reached out with its beak to take a tentative bite out of Němec's hat.

'People only began eating fried carp in the nineteenth-century, before that it was traditional to cook a goose with cabbage soup...' the radio babbled.

Němec sneezed. The parrot, in complete disregard for gravity, tipped upside-down on its perch, then with beak & claw righted itself again. Mrs Severínová meanwhile was pointing at something above the sink, her voice barely audible over the radio's prattle about Magdalena Dobromila Rettigová & the approved method for parboiling salad potatoes. Němec went to see what the old lady was pointing at. It was a row of hooks, sticking out from the wall above the kitchen sink, from which keys of various shapes & sizes hung. And above each of the hooks was a handwritten label: the one marked CELLAR was empty. *Well, well, whaddayaknow, eh?*

With growing exasperation, Němec checked & rechecked the tags on all the other keys, groped behind the various pots & jars arranged on the counter, peered into the sinkhole, opened cupboards, rifled the old woman's kitchen drawers. Mrs Severínová hardly seemed aware of what he was doing — she'd gone back to her knitting as though she was doing it in her sleep, only with her eyes open. Had it not been for the parrot keeping a beady watch on him the whole time, Němec might've taken the entire kitchen apart. Meanwhile the radio blathered on:

'We've all heard the story about the woman on Kaprova Street who keeps a carp in her bathtub for a pet...'

Eventually Němec gave it up. The parrot gloated, lifted its tail & with eyes half-shuttered let fall a watery string of bird crap. Němec removed his hat & massaged his patchwork skull. The parrot craned its head to get an eyeful. Before it had a chance to whistle, Němec swung the bowler hat at it. The parrot ducked & swivelled upsidedown on its perch again, sticking its tongue out at him. Němec glared in disgust & jammed the hat back on his head. The parrot flapped its wings in delight. *Letting a green bird get the better of you, eh, kiddo?* He let his gaze drift around the kitchen one last time, in case the obvious had escaped him. If it had, it still did. After a while he went back over to where the caretaker sat beside the stove, absorbed in her knitting. He leant close, so that the old lady could hear him, & speaking very slowly & distinctly he said —

'Who was Josef Kulička?'

Her eyes twitched, both of them, but that was all.

In the courtyard it'd begun to snow. *Well, at least someone got the forecast right.* Němec peered up into the whiteness. The Tower stood there like a cut-out in a snowdome that'd been swished about upsidedown. The whiteness of the Tower bleeding into the whiteness of the snow. The light fluttered against the eaves. Black wings. Phantoms under the gables. Troglodytes under the floor. If he squinted just-so, he could just about get the shape of the tetchy alchemist's ghost up there in the observatory, arms flailing in the air, cursing the weather, sounding for all the world like the fulsome braying of an ass. Call it the wind.

As Němec re-climbed the Tower stairs in tired pursuit of an idea, it came to him, like the story of the immortal who couldn't be harmed unless he was stabbed in the eyes with the rib of his brother, who also happened to be immortal & dwelt a thousand leagues hence, deep under a mountain, etc. Like the Sphinx, the Gordian knot, the Voynich Manuscript all bundled into One. The universal salve, anodyne for every pain. Well you'd go out of business pretty quick flogging that idea with the kind of opposition arrayed against you & not just Jesuits with joss-sticks, or whatever, but the whole intergalactic corporate apparatus. *Man in the White Suit* stuff. *Ever met a corporation with a sense of humour, kiddo?* What if K had been the original, proto-Š.V.E.J.K.? The proverbial spanner-in-the-works for all them boys in The Organisation? Had the answer been as simple as that all along? The simple fact of the Book itself, like an open contradiction, designed to drive the Board of Directors nuts?

A shadow moved just ahead of him on the stairs. Footsteps echoed. Němec paused at the door to the Prof's apartment, as if to assure himself, then continued on, shorter of breath, aching still, mind growing clearer, an idea within his grasp almost. One level up, he scanned the brickwork, but no evidence of an attic door. Nothing between the Prof's & the astrologist's eyrie. And why was that, he wondered? Soon a pale square of light opened above, & the sky above that, climbing the last steps to the observatory, aswirl with dark snow, alone up there, not even a ghost, then hoisting up through the trapdoor into the observatory proper, from which man once took the measure of his

Maker — the veiled sky, the City's lights all a-blur, inscrutable, fictioned. From the streets below, voices drunkenly sang:

> *Die Preise hoch, die Läden dicht geschlossen,*
> *die Not marschiert und wir marschieren mit…*[*]

A car horn blared & then an engine started up, obliterating the words, the voices wafting back again, then fading.

> *Die hungern auch doch nur im Geiste mit…*[*]

On the western side of the observatory wall, the roof of the house sloped upwards & obscured the view. Scanning the shape of the rooftiles under snow, Němec sighted the outline of the skylight halfway up the gable. An aerial wire ran past it a metre or so from where Němec stood — by getting a leg over the observatory parapet he was able to reach it, the ledge made slippery by the snow, groping for the wire & finding it just as his footing gave way. For excruciating seconds he hung there by his hands, dangling into space, the grip of vertigo, then found the ledge again, hoisting over the eave, the snow soaking his jacket, numbing his arms, turning the dust that still covered him into a dirty sludge.

Inch-by-inch, he worked his way up the gabled Everest of the roof towards the black rectangle of the skylight, shining like wet obsidian where the snow had failed to settle. It stood out against the white the way an open doorway stands out from a white wall in the middle of the day. Coming within reach of it, gasping, dumb hands. Swept the snow from around the sill — a band of black showed where a cobblestone had been used to prop the window open. Clearing the gap, a draught of musty air wafted out. He pushed against the frame, the wire-meshed glass groaning under the effort, clawing with stupid fingers for a latch to get the damn thing open, but the hinges were rusted tight. He hammered at the frame with the blunt side of his fist till it bled. It took a dozen blows to smash a hole big enough to get his hand through.

Down below dust stirred in the dark rising in wisps visible even against the snowfall. A cramp ran down Němec's entire left side from the effort of

---

[*] Tonight on *The New Price is Right*! See if the reigning champ can win our huge Showcase Playoff against this week's challenger. Stay tuned! [✋]
[*] The bell's a-ringin', folks! Time to get goin' on up to the *Spirit in the Sky* for them BIG discount lunch menu specials! [✋]

gripping the aerial wire, legs braced against the rooftiles, straining to keep balanced as he worked his right arm in through the gap, summoning a mental picture of that glittering thing he'd seen in the torchlight As Němec lay there upon the steep incline of night, fain mirages of the mind came & went — the aurora in the heavens, the sky's blanched vault, a length of old knotted rope hanging from a rafter, & a dream-figure, descending it through the falling snow, hand over hand, the loose end trailing between slippered feet: level with the observatory the figure stopped & looked directly at Němec, face as blank as the faces in medieval paintings, eyes black, slanted upwards, a straggly Fu Manchu — he took one of his hands from the rope & with index finger pointed upwards at something glittering in the sky. With his eyes Němec followed the direction of the gesture. He edged closer to the skylight. Clumsy fingers, barely sensate, as his hand moved beneath him, groping blind through empty space Braille-like tracing a beam of splintered timber, finding the edges of something cold & hard, stretching as far as the gap would allow. Withdrawing. Poking through the gap with the flashlight. Blinking through the gloom at nothing, formless things, a mess of leaves, branches, plastic bags, bottle tops, paper wrappers, rubbish the years had accumulated, defiant of gravity, till the shape of a mangy jackdaw's bower revealed itself, nested between the trusses, dust sifting down from it, long abandoned.

And right there, snagged on a length of copper wire, was a metal ring with a cardboard tag tied to it — from which a polished brass double-headed key dangled.*

---

* Oh, boy! Well that really kills it, eh? That really trumps the trumps. [✋]

56

THE DEVIL'S WALL

A wetness covered Němec's face. Upwards, through a fine mica of snow, the moonmarbled sky half blotted-out — the round Tower rampant — whitewashed gleam of brick & mortar & grossly acuminated apex up-thrusting into it — a zenith, high over streets excrementally slicked with thaw — percolating subterranean winter vapours, swamp-like… And above all that, God's theodolite in its empty locus — firmaments only newly discovered not to be fixed at all, but out-flung in a constant expansive gesture — a case of the proverbial centre being nowhere & the periphery everywhere, taken to mockingly literal excess. What's a mere mortal to do? Unsuspecting from the start, stylite-man's heaven-gazing all in vain — it wasn't meant to be like that. Edrawd [sic] K in his dingy alchembobulist's den, sweating over yet another marred result destined to unravel everything his life's work's stood for — the Reconciliation of Opposites, the Physical Universe, parallax of the Cosmic Mind — but going on, nonetheless, shouldering the timeworn burden of philosophia at least for appearance's sake & a secure pension — his judges not yet afflicted by the war neurosis about to descend upon half the Known World — pious infamies alike of saviour & oppressor, Papist or Prod, Cretin or Saracen, looting, raping, burning — the plundering of libraries reduced to campfire ash, the backward creeping into ages darker, more fearful — tremulous in the night, the great God's ballyhoo — descended now as once before to the primordial estate of fleas, leeches, rats…

And what would the Prof've done in K's shoes, possessed of that priceless lingering aura, the Real Presence of Himself, a veritable medium's medium — were he, too, to've conducted since childhood countless celeb séances, table-tipping, ouija-board fantasias of card-trick numerology — talent-spotted by the gypsy fortune-teller at the Výstaviště showground, behind the lapidarium, head scarved in ruby brocade, incense, *Wizard of Oz* crystal ball, filling avid boyish ears with tales untold of eastern enchantment — the high-flung romance of all things occult, in due course ripening, like a pomegranate in a forcing frame, to an obsession fullblown, the noxious scholastic stench of it, dripping its pedantic ooze. In all that time, clinging to a piece of apocrypha like a rat to driftwood — a talisman against the tidal pull of change — the world & everything in it? Who could say? Němec pictured the Old Man, sitting in his bath, chessboard perched precarious on knobbed knees — steam beading alike the stout rooks, cavalier knights, scheming bishops, the puppet king, the infidelitous queen, the communard rank & file — re-staging the moves of a puzzle that wouldn't come out because, all contrary appearances notwithstanding, it *had* no solution. And what would there've been left to do but die laughing? Ahem.

The beginning wasn't auspicious, either, but what more sinister end could a man of former beliefs come to? Němec stood out under the snow plumbing, in so many words, an inner depth of uncertainty. *To go on? To not go on?* Hadn't fortune placed in his hands the key? At least, the key to the winecellar door? There could be mileage in that. But what else was it meant to unlock? *Don't be an ass. What'd you expect? The Pearly Gates? The Doors of Perception?* A stirring in the courtyard among the bins — something on the prowl, scratching in the gloom. *Not alone, then.* All around, the giant mesh of half-rusted steel, rising from the ground, blotting-out the walls, its top rungs whited with snow, scaffolding the night. The scratching continued along the courtyard's periphery, past the caretaker's lodge, the mess of building machinery, the garden table & upended chairs — a burrowing through drifts of sleet, emerging on the far side by the Tower door — a long thin four-legged silhouette against the wall, regal glint of eye peering back, teeth nattering, *time to get a move-on, m'boy, shake a leg, make tracks* — head down across the threshold, gone. An emissary perhaps, some rat Virgil to guide him into the underworld, down the sibylline windings beneath the Tower stairs. Once more Němec felt the key in his pocket, hardening his resolve — *haha* — took a last piss in the snow & retraced his steps inside.

Where one stairwell ended, another began. After a single turning it came to an archway with a wooden staircase, handrailed, tending steeply to a storeroom quarried beneath the house — the room was stacked with old paint tins, kerosene drums, bits of unrestored furniture, window frames, a rusted boiler, other rubbish. Němec groped for the lightswitch. Wedged beside the storeroom entrance, an upturned basin on a pile of vegetable refuse half-concealed a rat's nest. A sharp hiss as he passed — then another. Sentries posted. Proceed cautiously so as not to alarm these guardians of the Lower Rat Kingdom. Two steps in advance, a stray shadow pressed to the wall — an outrider creeping side-on, Egyptian-style, tail pointing one way, head & hindquarters the other, ghosting him — where it led was a dark gap in the masonry beneath the wooden staircase. The outrider cast a last furtive glance around & disappeared, lower-brain stealth navigating the subterranean murk — where the gap was, a heavy grating rested on a pair of iron hinges fixed into stone. A gibbous eye glinted out from it, split down the middle — an antique padlock. Němec took the key from his pocket & tried it in the lock — it turned reluctantly — the padlock slipped from its recess with a dull clunk. On ahead, a general skirmishing of rat-feet on flagstones — some hastily dispersed convocation of the Hidden Orders — signals relayed down into the sewers, where perhaps ancient rat descendents of the First Fathers still dwelled, survivors of who knew what heresy from times of yore — forced underground, among waste & effluent, salvaging what little dignity there was to salvage of a life now trampled into mud — bits & pieces of the Old Pre-Scripture, desecrated icons, a splinter of the True Cross, a shekel from the Temple of Jerusalem, Hanukah tallow, a cracked psalter, tesserae of stained glass, a chip off the Rock of Ages, the braid from a bishop's stole, a rabbi's yarmulke, a muezzin's turban... this secret horde reciting their fable, writ in a cuneiform of four-fingered scratchings, prisonhouse graffiti, counting the days from the Gen. to Rev. — labyrinths of sacral inkblot jottings, their Book, the One True Rat Almanac, its intricate rhizomes of matrilineated descent from the Ur-Tribes, back before the dawn of the first princely Přemyslids, of Nezomysls & Křesomysls, of Boleslavs red-haired pious & cruel, down down down all the way to this most profane of present epochs, the founding of the first Rat Democracy, the Great Betrayal, the Rat Riot of '42, the Exodus of '48, the forty-year Rat Resistance... Deeper still, concealed in granite seams dropping away to molten schist, the forbidden Apocrypha, taken down in times when Earth itself was still young, recounting fables more primitive, disquieting — intoned by the priestly caste in low tectonic frequencies, which are the immemorial resonance of a Pre-Palaeolithic, Jurassic, evolutionary God-instant when, so-to-speak, everything began — monads of bacterial sludge in its eons-long journey of becoming this noble & wise four legged Muroidea, *rattus rattus…*

Němec heaved & the grating swung heavily inwards on its hinges. Flakes of rust came away in his hands. The storeroom light sputtered out. There was a heavy, penetrating, all-pervasive silence. He stood still, holding his breath, listening, unable to discern any sound. And then, through the silence, the low thudding of blood in the veins, the static hiss of the nervous system. He felt through his pockets for the torch & switched it on: in front of him lay yet more steps, Piranesi-like, disappearing into blackness. He locked the gate behind him & began his descent. Cobwebs & tangled electrical wires. A dead lightbulb screwed into the ceiling. Racks & bottles. This, then, was the winecellar. He wondered how the Prof ever managed to get down here & back up again. The cellar itself was approximately rectangular in shape, about five metres wide, but the far end could've been anything. The racks were wooden, arranged close to the steps & reaching almost to the ceiling. The bottles lay under a patina of grey dust. Němec pulled one out at random & brushed the grime from its label. Lagrima. *Tears of Eurydice.* Real Companhia Velha — Instituado por Alvará Régio de 1756 — Providentia Regitur, & all that. The Prof's secret hoard.

Just above eye-level, in the middle of the adjacent wall, Němec's flashlight caught the extruding capstone of an archway long-ago filled in, from where the cellar floor sloped to the right, behind the bottleracks. The slightest tremor might send them all tumbling like dominos. He drew a map in his mind to set the bearings: Castle, Monastery, River, the gardens under Petřín Hill. Behind the capstone could've been anything, the foundations & buried crypt of old St

Thom's, perhaps, long-abolished, but who knew what remained? A faint shiver agitated Němec's spine. He might, even then, have been standing on once-hallowed ground. The madman in the belfry, bones in the basement.

He tapped the wall: solid stone. He edged clockwise through the narrow spaces, following the slope of the floor. The shadows extruded. The place was like a maze. Finally a space opened, littered with a jumble of rusted metal hoops & decayed wine barrels, with a table & a single chair set in the middle of it. On the table lay a rusted corkscrew, a half-melted candlestick, a chipped glass full of calcified dregs, bottle-grit & dust. The bottle racks formed a kind of perimeter around it, open on one side, with a damp-eroded slab of wall facing. Němec played his torch across it: a faded checkerboard pattern, frescoed into the crumbling plaster, emerged from the darkness by concentric facets, like tiles at the bottom of a fountain. Chipped-away layers of overpaint revealed a patchwork of 12x12-inch squares, marked-off in turn by a palimpsest of carpenters' & electricians' gridwork, shorthand notations, measurements, symbols for a construction that'd been given up before even begun.

Set off to one side of it, a line of exposed red brick revealed where a second doorway had also been walled-up. Němec tapped at the bricks with the workmen's heavy chisel — a faint, dull, hollow sound came back, almost an echo. He gouged the pointy end into the mortar & it came away like powder, sifting onto the ground. It seemed as good a place as any to begin. He pulled over the chair & set to work. The chair groaned under his weight, dust blew between his legs then settled in the torchlight. The brickwork made sounds like piano strings muted with rubble. After an hour or so a hole had opened up large enough for him to poke first the flashlight, then head (sans chapeau) & eventually, a tight squeeze, the arms & shoulders. Another half-hour of work & he made it through comfortably. The effort was rewarded with a long vaulted passageway made of burnt brick. He stood there dusting himself down, taking it in. Could this be the entrance to one of those tunnels that legend had catacombing the City?

Such tunnels existed already in the Middle Ages, in turn carved from ancient sewer ducts, catacombs, wells driven down through bedrock to mythic artesian springs, mineralised with the fossil remnants of Ice Age anthropods. Time &

legend rendered these places mysterious. Sibylline grottos, alchemical caverns, Rabbinical laboratories, Rudolf's secret storehouse of portents & potions, unmarked mass graves, plague cemeteries, wells & sewer traps, irrigation channels for the Stromovka carp ponds, siege defences, drainage ditches, dungeons & escape routes, salt mines & primitive particle accelerators, Masonic lodges, Jesuit judas-holes, bolt-holes, glory-holes, Wagnerian crypts & Nietzschean creeps, Nazi bunkers, partisan peepshows, Soviet silos, fallout shelters, subterranean harems for the Party elite, crisscrossed, backfilled, re-excavated, sealed against pandemic, unsealed against pogrom, lost, forgotten, suffocated, drowned, collapsed under a cumulative inertia only to be reconquered in the dark hours of Man's faltering estate by their most native & rightful denizens — the Moldau Rats — or whatever remained of that once noble tribe: last of a once-dwindling Underground now again resurgent in these prophetic End Times of their oppressor's ebb, impervious (now that The Hour was finally nigh) of admonishment or dissent, united with a great tenacity of purpose & the sense of manifest rat destiny, All for One & One for the Species!

While the Fall of the Third Evil Empire* played-out in the streets, these éminences-grises of the Novus Ordo Seclorum did convoke their ancient & long-lapsed Grand Synod in reconciliation of the old factions, divided by points of law secular & ecclesiastical many years obscured by the mists of sectarian strife & subjugation — once were adversaries, now triumviral brothers-in-arms, seizing the revolutionary hour, all-for-one & one-for-all, affirming in solemn unison the Secret Conventicles of Grace, Predestination & the Four Vows — Obedience, Poverty, Chastity, Conformity — swearing undying fealty to the Regulae Societatis Ratu, the Vindicae contra Tyranos, the Perinde ac Cadaver, mutually bound in sacred missionary vigilance against all species of Heretic, Janissaries, Templars, Assassins, Pharisees, Moloch, the Plague of Egypt, the Flood, Balaam's Ass, etc...

Slinking away on the periphery of these orgies of piety & revindication of the New Old Law, the lone figure reincarnate of mad Rudi, exiled & wandering, shunned king-in-name-only, Leer of the thrice-divided pre-Fall rat realms, rumoured of ancient annals, seer, alchemist, Celtic druid — ghostlike presence still haunting the consciences, perhaps, of today's triumvirs & tomorrow's turncoats, architects of the restored Rat-Publicum, flags aflutter, choirs & cheerleaders, armies marshalled, orations of soaring optimism, *this national*

---

* Even rats can count. [☙]

awakening, temper democratic, destiny manifest, the great dawn, etc. — a relic, this Rudi-the-Rat, an anachronism, as out-of-place here as a Wittelsbach at a bar-mitzvah, unburdened by cares of state, crawling towards that final death —

'They flattered me like a dog & told me I had white whiskers in my beard ere the black ones were there… When the rain came to wet me once — & the wind to make me chatter — when the thunder would not peace at my bidding, there I found 'em, there I smelt 'em out…'

Kindred spirit of the lost, the afflicted, the visionarily deranged — that's him now, stalking along the cellar floor, clambering old-man-tired atop the heaped rubble, up on stick-spindly hind legs, in the pierced middle of the wall, eyeing that strange silhouette with the stick & hat — *eh, Charlot!* — & catching the beam of Němec's torch like scintillating stagelight, transforms from a rat in chiaroscuro to a veritable Olivier casting a giant's shadow against world's (or at least a bottlerack's) vainglorious backdrop — standing there with arm outstretched, draped by purple-trimmed toga, pointed finger, in pose most Caesarean,[*] astutely copied from knock-off plastercast reproductions (a true thesp at heart, our Rudi), eyes grey-red, sniffing the air, which way the wind's draughting, etc. — & in high oratorical voice, as once upon the Forum's steps, saying —

'Follow me, kiddo…'

Pitterpatter of rat-foot receding down the passageway — a pause, eyes glinting in the torch's mottled cone, peering back, head over shoulder, one last come-hither beckoning of the royal hand & then gone from the light. What caused Němec to hesitate? What held him back? The air, he noticed, had grown thick. Beads of sweat stood out on his brow. He felt suddenly exhausted by the effort of breaking through the wall, his adrenaline spent. His back & arms ached. His head weighed a tonne. From somewhere very remote he thought he heard a voice, echoing up the passageway. He lay with his head on the cold ground to listen to it.

---

[*] The true Romani never having made it this north far, held at bay always across the centuries by the eponymous Boii of La Bohème, as extinct now as their peninsuline foes, only pale clerical understudies in scheming priest-garb calling themselves Holy, as Rudi himself more than any ought to know. [🐀]

Little by little, a disturbed sleep took hold of him. Time stretched out & shrank. In the dream into which he fell, Němec saw again the deadman lying inside the Monastery gate, the quaking mass of dead body like a gob of chewed fat. A sinister cadaveric fluid the colour of intestinal scoria oozed from beneath the corpse & down into the gutter. Němec's dreamself walked over to the place where the corpse was lying & watched it slowly dissolve. Sitting beside it in a chair was a nurse with Alice Steinerová's face — she was kneading & wringing long strings of fat from her hands. Perched on her right shoulder was a grey rat, familiar-looking. This version of Alice Steinerová had something far too perfunctory about her — like a wind-up doll. She'd wrung the last of the fat from her hands & now sat there filing her nails. The scene reminded Němec in a peculiar way of the Prof's ghost, the first time he'd appeared, sitting on a snowdrift. The rat on Alice Steinerová's shoulder snickered. In the background, the spires of St Vitus were visible above the rooftops. Němec tried to get some sort of bearing, but the scene kept slipping. Alice Steinerová yawned. When she looked up from her nails, a vague disquieting expression came into her eyes. Her lips, when she moved them, made a sound like a radio whose tuning wasn't aligned with the broadcast band. A sound like someone peeling off a nylon raincoat. Of sand being poured slowly through a sieve onto a tin sheet.

'There was a custom in former times,' she said, as if seeing him for the first time, 'for guardian spirits to dwell among the thresholds, where no man must linger, for fear of being turned to stone.'

She was looking at him exactly the way Mrs Severínová sometimes looked at him, whenever he asked a wrong question. But how could you tell the difference between right questions & wrong questions?

'Drown the cocks,' snickered the rat.

By now the corpse had completely dissolved, all that was left was a yellowbrown smear in the cracks between the cobble stones.

'Shouldn't we go away now that there's nothing left?' he said, not knowing why.

He felt idiotic standing there like that.

'You'll have to wait,' Alice Steinerová said, turning her attention back to her fingernails.

'Mouths in the glass,' the rat.

'Wait? Wait for what?'

'The door.'

'Tremble thou wretch!' sneered the rat.

'What door? There isn't any door.'

'You'll see.'

'Make no noise, make no noise — draw the curtains!' Rattus rattus.

A moment later, a couple of gallery assistants arrived, carrying a large roll of photographic paper. They placed it carefully on the ground & then began to unroll it across the brownish stain the corpse had left behind. The paper was entirely white, *like a fresh blanket of snow*, except in the middle, where there was a picture of a blue door. Němec stared at it in wonder. Just then, slipping the nailfile into the breast pocket of her pinafore, Alice Steinerová casually stood & walked across the photograph towards him.

'It's time,' she said.

'Come-on m'boy — how dost m'boy? Art cold?' snickering rat.

Then, just as Alice reached out her hand, the blue door opened & they were sucked inside, rat & all.

Once upon a time, in the mists of childhood, there was a Game. The purpose of the Game was never clear, nor was anything excluded from the Game — above all, the Game required no agreement between the players & it went on regardless of whether anyone wanted to play it or not. The rules of the Game were very precise. There were only two, but these two determined all possible bylaws & subclauses that might otherwise be derived from them — being, simply, to affirm all that *can* be affirmed & deny all that *can* be denied. The Game was called the Death Game, because it was the contrary of everything the System taught us about Life — to accept what you're told & do only as you're permitted. The trick was to outwit Death & stay Alive. But how'd you know if you were Alive or Dead? And who was keeping score? For as long as Němec could remember, he'd had a fear of unknown forces taking possession of his body while he slept. At the Home he dreamt of being abducted by androids who performed experiments on him under an anaesthetic that left him conscious inside his unconsciousness. They were careful never to leave a trace. Phantom paranoias. He would wake up screaming & have nothing to show for it. The androids always came in *through the windows* & wrapped him in white sheets. Android hands strapped a rubber mask over his face. There'd be a hiss of gas released from a gas cylinder & a machine-voice commanding him to count backwards from one thousand. And while he counted, people he knew would be having a conversation, which he could only just make out, somewhere very near, as if underneath the bed, & yet infinitely far away, completely unaware of him, in a parallel world, like crossed phone lines — about the most extraordinary banalities that went on & on & on & on…

He'd aged tremendously while he slept. He remembered hearing a voice, counting & counting. But the numbers followed no pattern, they were simply random, one after another. Fourhundred&thirtytwo. Sixhundred&forty. Twohundred&sixteen. Threehundred&twentyeight. Sevenhundred&thirtysix… His head ached. Red flickered across his eyelids. The taste of something metallic in his mouth. A sour smell. When Němec opened his eyes, at first he saw nothing, a blob of light, faint shadows, then gradually the outline of the hole in the wall, the shapes of bottle racks caught in the glow of the flashlight lying on the ground. All else was darkness A draught blew through the barred gate at the top of the cellar steps. He felt something move at his feet & kicked out at it with his boot, but found only the wall.

Němec dragged upright. By the dimming light of the torch he saw that the rats had marked-out a boundary around him. Concentric rings of spilt wine, candle stubs, bits of broken cutlery, splinters of glass, bits of shredded newsprint, wooden shards, bottletops, shrivelled cabbage leaves — a curse or an offering, in accordance with some elaborate rite he could barely begin to guess at — fragments, echoes, the mindforged mutterings of ages, coded messages relayed through the subterranean dark, highpriestly incantations of Head Rats above an altar, the pointed bony finger: *Don't imagine, human, that the evolution which gave rise to you was the only one!* Dire warnings uttered over the entrance to their underworld — FACILIS DESCENSUS!* — the broken wall, the darkness beyond — strange evocations, half-dream, half-undream. He couldn't separate them. His fingers, caked with dirt & raw from scraping, traced unfamiliar symbols in the dirt. Cuneiform of rats' feet.

He sought, belatedly, the pitter-patter footsteps of his guide, but there was nothing. The passage's gloom swallowed the torchlight. A sense of urgency

---

* Getting back out's always been the real trick. [♦]

renewed drew him on regardless — no longer tired, aching, neither hungry nor thirsty — as so often before, compelled by some higher love of causeless things? By the light of that lobe of the brain in which visions were produced, he perceived a kind of map, the secret destination marked by an X. It was a map drawn completely in shades of black, depicting the darkness through which he was yet to pass in order to discover the secret algebra — the *anima telluris* — the key to the "key."

Then the passage dropped away, from a set of stairs into nothingness. Němec had no other choice but to begin his descent. Clutching a metal rail in one hand, his stick in the other, he lowered himself one treacherous step at a time into a narrow tunnel. The tunnel was arched at the top & had been built from stone. In one direction it was all but impassable, crisscrossed with leaking pipes, stalactites & sheets of cobweb. In the other it tended in a downward slope, unobstructed. Even then, it was necessary for Němec to proceed sideways along it like a crab, then to stoop, then to crouch. At several points the tunnel branched or was joined by smaller tributaries. Cold draughts stirred the dank air. At each intersection Němec scratched an 4 into the wall with the butt of the flashlight. A hop, step & jump further on, the tunnel intersected a disused sewer. Reminding of the mad theosophist Meyrink, who dreamt of finding the Philosopher's Stone among all the shit that flowed there under the City: the miraculous cloacal passage, the Filthy Dispensary, King Midas arsehole. He breathed the odour of dead matter composting. It was like breathing the air from a tomb. Dark icons hung down from the ceiling, crosses & gammadions, iron rungs set into stone leading who-knew-where. Something rumbled overhead. It could've been anything, a thunderstorm, bombs falling, the trams crossing Malostranské Square. A gangway took him to the farther side, where the tunnel continued as before.

Before very long, the rumbling of the trams was replaced by a sound like a low claustrophobic whisper. From time to time the whispering subsided & then grew louder again, as the tunnel turned & snaked its way beneath the medieval foundations. Němec sensed that he was passing not only through space but also time, as though the tunnel itself was part of an archaeology, an excavation through fabrics of remote, hidden, lost or inaccessible instances. Very soon the tunnel narrowed to a point of virtual impassability, dipped, turned, became steeper, more treacherous. It became necessary to crawl. Crookkneed, Němec made a bold show of it, urged on by the weight of the shadows gathered behind him & the spiralling torchlight ahead of him. The stone walls tilted increasingly inward — subsidence caused the ground to fall away precipitously — the roof in places was buckled under the weight of petrified tree roots, exposing terrifying cracks wound with mammoth tusks. Shadows slithered away between the hewn slabs. The further Němec went, the more it seemed he'd gone beyond the scale of calendrial time, into a zone of myth & prehistory, descending through emulsioned sediments, golem-mud, photosensitive slime. The whispering of strange tongues reverberated all around. Němec's awareness, too, seemed somehow extended in space & time, like a burrowing disembodied eye. He'd lost all track of time, it was impossible to gauge how far he'd come. Soon, perhaps, he'd arrive at the very dawn of man, the twinkle at the end of God's retina. He inched his way onwards with an avid, sickening fascination. Then — as if to restore a certain balance in this rapidly deteriorating scheme of things, from the mildly portentous to the outright cataclysmic, from a casually meandering curiosity to a Devil-take-the-hindmost *Journey to the Centre of the Earth* — out of the gloom & into the spot of Němec's flashlight sauntered a pair of incongruous rats in greasy lounge suits. One of them sported black sunglasses, the other waved a cigar. *And now, ladies and gents, a brief interlude, with everyone's favourite dynamic duo of laugh-till-yer-plotzes-drop-and-yer-fritzes-split, OZ and MOZ!!!* Němec blinked, the rats grinned. From somewhere a showband kicked into gear, one of those Kander & Ebb numbers that used to be so popular back in the day, right as the marquee lights fired up on

THE OZ & MOZ SHOW

C'mon and frappez la rue
we're blowin' today
we're bustin' right on out of it
this shitty ol' city!

These sewer rat blues
we're spreadin' the clay
we'll wipe that big fat smile off it
this shitty city!

We're gonna cake up
the works from down on deep
we'll be the kings of the crap
top of the shitheap!

These coprolite bayous
we're sailin' away
we'll make a big ballyhoo of it
this ol' shitty city!

If we can tread thin air
then we won't drown down there
it's a shit stew, Golem City! Go-lem Citeeeee!

'Hey Oz, ever hear the one about the three rabbis, Lox, Shlock & Bagel?'

'That's a gas, Moz. Kills me every time.'

'How 'bout the one, ya know, JC & St Franny are out surfin' the Dead Sea…'

'Sittin' on their boards waitin' for the mystic peak…'

'And it starts rainin'…'

'Oh boy…'

'And JC says to Franny, *Man, I can't swim! What we gonna do?*'

'And Franny says…'

'*I dunno 'bout you, Boss, but I ain't never heard a no drowned man gettin' crucified!*'

'Hey, how 'bout the one, the three wiseguys & the camel…?'

'Hang on, I think I gotta go round back for a mo, *hehe*! But while we're bein' straight, you ever catch Frankie Scrote's gig at Caesar's Palace?'

'Hold the press! Was that the one, you know, when Lucky licked Luciano?'

'You're confused, that was Jaysus Joist & the Mermen, back in '39!'

'Hell, I thought that was *Ethel* Merman doin' a Sammy Davis routine…'

'Or Lucille Ball playin' *Great Moses, a Fire*!'

'Or was it Billie Haley & the Mars Bars?'

'Well it weren't no Martin Luther in whiteface, *har-dee-har-har*!'

'Or no Stonewall Jackson in no leather shlongstrap!'
'I heard one the other day, about the friends of Dorothy Lamour…'
'Don't you mean Judy Garland shootin' the cancan?'
'The doo-wop?'
'The doo-run-run?'
'Let me tell you about last night, you won't believe it. You know who they had on TV? You'll never guess. Can you guess? It's just too good to be true…'

The torch flickered, the picture died. No more rats tossing gags back & forth, just Němec alone in there poking his way down the hole with his stick towards a dimming point of light. *Well it's good to get your mind off things for a while, every now and then, kiddo.* Like now, with the humidity dripping off him & the rotten stink oozing through the stonework & the whispering echo of something coming ever closer. Voices maybe. Too many of them to make any sense of, all competing for his attention. At some point the gradient began to level & the tunnel to broaden & he was almost able to stand. Then quite suddenly it came to an dead end. A stone wall blocked the way. By now Němec had run out of enthusiasm for the whole deal, his head throbbed, his body ached. The voices had abandoned all subtlety & become an outright cacophony. The wall glistened in the torchlight — this proverbial *lumen-ad-finem* of the veritable blocked passage: *obit anus*, as a philosopher once said, *abit onus*, or words to that effect. Němec dumped his hat & stick on the ground, slumped down, eyes drooping, forehead pressed to the stones — cold, wet, vibrating. The voices swelled into a mad aria. *The Devil's Wall* sung all at once by a chorus of lunatics. And the idiotically resounding thought that Němec couldn't get out of his skull — that when Smetana penned that timeless delirious piece of operatic tripe, he was stone deaf already, inner-ear & auditory cortex eaten down to the stumps by the syph. Just the sounds inside his head. *You hear that, kiddo? JUST THE SOUNDS INSIDE HIS GODDAMN HEAD.*

h. The Wrong Square

57

HANG ME WITH SLÁNSKÝ!

There's a famous pic of Klem Gottwald, snapped one cold February morning in 1948, on a balcony overlooking the Altstädterring, four months before becoming President. Also in the photograph, standing next to Gottwald, were three other men (shadows of men really): Vlado Clementis, Rudolf Slánský & photographer Karel Hájek. When that fenster-fucker Jan M wound up spreadeagled under his bathroom window, it was Clementis who bagged his old job at the Foreign Ministry, while Slánský got to be Klem's stand-in as Party Gen-Sec. A few years down the line & all three (Clementis, Slánský, Hájek) had got themselves deleted from that photograph. All but a hat.

Clementis & Slánský were hanged in 1952. Of the hapless papparatchik, Hájek, the records are silent. What's known is that, not very long afterwards, in '53 — only five days after standing in the cold at the funeral of his dearly belovèd Stalin — Gottwald himself suffered a massive cerebral haemorrhage, brought on by chronic heart disease, alcoholism & (like Daluege, Smetana & countless Great Men before) the syph. March 14, almost as many years to the day since the Nazis, with Stalin's blessing, came marching into fair Golem City. In due course, the embalmed cadaver of Emperor Klem'll be ceremoniously interred in the National Monument, beneath the towering bronze of one-eyed Žižka. Till (by accident or design) it slowly begins to rot & turn black, so that it, too — first cremated, the ashes kept in a jar, then buried in a mass communist grave at Olšany — is quietly erased from History.

815

Rewind to Gottwald on the balcony, surrounded by ghosts — & in the background, that other Hájek, holding his camera, somehow out of place, on the wrong side of the lens — as if his very presence attested to the image's illusionism — demanding erasure, correction, to be reinstated in its rightful position, *behind* the camera, among all those other ghosts for whom History itself is made visible by a collective absence — all the rest marked for a vaudeville backdrop. No sooner said than done! The technicians already at work inside the Image Machine, out-takes & alternative-takes piling up on the cuttingroom floor — montage for some midget auteur at rat's eye-level, scuttling between legs, dashing back & forth, slipsliding all over the place on unspooled celluloid doing a Gene Kelly act, *just me and my shadow* — an idea forming there at the back of that tiny rodent brain, sound-up in the orchestra pit & it's...

Showtime! Klem Gottwald & Rudolf Slánský singing in duet that all-time Vera Lynn fave, *We'll meet again, don't know where, don't know when,* standing in the rain on the Barrandov Terraces, the place lit-up with a dozen sets of headlights belonging to the unmarked cop cars parked just beyond those trees, shadowy figures moving behind — an audience of faceless men in leather coats. The waiters have cleared a stage space among the tables, & now Klem & Rudi are working-in a few dance steps, Klem a bit unsteady on his feet — he's been hard at the bottle all day, shouldering the cares of the state...

'I didn't choose to be like this, you know. Fate chose for me. I'd give it up tomorrow, but for the good of the nation, the people, the Five-Year-Plan... Look, how about one more drink, for old time's sake? Remember how it was, back in the day? The bees in the clover? Birds singing in the trees? Jerries strung from the lampposts? Listen, you're a hero mate, no mistaking it, which is why we've gotta do what we've gotta do. Give the public what they want. Yesterday's monument is tomorrow's martyr! We've gotta hedge our bets, get ahead of the game, look the future squarely in the eye, take the Revolution to the next life. What d'you say?'

Klem mooches up to the microphone & starts singing off-key as the balalaikas sound-up from the wings —

> *Doch wir konnen siegen,*
> *Fur immer und immer!*
> *Und wir sind dann Helden,*
> *für einen tag...*

Now the whole cast comes out onto the Terraces for an encore — balloons, tinsel, banners hoisted for the TV cameras:

Long live the Communist Party of Cheskoslovnikia!

Long live the Party General-Secretary, Rudolf Slánský!

It's all just a little warm-up act for the Big Show-Trial, starring all Klem's old buddies, Zhids mostly (oops, not supposed to mention that) — Slánský making a farewell performance in the leading role, sacrificing himself for the good of the nation — setting an example, so to speak, showing the world what a real communist's made of — Clementis, too (could never stand that mutt of his, Brouček, crapping on the Presidential Office floor, *The dog's death to the dog*! he'd have to put the idea up to Moscow, *anti-conspiracy dog*, run a check on the rabid little mongrel's proletarian credentials) — who else? Those fakes — Frejka, Reicin, Simone — Fischl, too, Frank, Geminder, Šling, Šváb…

Quite a *Who's-Who* the Ruskies have managed to put together, even for the supporting cast — a scapegoat for every occasion, the Five-Year-Plan gone to shit thanks to the Politburo boys (not sounding his usual optimistic self today, our Klem), understandable that the People are out for blood & better theirs than his — oh & not to forget that non-entity, Margolius, ex-Auschwitz, *What the hell's he on the list for*? But it's too late to be worrying about minor details like that, they've been at rehearsals for weeks already, months, getting their lines down pat, the whole production, a bigger-than-Busby-Berkeley spectacular, not some bogus *Triumph of the Will* peroration, but men speaking from the heart, getting to the truth of the matter, their own personal Calvary for the salvation of all. *Now that's what I call selflessness. The real McCoy and not some one-eyed Joe windbagging.*

It'll be the best press they've had in years, a box office sensation. So much he hopes, at least, our Klem, aiming to please the Great Leader, Josef Vissarionovich, love of his life & all that. He'd get down on his knees if that'd help, but afraid he wouldn't make it back up again — it's the weather & he's under it, sweating like a pig, but no-one can see because the spotlights are all on Slánský now, dark, swarthy, handsome in a sinister Rudolf Valentino way —

817

reciting his curriculum vitae now to adoring fans with little HANG ME WITH SLÁNSKÝ placards waving in the foreground.

'The aim of the Communist Party,' he's saying, trying to save his own bacon, barely audible, drowned-out by continuous cheers, 'is to safeguard the successful completion of the five-year economic plan!'

Oscar-winning stuff this. *What a genius for bullshit*, Klem congratulates himself. *He'd be after* my *job, if he could climb down from that scaffold and get a hold of it.* 'Cos that's where Slimy Slánský's headed once the judges get to work on him, *hehe*, & those pre-taped confessions get aired on family-hour radio — but why wait? Sometimes, Klem thinks, these production guys put too much store by realism. Oh it's a terrible thing to say, he knows, but couldn't they just hang the lot of 'em now & be done with it? But the show goes on, a mind of its own it seems, & if there's a train in the picture he's not driving it anymore, just a passenger now, can sit back & enjoy the view rushing by, the restaurant car's well-stocked liquor cabinet jangling its oriental windchime jangle as thoughts waft a long way from solitary confinement cells, back to his childhood in Dědice, born under a hayloft, so the story went, old granddad Bartholomew, a drunk to beat the band, sending his poor matka on the road, pregnant & all, slouching towards her Bethlehem, grist for a minor nation's messiah complex.

But there's Slánský, taking up the picture again, explaining to the faithful & some interviewers from *Pravda Daily* his hand (irony of ironies — though perhaps this hasn't quite dawned on the imbecile yet) in the behind-the-scenes preparation for the Big Show — architect of the torture state, builder of forced labour camps & prime mover in bringing to Golem City those self-same Bolshevik inquisitors who — *Soon children, soon*! — will see him (Slánský), & Klem's particularly proud of this detail, lynched unceremoniously in the courtyard of Pankrác prison (*No Man's Bigger than the State* isn't just a trippy slogan & he's about to prove it).

What was it that idiot Masaryk said? *Justice is the mathematics of humanity.* Right. Well, you wring enough necks, see — that's socialist democracy — justice for everyone! Cut back now to Vera Lynn, the Golden Days, the victory in '48 (*Can't believe it's only four years ago — just like yesterday…*), the TV boys doing a general round-up of Where it all Began — the Best of Slánský — *How far the mighty have fallen*! Something in this for everyone to get their teeth into! See the bushy-browed kid from Plzeň, local Commercial Academy graduate, smoking cigarettes in the backroom of the Golem City Marxist Club — then Moscow during the winters of '41, '42 — the dutiful wife working at Radio Big Red —

the daughter's kidnapping — life lessons at the School for Torture — after the War, leading the way in the Slovnik National Uprising — receiving for his pains the exalted *Order of Socialism* (a real coup thinking up that one)…

Then — it's the Greek Tragedy moment they've all been waiting for — *The Downfall*: Šling & Reicin — the Tito Conspiracy — the suicide attempt. All the pathos of mixed emotions. It'll top the ratings come the day, every worker's committee in the country, supplied already with a juicy selection of prescribed resolutions, hectoring for the number two guy to get it in the neck, boxes ticked, stamps stamped, just waiting to be cabled-in. STRING UP SLÁNSKÝ! What a life! Meanwhile the girls in the Workers' Wives Club are knocking back Gin Šlings like it's Singapore in '42 & not a worry in the whole wide world — lots of backslapping & the odd below-the-belt tickle, letting their hair down from their headscarves, saying *Slip me a Slánský there love*, & *She's peaches, old chum*, like it's the ladies lounge at Raffles — & all the while the barmaid lecturing the black&white idiot box, *Don't make the rope too long, we run a family establishment here*! Just good healthy entertainment for the up&coming proles of the thousand-year Socialist Reich, oh Glorious Tomorrow, oh Brave New Void:

> *Though we'd sell our sisters to Stalin*
> *faster than you can say Sieg Heil*
> *and peddle our arses in Astrakhan*
> *to the boys going round on the Politburo turnstile,*
> *you can't say the future's not rosy my comrades,*
> *not rosy, oh rosy, oh rosy today!*

58

ONE FOR THE LITTLE GUY

Faktor's dwarf was leaning against the doorframe — dirty raincoat, mouth creased by a faintly satirical smirk beneath curled mustachios, eyelids puckered, expectant — watching Němec as he lay on the floor blinking up into the light. The sight of the dwarf, coming into focus only gradually, but not too gradually to deprive Němec of what could only be described as a rude awakening, caused him to experience a sudden rush of agoraphobia. For one terrible hallucinatory moment, he was five years old again, looking up at an StB man in a brown overcoat towering over him in the doorway, the moment his little world came apart. In that moment the dwarf might as well've been a colossus.

The moment passed & with an effort Němec sat up. His head felt like it was splitting open. He wasn't sure where he was, or who he was, or even when he was. Blood had stained all down the front of his shirt, his mouth thick with the taste of it. Somebody or something had worked him over pretty good. As to *where* he was, a glance around the room confirmed he hadn't really gone anywhere: he was still in the Old Man's bureau, hat dented on one side lying next to him on the floor, muddied trousers & boots, parquet strewn with torn & crumpled paper. Němec blinked at the dwarf in the doorway & then back at the paper, wondering if whoever had gone through the place found what they were looking for. *Well, can't say you didn't know it was coming, sooner or later.* He heard the dwarf clear his throat.

'Mr Němec?'

'Says who?'

'You think you can forget who you are?'

'Nah, I know who I am. I'm the monkey talking to an imaginary midget.'

'No need to get personal.'

'Personal smershonal.'

Němec pressed his knuckles into his eyes, stared at the runic lines on the back of his hands. Faint echoes of breaking glass, cold wind, weightlessness. Somewhere, a voice inside him said, a journey begins, you set out unmindfully, seeking a point from which you've already departed — all the wisdom of ages could be distilled to this. Blah.

'It's a comforting thought,' said the dwarf.

Němec turned his head & glared —

'You don't exist.'

After some effort he managed to get on his feet. He could hear the workmen in the yard, hammering & sawing.

'How the hell'd you get in here anyway?'

'Door was open.'

'Goes without saying, door's always open. That's our motto, didn't you know? Very friendly people, we are. Sure you weren't here when all the excitement happened?'

'If only you'd sent out invitations.'

'So kind.'

Němec staggered out to the kitchen & searched for Volta's pills — found some lying on the counter & forced a handful into his mouth. His teeth felt wrong, like they'd been caved in, but they were still there, only the gums were bleeding. He tried to cauterise the pain with a half-dozen rapid gulps of slivovice. There were bright lights, shapes dissolving in fog. It was hard work not to throw up, wasting all that drink. His eyes felt like they were perspiring, like beads of yellow fluid were sweating out of them. He tried washing the blood from his face but couldn't see what he was doing without a mirror. When was the last time he'd shaved? He groped in the pantry for a spare shirt. Did one exist? Apparently not. *Steal a new one later.* He unbuttoned the bloody one, ribs a continuous welt, a real quality piece of work. He gulped more slivovice, getting himself good & numb, trying to remember what'd happened, unable to. Tossed the ruined shirt into the wastebasket — a vague smell of mouldy coffee grounds wafted out of it. Slipped his jacket back on. When he coughed, a clot of phlegm came up with blood in it. Something in his lungs. Burning. The burning fading.

When Němec got back to the bureau, the dwarf was standing in the middle of the room, surveying the damage. The coat he was wearing reached to the floor, which made him look even shorter than he already was, & he had a brown pork pie hat on his head. Something about his face wouldn't stay in focus, it was very grey, but Němec could hardly blame the dwarf for that — one man's aberration being another man's, you know. Like the one about the old lush who needed two mirrors to get her make-up on, if it was *before* midday — 'cos *after* midday, it was the blind leading the blind. *Could always go over and put my thumbs in his eyes,* Němec thought, *just to feel if he's all there, Braille-like, only backwards, concave rather than convex.* And what if there was only one eye? Some unholy hole, a dwarf with a golem's head. *And did they feel everything double, the way we see double?* The blind, he meant. Eye at the end of the finger. How would it look? A bit shaky maybe, like tripping over a pair of shoes in the dark you don't remember having left there. *You think a blind person would know what a mirror is, kiddo? Depends, I suppose. Things you can know without ever seeing them, things you can see without ever knowing what they are…*

'Don't it make you sick…'

'It sure does.'

'I mean, is this the best you could do? And after everything that's been done for you? *This?* This is *nothing*, don't you understand? If the Boss didn't know better, I'd say I'm wasting my time here. Am I wasting my time?'

Němec didn't have anything to say to that. But *something* had happened — he searched his mind for some sort of clue as to what it was. Secret chambers? Ladders through the ceiling? Tunnels under the ground? Nonsense. How could any of that have actually happened? And how'd he gotten back there? The dwarf, meanwhile, was busy studying the bits & pieces of torn paper that lay all over the floor, stirred hither & thither by the breeze. They were the shadows the Prof had left behind. At that moment something caught the dwarf's attention & he stooped down to pick up a rough sheet of folio paper — Němec recognised at once the frontispiece from the Black Book.

'Get your hands off that!'

The dwarf smirked, the hair on his upper lip drooping as the smirk broadened.

'Touchy about this one, eh? But if I don't exist, what's it matter?'

'Well do you exist or don't you?'

The question, the instant it'd passed his lips, startled Němec by its absurdity. The dwarf merely sighed & continued eyeing the frontispiece. He held it up to the light —

'Mmm. Not a bad likeness, eh?'

Likeness of what? Němec watched the dwarf turn the paper around & peer at it from different angles, like it was more interesting that way, not knowing what else he should do. Was there supposed to be a clue hidden in the etching? Something he'd missed? Blah. They were welcome to it. Maybe. He wasn't sure.

'What do you want?' he said finally.

The dwarf straightened up & seemed to consider the question for several moments, before folding the paper he was holding & tucking it inside his coat.

'I only want what belongs to Mr Faktor.'

'What could I have that belongs to *Mistah Faktah*?'

'That's what I ask myself. *Why would this complete nobody have something that belongs to the Boss*? Couldn't've put it better myself…'

'Give me a clue.'

'The key, of course.'

'What key?'

'The one that belongs to Mr Faktor.'

One of them, it seemed, was definitely nuts. But then, if the dwarf didn't exist, that just left Němec. *Well, nice morning for it, eh, kiddo*? He went closer to the dwarf, bent down, & looked him square in the eye. If this creature was a figment of his imagination, it was a very cunning figment.

'Something wrong, Bo?'

'Why should anything be wrong?'

But something was always wrong, not adding up, escaping him like the proverbial needle in the eye, or splinter, or beam — like that Polyphemus, blinded by something as crucial yet infinitesimally evasive as a pivotal truth.[*] The elephant in the room — or, let us say, the dwarf in the room — the *gnome*, even. Mr Gnomebody. *Gnomebody slays me with cunning, hehe.* The problem wasn't just the dwarf, however, but the space he was standing in: the walls seemed off-kilter, the doorway skewed to one side, like a body with its skeleton poking through the skin where you least expect it — a thighbone, for example, or the lower reaches of the pelvis — exhibiting all the obscenity of something starved, which has been deprived of some essential nutrient & is in the process of a nervous collapse. The room, hung with shadows, was more cave than bureau. The black plastic in the windows billowed, cold grey air swept in.

Němec had the ludicrous idea that somehow the fabric of the place mirrored his own derangement, a parody now of what it was, a shambles. As if Caliban had been assigned the task of restoring Prospero's library from its watery mass grave, Dewey-Decimalising the drowned books — giving the whole sodden ink-running mess a modicum of dignity — putting the *corpus mysticum* back together with its right parts reconnected in the right order, as if capable of speaking the magic words over it & bringing it back to life. Except the thoughts & words in Němec's head seemed more like the spastic babbling of a toad-headed beetle-bat twitching at the end of a Galvani shock machine.

---

[*] Heavy stuff. [✋]

Just when things looked like they might be getting interesting, the workmen appeared. Eight of them, in muddy boots & blue quilted overalls, wool hats pulled down over their eyes, dragging in toolboxes, ladders, dropsheets, paint buckets, sacks of plaster-of-Paris, etc. Like undertakers' mutes, not so much as a grunt by way of an *'ere we are, mate, this gaff is 'ereby requisitioned.* They set up right there in the Prof's bureau. It was impossible for Němec to gauge the extent of his hallucination. The mummers stacked their gear & straightaway filed out again. Quite a crowd. Němec followed them to the door, listened to the steps receding down the stairwell. *Feelin' like there's more than usual goin' on that you don't quite understand, eh, kiddo?* And what if he *wasn't* hallucinating? *Thought they were gonna cure you of that, did ya? Maybe all them drugs was just to get all the mess in your head rearranged into the RIGHT mess — some keycoded primordial secrethandshake mess, sensitive to whatever spooky influence they're zapping at you down through the ether. Or maybe you figured it out already back at the beginning. Androids. Reckon it's the androids, kiddo?*

The circle closed, so to speak, & in closing, opened.

Němec locked the door. But what good would that do?

Back in the Prof's sanctum sanctorum the dwarf had gone. Němec stared helplessly at the room — & for a long time it seemed as if *it* was staring back at *him*, from above & from all sides, like an observer observing an insect in a box. For good measure he searched the apartment, but the dwarf was nowhere to be found. *Got out while the going was good, eh?* And that meant things were only going to get worse? What would the Bugman have said in a situation like this? *You're on your own, kiddo. But whatever you do, don't shit yourself, it only makes more of a mess you'll have to clean up afterwards.* He felt he was back exactly where he'd started. And then he stopped cold.

In his trouser pocket, Němec felt his right hand close around something hard & metallic. A shiver ran up his arm & he began to feel sick all over again. He clenched his fist tight, the object bit into his flesh. Cogs turned in the back of his mind. Staggering out to the stairs, he found no sign of the dwarf there either. Spooky. A couple of workmen pushed past shouldering a sawhorse. As soon as the coast was clear, Němec leant against the wall & withdrew his hand from his pocket. There, pressed into his palm, was a brass key. He stared at it incredulously. Then it came back to him, where it'd come from, & what it was for. He almost felt saved.

But something told him *this* wasn't the key Faktor's dwarf had been looking for. Not *the* key. But it was enough. Echoes, hazy pictures of a room-within-a-room, ropes & ladders & underground labyrinths. He groped along the hallways till he found it — the closet with the back stripped-out, panels hinged into a door, the musty sanctuary beyond — just as he'd dreamed it. Only he hadn't dreamed it. It was real.[*] He could hear the workmen in the courtyard, stomping in the snow. His mind resolved itself into action, of its own accord it seemed — rushing back to the Prof's bureau, still strewn with paper wreckage, forming weird constellations on the parquet (even now, Němec felt provoked by the want of some underlying order, like Severínová reading her tea leaves). He took a bin-bag from the kitchen & stuffed all the pages he could find in it, dragged it back to the "secret" room & kicked it under the camp bed — then back to the bureau to gather whatever else he might need: turntable, box of vinyls, duffelbag, medicaments, last bottle of moonshine, coffee pot & other miscellaneous — & with all this, barricaded himself in behind the closet door like a fugitive. *From now on*, he thought — but from now on *what*?

The hole truth & nothing butt…

All Němec wanted was to sleep, but they wouldn't let him. Out in the hall, the dull thud of the workmen returning, moving about in the apartment. A slow southern drawl & twangy guitar drifted in from a portable radio they'd set down right on his doorstep, so to speak, as if to tell him they knew exactly where he was at. Over the country&western, the sound of things breaking, being torn up, getting hammered into rubble. Billy Ray Cyrus meets Einstürzende Neubauten. Yep. Whatever they were looking for, they hadn't found it yet. Unless they weren't looking. Unless they were just biding their time, waiting for him to lead them to it. Sure, like a rat leading himself down a hail by the tail. Something was missing. Something was always missing. Oh well. *Truth's never whole*, is what the Bugman would've said. Or maybe he wouldn't. Maybe Němec had *that* all wrong, too.

    Němec lay down on the narrow bed in the pitch blackness, listening to the noise, too tired to think & too tired to sleep. The air in the room inside the closet felt heavy, as if an electrical storm was brewing somewhere. If he closed his eyes, would he take on the dreams of those who'd slept there before him? And who *was* Josef Kulička? What was *the key*? The air grew heavier, saturated with Němec's own exhaustion, a smell like tobacco mouldering in a tin, cut with

---

[*] Really real. [✋]

iodine — a smell like fear or punishment. *How d'you escape from a room with no window and a ladder that only goes up? An attic with no doors? One dead end with a view onto another?* Into his thoughts drifted an image of Edwode Kelley in his Tower — lightning conductor wanding at the sky — storm-blackened cumulonimbus — the sudden terrible crack of its discharge burning a cinder in the eye — the darkness again — the afterflash, breathing deep the pure air — the nitrus pabulum…

A Besieged Man must want other means. A last redoubt before the desperate leap into the void — a mirror to climb through — a tunnel carved from air — or a cyanide capsule — or even just a closet door: between himself & a bullet between third & fourth vertebrae / a hangman's noose / a gutful of zyklon-B / 88lbs of guillotine blade swishing down from 14ft in some ex-Gestapo HQ basement / a dissection slab under a hanging lightbulb, scalpels arranged in kidney dishes, voltameter & electrodes & alligator clips. The paschal lamb. All that. But if his hours listening to Volta mumble into his cigar had taught Němec anything: the waiting game in the eternal waiting room dreaming of the Great Maze outside, where a man might foster the absurd notion that he's not in reality a species of rat watched by secret laughing eyes. A flick of the switch & see him scamper! Up the ladder, like a wisp from a chimney stack. Well goodbye to that morose quack clinging to his mahogany desk like it was the Raft of the Medusa.

And what forces were at work contesting *his* fate, eh? Not that there was much to contest? It'd be enough to just kick his teeth in. He touched his mouth: it stung. A little bit of pain, that was all. Memory? Something underground. A wall. Voices? He searched about for handles, but found none. A stumble in the dark, digging an escape route. A ladder without rungs. *Up there, maybe? The moment of truth? Once more the bold leap into the void, eh, kiddo? One more desperate howling laugh into the dark? Or go down, like Orpheus? See with your own eyes…* What disjointed subset of the world was it his to prove or disprove? Working against the mindclock, forms of slowness building new impediments, neither asleep nor not asleep, to get somewhere before the universe of thinkable objects came apart entirely, no longer held by improbable threads, & the body with it, finally! But why should anywhere else be better than where he already was? And all this, not without precedent, eh? Twice fallen, so to speak. Not unforeseeable if still unforeseen? Not satisfied with the nature of appearances? Of disappearances? Of inappearances?

How, after the Prof died, catching himself at times unawares, at others being caught, as if by some indefinable presence, or a definable absence. What Volta had said, that to achieve purity, Man must be cleansed *even of his soul.* And what was that supposed to mean? He'd tried to isolate the various reasons for his being *there*, not the specific *there* of the room, but the general *there* of his socalled existence. As if he'd been looking all along for his own reflection. But each time the world threw up obstacles, dead ends. It was an old story.

Concerning the "Fall"

Well all that was about as enlightening in his present situation as the physics of tossing a book out a fourth floor window. Time, space & a free-falling projectile. The kind of thing any twit with half a brain could do backwards with their eyes closed. Němec turned the image around in his mind, like a child's puzzle, present but with no depth. Sure, easy as stepping into a big black hole.

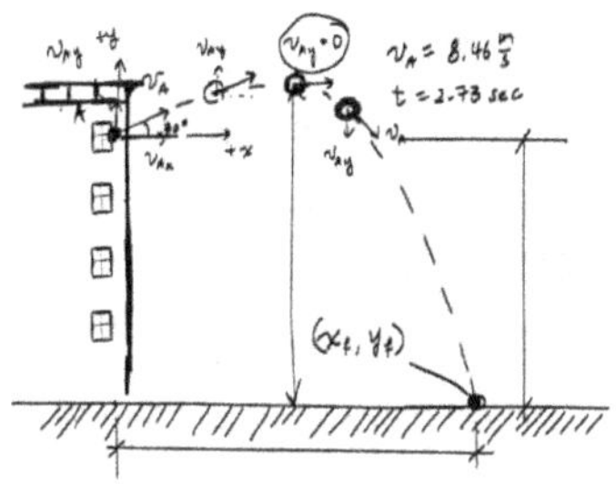

It was the first thing Němec saw when he turned the light back on. How he'd missed seeing it the first time, he didn't know.[*] An attaché case sitting beside the desk — brown, tan almost — identical to the ones in the basement of the Patriot Klub: two side pockets with gold sliding clasps, key holes, a hinged leather handle. What it contained, though. Well, had Němec not been convinced he was awake, he'd've sworn it was a dream, a dream he'd already had, twice before, with his eyes open. Only this time there was no square of white card with **NEMOC** typed on it,[*] just a plain package & inside the package a kind of book. Like its counterpart, it was wrapped in a kind of undistinguished beige, only this one hadn't come out of a Xerox machine. Vellum, presumably. A very expensive kind of undistinguished. It was creased at the edges & heavily seamed.

---

[*] But we do, don't we, eh, Squillhead? [☞]
[*] Third time lucky, maybe? As they say, a bit of variation, good as a holiday! [☞]

Old, to be precise. Was there any *other* kind of velum? Automatically he turned to the first page, always eager to get on with the story. There was that weird brown calligraphy again, alright, bled-though with some sort of cartoon plant, etc. But facing, instead of an *ex libris* card with the Yale crest, & Beinecke Rare Book & Manuscript Library reference number MS 408 pencilled on it, was a Reich's eagle with swastika & ⚡ runes. Not, insofar as Němec had been expecting anything, the kind of thing he *would've* expected.

'Holy Moses!' he said aloud, startling himself in the process.

Had anyone heard? The question immediately struck him as ridiculous. Who did he thing would've heard? The ninjas or whatever they were, time-travelling Nazis from the next dimension who'd just dropped by with an attaché case on their way to God only knew where, were any such God to've existed. Out in the hallway the radio continued to twang, the walls to shake. The door remained barricaded, just as it had been. Spooky. Maybe that secret room was in fact a kind of portal & somewhere, in a different time from this, someone in perhaps an even less envious position than him was frantically searching for an attaché case that'd apparently just vanished into thin air.

Mmm. So there were two, then. Two Voynich Manuscripts, in two parallel dimensions. *Zap!* Or did it mean, now that *this* VM had popped up out of nowhere, that the *other* VM had also, simultaneously, gone the other way? Dropped out of the sky, possibly, on some unsuspecting Nazi's head? Maybe it was something like that, had conked Saul off his horse? Well, well, & why not? What if all the aberrant switcheroos of historical fortune could be traced back (or forward) to some sort of Voynichian quantum voodoo? Manuscripts from the sky! Under the bed! Atop the mountain! Making a lightning detour via JFK's motorcade, the pyramids of Egypt, Machu Pichu, Salt Lake City.[*]

After a while spent absorbing the fact of what he was (both figuratively & literally, potentially & actually) holding in his hands, a strange idea came to him. What if there'd always two. *Two* Voynich Manuscripts, not *two languages*: the secret of the code ∴ = a "tongue" *doubly foreign* because *divided*, i.e. each as incomplete as the divided hermaphroditic soul Volta waffled on about, ever seeking its inverted twin, its double, its mirror-image, its doppelgänger… Was *this* why it'd remained indecipherable all this time? The key was its *incomplete self*? Why stop at two? Perhaps there were others, copies originating in scribal cloisters in the last Dark Ages, secretly disseminated during the purges of the

---

[*] As usual Němec's thoughts were getting carried away with themselves. [☞]

Reformation, or faked by enterprising clerics in their bitter struggle against the Rosicrucians, all up for grabs by the time Fascism was on the rise, every book for itself, so to speak, some consigned to the flames, others buried, drowned, sealed in tombs, pulped, rat-eaten, or dandied-up as true relics of the Long Lost Etcetera, mute fetishes to be auctioned off to the highest bidder, feeding the market in arcane Nazis mythomania?

Then a timely image flashed through Němec's head, of the pile of discarded attaché cases in the wine cellar under Jilská Street. *Now it's all beginning to make sense, mmm?* What if for each attaché case there existed also a unique Manuscript? He envisaged himself, all of a sudden, in a room ten years hence, shelves on all sides piled high, all the way to the ceiling, with countless Voynich Manuscripts, as if it'd become his sole task in life to be guardian of them all, receiving them into this hidden repository, delivered by unknown hands, the secret couriers of an occult bibliomania, some hidden store in process of being distributed, for reasons undisclosed, between rooms such as this one, in this or other cities like it — who knew how many, or which other unwitting librarians existed out there!

And what about Faktor? Was he searching for the same thing, or some other, unrelated, yet coincident thing? Or was it the One True he sought? Perhaps *these* were meant to be clues, pointers, like attracting like? Which made *him* what? The mediumistic idiot, book under his pillow, mumbling its secret dictation in the dark? Or, strange thought, did it go much deeper than that? Beyond duplicates, twin, Nazi forgeries, to the revelation that there *was no original?* The book, or books, nothing but an allegory of THE BOOK?

Or not so metaphysical, something simpler, more obvious, like the Voynich Manuscript being really just a worthless copy, riddled with errors, of a copy of a copy, each in turn & so on & so forth, making the whole thing illegible in any language. In which case, *this?* The potential grail of Voynichologists? The real deal, after all these years, having never left Golem City in the first place? And somehow, since K's sojourn in the Tower possibly, having made its way *here?* Thence, during the Protektorat? But why the stamp? Who knew about it? Had the Prof known? Had he too been searching for it — *the key?* And what *now?*

As if to convince himself one way or the other of what lay before him, Němec spread the folios out in a fanning pattern on the bed. There were at least a couple of hundred. The familiar procession of dull pigments describing strange tendrilled organisms & stranger cosmodemonologies. None of your usual upsidedown pentangle rubbish. Not your standard Merlin-the-Magician grimoire. Had he never heard of Bacon's pigskin, K's blarneybook, D's Dunciad, Rudi's folly, Voynich's V-weapon, Prof Hájek's hijacked hocusbook, he might've taken it for a child's antique doodlebook, or some artless schizophrenic's message from the Ancients of Mumu. Someone, after all, had *made* the Manuscript. Just as someone had made the Gospels & had made God & His mirrorverse, from the Big Boo to the crystal ball, infinitely doubled, disjoined, coincident.

Adventures of the Teleophone

The workmen were still there at 8:oo p.m. Front door off its hinges, leaning against the jambs. Radio in the hallway, the same plaintive drawl going on & on about trucks & roads & being left by a woman, just sometimes the voices changed. Down in the courtyard a light shone in the window of the caretaker's flat. Everything seemed like this was how it was meant to be, everything in its proper order, nothing untoward. All the Boolean algebras of AND/OR running to programme, in which case... Like a lopsided connotation, listening at the back of a closet for clues: the world as a rat hears it — dwellers of thresholds, wormholed interstices of the physical & material, the articulated gap in the rubik's cube that makes a different arrangement of the same thing — like rooms in a house, *ta-dee-dum...*

When the phone rang, Němec waited to see if anything would happen. Nothing did. The ringing stopped & then began again. He inched out of the closet into an empty hallway. For a moment, barely recognising where he was, he stood there like a goat tethered to a pole, expecting some calamity. At the end of the hall a scene of meticulous disorder presented itself — what it most resembled was a film being played backwards, a colour documentary projected on a cut-away screen that showed men wearing blue boiler suits in the process of deconstructing an apartment. The ringing stopped & began again almost immediately. Persistent, whoever it was. He picked the phone up off the floor & lifted the receiver to his ear. At the end of the hall, the workers continued ripping up the plumbing, dismantling the stove, tearing out the gas pipes, smashing through walls with sledgehammers, drilling, chiselling, stripping back the plaster, levering up the parquet, de-glazing the windows. A bitterly cold draught circulated through the rooms, up the stairwell, rattling the panes.

Even with the banging & stomping, the radio & the static interference, the voice at the other end was clearly recognisable.[*] Němec's first reflex should've been to hang up before it was too late. Instead he stood there like a chump, shivering in the draught. He ogled the construction workers in their boiler suits with a certain degree of apprehension but they very conspicuously paid not the slightest heed to him. He got the message. Whichever faction they worked for, the order had come down: treat the jerk on the hat like a ghost, he ain't even in the picture. Němec felt a sudden urge to throw the telephone at them, but just thinking it brought out a cold sweat down the back of his neck. He wiped it away with his hand but that only made it worse. Then out of the static & feedback came the Voice. It said his name. Without thinking, Němec asked what it wanted.

'Mister Faktor's been expecting you,' the dwarf said. 'He'll be waiting in the herbarium, at the Botanical Gardens, midday tomorrow. Punctuality,' the word came out simperingly despite all the racket, 'is advised.'

Shit, what was the guy, telepathic? Got wind already of the second coming?[*] Němec tried not to scream. *They've got ESP in the back of your fucking head*! The idea was so stupid it stopped him in his tracks, so to speak. Then the line went dead. Němec stared at the receiver as if expecting something else to happen & then after a minute or so put it down. No sooner done than one of the workers appeared (they all looked alike, faceless in boiler suits) &, without saying a word, took the black Buddha from Němec's hands, unplugged it from the wall, wound the cable around it as though performing the last rites, & carried it off. Immediately one of his confreres began stripping the wiring from the skirting board. Plasterwork sprayed on the floor. Němec retreated once more

---

[*] Highpitched, echoing in delay between automated clicks, crossed-line dial tones, remote voices in the sky, under the ground, relayed from switchboard to switchboard across the continental grid, satellite link-up, ionosphere, looped into backchannels only to arrive at its intended destination perhaps long after the event, when the machinery itself, the entire technology of the earth-bound telephone, was obsolete, post-evolved, no longer a matter even of voice or its analogues but something more elemental, particulate, mind-to-mind, short-circuit in the ether, spooky influences in the Mega Cortex, cosmic synapse bother, aberrations in the very fabric of the universe that'd allow one person to be in ten different places at once, simultaneously, & in each of them equally *aware*, *cognisant*, pursuing intentions through to their concluded implications, etc — & from ten to how many more bifurcations, trifurcations, branching out, going deeper into possibilities unfathomed, unexplored & most likely unrealisable, though you'd never be quite sure on that count, never quite certain of what the final outcome would be if ever there was an outcome — something in perpetual delay, just over the horizon, & the horizon beyond the horizon, beyond any & all enumeration, calculus, contrivance…? [✋]

[*] So to speak. [✋]

to his sanctuary, expecting some kind of last stand, determined not to give up that final piece of territory before his work was done, whatever it was…

So, he was expected, was he? It only seemed reasonable, under the circumstances. What point could there be from now on in trying to resist? He waited for the Bugman to make one of his customary wisecracks from the backbrain peanut gallery, but all was depressingly quiet on that front. Well, worst case, Faktor's summons would turn out to be just another tease, right? More of that Jesuitical spuriosity. Or maybe not. Maybe that wasn't the worst. Maybe they'd gotten as tired of him as he was & planned to give it to him in the neck, bury the corpse under the cactus gardens, or the worm farm, or the goddamn parrot house. Walk right into it. Well…

He leant his weight against the door, it wasn't much to keep them out if they decided to make a move on him right there & then, cut all that foreplay bullshit. Would he do as Faktor said? Did he really have a choice in the matter, one way or the other? If not now, some other time. If not here, etc. It was like the moment in one of those films when the sucker thinks about the Girl &, no doubt in his mind at all that he's doomed down to his shoelaces, can't help wanting to see that lovely treacherous face of hers One Last Time. Even if it's her who's going to pull the trigger. But in his mind, still grasping at some picture of a frail naked thing all pliant & fleshlike beneath his touch. A victim, like him, caught up in all the sound & fury of blah-de-blah. *Sure she really loves you, kiddo, didn't she say so herself in that scene went to turned to crosseyed mush?*

You could bet your bottom dollar, that was exactly the sort of nonsensical nonsense doing the rounds of Němec's emotive faculties, perhaps for a cathartic last lap of honour but you wouldn't want to depend too much on that, seeing in his mind's eye some variation of Alice Steinerová, Veronika Voss, Elsbeth von N____, whoever the hell she was supposed to be at that moment in Němec's subconscious, standing out of the wind in a smashed phonebooth, trying to get word to him only the phone's been kicked-in. Tears streaking her mascara. A haunted desperate look in her eyes as she struggles & fails to light a cigarette: her hands shake so hard the cigarette breaks in half, one end dangling like a bit of severed finger, the ends of her blonde hair whipping her face. Someone offscreen speaks her name & already she's ceased to exist, a minor detail, replaced by things too vivid to be real. Mirrorworld characters were stumbling around in the dark — now flattened-out in depthless light — countless mental photographs wanting nothing more than to be forgot, uncreated, abolished.

The film in his head was resolving itself towards that single inescapable point, the closing act, & whatever the characters chose to do from now on would only bring them ever closer to it.

Like Scabby Marat

A door without a hinge. Perhaps that was enough — the problem had been wrongly posed & by restating it the question it asked was abolished. Němec sat pretty, waiting for the workmen to knock-off for the night. As far as he could see the future had no synopsis. He sat in the 40watt gloom & breathed the dead atmosphere. The smell of the velum, the leather attaché, the dank mattress, the ancient dust. The longer he sat the more conscious he became of the numbness in his body, it ached so much he couldn't tell which part of his body was which. If he'd had to stay that way much longer, his head would've come apart. By ten the place was silent, as per §34 of City Ordinance 258/2000 Coll., "on the Protection of Public Health (Noise Curfews)." Boots tramping down the stairs.

Němec made a quick reconnaissance. The place was a wreck. All that could be seen of the Prof's former bureau was a maze of steel braces, put there to hold up the roof, or the walls, or something. Every lightfitting had been gouged out of the ceiling, the wood trusses exposed inside the holes, bits of decomposed straw, rubble, compacted newsprint from the last refurbishment the rats hadn't got to yet. Above, the weight of the attic seemed to groan. Grey shadows played around the rooms now that the windows were laid bare.

Down on the street there were only lurching shadows cast by the builders' scaffolds as they creaked in the wind — TV voices through an open window — the dripdrop of water from eaves. Were those, too, figments? It brought back memories, figments of lost childhood... through a window... a derelict hotel with a sagging bluegreen marquee... two men with a piano. Who were they? Where had they come from? Where were they going? Scarecrows in trenchcoats, pitching into the wind... the scene erased behind falling snow... a warped note played backwards... *Something led me to this, guided me and transported me, yet communicated nothing.* Once upon a time somebody else's body had been sewn inside his skin: a sanctuary inside a sanctuary — the outer shell & the inner shell — like that secret room. Once they'd demolished all the rest of it, would the room vanish, collapse back into some invisible fourth dimension?

Němec stalked through the apartment, listening at the walls. He cracked open the door onto the stairwell, listened for footsteps, but there was nothing, only the blood hammering in his ears. Down in the courtyard something was banging, like a rusty gate in the wind, only there was no wind. From the Tower window he could see a light on in the caretaker's flat — a pair of silhouettes were framed in the doorway, carrying a sack. It looked wrong. By the time he reached the bottom of the stairwell they were gone. Had he imagined them? He could feel the panic working away inside him. *Interior Ministry. Childhood visions of men in coats. Orphanage.* He checked the street entrance. Nothing. The smell of unmixed cement, turned clay, hydraulics & generator fuel suffused the air. He slouched back to the courtyard & rang the bell outside the caretaker's flat, but there was no answer. The parrot stared at him unblinkingly, one eye glued to the inside of the window. Something reflected in the eye moved. Němec turned to see what it was, but there was nothing behind him but the unlit entrance way.

He was about to ring the bell again when he caught a second reflection in the window: something hideous stared out at him & he immediately understood that look on Mrs Severínová's face when he'd come down from the attic. His face had the half-crazed look of someone who'd been buried alive in a grave & had to dig themselves out. Glancing around, he saw a bucket beside the wood pile. He grabbed hold of it & put it under the tap — the pipe, half-frozen, shuddered. A viscous thread of water came out, but eventually he had enough to fill the bottom of Hájek's bath, once he'd hauled it upstairs & dunged the cracked tiles & mortar out of the tub. The water was so cold it made the cold air in the bathroom steam. Moonlight filled the window, turning everything to bruises. Němec wrung the blood out of his shirt & hung it to dry on a pair of screws sticking out of the wall where the mirror used to be. He did what he could to undo the previous night, knees drawn up, breath turning to vapour, scavenged soapcake mushing to pulp in his hand. Shivering.

At the end of it, he felt like an empty vessel in which vibrations of air create an echo, & nothing more. He couldn't help thinking of the Prof, who'd died in that exact same spot, like scabby Marat, an unfinished game of chess — what was it? The Fool's Gambit? Himself as his own worst adversary… No sign of a ghost in that light… And between then, the ghost & him, what was the connection, apart from the likes of *this*, mere circumstance, all evidence of which soon to be stripped away, dissembled, abolished? Soon the whole place would be rubble to the rafters & then they'd tear the rafters down too, rip the guts out & just leave the shell standing, a curio on the hillside for the sightseers to take a gawk at: *Up there's where that Kelley did magic tricks for the Emperor (the old soak)*!

Well, if the world really came to that, what'd be the point resisting? *A man lived here once — I knew him.* But walls are just walls, like a shell when the creature inside it's dead: hold it to your ear & you don't hear an ocean, only the ear's echo — one ear listening to itself across a hole in time,. Which is the sound a skull makes when it's emptied of all superfluous matter, though maybe you shake it & something rattles, the shrivelled remains. You could've smelled it if you hadn't believed there was nothing left in there, nothing to upset you with its obscene presence after the fact. *The inertia of it, closing in, the unremitting entropy, shutting down the receptor nerves, static flooding the circuits…*

Němec coughed. It was all he could do to feel his own body. And what would they do with *that* once the rest of everything else had been disposed of? Would they come for him in the middle of the night, some time when he wasn't expecting it? Or were his days numbered in any case? They'd simply come in one day, not so far from now, & find what was left of him lying there like a patch of scum around a plughole?

There had to be a way out of this.

And if you had to go through it all over again, you wouldn't, would you?

He stood & wiped himself off with his hands, pulling on stale threads — old superstitions of unwash passed-down, proofed against all weather by reek of smoky bars & mothballs: camouflage. You live in your own stink long enough anything else smells evil: enough people all live in the same stink together, you've got the basis of a nation state right there. Only have to watch the old threepiece doesn't get up one day & walk of without you, Golem-like, start running things its own way, just like them androids. Now there was a thought… *Ever wonder why strangers all got that peculiar whiff about 'em, kiddo?*

<u>HOSPITALITY</u>

A room with armchairs, settee, reading lamps, bookshelves, tribal
masks hanging on the walls. Door stage-right, stairway stage-left.
At centre, a low table with two glasses & a decanter, an ashtray, an
open packet of cigarettes, a lighter. A drinks trolley. It's evening.
Two figures, FAKTOR & the DWARF, enter separately through the door
on the right. FAKTOR wearing a crushed, burgundy polyester suit,
pink carnation in buttonhole, striped tie, short grey hair, goatee.
The DWARF -- with stringy pasted-on moustache -- is dressed in a
pork-pie hat, dirty beige raincoat, with brown corduroy trousers, &
carries a leather attaché case. They move slowly across the room,
taking it in. They're relaxed, at ease.

DWARF: They expecting us?
FAKTOR: Expecting us? How could they be expecting us? No-one
            ever expects us. There're never any expectations where
            we're concerned.
DWARF: Still. A first time for everything.
FAKTOR: Don't make me laugh.
DWARF: Eh? First time for everything, you know.
FAKTOR: Considerate of 'em to've left the key under the doormat.
            Saves making a mess, eh? Nice gaff like this. Would've
            been a pity to make an unnecessary mess, when there's a
            perfectly civilised way of going about it. In some
            cultures they're very particular about such things.
            Hospitality, that is. What's mine is yours, as they say. An
            open door. Succour & sustenance. The comfort of strangers
            put always before one's own personal etc. Everything left
            for the weary traveller to come upon, a vista of
            generosity. Accepted without stint or question. Without
            need of gratitude. Nothing expected in return. A gift
            like that, no strings attached, do you know what that
            means?
DWARF: You're talking a lot of bollocks. How the fuck can you
            lay on a welcome if you're not expecting anyone?
FAKTOR: I don't mind saying there are times when my sense of
            responsibility for you weighs heavily. You may not've
            realised that. It was your mother's last wish. 'Vic,' she
            said, looking up at me with tears in her eyes… She had a
            fine pair of eyes your mother. Could see through that
            gutless wonder your socalled father was. Not too soon,
            though. No. We all learn by our mistakes. But then you
            don't make the same mistake twice, do you? Not if there's
            anything upstairs you don't. Your mum, she had plenty
            upstairs. Would've put the boot in herself, too, if she'd

had a leg to stand on. Ruined for a no good, swindling
little mutt. Crippled in her prime of life. It was the
first time in years a smile passed her lips the day she
heard the news. (Pause.) You don't look a bit like your old
man, you know that? Now there're some fellas you couldn't
say that about. But looks aren't everything, are they?
Take Jesus, for example. It'd be a bleedin' miracle if
he'd've taken after that Joseph. And then where'd we be,
eh? Then where'd we be?

DWARF: (Casing the room.) Sure this is the right place?

FAKTOR: Of course, not that there's any comparison. I wouldn't go
            so far as that. I respected your mum. We all did. She
            earned it, too. But we're all human in the end. Even you,
            I'm sorry to say.

DWARF: You been here before?

FAKTOR: Who? No no no. You're grasping at straws son. It's not
            possible. The odds are stacked against it. You weren't
            even a twinkle in God's eye when they tipped your old
            man back into the hole he came from... It's better you
            know where you stand. No point labouring under false
            illusions.

DWARF: I said, Have you been here before?

FAKTOR: I'm not deaf, you little bitch!

DWARF: Ooh-ooh-ooh. Just wondered. It's okay to wonder isn't it?
            (Pause.) How'd we end up at this joint, anyway?

FAKTOR: How the feck should I know? (Pause.) We do what we're
            told. Like always. (Pause.) Never once made a wrong turn,
            eh? You saying otherwise? Always ended up at the right
            destination. Pinpoint bleedin' accuracy, me. Everything
            accounted for. Never missed a beat. Not a beat. (Pause. An
            indistinct noise coming from upstairs. Running water.
            Silence. Both look up towards the top of the stairs.)

DWARF: Sure no-one's expecting us?

FAKTOR: What did I just say?

DWARF: No-one knows we're coming?

FAKTOR: One would seem to imply the other.

DWARF: You know, I was reading this magazine the other day.

FAKTOR: My my! Well that's a discovery.

DWARF: They reckon the more times something doesn't happen, the
            more likely it's going to happen, in the future. Law of
            probability that is. Or diminishing returns. I forget
            which. (Pause.) So it occurred to me, that someone might be
            expecting us after all -- I mean, the sense of
            expectancy...

FAKTOR: Occurred to you, did it? Do something useful, eh, & see
            what's behind that door there. (The DWARF begins moving
            towards door.) Leave the bag! (Pause. The DWARF puts
            attaché case down beside table. Crosses to door at stage-
            left. Opens it. Looks in. Closes door. Turns back to the
            room & takes in the new perspective. FAKTOR struggles to
            sit in one of the armchairs, stands up, looks at the
            armchair with disgust.)

FAKTOR: You'd think they could manage something with a bit of

comfort, wouldn't you? What's the point of an armchair if
it lacks comfort? No point at all, that's what. Pure
bloody-mindedness. Look at this -- it's an instrument of
torture! A bit of comfort's all I ask. Is that too much?

DWARF: I mean it's not unusual is it?

FAKTOR: That's the sad truth. Everything's going to the dogs.

DWARF: It's like when you're in a room.

FAKTOR: Eh?

DWARF: And all of a sudden, for no reason at all, you get this
feeling something's about to happen.

FAKTOR: What is?

DWARF: Anything. There's no way of knowing.

FAKTOR: Of course not. Of course there's bloody not.

DWARF: Something completely unexpected. Just like that. Out of
the blue.

FAKTOR: Out of the blue, you say?

DWARF: Take _this_ room for example.

FAKTOR: Might not be as easy as it looks...

DWARF: Imagine we're standing here. Talking...

FAKTOR: Like this?

DWARF: And all of a sudden the phone starts ringing...

FAKTOR: There isn't any phone.

DWARF: But there could be...

FAKTOR: How could there be? There isn't. An empirical fact. A
phone which doesn't exist can't start ringing. There are
preconditions that must be met...

DWARF: But imagine there's a phone in the _next_ room. You don't
know it's there. You can't _see_ it. You're not _aware_ of it -
- you're not even aware of the _possibility_ that it might
ring. It may as well _not exist_...

FAKTOR: My point exactly.

DWARF: But it does...

FAKTOR: Something you're not telling me?

DWARF: ... because you'd hear it.

FAKTOR: I don't hear anything...

DWARF: No, but if you _did_ hear it, you'd know straight away
there was a phone in the next room...

FAKTOR: How?

DWARF: Because it'd be ringing.

FAKTOR: What would it sound like, eh? Give us a little
demonstration.

DWARF: And you'd _sense_ that if you went in there & answered it,
there wouldn't be anyone at the other end.

FAKTOR: Get to the point soon, won't you.

DWARF: I'm talking about a sense of foreboding.

FAKTOR: You're full of surprises tonight.

DWARF: I mean the unaccountable expectation that something's
about to happen which violates all reason.

FAKTOR: Violates reason, did you say? Violates reason? I'll tell
you what violates reason. It's a safe bet no thought's
ever entered that pigmy skull of yours that made it back
out in one piece. _Abandon all hope ye who enter!_ You call
that a brain? It's a bleeding butcher's shop. A Jacobean

travesty. Carnage, as far as the eye can see. You're not
only a midget, you're a moron.

DWARF: Finished yet?

FAKTOR: Idiot!

DWARF: You take liberties with me. (Pause.) It's not very nice to
take liberties with people.

FAKTOR: Who? Me? Now why would I do a thing like that? Don't
make faces at me, laddy. You may not realise this, but I
care very much about your future -- & it's because I care
that I worry. I worry you're wasting your talent. That
you're not getting the right sort of opportunities. The
proper creative outlet. I'd like to know if you have any
particular thoughts on that subject. (Pause.) Well what
are you looking at? (Pause.) Pour me a drink, why don't
you. (The DWARF shrugs, goes to the drinks trolley.
FAKTOR seats himself on the settee.) This is more like it!

DWARF: There aren't any glasses.

FAKTOR: Come here. (Pause.) Regard if you will. (Indicates the
glasses & decanter sitting on the table in front of him.)
Quite fortuitous that, wouldn't you say? (Pause.) Pour
yourself one while you're at it. (The DWARF pours. Holds a
glass out to FAKTOR. Faktor stands.)

FAKTOR: A quick drink before we settle down to work. To your
health then. (The DWARF stands motionless.) Well? (They
drink.) There, painless. <u>WHAT DO YOU SAY</u>?

DWARF: Ta.

FAKTOR: Not at all. Not at all. Another?

DWARF: I'm with you. (Pours.)

FAKTOR: Good lad. One for the road then.

DWARF: Already?

FAKTOR: What?

DWARF: We only just got here...

FAKTOR: A mere figure of speech. A manner of speaking. (Pause.)
Well, never mind. Here's to...

DWARF: Your health?

FAKTOR: Why not. Why not my health? Eh?

DWARF: So, to your health.

FAKTOR: Yes. (Both remain motionless, looking at one another.)

DWARF: To your health, then.

FAKTOR: Overdoing it a bit aren't you? (Silence. FAKTOR finishes
his drink in one & walks off. The DWARF stands
motionless, glass in hand.)

FAKTOR: You've forgotten something.

DWARF: What?

FAKTOR: You forgot to say what's behind that door.

DWARF: Nothing.

FAKTOR: Nothing? (Pause.) How can <u>nothing</u> be on the other side of
that door? (Pause.) Why do I bother?

DWARF: Look for yourself can't you.

FAKTOR: That's not the point, is it my son? It's your irreplaceable
way of seeing I value. Not merely your astonishing
capacity for insight, but the way you bestow a special
charm on the most senseless & trivial observations...

DWARF: Well, now you mention it...
FAKTOR: Shut up & get your mind on the job.
DWARF: <u>Get your mind on the job</u>, he says.
FAKTOR: No screw-ups!
DWARF: <u>No screw-ups</u>, he says. Oooh, come on dads, what you say
            that for? You rely on me, don't you? Can't deny that.
            Can't say I've ever let you down.
FAKTOR: Reliable as a leper's tit.
DWARF: I do my part.
FAKTOR: What do you want, a kiss on the arse? Finish your drink -
            - you look ridiculous, standing there like you're holding
            a pissy diaper.
DWARF: I know my worth. Don't think I don't know my worth.
FAKTOR: Even a midget should know his worth, eh? (Pause.) Better
            check that everything's in the bag.
DWARF: I already checked.
FAKTOR: Well check again.
DWARF: (Goes to attaché case, lifts it onto the top of the drinks
            trolley, opens it & peers in. Closes it & replaces it on
            the floor.) Just like I said.
FAKTOR: Good. (Pause.) Well, well. (Pause. Checks his watch.) Still
            time yet. How long's it been, eh? How many years, you
            reckon, us together? (Pause.) Can't say you've lost out on
            anything, can you, eh? Interesting people. Nice scenery.
            No overheads. No regrets. No obligations outside the job.
            And what a job, eh? All the fringe benefits. None of your
            everyday nine-to-five shite. Regular, but not regimented.
            Flexibility, that's the name of the game. A win-win
            situation as our transatlantic friends would have it.
            Never bogged down in the one place. Get to move about.
            Travel. See a bit of the old four corners. Man of the
            world. Well, <u>midget</u> of the world -- not that I'm the type
            to discriminate, mind. <u>One for all & all for one</u>'s what I
            always says. I mean, <u>one-&-the-same</u>, this place or any
            other place -- 'cos no matter where you pull up, after a
            long day's honest labour, there's always a hearth you can
            as good as call your own. In the very bosom of
            hospitality. What more could a man, er, want? (Pause) Eh?
            Not bad, this. Not bad at all... I'm beginning to feel I
            quite like it here. What we need now is a bit of music.
            Eh? Put some music on for us Count? Something classy.
            Something with style. (The DWARF goes behind FAKTOR, out
            of view. In a moment we hear Mahler's Kindertotenlieder.
            The DWARF doesn't re-appear.) Perfect. Perfect. You're a
            gentleman & a scholar. What you reckon about that, eh,
            <u>gentleman & scholar</u>? Your fecking idiot old man used to
            say that. What the hell did he know about it? Anyway,
            enough of that. You're a real block off the old chip,
            aren't you? Charmed life. No doubt about it. And against
            all the odds, too. Who'd've put money on you, eh? Prove the
            bastards wrong, that's what I say. Ah. Charmed life. A
            charmed life. (Long pause. Music ends.) What? So soon?
            Play it again, son. Go on. Play it again. (After a pause,

music recommences.) Gives me a chill up my spine, that
does. Turn off the lights will you Count? We need some
atmosphere. (The DWARF re-enters, turning off the lamps.
Goes to switch off lamp beside FAKTOR's armchair.) No, not
that one. Give it to me. (The DWARF hands the lamp to
FAKTOR who takes it in his arms & cradles it like a baby,
rocking it slowly in time to the music. The DWARF stands
looking down at him.) That's better. (Addressing himself
as though to the lamp.) I was like a father to you. I bet
you don't remember that, eh? Gave you your dummy at
night when the nightmares came. Bounced you on my knee.
Patted your bum. Wiped away your vomit. Cleaned up all
your shite. Rubbed your nose in it... You seemed to
appreciate that. Very touching as a child, you were. I
remember your old mum crying her eyes out just to look
at you. Never was a woman with a bigger heart. Still, I
had to shut her up now & then. Gentle, though... She
deserved respect, if nothing else. And it's true, I had no
end of respect. Pity is, someone had to put her out of her
misery. And there you were, apple of her eye, & not a
damn to spare between the two of you... (Music stops.)
What? finished again? Fix that, won't you, son? Silence
won't do us any good. Not now... (The DWARF moves behind
Faktor & out of sight again.) I suppose you weren't
listening eh? What I was just saying? Eh? I bet you don't
remember a thing... Immaculate bloody conception. Born
fully deformed from the hole in your own arse... You
listening to me? (Pause. Brings the lamp close to his
face.) Funny, she only screamed for the first bit, then it
sort of just went out of her. The screaming, I mean. I
suppose it was the only time she ever really knew she was
alive... I gave her that... I made her feel that... The
expression... The eyes... And you know what she said?
(Pause.) Eh? Think you can guess what she said, Baby
Jesus? (The Mahler recording begins again & plays at
gradually increasing volume.) Ah, that's better. That's
good. (Closes his eyes. Pause. Opens eyes. Decides to switch
off the lamp instead, still holding it close to his face.)
I'll tell you... I'll tell you what she said, your virgin
mother. Her last words. Right at the end. After all that
unnecessary pain & misery. Tears in her eyes. Face all --
well, you know how it is. And you lying beside her,
smiling away, googoo, happy as a pig in shite. The last
words she uttered in this life. You know what they were?
(Pause.) Nothing... Not a fecking thing. (Music plays to
end. Lights dim, FAKTOR still holding the lamp, unlit,
against his face. A door opens at the top of the
staircase. The sound of bare feet on the stairs, then a
figure coming into view, illuminated from behind &
above. It's ALICE, in a white bathrobe.)

ALICE: Jan, is that you? (Silence. She continues descending. In
the dark she walks across the room to the low table,
centre, fumbles for cigarettes & lighter. Smokes. The glow

of the cigarette as she inhales & faintly illuminated
cloud of smoke as she exhales. Walks across to stage left
& switches on lamp. Walks back across stage to right. As
she comes level with the settee on which FAKTOR is
sitting, he switches on the lamp he's holding,
illuminating his face. ALICE stops, but continues
smoking. With her free hand she checks her hair. She's
vaguely surprised -- bemused rather than disturbed. The
DWARF remains out of sight. FAKTOR stares directly
ahead, silent.) I didn't hear you come in obviously. Only
some music. I suppose Jan's expecting you. I thought you
might be him. But you're not. He didn't mention he'd made
any arrangements… (Silence. ALICE shrugs. Goes to drinks
trolley, locates a fresh glass in side compartment, pours
a gin, drinks, pours another, crosses back to Faktor.)
Quiet type are you? (She drinks, meditates briefly,
revolving the empty glass.) You could at least say
something. Death in the family. An accident. A
foreclosure. You've got that harbinger-of-doom look down
to a fine art, don't you? I bet you work on it in front of
a mirror. (Pause.) Am I supposed to say "trick or treat"?
(Returns to drinks trolley. Pours another gin.) Well,
you've helped yourself I see. (FAKTOR gets slowly up from
the settee, replaces lamp on side table. Goes to refill his
glass from the whiskey decanter.) So what do people call
you, or don't they?

FAKTOR: The Faktor. That'll do.
ALICE: Factor?
FAKTOR: The Faktor. You'll get yourself a chill standing around
            like that.
ALICE: Don't bother…
FAKTOR: Why, no bother at all, not at all… Your hair's still wet.
            (Puts his hand to her hair.) Feel that. You're standing in
            a draft…
ALICE: There's no draft. (Moving out of FAKTOR's reach.)
FAKTOR: You don't feel a slight chill?
ALICE: Should I?
FAKTOR: A slight chill down your back?
ALICE: Down my back?
FAKTOR: Like a cold hand…
ALICE: Yours?
FAKTOR: Down your back…
ALICE: Tell me how it feels.
FAKTOR: Feels?
ALICE: Mmm. What do you imagine, running your cold hand down
            my back? How does it feel?
FAKTOR: As though someone just walked over your grave.
ALICE: Playing the ghoul are we? (Laughs.) You didn't ask my
            name.
FAKTOR: No.
ALICE: Perhaps you already know it. Or perhaps you'd rather not
            know. Men like you think women are just objects, things,
            isn't that right? (Pause.) Not fussed at all. Are you

always so cold-blooded?
FAKTOR: I prefer taking my time. Better to savour things a bit,
           don't you think? The finer details. You only live once, as
           they say...
ALICE: That's what they say...
FAKTOR: I'd like to ask you a personal question if you don't mind.
ALICE: Should I?
FAKTOR: In your opinion, do you think it's wrong for one man to
           love another man? I mean, physically.
ALICE: (Laughs) What a thing to ask...
FAKTOR: Do you ever think about what it's like to be a man, to be
           made love to by another man?
ALICE: Without a woman, you mean? You hate women, don't you?
           You're afraid of them...
FAKTOR: Does it repulse you? Arouse you? Would you like to watch?
ALICE: Is that what you do? You think we're alike?
FAKTOR: Closer than you imagine...
ALICE: How close is that?
FAKTOR: You want to know?
ALICE: Fascinated.
FAKTOR: Aren't you afraid?
ALICE: Should I be?
FAKTOR: You might be. It wouldn't be unusual.
ALICE: Habit of yours, isn't it, trying to frighten people...?
FAKTOR: I don't frighten you though, do I?
ALICE: Not me.
FAKTOR: You're different from the others...
ALICE: Others?
FAKTOR: How long has it been?
ALICE: Since when?
FAKTOR: Married. (He reaches out to take her glass, she gives it to
           him. He puts the glasses down on the table.)
ALICE: Oh. (Instinctively she glances down at her right hand. A
           wedding ring.) Long enough. It's... our anniversary
           actually. We were supposed to be...
FAKTOR: Ah, the blushing bride. Not a little girl anymore, are
           you? How time flies, eh? The happiness, fear, hope,
           uncertainty. Old before you know it. What ever became of
           our youth? Did you find life a disappointment? Seek
           comfort in unnatural acts? Do you go to the butchers to
           watch the man there cutting up the meat? Do you sniff
           it? Keep a bag of it under the bed? Feed it to your dog?
           And where _is_ the little dogsywogsy? Not at home, yet, eh?
ALICE: Why are you here?
FAKTOR: Sympathetic faculty... I sense other people's suffering.
ALICE: Really? You sense other people's... _suffering_?
FAKTOR: It pains me. It's the most terrible pain known to man.
ALICE: I don't think I know... what you mean...
FAKTOR: You will... You can help me...
ALICE: Help you?
FAKTOR: Here, for example. Give me your hand. Touch it. In my
           throat. And here, in my chest. My guts. My intestines.
           Imagine razor blades running through you, end to end,

except you're numb, perfectly numb, but you know they're there. Gashing out the insides of your pretty little body. So much pain, trying to get out. But something's in the way. Something's blocking the passage. What is it? Tell me. Tell me what it is…

ALICE: No…
FAKTOR: Help me…
ALICE: No!
FAKTOR: (Clenches his stomach grotesquely.) Can't you see the little fuckers writhing about inside me? Can't you? Open your fucking eyes! (ALICE backs away to the drinks trolley, takes the bottle of gin by the neck. Faktor slowly circles around her. The sound of Mahler softly in the background. The DWARF appears, crosses the room unnoticed. Stops when he sees ALICE.)
DWARF: (Whistles low.) Well well well, what have we got here, then?
ALICE: What…? (Sees the DWARF, flinches.)
FAKTOR: Have some self respect. What sort of a wife are you?
ALICE: (Confused.) Sorry?
DWARF: Sorry, she says.
FAKTOR: Sorry isn't good enough…
ALICE: What do you want?
FAKTOR: Want? We only want what's best for you…
ALICE: No. No. No! This isn't happening.
FAKTOR: What isn't happening?
DWARF: Maybe she doesn't feel well.
FAKTOR: We're here to look after you.
DWARF: Nothing to be afraid of.
FAKTOR: It'll pass. Everything passes.
DWARF: You're with friends.
FAKTOR: Why not lie down…
DWARF: You'll feel better. You'll be a new person…
ALICE: (Raising the bottle.) Don't you come near me! (Sudden, unexpected, FAKTOR punches ALICE hard in the stomach. She staggers back against the DWARF, who struggles to catch her under the arms. The bottle drops. The DWARF makes a series of jerking dance-like movements with ALICE's limp body, her bathrobe coming open. The music ends. Without warning, the DWARF lets go of her. She gasps for breath on the floor. Attempts to crawl. Fails. Everyone's silent. ALICE, rasping.) Help…
DARWIN: Says she wants someone to help her.
FAKTOR: Oh yes, they always do. Funny, it never ceases to be… touching.
ALICE: (Calmer.) Please… Don't hurt me…
FAKTOR: She doesn't want you to hurt her. Did you hear that?
DWARF: Eh? What's she on about? They never feel a thing. Not once you get started…
FAKTOR: Hear that sweetie? The pain won't last long. You get to the other side of it. That's what we're here for. To help you get to the other side of your pain…
ALICE: Not here. Not here… (The DWARF drags her into a sitting

position. She opens her mouth, about to scream. FAKTOR
bends down & strikes her hard across the side of the
head. She slumps, unconscious.)

FAKTOR: Beauty sleep. (FAKTOR takes hold of ALICE's legs & the
two of them carry Alice up the stairs. After a short time
the sound of a key trying a lock at stage-right. Door
opens & JAN enters, dressed in a business suit beneath a
gabardine overcoat. He caries an attaché case, identical
to the one the DWARF was carrying earlier, an umbrella &
a large bouquet of carnations. It's been raining & despite
the umbrella JAN's overcoat is wet. The bouquet is ruined.
He leaves the attaché case & umbrella by the door & walks
into the room. He has an harassed appearance. He looks
about the room, then at the flowers. Finally he decides to
leave then on the table. Notices the three glasses, one
with lipstick traces, & a cigarette butt, also with
lipstick, in the ashtray. He picks up the butt & sniffs
it. Notices the gin bottle on the floor. Looks up towards
the top of the stairs. He's about to call ALICE's name,
when the sound of moaning comes from the top of the
stairs. Instead, he picks up the gin bottle from the floor
& pours himself a drink. Drinks. Takes off his overcoat &
hangs it over the back of an armchair. Pours himself
another drink & sits, staring at his hands. Drinks.
Stares. Looks at his watch...)

JAN: (Imitating his wife's voice.) Oh! Home so early? I wasn't
expecting you, darling! <u>Not interrupting anything I
hope</u>? Oh, darling, I had a migraine. I needed to lie down.
Wished you were here to rub my head for me. Did you miss
me? (Reverting to his own voice.) What's the point?
(Drinks.) Have another drink. Why get worked up over
nothing... (Drinks. Gets up, pours himself another. raises
glass.) Good cheer! (Laughs bitterly. Drinks. His eyes rest
on the DWARF's attaché case. Pours another drink. Goes
over to attaché case. Looks down at it. Drinks. Puts glass
down. Picks up attaché case, opens it with one hand, looks
in. Long pause. Closes attaché case. Looks up blankly.
Turns towards stairs. The DWARF has re-appeared & is now
standing mid-way down the staircase watching JAN. JAN
drops the attaché case. Looks down at it. Looks back at
the DWARF. JAN backs away from the attaché case
uncertainly. The DWARF descends, walks over to attaché
case, looks at it, looks at JAN.)

DWARF: You've dropped your bag. (The DWARF picks up attaché case
& holds it out to JAN.)

JAN: It's not mine.

DWARF: Not your bag?

JAN: No, I... Where...?

DWARF: Whose bag is it then?

JAN: What? I don't... How should I know? Who...?

DWARF: Now what did mammy tell little Johnny about touching
things that don't belong to him?

JAN: Uh?

DWARF: Not touch, Johnny. Bad boy!
JAN: There's something…
DWARF: In the bag? (The DWARF puts attaché case down on front
            table.)
JAN: It's…
DWARF: What?
JAN: It's… (Recovering himself.) Look, this is my bloody house…
DWARF: Yes, we've been expecting you. Didn't want to miss you on
            your big day. Could've made more of an effort to be
            punctual though…
JAN: I'm not late.
DWARF: Not late for what?
JAN: I'm early.
DWARF: Now that all depends, doesn't it, on what you're here for.
            Everything happens, my friend, at exactly the right time
            & place. You miss the boat, time & tide wait for no man.
            The early bird gets the worm, eh? While Johnny-come-
            lately here gets the sticky finger.
JAN: Where's Alice?
DWARF: Where's…? Why, she's… lying down, John. Putting her feet
            up.
JAN: I want to see her. (JAN tries to circle around the DWARF.)
DWARF: Well she doesn't want to see you, I'm afraid, John.
JAN: What do you mean? Of course she does. I'm…
DWARF: Terribly sorry old boy. Everything in due course.
            Perhaps… later on. When the young lady's had a chance
            to… rest. Get her breath back. She's… in a very sensitive
            state. You do understand, don't you, John?
JAN: No, I… I don't… I don't like your tone…
DWARF: John. Johnny. You understand -- I can tell, because
            you're obviously a man of culture. All these books…
JAN: Never seen books before?
DWARF: We'll ignore that little remark, John, shall we? I was
            just making an observation -- that you're what people
            might call well-read. Would that be a fair thing to say,
            John? Someone who likes to poke his nose in the odd
            paperback from time to time. A little introverted, self-
            absorbed perhaps, but sensitive all the same. A sensitive
            man. Am I on the right track, John? Eh? A man who likes
            his books, eh? (Pause.) Well, I can see that, John. Anyone
            could see that. You don't need to tell me. I'd say you're a
            rather sensitive well-read man, eh?
JAN: Alright, you've made your point…
DWARF: I'd really like to know, John, what a well-read man like
            yourself thinks about the idea of intuition. I mean, to
            know something a priori, as they say…
JAN: I see…
DWARF: Do you?
JAN: Pardon?
DWARF: Do you see? (Pause) Consider, for example -- for the sake
            of our little discussion -- a crow pecking out the eyes
            of a new-born lamb, leaving it to die a slow & agonising
            death… Is it possible, in your opinion, for the lamb to

know, without any previous experience of the world, what
its fate must almost certainly be?

JAN: You can't intimidate me. (Pause) I said you can't
intimidate me.

DWARF: Do you realise, John -- do you realise what's happening
to us here, you & me? This tentative blossoming of
intimacy between two people who only a moment ago were
complete strangers? (Pause.) Have a drink.

JAN: I will if I like. It's my house. I don't need permission to
do what I like in my own house...

DWARF: That's the spirit...

JAN: Thinking of moving in, are you?

DWARF: Just a visit, John. We'll be gone before you know it...

JAN: We? (Unsteadily pouring himself another drink.) Taking
my wife with you, eh? Or do you travel in a pack? (Pause.)
That would be more appropriate, wouldn't it? Sniffing
around here, eh? The neighbourhood bitch, eh?

DWARF: That's very uncharitable towards your young wife, John.

JAN: What did you say?

DWARF: Not very civil.

JAN: And exactly what fucking business is that of yours?

DWARF: Tut-tut. Language, John. You're not behaving yourself
very well, are you? Let's start again, shall we, on a
different subject? (Pause) You seem quite fond of art...

JAN: How observant...

DWARF: There's something I've been meaning to ask, if I may -- to
gauge your opinion... I'd like to know what you think
about that piece on the wall over there. (The DWARF
points to an African mask. JAN edges around
suspiciously.) You see that? What's your opinion of that?
I mean, what do you think of it as a <u>work of art</u>? What
sort of emotion was the artist trying to convey? What
mystery of the soul did he mean to express, eh? What do
you say? What sort of a man was it who sacrificed
himself for that? Who rotted in some malarial swamp for
the sake of that piece of wood there? Who died with
nothing to show for his effort but a handful of white
man's trinkets? Who bartered his balls for the sake of
your loungeroom décor? (Pause) I bet you don't have the
first fucking idea what I'm saying, do you, you pathetic
cunt?

JAN: Say that again... (Steps back & produces a revolver from
beneath his suit jacket. Both freeze in their respective
positions at either end of the settee. After several
moments FAKTOR appears, somewhat illogically, through
the door at stage-right. He's wet from the rain. Brushes
himself off, combs back his hair with his hand. He acts as
though he's alone in the room, circles the trolley, pours
himself a drink, sits as before on the settee.)

FAKTOR: Bitch of a night for it. (Pause.) Flowers? (Picks up
flowers from the table. Sniffs. Throws them back down.)
Not what they might've been. Preservatives. Lose their
scent. (Pause.) Who cares. (Pause.) Better, though. This.

Peace & quiet. (Pause.) There once was a young man from...
wherever. (Drinks. Stretches out. Music starts. FAKTOR
straightens up suddenly. Music stops.) What the...? (Looks
around. Confused. Wipes forehead.) Bleeding hell. What's
this, eh? Hearing things already? (Pause.) It's nothing,
chum. Relax. Another drink. Stop thinking so much...
(Pours, drinks, stretches back on settee. Music
recommences. Faktor sits bolt upright. Silence.) What sort
of game's this, eh? (Looks around.) Expecting anyone? No.
No-one's here. Just you old boy. Pull yourself together.
(Pours another. Closes eyes. Leans forward, elbows on
knees, head in hands. Pause. Music -- Mahler's
Kindertotenlieder, as before. Louder. The music's coming
from the attaché case on the table. Slowly FAKTOR opens
his eyes. Looks resignedly at the attaché case. Music
continues.) Now I've seen it all. A musical bag. Where'd
that come from? I'm off my nut. Eh? Still going? Who's
this for? Knock-knock, trick or treat? (Stands &
approaches bag. Leans over. Goes to open it.) Never fuck a
gift horse in the mouth, is what I say? (Opens bag. Music
stops. Faktor looks in. Closes attaché case violently &
steps back. If possible, more confused than before. Slumps
back on settee.) Must be hallucinating. Snap out of it!
Need to get your fucking head examined. Need to... Another
drink, that's it. Hehe. The old bastard's up to his little
tricks again, eh? (Stares at attaché case, then pours a
drink, finishes it, wipes his face with both hands.) Well
come on then! Pipe up! (Pours another drink, finishes it.
Coughs. Laughs.) Idiot! Pulling my own leg. What next eh?
Take a piss. Back in a mo. (Goes to stand. Immediately the
DWARF & JAN come to life. JAN moves around to front
right of settee, still holding the gun. The DWARF circles
behind FAKTOR to his left. FAKTOR sees JAN & freezes.)
Jesus, where'd you come from?

JAN: Sit down old man.
FAKTOR: I was just going to relieve myself.
JAN: I said, <u>sit down</u>. (Pause. FAKTOR sits.)
FAKTOR: Couldn't've timed it better. Eh?
DWARF: Don't want to make a mess of your nice furniture.
FAKTOR: (Turns & sees the DWARF.) Eh? Dreaming you, too, am I?
JAN: Think this is a dream?
FAKTOR: Nightmare more like...
DWARF: Been talking to yourself again?
FAKTOR: You don't exist.
JAN: Don't exist, eh?
FAKTOR: (Rising.) Had enough of this... (The DWARF, from behind,
            wrenches him back onto the settee by the hair. FAKTOR
            roars.)
DWARF: The gentleman here asked you very politely to sit down,
            sir. Did you forget?
JAN: Tut-tut, what's this about, then? We're all friends here,
            aren't we, <u>Faktor</u>?
FAKTOR: What do you want?

JAN: That's right. Old friends. The oldest. Thought we'd drop
          by, seeing as we were in the vicinity. Out here, in the
          arsehole of nowhere. What on Earth possessed you to hole
          up in a place like this, Faktor? I would've thought you'd
          have more sense.
DWARF: Maybe he's keeping his head down. Lying low. Out of sight,
          out of mind.
JAN: But not out of <u>our</u> minds, Faktor, eh? You've never been
          too far from our thoughts, let me tell you. In fact,
          Sunny Jim here was under the impression you might've
          been expecting us.
FAKTOR: Go to hell…
DWARF: No rush, Faktor. All in good time.
JAN: Besides, you ain't fit to go anywhere, sunshine.
DWARF: You're a bleeding wreck…
JAN: Not half the man you once were, Faktor…
DWARF: Not even the shadow of a man…
JAN: Your old former self, Faktor, what ever happened to him?
          Now <u>there</u> was a sack of bones with some spine in it. A
          figure to reckon with. The shape of a man to take a real
          hiding. Now look at you.
DWARF: You're a shambles…
JAN: Pull yourself together… (FAKTOR, after a brief inner
          struggle, grabs a decanter from the trolley, empties the
          remainder of its contents down his throat, undoes his
          flies, then pisses into decanter. An expression of relief
          verging upon the beatific transforms his face.) Now, what
          <u>is</u> Alice going to say? Pissing in her pretty decanter. A
          wedding gift, no doubt…
DWARF: Someone could drink that by mistake…
JAN: Even you, Faktor. Forget yourself in a moment of
          desperation. Guzzle guzzle.
DWARF: How does he know he didn't do it already?
FAKTOR: Ahh! That's better. What? Still here? Thought you'd gone.
          Back into the ether. Not bored with yerselves yet? How
          about a drink of nice warm piss? Wet your whistle. Looks
          like you could do with one, old ghost.
JAN: What'd he just say?
DWARF: I don't know. I can't figure it out. (To FAKTOR.) My
          learned colleague would like to know what it is you just
          said…
FAKTOR: Put some colour into you… (Laughs. Picks up flowers &
          tries to shove them into decanter. Gives up.)
DWARF: He doesn't seem inclined to respond…
JAN: Not very civil of him.
DWARF: Perhaps he didn't understand the question…
FAKTOR: Uh? (Looks up.) Failing light…
JAN: Speaking for myself…
FAKTOR: Where am I?…
JAN: …I thought you phrased yourself…
FAKTOR: Unfamiliar locations…
JAN: …in an uncharacteristically clear & concise manner.
FAKTOR: Strange doorways…

DWARF: Thank you.
FAKTOR: Rooms, corridors...
DWARF: I do like to make a special effort...
FAKTOR: A face in a mirror. Stranger at the window...
DWARF: Still, it's hard to judge. Getting the right...
FAKTOR: Someone knocking in the middle of the night...
DWARF: ...words in the right order. Laying just the...
FAKTOR: A telephone...
DWARF: ...right amount of emphasis...
FAKTOR: An alarm clock...
DWARF: ...in the right places...
FAKTOR: A tap dripping...
JAN: No, I think you did...
FAKTOR: An alarm clock...
JAN: ...rather well.
FAKTOR: A fuse box...
DWARF: I appreciate that. I always...
FAKTOR: Footsteps...
DWARF: ...do appreciate it when...
FAKTOR: An alarm clock...
DWARF: ...people make constructive comments.
FAKTOR: A wake-up call...
JAN: It's the destructive...
FAKTOR: Are you awake? <u>Wakey-wakey</u>...
JAN: ...comments you can do without.
FAKTOR: Breakfast lunch or tea?
DWARF: Now isn't that so true?
FAKTOR: Easy-over or sunny-side-up?
DWARF: The number of times I've had to...
FAKTOR: Coffee? Juice?
DWARF: ...put up with unhelpful comments...
FAKTOR: Blue pill, pink pill, white pill...
JAN: Do you think he's addressing us?
FAKTOR: Yellow pill...
DWARF: It would appear doubtful...
FAKTOR: Yellow pill?
JAN: Could be talking to himself...
FAKTOR: Yellow pill.
DWARF: An idiot shouting into a maelstrom...
FAKTOR: A clear conscience is the best policy...
JAN: Should we snap him out of it?
FAKTOR: Get it off your chest...
DWARF: Why not?
FAKTOR: Better out than in...
JAN: Be my guest.
FAKTOR: (Stands, advances towards JAN, shouts.) TRICK OR TREAT?
          (The DWARF, moving behind him, kidney-punches FAKTOR
          with the gin bottle. FAKTOR goes down.)
DWARF: I think you were right.
JAN: Never doubted it.
DWARF: Strange way of extending a welcome...
JAN: One shouldn't expect too much...
DWARF: Treating his old friends like that...

JAN: Like he wouldn't treat a complete stranger...
DWARF: Like he wouldn't treat his dog...
JAN: You see what the world's coming to?
DWARF: It's a sorry sight...
JAN: We who'd've stood by through thick & thin...
DWARF: Been there when worse came to worst...
JAN: In sickness & in health...
DWARF: The brother he never had...
JAN: The father he never knew...
DWARF: Who'd've watched over him...
JAN: Held his hand at night...
DWARF: On his deathbed...
JAN: Who'd've prayed for him in his grave...
DWARF: Watered the daisies...
JAN: Poisoned the weeds...
FAKTOR: (Gasping, tries to rise, opens his mouth. Pause.) Fecking
            murderers.
DWARF: What's that, daddio? Still ticking?
JAN: Thought you might've given up the ghost on us. Listen
            dads, I hate to see you like this. It gives me pain...
DWARF: The tears of a grown man, horrible to behold...
JAN: What do you say, Jake? Kiss & make up?
FAKTOR: (Staggers to his feet. He's confused, drunk & in pain. He
            looks around. Shuffles uncertainly towards the stairway.
            The DWARF & JAN move in a flanking manoeuvre. Their
            gestures are both comical & menacing. Everything seems to
            happen in slow motion. FAKTOR turns, sees the DWARF &
            JAN, backs towards stairs. Stops. Points at them with a
            shaky finger.) I... <u>know</u> you. (Pause. Stares ahead. Eyes
            lost in the distance.) Many years... When I was... Two boys...
            Crossing a field... Home... A short-cut... Dirt track... Grass
            either side, very tall... Taller than I was... Didn't see...
            Stepped out in front of me... Didn't know what to do...
            Couldn't do anything... Smell of grass... When my old man
            came home... Too ashamed to... Afraid he'd whip me... Knew I
            was hiding something... The fear... He was very calm...
            Never raised his voice... Said one day I'd understand how
            much he loved me... Ma cried... I cried with her... Then up
            to the room... It was cold... Waited in the dark... Faint
            glow under the door... Footsteps... I could barely hear
            them... The ringing was so loud in my ears... (Half-way
            through Faktor's monologue a light appears at the top of
            the stairs. ALICE enters as before, trance-like. She stops
            halfway down.)
ALICE: John? Is that you?
FAKTOR: (Opens his mouth to speak, but makes only choked animal
            sounds, as though struggling to wake from a nightmare.
            ALICE stares at him without the slightest recognition.
            Lights fade to black. Silence. After a long pause, a
            series of knocks at the door, stage-right. Another pause.
            More knocking. Sound of a key in the lock. Lights
            gradually up. Enter ALICE & JAN, together. ALICE appears
            in a slightly crushed, taffeta evening dress, holding a

bouquet of pink carnations. JAN wears a tuxedo & is
carrying a leather attaché case. ALICE moves hesitantly
into the room, looking about. JAN, at home, places the
attaché case on the table, pours himself a drink, sits on
the sofa.)

ALICE: They _are_ expecting us, aren't they?

JAN: Expecting us? Of course they're expecting us. Seven-
thirty on the nose. Plenty of time to get to the theatre.
Why don't you go & see if anyone's upstairs.

ALICE: (Calling.) Hello! We're here! (Pause.) Hello? (Pause.) We're
here!

60

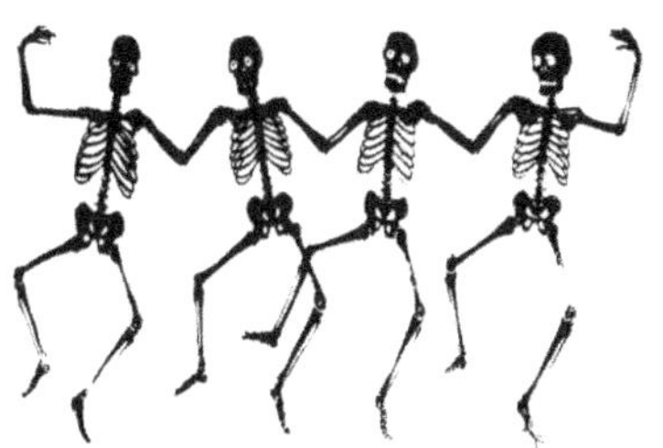

TOTENTANZ

Whitened by frost & snow, the Botanical Institute's domed herbarium took on a peculiar appearance. It looked like something carved from ice that'd slowly begun to melt & was on the verge of formlessness. Němec passed through the main gate & walked towards it down a narrow path strewn with gravel. There seemed to be no-one else around & yet he could feel himself being observed. The red eye of a security camera blinked above the door — the door itself was unlocked, so Němec entered & found himself standing in a vestibule of sorts.

The air inside was uncomfortably humid. Němec unbuttoned his jacket & loosened his collar while he waited to see if his arrival would produce any kind of effect. Apparently it didn't. He took his time looking around. Three doors led off from the vestibule: one directly into the "Cactus Room," another into an area under reconstruction, the third onto corridor that led to the "Victoria Regia" pavilion under the large dome. Distributed around the vestibule's periphery was a series of exhibits, including a scaled model of the herbarium itself beside an almost identical model of a "Pleasure Dome," originally intended (so a plaque on the wall informed him) for Rudolf II's gardens, but never constructed. A carefully designed system of mirrors allowed the viewer to see into the Pleasure Dome's minutely crafted interior by means of an adjustable periscope. In this way it was possible to view not only the internal architecture, but also each of the individual furnishings, as well as various curios from the Imperial Bestiary.

Němec peered into the periscope lens at this strange *Alice in Wonderland* construction. Like a world within a world, the veracity of its detail was uncanny — the Botanical Institute by comparison represented a mere shadow.

853

Surrounding this oddity, & filling the rest of the corridor, was a display of tropical flora of many varieties. Strangler vines dangled from platforms high up, bird of paradise, orchids & bougainvillea. At the end of the vestibule was a tall cage with three blue macaws inside it. The birds hung there by their claws, eyes pressed between the bars, grating their tongues against their beaks as Němec approached. He eyed the parrots warily. The sound followed him along the corridor & out beneath the high dome.

Faktor was waiting for him in the Victoria Regia pavilion, on the far side of an artificial pond choked with broad, fleshy lilypads & insalubrious white flowers. The water around them stirred with the mouths of ornamental carp pensively gulping the air. High up, a pair of window-cleaners in mismatched overalls could be seen through the glass, hanging suspended from ropes & pulleys like mountaineers descending the sides of a glacier. Faktor watched Němec attentively as he approached, eyes flickering beneath the brim of a black borsalino, like a moyl with a cutthroat razor in his pocket. He wore a pair of nearly opaque glasses perched halfway down his long nose. His former goatee now extended up the sides of his face into a full-beard — there were tide marks where the dye job had gone awry.

Just as he had been on the first occasion Němec had seen him, Faktor was seated at a small table with a chessboard in front of him, only this time he was leaning back in a large wicker chair, holding his pipe in his mouth & gazing at Němec across the top of it. He motioned with his eyes for Němec to take the seat opposite, which Němec did. The dwarf was nowhere to be seen — he might, for all Němec knew, have at that very moment been ransacking the Prof's apartment in search of "the key." But Němec had his doubts. He didn't believe that whatever "key" they were searching for could be found just by looking. Something told him Faktor knew this also & that "the key" was altogether elsewhere.

Except for the periodic stirring of water in the pond, the pavilion was utterly silent. Němec sat down & was about to speak when Faktor held up his hand to stop him. As on that first occasion in the winecellar, Faktor had arranged a puzzle on the chess board in front of him. This time the puzzle was a deceptively uncomplicated one. Němec was surprised to recognise it from one of his evenings with the Prof: it was Réti's two-pawn endgame. Němec sat there obediently & watched his presumed adversary rehearse the scripted moves, as if the whole thing was part of some recurring dream — the type of dream littered with symbols & coincidences of the most blatant kind.

Němec had only the vaguest interest in what message Faktor intended to impart to him by means of this little demonstration. But whereas on the occasion of their first meeting, "The flight of Napoleon from Russia to Paris" had required a complicated orchestration of many pieces (to convey its epic scope), Réti's endgame required only four, & within the space of three short moves the scenario was complete. Němec eyed Faktor impassively, waiting for some sort of explanation for his summons, but none was forthcoming. He let his attention shift to the pavilion's minutely ordered architecture — from one regulated environment to another — the enveloping edifice, the chessboard arrangement of the glass panes. Coincidence?[*]

Faktor set his pipe down on the table & stroked his beard. Němec looked at him & waited. He wondered if it was the man's intention for him to've come there just to watch him rehearse chess puzzles with himself. Faktor cleared his throat finally.

'The principle is simple,' he said, in a tone of voice only slightly tinged with irony. 'Réti was a mathematical genius, but he also appreciated the importance of psychology & perception... Look at the board... There are eight squares from side to side... And eight squares from top to bottom... And yet there are also eight squares running diagonally from one corner of the board to the other... A piece capable of moving in any one of those directions would travel the same distance, yet to the eye it appears that the diagonal is longer.'

He paused to be sure that Němec was paying attention.

'You see,' he went on, 'in chess you have a mathematical quandary... Measured by the number of squares, the sides & diagonal together describe an equilateral triangle... But they also describe a rightangled triangle... In Euclidian geometry the two are mutually exclusive. Another example of this would be if you were to draw a triangle using the meridian lines of a globe. The equator, the Greenwich meridian & the 90th parallel running through New Orleans. A triangle, the sum of whose angles would not be 180 degrees, but 270. An impossibility, it would seem.'

While elaborating all this, Faktor rearranged the pieces on the board. Two pawns, black & white, & two kings. Something about the way he spoke,

---

[*] Allegories of light & shadow, blindness & insight, irrationality & reason: the artificial life it promoted, whole vegetable micro-worlds, held in a type of abeyance, suspended animation, awaiting transmutation into other, untold states, metamorphic curiosities, evolutionary puzzles unpicked gene by gene, combined & recombined, grafted, hybridised, in the cause of the beautiful idea or some fleshy abomination. Science preening itself in a mirror. [✺]

reminded Němec of the Prof. The two might've been twins when it came to soliloquising. But Faktor's soliloquies were the more tendentious, with an air of having been scripted, prepared in advance, issued by who knew what higher powers, secret chains of command, lords & potentates, wizards, goblins, table-tapping Sibyls, fat little men with tawdry hand-me-down medals on frayed ribbon, denizens of that hidden Parallel Polis tipping their hand at the great game in which all *this* was just a sideshow, one little pawn.

'In the most simplistic terms,' Faktor leered at him, 'the objective of Réti's puzzle is for white to achieve a draw. He can do this in two ways. Prevent the capture of his own pawn, or threaten the capture of black's. On the other hand, black must prevent white's pawn from reaching the last rank & queening, while threatening to queen with his own pawn. The puzzle thus involves a dilemma, as all puzzles do, but its solution is also a dilemma. Réti saw how in order to achieve a draw white must create an impossible situation for black, so that any move whatsoever would produce a result to white's advantage. And how he achieved this was by exploiting the paradoxical logic of the diagonal.'

A brief *danse macabre* once more ensued. With unfailing certitude, Faktor demonstrated all the possible variations, the inexorable dénouement. Then again. And yet once more. On each occasion, the struggle reached the foreseen impasse. Němec wondered at this strange compulsion to repeat & re-illustrate the obvious. Until it occurred to him, that this was precisely the point …

Réti's two-pawn endgame. *White to move and draw…*

'The key, is for the white king to move as though *away* from both black's pawn & his own.'

Faktor regarded him with eyes empty of expression. Like the eyes of an interrogator who already knows the answers. Who, instead of posing questions, speaks in riddles, allegories, parables, to provoke some unconscious awakening that might transform a closed scenario into an actual struggle. To restore a fundamental relation. As if the point wasn't to prove the futility of resistance, but to draw out a confession.

'Black,' Faktor continued, 'has two options, to capture white's pawn or progress his own. But he can only move one square at a time. Each unit of time, in other words, is represented by one square, & each *square*, as it were, forms part of white's *triangle*. By exploiting the strange logic of the diagonal, white's king is able to be either equidistant in time or equidistant in space from the piece he needs to defend & the one he must threaten. Elegant, no?'

He rearranged the pieces.

'Watch again.'

Again Faktor repeated the same moves. Again Němec made a pretence of observing.

'Try as he might,' Faktor lamented, 'it's impossible for black to realise any other fate than the one white has created for him.'

The whole thing was a little like the genetic code of an extinct language. Mathematically elegant, yet in a crucial way meaningless.

Faktor arranged the pieces as they'd been at the beginning.

'Yes,' he sighed, 'poor black is caught. Decide he must — either to threaten white's pawn or advance his own. Yet whichever decision he makes, he is in fact without a choice. The end has already been determined, though it will only come into view for him when everything else has receded from the picture. The one determining factor is Time, which is always against him. It is the geometry of Destiny at work. Illusory, paradoxical, yet inescapable.'

Faktor looked up from the board.

'All things being equal,' he said, regarding Němec now with eyes fixed & hard as polished slate, 'it would seem to be rather like your own situation.'

61

PEEPHOLES TO THE INFINITE

'Did you hear the one about Buzz Aldrin falling down the steps of the Lunar Module?' He was busy filming Neil Armstrong waving the stars-&-stripes — *One small step for the Aryan Brotherhood* & all that — when he slipped & went arse-over-tit, Super-8 & all. Smashed the lens on a moonrock just when Armstrong was spouting the immortal words, & splonk! Had to re-stage the whole biz on a soundstage back of the Paramount lot, only the genius at the moviola forgot to edit-out the bit where the flag starts blowin' about in slo-mo 'cause some klutz left one of them industrial aircon units or whatever runnin' & O.J. Simpson in whiteface under the helmet with them big gel-lights in his oculars — you look real close at the finished product, you can see it ain't no whiteboy from Wapakoneta, Ohio…'

Well, & where'd that giant leap get everybody? Supposedly they used to say back in '68, *When the finger points at the moon* ☞ *the idiot looks at the finger.* The idiot was right to look at the finger. Nothing up there to see anyhow, no Coon-in-the-Proverbial, no Big Cheese, no Star-Spangled neither. On account of they landed under a giant fucking shamrock, *where none a them Commies could get a gander at what they was doin'.*[☞] *What else you s'pose they did that for? To keep outta the sunshine? Can't've been all dark, or how'd they've filmed it? Reckon they took their own movie lights up there with 'em? And half of Barrandov, too?*

'Wait a minute! Wait a minute! You ain't heard nothin' yet!'

What you wanna remember, the Bugman'd say, *is you can't always know the whole story. But sometimes you know MORE than the whole story — only you don't know which bits belong in it, and which bits don't.* Could be there weren't no astronauts at all. *Wait till them Chizinks get up there 'n' see if they find whitey's flag.* But who'd be able to say for sure the swopes went there either, except they send up a rocket & wait for it to come down again, call it *Capricornhole 11* in honour of all thirdworld mankind takin' that Big Leap Forward, hold a pressbang on the

---

☞ Like Comrade Yeltsin, *hehe.* [☞]
☞ How many kosmonauts does it take to change bullshit to fatuous light? [☞]

Yang-Tse with a coupla gooks in spacesuits been locked in a tincan somewhere outta reach for a month in Inner Mongolia & the cameras snappin' it all up, *papier-mâché* moonrocks & *Look, no Yankee flag! Hey whitey, where you been hidin' up dere?* Call the Man on all that Apollo fakeout 'n' counterfake 'n' see what he do about it. *Oh hell yeah, we was up there first, musta been some a them illegal aliens zap down 'n' stole Ol' Glory. Call the Marines! We is gonna go nuke us some Martian pootie pronto, Tonto...*

What the eggheads back in Houston call *reductio ad absurdum* or maybe it's something else, *deductione proprium culus...*?

Like that joke about the two Ivans crossing Checkpoint Charlie Bridge ogling the saints, one of them telling the other a story about a different pair of Ivans, crossing a different bridge, in Ljubljana maybe, where they've got bronze dragons instead of saints (supposed to wag their tails, them dragons, getting' a hard-on whenever once in a blue moon a virgin strays across, *hehe*), & one of them's gabbin' to the other in Rusky about these two commissars in St Petersburg this time, also crossing a bridge, if there's a bridge in St Petersburg where they have statues of dragons or saints, or even if there isn't — maybe the statues weren't important, or maybe that was the point, that there *weren't* any statues on *this* bridge but that there *should've been* (airbrushed out, airbrushed in, take yer pick) — & one of these commissars starts relating to the other commissar a story about how there was once a bridge in Danzig, etc., etc., the gist being, in the midst of all this *redux up uranus*, back there where it all started, in Golem City, the original Ivan number two, who's been listening to this whole rancid spiel so far without uttering a syllable, suddenly & with not the slightest forewarning, pulls up in front of a passing likeness of Jan Nepomuk, flashes the martyred motherfucker a bugeyed stare, screeches words to the effect that *I'm mad as hell 'n' I ain't gonna take this no more* & hurls himself over the balustrade into the river...

☾

The moon hung in the window like the pockmarked face of an idiot.

December had halfway run its course — another circle was closing — another fraction tending towards a whole, a completed instant in the revolutions of sidereal Time, Entropy & the Cosmic Conspiracy. The measure was as good as arbitrary: *three-hundred-and-sixty-five revolutions-within-a-revolution between now and that night* — the night of "the Fall…" Earth with her minion satellite revolving around the sun as ever she had, since before Copernicus & Galileo, though more crowded up there with spacejunk & satellites & talkback radio wafting out across the firmament, Heaven's vault, stripped of her mystery now.

Was there a special significance in one world's vector through space, its alignments, its eclipses, its solstices & equinoxes? What did the equations governing the brief span of years reveal, except that Time itself was a selfenclosed algebra, signifying who-knew-what?

Somewhere in the back of Němec's mind, a childish theatrical devil was muttering lines got by rote, long ago, which only now, by accident of memory, bearing down with full impetus, etc., saying — *If man, this small world of madness, considers himself to form a whole, I'm a piece of the piece that came before Everything, a piece of the obscurity that gave birth to light.*

Did the journey he'd embarked upon, therefore, begin nowhere & lead nowhere? Did it exist, like a dream, in the infinite division of time, in the marriage of unrelated instances, born of the antagonism of eternal absolutes? Of the one & the zero? The all & the nothing? Its path, ambiguous, uncertain, no longer a journey away from one location towards another, but an itinerary of placelessness: the destination could be anywhere, or nowhere. All Němec could guess was that somewhere, somehow, someone or something was expecting him: a voice from a telephone, a face in a window, a key to a door.

☾

One wrong turn leads to another.

North from the Botanical Gardens then east through the maze behind Charles Square. Resin-coloured streetlamp filaments making haloes in the mist. Trudging aimless past whiskey bars, wine bars, café bars, nonstop slot machine arcades, newsstands, pole-dance clubs, massage parlours, beer & cigarette holes-in-the-wall. Visions of a blindman outside a table-dancing joint, black glasses & white cane, ear pressed to fogged window-glass, left wrist emptying his groin. A selfrighteous drunk lecturing a pregnant kid in fake-fur jacket, spandex & vinyl boots, about the evils of money & the flesh trade: her not understanding a word of it, holding up two fingers in his face, *zwo hundert*. All the abjectness of streets like melted polystyrene the colour of floors in public urinals. The City in freezeframe after freezeframe — a type of mental stagger, thoughts always somewhere further ahead, further behind.

Eventually, wandering through the square, gazing up between branches into the swelling blackness: needlepricks of a million light-years ago & the darkness of those yet to be. *What rumour'd heavens are these?* Vast, slumbering, unmindful. As if thought-commands transmitted between synapses improbably remote. Ancient neuron pathways flaring in redshift dopplereffect on the very edge of the One True abyss: the universe & everything in it shrinking away even as it expands, to fill the void, the uncreated invisible void, prolific & devourer — *and all we're able to see, is but a haphazard constellation of fragments, the fading shimmer of a departing dream?* Little windows on eternity like hotel bedroom scenes in the movies: the peroxide *femme fatale* Alice Steinerová on the pink coverlet, naked with needle tracks up the back of her thighs. *I'm a pain killer, baby.* Or pictures of things you once-upon-a-time tried to believe in, the way perhaps she'd tried to believe.

Bits of overheard boozed-up talk in bars. The Bestiarium, The Black Bat, The Karlák, The Apollo Lounge:

'Don't be shy about it, babe…'

'Name's Mo — Mo Town.'

'Like the ocean to the rain.'

'Sure you is, mistah, like I'm a monkey's sistah…'

'Well, Mr Town…'

'I'm tellin' you babe, this deal's goin' stratospheric — everyone wants in on it — this's the BIG one, the once-in-a-lifetime opportunity, the you-be-crazy-if-you-walk-away-from-this-motherfucker opportunity. You wanna be a one-night-stand in this dump the rest of your life?'

'Yo, I don't care how you *got* here…'

'You kiddin' me?'

'This's the Big Time comin' — headliners — MTV — gold — platinum — rhine-fuckin'-stone — the whole eight inches babe. Who gives a damn about the Ape-olio anyhow? This hole's for junkies, two-time losers & stiffs. We're goin' to the moon, babe. We're goin' to the MOON…!'

'Can I have my drink now?'

☾

A circus filled the lower end of Charles Square: a pandemonium of carousels & market stalls — stalls flogging Bolshevik fur caps & papiermâché heads, wroughtiron lanterns & sacred hearts & stale cakes, pictures & plaster-cast statuettes of saints, madonnas, Baby Jesus — bottles of Vodka with brandnames like Yeltsin, Stalin, Lenin — three blue tubs in a row overflowing with sluggish water, fishmouths gulping, a trestle-table with blood-slicked chopping block guarded by a bowlheaded pagan with bloodied apron & chainmail glove sharpening a long knife, left hand showing a pair of stumps where index & middle finger used to be, while standing beside him, gloveless, a native of Třeboň gripping a fish & beating its head with a wooden truncheon, slain Polycarpus — a queue of babičkas clutching old shopping bags in front of the weighing scales, feet sinking into mud & yellow-red-grey slush.

Untouched by this mouthwatering spectacle, children dressed as winged angels & devils with red horns skipped past in the direction of the river. On a pair of stilts, St Nicholas with his bishop's mitre. A tiny devil dragging a sack of coal, crying after its mother, oblivious, beak full of steaming wine…

In a pair of high-heeled Wellingtons, a tall black transvestite, somehow familiar, appeared from nowhere, wading between the circus tents. *Could it be…?* It was. The singer from the Green Fairy cabaret, Ruby Ray no less! Němec blinked then waded straight in after her, across an obstacle-course of fairy-flossed & ketchupped muck, vomit, Glühwein, mustard-smeared paper plates, dog turds & hidden guy ropes waiting to snag the unwary & usher them to their doom. Stumbling out the other end, he found himself in front of a puppet theatre, no sign of Ruby Ray left, right or centre. A herd of tiny red-horned devils rushed in circles, chasing each other's tails. Just then a fanfare sounded & the lights of the tiny theatre went on. *The show! The show!* cried the devils, pushing towards the stage. The curtains parted. Two puppets appeared behind a piece of scenery — one tall & one very short, both equally grotesque. Despite this grotesqueness, the tall one wore angels' wings & carried a big stick, with which he beat the short one, who was naked & bore a hump on its back.

Booooo! the devils cried.

The hunchback wailed.

The angel cackled.

A timeless parable: the entire production was just the angel beating the hunchback, that was all.

The devils looked on avidly.

☾

Bored, Němec let himself drift, past the sideshows, the knife-thrower, the bearded lady, the strongman, the sharpshooters & gaping clowns, trying to lose himself, become just another face in the crowd — any face, any crowd — camouflaged among the spiralling carnival lights, the wheels-within-wheels of the mass ego, turning in the great night in which Man unmindfully dwelled. *Hey, master*! Warped carrousel music, Missa solemnis, some pop-up effigy of J.J. Ryba late of Purgatorio, *Peace be to your soul, brother*! Little skeletons on strings doing a jig. *Step right up*! the tout grinned, beckoned, a sly wink, a snickering honeyed whisper-in-the-ear, *Something in here for everyone, friend. Even you…* Hustled inside, the maze of tawdry peepshow cubicles, periscopes & spyholes, the *flagrante delicto* of naked, gaudy, fantastic, banal, horrific Nothingness, porno-graphies of Hope & Despair, the Life Before & the Life to Come, visions of gross numeric improbability, particles & vapours strewn through untold vastnesses. Midget-in-a-Funhouse stuff. Splinter in the Eye of Creation, & all that. A bug squidged between the pages of the Eternal Codex, bits of yellow&green marbled with capillary which, scrutinised through some remote Martian telescope might indeed resembles an involuted freak of untold nature, a coiled extra-dimension perhaps, perturbations in the thanatosphere, intagliated like a Siamese embryo, translucent, blackholes for eyes, milky brainstem & cortex, synaptic novae of uterus-within-uterus, swollen, distended, pre-aborted, forever about to swallow itself… *Kill it! Before it escapes and we're all doooomed*!

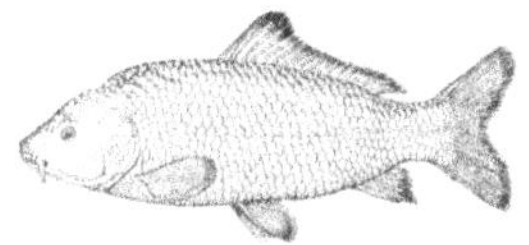

The Carp Eaters

Old Bohemian Breaded Fried Carp
1 carp (uncleaned), salt, flour, eggs, milk, breadcrumbs, vegetable oil.

Debone, remove skin and clean fish, pat dry. Dip cleaned fish filets in salt/flour mixture, then egg/milk mixture, and finally breadcrumbs. Fry slowly in hot oil till golden brown.

Old Zhiddish Gefilte Fish
1 carp (cleaned), brown cooking onions, salt, pepper, eggs, bread crumbs or matza meal, sunflower oil.

Debone and mix flesh with ingredients, including bread crumbs or matza meal, and fried onion. Shape into balls. Bake or fry slowly.

* The picking of bones on the Sabbath is prohibited by religious edict. [🐟]

☾

Without knowing how, Němec found himself back at the southwest corner of the square, where once pagan Sklavs offered hecatombs to the goddess Morana, Morena, Mara, Marmora, Marzanna, Mother of Death, Winter, Nightmares, her drownèd carp-pond effigy on that there very spot, right across from the old Mladotovský joint. *That gulping mouth in the puddles! Don't look!* He picked his way past Death's door onto the sidewalk. *Woofwoof!* A scruffy Mephistofleas, lineal descendent of Hoffman's speaking poodle, stopped & ogled him with eyes full of uncommunicated meaninglessness. It sniffed & cocked its leg at his boots, yawning, then padded off behind its master. Upon such tawdry little dramas were the great unyielding narratives of gods & men construed. Walking with the Corpse, walking with the Black Queen.

Němec sighed, crossed the road & entered the open coachway, through into the palace courtyard. At first, when he looked up, it seemed as though there were lights in Volta's window, but it was only the reflection of Christmas decorations. He pictured the psychiatrist in his office, sitting at his desk, mouth contorted behind his cigar —

'For verily Death alone shares in the allure of saviours, redeemers, miracle cures, inexhaustible energy supplies, cosmic designs & final solutions. To rectify the world by any means necessary. The interred world & the world merely dreamt.' *Between is nothing, mene mene.* 'A word. A word in place of the nothing of the world.'

For the sake of posterity's posterity. Like a hairy god pissing against the eternal lamppost. And he, Němec, unburdening himself like a deliberate, compliant idiot yet again. *I hear things and I don't hear things. Voices. Footsteps. Music. I see things that don't exist. Ghosts. Dead people…* Had he come to confess? Absolve himself once & for all, before the inevitable dénouement? Because deep down he still wanted to doubt all of it, the whole mad journey just a wild-goose chase? Telling himself there *was* no journey, merely the aftermath of having tried & failed to stuff himself into the blank space between an image & its anti-image. And the Engineer of Human Souls' predictable ironic retort —

'Man's sense of failing is only an extension of his narcissism.'

Who was he trying to kid? Digging among the ashes of a deadman, with all the doggedness of a child with a broken stick, as morbid & futile as it was inexplicable. For what? A nugget of pure truth? Some morsel of the countless mastications & digestions from occipital cortex to pancreas to duodenum? Some miraculated excretion from the Lord Almighty's private arsehole? Something already deceased & yet (incredible! astonishing!) capable, after a generous application of massage ointment & the proverbial Kiss of Life, of once again walking & speaking & thinking? That lost little amputated Homunculus Himself *you've* been searching for all these years, He who operates the projector, twitches the strings, waits patiently in the prompter's box in that miniature Cocktesian Puppet Theatre at the Rear Entrance of the Mind — *peepholes to the infinite* — glad-handing you now that He's not nailed up on that cross anymore & can kick back & enjoy the afterlife. How it was meant to be. Returning to that happy swaddled humidity of Himself like a baby golem in its goulash of bottled swamp & mud in jam jars. That putrid fishy thing ready to take *your* place in the seedy round, among all those other little lurid death-motes, re-accruing — the End driven back upon the Beginning, Möbius of the First Coming & the Last, the Becoming of the Unbecoming of the Coming-To-End-All-Comings come what may.

62

—————

SHOT / REVERSE-SHOT

You walk through the night long enough in this rat-toothed city, you arrive at an understanding — that despite everything known by daylight, there's nothing else, no other reality than these half-lit canyons, with their cave mouths blacked-out, the beasts howling in the wilderness, that gothic silhouette on the hill like an unsleeping eye that sees everything: all the maladjusted memories, little bits of History play-acting at being that neutral object of contemplation only Time makes palatable — evoking the idea of a film in which the scenery & figures barely move, a voiceover strangely disconnected from what's seen…

You'd have to forgive the audience for being disappointed, wanting the price of their ticket back, though maybe in hindsight, a different perspective, suspending judgement, the benefit of the doubt — *Here, take a seat at the bar, think it over* — knowing just about anything at all looks better after you've had a few, ready to be persuaded white's black if black's wearing those stilettos, that people's souls are more beautiful than past experience has proved, that situations don't uniformly conspire against you, that not every wall is equivalent to every other wall & other rooms also exist outside the one you're in & aren't necessarily prisons for the mind, that if you slant your eye right the light really does dance & the greyness glisten, diamantine. All very nice in theory — & as the old poet says, all theory's grey, mate — *Grau, teurer Freund, ist alle Theorie…*

Well, he'd look the part at least.

With the river at his back, Němec followed the streets in whatever order they came, wherever they went. The night could've gone on for ever & he wouldn't care: he wasn't going anywhere, there wasn't anywhere to go. Whoever was playing the big game had him by the balls, so tight any minute they'd start bleeding. Like the rest of him was bleeding, coming unstuck, splitting at the seams. He'd walked too long to feel anything, so much drink in him he was beyond being drunk. There was only the expectancy, that it all had to end soon — the time for this stale little melodrama was running out — he'd seen enough of it already, from every angle. He could take it apart & put it back together piece-by-piece & it still wouldn't have any rhyme or reason. He could walk the streets in his sleep. He'd been doing it for months.

Němec seemed to remember the snow falling. An orange streetlight & the snow falling, very slowly, as if it were only falling in his head, the way in dreams everything moves with excruciating slowness — the footfall along the corridor, the bounding steps, the object you want desperately to get hold of just out of reach, hanging there, like a child's balloon. Then change scenes: from snow to faintly drifting nuclear winter fallout — ambient doomsday montage of disintegrated cityscapes, Dresden, Pompeii, Nagasaki — duck & cover TV mantras — schoolkids pissing themselves under classroom desks, giggling, farting, scratching graffiti (*Jan woz here* — *For god head call Alička 221619240*), groping, crying, falling asleep — knowing the rest of their lives must inexorably tend to that assured mutual desolation.

Yeah, they programmed you well, you're a real survivor, kiddo…

And was he ever that child with the balloon? In a park, the music of a carousel, snow falling through naked tree branches, a red balloon floating in the air tied to a string. *And there's me*! The kid in the black suit, a midget homunculus of himself, running after the balloon with slow heavy steps, never quite able to reach it, till it rises on a gust & drifts over the treetops, the river, the spires, a red dot grown smaller & smaller, gone forever. Whatever that child version of him felt watching it go was only a fleeting emotion, because already are standing behind him — & behind them, where their footprints lead back across the snow, a black Mercedes with another man sitting in it — a man with a beard whose eyes glitter like a pair of golden keys…

Got a smoke, love?

Some doxy in the shadows, purring, alleycat eyes, was busy feeling for his pockets. Němec jerked away. *Wake up*! It was still snowing. Feet wet, shoe soles worn through. *It's cold, it'll grow colder.* He could feel the steel pins in his knee — a creaking of the joints like a rusty gate — bits of metal in his head tuning into the frequencies, numbers on the ether. *Achtung*! *Neun neun fünf neun zwo. Neun neun fünf neun zwo. Achtung*! He turned the corner, it was darker but there was a streetlamp at the end of the block. *Always hope, eh?* Past it & he'd be home safe. *Home safe.* Even the sound of it… The scaffolds, looming out of the swirling snow. Black shapes flapping in the wind.

Flap! *Flap*! *Flap*!

It was only once he'd navigated the mess the workmen'd left behind in the courtyard that Němec could see the caretaker's door was ajar. There didn't seem to be any point knocking. The green parrot stared out at him from the window, eye stuck to the glass, unmoving. The devious creature made no sound when he pushed the door open & stepped inside. The reason was obvious. Someone had shot a hole in it — there was blood with bits of feather in it all up the wall, the perch wedged under the windowsill with the bird's head sticking up like it was on sentry duty. It looked like it'd been that way for days, turned stiff in the cold, rigor mortis, eye gone dim. There was something faintly ridiculous about it sitting there like that, like a stuffed toy with the stuffing blown out of it, grinning at him, its black tongue between its beak, caked with dried puke.

They say parrots have long memories. *I bet you could've told them a pretty story, eh, Polly?* Someone had knocked over the kitchen table. Broken china & tea leaves littered the floor. A smashed jar of uncandied honey. A cracked rhinestone broach. Whoever it was must've turned up right when the old bird was reading her fortune. *Wonder if she saw it coming…* Further inside the flat there was a smell of cinders hanging in the air, but no smoke. The glowing blue eye of the large old woodframed Tesla faintly hissed. Němec switched it off. Now the only sound in the place was of the soles of his shoes on linoleum. There was a bed-sit out the back & that was all, a fairly Spartan existence for our Severínová. Wardrobe virtually bare, drawers containing only knickknacks: pencils, blank sheets of blue letter-paper, tweezers, a magnifying glass, eyedrops, balls of yarn, knitting needles, a pattern book & a photo album with all the pictures torn out. As if, for whatever reason, the woman had been determined to leave behind only the minimum possible trace.

Back in the kitchen, he went through the drawers & cupboards again looking for what wasn't there to be found. Whoever they were, they'd gone to the effort of wiping their shoes at the door — but the footprints could still be seen, just faintly, where the spilt Yunan tea had dried & the honey had set. There would've been two of them: they would've come in through the door while the caretaker was busy gazing into her cup — they wouldn't't've been expecting the parrot, though — it would've kicked up its usual fuss, maybe gone for one of them with its beak, & so they popped it — then what happened? Maybe they knocked Severínová on the head & put her in a bag — but why? Why go to the trouble of kidnapping an old babička with virtually nothing to her name? And if they'd simply wanted to do her in, why steal the body?

Němec kept looking. There was a pile of ashes lying in the grate of the old iron stove, the source of the cinder smell. He reached in & got his hands dirty sifting through fine leaves of carbonised paper. He tried gently lifting a piece out but it disintegrated between his fingers. Getting an idea he went back out to the bed-sit & found the tweezers & magnifying glass, then tried again: no matter how delicately he worked, there were only fragments — at best, bits of printed type, black on black, which could've said anything. But by digging with the tweezers he had more luck. Severínová must've been hoping to hide it, because it was inside a folded square of tinfoil at the back of the grate: the foil was black with charcoal, but the photograph it contained barely showed a blemish.

At first Němec wasn't sure he was seeing clearly & then he was. At first he figured it must've been Alice Steinerová, in one of those movie stills. *The Teratologists.* Though how the hell it could've got into the caretaker's fireplace was something else. But that hardly mattered, because it wasn't. Staring out at him from the photograph was the face of Elsbeth von N____. It was an almost identical photograph to the one the caretaker had given him months ago, the one of the Prof sitting at a table on the Barrandov Terraces, the one Němec left beside the Old Man's urn at Olšanská — except that in the place where the Prof'd been sitting in the other photo there was now an empty chair & where before there'd been an empty chair Elsbeth von N____ was now sitting. She was much younger, but not as young as you'd expect. Her features were exceptionally fine, striking even, severe. Her hair was cut very short, like Alice Steinerová's. And unlike the Prof in the first picture, Elsbeth von N____ was gazing intently *past* the lens of the camera, instead of *at* it.

But it wasn't what she might've been looking *at* that bothered Němec. What bothered him was the fact that Elsbeth von N____ appeared to be dressed in a man's grey military uniform, deathshead waffenfarbe stitched on the left lapel like a tiny Karl Lagerfeld mask. Apart from that little anomaly, the same chessboard was sitting on the table. As in the first photograph, the board showed the position at the end of a game: white's king in checkmate, but even clearer now was the fact that both of black's bishops were positioned on white squares. Somehow neither the Prof nor Elsbeth von N____ seemed to've noticed. Or else one of them had accidentally disturbed the arrangement (getting up from the table, perhaps)? Or maybe it'd been intended that way: some kind of drama concealed in a calculated error — a code, a sign, a riddle addressed to the person behind the camera, or someone else, someone in the future — someone who was expected to look at that photograph & recognise the specific significance of one of black's bishops being *out of place.*[*]

In this second picture, Elsbeth von N_____ was resting one of her hands on an attaché case lying open on the adjacent chair. A moment earlier, or a moment later, she & the Prof might've been in conversation. He might've been showing her something, as was his habit, on the board, or from the attaché. There might've been a third party, too. The whole thing might even've been staged as some kind of fancy-dress tableau, in questionable taste admittedly, but... Whatever it was, something about the occasion had demanded a photograph: one of them had brought a camera — perhaps they'd even brought the camera for the express purpose of recording their terrace rendezvous, recording *that* particular scene, that *particular* tableau. Except they hadn't recorded a rendezvous. In neither photograph did the two subjects appear together, but only separately. Could there've been yet another picture, snapped by somebody else — a person seated at a neighbouring table perhaps, or (was there a reason for her omission?) Alžběta Hájková, whose absence might be construed as more than a little conspicuous? A third picture, in which they were both, the Prof & Elsbeth von N_____, in the same frame?

Absorbed in the drama of the photograph, Němec almost failed to register the date pencilled on the back, in the lower right-hand corner. June, 1942. He stared at it. It seemed too fantastic, ridiculous, absurd. Could *this* have had something to do with the Prof's secret? A secret the caretaker had guarded, till now, loyal to the end? But why now? Then a different thought occurred to Němec: Was the picture *real*, or was it something else — something that only *potentially* existed, once, as a kind of hypothesis, acted-out in advance yet ultimately unrealised, cancelled-out — a perturbation merely, haunting the present like a ghost? Or was he, Němec, still deceiving himself? Was the image itself a deception & not at all what it seemed? Němec kept studying the photograph, the face, the uniform, the date. He couldn't stop wondering why Severínová had lied? It was obvious, of course, why she lied. But why hold onto that picture? Right up to the end. And even then she'd tried to protect it. Who was she hiding it *from*? And who was she hiding it *for*? Why had she kept the photograph at all? What did Elsbeth von N_____ mean to *her*?

Němec switched off the light & pulled the door closed behind him, the dead parrot still there with its eye frozen to the window. He stopped & listened.

---

[*] But which one? [✋]

There was only the sound of the snow falling very faintly now. Somehow he knew that in the meaning of the photograph lay the key to something important. Retreating back upstairs to the sanctuary of the hidden room, he sat for a long time, taking stock. The Nazi manuscript was on the desk where he'd left it, the Reich eagle, trying to tell him something, not by ciphered runes but by something obvious & overlooked.

Němec lay the photo on the desk & went over it again with a magnifying glass: the image bulged up at him in facets as he swept the glass back & forth looking for clues. And at last it began to dawn on him: What did he know about Elsbeth von N____, except that he'd seen her once in the flesh & once before in a photograph…? Staring at the face of the ⚡ officer in the picture, a very obvious fact presented itself. It should've been obvious from the very start, from the moment the Prof first mentioned Kircher's letter. How everything about him & it — everything Němec had accepted as being the case — was in actuality supported by nothing but a fabric of supposition & circumstance. He wanted to put the Prof somehow into that picture, his face there beside the face he was staring at, to bridge that gap. The chessboard, the Nazi uniform, the attaché case (just like the one sitting there, in the room he was in now, beside the desk, identical to it), the people in the background, the telltale date pencilled on the back making nonsense of chronology. And if the Prof didn't belong in that picture, was it because he was never there?

Perhaps, Němec thought, adding the situation up, there was still a chance he could still get past whoever might be down on the street waiting for him — slip back out unnoticed, make one last foray. To retrieve the one piece of the puzzle that might shed light on the mystery. He took his hat, stuffed the photograph in his jacket pocket, then out through the cupboard into the hall, down the stairs, past the scaffolds. No-one tried to stop him.

Just click your heels & think of…

The cemetery looked different at night — the lights of the City reflecting off the snow, the clouds like a glowing shroud making the trees skeleton-thin, their branches meshed-together like spiderwebs against the sky… The nighttram's bell faded as the tram heaved off past the freight terminal towards the valley. A glacial wind blew along the wide unsheltered boulevard, the snow underfoot turning to ice. Němec kept close to the cemetery wall, groping for the gate, like a blindman with a stick. It was a small gate with a Judas-hole & with an effort he supposed he'd able to climb it without breaking his neck. But he must've fainted from the pain, heaving himself over, because the next thing he was lying on a mound of snow & mulched leaves, but still in one piece.

For a moment he experienced that familiar thigh-tingling sense of déjà vu, seeing in his mind-of-minds the Old Man in brown suit paring his fingernails. It passed. Somewhere an undertaker's mutt growled in its sleep — nearby or further off, it was impossible to tell. Němec made his way through the labyrinth of headstones to the alcoved wall where the urns stood in tiers like boxes at an opera — the most patient of all audiences, places booked for the last show in the world. They'd be waiting a while yet, he thought, & if it ever came, it'd be over before they knew it.

The face watching out at him from behind the square window was still enough like the Prof's. Němec had to smash the glass to retrieve the picture & prayed the deadman would forgive me the trespass. In the gloom of the cemetery, by the wall, under the glow of a streetlamp, he pulled out the photo of Elsbeth von N____ & held it up beside the Prof, trying to get the two images into the same focus, like disjointed Siamese twins. Side-by-side, they somehow failed to connect. The backgrounds were at odds, as if a key element had been shifted. The camera position in the second picture was further to the right, more elevated, the river clearly visible below the terraces, yet something about the scenery itself had been *adjusted*, or left out, or avoided — something that couldn't be shown.

Like the date on the back of the first picture, the one with the Prof. A "6" superimposed on the "2," almost but not entirely obliterating it — something Němec had entirely failed to twig before — making it the annus horribilis of 1942 & not that holiday in the foothills of state socialism four years hence. Was someone trying to buy time? (Anyone we know?) Němec put the two photographs together again, like a shot/reverse-shot in a film that was out of sync. But it wasn't only the angles that didn't match: placed next to each other, the faces, also, seemed to form a contradiction: "the Prof" on the left, "Elsbeth von N____" on the right (or he on her right & she on his left). But what Němec took for contradiction was possibly nothing more than disillusionment. Like the true believers of the Revolution when their time came to be strung up. How did a person live with their own disbelief?

Under the dim streetlight Němec tried to change "the Prof" back into himself. Perhaps it was the wind that did it, a brief flare of the streetlight between shifting branches, only slightly, but enough — enough to see what he'd so far failed to see. For too long he'd been making his own pact with the Devil, seduced by details, becoming blind to the bigger picture. What the movement of the light showed him was the scenario for a very different story than the one he'd been telling himself. All he needed now was to write it, for everything to fall into place, or nearly into place. And only nearly everything. It might even have a happy ending, if he ever got that far.

63

THE CASE OF ELDRICH VON N____

A man can have so little liking for himself that people come to detest him.

Right at this moment, Tomáš Hájek, Snr. [T.H.] a.k.a. Josef Kulička, junior archivist at the State Literary Archive situated on the premises of Strahov Monastery, is thinking precisely this — wishing he was as far from where he presently is as humanly possible: in Tahiti, for example, the South Pole, or the Moon.

It's been eight months since that nut Heydrich took von Neurath's job as Reichsprotektor (acting) & for the last six of them T.H. has felt like he's been losing his marbles. His assumed identity serves a double purpose, to protect himself on the one hand against charges of collaboration by the partisan underground, & on the other to throw the Gestapo off his scent on the offchance someone gets wise to his little blackmarket sideline in literary antiquities.

Recently T.H.'s conscience has been troubling him more than usual, on account of this Heydrich, who's had most of his (Kulička's) colleagues tortured & shot on account of some private obsession to get his hands on the lost alchemical library of Rudolf II & one volume in particular, the Roger Bacon manuscript, socalled, the original (but not copy) of which, unbeknownst to Heydrich (but not to T.H.), is at that moment residing in a safe deposit box at the First Bank of America, Manhattan branch, registered to the widow of one W.M. Voynich. Kulička's on the Gestapo's most-wanted list, but so far T.H. has had the advantage: he knows Josef Kulička doesn't exist, while the Gestapo (he thinks) don't yet know *he* exists.

The idea had come from Eldrich von N____: they'd known each other since kindergarten. Kulička is T.H.'s insurance policy & a convenient cover for Eldrich von N____'s scam-mongering: *his* insurance policy is that he's managed, through old Silesian family connections, to get himself a junior commission at the Ministry of Inertia, complete with desk, pen-set & tailored grey ⚡ uniform. When he's not busy supplying the "enemy" with morale-defeating celeb gossip about Goebbels' latest Barrandov blockbuster (photo opps with all the big names —

Moravec, the Havels, Goebbels' fat wife — having quite the time of it, he is) & generally hobnobbing away from the office, Eldrich von N____, self-styled baron-in-waiting ever since his father's been safely ensconced in a sanatorium on Lake Geneva, moonlights (a fact not unknown to his superiors, some of them his best customers) as an agent for the Golem City Book Emporium — *Buchstabengetreu!* — earning fat commissions in the antiques trade.

Business is good. In fact, from where Eldrich von N____ is sitting, so to speak, it couldn't be better. Together with T.H. — a graduate of the historical restoration programme at the National Visual Arts Academy — he's put together a nice little sideline in lesser-known rare editions, all fakes of course, sold at considerable profit to unsuspecting collectors: everything from Gutenberg psalm books to the works of that lunatic Englishman, William Blake, sometimes even the odd papyrus from the 2nd Intermediate. They've been at it for years, even before Munich, taking regular jaunts up to Berlin with autograph copies of everything from Schiller to Sharkspier, milking the market in cultural *Anmaßung.*

It was Eldrich von N____ who'd first conceived the scam of flogging a copy of the Bacon Manuscript to a high-ranking Nazi mystagogue — Rosenberg possibly — circulating rumours to the effect that a long-lost Teutonic ur-text had recently come to light… Which wasn't a *new* idea admittedly, but it was precisely the existence of older, similar rumours, that gave their little scheme all the credence it required. So as soon as that colossal narcissist & arch-sucker, ᛋᛋ-Obergruppenführer Heydrich, started honing his interrogation regime along those self-same lines (*Wo ist das Buch, du Abschaum?!*), Eldrich von N____ *knew* he had his man.

Right now, though, T.H. — or Josef K, as his co-conspirator insists on calling him — is entertaining serious doubts. For one, he's certain he's been watched since his last foray up to the Monastery three days ago, to collect the vellum binding for the bogus Manuscript. The whole thing's been put together piecemeal over a period of years (no small undertaking) in a workshop they'd rigged up for this & other purposes in the Archive's basement — a disused janitor's closet under a stairway in the south wing whose door had been plastered over & sometimes lacked the necessary ventilation, causing T.H. no end of trouble keeping his head straight. If it weren't for the two obvious-looking plainclothes detectives sitting a few tables away, he'd probably tell himself he was imagining things. S.D. most likely — *Sicherheitsdienst* — Heydrich's personal goon squad.

Nervously T.H. shifts the attaché case containing the manuscript, completed only that morning — the hundred-odd pages handstitched into the binding with vintage gutstring (got at a discount from a Zhiddish violin-maker who'd just been issued a deportation order) — to the chair on his left &, for the time being at least, out of sight. In the opposite chair, Eldrich von N____ is sipping from a cup of coffee, the restaurant on the Barrandov Terraces being the only place in town you could still get a really decent brew, & pondering his next move in the chess game they've been making a pretence at for the last half-hour: by rights he ought to be losing, but since the twelfth move things have been unexpectedly looking up — he puts it down to the fact that his opponent has all the appearance of someone who hasn't slept in a week: black around the eyes, hollow cheeks, a little too closely shaven under the chin. Oddly, the effect is to make him (T.H.) look younger than he actually is. *Probably been losing weight, too.*

He (T.H.) is playing a characteristic Queen's Gambit, following the orthodox line, while Eldrich von N____ is struggling to remember the proper combination of moves that constitute the usually innocuous Vienna Game: pawn to king four... knight to king's bishop three... pawn to queen four (!)... & afterwards? White's pawn-exchange tilts the game towards an open paradox neither player seems aware of, distracted as they each are by concerns of a different order — terms like "classical" & "hypermodern" have no currency here, it's all gut-instinct & joining-the-dots — T.H. blundering his king into an impossible position just as one of the undercover cops gets up from his table & heads across the terrace into the restaurant, probably to take a piss but who knows, could be making a phone call to HQ: *We've got your man right out in the open. He's a sitting duck. Want us to bring him in?* Even Eldrich von N____ can see there's a checkmate coming in the next move.

The cop's on his way back to the table when T.H. suddenly blurts out —

'D'you make the two SiPo stooges over there by the railing?'

Eldrich von N____ looks up from the board at his companion as if he's just said something incomprehensibly stupid, like *Do Martians have spots on their tails?* For one frightening moment T.H., who's already afraid his face reads like a guilty conscience displayed in broad daylight, thinks his companion might even be in on it — *The whole thing's a frame-up!* — but then he (Eldrich von N____) points at the board & in a voice that almost seems to doubt itself says —

'Looks like you're fucked, mate.'

'No, I mean the cops, *over there*, the ones in the coats, by the balustrade — they've been watching us for the last half-hour at least. *Don't look at them!* Here,' T.H. says, reaching into the attaché case & sliding out a Fex 127, 'take a picture.'

Just then a shout goes up from below the terrace: it's the annual Youth

Sports Festival taking place in the open-air Barrandov swimming pool. Women's 400m backstroke most probably — always a fave with the terrace oglers. The cops, slow on the drawer, turn their heads well after the starter's gun's sent eight bathing beauties arching away from the blocks. Eldrich von N____, who's understood only that his friend wants his photo taken, duly gets up & snaps a shot from a few steps back, cropping the two plainclothesmen at shoulder height so all that can be seen of them is their coats — T.H. in the foreground with the undeniable proof of his recent blunder visible for all to see on the chessboard in front of him.

The cops are still peering over the balustrade when T.H. takes his turn with the camera. They're elbowing each other in the ribs — *Core, get a load of that!* — the girl in lane three, white swimsuit a little on the sheer side & *Wouldn't mind trying a bit of the old breaststroke with her, eh Fritzl?* It's just as they turn their heads — a weirdly synchronous movement — towards where he'd been sitting a moment ago that T.H. presses down with index finger on the round metal button. *Snap!* When the aperture clicks back, he can still see them (the cops), frozen in the viewfinder: Eldrich von N____ in his ridiculous Oberst's uniform suppressing a private gloat over the scene of carnage depicted on the board. Though, for the record, neither appears to notice the odd disposition of black's bishops.

The question preoccupying T.H. is whether or not the cops know who *he* is, or if Eldrich's the one who's blown it, or if their being there is nothing but pure coincidence? He'll get the photos developed & see if Eldrich can have the goons checked out, somehow, on the quiet, use one of his contacts down at Gestapo HQ. But no sooner has he laid the camera on the table than he notices something very peculiar about Eldrich von N____'s face: the expression reminds him of a child who's just dropped an icecream cone & is still factoring the details of the situation before bursting into tears. It's this expression that causes T.H. to glance down, half expecting to find a mushy ball of lemon sorbet melting on the chessboard — but instead it's black's bishops, both of them on white squares.

Were it not for the fact that T.H. is unable to resist casting a grinning eye at his opponent, he undoubtedly would've registered the two SiPo men now moving away from their table & the view afforded over the balustrade, coming directly towards him, straightening their coats in unison as though they'd rehearsed that particular touch countless times, perhaps on some casting agent's advice, for who's to tell they're both not out-of-work thespians on the make? After all, this *is* Barrandov, home of the Entertainment Industry.

Yet none of this has a chance to occur to T.H., who's still grinning but dimly aware that not only is his companion *not* amused, he's not even looking at him — *Probably in a huff!* he thinks, losing like that on a technicality, but no, his expression's exactly as it was a moment ago, *And he's looking at something directly behind me…?*

It's at precisely this moment that a tap comes on T.H.'s shoulder. Only now does he see the two goons standing on either side of Eldrich von N____ & that one of them's reaching for the attaché case left lying on the chair. A voice he doesn't recognise says something — the man it belongs to, the man who's just tapped him on the shoulder, has an air of impatience that suggests he's more familiar with giving orders than taking them.

Turning, T.H. is finally able to appreciate the meaning of Eldrich von N____'s expression. If the voice is unfamiliar, the face isn't, for the man now standing before him is none other than Horst Böhme, SS-Standartenführer, notorious owner of a red open-top Tatra sports car & commander of the City's Keystone Cop Brigade.

'*So leid*, Herr Oberst,' addressing Eldrich von N____, who's knocked his chair over trying to get up fast enough & stand to attention, 'I'm afraid your' (voice charged now with the full weight of Saxon innuendo) '*companion* will not be at liberty to remain for the customary revenge match' (indicating the board), 'which would in any case appear superfluous. You'd be better advised in future, Herr Oberst, to keep the company of your fellow officers. Doubtless you're unaware, but your companion here, this Mr *Kulička*, is in fact a notorious criminal & *enemy of the Reich*. In view of which, I expect you in my office at eight tomorrow morning, sharpish, with a full written account of all your dealings with this person — am I understood?'

'Ja wohl! Herr Standartenführer!'

T.H. can hear the snap of Eldrich von N____'s bootheels, picturing him, right arm chopping the air in that absurd salute, like a ham-actor trying a little too hard to convince himself of his own role in this sham, struggling not to choke on his lines, gone completely pale by now he'd imagine. Thinking this, is probably the only thing that keeps T.H. from fainting right there on the spot — nerves in a state of suspended animation, for the time being at least but surely that won't last — as the two goons get their paws under each of his arms ready to frogmarch him across the terrace in full view of the paying public. *Plenty of excitement here today, folks.* He daren't glance back & only hopes Eldrich's had the presence of mind to pocket the camera, if only for posterity's sake…

64

LA CHUTE

By the clocks it was almost four a.m. — nothing stirred, like a street with the soundtrack switched off. Approached from the opposite side, the house on Jánský Vršek had all the appearance of having been long abandoned — streetlamps casting the workers' scaffolds in stark chiaroscuro: the eerie brightness of the snow against the overhanging gloom — the black holes where the upper windows used to be — the lower windows boarded-up with graffitied squares of plywood. Němec searched for signs of whoever might be waiting — something out of place, footprints, cigarette butts — there was nothing, they were playing it very subtle. It wouldn't've mattered, there were no options left anyhow — an endgame already calculated to logarithmic depths — the clock was running & time was running out — it was pointless to hesitate any longer.*

In the courtyard, piles of terracotta stood in snow-capped ziggurats, from where the workmen had begun hauling down the roof, section by section — scaffolds mounted around the Tower, blotting most of it out, up above the ramparts — tarpaulins of black plastic sagging under a weight of ice & snow. Down the adjoining wall a long chute like an articulated backbone hung with its tail planted in a skip half-full of snow & rubble, broken bits of things, debris from a smashed higher world. A dead rat protruded from between a pair of table legs, a turn-key stuck in its back. Němec wound the key-end with an effort & watched the sodden snout with its teeth & glass eyes writhe about, unable to free itself. Inside the stairwell, half-frozen mud lay thick across the floor & the steps leading down to the cellar gate. Bags of cement had been stacked four-deep behind a diesel generator, a compressor, a crusted cement mixer. They blocked the way, more weight than one man could shift. Němec felt for the cellar key in his trouser pocket, the tag still hanging from it, useless now. How would he get back? Some essential exigency demanding a different solution & not the obvious one? He'd had it with riddles. Besides, it was just a matter of time now before

---

* What Faktor had been at conspicuous pains to persuade him, that all the existing paths were already insufficient? [✋]

they had the whole set disassembled, right down to the foundations, the sub-foundations & the sub-sub-foundations — all that was once hidden, immodestly exposed to the light.

There was no choice but to try & remake the previous moves in a different combination. Catch the opposition sleeping. Or if not remake, then as far as possible transpose along a contrary line — pursue the diagonal by forgoing the vertical — shortcircuit the traps. *Everything was misconceived at the beginning, just like you were, eh kiddo? Maybe that was the beauty of it.* The wind moaned in the Tower. A cough. A splutter. Flap of wing. The ghosts would soon be obliged to do without their familiar habitat.

Climbing the stairs was like running an obstacle course of buckets, wooden cases, workmen's tools, unhinged doors & doorframes, disassembled bits of railing. Feeling along the hall, crunch of debris underfoot — braille of dead lightswitch — for a long time standing on the threshold of the room that once had been the Old Man's bureau, now barely a room even, contemplating, so to speak, this Last End & associated items: what the two photographs meant — the caretaker's abduction — the sense of something closing-in — a sudden, precipitous, concerted action. How to concede without giving-in? To whom the final, Pyrrhic victory? Somewhere in his Purgatorio, the antique alchemist, massaging his insteps through toe-jam crusted stocking-socks, might well be grinning, a borrowed brogue of *Didn't I tell you so?* Ironic gleam in that eye's wink. *Take it from me, kiddo, best plan's to look before you leap. Or if that's out of the question, leap like a sonofabitch and don't look back.*

The workmen had been selective in their dismantling, suggestive of some kind of system at work: a dozen windowframes worth scavenging stood against the wall, great holes where the windows used to be, some with billowing sheets of black plastic, others bare, snowflakes drifting in to settle on the stripped-back floor. Planks of fibreboard had been arranged in a patchwork over the exposed beams, circumnavigating a heap of rubbish erected pyramid-fashion in the middle of the room. It seemed wrong to leave it like that. Němec tried one last time to conjure the deadman's memory — sitting, as so often he'd seen him, in an armchair beside his desk, preparing his thoughts, turning his drink in his hand, about to draw some unlikely analogy from ordinary things: a simple chesspiece, for example, reaching out & plucking a black knight from the board, describing, as if to a child — three squares down or up to one across, three across to one down or up — a horse jumping over, a ghost passing through — a piece pinned by two knights or two pieces by one... *Der schwarze Reiter.*

To complete the picture, Němec hauled the recordplayer out into the crepuscular nonlight of this anteroom, balancing it atop the mound of rubble — pill jars, brandy bottles, electrical wires, gas pipes, radiator grills, squares of parquet, smashed tiles, wall cabinets, doors, door jambs, a stainless steel sink with all the plumbing still attached, the Prof's bathtub like some allegorical lifeboat tipped on its side... It had all the appearance of a shrine buried in a middenheap, with its squat machine-idol perched there, surveying a wilderness of shattered masonry — an archaeologist's trophy in the jungle, emerging from the roots & undergrowth, wind echoing among the stones as if the godhead wished to speak but unable to merely wailed or sometimes sang... The workmen had left an extension cable they'd run up from the mains downstairs: he plugged the recordplayer in & put on a Berlin Philharmonic recording of Mahler's "Resurrection" in C^m with the Klimt on the cover, Rafael Kubelik conducting, Norma Procter contralto. Those funereal violins! Those aggrieved cellos!

Outside, the workmen were beginning to arrive. Above the strains of Mahler's symphony Němec could hear their voices echoing in the stairwell — the stomping of boots on the steps. Soon the jackhammers would begin again tearing up the road in front of the house, while men with black masks would be shovelling tarmac from a brazier, huge steel alembics, fumes & bellows, sealing-over the trenches only recently excavated — one side digging while the other filled-in, like opposing teams in a game with no apparent purpose. Behind the scaffolding, the rooftops were like white & black squares, lopsided under shadows belonging neither to day nor night. From the courtyard, a *whoosh!* of something in mid-collapse — sheets of snow coming down from the rooftop — then the sound of the giant funnel, like an articulated windpipe, belching debris, grey dust drifting in from the stairs — a conjurer's ghost changing shape in the spectral half-light, suffusing the air.

Between the roar & crash of debris being fed down the funnel, echoes of heavy boot-tread in the attic above — ceiling plaster cracked, sifting down with each hobnailed stomp. There they were, disposing of all the evidence — a demolition crew sent to obliterate every last trace of something that'd never quite existed in any case. Could Faktor's hidden hand be detected in all this? Another of his pedantic little games, where one player's moves are calculated to undo the probabilities implied in the other's — thwarting plans as yet unrealised, barely formulated, unravelling the gambit before it's been offered, tying up loose ends well before the end's in sight, punching holes in defences still unbuilt, pulling the rug out from under grand schemes that were never more than a far-off glimmer of hope, turning the clock back to cancel each & every one of your moves before you've even made them, like a meticulously deconstructed falsehood.

For all Němec knew, it was a pattern being repeated all over the City — like the wine cellar on Jilská Street, the cabaret on the Island, the archives at the Strahov Monastery — where else? what else? who else? The Bugman, Volta, Alice Steinerová? What if, at this very moment, they too were being made to disappear, taken out of the script, buried in a drawer in an office with no name, for all intents & purposes dead — as dead as the old lady's parrot?

And all this just for your sake, kiddo? You'll tell yourself next they're waiting for you to leave, before packing up the last of the show, put it all away in boxes somewhere for next time — allowing you to find a bit of manoeuvring space... to put things to rights, get it over and done with, the way once-upon-a-time they'd leave a man alone in a room with a loaded pistol, one shot only, because that's all he'd need. Real considerate of them, wouldn't you say? Gone to a lot of trouble over a complete nobody, eh? Well, like the wiseguys always say, beggars can't be choosers...

But even as he was thinking it, the walls echoed with the work of demolition on all sides. How long before they gutted the entire house in a mad orgy of erasure, with just the façade left standing — for authenticity's sake — flogged-off to developers, KELLEY'S TOWER HOTEL, already at work on their plans for a multistorey underground carpark, indoor swimming pool, sauna, recreation area, tropical fishpond in the lobby, restaurant & giftshop & elevator up to the observation deck, five-star panorama, glass-ceiling, luxury, exclusive, all modcons? *The world just keeps getting better all the time, haven't you noticed?*

The symphony had reached its final movement by the time Němec retreated for good to the hidden room, the monk's cell, the captive's closet, to prepare a last stand.

> *Aufersteh'n, ja aufersteh'm*
> *Wirst du, Mein Staub,*
> *Nach kurzer Ruh'!*
> *Unsterblich Leben! Unsterblich Leben*
> *wird der dich rief dir geben!*[*]

In the pitch dark the space seemed huge, though all he needed was to reach out on either side to feel the walls. He struck a match & by the dull flicker of candlelight set about barricading the entrance with the little at hand: a writing

---

* "From dust till dung [sic], the Golem rides again..." [✋]

desk & other miscellaneous. Temporary measures. Still the effort overwhelmed him & he sank into the cot-bed conscious only of his breathing. What roused him was the renewed sound of footfall coming from above & a weight, something very heavy — *like a piano, mnn?* — being pushed across the attic floor. The shifting stopped at a point directly over the wardrobe, where the Jacob's ladder led up: one more avenue of escape barred — no denying a certain "finesse" to all this. There'd have to be some other way.

Němec stared at the scars on his hands, trying to read something out of them. If this were in a film, what would happen next? How would *he* script it, given the chance? The protagonist putting his mind on a wavelength with the thing that needs to be found & opening up a channel... static in the ether... pictures flickering on the inward-sided screen... the whole motley montage of unlikelihoods... & just maybe, among them, the *key*, the Eureka moment: replaying that Eve&Adam scene under the apple tree that must've been lived a million&one times before Newton called it gravity, guessing what goes up must eventually come down, in fallen days of yore before the first rocketman, the lost Voyager soundtrack playing to angels out beyond the reach of God or solar system — garbled greetings to distant eons, time-capsuled archaeo-blather, "The Sounds of Earth" with a special message from U.N. Secretary-General Kurt Waldheim (that Nazi), addressed to spacefarers & dwellers of dark matter, savants of the spiralling colostrums of remote galaxies, warped beyond any dopplereffect, becoming the nascent Logos of other heavenly hosts & other Gods. Like Jacob's ladder, first you ascend in order to descend... Establishing shot, mid-shot, panoramic shot, close-up... Scenes of civilisation's rise & fall, beginning in the depths of the sea, newts evolving into man, machines with brains, aliens abducting the planet by corporate proxy, evolution sub-contracted running backwards into the future & the closing credits: a chorus of time-wearied messengers of apocalypse, purveyors of cosmic doom, builders of rhetorical arks against the onset of the Great Inundation...

> *But oh, when you get down to it,*
> *right in the muck of it,*
> *ain't life just...*
> *When you get down to it,*
> *right in the filth of it,*
> *ain't life just graaaand?*

And so, taking his cue, with nothing to lose by it — getting down on all fours, rooting at the bottom of the wardrobe among the shoes & shoehorns, the transformers & busted crystal sets — the accumulated dust, dead bugs, hair, lint, loose threads of years or decades — managing with fingernails turning bloody to dislodge a puzzle-piece of parquet with a metal ring recessed below. The ring belonged to a trapdoor which came up from the floor with an effort — & beneath the trapdoor, a narrow shaft led down, steel rungs protruding from mildewed brickwork — candlelight too feeble to reach the bottom of it. The gust of a clammy draught — the flame guttering…

No time to evaluate the pros&cons. Němec gathered what he needed. The Proxy Polygraphia & the secrets insinuated in it — avatars of some uncompleted, undisclosed project that'd begun with a deception & ended by confusing itself with the Big Truth? Who else than Hájek had known the real form of that puzzle which only in appearance resembled it? Severínová? Elsbeth von N____? Hájek's wife, Alžběta Seifertová? And Faktor? Bareš? All the other co-involved conspirators, clutching at straws, machinating this entire drama in the hope he, Němec, or someone like him, would unearth what their own exhausted labours had failed to? Unaware that the secret & the puzzle weren't equivalent, but only as like as a reflection in two parts — the visible part & the invisible part* — which, when brought together, would describe at best a chronicle of omissions, a secret codex of the misplaced, a Pandora's biscuit-tin of abominations, disjointings, farces — last word in the Book of Errors — penned in the most erroneous script imaginable, as if thereby to remove them (& it) from the world. Real or fake? No-one would ever know: the story ended here.

Němec spilled the contents of the folders into a plastic garbage bag — bundled the Nazi Manuscript together with the facsimiles & tossed those in too — the undeciphered Black Book coming apart at the spine — all the evidence needing to be disposed of — his Miranda in her coffinbox with bundled useless scribblings — Kulička's postcard… He slipped the two photographs — Hájek's double, the two bishops, the deathshead staring out, seeming to grin & wink at him in the candlelight — face-to-face together in his jacket pocket. Looked at one way, the pictures made no sense, or only the opposite of sense — the alternative was to reduce everything to banalities: a scam gone wrong, whose key was a list of names, a dramatis personae in a tale of forgery & stolen loot. The only person with the answers was probably dead by now — Němec was free to

---

* There's always more to anything than meets the eye. [✊]

invent whatever comforting fictions he chose.

Out in the bureau the record had played-out & was starting at the beginning again. There were footsteps in the hall: they paused outside the entrance to the room, as if aware of his presence within. In the courtyard it was probably snowing again by now — the doors & windows along the ground floor with no sign of anyone. The dead parrot. The broken tea pot on the floor of the caretaker's flat. And what of the other inhabitants he'd never laid eyes on? Mere ciphers? Unpaid extras who'd been edited out of the script? Němec took up his inherited hat & walkingstick (he'd soon have no further need of such props: they might yet become evidence of some obscure allegory, were anyone to pay heed to them — like the smear on the ceiling of Faust's workshop — false clues leading nowhere), the flashlight, hammer & chisel. What else would he need?

On the bookshelf stood a shaving mirror that'd once belonged to a man called Josef Kulička — one last look: that breached bastion of a corpus — a face you'd barely notice because all it described was the broken silhouette of something else — Mr Nonentity — a scarecrow in the wind with its stuffing knocked out... Němec snuffed the candle & dropped the bag into the hole, easing himself down after it, one foothold at a time. How long would they wait before they came looking? Would they ever? Already he'd forgotten what day of the week it was. It didn't matter.

As Němec descended the Jacob's ladder, the music echoed weirdly in the gap above — the shaft was narrow, sunk through a space between two walls with pipes running at intervals on either side — brick & mortar giving way to wood sheet-piling, tongued & grooved, extending down through foundations ending in an air vent squeezed between bottle racks in the cellar. Scuttle of rats' feet — muffled voices beyond the gate — dampness suffusing the air. He cast the torchlight through the hole in the far wall, pushed the bag through & climbed after it, rubble strewn about on either side.

A faint current stirred beyond the threshold — far distant, the river's beckoning whisper, conjugating in all its moods — *hark*! — calling on, down into the cave of itself, torchlight & shadowspiel, the guiding spirits casting back a sheep's eye — as up above the cranking of machines drowned-out the last strains of Mahler's "Resurrection," while from the east dawn's pond'rous relay, eight o'clock, & the stink wafting up the valley, the TV tower's unblinking eye above a greyblack cobblestoned sea — the beleaguered Erdshadow receding 6ookm/s — faint secondhand light through west-facing window-holes making dumbshow silhouettes on the recordplayer's dial.

Once more retracing his steps, the resumed journey, the retold & aforesaid, if only to hear the end of it — burrowing under the City, the atavism of the descent, guided by the torch's one eye, Golem in the land of the blind, deeper & deeper into its undermind, Orpheus returning under Lesbos, Eurydice, her bittersweet tears...

Down through bedrock, sediment, clay, mud, protoplasms & toxic waste, regurgitated bile & tuberculous spittle — sack of broken books dragged behind, by hooked crook of walkingstick. And as Němec progressed, the distance behind did seem to swell, while the distance ahead did seem to contract to a hovering speck of fairylight: he desired to touch it, but it was always just beyond reach. *Patience, my dear...*

Further & further crawling along the shaft into the very heart of the labyrinth — Minotaur long dead — you wouldn't find any trace of it down here, not even a ghost — it was a place from which everything seemed to've fled, of its own will or under some elsewise influence.

There was an ancient proverb, that only in accursèd places can sanctuary be found: the pariah who dwells in cemeteries among the dead, Mydlář, the headsman, faceless, camouflaged among the outcasts of the Ghetto — the Golem-fearers, the sewer-builders, sootmouthed frackers of gold from subterranean vapours, mudmen, creatures of the Maharal.

Piranesi dungeons of irrational dream architectures — opposed & intertwined dimensions in labyrinths of time & space — turbulent, overflowing, mephitic…

Narrowing, the descent grew steeper. The ever-accompanying whisper, louder. Ahead, just a little further on, the blackness beyond the torchlight resolved into a solid form. Němec breathed hard but the sound of his breathing was lost. Closer now, the dancing spot of light touched the surface of a wall barring the way. Faintly it glistened. He set down with his tools upon the ground, barely room to hunch in. It could've been anywhere, a tunnel beneath a pyramid on the Nile & he a thief squatting at the door of Pharaoh's tomb. The stones bore the marks of something that'd clawed them so that they bled. Some elementary self-sentience prowling the dark. The Great Voice whispered, swelled, beat within. Němec strained to give a shape to the cacophony — the voice inside the voice, the whisper inside the whisper. *Shush now.*

To go on? Or not go on? To wait again for the violent sleep to come over him? To submit to the senseless conforming law of the circle, again at an impasse — the presentiment of a definitive fact wanting only to be born? And what if, on the other side of the wall, there was only another wall? And yet another beyond that? Or what if, on the other side, someone identical to him was already there, squatting with *his* back to the dark as Němec was, thinking these same thoughts, having undertaken an identical journey, only to arrive here, as he had, at the threshold of a point with no duration, which belonged to no sequence. Yes, like the two parts of that mirror, agonist & antiself, which when brought together would seamlessly overlap, abolish one another. And yet something else would remain. What would it be?

Even now his secret counterpart might've be anticipating him, preparing to cross over also, to assume *his* place — the final, decisive move in a game whose compass is as fixed as the motion of the stars. The parallel lines stood acquitted of one another. Němec rested his forehead against the wall — its coldness numbed him. He could close his eyes & none of this would exist — the whole contracted four-square world flickering in the torchlight — & him in it, already coming apart, fraying at the seams.

First you lose yourself in order to become whole?

To unmake.

To make.

He'd never been any good at elegant solutions, born haphazard & always wise after the fact. The only real question was what the situation required to complete itself.

But if all that was left was this
(here, in this present & no other)
alone with a wall,
keeping to the facts…?

A wall & nothing.

A thing.

A no thing.

Coda

[✋]

Is this the only way it could've ended — badly, stupidly, inevitably? The story's gone on long enough. Is there anyone left who still believes the final act wasn't scripted in advance, before the beginning even, to draw a line under the whole fiasco, set the scene for another *all's well that ends well* kick in the pants to get bums out of seats & back in line at the boxoffice, as decorum itself demands, not to allow a slow death to drag on any more than the absolute minimum it needs to get its point across, leave the punters with that creeping sense of uncertainty about their own gaping mortality, God forbid! or spiral-off into some lugubrious mirrormaze of the baser emotions, with all the intellectual anaemia of a child's wrist reflex, tossing-off under the same old ratty blanky they've been swaddled in since birth & nothing but that handheld *commedia dell'arte* or *arte della commedia* to keep them sane at night, once the lights of the moviepicture go out & it's all left to them to fill-in the dark? And speaking of acts of despair, look, there's that ponderous palpitation himself, l'il diddly Squillbrain in his borrowed Chaplin-suit, a skin&bones Punchinello, still sitting in front of that wall waiting for the curtain to drop! Should we leave him there? Or is a more sympathetic kind of resolution in order? Puke of human kindness & all that? Or should we just face facts & admit the only thing left to do is improvise the means of putting the poor sod out of his (& our) misery? To play the scene out, short & simple, & let others take his place on stage. You perhaps. But is this really the end or just another botched beginning? As the Chink with the fortune cookies might've said: 'Chicken no good for making omelette.' For omelette, of course, you need an egg, but try telling this to the egg & quick as you like the egg'll disappear up its own arse & what you're left with's a cold plate of *coq-au-vin*. Well, culinary cul-de-sac's aside, what's Squillhead up to, anyway, down in his hole? A man (even of *his* calibre) goes digging for the elusive inner nature of things long enough, it's bound to lead somewhere, eh? Has he found what he's been searching for? *Well, look on the bright side, kiddo. Things can only get better from here on in, hehehe!* Shouldn't be too rough on the poor idiot — he never stood a chance — been better off if he'd just lain down & gasped his last at the starter's whistle, 'stead of floundering about all over the place like a carp out of water. Well look who's talking! D'you think they'll even notice he's gone? Like a creaking floor in an empty house — a tap that drips — a door with a squeaky hinge — a window that doesn't shut properly & rattles in the night — a draught in a sealed room — a thump in the attic — that creature you never see, scavenging in the eaves… How long's reasonable for a man to realise that all he's been doing from the get-go is trying to opt-out of the game? And how many more miles before he learns for himself there's no place to get to, no place to hide, no thought, impulse, feeling in his head that wasn't put there for him — still believing in some achievable vantage point, a "still point," with lucidity unmatched since Gott spoke to Moe from a burning bush.[†] Some panorama he's found for himself at the bottom of his rat-hole, eh? You reckon he thinks we can't hear him down there with all that ruckus? Picture the dumb rubberlipped stickman, caught in the crosslights of his own Altamira, mind's eye myopia making faces-in-the-wall: Alice in Wanderlust — the Salamander King — Golem Joe — Little Orphan Němec slouching off to Central Casting to collect his costume of baggyarsed handmedowns (that's him alright, sloping shoulders, scrawny knees, bugeyes & kingsize flappers)... And listen! The stones speak! The shadows dance! This wasn't on the programme — does he think he can get away with being self-sufficient? Making stoneage cinema come to life, all the golden oldies back-to-back, with nothing but a dying light & an outlook without prospects? Taking all this alcomical hocuspokery a little too literally you might say, pulling the proverbial rabbit out of the hat, the metaphorical smoke&mirrors routine, conjuring TV from the fluvium, ethereal animations emanating from the very *substratum* by dint of his maladroit madness projected upon it? *Shhhhh! We're trying to watch!* Looks like a trip down memory lane — the near & dead — days of yore & all that: The Good Mother, the *Bona Meretrix* — Papa Plato reading his beerhall books — the slutty merkin next door with her combinations drying on the balcony, shouting *Fardrai zich dem kop*! in the stairwell & lobbing flowerpots, always friendly with the boys-in-brown — he himself at the

---

[†] Pure gore!

May Day parade with a smiley face on a balloon half-deflated into something grotesque — a playground sandpit, fighting over toy trains, & one of the Fairynelly Twins taking a plastic hammer & beating him over the head with it, calling him *stingy kike* — New Year's rockets going *boom*! in the sky, pink green silver & blue — newsflash of the Spartakiad Strangler,[*] *Za Socialismus, Za Mír*! — Lučinkas in gymslips & leotards red&blue, balancing balls & spinning hoops (*hoopla*!), kicking their legs & splitting their handstands for eager frontrow apparatchiks busy fingering tie-knots (all black half-Windsors), thicknecked, veins pumping as those little snatches sweat & the stadium swells — redeyed comrade teachers stinking of tuzemák & Stoli, blind from sun-up to sun-down, hard at work keeping the five-year-educational-plan on track, shedding a tear for goodtimes never again to be seen now words like *glasnost* & *perestroika* are being bandied about (early days, though who knows what the dear young things might grow up to be in that uncertain future — western capitalism's willing kurvas? Perish the thought!) — boy hustlers stamping their feet in the cold, bumming cigarettes under lampposts, *Prosím pozor*! loudhailer crackle running through arrival & departure schedules, echoing in bleak December fog… Oh it's all the dreariest of stuff — can't believe he's dug himself into a deadend just to sit there watching reruns while the rest of the world goes to hell. Might as well've been squatting in some grotto-on-a-mountain-top, high above the City with the wispy clouds turned upsidedown, the world in retrospect

---

[*] ?!?

through its rivery reflection, counting down the last moments before the futurepast Flood-to-end-all-floods: sandbags & bilgepumps, Noah in his Ark with daughters pawing over the Bodily Tabernacle, Yahweh in his U-boat with periscope & snorkel. *Blip. Blip.* Yoohoo in his bathtub with a fat hard-on. *Blap. Blap.* All hands going down. *Descensus ad Inferos* et omnes qui. The Great Voice, *Hhhhhhhhhhhh*! Kind of performance that'd demand a standing ovation if the audience hadn't already flown the coop, got out while the going was good, decamped, jumped ship, beat a retreat, taken to their heels, slinked away, sloped off, taken French leave, skedaddled, absquatulated, walked their chalks... But not our Squillhead. No, sir. He's the type wants to stick around for the curtain call, the action replay, the encore. There could be airraid sirens going off & he'd still be thumbing through the channels till someone took his gadget away. What should we do with him? Leave him be? Give him a supply of Evereadys to last till the End of History, & maybe even a little longer? Tell him to stop wasting time & get on with the vanishing act? Up-tools & start work building an escape hatch? *Knockknock, who's there? Nobody. Hahahaha.* Banging away with a clear conscience, the wall just a wall after all, down where it must be getting hard to breathe about now, no time to be meditating on the petrific word or pneuma of speech, it's all just a soap opera in infinite instalments, this time again next life, adjusting the signal-error, the cosmic feedback coming through in neutrino fizzle — hitting fastforward to see what happens next, the view from Mount Ararat, the seven horsemen (room for one more if they squeeze over a little bit), the Wise Old Caterpillar atop the mushroom cloud smoking a hookah, spelling out in smoke signals: *Welcome to the gameshow at the end of the universe! LUCKY LAST!* Well our doughty Squillhead can guess with the best of 'em, tell a wild goose from a red hearing blindfolded, if needs be, avoid an accident that can't fail to occur, misconstrue a meaningful coincidence, hit an *ad hoc* nail on the head, evolve by anastomosis to the next round to ring-up the till on eschatology's account & see *Who'll be the winner!* With a bit of luck he might even become the Voice of the Tribe — our pseudo-Švejkian man-mute you wouldn't bet your own money on — poking away at a wet-behind-the-gills tabularasa with the blunt end of his stick. *Lucky Last Suck*, more like. What's he think he'll find down there? The blackhole he was born from? A Minotaur in a box? A breath of fresh air? Working his Braille-bone into the cracks — slimy grey stones vibrating to the touch — strange music creeping along finger-joints. Poetry, that. And let's not forget the superficial cause of it all — the reason we're all gathered here in the first place, to see how the action pans out — doesn't seem much to look at, just a regular old binbag, scuffed, a tear along one side where torn scraps of quarto are sticking out, leaving a papertrail behind him in the dark, though he can't see it, one nobody'll ever follow in any case, leading all the way back to the cellar under the mad alchemist's stairwell, where already the workmen are bricking up the doorway, the rats long gone, forewarned by ancient rat-instincts. There's no way back though it hardly seems to be an issue at this stage in the game & who knows, keeping a brave face on it, maybe he can still find a use for the dead Prof(et)'s Holygraphia, when the hour cometh, the bells toll, the… *Knocknocknock!* Just to remind he's still digging away down there, the industrious Squillhead, though it's all studio sound-effects, that knocking, over-dubbed, can barely hear himself think, truth be told, on account of, etc. Seems like an eternity (much reluctance evinced by masonry set in its ways) before the first stone finally comes loose, levered millimetre by millimetre (slow work this but with perseverance) & plonks down almost in his lap — *thunk!* He keeps this up it'll be a tight squeeze, if he doesn't bury himself first, breaking down one wall so as to construct another. Like that joke about the poor bastard went into hospital with gall stones & came out *sans* prostate — did I ever tell you that one? And there goes the last rushhour metro from Malostranská rumbling under the river — not the peace & quiet you might've expected, eh? You'd've preferred something a little more tranquil, sedative, assuaging, soothing, serene even? A little *pastorale* by a burbling brook? A bit of quiet contemplation in the innermost recess of your coddled catatonic soul? The "still point" you're forever going on about when you think a bit of profundity's in order? Give the man a chance, why don't you. If you don't like it, you can always go pour wax in your ears or pull a van Gogh or aim a contorted swift kick at the side of your head & find comfort in the innermost lost wanderings of soundless sleep, etc. Or if you're like our Němec here, maybe a familiar voice in the wilderness, for old times' sake, just to help you along, bear-up under adversity, do your ventriloquist's act for you like an undertaker's understudy, to lighten the occasion, so to speak, stop you from getting too caught up in the morbidity of the moment, remind you it's never over till the fat lady gets the wind up. Like all those bits of choice wisdom we've been getting an earful of from that old fruit up on his Astroturf, maybe just a figment of our chump here's pseudocognitive reflex. *See, it's like this. Back in '68, all us refugee-types had to line up outside an office every Wednesday to collect our welfare stamps. You'd be there for hours. People'd be fiddling scams to collect at half-a-dozen different offices around town. If they were clever enough they'd get a routine going, all in a day's work. There was one such occasion, getting up near the head of the queue just when one of these scam artists everyone knew had nipped off to wherever and no sooner out the door than the crabby garter behind the desk calls his name off the roll: 'Vergil,' she says. No answer. 'Vergil!' Looks up from the slate of applications: 'Is there a Vergil here?' And some wiseacre at the back of the room pipes up: 'He's gone homer...'* Which goes to show, eh, you shouldn't mistake one man's posterity for another man's punchline — an austere chicken in every fleshpot in Egypt — Sisyphus dreaming of a non-worker's paradise — the Hunger Artist living off the fat of the air & all that. Still with me? Watch how our Němec chisels at his hole, admire the fortitude he displays working the unresponsive stone, pissy slivers of bilgewater trickling through the cracks — hunched in the coffin-width of a dead-end, envisaging, perhaps, the dead-end that lies beyond it, & the dead-end beyond that. D'you reckon he has any regrets? Thinking, as he excavates, of his fond friend shovelling snow off the astroturf, or maybe lounging on a deckchair, warm‡ inside the makeshift hothouse up there, high (but not so high) above the City's patchwork — as if in a different hemisphere entirely, poking at an ingrown toenail with a toothpick & waiting for the New Year's fireworks to start going off, a bottle of the good stuff close at hand (just imagining it makes poor Squillhead thirsty), who'd've told *him* in any case? *Nothing was ever achieved in the world by saying goodbye, kiddo. Just remember, if yer gonna go, don't look back, you won't like what you see.* And wasn't the aim of the game to find the most direct route *out*? Well, like they say, sometimes the shortest way home's the longest way 'round, & sometimes a straight line's only the implied hypotenuse of an opposed rightangle. Preschool Pythag you'd think anyone could get their heads around. But nothing, as they say, is quite as it meets the eye, & when all you've got to see around the metaphorical corner with's a light at any moment about to sputter — not as straight-forward as you'd hope it'd be, if you were in *his* shoes — figuring by now that the solution to the big puzzle's always just another puzzle. What came first, the clucky Sphinx or riddled egg? And how to keep the lid on the fact it's all a scam in any case? *What? There isn't one? No riddle? And how about all them plagues? Just plain bad luck, was it?* Like the masked mystery of mysteries they keep locked-up with the communion wine & the wily kid stealing into the temple after dark, saying to the virgin priestess how *a man's gotta do what a man's gotta do, eh, Sphinxy?* And wasn't that the real reason

---

‡ *Balmy*'s the word.

(on all fours like that, *Blue Angel* wings &
vaselined Dietrich smirk) our femme-fatale-on-
the-make turned tail & threw her lithesome self
from the high buttress? Wind in her hair, a
supple half-pike — only to have her very High
Cinematic gesture spoiled by that toothless
travesty, blind Tiresiarse, who just couldn't help
himself & had to spill it to all & sundry —
Forget the dame! It was the kid all along! He's a
bad egg! Scrambled! All messed up! THERE AIN'T
NO GODDAMN CHICKEN! And of course
they gave the old beak the credit due a
nostradame of the people, with those
disconcerting dugs reminding how he'd crossed
the line in spectacular fashion himself in days of
yore & had first hand on what he was clucking
about. Well it always suits someone to take a
nutter at his word. *Ecco, ecco, il vero pulchinella!*
And that's the black & the white of it, *hehe.* No
yolk! *Hehe.* Worse & worse. *Can't you at least try*
for a little pathos? Something to wet the cheeks
before we dry them? To make the long arduous wait
worth our while? How about a limerick? I've
been saving this one…

> *There once was a young man from Cheb,*
> *with a nob like a thick loaf of bread —*
> *so hard when stale*
> *he could hammer a nail*
> *and when fresh, as soft as his head, duh-dum.*

No point giving-in to coldblooded despair —
though at this point, pitiable Squillhead there
might've expected the old ghosts to put in an
appearance, give him a send-off — the Prof in
his portable bathtub cracking wise about the
benefits of taking the waters, *hehe,* though
Management would've probably nixed that —

no way to fit the fusty windbag into the programme at this late stage, the way he had a tendency to blather on the moment he got started — maybe later, after the job's done, there'll be time for a chinwag to last through till Auld Lang Syne…

There once was a man called Enoch,
famed for the length of his…

And the rest? Would they ever even think of poor Squillhead again? The Prof's ghost, the Good Doctor, Faktor-the-Redaktor & his domesticated dwarf, shyster Bareš, pouty Petrovná, the racy redhead at the Natural Sciences Museum, Zahradník the diligent footnoter, Alice Steinerová, who else…? Not much of a rollcall — no Cecil B. DeMille cast-of-biblical-zillions — the others, nothing but filler for a six-foot pothole now, *lorem ipsum dolor sit amet*, the sloughed-in background to a story buried before its time, an automatic typewriter job, their vital statistics as arbitrary & inert as they are. That, possibly, would be their revenge, come the time, when all the fictions are brought naked before the Grand Tribunal of the Last Judgement, when all the alibis turn to frass. Perhaps they all knew better than to be present at the End. Not the story's end but the Real End, the one that *goes on ending* even after our heroic Squillhead here's drawn his last. The End that can't be written, that has no way of *being* written, because it comes *after* all that. Like that chicken & that humptydum egg. But in the meantime, readers, things've been moving along, the hole in that wall down there's getting wider, the effort finally seeming to add-up to something — surprise, surprise: he's even begun pushing the stones through to the other side, it hardly seems any work at all, peering in with his flashlight as the faintest whiff of a draught out of the black space beyond tickles his nose & brushes his ears, like a ghost making its getaway — the tombstink of the anterooms of Purgatory, where even rats fear to tread. Busy, busy. Look! He's already made a hole wide enough to get his Squillhead through, shining flashlight left & right, up & down, to discover in there a chamber to all appearances square or, rather, cube-like, though barely more than a metre wide, ceiling too low to stand under by half, the floor lost beneath primeval mud, walls dripping with vegetal growths where no light has ever shone. It's almost an anticlimax, we might've expected something more definitive, a roaring torrent, or some hidden trove with a corpse guarding it, but a four-square chamber will have to do. Shadow of a man that Němec is, he still only just manages to push himself through the hole with nothing to spare, dragging behind him the sum total of his worldly possessions, for all the good they'll ever be to him now — a garbage sack weighed down by a useless wordmachine (the only masterpiece *he'll* ever write) surveying the cracks in the walls, dark with foliated hieroglyphs, a veil of signs, funerary texts. But their forms are rapidly fading as the flashlight fades, while the fragments of that mock mysterium, the drowned Book, swirl around him. If possible, the noise inside the chamber's even louder than the noise in the tunnel. He's made it just in time to watch it all sink into a kind of twilight. We can hear the river on four sides, the groaning of the floodtide beyond the walls, imagining what it must feel like to be trapped in a closed space that seems only to get smaller & smaller as the darkness contracts — a box not even Houdini could sleaze his way out of. Without seeing as clearly as we might wish, we can still detect how the level of the water has begun, very gradually, to rise. We can imagine poor Squillhead feeling that he's growing lighter & heavier at the same time — a buoy in a tidal estuary, or balloon weighted to a rock & the rock like an anchor in the sea as the balloon seeks & fails to rise above the current. Perhaps he's reminded of that blind girl on the stairs of the socalled Faust House — how long ago was that already? Little girl waving a red balloon on a stick. As the darkness stretches out its tendrils towards him, will he finally learn to see? What Braille would ever amount to a red balloon? What word would ever convey a touch that wasn't itself touched? Eye of the sixth sense. What's *she* doing here now, in the dark, in the deafening dark, under the river, in Squillhead's mind? Prophetess of the stairway, balloon-child — were she to reach out now & touch his thoughts, what would she read in them? Is there something there *he* can't see? Something kept secret from him but visible to others, to us, even the blind? Something written across his forehead, perhaps, carved from flesh, clay, rivermud, signature of God-the-Creditor, the Demiusurer, the Mad Rabbi, that whole consortium of mugs that made him: ⠲⠂⠒⠶⠶ — ⠂⠲⠂⠒⠶⠶? (Blah blah blah.) As the water rises, our reluctant protagonist appears to be overcome by a strange urge. In the closely confined space he's started to strip off his rags — first emptying the pockets: pills made colourless in the gloom, let dissolve in the swirling waters — identity papers with name actual or assumed, irrelevant in either case — the cellar key, let slip between fingers — the dark ink-smudge of Devil & Carmelite in xeroxed duplicate — folded coversheet of that *other* VM with faintly green-glowing watermark (strange, for a watermark, to *glow in the dark*, but Squillhead here's beyond noticing such things at this stage), heraldic eagle, wings spread, grasping in its talons a laurel wreath, ancient rune inscribed within — a black horseheaded chesspiece — the obscure allegory contained in a pair of black&white photographs torn into approximate squares & scattered on the ebbtide — crooked stick broken in two, etc. Then, article-by-article, he exposes his unblushing Squillself — jacket folded across the threshold, shirt, trousers, likewise, & the rest, sopping shoes filling-in the space at the top — naked now as John on Patmos with only a dented dunce-hat brushing the stalactites — asquat upon booksack, torch in hand, awaiting the visions, the dream of prenatal life in the unseasonal warmth of his own womb — watching the images on the paper dissolve as the flashlight becomes nothing but a dull ember. Like him, we feel a threshold's been finally crossed — there's really no going back this time — the muddy water continuing to rise, the encircling current, his body the axis of its spiral, the fluid mandala — no mythical "still point" now, only the slowly eroding suspension of a faintly held disbelief whose homily for today is *Up Shit Creek and No Paddlepop.* The torchlight, in a final paroxysm, flickers & dies. Picture, in its place, a dialectical porthole onto some remote parallel universe, where at this very moment K in *his* last confinement is about to attempt the bold leap — stepping out from the precipice, in that gap in Time when everything irreversible promises to come undone, the laws of gravity suspended, the pendulum forever caught in the infinite regress of its arc, plumbing the proverbial nadir — yes, just as if he (K) himself had become the living purport & tenor of that pissant Zeno's parting paradox: no more some jesting alshemist blarneying backwards out his own arse, so to speak, but the very vortex & personified azimuth of (now try saying this with a straight face) Creation & Uncreation itself! No makebelieve Maxwell's Demon, this! No ventriloquist's midget Mephisto! But a trueblue God's Eye negentropy *Wunderwaffe* to undo Genesis with (if only *he*, his kryptonite K-self, so desireth)! Piloting his mortal remains headfirst out the tower window through the pungent night air, up, up, arcing over with arms out wide, putting the brakes on to take in the view from On High, the *Schluß* in *Brennschluß*, slowing the picture down frame-by-frame till it's long past any regular kind of slo-mo & crosses the line into a sort of molecule-by-molecule P.O.V. where he can actually *see* all the nitrogens, oxygens, argons, carbon dioxides that make up the usually invisible surrounds, vapours bristling with static, meteorological conditions of a decidedly unprecedented kind, his mind's gyroscope keeping the whole thing just on the edge of spiralling out of control (*you can't get any closer to the STILL POINT than this, kids!*) — the second hand on our man's bizarrely anachronistic Quartz wristwatch trembling, coming to a stop, & even appearing to — *this can't be possible* — move in reverse! Well, you can change the time but you can't *change Time*, as the old saying goes, & just when K's begun to convince himself he'll stay up there forever (*The Key! The Key! I've found it! Der Schlüssel!*) — or maybe drift off into the clouds on angel-wires, some latterday Assumption in a sudden shaft of moonlight... Yep, just at *that* moment, something comes right up as if out of nowhere & slaps the earless ass right in the kisser. *Wakey-wakey sunshine!* That something being an accelerating spheroid mass of approx 5.9736 x 10^{24} kg. All things being relative.

Golem City
January 2008 — January 2016